ZAP
ZAP

Unidentified Flying
Bovine spotted
flying over Shinjuku
while shooting laser
beams from its eyes
and spinning at high
speed!

I'm still in a daze from all the things that have happened to me one after another since I became a published manga artist. It's all happening so quickly! It's the unexpected events that make life thrilling.

—Hiromu Arakawa, 2004

Born in Hokkaido (northern Japan), Hiromu Arakawa first attracted national attention in 1999 with her award-winning manga *Stray Dog*. Her series *Fullmetal Alchemist* debuted in 2001 in Square Enix's monthly manga anthology *Shonen Gangan*.

FULLMETAL ALCHEMIST
3-in-1 Edition

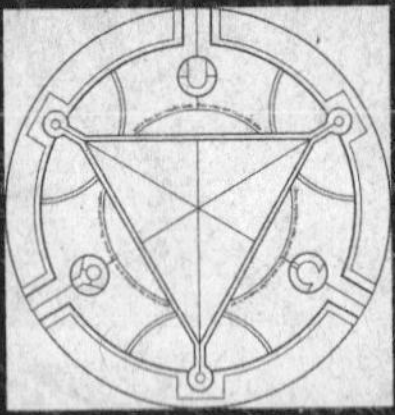

VIZ Media Omnibus Edition Volume 3
A compilation of the graphic novel volumes 7–9

Story and Art by Hiromu Arakawa

Translation/Akira Watanabe
English Adaptation/Jake Forbes
Touch-up Art & Lettering/Wayne Truman
Manga Design/Amy Martin
Omnibus Design/Yukiko Whitley
Manga Editors/Jason Thompson, Urian Brown
Omnibus Editor/Alexis Kirsch

Printed in the U.S.A.

Published by VIZ Media, LLC
P.O. Box 77010
San Francisco, CA 94107

10 9 8 7 6
Omnibus edition first printing, October 2011
Sixth printing, December 2015

鋼の錬金術師

FULLMETAL ALCHEMIST

荒川弘

HIROMU ARAKAWA

7

□ アルフォンス・エルリック

Alphonse Elric

□ エドワード・エルリック

Edward Elric

□ アレックス・ルイ・アームストロング

Alex Louis Armstrong

□ ロイ・マスタング

Roy Mustang

OUTLINE
FULLMETAL ALCHEMIST

Using a forbidden alchemical ritual, the Elric brothers attempted to bring their dead mother back to life. But the ritual went wrong, consuming Edward Elric's leg and Alphonse Elric's entire body. At the cost of his arm, Edward was able to graft his brother's soul into a suit of armor. Equipped with mechanical "auto-mail" to replace his missing limbs, Edward become a state alchemist, serving the military on deadly missions. Now, the two brothers roam the world in search of a way to regain what they have lost.

The Elric brothers return to their old alchemy teacher, Izumi Curtis, who once attempted the abhorred practice of human transmutation. Ed, Al and Izumi have all paid for their sin with a part of themselves but despite losing his entire body, Al has no memory of "the truth" which the others glimps when they were "taken." Now Izumi looks for a way to unlock that memory, which may be the key to restoring the boys' bodies. Meanwhile far away, the assassin Scar recovers from his wounds in a refugee camp

鋼の錬金術師
FULLMETAL ALCHEMIST

CHARACTERS
FULLMETAL ALCHEMIST

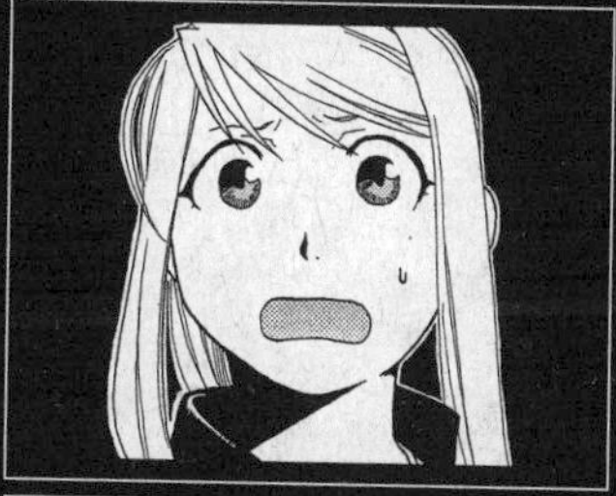

ウィンリィ・ロックベル

Winry Rockbell

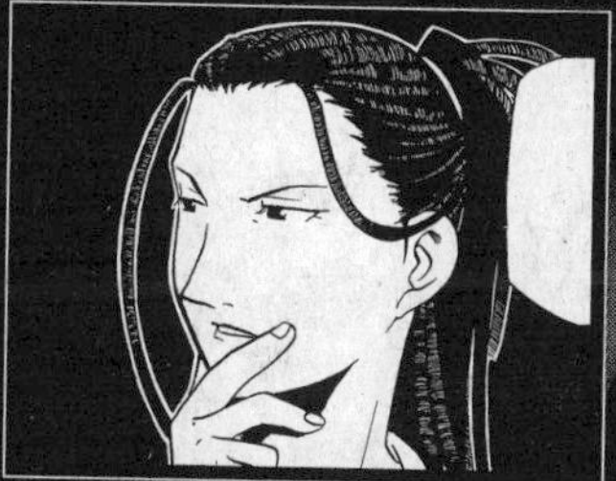

イズミ・カーティス

Izumi Curtis

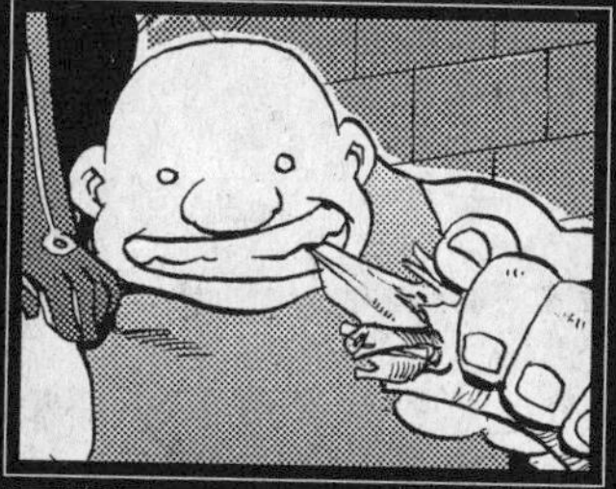

グラトニー

Gluttony

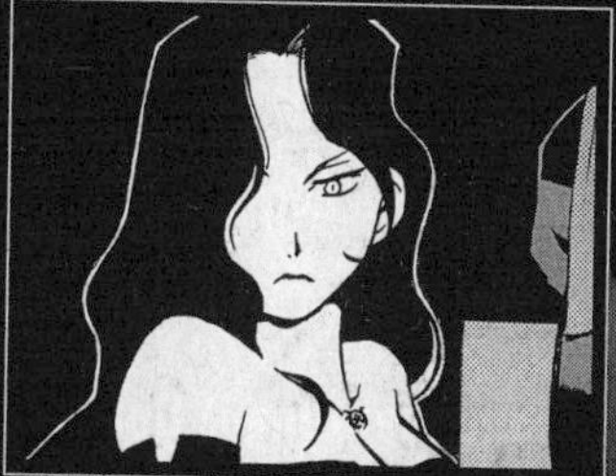

ラスト

Lust

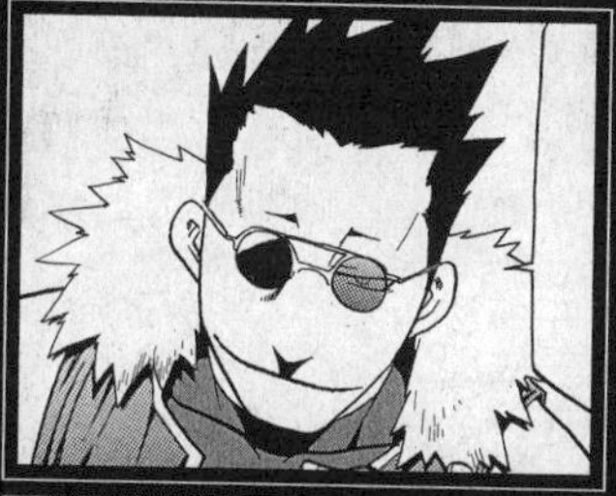

グリード

Greed

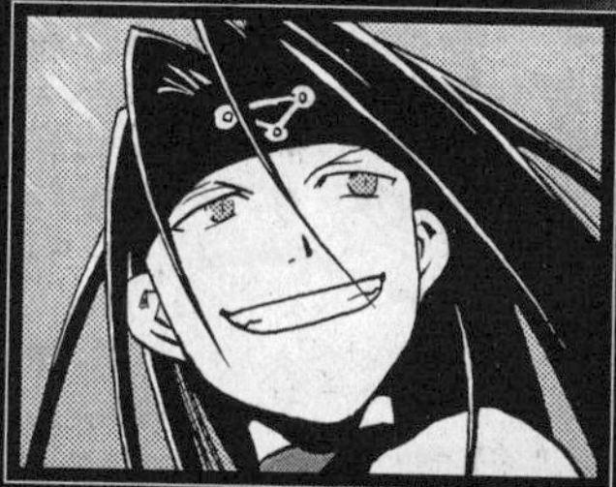

エンヴィー

Envy

CONTENTS

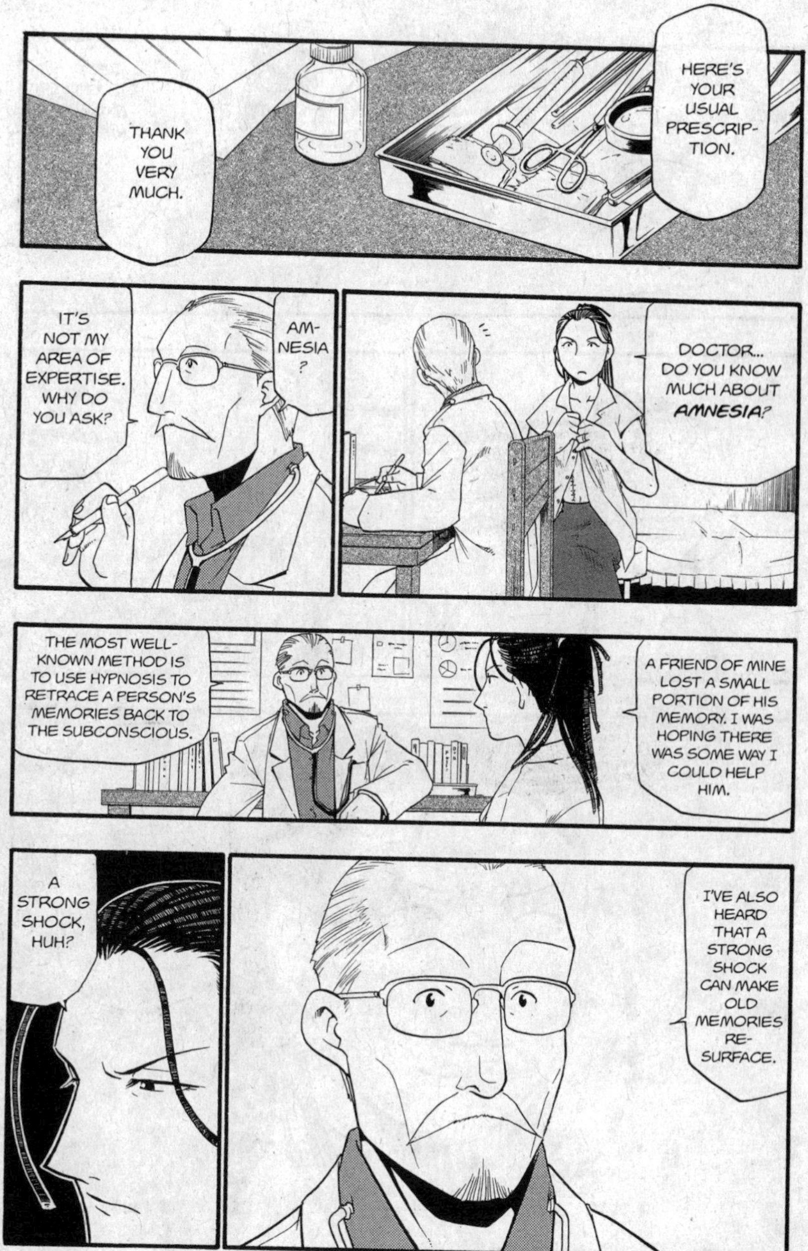
HERE'S YOUR USUAL PRESCRIPTION.
THANK YOU VERY MUCH.
DOCTOR... DO YOU KNOW MUCH ABOUT *AMNESIA*?
AMNESIA?
IT'S NOT MY AREA OF EXPERTISE. WHY DO YOU ASK?
A FRIEND OF MINE LOST A SMALL PORTION OF HIS MEMORY. I WAS HOPING THERE WAS SOME WAY I COULD HELP HIM.
THE MOST WELL-KNOWN METHOD IS TO USE HYPNOSIS TO RETRACE A PERSON'S MEMORIES BACK TO THE SUBCONSCIOUS.
I'VE ALSO HEARD THAT A STRONG SHOCK CAN MAKE OLD MEMORIES RESURFACE.
A STRONG SHOCK, HUH?

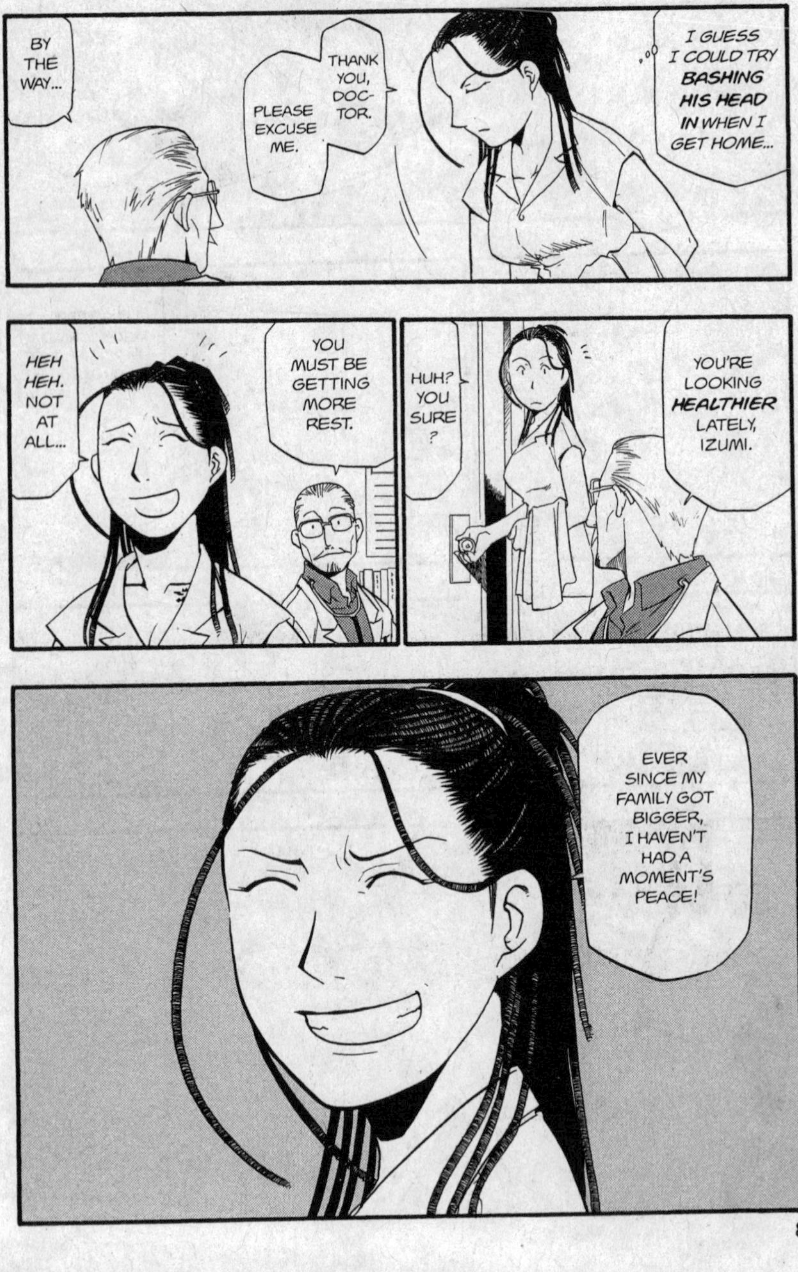
I GUESS I COULD TRY **BASHING HIS HEAD IN** WHEN I GET HOME...
THANK YOU, DOCTOR.
PLEASE EXCUSE ME.
BY THE WAY...
YOU'RE LOOKING **HEALTHIER** LATELY, IZUMI.
HUH? YOU SURE?
YOU MUST BE GETTING MORE REST.
HEH HEH. NOT AT ALL...
EVER SINCE MY FAMILY GOT BIGGER, I HAVEN'T HAD A MOMENT'S PEACE!

Chapter 26: To Meet the Master

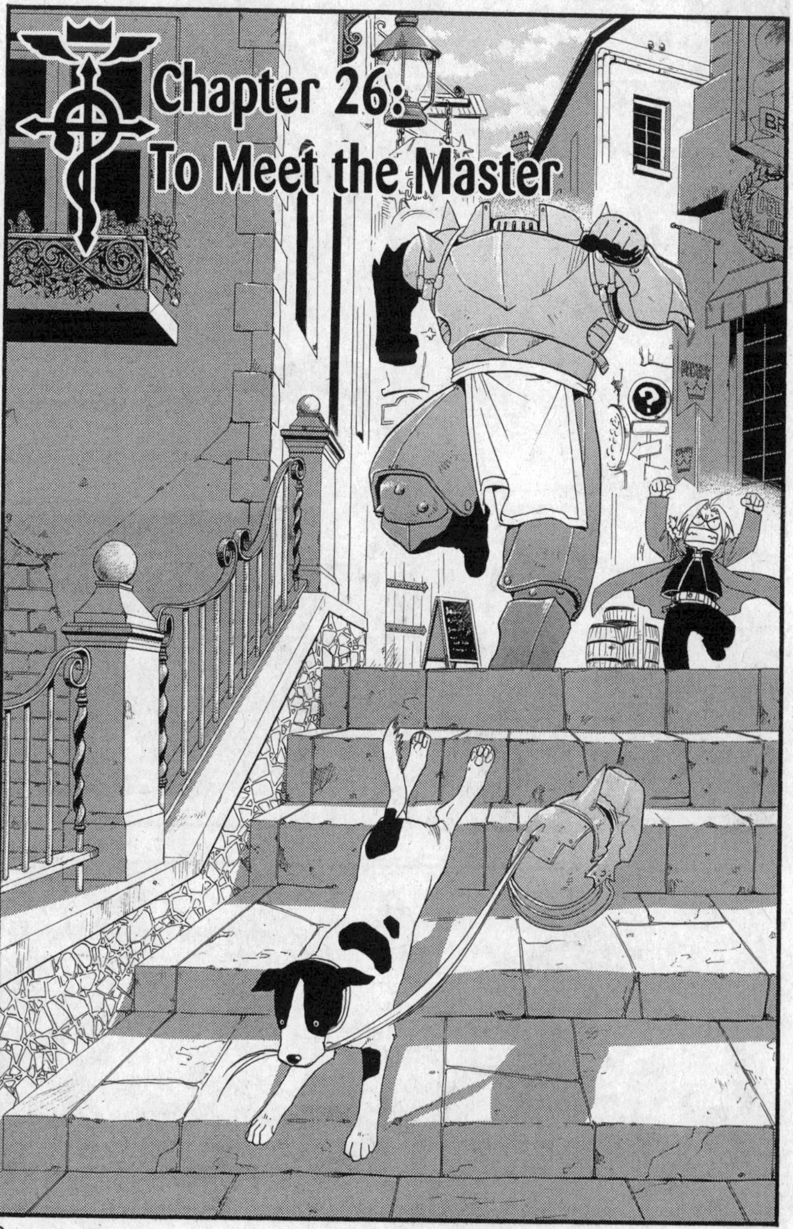

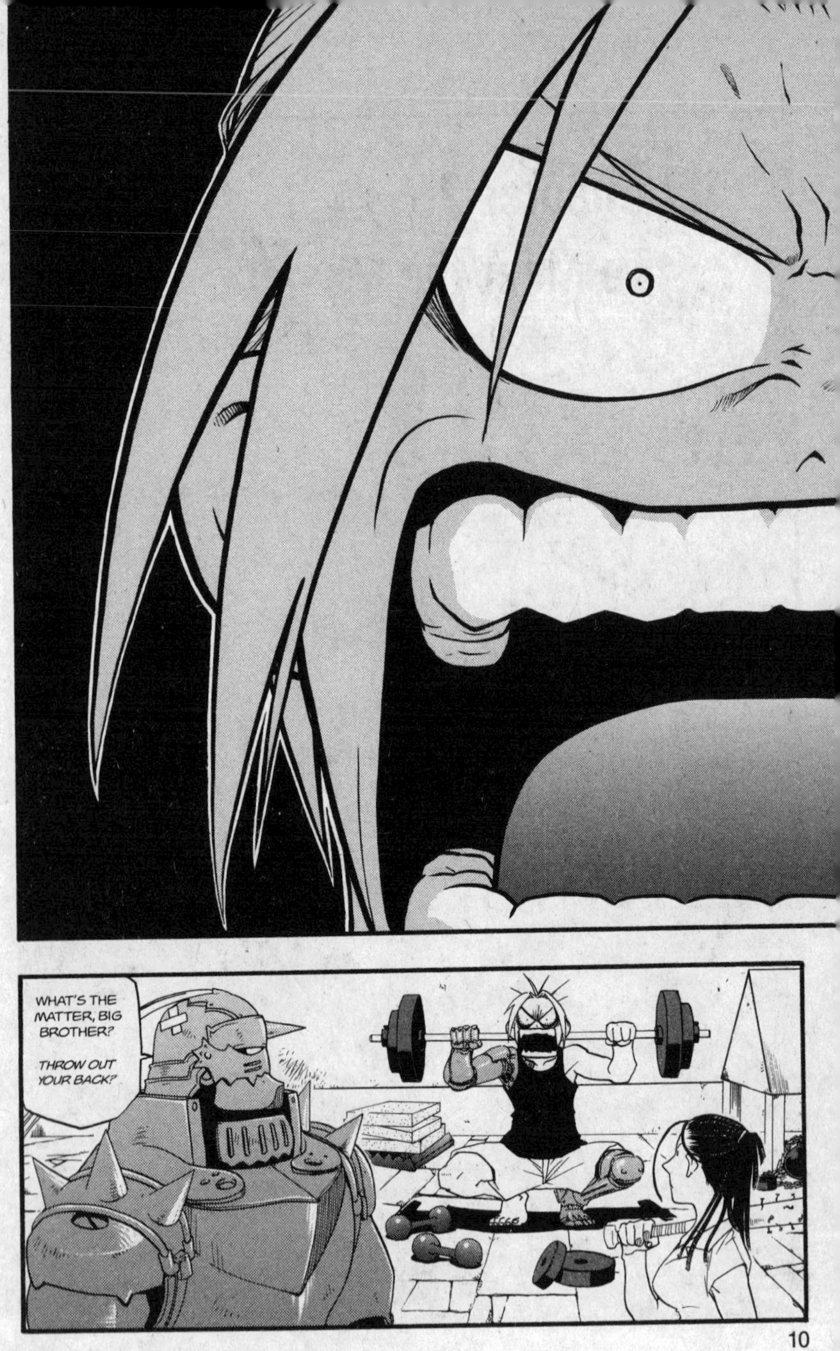
WHAT'S THE MATTER, BIG BROTHER?
THROW OUT YOUR BACK?

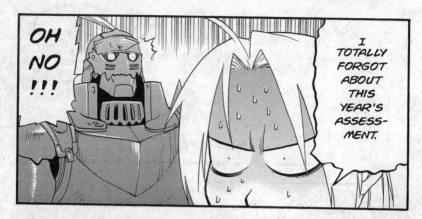

I TOTALLY FORGOT ABOUT THIS YEAR'S ASSESSMENT.
OH NO!!!
THIS YEAR'S WHAT?
THE ANNUAL ASSESSMENT FOR STATE ALCHEMISTS!
EVERY YEAR WE HAVE TO PASS AN ASSESSMENT OR THEY'LL TAKE AWAY OUR LICENSE.
I'VE BEEN SO BUSY LATELY, I FORGOT ALL ABOUT IT!
THIS ISN'T GOOD. NOT GOOD AT ALL...
GREAT! YOU CAN USE THIS OPPORTUNITY TO QUIT BEING THE MILITARY'S DOG.
I'LL GO AHEAD AND LET MILITARY HQ KNOW YOU WON'T BE SHOWING UP.
STOP!!
I'VE BEEN MEANING TO GO TO HEADQUARTERS, ANYWAY.
SURE HAVE!
FEH!
RAMEN HOUSE! HELLO!

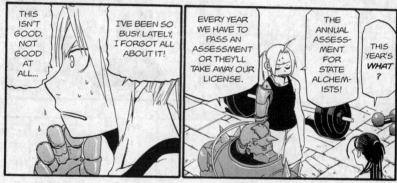

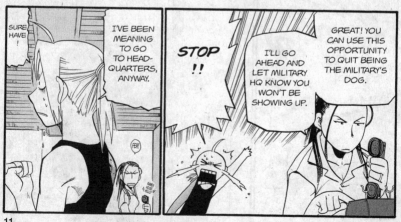

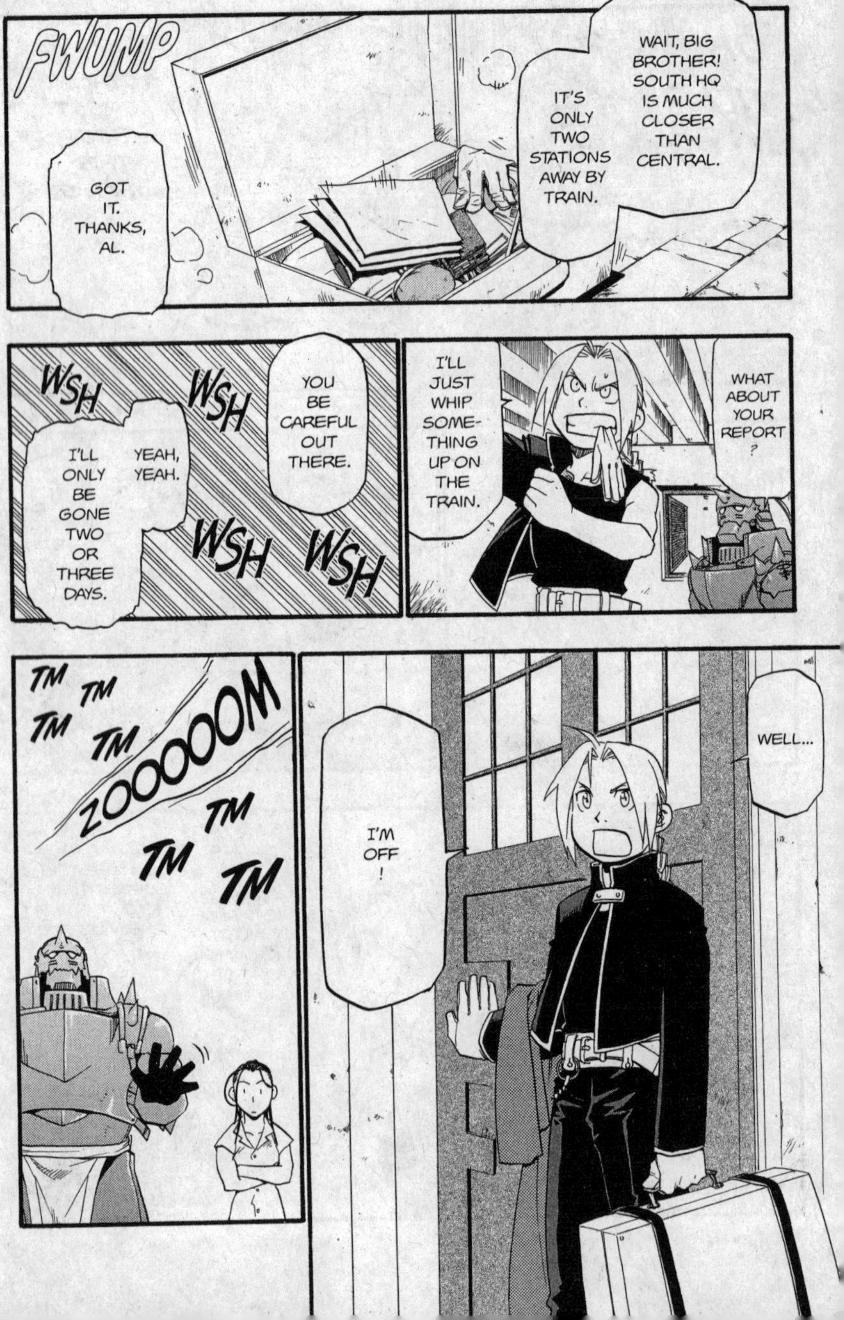
WAIT, BIG BROTHER! SOUTH HQ IS MUCH CLOSER THAN CENTRAL.
IT'S ONLY TWO STATIONS AWAY BY TRAIN.
FWUMP
GOT IT. THANKS, AL.
WHAT ABOUT YOUR REPORT?
I'LL JUST WHIP SOMETHING UP ON THE TRAIN.
YOU BE CAREFUL OUT THERE.
WSH WSH
YEAH, YEAH.
I'LL ONLY BE GONE TWO OR THREE DAYS.
WSH WSH
WELL...
I'M OFF!
TM TM TM TM
ZOOOOOM
TM TM TM

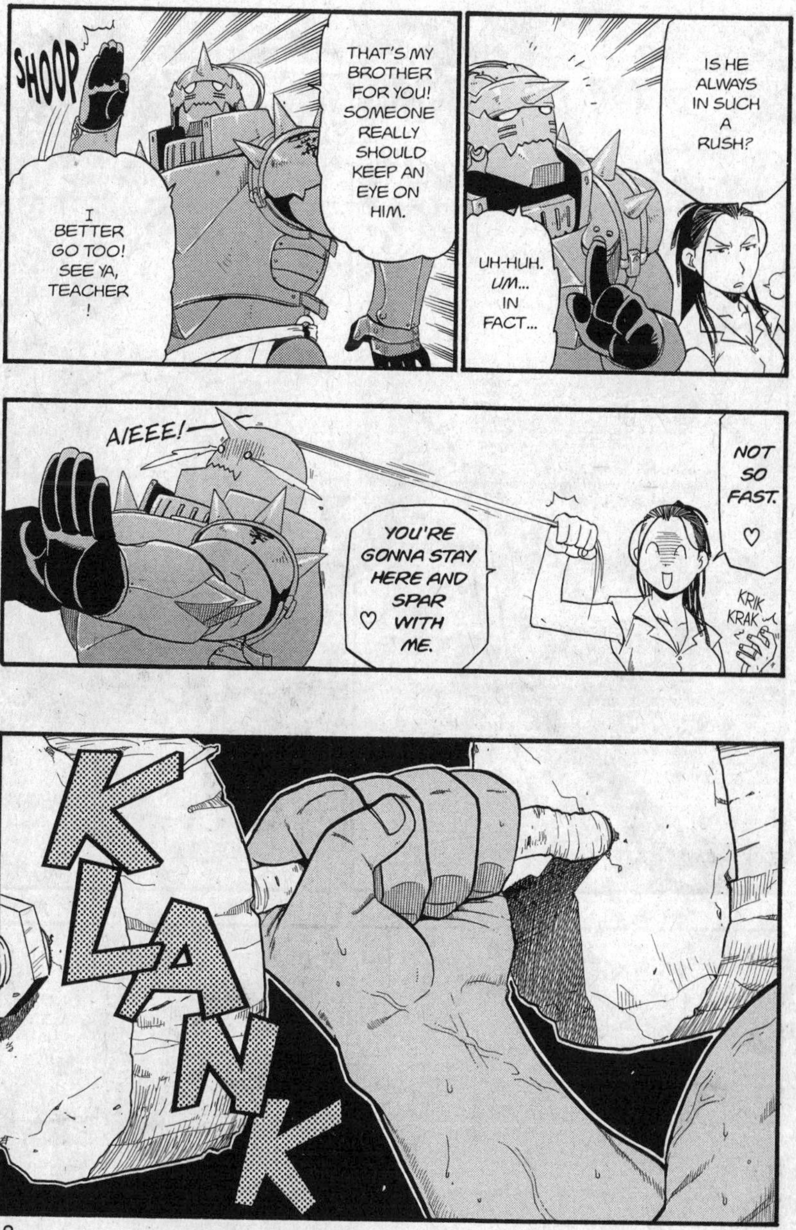
IS HE ALWAYS IN SUCH A RUSH?
UH-HUH. UM... IN FACT...
THAT'S MY BROTHER FOR YOU! SOMEONE REALLY SHOULD KEEP AN EYE ON HIM.
SHOOP
I BETTER GO TOO! SEE YA, TEACHER!
NOT SO FAST. ♡
YOU'RE GONNA STAY HERE AND SPAR WITH ME. ♡
KRIK KRAK
AIEEE!
KLANK

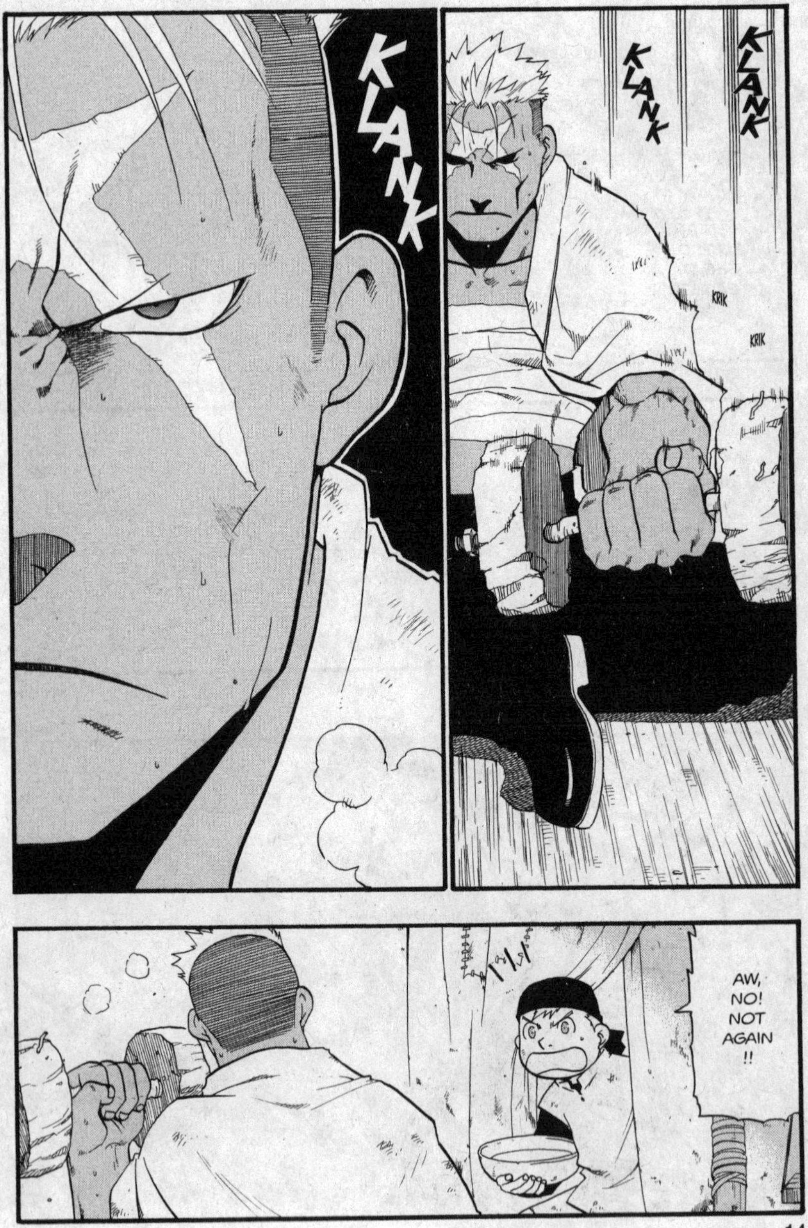
KLANK
KLANK
KRIK
KRIK
KLANK
AW, NO! NOT AGAIN!!

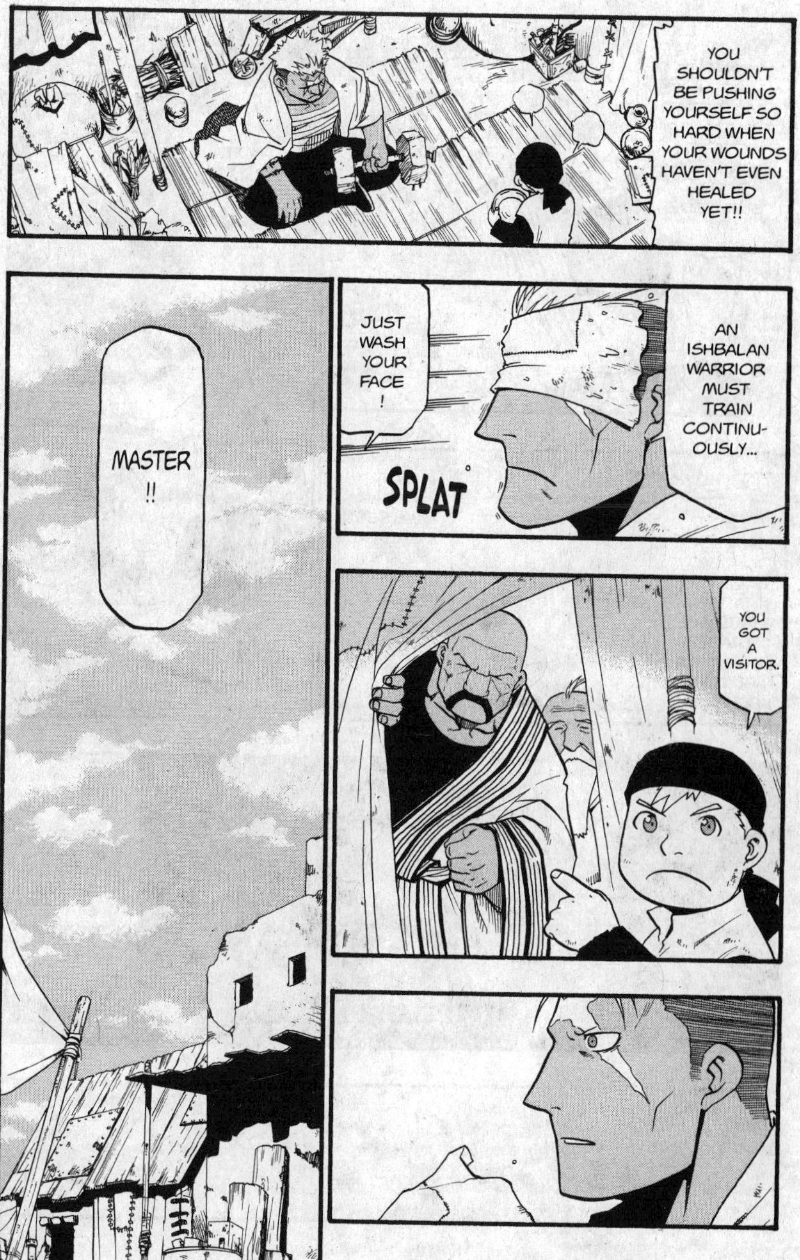
YOU SHOULDN'T BE PUSHING YOURSELF SO HARD WHEN YOUR WOUNDS HAVEN'T EVEN HEALED YET!!
AN ISHBALAN WARRIOR MUST TRAIN CONTINU-OUSLY...
JUST WASH YOUR FACE!
SPLAT
YOU GOT A VISITOR.
MASTER!!

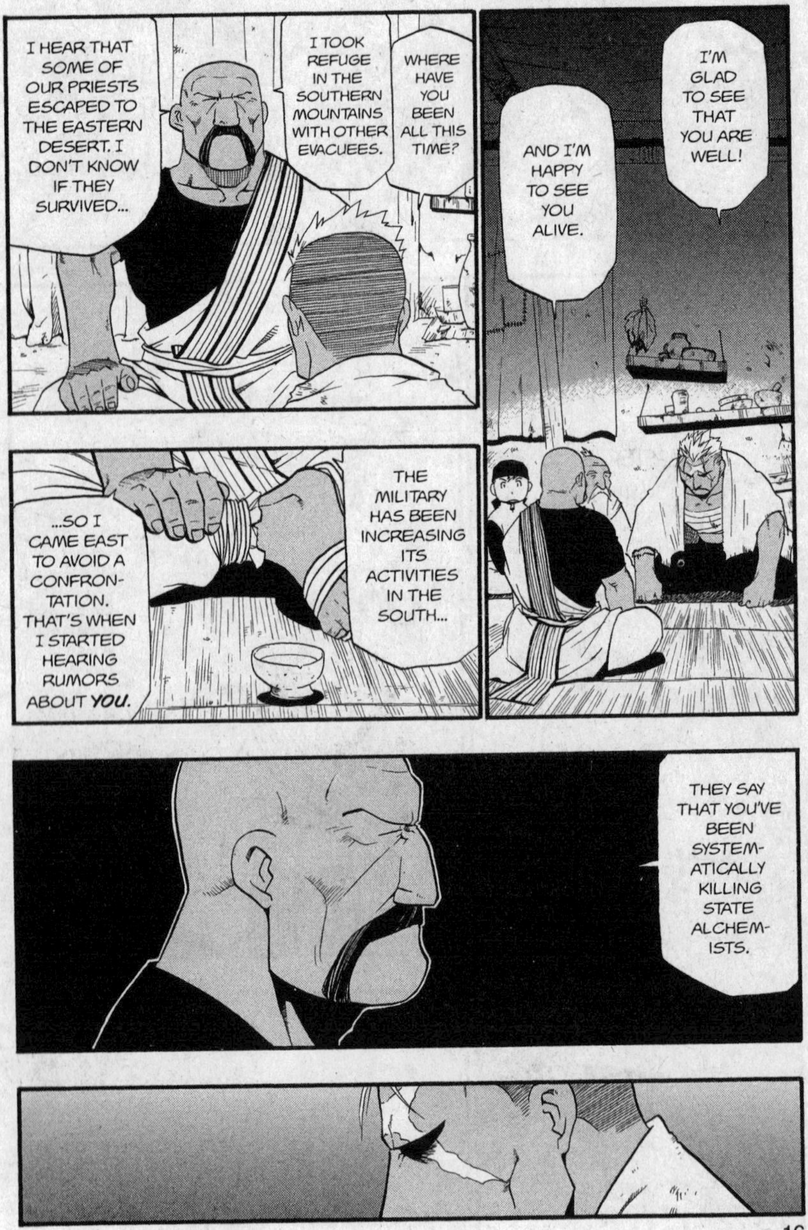
I'M GLAD TO SEE THAT YOU ARE WELL!
AND I'M HAPPY TO SEE YOU ALIVE.
WHERE HAVE YOU BEEN ALL THIS TIME?
I TOOK REFUGE IN THE SOUTHERN MOUNTAINS WITH OTHER EVACUEES.
I HEAR THAT SOME OF OUR PRIESTS ESCAPED TO THE EASTERN DESERT. I DON'T KNOW IF THEY SURVIVED...
THE MILITARY HAS BEEN INCREASING ITS ACTIVITIES IN THE SOUTH...
...SO I CAME EAST TO AVOID A CONFRONTATION. THAT'S WHEN I STARTED HEARING RUMORS ABOUT YOU.
THEY SAY THAT YOU'VE BEEN SYSTEMATICALLY KILLING STATE ALCHEMISTS.

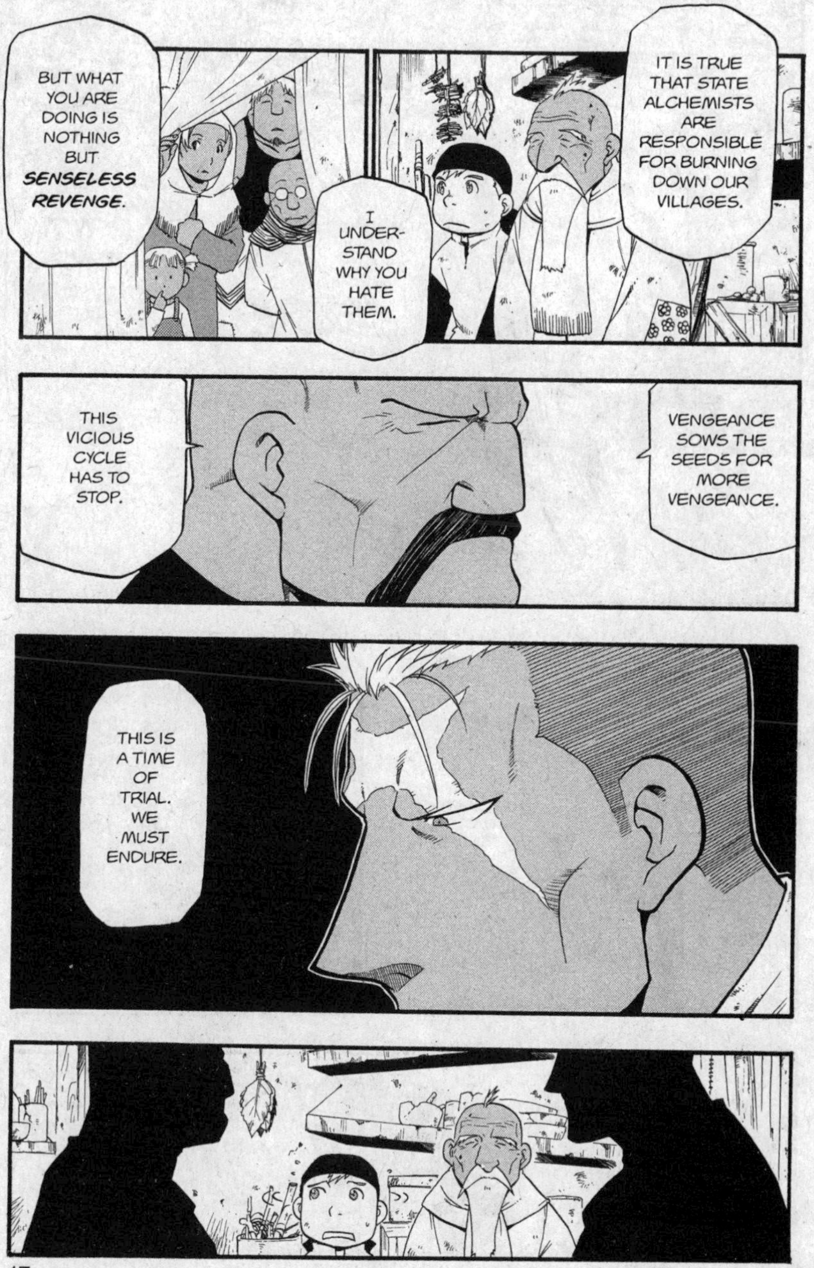
IT IS TRUE THAT STATE ALCHEMISTS ARE RESPONSIBLE FOR BURNING DOWN OUR VILLAGES.
I UNDERSTAND WHY YOU HATE THEM.
BUT WHAT YOU ARE DOING IS NOTHING BUT ***SENSELESS REVENGE***.
VENGEANCE SOWS THE SEEDS FOR MORE VENGEANCE.
THIS VICIOUS CYCLE HAS TO STOP.
THIS IS A TIME OF TRIAL. WE MUST ENDURE.

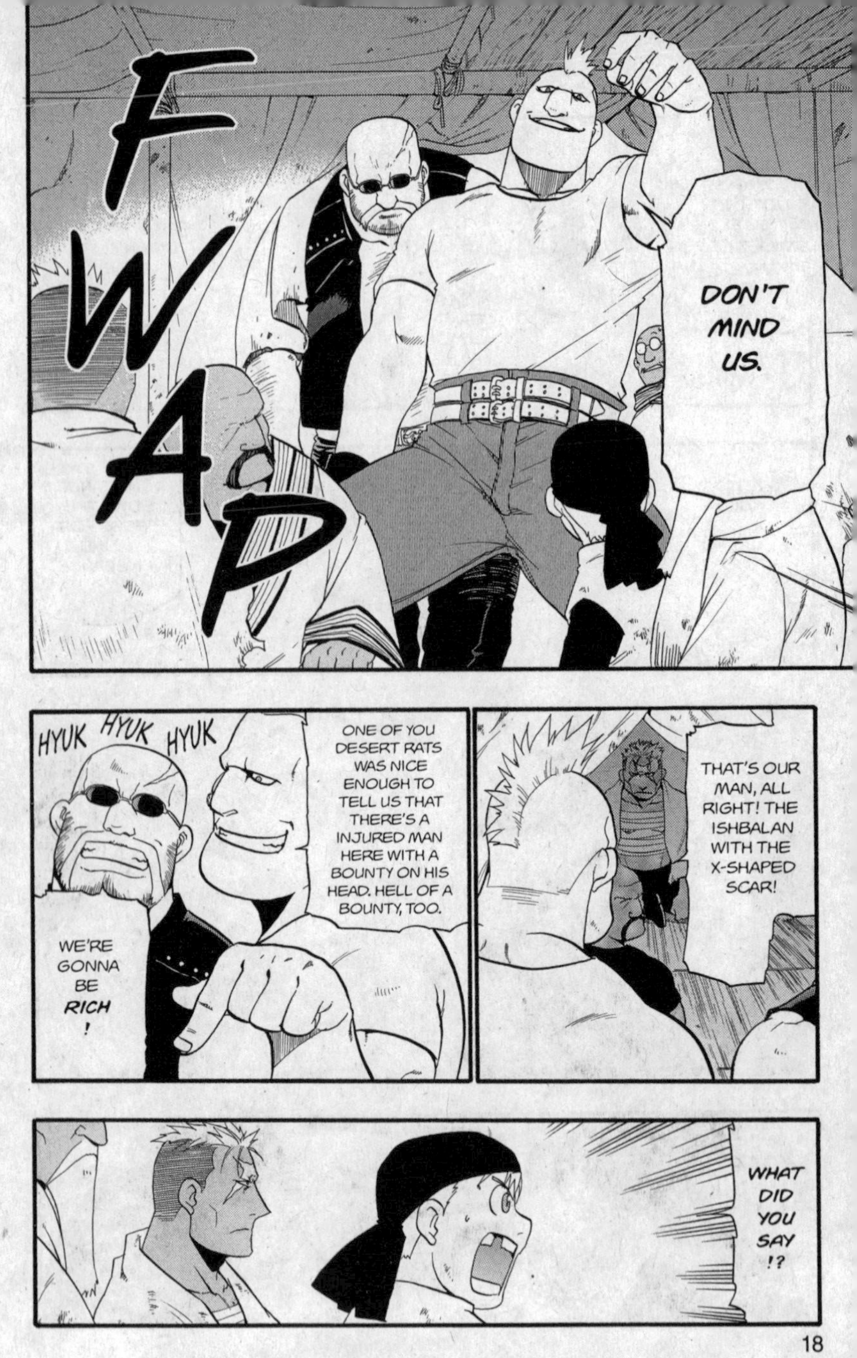
DON'T MIND US.
FWAP
THAT'S OUR MAN, ALL RIGHT! THE ISHBALAN WITH THE X-SHAPED SCAR!
ONE OF YOU DESERT RATS WAS NICE ENOUGH TO TELL US THAT THERE'S A INJURED MAN HERE WITH A BOUNTY ON HIS HEAD. HELL OF A BOUNTY, TOO.
HYUK HYUK HYUK
WE'RE GONNA BE RICH!
WHAT DID YOU SAY!?

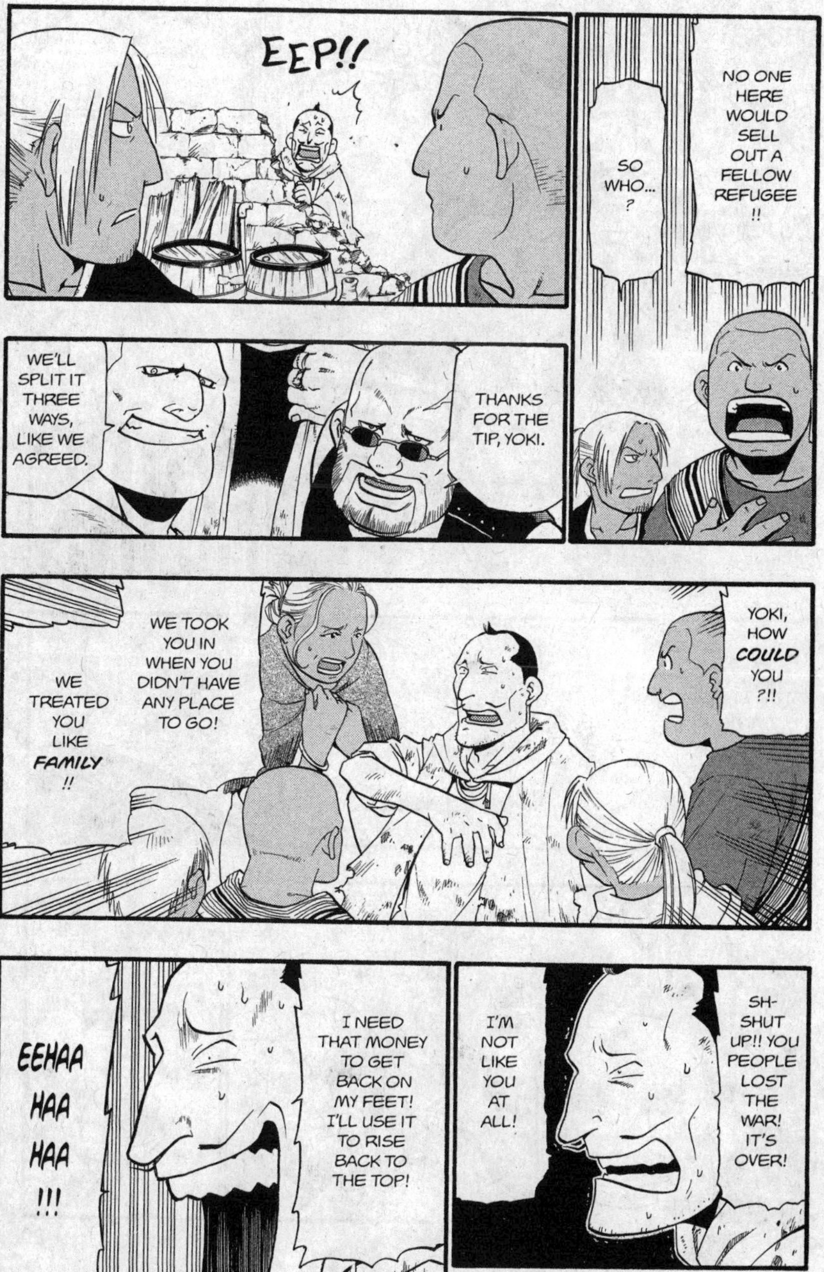
NO ONE HERE WOULD SELL OUT A FELLOW REFUGEE!!
SO WHO...?
EEP!!
THANKS FOR THE TIP, YOKI.
WE'LL SPLIT IT THREE WAYS, LIKE WE AGREED.
YOKI, HOW **COULD** YOU?!!
WE TOOK YOU IN WHEN YOU DIDN'T HAVE ANY PLACE TO GO!
WE TREATED YOU LIKE **FAMILY**!!
SH-SHUT UP!! YOU PEOPLE LOST THE WAR! IT'S OVER!
I'M NOT LIKE YOU AT ALL!
I NEED THAT MONEY TO GET BACK ON MY FEET! I'LL USE IT TO RISE BACK TO THE TOP!
EEHAA HAA HAA!!!

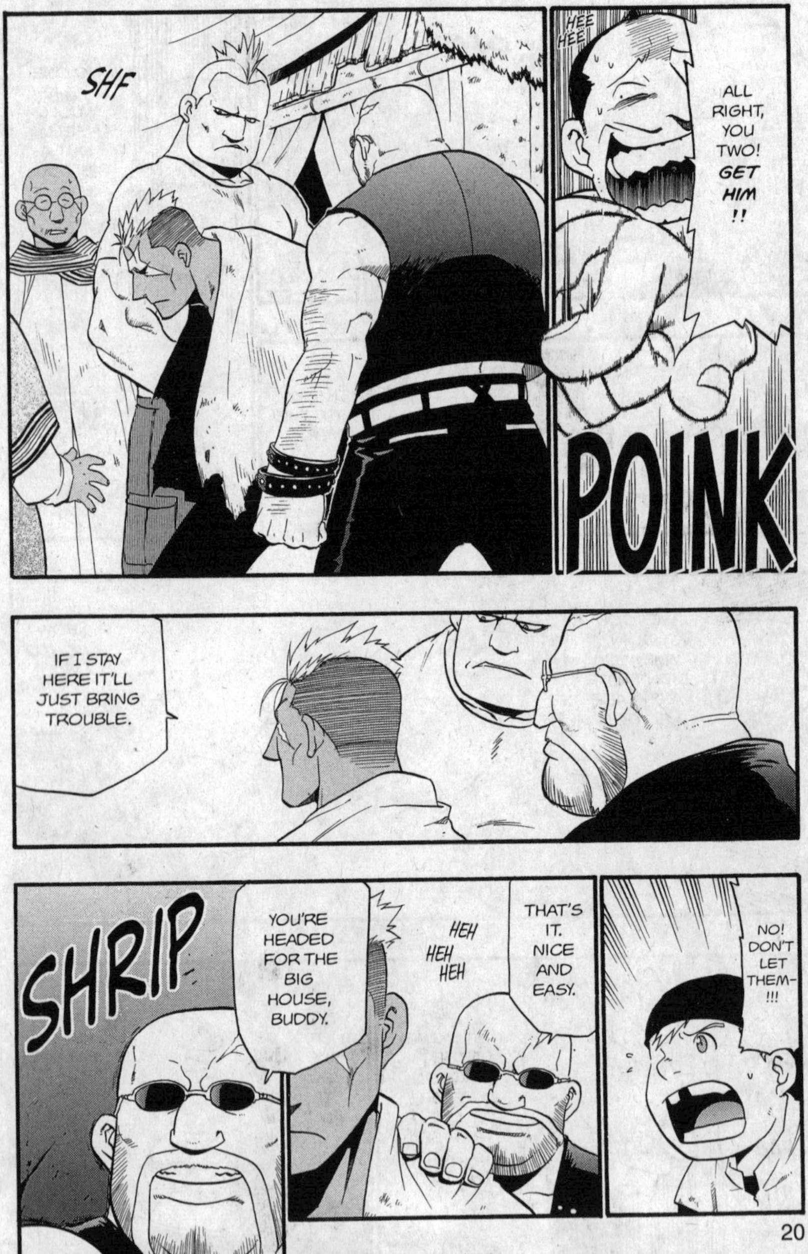
HEE HEE
ALL RIGHT, YOU TWO! GET HIM!!
POINK
SHF
IF I STAY HERE IT'LL JUST BRING TROUBLE.
NO! DON'T LET THEM-!!!
THAT'S IT. NICE AND EASY.
HEH HEH HEH
YOU'RE HEADED FOR THE BIG HOUSE, BUDDY.
SHRIP

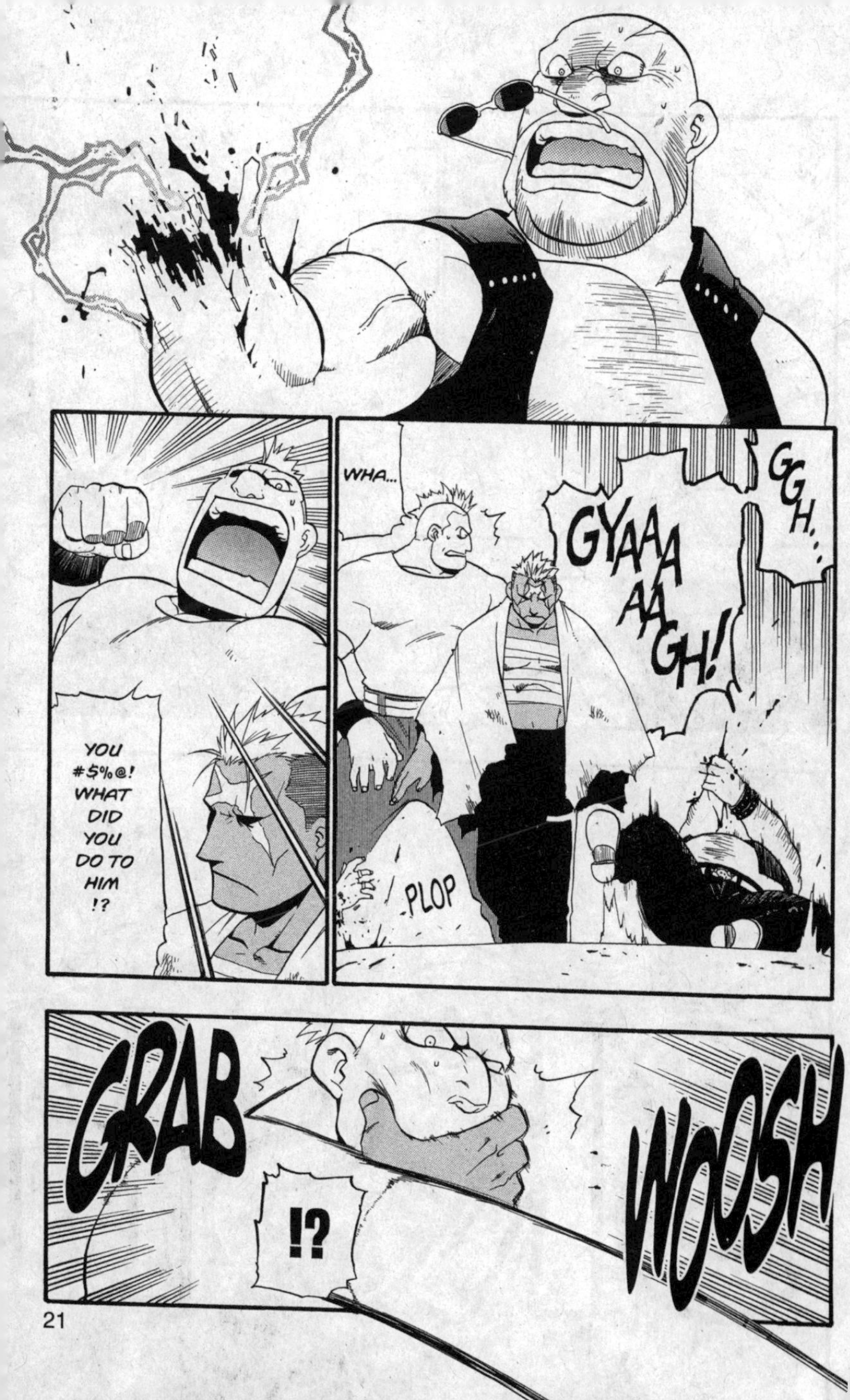
GGH...
GYAAAAAGH!
WHA...
PLOP
YOU #$%@! WHAT DID YOU DO TO HIM!?
WOOSH
!?
GRAB

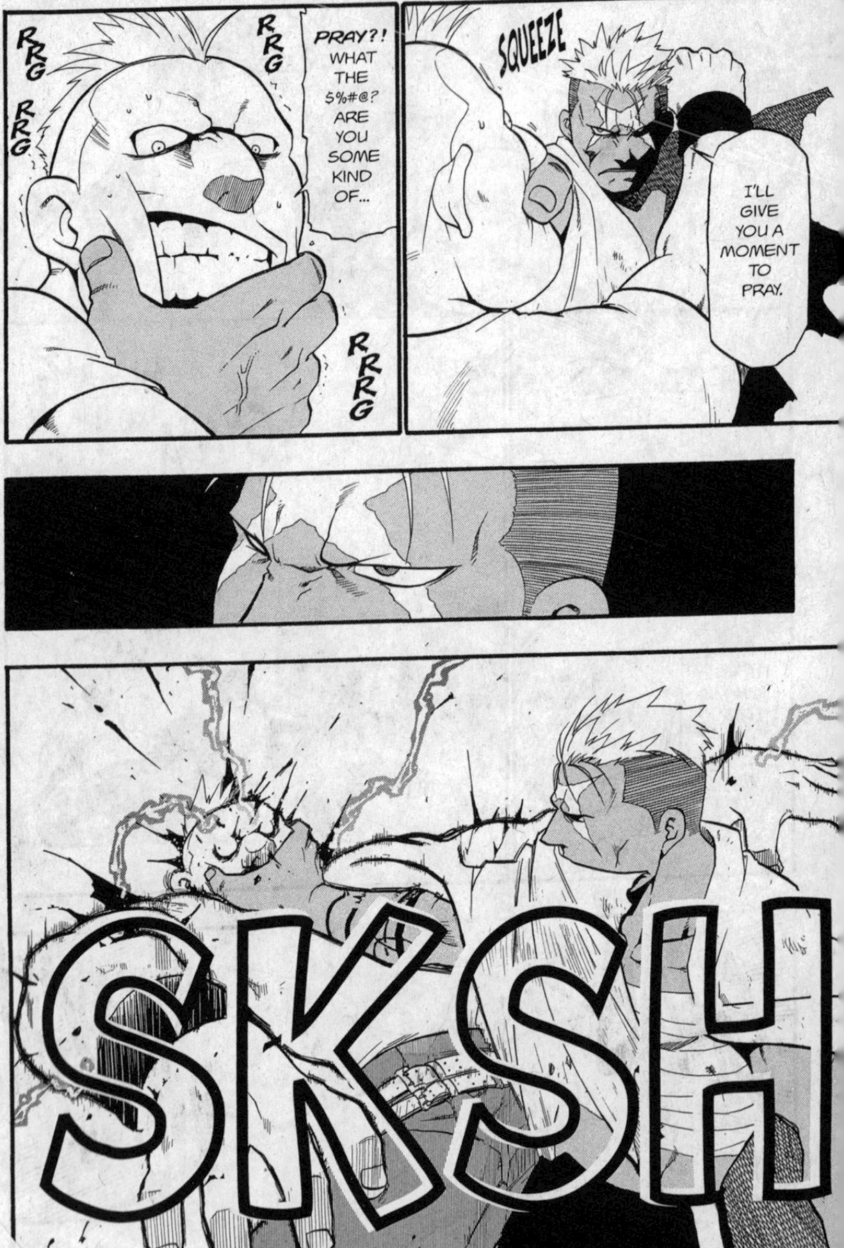
SQUEEZE
I'LL GIVE YOU A MOMENT TO PRAY.
RRG
RRG
RRG
PRAY?! WHAT THE $%#@? ARE YOU SOME KIND OF...
RRRG
SKSH

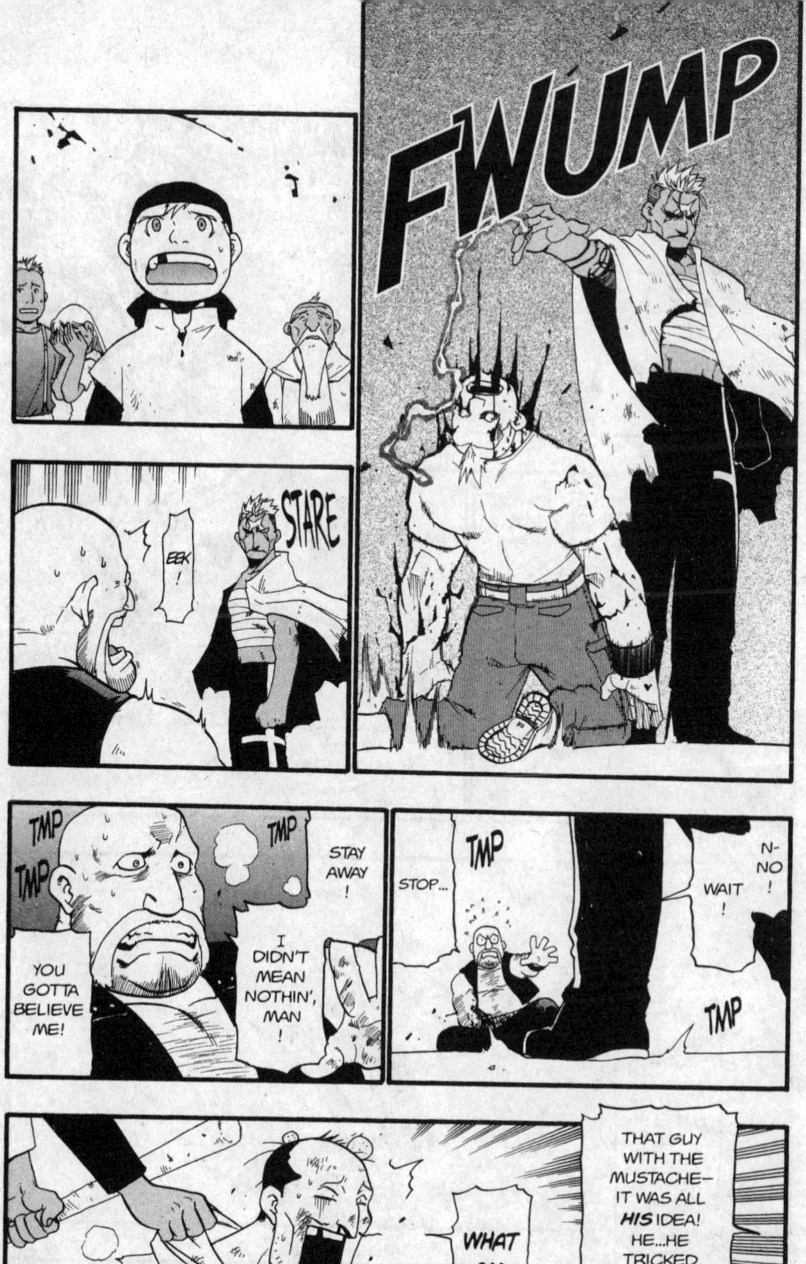

FWUMP
STARE
EEK!
N-NO!
WAIT!
TMP
STOP...
TMP
TMP
STAY AWAY!
I DIDN'T MEAN NOTHIN', MAN!
TMP
TMP
YOU GOTTA BELIEVE ME!
THAT GUY WITH THE MUSTACHE— IT WAS ALL ***HIS*** IDEA! HE...HE TRICKED ME!
WHAT ?!!

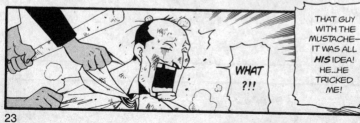

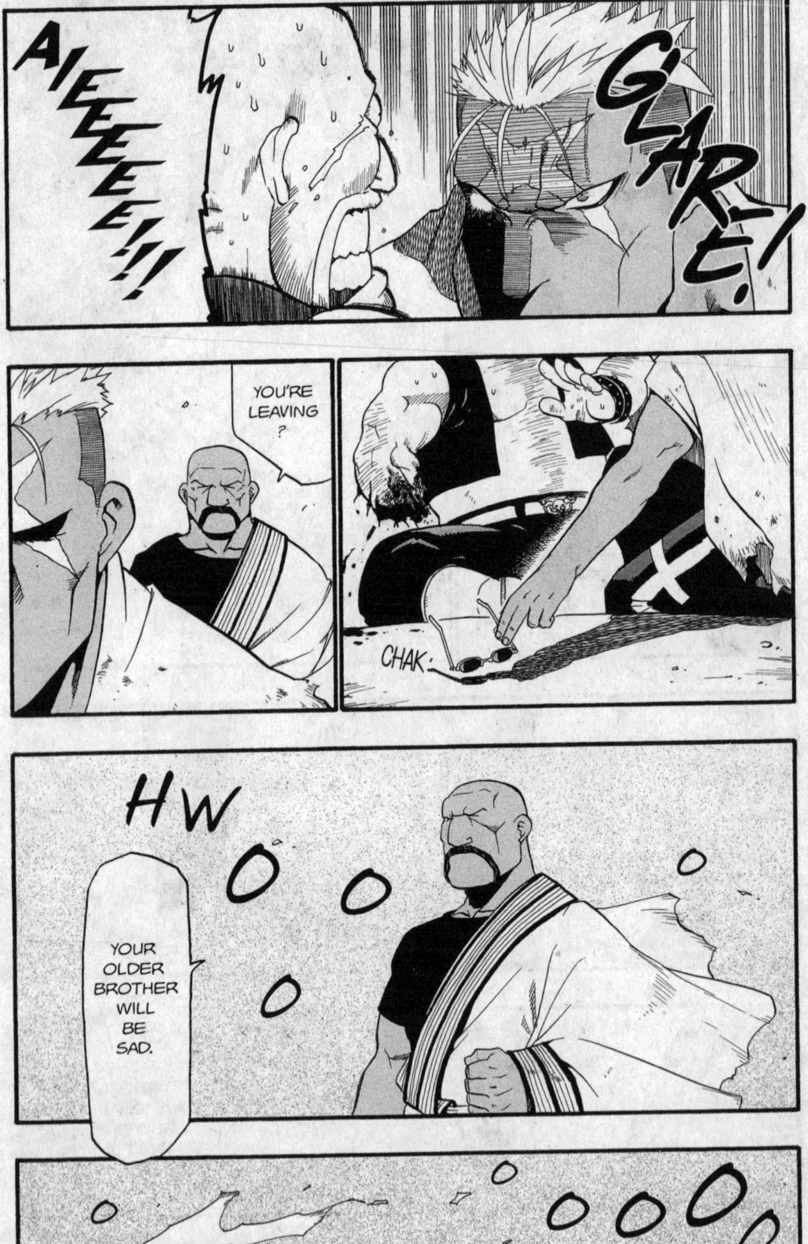
GLARE!
AIEEEEE!!!
CHAK
YOU'RE LEAVING?
HWOOO
YOUR OLDER BROTHER WILL BE SAD.
OOOOOO

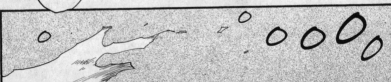

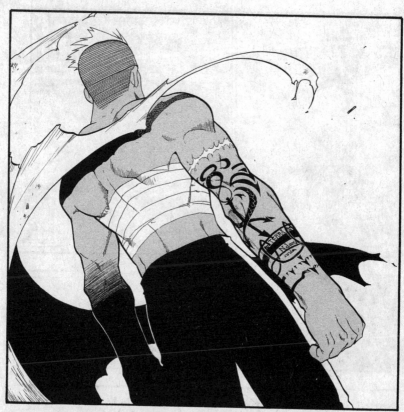

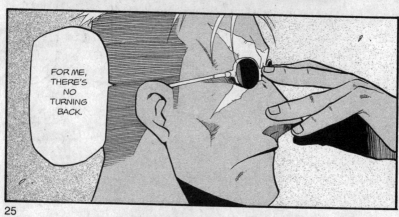

FOR ME,
THERE'S
NO
TURNING
BACK.

POF

TUP TUP

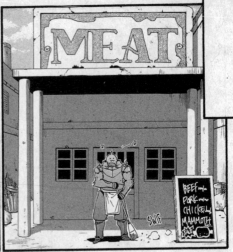

MEAT

BEEF
PORK
CHICKEN
MAMMOTH

SWIF

?

ALL
RIGHT,
WHO'S
THE
LITTER
BUG...
?

TSK

TSK

CRINK

26

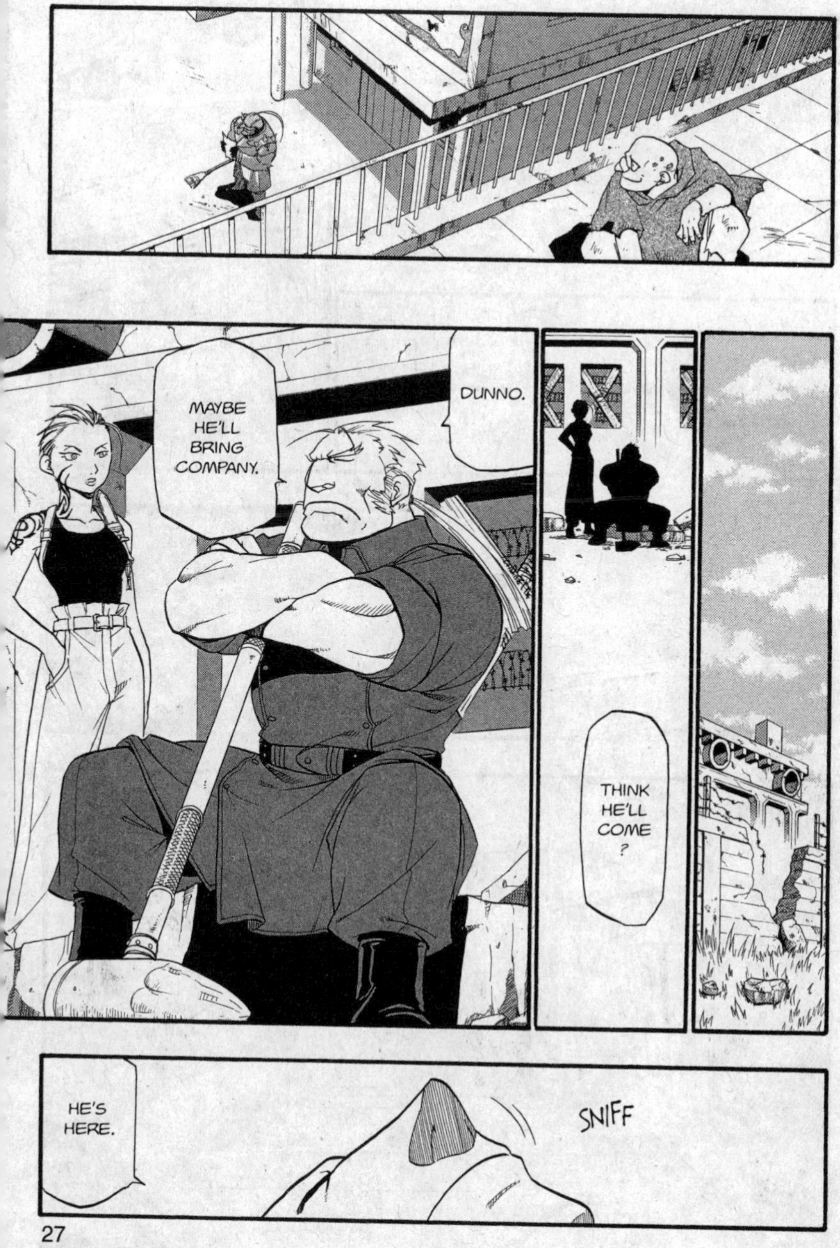
THINK HE'LL COME?
DUNNO.
MAYBE HE'LL BRING COMPANY.
SNIFF
HE'S HERE.

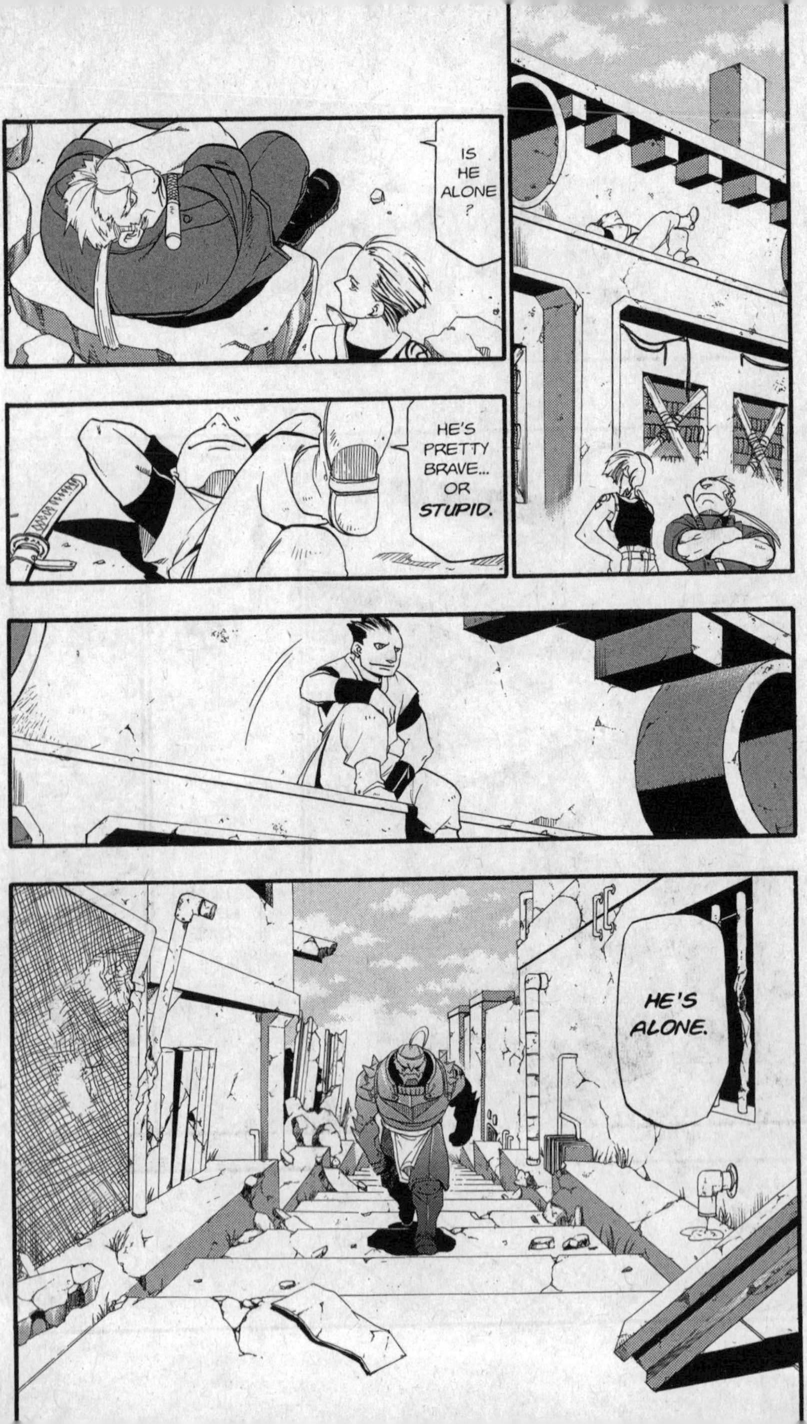
IS HE ALONE?
HE'S PRETTY BRAVE... OR STUPID.
HE'S ALONE.

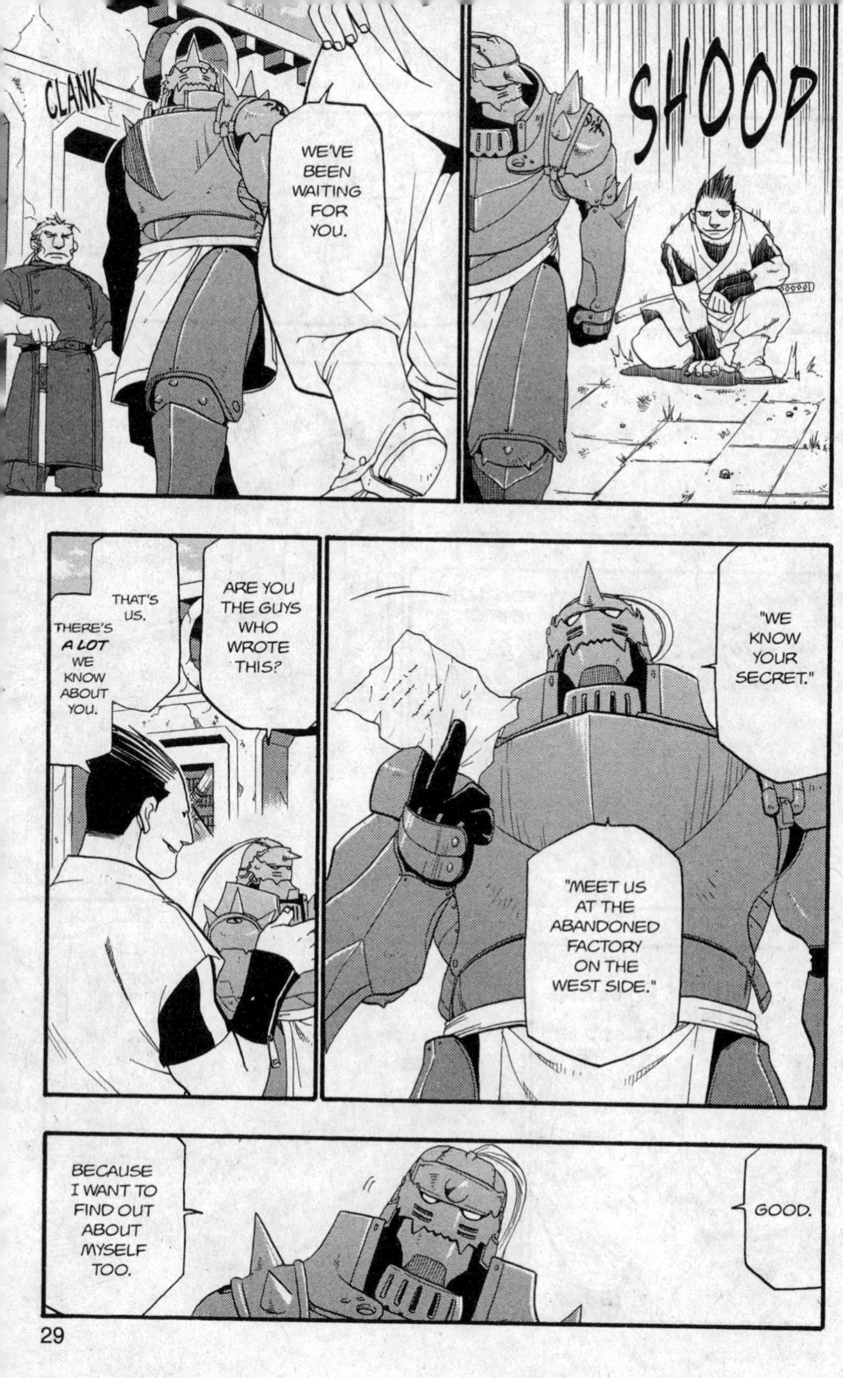

SHOOP
CLANK
WE'VE BEEN WAITING FOR YOU.
"WE KNOW YOUR SECRET."
"MEET US AT THE ABANDONED FACTORY ON THE WEST SIDE."
ARE YOU THE GUYS WHO WROTE THIS?
THAT'S US.
THERE'S ***A LOT*** WE KNOW ABOUT YOU.
GOOD.
BECAUSE I WANT TO FIND OUT ABOUT MYSELF TOO.

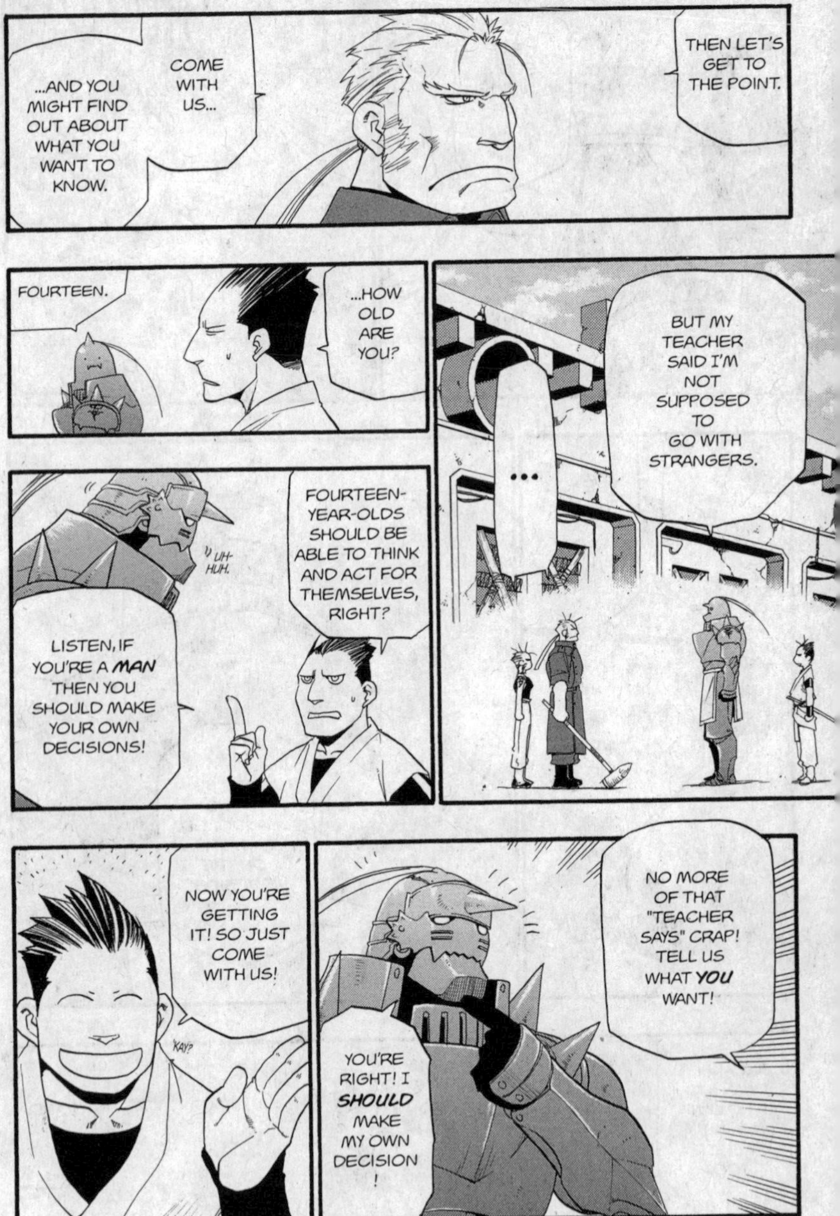
THEN LET'S GET TO THE POINT.
COME WITH US...
...AND YOU MIGHT FIND OUT ABOUT WHAT YOU WANT TO KNOW.
BUT MY TEACHER SAID I'M NOT SUPPOSED TO GO WITH STRANGERS.
...
...HOW OLD ARE YOU?
FOURTEEN.
FOURTEEN-YEAR-OLDS SHOULD BE ABLE TO THINK AND ACT FOR THEMSELVES, RIGHT?
UH-HUH.
LISTEN, IF YOU'RE A *MAN* THEN YOU SHOULD MAKE YOUR OWN DECISIONS!
NO MORE OF THAT "TEACHER SAYS" CRAP! TELL US WHAT *YOU* WANT!
YOU'RE RIGHT! I *SHOULD* MAKE MY OWN DECISION!
NOW YOU'RE GETTING IT! SO JUST COME WITH US!
'KAY?

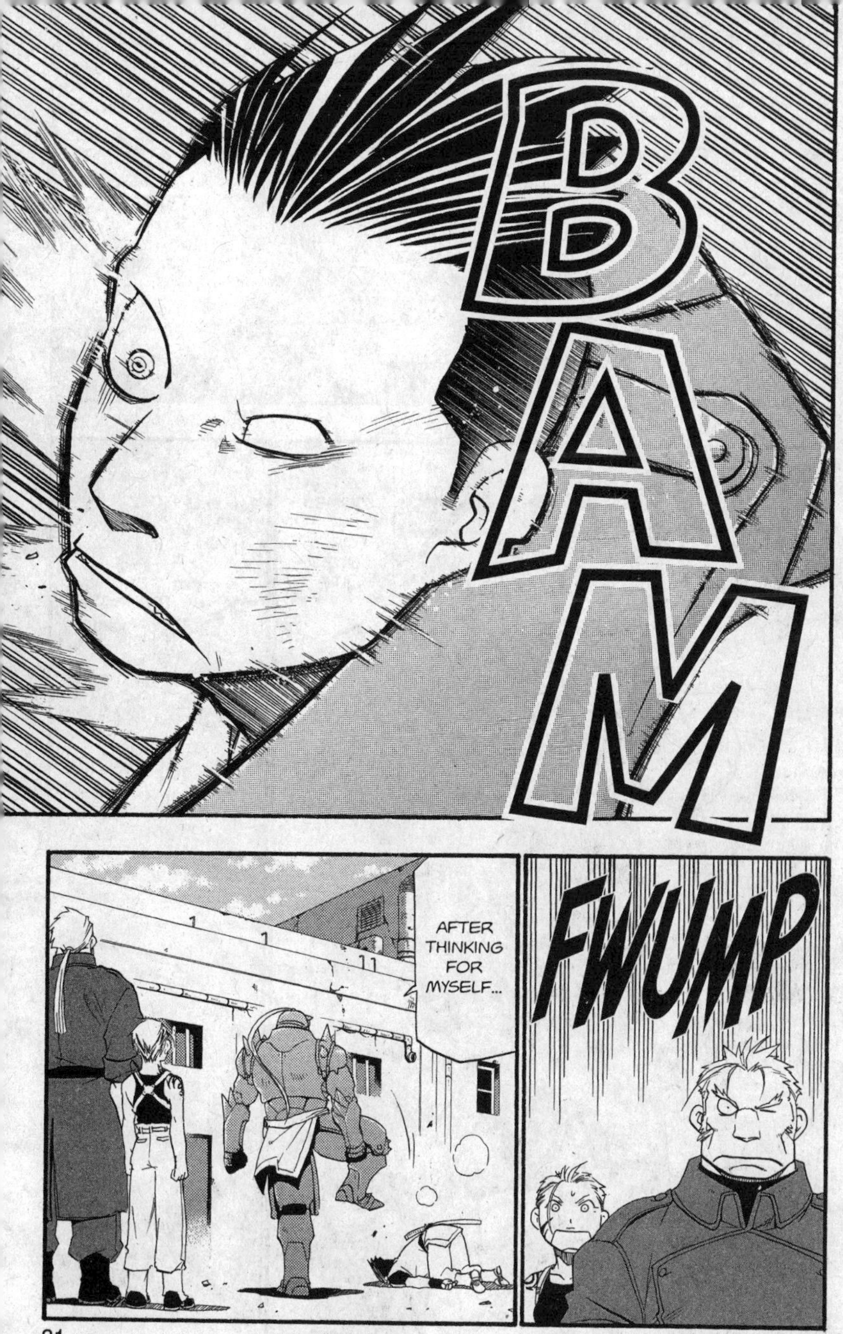
BAM
FWUMP
AFTER THINKING FOR MYSELF...

...I'VE DECIDED TO **MAKE** YOU GUYS TELL ME.

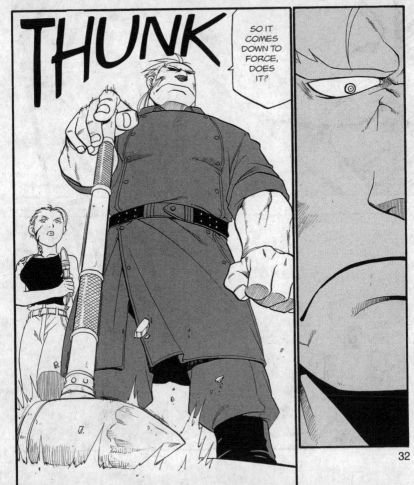

THUNK

SO IT COMES DOWN TO FORCE, DOES IT?

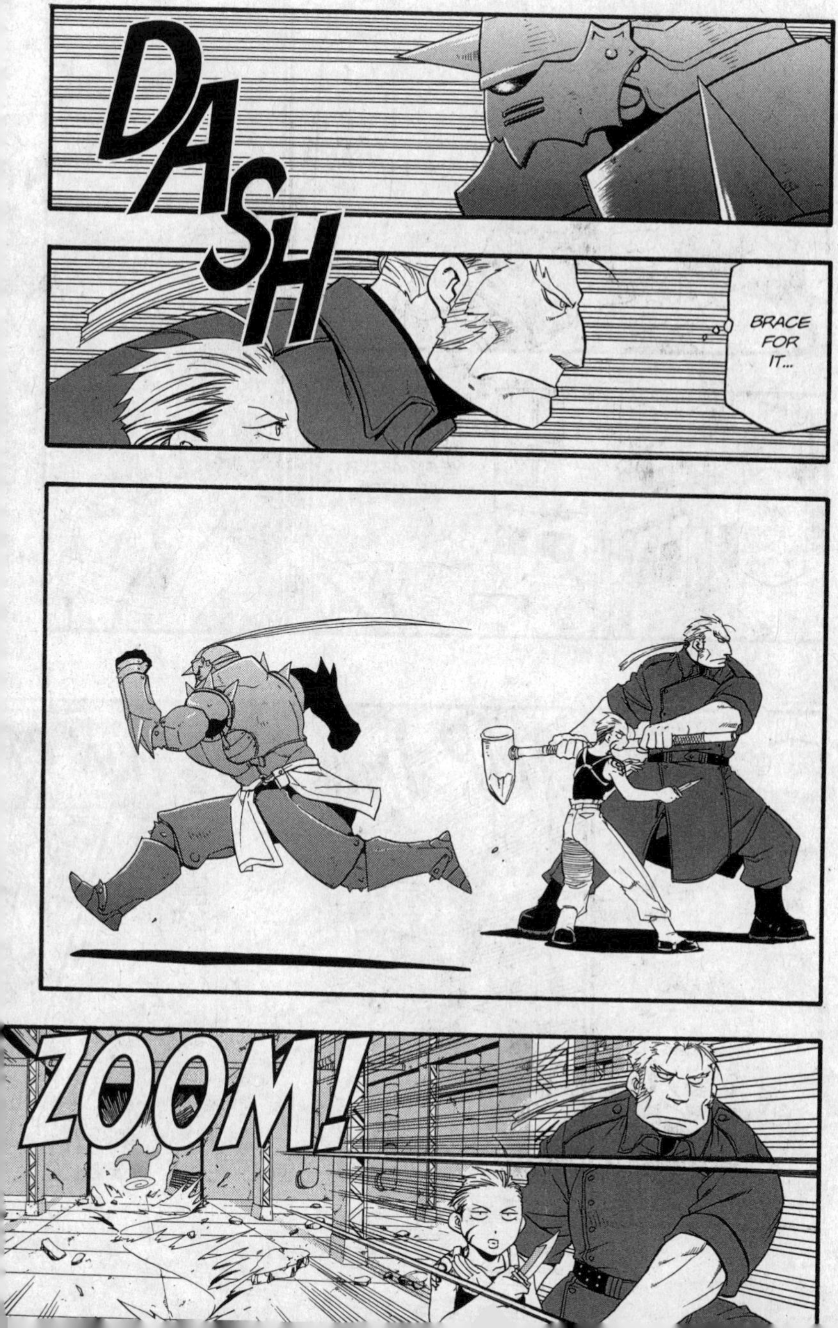
DASH
BRACE FOR IT...
ZOOM!

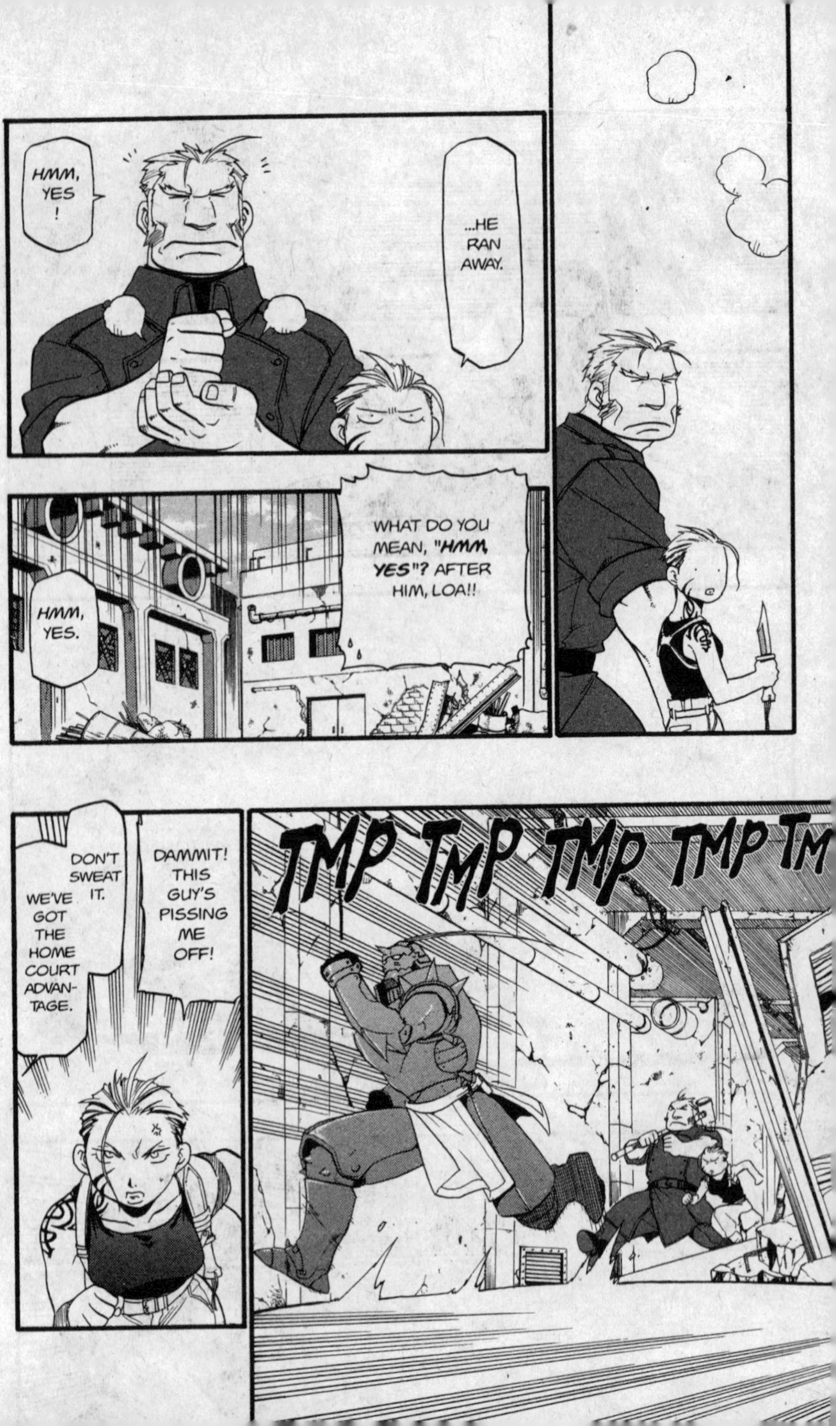
...HE RAN AWAY.
HMM, YES!
WHAT DO YOU MEAN, "HMM, YES"? AFTER HIM, LOA!!
HMM, YES.
TMP TMP TMP TMP TM
DAMMIT! THIS GUY'S PISSING ME OFF!
DON'T SWEAT IT. WE'VE GOT THE HOME COURT ADVANTAGE.

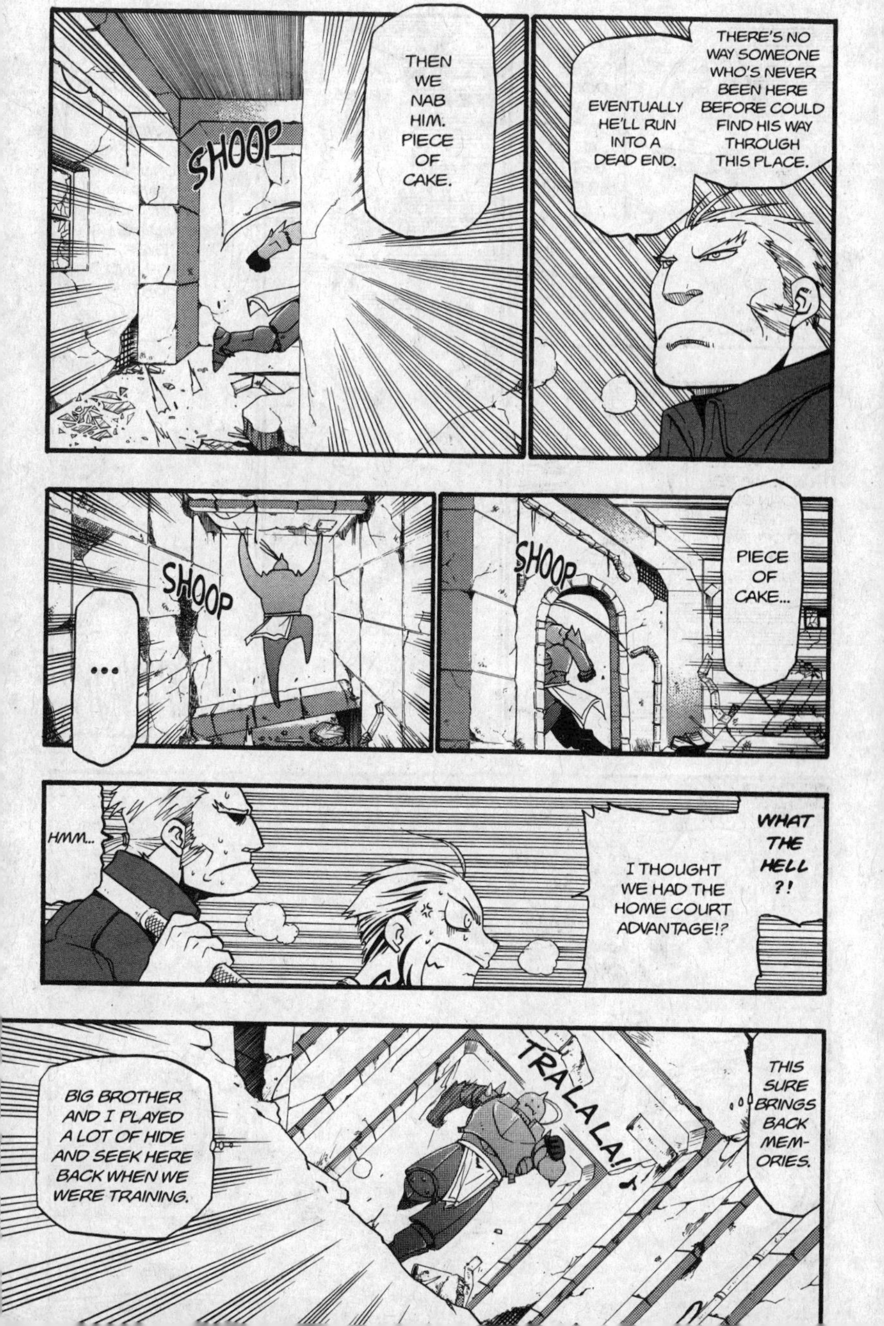
THERE'S NO WAY SOMEONE WHO'S NEVER BEEN HERE BEFORE COULD FIND HIS WAY THROUGH THIS PLACE.
EVENTUALLY HE'LL RUN INTO A DEAD END.
SHOOP
THEN WE NAB HIM. PIECE OF CAKE.
PIECE OF CAKE...
SHOOP
SHOOP
...
WHAT THE HELL?!
I THOUGHT WE HAD THE HOME COURT ADVANTAGE!?
HMM...
THIS SURE BRINGS BACK MEMORIES.
TRA LA LA! ♪
BIG BROTHER AND I PLAYED A LOT OF HIDE AND SEEK HERE BACK WHEN WE WERE TRAINING.

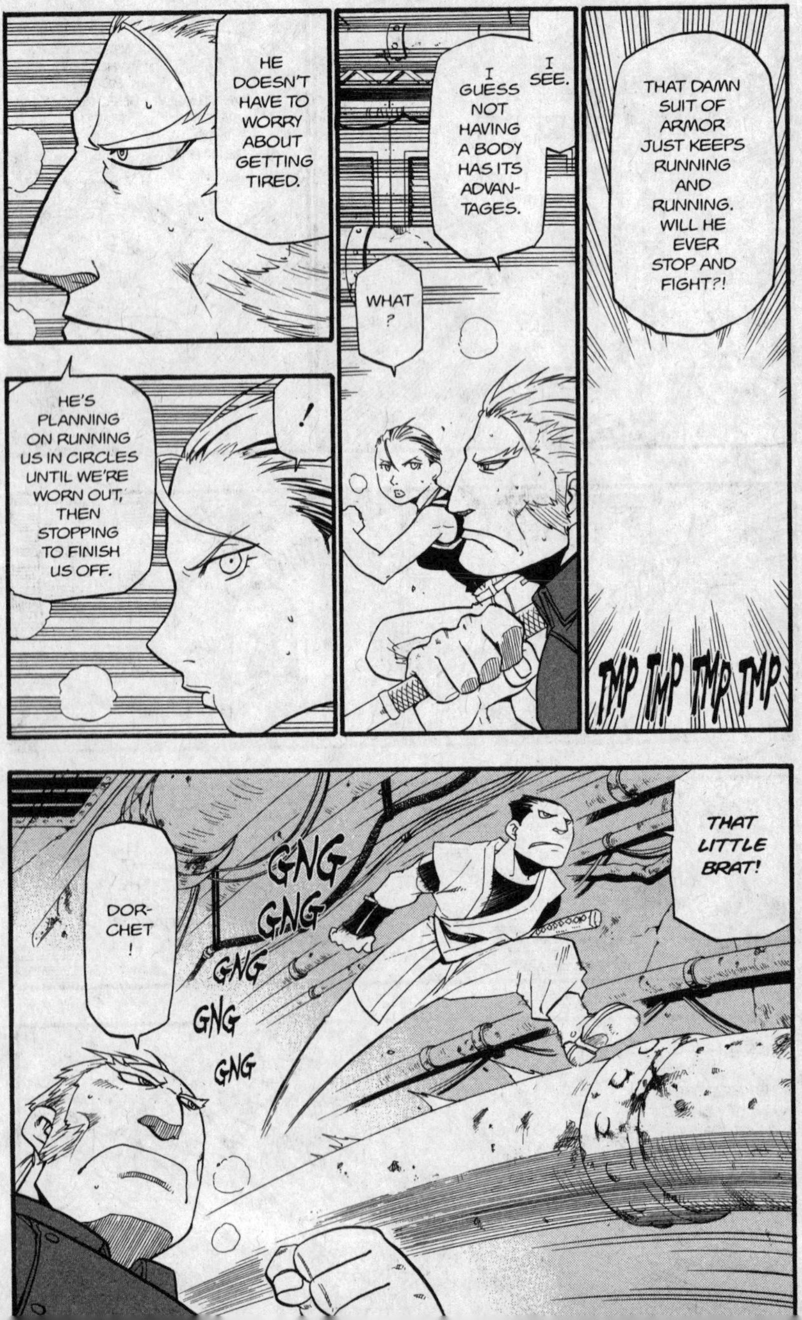
THAT DAMN SUIT OF ARMOR JUST KEEPS RUNNING AND RUNNING. WILL HE EVER STOP AND FIGHT?!
TMP TMP TMP TMP
I SEE.
I GUESS NOT HAVING A BODY HAS ITS ADVANTAGES.
WHAT?
HE DOESN'T HAVE TO WORRY ABOUT GETTING TIRED.
!
HE'S PLANNING ON RUNNING US IN CIRCLES UNTIL WE'RE WORN OUT, THEN STOPPING TO FINISH US OFF.
THAT LITTLE BRAT!
GNG
GNG
GNG
GNG
GNG
DOR-CHET!

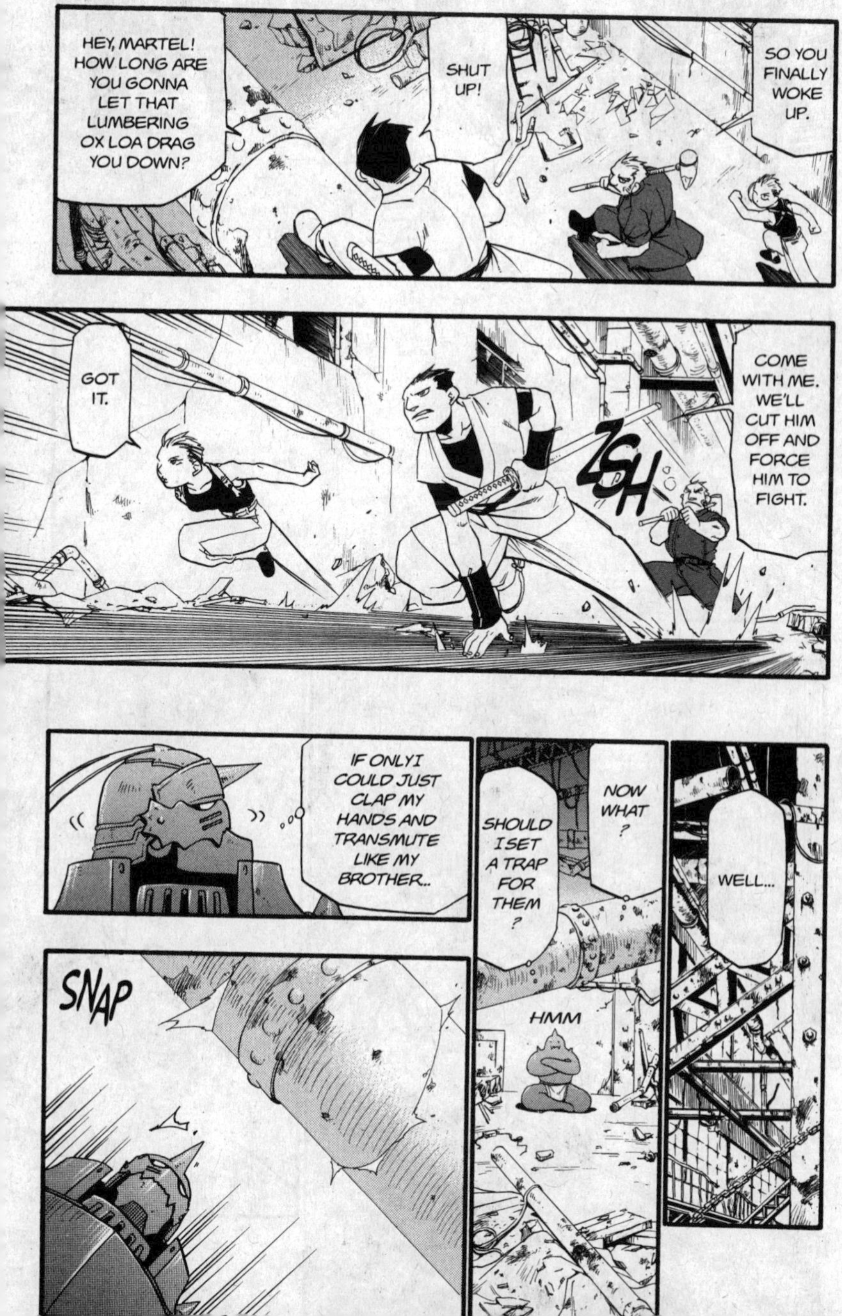
SO YOU FINALLY WOKE UP.
SHUT UP!
HEY, MARTEL! HOW LONG ARE YOU GONNA LET THAT LUMBERING OX LOA DRAG YOU DOWN?
COME WITH ME. WE'LL CUT HIM OFF AND FORCE HIM TO FIGHT.
ZSH
GOT IT.
WELL...
NOW WHAT?
SHOULD I SET A TRAP FOR THEM?
HMM
IF ONLY I COULD JUST CLAP MY HANDS AND TRANSMUTE LIKE MY BROTHER..
SNAP

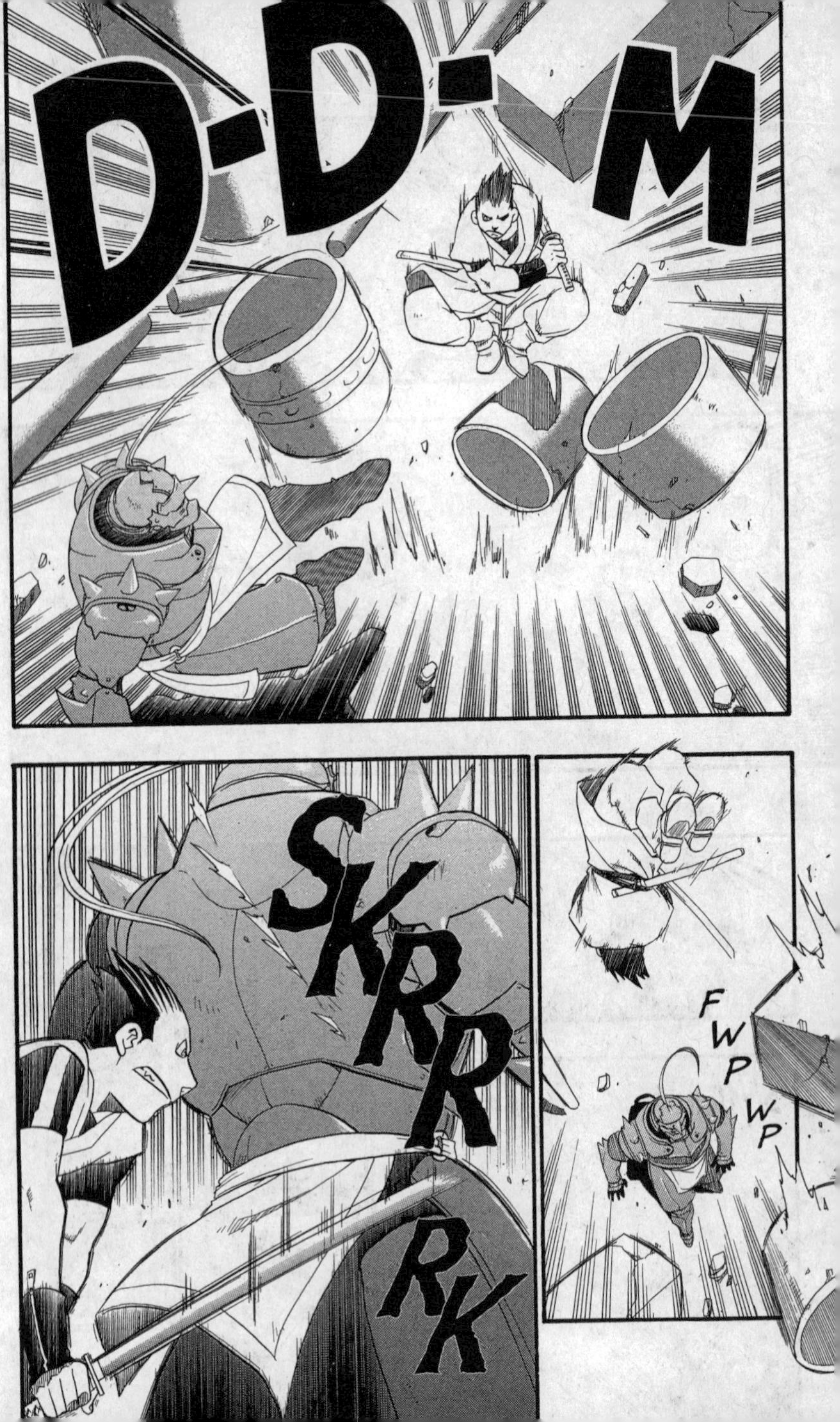
D-D-M
FWP WP
SKRRRK

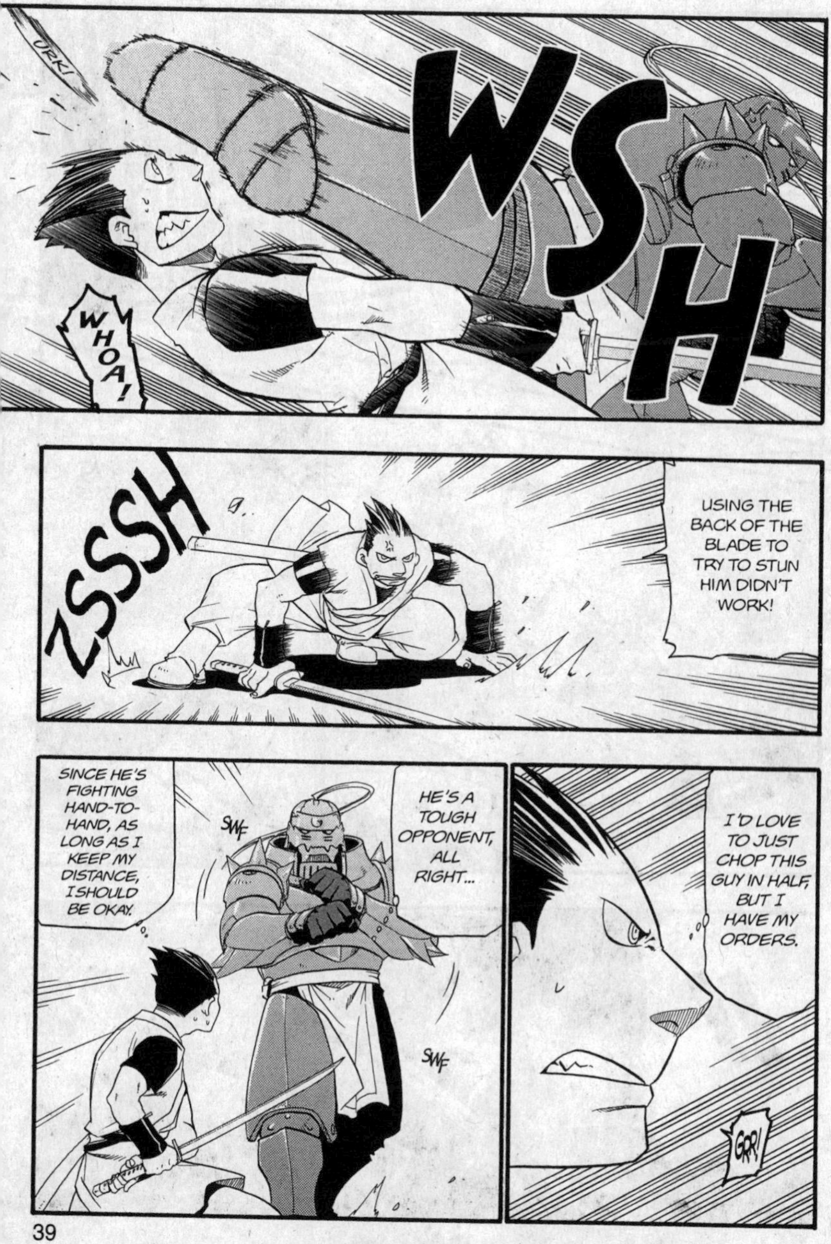
WSH
URK!
WHOA!
USING THE BACK OF THE BLADE TO TRY TO STUN HIM DIDN'T WORK!
ZSSSH
I'D LOVE TO JUST CHOP THIS GUY IN HALF, BUT I HAVE MY ORDERS.
GRR!
HE'S A TOUGH OPPONENT, ALL RIGHT...
SWF
SINCE HE'S FIGHTING HAND-TO-HAND, AS LONG AS I KEEP MY DISTANCE, I SHOULD BE OKAY.
SWF

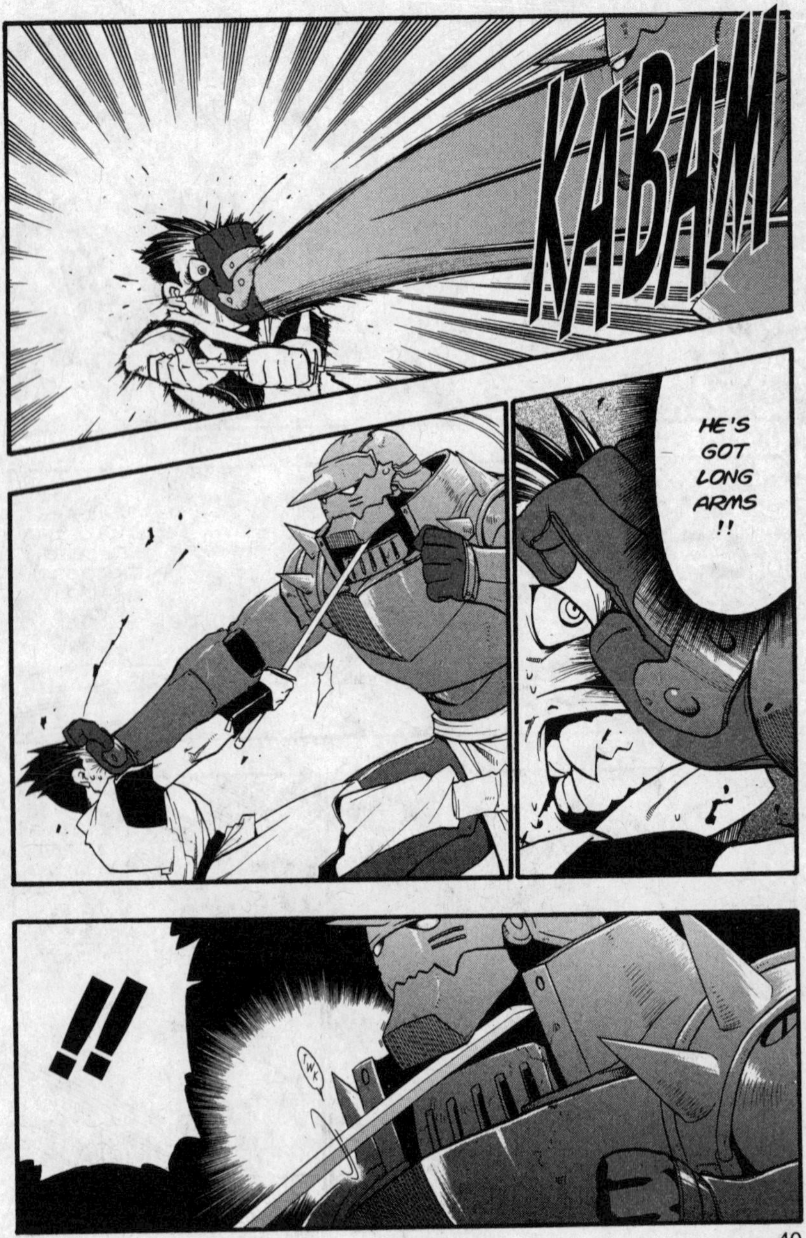
KABAM
HE'S GOT LONG ARMS !!
!!
TWK

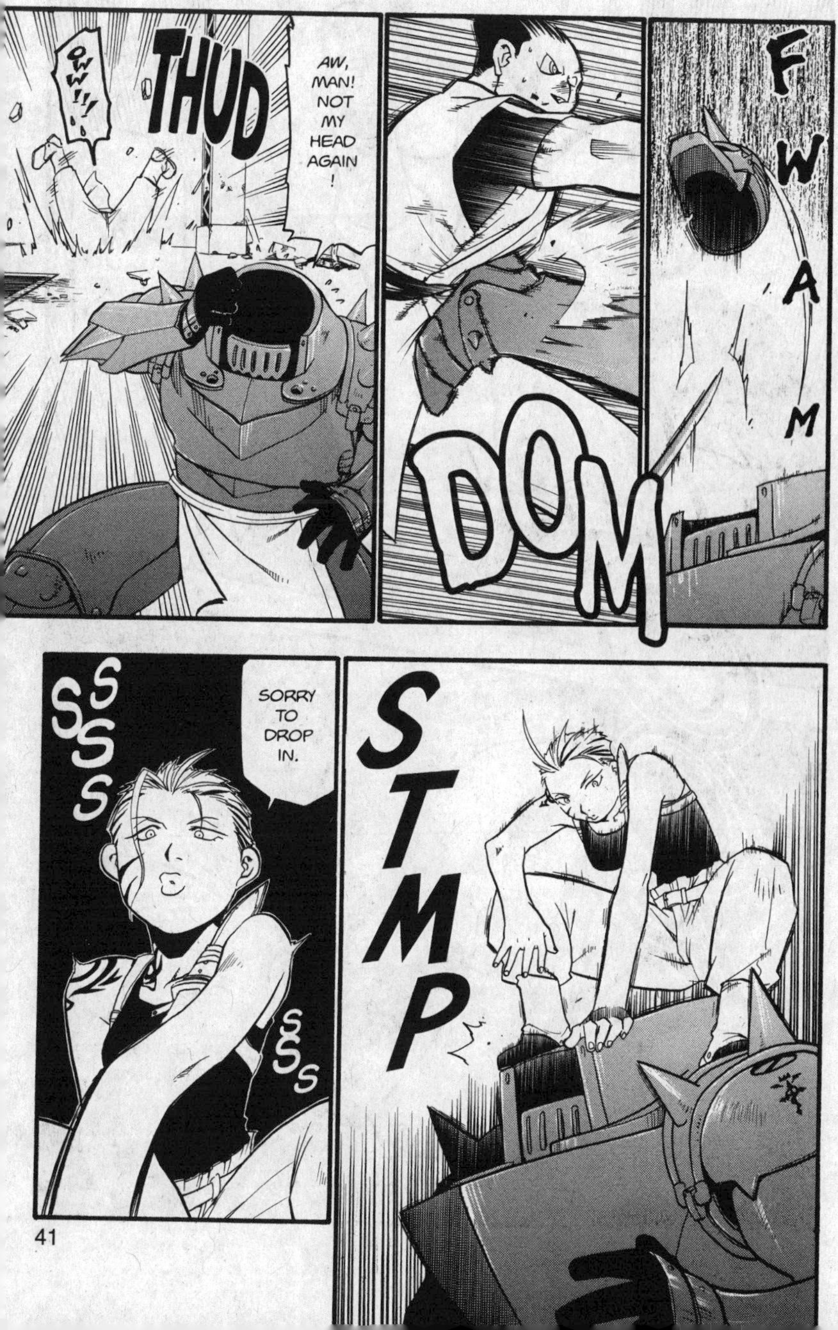
FWAM
DOM
AW, MAN! NOT MY HEAD AGAIN!
THUD
OWW!!!
STMP
SORRY TO DROP IN.
SSSS
SSS

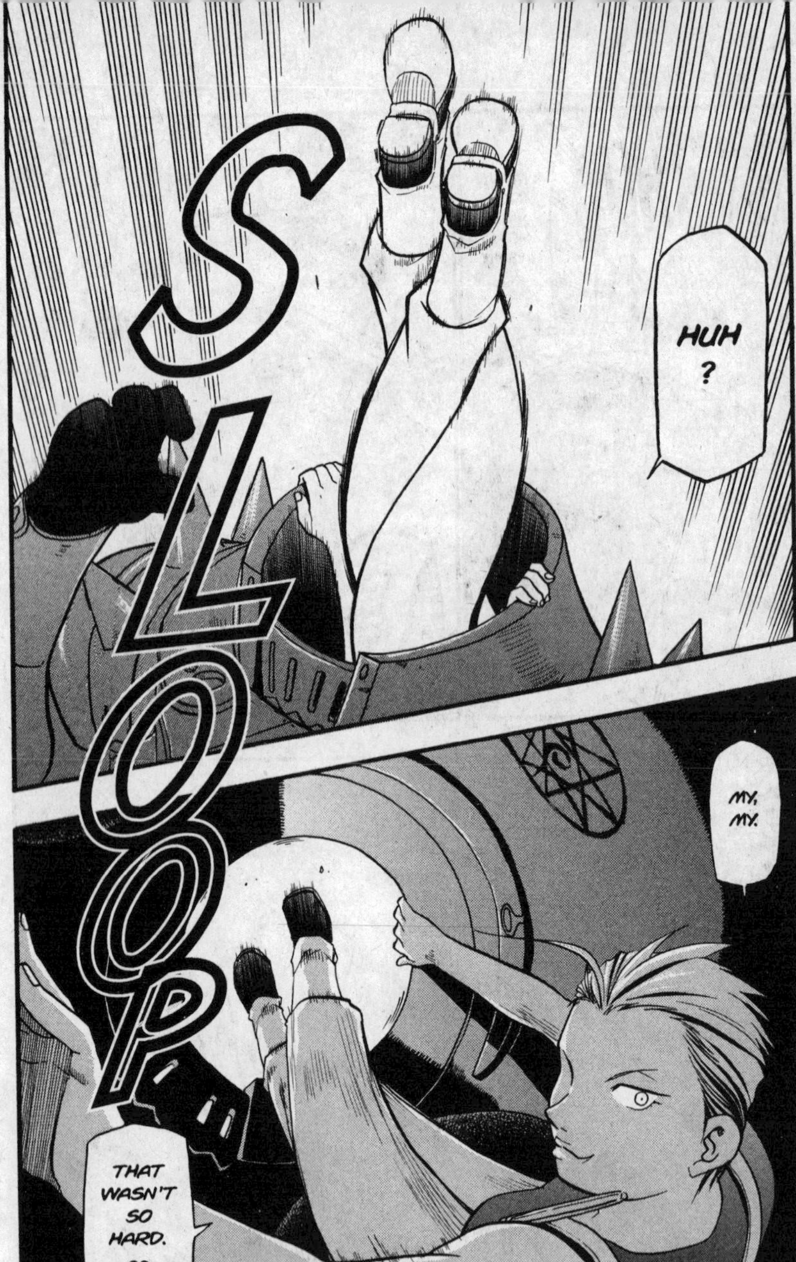
HUH ?
SLOOP
MY, MY.
THAT WASN'T SO HARD. ♡

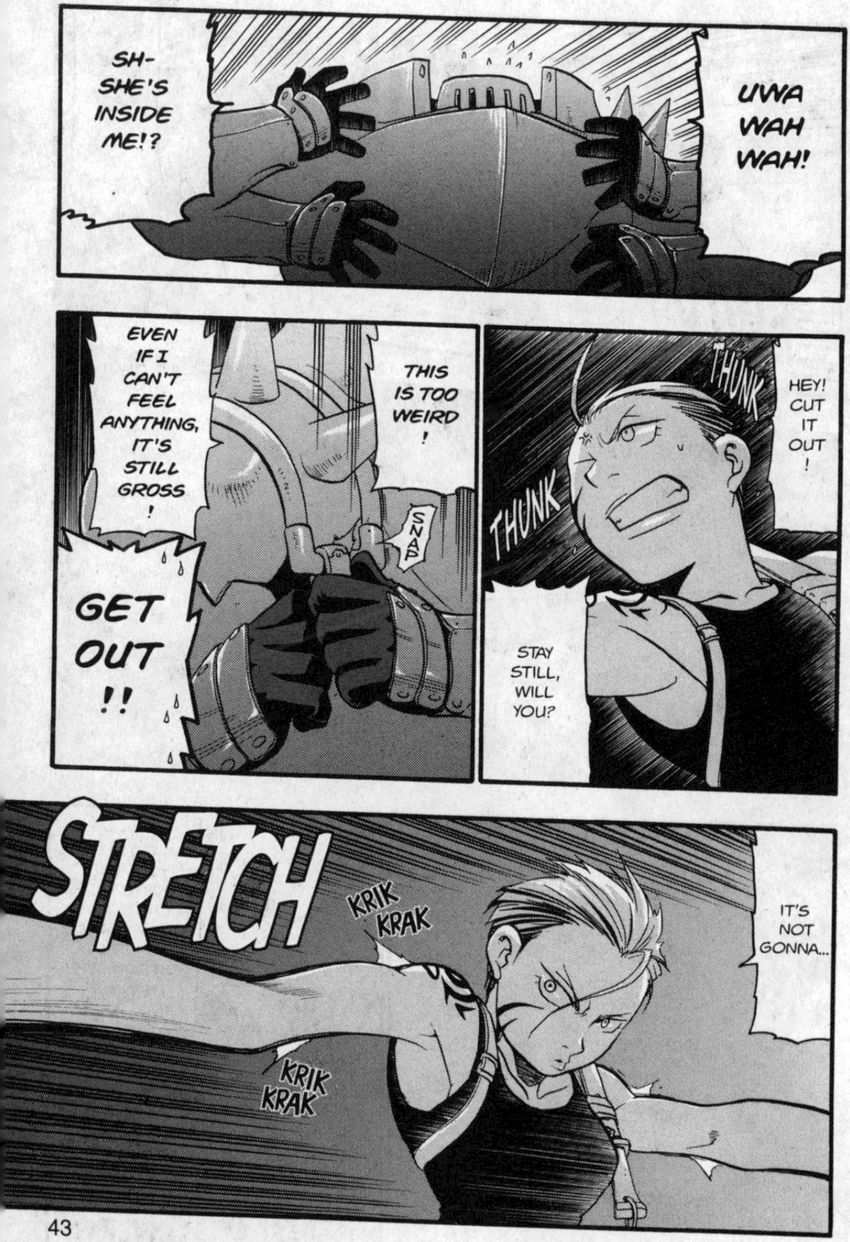
UWA WAH WAH!
SH-SHE'S INSIDE ME!?
THUNK
HEY! CUT IT OUT!
THUNK
STAY STILL, WILL YOU?
THIS IS TOO WEIRD!
EVEN IF I CAN'T FEEL ANYTHING, IT'S STILL GROSS!
SNAP
GET OUT!!
IT'S NOT GONNA...
STRETCH
KRIK KRAK
KRIK KRAK

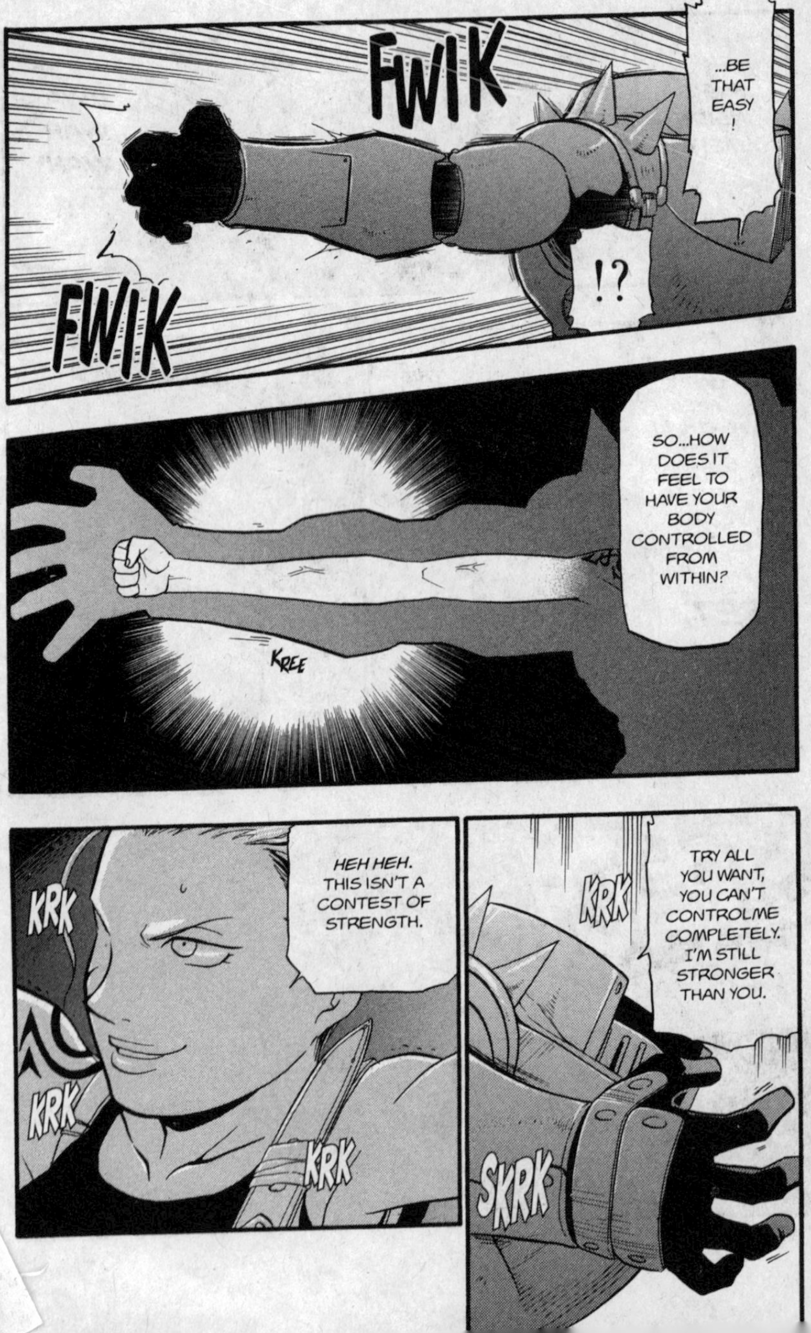
...BE THAT EASY!
FWIK
FWIK
!?
SO...HOW DOES IT FEEL TO HAVE YOUR BODY CONTROLLED FROM WITHIN?
KREE
TRY ALL YOU WANT, YOU CAN'T CONTROLME COMPLETELY. I'M STILL STRONGER THAN YOU.
KRK
SKRK
HEH HEH. THIS ISN'T A CONTEST OF STRENGTH.
KRK
KRK
KRK

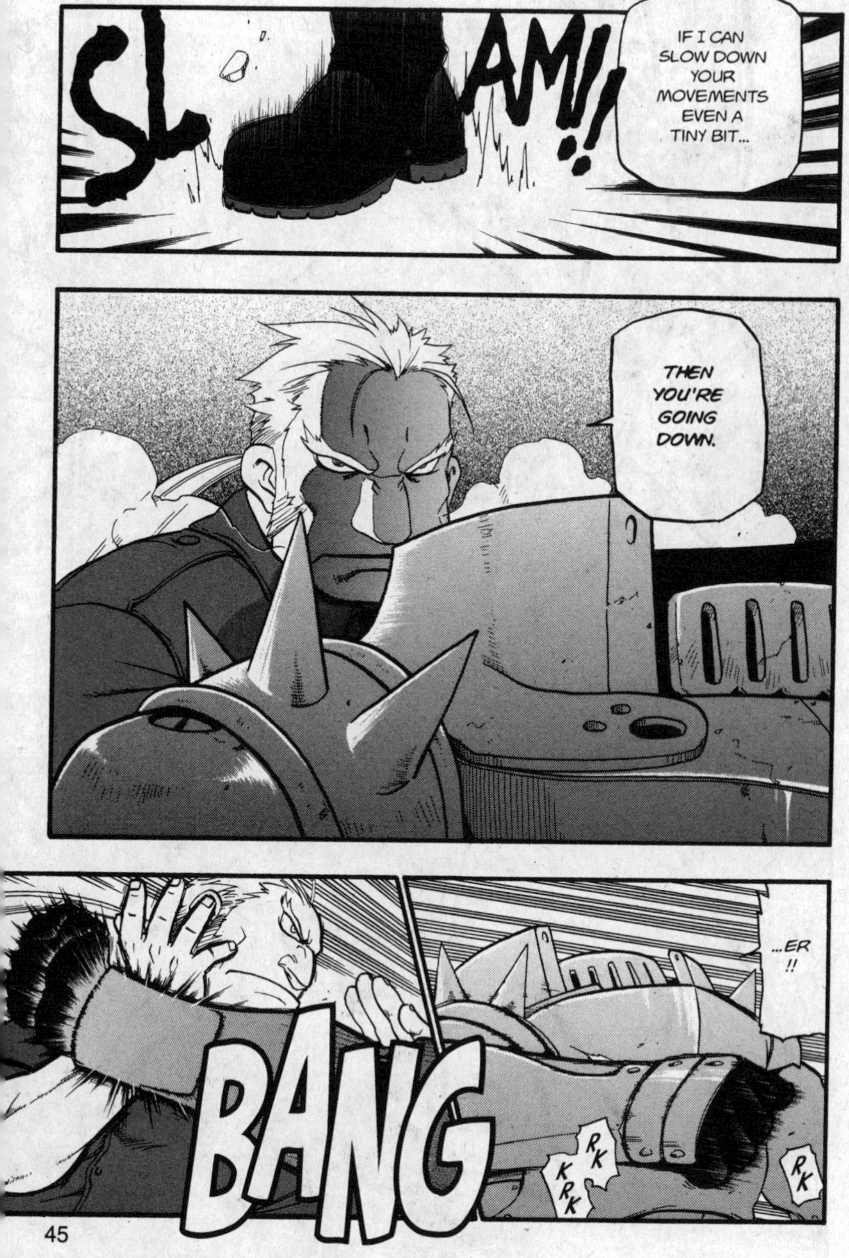
IF I CAN SLOW DOWN YOUR MOVEMENTS EVEN A TINY BIT...
SL AM!!
THEN YOU'RE GOING DOWN.
...ER !!
BANG
RK
RK KRK

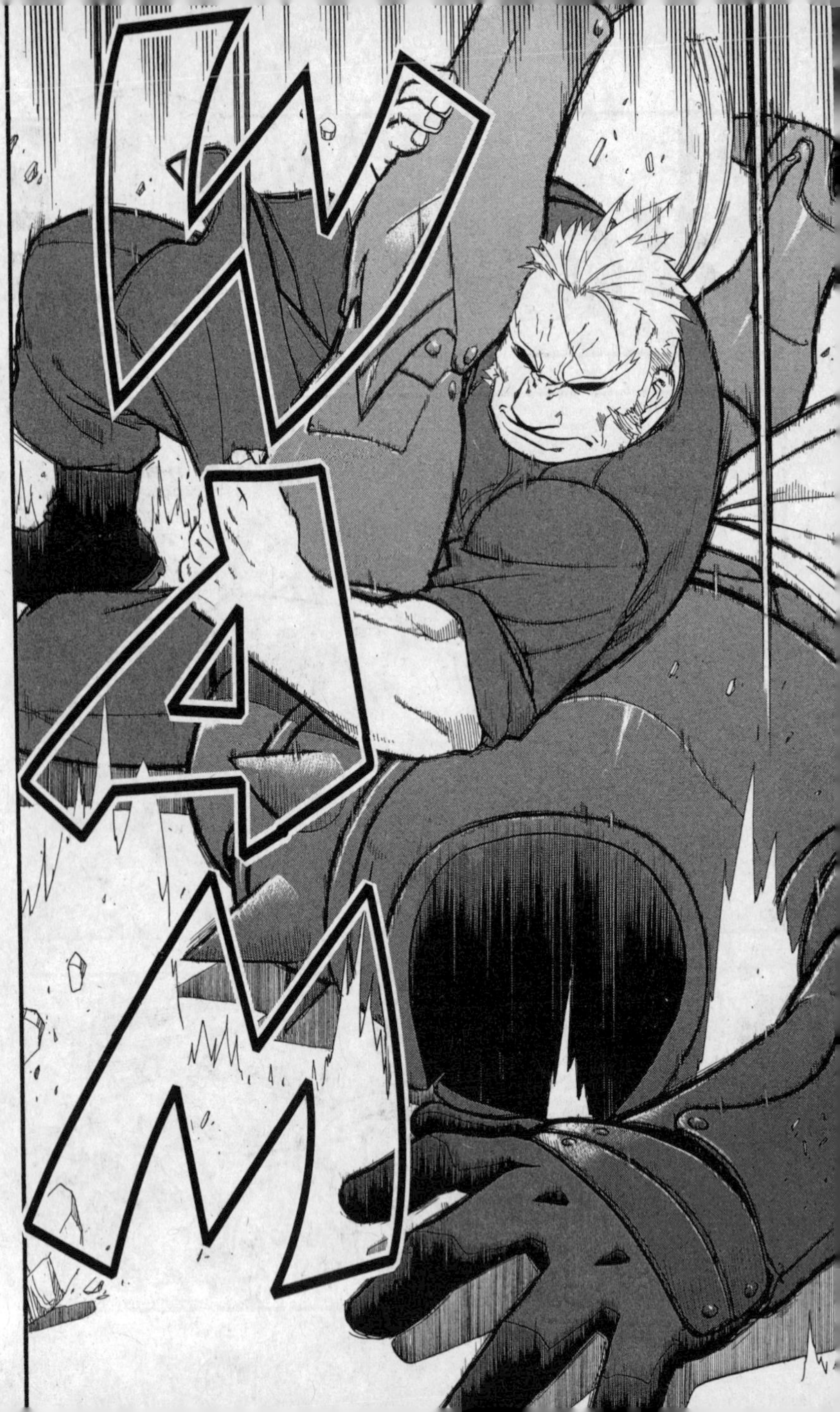
WAM

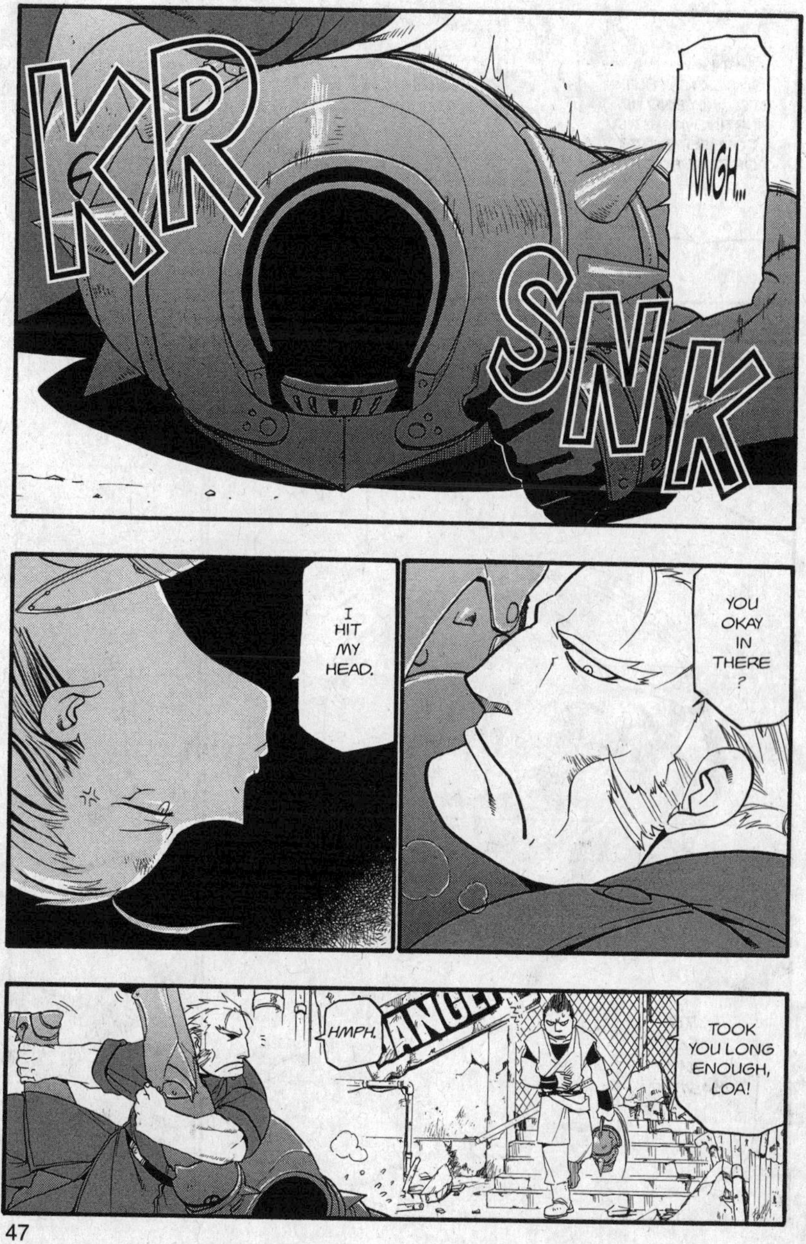
NNGH...
KR
SNK
YOU OKAY IN THERE?
I HIT MY HEAD.
TOOK YOU LONG ENOUGH, LOA!
HMPH.

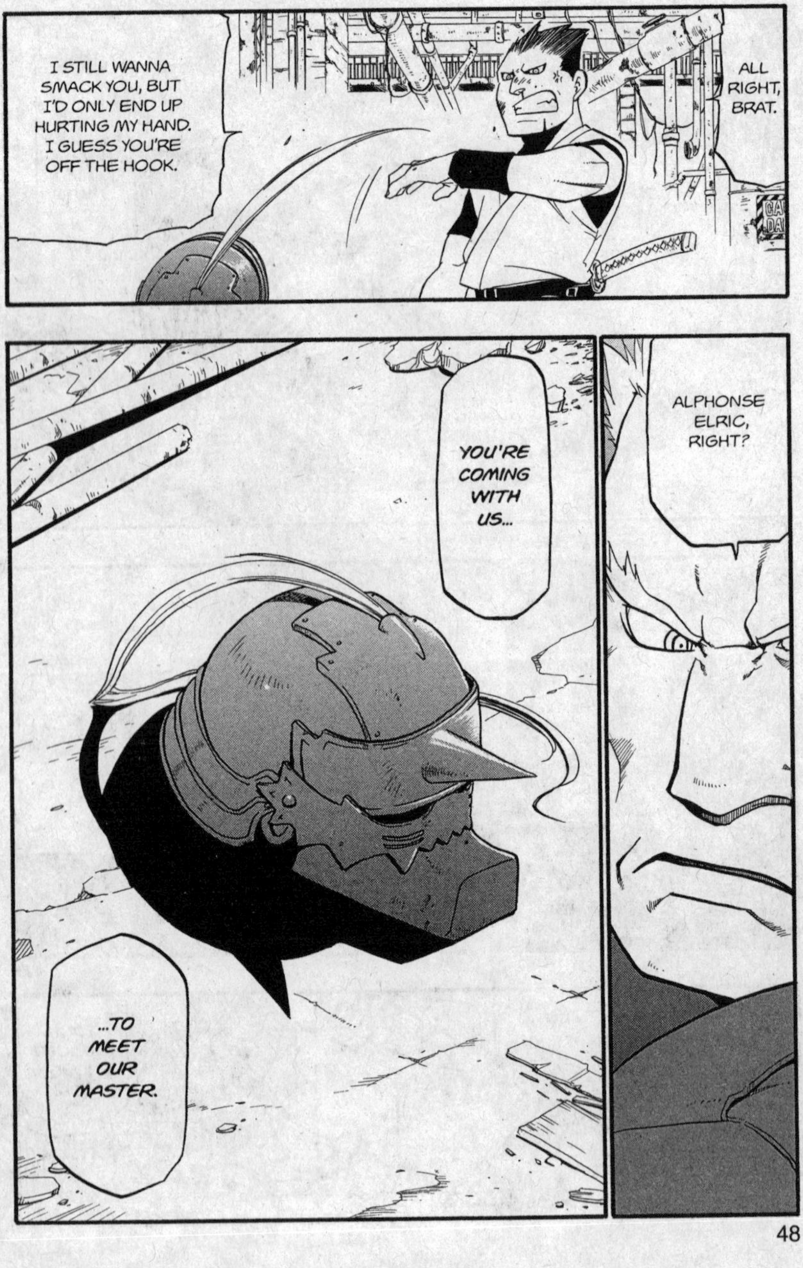
ALL RIGHT, BRAT.
I STILL WANNA SMACK YOU, BUT I'D ONLY END UP HURTING MY HAND. I GUESS YOU'RE OFF THE HOOK.
ALPHONSE ELRIC, RIGHT?
YOU'RE COMING WITH US...
...TO MEET OUR MASTER.

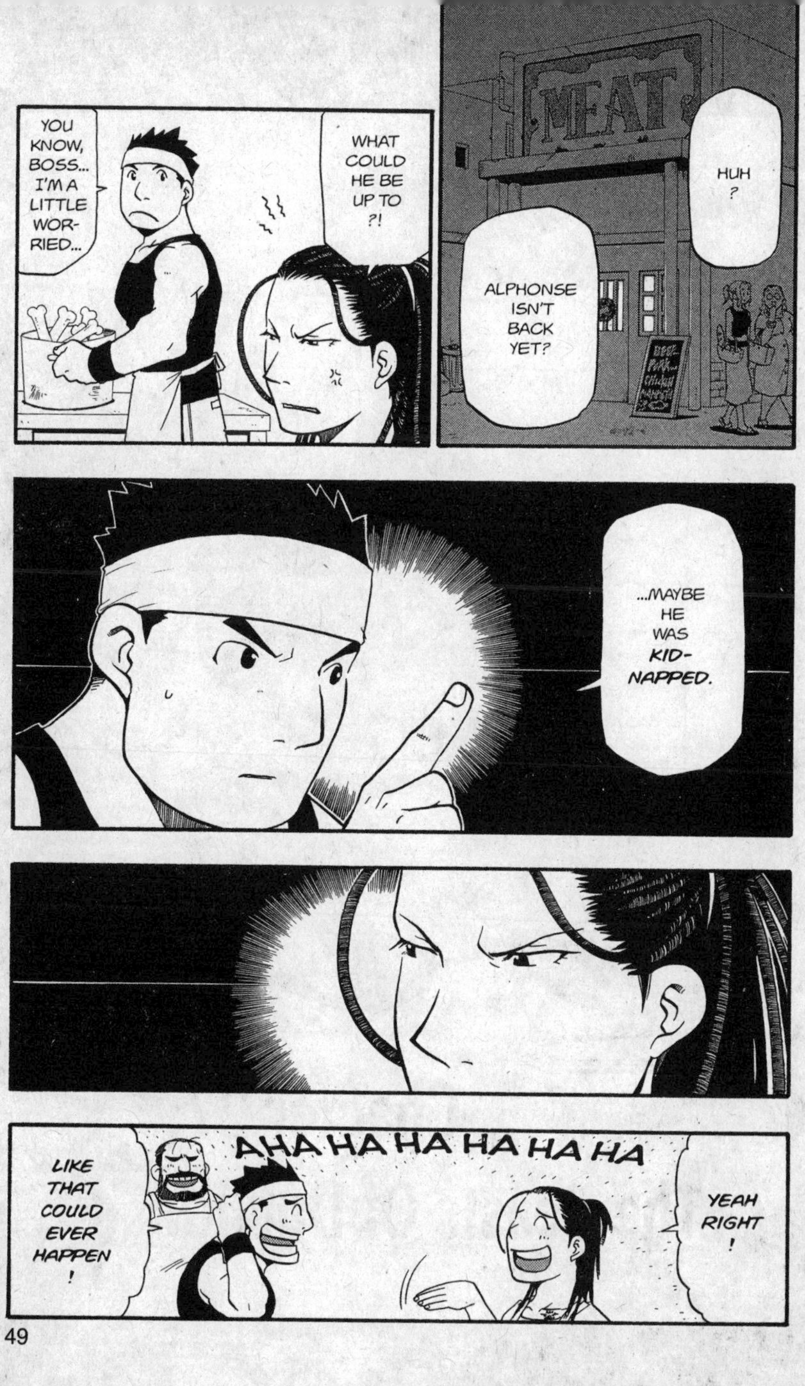
MEAT
HUH?
ALPHONSE ISN'T BACK YET?
WHAT COULD HE BE UP TO?!
YOU KNOW, BOSS... I'M A LITTLE WORRIED...
...MAYBE HE WAS KIDNAPPED.
AHA HA HA HA HA HA HA
YEAH RIGHT!
LIKE THAT COULD EVER HAPPEN!

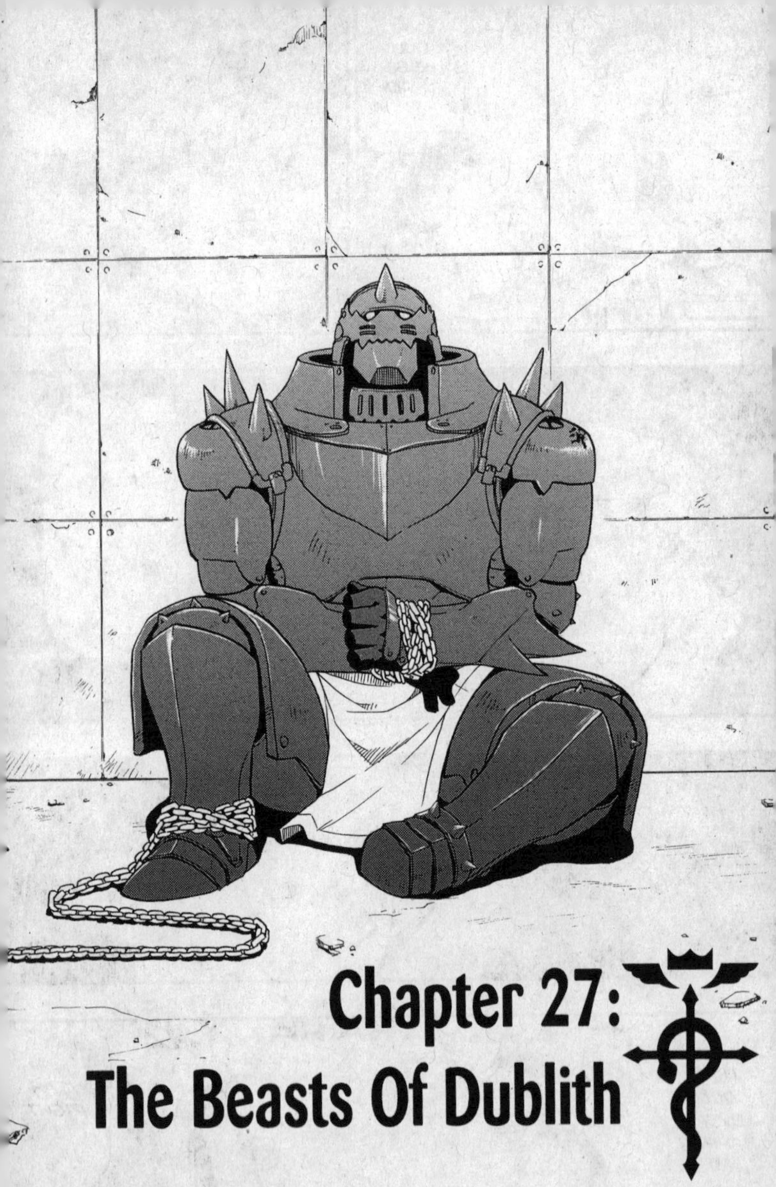

Chapter 27: The Beasts Of Dublith

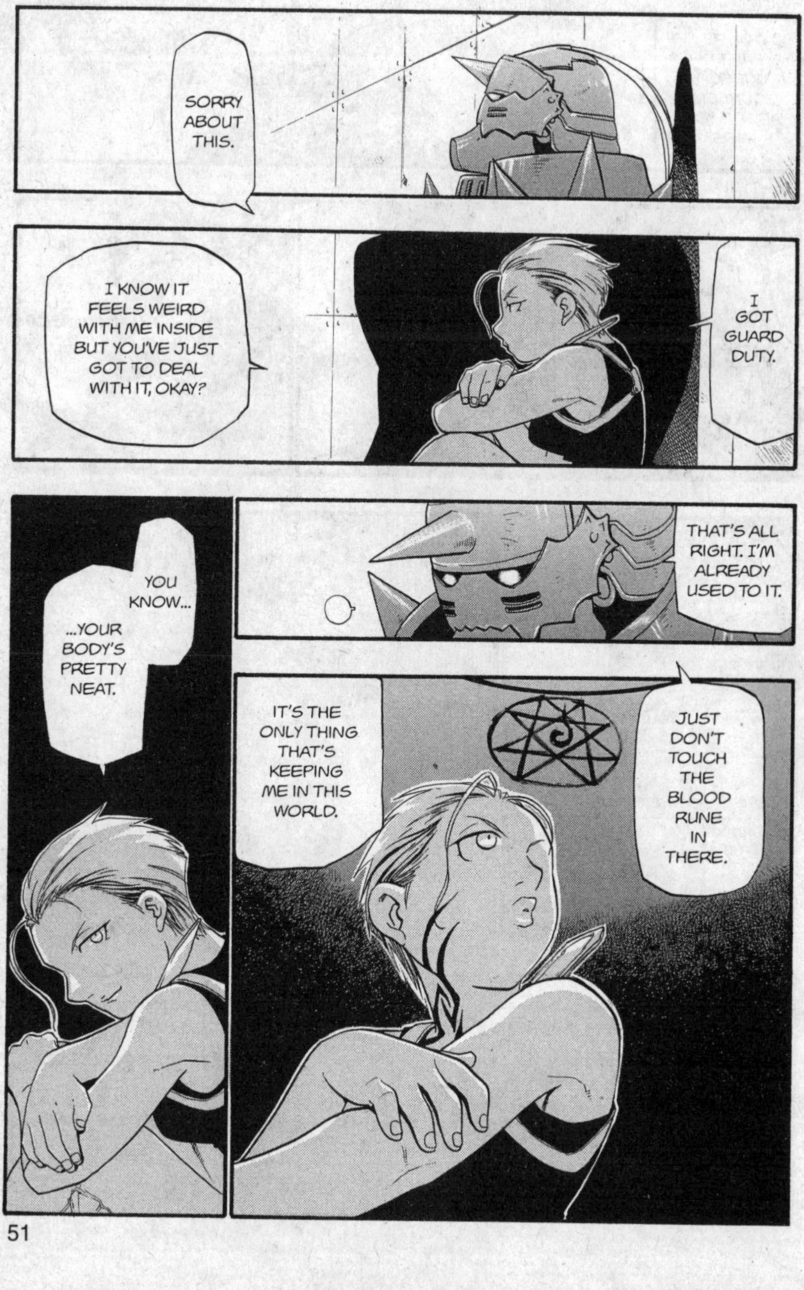
SORRY ABOUT THIS.
I GOT GUARD DUTY.
I KNOW IT FEELS WEIRD WITH ME INSIDE BUT YOU'VE JUST GOT TO DEAL WITH IT, OKAY?
THAT'S ALL RIGHT. I'M ALREADY USED TO IT.
JUST DON'T TOUCH THE BLOOD RUNE IN THERE.
IT'S THE ONLY THING THAT'S KEEPING ME IN THIS WORLD.
YOU KNOW...
...YOUR BODY'S PRETTY NEAT.

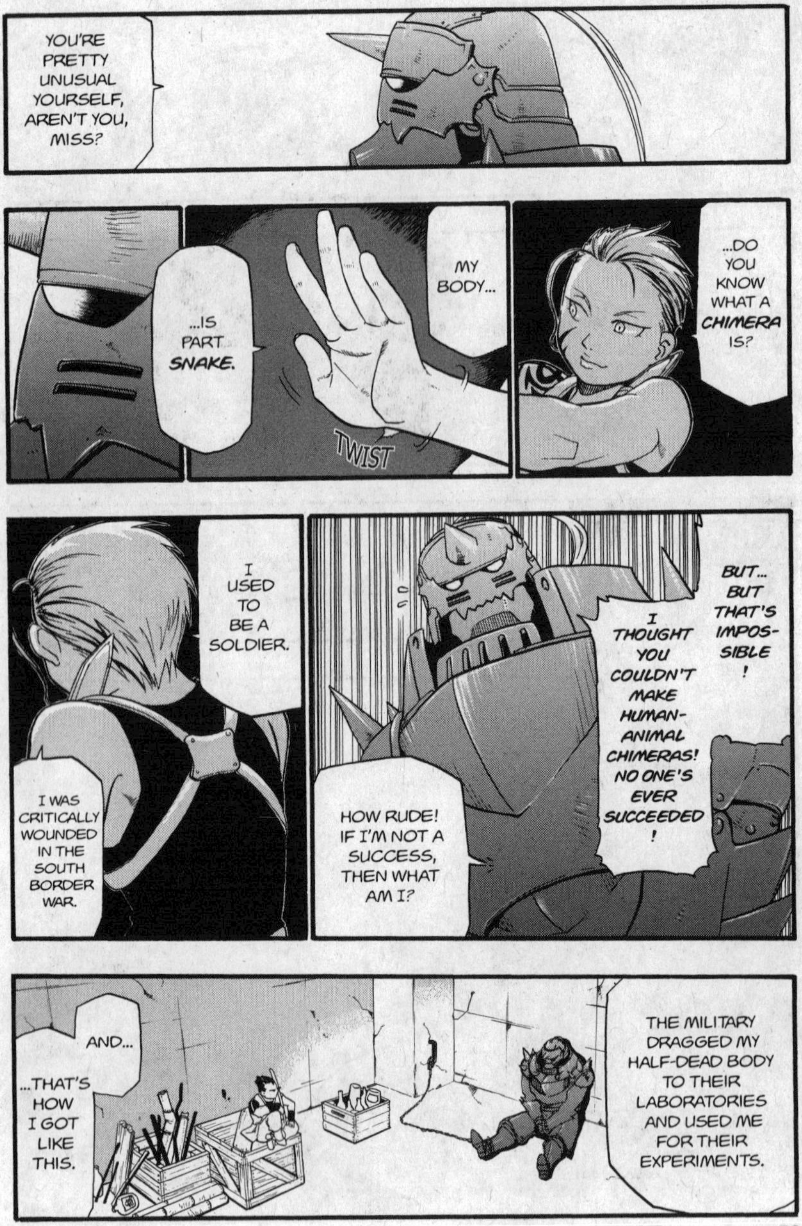
YOU'RE PRETTY UNUSUAL YOURSELF, AREN'T YOU, MISS?
...DO YOU KNOW WHAT A CHIMERA IS?
MY BODY...
...IS PART SNAKE.
TWIST
BUT... BUT THAT'S IMPOSSIBLE!
I THOUGHT YOU COULDN'T MAKE HUMAN-ANIMAL CHIMERAS! NO ONE'S EVER SUCCEEDED!
HOW RUDE! IF I'M NOT A SUCCESS, THEN WHAT AM I?
I USED TO BE A SOLDIER.
I WAS CRITICALLY WOUNDED IN THE SOUTH BORDER WAR.
THE MILITARY DRAGGED MY HALF-DEAD BODY TO THEIR LABORATORIES AND USED ME FOR THEIR EXPERIMENTS.
AND...
...THAT'S HOW I GOT LIKE THIS.

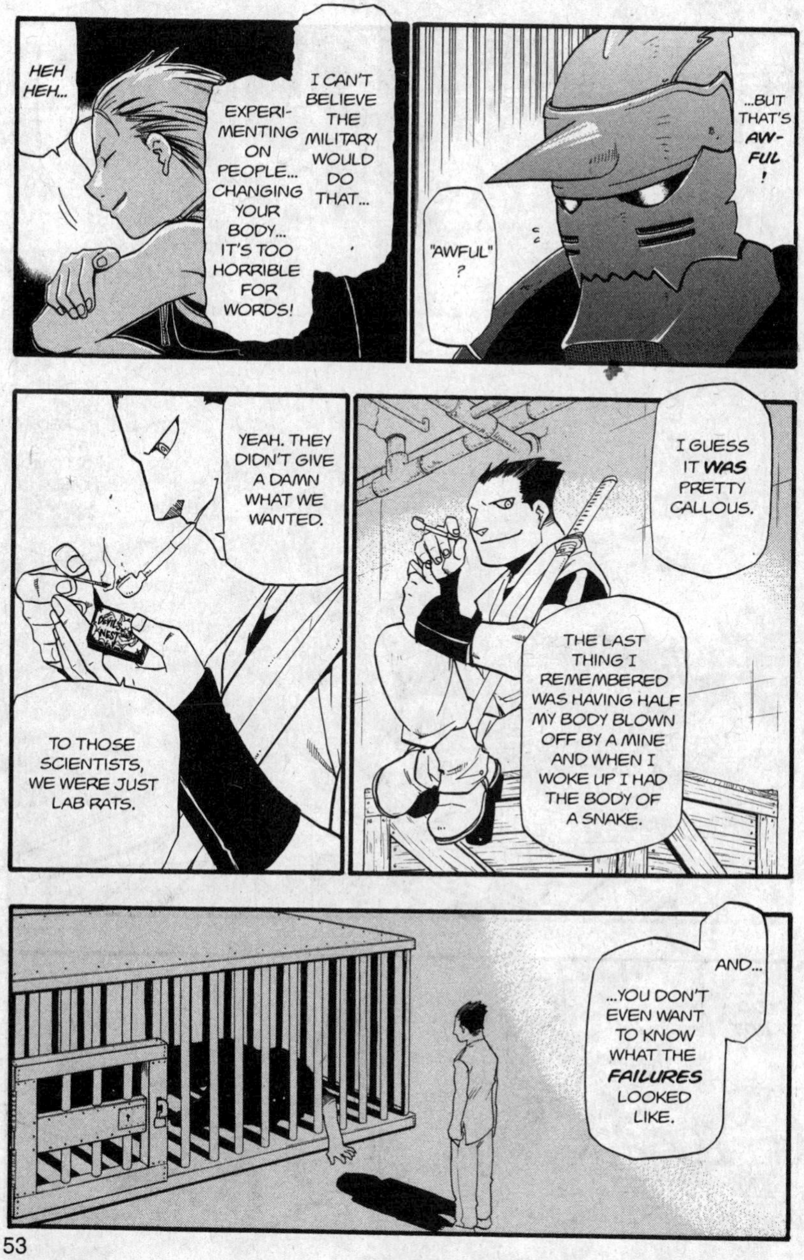
...BUT THAT'S **AWFUL**!
"AWFUL"?
I CAN'T BELIEVE THE MILITARY WOULD DO THAT...
EXPERIMENTING ON PEOPLE... CHANGING YOUR BODY... IT'S TOO HORRIBLE FOR WORDS!
HEH HEH...
I GUESS IT **WAS** PRETTY CALLOUS.
THE LAST THING I REMEMBERED WAS HAVING HALF MY BODY BLOWN OFF BY A MINE AND WHEN I WOKE UP I HAD THE BODY OF A SNAKE.
YEAH. THEY DIDN'T GIVE A DAMN WHAT WE WANTED.
DEVIL'S NEST
TO THOSE SCIENTISTS, WE WERE JUST LAB RATS.
AND...
...YOU DON'T EVEN WANT TO KNOW WHAT THE **FAILURES** LOOKED LIKE.

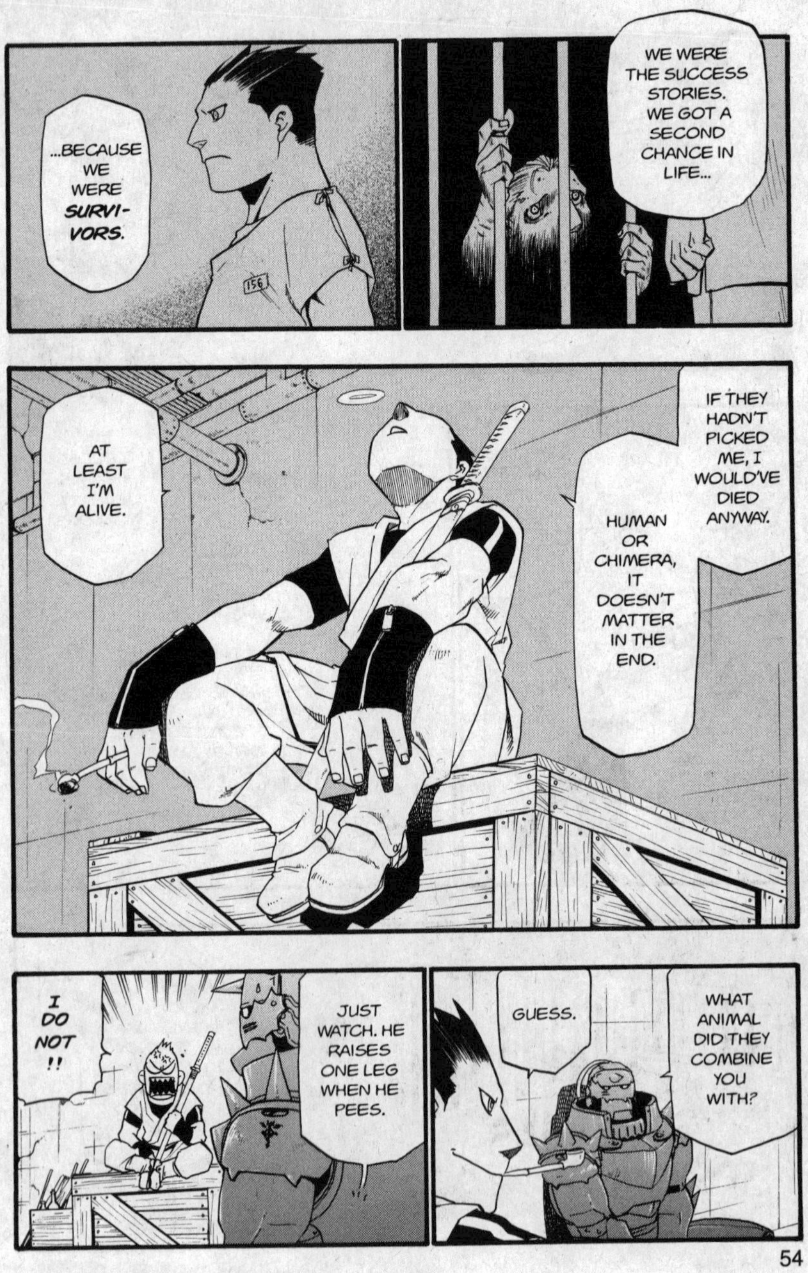
WE WERE THE SUCCESS STORIES. WE GOT A SECOND CHANCE IN LIFE...
...BECAUSE WE WERE SURVIVORS.
IF THEY HADN'T PICKED ME, I WOULD'VE DIED ANYWAY.
HUMAN OR CHIMERA, IT DOESN'T MATTER IN THE END.
AT LEAST I'M ALIVE.
WHAT ANIMAL DID THEY COMBINE YOU WITH?
GUESS.
JUST WATCH. HE RAISES ONE LEG WHEN HE PEES.
I DO NOT!!

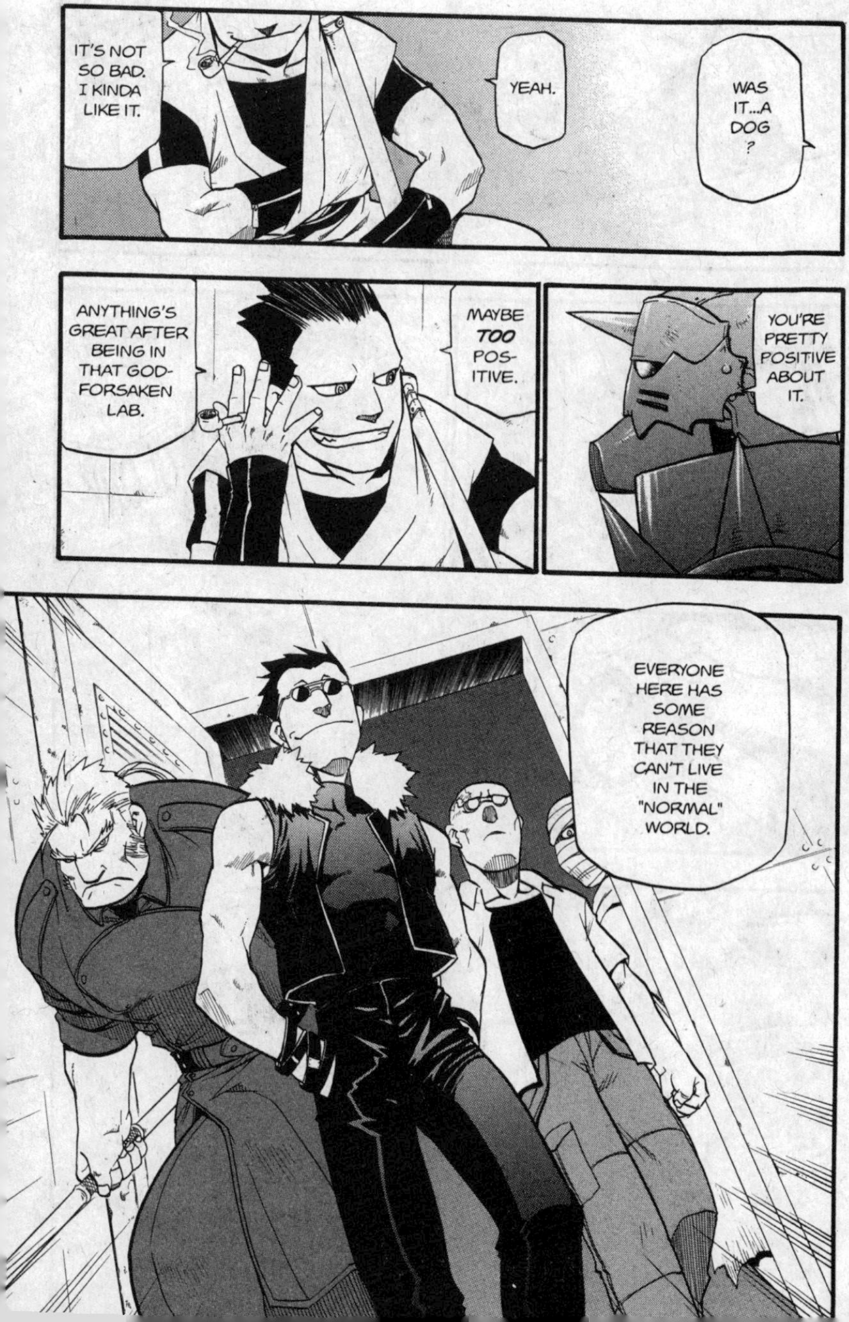
WAS IT...A DOG?
YEAH.
IT'S NOT SO BAD. I KINDA LIKE IT.
YOU'RE PRETTY POSITIVE ABOUT IT.
MAYBE *TOO* POSITIVE.
ANYTHING'S GREAT AFTER BEING IN THAT GOD-FORSAKEN LAB.
EVERYONE HERE HAS SOME REASON THAT THEY CAN'T LIVE IN THE "NORMAL" WORLD.

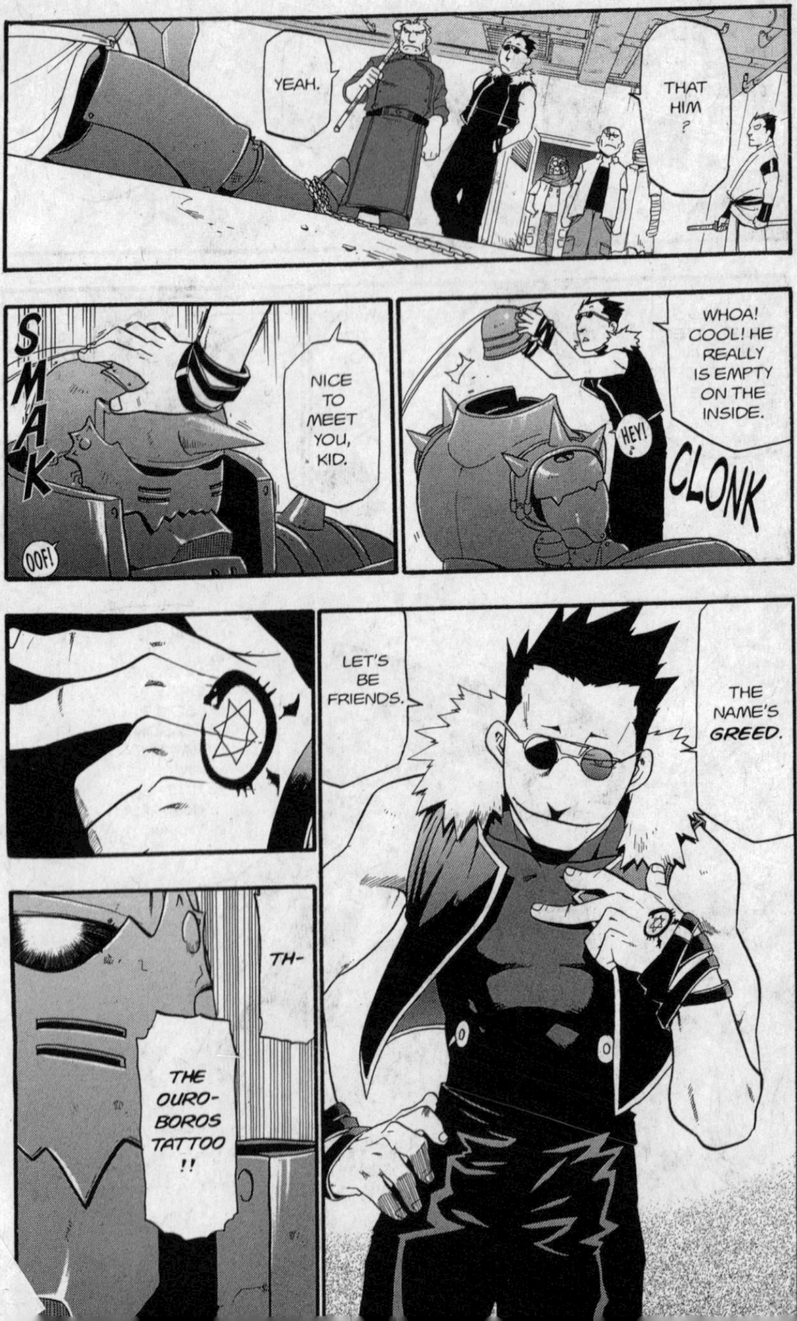
THAT HIM ?
YEAH.
WHOA! COOL! HE REALLY IS EMPTY ON THE INSIDE.
CLONK
HEY!
SMAK
NICE TO MEET YOU, KID.
OOF!
THE NAME'S *GREED*.
LET'S BE FRIENDS.
TH-
THE OURO-BOROS TATTOO !!

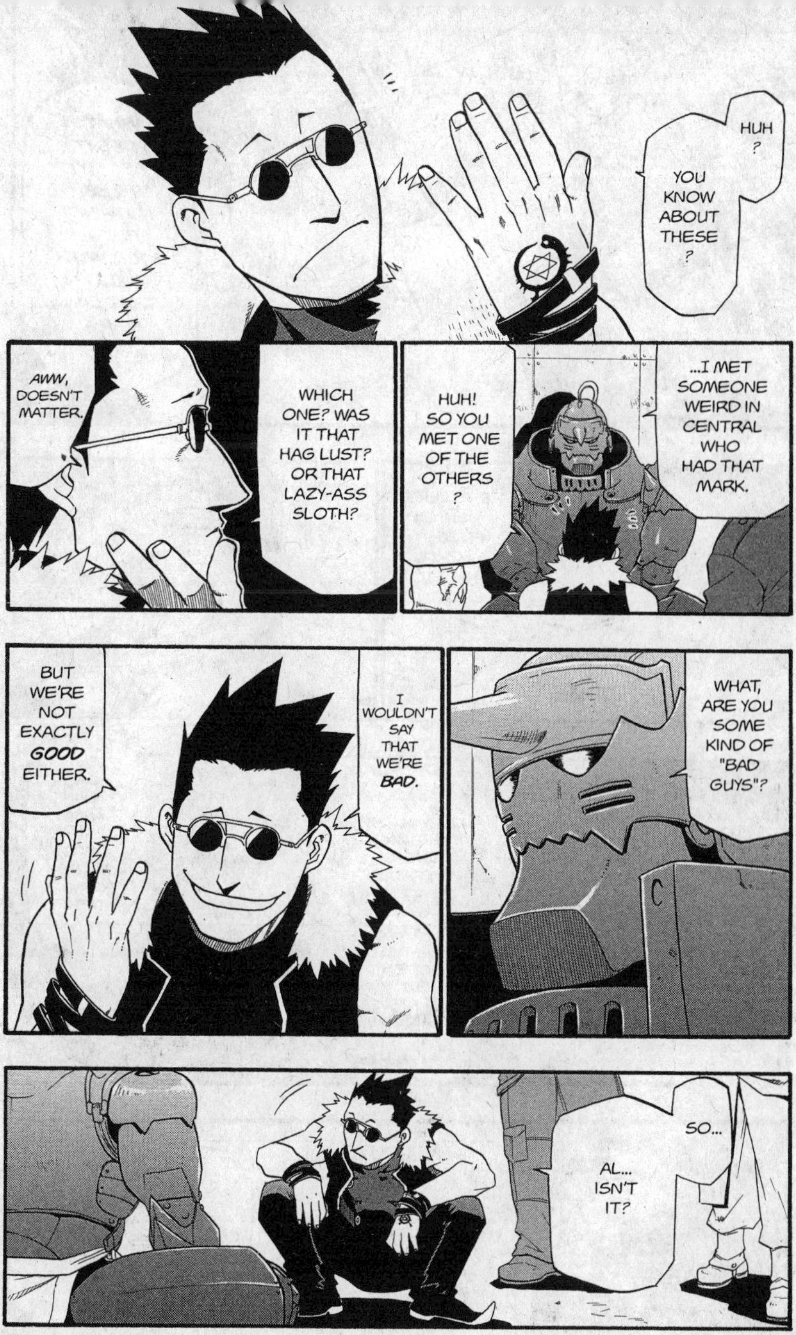
HUH?
YOU KNOW ABOUT THESE?
...I MET SOMEONE WEIRD IN CENTRAL WHO HAD THAT MARK.
HUH! SO YOU MET ONE OF THE OTHERS?
WHICH ONE? WAS IT THAT HAG LUST? OR THAT LAZY-ASS SLOTH?
AWW, DOESN'T MATTER.
WHAT, ARE YOU SOME KIND OF "BAD GUYS"?
I WOULDN'T SAY THAT WE'RE *BAD*.
BUT WE'RE NOT EXACTLY *GOOD* EITHER.
SO...
AL... ISN'T IT?

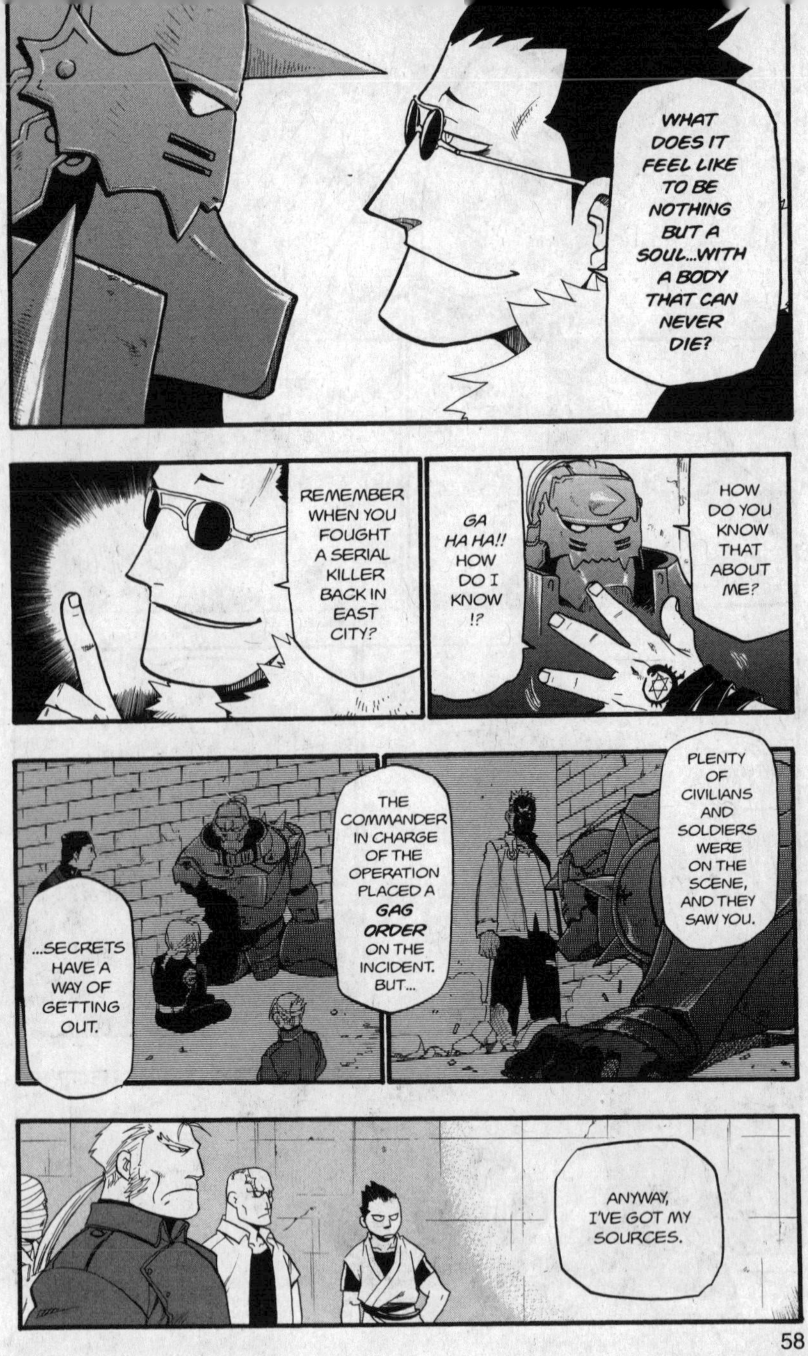
WHAT DOES IT FEEL LIKE TO BE NOTHING BUT A SOUL...WITH A BODY THAT CAN NEVER DIE?
HOW DO YOU KNOW THAT ABOUT ME?
GA HA HA!! HOW DO I KNOW !?
REMEMBER WHEN YOU FOUGHT A SERIAL KILLER BACK IN EAST CITY?
PLENTY OF CIVILIANS AND SOLDIERS WERE ON THE SCENE, AND THEY SAW YOU.
THE COMMANDER IN CHARGE OF THE OPERATION PLACED A **GAG ORDER** ON THE INCIDENT. BUT...
...SECRETS HAVE A WAY OF GETTING OUT.
ANYWAY, I'VE GOT MY SOURCES.

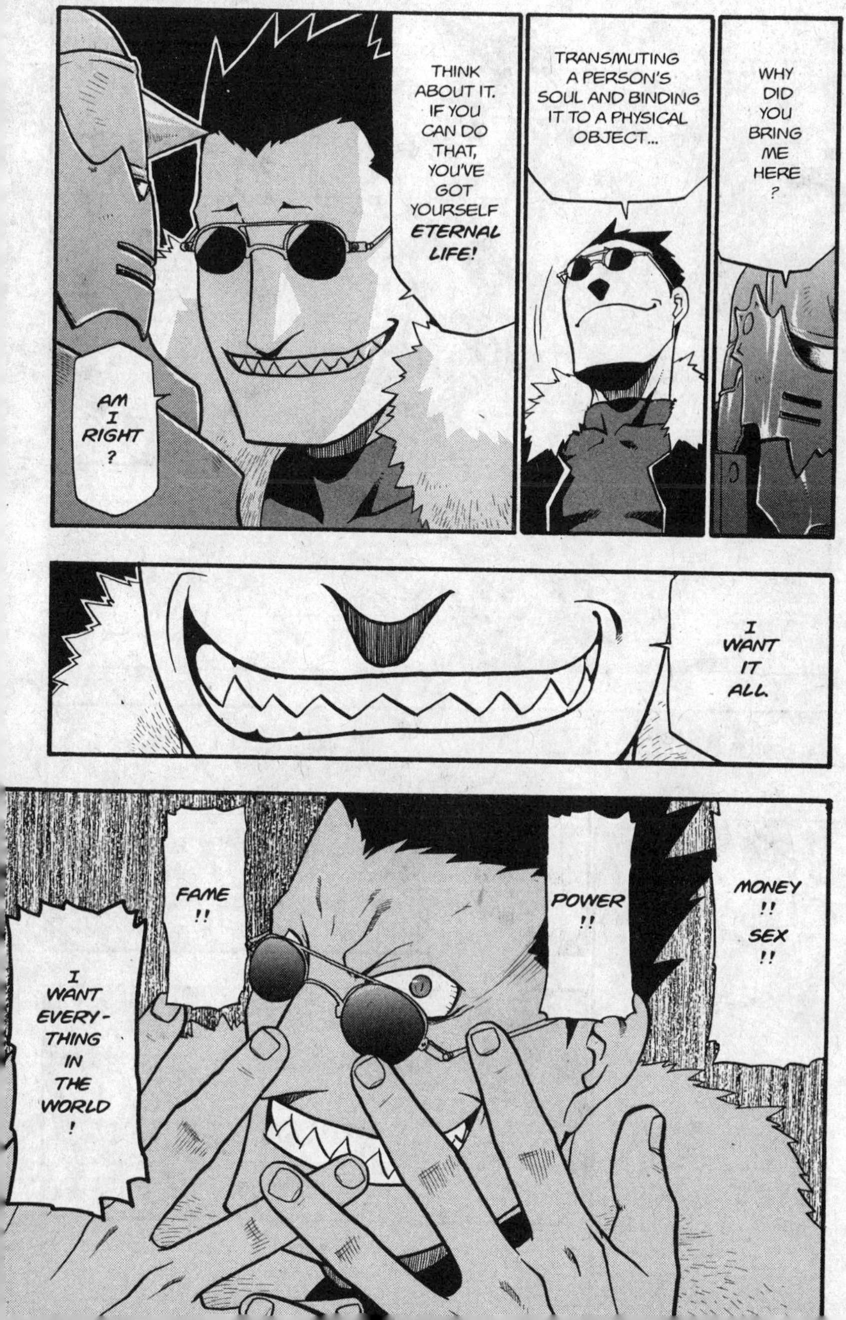
WHY DID YOU BRING ME HERE?
TRANSMUTING A PERSON'S SOUL AND BINDING IT TO A PHYSICAL OBJECT...
THINK ABOUT IT. IF YOU CAN DO THAT, YOU'VE GOT YOURSELF ETERNAL LIFE!
AM I RIGHT?
I WANT IT ALL.
MONEY!! SEX!!
POWER!!
FAME!!
I WANT EVERY-THING IN THE WORLD!

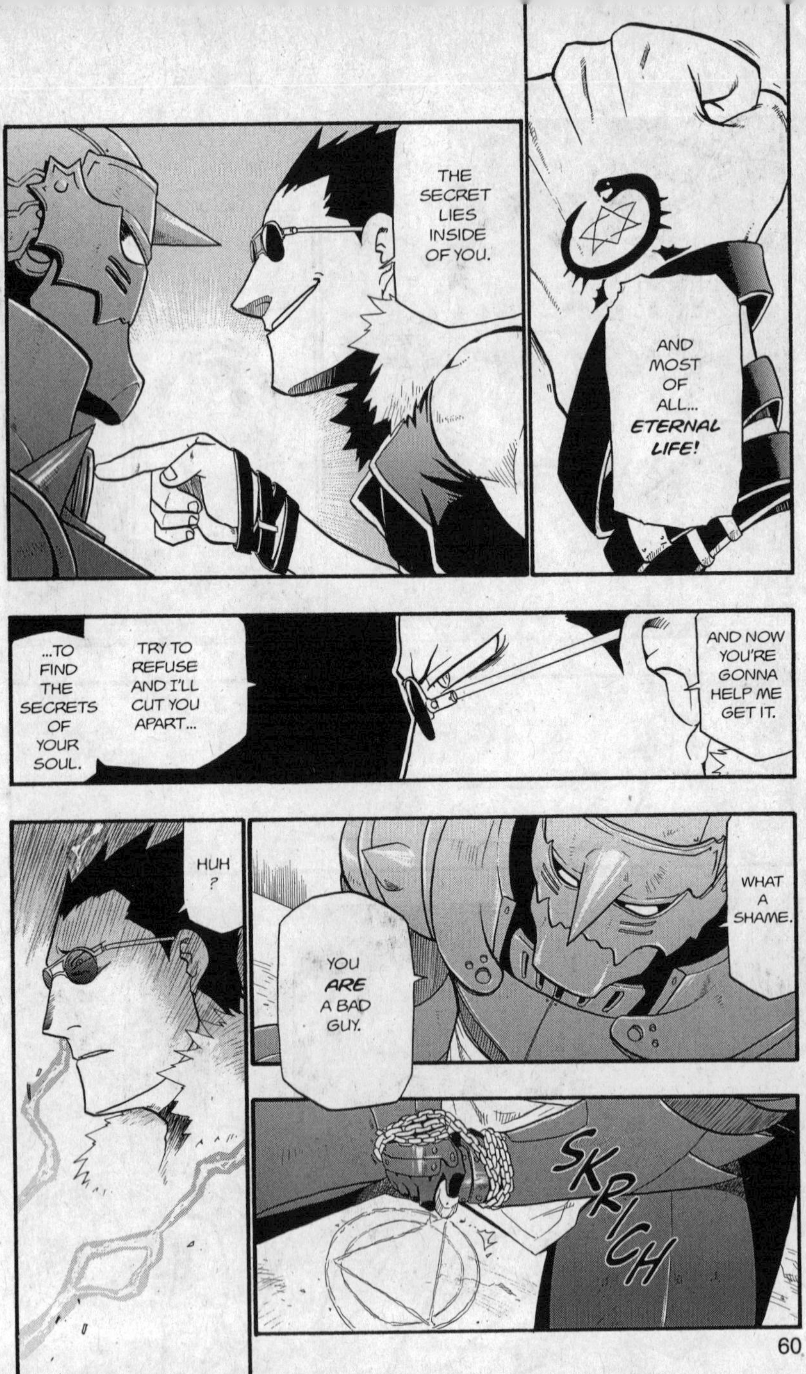
AND MOST OF ALL... **ETERNAL LIFE!**
THE SECRET LIES INSIDE OF YOU.
AND NOW YOU'RE GONNA HELP ME GET IT.
TRY TO REFUSE AND I'LL CUT YOU APART...
...TO FIND THE SECRETS OF YOUR SOUL.
WHAT A SHAME.
YOU **ARE** A BAD GUY.
SKRICH
HUH?

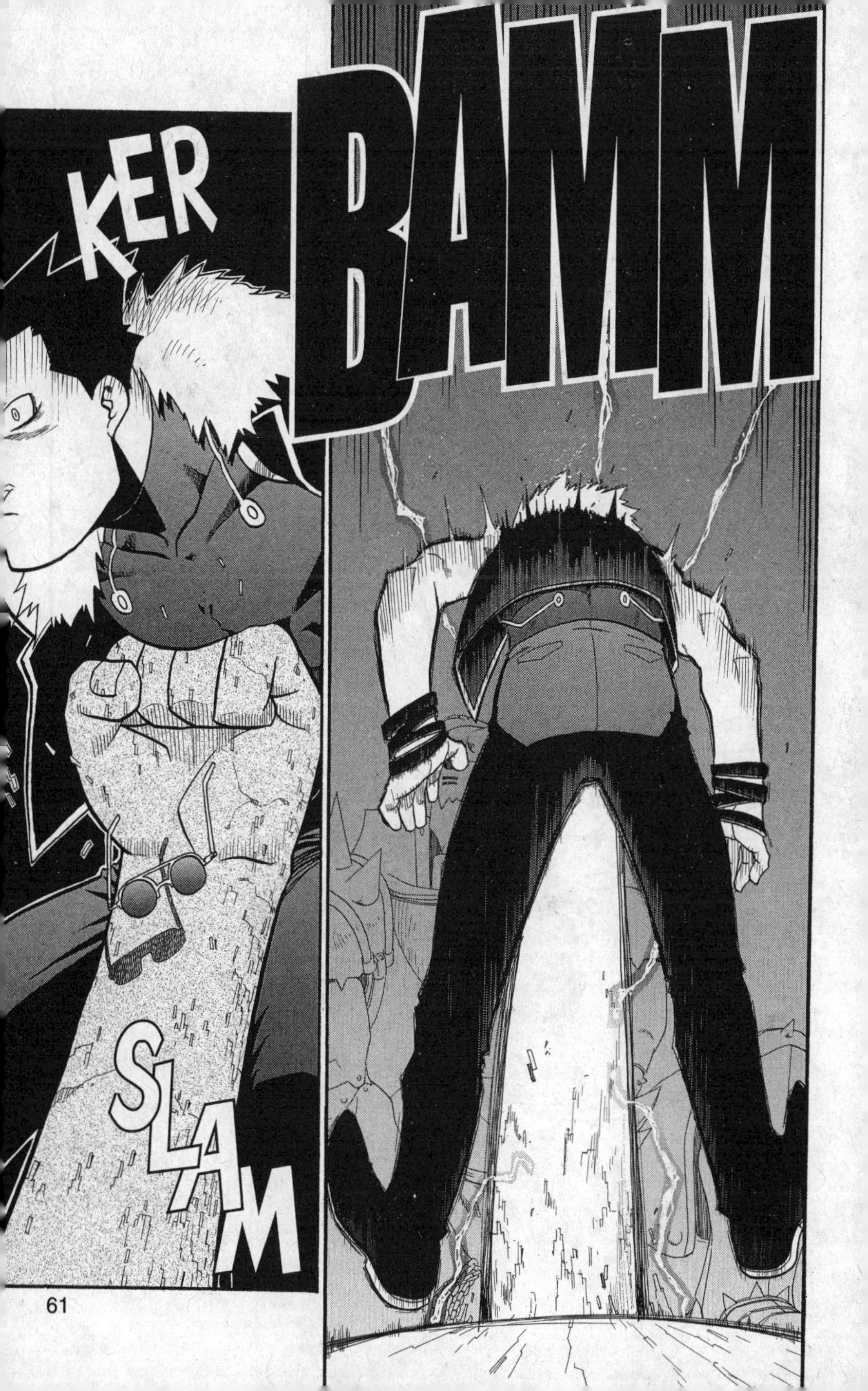
KER BAMM
SLAM

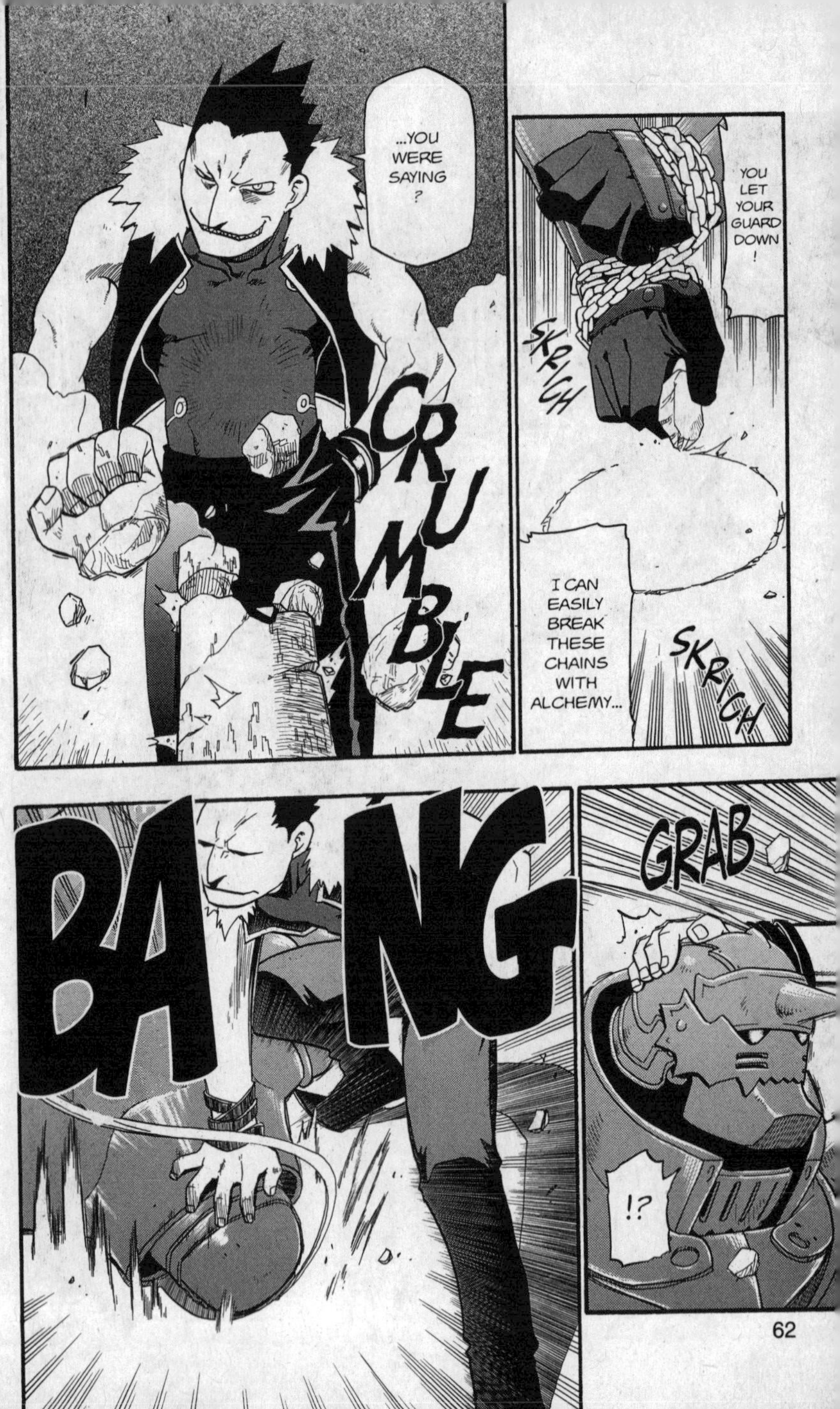
YOU LET YOUR GUARD DOWN!
SKRICH
I CAN EASILY BREAK THESE CHAINS WITH ALCHEMY...
SKRICH
...YOU WERE SAYING?
CRUMBLE
GRAB
!?
BANG

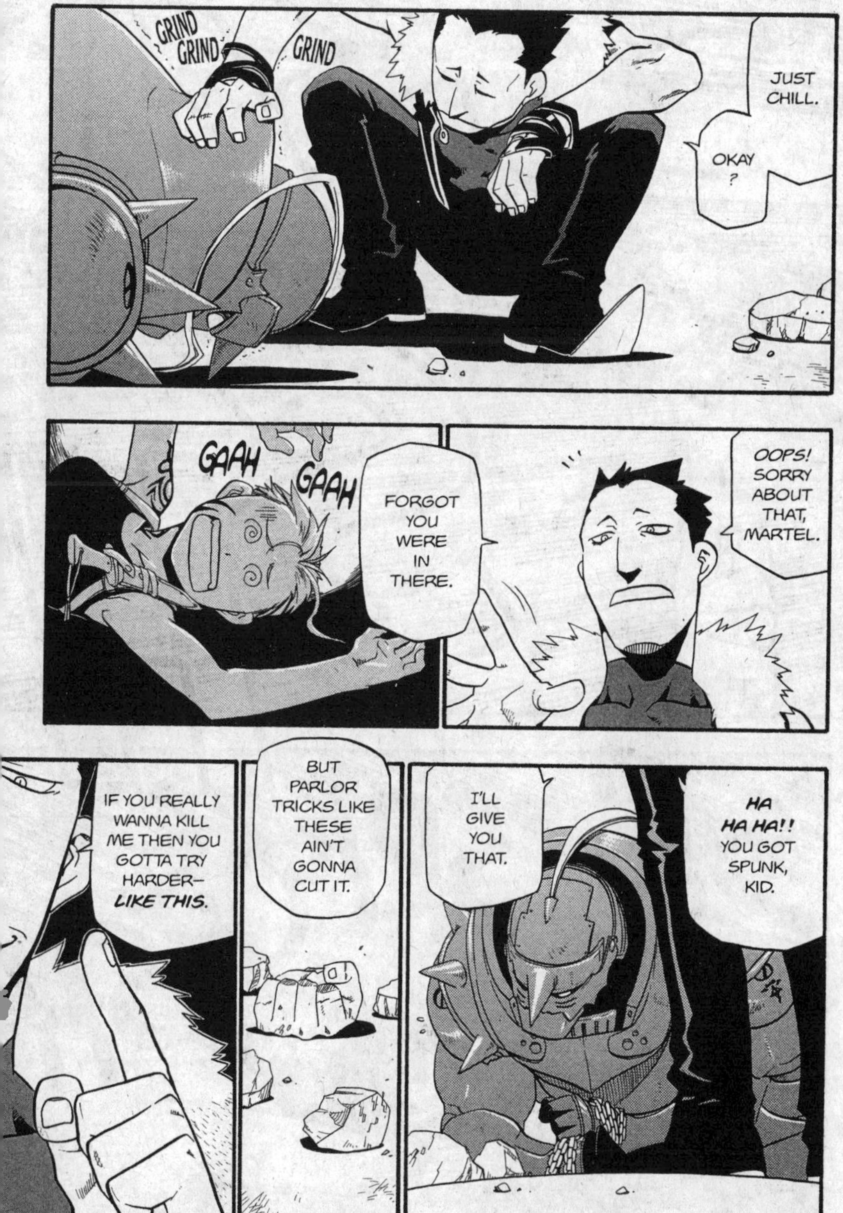
JUST CHILL.
OKAY ?
GRIND
GRIND GRIND
OOPS! SORRY ABOUT THAT, MARTEL.
FORGOT YOU WERE IN THERE.
GAAH
GAAH
HA HA HA!! YOU GOT SPUNK, KID.
I'LL GIVE YOU THAT.
BUT PARLOR TRICKS LIKE THESE AIN'T GONNA CUT IT.
IF YOU REALLY WANNA KILL ME THEN YOU GOTTA TRY HARDER— LIKE THIS.

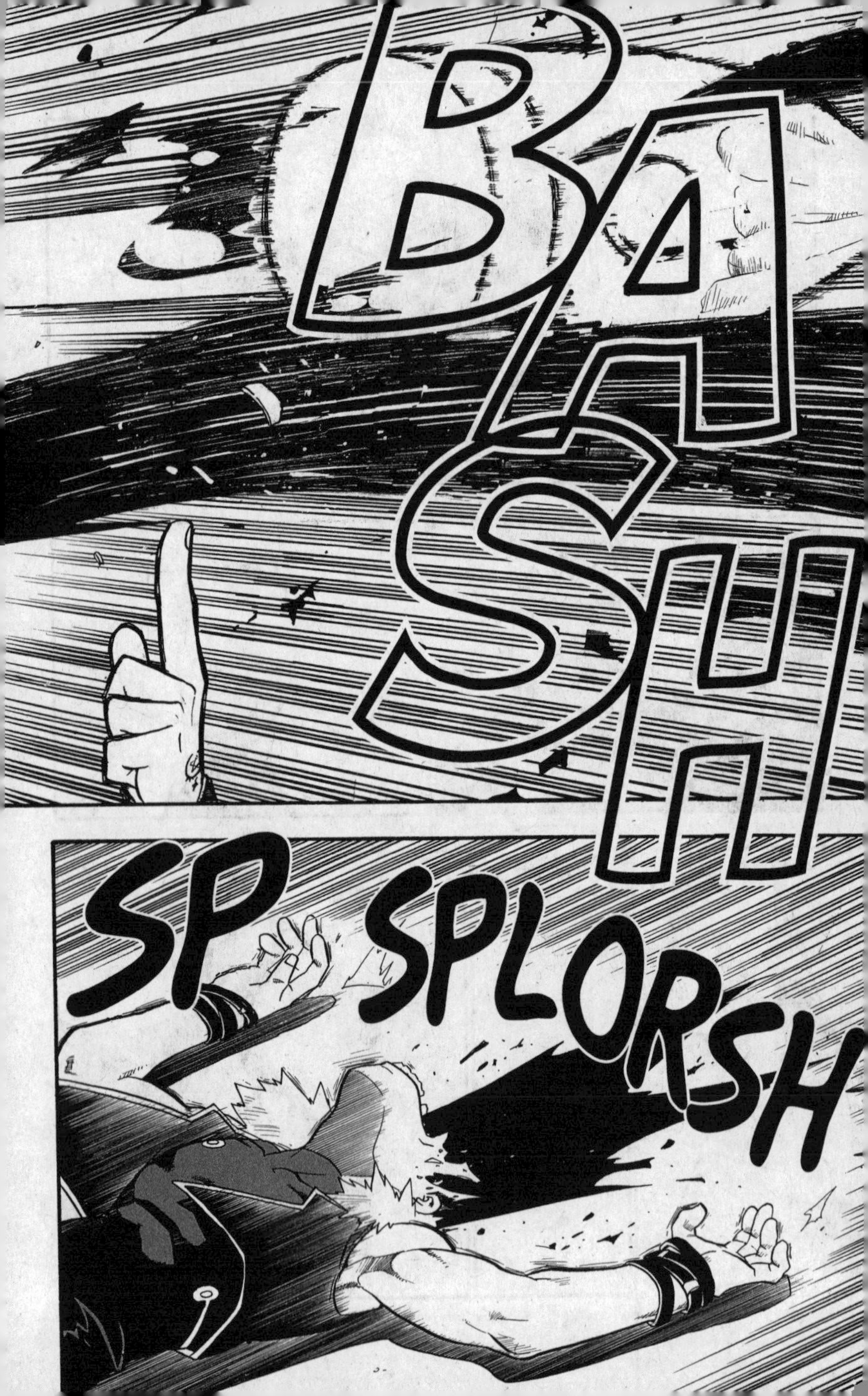
BASH
SP SPLORSH

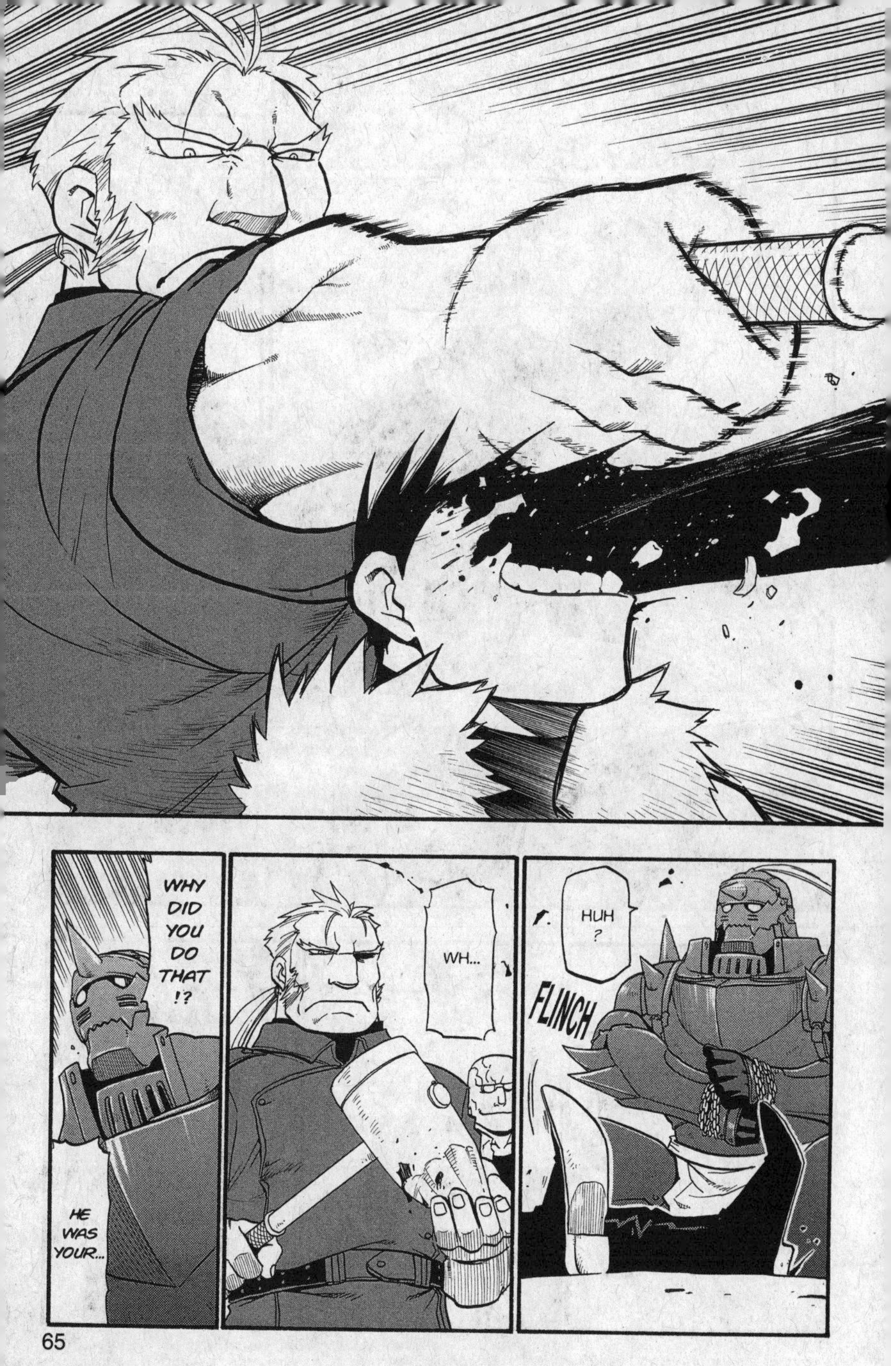
HUH ?
FLINCH
WH...
WHY DID YOU DO THAT !?
HE WAS YOUR...

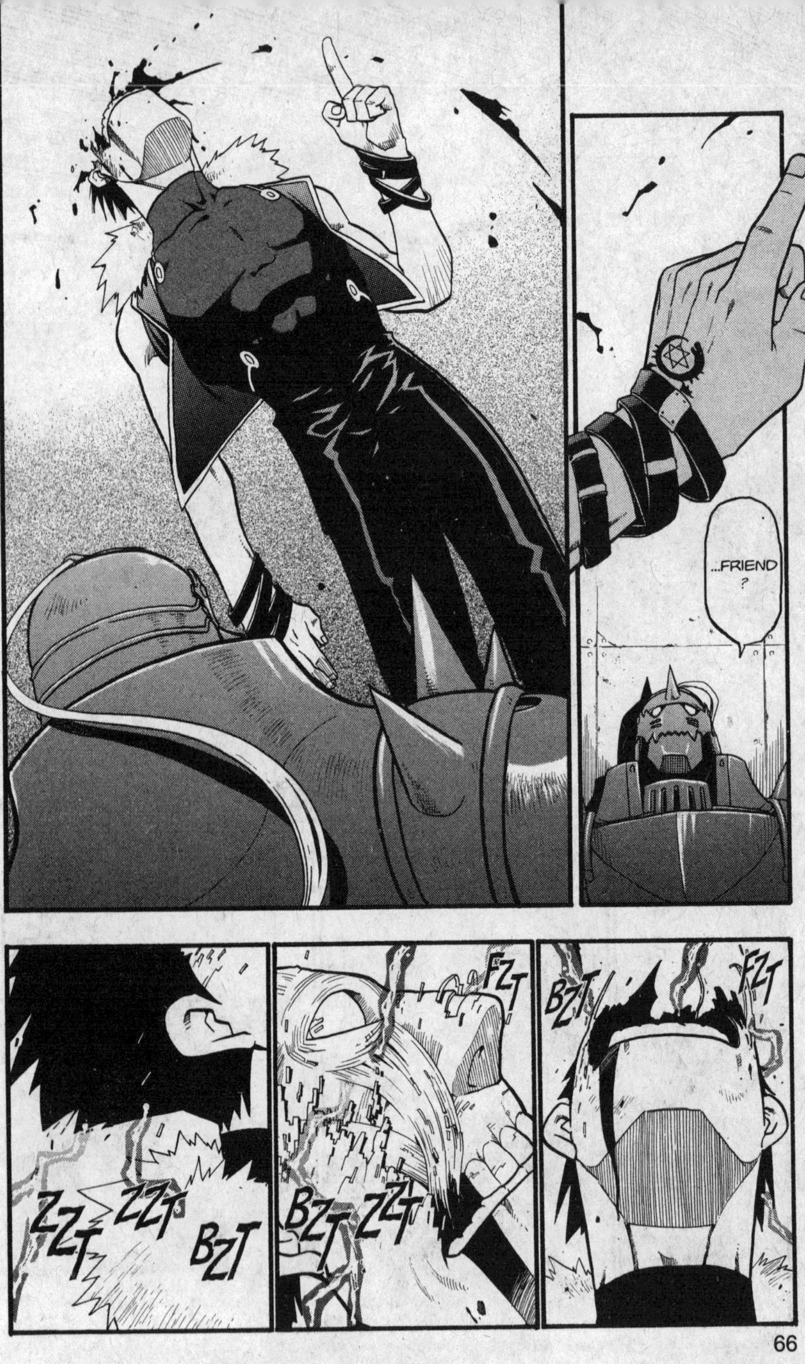
...FRIEND ?
BZT
FZT
FZT
BZT
ZZT
ZZT
ZZT
BZT

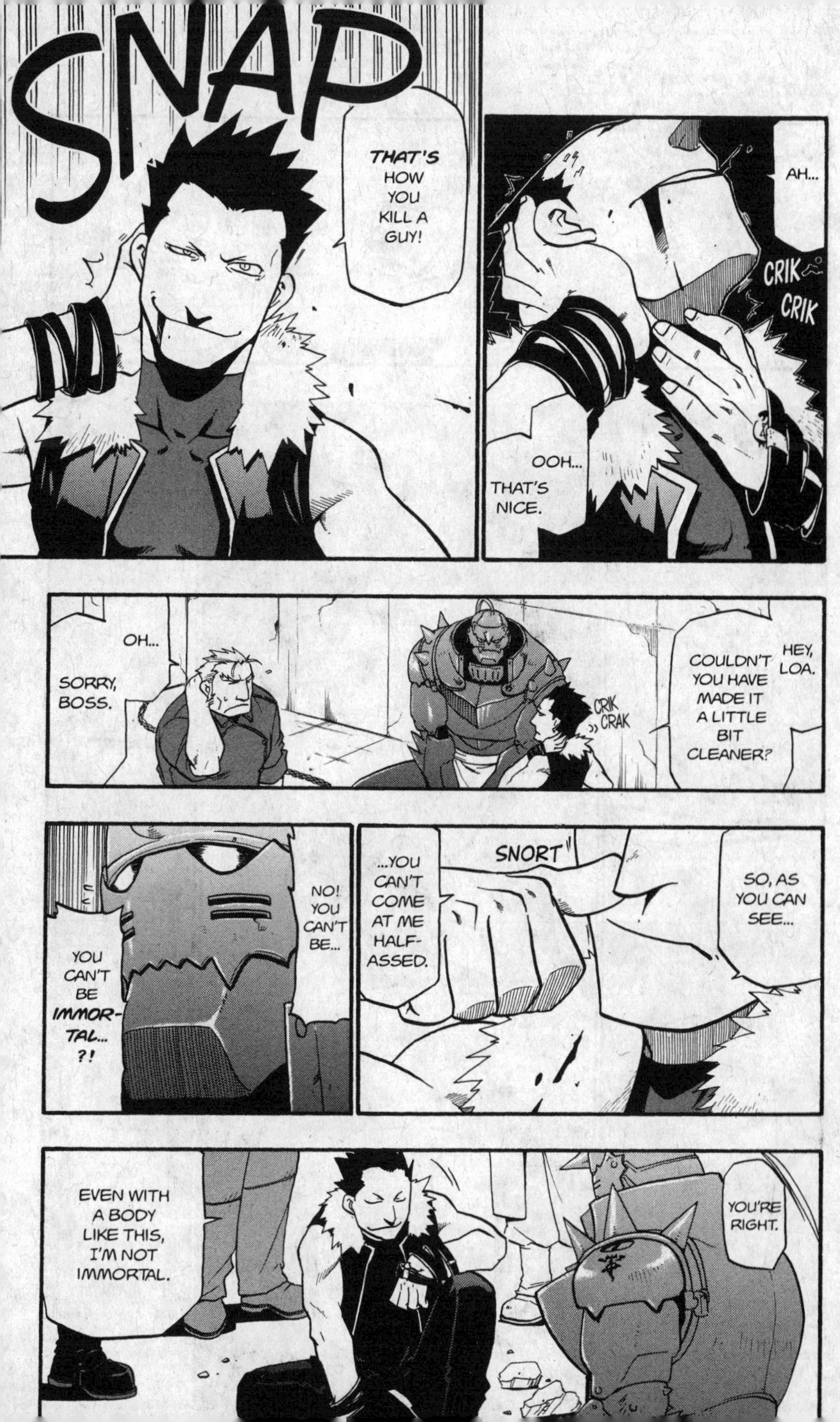
AH...
CRIK CRIK
OOH... THAT'S NICE.
SNAP
THAT'S HOW YOU KILL A GUY!
HEY, LOA.
COULDN'T YOU HAVE MADE IT A LITTLE BIT CLEANER?
CRIK CRAK
OH... SORRY, BOSS.
SO, AS YOU CAN SEE...
SNORT
...YOU CAN'T COME AT ME HALF-ASSED.
NO! YOU CAN'T BE...
YOU CAN'T BE IMMORTAL...?!
YOU'RE RIGHT.
EVEN WITH A BODY LIKE THIS, I'M NOT IMMORTAL.

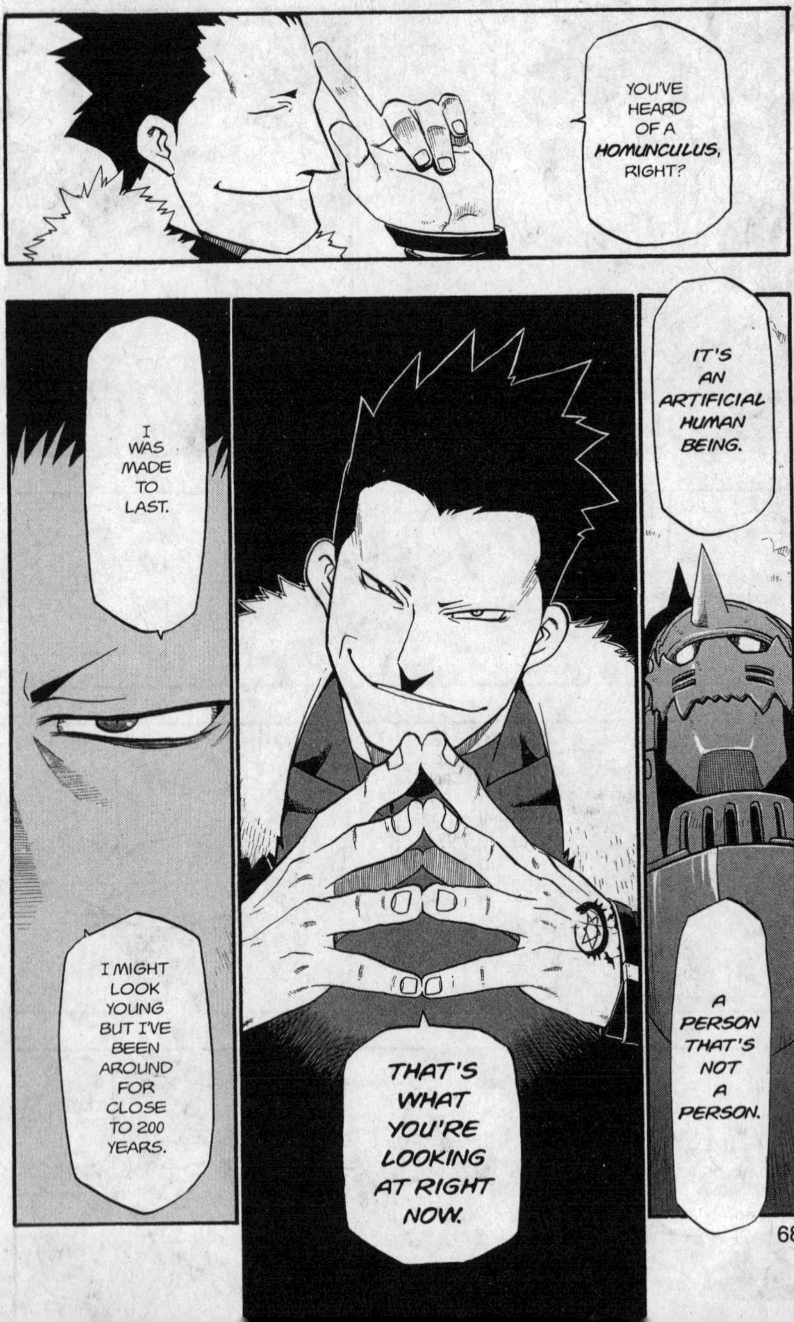
YOU'VE HEARD OF A HOMUNCULUS, RIGHT?
IT'S AN ARTIFICIAL HUMAN BEING.
A PERSON THAT'S NOT A PERSON.
THAT'S WHAT YOU'RE LOOKING AT RIGHT NOW.
I WAS MADE TO LAST.
I MIGHT LOOK YOUNG BUT I'VE BEEN AROUND FOR CLOSE TO 200 YEARS.

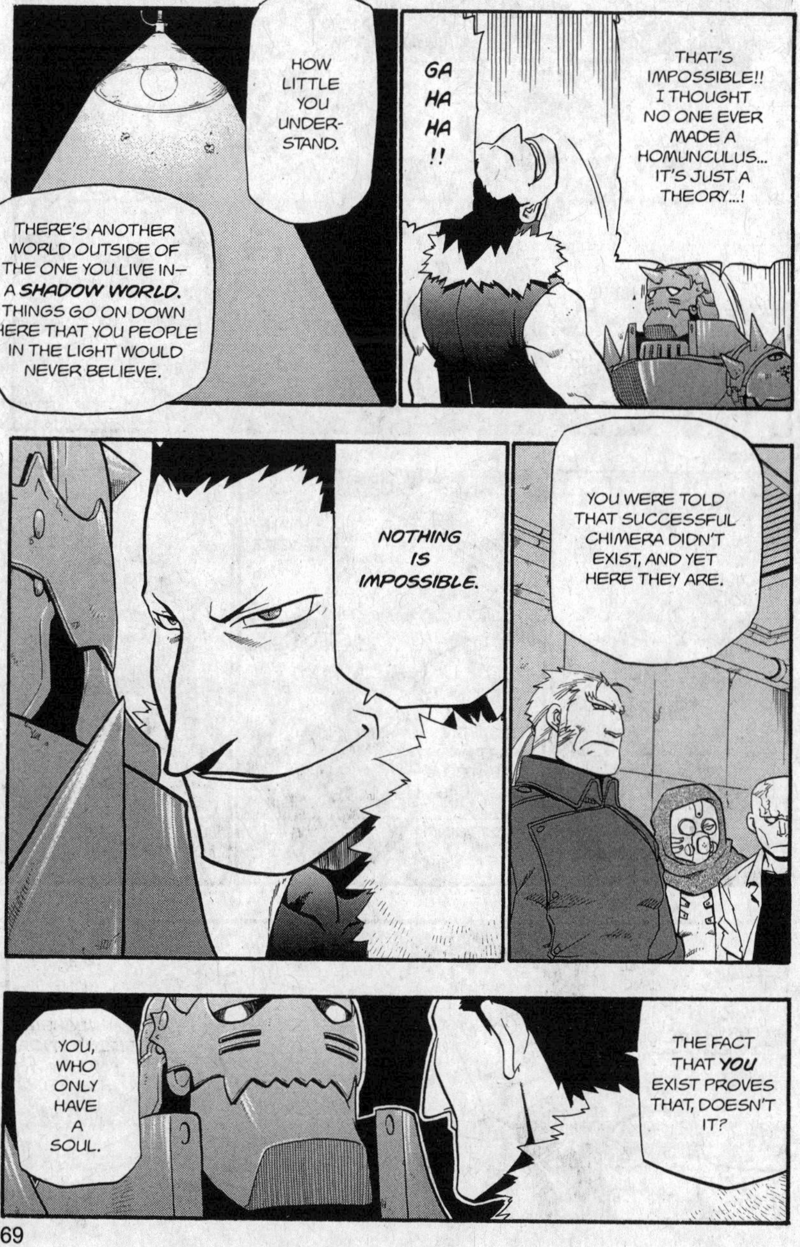
THAT'S IMPOSSIBLE!! I THOUGHT NO ONE EVER MADE A HOMUNCULUS... IT'S JUST A THEORY...!
GA HA HA!!
HOW LITTLE YOU UNDER-STAND.
THERE'S ANOTHER WORLD OUTSIDE OF THE ONE YOU LIVE IN— A **SHADOW WORLD.** THINGS GO ON DOWN HERE THAT YOU PEOPLE IN THE LIGHT WOULD NEVER BELIEVE.
YOU WERE TOLD THAT SUCCESSFUL CHIMERA DIDN'T EXIST, AND YET HERE THEY ARE.
NOTHING IS IMPOSSIBLE.
THE FACT THAT **YOU** EXIST PROVES THAT, DOESN'T IT?
YOU, WHO ONLY HAVE A SOUL.

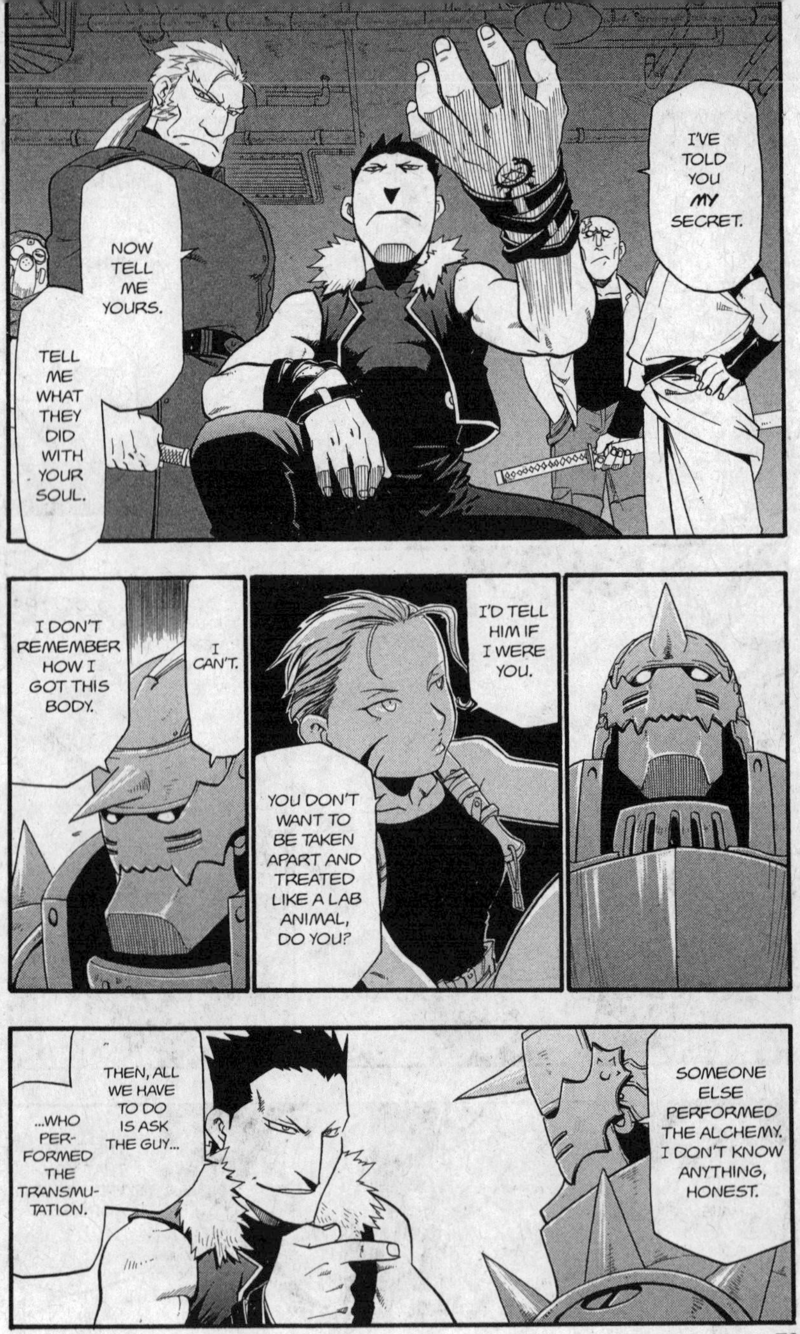
I'VE TOLD YOU MY SECRET.
NOW TELL ME YOURS.
TELL ME WHAT THEY DID WITH YOUR SOUL.
I'D TELL HIM IF I WERE YOU.
YOU DON'T WANT TO BE TAKEN APART AND TREATED LIKE A LAB ANIMAL, DO YOU?
I CAN'T.
I DON'T REMEMBER HOW I GOT THIS BODY.
SOMEONE ELSE PERFORMED THE ALCHEMY. I DON'T KNOW ANYTHING, HONEST.
THEN, ALL WE HAVE TO DO IS ASK THE GUY...
...WHO PER-FORMED THE TRANSMU-TATION.

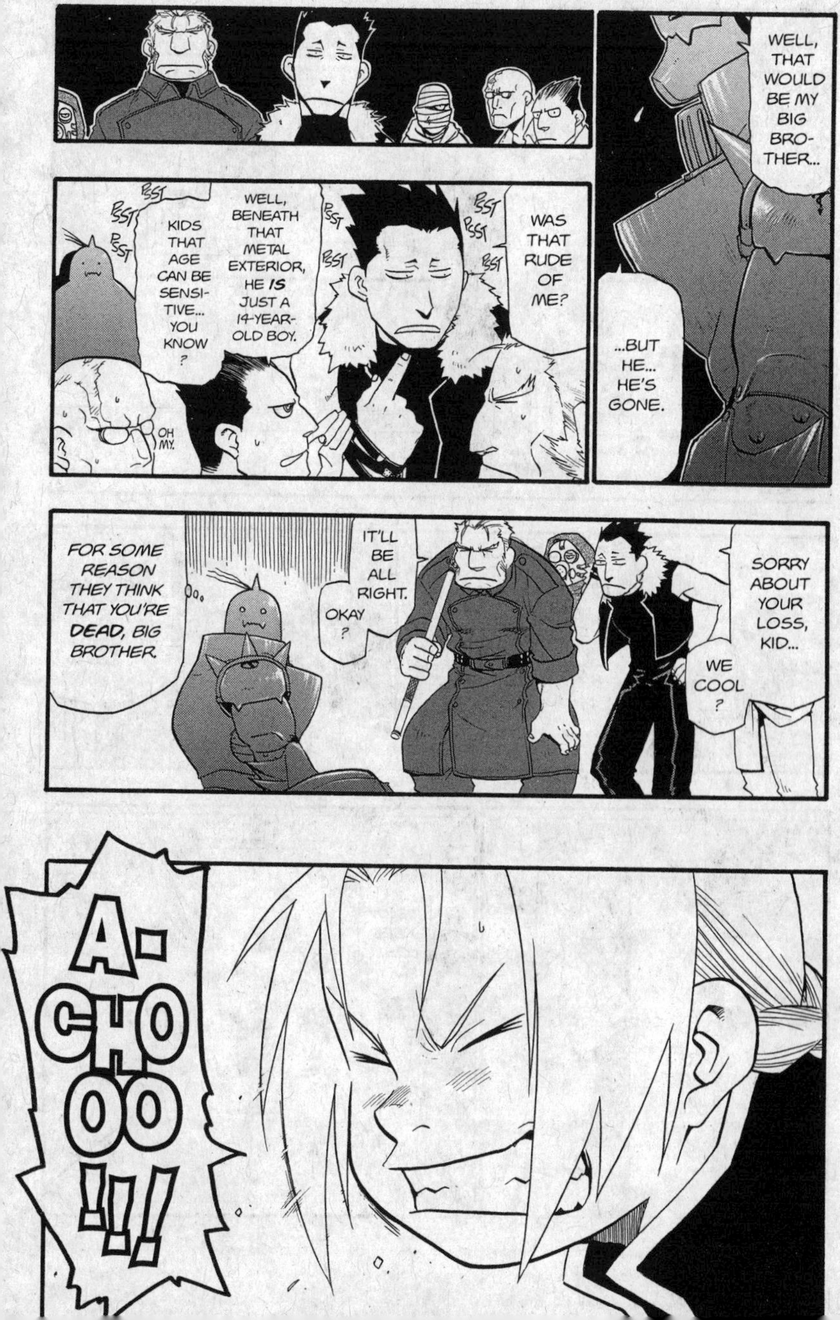
WELL, THAT WOULD BE MY BIG BROTHER...
...BUT HE... HE'S GONE.
WAS THAT RUDE OF ME?
PSST PSST PSST
WELL, BENEATH THAT METAL EXTERIOR, HE *IS* JUST A 14-YEAR-OLD BOY.
KIDS THAT AGE CAN BE SENSITIVE... YOU KNOW?
PSST PSST PSST
OH MY.
SORRY ABOUT YOUR LOSS, KID...
WE COOL?
IT'LL BE ALL RIGHT.
OKAY?
FOR SOME REASON THEY THINK THAT YOU'RE ***DEAD****, BIG BROTHER.*
A-CHOO!!!

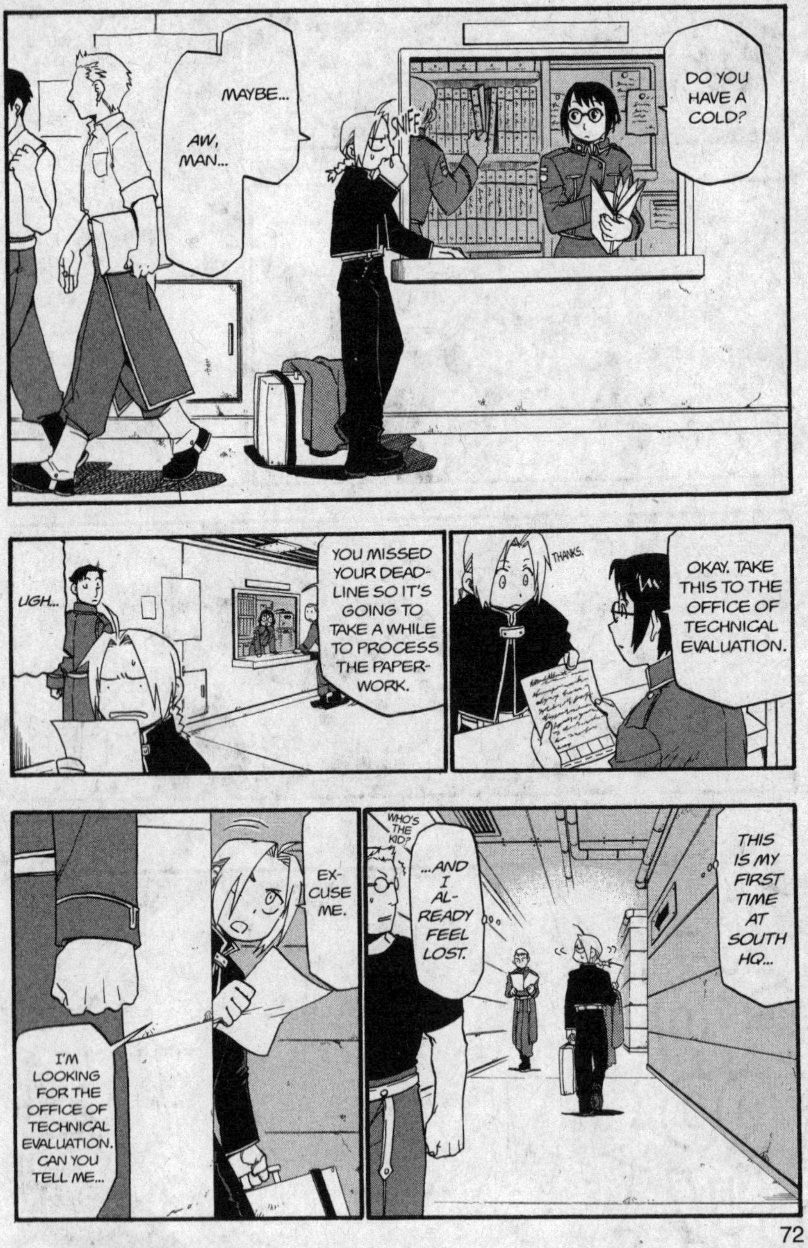
DO YOU HAVE A COLD?
SNIFF
MAYBE...
AW, MAN...
OKAY. TAKE THIS TO THE OFFICE OF TECHNICAL EVALUATION.
THANKS.
YOU MISSED YOUR DEAD-LINE SO IT'S GOING TO TAKE A WHILE TO PROCESS THE PAPER-WORK.
UGH..
THIS IS MY FIRST TIME AT SOUTH HQ...
...AND I AL-READY FEEL LOST.
WHO'S THE KID?
EX-CUSE ME.
I'M LOOKING FOR THE OFFICE OF TECHNICAL EVALUATION. CAN YOU TELL ME...

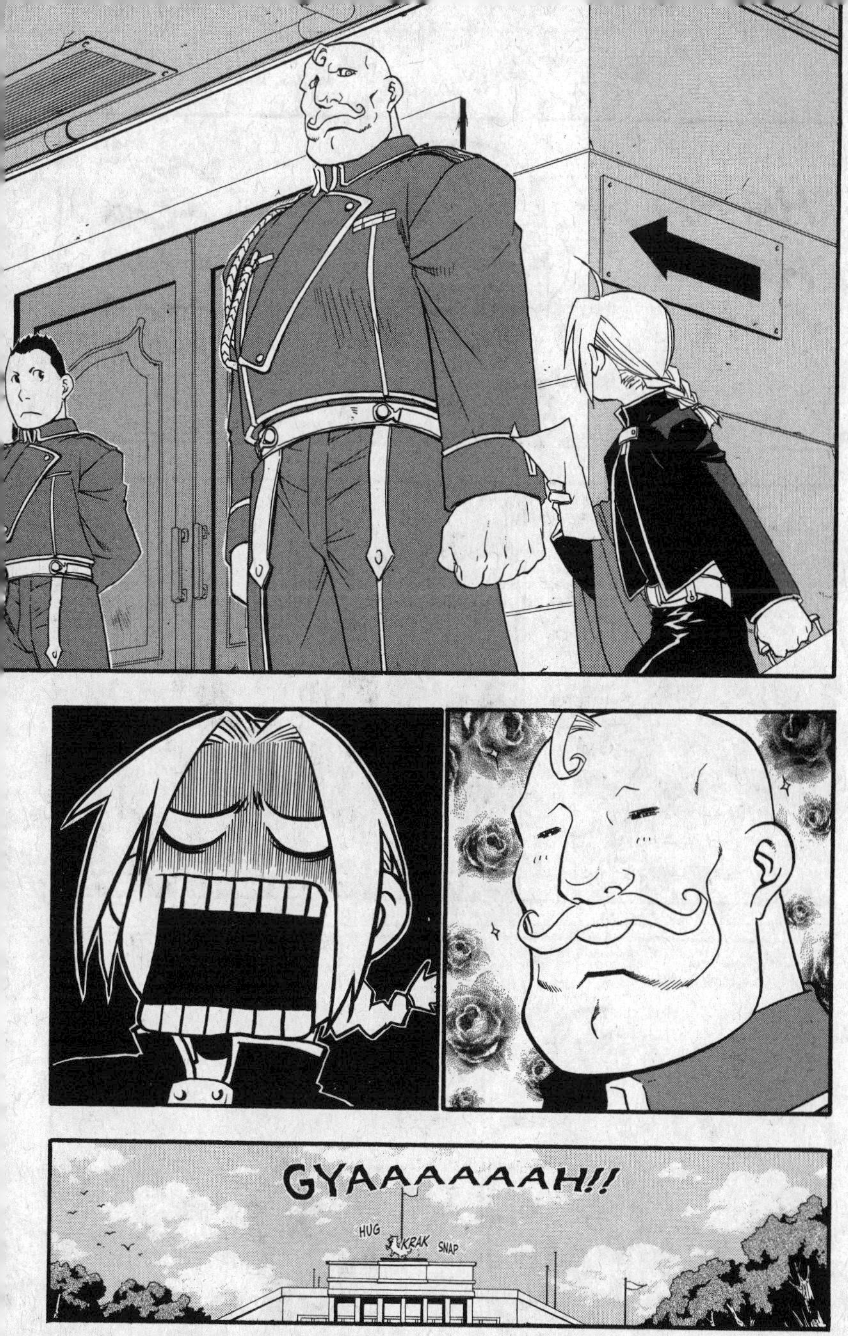
GYAAAAAAH!!
HUG
KRAK
SNAP

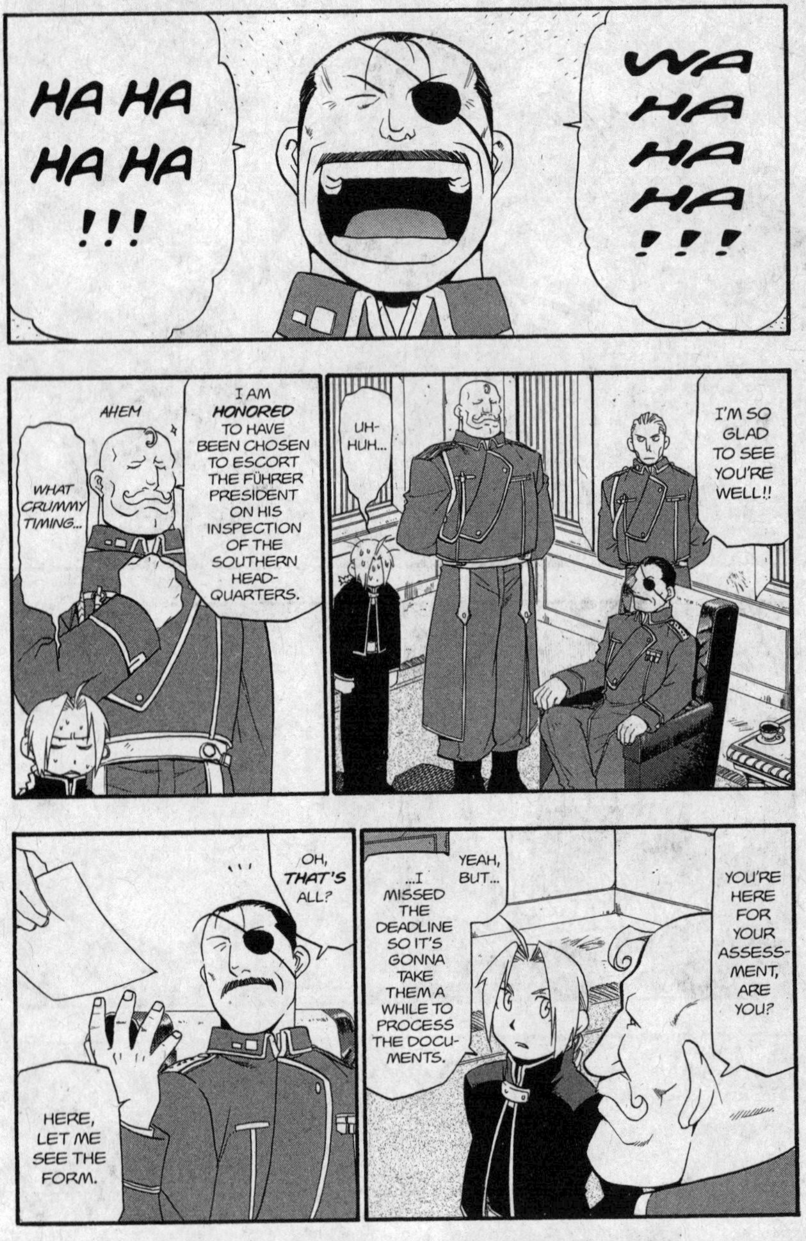
WA HA HA HA !!!
HA HA HA HA !!!
I'M SO GLAD TO SEE YOU'RE WELL!!
UH-HUH...
I AM HONORED TO HAVE BEEN CHOSEN TO ESCORT THE FÜHRER PRESIDENT ON HIS INSPECTION OF THE SOUTHERN HEAD-QUARTERS.
AHEM
WHAT CRUMMY TIMING...
YOU'RE HERE FOR YOUR ASSESS-MENT, ARE YOU?
YEAH, BUT...
...I MISSED THE DEADLINE SO IT'S GONNA TAKE THEM A WHILE TO PROCESS THE DOCU-MENTS.
OH, THAT'S ALL?
HERE, LET ME SEE THE FORM.

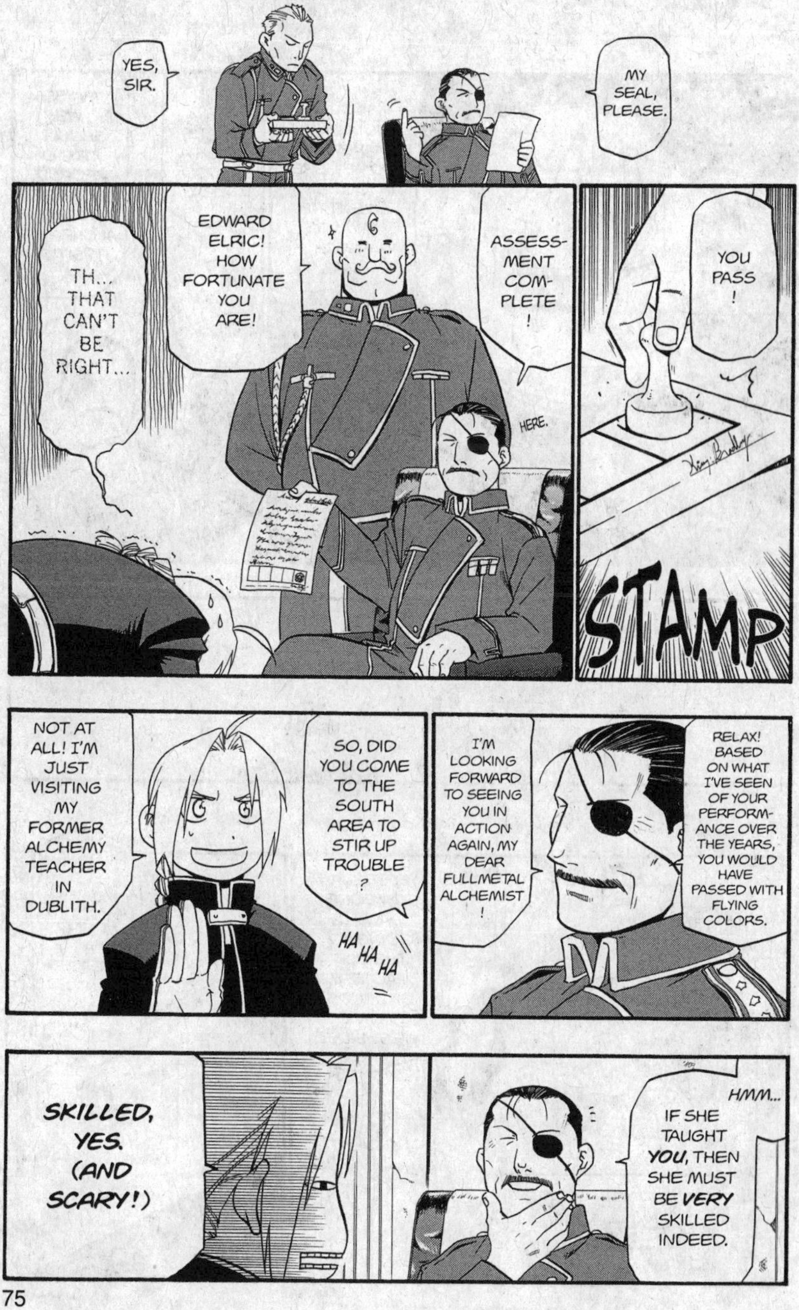
MY SEAL, PLEASE.
YES, SIR.
YOU PASS!
STAMP
ASSESSMENT COMPLETE!
HERE.
EDWARD ELRIC! HOW FORTUNATE YOU ARE!
TH... THAT CAN'T BE RIGHT...
RELAX! BASED ON WHAT I'VE SEEN OF YOUR PERFORMANCE OVER THE YEARS, YOU WOULD HAVE PASSED WITH FLYING COLORS.
I'M LOOKING FORWARD TO SEEING YOU IN ACTION AGAIN, MY DEAR FULLMETAL ALCHEMIST!
SO, DID YOU COME TO THE SOUTH AREA TO STIR UP TROUBLE?
HA HA HA
NOT AT ALL! I'M JUST VISITING MY FORMER ALCHEMY TEACHER IN DUBLITH.
HMM...
IF SHE TAUGHT YOU, THEN SHE MUST BE VERY SKILLED INDEED.
SKILLED, YES. (AND SCARY!)

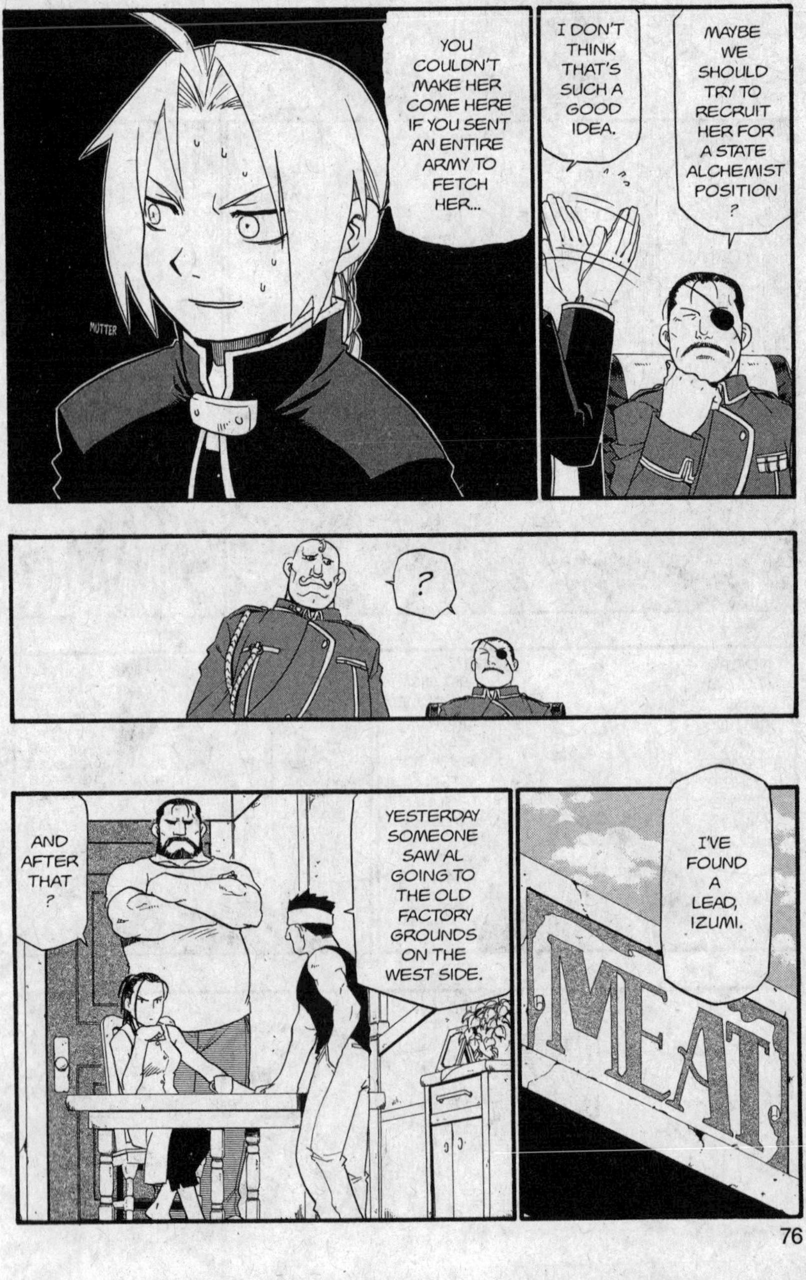
MAYBE WE SHOULD TRY TO RECRUIT HER FOR A STATE ALCHEMIST POSITION?
I DON'T THINK THAT'S SUCH A GOOD IDEA.
YOU COULDN'T MAKE HER COME HERE IF YOU SENT AN ENTIRE ARMY TO FETCH HER...
MUTTER
?
I'VE FOUND A LEAD, IZUMI.
MEAT
YESTERDAY SOMEONE SAW AL GOING TO THE OLD FACTORY GROUNDS ON THE WEST SIDE.
AND AFTER THAT?

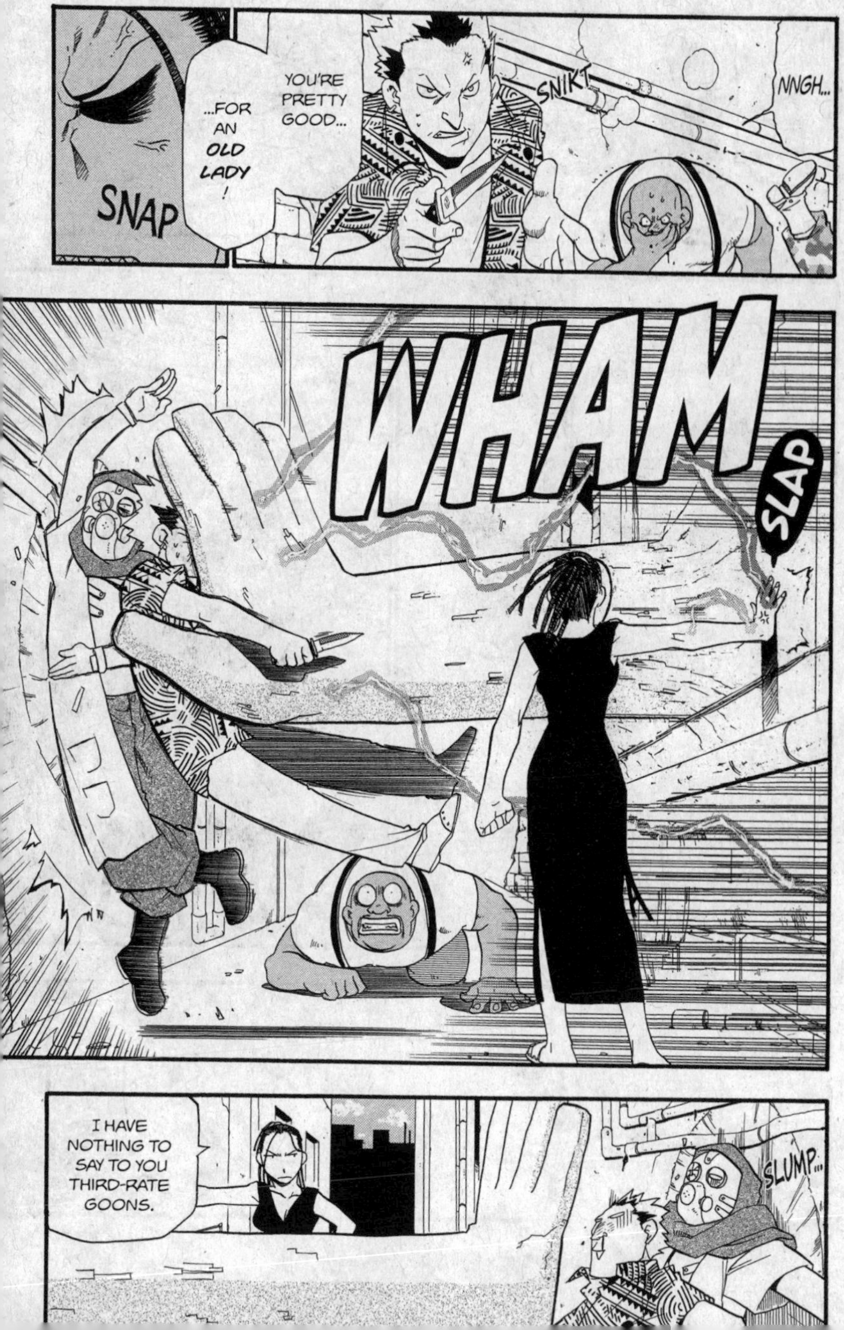
NNGH...
SNIKT
YOU'RE PRETTY GOOD...
...FOR AN OLD LADY!
SNAP
WHAM
SLAP
SLUMP...
I HAVE NOTHING TO SAY TO YOU THIRD-RATE GOONS.

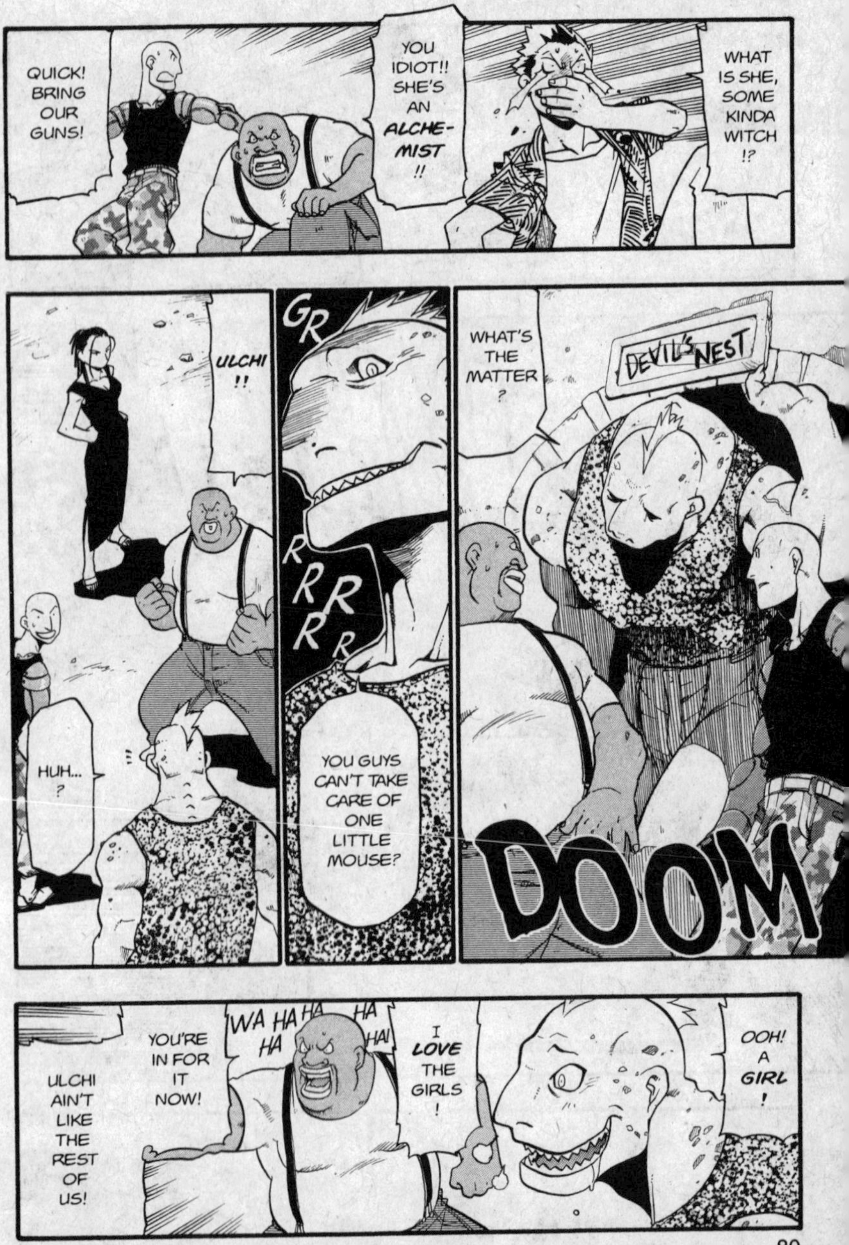
WHAT IS SHE, SOME KINDA WITCH !?
YOU IDIOT!! SHE'S AN ALCHE-MIST !!
QUICK! BRING OUR GUNS!
DEVIL'S NEST
WHAT'S THE MATTER ?
DOOM
GR
RRRRR
YOU GUYS CAN'T TAKE CARE OF ONE LITTLE MOUSE?
ULCHI !!
HUH... ?
OOH! A GIRL !
I LOVE THE GIRLS !
WA HA HA HA HA HA!
YOU'RE IN FOR IT NOW!
ULCHI AIN'T LIKE THE REST OF US!

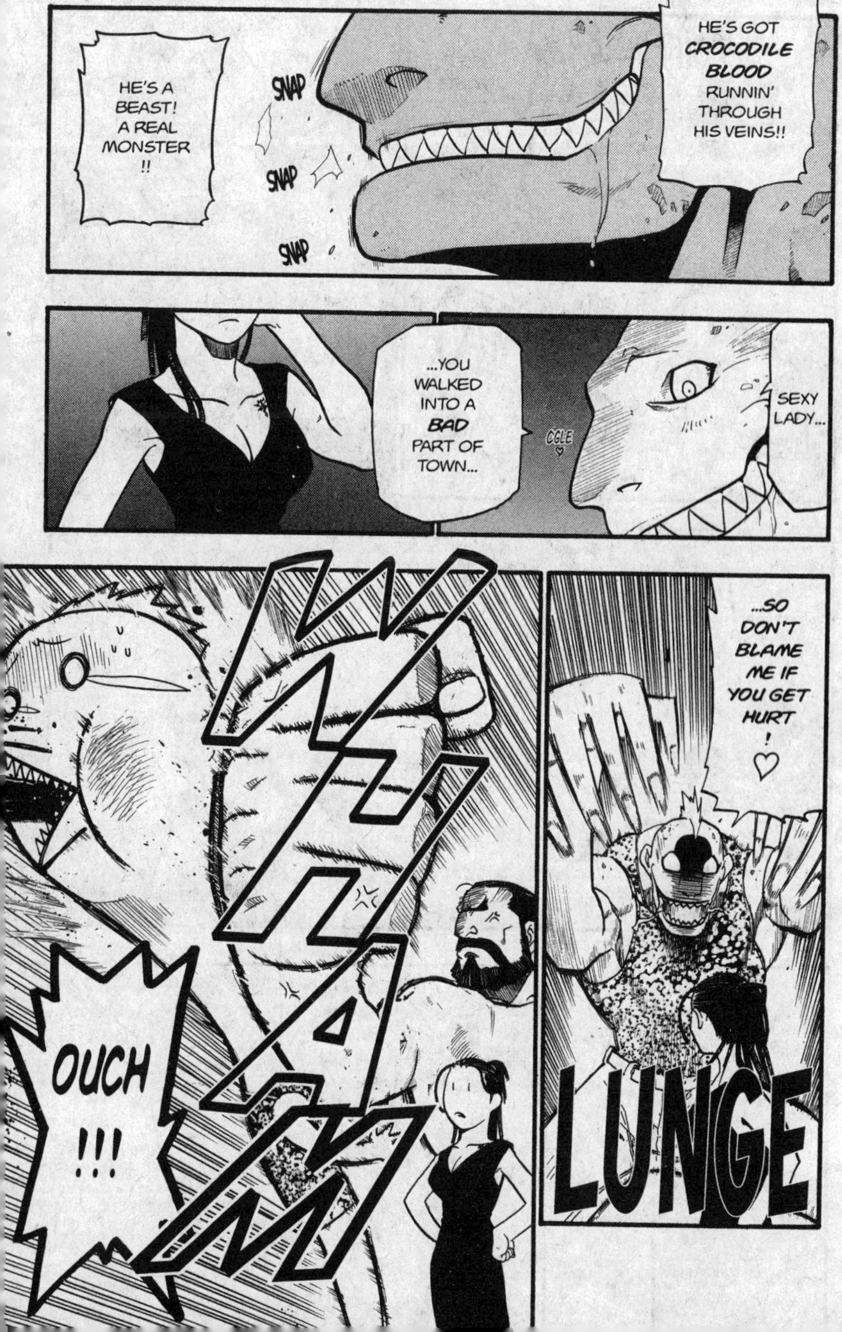
HE'S GOT **CROCODILE BLOOD** RUNNIN' THROUGH HIS VEINS!!
SNAP
SNAP
SNAP
HE'S A BEAST! A REAL MONSTER !!
SEXY LADY...
CGLE ♥
...YOU WALKED INTO A **BAD** PART OF TOWN...
...SO DON'T BLAME ME IF YOU GET HURT! ♥
LUNGE
WHAM
OUCH !!!

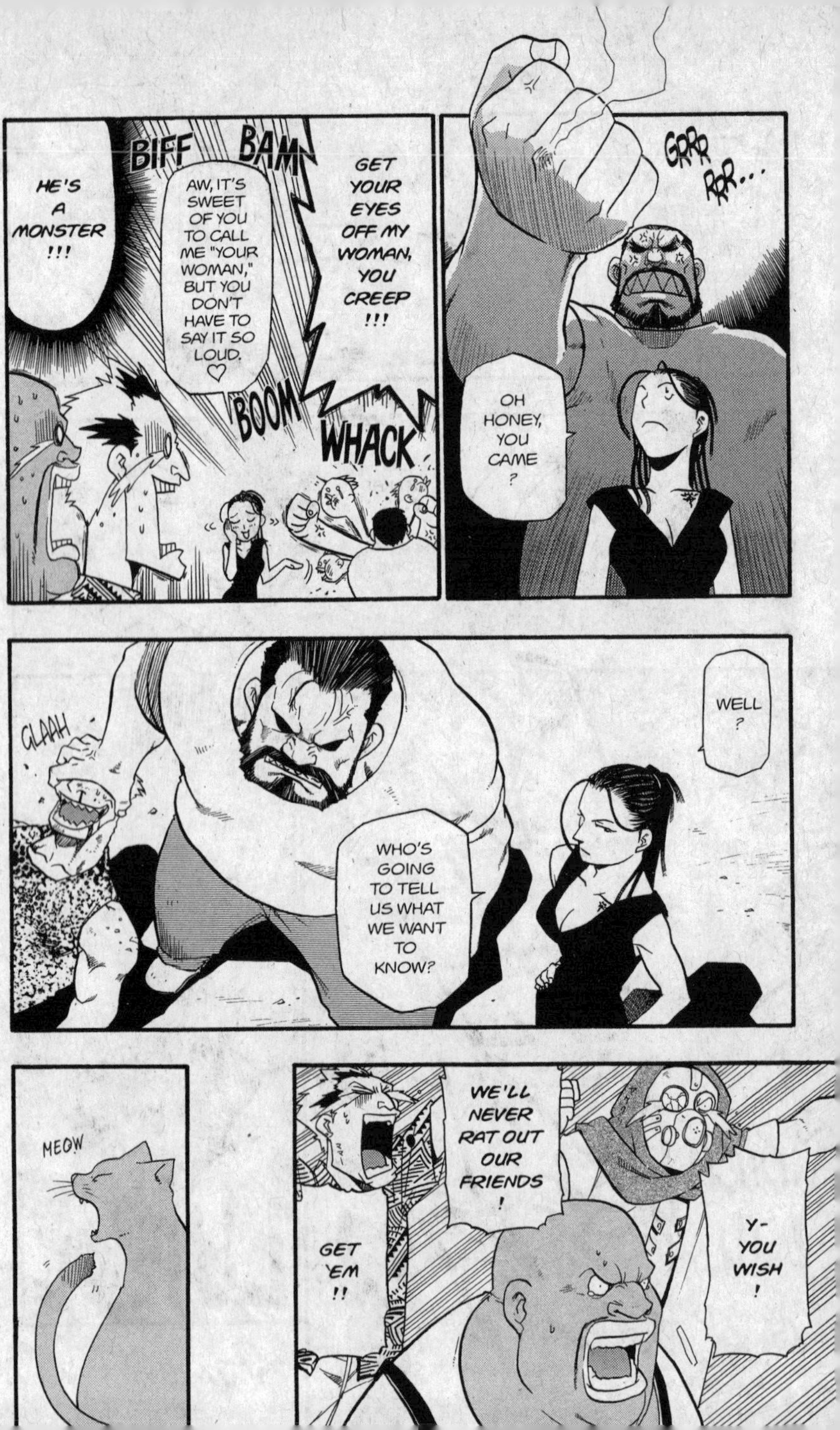
GRRR RRR...
OH HONEY, YOU CAME?
GET YOUR EYES OFF MY WOMAN, YOU CREEP!!!
BAM
BIFF
AW, IT'S SWEET OF YOU TO CALL ME "YOUR WOMAN," BUT YOU DON'T HAVE TO SAY IT SO LOUD. ♡
HE'S A MONSTER!!!
BOOM
WHACK
WELL?
WHO'S GOING TO TELL US WHAT WE WANT TO KNOW?
GLAAH
Y-YOU WISH!
WE'LL NEVER RAT OUT OUR FRIENDS!
GET 'EM!!
MEOW

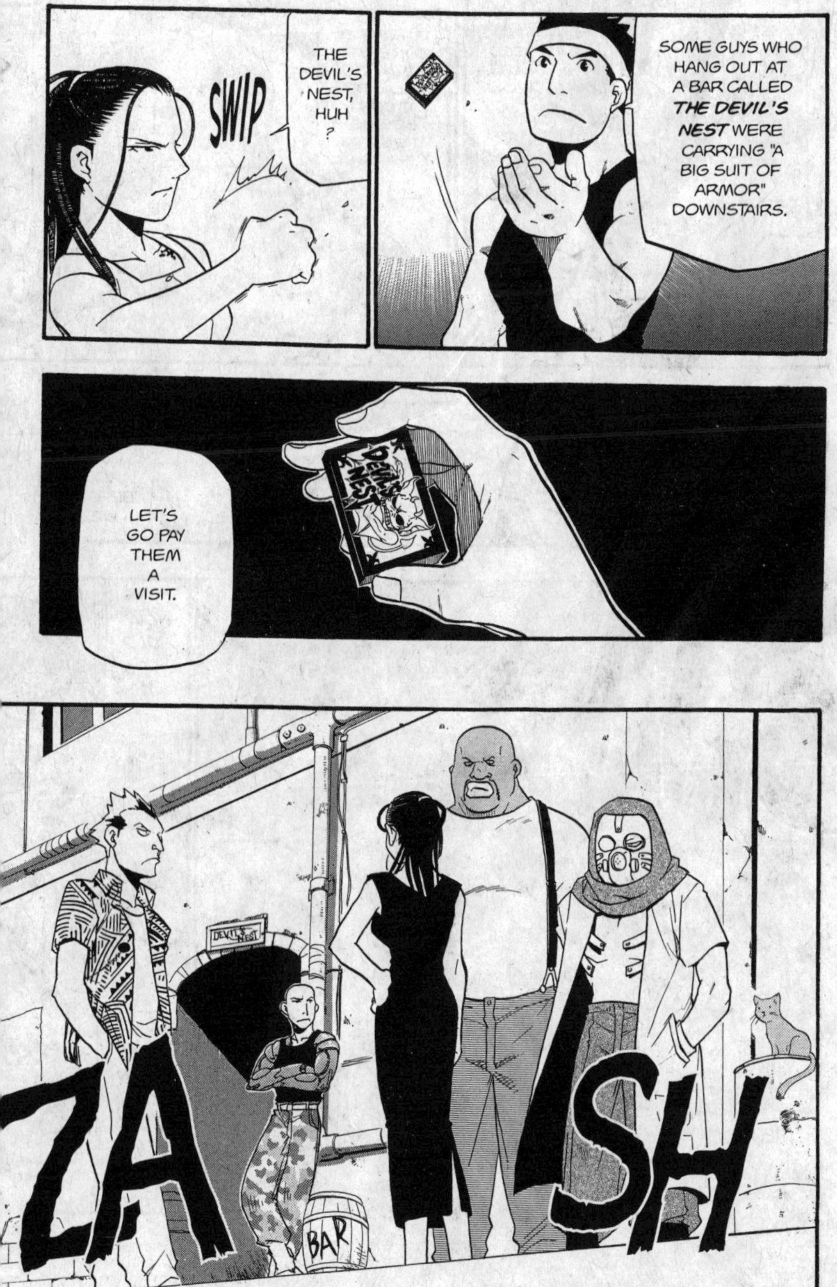
SOME GUYS WHO HANG OUT AT A BAR CALLED **THE DEVIL'S NEST** WERE CARRYING "A BIG SUIT OF ARMOR" DOWNSTAIRS.
SWIP
THE DEVIL'S NEST, HUH?
DEVIL'S NEST
LET'S GO PAY THEM A VISIT.
DEVIL'S NEST
BAR
ZASH

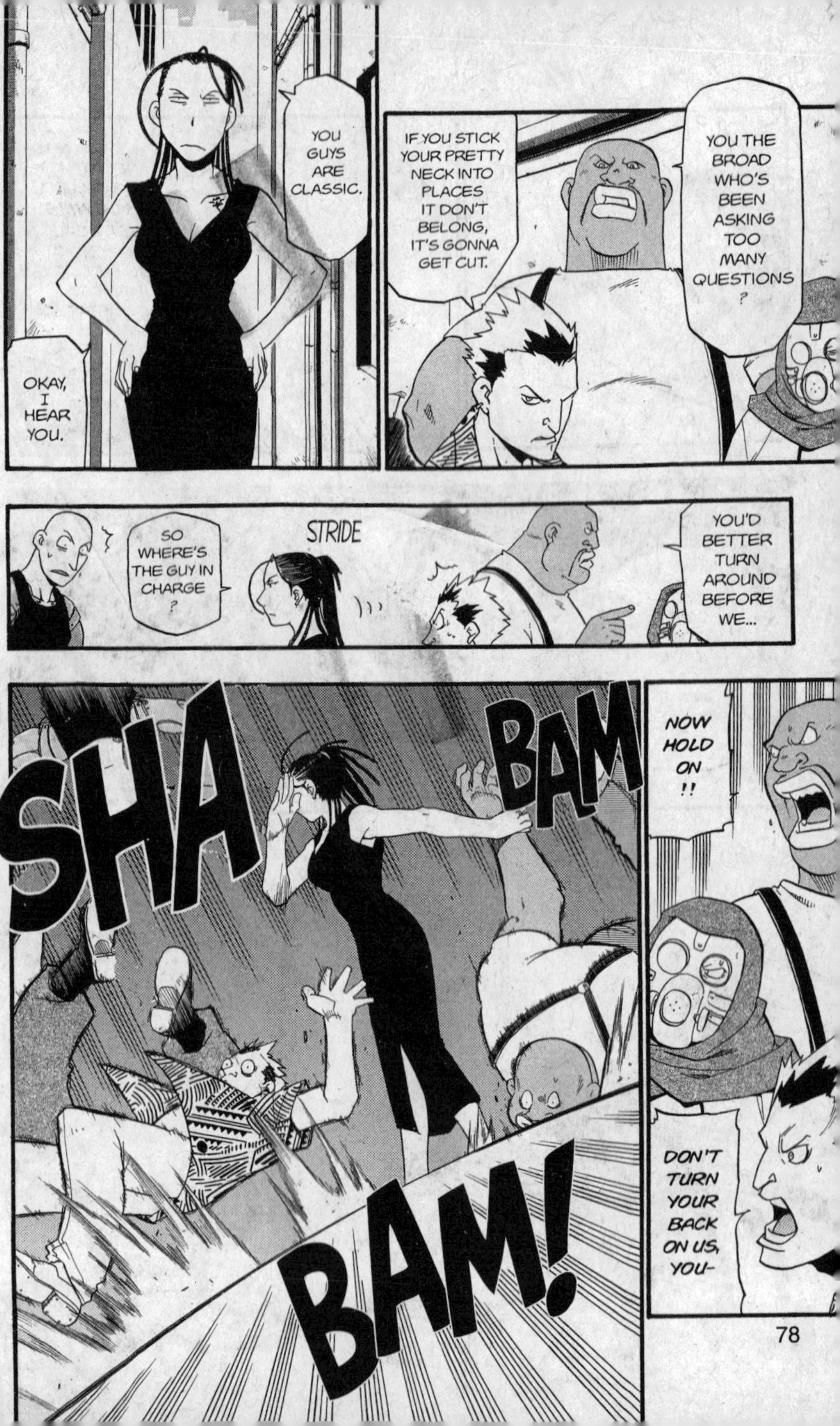
YOU THE BROAD WHO'S BEEN ASKING TOO MANY QUESTIONS?
IF YOU STICK YOUR PRETTY NECK INTO PLACES IT DON'T BELONG, IT'S GONNA GET CUT.
YOU GUYS ARE CLASSIC.
OKAY, I HEAR YOU.
YOU'D BETTER TURN AROUND BEFORE WE...
STRIDE
SO WHERE'S THE GUY IN CHARGE?
NOW HOLD ON!!
DON'T TURN YOUR BACK ON US, YOU-
BAM
SHA
BAM!

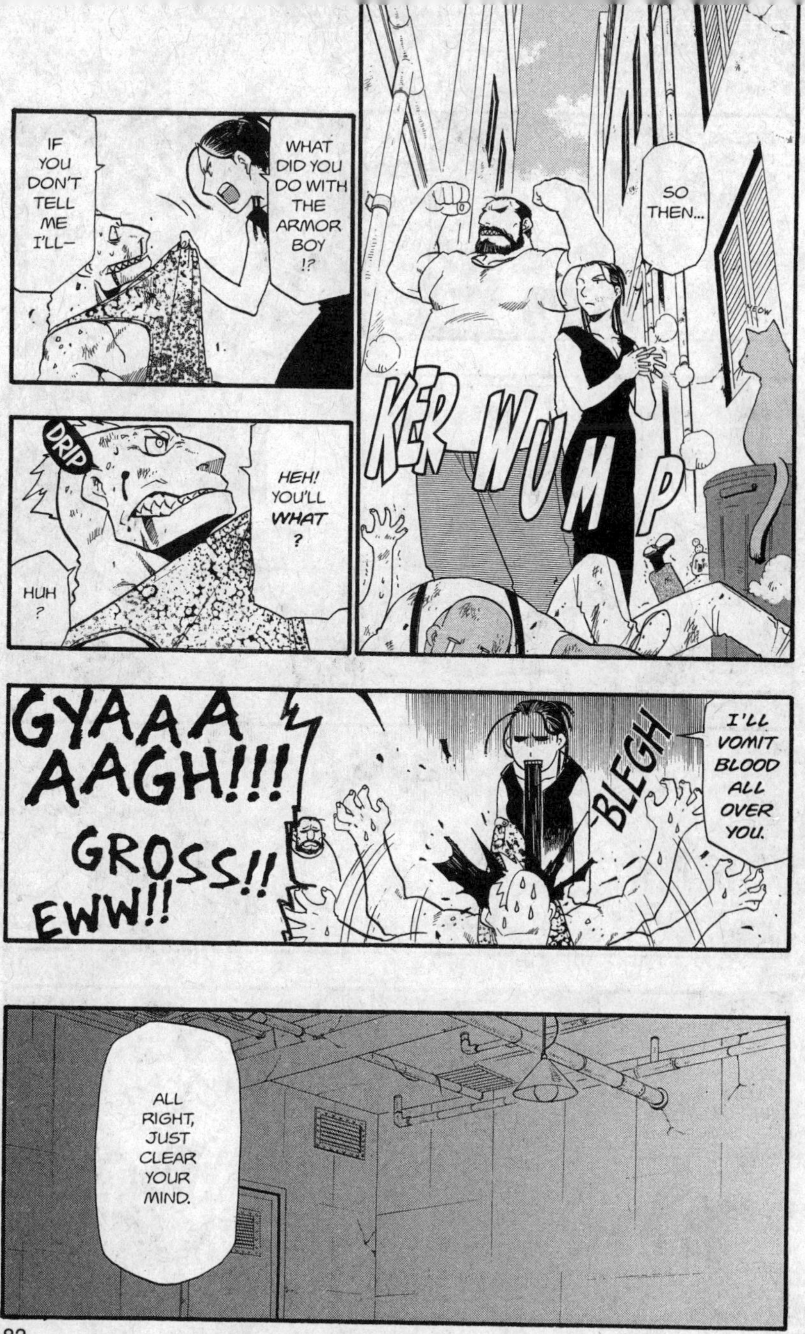
WHAT DID YOU DO WITH THE ARMOR BOY !?
IF YOU DON'T TELL ME I'LL—
DRIP
HEH! YOU'LL *WHAT* ?
HUH ?
SO THEN...
KER WUMP
MEOW
GYAAA AAGH!!!
GROSS!!
EWW!!
BLEGH
I'LL VOMIT BLOOD ALL OVER YOU.
ALL RIGHT, JUST CLEAR YOUR MIND.

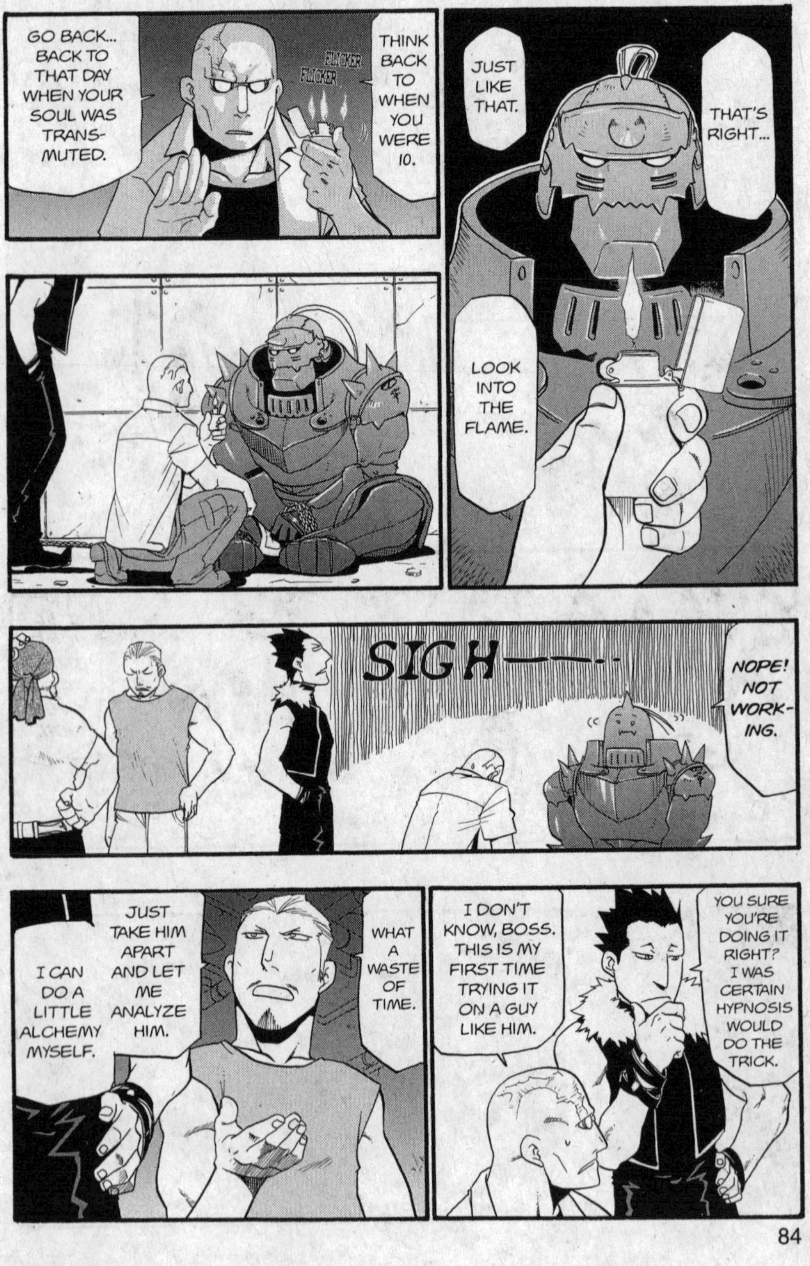

THAT'S RIGHT...
JUST LIKE THAT.
LOOK INTO THE FLAME.
THINK BACK TO WHEN YOU WERE 10.
FLICKER
FLICKER
GO BACK... BACK TO THAT DAY WHEN YOUR SOUL WAS TRANS-MUTED.
NOPE! NOT WORK-ING.
SIGH———..
YOU SURE YOU'RE DOING IT RIGHT? I WAS CERTAIN HYPNOSIS WOULD DO THE TRICK.
I DON'T KNOW, BOSS. THIS IS MY FIRST TIME TRYING IT ON A GUY LIKE HIM.
WHAT A WASTE OF TIME.
JUST TAKE HIM APART AND LET ME ANALYZE HIM.
I CAN DO A LITTLE ALCHEMY MYSELF.

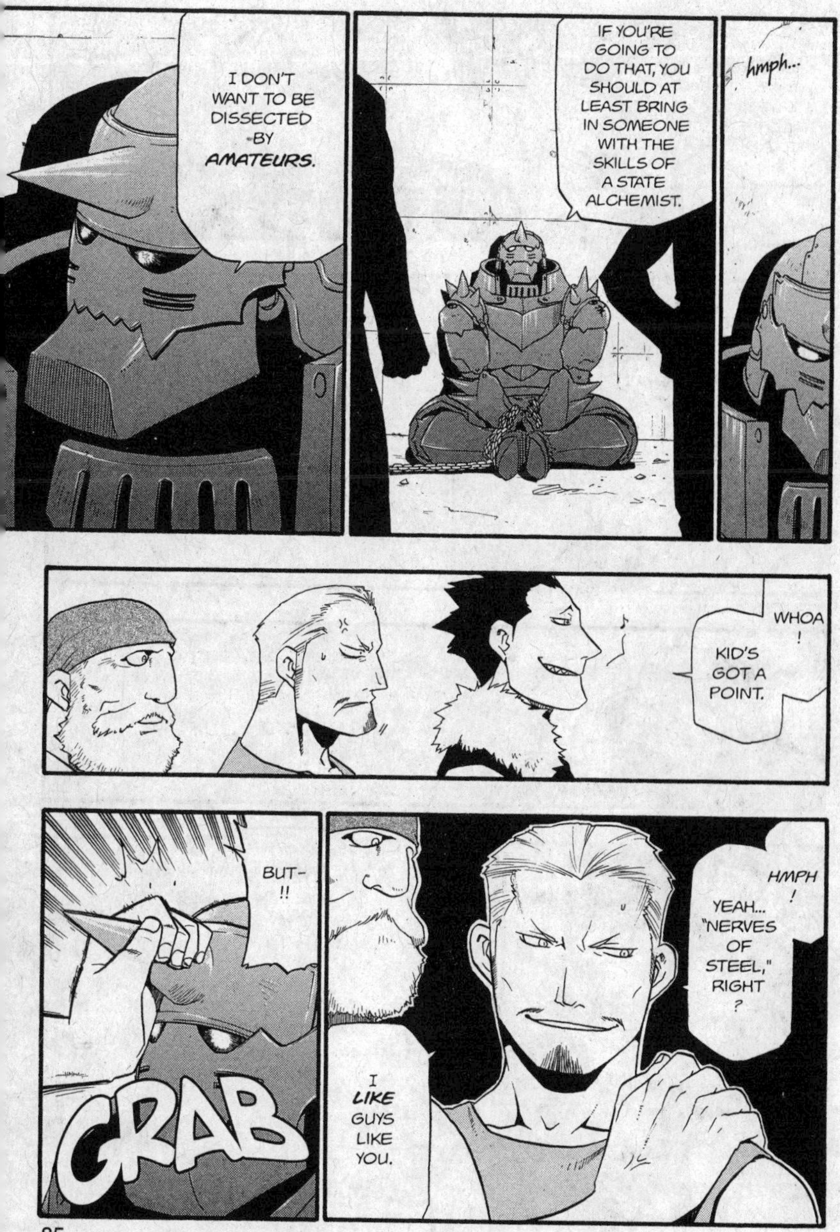
hmph...
IF YOU'RE GOING TO DO THAT, YOU SHOULD AT LEAST BRING IN SOMEONE WITH THE SKILLS OF A STATE ALCHEMIST.
I DON'T WANT TO BE DISSECTED BY AMATEURS.
WHOA! KID'S GOT A POINT.
HMPH! YEAH... "NERVES OF STEEL," RIGHT?
I LIKE GUYS LIKE YOU.
BUT-!!
GRAB

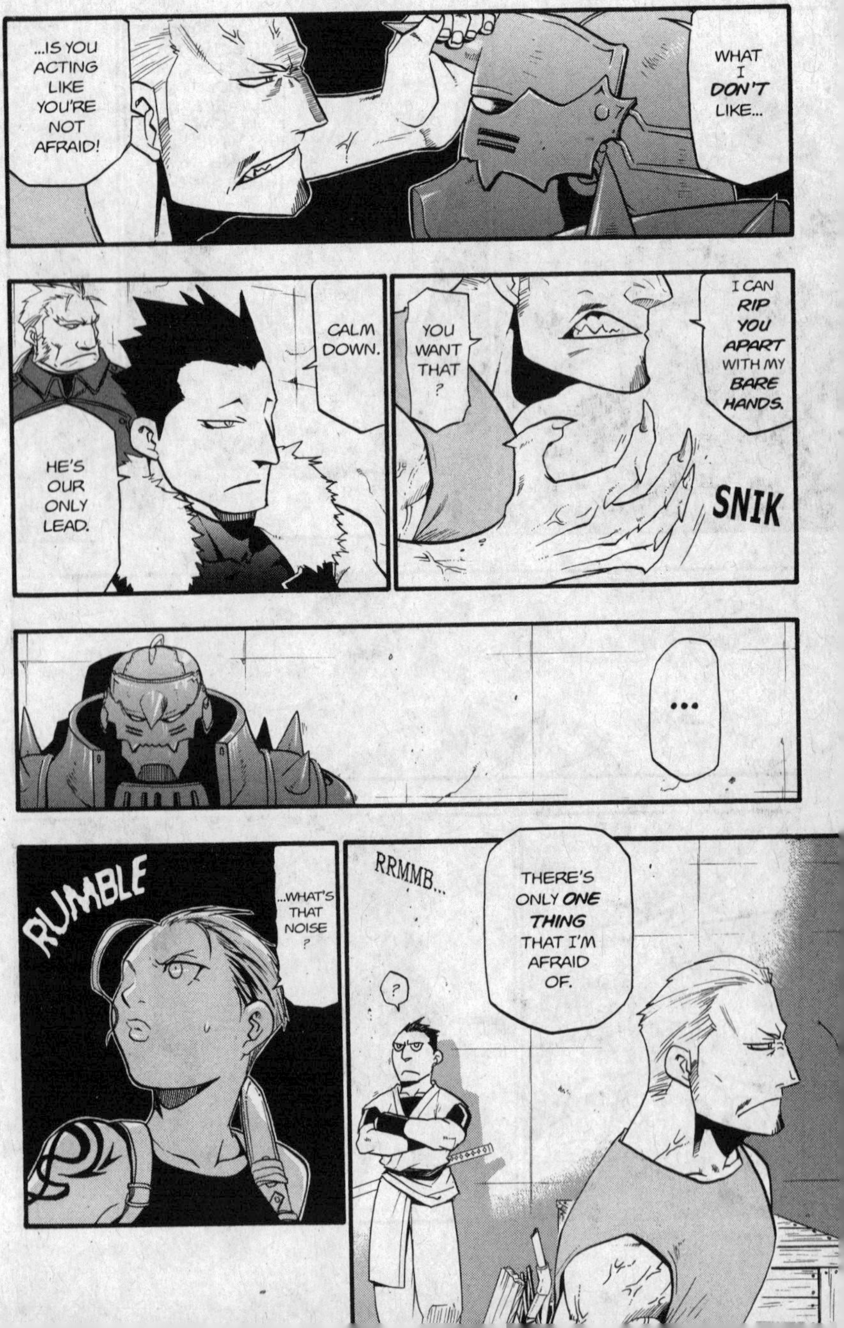
WHAT I DON'T LIKE...
...IS YOU ACTING LIKE YOU'RE NOT AFRAID!
I CAN RIP YOU APART WITH MY BARE HANDS.
SNIK
YOU WANT THAT?
CALM DOWN.
HE'S OUR ONLY LEAD.
...
RRMMB...
THERE'S ONLY ONE THING THAT I'M AFRAID OF.
?
RUMBLE
...WHAT'S THAT NOISE?

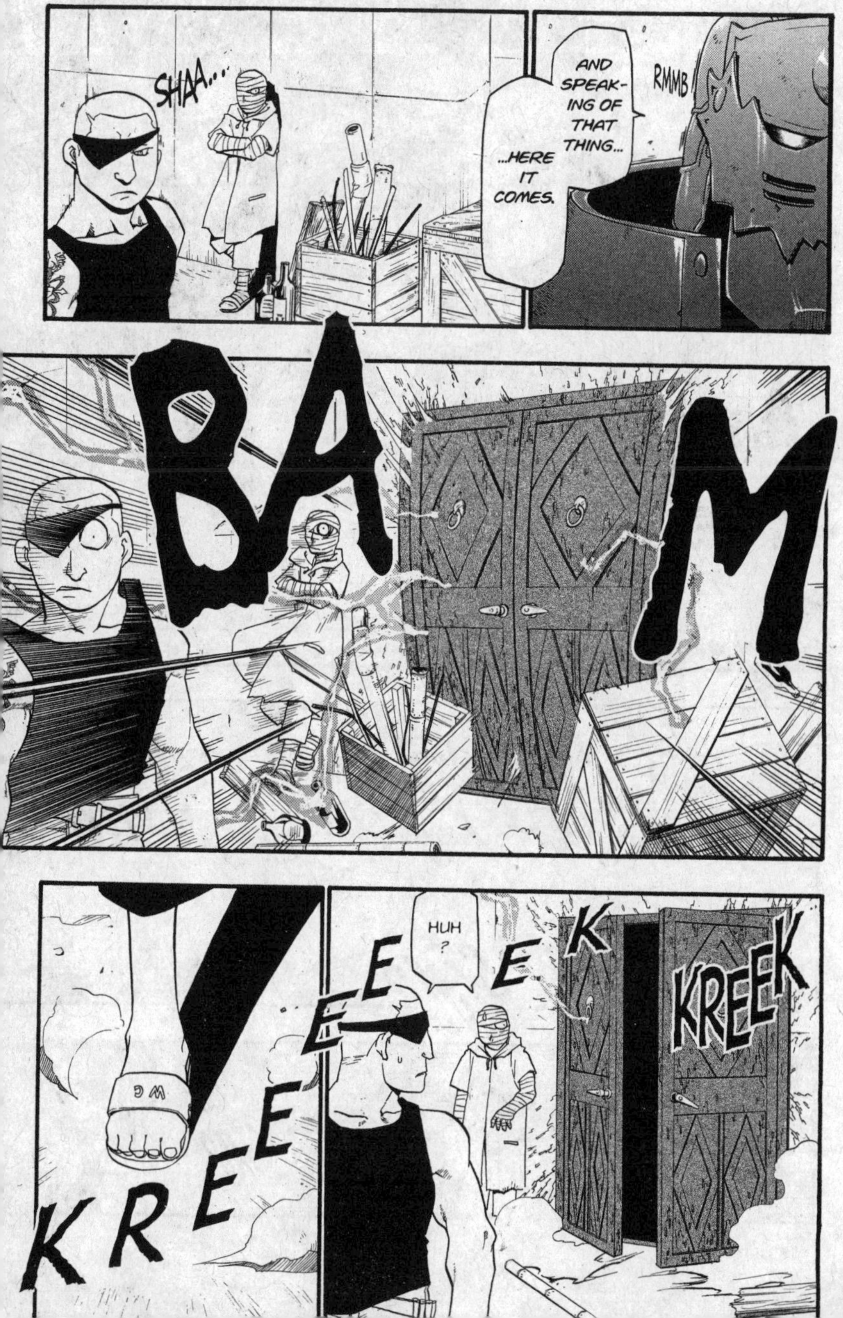

RMMB
AND SPEAKING OF THAT THING...
...HERE IT COMES.
SHAA...
BAM
KREEK
HUH?
KREEEEEK

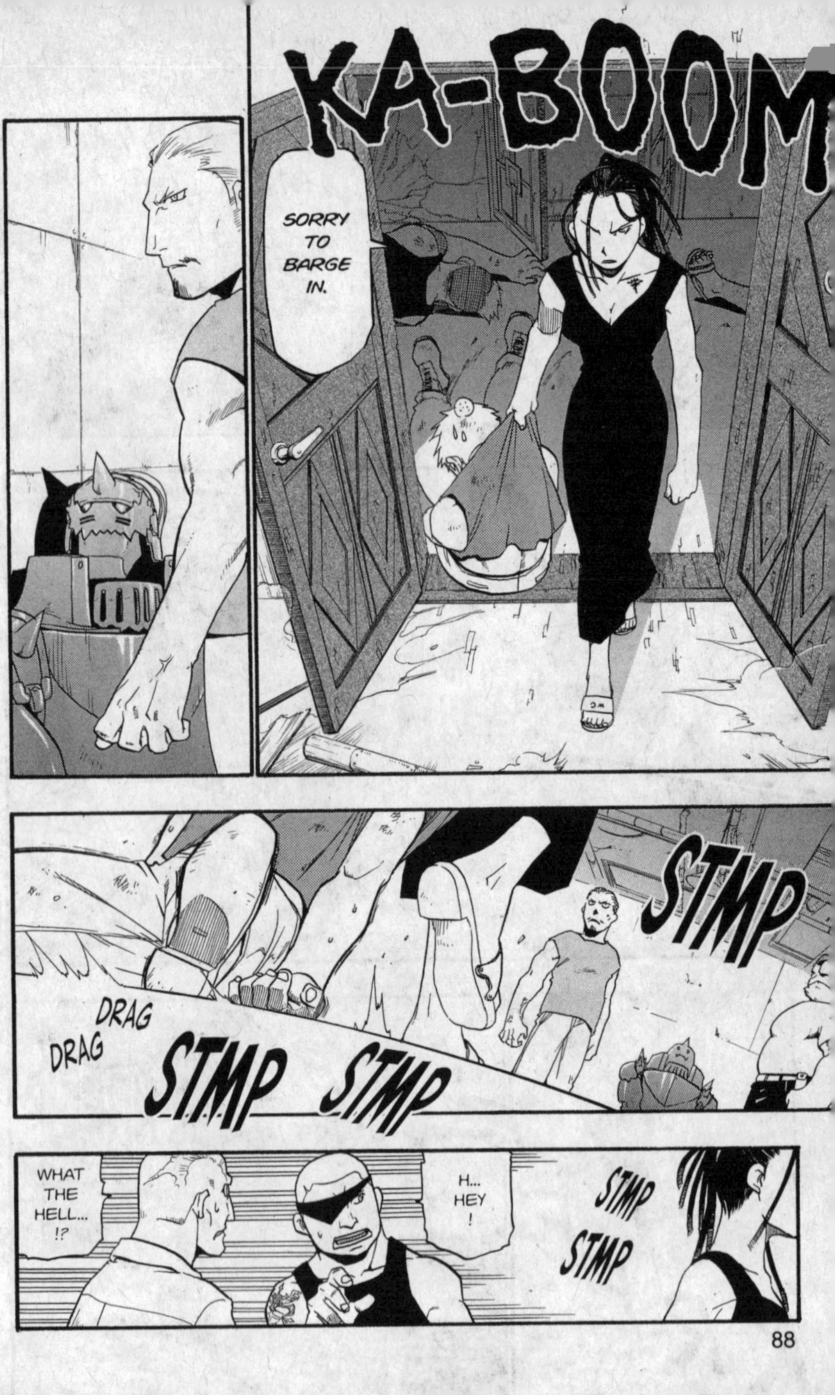
KA-BOOM
SORRY TO BARGE IN.
STMP
DRAG DRAG
STMP STMP
STMP STMP
H... HEY!
WHAT THE HELL...!?

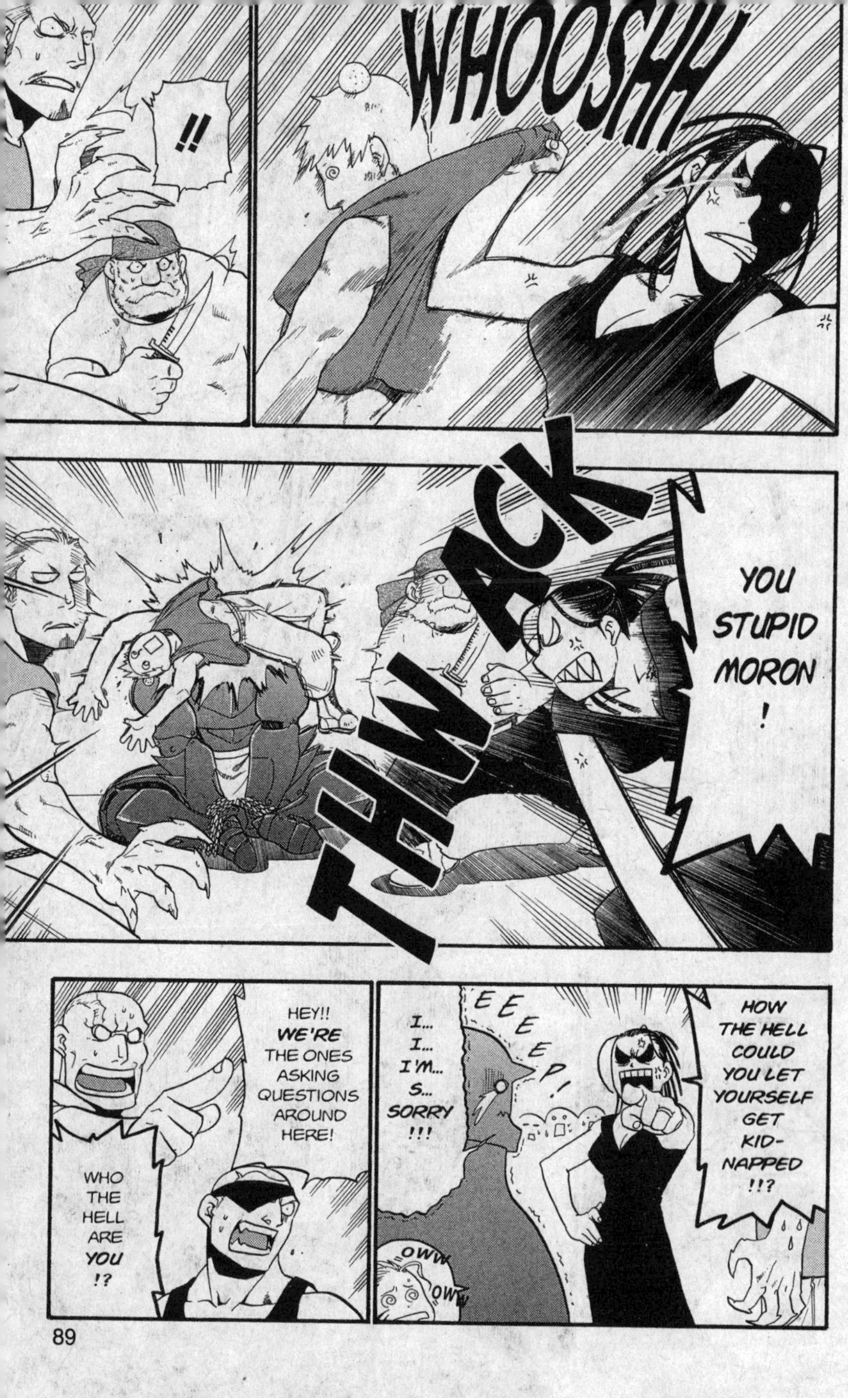
WHOOSHH
!!
THWACK
YOU STUPID MORON!
HOW THE HELL COULD YOU LET YOURSELF GET KID-NAPPED!!?
EEEEEP!
I... I... I'M... S... SORRY!!!
OWW OWW
HEY!! WE'RE THE ONES ASKING QUESTIONS AROUND HERE!
WHO THE HELL ARE YOU!?

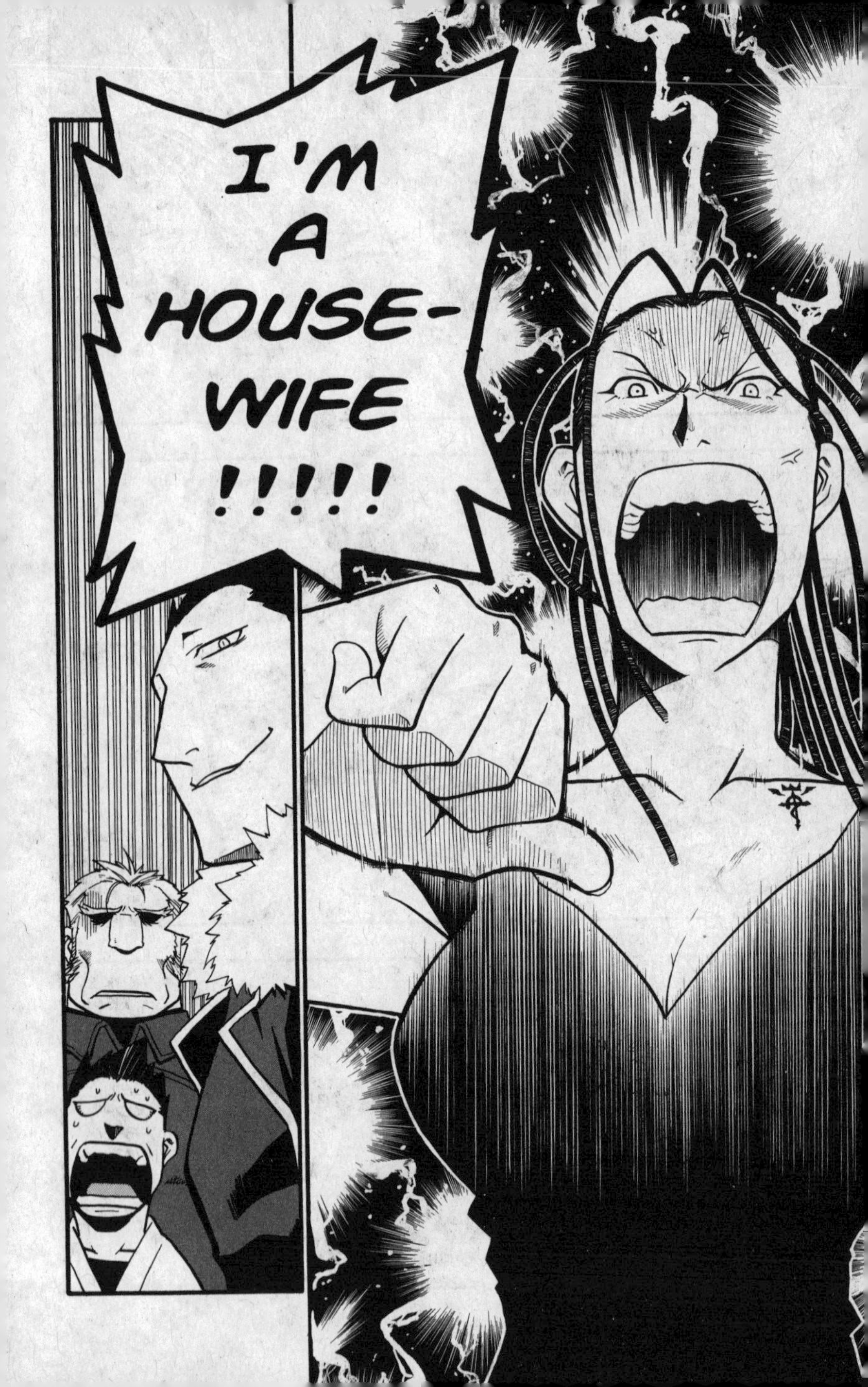
I'M A HOUSE-WIFE !!!!!

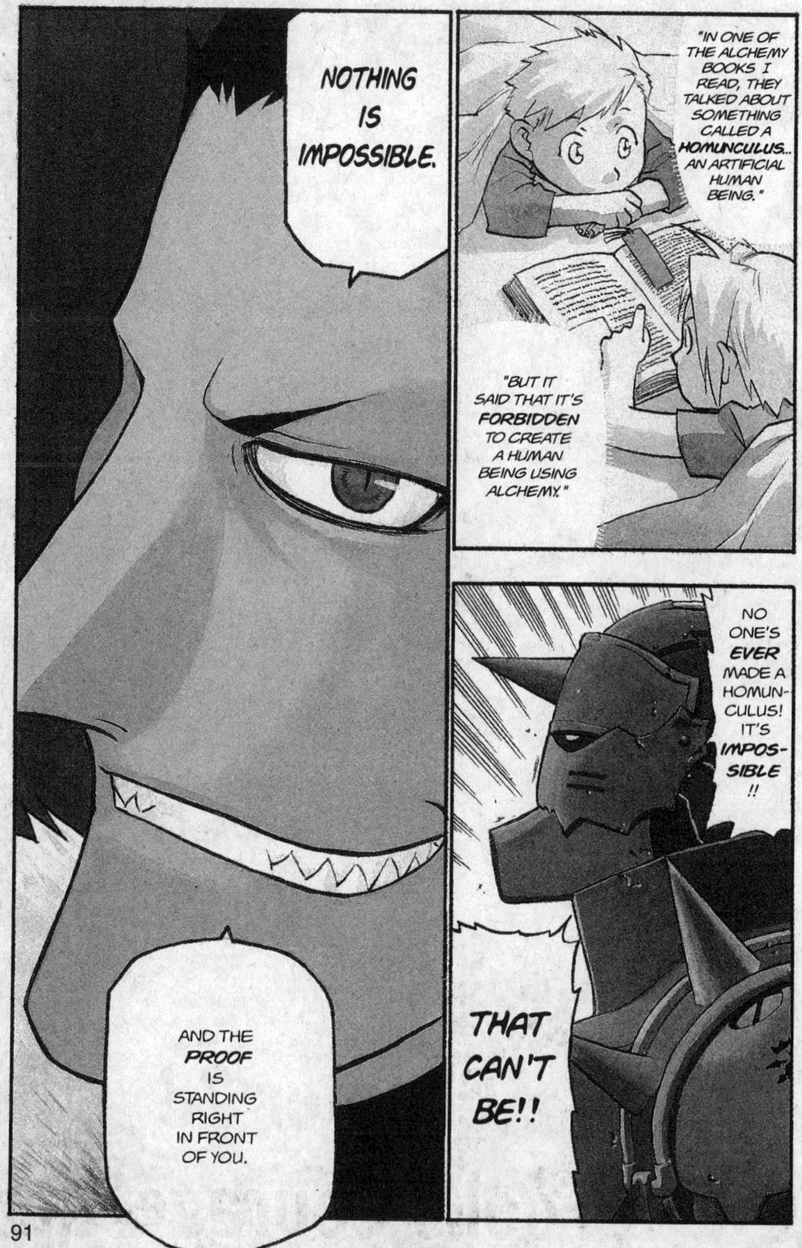
"IN ONE OF THE ALCHEMY BOOKS I READ, THEY TALKED ABOUT SOMETHING CALLED A HOMUNCULUS... AN ARTIFICIAL HUMAN BEING."
"BUT IT SAID THAT IT'S FORBIDDEN TO CREATE A HUMAN BEING USING ALCHEMY."
NO ONE'S EVER MADE A HOMUNCULUS! IT'S IMPOSSIBLE!!
THAT CAN'T BE!!
NOTHING IS IMPOSSIBLE.
AND THE PROOF IS STANDING RIGHT IN FRONT OF YOU.

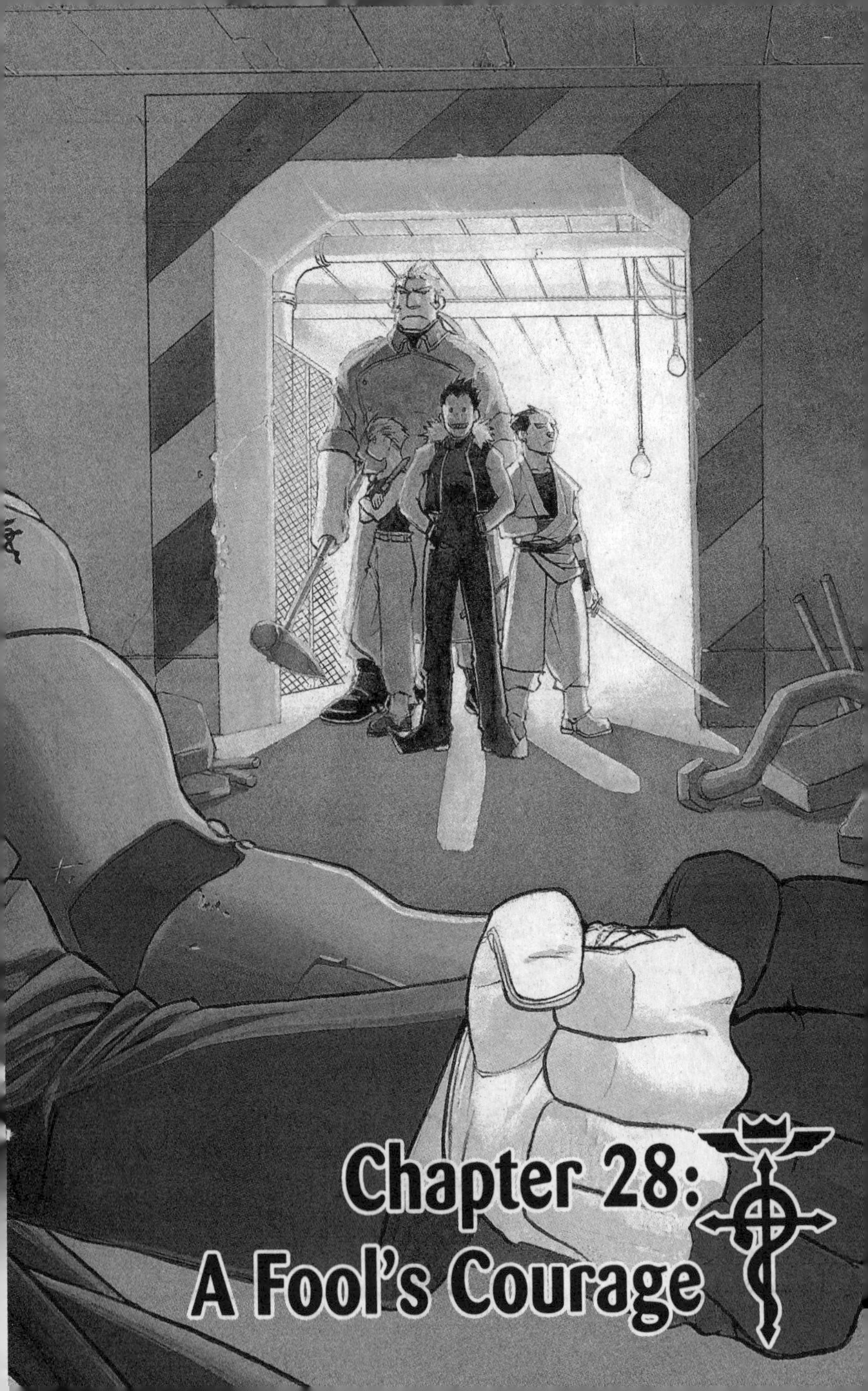
Chapter 28:
A Fool's Courage

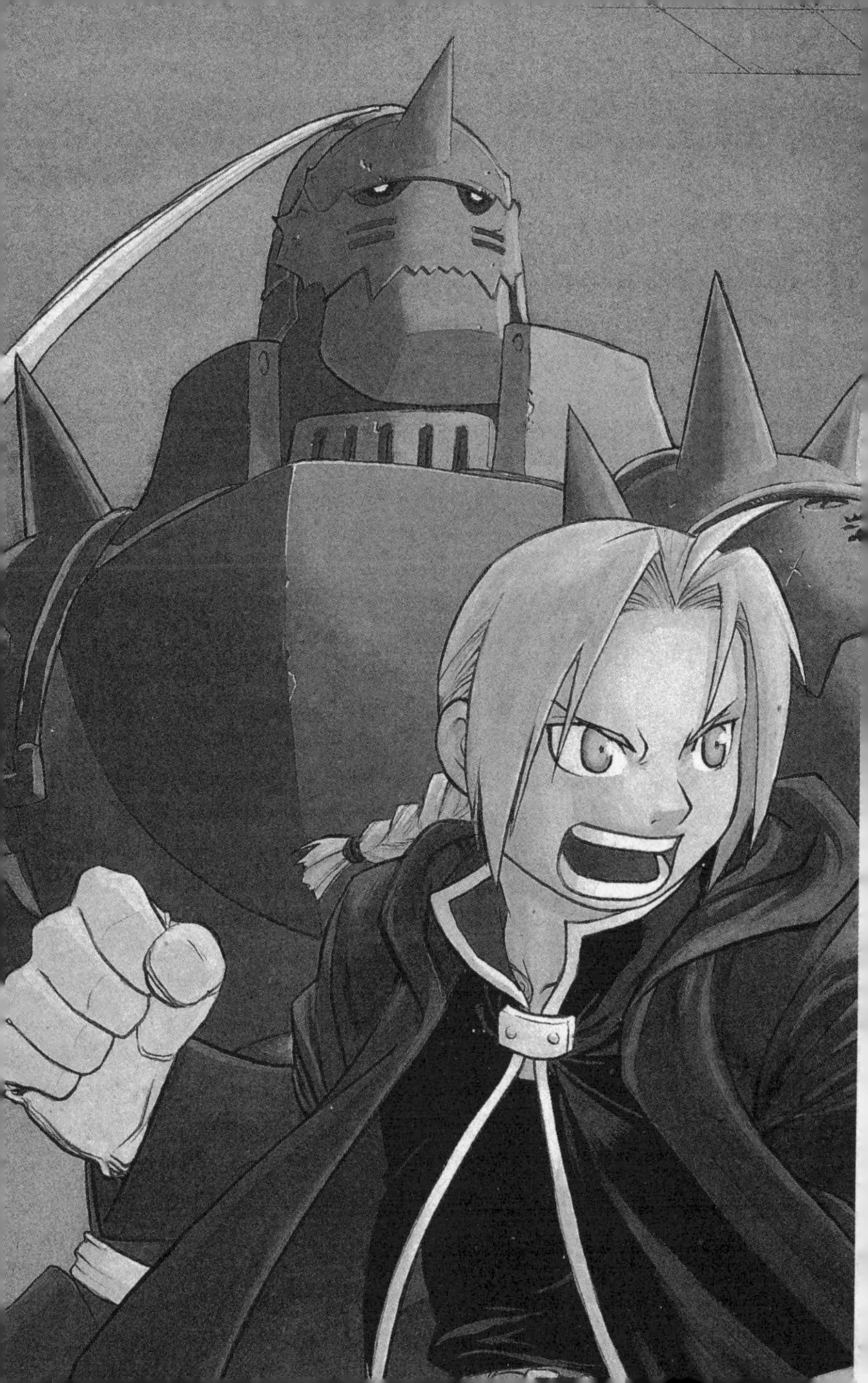

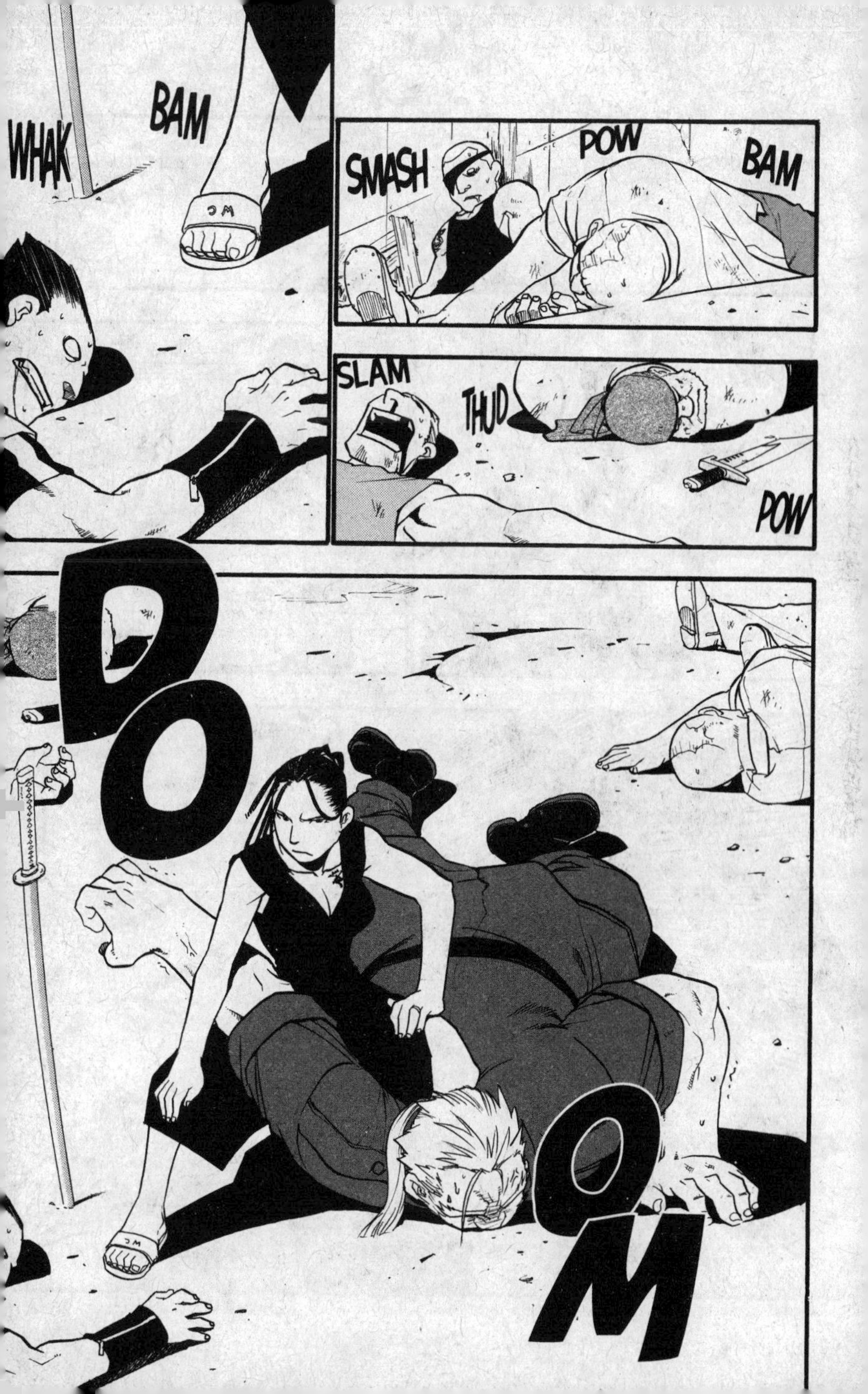
BAM
POW
SMASH
SLAM
THUD
POW
BAM
WHAK
DOOM

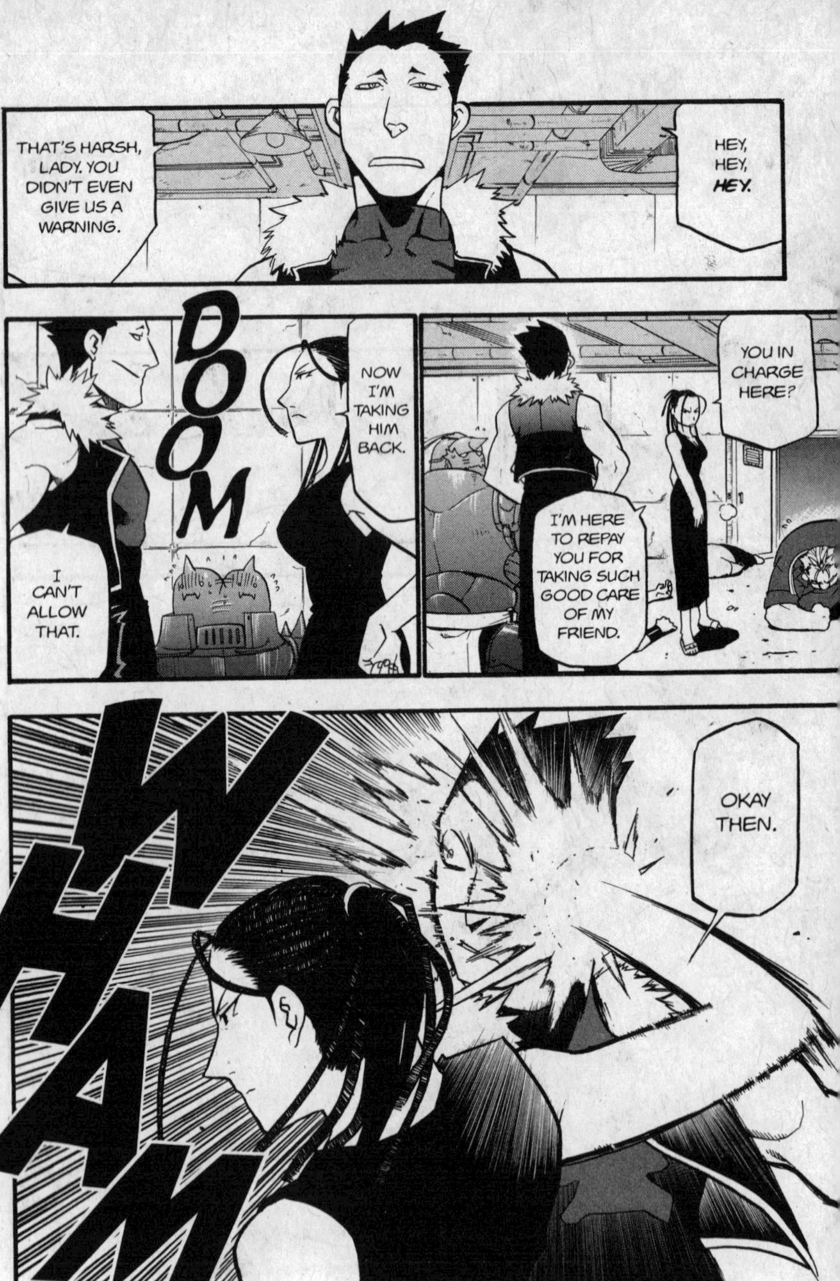
HEY, HEY, HEY.
THAT'S HARSH, LADY. YOU DIDN'T EVEN GIVE US A WARNING.
YOU IN CHARGE HERE?
I'M HERE TO REPAY YOU FOR TAKING SUCH GOOD CARE OF MY FRIEND.
NOW I'M TAKING HIM BACK.
DOOM
I CAN'T ALLOW THAT.
OKAY THEN.
WHAM

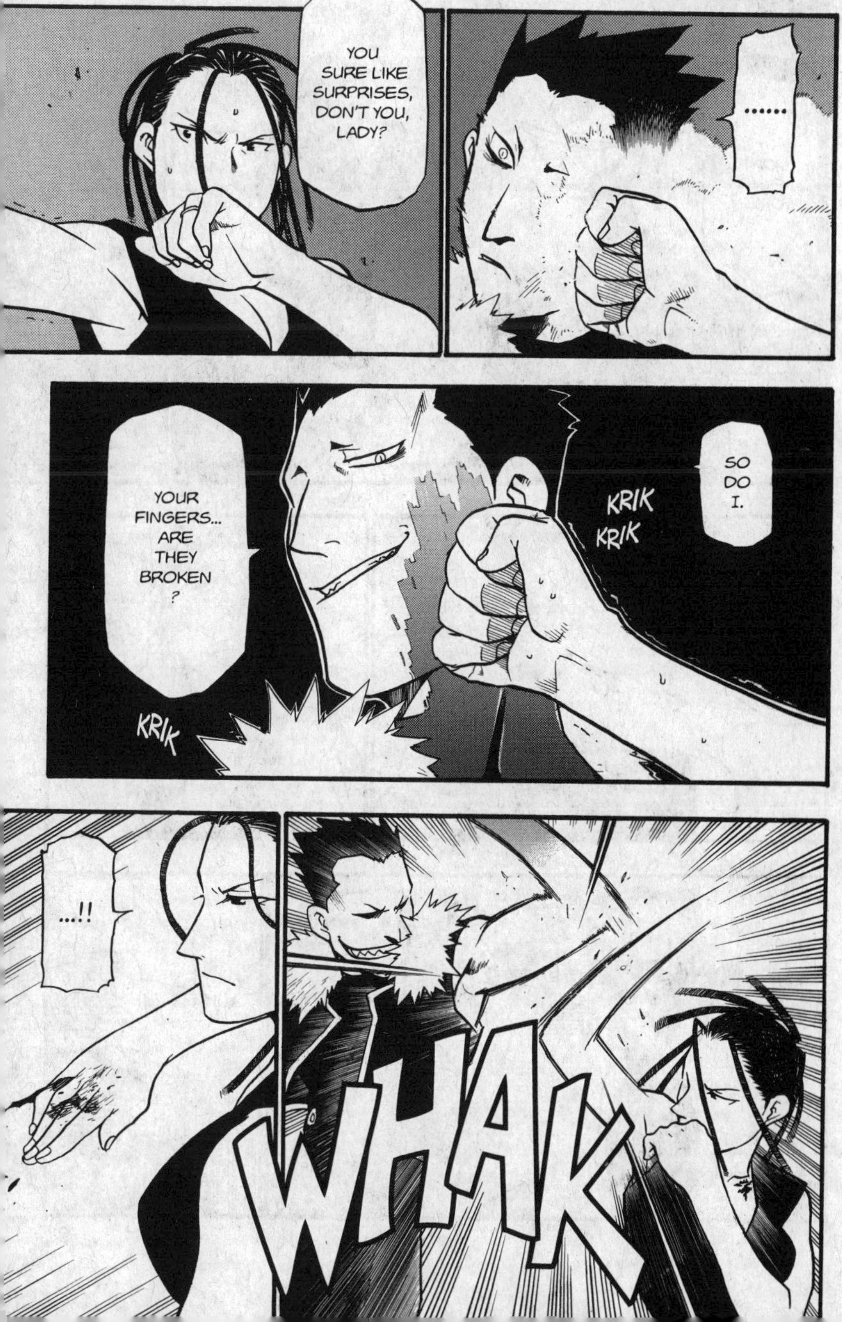

......
YOU SURE LIKE SURPRISES, DON'T YOU, LADY?
SO DO I.
KRIK KRIK
YOUR FINGERS... ARE THEY BROKEN?
KRIK
WHAK
...!!

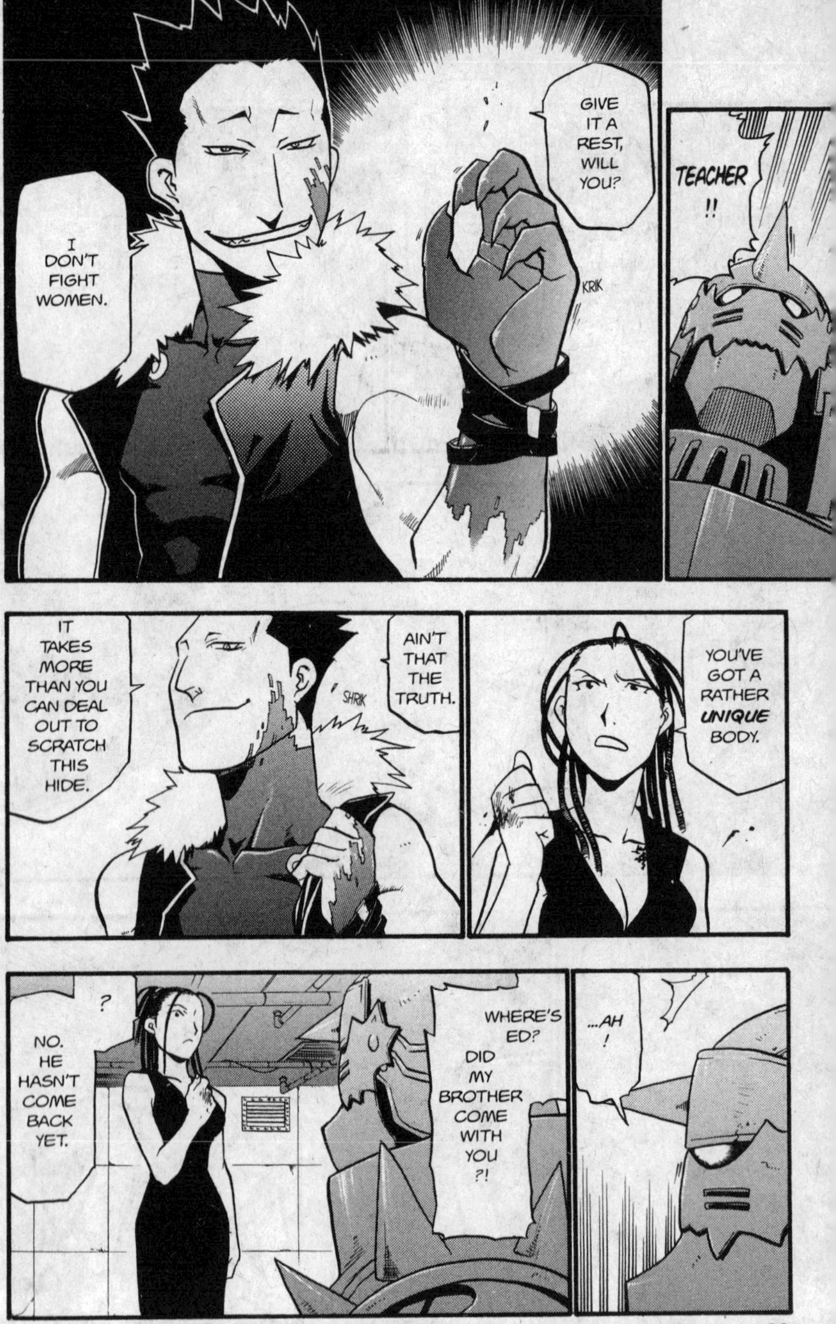
TEACHER !!
GIVE IT A REST, WILL YOU?
I DON'T FIGHT WOMEN.
KRIK
YOU'VE GOT A RATHER *UNIQUE* BODY.
AIN'T THAT THE TRUTH.
SHRIK
IT TAKES MORE THAN YOU CAN DEAL OUT TO SCRATCH THIS HIDE.
...AH!
WHERE'S ED? DID MY BROTHER COME WITH YOU?!
?
NO. HE HASN'T COME BACK YET.

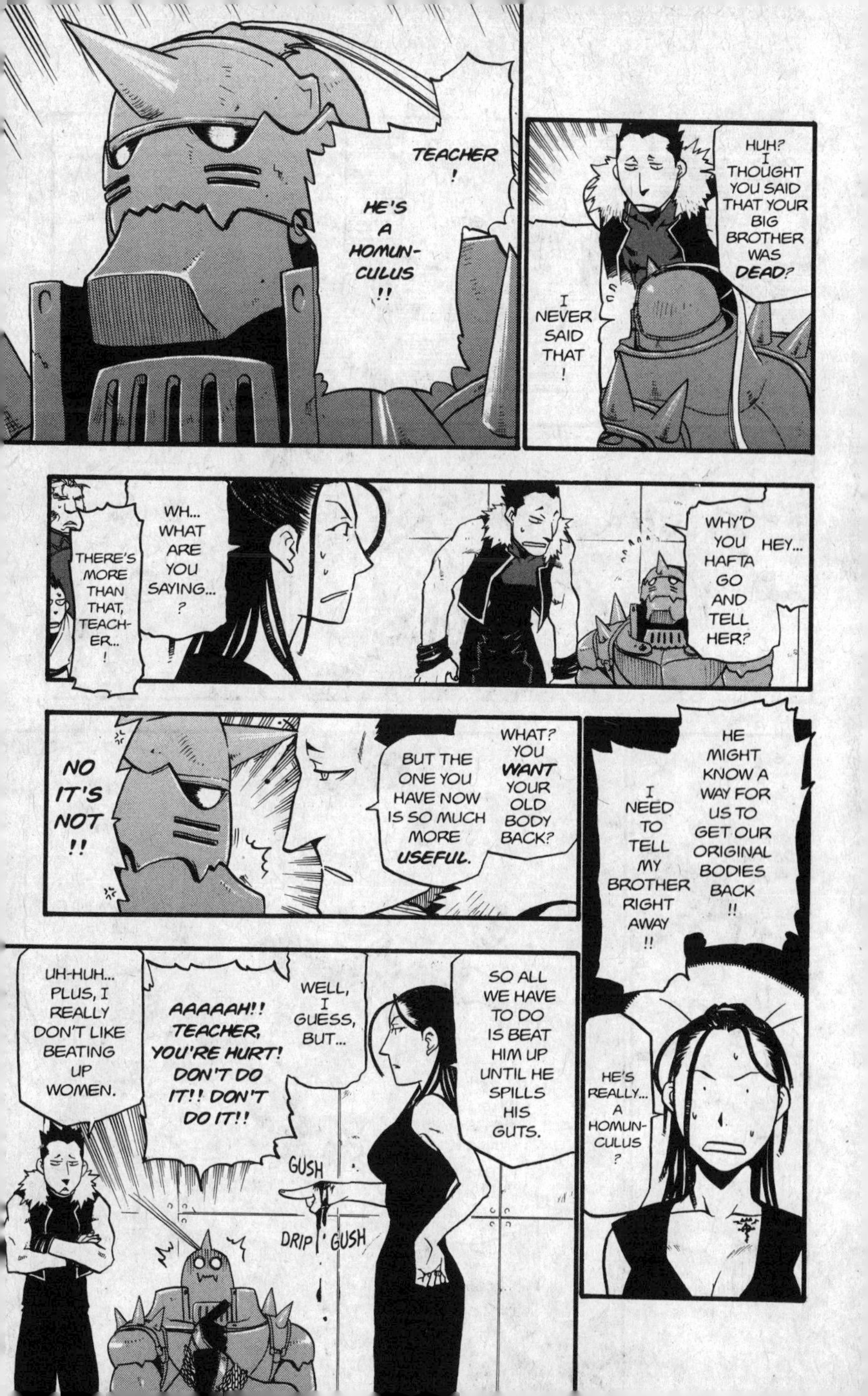
HUH? I THOUGHT YOU SAID THAT YOUR BIG BROTHER WAS DEAD?
I NEVER SAID THAT!
TEACHER!
HE'S A HOMUNCULUS!!
HEY...
WHY'D YOU HAFTA GO AND TELL HER?
WH... WHAT ARE YOU SAYING...?
THERE'S MORE THAN THAT, TEACHER...!
HE MIGHT KNOW A WAY FOR US TO GET OUR ORIGINAL BODIES BACK!!
I NEED TO TELL MY BROTHER RIGHT AWAY!!
HE'S REALLY... A HOMUNCULUS?
WHAT? YOU WANT YOUR OLD BODY BACK?
BUT THE ONE YOU HAVE NOW IS SO MUCH MORE USEFUL.
NO IT'S NOT!!
SO ALL WE HAVE TO DO IS BEAT HIM UP UNTIL HE SPILLS HIS GUTS.
WELL, I GUESS, BUT...
GUSH
DRIP
GUSH
AAAAAH!! TEACHER, YOU'RE HURT! DON'T DO IT!! DON'T DO IT!!
UH-HUH... PLUS, I REALLY DON'T LIKE BEATING UP WOMEN.

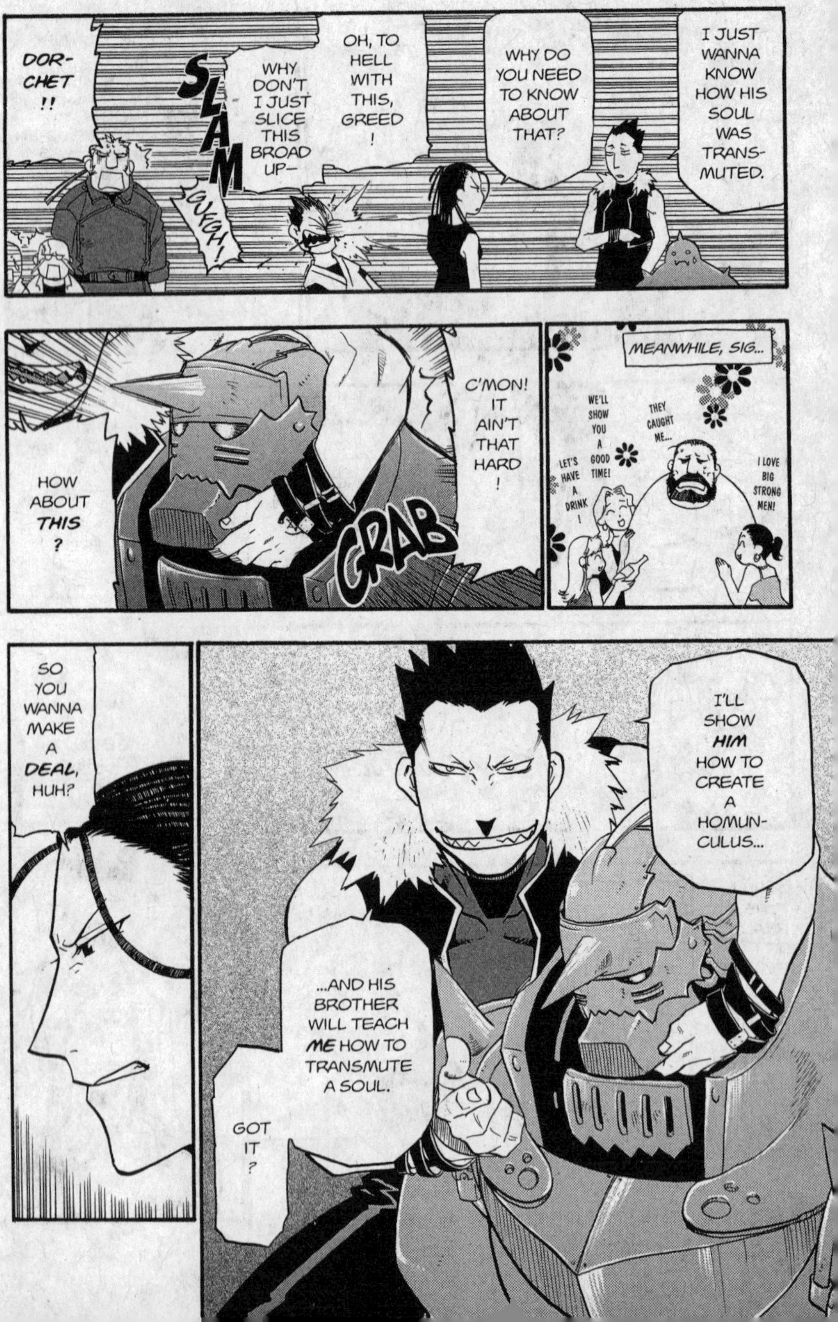

I JUST WANNA KNOW HOW HIS SOUL WAS TRANSMUTED.
WHY DO YOU NEED TO KNOW ABOUT THAT?
OH, TO HELL WITH THIS, GREED!
WHY DON'T I JUST SLICE THIS BROAD UP—
SLAM
GUKGH!
DOR-CHET!!
MEANWHILE, SIG...
THEY CAUGHT ME...
I LOVE BIG STRONG MEN!
WE'LL SHOW YOU A GOOD TIME!
LET'S HAVE A DRINK!
C'MON! IT AIN'T THAT HARD!
GRAB
HOW ABOUT THIS?
I'LL SHOW HIM HOW TO CREATE A HOMUNCULUS...
...AND HIS BROTHER WILL TEACH ME HOW TO TRANSMUTE A SOUL.
GOT IT?
SO YOU WANNA MAKE A DEAL, HUH?

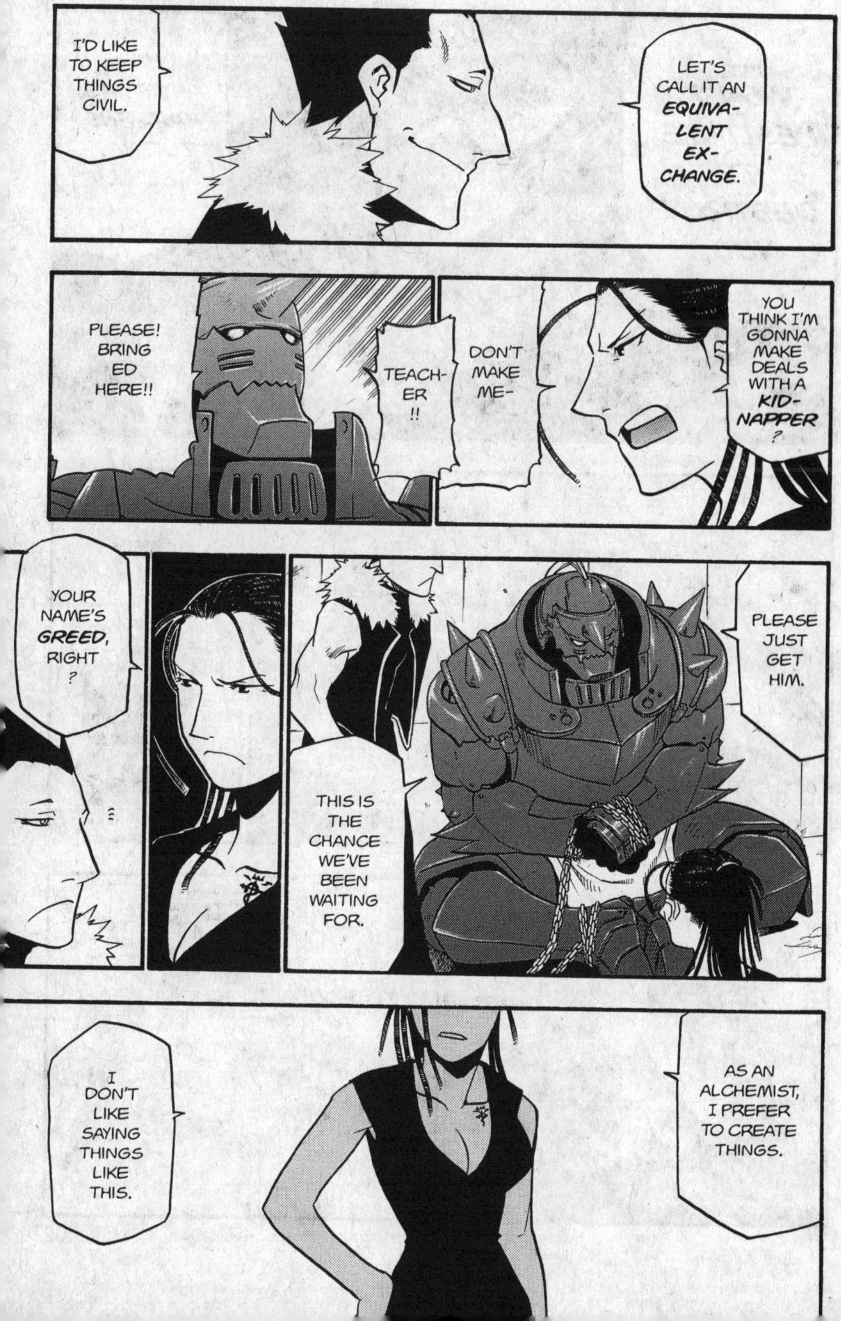
LET'S CALL IT AN **EQUIVALENT EXCHANGE.**
I'D LIKE TO KEEP THINGS CIVIL.
YOU THINK I'M GONNA MAKE DEALS WITH A **KIDNAPPER**?
DON'T MAKE ME-
TEACHER!!
PLEASE! BRING ED HERE!!
PLEASE JUST GET HIM.
THIS IS THE CHANCE WE'VE BEEN WAITING FOR.
YOUR NAME'S **GREED**, RIGHT?
AS AN ALCHEMIST, I PREFER TO CREATE THINGS.
I DON'T LIKE SAYING THINGS LIKE THIS.

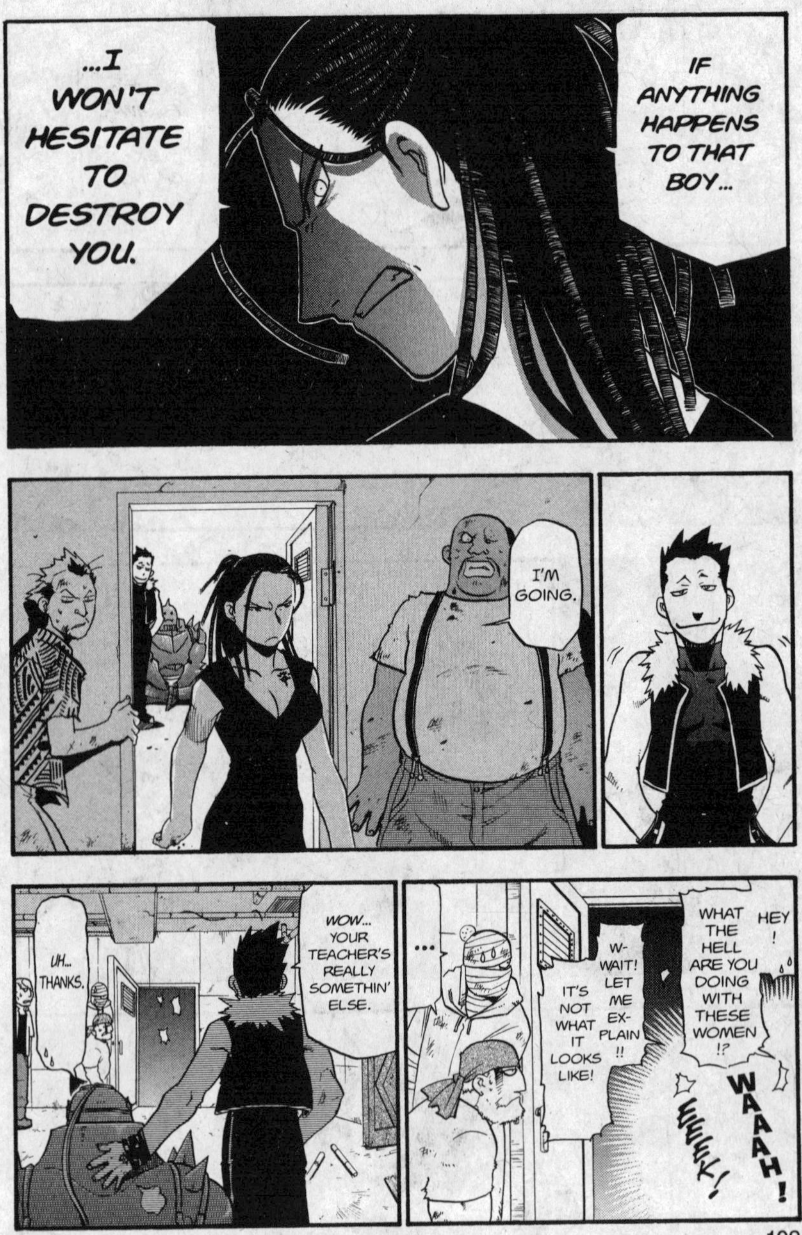
IF ANYTHING HAPPENS TO THAT BOY...
...I WON'T HESITATE TO DESTROY YOU.
I'M GOING.
HEY!
WHAT THE HELL ARE YOU DOING WITH THESE WOMEN!?
W-WAIT! LET ME EX-PLAIN!!
IT'S NOT WHAT IT LOOKS LIKE!
...
WAAAH!
EEEEK!
WOW... YOUR TEACHER'S REALLY SOMETHIN' ELSE.
UH... THANKS.

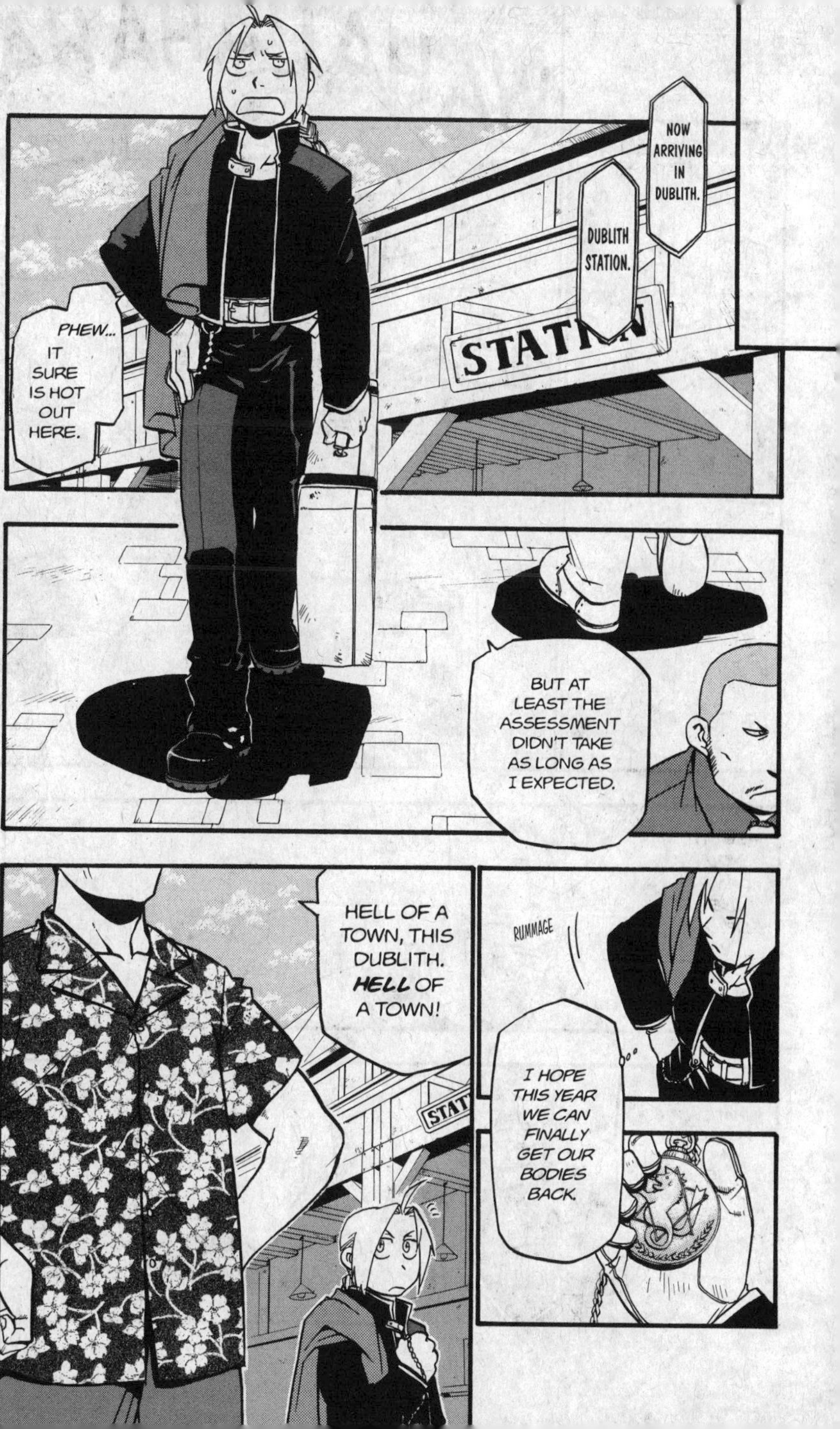
NOW ARRIVING IN DUBLITH.
DUBLITH STATION.
PHEW... IT SURE IS HOT OUT HERE.
BUT AT LEAST THE ASSESSMENT DIDN'T TAKE AS LONG AS I EXPECTED.
RUMMAGE
I HOPE THIS YEAR WE CAN FINALLY GET OUR BODIES BACK.
HELL OF A TOWN, THIS DUBLITH. **HELL** OF A TOWN!

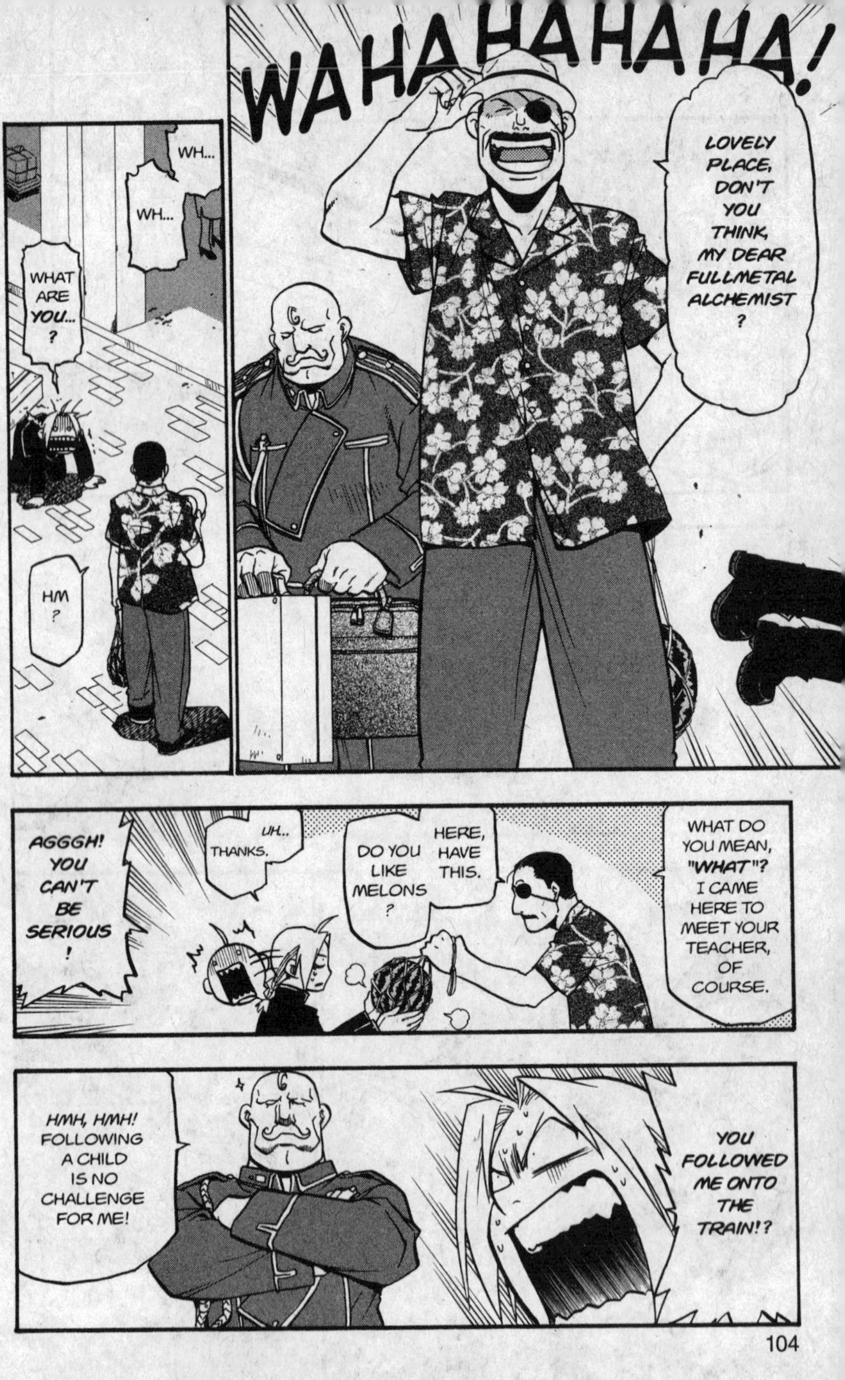
WAHAHAHAHAHA!
LOVELY PLACE, DON'T YOU THINK, MY DEAR FULLMETAL ALCHEMIST?
WH...
WH...
WHAT ARE YOU...?
HM?
WHAT DO YOU MEAN, "WHAT"? I CAME HERE TO MEET YOUR TEACHER, OF COURSE.
HERE, HAVE THIS.
DO YOU LIKE MELONS?
UH.. THANKS.
AGGGH! YOU CAN'T BE SERIOUS!
YOU FOLLOWED ME ONTO THE TRAIN!?
HMH, HMH! FOLLOWING A CHILD IS NO CHALLENGE FOR ME!

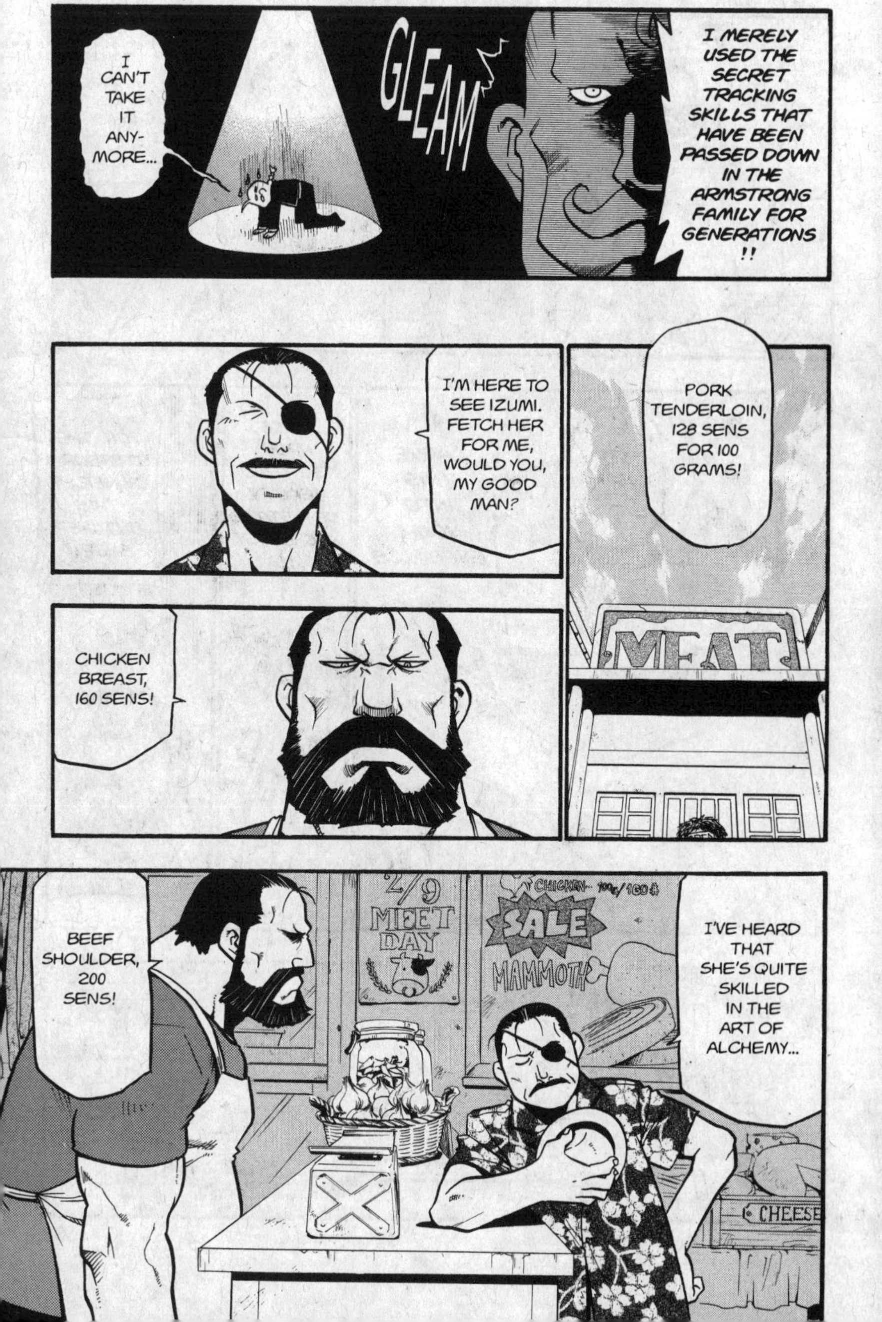
I MERELY USED THE SECRET TRACKING SKILLS THAT HAVE BEEN PASSED DOWN IN THE ARMSTRONG FAMILY FOR GENERATIONS !!
GLEAM
I CAN'T TAKE IT ANY-MORE...
PORK TENDERLOIN, 128 SENS FOR 100 GRAMS!
MEAT
I'M HERE TO SEE IZUMI. FETCH HER FOR ME, WOULD YOU, MY GOOD MAN?
CHICKEN BREAST, 160 SENS!
I'VE HEARD THAT SHE'S QUITE SKILLED IN THE ART OF ALCHEMY...
CHICKEN
SALE
MAMMOTH
2/9 MEET DAY
BEEF SHOULDER, 200 SENS!
CHEESE

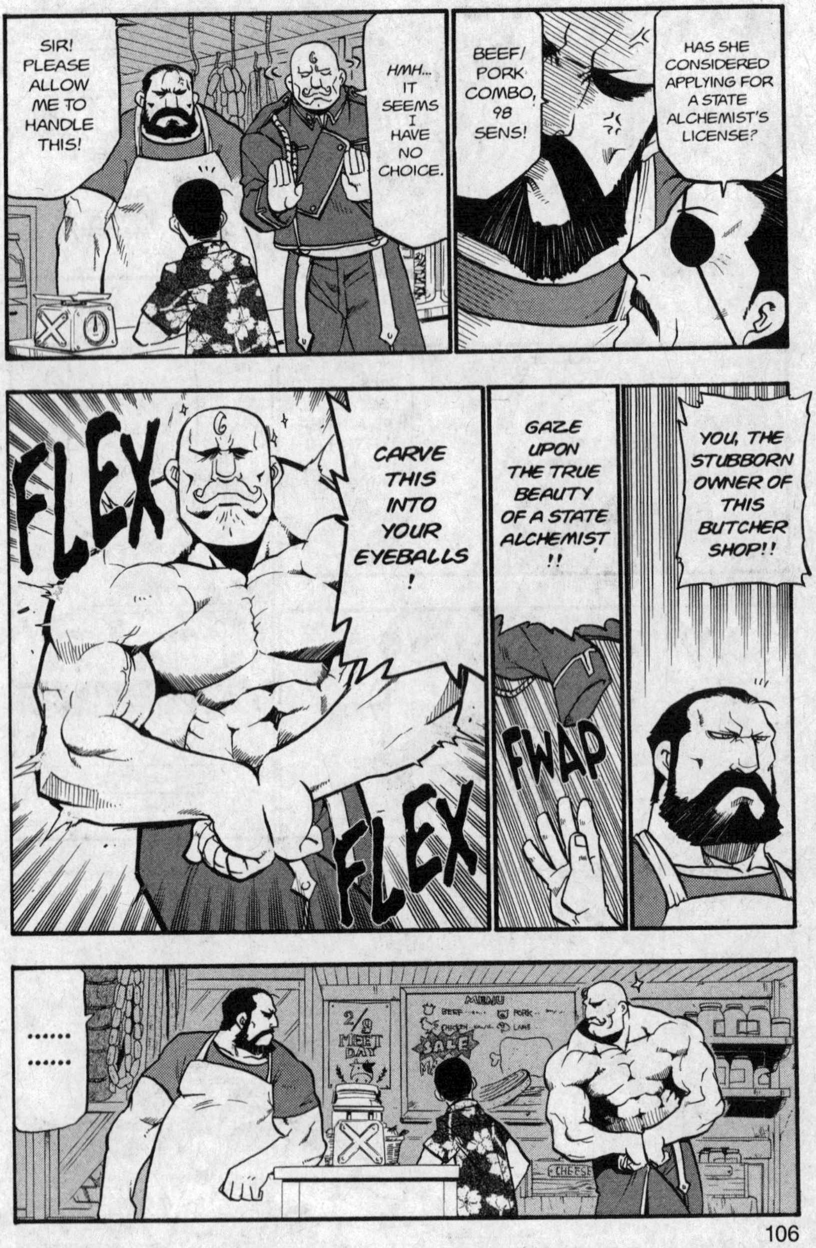
HAS SHE CONSIDERED APPLYING FOR A STATE ALCHEMIST'S LICENSE?
BEEF/PORK COMBO, 98 SENS!
HMH... IT SEEMS I HAVE NO CHOICE.
SIR! PLEASE ALLOW ME TO HANDLE THIS!
YOU, THE STUBBORN OWNER OF THIS BUTCHER SHOP!!
GAZE UPON THE TRUE BEAUTY OF A STATE ALCHEMIST!!
FWAP
CARVE THIS INTO YOUR EYEBALLS!
FLEX
FLEX
MENU
BEEF
PORK
SALE
2/9 MEET DAY
CHEESE
......
......

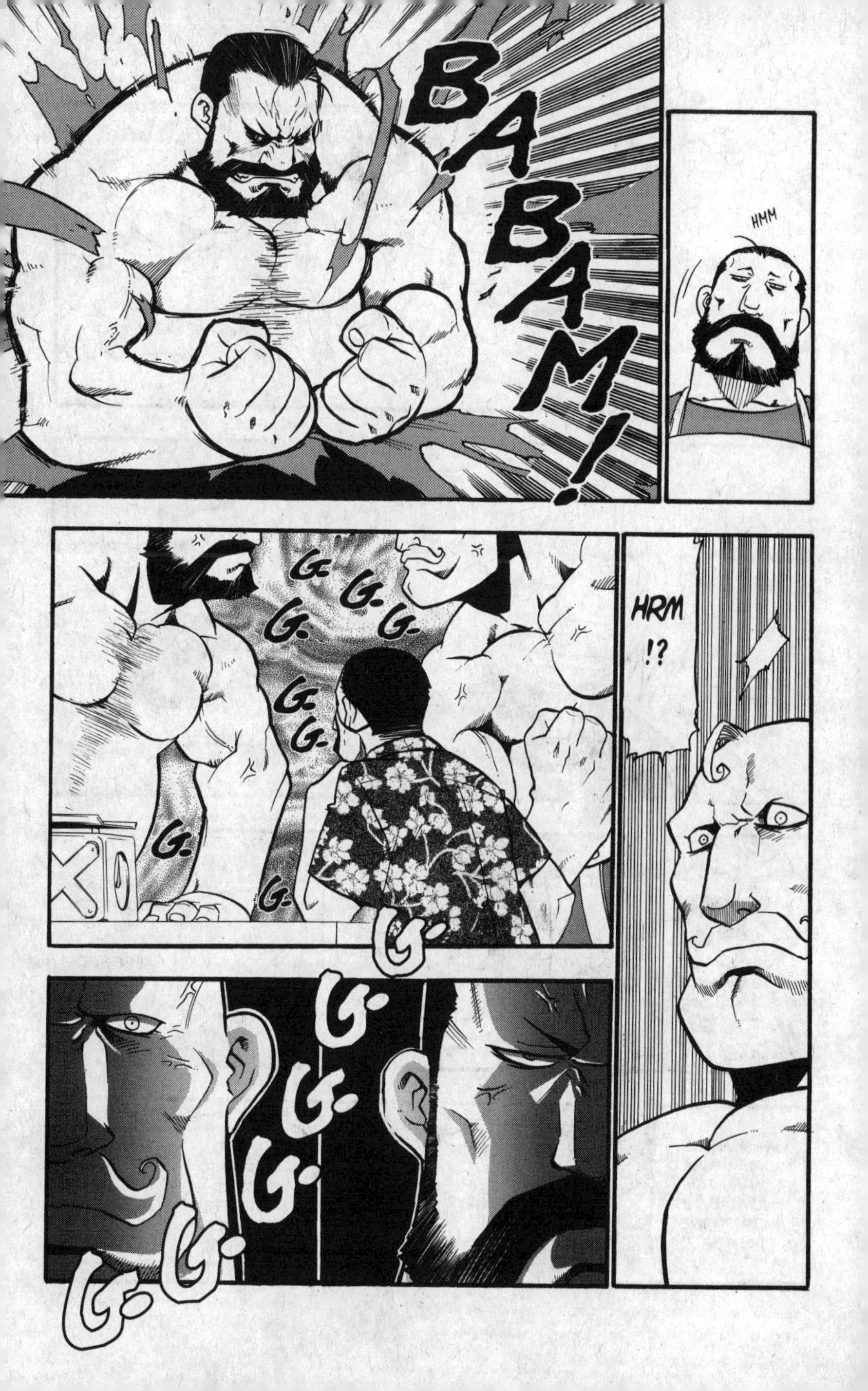
HMM
BABAM!
HRM
!?
G- G- G- G- G- G- G- G-
G- G- G- G- G- G- G-

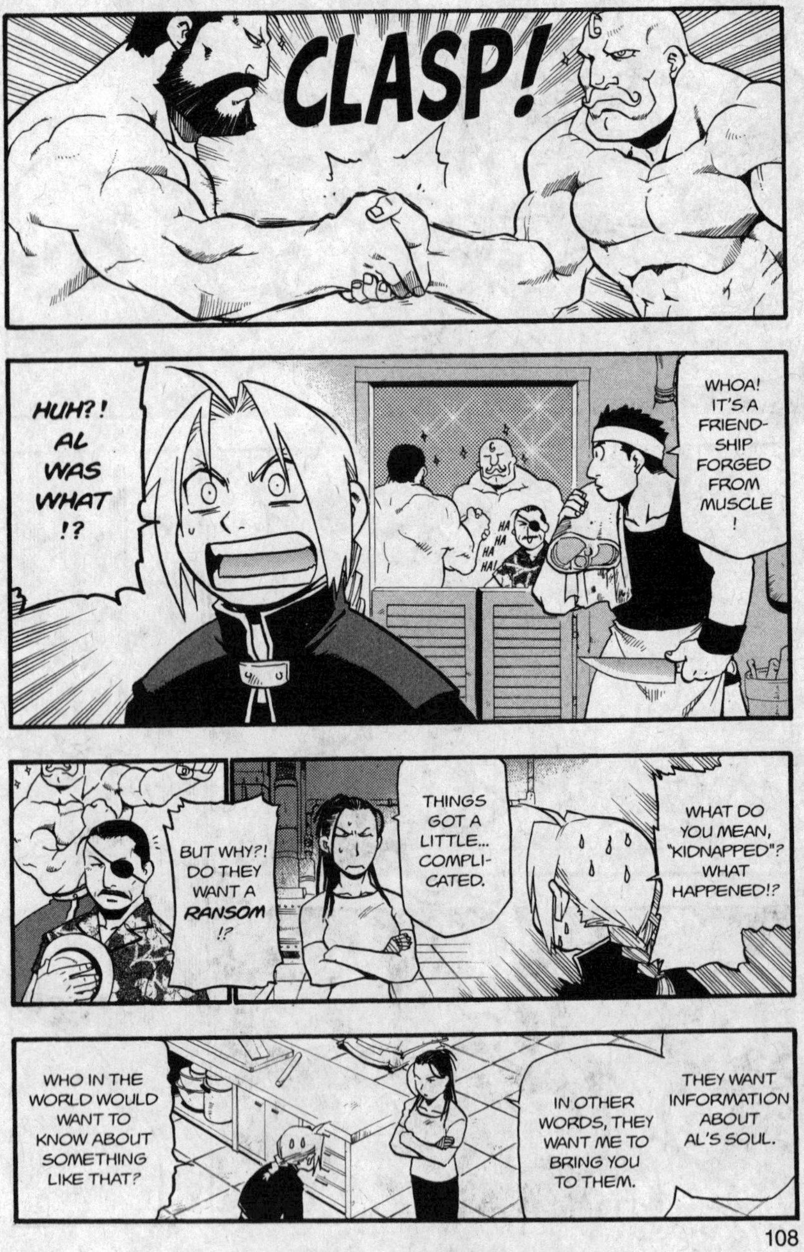
CLASP!
WHOA! IT'S A FRIEND-SHIP FORGED FROM MUSCLE!
HA HA HA HA!
HUH?! AL WAS WHAT!?
WHAT DO YOU MEAN, "KIDNAPPED"? WHAT HAPPENED!?
THINGS GOT A LITTLE... COMPLI-CATED.
BUT WHY?! DO THEY WANT A RANSOM!?
THEY WANT INFORMATION ABOUT AL'S SOUL.
IN OTHER WORDS, THEY WANT ME TO BRING YOU TO THEM.
WHO IN THE WORLD WOULD WANT TO KNOW ABOUT SOMETHING LIKE THAT?

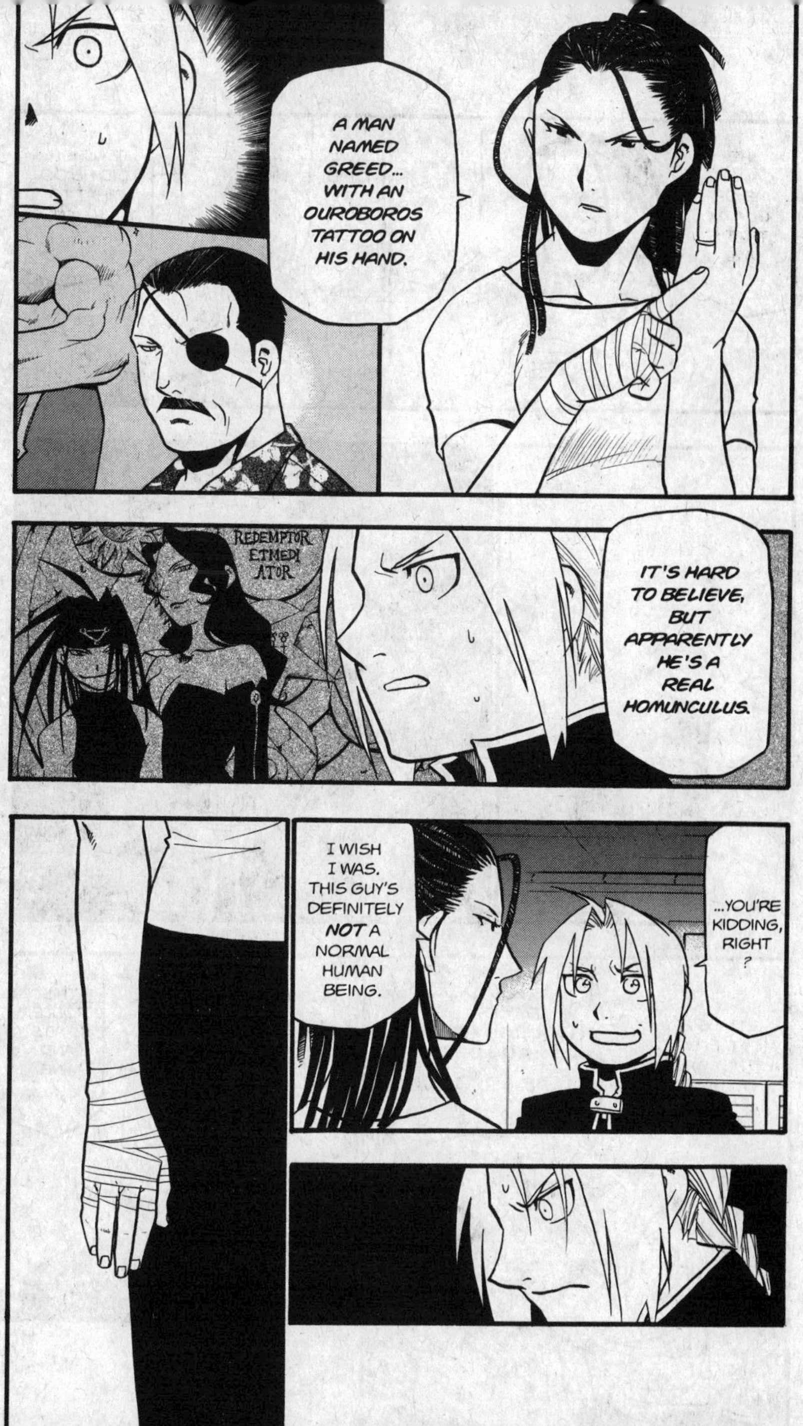
A MAN NAMED GREED... WITH AN OUROBOROS TATTOO ON HIS HAND.
IT'S HARD TO BELIEVE, BUT APPARENTLY HE'S A REAL HOMUNCULUS.
REDEMPTOR ET MEDI ATOR
...YOU'RE KIDDING, RIGHT?
I WISH I WAS. THIS GUY'S DEFINITELY NOT A NORMAL HUMAN BEING.

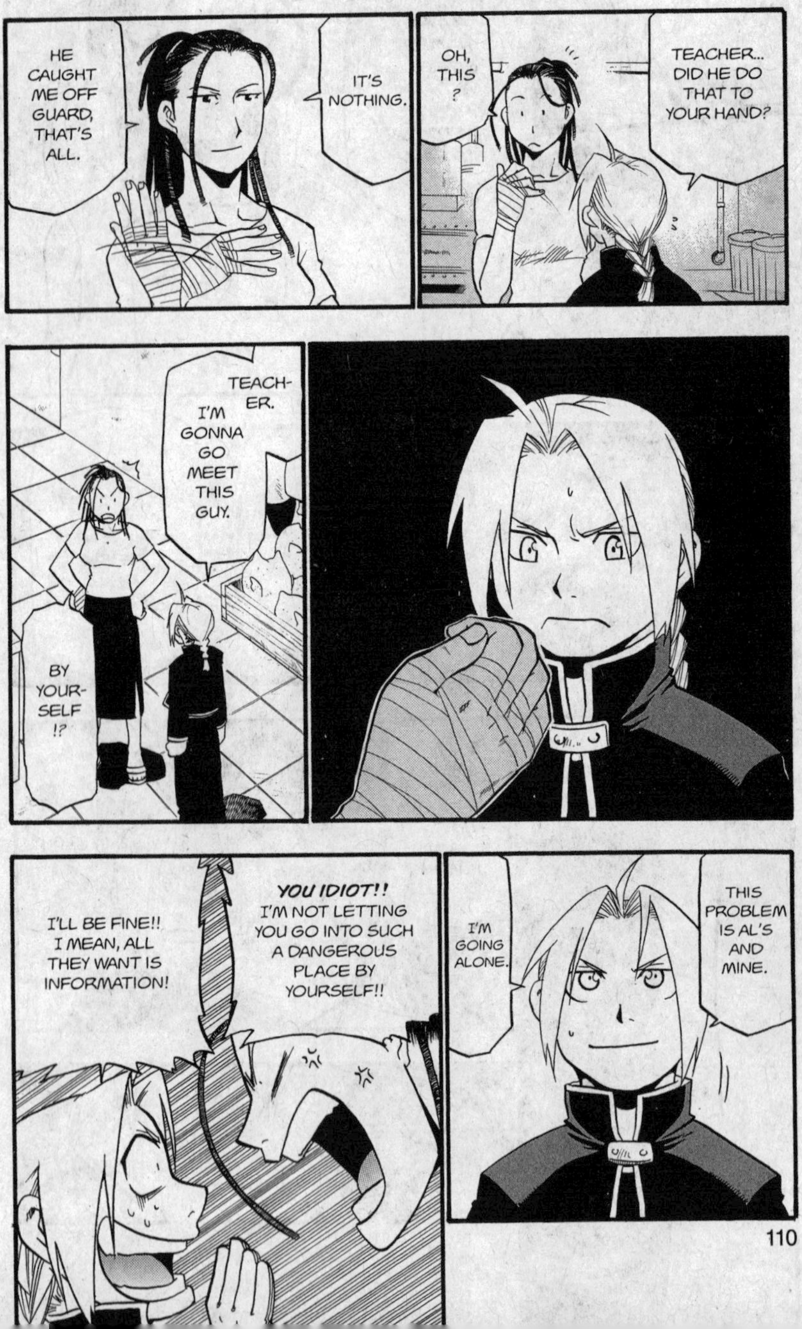
TEACHER... DID HE DO THAT TO YOUR HAND?
OH, THIS?
IT'S NOTHING.
HE CAUGHT ME OFF GUARD, THAT'S ALL.
TEACHER.
I'M GONNA GO MEET THIS GUY.
BY YOURSELF !?
THIS PROBLEM IS AL'S AND MINE.
I'M GOING ALONE.
YOU IDIOT!! I'M NOT LETTING YOU GO INTO SUCH A DANGEROUS PLACE BY YOURSELF!!
I'LL BE FINE!! I MEAN, ALL THEY WANT IS INFORMATION!

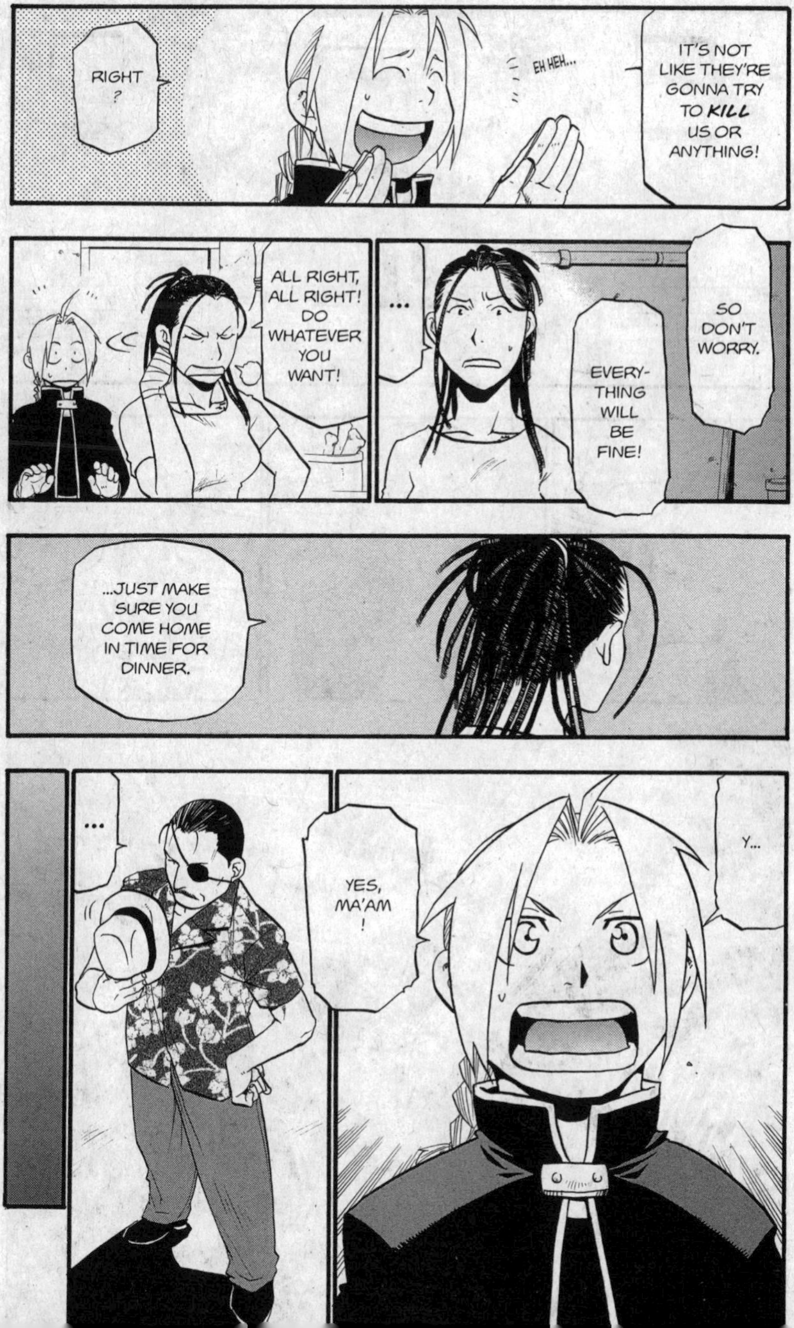
IT'S NOT LIKE THEY'RE GONNA TRY TO **KILL** US OR ANYTHING!
EH HEH...
RIGHT?
SO DON'T WORRY.
EVERY-THING WILL BE FINE!
...
ALL RIGHT, ALL RIGHT! DO WHATEVER YOU WANT!
...JUST MAKE SURE YOU COME HOME IN TIME FOR DINNER.
Y...
YES, MA'AM!
...

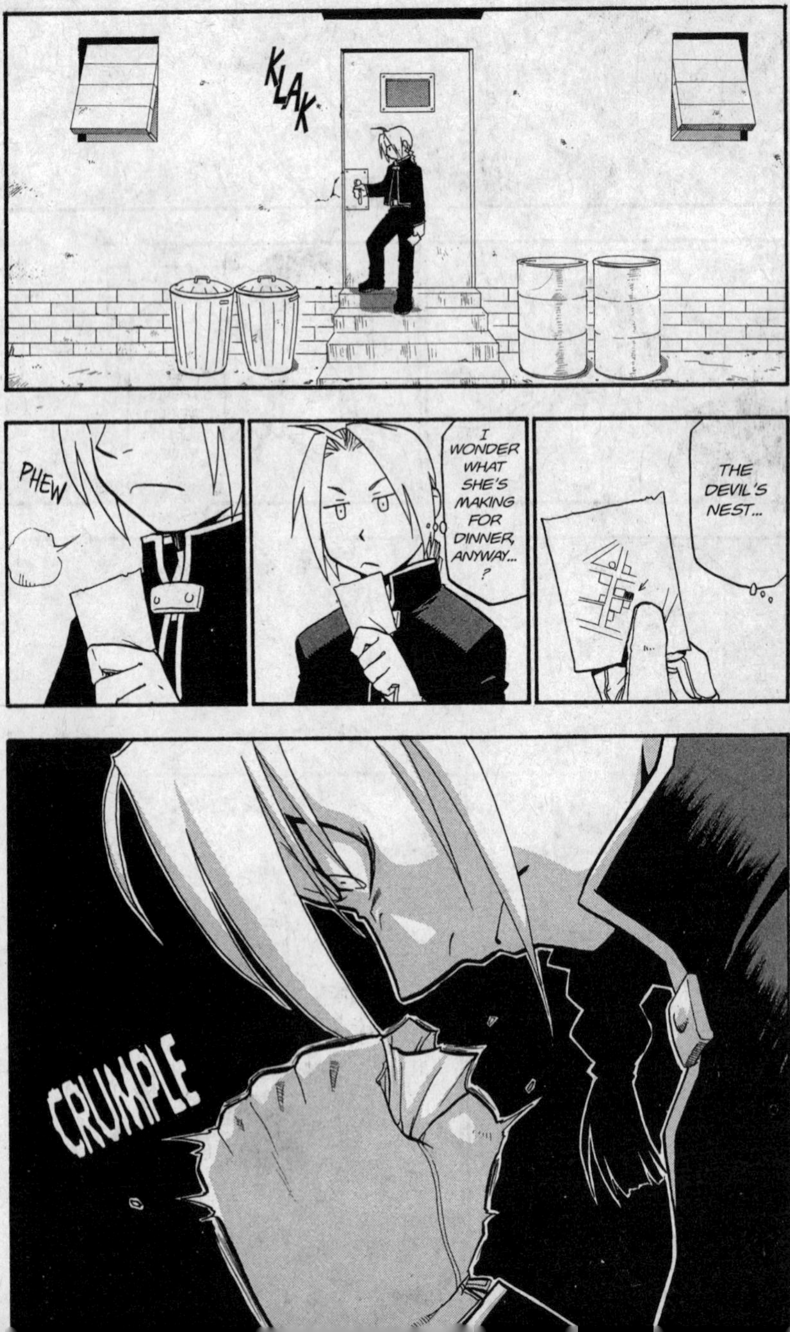
KLAK
THE DEVIL'S NEST...
I WONDER WHAT SHE'S MAKING FOR DINNER, ANYWAY...?
PHEW
CRUMPLE

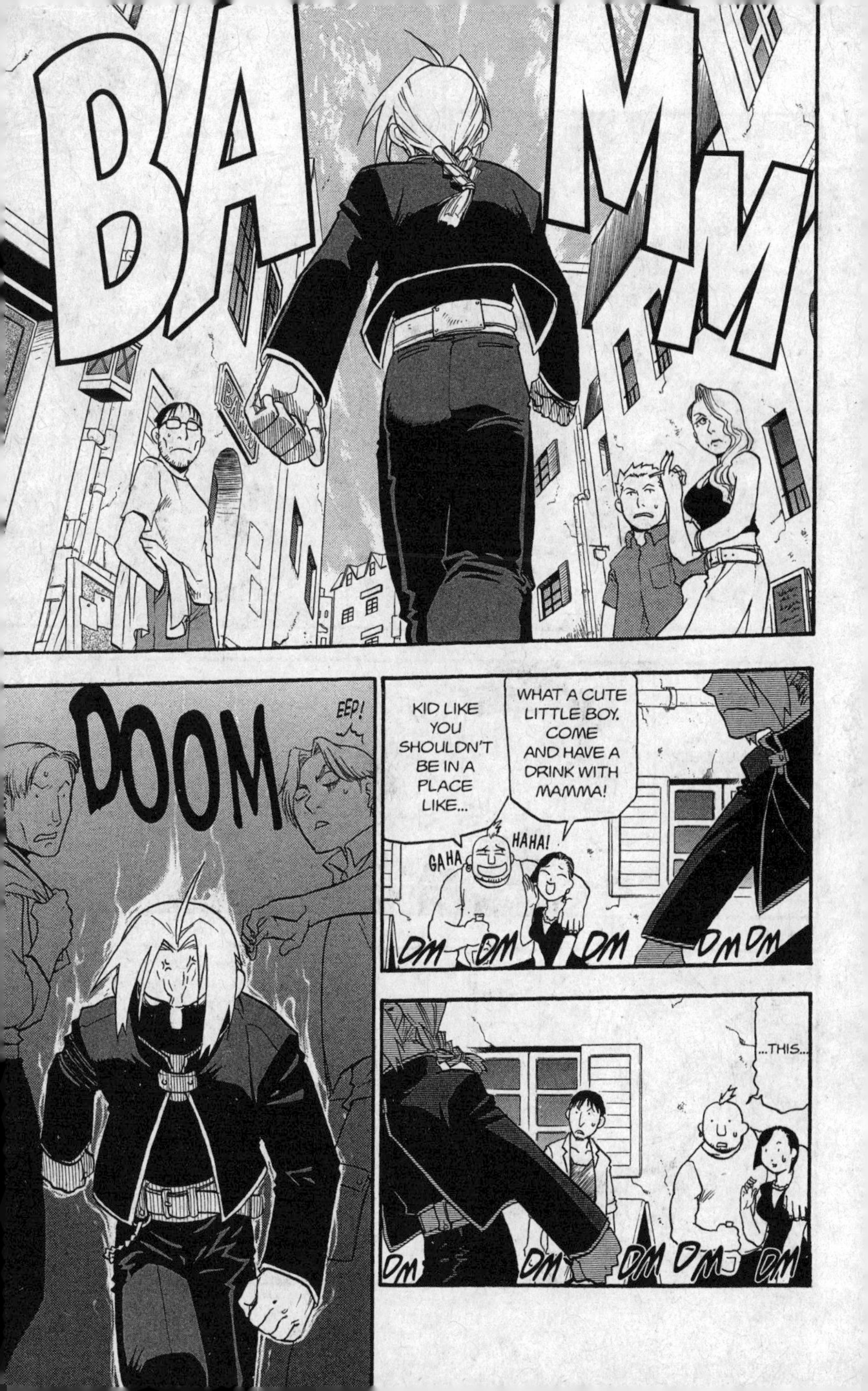
BAMM
WHAT A CUTE LITTLE BOY. COME AND HAVE A DRINK WITH MAMMA!
KID LIKE YOU SHOULDN'T BE IN A PLACE LIKE...
HAHA!
GAHA
DM DM DM DM DM
...THIS...
DM DM DM DM DM
EEP!
DOOM

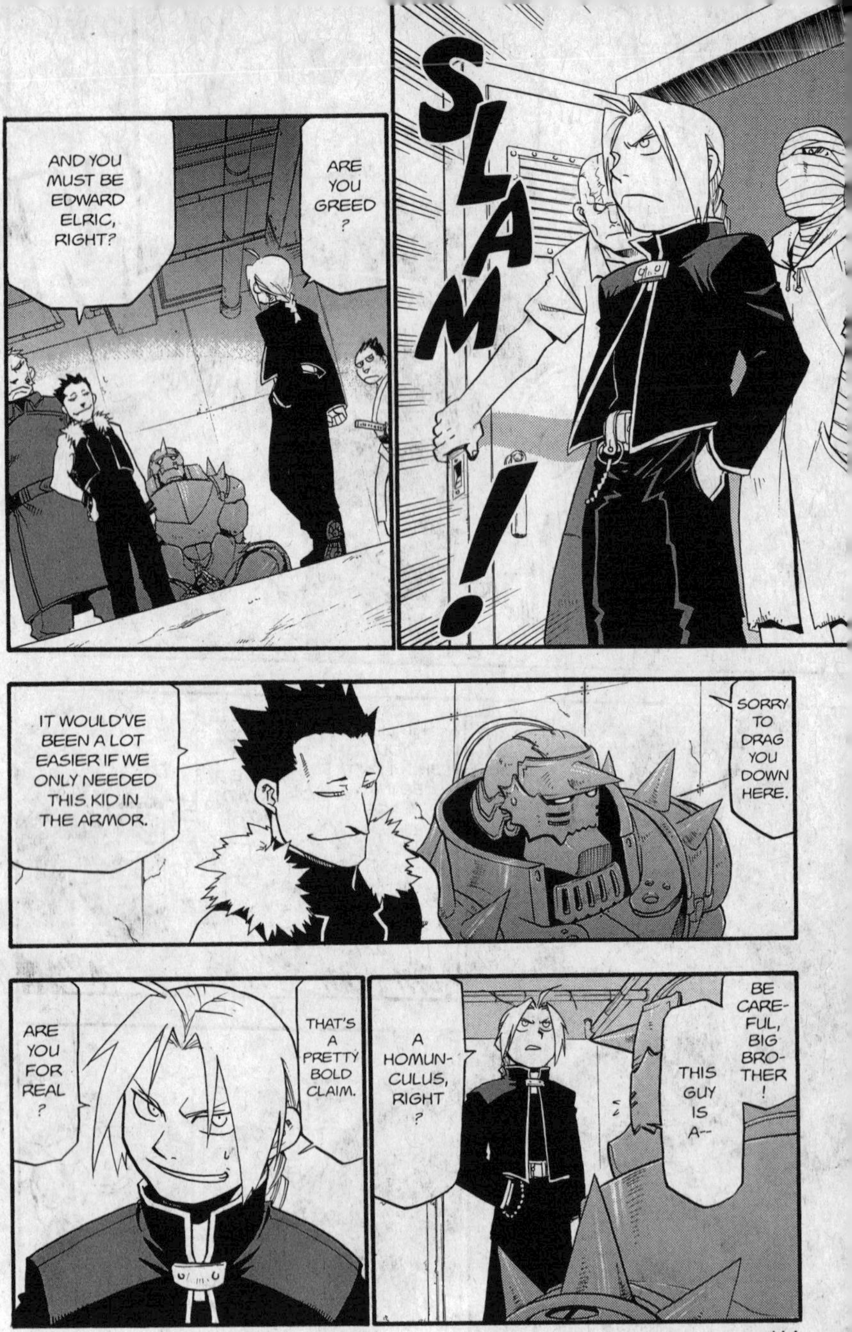
SLAM!
ARE YOU GREED?
AND YOU MUST BE EDWARD ELRIC, RIGHT?
SORRY TO DRAG YOU DOWN HERE.
IT WOULD'VE BEEN A LOT EASIER IF WE ONLY NEEDED THIS KID IN THE ARMOR.
BE CAREFUL, BIG BROTHER!
THIS GUY IS A--
A HOMUNCULUS, RIGHT?
THAT'S A PRETTY BOLD CLAIM.
ARE YOU FOR REAL?

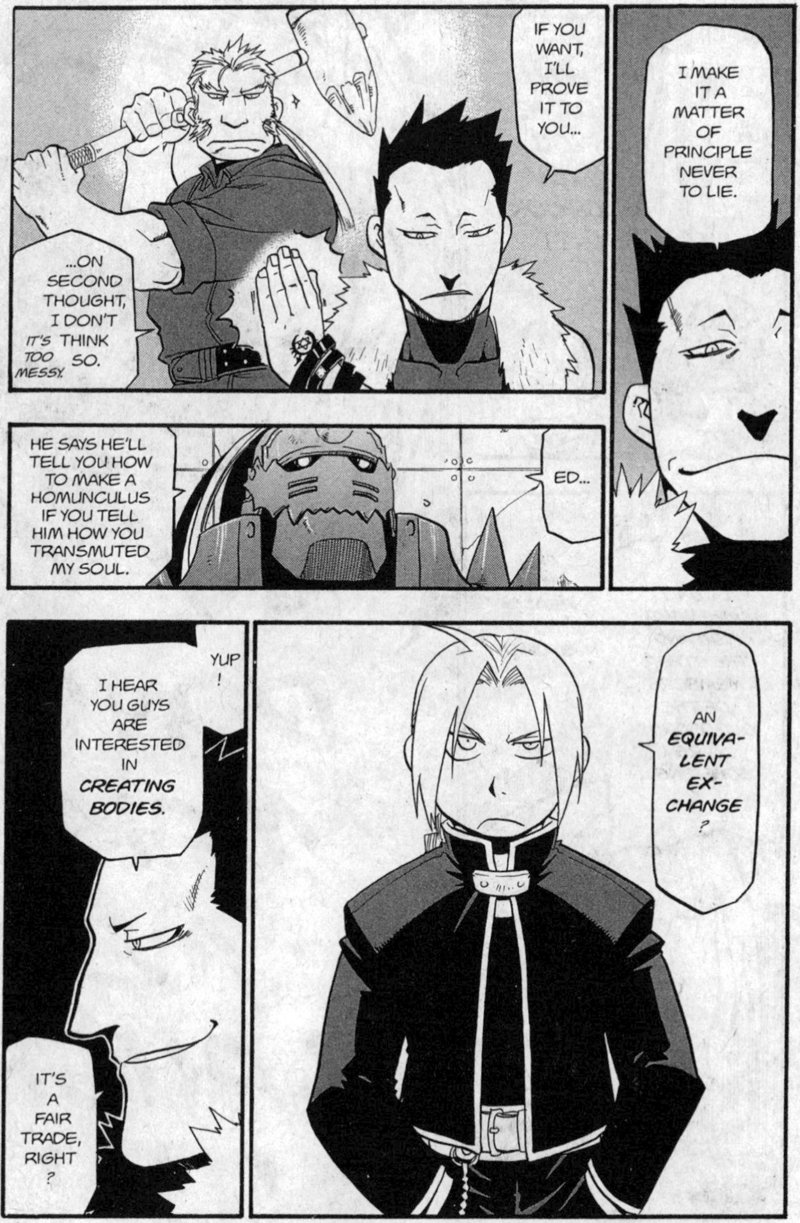
I MAKE IT A MATTER OF PRINCIPLE NEVER TO LIE.
IF YOU WANT, I'LL PROVE IT TO YOU...
...ON SECOND THOUGHT, I DON'T THINK SO.
IT'S TOO MESSY.
ED...
HE SAYS HE'LL TELL YOU HOW TO MAKE A HOMUNCULUS IF YOU TELL HIM HOW YOU TRANSMUTED MY SOUL.
AN EQUIVALENT EXCHANGE?
YUP!
I HEAR YOU GUYS ARE INTERESTED IN CREATING BODIES.
IT'S A FAIR TRADE, RIGHT?

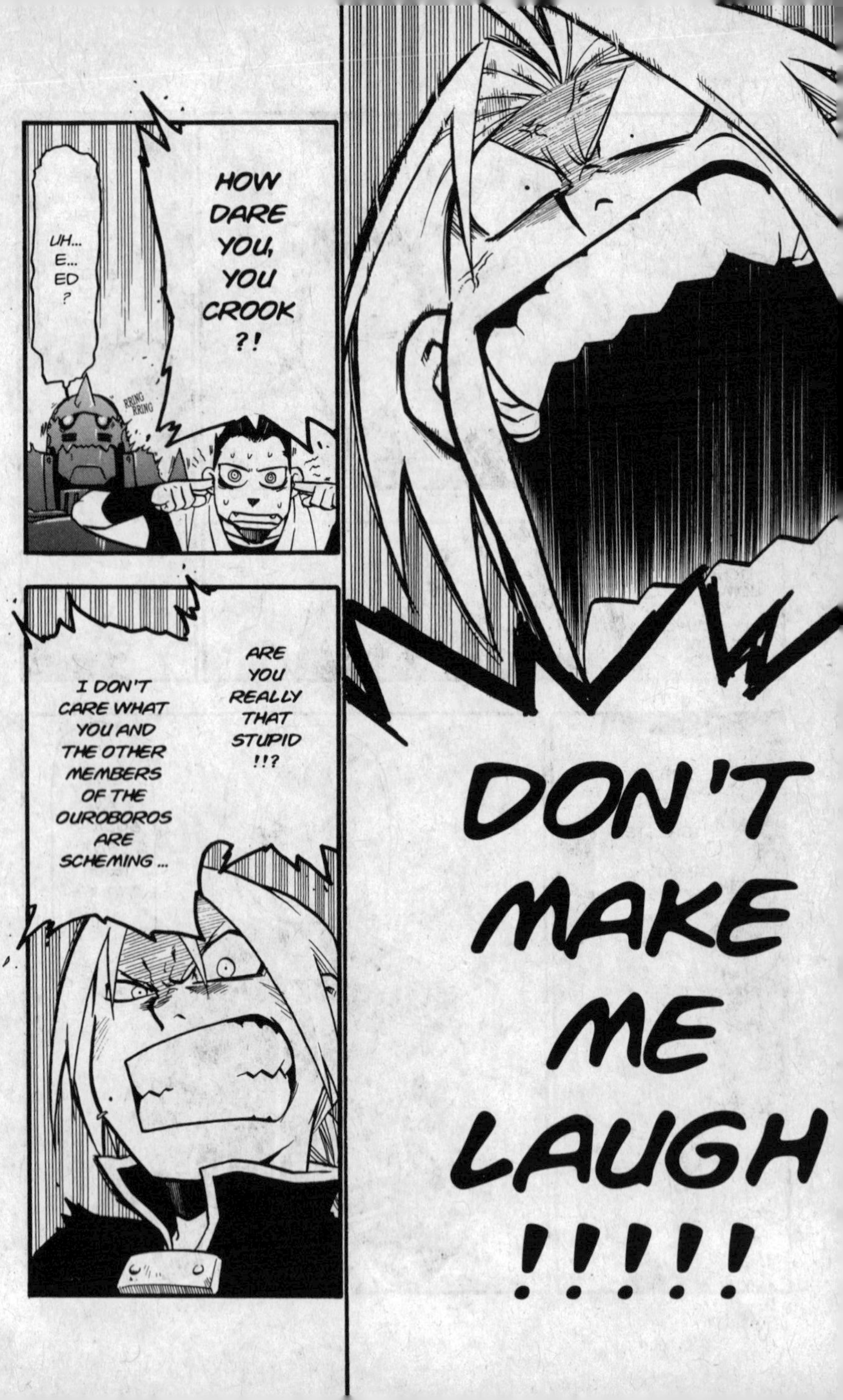
DON'T MAKE ME LAUGH!!!!!
HOW DARE YOU, YOU CROOK?!
UH... E... ED?
RRING RRING
ARE YOU REALLY THAT STUPID!!?
I DON'T CARE WHAT YOU AND THE OTHER MEMBERS OF THE OUROBOROS ARE SCHEMING...

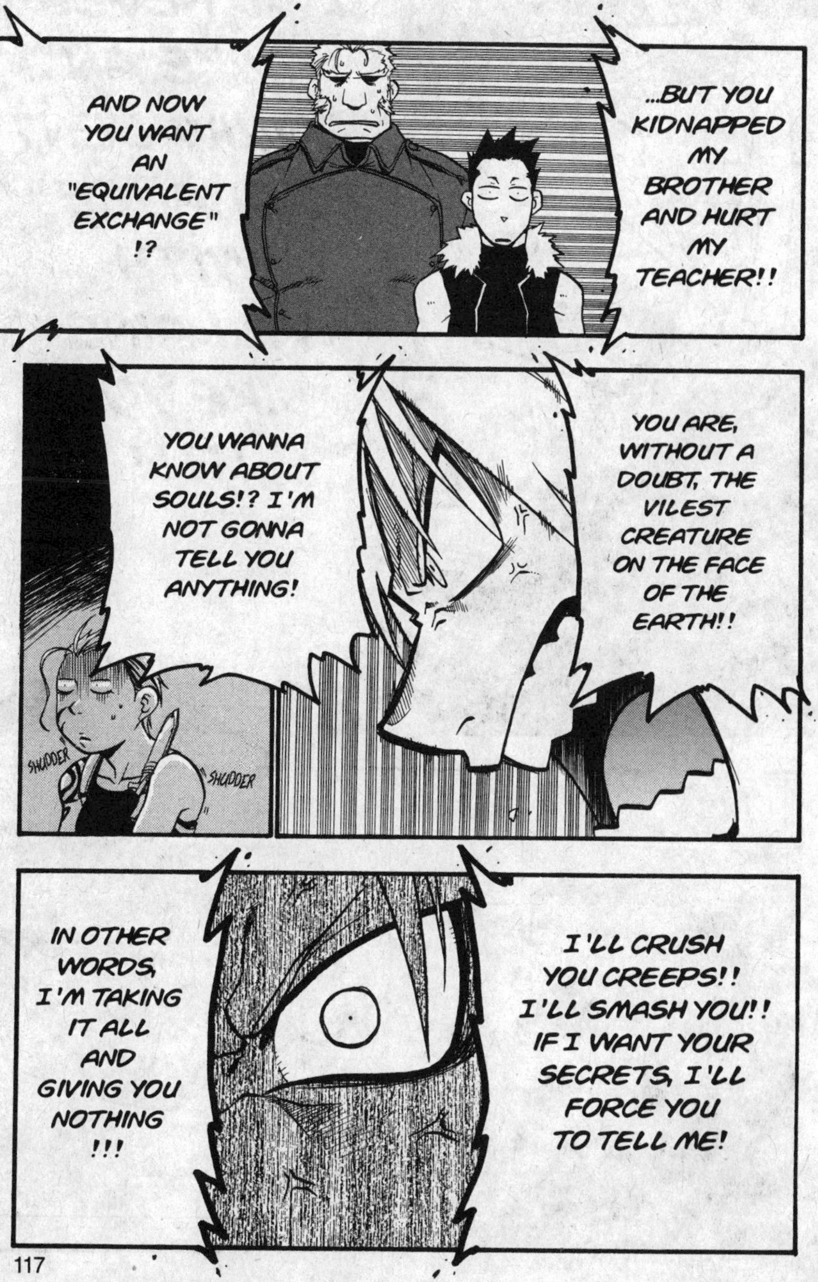

...BUT YOU KIDNAPPED MY BROTHER AND HURT MY TEACHER!!
AND NOW YOU WANT AN "EQUIVALENT EXCHANGE" !?
YOU ARE, WITHOUT A DOUBT, THE VILEST CREATURE ON THE FACE OF THE EARTH!!
YOU WANNA KNOW ABOUT SOULS!? I'M NOT GONNA TELL YOU ANYTHING!
SHUDDER
SHUDDER
I'LL CRUSH YOU CREEPS!! I'LL SMASH YOU!! IF I WANT YOUR SECRETS, I'LL FORCE YOU TO TELL ME!
IN OTHER WORDS, I'M TAKING IT ALL AND GIVING YOU NOTHING !!!

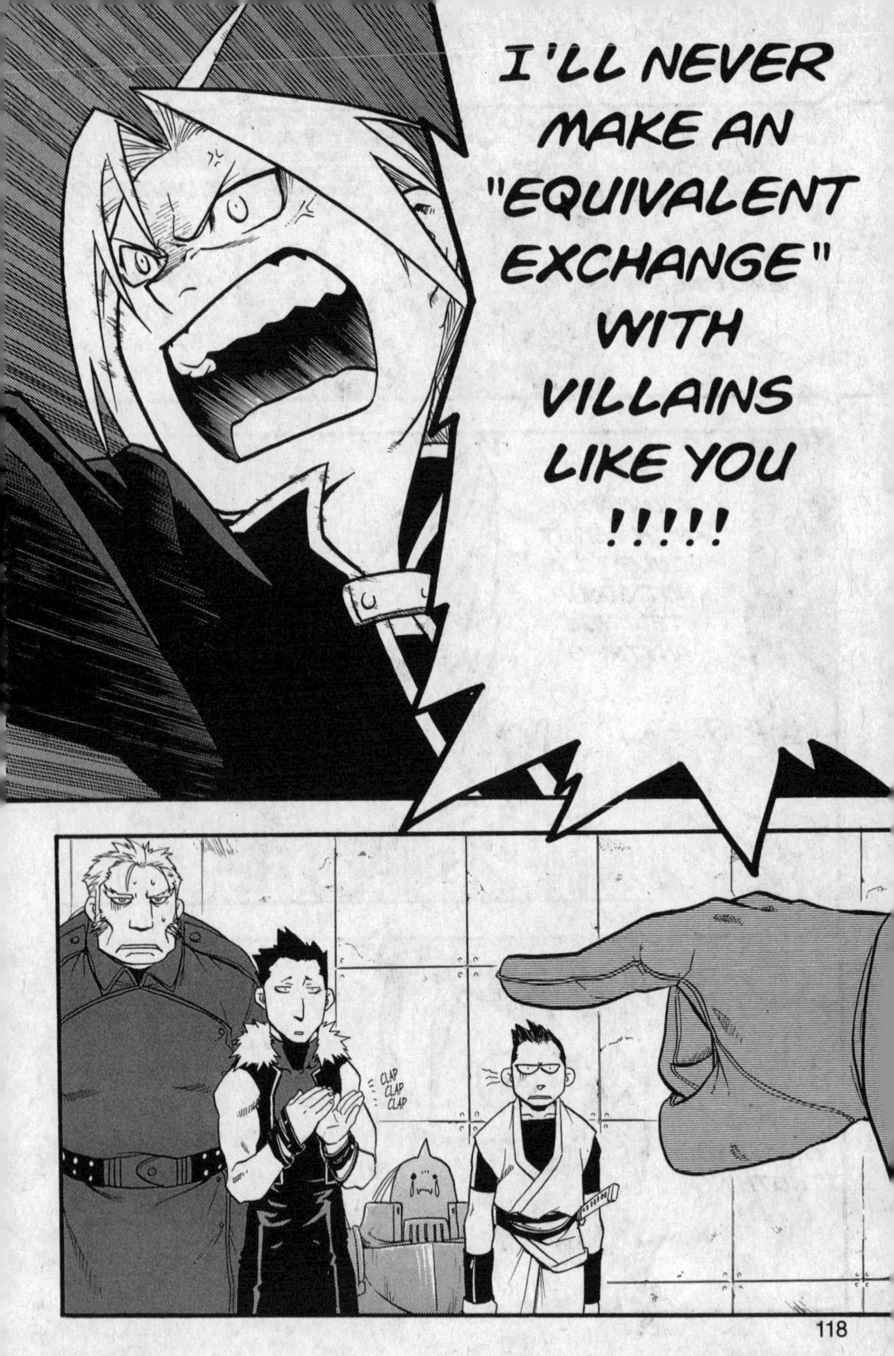
I'LL NEVER MAKE AN "EQUIVALENT EXCHANGE" WITH VILLAINS LIKE YOU !!!!!
CLAP CLAP CLAP

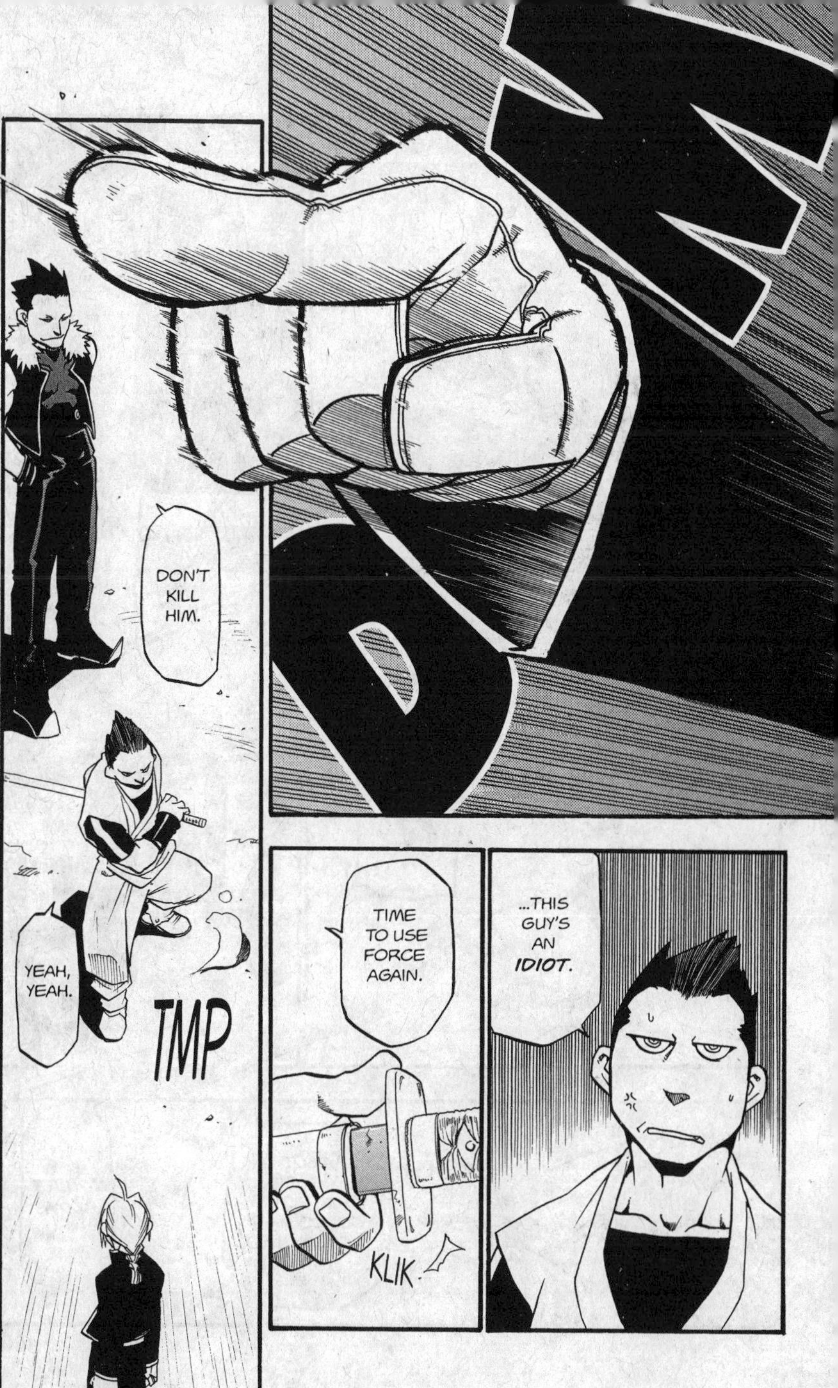
...THIS GUY'S AN *IDIOT*.
TIME TO USE FORCE AGAIN.
KLIK
DON'T KILL HIM.
YEAH, YEAH.
TMP

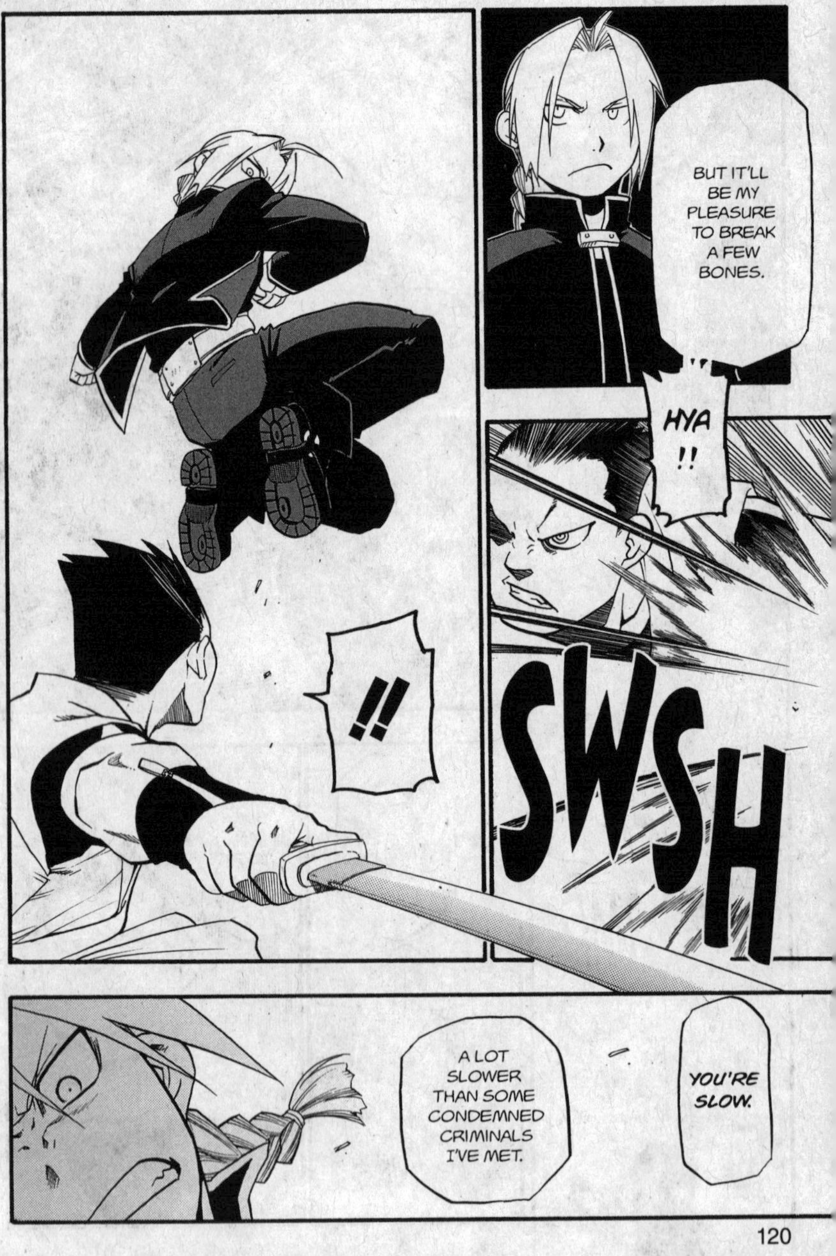
BUT IT'LL BE MY PLEASURE TO BREAK A FEW BONES.
HYA !!
SWSH
!!
YOU'RE SLOW.
A LOT SLOWER THAN SOME CONDEMNED CRIMINALS I'VE MET.

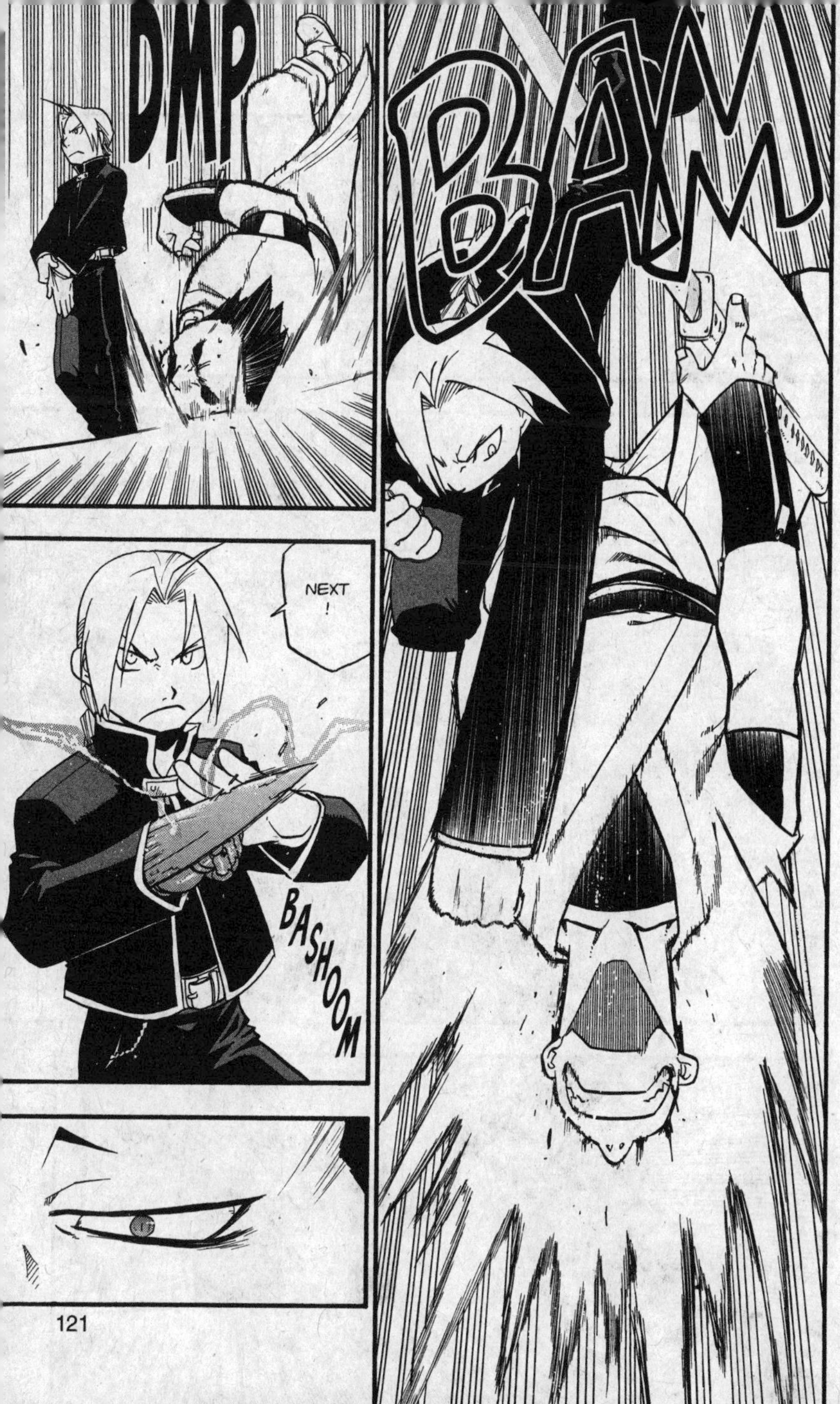
BAM
BAM
DMP
NEXT!
BASHOOM

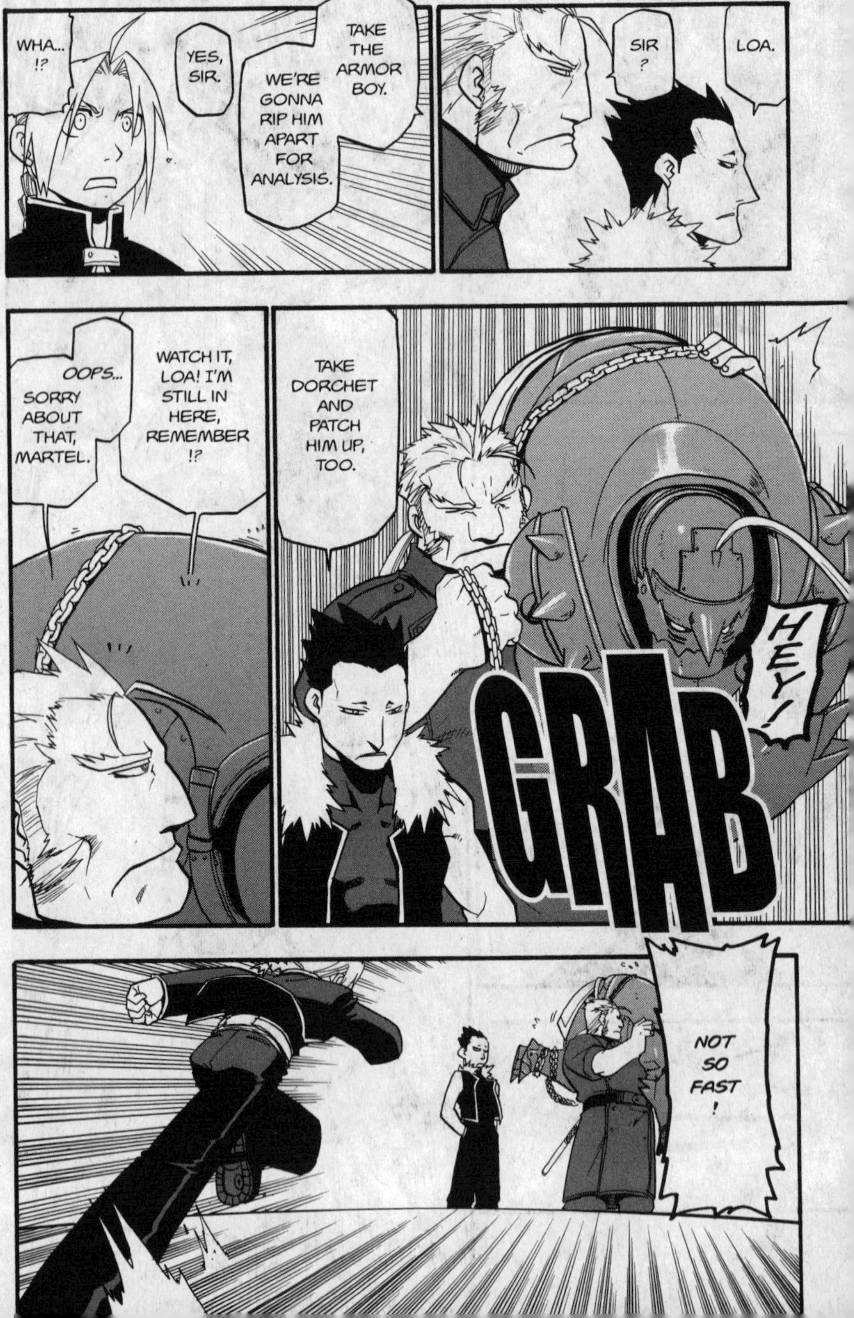
LOA.
SIR?
TAKE THE ARMOR BOY.
WE'RE GONNA RIP HIM APART FOR ANALYSIS.
YES, SIR.
WHA...!?
TAKE DORCHET AND PATCH HIM UP, TOO.
HEY!
GRAB
WATCH IT, LOA! I'M STILL IN HERE, REMEMBER!?
OOPS... SORRY ABOUT THAT, MARTEL.
NOT SO FAST!

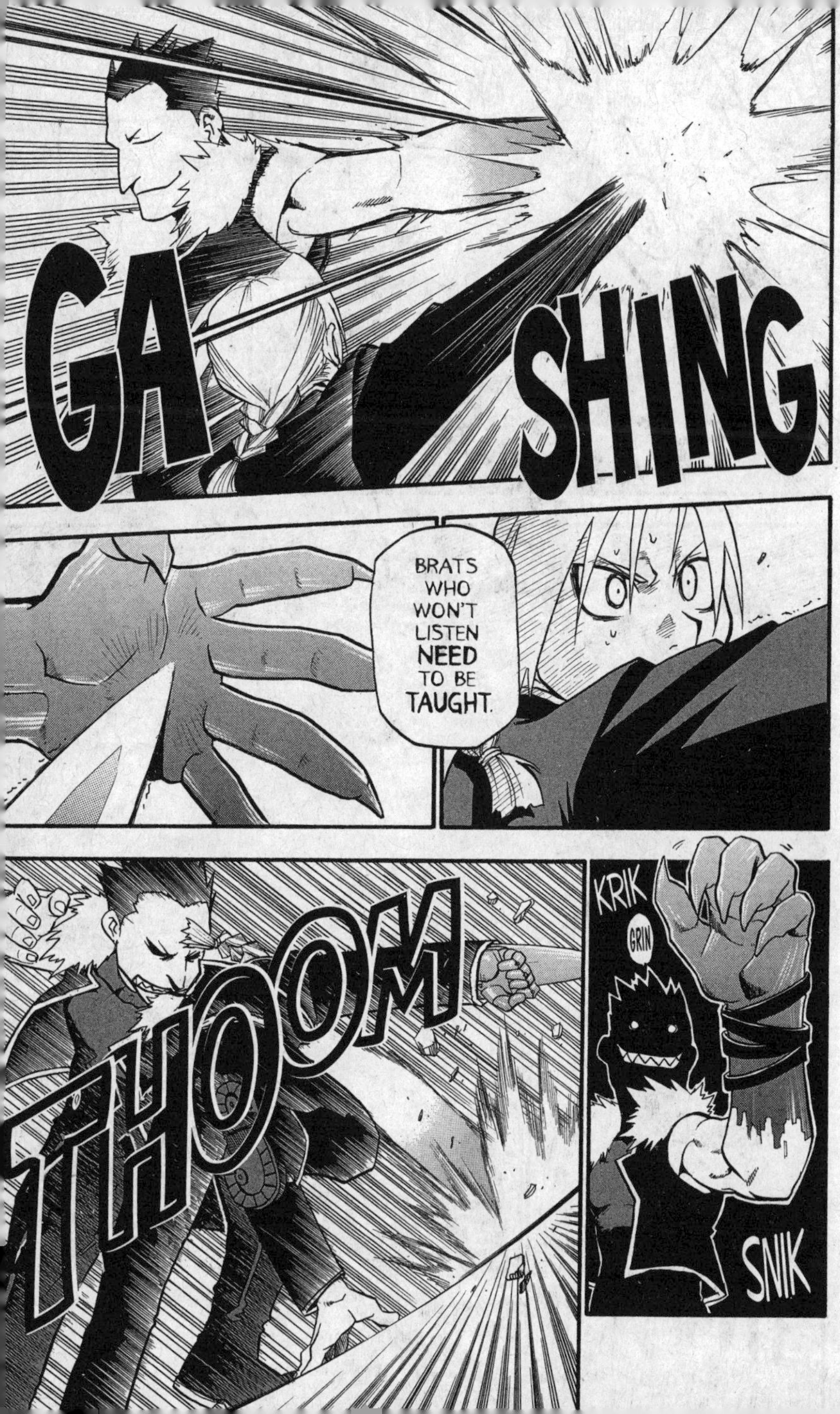
GA SHING
BRATS WHO WON'T LISTEN NEED TO BE TAUGHT.
KRIK
GRIN
SNIK
THOOM

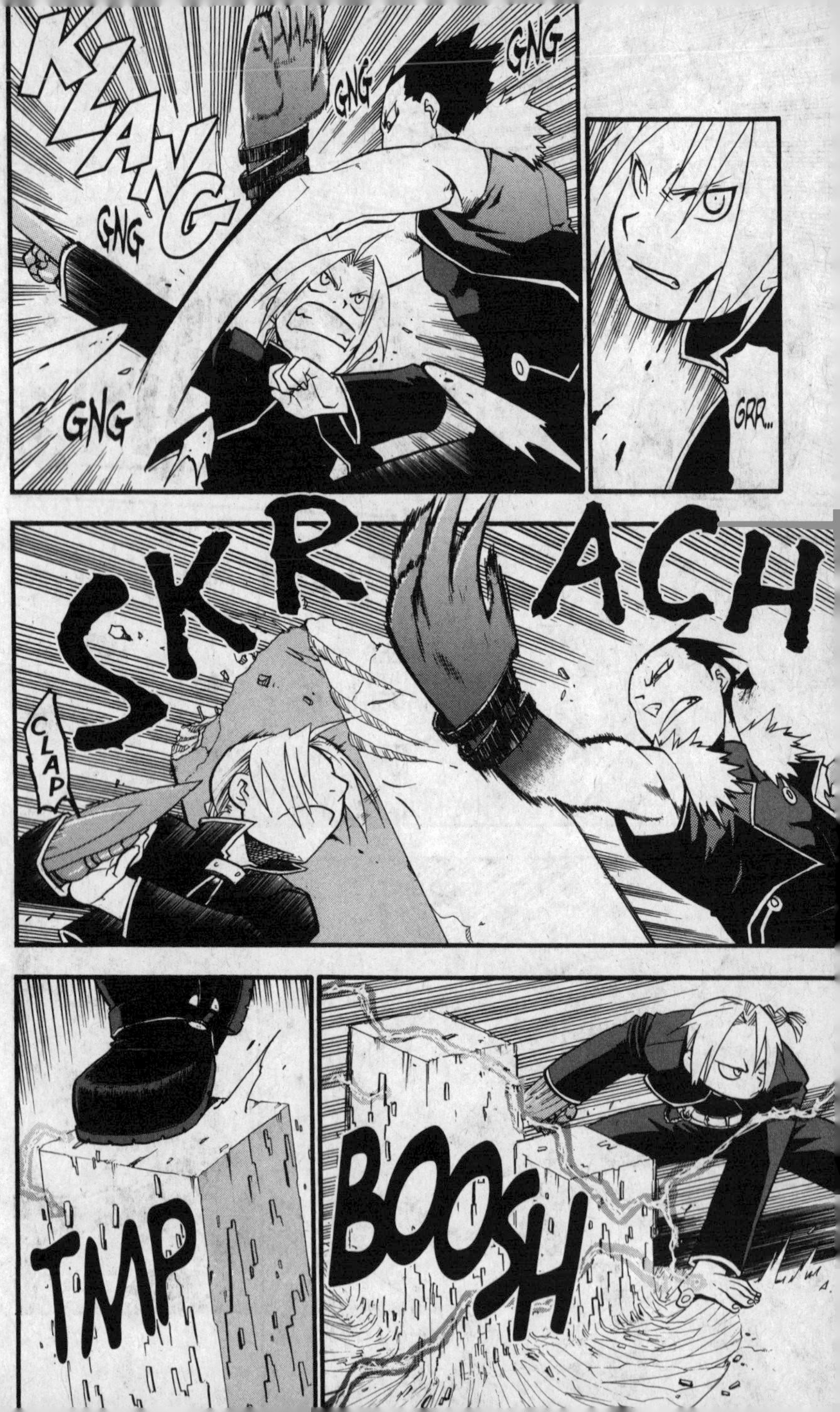
GRR...
KLANG
GNG
GNG
GNG
GNG
SKRRACH
CLAP
BOOSH
TMP

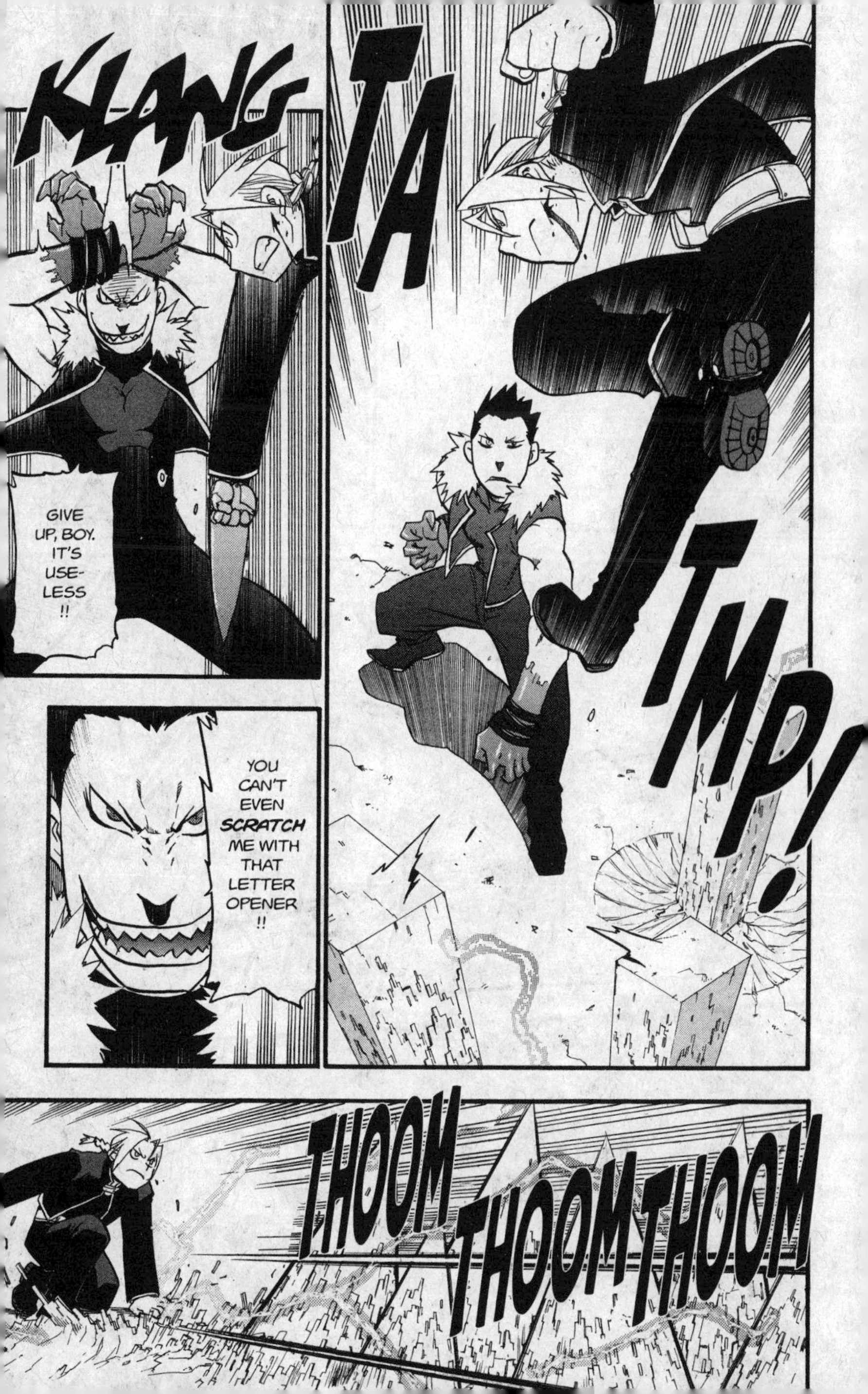
TA
TMP!
KLANG
GIVE UP, BOY. IT'S USELESS !!
YOU CAN'T EVEN SCRATCH ME WITH THAT LETTER OPENER !!
THOOM THOOM THOOM

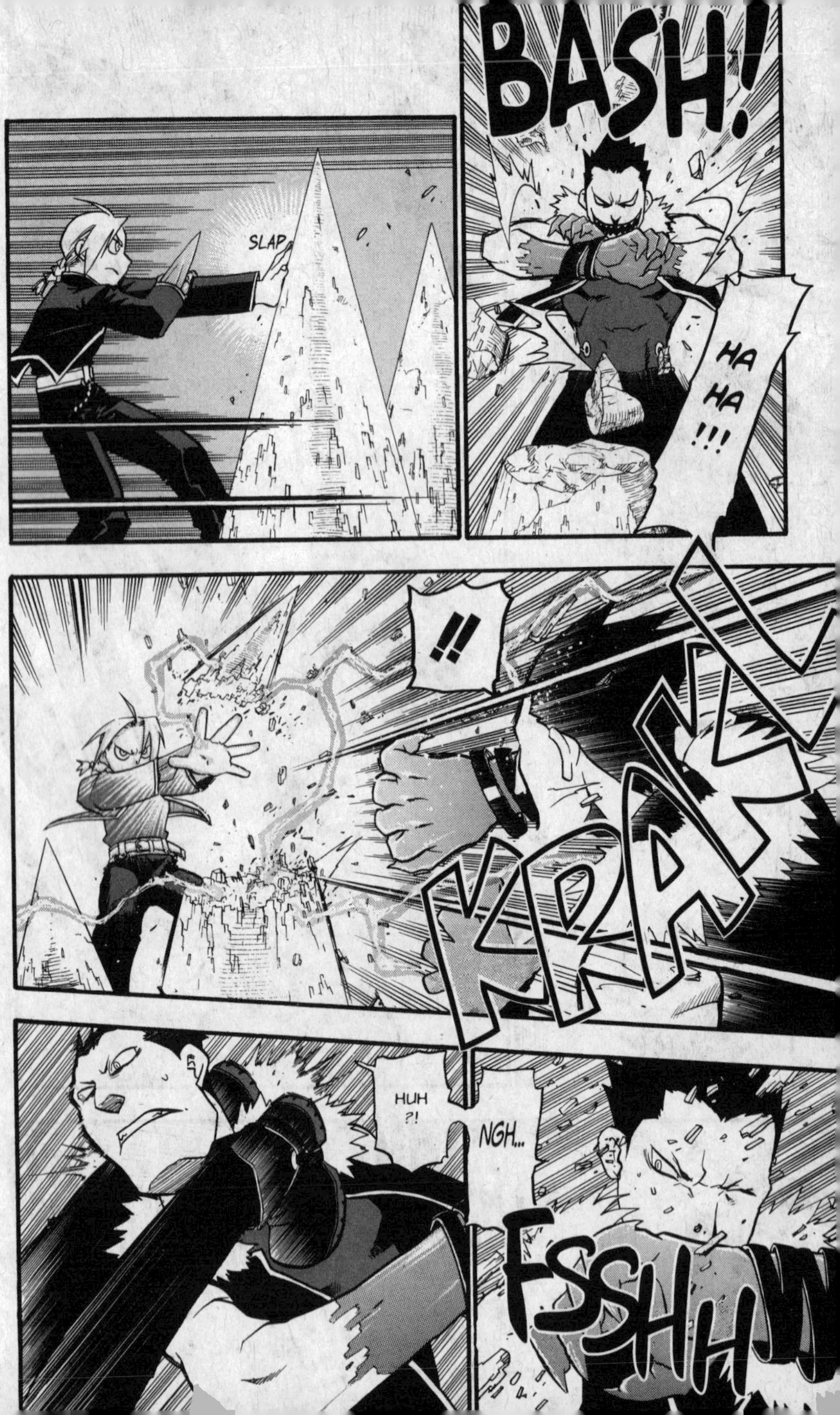
BASH!
HA HA !!!
SLAP
!!
KRAK
NGH...
FSSHH
HUH ?!

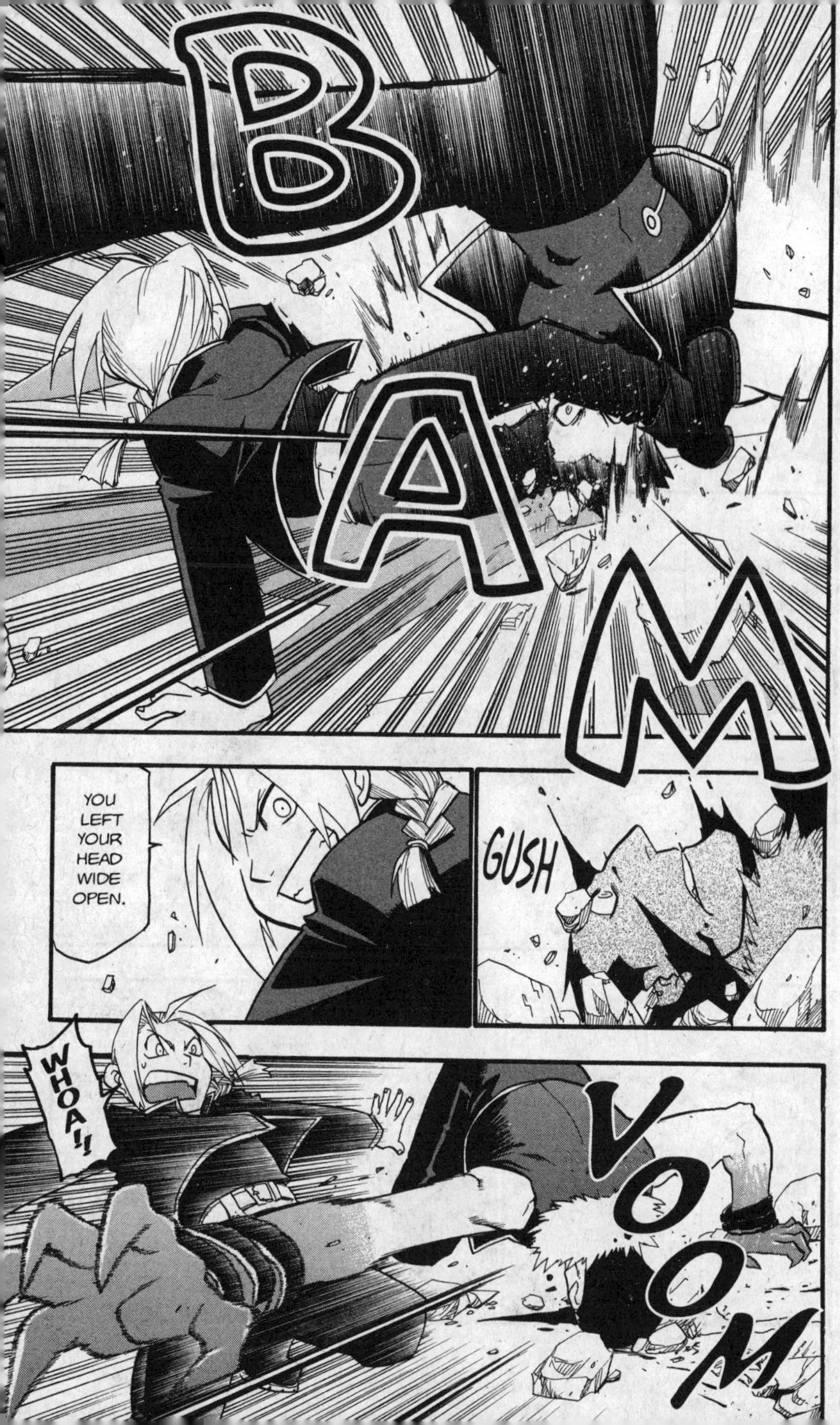
BAM
GUSH
YOU LEFT YOUR HEAD WIDE OPEN.
VOOM
WHOA!!

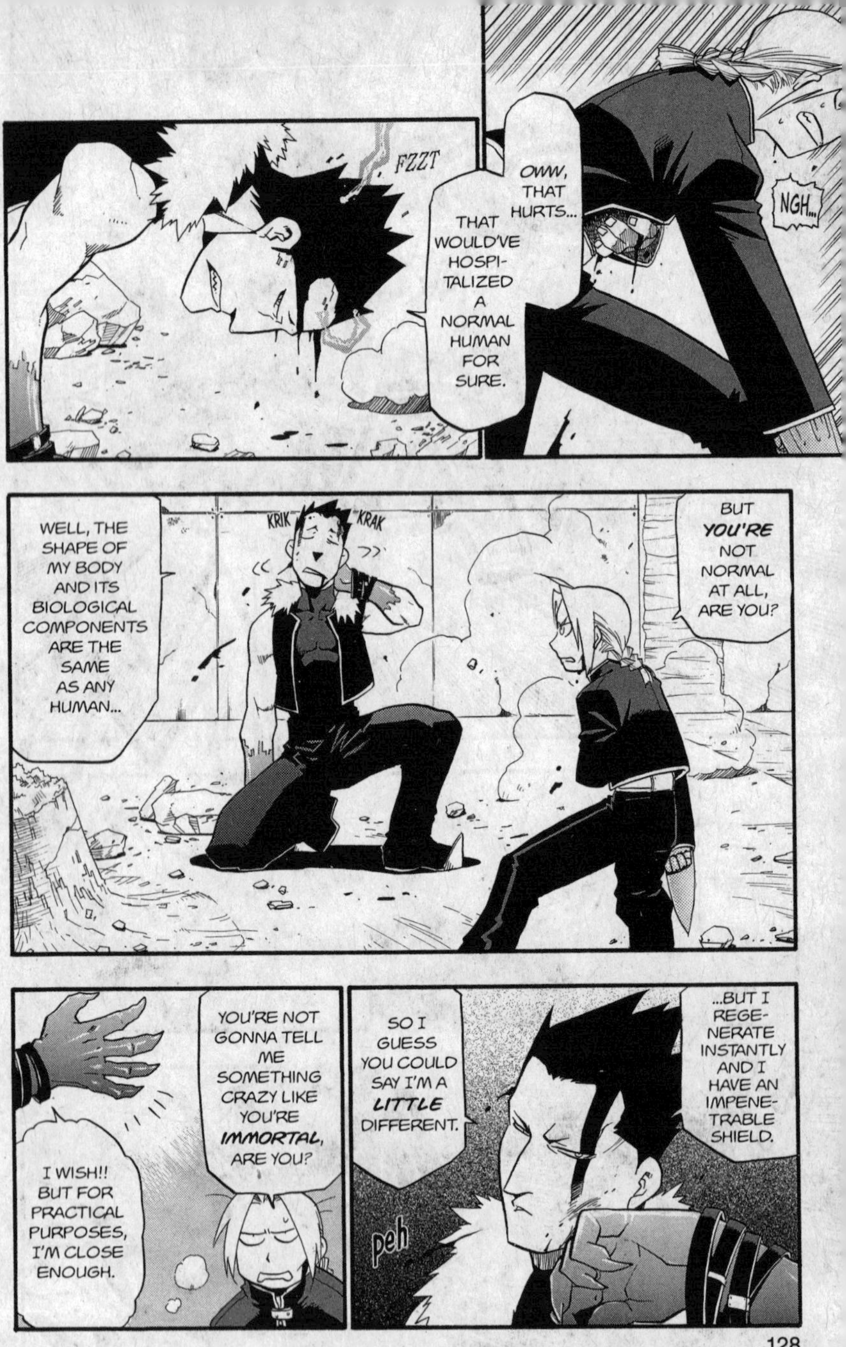
NGH...
OWW, THAT HURTS...
THAT WOULD'VE HOSPITALIZED A NORMAL HUMAN FOR SURE.
FZZT
BUT *YOU'RE* NOT NORMAL AT ALL, ARE YOU?
KRIK KRAK
WELL, THE SHAPE OF MY BODY AND ITS BIOLOGICAL COMPONENTS ARE THE SAME AS ANY HUMAN...
...BUT I REGENERATE INSTANTLY AND I HAVE AN IMPENETRABLE SHIELD.
SO I GUESS YOU COULD SAY I'M A *LITTLE* DIFFERENT.
peh
YOU'RE NOT GONNA TELL ME SOMETHING CRAZY LIKE YOU'RE *IMMORTAL*, ARE YOU?
I WISH!! BUT FOR PRACTICAL PURPOSES, I'M CLOSE ENOUGH.

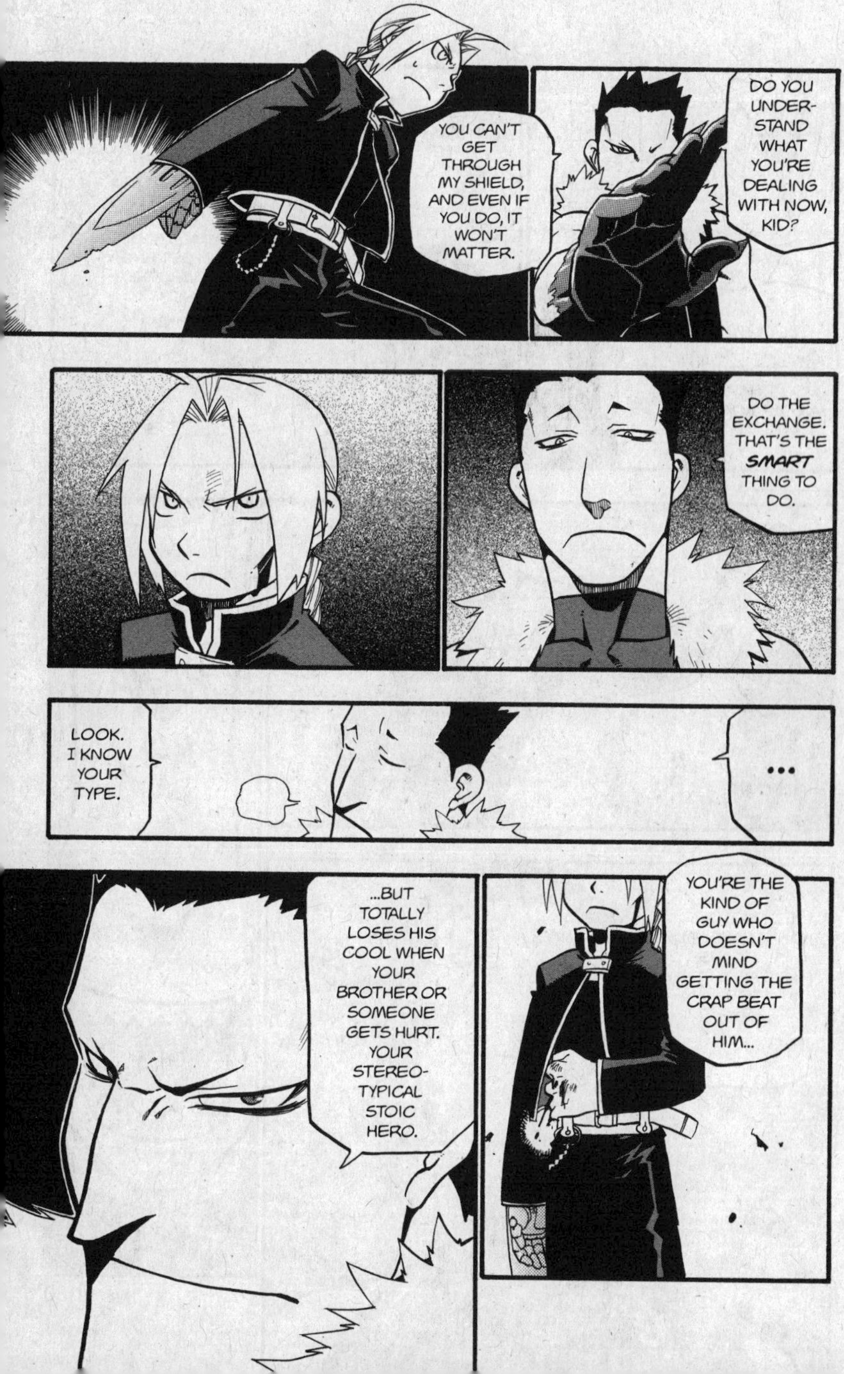
DO YOU UNDERSTAND WHAT YOU'RE DEALING WITH NOW, KID?
YOU CAN'T GET THROUGH MY SHIELD, AND EVEN IF YOU DO, IT WON'T MATTER.
DO THE EXCHANGE. THAT'S THE SMART THING TO DO.
...
LOOK. I KNOW YOUR TYPE.
YOU'RE THE KIND OF GUY WHO DOESN'T MIND GETTING THE CRAP BEAT OUT OF HIM...
...BUT TOTALLY LOSES HIS COOL WHEN YOUR BROTHER OR SOMEONE GETS HURT. YOUR STEREO-TYPICAL STOIC HERO.

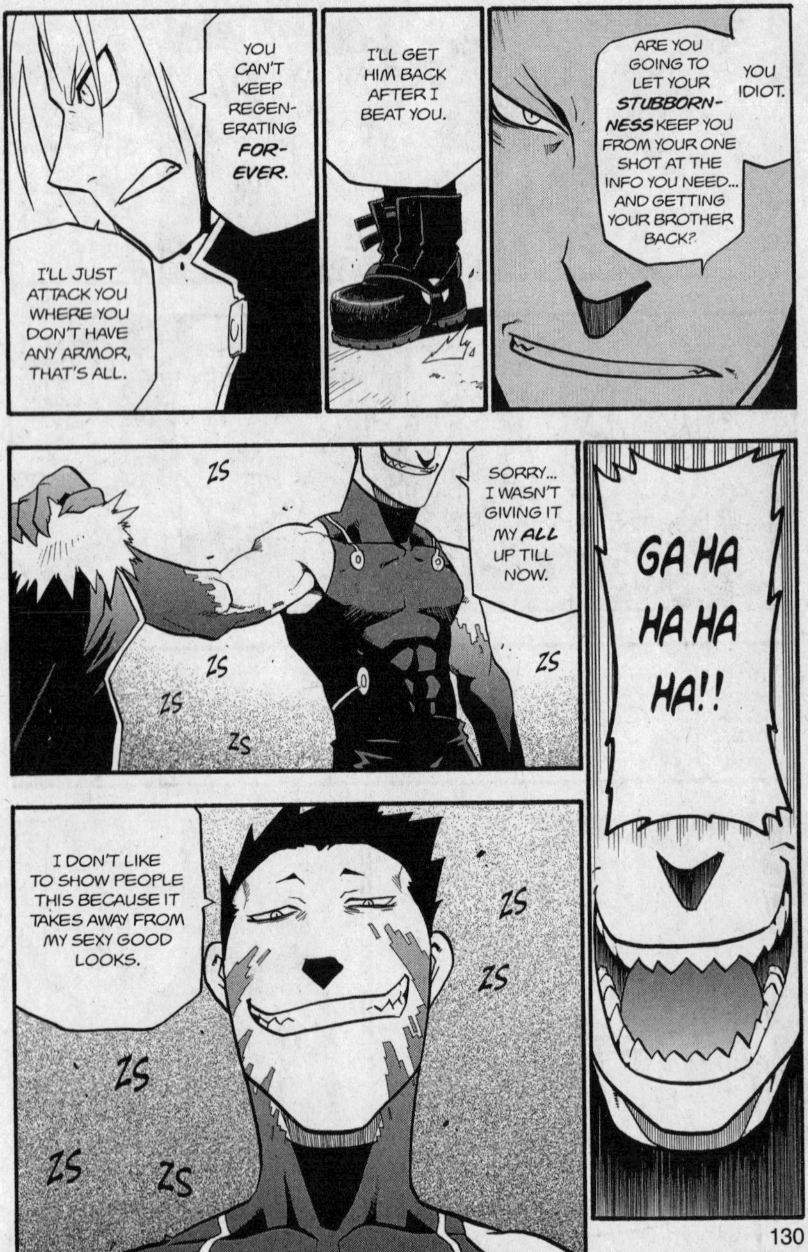

ARE YOU GOING TO LET YOUR STUBBORN-NESS KEEP YOU FROM YOUR ONE SHOT AT THE INFO YOU NEED... AND GETTING YOUR BROTHER BACK?
YOU IDIOT.
I'LL GET HIM BACK AFTER I BEAT YOU.
YOU CAN'T KEEP REGEN-ERATING FOR-EVER.
I'LL JUST ATTACK YOU WHERE YOU DON'T HAVE ANY ARMOR, THAT'S ALL.
GA HA HA HA HA!!
SORRY... I WASN'T GIVING IT MY ALL UP TILL NOW.
ZS
ZS
ZS
ZS
ZS
I DON'T LIKE TO SHOW PEOPLE THIS BECAUSE IT TAKES AWAY FROM MY SEXY GOOD LOOKS.
ZS
ZS
ZS
ZS
ZS

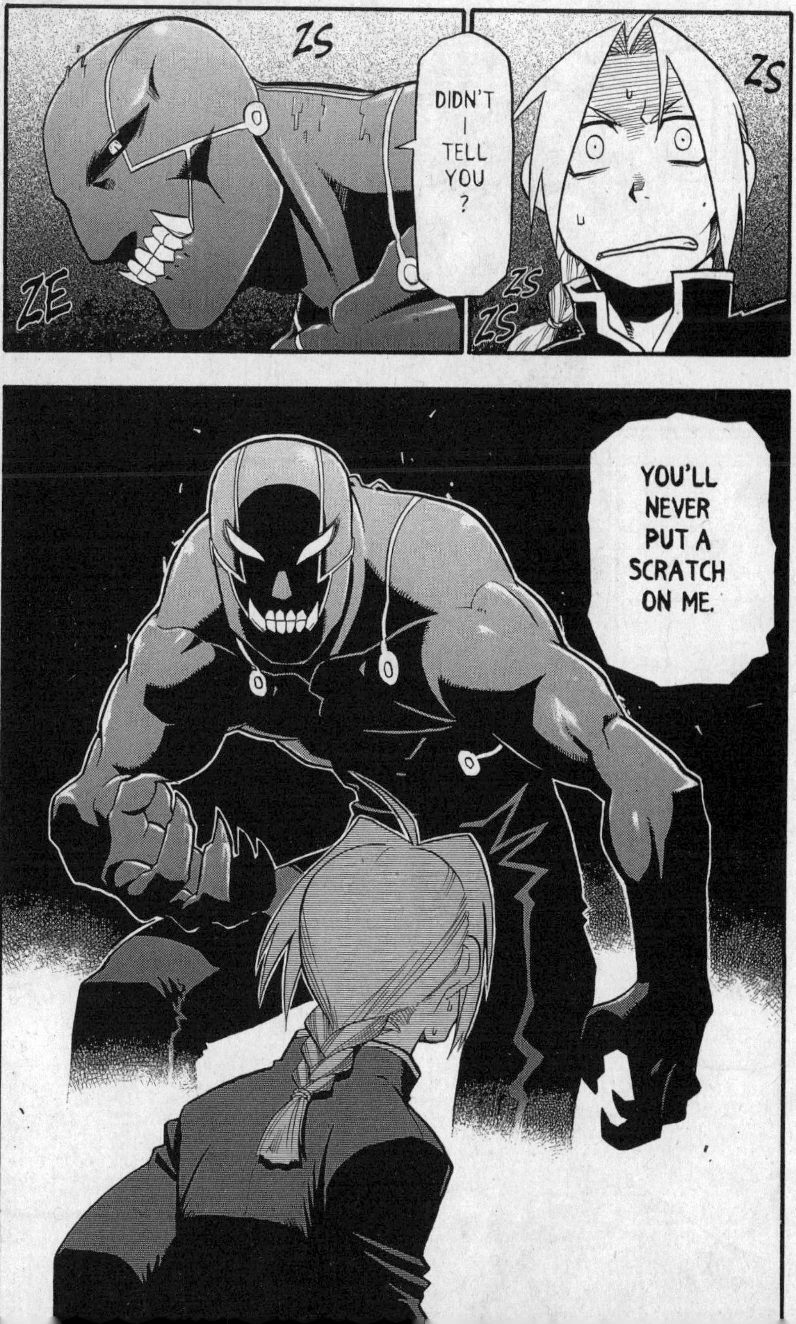
ZS
ZS
ZS
ZS
DIDN'T I TELL YOU?
ZE
YOU'LL NEVER PUT A SCRATCH ON ME.

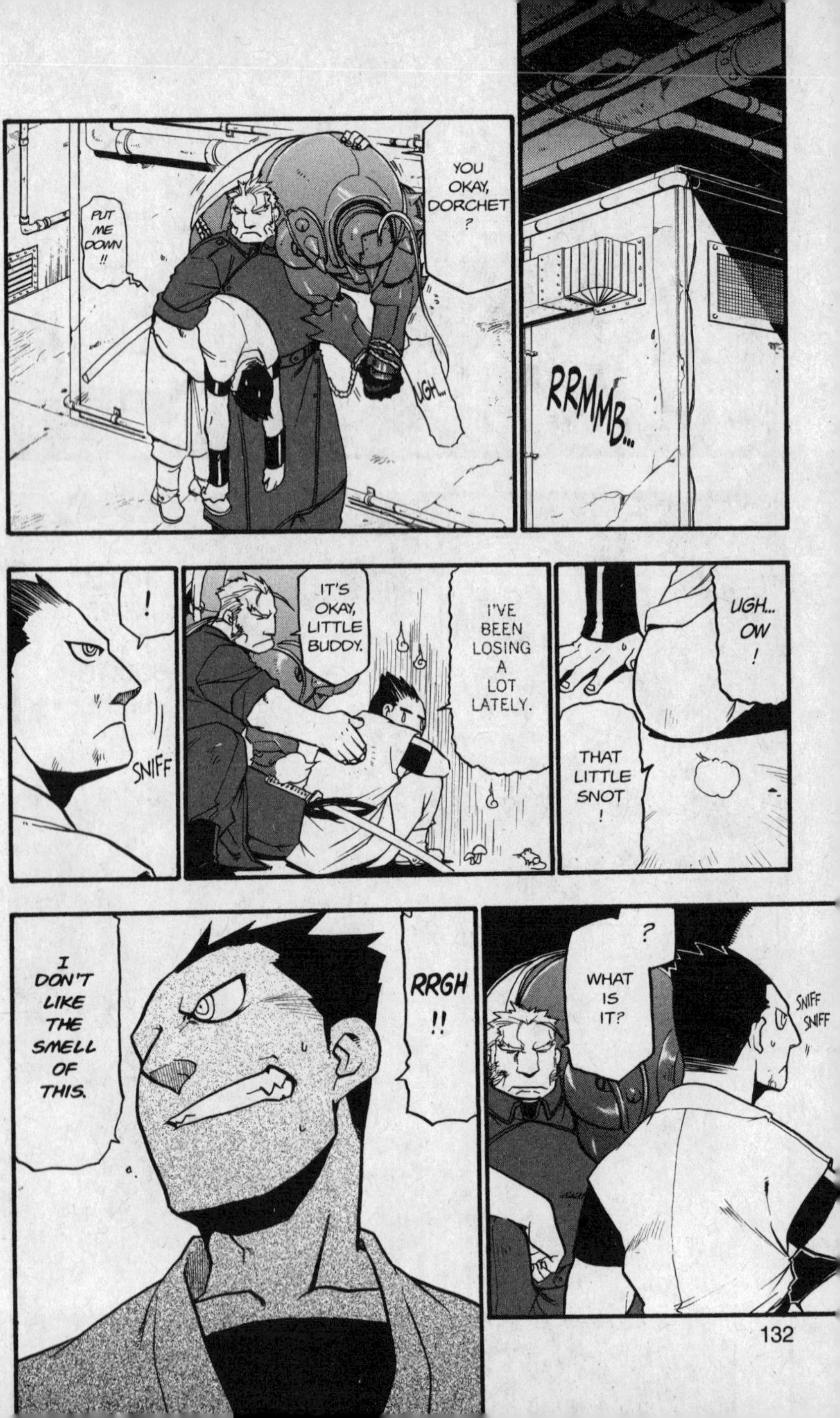
RRMMB...
YOU OKAY, DORCHET?
PUT ME DOWN!!
UGH...
UGH... OW!
THAT LITTLE SNOT!
I'VE BEEN LOSING A LOT LATELY.
IT'S OKAY, LITTLE BUDDY.
!
SNIFF
?
WHAT IS IT?
SNIFF SNIFF
RRGH!!
I DON'T LIKE THE SMELL OF THIS.

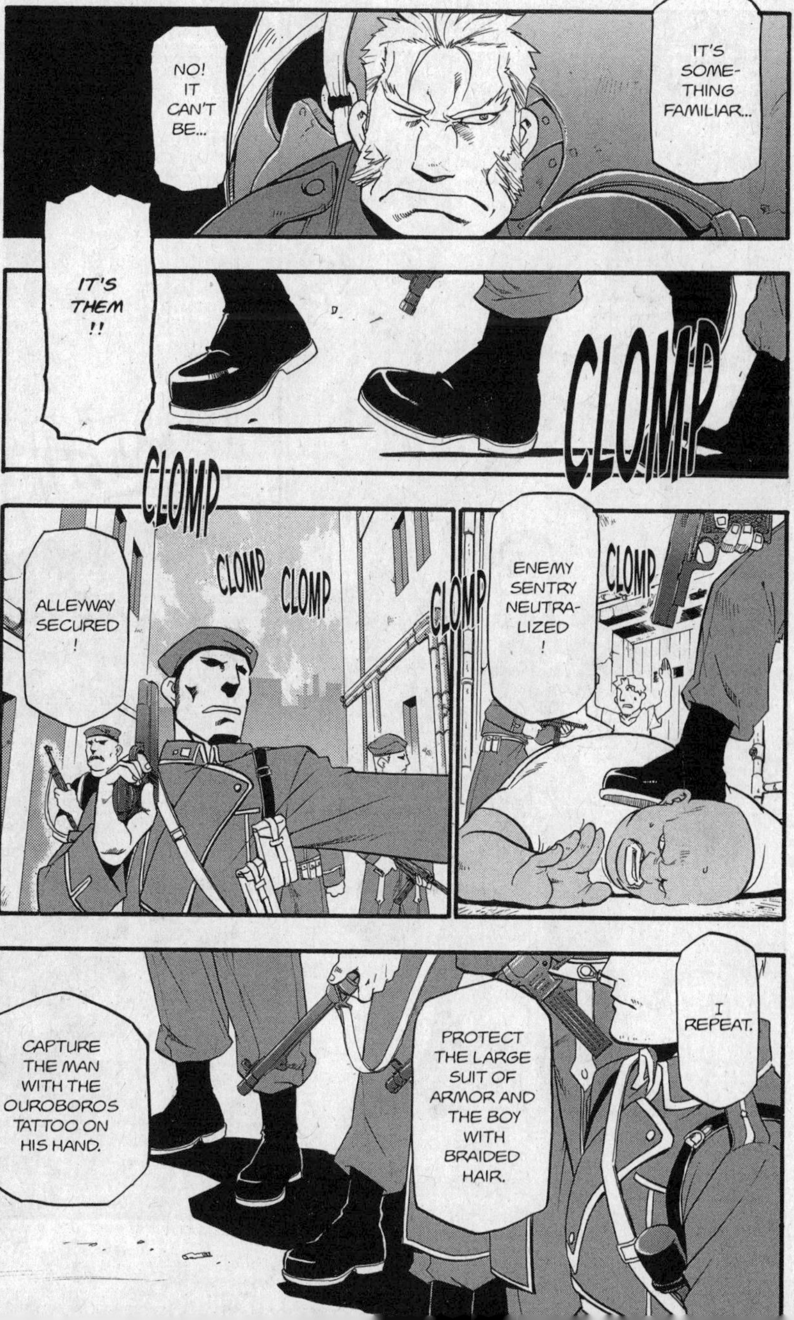
IT'S SOMETHING FAMILIAR...
NO! IT CAN'T BE...
IT'S THEM!!
CLOMP
CLOMP
CLOMP
ENEMY SENTRY NEUTRALIZED!
CLOMP
CLOMP
CLOMP
ALLEYWAY SECURED!
I REPEAT.
PROTECT THE LARGE SUIT OF ARMOR AND THE BOY WITH BRAIDED HAIR.
CAPTURE THE MAN WITH THE OUROBOROS TATTOO ON HIS HAND.

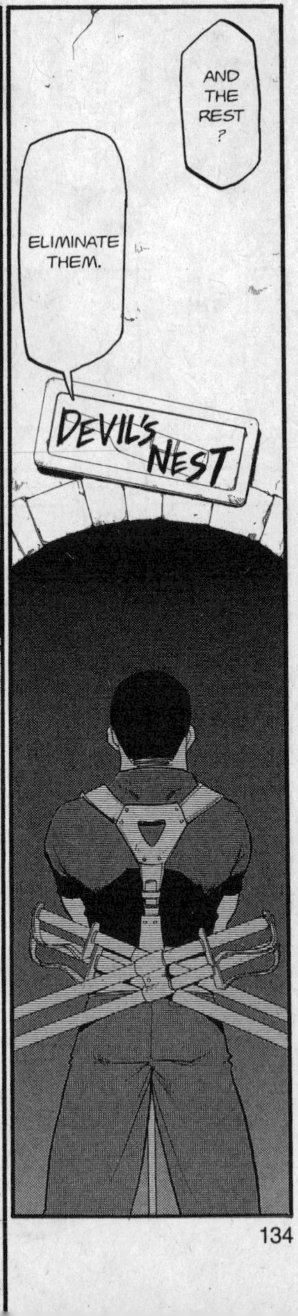
AND THE REST?
ELIMINATE THEM.
DEVIL'S NEST

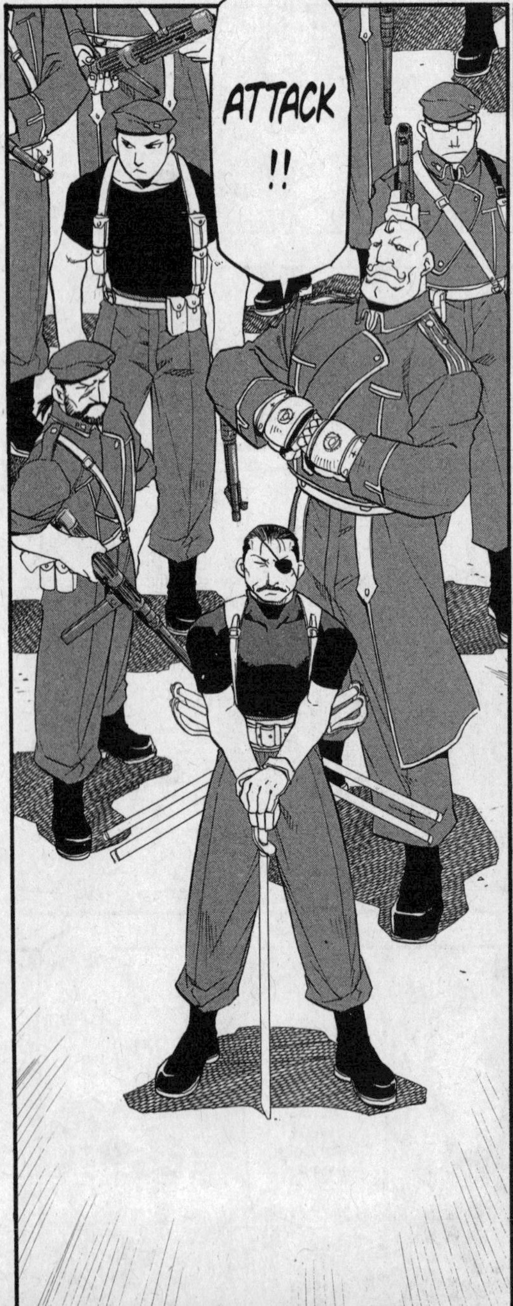
ATTACK!!

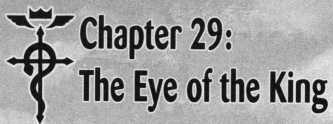

Chapter 29:
The Eye of the King

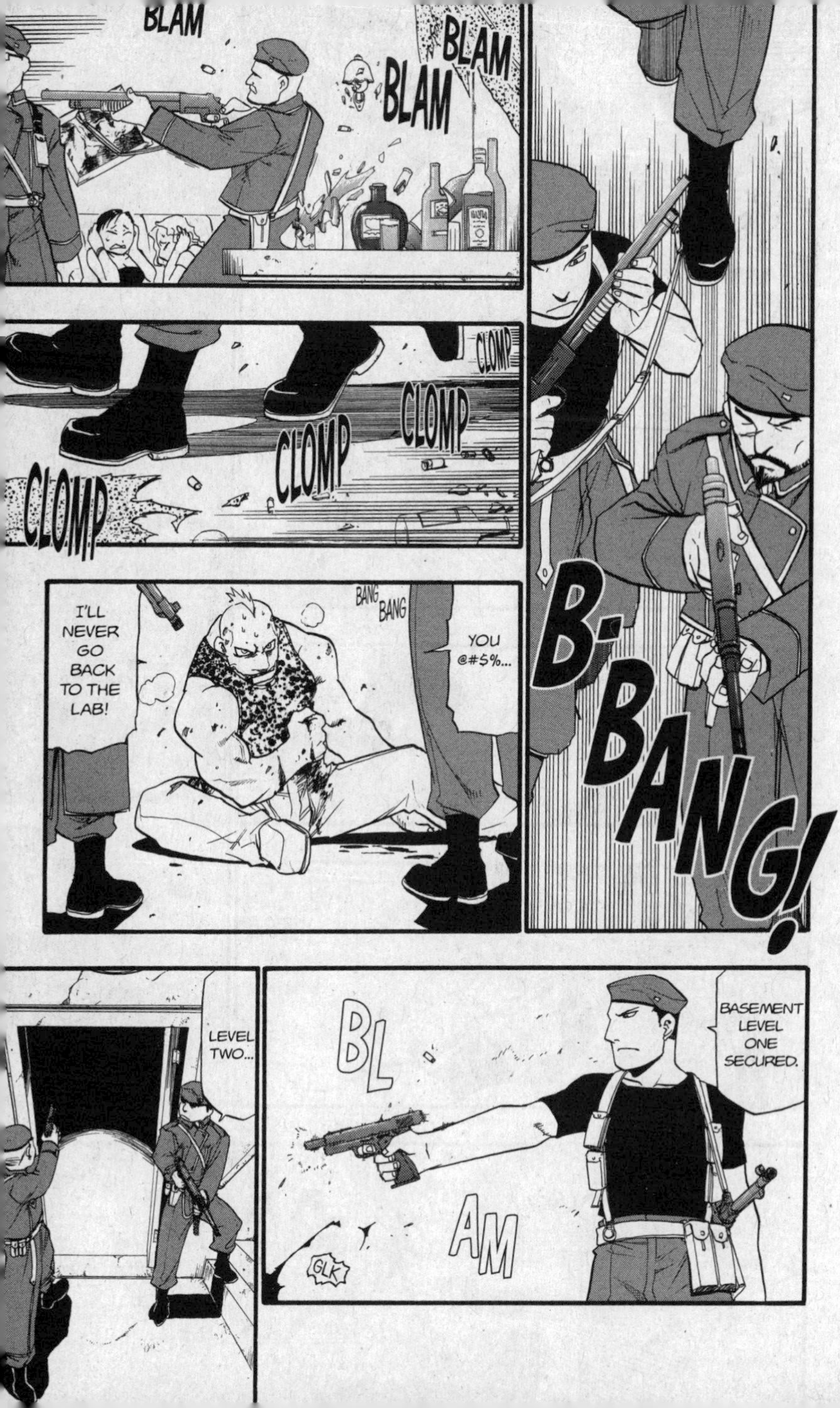
B-BANG!
BLAM
BLAM
BLAM
BLAM
CLOMP
CLOMP
CLOMP
CLOMP
BANG BANG
YOU @#$%...
I'LL NEVER GO BACK TO THE LAB!
BASEMENT LEVEL ONE SECURED.
BLAM
GLK
LEVEL TWO...

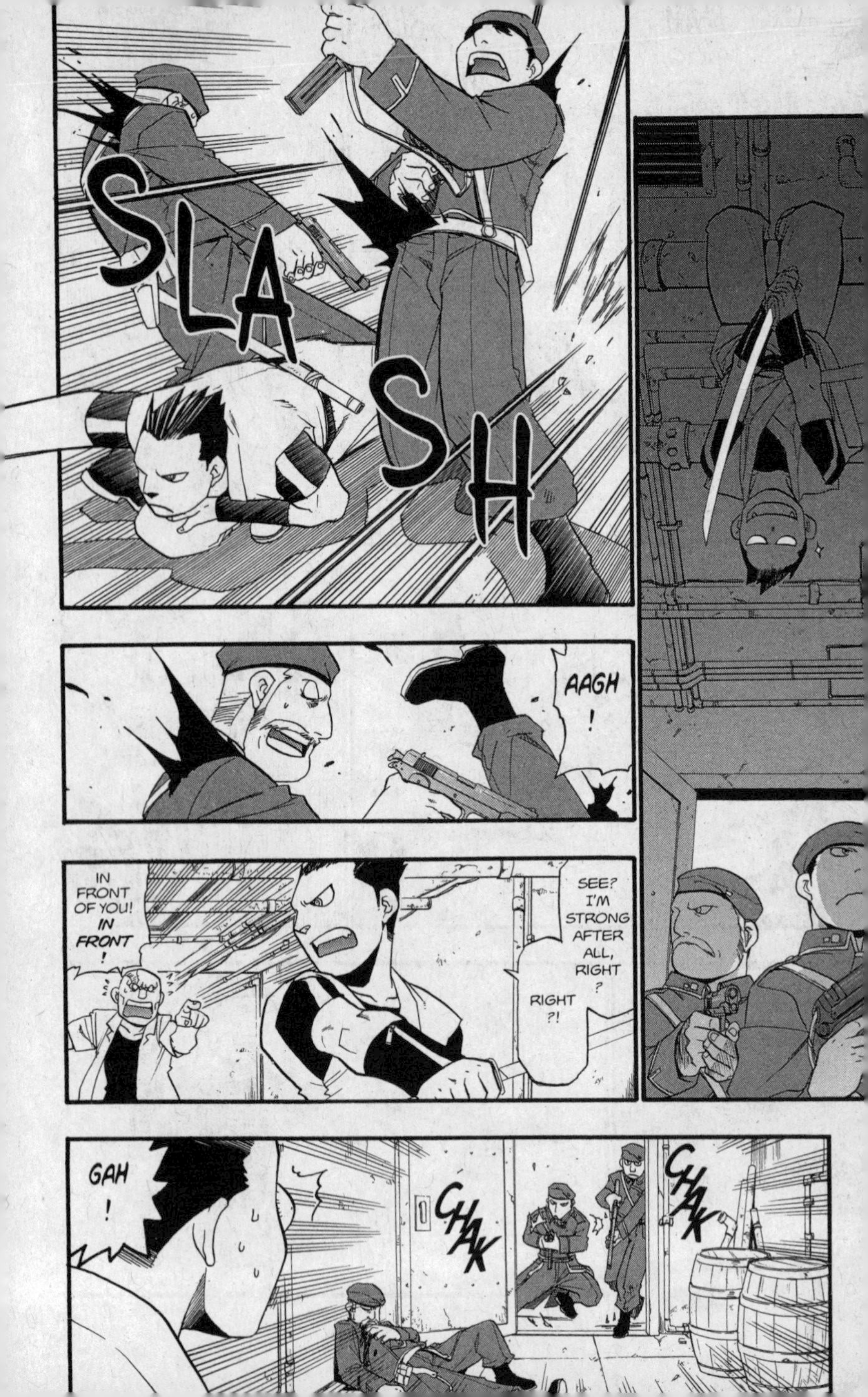
SLASH
AAGH!
SEE? I'M STRONG AFTER ALL, RIGHT?
RIGHT?!
IN FRONT OF YOU! IN FRONT!
CHAK
CHAK
GAH!

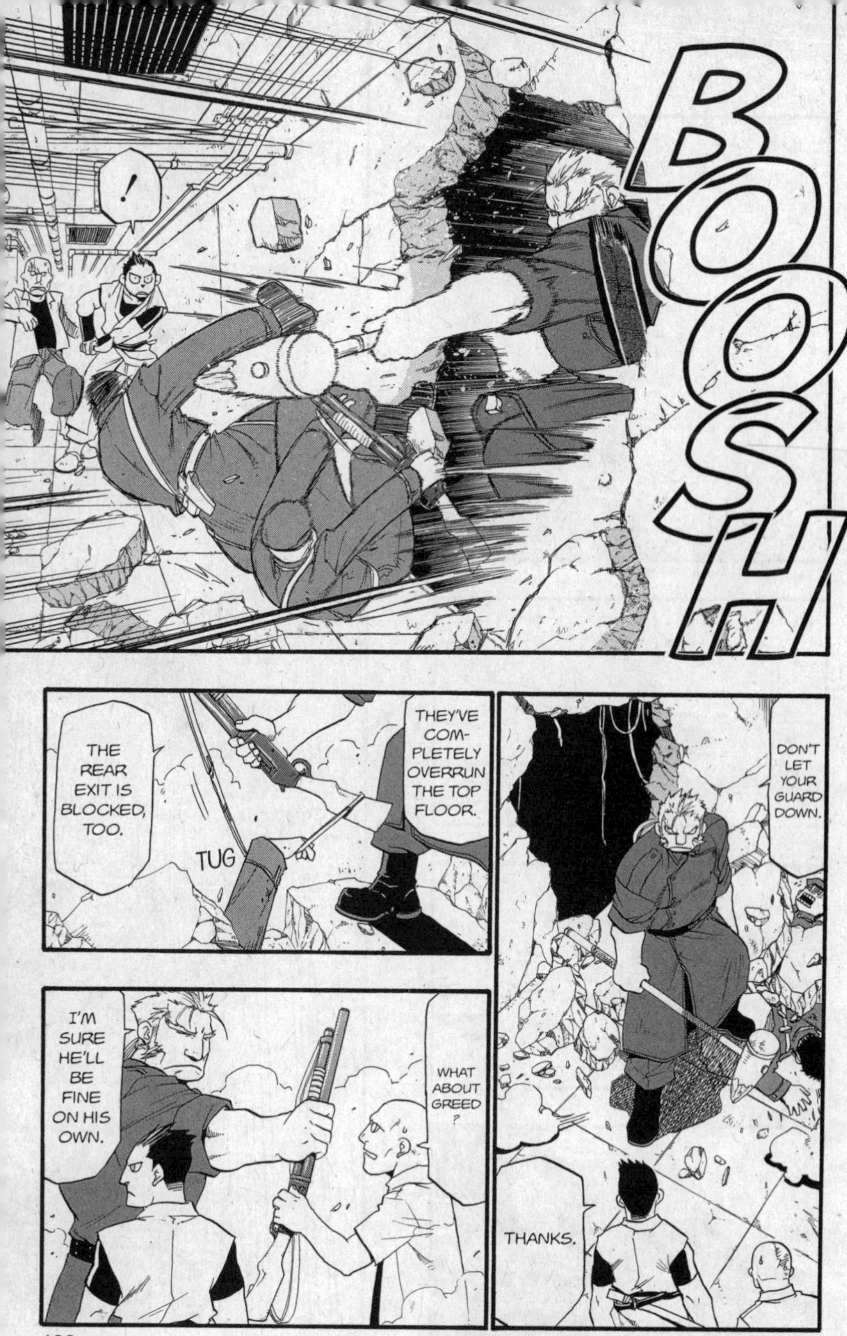
BOOOSH
!
DON'T LET YOUR GUARD DOWN.
THANKS.
THEY'VE COMPLETELY OVERRUN THE TOP FLOOR.
THE REAR EXIT IS BLOCKED, TOO.
TUG
WHAT ABOUT GREED?
I'M SURE HE'LL BE FINE ON HIS OWN.

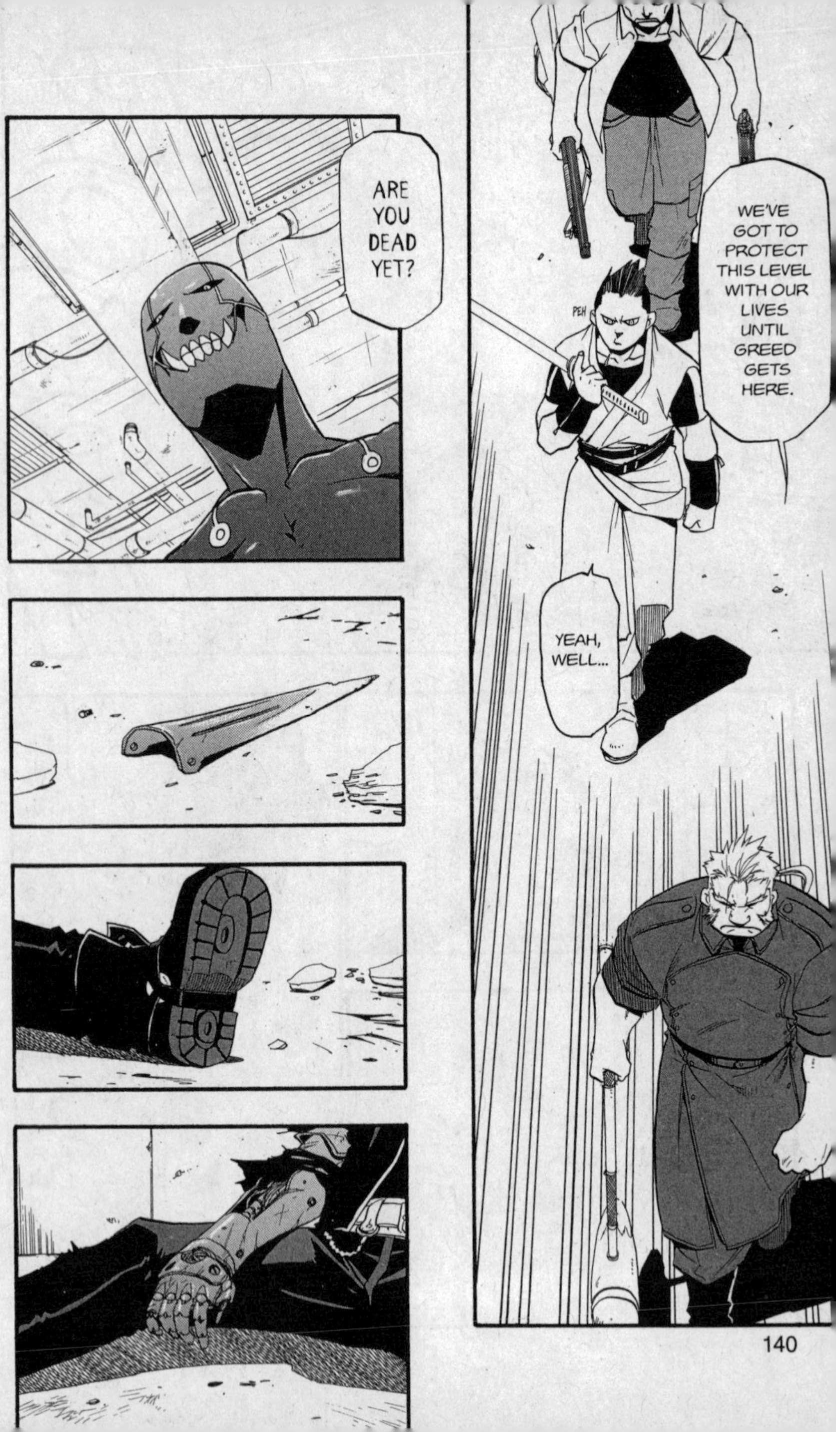
WE'VE GOT TO PROTECT THIS LEVEL WITH OUR LIVES UNTIL GREED GETS HERE.
PEH
YEAH, WELL...
ARE YOU DEAD YET?

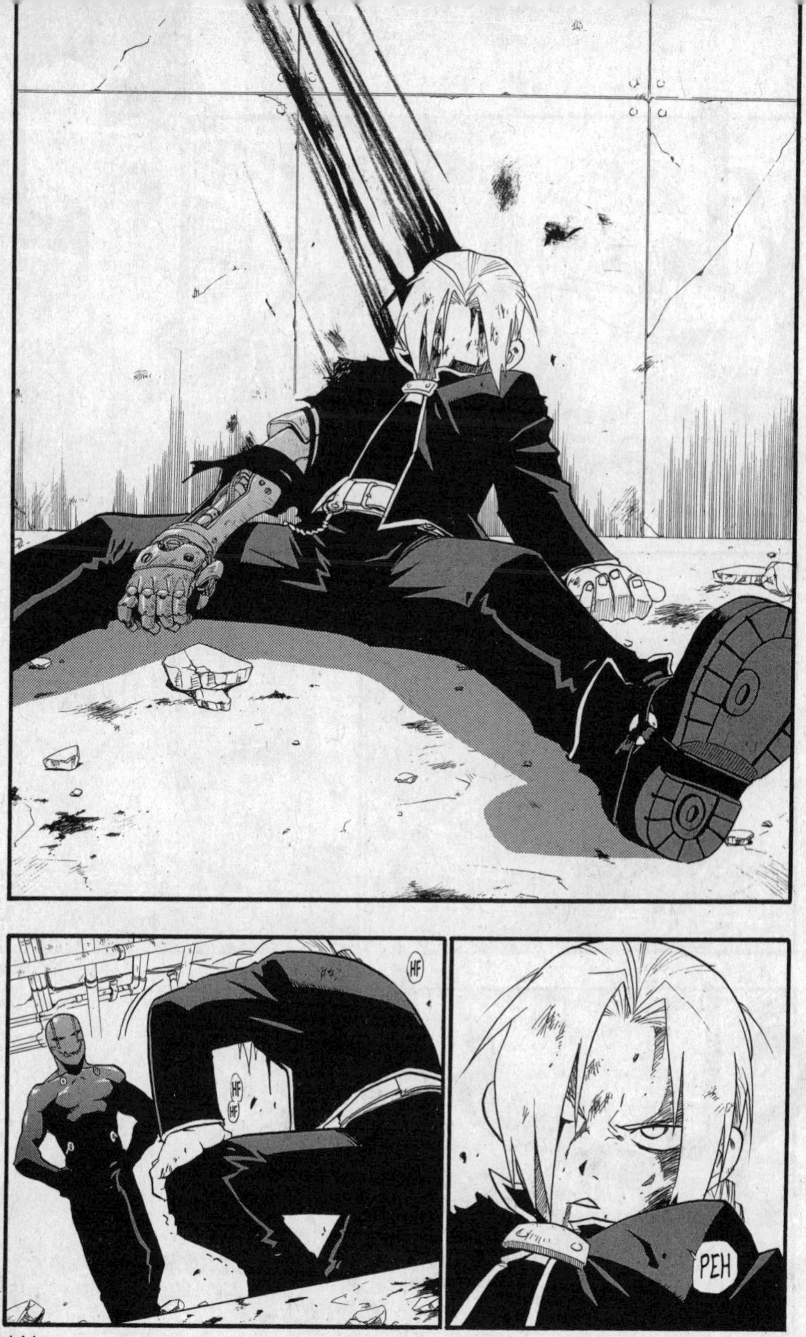
PEH
HF
HF
HF

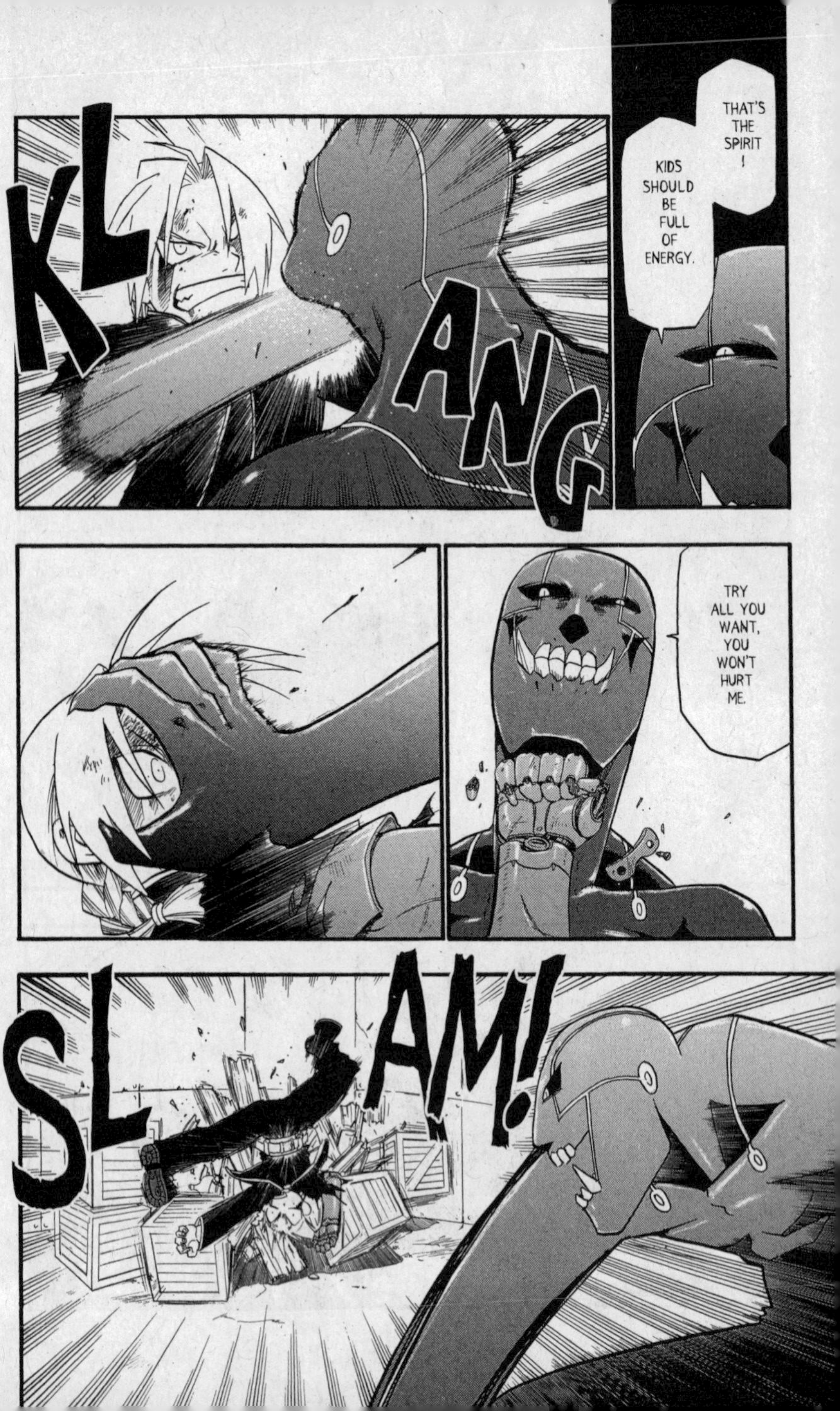
THAT'S THE SPIRIT!
KIDS SHOULD BE FULL OF ENERGY.
KLANG
TRY ALL YOU WANT, YOU WON'T HURT ME.
SLAM!

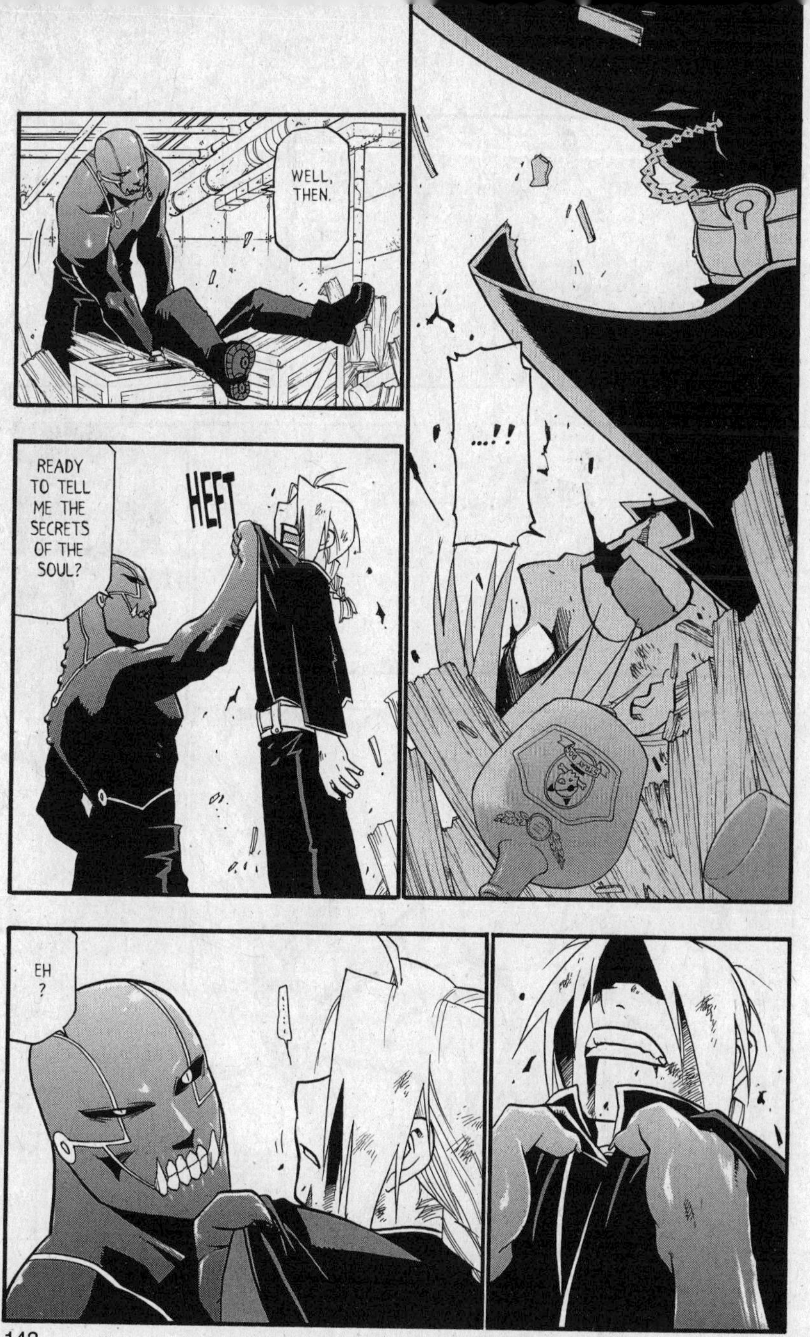
...!!
WELL, THEN.
HEFT
READY TO TELL ME THE SECRETS OF THE SOUL?
EH ?

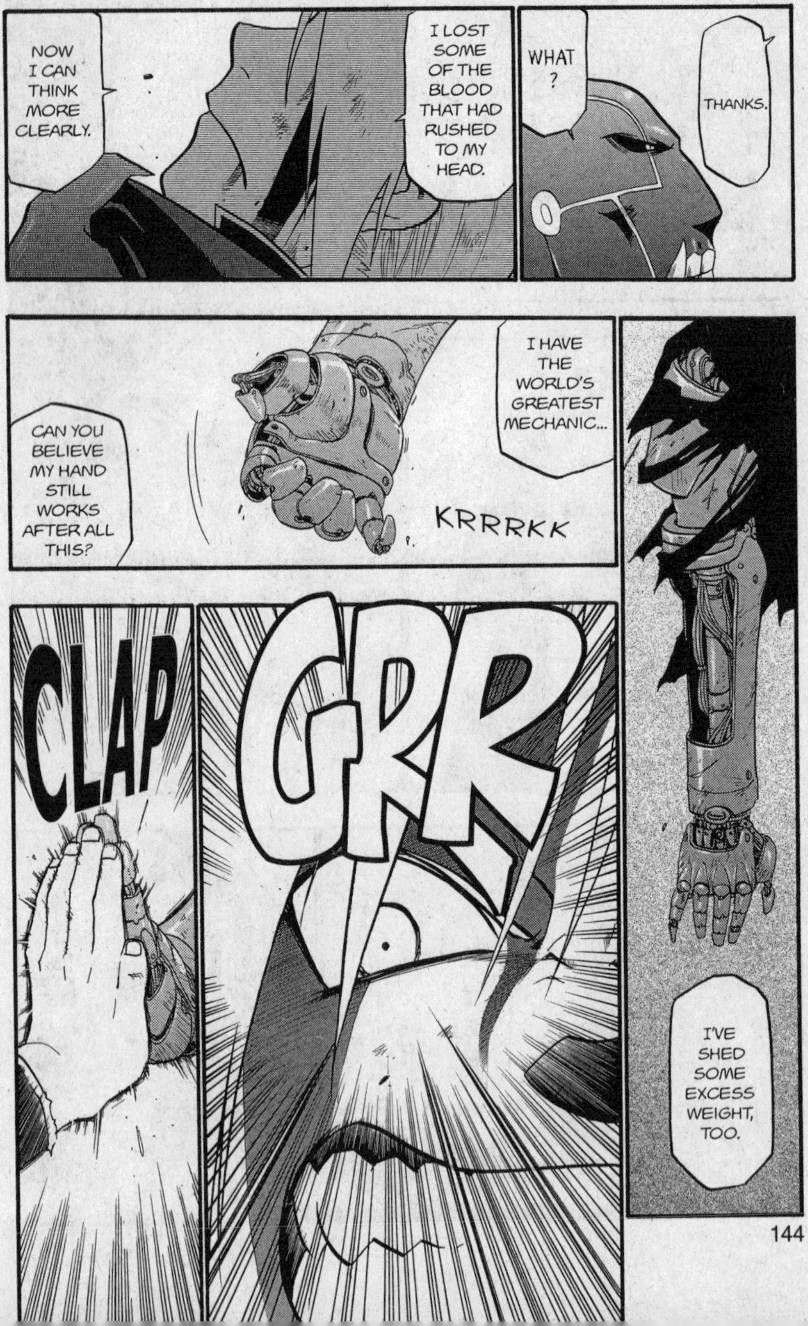
THANKS.
WHAT ?
I LOST SOME OF THE BLOOD THAT HAD RUSHED TO MY HEAD.
NOW I CAN THINK MORE CLEARLY.
I'VE SHED SOME EXCESS WEIGHT, TOO.
I HAVE THE WORLD'S GREATEST MECHANIC...
CAN YOU BELIEVE MY HAND STILL WORKS AFTER ALL THIS?
KRRRKK
GRR
CLAP

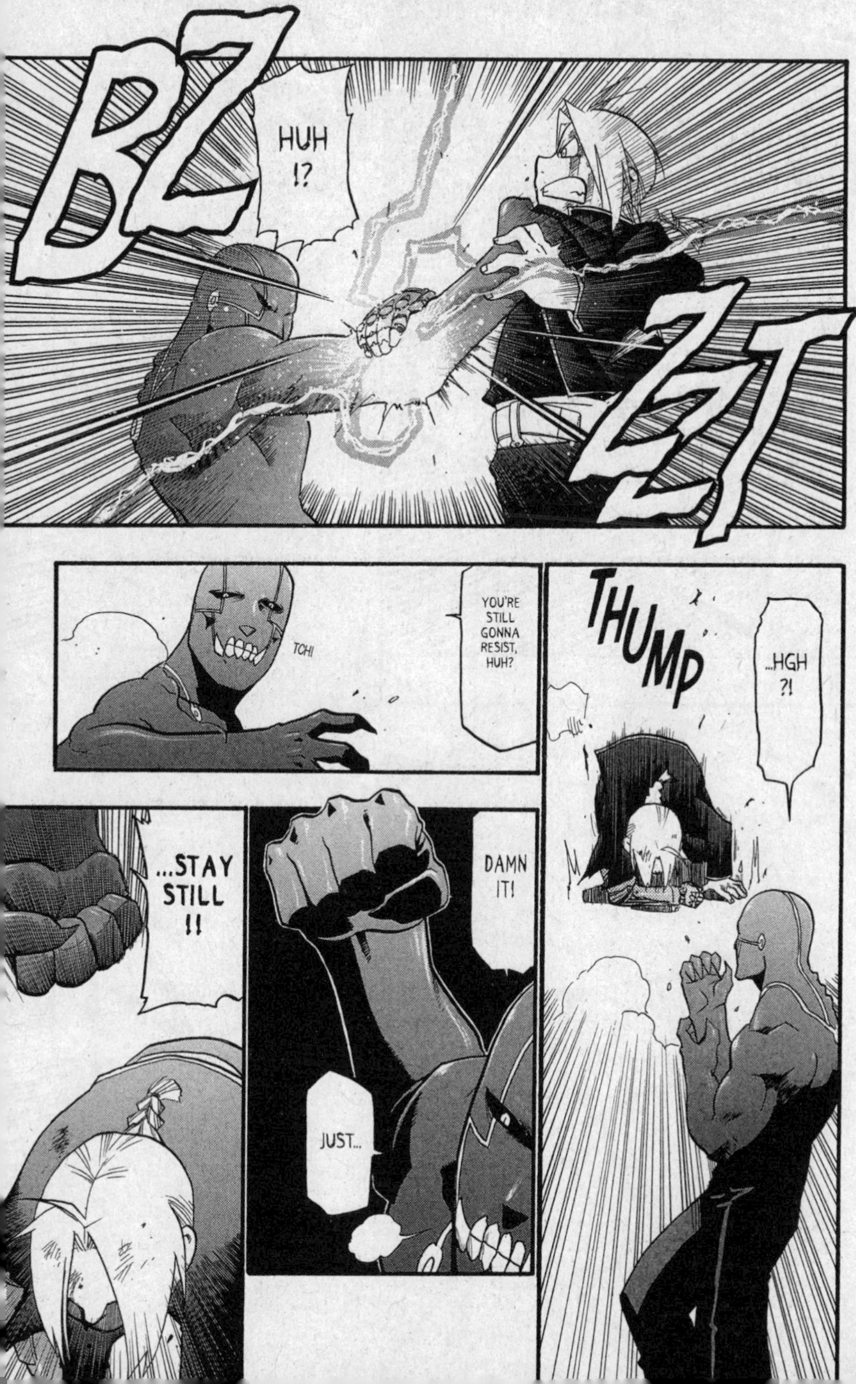
BZ
ZZT
HUH !?
THUMP
...HGH ?!
YOU'RE STILL GONNA RESIST, HUH?
TCH!
DAMN IT!
JUST...
...STAY STILL !!

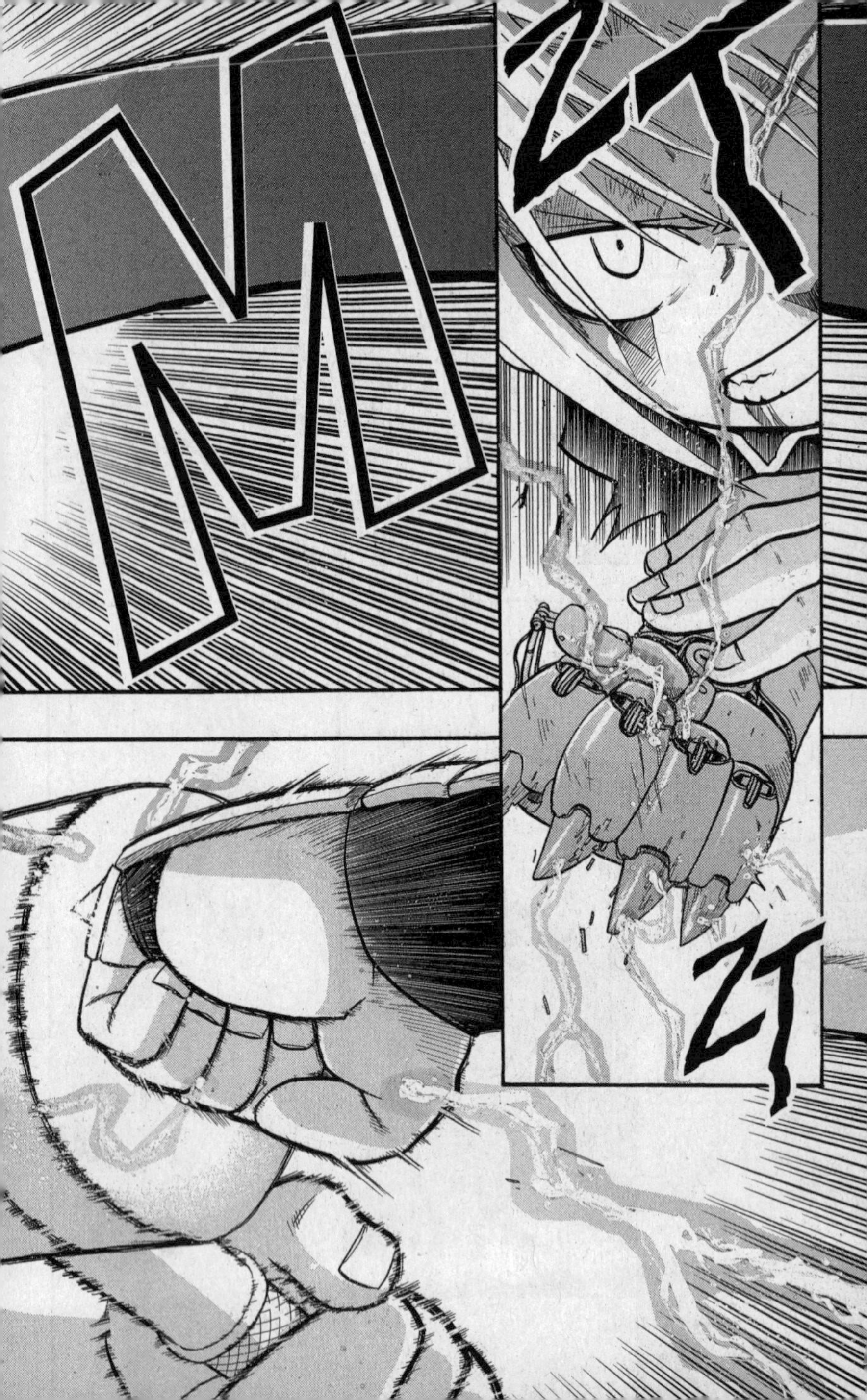
ZT

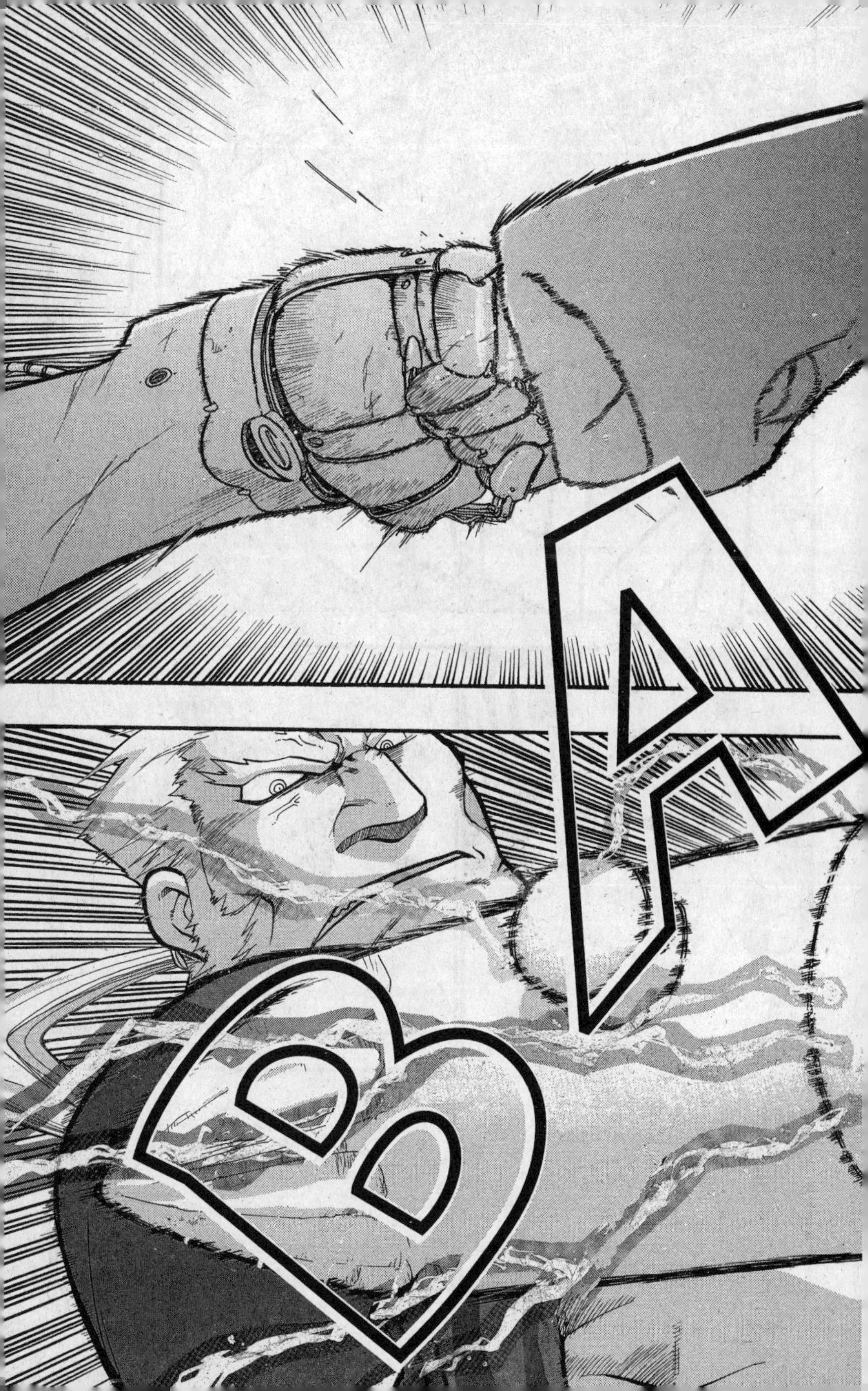
BA

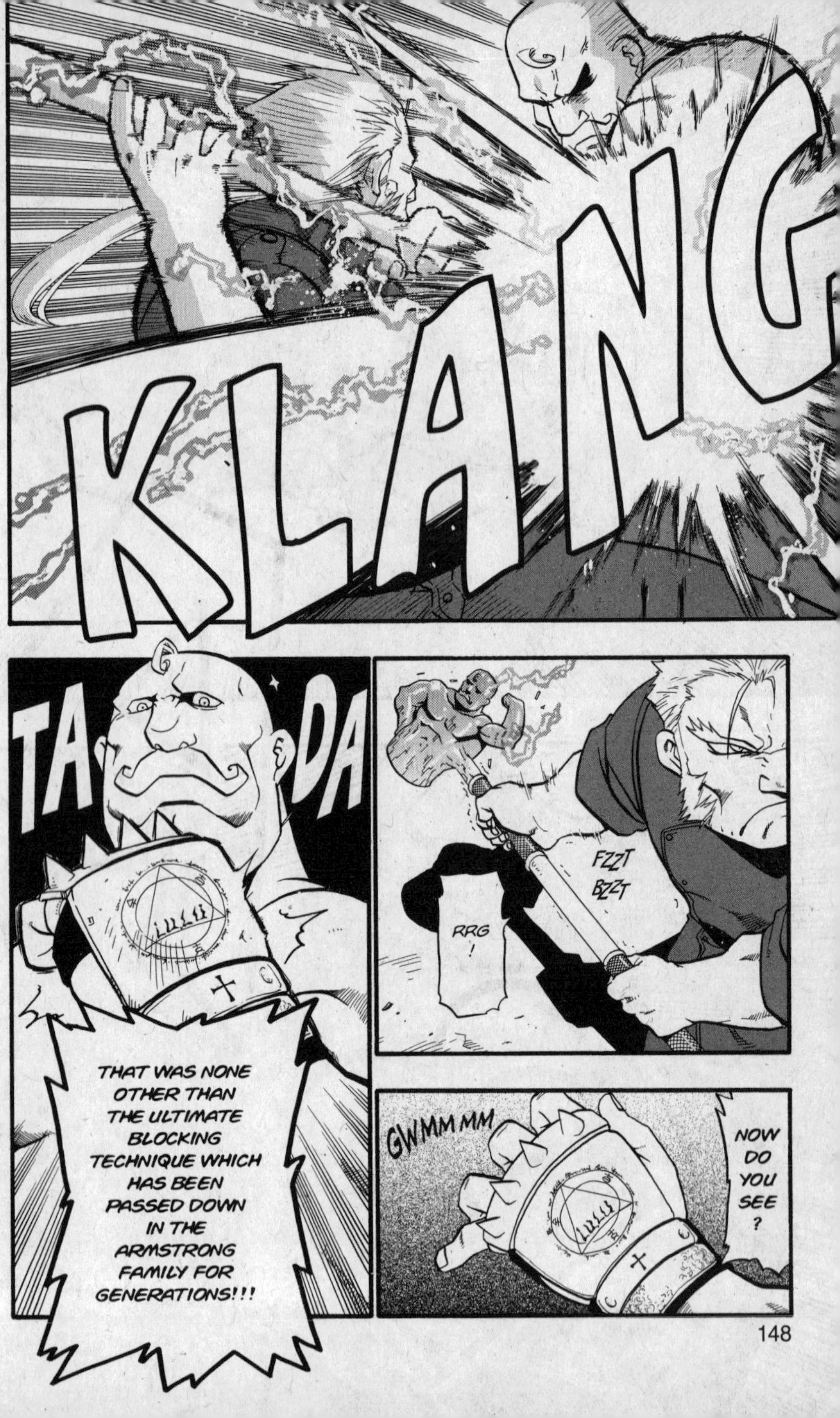
KLANG
FZZT
BZZT
RRG!
GWMMMM
NOW DO YOU SEE?
TA DA
THAT WAS NONE OTHER THAN THE ULTIMATE BLOCKING TECHNIQUE WHICH HAS BEEN PASSED DOWN IN THE ARMSTRONG FAMILY FOR GENERATIONS!!!

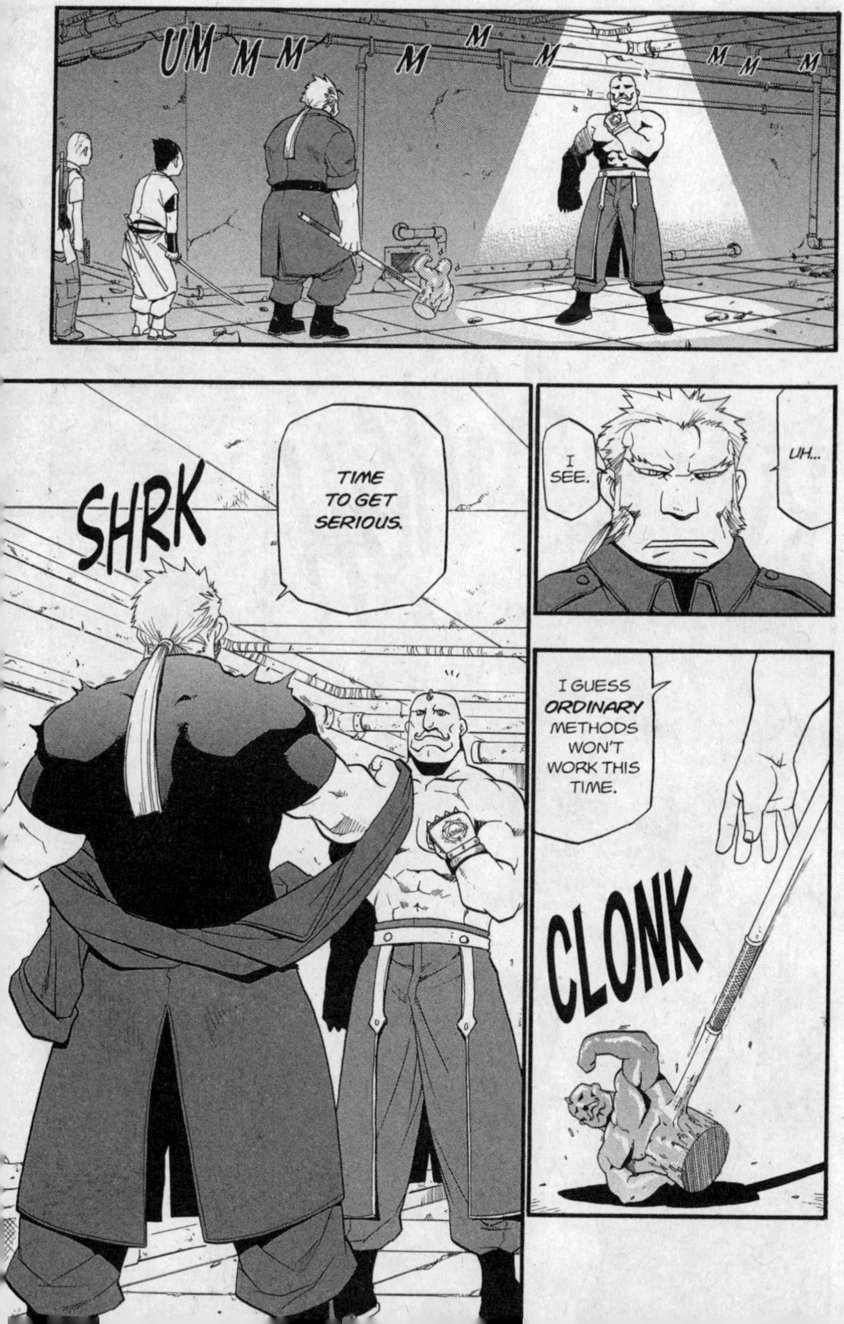
UMMMMMMMMM
UH...
I SEE.
I GUESS ORDINARY METHODS WON'T WORK THIS TIME.
CLONK
TIME TO GET SERIOUS.
SHRK

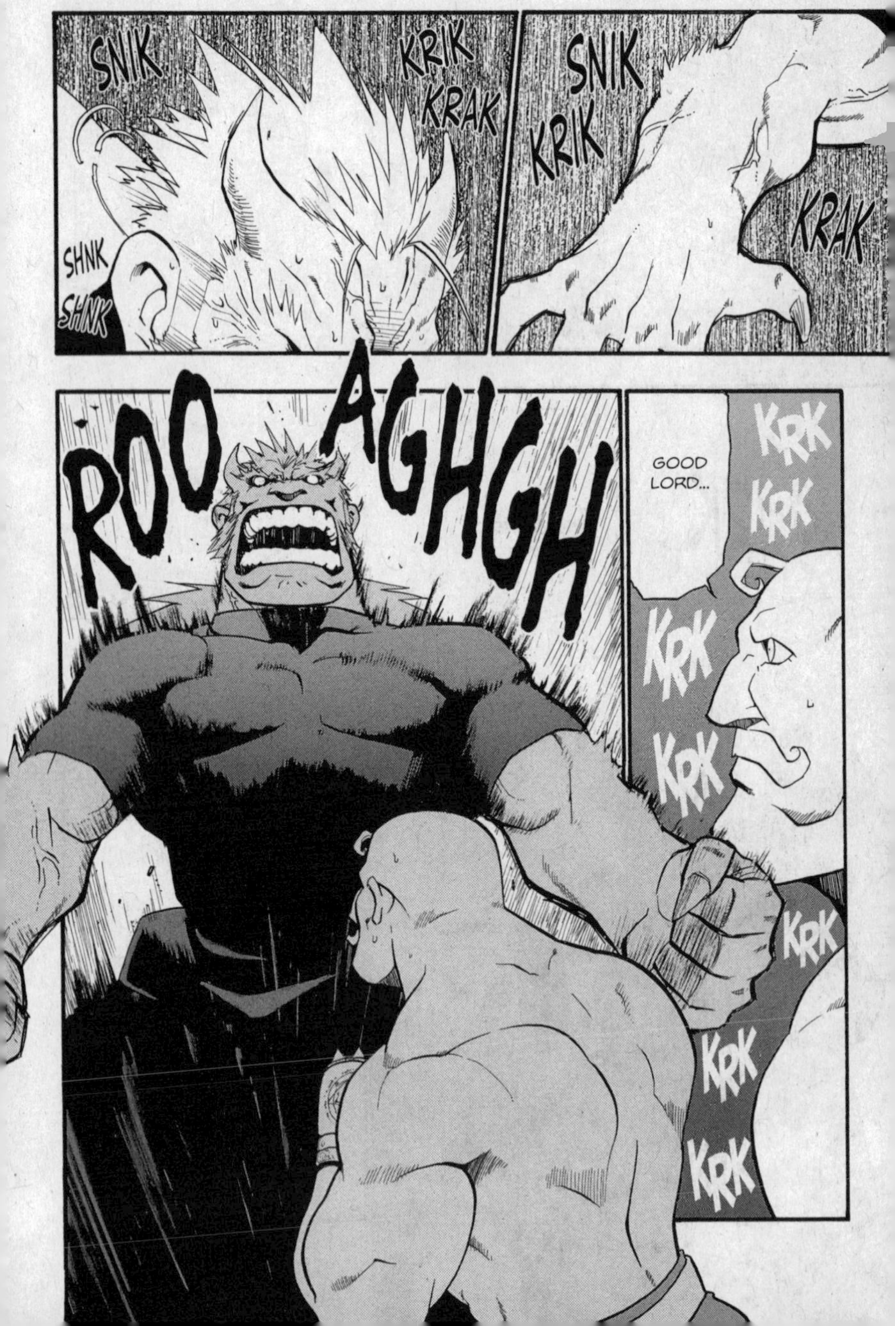
SNIK
KRIK
KRAK
SNIK
KRIK
KRAK
SHNK
SHNK
GOOD LORD...
KRK
KRK
KRK
KRK
KRK
KRK
KRK
ROO AGHGH

DM
HMH!
BAM BAM BAM
WSH
VOOM
WHAM
HRMH!
GMP

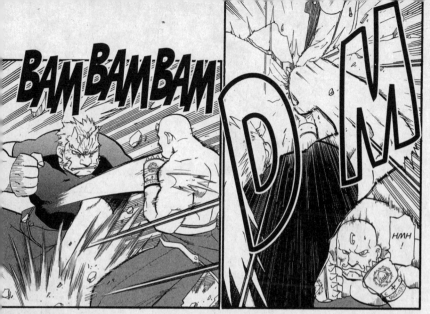

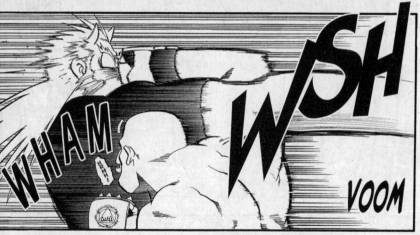

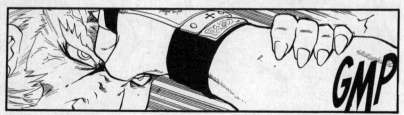

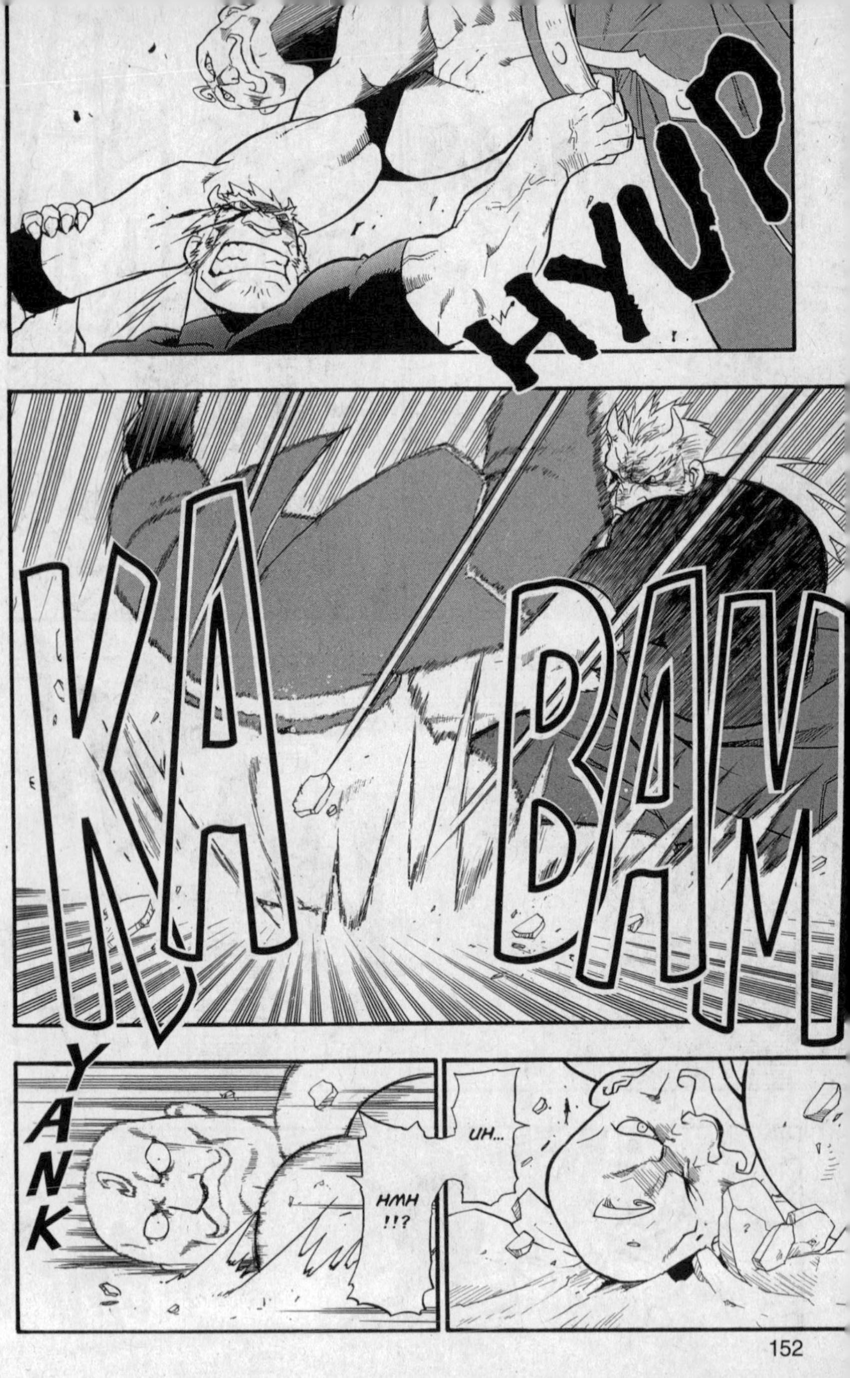
HYUP
KA BAM
UH...
HMH !!?
YANK

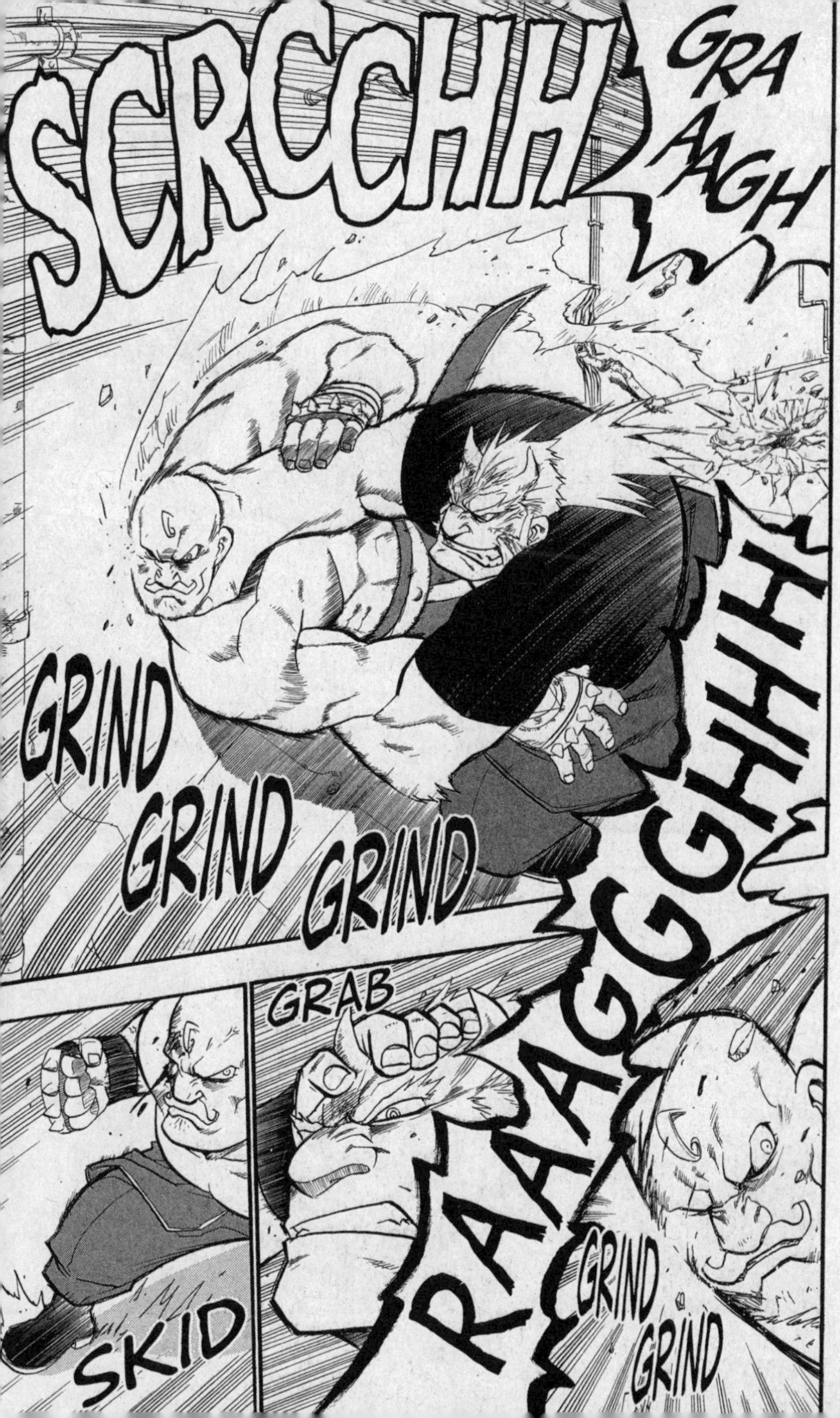
GRAAAGH
SCRCCHH
GRIND GRIND GRIND
RAAAGGHHH
GRIND GRIND
GRAB
SKID

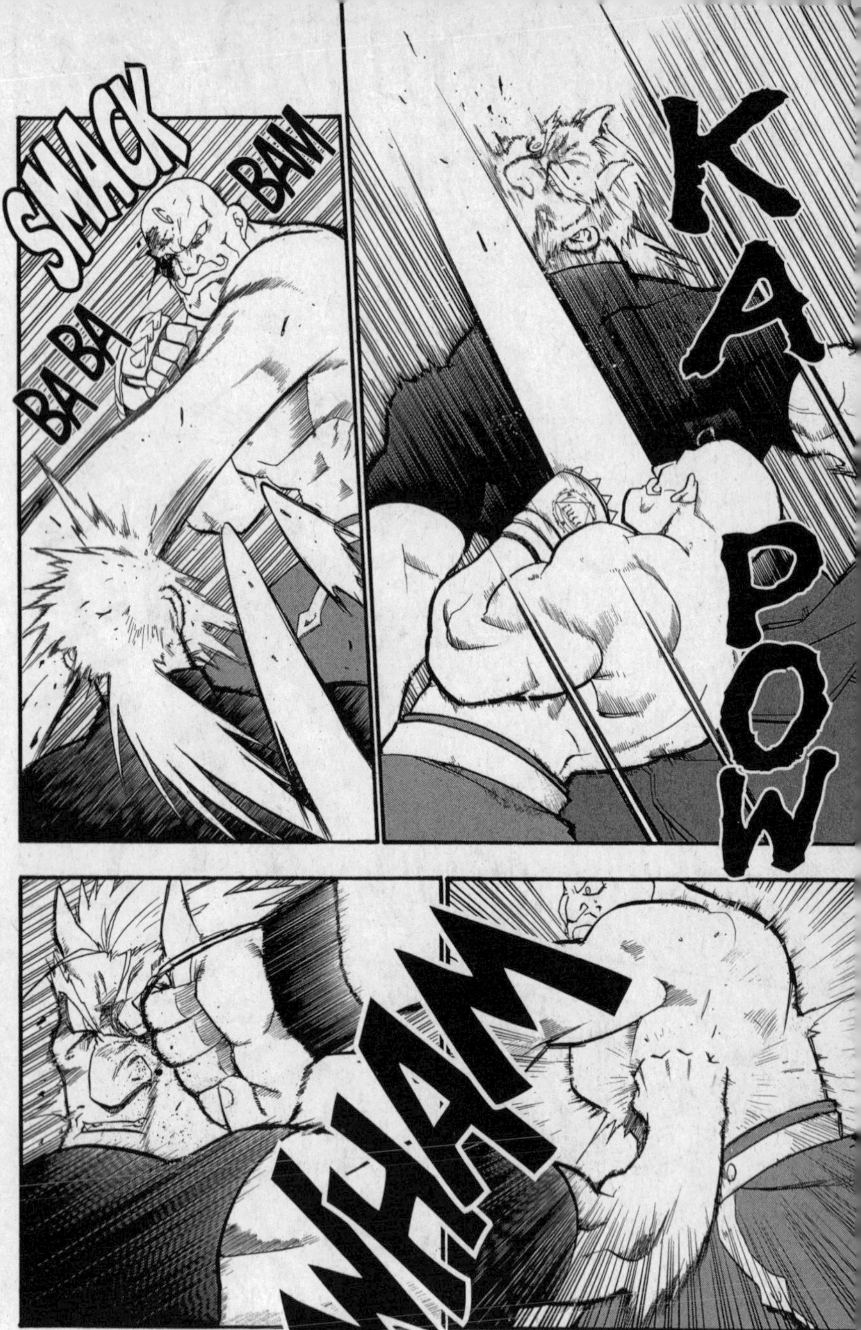
KA
POW
SMACK
BAM
BA BA
WHAM

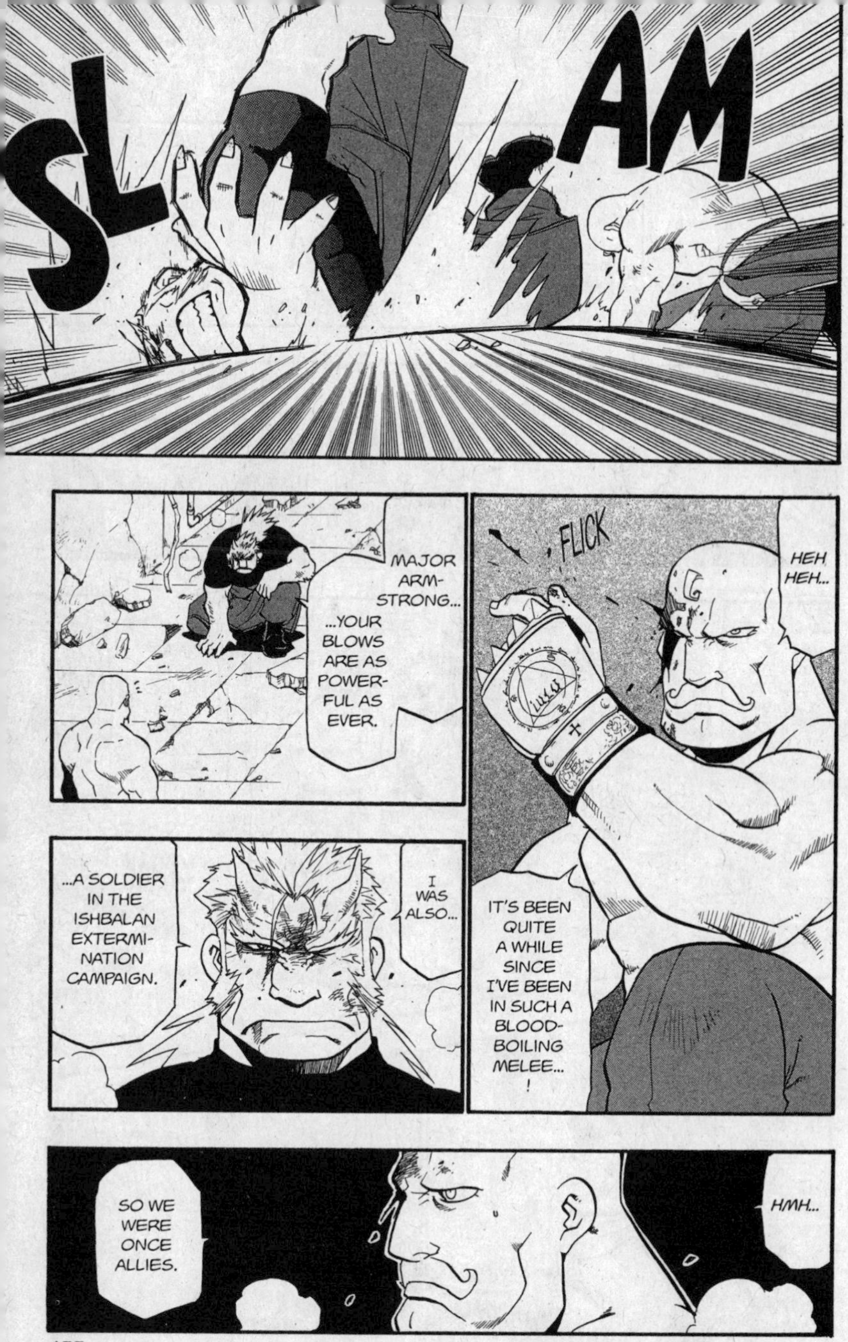
SLAM
FLICK
HEH HEH...
IT'S BEEN QUITE A WHILE SINCE I'VE BEEN IN SUCH A BLOOD-BOILING MELEE...!
MAJOR ARM-STRONG...
...YOUR BLOWS ARE AS POWER-FUL AS EVER.
I WAS ALSO...
...A SOLDIER IN THE ISHBALAN EXTERMI-NATION CAMPAIGN.
HMH...
SO WE WERE ONCE ALLIES.

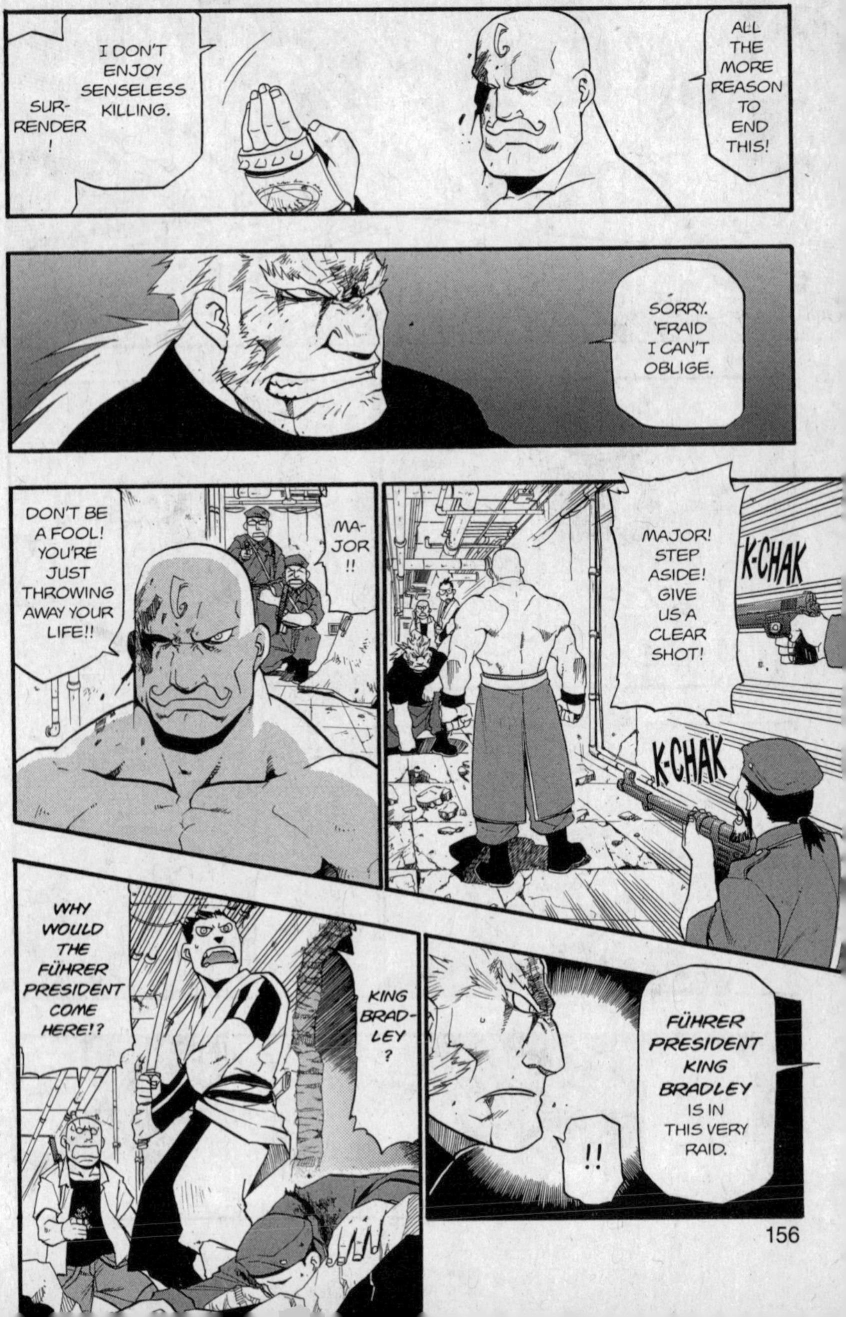

ALL THE MORE REASON TO END THIS!
I DON'T ENJOY SENSELESS KILLING.
SURRENDER!
SORRY. 'FRAID I CAN'T OBLIGE.
MAJOR! STEP ASIDE! GIVE US A CLEAR SHOT!
K-CHAK
K-CHAK
MAJOR!!
DON'T BE A FOOL! YOU'RE JUST THROWING AWAY YOUR LIFE!!
FÜHRER PRESIDENT KING BRADLEY IS IN THIS VERY RAID.
!!
KING BRADLEY?
WHY WOULD THE FÜHRER PRESIDENT COME HERE!?

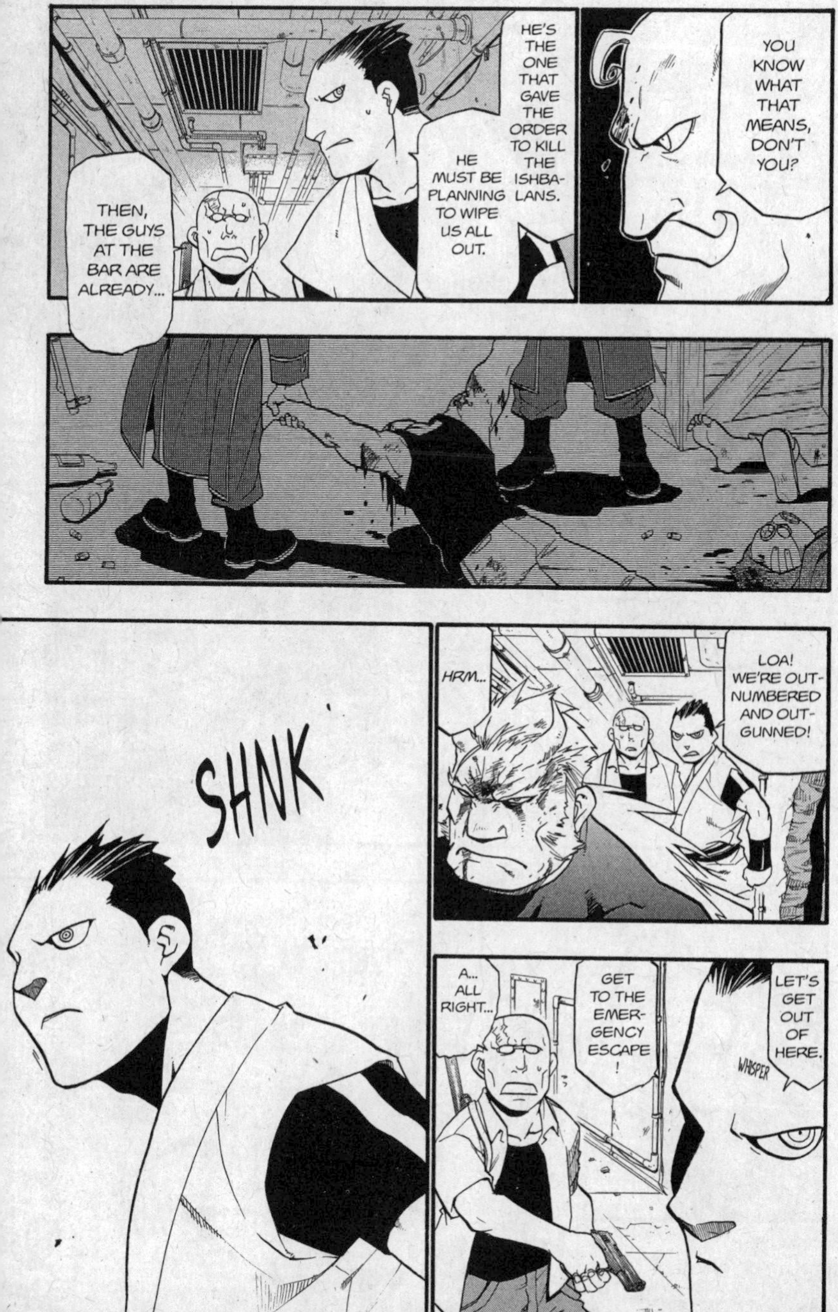
YOU KNOW WHAT THAT MEANS, DON'T YOU?
HE'S THE ONE THAT GAVE THE ORDER TO KILL THE ISHBALANS.
HE MUST BE PLANNING TO WIPE US ALL OUT.
THEN, THE GUYS AT THE BAR ARE ALREADY...
LOA! WE'RE OUTNUMBERED AND OUTGUNNED!
HRM...
LET'S GET OUT OF HERE.
WHISPER
GET TO THE EMERGENCY ESCAPE!
A... ALL RIGHT...
SHNK

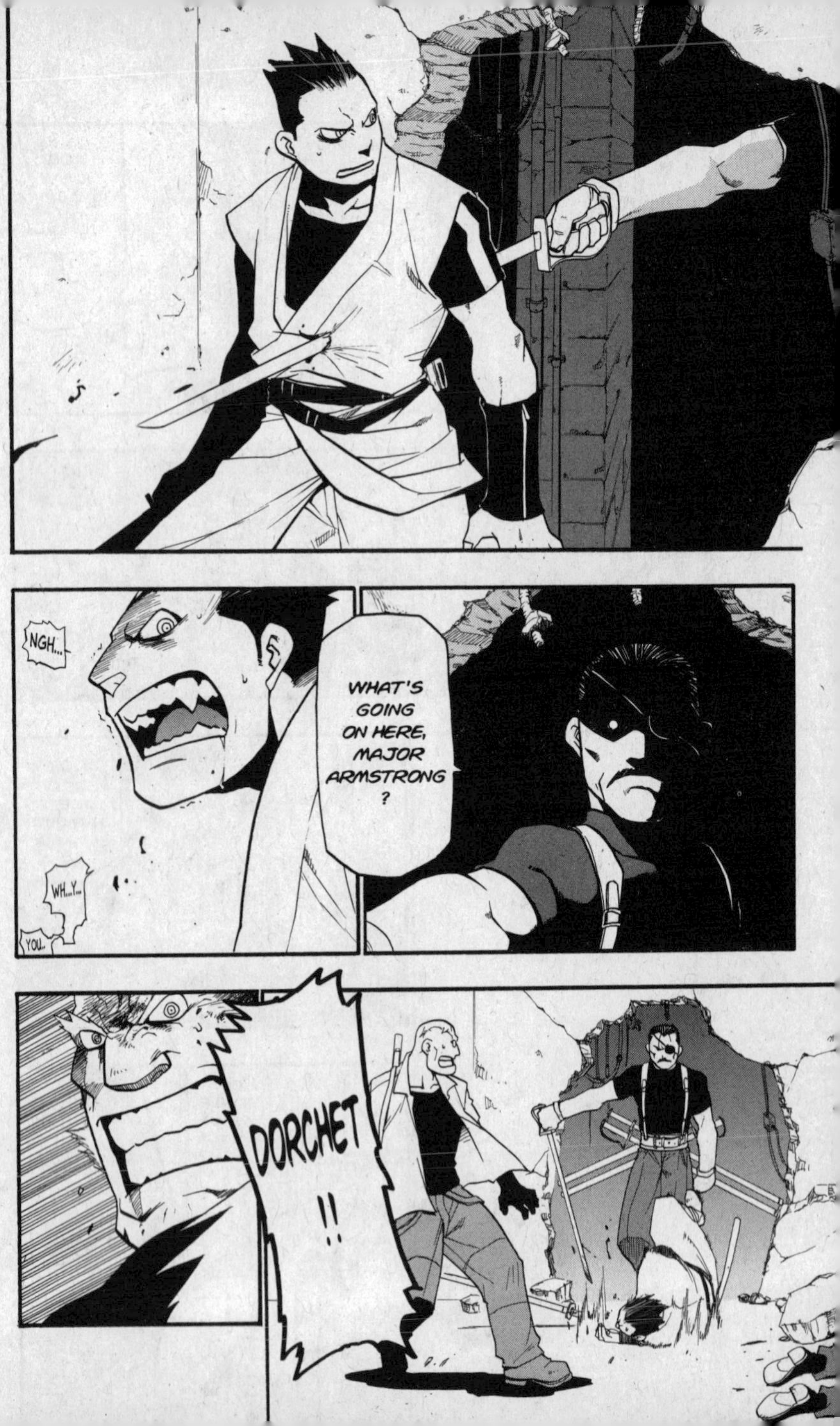
WHAT'S GOING ON HERE, MAJOR ARMSTRONG?
NGH...
WH...Y...
YOU..
DORCHET !!

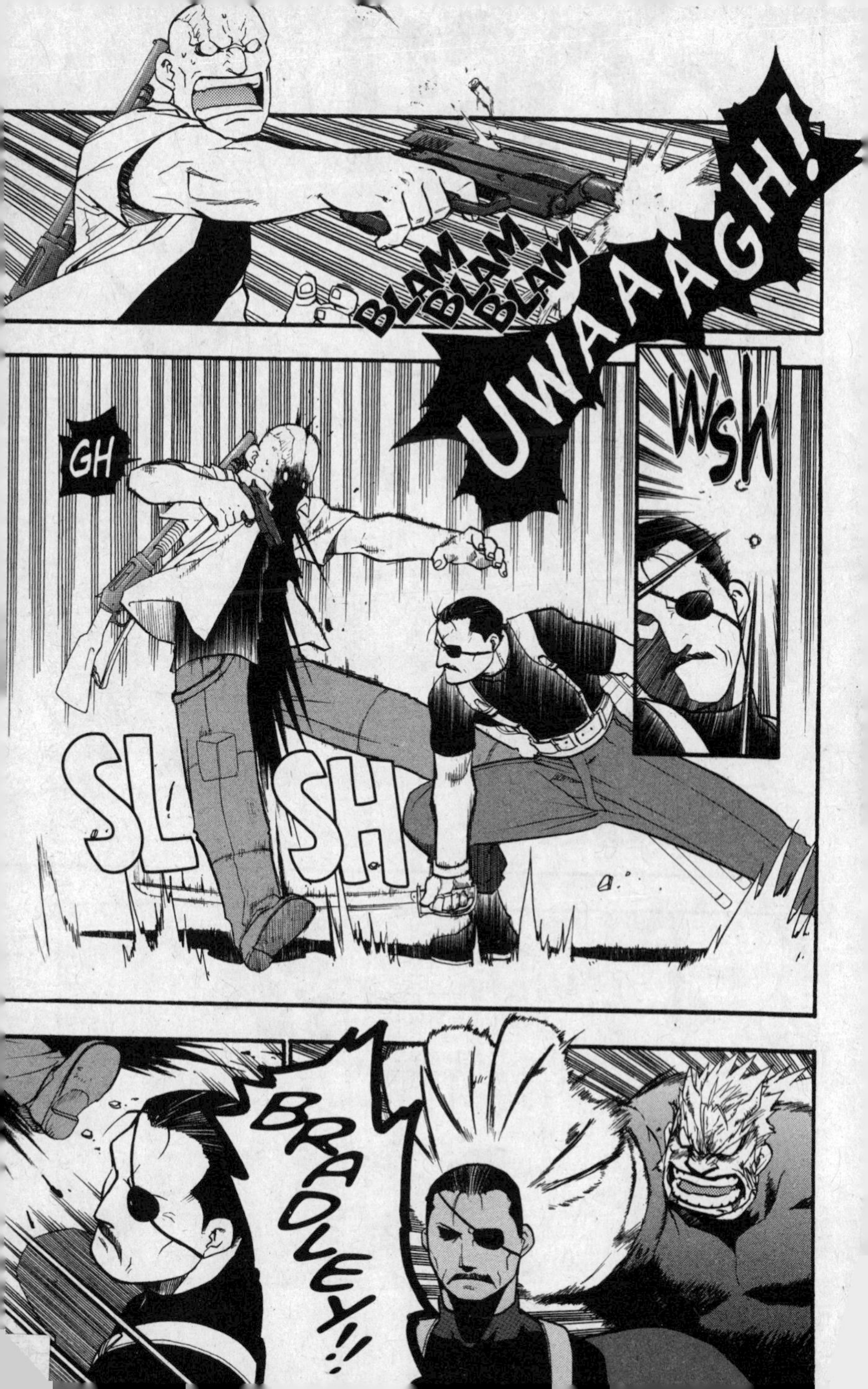
BLAM BLAM BLAM
UWAAAGH!!
Wsh
GH
SLASH
BRADLEY!!

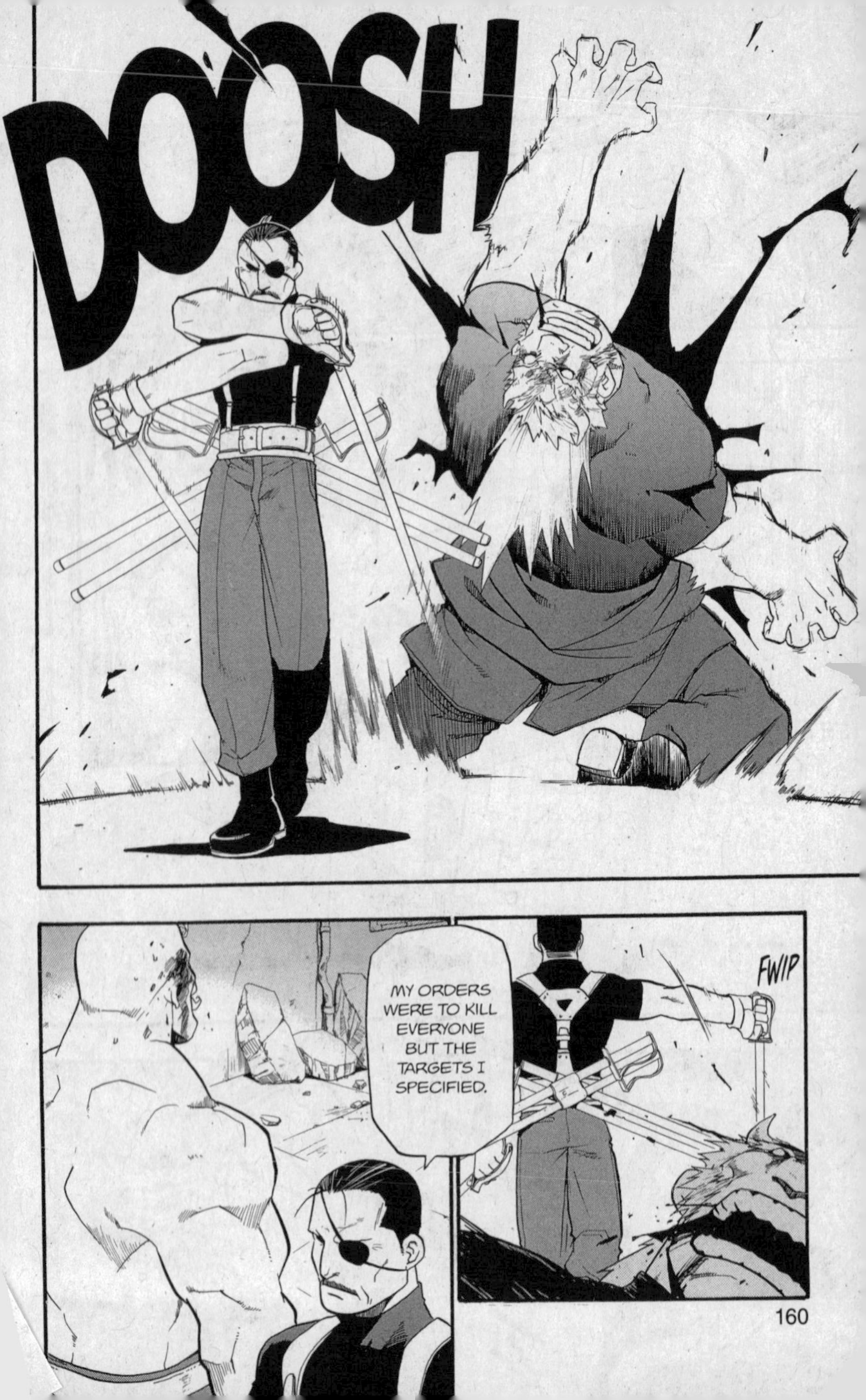
DOOSH
FWIP
MY ORDERS WERE TO KILL EVERYONE BUT THE TARGETS I SPECIFIED.

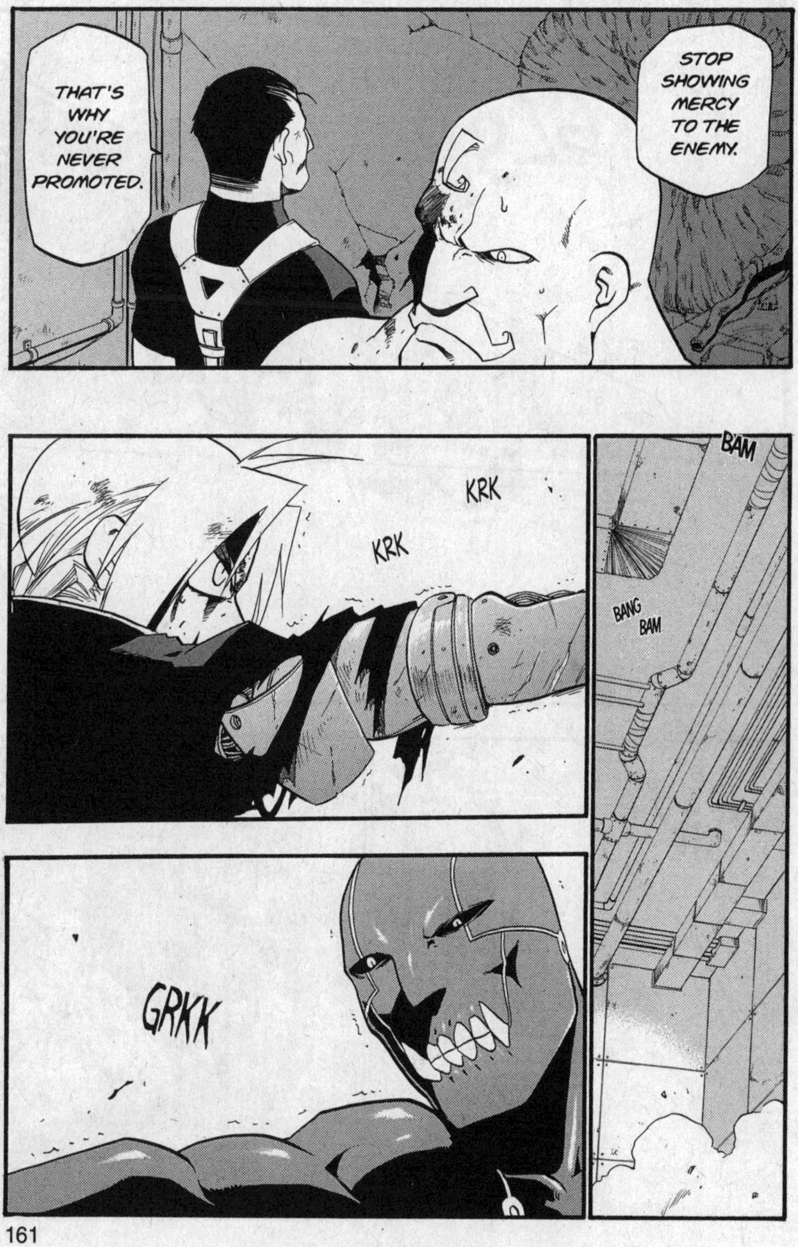
STOP SHOWING MERCY TO THE ENEMY.
THAT'S WHY YOU'RE NEVER PROMOTED.
BAM
BANG BAM
KRK
KRK
GRKK

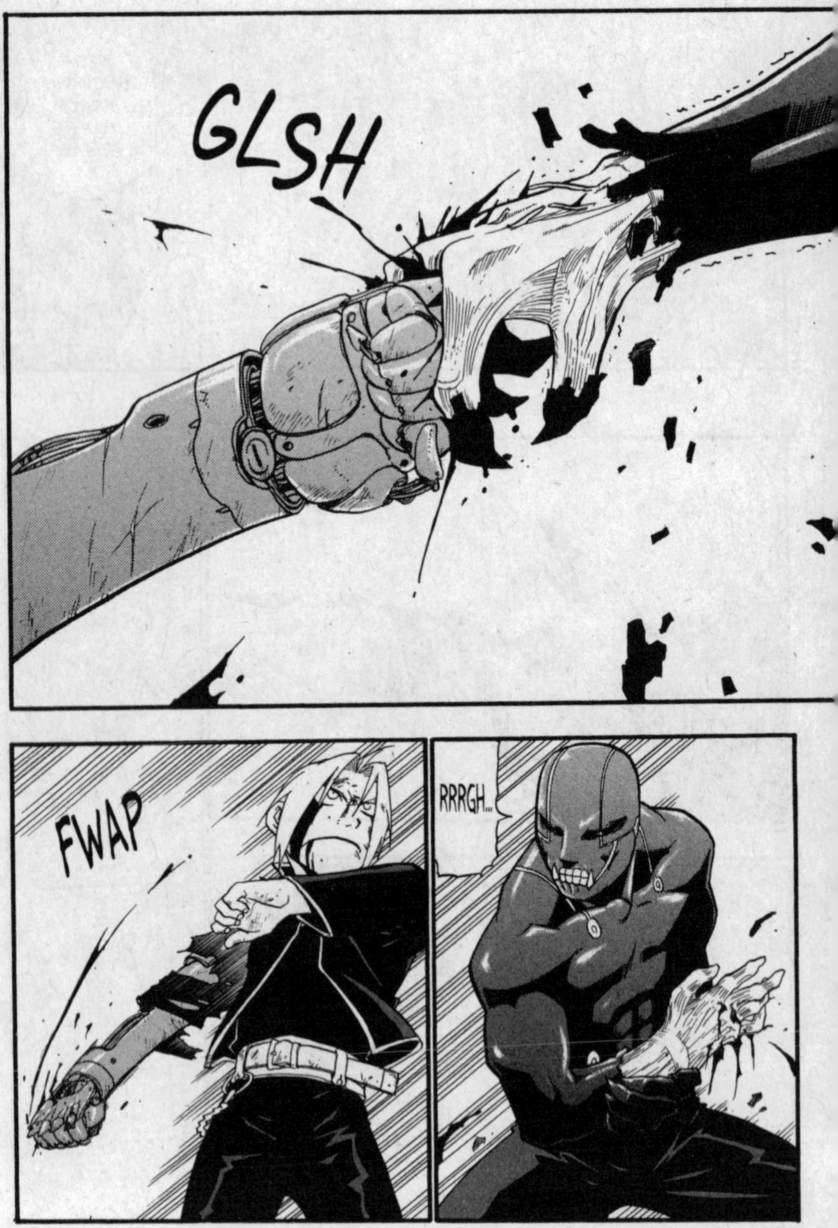
GLSH
RRRGH...
FWAP

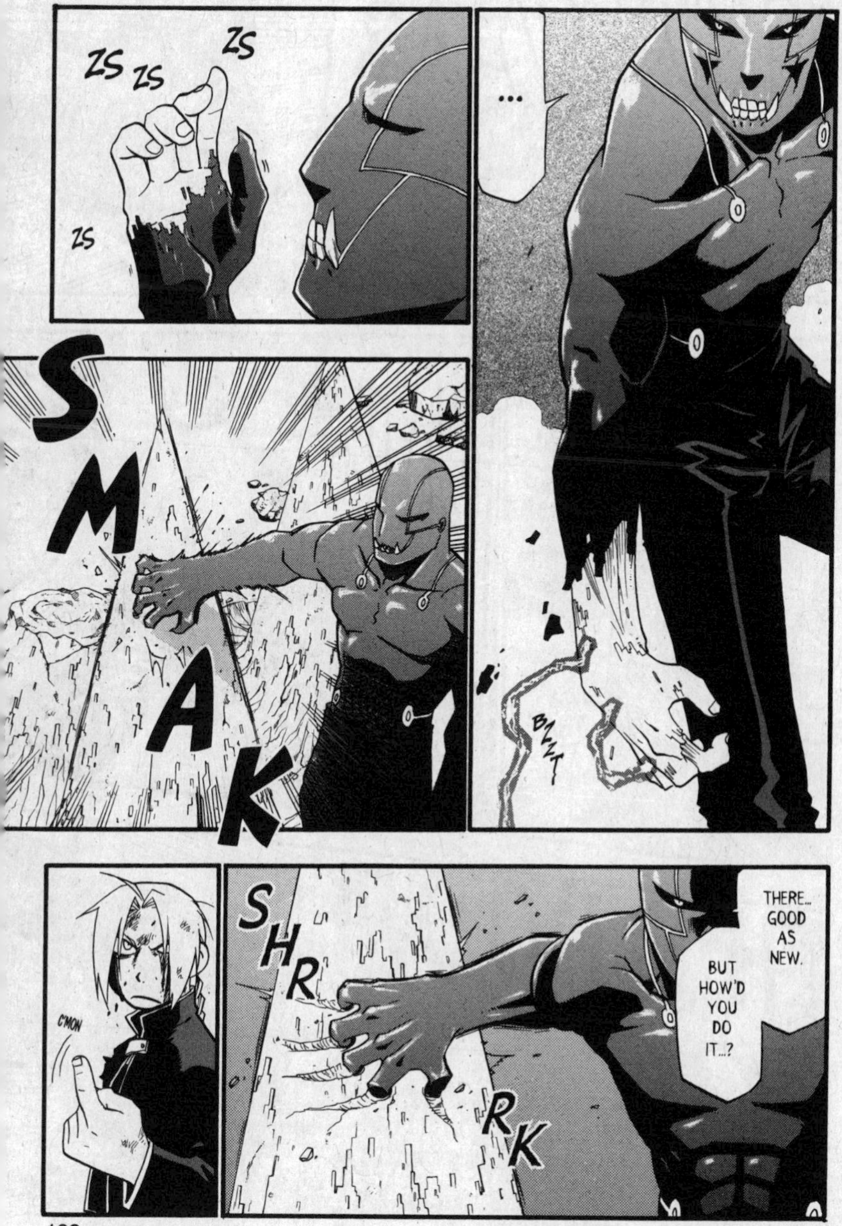
...
BZZT
ZS ZS ZS ZS
SMAK
SHRRK
THERE... GOOD AS NEW.
BUT HOW'D YOU DO IT...?
C'MON

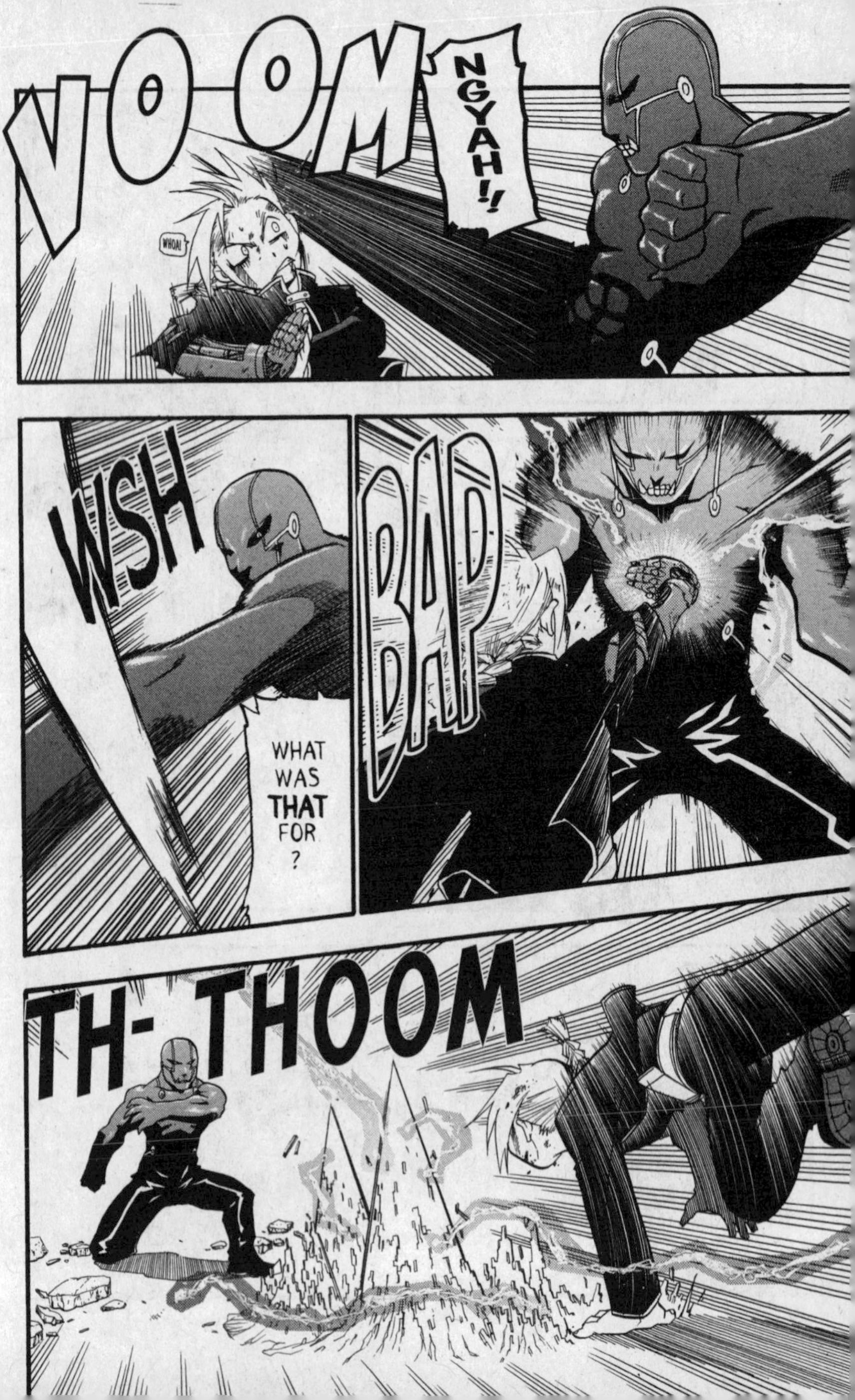
NGYAH!!
VOOM
WHOA!
BAP
WSH
WHAT WAS THAT FOR?
TH- THOOM

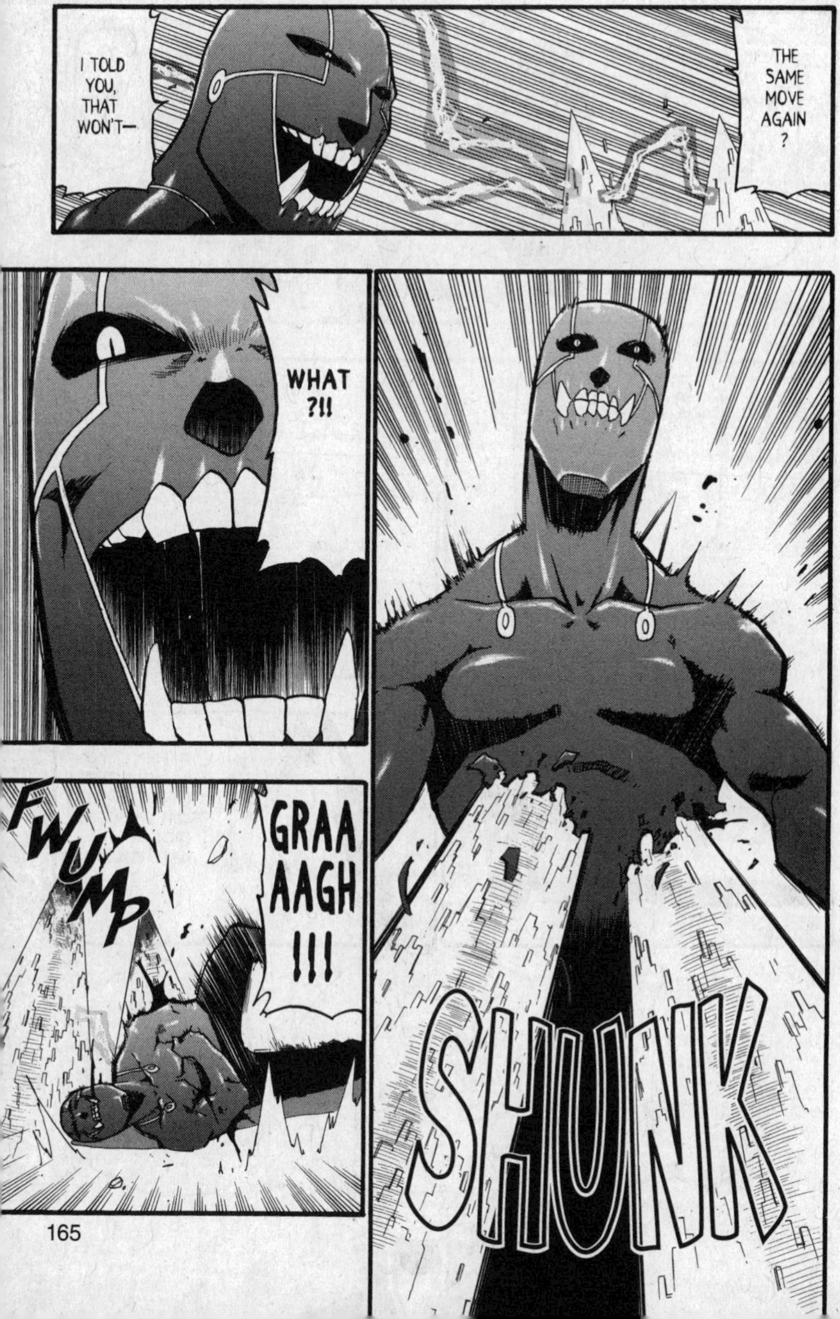
THE SAME MOVE AGAIN?
I TOLD YOU, THAT WON'T—
SHUNK
WHAT?!!
GRAAAAGH!!!
FWUMP

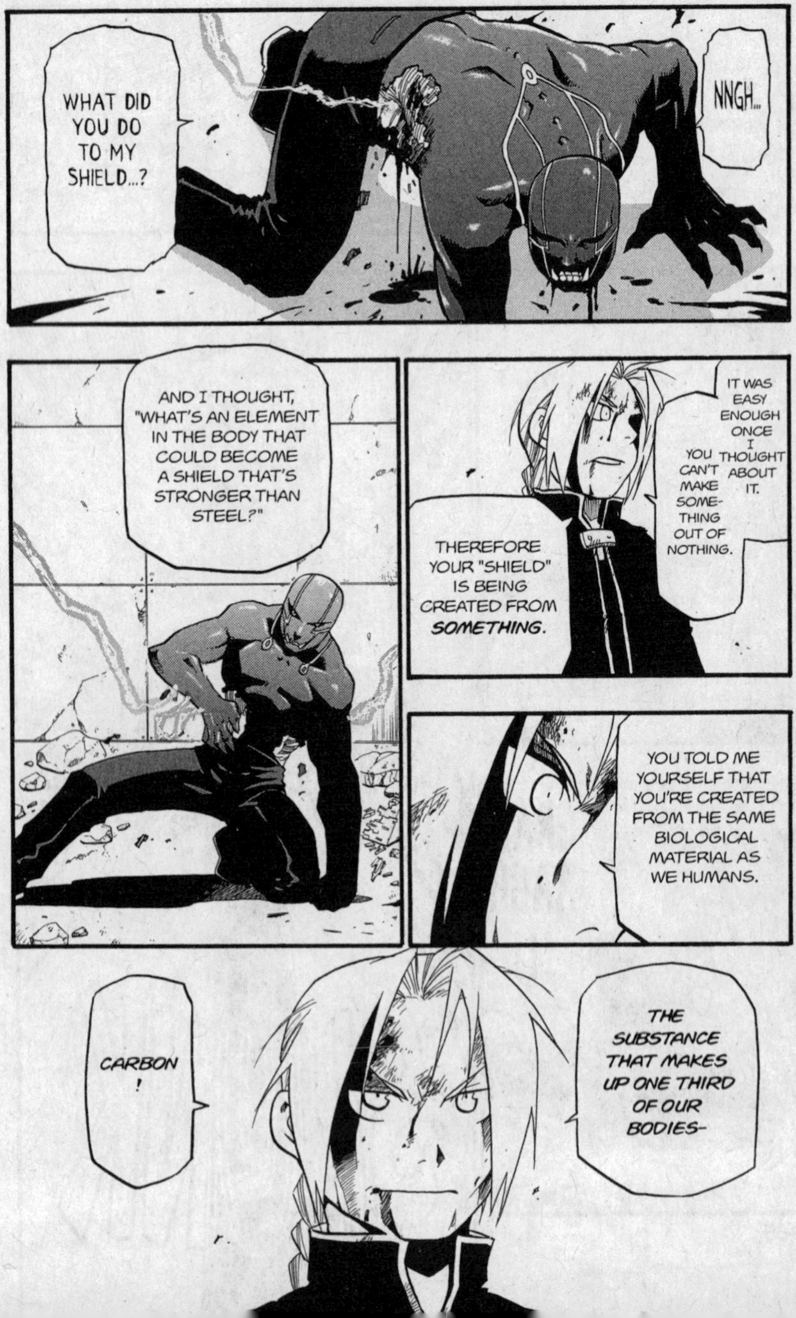
NNGH...
WHAT DID YOU DO TO MY SHIELD...?
IT WAS EASY ENOUGH ONCE I THOUGHT ABOUT IT.
YOU CAN'T MAKE SOMETHING OUT OF NOTHING.
THEREFORE YOUR "SHIELD" IS BEING CREATED FROM *SOMETHING*.
YOU TOLD ME YOURSELF THAT YOU'RE CREATED FROM THE SAME BIOLOGICAL MATERIAL AS WE HUMANS.
AND I THOUGHT, "WHAT'S AN ELEMENT IN THE BODY THAT COULD BECOME A SHIELD THAT'S STRONGER THAN STEEL?"
THE SUBSTANCE THAT MAKES UP ONE THIRD OF OUR BODIES-
CARBON!

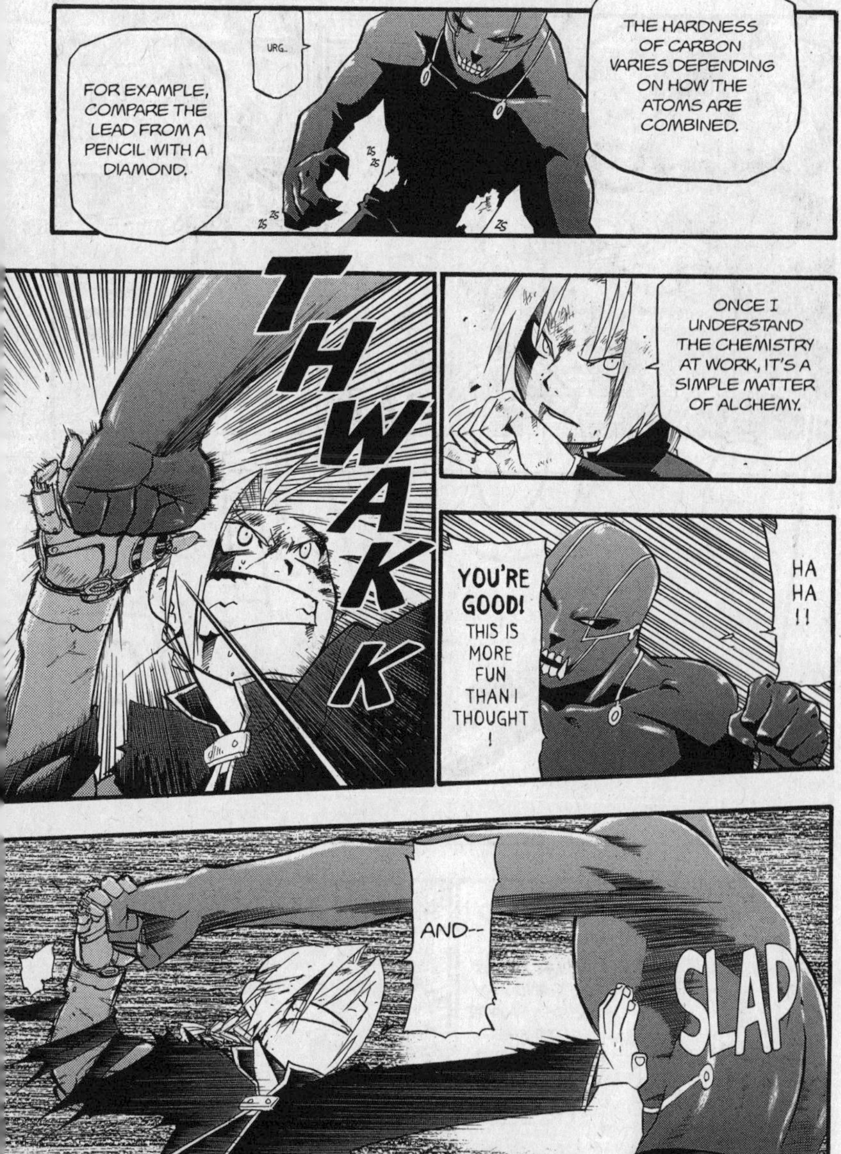
THE HARDNESS OF CARBON VARIES DEPENDING ON HOW THE ATOMS ARE COMBINED.
URG..
FOR EXAMPLE, COMPARE THE LEAD FROM A PENCIL WITH A DIAMOND.
ZS ZS
ZS ZS
ZS
ONCE I UNDERSTAND THE CHEMISTRY AT WORK, IT'S A SIMPLE MATTER OF ALCHEMY.
HA HA !!
YOU'RE GOOD! THIS IS MORE FUN THAN I THOUGHT!
THWAKK
AND--
SLAP

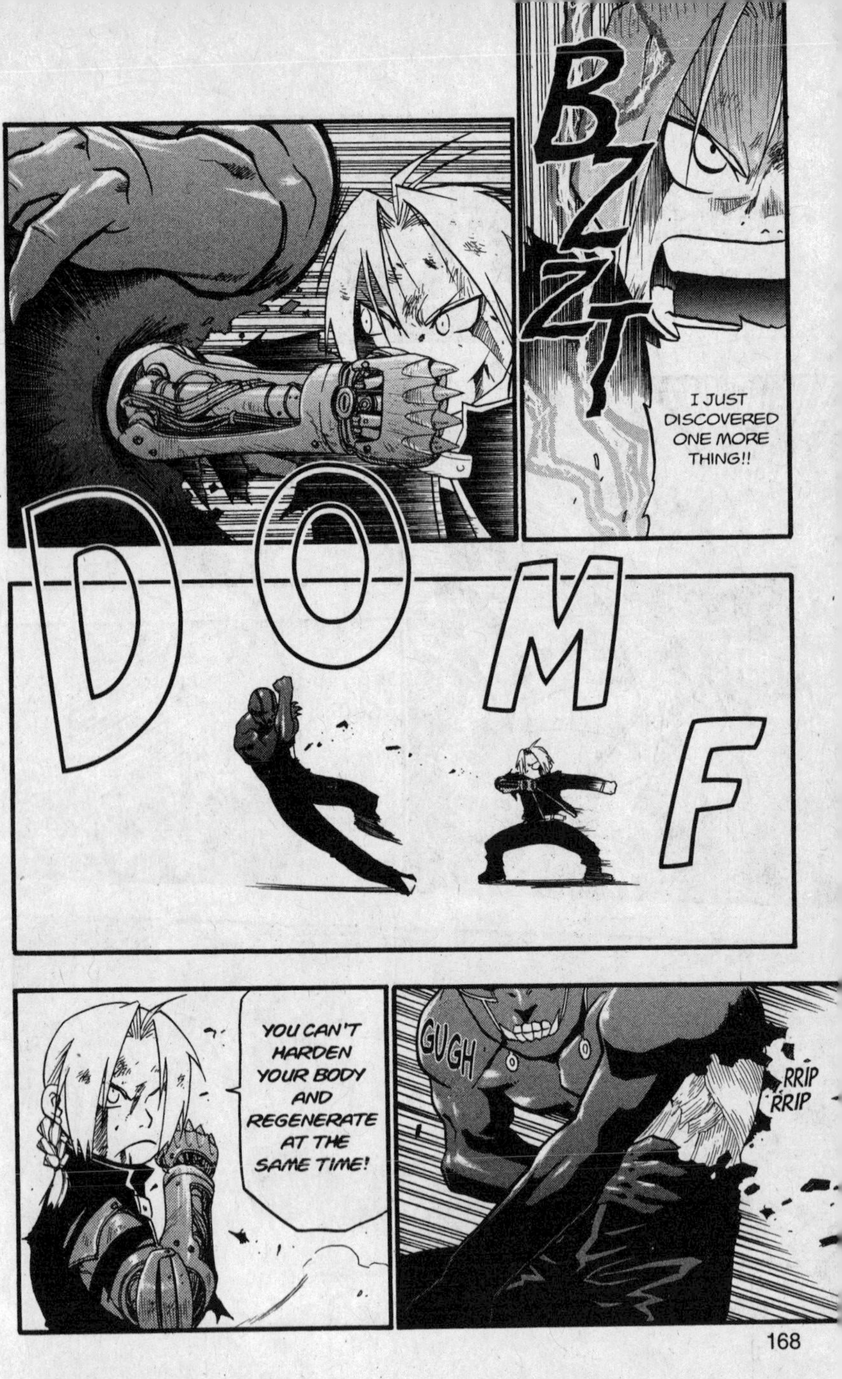
BZZT
I JUST DISCOVERED ONE MORE THING!!
DOMF
GUGH
RRIP RRIP
YOU CAN'T HARDEN YOUR BODY AND REGENERATE AT THE SAME TIME!

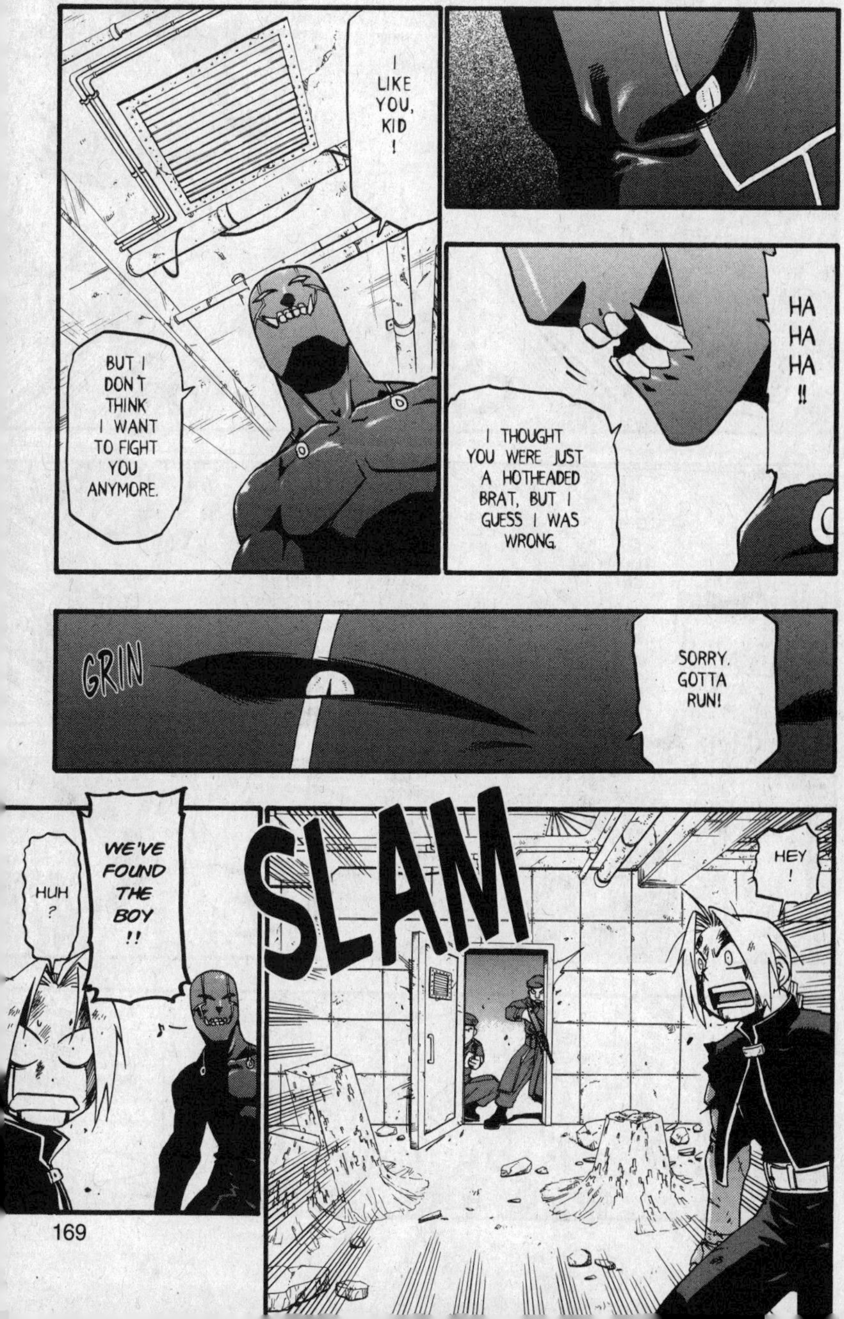
HA HA HA!!
I THOUGHT YOU WERE JUST A HOTHEADED BRAT, BUT I GUESS I WAS WRONG.
I LIKE YOU, KID!
BUT I DON'T THINK I WANT TO FIGHT YOU ANYMORE.
SORRY. GOTTA RUN!
GRIN
HEY!
SLAM
WE'VE FOUND THE BOY!!
HUH?

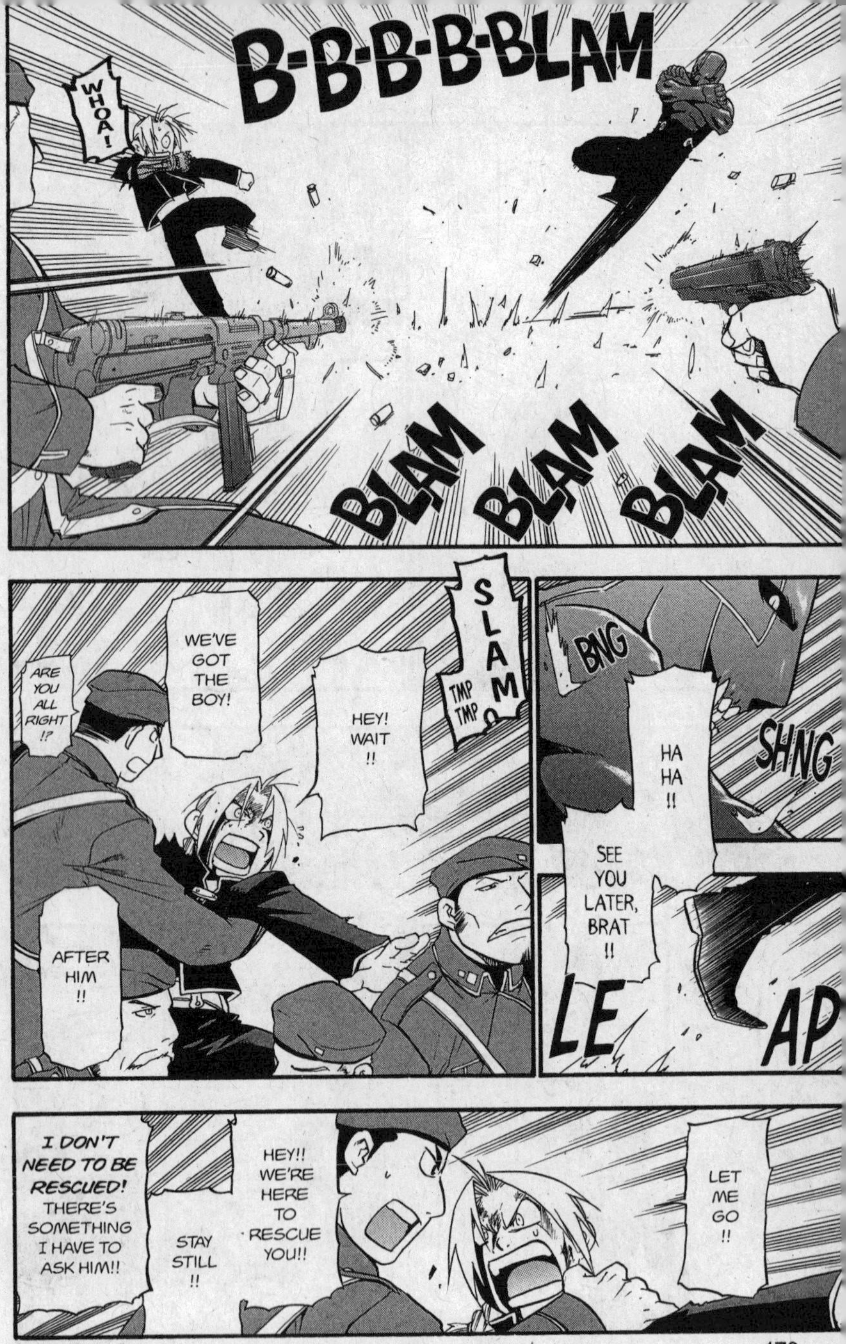
B-B-B-B-BLAM
WHOA!
BLAM BLAM BLAM
BNG
SHNG
HA HA!!
SEE YOU LATER, BRAT!!
LEAP
SLAM
TMP TMP
HEY! WAIT!!
WE'VE GOT THE BOY!
ARE YOU ALL RIGHT!?
AFTER HIM!!
LET ME GO!!
HEY!! WE'RE HERE TO RESCUE YOU!!
STAY STILL!!
I DON'T NEED TO BE RESCUED! THERE'S SOMETHING I HAVE TO ASK HIM!!

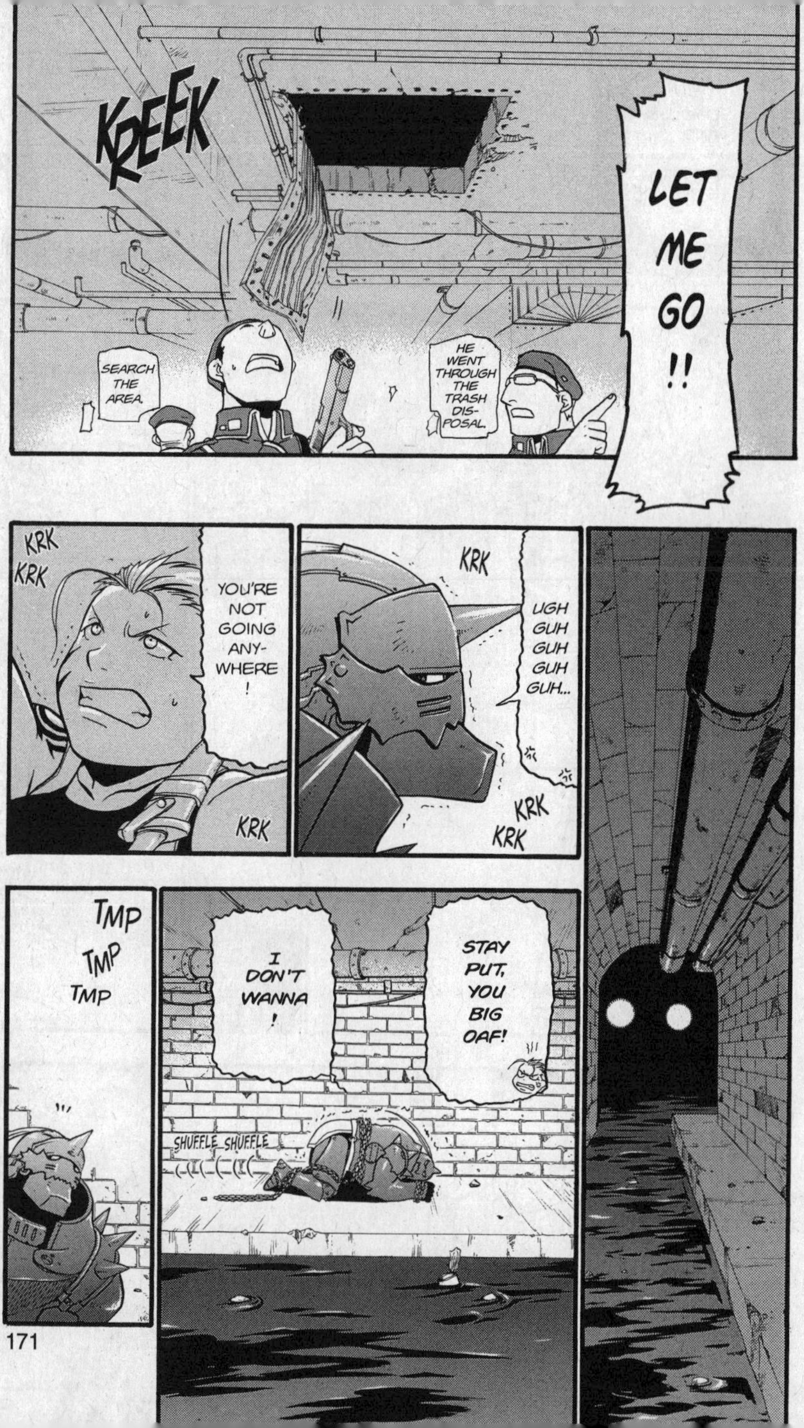
LET ME GO!!
KREEK
HE WENT THROUGH THE TRASH DISPOSAL.
SEARCH THE AREA.
KRK
UGH GUH GUH GUH GUH...
KRK KRK
KRK KRK
YOU'RE NOT GOING ANYWHERE!
KRK
STAY PUT, YOU BIG OAF!
I DON'T WANNA!
SHUFFLE SHUFFLE
TMP TMP TMP

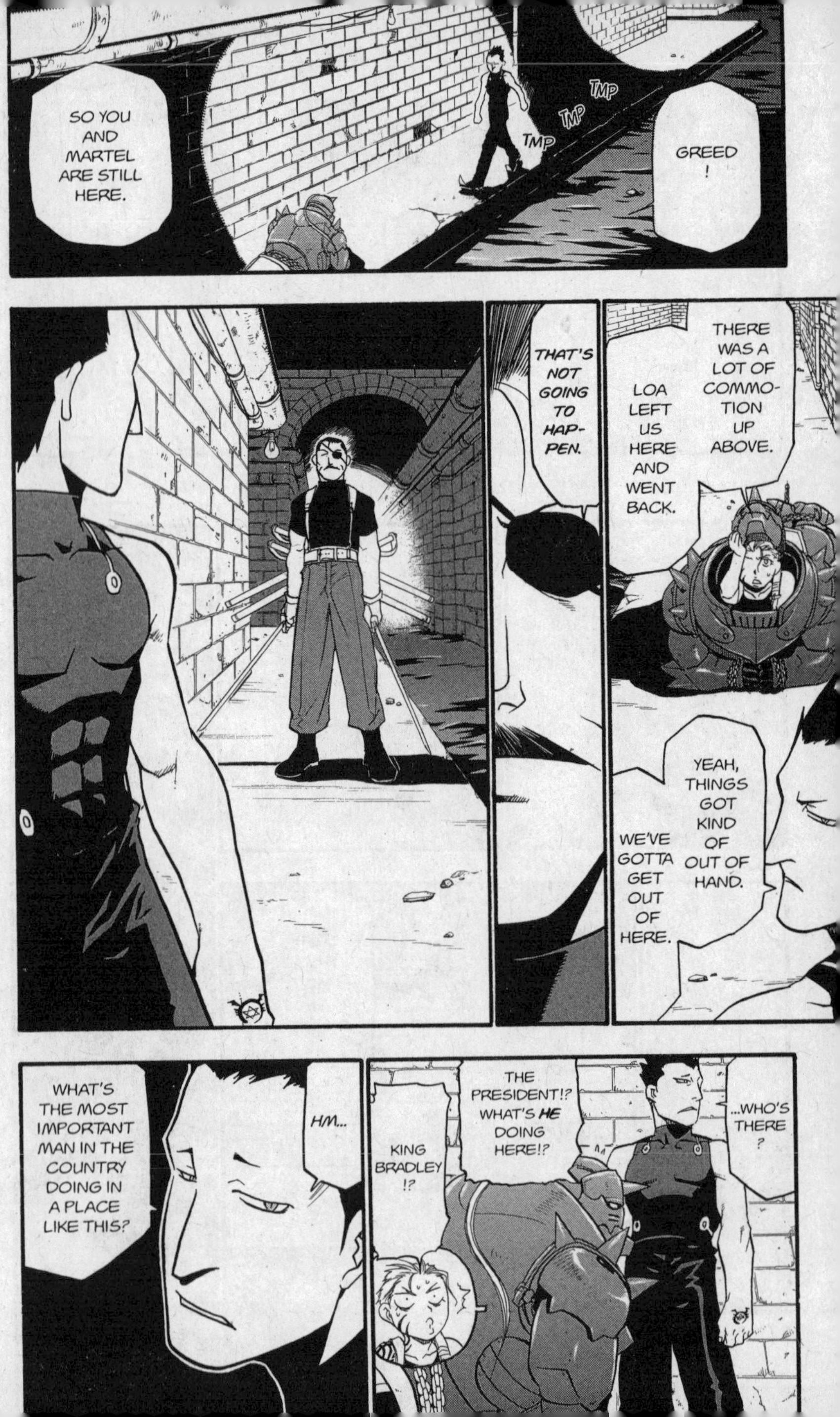
TMP TMP TMP
GREED!
SO YOU AND MARTEL ARE STILL HERE.
THERE WAS A LOT OF COMMOTION UP ABOVE.
LOA LEFT US HERE AND WENT BACK.
YEAH, THINGS GOT KIND OF OUT OF HAND.
WE'VE GOTTA GET OUT OF HERE.
THAT'S NOT GOING TO HAPPEN.
...WHO'S THERE?
THE PRESIDENT!? WHAT'S HE DOING HERE!?
KING BRADLEY!?
HM...
WHAT'S THE MOST IMPORTANT MAN IN THE COUNTRY DOING IN A PLACE LIKE THIS?

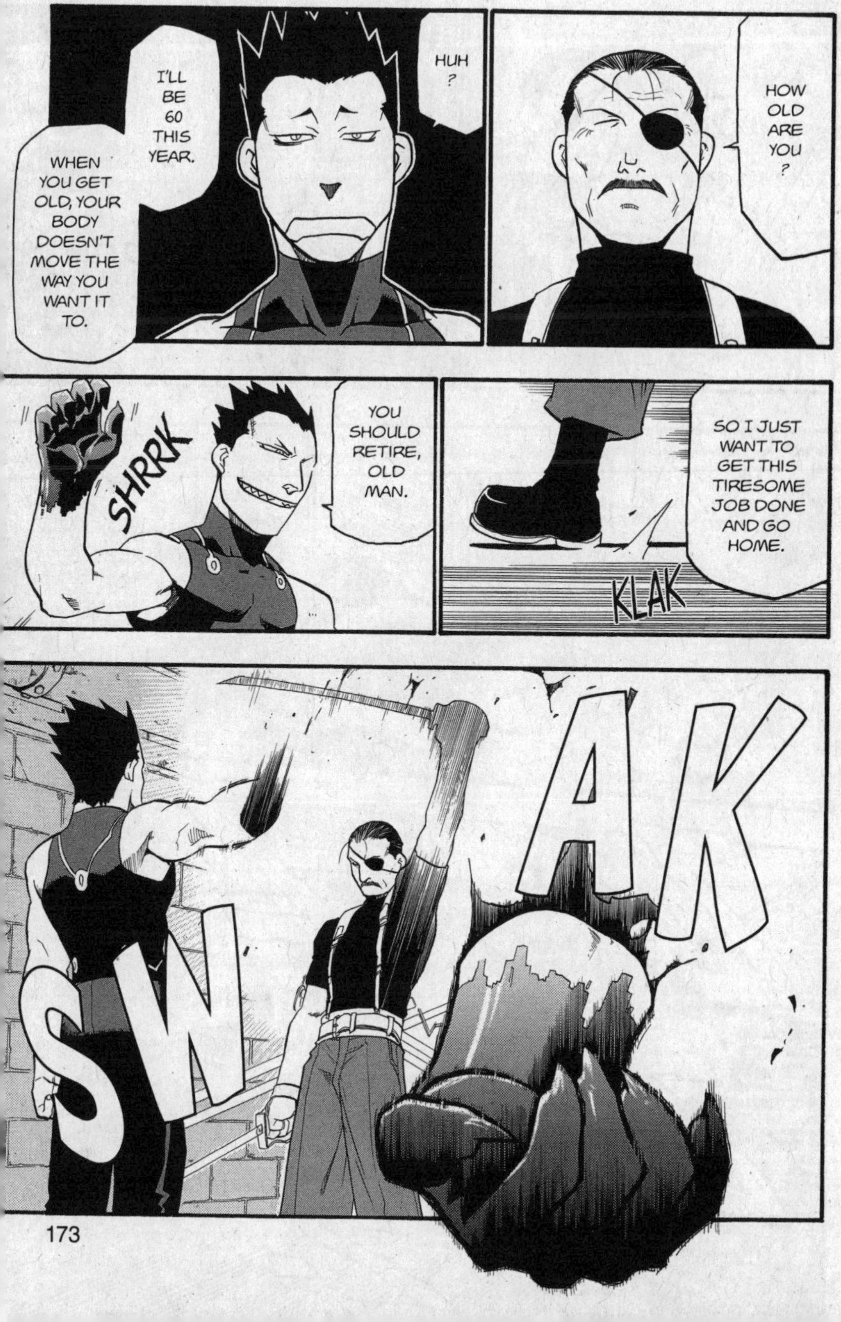

HOW OLD ARE YOU?
HUH?
I'LL BE 60 THIS YEAR.
WHEN YOU GET OLD, YOUR BODY DOESN'T MOVE THE WAY YOU WANT IT TO.
SO I JUST WANT TO GET THIS TIRESOME JOB DONE AND GO HOME.
KLAK
YOU SHOULD RETIRE, OLD MAN.
SHRRK
SW
AK

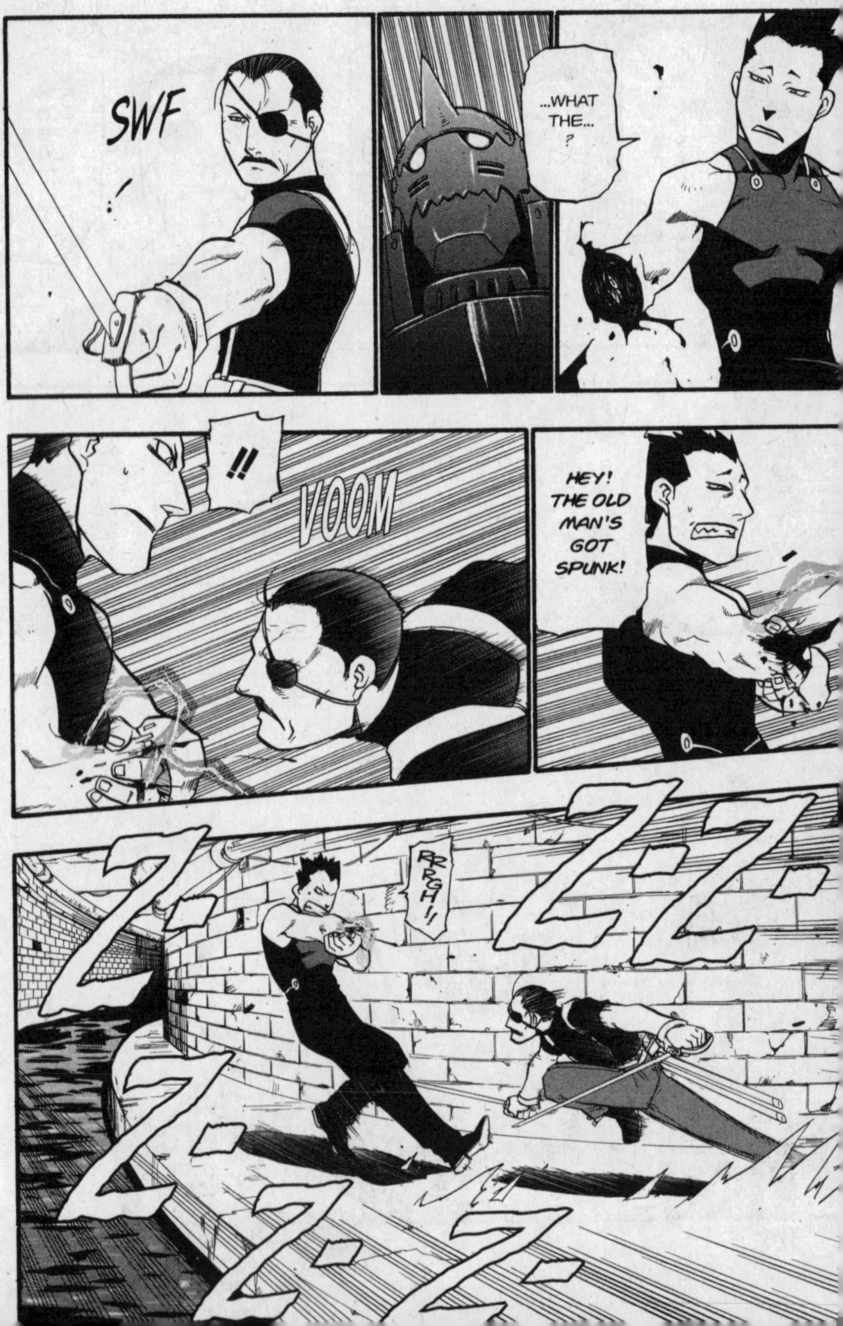
...WHAT THE... ?
SWF
HEY! THE OLD MAN'S GOT SPUNK!
!!
VOOM
Z-Z-
RRRGH!!
Z-Z-Z-

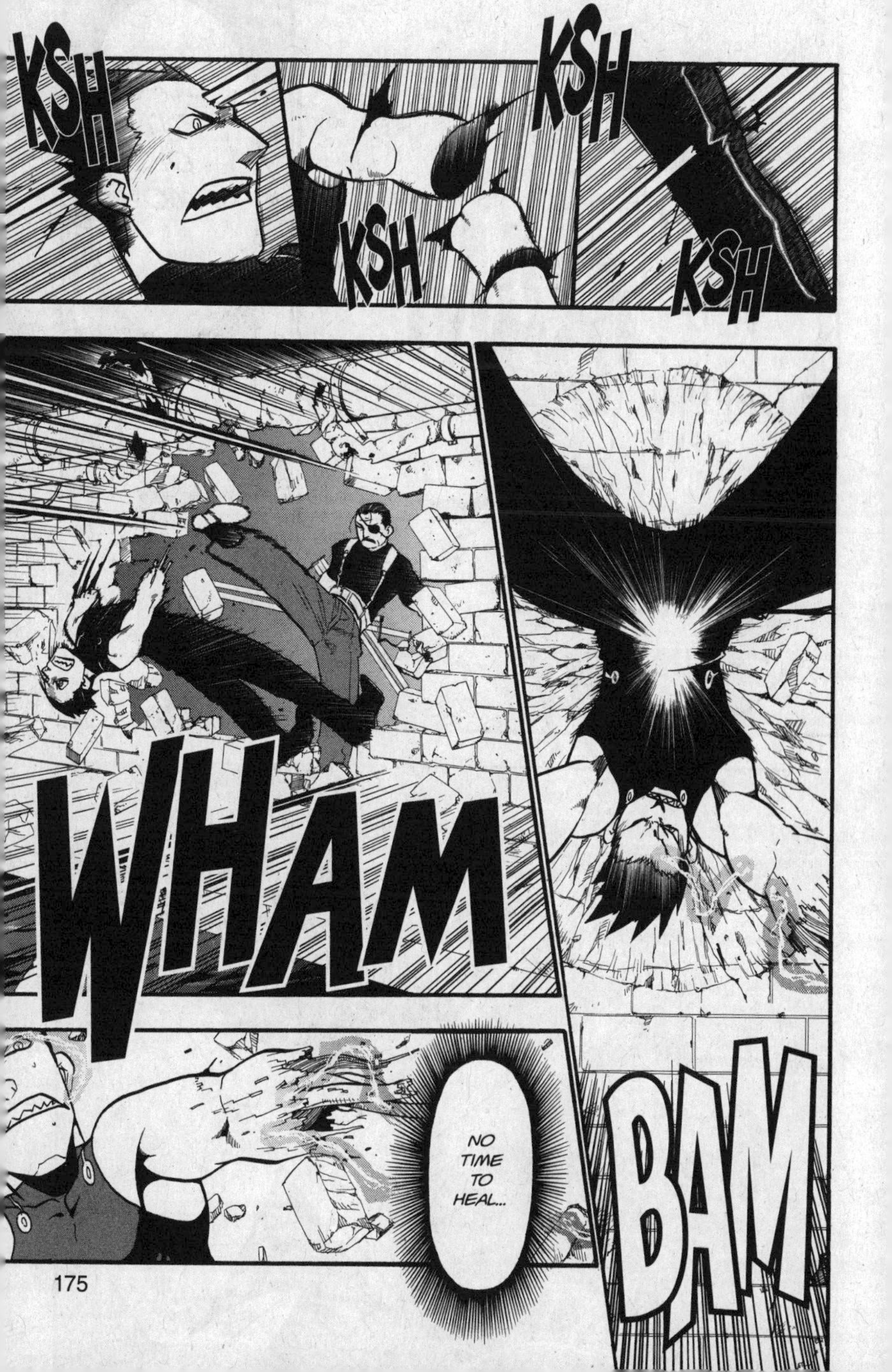
KSH
KSH
KSH
KSH
BAM
WHAM
NO TIME TO HEAL...

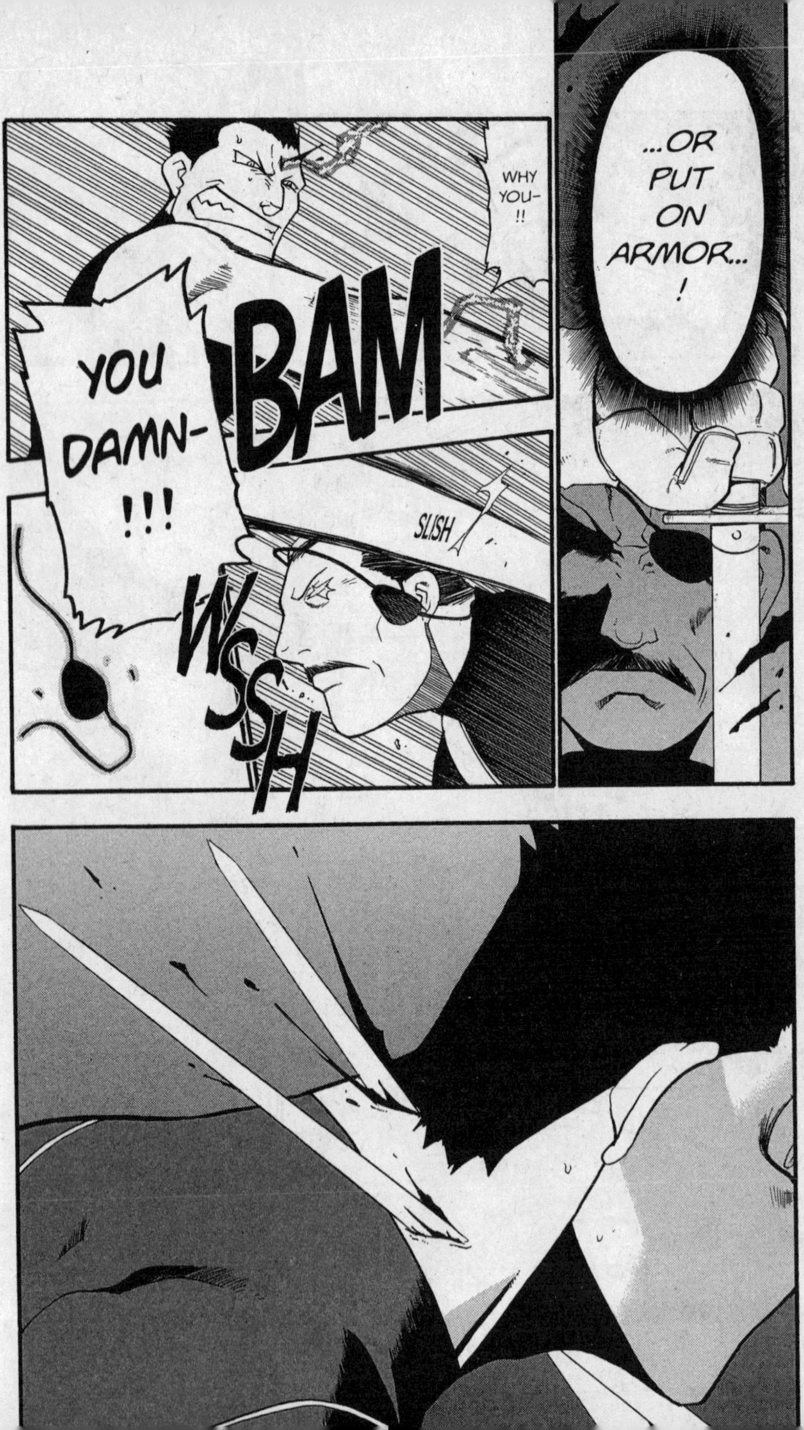
...OR PUT ON ARMOR...!
WHY YOU-!!
YOU DAMN-!!!
BAM
SLISH
WSSH

THIS MANGA WAS ORIGINALLY PRINTED IN MONTHLY **SHONEN GANGAN**, SEPTEMBER THROUGH DECEMBER 2003.

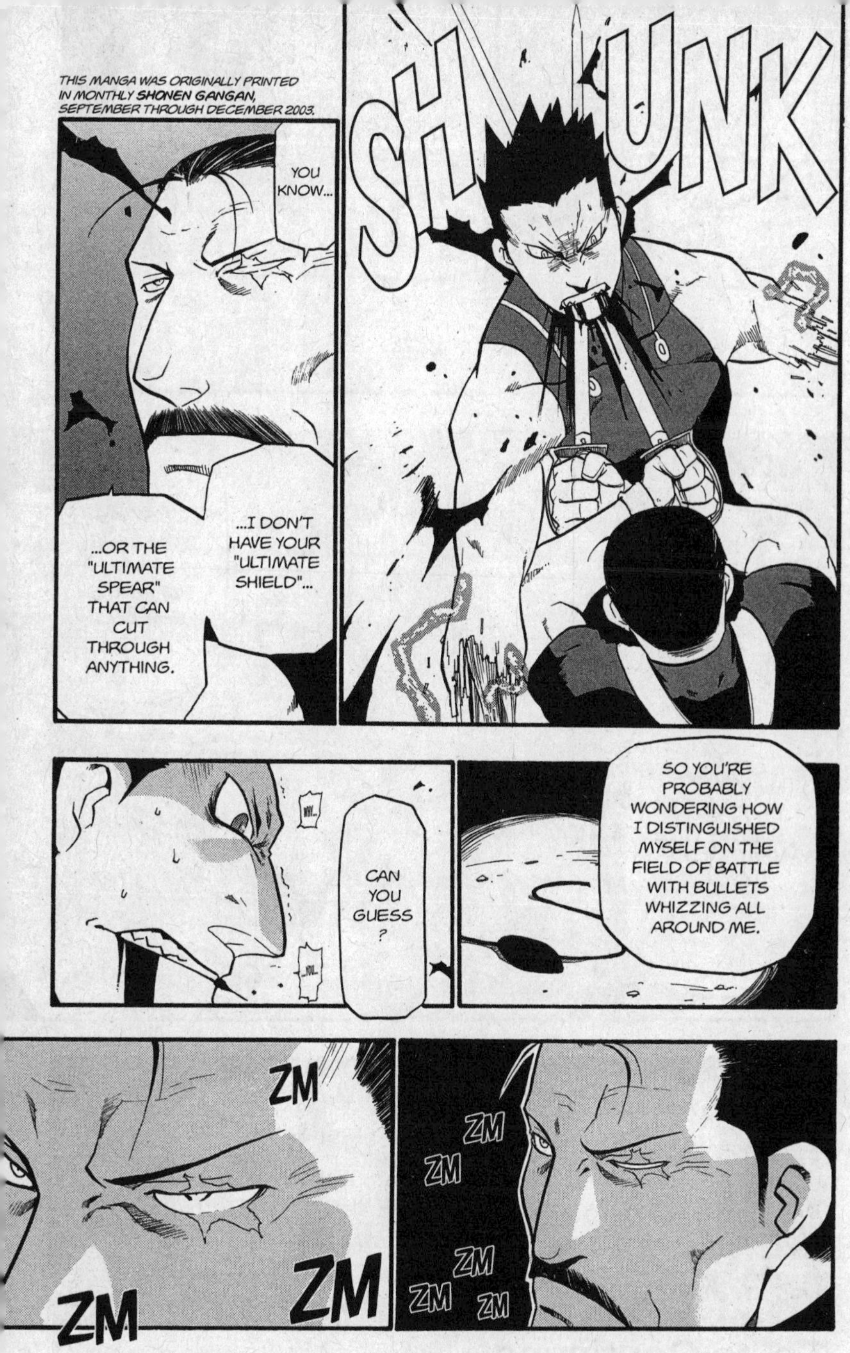
SHUNK
YOU KNOW...
...I DON'T HAVE YOUR "ULTIMATE SHIELD"...
...OR THE "ULTIMATE SPEAR" THAT CAN CUT THROUGH ANYTHING.
SO YOU'RE PROBABLY WONDERING HOW I DISTINGUISHED MYSELF ON THE FIELD OF BATTLE WITH BULLETS WHIZZING ALL AROUND ME.
CAN YOU GUESS?
WHY...
...YOU...
ZM
ZM
ZM
ZM
ZM
ZM
ZM
ZM

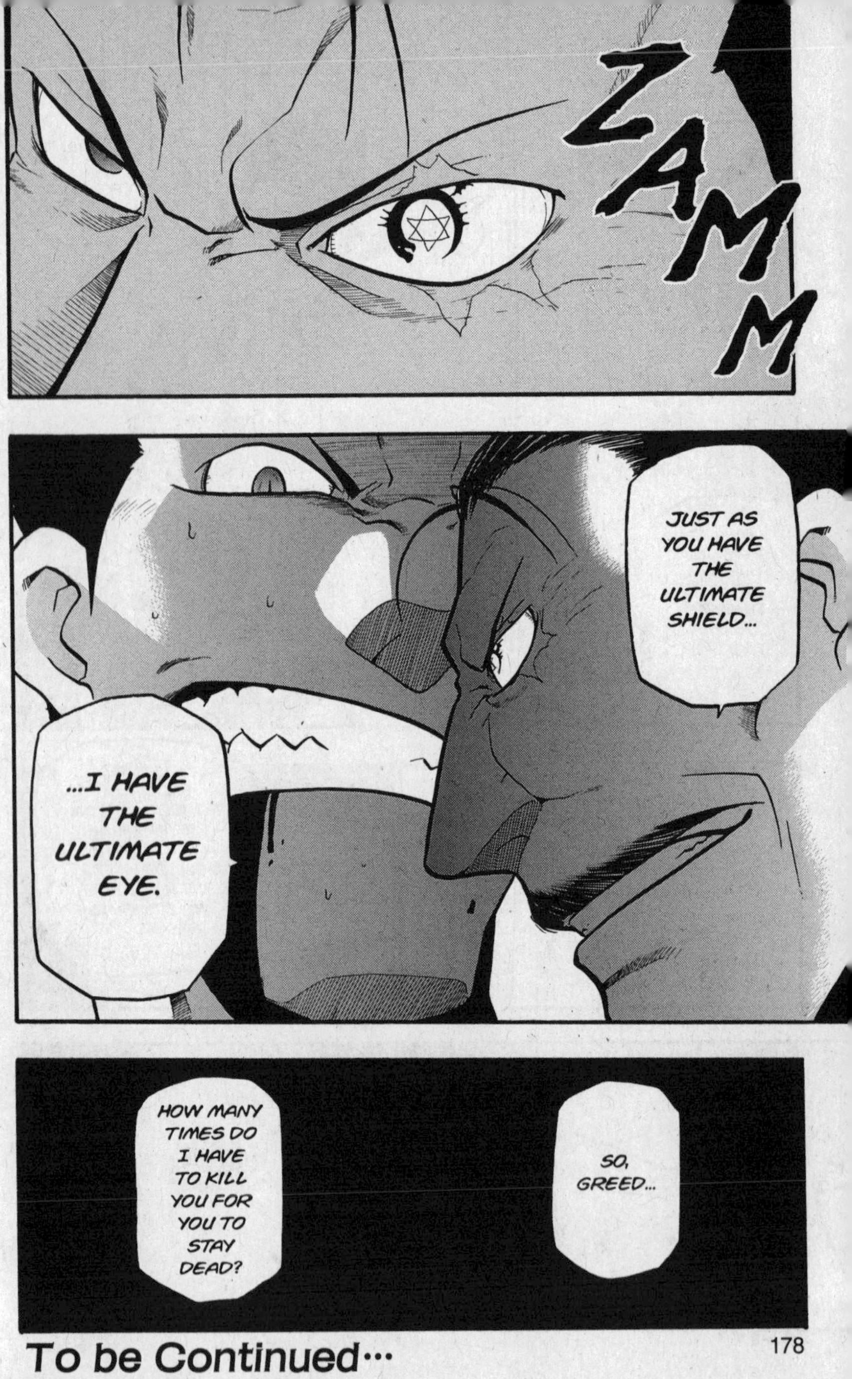
ZAMM
JUST AS YOU HAVE THE ULTIMATE SHIELD...
...I HAVE THE ULTIMATE EYE.
SO, GREED...
HOW MANY TIMES DO I HAVE TO KILL YOU FOR YOU TO STAY DEAD?

To be Continued...

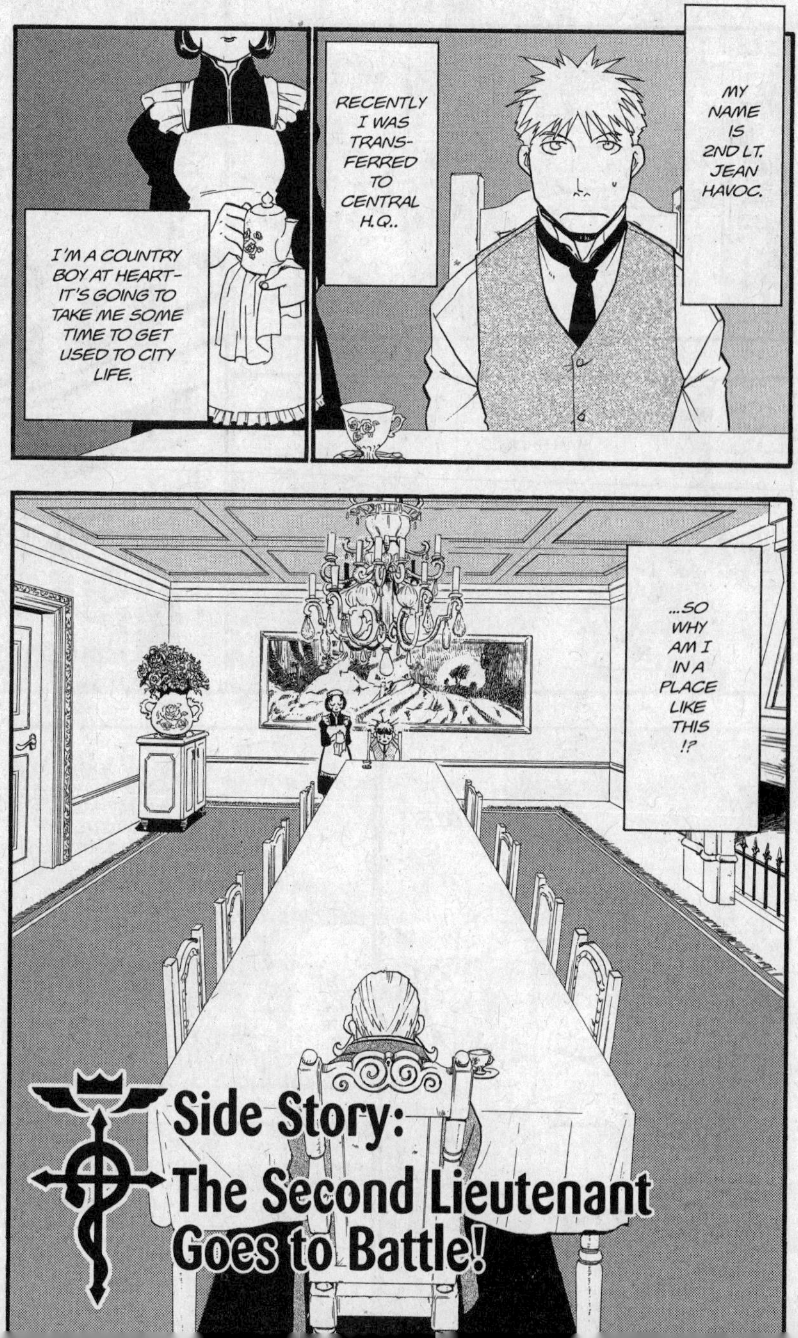
MY NAME IS 2ND LT. JEAN HAVOC.
RECENTLY I WAS TRANS-FERRED TO CENTRAL H.Q..
I'M A COUNTRY BOY AT HEART-IT'S GOING TO TAKE ME SOME TIME TO GET USED TO CITY LIFE.
...SO WHY AM I IN A PLACE LIKE THIS!?

Side Story: The Second Lieutenant Goes to Battle!

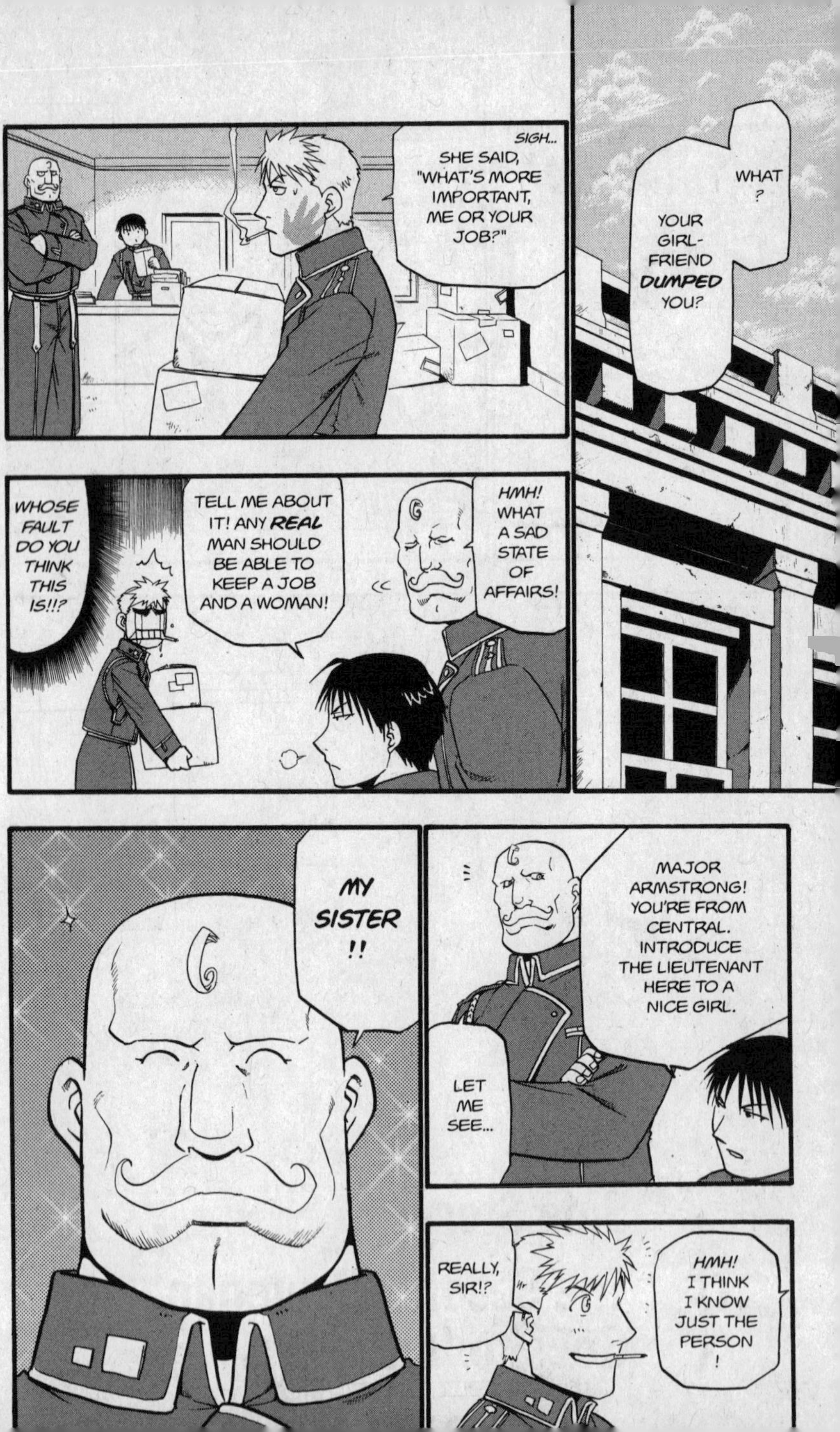
WHAT?
YOUR GIRL-FRIEND DUMPED YOU?
SIGH... SHE SAID, "WHAT'S MORE IMPORTANT, ME OR YOUR JOB?"
HMH! WHAT A SAD STATE OF AFFAIRS!
TELL ME ABOUT IT! ANY REAL MAN SHOULD BE ABLE TO KEEP A JOB AND A WOMAN!
WHOSE FAULT DO YOU THINK THIS IS!!?
MAJOR ARMSTRONG! YOU'RE FROM CENTRAL. INTRODUCE THE LIEUTENANT HERE TO A NICE GIRL.
LET ME SEE...
HMH! I THINK I KNOW JUST THE PERSON!
REALLY, SIR!?
MY SISTER!!

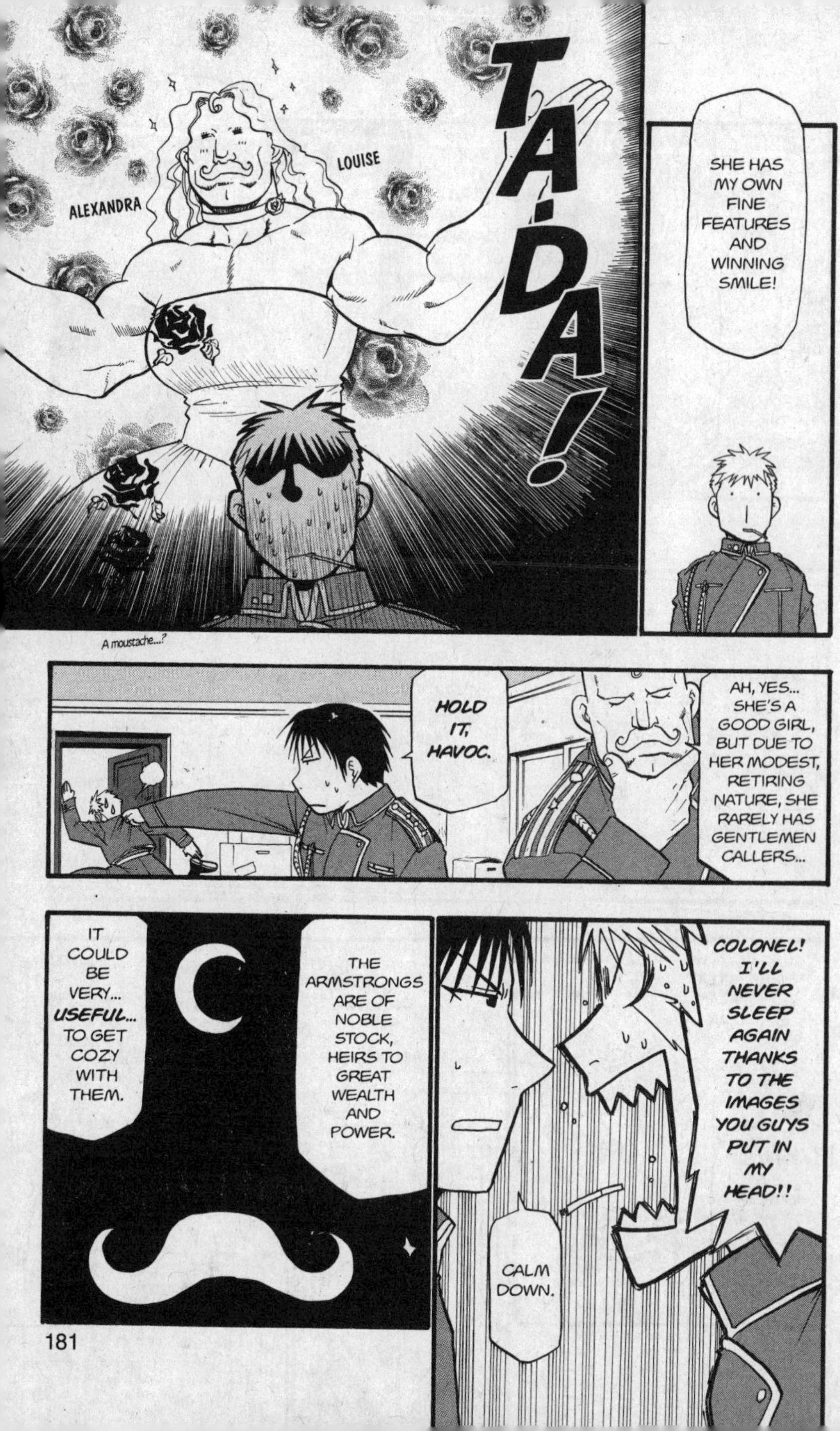
SHE HAS MY OWN FINE FEATURES AND WINNING SMILE!
TA-DA!
LOUISE
ALEXANDRA
A moustache...?
AH, YES... SHE'S A GOOD GIRL, BUT DUE TO HER MODEST, RETIRING NATURE, SHE RARELY HAS GENTLEMEN CALLERS...
HOLD IT, HAVOC.
COLONEL! I'LL NEVER SLEEP AGAIN THANKS TO THE IMAGES YOU GUYS PUT IN MY HEAD!!
CALM DOWN.
THE ARMSTRONGS ARE OF NOBLE STOCK, HEIRS TO GREAT WEALTH AND POWER.
IT COULD BE VERY... USEFUL... TO GET COZY WITH THEM.

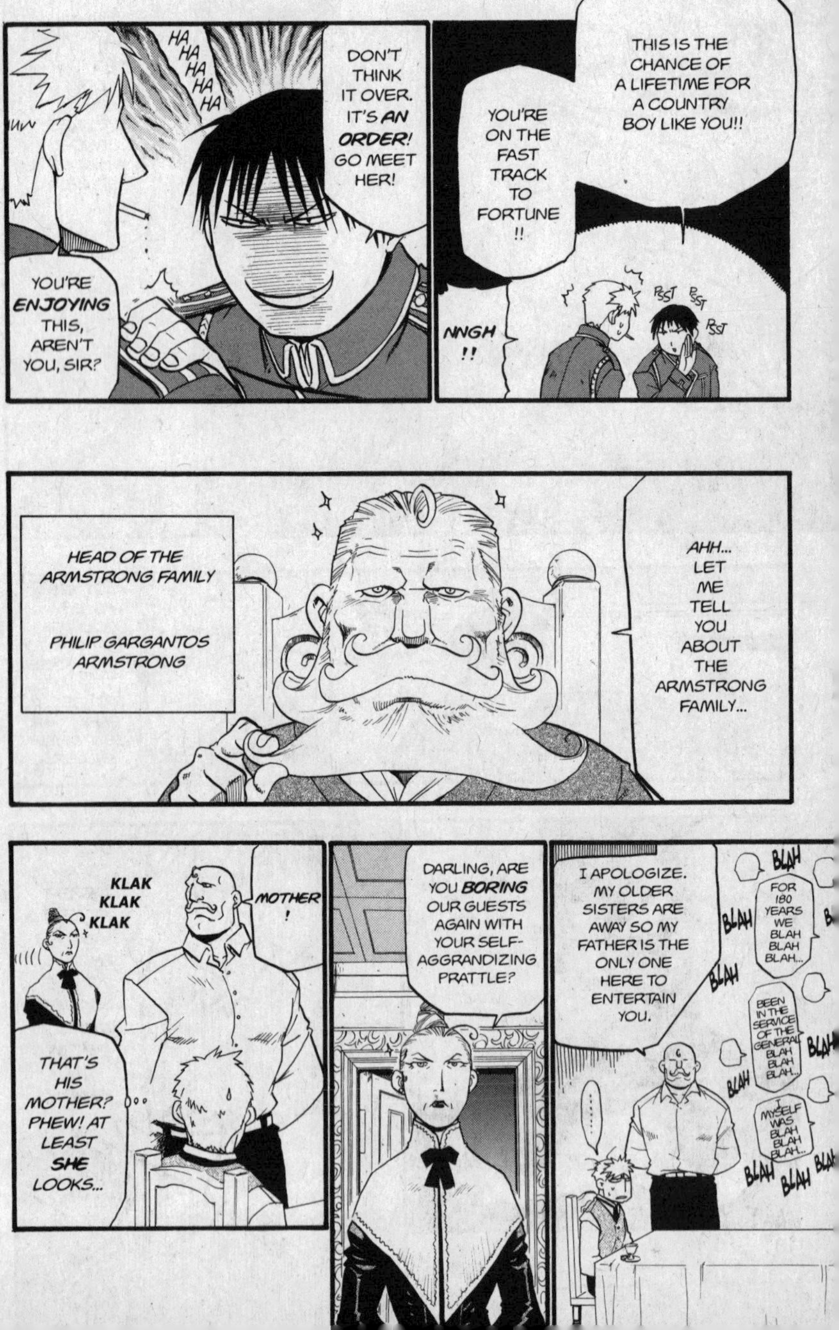
THIS IS THE CHANCE OF A LIFETIME FOR A COUNTRY BOY LIKE YOU!!
YOU'RE ON THE FAST TRACK TO FORTUNE !!
NNGH !!
PSST PSST PSST
DON'T THINK IT OVER. IT'S AN ORDER! GO MEET HER!
HA HA HA HA HA
YOU'RE ENJOYING THIS, AREN'T YOU, SIR?
AHH... LET ME TELL YOU ABOUT THE ARMSTRONG FAMILY...
HEAD OF THE ARMSTRONG FAMILY
PHILIP GARGANTOS ARMSTRONG
I APOLOGIZE. MY OLDER SISTERS ARE AWAY SO MY FATHER IS THE ONLY ONE HERE TO ENTERTAIN YOU.
FOR 180 YEARS WE BLAH BLAH BLAH...
BEEN IN THE SERVICE OF THE GENERAL BLAH BLAH BLAH...
I MYSELF WAS BLAH BLAH BLAH...
BLAH BLAH BLAH BLAH BLAH BLAH BLAH BLAH
DARLING, ARE YOU BORING OUR GUESTS AGAIN WITH YOUR SELF-AGGRANDIZING PRATTLE?
MOTHER !
KLAK KLAK KLAK
THAT'S HIS MOTHER? PHEW! AT LEAST SHE LOOKS...

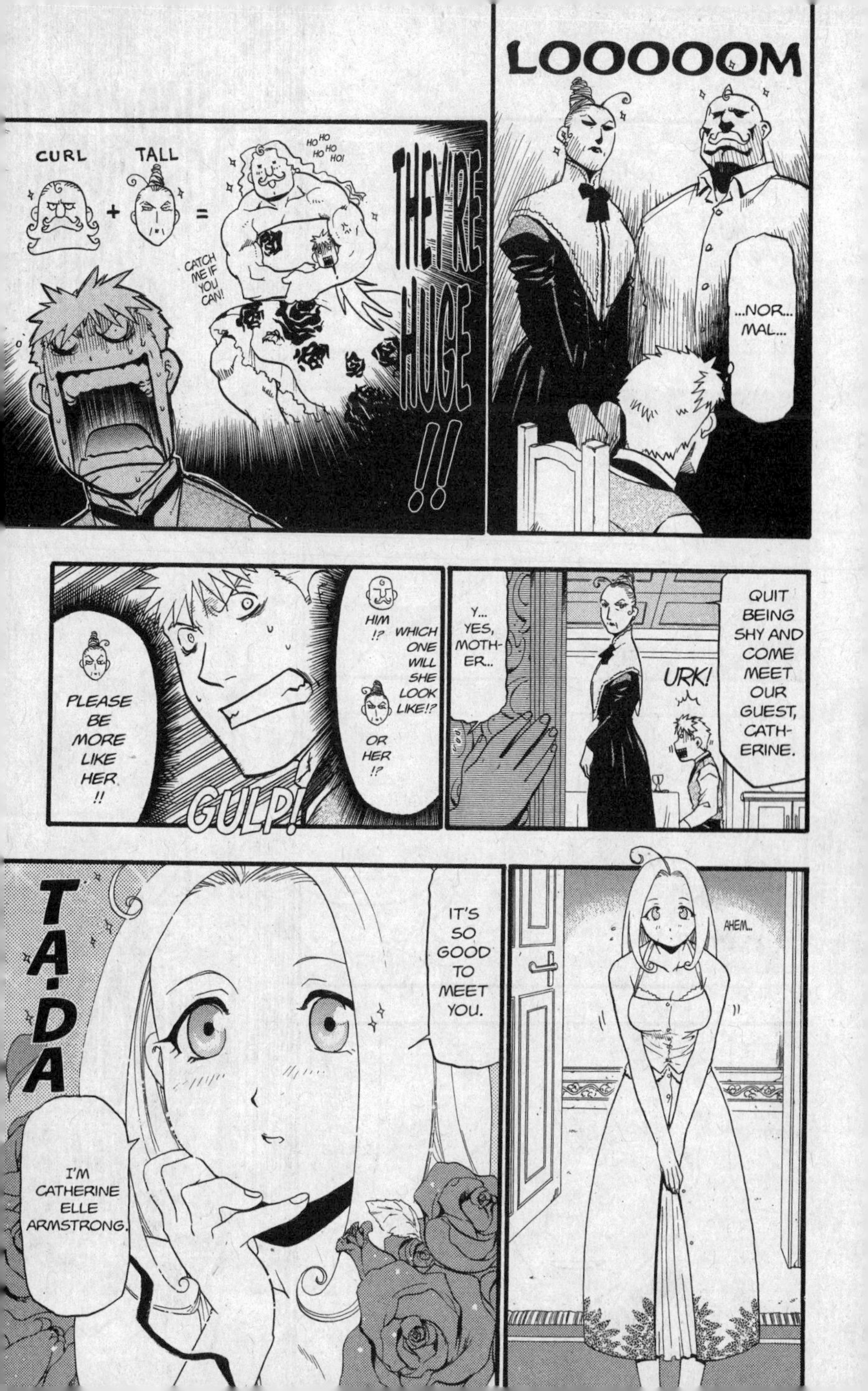
LOOOOOM
...NOR... MAL...
CURL
TALL
HO HO HO HO HO!
CATCH ME IF YOU CAN!
THEY'RE HUGE !!
QUIT BEING SHY AND COME MEET OUR GUEST, CATHERINE.
URK!
Y... YES, MOTHER...
WHICH ONE WILL SHE LOOK LIKE!?
HIM !?
OR HER !?
PLEASE BE MORE LIKE HER !!
GULP!
AHEM...
TA-DA
IT'S SO GOOD TO MEET YOU.
I'M CATHERINE ELLE ARMSTRONG.

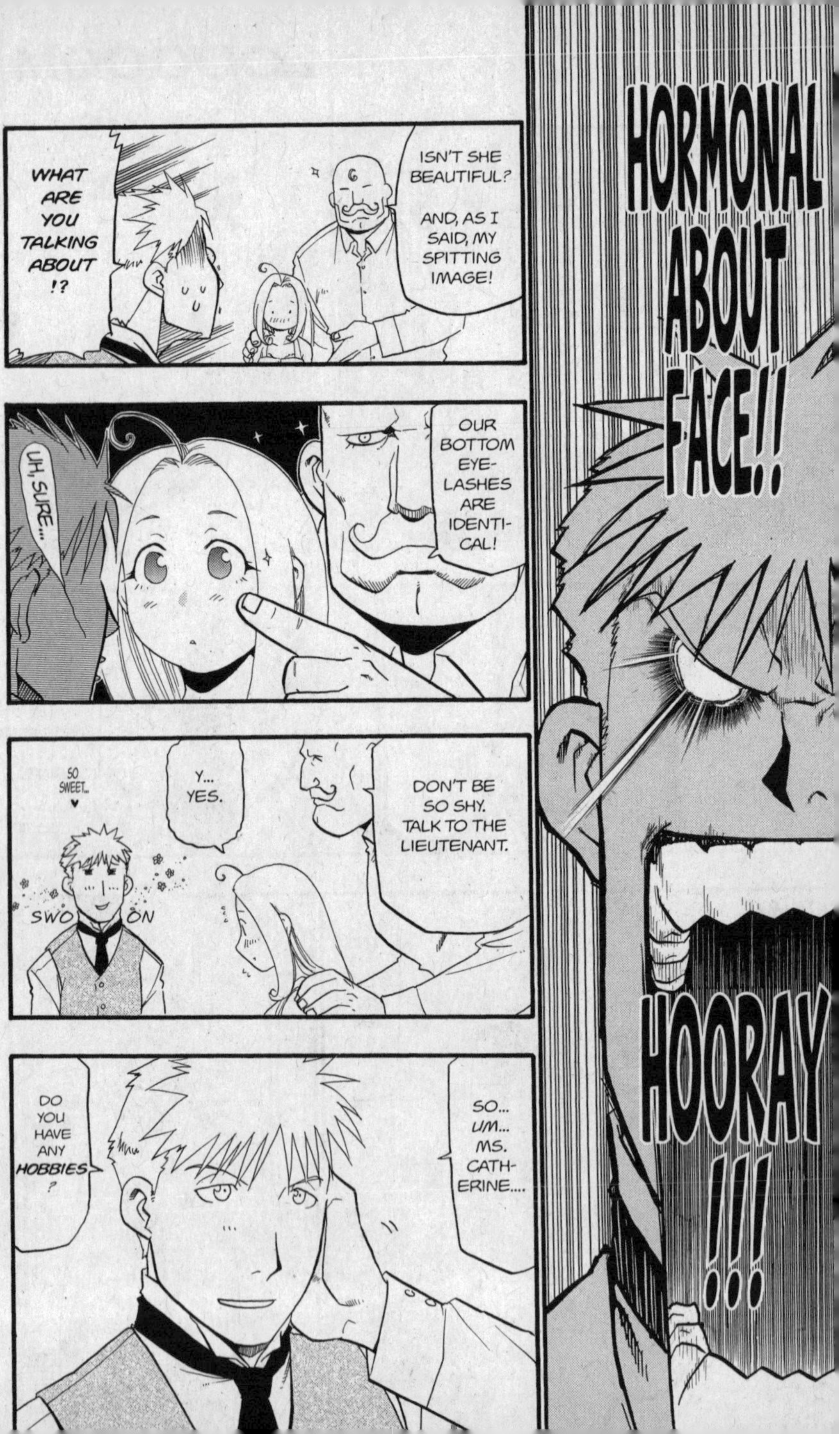
HORMONAL ABOUT FACE!!
HOORAY!!!
ISN'T SHE BEAUTIFUL?
AND, AS I SAID, MY SPITTING IMAGE!
WHAT ARE YOU TALKING ABOUT!?
OUR BOTTOM EYE-LASHES ARE IDENTI-CAL!
UH, SURE...
DON'T BE SO SHY. TALK TO THE LIEUTENANT.
Y... YES.
SO SWEET...
SWOON
SO... UM... MS. CATH-ERINE....
DO YOU HAVE ANY HOBBIES?

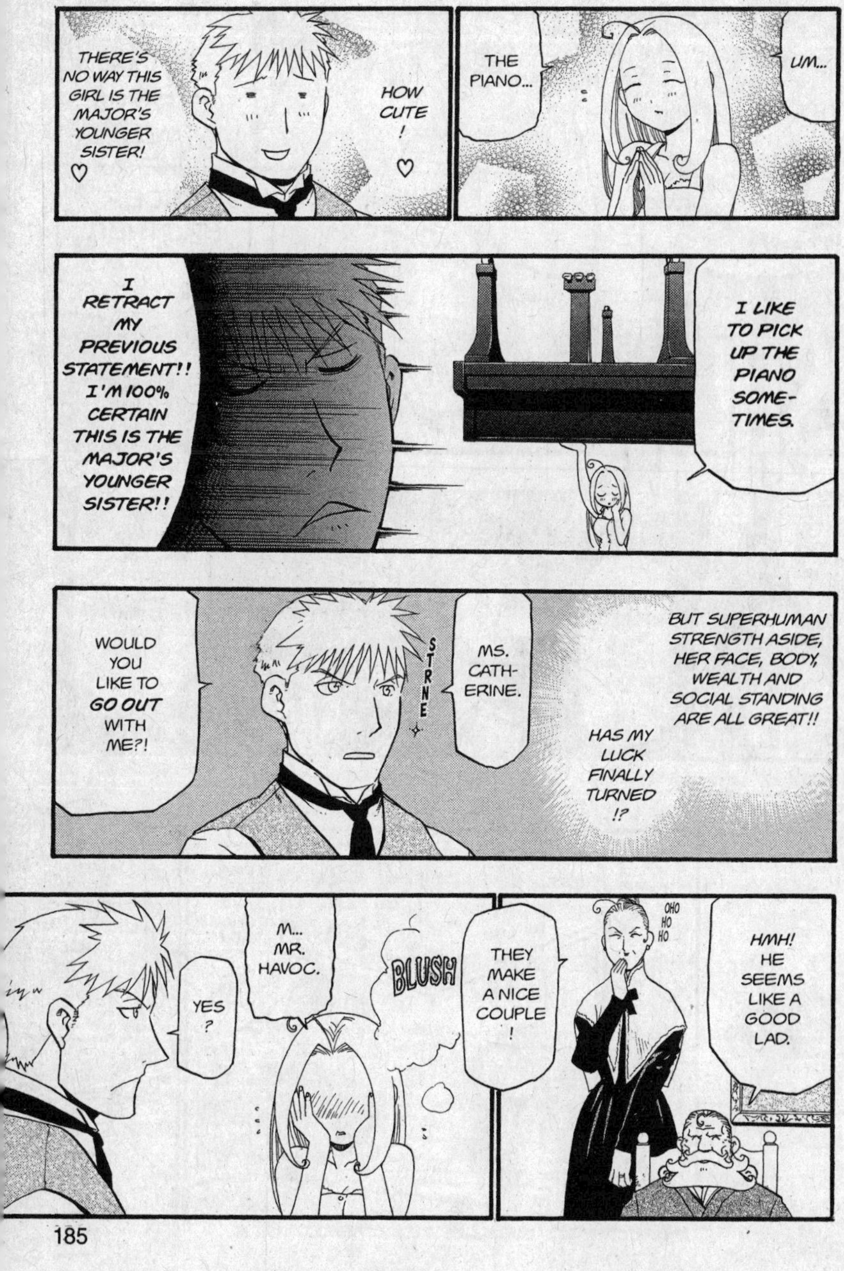
UM...
THE PIANO...
HOW CUTE!
THERE'S NO WAY THIS GIRL IS THE MAJOR'S YOUNGER SISTER!
I LIKE TO PICK UP THE PIANO SOMETIMES.
I RETRACT MY PREVIOUS STATEMENT!! I'M 100% CERTAIN THIS IS THE MAJOR'S YOUNGER SISTER!!
BUT SUPERHUMAN STRENGTH ASIDE, HER FACE, BODY, WEALTH AND SOCIAL STANDING ARE ALL GREAT!!
HAS MY LUCK FINALLY TURNED!?
MS. CATHERINE.
STRNE
WOULD YOU LIKE TO GO OUT WITH ME?!
HMH! HE SEEMS LIKE A GOOD LAD.
OHO HO HO
THEY MAKE A NICE COUPLE!
BLUSH
M... MR. HAVOC.
YES?

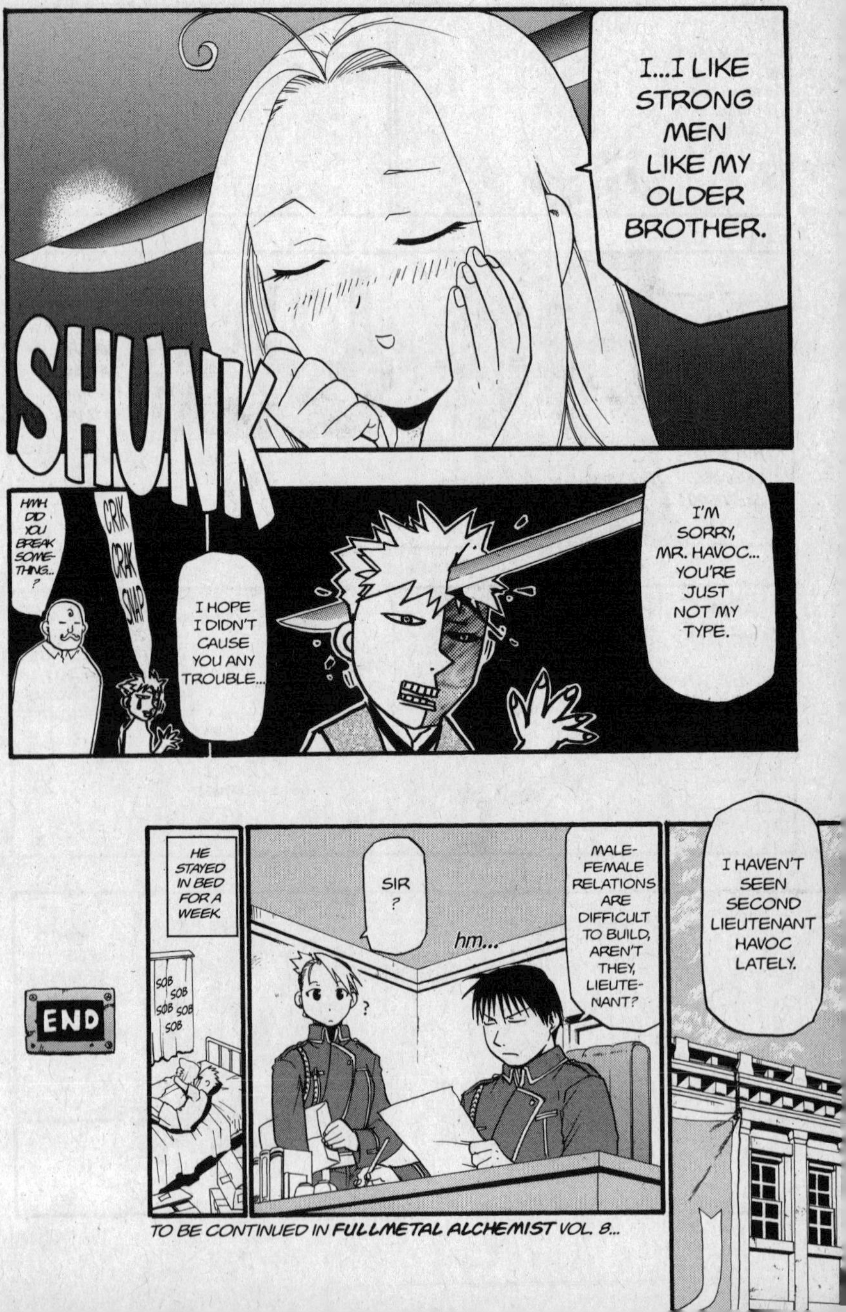
I...I LIKE STRONG MEN LIKE MY OLDER BROTHER.
SHUNK
I'M SORRY, MR. HAVOC... YOU'RE JUST NOT MY TYPE.
I HOPE I DIDN'T CAUSE YOU ANY TROUBLE...
CRIK CRAK SNAP
HMH DID YOU BREAK SOMETHING...?
I HAVEN'T SEEN SECOND LIEUTENANT HAVOC LATELY.
MALE-FEMALE RELATIONS ARE DIFFICULT TO BUILD, AREN'T THEY, LIEUTENANT?
hm...
SIR?
HE STAYED IN BED FOR A WEEK.
SOB SOB SOB SOB SOB
END

*TO BE CONTINUED IN **FULLMETAL ALCHEMIST** VOL. 8...*

CRUEL GIRL

I'VE FINISHED UPGRADING ED'S ARMS WITH THE ROCKET PUNCH ABILITY!!
WHAAT !!?
WHEN DID YOU DO THAT !!?
FIRE !!
VOOM
CLICK
WAGH !!!
GLEAM
IMPOSSIBLE TO RETRIEVE
HOW COULD YOU DO THAT TO MY NEW INVEN-TION !!?
POW
HOW IS THIS MY FAULT ?!

FULLMETAL ALCHEMIST 7

SPECIAL THANKS TO...

KEISUI TAKAEDA-SAN
SANKICHI HINODEYA-SAN
MASANARI YUBEKA-SAN
JUNSHI BABA-SAN
AIYAABALL-SAN
JUN TOKO-SAN
YOICHI SHIMOMURA-SHI (MANAGER)

AND YOU!!

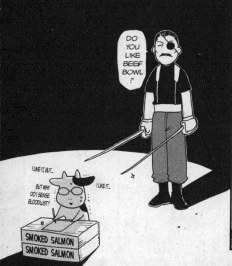

DO YOU LIKE BEEF BOWL ?
I LIKE IT...
I LIKE IT, BUT...
BUT WHY DO I SENSE BLOODLUST?
SMOKED SALMON
SMOKED SALMON

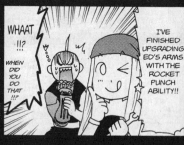

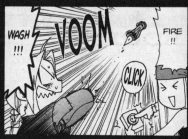

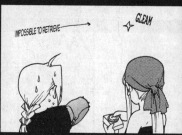

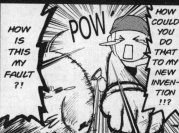

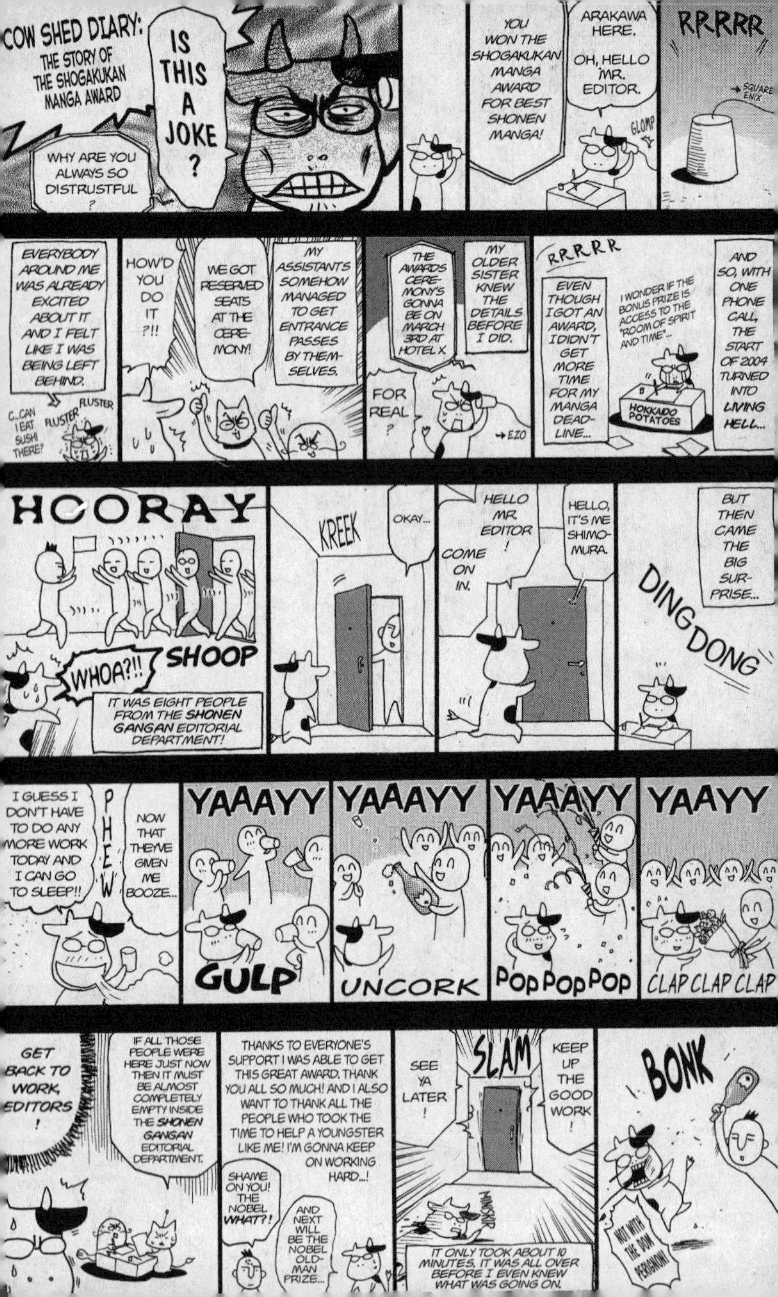
RRRRR
SQUARE ENIX
ARAKAWA HERE.
OH, HELLO MR. EDITOR.
GLOMP
YOU WON THE SHOGAKUKAN MANGA AWARD FOR BEST SHONEN MANGA!
IS THIS A JOKE?
COW SHED DIARY: THE STORY OF THE SHOGAKUKAN MANGA AWARD
WHY ARE YOU ALWAYS SO DISTRUSTFUL?
AND SO, WITH ONE PHONE CALL, THE START OF 2004 TURNED INTO LIVING HELL...
RRRRR
EVEN THOUGH I GOT AN AWARD, I DIDN'T GET MORE TIME FOR MY MANGA DEADLINE...
I WONDER IF THE BONUS PRIZE IS ACCESS TO THE "ROOM OF SPIRIT AND TIME"...
HOKKAIDO POTATOES
MY OLDER SISTER KNEW THE DETAILS BEFORE I DID.
THE AWARDS CEREMONY'S GONNA BE ON MARCH 3RD AT HOTEL X.
FOR REAL?
→EZO
MY ASSISTANTS SOMEHOW MANAGED TO GET ENTRANCE PASSES BY THEMSELVES.
WE GOT RESERVED SEATS AT THE CEREMONY!
HOW'D YOU DO IT?!!
EVERYBODY AROUND ME WAS ALREADY EXCITED ABOUT IT AND I FELT LIKE I WAS BEING LEFT BEHIND.
FLUSTER FLUSTER
C...CAN I EAT SUSHI THERE?
BUT THEN CAME THE BIG SURPRISE...
DING DONG
HELLO, IT'S ME SHIMOMURA.
HELLO MR. EDITOR!
COME ON IN.
KREEK
OKAY...
HOORAY
SHOOP
WHOA?!!
IT WAS EIGHT PEOPLE FROM THE SHONEN GANGAN EDITORIAL DEPARTMENT!
YAAYY
CLAP CLAP CLAP
YAAAYY
POP POP POP
YAAAYY
UNCORK
YAAAYY
GULP
NOW THAT THEY'VE GIVEN ME BOOZE...
PHEW
I GUESS I DON'T HAVE TO DO ANY MORE WORK TODAY AND I CAN GO TO SLEEP!!
BONK
NOT WITH THE DOM PERIGNON!
KEEP UP THE GOOD WORK!
SLAM
SEE YA LATER!
IT ONLY TOOK ABOUT 10 MINUTES. IT WAS ALL OVER BEFORE I EVEN KNEW WHAT WAS GOING ON.
THANKS TO EVERYONE'S SUPPORT I WAS ABLE TO GET THIS GREAT AWARD. THANK YOU ALL SO MUCH! AND I ALSO WANT TO THANK ALL THE PEOPLE WHO TOOK THE TIME TO HELP A YOUNGSTER LIKE ME! I'M GONNA KEEP ON WORKING HARD...!
AND NEXT WILL BE THE NOBEL OLD-MAN PRIZE...
SHAME ON YOU! THE NOBEL WHAT?!
IF ALL THOSE PEOPLE WERE HERE JUST NOW THEN IT MUST BE ALMOST COMPLETELY EMPTY INSIDE THE SHONEN GANGAN EDITORIAL DEPARTMENT.
GET BACK TO WORK, EDITORS!

Everyone from Devil's Nest
There's too many of them...
In Memoriam

I feel a draft !!!
THE TRUTH TOOK MY BOXERS!

HA HA HA HA HA
EAR
EAR
LEFT HAND
RIGHT HAND
BUTT
THE BRADLEY SCHOOL'S ULTIMATE SWORDFIGHTING TECHNIQUE:
Five Sword Style!!!

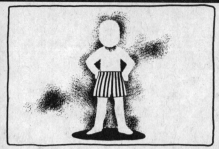

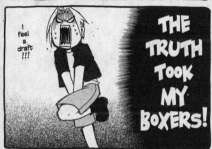

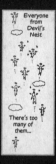

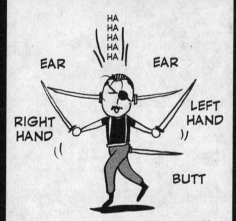

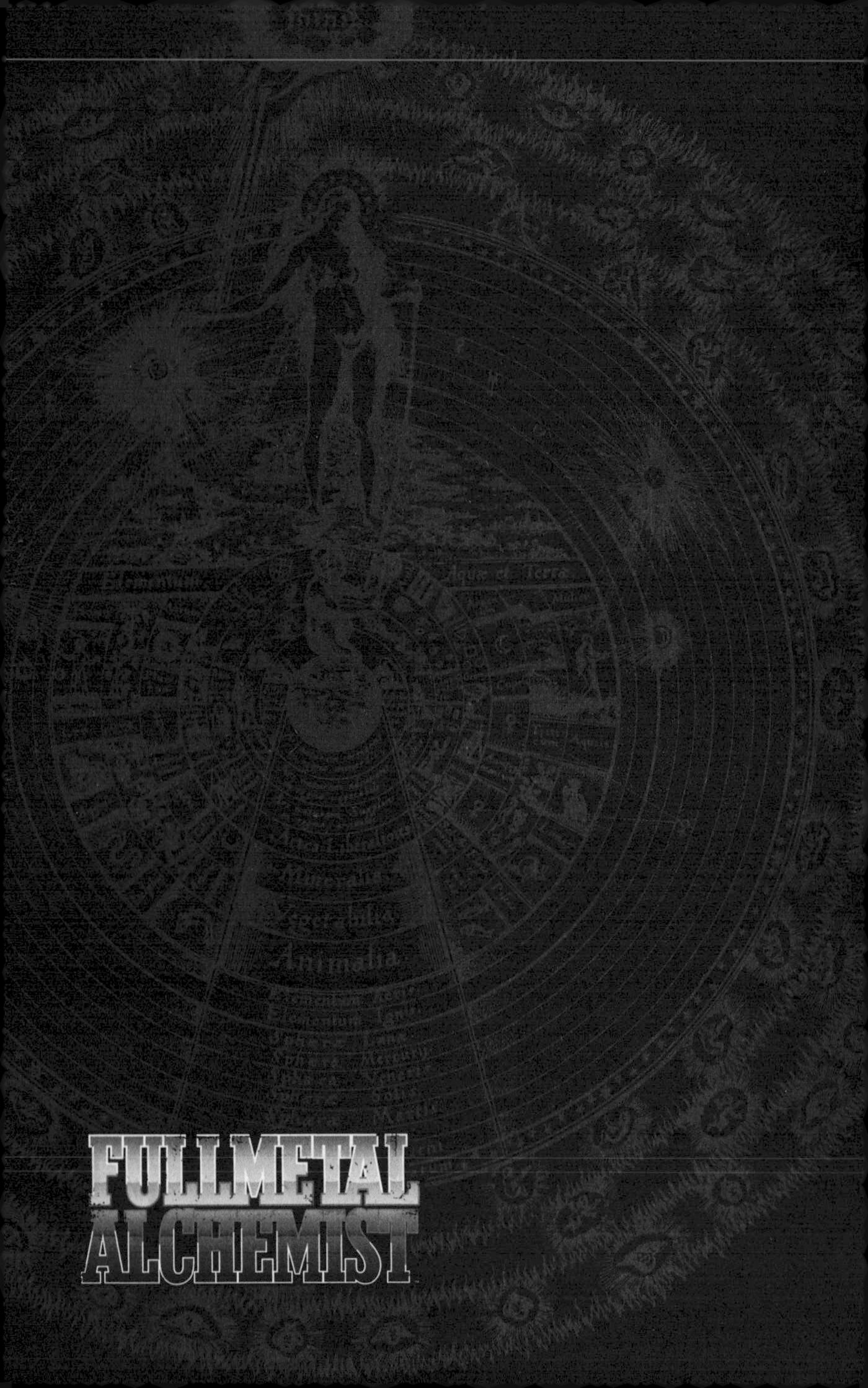
FULLMETAL
ALCHEMIST

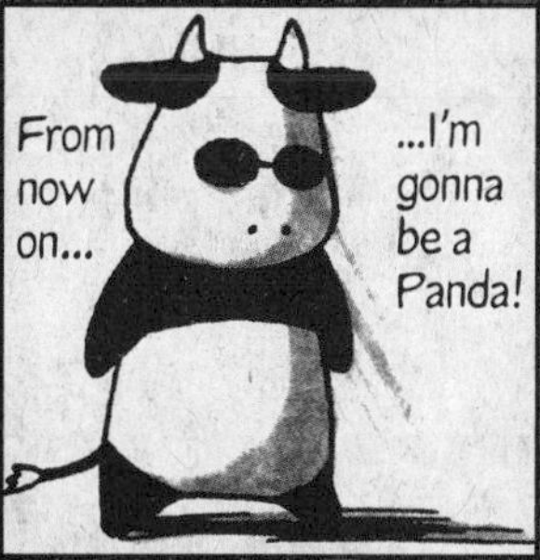
From now on...
...I'm gonna be a Panda!

I always draw ridiculous-looking self-portraits for this series, so I have a really hard time when I need to choose one for other magazines. It's regrettable how they always use the "underwear" picture from volume one. Really regrettable.

—*Hiromu Arakawa, 2004*

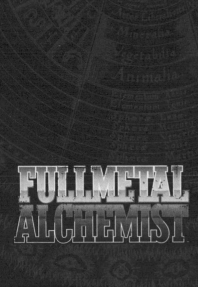

FULLMETAL
ALCHEMIST

鋼の錬金術師

FULLMETAL ALCHEMIST

8

荒川弘

HIROMU ARAKAWA

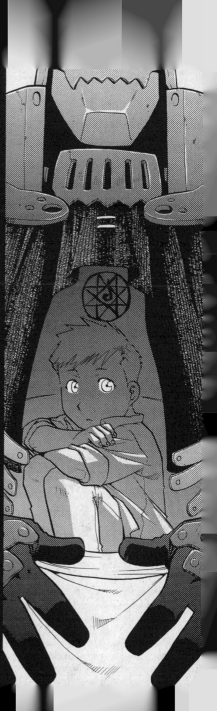

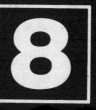

■ アルフォンス・エルリック

Alphonse Elric

■ エドワード・エルリック

Edward Elric

■ アレックス・ルイ・アームストロング

Alex Louis Armstrong

■ ロイ・マスタング

Roy Mustang

OUTLINE
FULLMETAL ALCHEMIST

Using a forbidden alchemical ritual, the Elric brothers attempted to bring their dead mother back to life. But the ritual went wrong, consuming Edward Elric's leg and Alphonse Elric's entire body. At the cost of his arm, Edward was able to graft his brother's soul into a suit of armor. Equipped with mechanical "auto-mail" to replace his missing limbs, Edward becomes a state alchemist, serving the military on deadly missions. Now, the two brothers roam the world in search of a way to regain what they have lost...

Having reunited with their former teacher, Izumi Curtis, the boys now seek a way to recall Al's lost memories of losing his physical body, which may be the key to changing the brothers back to normal. Little do the Elrics know that they, too, are being hunted. Greed, a homunculus who bears the Ouroboros tattoo, kidnaps Al to find the secrets of merging a soul with a suit of armor. When Ed tries to rescue his brother, the situation turns violent. Soon, chaos ensues as Führer President Bradley himself leads an assault on Greed's underground lair...

鋼の錬金術師
FULLMETAL ALCHEMIST

CHARACTERS
FULLMETAL ALCHEMIST

ウィンリィ・ロックベル

Winry Rockbell

キング・ブラッドレイ

King Bradley

グラトニー

Gluttony

ラスト

Lust

グリード

Greed

エンヴィー

Envy

CONTENTS

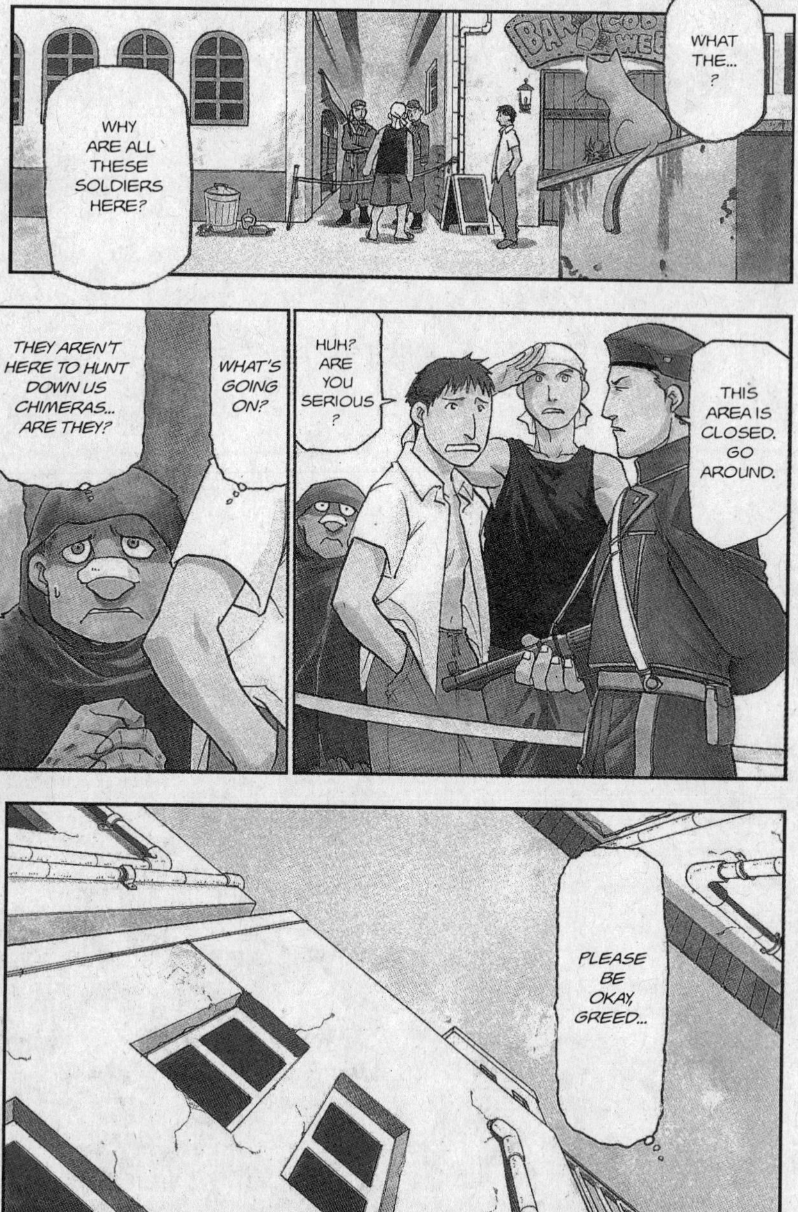
WHAT THE...?
WHY ARE ALL THESE SOLDIERS HERE?
THIS AREA IS CLOSED. GO AROUND.
HUH? ARE YOU SERIOUS?
WHAT'S GOING ON?
THEY AREN'T HERE TO HUNT DOWN US CHIMERAS... ARE THEY?
PLEASE BE OKAY, GREED...

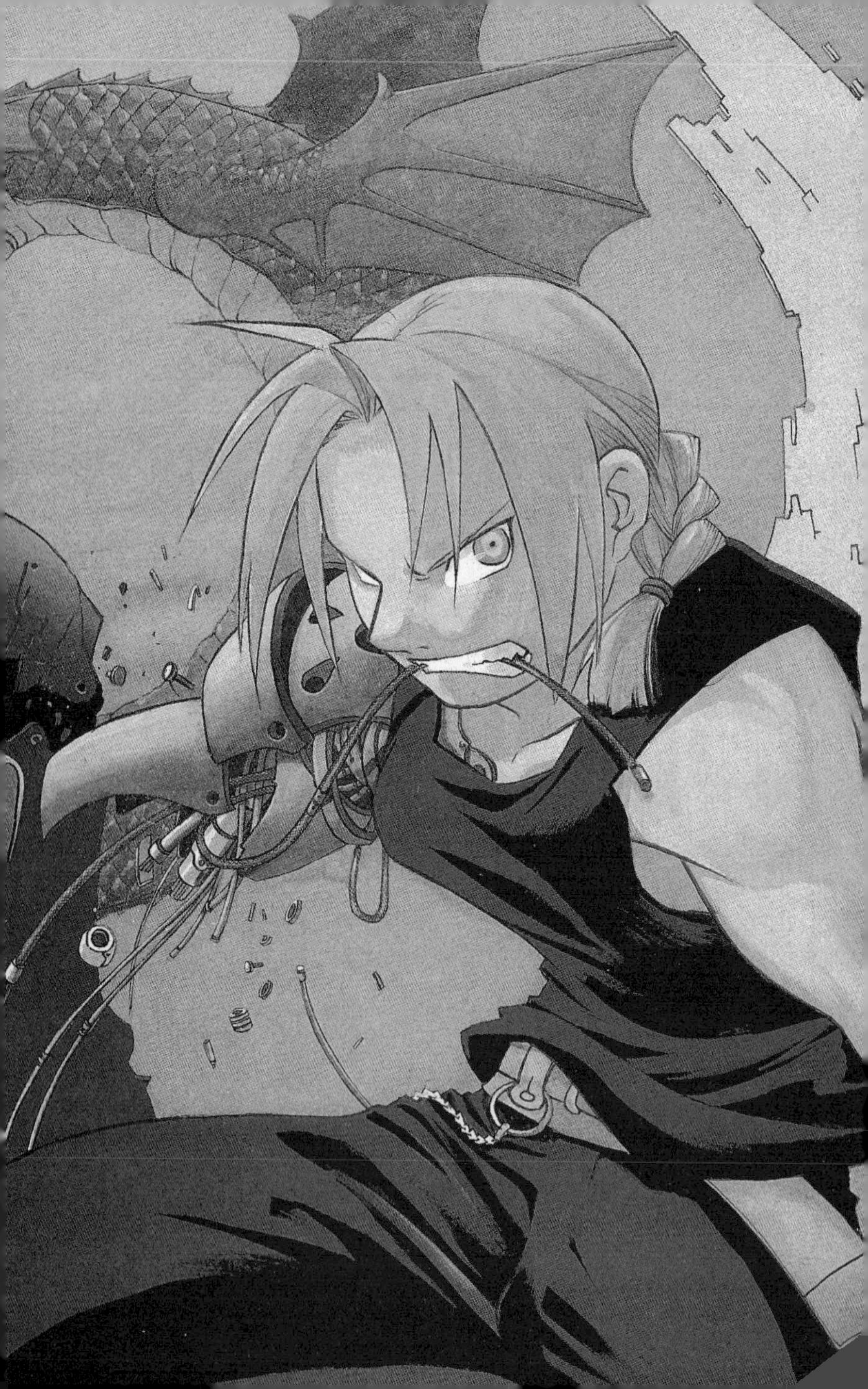

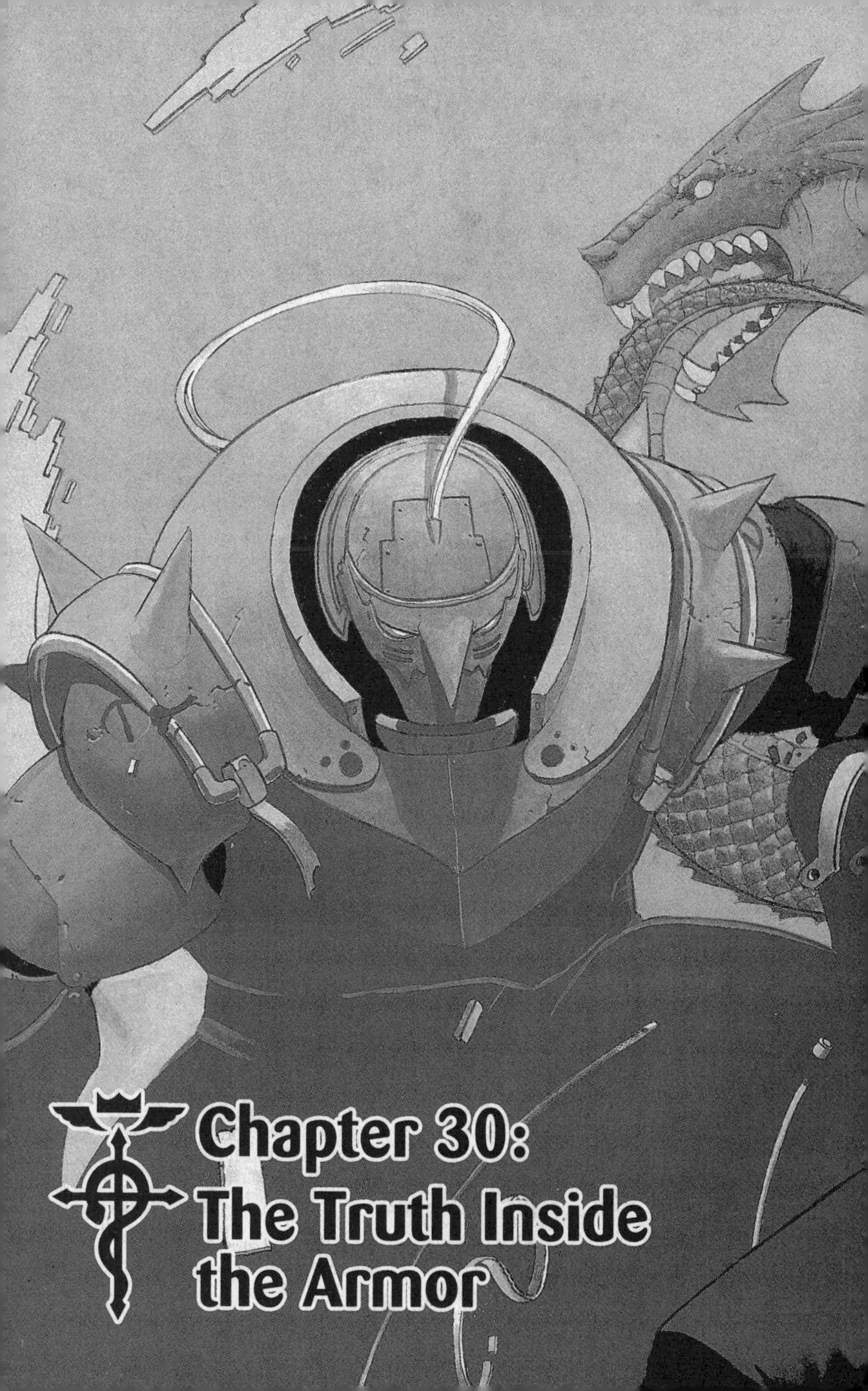
Chapter 30:
The Truth Inside the Armor

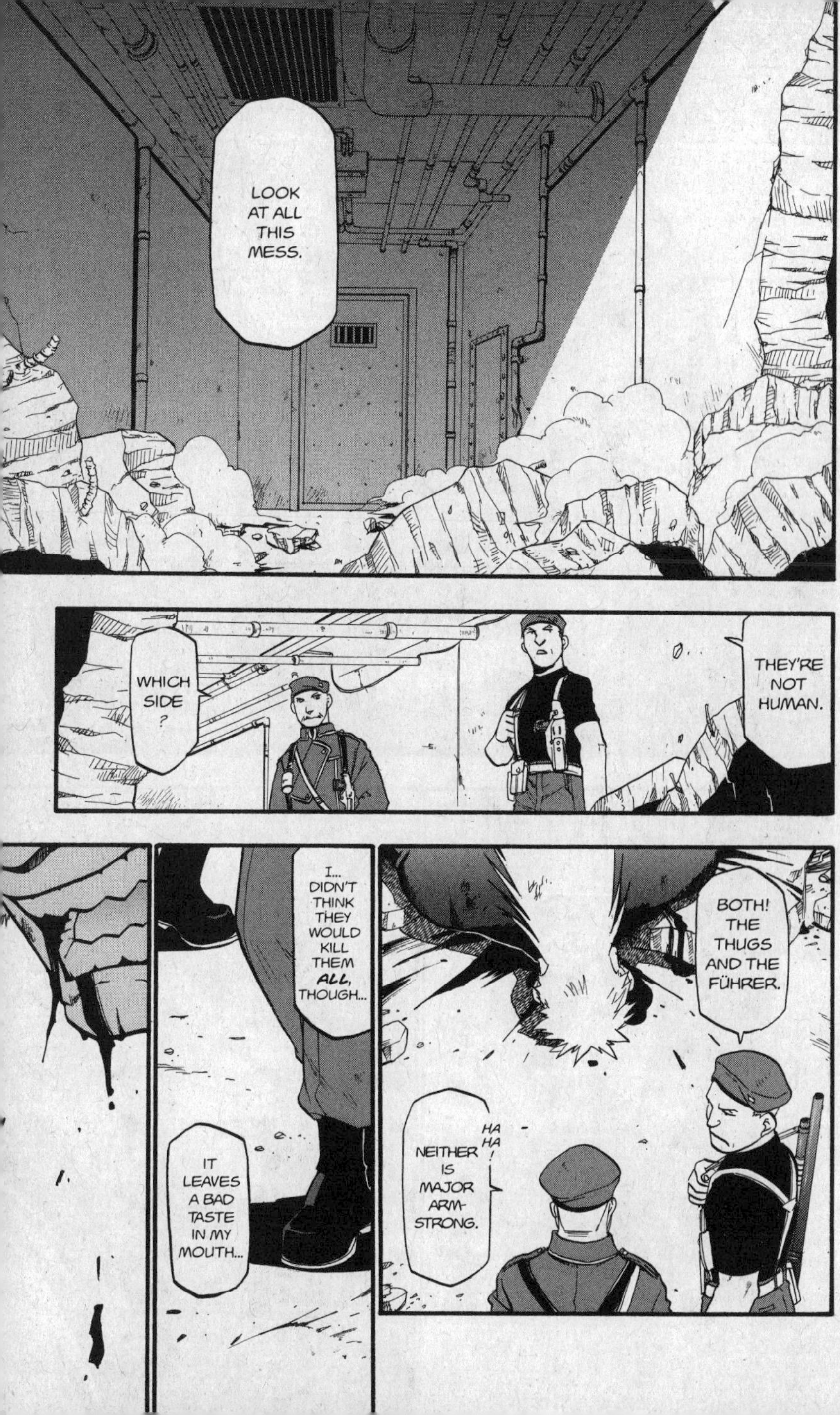
LOOK AT ALL THIS MESS.
THEY'RE NOT HUMAN.
WHICH SIDE?
BOTH! THE THUGS AND THE FÜHRER.
HA HA!
NEITHER IS MAJOR ARMSTRONG.
I... DIDN'T THINK THEY WOULD KILL THEM ALL, THOUGH...
IT LEAVES A BAD TASTE IN MY MOUTH...

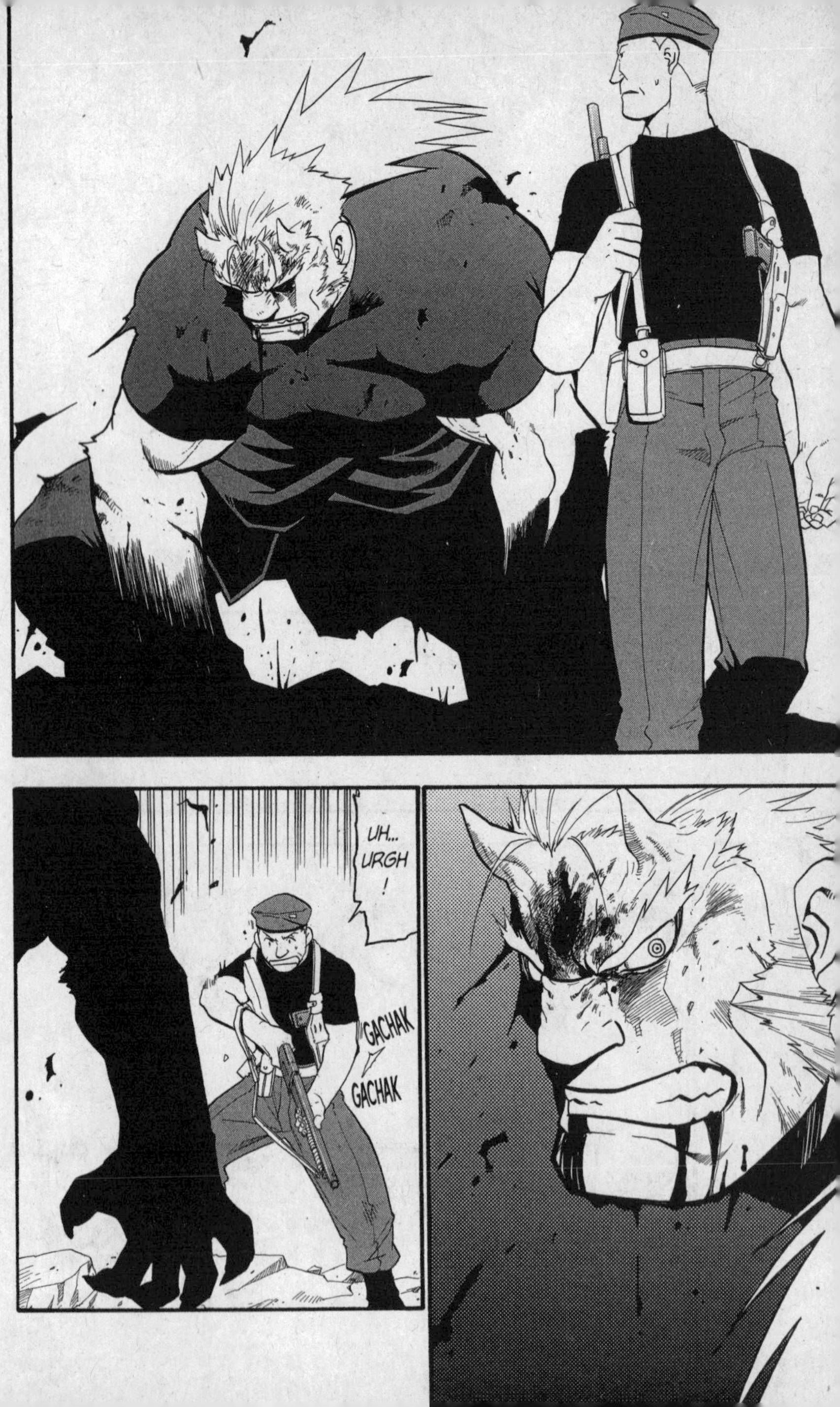
UH... URGH!
GACHAK
GACHAK

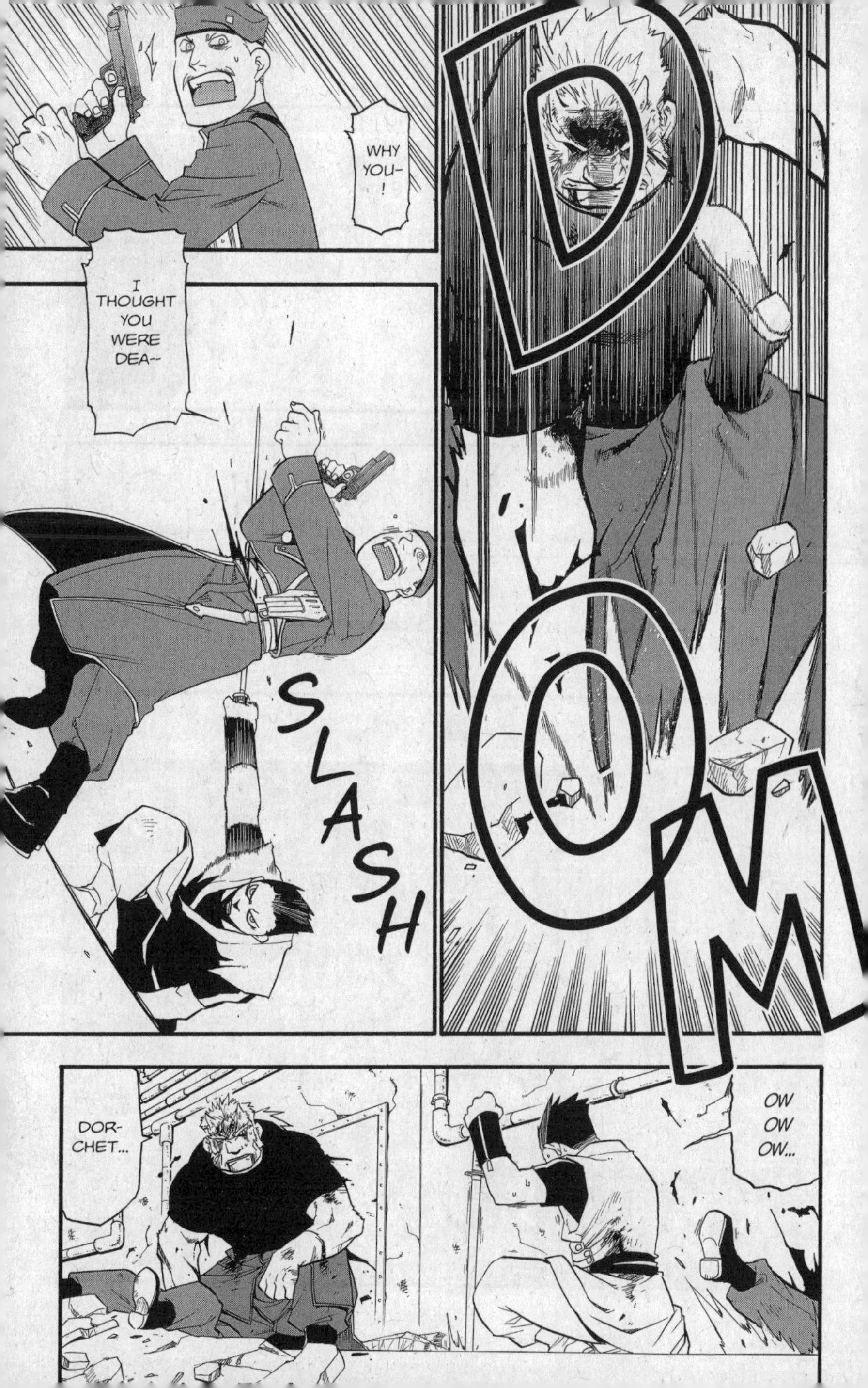
DOOM
WHY YOU-!
I THOUGHT YOU WERE DEA--
SLASH
OW OW OW...
DOR-CHET...

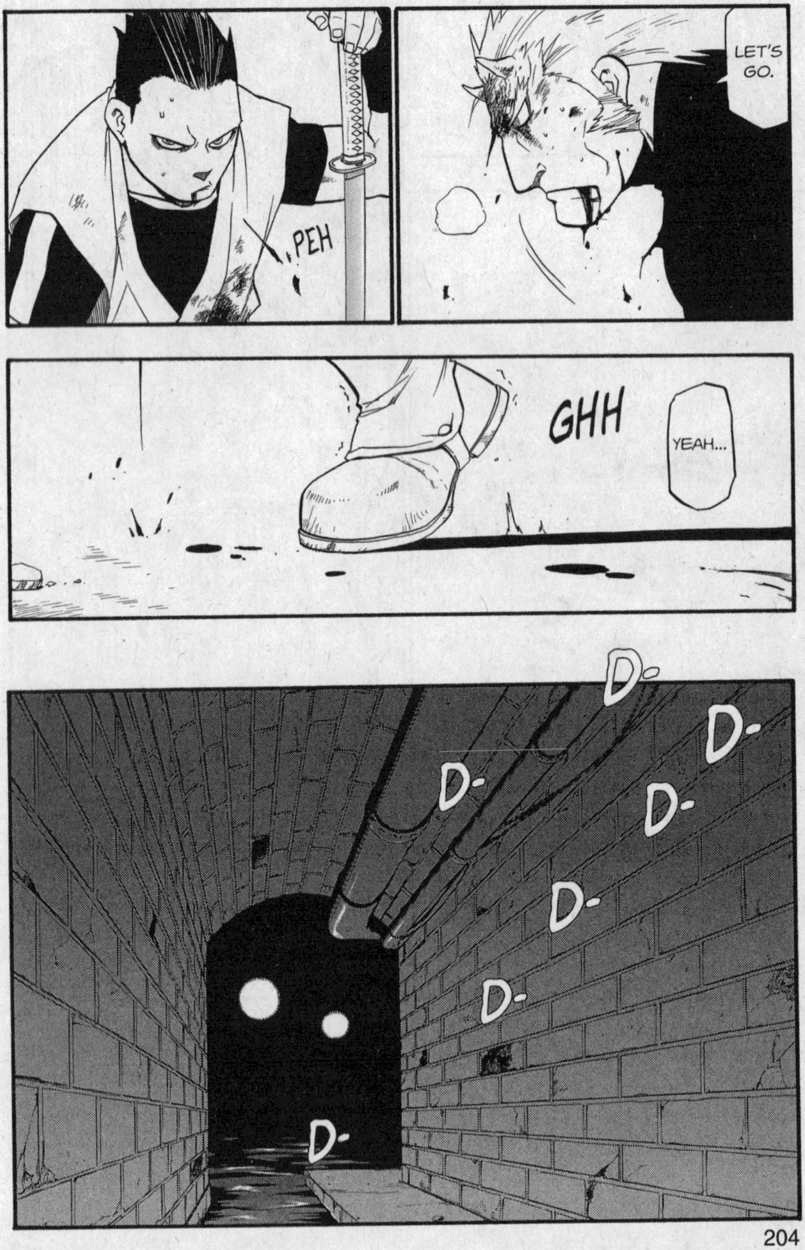
LET'S GO.
PEH
YEAH...
GHH
D-
D-
D-
D-
D-
D-
D-

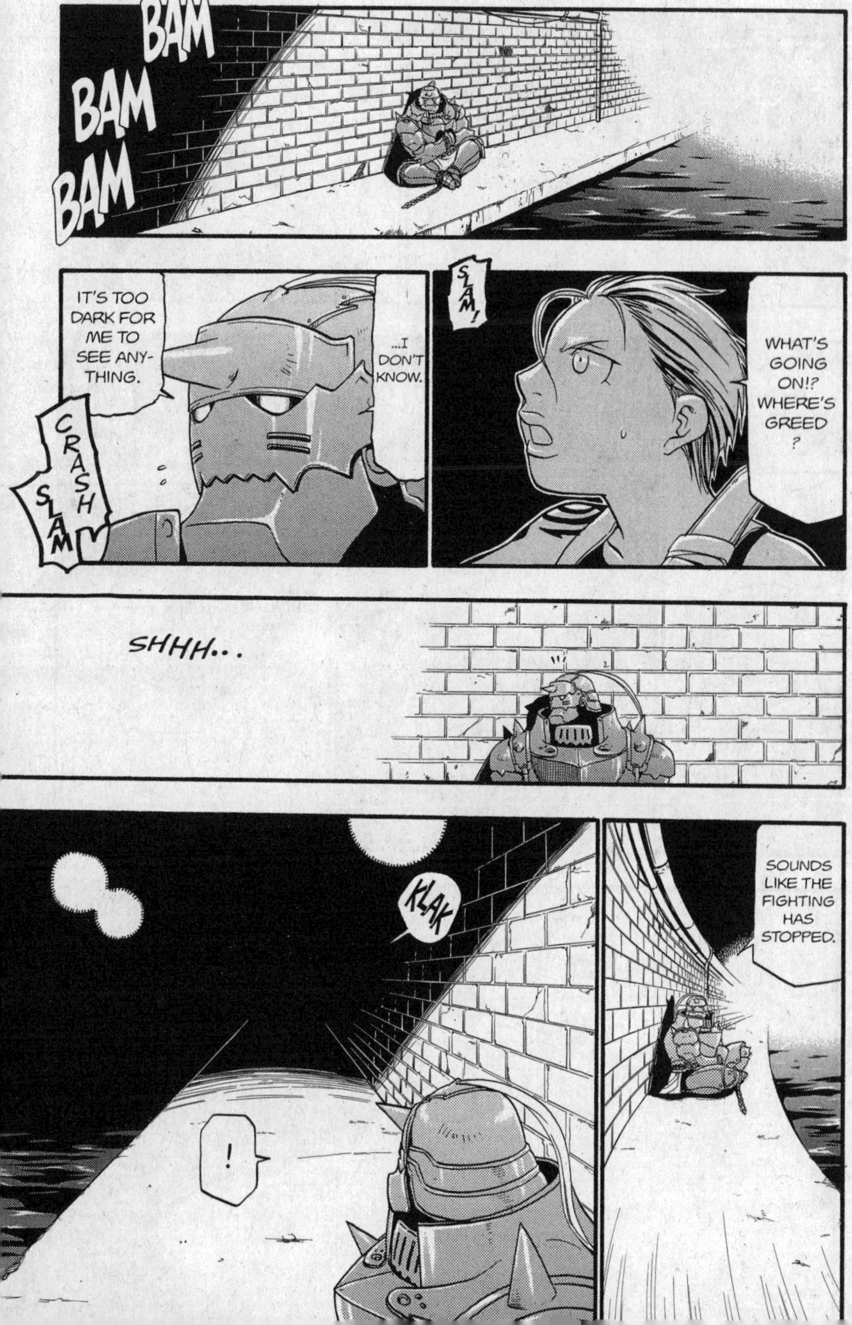
BAM
BAM
BAM
SLAM!
WHAT'S GOING ON!? WHERE'S GREED?
...I DON'T KNOW.
IT'S TOO DARK FOR ME TO SEE ANY-THING.
CRASH
SLAM
SHHH...
SOUNDS LIKE THE FIGHTING HAS STOPPED.
KLAK
!

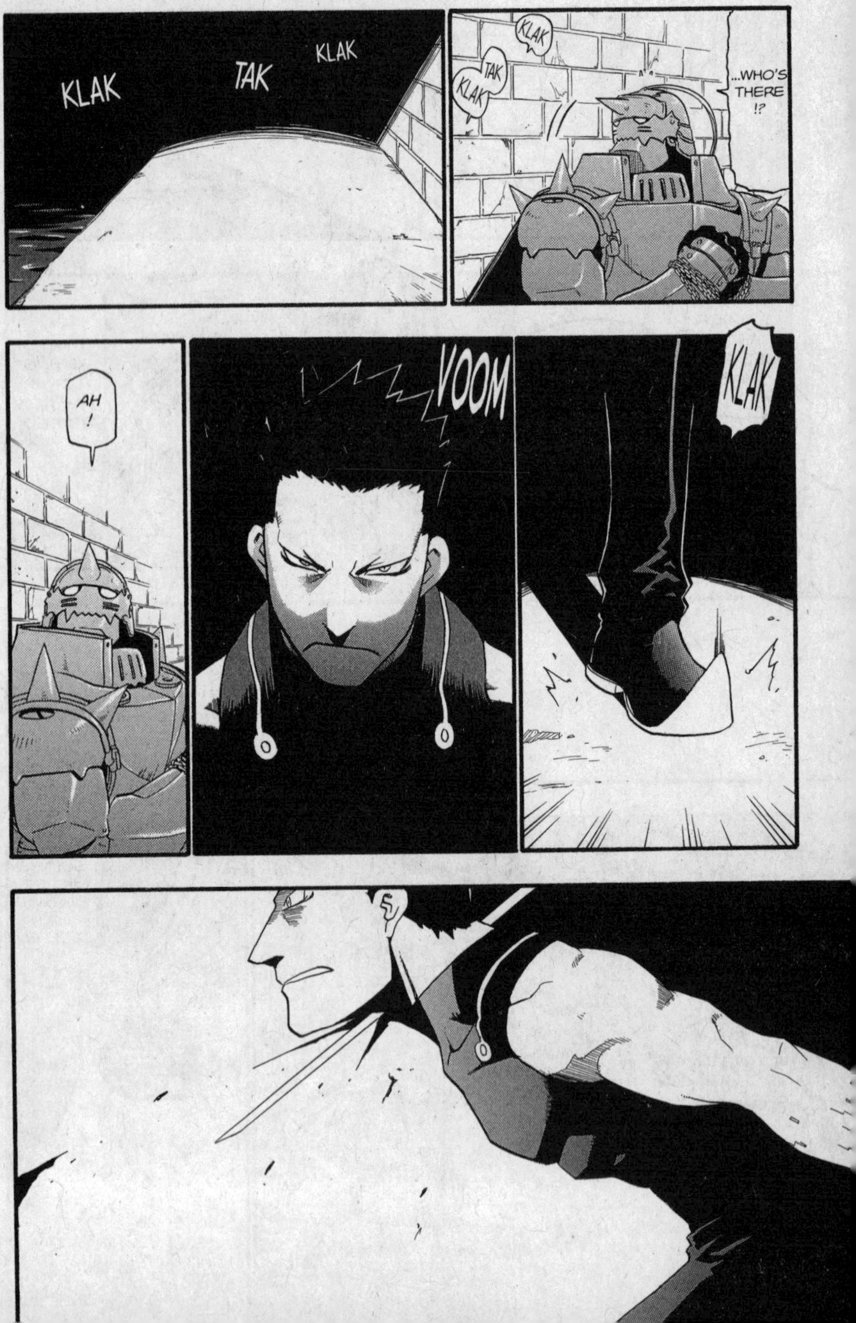
KLAK
TAK
KLAK
...WHO'S THERE !?
KLAK
TAK
KLAK
KLAK
VOOM
AH!

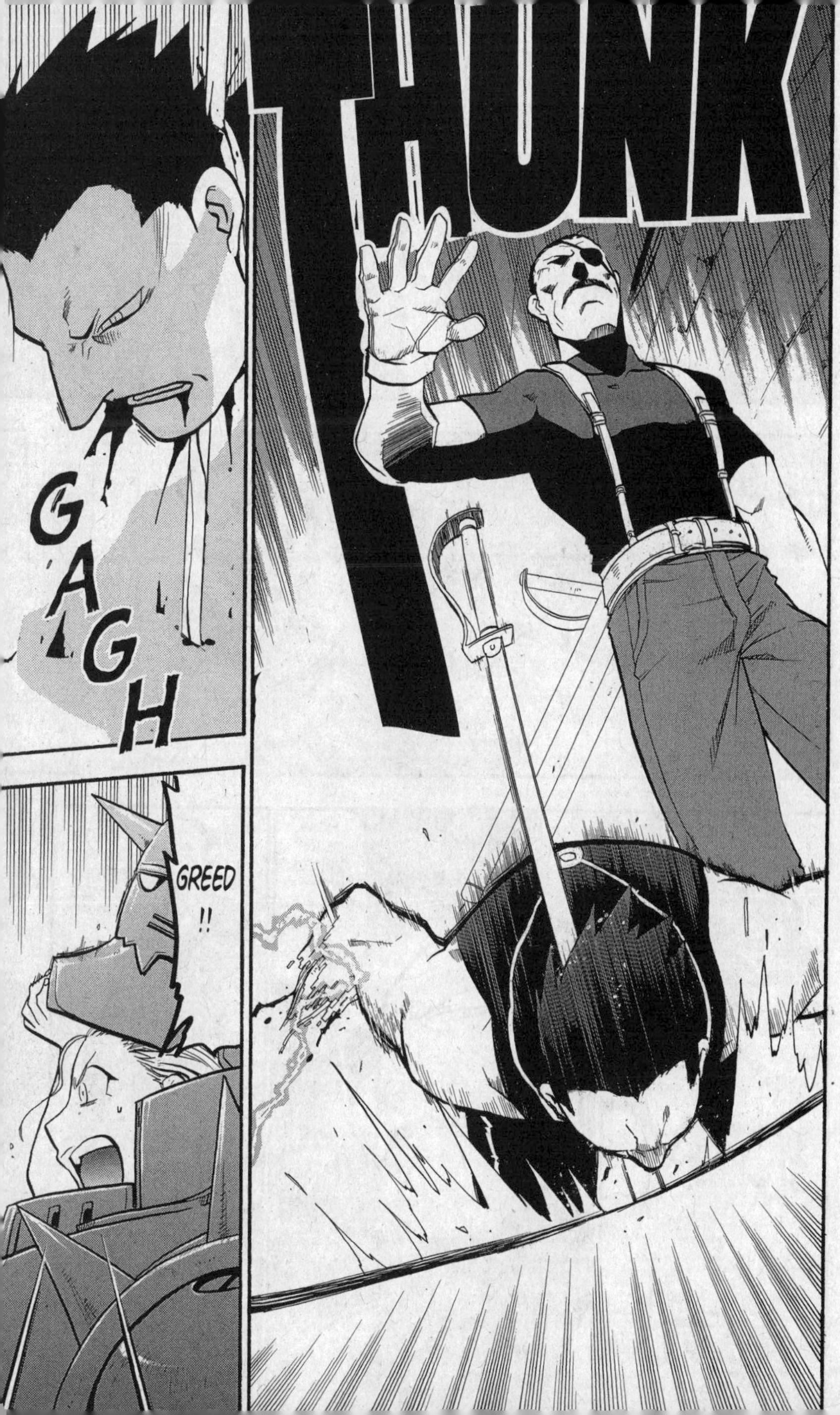
THUNK
GAGH
GREED!!

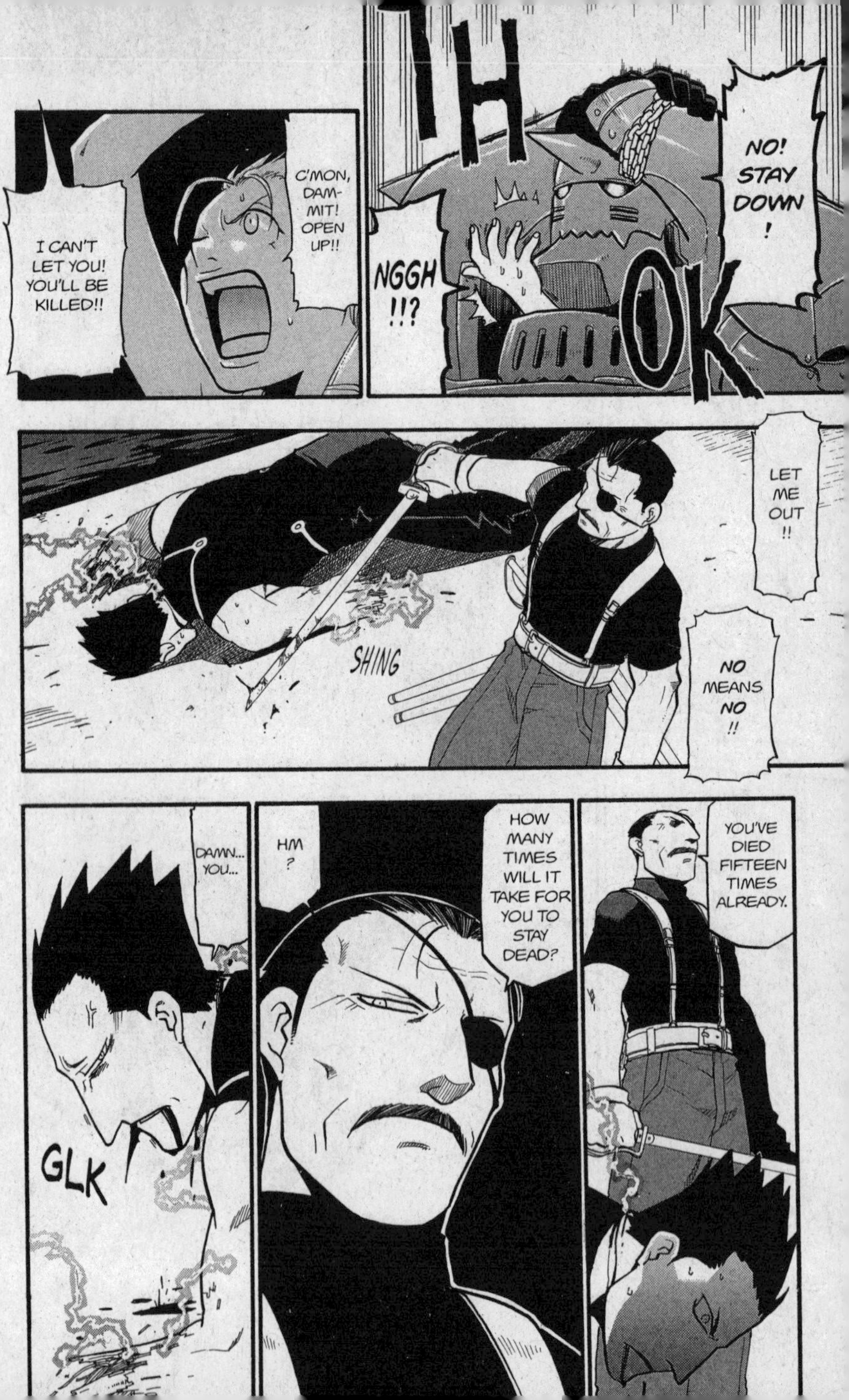
IH
OK
NO! STAY DOWN!
NGGH!!?
C'MON, DAM-MIT! OPEN UP!!
I CAN'T LET YOU! YOU'LL BE KILLED!!
LET ME OUT!!
NO MEANS NO!!
SHING
YOU'VE DIED FIFTEEN TIMES ALREADY.
HOW MANY TIMES WILL IT TAKE FOR YOU TO STAY DEAD?
HM?
DAMN... YOU...
GLK

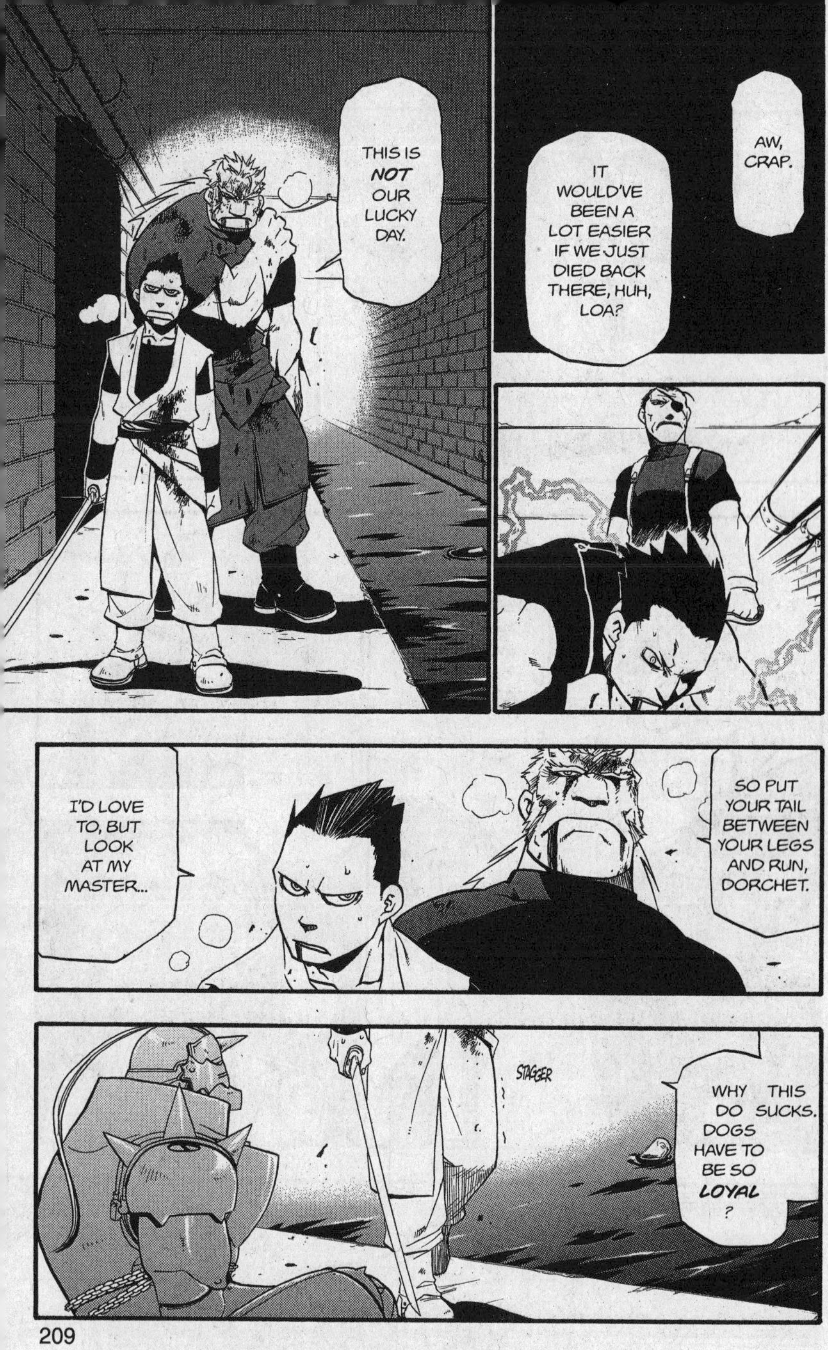
AW, CRAP.
IT WOULD'VE BEEN A LOT EASIER IF WE JUST DIED BACK THERE, HUH, LOA?
THIS IS ***NOT*** OUR LUCKY DAY.
SO PUT YOUR TAIL BETWEEN YOUR LEGS AND RUN, DORCHET.
I'D LOVE TO, BUT LOOK AT MY MASTER...
THIS SUCKS.
WHY DO DOGS HAVE TO BE SO ***LOYAL***?
STAGGER

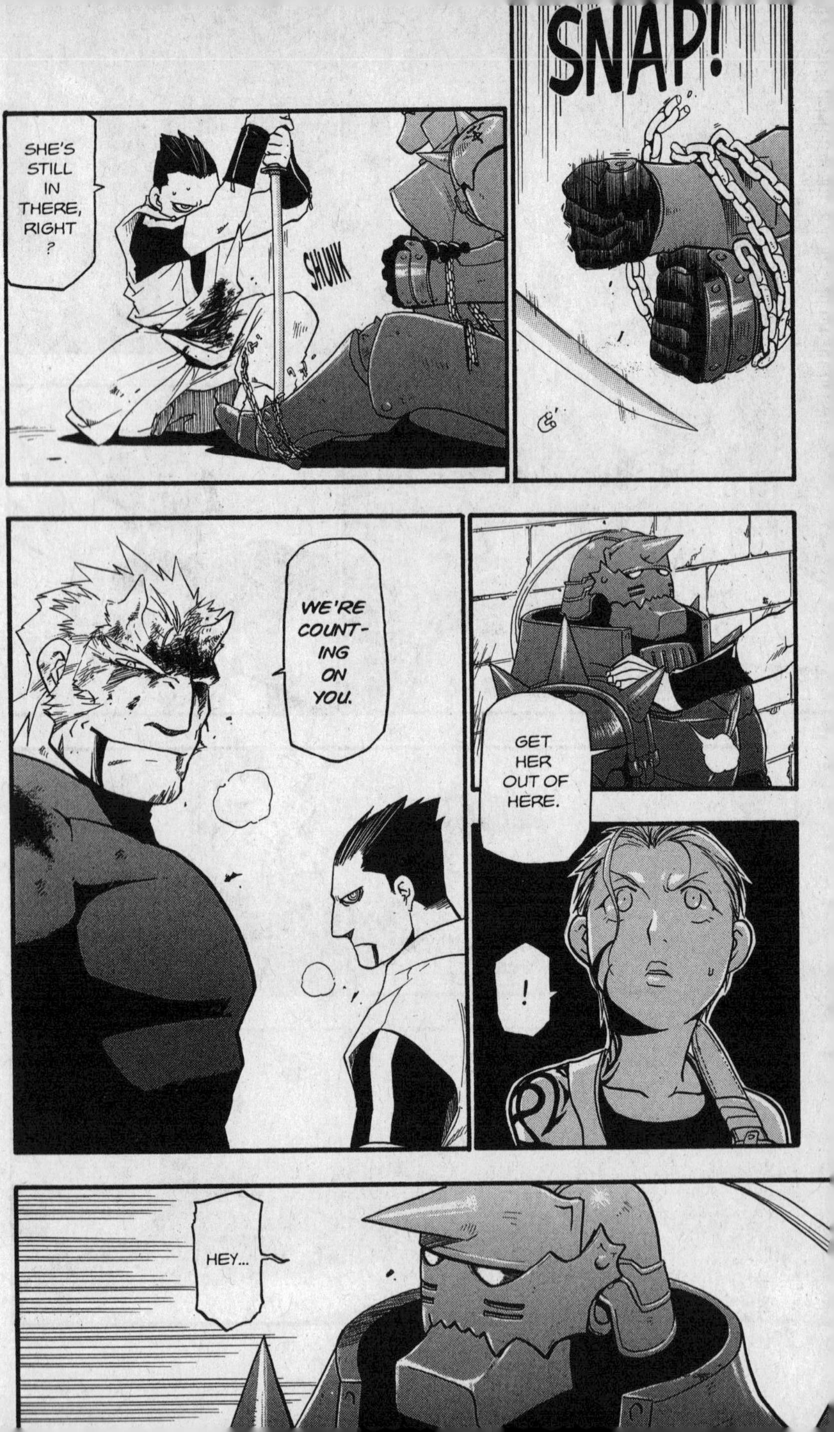
SNAP!
SHE'S STILL IN THERE, RIGHT?
SHUNK
GET HER OUT OF HERE.
!
WE'RE COUNTING ON YOU.
HEY...

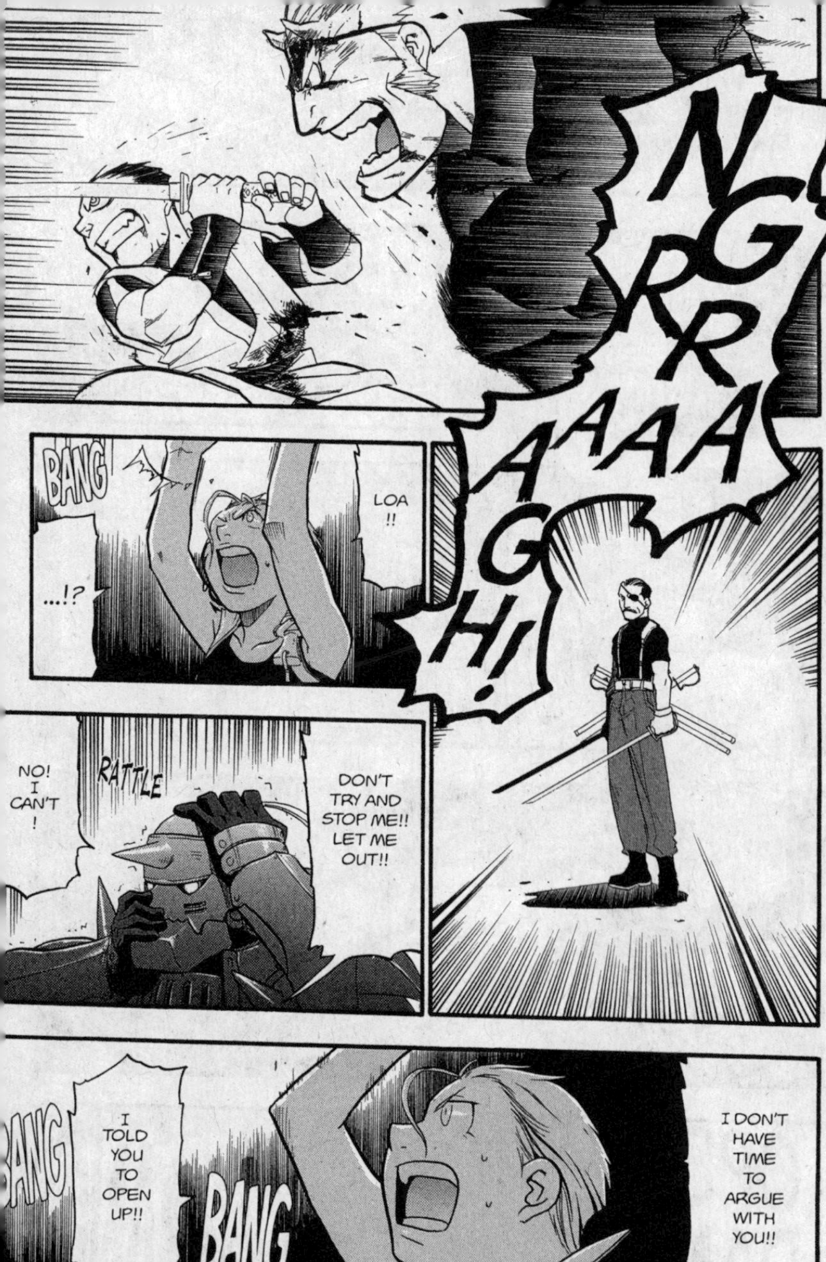
NGRRRAAAAAGH!!
LOA!!
BANG
...!?
DON'T TRY AND STOP ME!! LET ME OUT!!
RATTLE
NO! I CAN'T!
I DON'T HAVE TIME TO ARGUE WITH YOU!!
BANG
I TOLD YOU TO OPEN UP!!
BANG

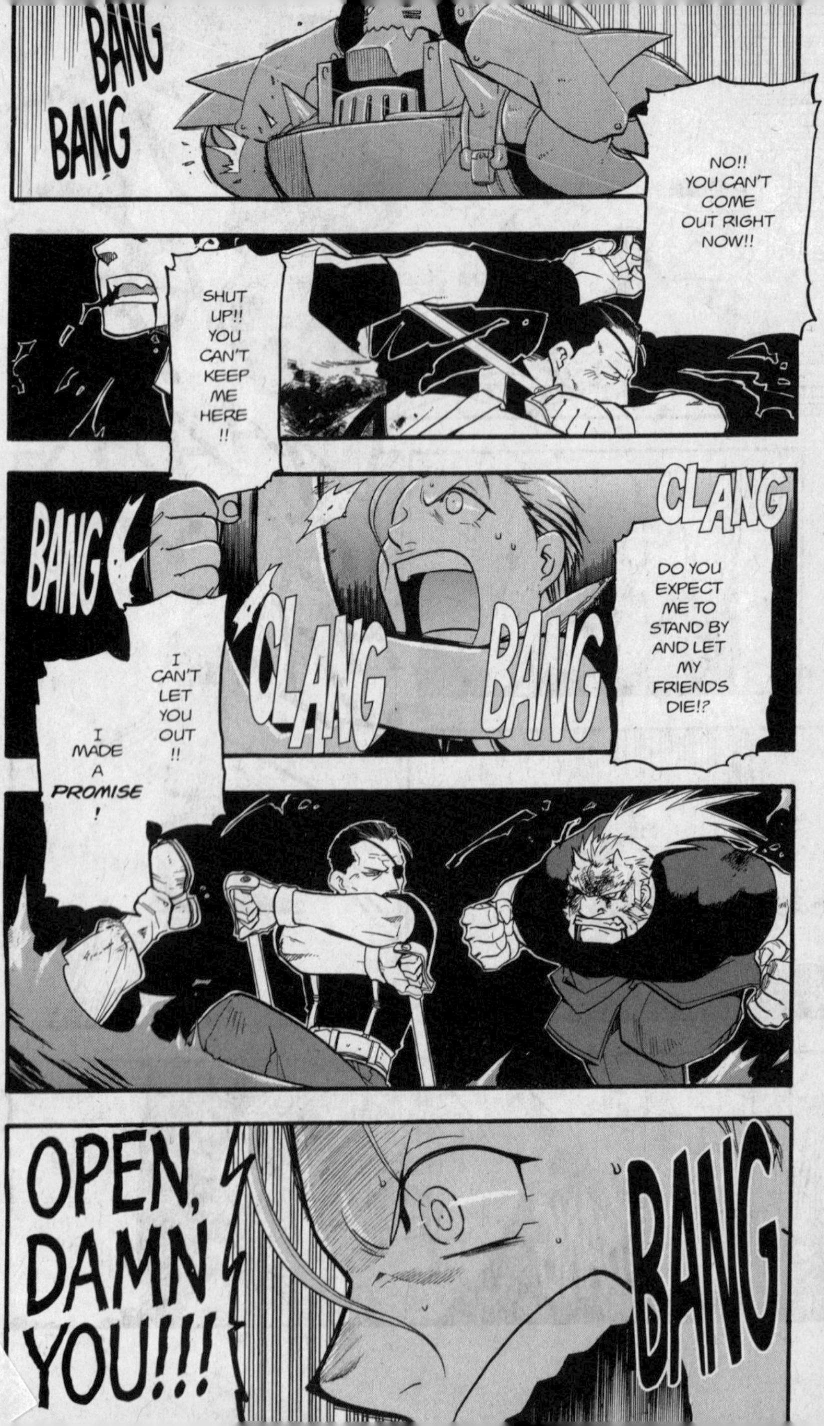
NO!! YOU CAN'T COME OUT RIGHT NOW!!
BANG
BANG
SHUT UP!! YOU CAN'T KEEP ME HERE!!
CLANG
DO YOU EXPECT ME TO STAND BY AND LET MY FRIENDS DIE!?
BANG
CLANG
BANG
I CAN'T LET YOU OUT!!
I MADE A PROMISE!
BANG
OPEN, DAMN YOU!!!

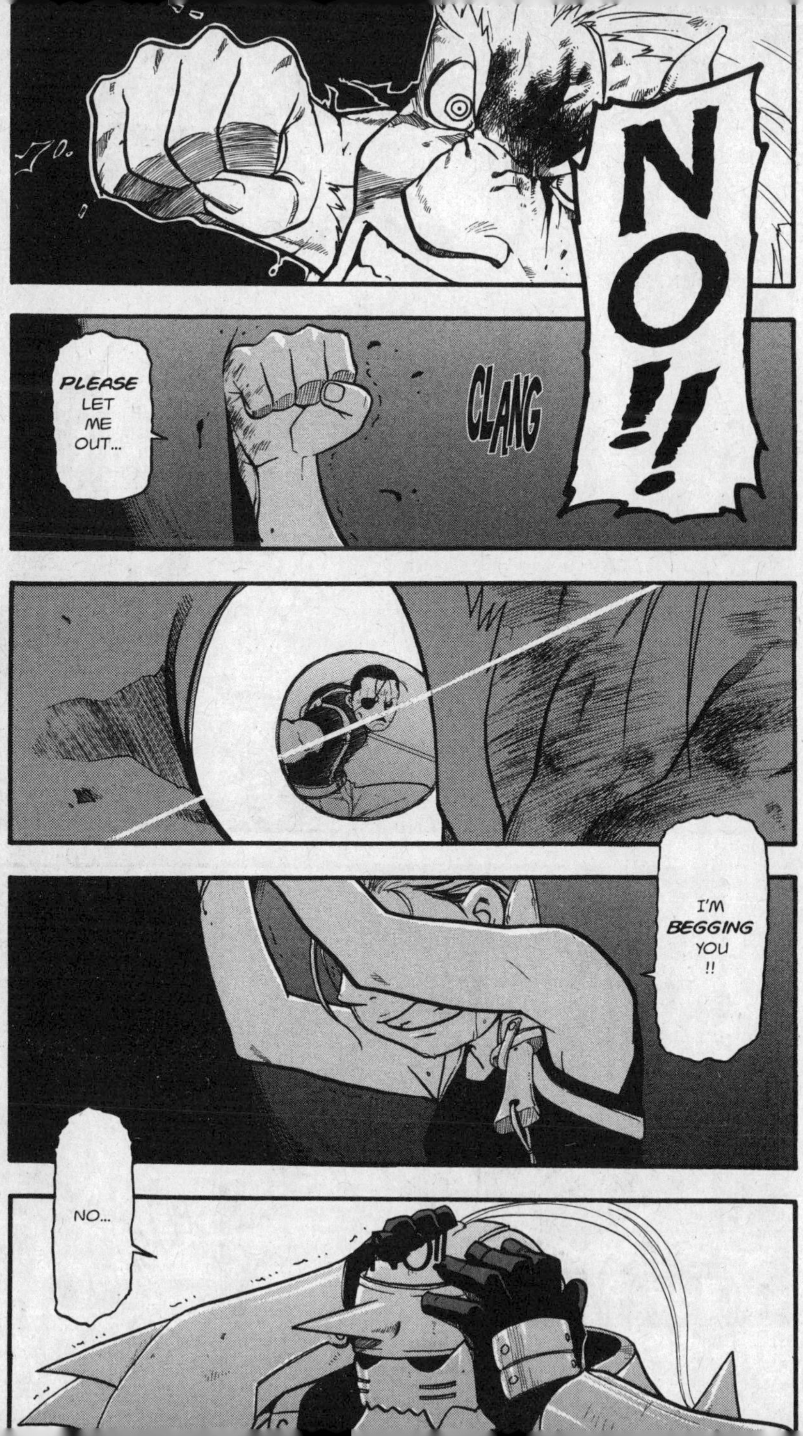
NO!!
CLANG
PLEASE LET ME OUT...
I'M BEGGING YOU!!
NO...

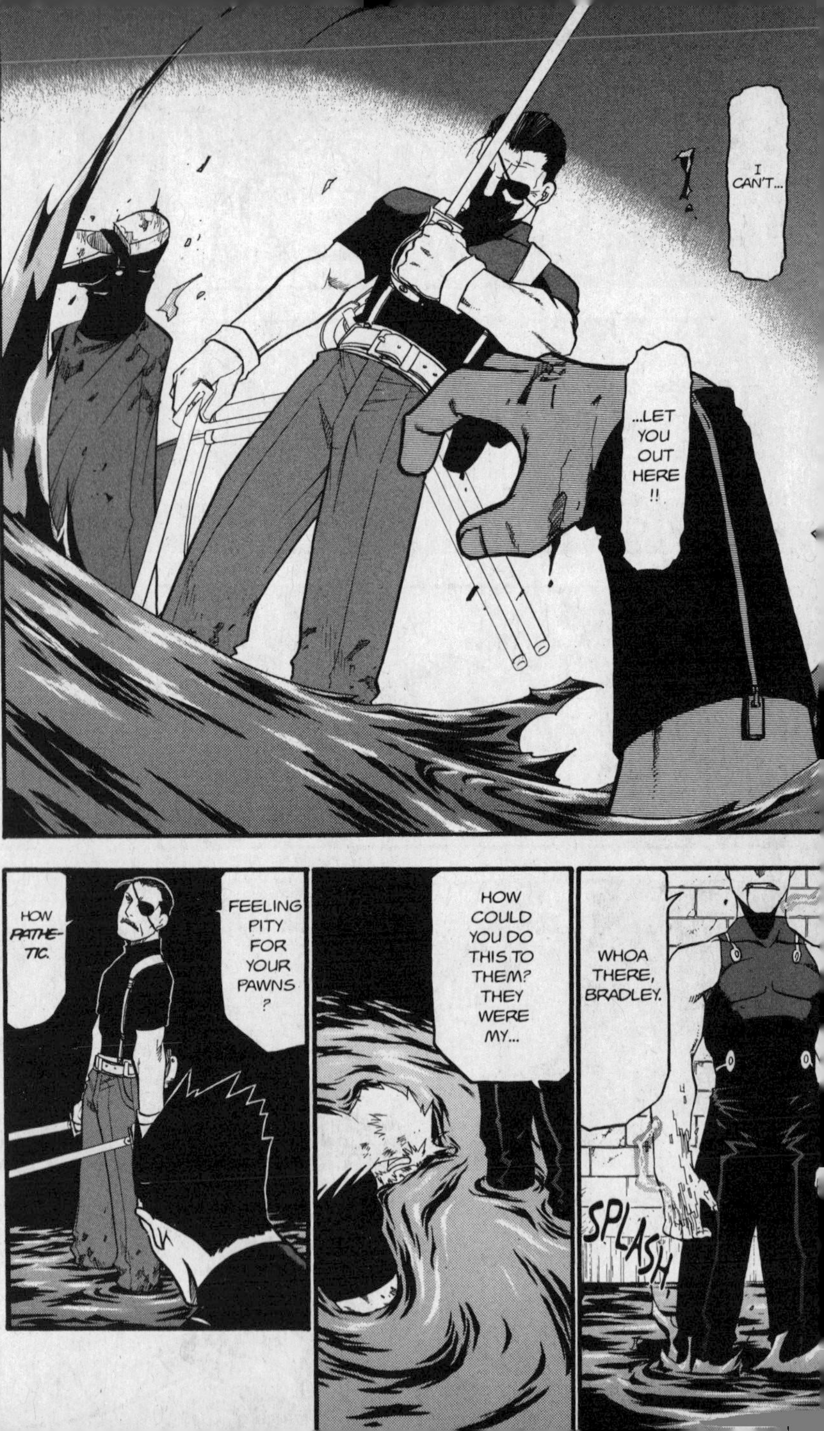
I CAN'T...
...LET YOU OUT HERE!!
WHOA THERE, BRADLEY.
SPLASH
HOW COULD YOU DO THIS TO THEM? THEY WERE MY...
FEELING PITY FOR YOUR PAWNS?
HOW PATHETIC.

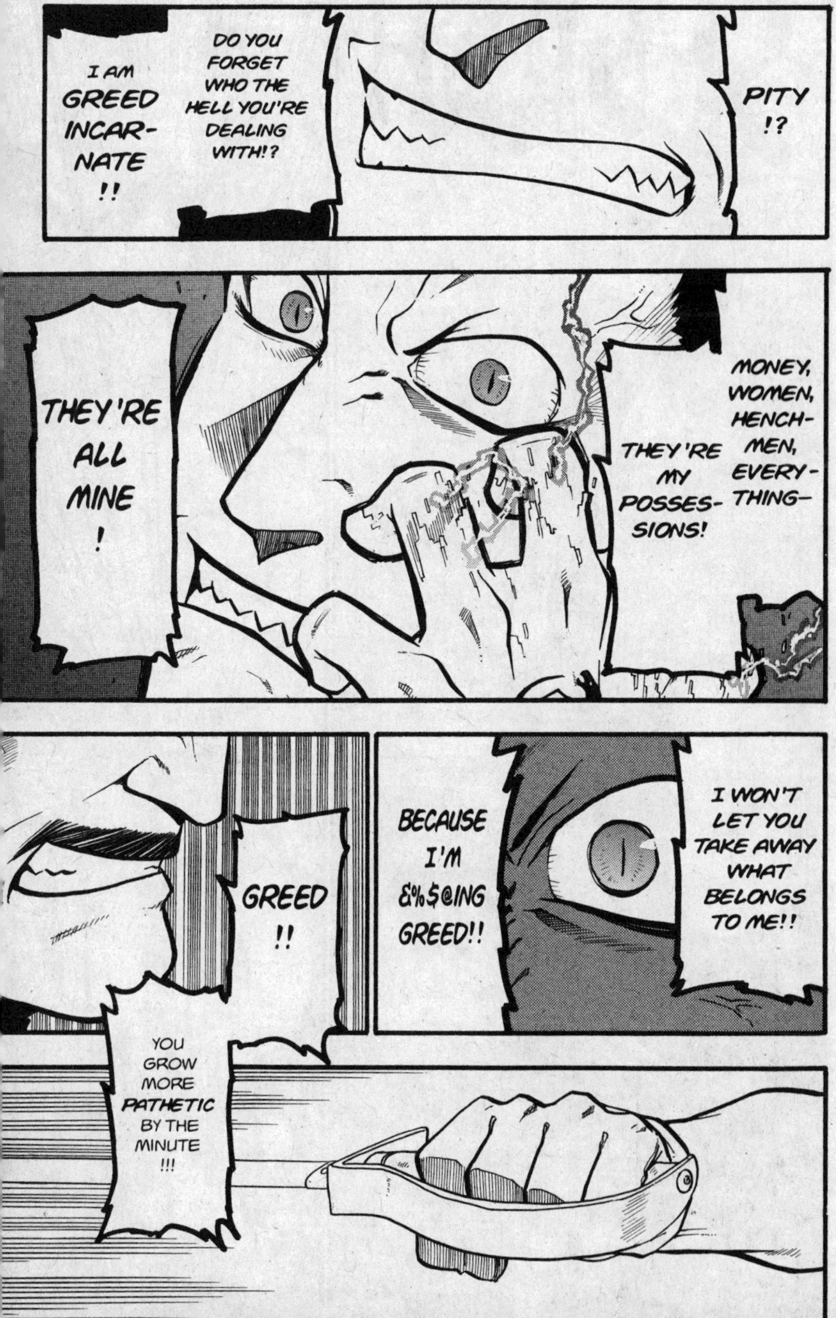
PITY !?
DO YOU FORGET WHO THE HELL YOU'RE DEALING WITH!?
I AM GREED INCARNATE !!
MONEY, WOMEN, HENCHMEN, EVERYTHING-
THEY'RE MY POSSESSIONS!
THEY'RE ALL MINE !
I WON'T LET YOU TAKE AWAY WHAT BELONGS TO ME!!
BECAUSE I'M &%$@ING GREED!!
GREED !!
YOU GROW MORE PATHETIC BY THE MINUTE !!!

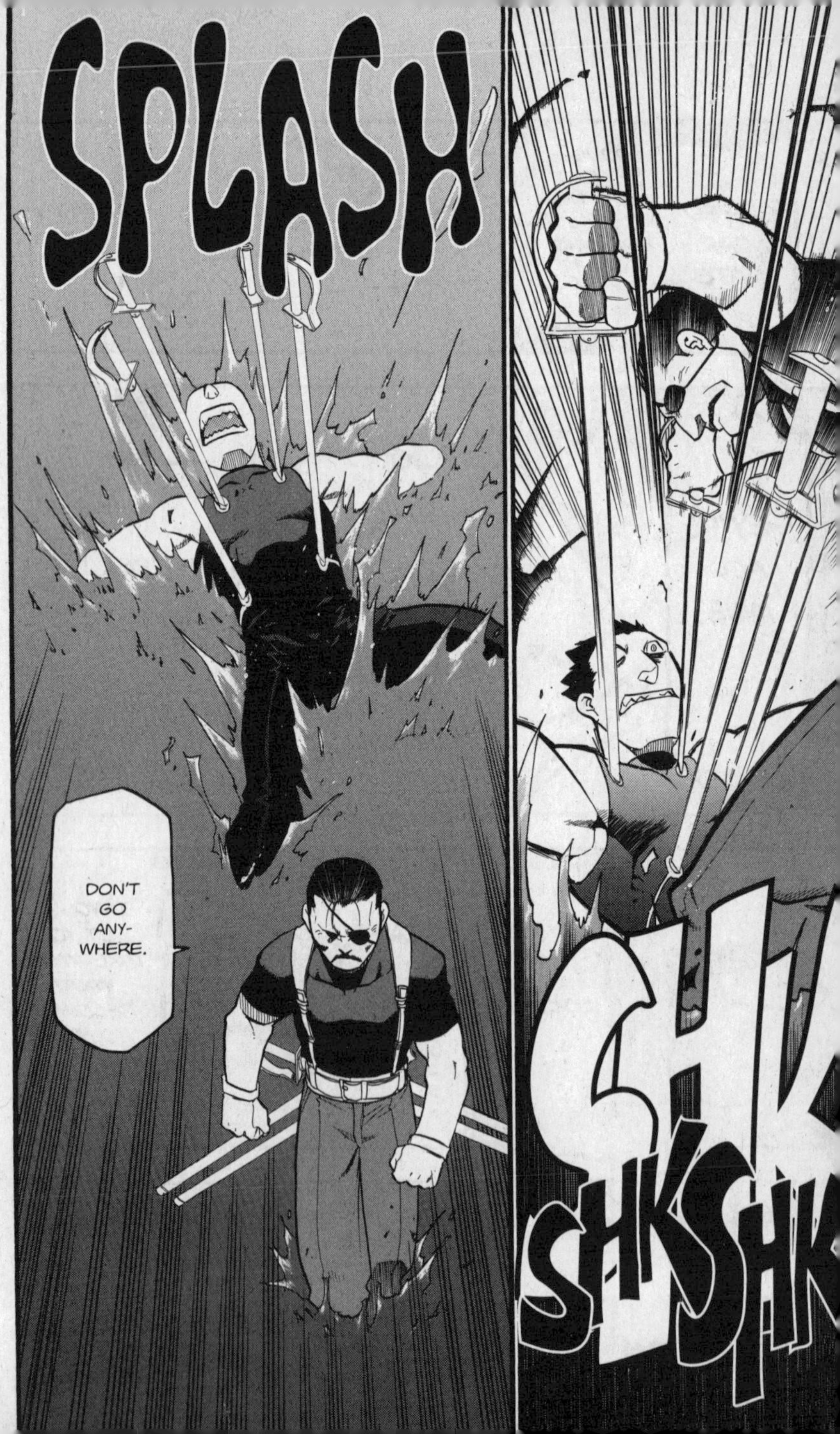
CHK
SHKSHK
SPLASH
DON'T GO ANY-WHERE.

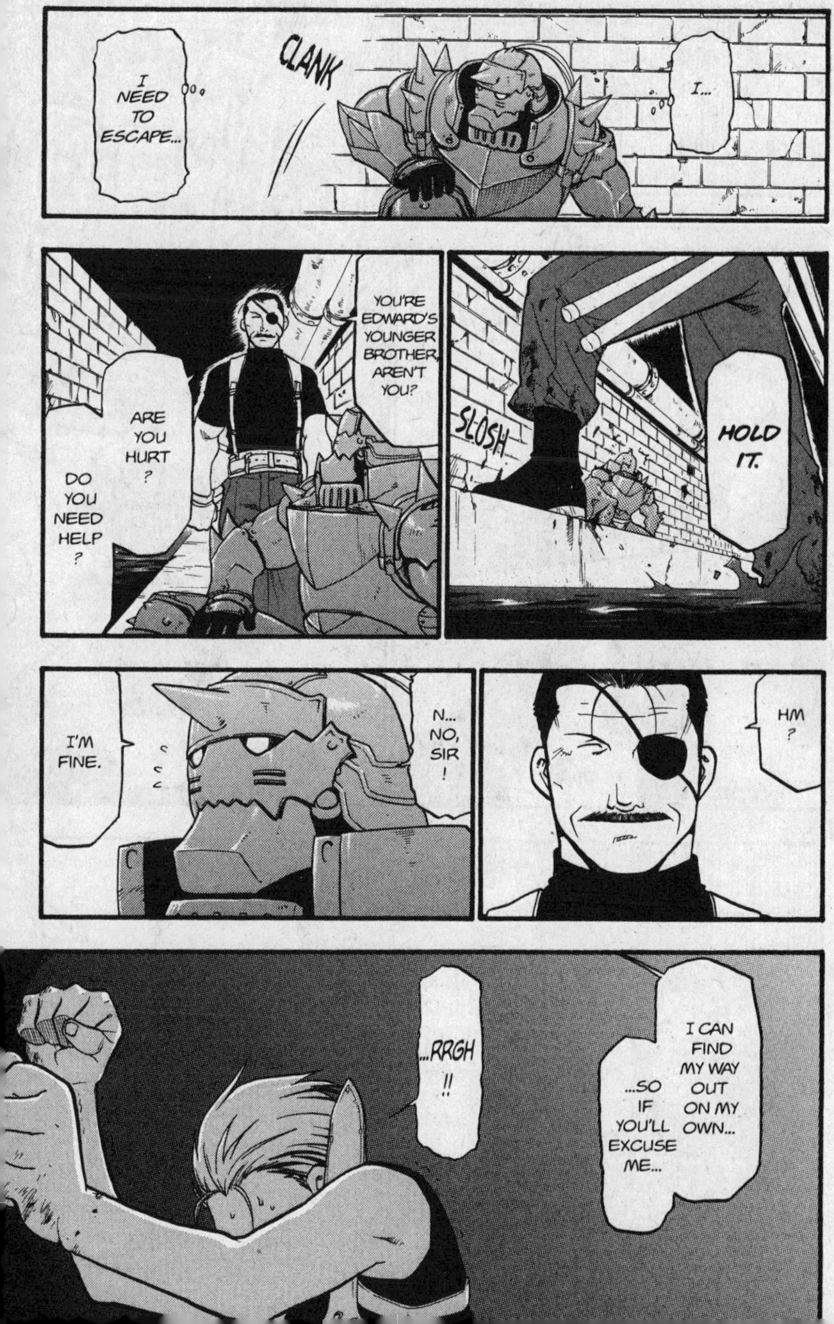
I...
CLANK
I NEED TO ESCAPE...
HOLD IT.
SLOSH
YOU'RE EDWARD'S YOUNGER BROTHER, AREN'T YOU?
ARE YOU HURT?
DO YOU NEED HELP?
HM?
N... NO, SIR!
I'M FINE.
I CAN FIND MY WAY OUT ON MY OWN...
...SO IF YOU'LL EXCUSE ME...
...RRGH!!

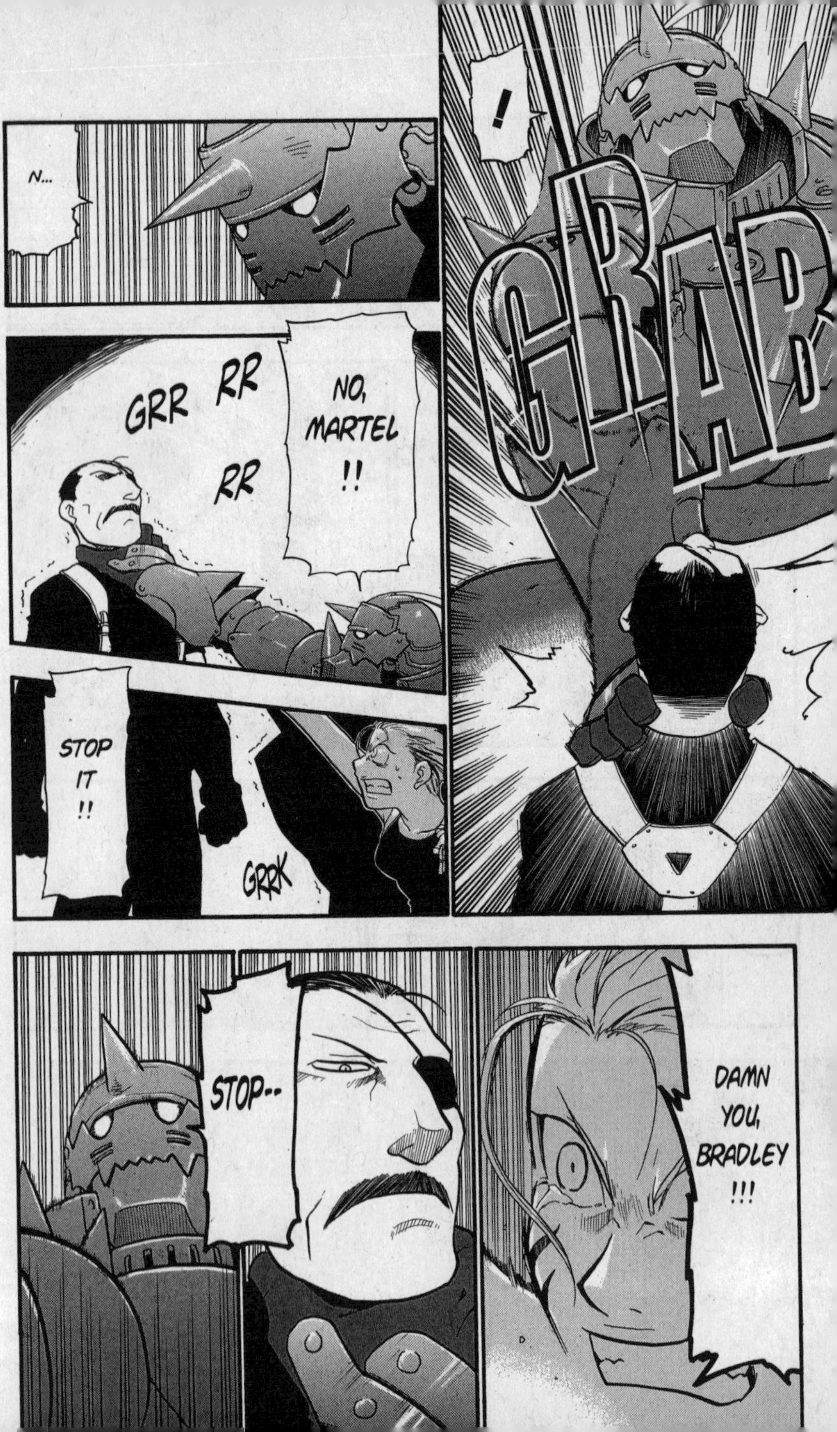
!
GRAB
N...
GRR RR RR
NO, MARTEL !!
STOP IT !!
GRRK
DAMN YOU, BRADLEY !!!
STOP..

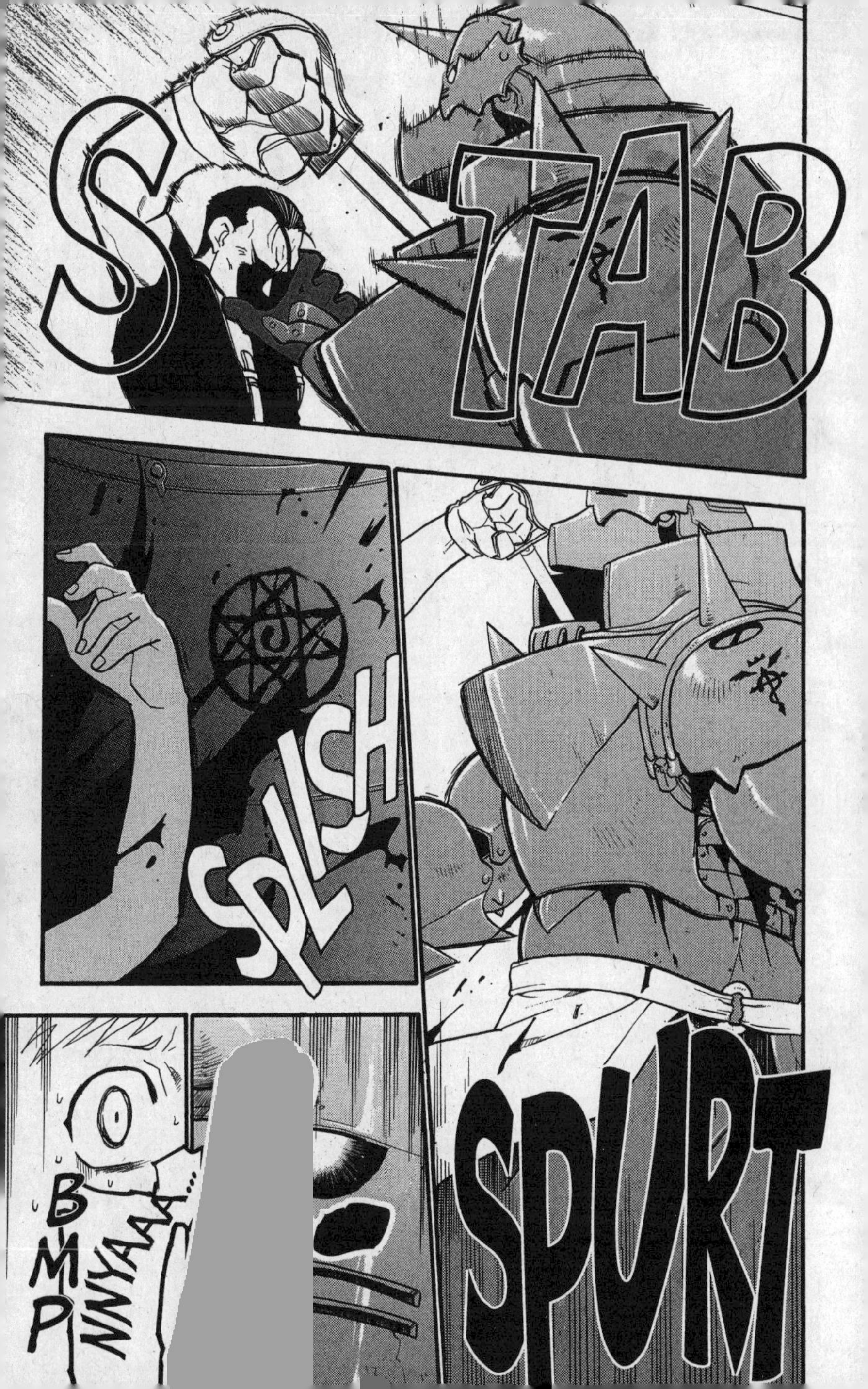
STAB
SPURT
SPLISH
NNYAAA...
BMP

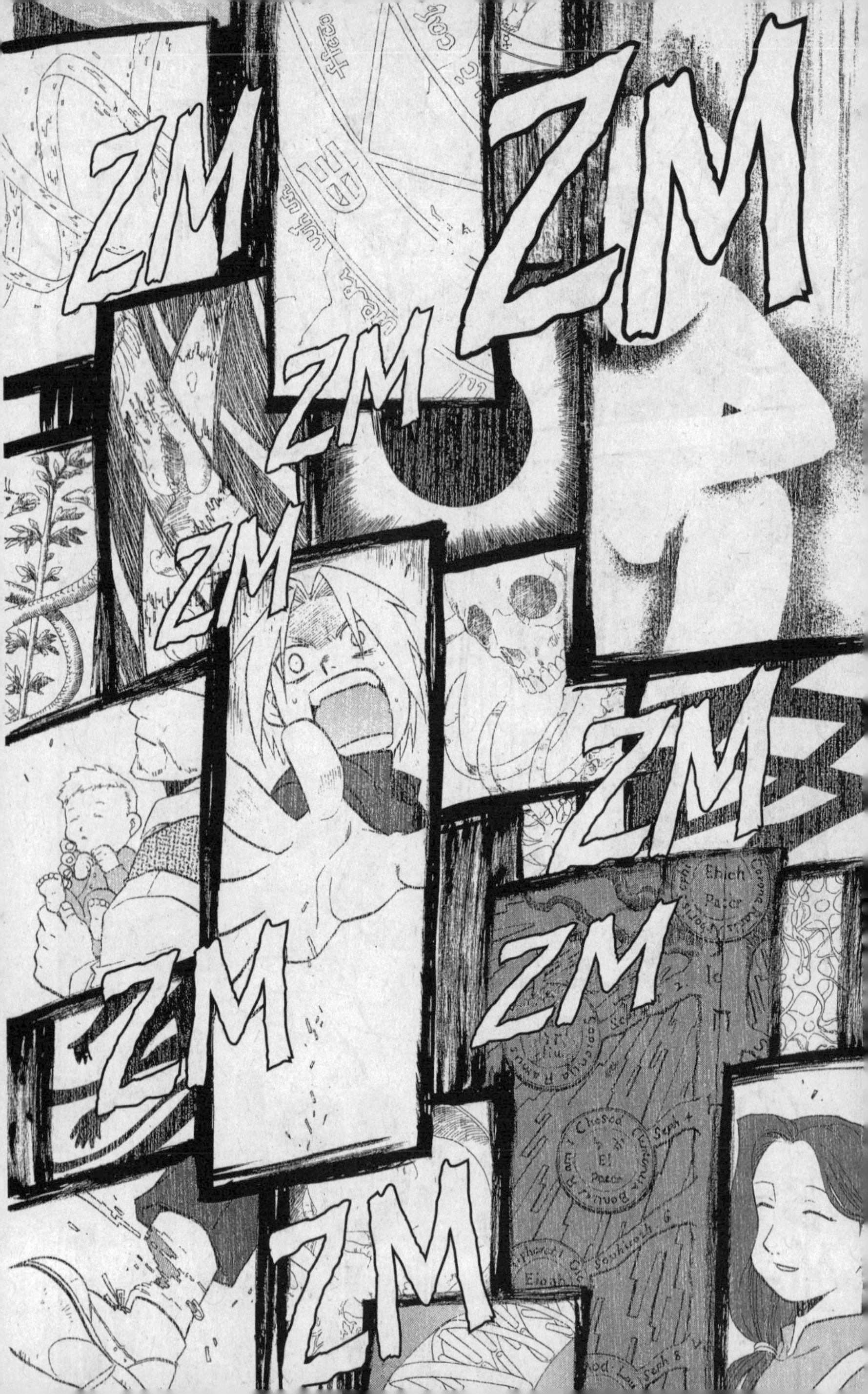
ZM
ZM
ZM
ZM
ZM
ZM
ZM
ZM

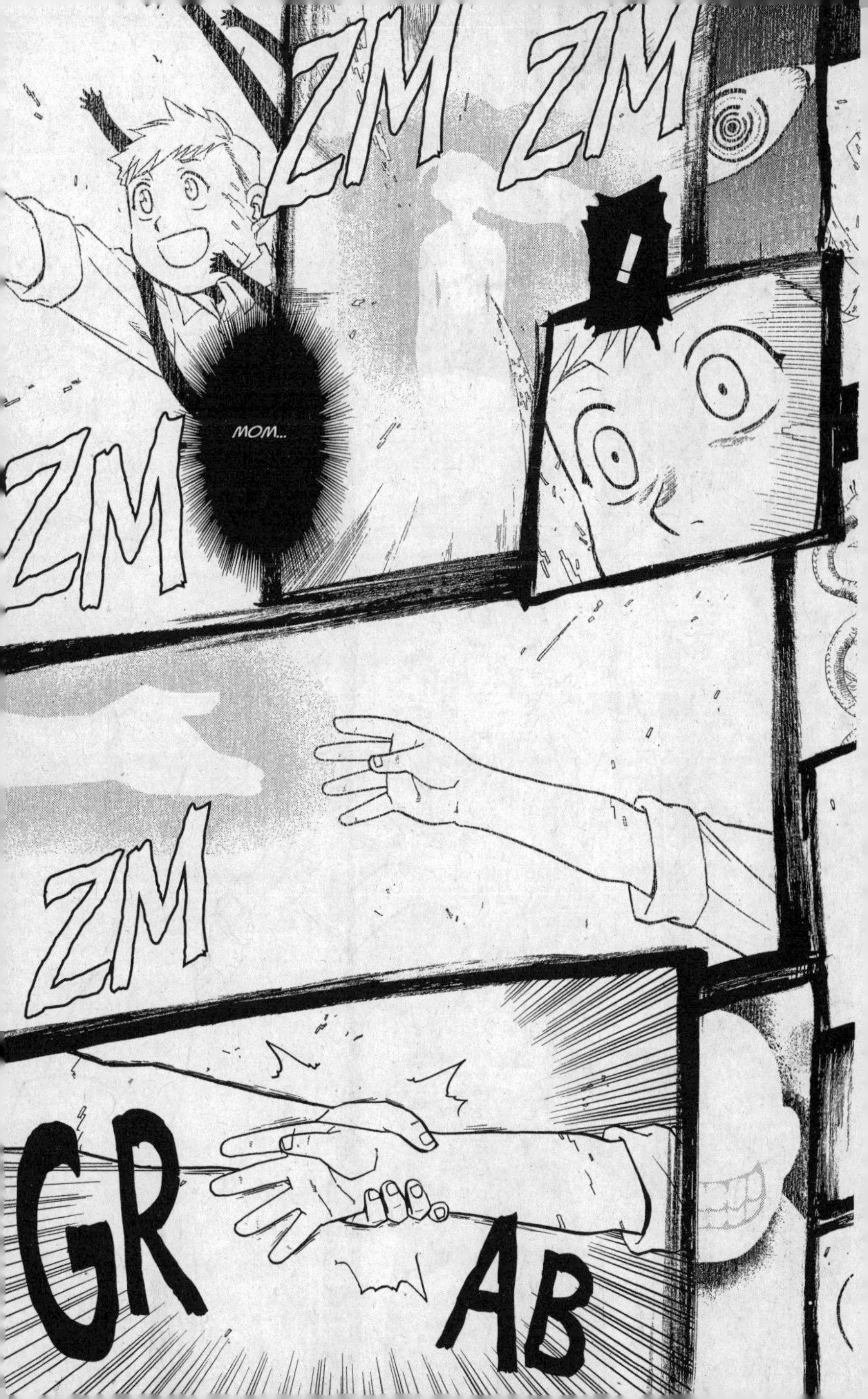
!
ZM ZM
MOM...
ZM
ZM
GR
AB

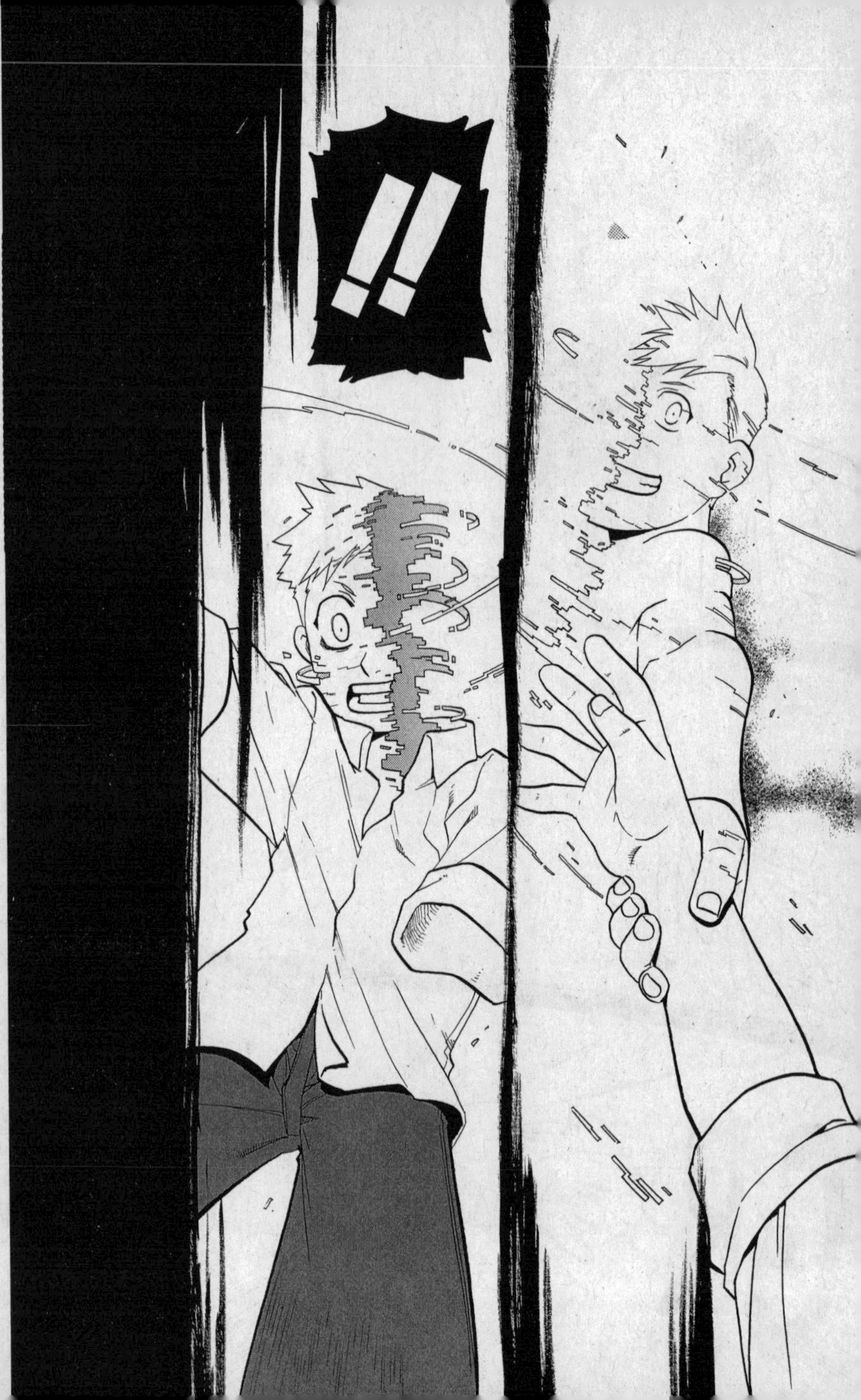
!!

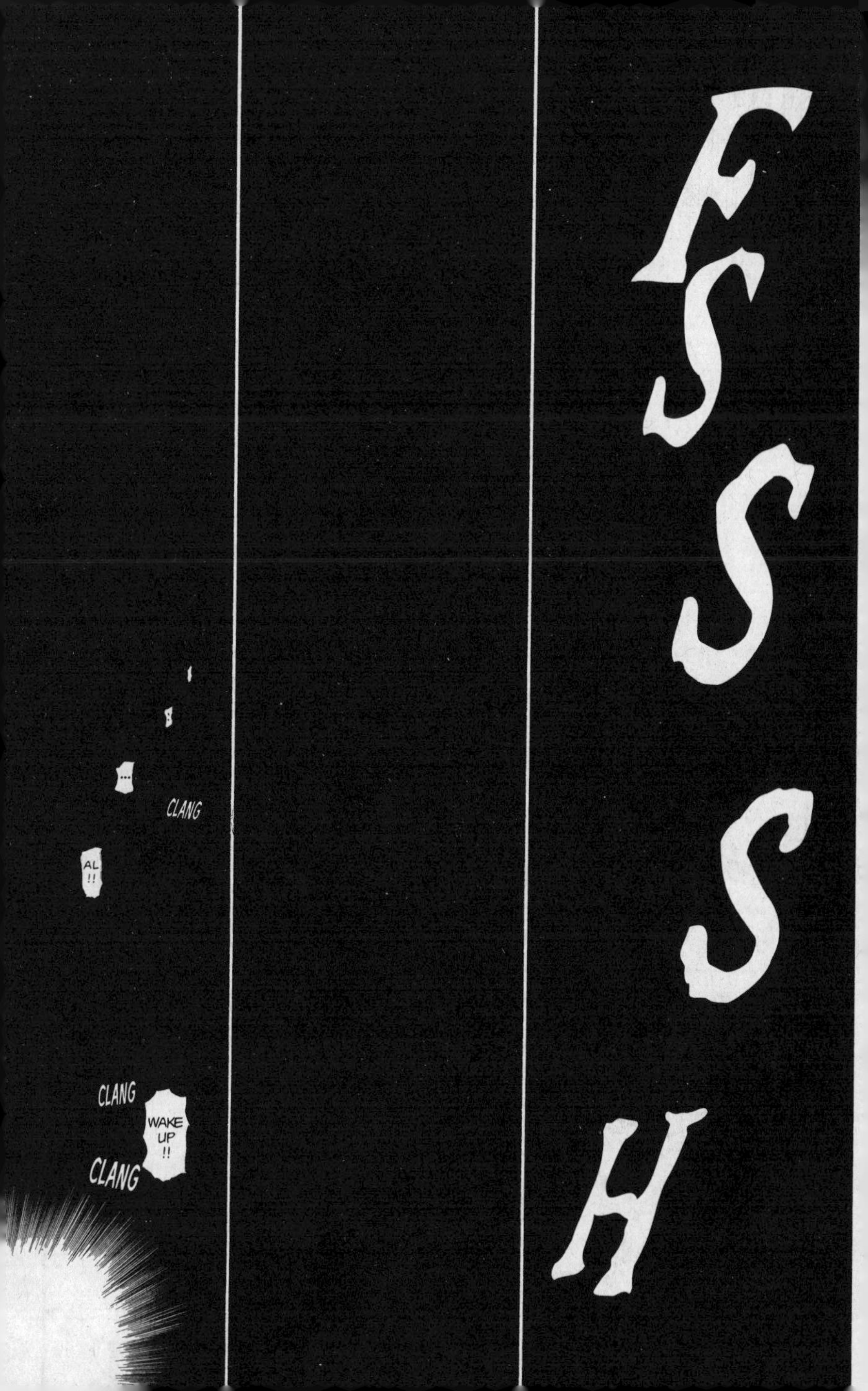
FSSSH
...
CLANG
AL !!
CLANG
WAKE UP !!
CLANG

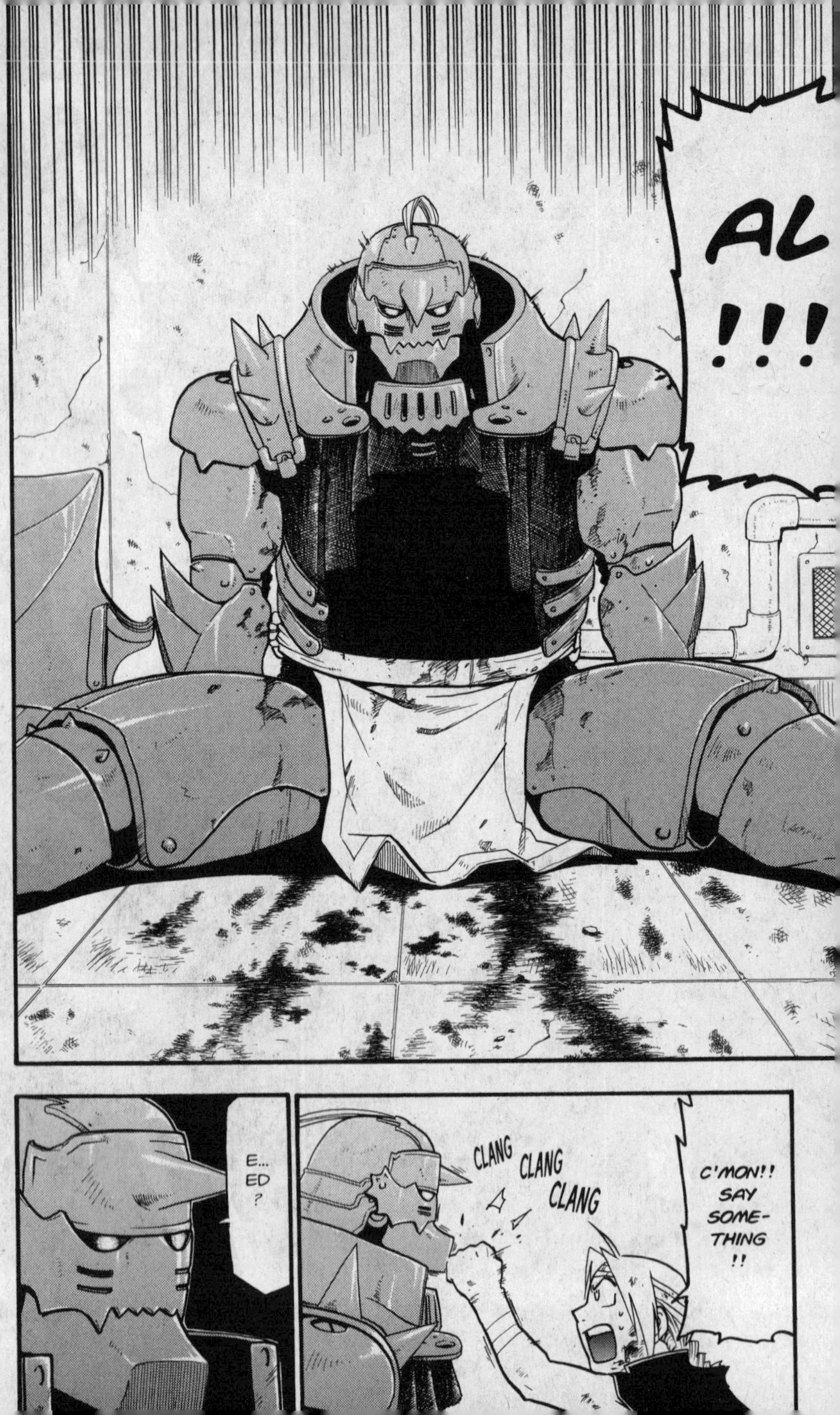
AL !!!
C'MON!! SAY SOME-THING !!
CLANG
CLANG
CLANG
E... ED ?

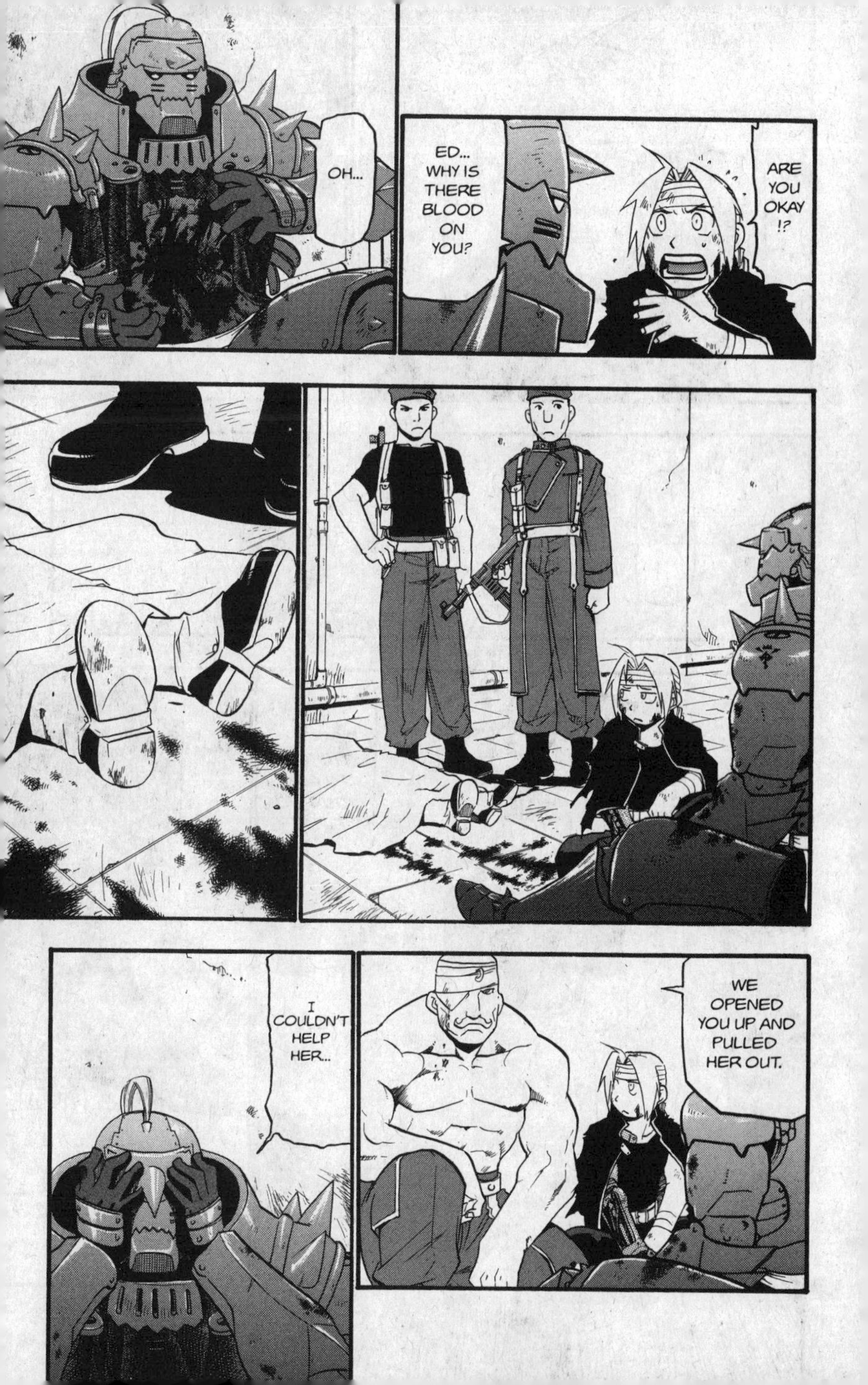
ARE YOU OKAY!?
ED... WHY IS THERE BLOOD ON YOU?
OH...
WE OPENED YOU UP AND PULLED HER OUT.
I COULDN'T HELP HER...

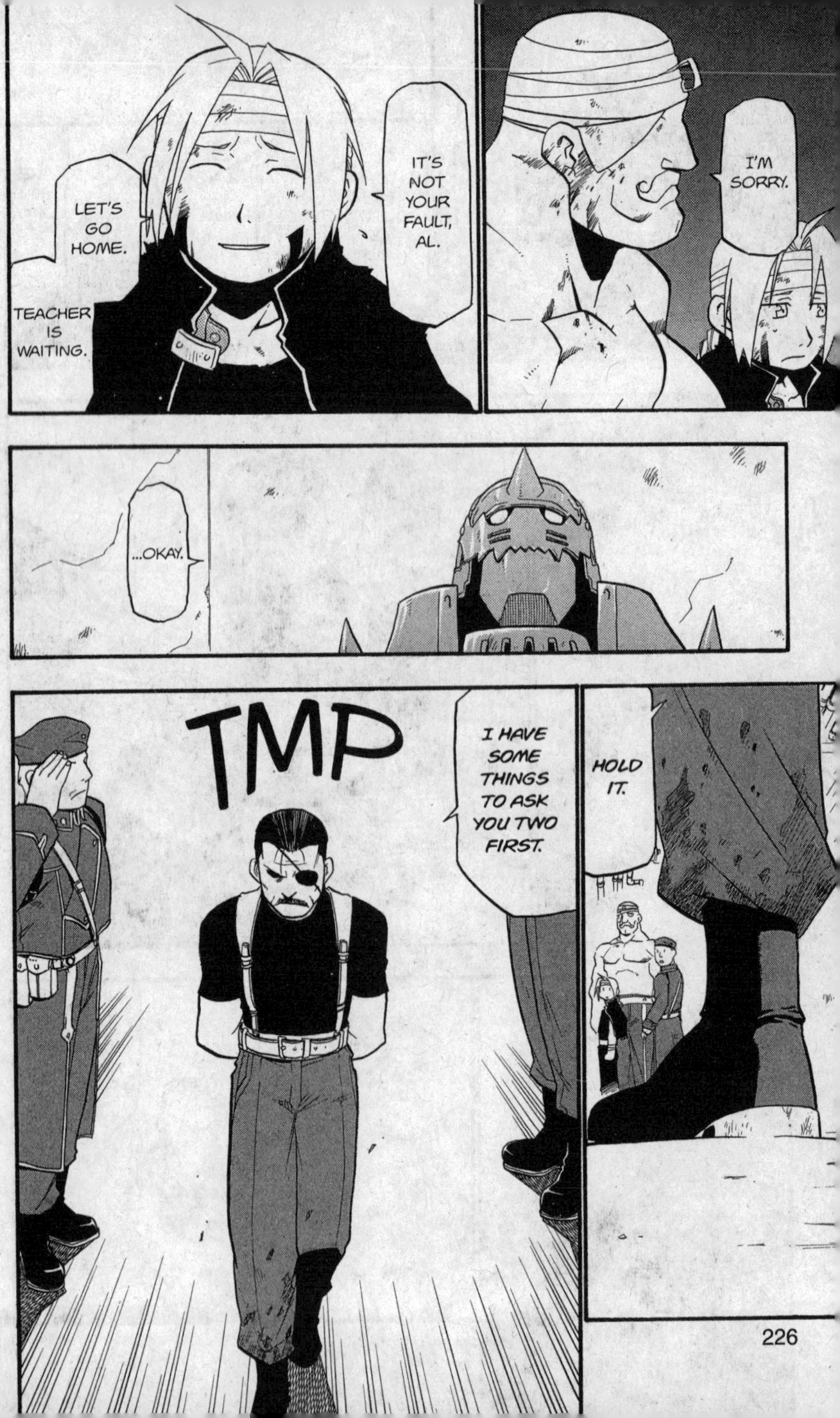
I'M SORRY.
IT'S NOT YOUR FAULT, AL.
LET'S GO HOME.
TEACHER IS WAITING.
...OKAY.
HOLD IT.
I HAVE SOME THINGS TO ASK YOU TWO FIRST.
TMP

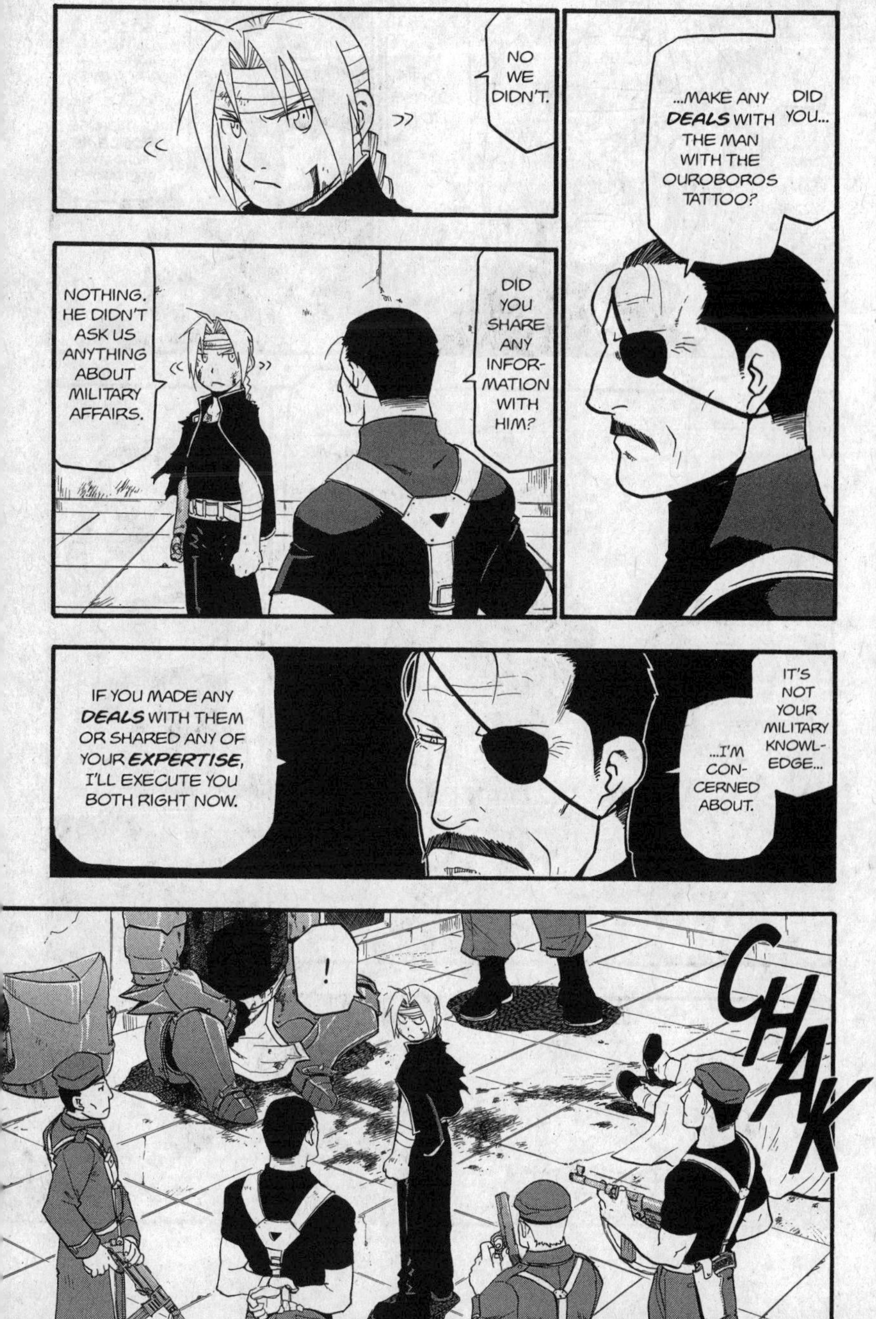
DID YOU...
...MAKE ANY **DEALS** WITH THE MAN WITH THE OUROBOROS TATTOO?
NO WE DIDN'T.
DID YOU SHARE ANY INFORMATION WITH HIM?
NOTHING. HE DIDN'T ASK US ANYTHING ABOUT MILITARY AFFAIRS.
IT'S NOT YOUR MILITARY KNOWLEDGE...
...I'M CONCERNED ABOUT.
IF YOU MADE ANY **DEALS** WITH THEM OR SHARED ANY OF YOUR **EXPERTISE**, I'LL EXECUTE YOU BOTH RIGHT NOW.
!
CHAK

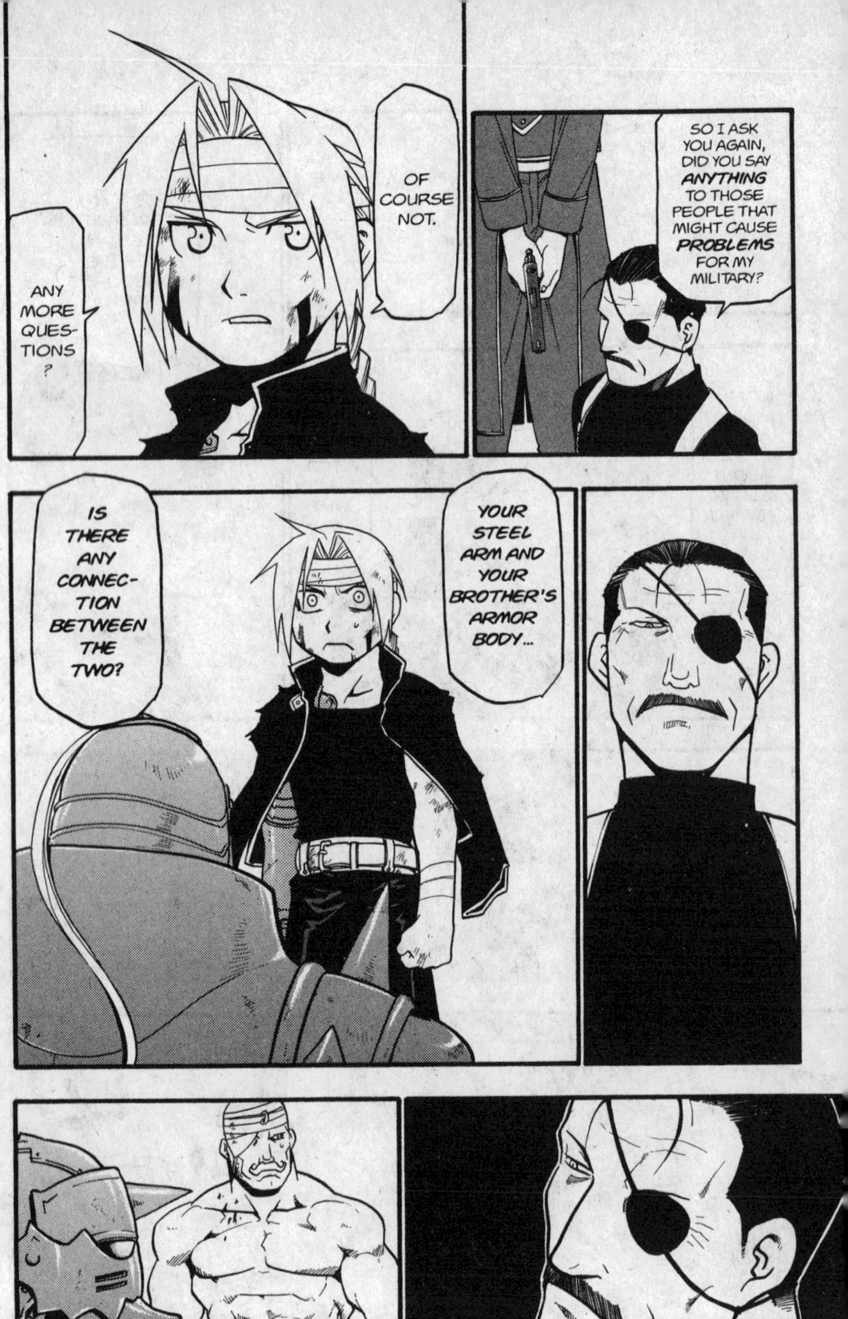
SO I ASK YOU AGAIN, DID YOU SAY ANYTHING TO THOSE PEOPLE THAT MIGHT CAUSE PROBLEMS FOR MY MILITARY?
OF COURSE NOT.
ANY MORE QUESTIONS?
YOUR STEEL ARM AND YOUR BROTHER'S ARMOR BODY...
IS THERE ANY CONNECTION BETWEEN THE TWO?

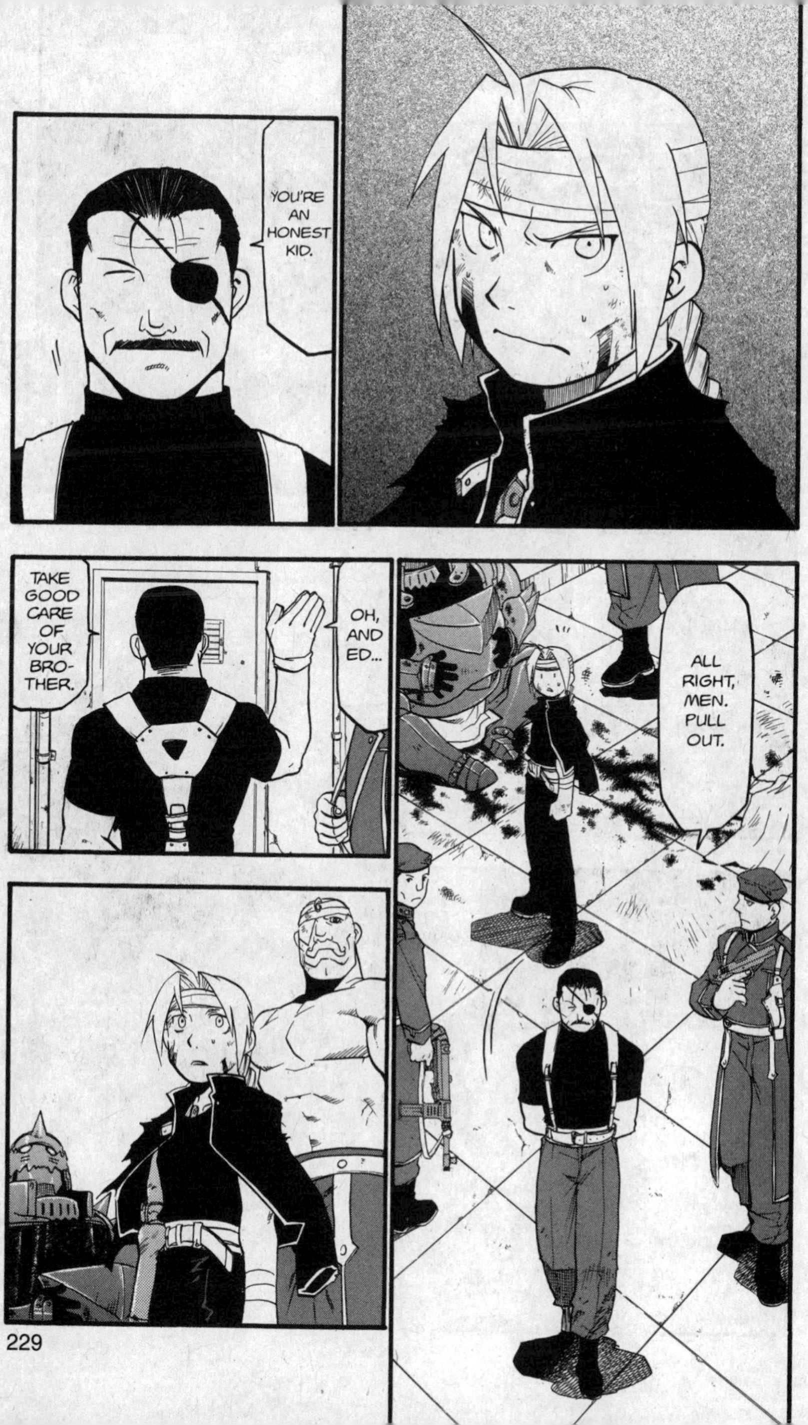
YOU'RE AN HONEST KID.
ALL RIGHT, MEN. PULL OUT.
OH, AND ED...
TAKE GOOD CARE OF YOUR BRO-THER.

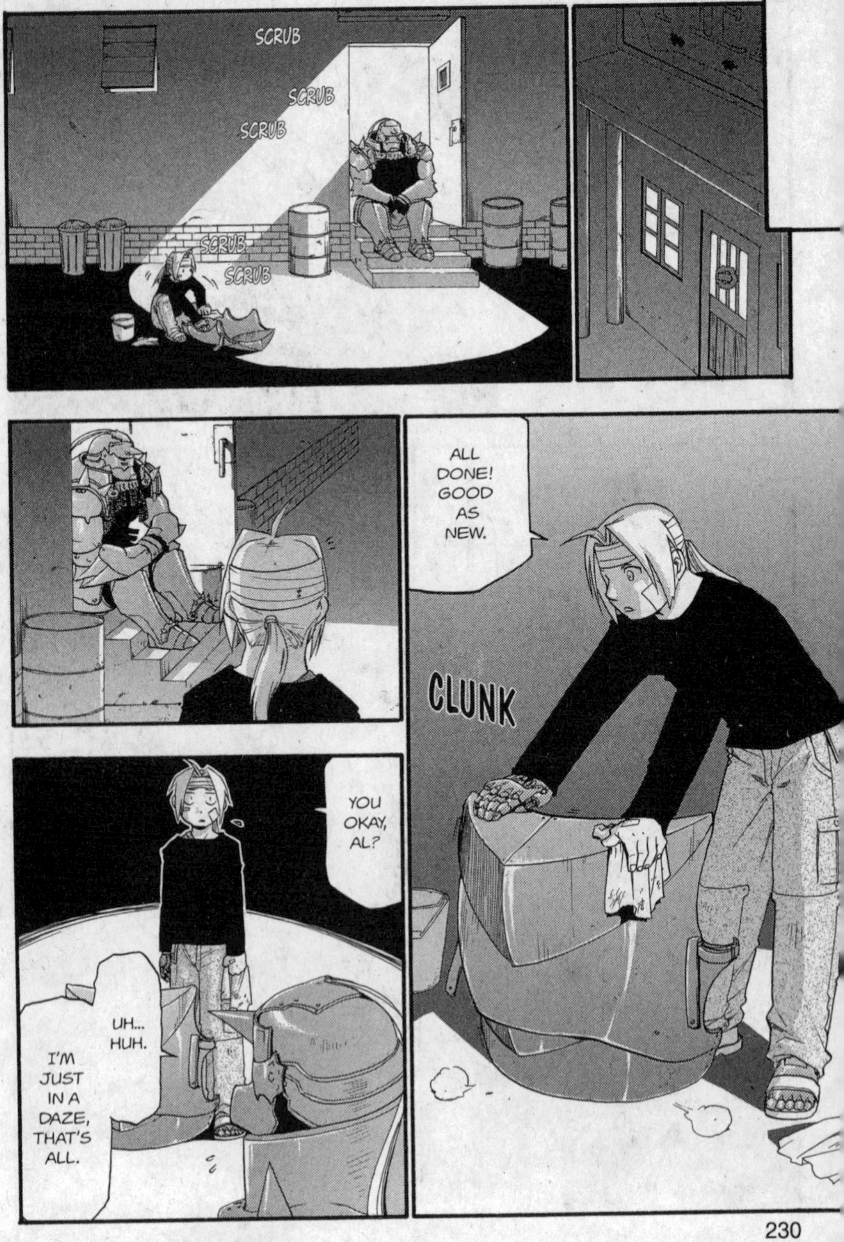
SCRUB
SCRUB
SCRUB
SCRUB
SCRUB
ALL DONE! GOOD AS NEW.
CLUNK
YOU OKAY, AL?
UH... HUH.
I'M JUST IN A DAZE, THAT'S ALL.

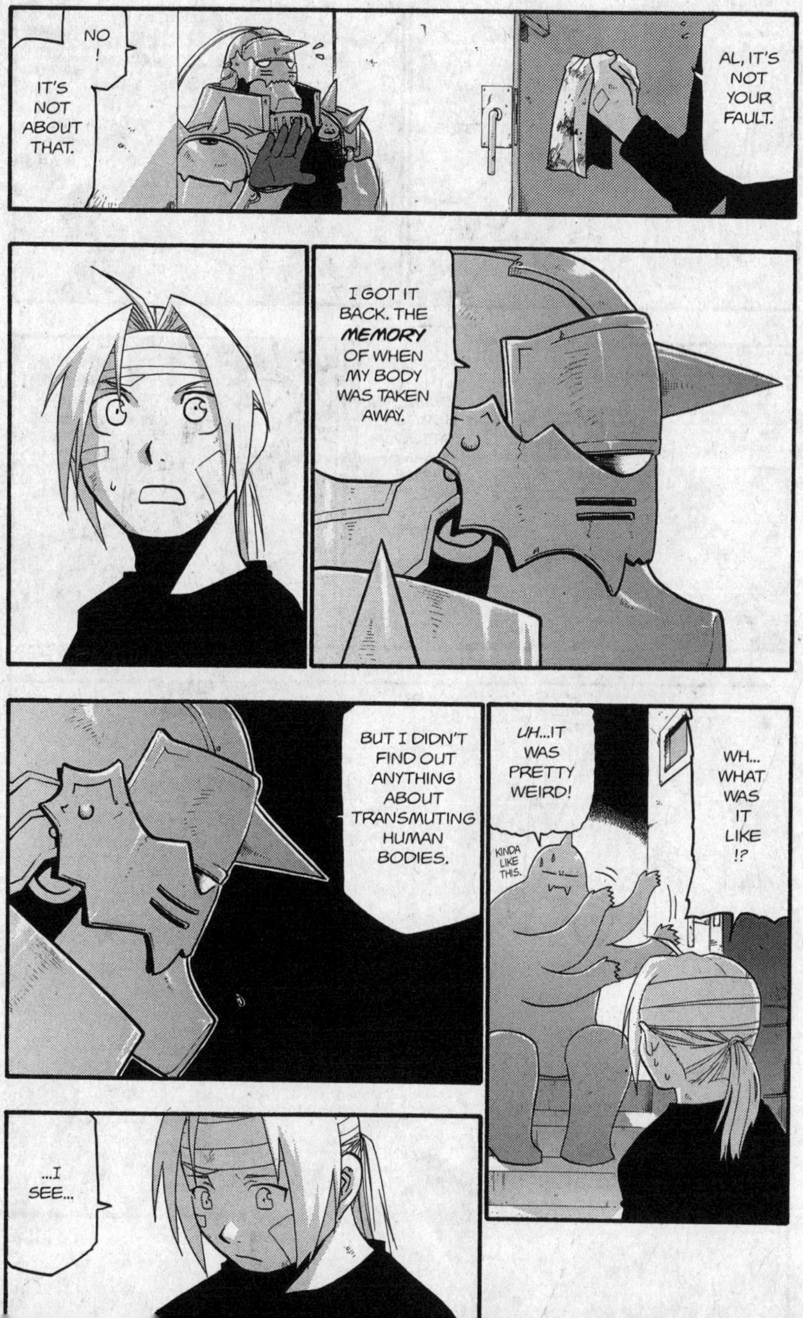
AL, IT'S NOT YOUR FAULT.
NO! IT'S NOT ABOUT THAT.
I GOT IT BACK. THE MEMORY OF WHEN MY BODY WAS TAKEN AWAY.
WH... WHAT WAS IT LIKE !?
UH...IT WAS PRETTY WEIRD!
KINDA LIKE THIS.
BUT I DIDN'T FIND OUT ANYTHING ABOUT TRANSMUTING HUMAN BODIES.
...I SEE...

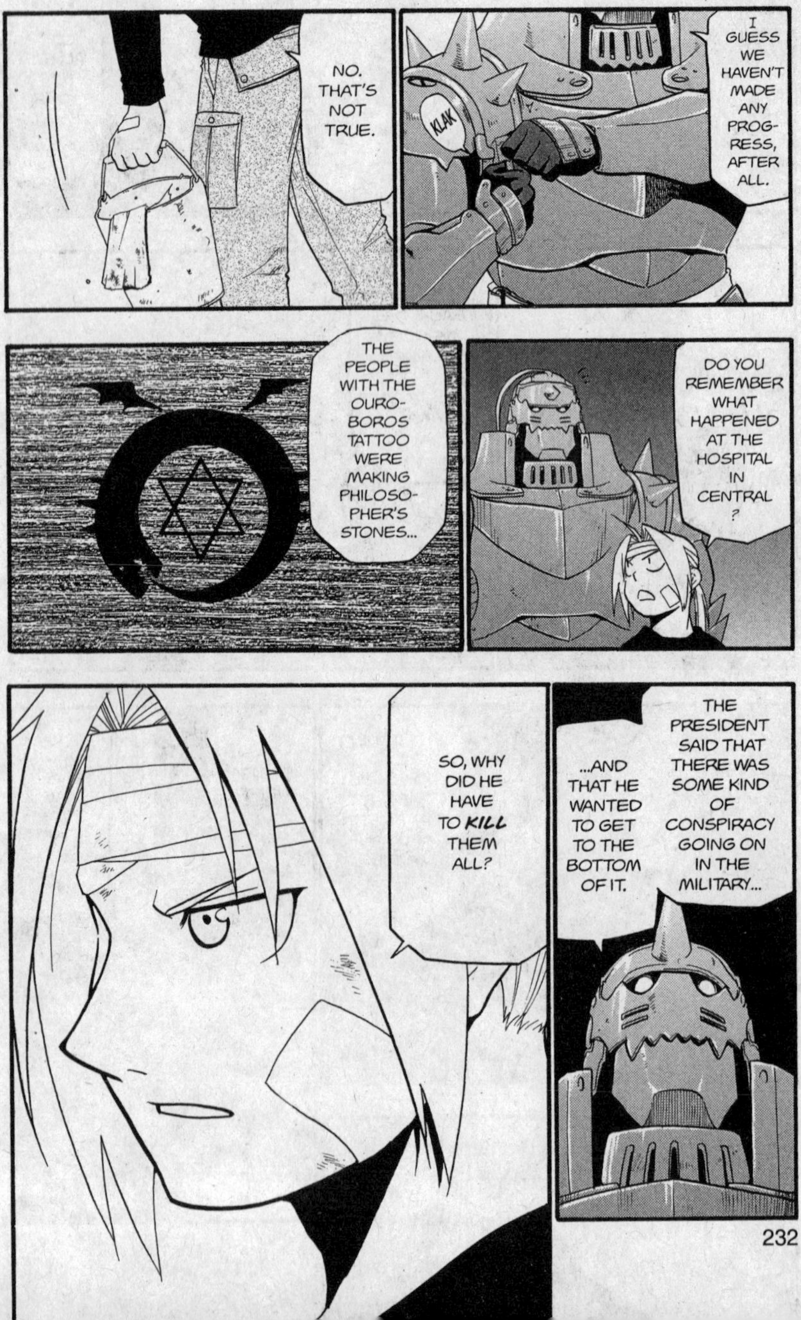
I GUESS WE HAVEN'T MADE ANY PROG-RESS, AFTER ALL.
KLAK
NO. THAT'S NOT TRUE.
DO YOU REMEMBER WHAT HAPPENED AT THE HOSPITAL IN CENTRAL ?
THE PEOPLE WITH THE OURO-BOROS TATTOO WERE MAKING PHILOSO-PHER'S STONES...
THE PRESIDENT SAID THAT THERE WAS SOME KIND OF CONSPIRACY GOING ON IN THE MILITARY...
...AND THAT HE WANTED TO GET TO THE BOTTOM OF IT.
SO, WHY DID HE HAVE TO KILL THEM ALL?

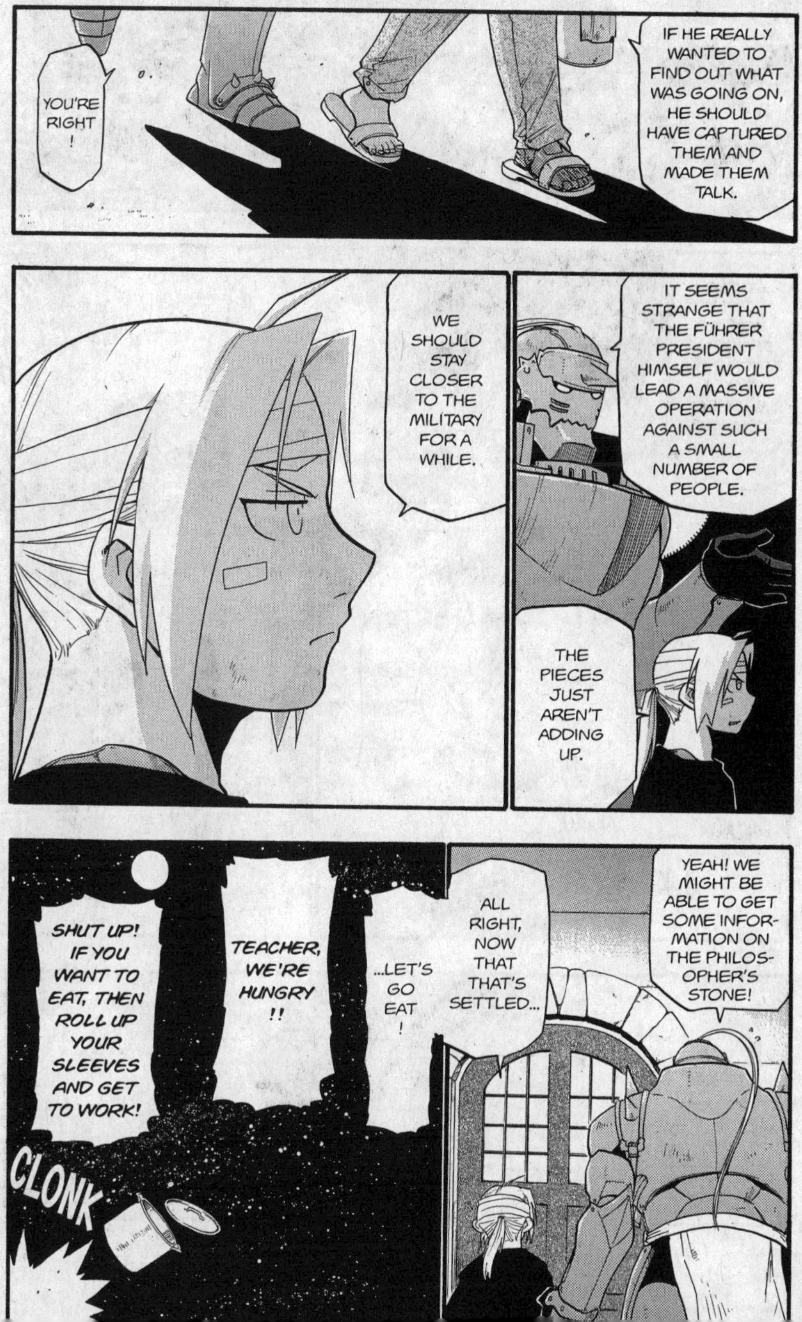
IF HE REALLY WANTED TO FIND OUT WHAT WAS GOING ON, HE SHOULD HAVE CAPTURED THEM AND MADE THEM TALK.
YOU'RE RIGHT!
IT SEEMS STRANGE THAT THE FÜHRER PRESIDENT HIMSELF WOULD LEAD A MASSIVE OPERATION AGAINST SUCH A SMALL NUMBER OF PEOPLE.
THE PIECES JUST AREN'T ADDING UP.
WE SHOULD STAY CLOSER TO THE MILITARY FOR A WHILE.
YEAH! WE MIGHT BE ABLE TO GET SOME INFORMATION ON THE PHILOSOPHER'S STONE!
ALL RIGHT, NOW THAT THAT'S SETTLED...
...LET'S GO EAT!
TEACHER, WE'RE HUNGRY!!
SHUT UP! IF YOU WANT TO EAT, THEN ROLL UP YOUR SLEEVES AND GET TO WORK!
CLONK

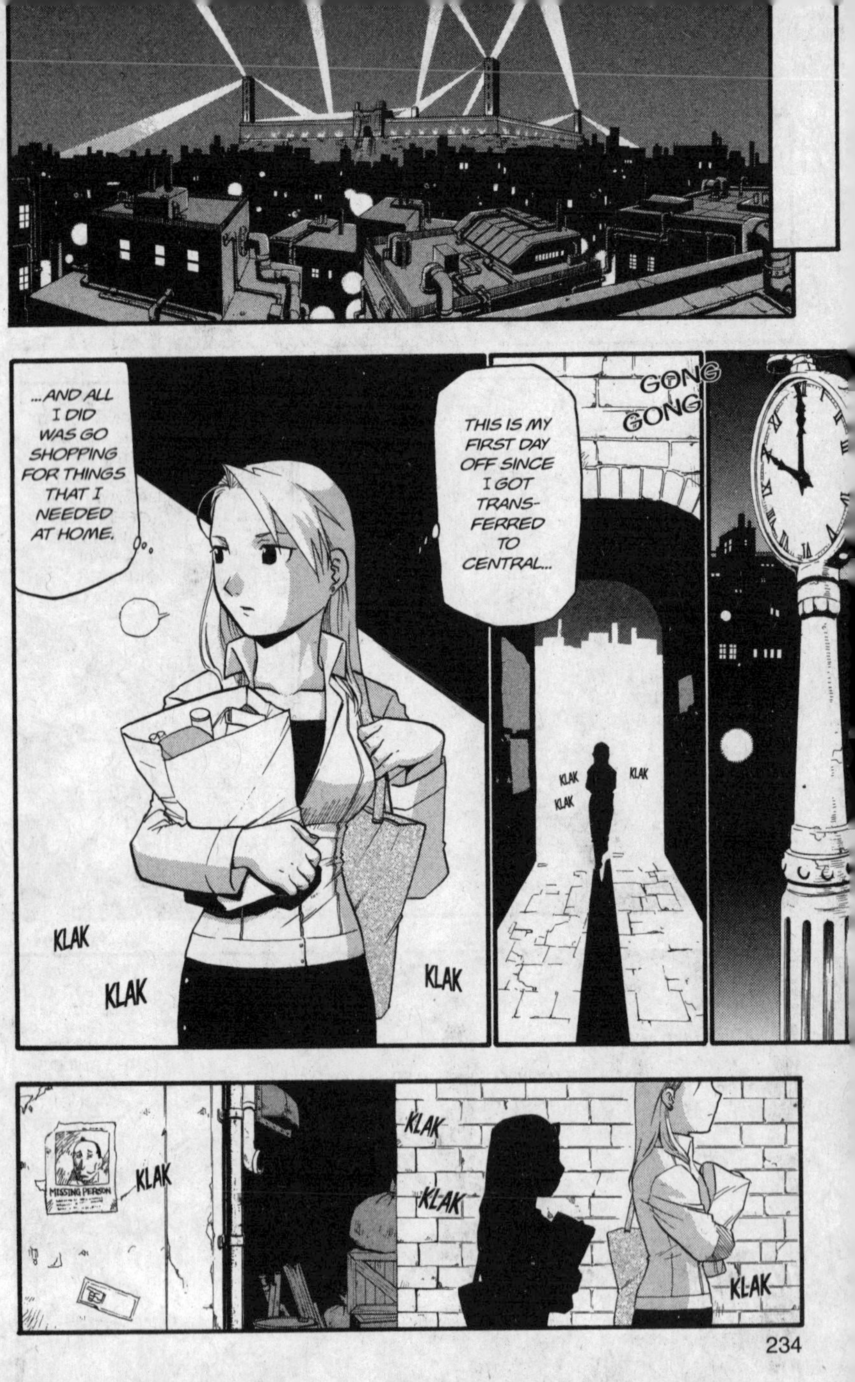
GONG
GONG
THIS IS MY FIRST DAY OFF SINCE I GOT TRANS-FERRED TO CENTRAL...
KLAK
KLAK
KLAK
...AND ALL I DID WAS GO SHOPPING FOR THINGS THAT I NEEDED AT HOME.
KLAK
KLAK
KLAK
KL-AK
KLAK
KL-AK
MISSING PERSON
KLAK

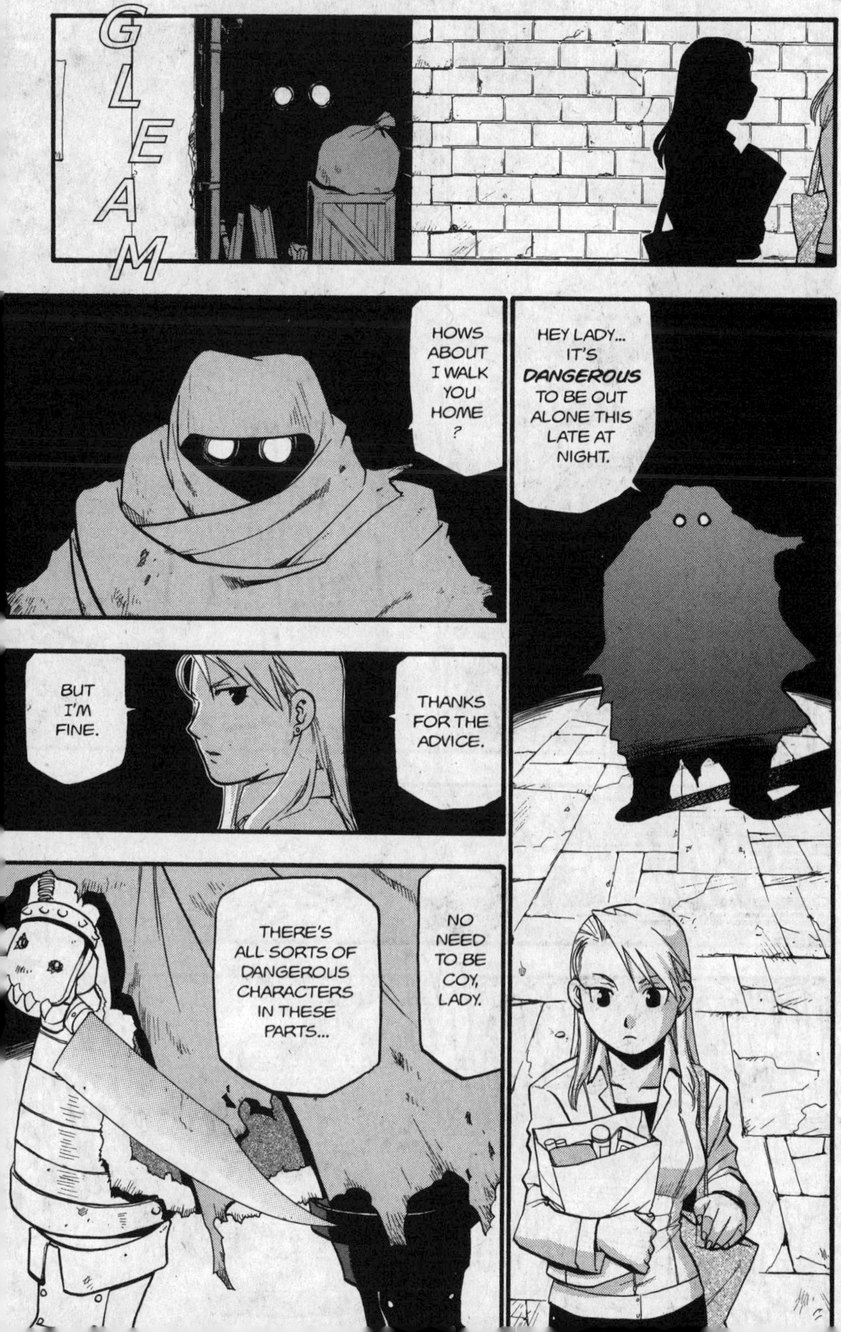
GLEAM
HEY LADY... IT'S DANGEROUS TO BE OUT ALONE THIS LATE AT NIGHT.
HOWS ABOUT I WALK YOU HOME?
THANKS FOR THE ADVICE.
BUT I'M FINE.
NO NEED TO BE COY, LADY.
THERE'S ALL SORTS OF DANGEROUS CHARACTERS IN THESE PARTS...

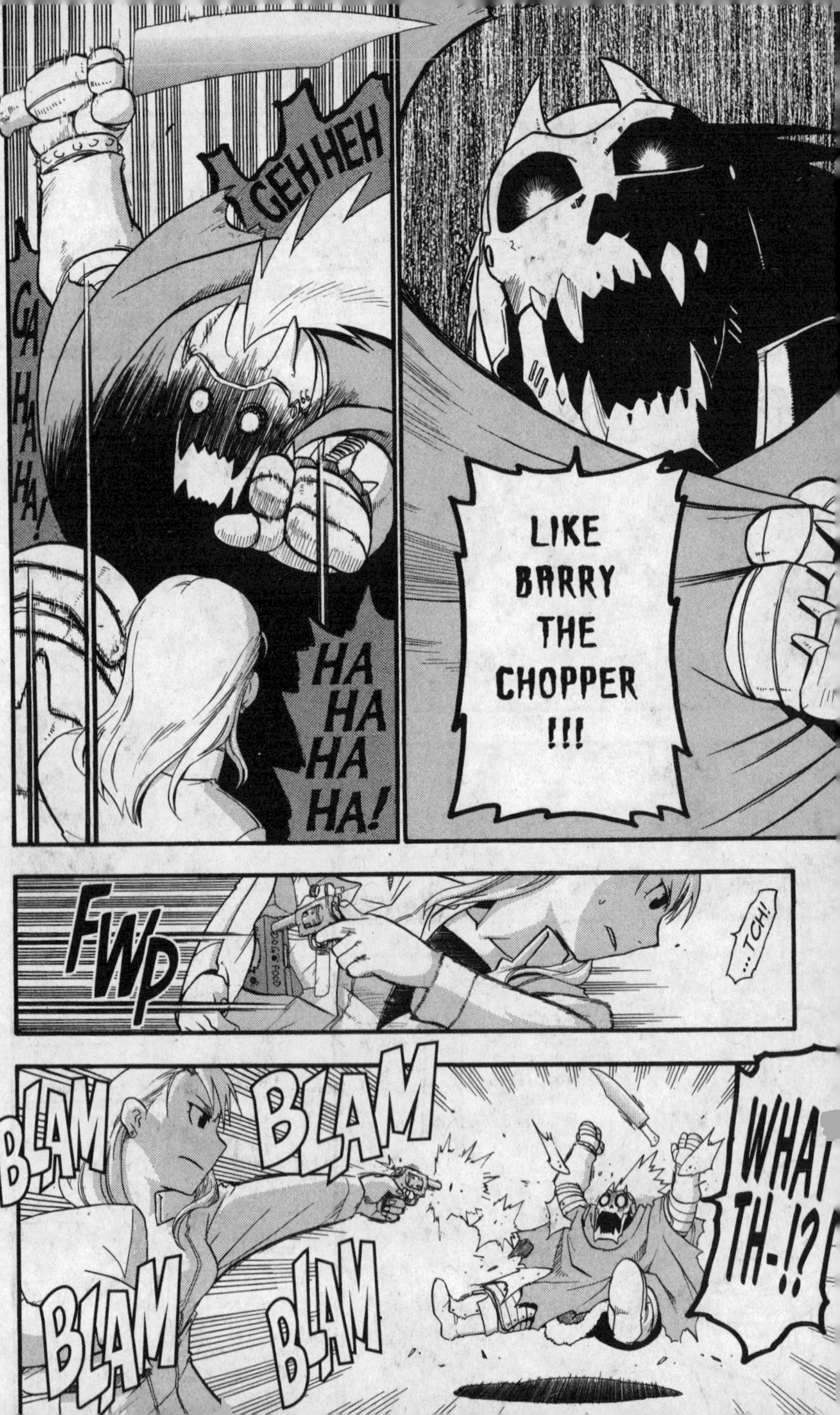
LIKE BARRY THE CHOPPER !!!
GEHHEH
GAHAHAHA!
HAHAHAHA!
...TCH!
FWP
WHAT TH-!?
BLAM
BLAM
BLAM
BLAM

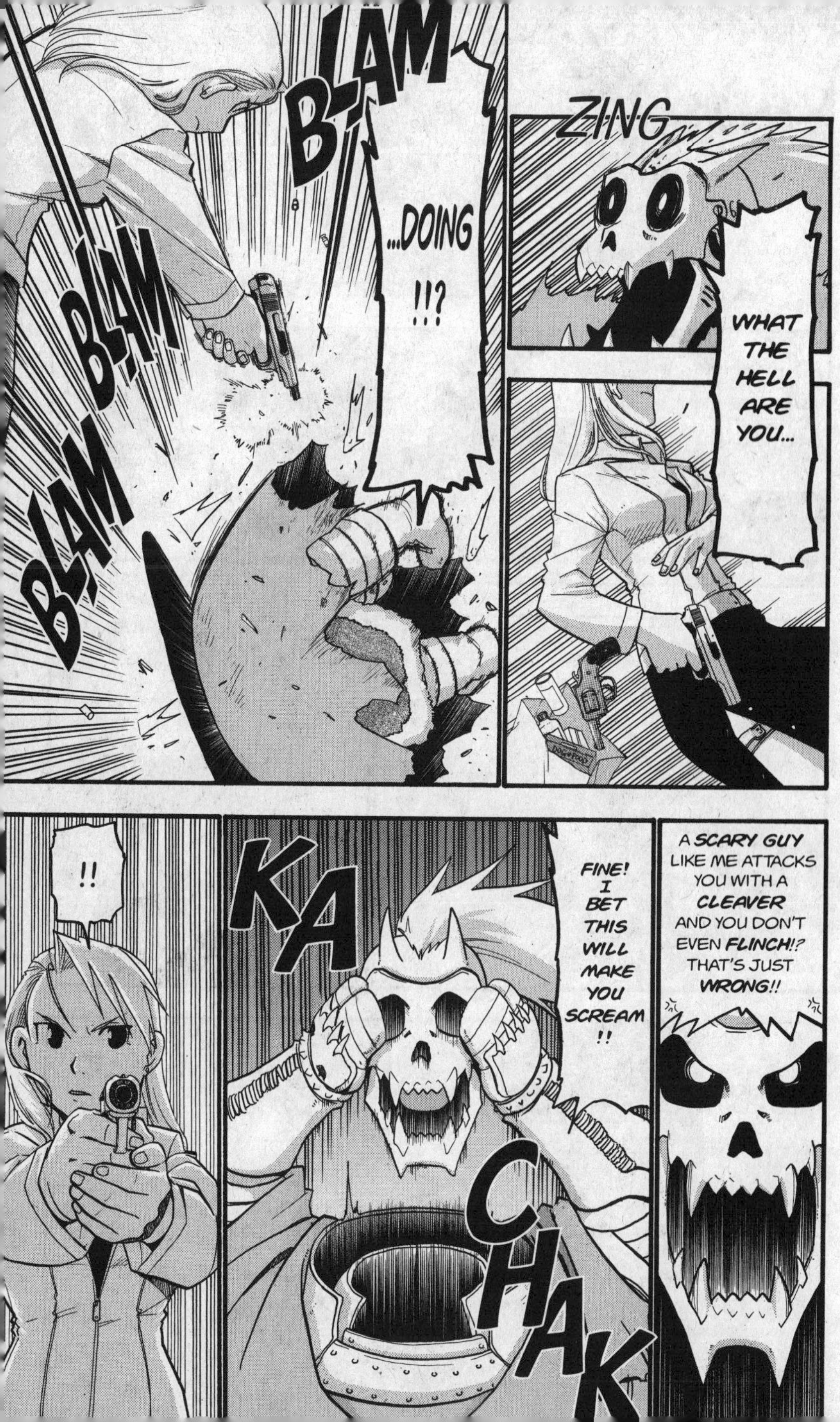
ZING
WHAT THE HELL ARE YOU...
BLAM
...DOING !!?
BLAM
BLAM
BLAM
A SCARY GUY LIKE ME ATTACKS YOU WITH A CLEAVER AND YOU DON'T EVEN FLINCH!? THAT'S JUST WRONG!!
FINE! I BET THIS WILL MAKE YOU SCREAM!!
KA
CHAK
!!

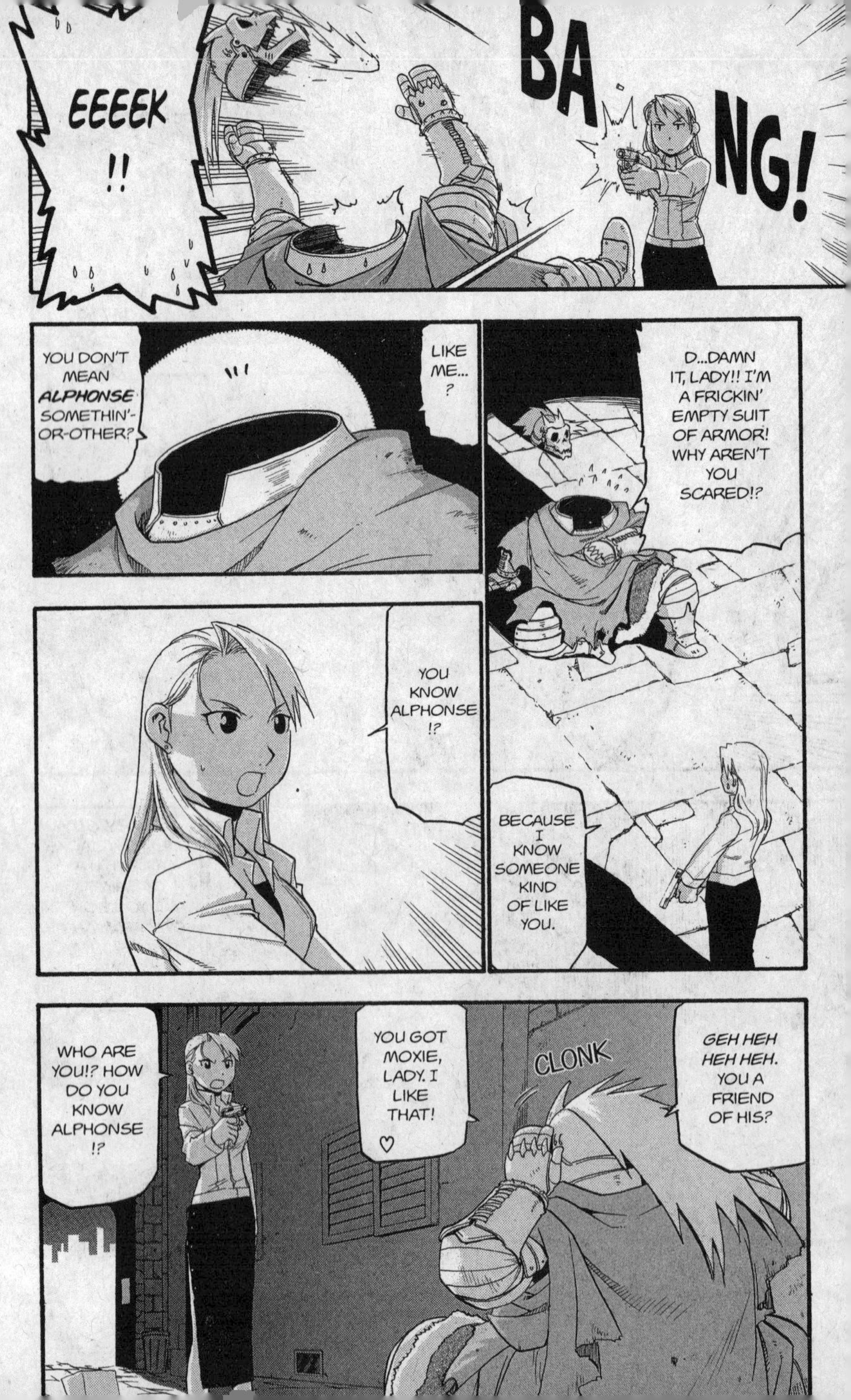
BA NG!
EEEEK !!
D...DAMN IT, LADY!! I'M A FRICKIN' EMPTY SUIT OF ARMOR! WHY AREN'T YOU SCARED!?
BECAUSE I KNOW SOMEONE KIND OF LIKE YOU.
LIKE ME...?
YOU DON'T MEAN ALPHONSE SOMETHIN'-OR-OTHER?
YOU KNOW ALPHONSE!?
GEH HEH HEH HEH. YOU A FRIEND OF HIS?
CLONK
YOU GOT MOXIE, LADY. I LIKE THAT! ♡
WHO ARE YOU!? HOW DO YOU KNOW ALPHONSE!?

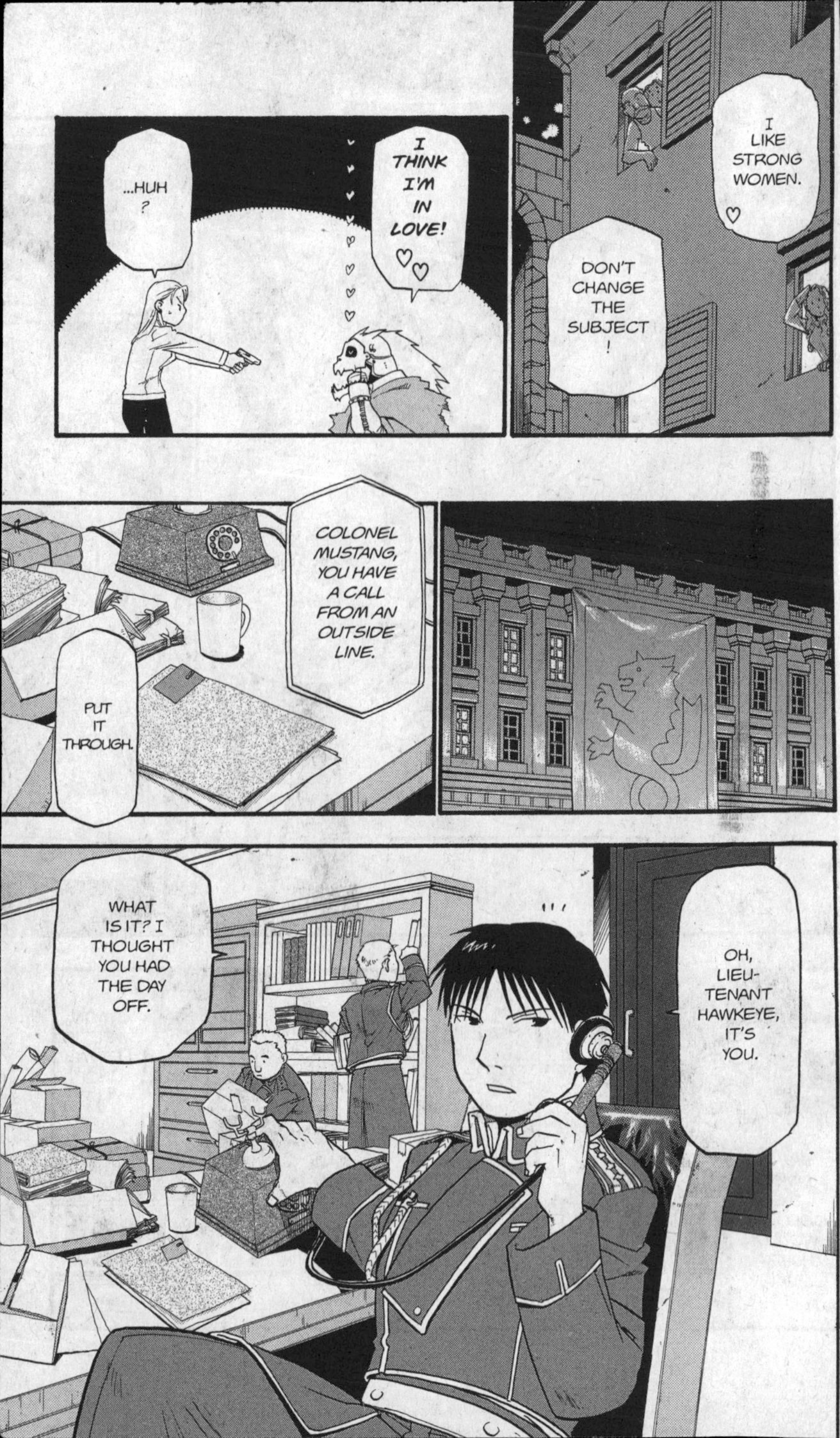
I LIKE STRONG WOMEN. ♡
DON'T CHANGE THE SUBJECT!
I THINK I'M IN LOVE! ♡♡
...HUH?
COLONEL MUSTANG, YOU HAVE A CALL FROM AN OUTSIDE LINE.
PUT IT THROUGH.
OH, LIEUTENANT HAWKEYE, IT'S YOU.
WHAT IS IT? I THOUGHT YOU HAD THE DAY OFF.

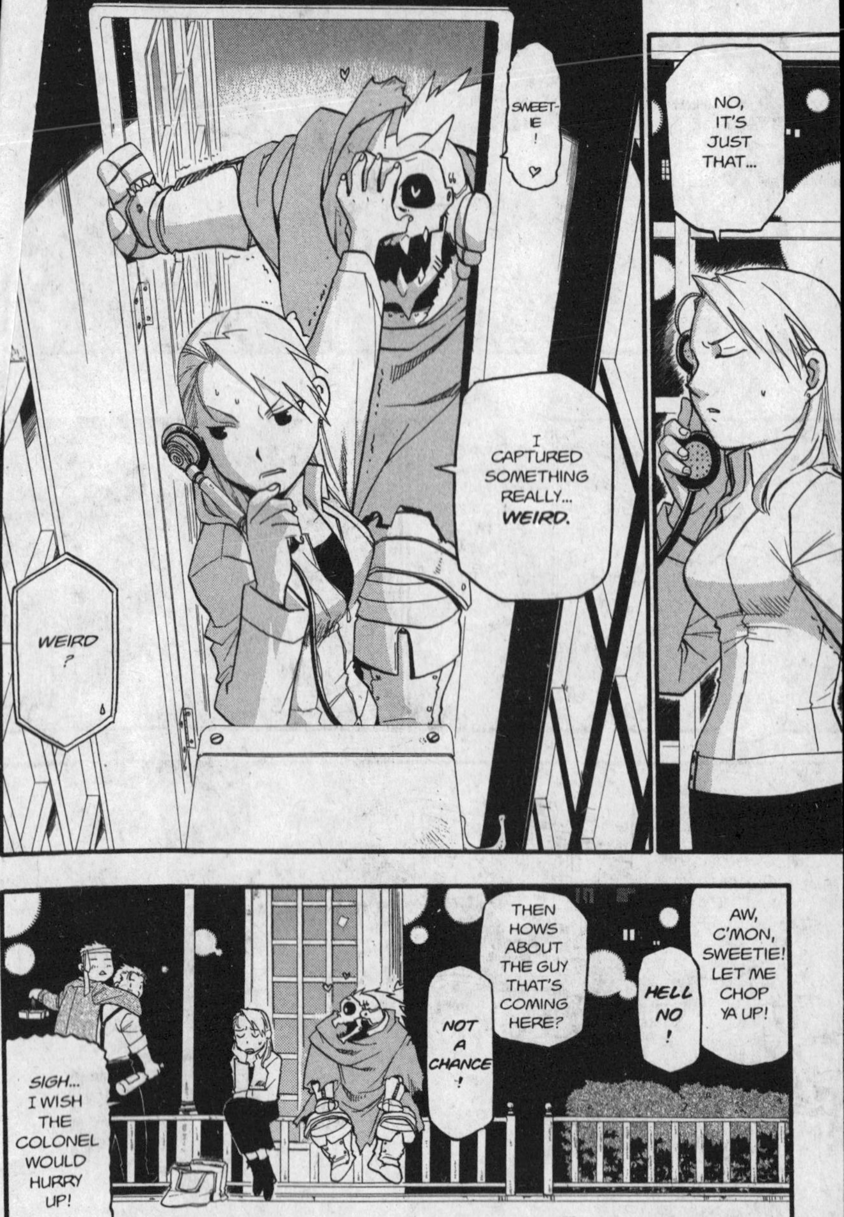
NO, IT'S JUST THAT...
SWEET-IE! ♥
I CAPTURED SOMETHING REALLY... WEIRD.
WEIRD?
AW, C'MON, SWEETIE! LET ME CHOP YA UP!
HELL NO!
THEN HOWS ABOUT THE GUY THAT'S COMING HERE?
NOT A CHANCE!
SIGH... I WISH THE COLONEL WOULD HURRY UP!

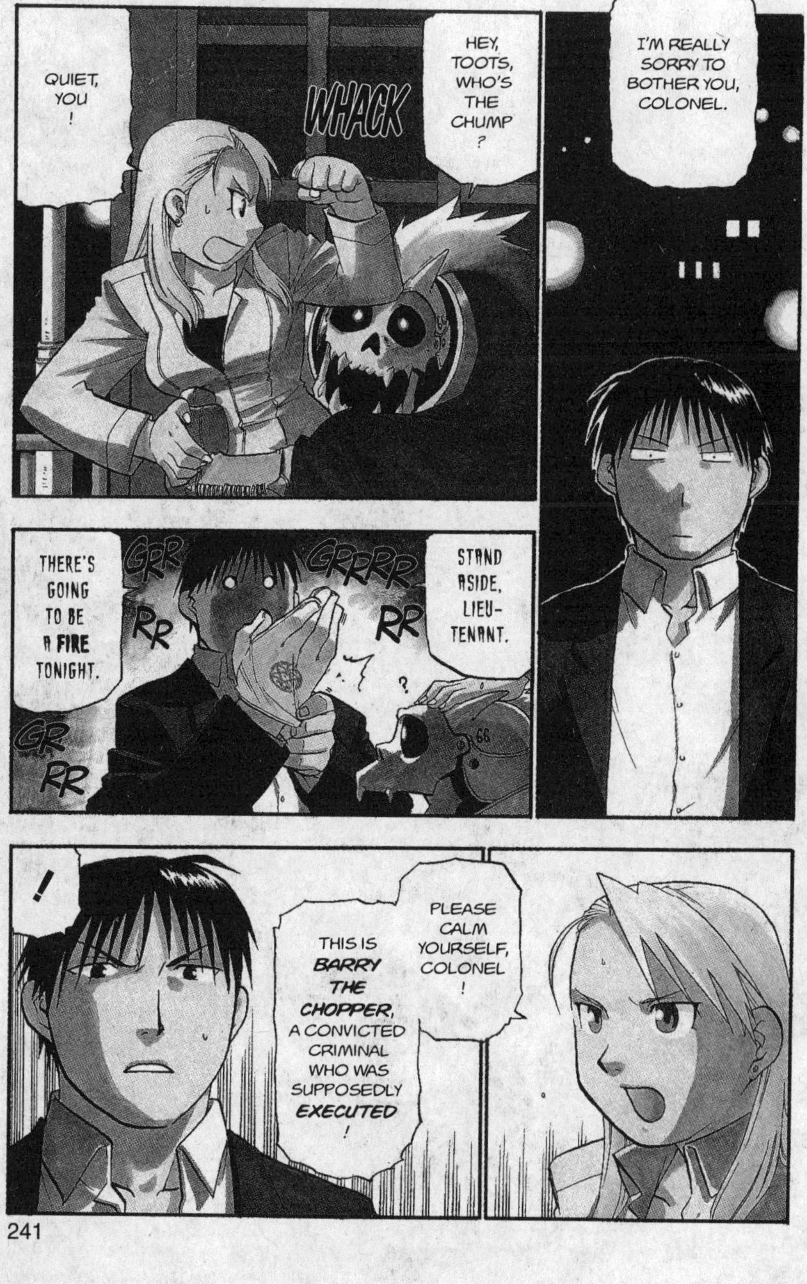
I'M REALLY SORRY TO BOTHER YOU, COLONEL.
HEY, TOOTS, WHO'S THE CHUMP?
WHACK
QUIET, YOU!
STAND ASIDE, LIEUTENANT.
GRRRR RR
GRR RR
THERE'S GOING TO BE A FIRE TONIGHT.
GR RR
PLEASE CALM YOURSELF, COLONEL!
THIS IS BARRY THE CHOPPER, A CONVICTED CRIMINAL WHO WAS SUPPOSEDLY EXECUTED!
!

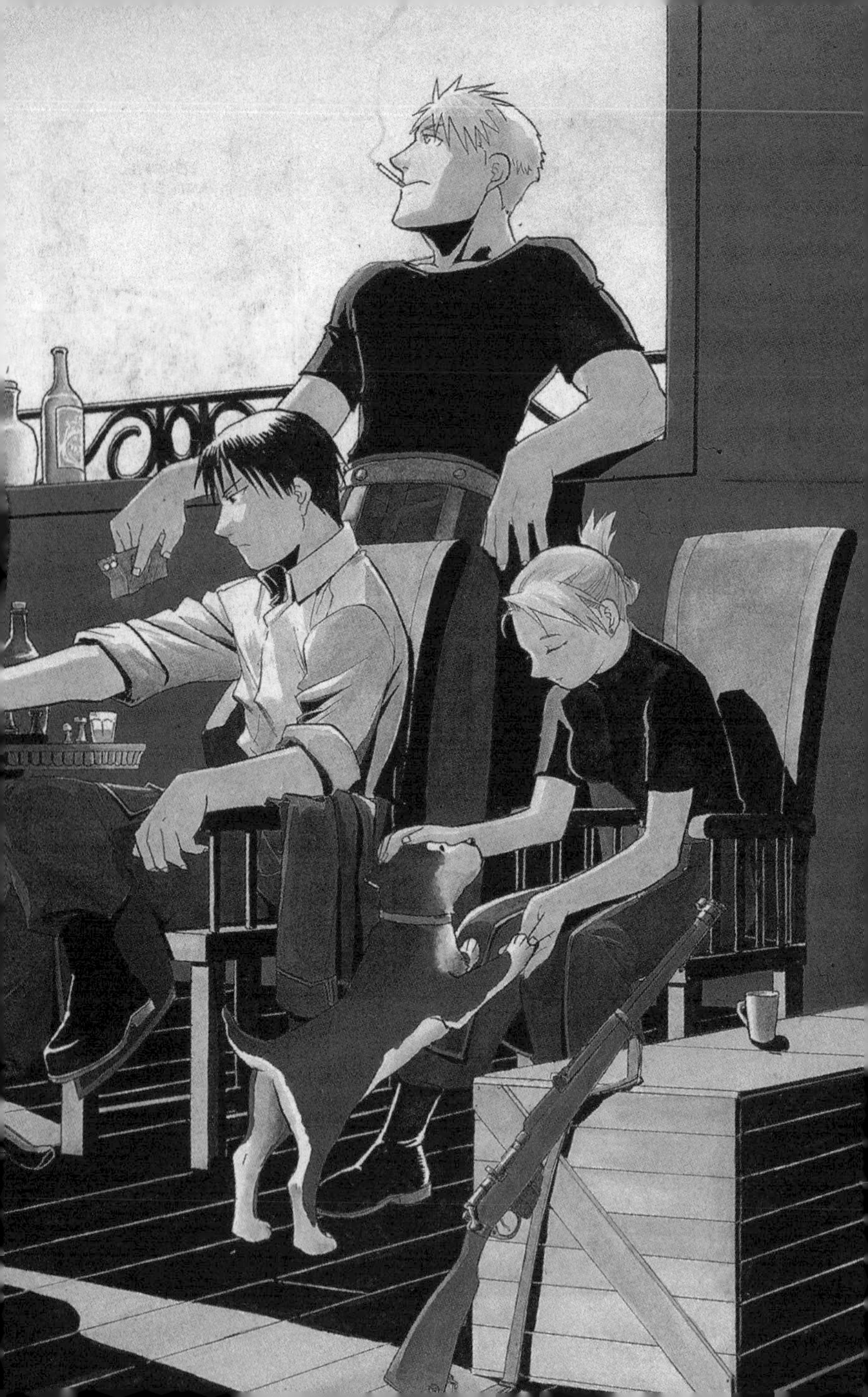

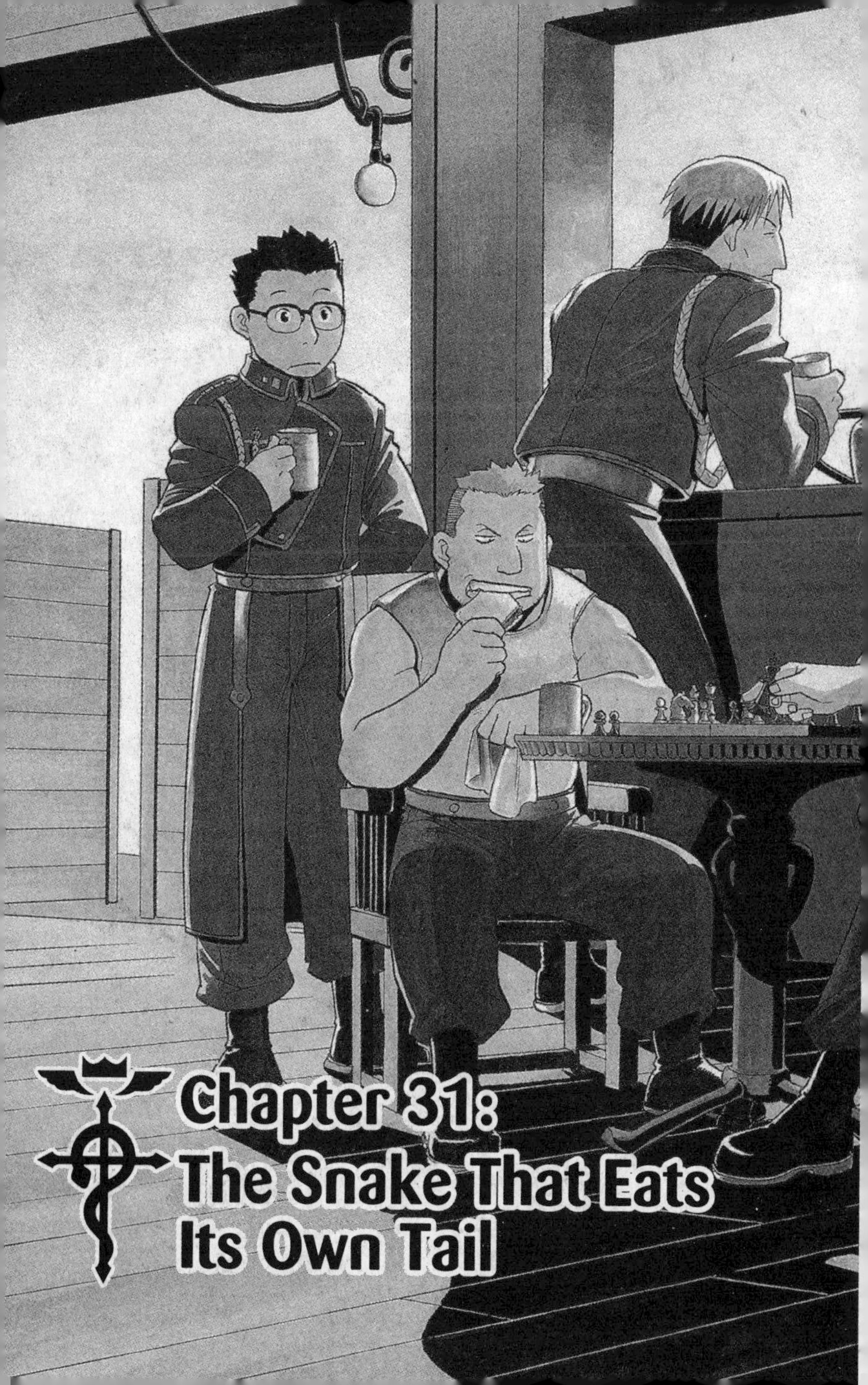
Chapter 31:
The Snake That Eats Its Own Tail

THERE ARE
WORSE
THINGS THAN
LIVING LIKE
A DOG...

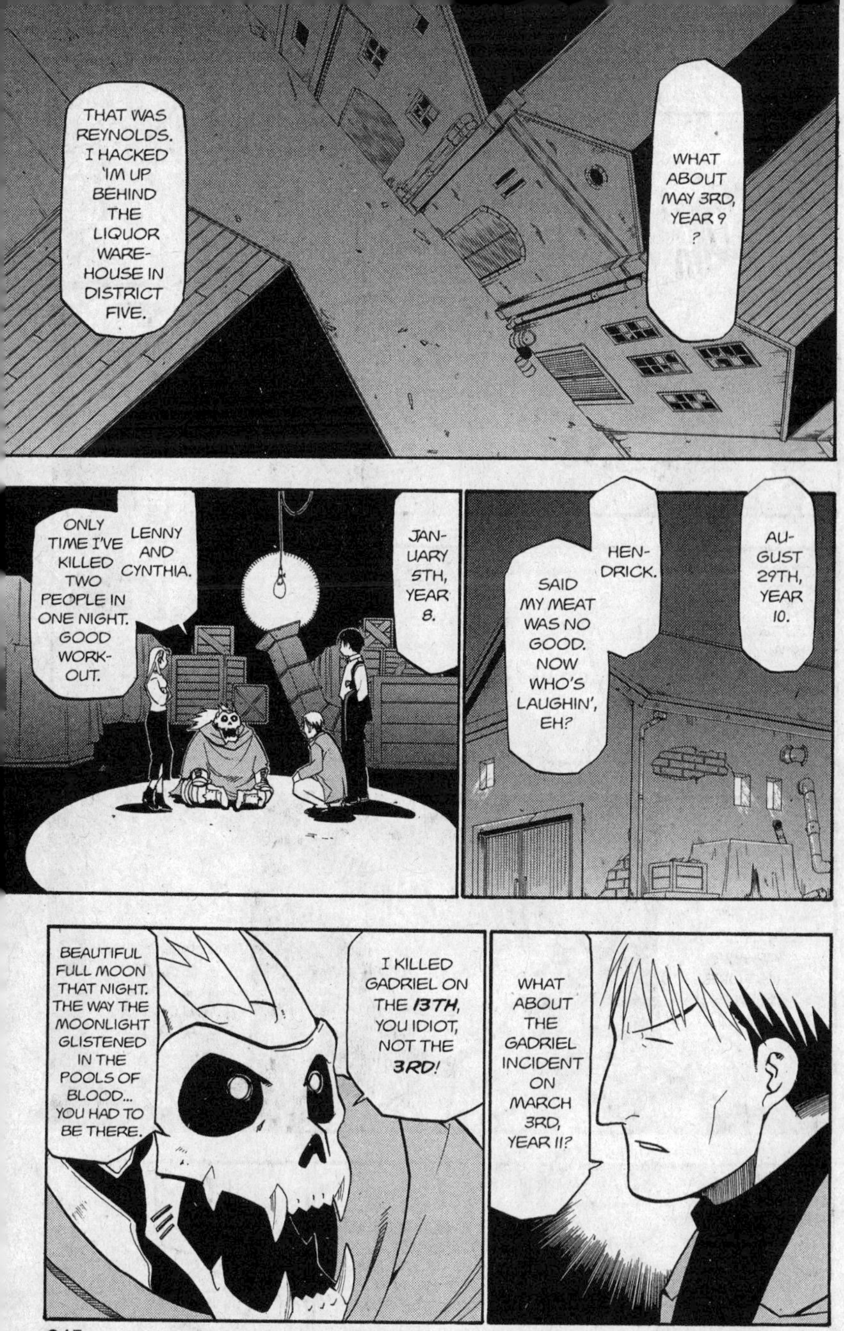
WHAT ABOUT MAY 3RD, YEAR 9 ?
THAT WAS REYNOLDS. I HACKED 'IM UP BEHIND THE LIQUOR WARE-HOUSE IN DISTRICT FIVE.
AU-GUST 29TH, YEAR 10.
HEN-DRICK.
SAID MY MEAT WAS NO GOOD. NOW WHO'S LAUGHIN', EH?
JAN-UARY 5TH, YEAR 8.
LENNY AND CYNTHIA.
ONLY TIME I'VE KILLED TWO PEOPLE IN ONE NIGHT. GOOD WORK-OUT.
WHAT ABOUT THE GADRIEL INCIDENT ON MARCH 3RD, YEAR 11?
I KILLED GADRIEL ON THE 13TH, YOU IDIOT, NOT THE 3RD!
BEAUTIFUL FULL MOON THAT NIGHT. THE WAY THE MOONLIGHT GLISTENED IN THE POOLS OF BLOOD... YOU HAD TO BE THERE.

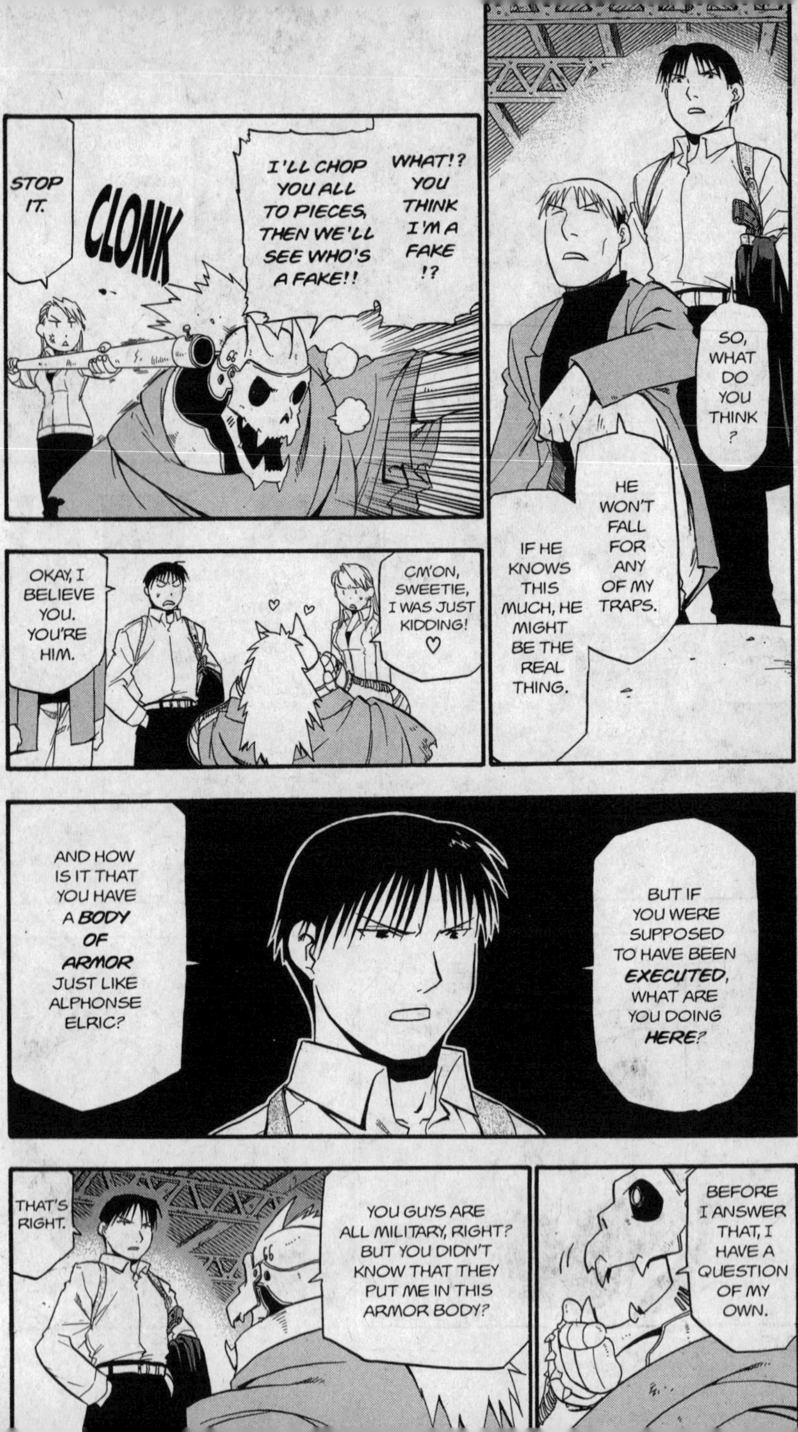
SO, WHAT DO YOU THINK?
HE WON'T FALL FOR ANY OF MY TRAPS.
IF HE KNOWS THIS MUCH, HE MIGHT BE THE REAL THING.
WHAT!? YOU THINK I'M A FAKE!?
I'LL CHOP YOU ALL TO PIECES, THEN WE'LL SEE WHO'S A FAKE!!
CLONK
STOP IT.
CM'ON, SWEETIE, I WAS JUST KIDDING! ♡
OKAY, I BELIEVE YOU. YOU'RE HIM.
BUT IF YOU WERE SUPPOSED TO HAVE BEEN *EXECUTED*, WHAT ARE YOU DOING *HERE*?
AND HOW IS IT THAT YOU HAVE A *BODY OF ARMOR* JUST LIKE ALPHONSE ELRIC?
BEFORE I ANSWER THAT, I HAVE A QUESTION OF MY OWN.
YOU GUYS ARE ALL MILITARY, RIGHT? BUT YOU DIDN'T KNOW THAT THEY PUT ME IN THIS ARMOR BODY?
THAT'S RIGHT.

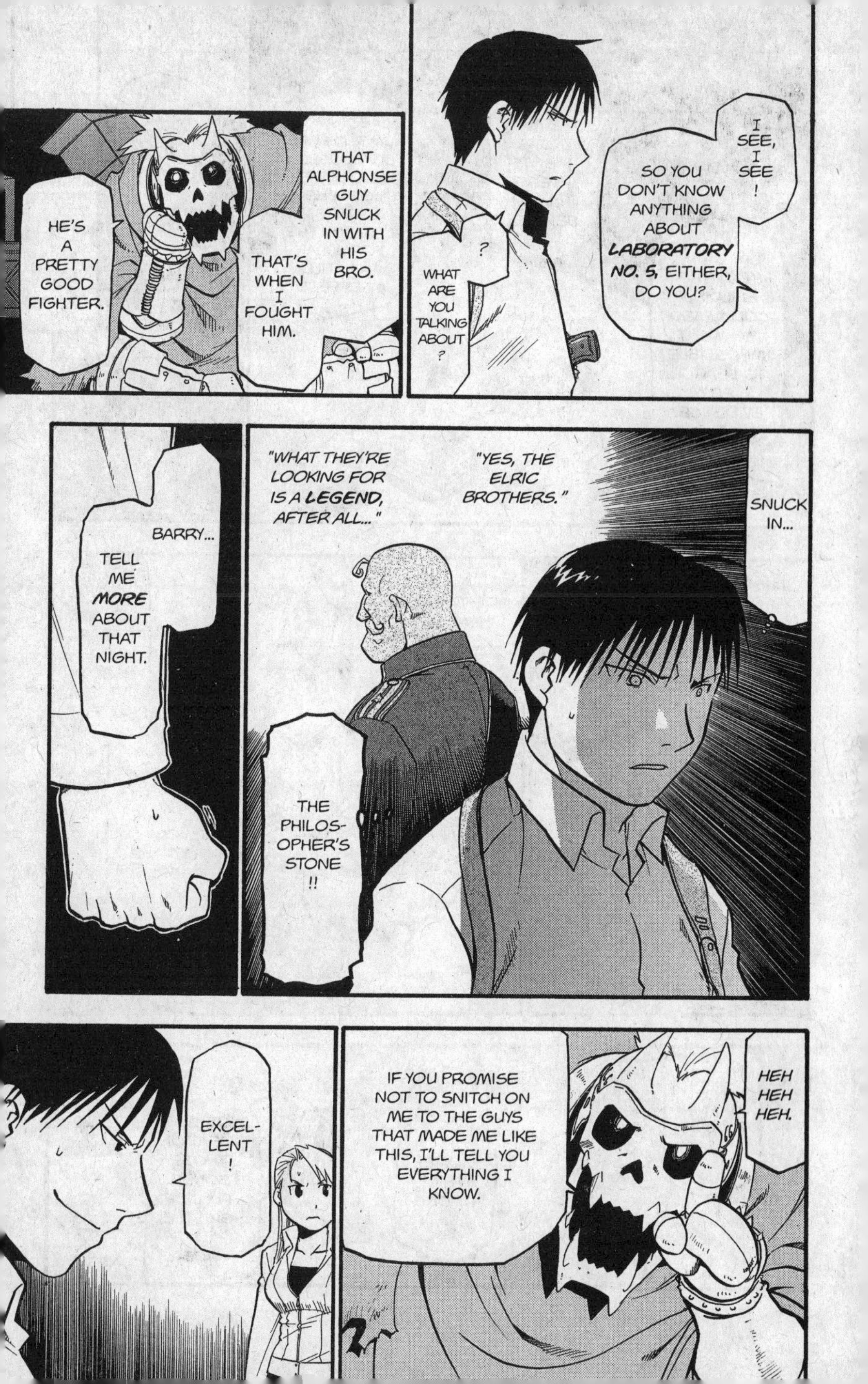
I SEE, I SEE!
SO YOU DON'T KNOW ANYTHING ABOUT LABORATORY NO. 5, EITHER, DO YOU?
?
WHAT ARE YOU TALKING ABOUT?
THAT ALPHONSE GUY SNUCK IN WITH HIS BRO.
THAT'S WHEN I FOUGHT HIM.
HE'S A PRETTY GOOD FIGHTER.
SNUCK IN...
"YES, THE ELRIC BROTHERS."
"WHAT THEY'RE LOOKING FOR IS A LEGEND, AFTER ALL..."
THE PHILOSOPHER'S STONE!!
BARRY... TELL ME MORE ABOUT THAT NIGHT.
HEH HEH HEH.
IF YOU PROMISE NOT TO SNITCH ON ME TO THE GUYS THAT MADE ME LIKE THIS, I'LL TELL YOU EVERYTHING I KNOW.
EXCELLENT!

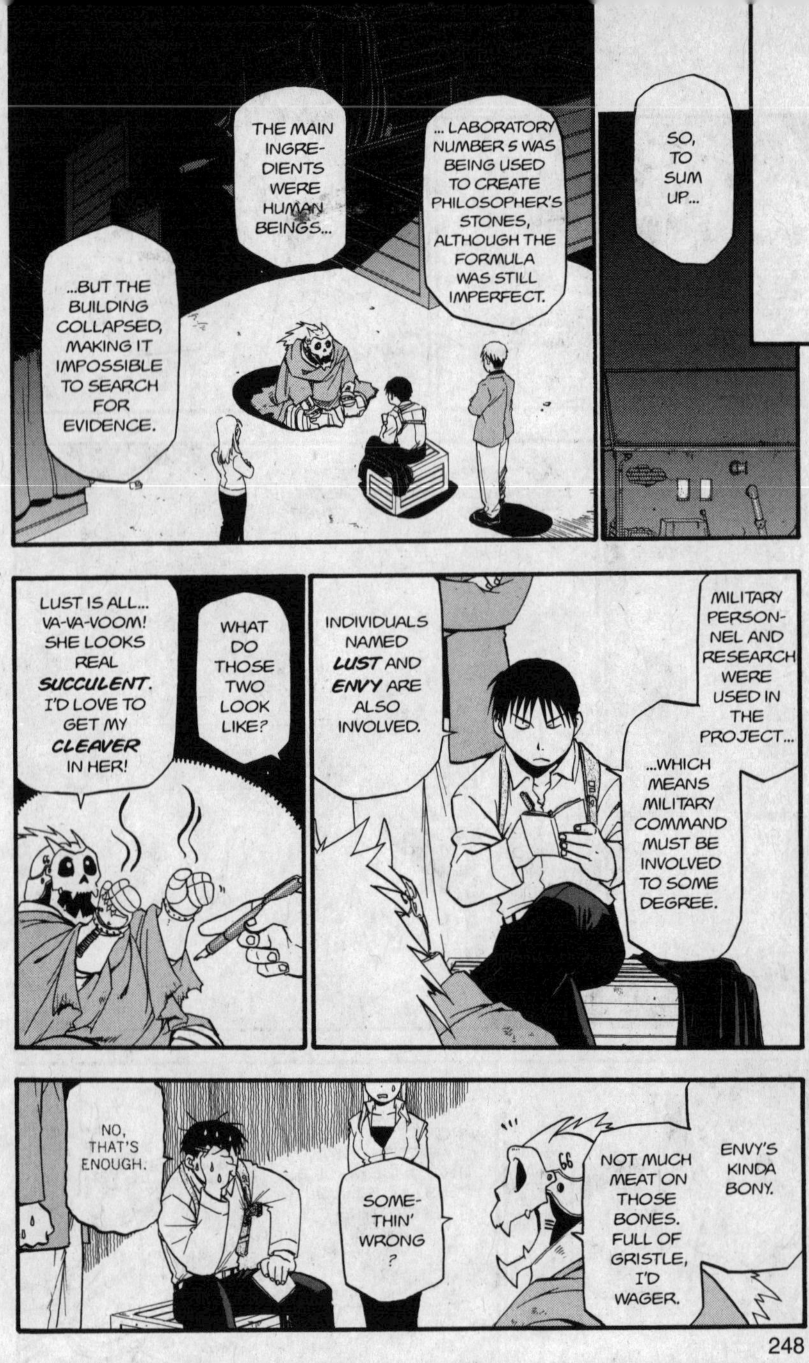
SO, TO SUM UP...
... LABORATORY NUMBER 5 WAS BEING USED TO CREATE PHILOSOPHER'S STONES, ALTHOUGH THE FORMULA WAS STILL IMPERFECT.
THE MAIN INGREDIENTS WERE HUMAN BEINGS...
...BUT THE BUILDING COLLAPSED, MAKING IT IMPOSSIBLE TO SEARCH FOR EVIDENCE.
MILITARY PERSONNEL AND RESEARCH WERE USED IN THE PROJECT...
...WHICH MEANS MILITARY COMMAND MUST BE INVOLVED TO SOME DEGREE.
INDIVIDUALS NAMED LUST AND ENVY ARE ALSO INVOLVED.
WHAT DO THOSE TWO LOOK LIKE?
LUST IS ALL... VA-VA-VOOM! SHE LOOKS REAL SUCCULENT. I'D LOVE TO GET MY CLEAVER IN HER!
ENVY'S KINDA BONY.
NOT MUCH MEAT ON THOSE BONES. FULL OF GRISTLE, I'D WAGER.
SOMETHIN' WRONG?
NO, THAT'S ENOUGH.

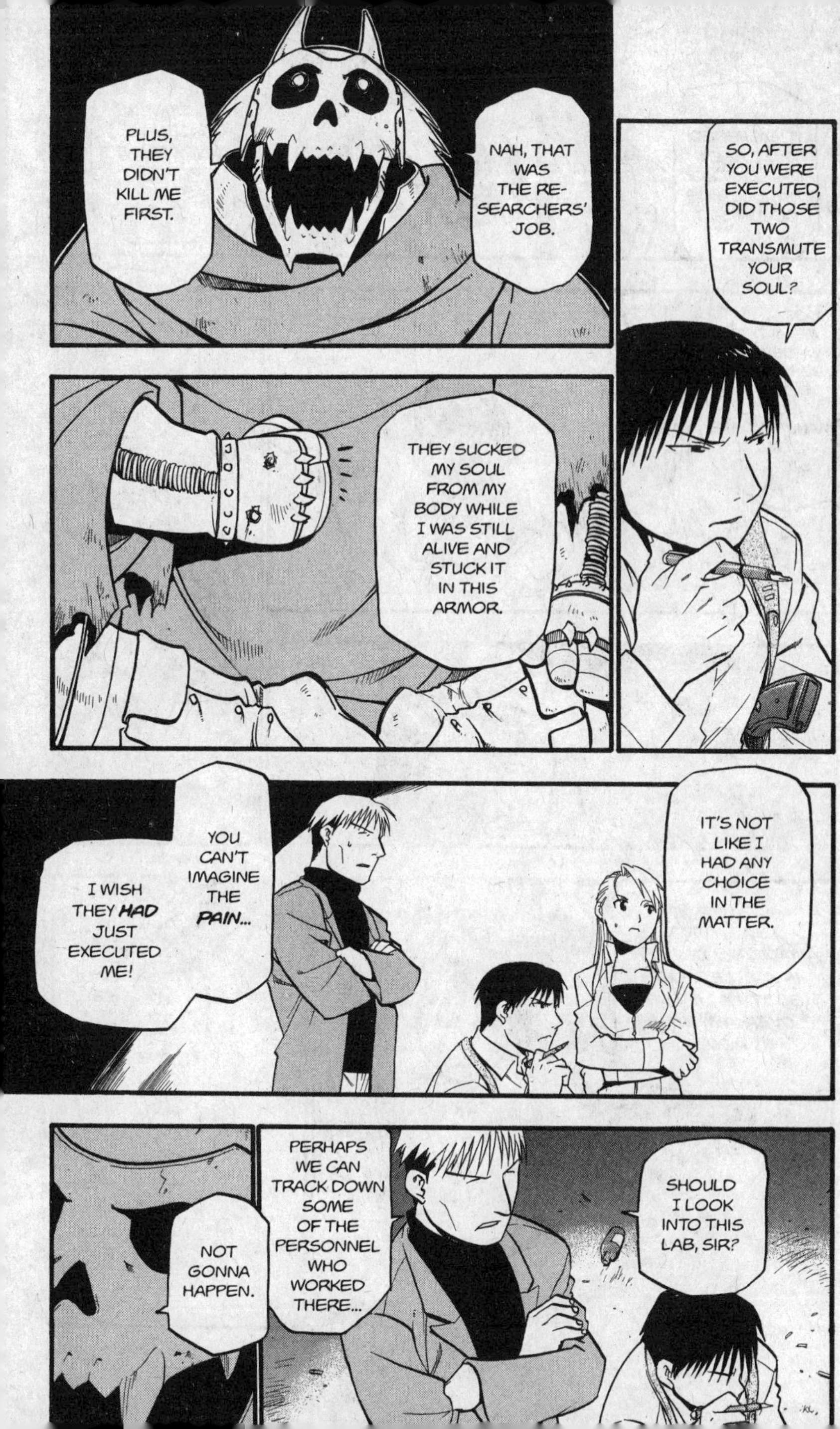
SO, AFTER YOU WERE EXECUTED, DID THOSE TWO TRANSMUTE YOUR SOUL?
NAH, THAT WAS THE RE-SEARCHERS' JOB.
PLUS, THEY DIDN'T KILL ME FIRST.
THEY SUCKED MY SOUL FROM MY BODY WHILE I WAS STILL ALIVE AND STUCK IT IN THIS ARMOR.
IT'S NOT LIKE I HAD ANY CHOICE IN THE MATTER.
YOU CAN'T IMAGINE THE **PAIN**...
I WISH THEY **HAD** JUST EXECUTED ME!
SHOULD I LOOK INTO THIS LAB, SIR?
PERHAPS WE CAN TRACK DOWN SOME OF THE PERSONNEL WHO WORKED THERE...
NOT GONNA HAPPEN.

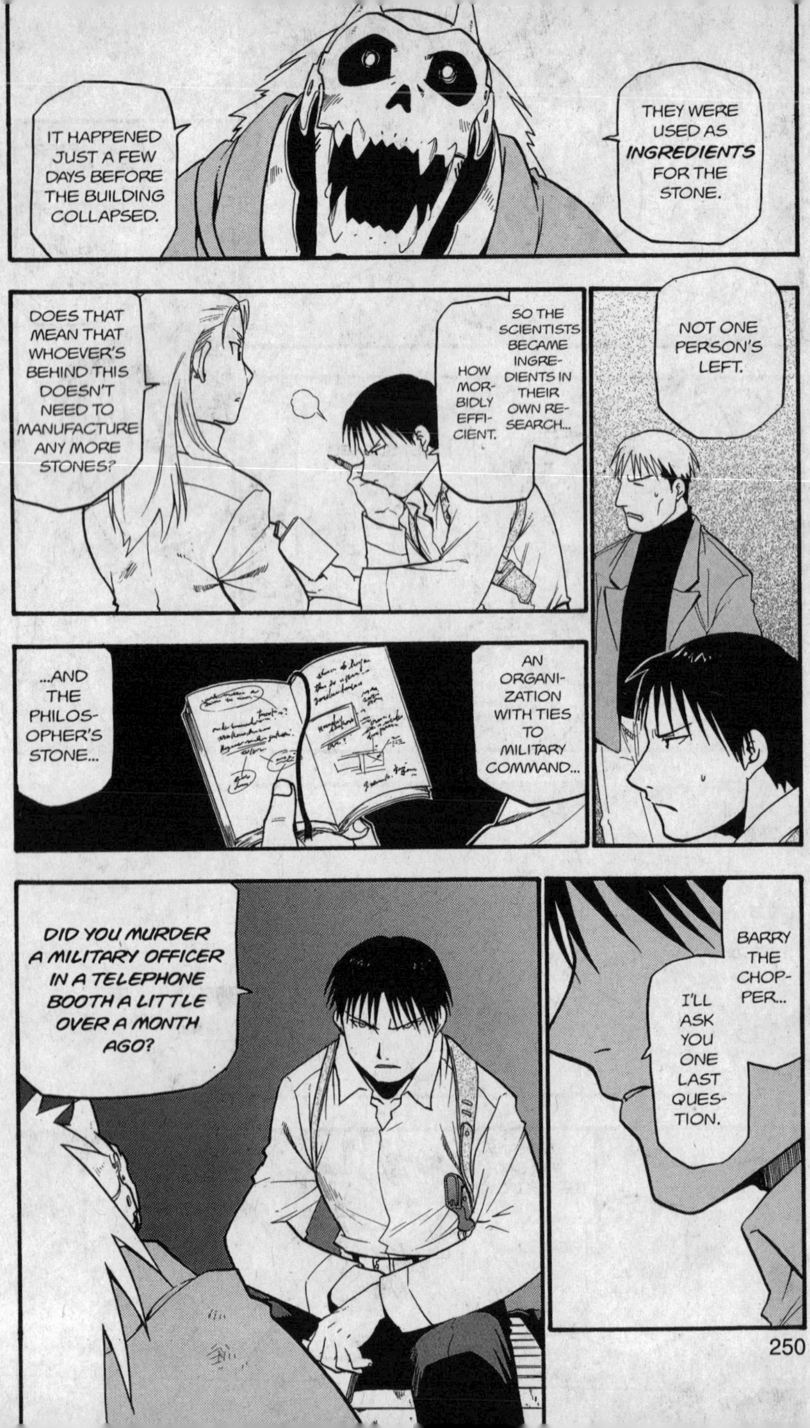
THEY WERE USED AS INGREDIENTS FOR THE STONE.
IT HAPPENED JUST A FEW DAYS BEFORE THE BUILDING COLLAPSED.
NOT ONE PERSON'S LEFT.
SO THE SCIENTISTS BECAME INGREDIENTS IN THEIR OWN RESEARCH...
HOW MORBIDLY EFFICIENT.
DOES THAT MEAN THAT WHOEVER'S BEHIND THIS DOESN'T NEED TO MANUFACTURE ANY MORE STONES?
AN ORGANIZATION WITH TIES TO MILITARY COMMAND...
...AND THE PHILOSOPHER'S STONE...
BARRY THE CHOPPER...
I'LL ASK YOU ONE LAST QUESTION.
DID YOU MURDER A MILITARY OFFICER IN A TELEPHONE BOOTH A LITTLE OVER A MONTH AGO?

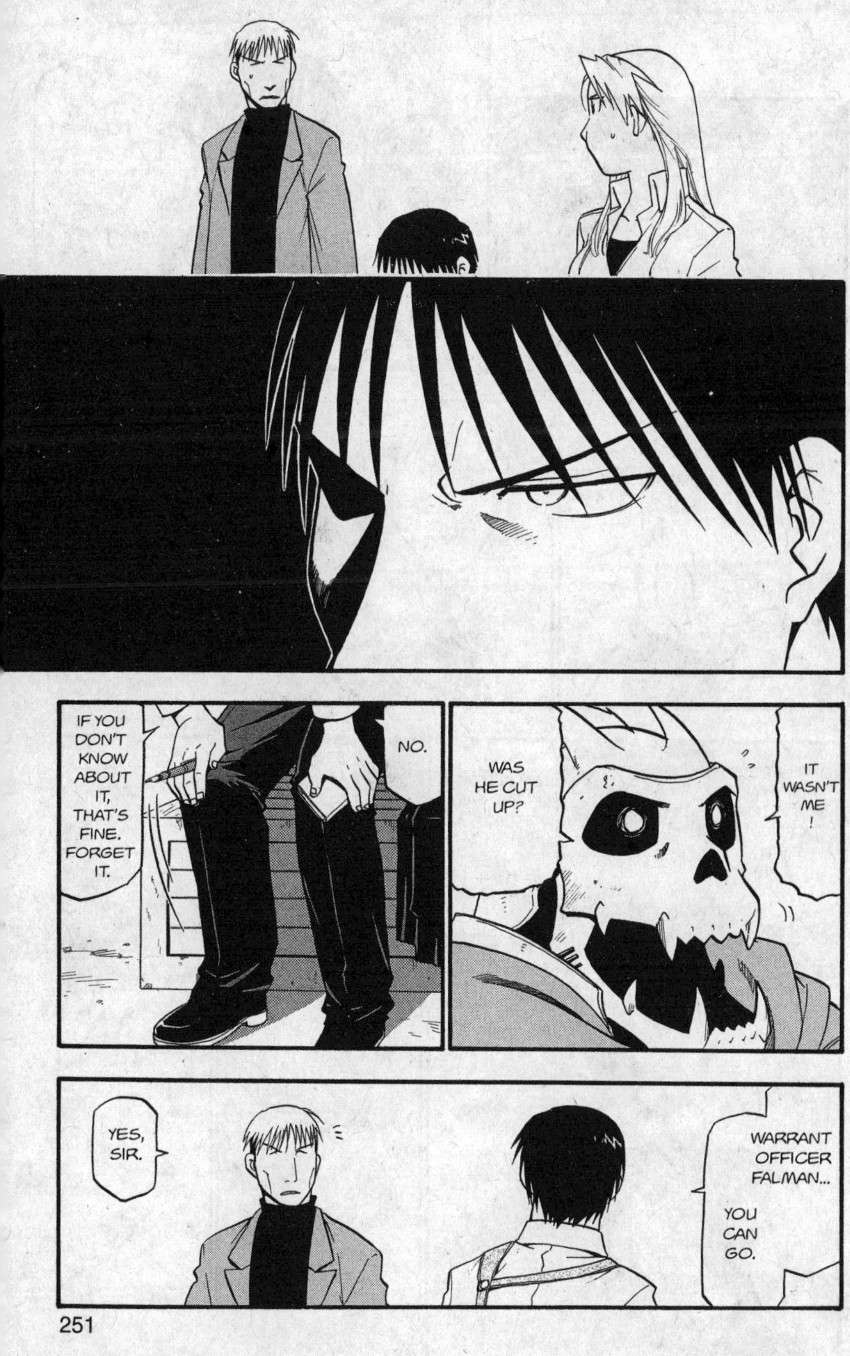
IT WASN'T ME!
WAS HE CUT UP?
NO.
IF YOU DON'T KNOW ABOUT IT, THAT'S FINE. FORGET IT.
WARRANT OFFICER FALMAN...
YOU CAN GO.
YES, SIR.

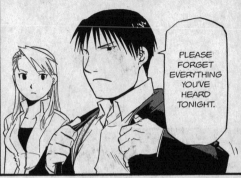

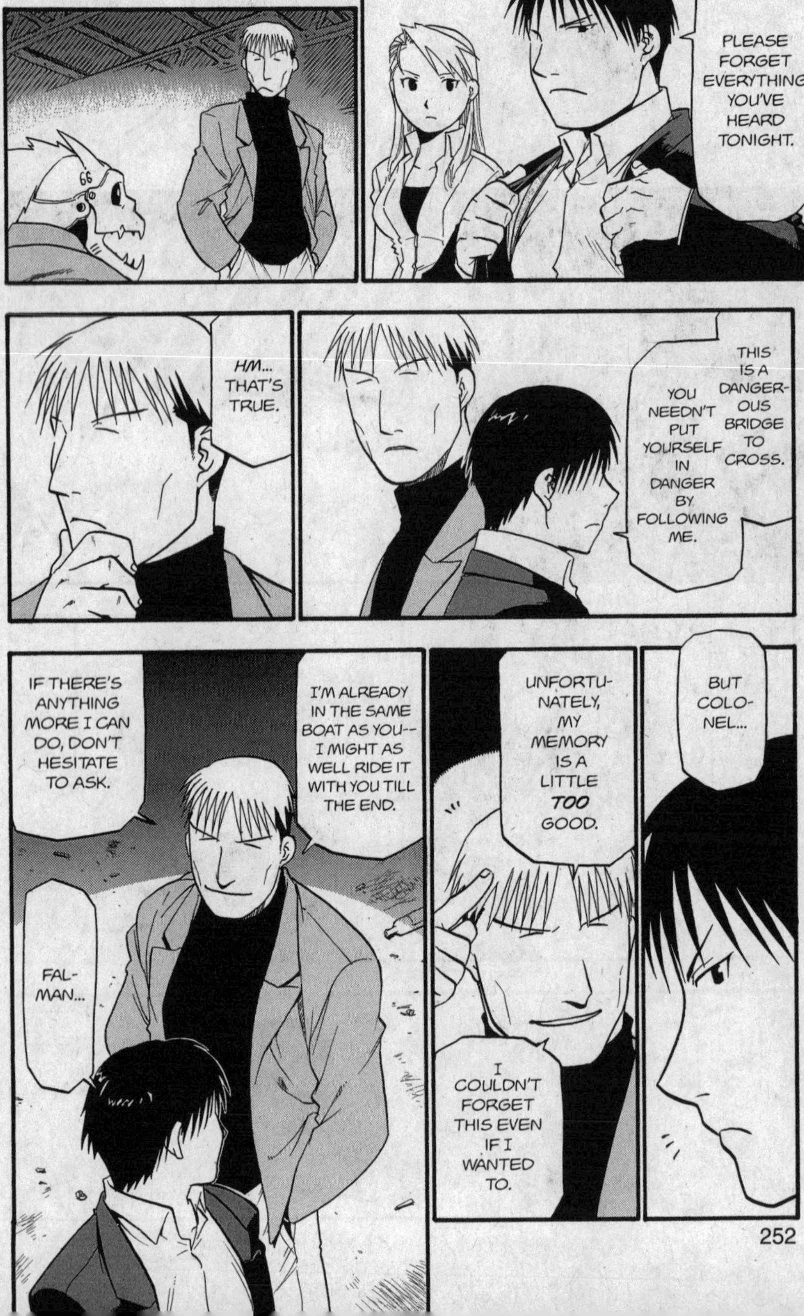
PLEASE FORGET EVERYTHING YOU'VE HEARD TONIGHT.
THIS IS A DANGEROUS BRIDGE TO CROSS.
YOU NEEDN'T PUT YOURSELF IN DANGER BY FOLLOWING ME.
HM... THAT'S TRUE.
BUT COLONEL...
UNFORTUNATELY, MY MEMORY IS A LITTLE *TOO* GOOD.
I COULDN'T FORGET THIS EVEN IF I WANTED TO.
I'M ALREADY IN THE SAME BOAT AS YOU-- I MIGHT AS WELL RIDE IT WITH YOU TILL THE END.
IF THERE'S ANYTHING MORE I CAN DO, DON'T HESITATE TO ASK.
FALMAN...

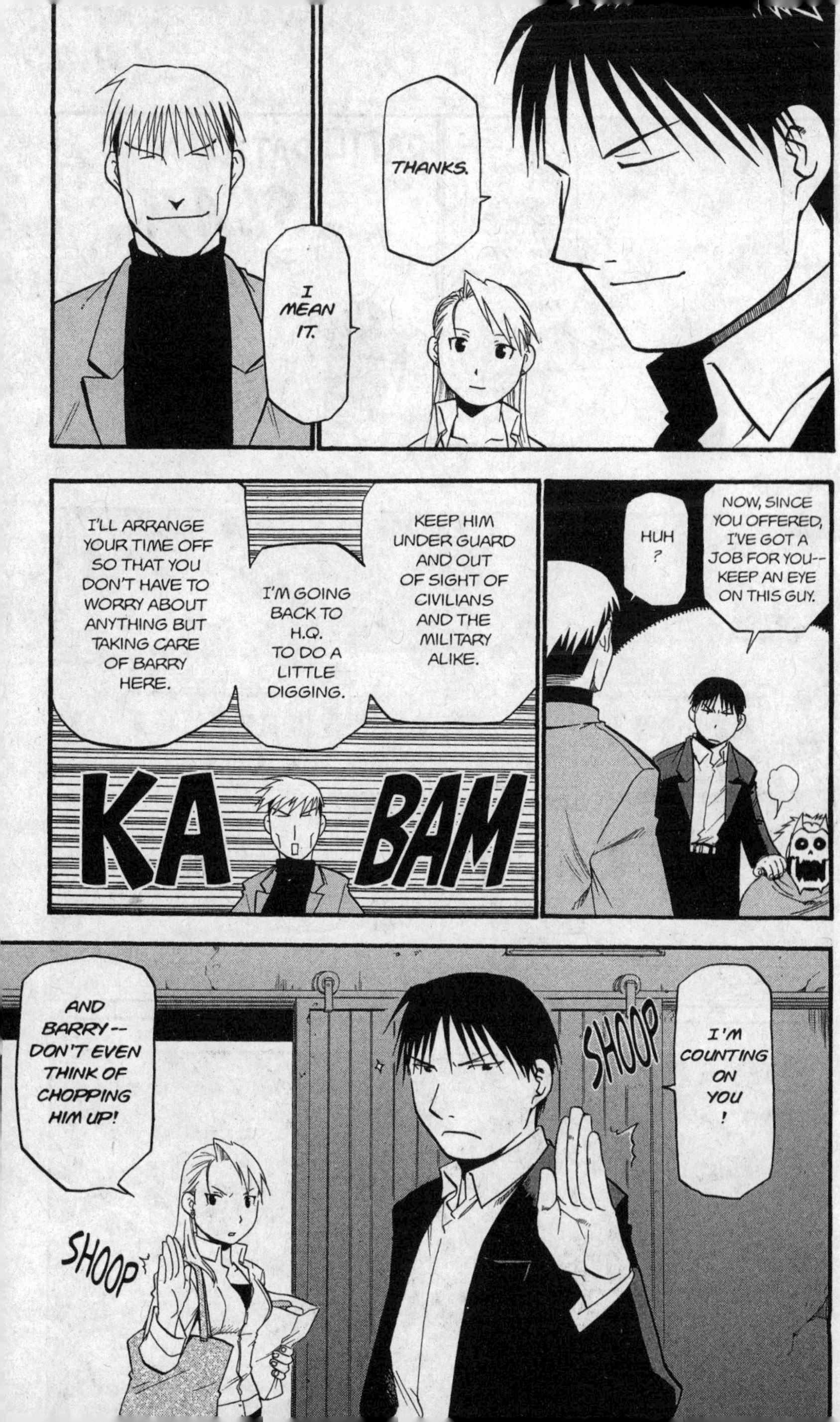
THANKS.
I MEAN IT.
NOW, SINCE YOU OFFERED, I'VE GOT A JOB FOR YOU-- KEEP AN EYE ON THIS GUY.
HUH?
KEEP HIM UNDER GUARD AND OUT OF SIGHT OF CIVILIANS AND THE MILITARY ALIKE.
I'M GOING BACK TO H.Q. TO DO A LITTLE DIGGING.
I'LL ARRANGE YOUR TIME OFF SO THAT YOU DON'T HAVE TO WORRY ABOUT ANYTHING BUT TAKING CARE OF BARRY HERE.
KA BAM
I'M COUNTING ON YOU!
SHOOP
AND BARRY-- DON'T EVEN THINK OF CHOPPING HIM UP!
SHOOP

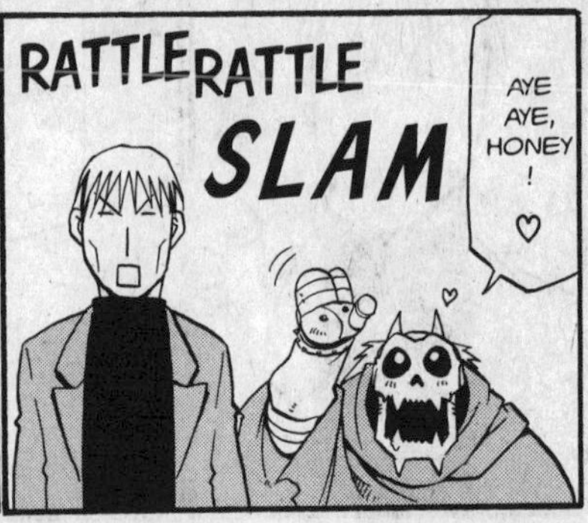
RATTLE RATTLE
SLAM
AYE AYE, HONEY! ♡

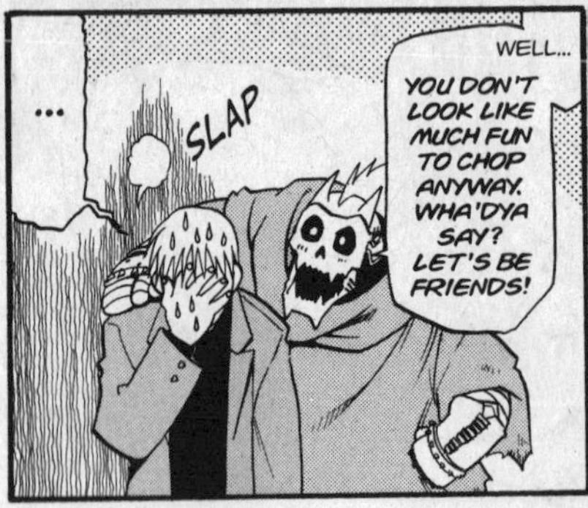
...
SLAP
WELL... YOU DON'T LOOK LIKE MUCH FUN TO CHOP ANYWAY. WHA'DYA SAY? LET'S BE FRIENDS!

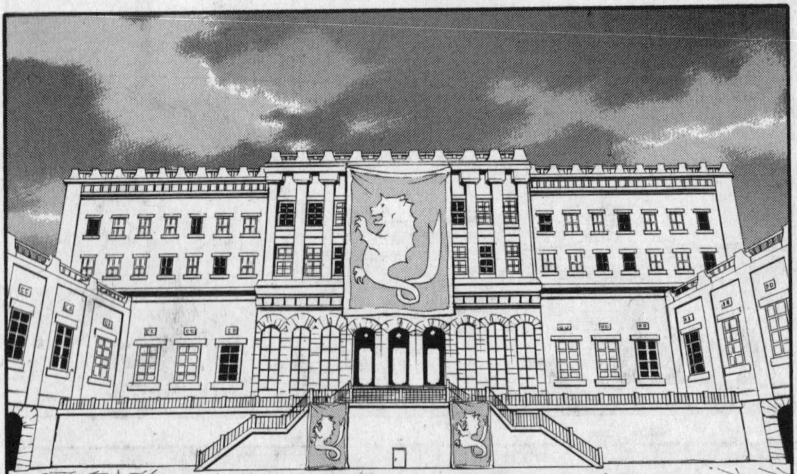

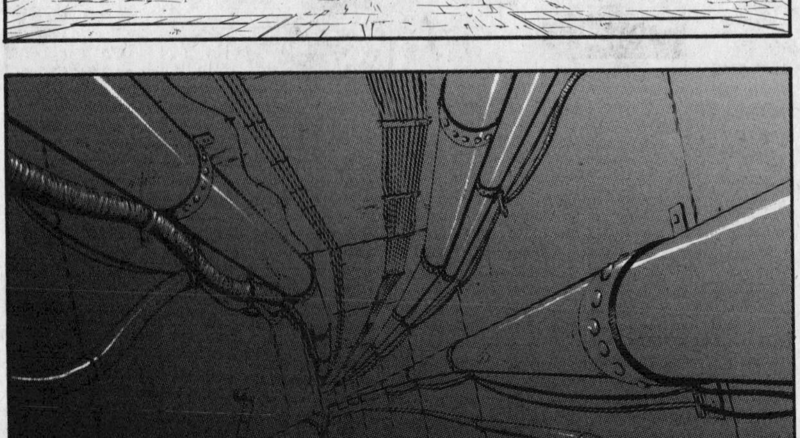

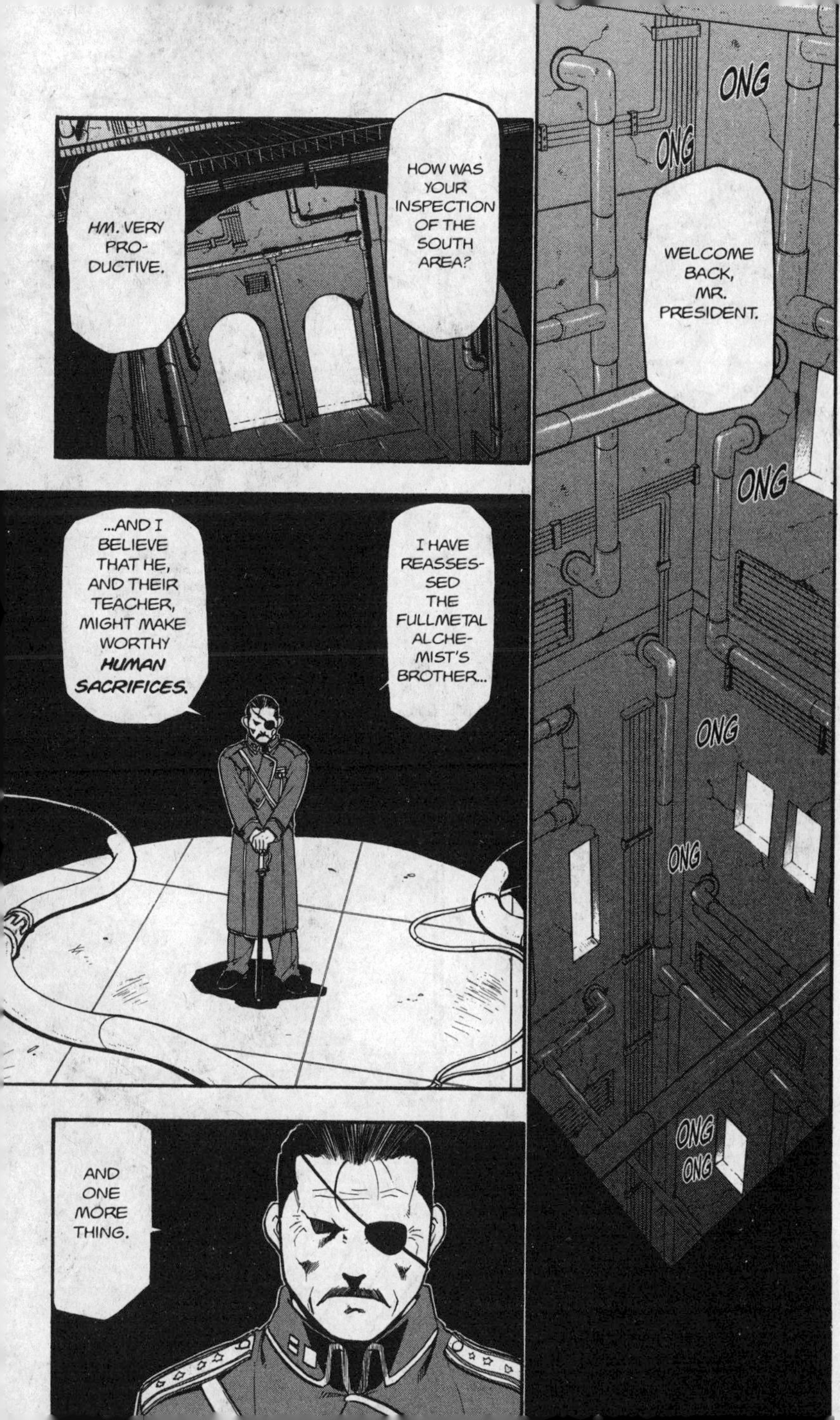
ONG
ONG
WELCOME BACK, MR. PRESIDENT.
ONG
ONG
ONG
ONG
ONG
HOW WAS YOUR INSPECTION OF THE SOUTH AREA?
HM. VERY PRO-DUCTIVE.
I HAVE REASSESSED THE FULLMETAL ALCHEMIST'S BROTHER...
...AND I BELIEVE THAT HE, AND THEIR TEACHER, MIGHT MAKE WORTHY **HUMAN SACRIFICES.**
AND ONE MORE THING.

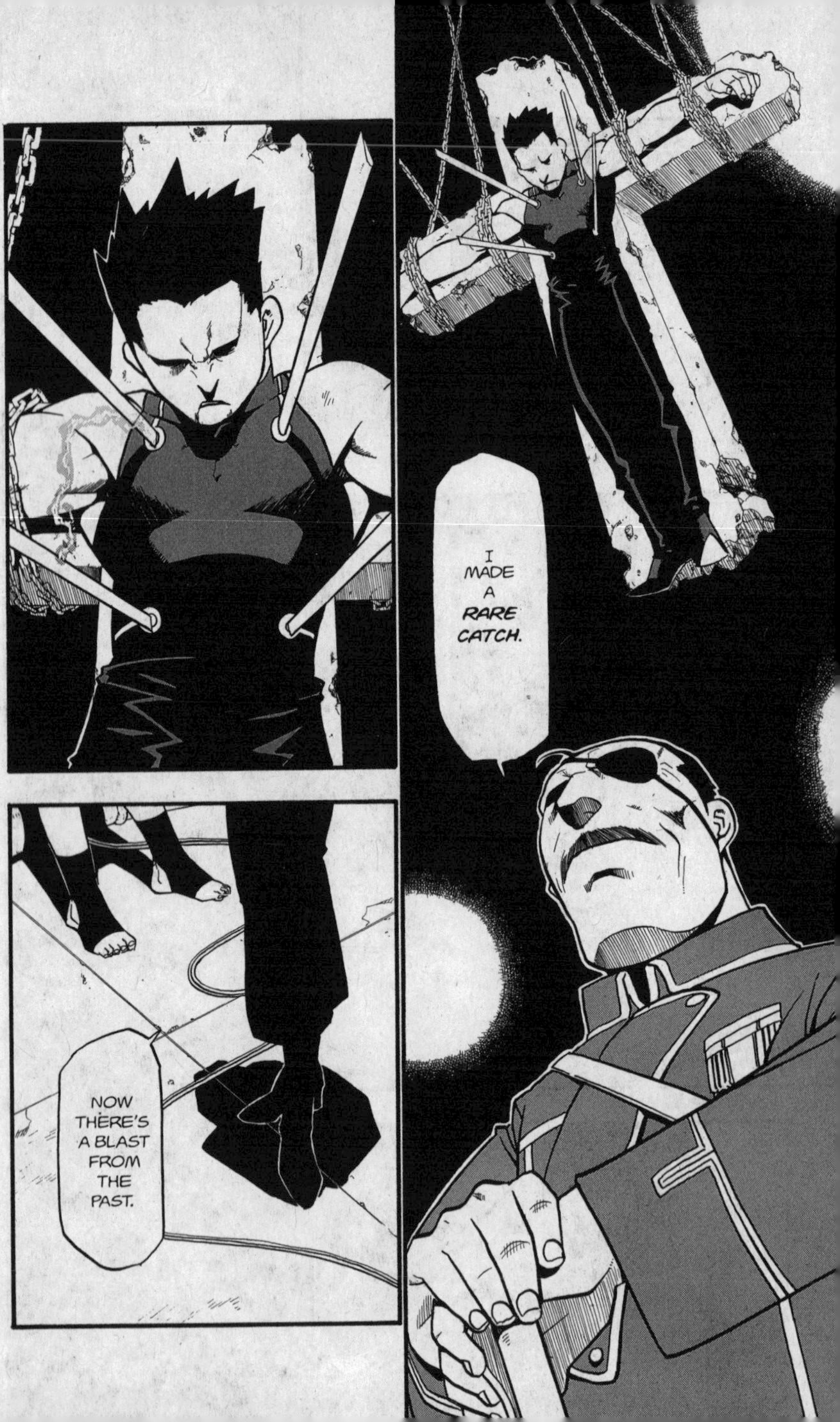
I MADE A RARE CATCH.
NOW THERE'S A BLAST FROM THE PAST.

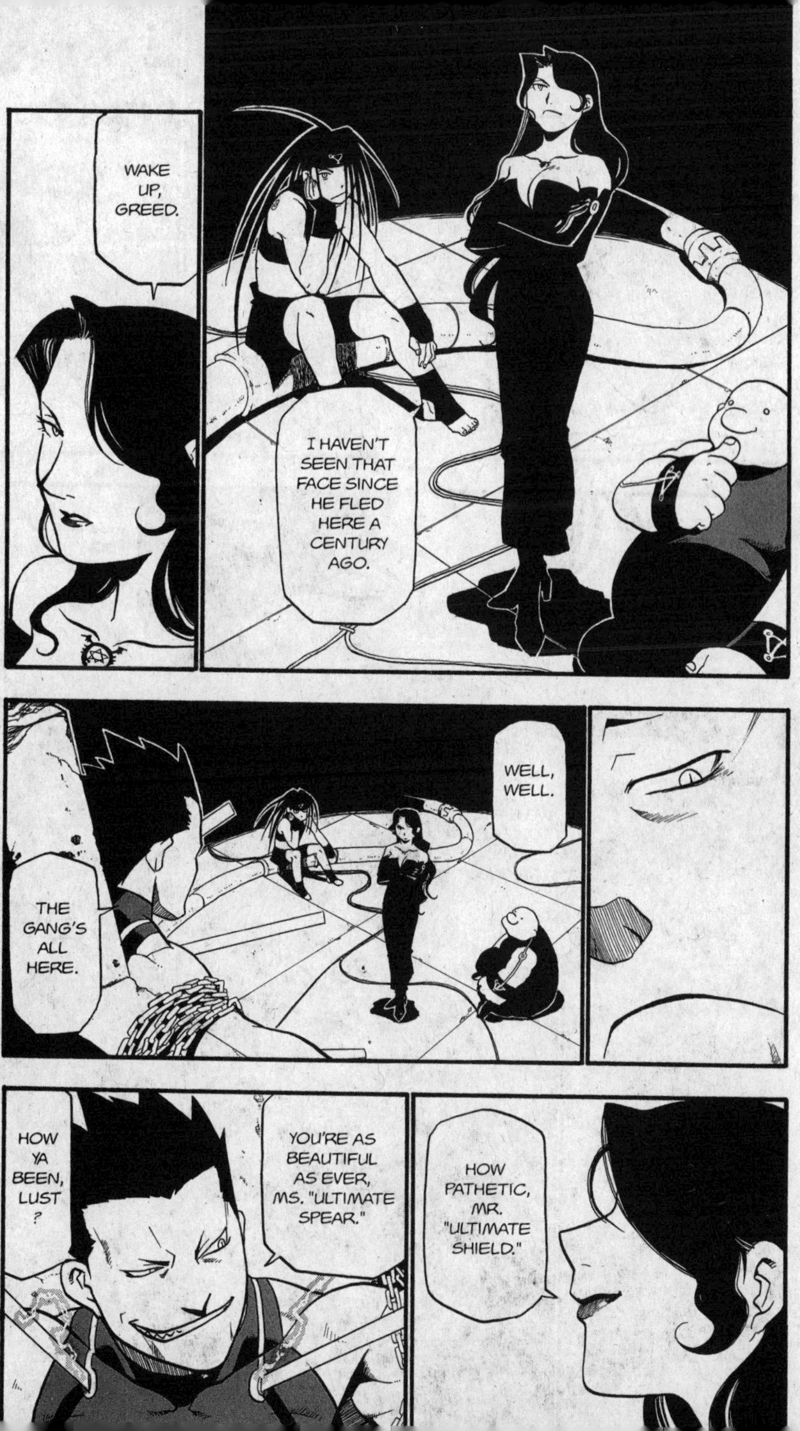
I HAVEN'T SEEN THAT FACE SINCE HE FLED HERE A CENTURY AGO.
WAKE UP, GREED.
WELL, WELL.
THE GANG'S ALL HERE.
HOW PATHETIC, MR. "ULTIMATE SHIELD."
YOU'RE AS BEAUTIFUL AS EVER, MS. "ULTIMATE SPEAR."
HOW YA BEEN, LUST?

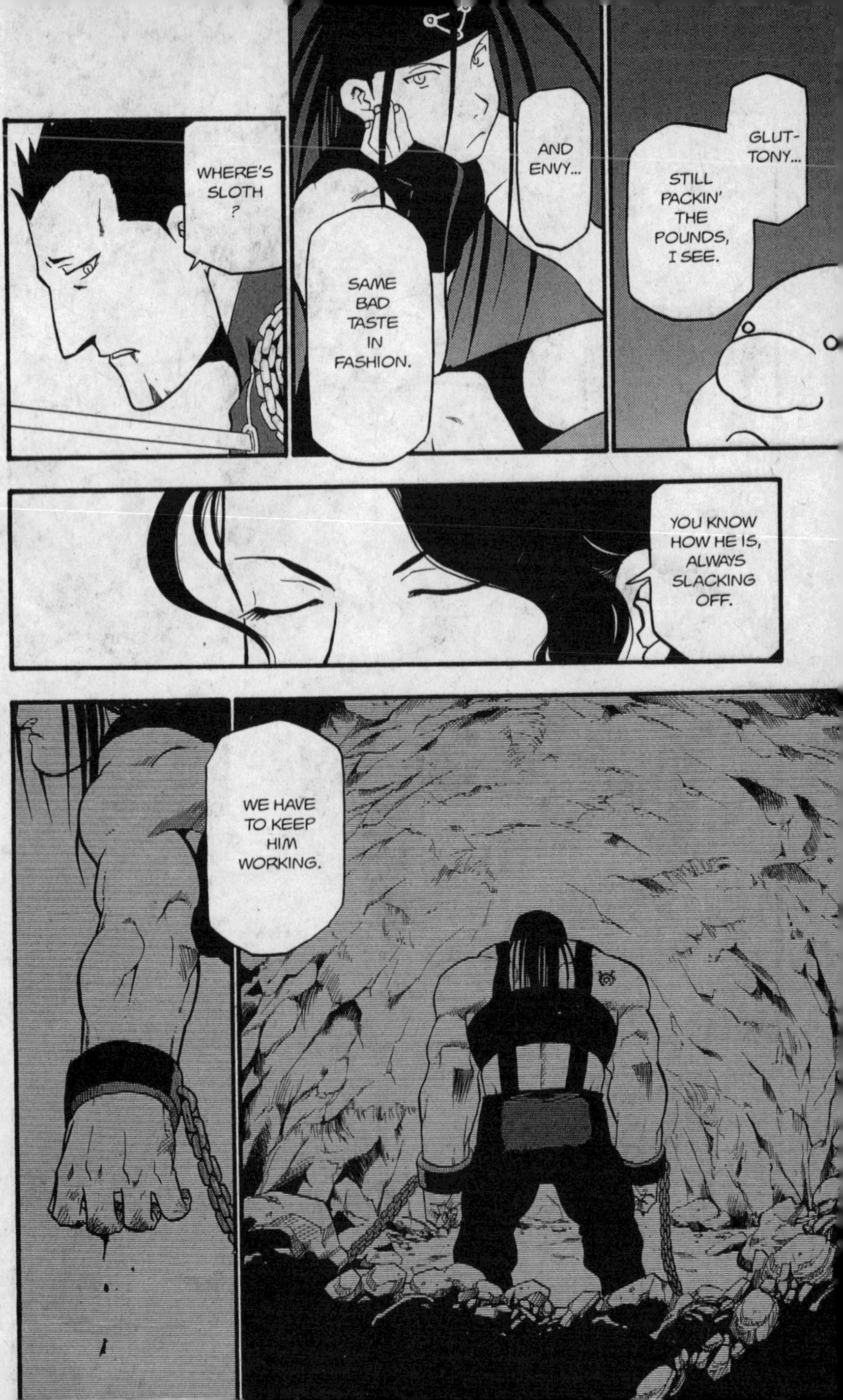
GLUT-TONY...
STILL PACKIN' THE POUNDS, I SEE.
AND ENVY...
SAME BAD TASTE IN FASHION.
WHERE'S SLOTH ?
YOU KNOW HOW HE IS, ALWAYS SLACKING OFF.
WE HAVE TO KEEP HIM WORKING.

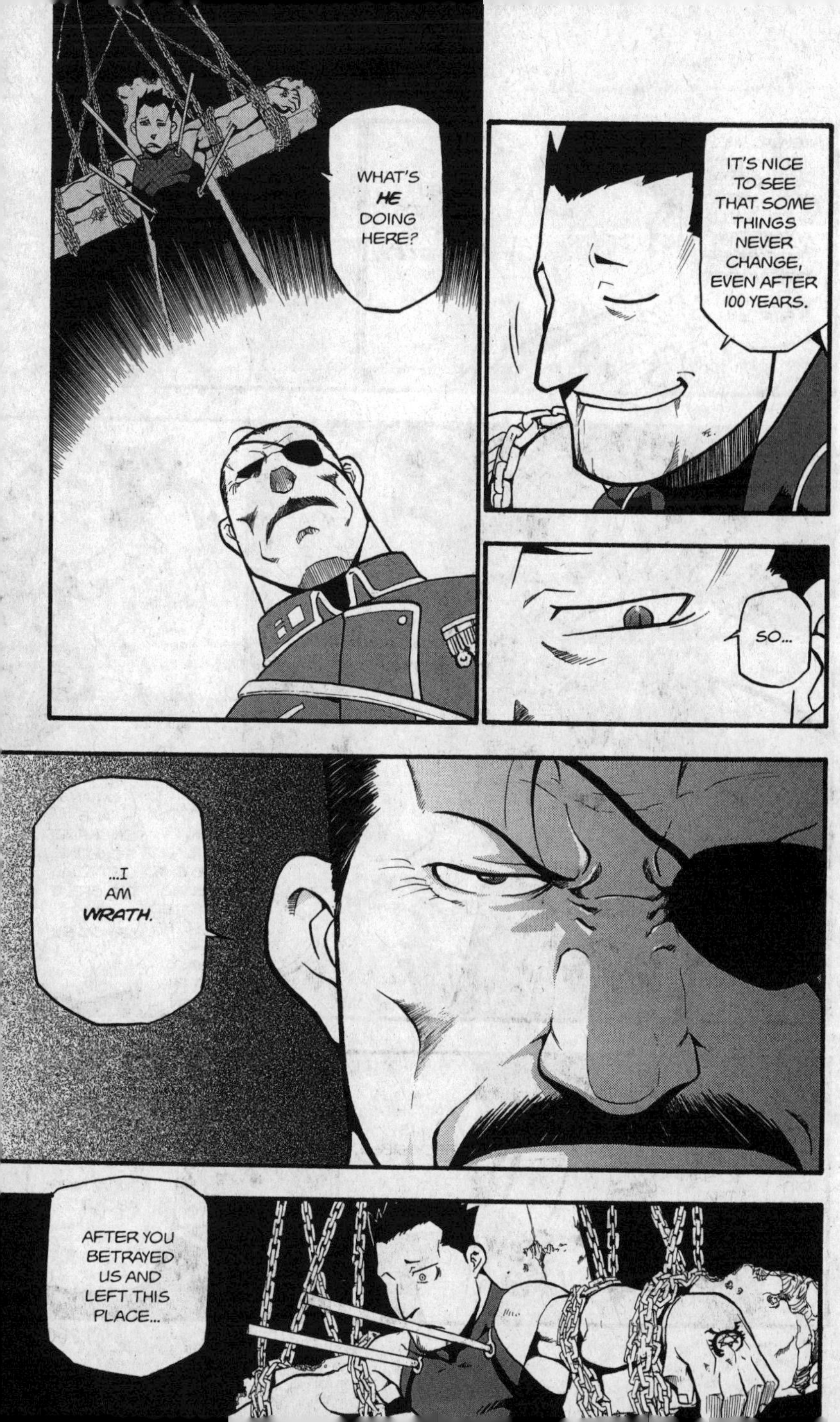
IT'S NICE TO SEE THAT SOME THINGS NEVER CHANGE, EVEN AFTER 100 YEARS.
SO...
WHAT'S HE DOING HERE?
...I AM WRATH.
AFTER YOU BETRAYED US AND LEFT THIS PLACE...

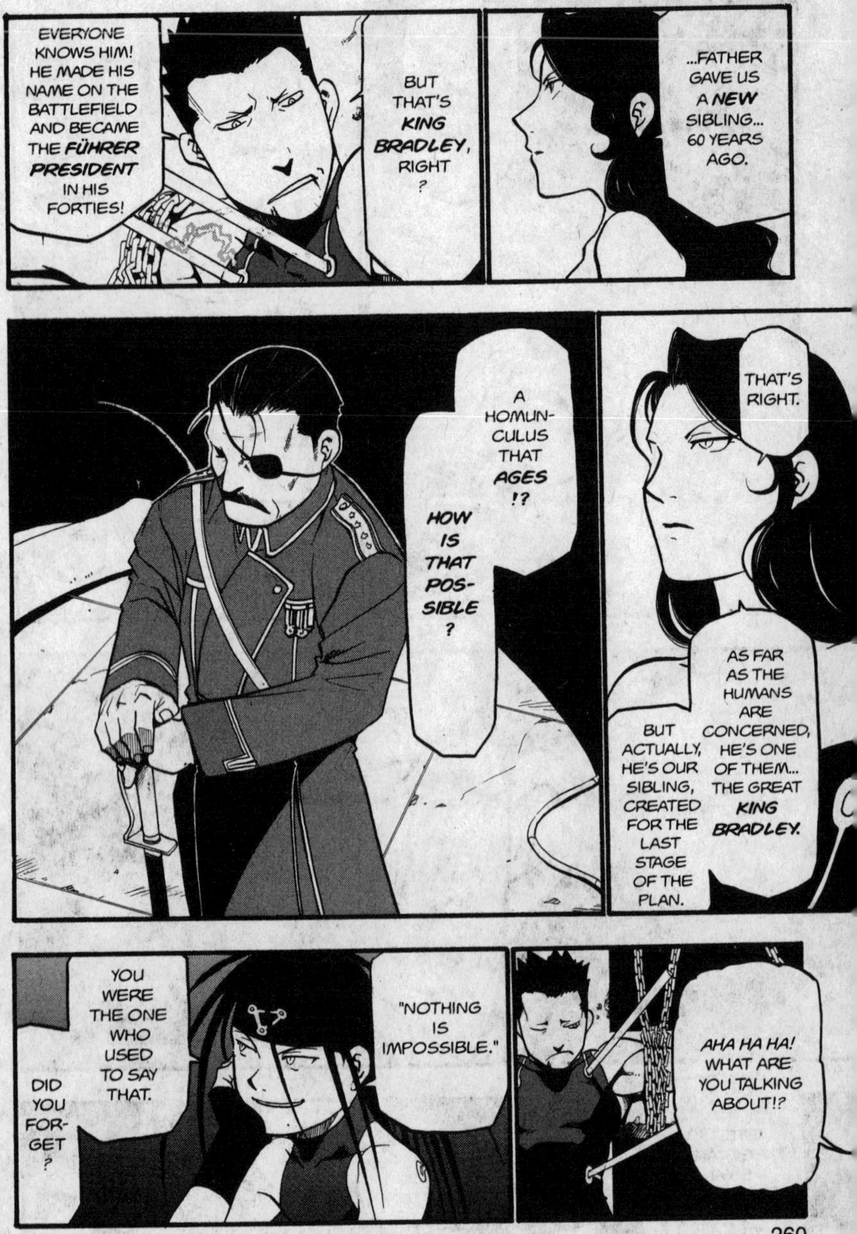
...FATHER GAVE US A NEW SIBLING... 60 YEARS AGO.
BUT THAT'S KING BRADLEY, RIGHT?
EVERYONE KNOWS HIM! HE MADE HIS NAME ON THE BATTLEFIELD AND BECAME THE FÜHRER PRESIDENT IN HIS FORTIES!
THAT'S RIGHT.
AS FAR AS THE HUMANS ARE CONCERNED, HE'S ONE OF THEM... THE GREAT KING BRADLEY.
BUT ACTUALLY, HE'S OUR SIBLING, CREATED FOR THE LAST STAGE OF THE PLAN.
A HOMUNCULUS THAT AGES!?
HOW IS THAT POSSIBLE?
AHA HA HA! WHAT ARE YOU TALKING ABOUT!?
"NOTHING IS IMPOSSIBLE."
YOU WERE THE ONE WHO USED TO SAY THAT.
DID YOU FORGET?

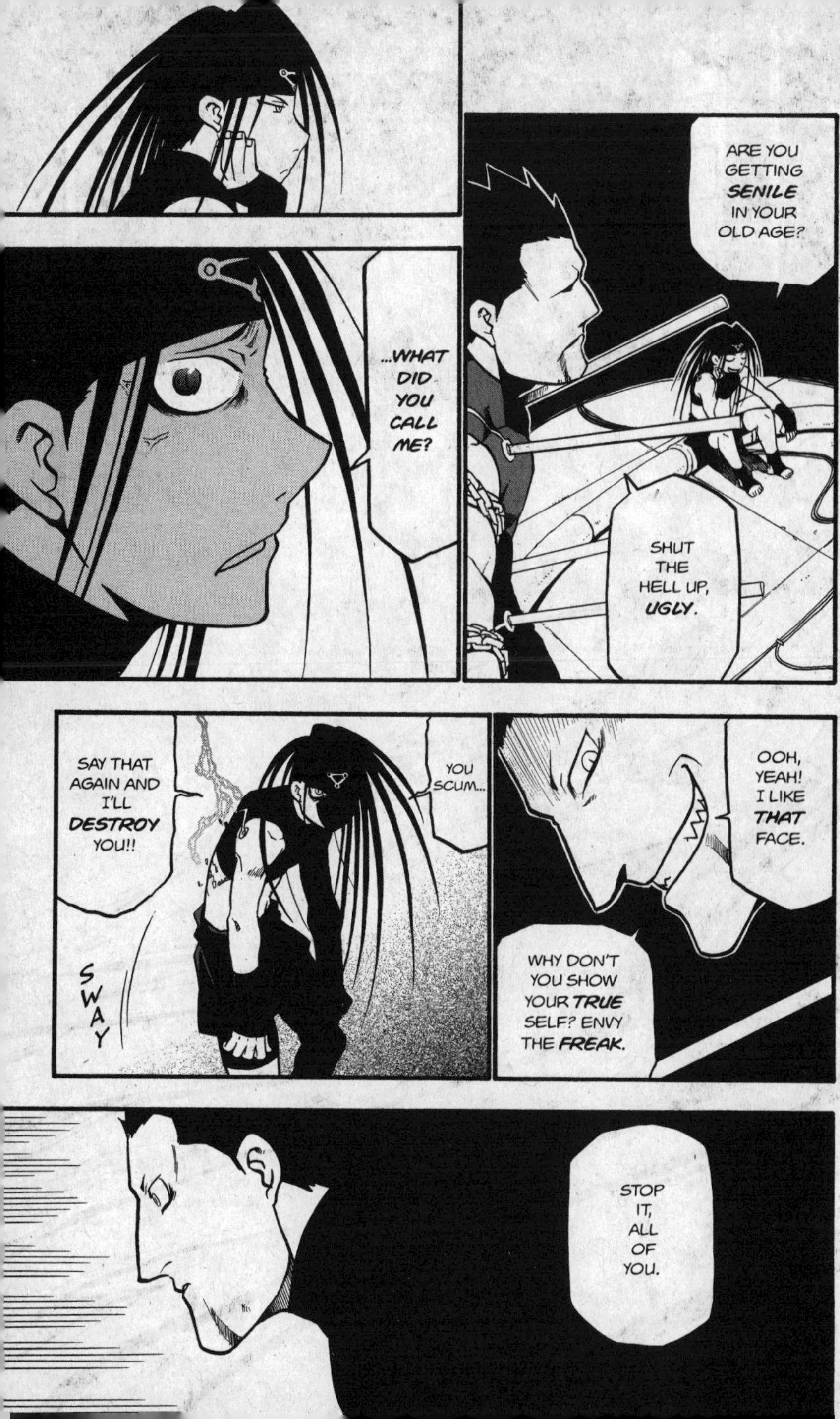
ARE YOU GETTING SENILE IN YOUR OLD AGE?
SHUT THE HELL UP, UGLY.
...WHAT DID YOU CALL ME?
OOH, YEAH! I LIKE THAT FACE.
WHY DON'T YOU SHOW YOUR TRUE SELF? ENVY THE FREAK.
YOU SCUM...
SAY THAT AGAIN AND I'LL DESTROY YOU!!
SWAY
STOP IT, ALL OF YOU.

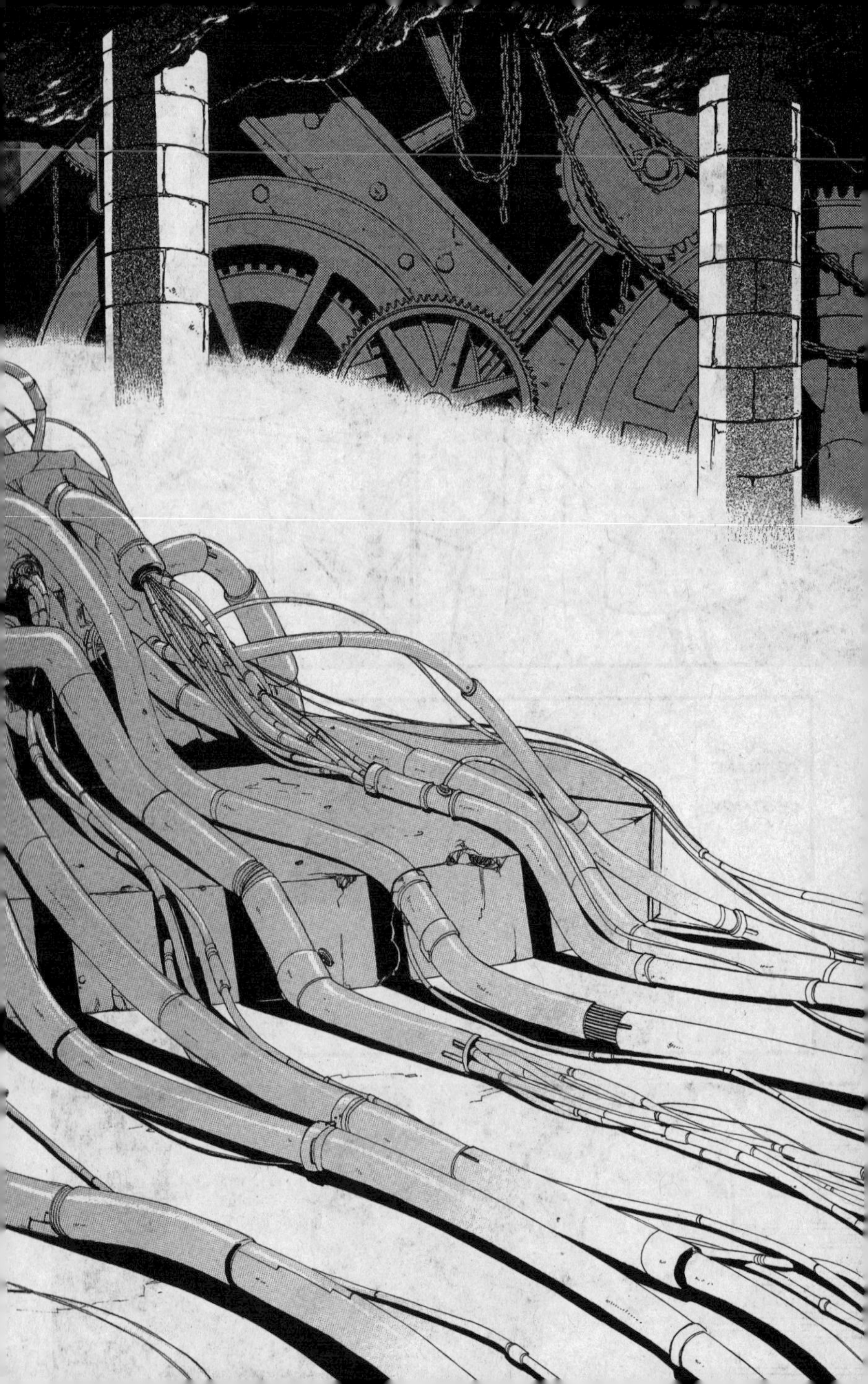

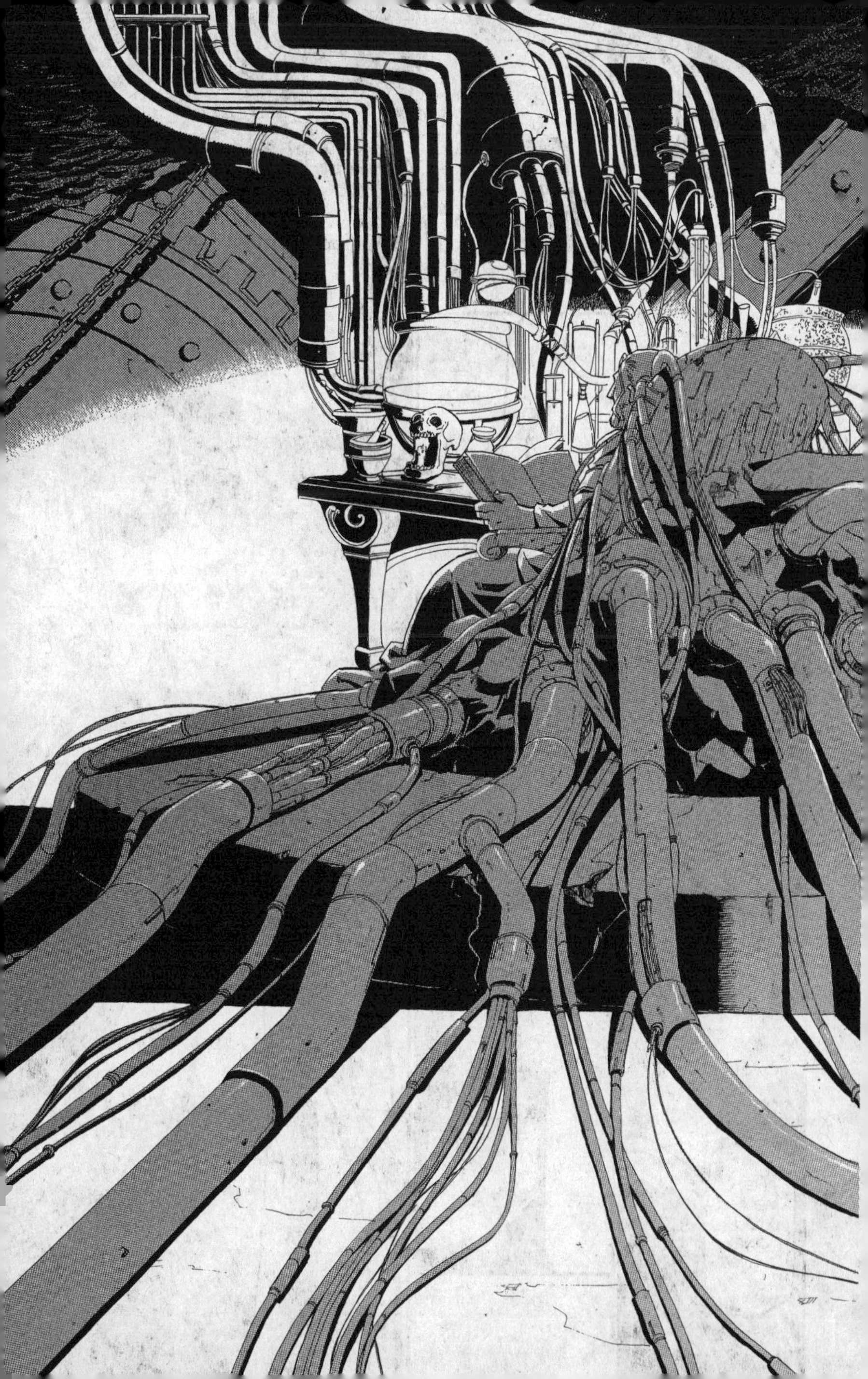

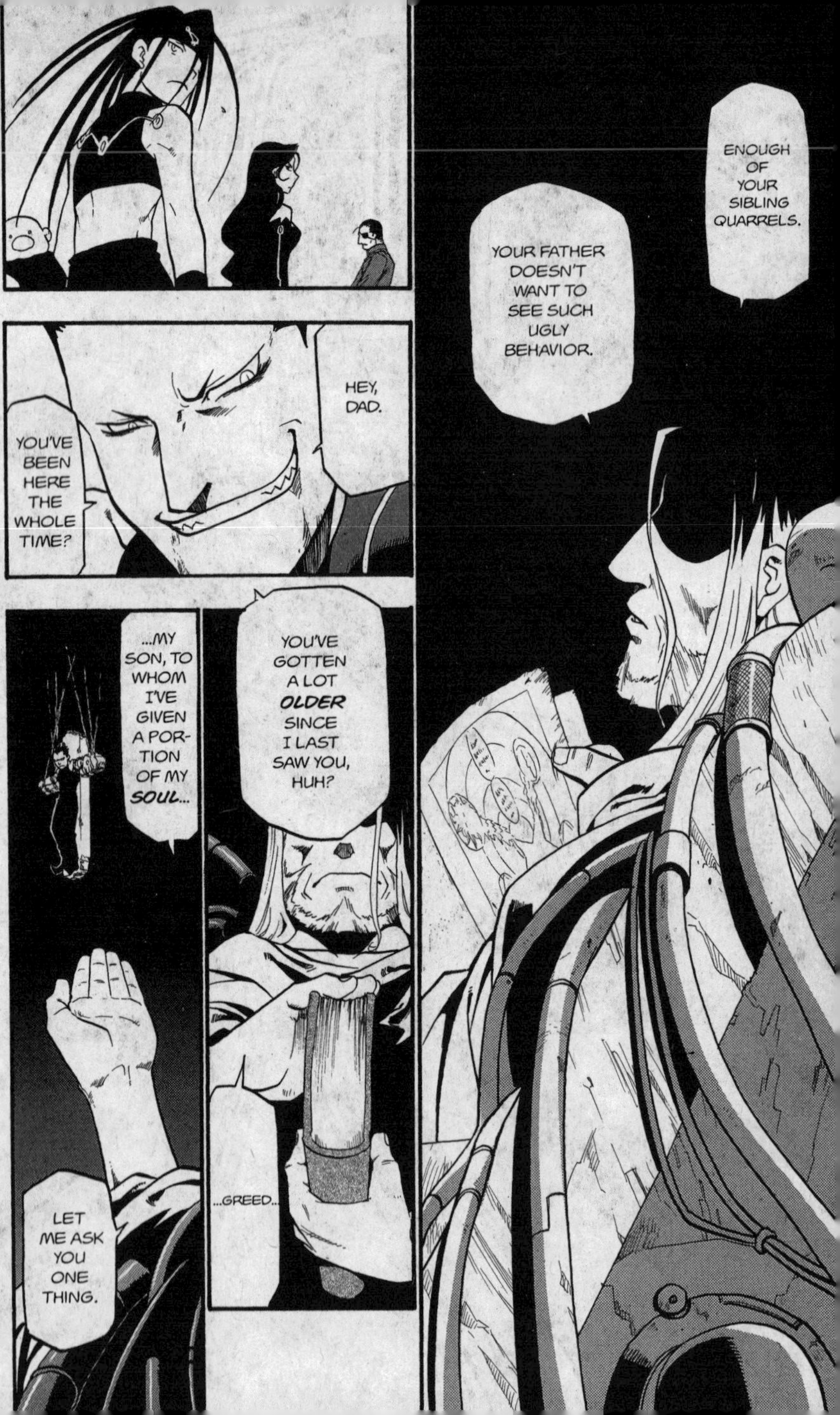
ENOUGH OF YOUR SIBLING QUARRELS.
YOUR FATHER DOESN'T WANT TO SEE SUCH UGLY BEHAVIOR.
HEY, DAD.
YOU'VE BEEN HERE THE WHOLE TIME?
YOU'VE GOTTEN A LOT **OLDER** SINCE I LAST SAW YOU, HUH?
...GREED...
...MY SON, TO WHOM I'VE GIVEN A PORTION OF MY **SOUL**...
LET ME ASK YOU ONE THING.

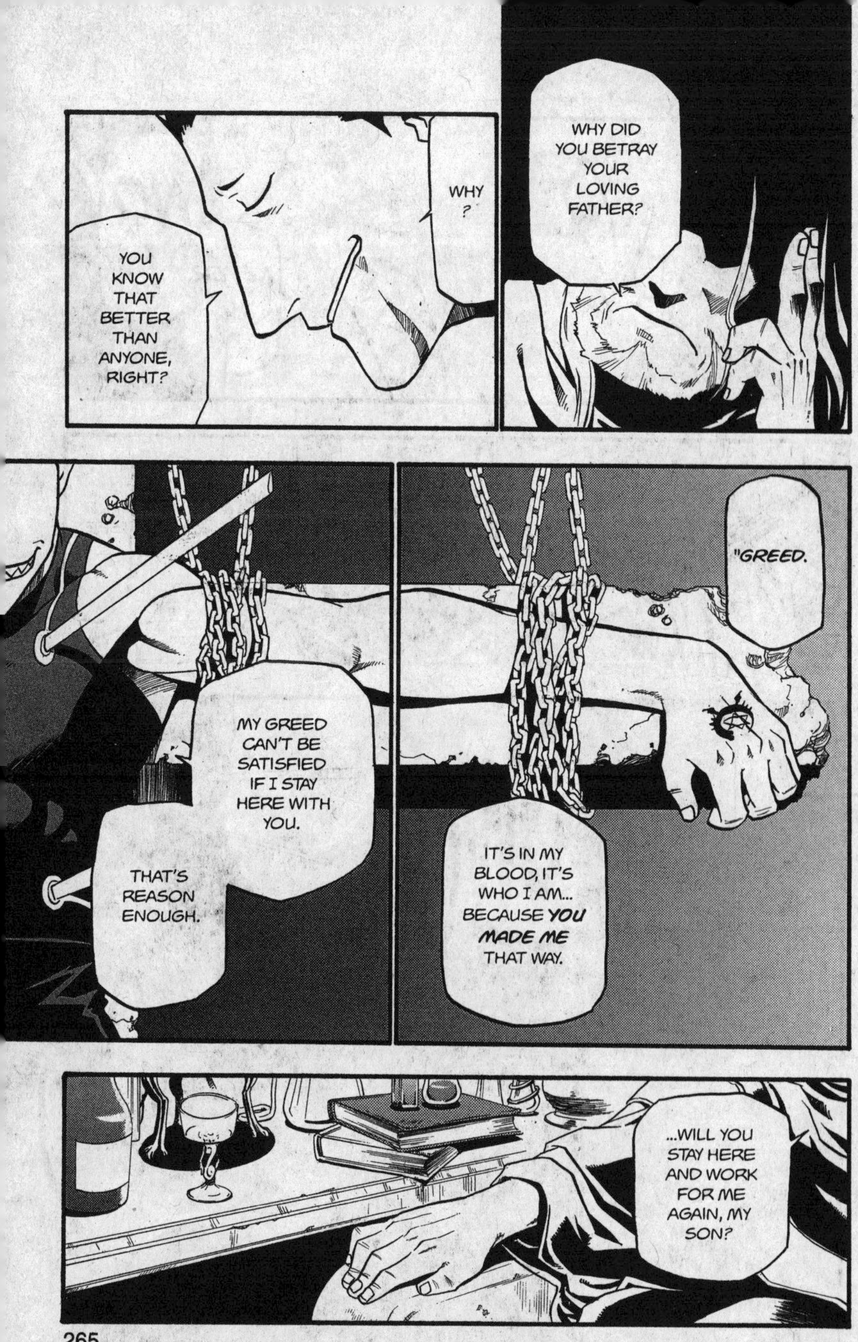
WHY DID YOU BETRAY YOUR LOVING FATHER?
WHY ?
YOU KNOW THAT BETTER THAN ANYONE, RIGHT?
"GREED.
IT'S IN MY BLOOD, IT'S WHO I AM... BECAUSE YOU MADE ME THAT WAY.
MY GREED CAN'T BE SATISFIED IF I STAY HERE WITH YOU.
THAT'S REASON ENOUGH.
...WILL YOU STAY HERE AND WORK FOR ME AGAIN, MY SON?

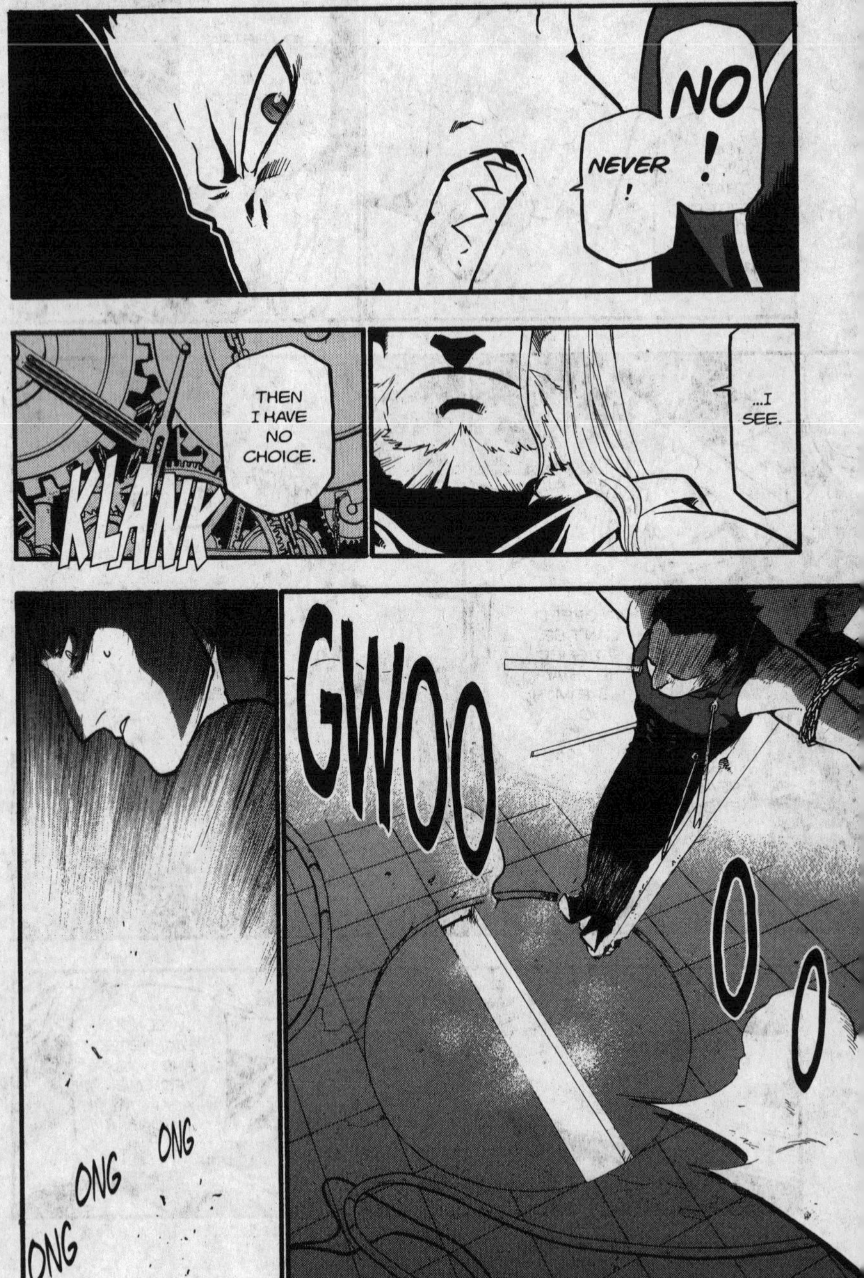
NO!
NEVER!
...I SEE.
THEN I HAVE NO CHOICE.
KLANK
GWOOOO
ONG ONG ONG

ONG
ONG
ONNG
D-
D-
D-
D-
D-
D-
D-
D-
GLUP
GLUP
KREEK
KLANK
...TALK ABOUT CHEESY...
CLINK CLINK

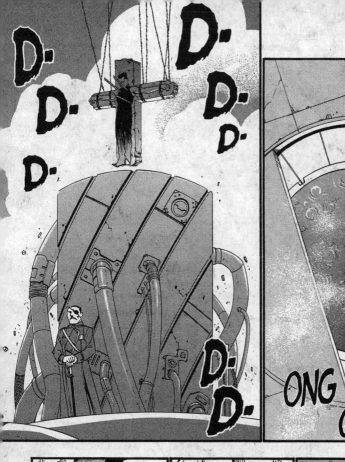

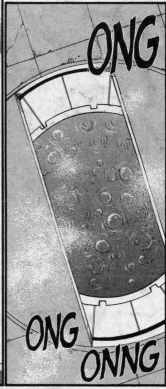

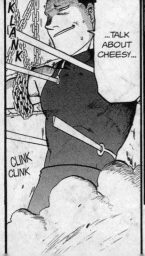

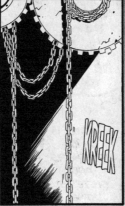

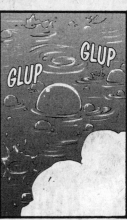

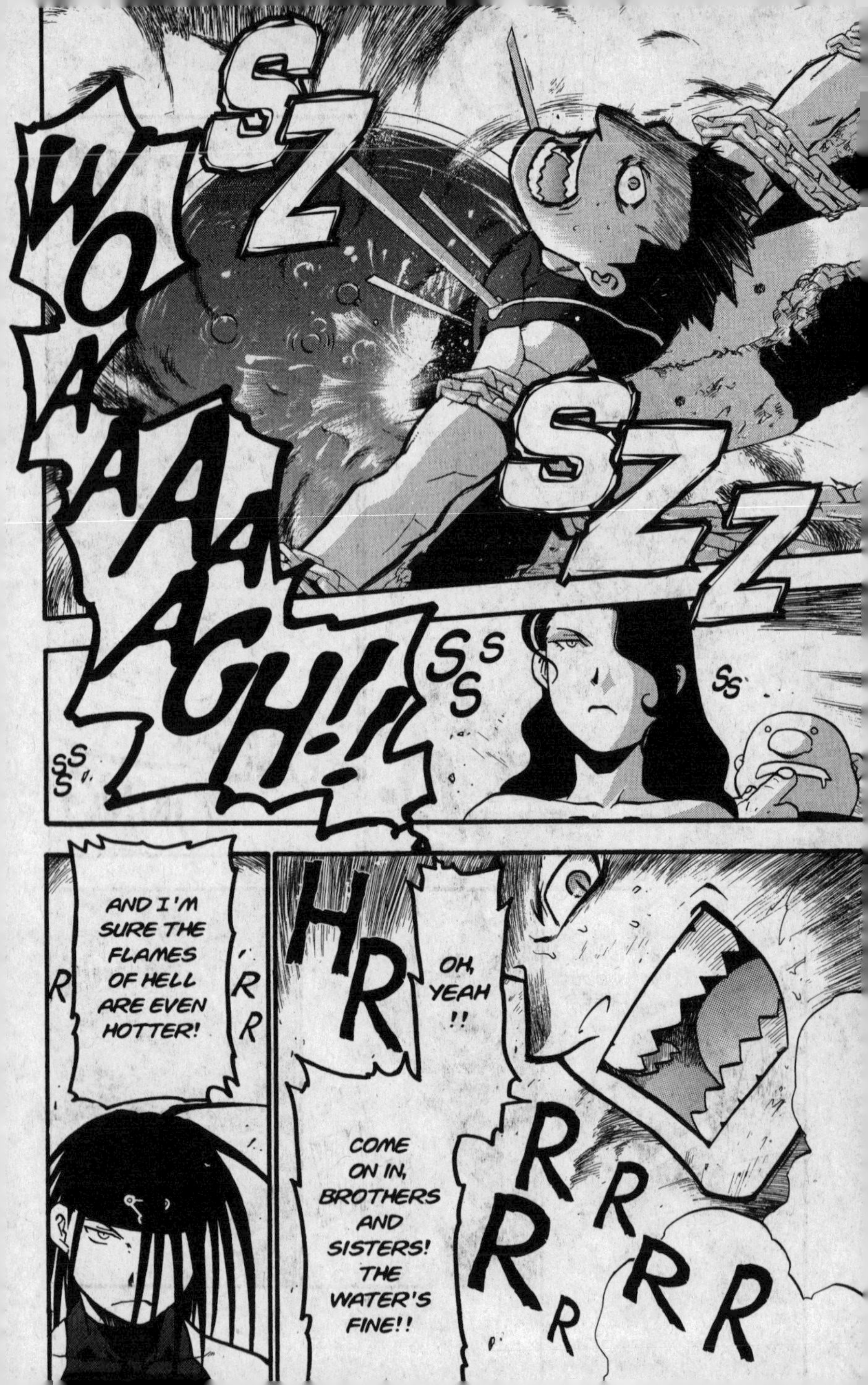
SZ
SZZ
WOAAAAACH!!
SSS
SS
SSS
HR
OH, YEAH!!
COME ON IN, BROTHERS AND SISTERS! THE WATER'S FINE!!
RRRRRRR
AND I'M SURE THE FLAMES OF HELL ARE EVEN HOTTER!
RRR

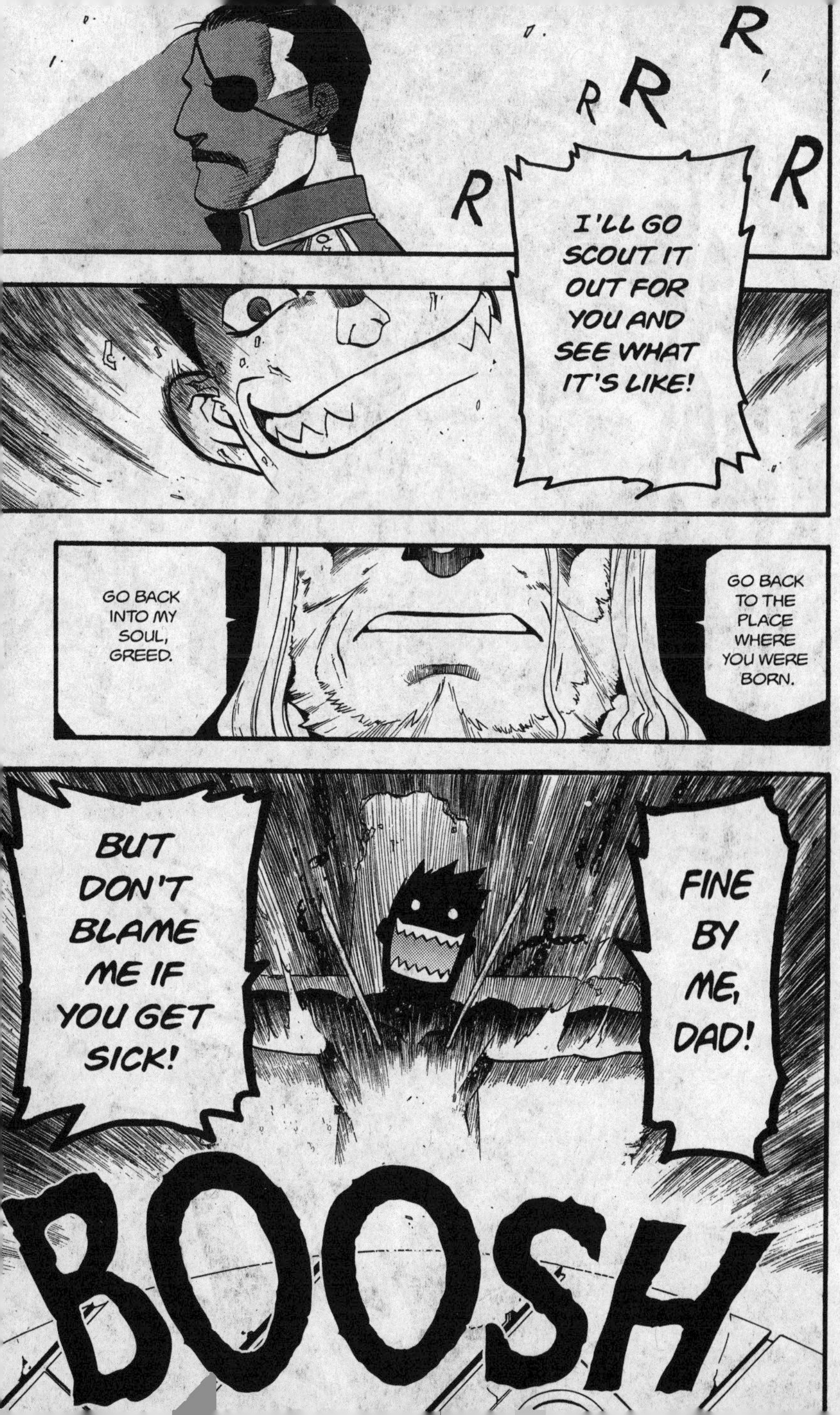
RRRRR
I'LL GO SCOUT IT OUT FOR YOU AND SEE WHAT IT'S LIKE!
GO BACK TO THE PLACE WHERE YOU WERE BORN.
GO BACK INTO MY SOUL, GREED.
FINE BY ME, DAD!
BUT DON'T BLAME ME IF YOU GET SICK!
BOOSH

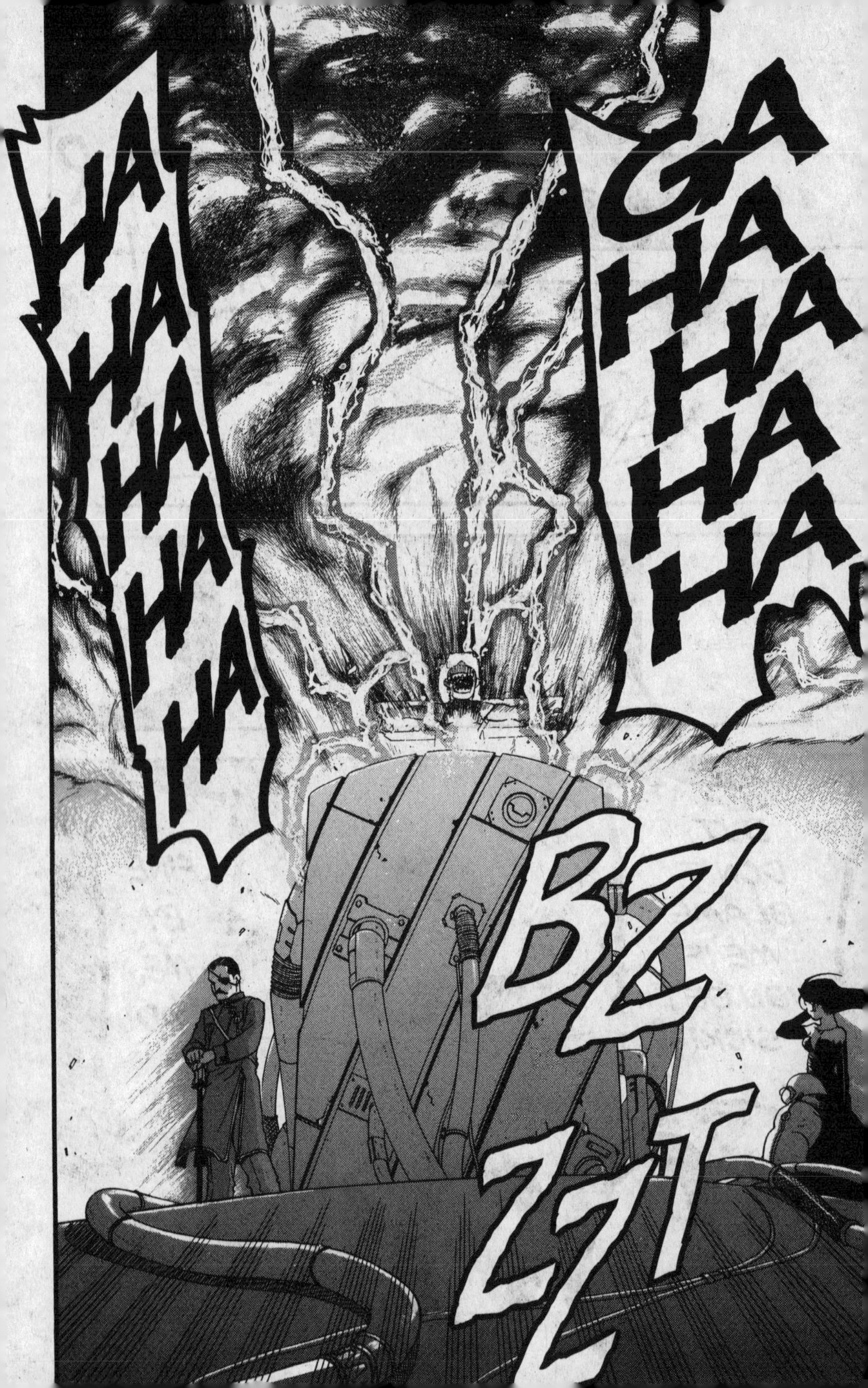
GA HA HA HA HA HA
HA HA HA HA HA HA
BZZZT

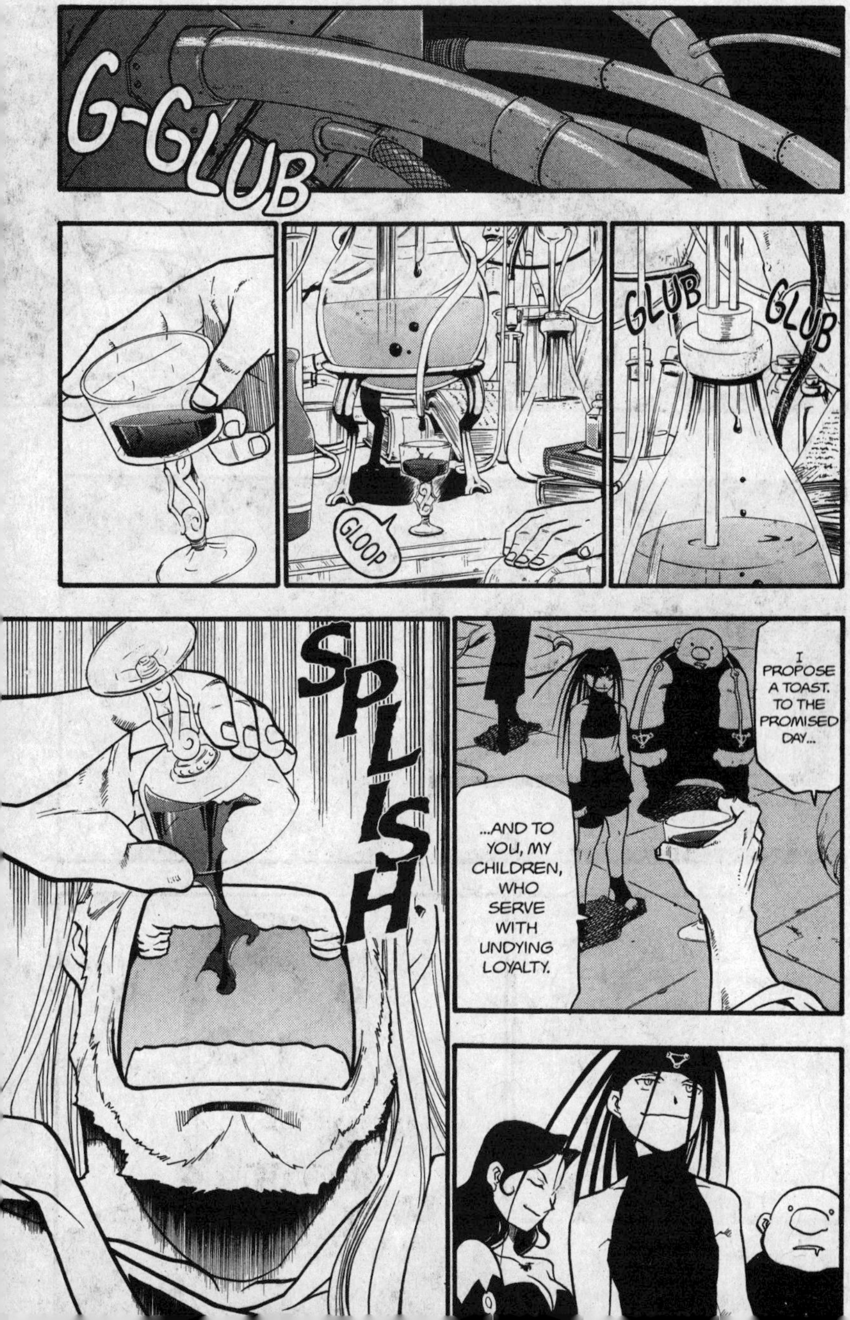
G-GLUB
GLUB GLUB
GLOOP
I PROPOSE A TOAST. TO THE PROMISED DAY...
...AND TO YOU, MY CHILDREN, WHO SERVE WITH UNDYING LOYALTY.
SPLISH

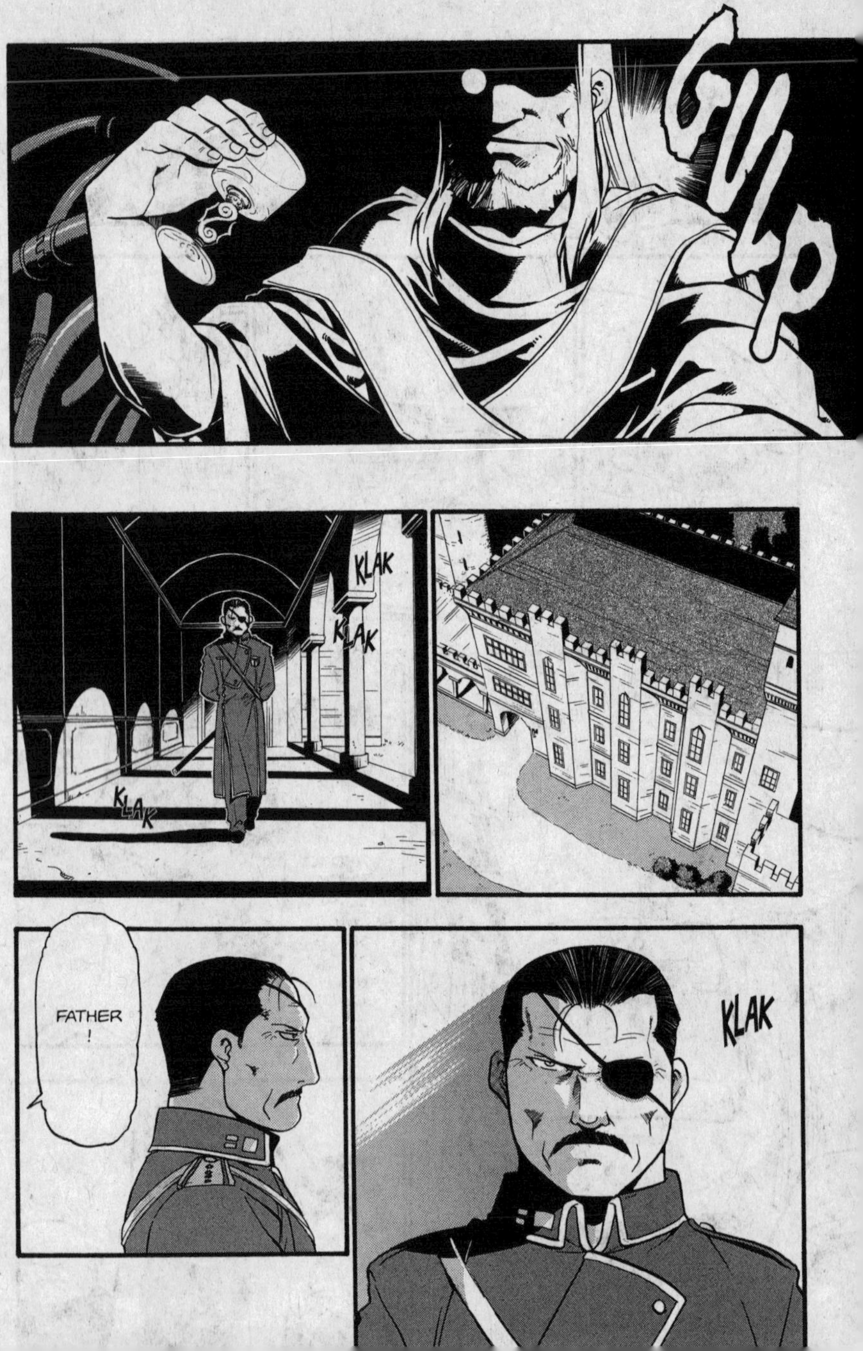
GULP
KLAK
KLAK
KLAK
KLAK
FATHER !

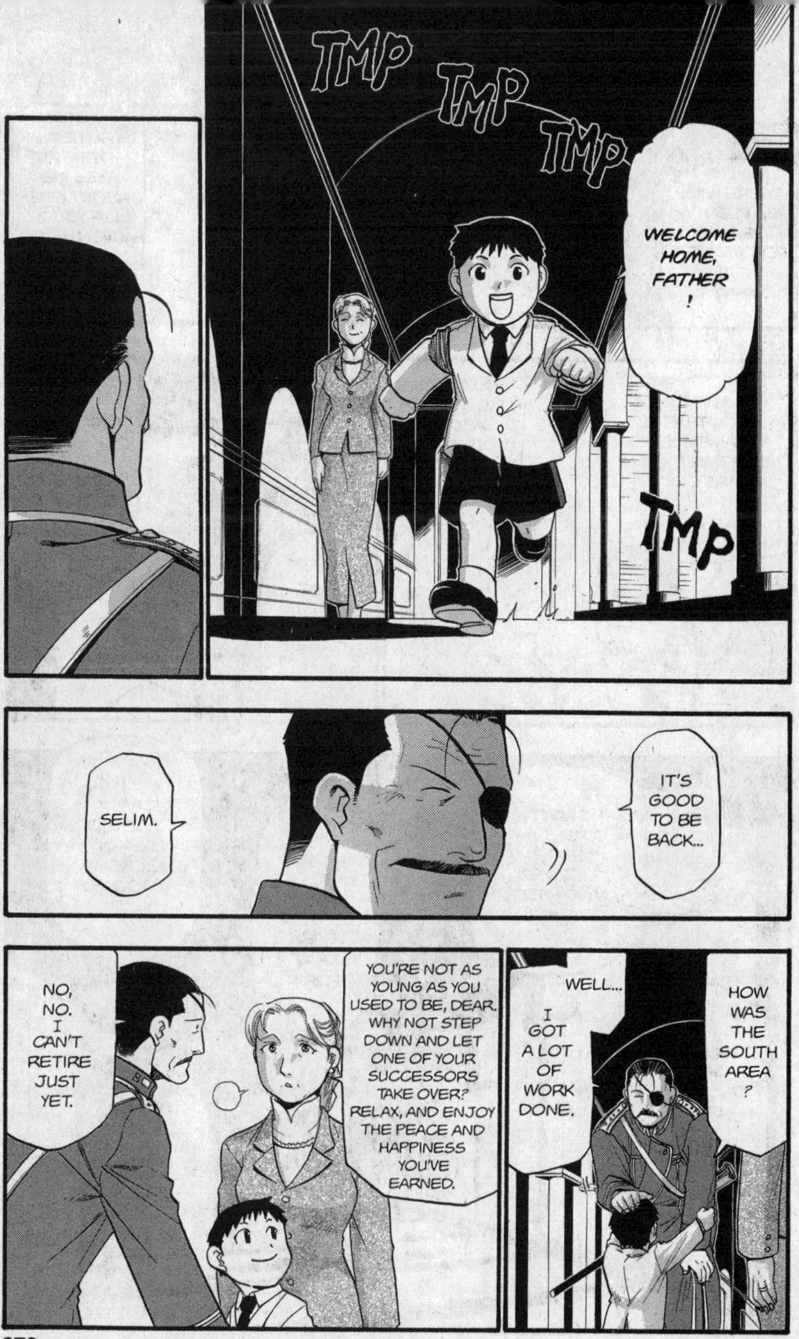
TMP TMP TMP
WELCOME HOME, FATHER!
TMP
IT'S GOOD TO BE BACK...
SELIM.
HOW WAS THE SOUTH AREA?
WELL...
I GOT A LOT OF WORK DONE.
YOU'RE NOT AS YOUNG AS YOU USED TO BE, DEAR. WHY NOT STEP DOWN AND LET ONE OF YOUR SUCCESSORS TAKE OVER? RELAX, AND ENJOY THE PEACE AND HAPPINESS YOU'VE EARNED.
NO, NO. I CAN'T RETIRE JUST YET.

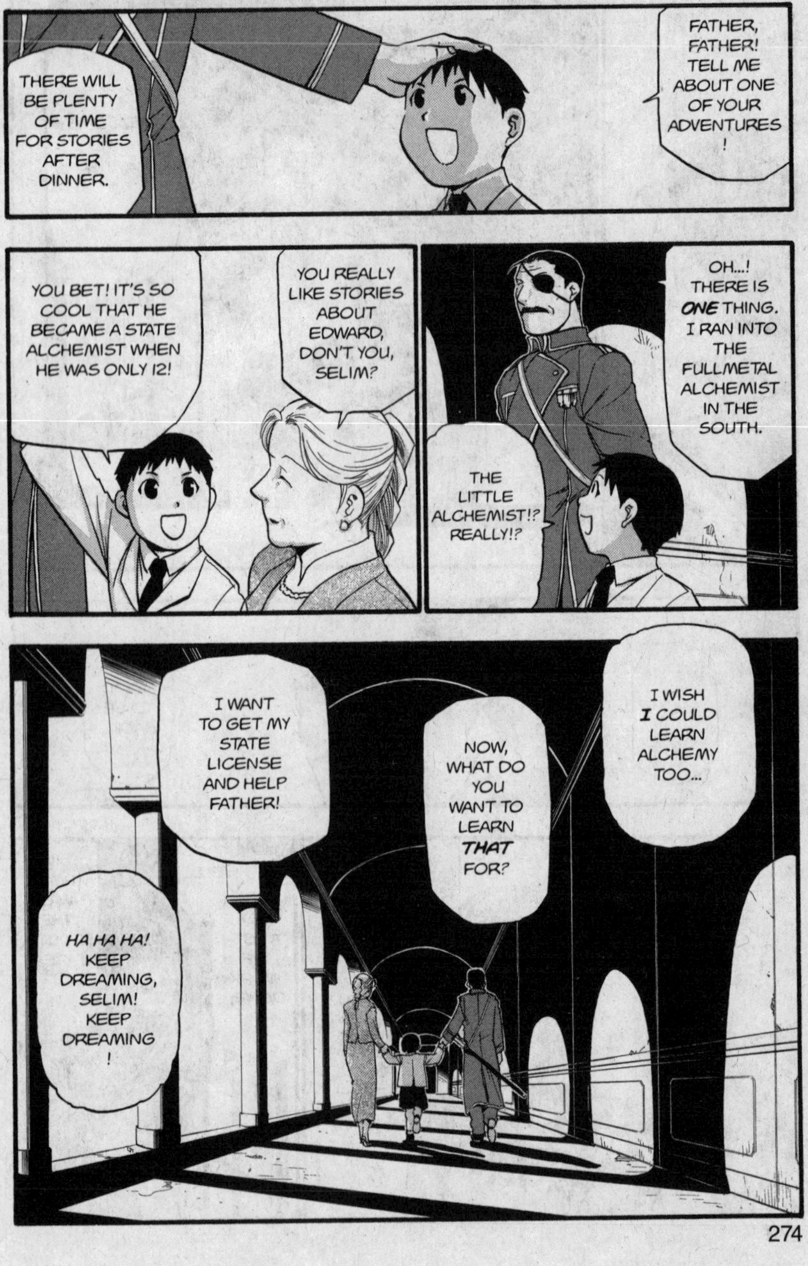
FATHER, FATHER! TELL ME ABOUT ONE OF YOUR ADVENTURES!
THERE WILL BE PLENTY OF TIME FOR STORIES AFTER DINNER.
OH...! THERE IS ONE THING. I RAN INTO THE FULLMETAL ALCHEMIST IN THE SOUTH.
THE LITTLE ALCHEMIST!? REALLY!?
YOU REALLY LIKE STORIES ABOUT EDWARD, DON'T YOU, SELIM?
YOU BET! IT'S SO COOL THAT HE BECAME A STATE ALCHEMIST WHEN HE WAS ONLY 12!
I WISH I COULD LEARN ALCHEMY TOO...
NOW, WHAT DO YOU WANT TO LEARN THAT FOR?
I WANT TO GET MY STATE LICENSE AND HELP FATHER!
HA HA HA! KEEP DREAMING, SELIM! KEEP DREAMING!

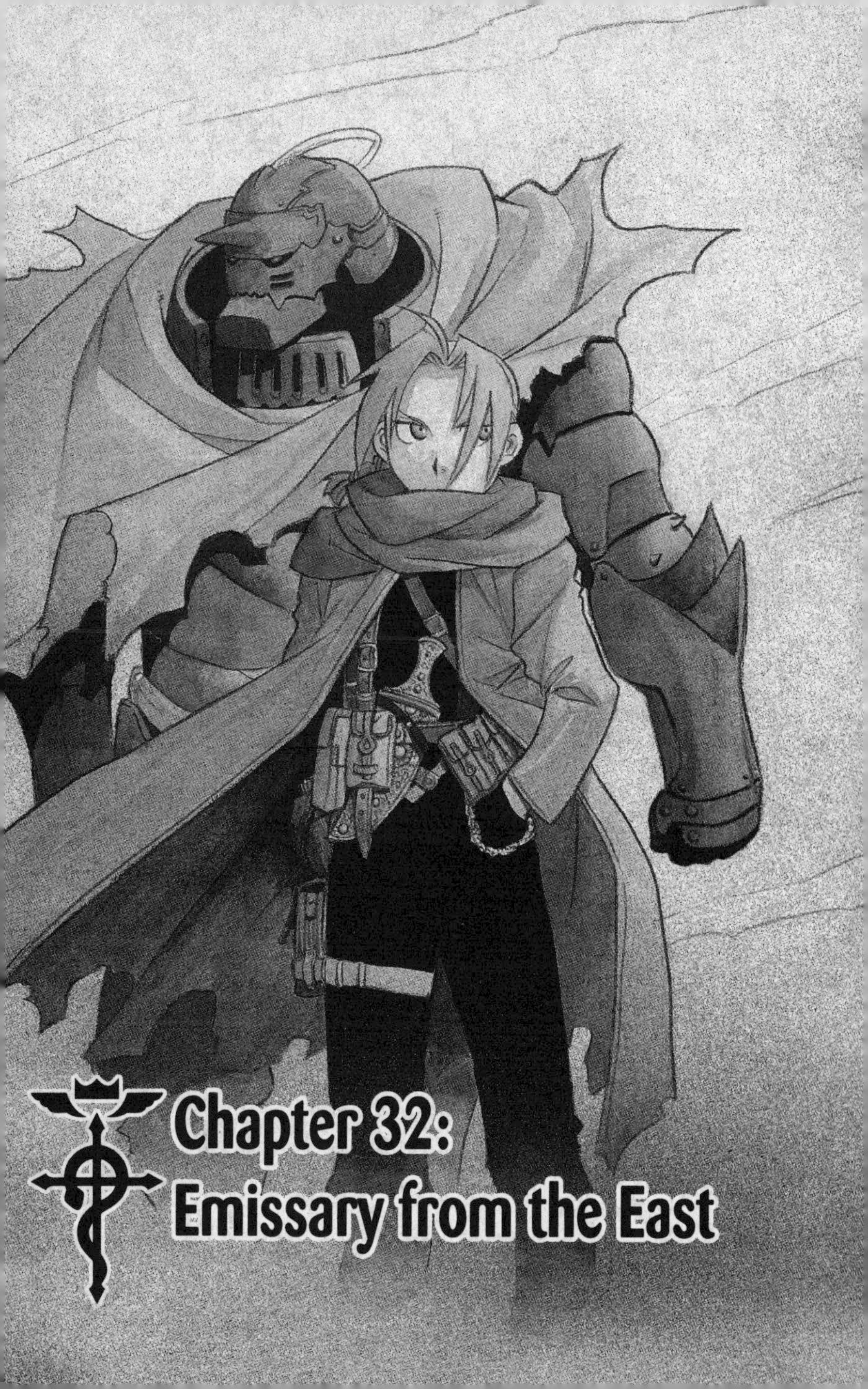

Chapter 32: Emissary from the East

FULLMETAL
ALCHEMIST

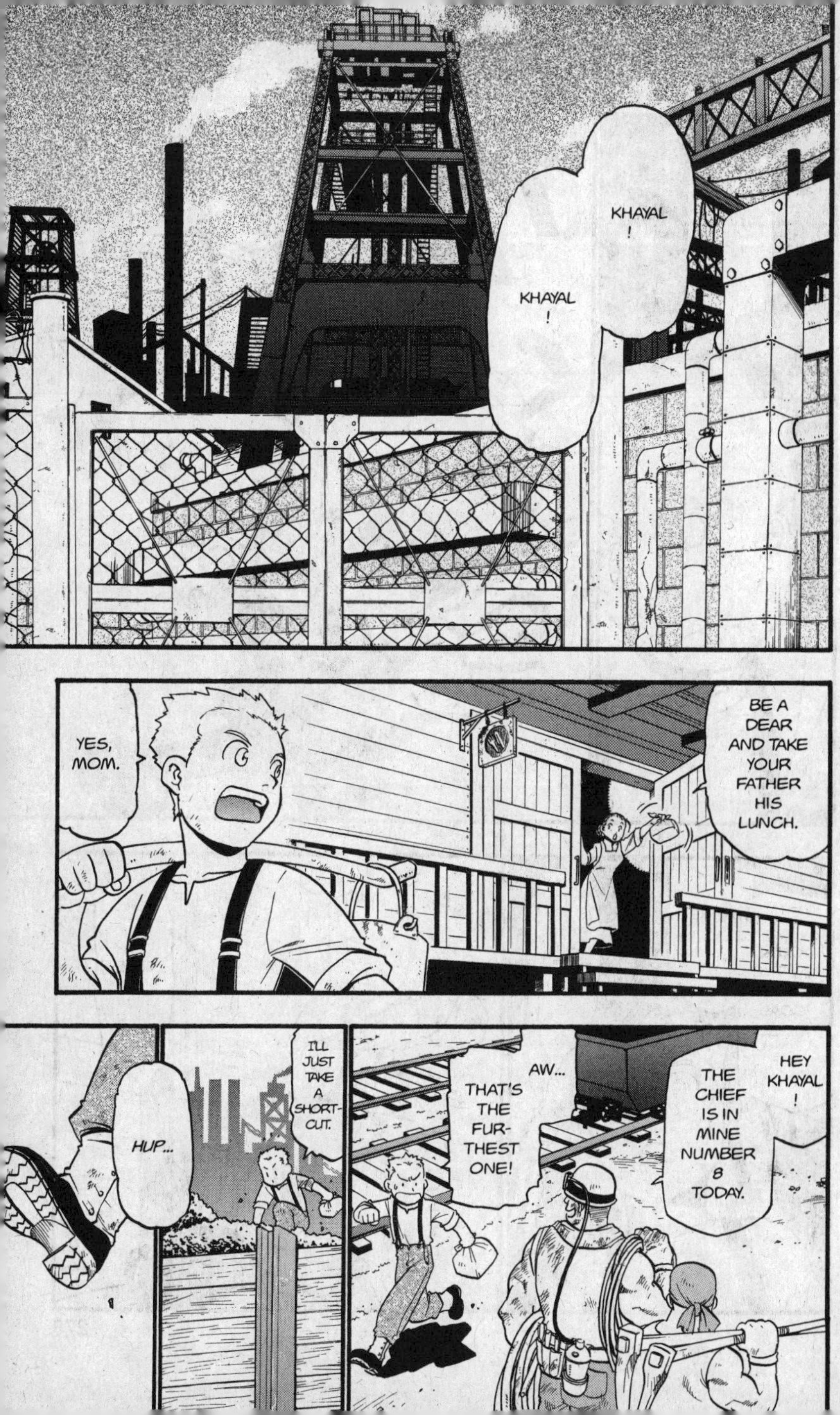
KHAYAL!
KHAYAL!
BE A DEAR AND TAKE YOUR FATHER HIS LUNCH.
YES, MOM.
HEY KHAYAL!
THE CHIEF IS IN MINE NUMBER 8 TODAY.
AW... THAT'S THE FURTHEST ONE!
I'LL JUST TAKE A SHORTCUT.
HUP...

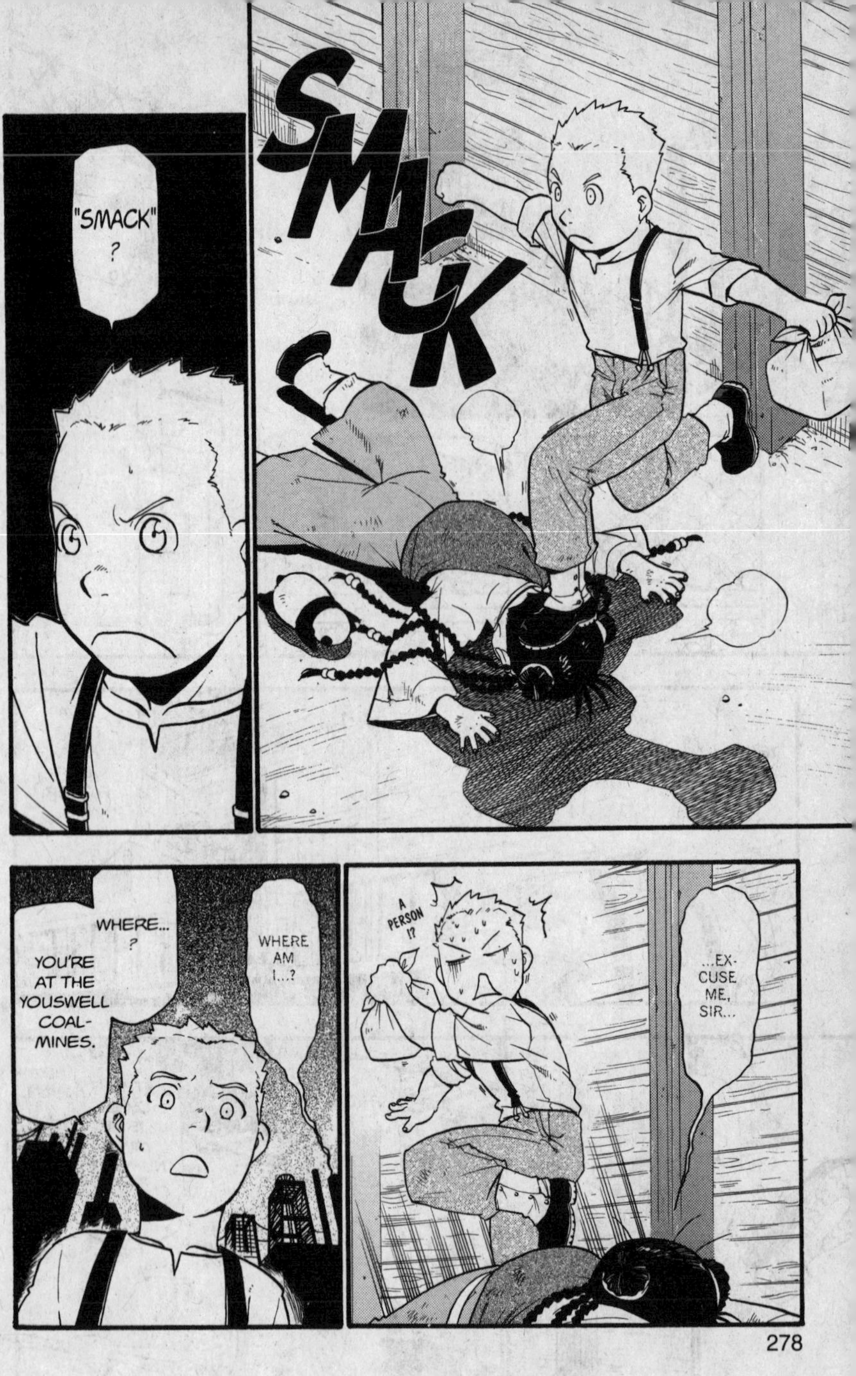
SMACK
"SMACK"?
...EX-CUSE ME, SIR...
A PERSON!?
WHERE AM I...?
WHERE...?
YOU'RE AT THE YOUSWELL COAL-MINES.

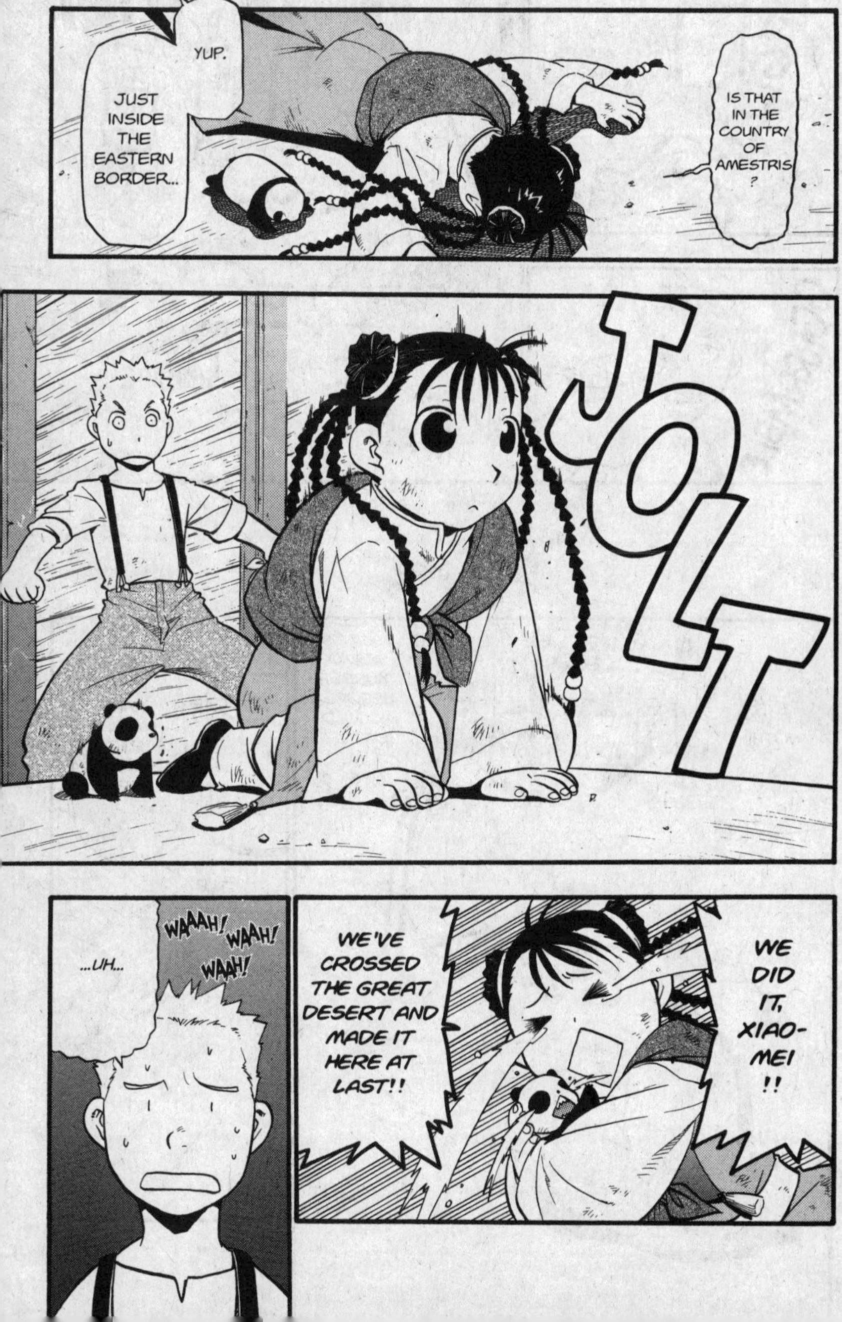
IS THAT IN THE COUNTRY OF AMESTRIS?
YUP.
JUST INSIDE THE EASTERN BORDER...
JOLT
WE DID IT, XIAO-MEI!!
WE'VE CROSSED THE GREAT DESERT AND MADE IT HERE AT LAST!!
WAAAH! WAAH! WAAH!
...UH...

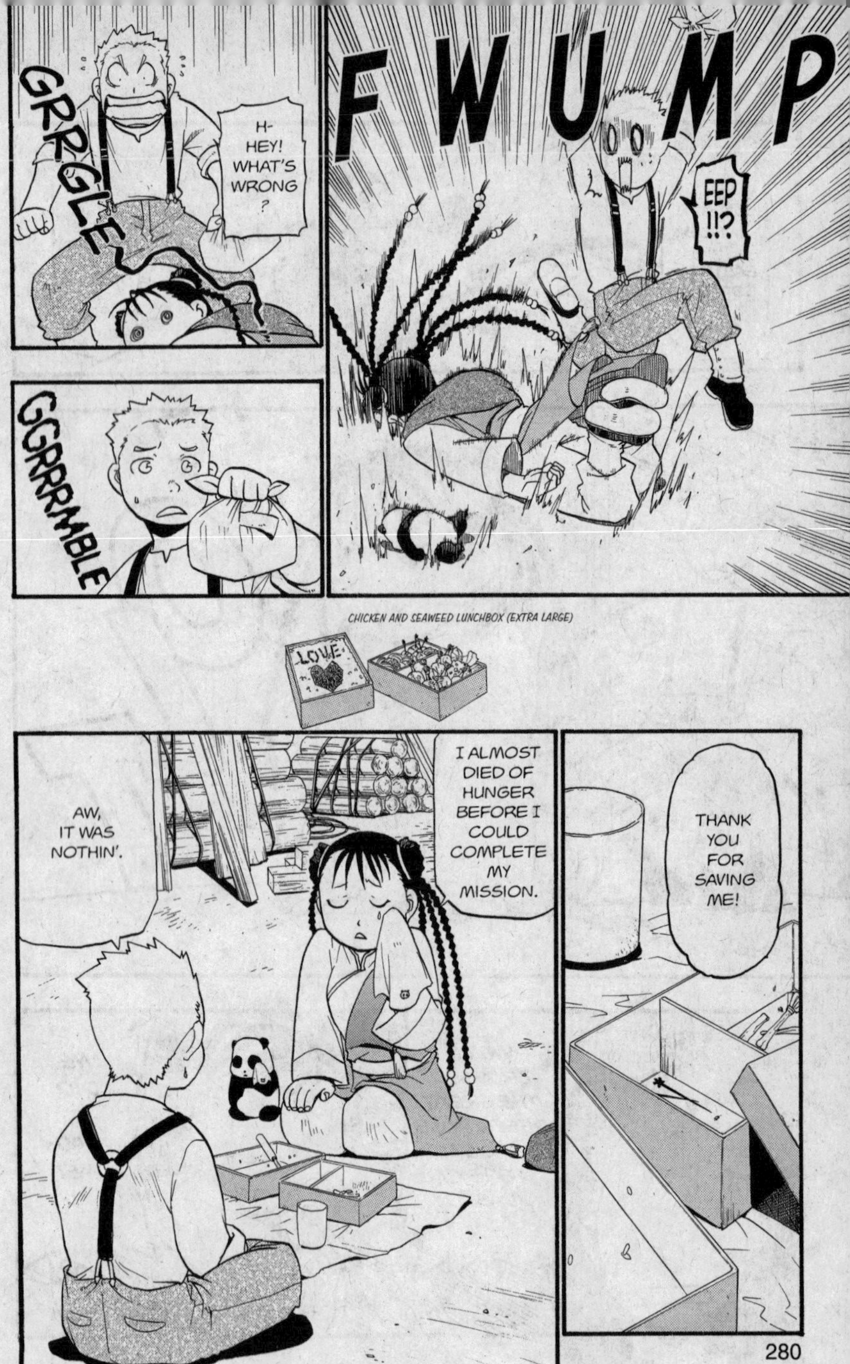
FWUMP
EEP!!?
GRRGLE
H-HEY! WHAT'S WRONG?
GGRRRMBLE
CHICKEN AND SEAWEED LUNCHBOX (EXTRA LARGE)
LOVE
THANK YOU FOR SAVING ME!
I ALMOST DIED OF HUNGER BEFORE I COULD COMPLETE MY MISSION.
AW, IT WAS NOTHIN'.

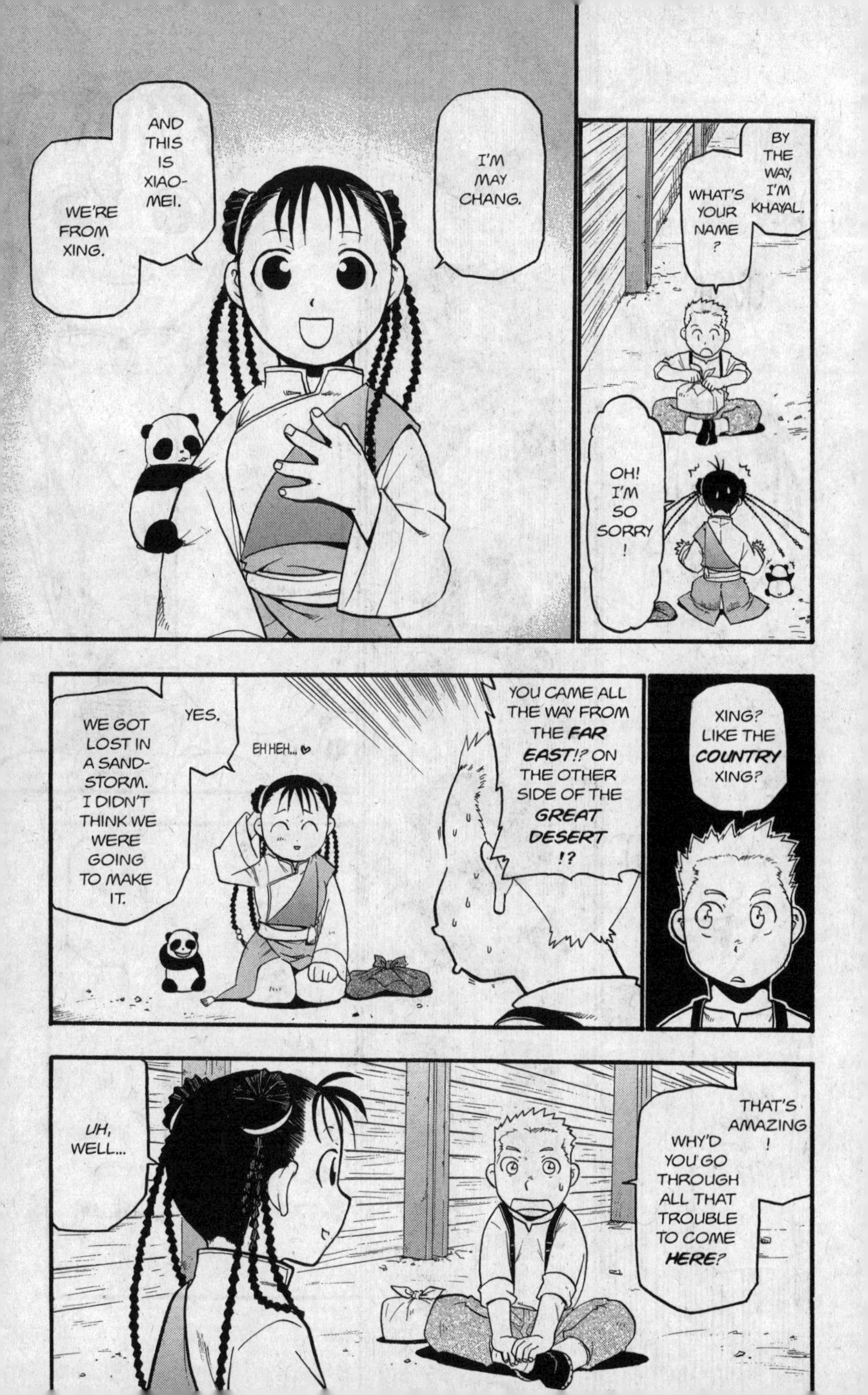
BY THE WAY, I'M KHAYAL.
WHAT'S YOUR NAME?
OH! I'M SO SORRY!
I'M MAY CHANG.
AND THIS IS XIAO-MEI.
WE'RE FROM XING.
XING? LIKE THE **COUNTRY** XING?
YOU CAME ALL THE WAY FROM THE ***FAR EAST!?*** ON THE OTHER SIDE OF THE ***GREAT DESERT*** !?
YES.
WE GOT LOST IN A SAND-STORM. I DIDN'T THINK WE WERE GOING TO MAKE IT.
EH HEH...
THAT'S AMAZING!
WHY'D YOU GO THROUGH ALL THAT TROUBLE TO COME ***HERE?***
UH, WELL...

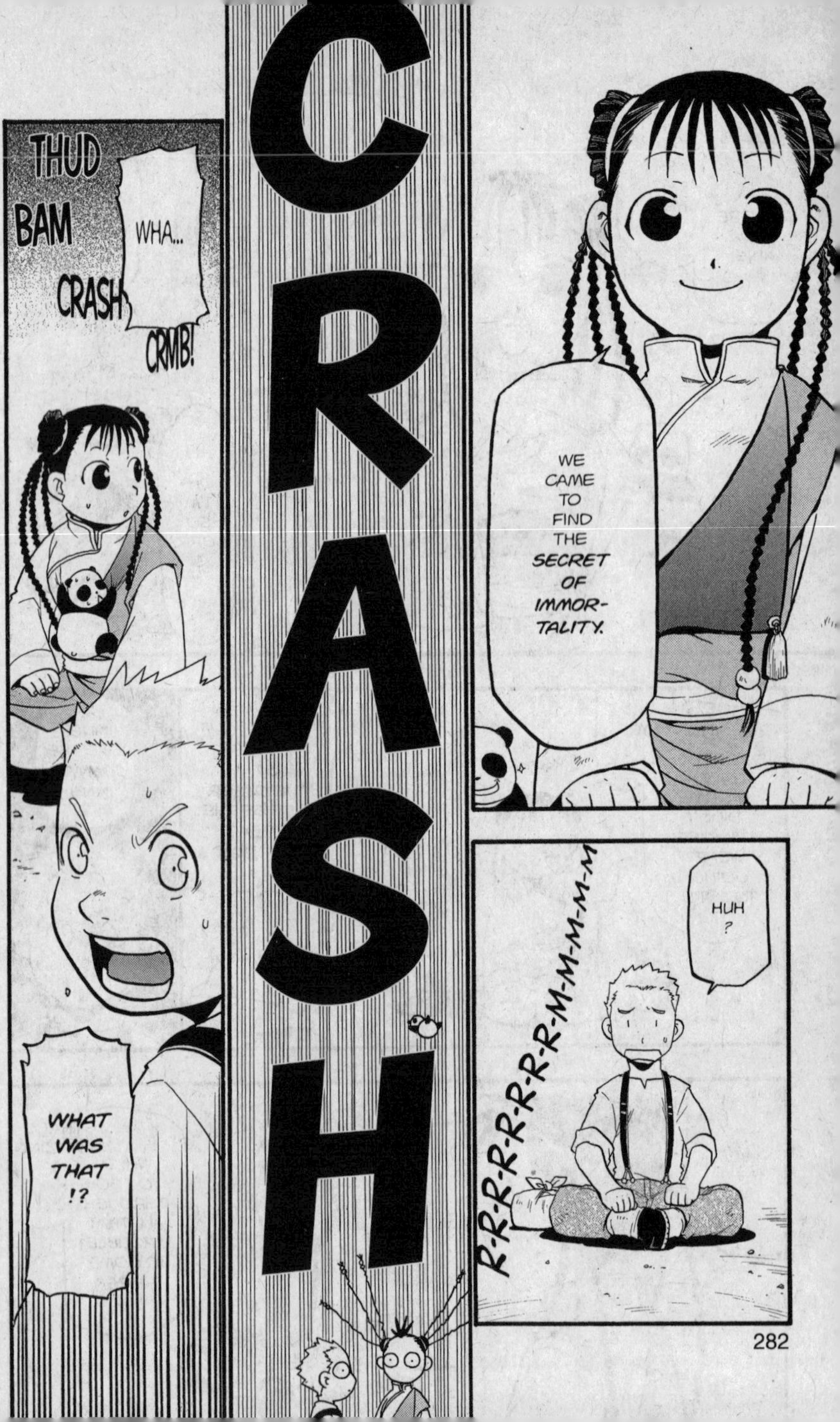
WE CAME TO FIND THE SECRET OF IMMORTALITY.
R-R-R-R-R-R-R-R-M-M-M-M-M-M
HUH?
CRASH
THUD
BAM
CRASH
WHA...
CRMB!
WHAT WAS THAT!?

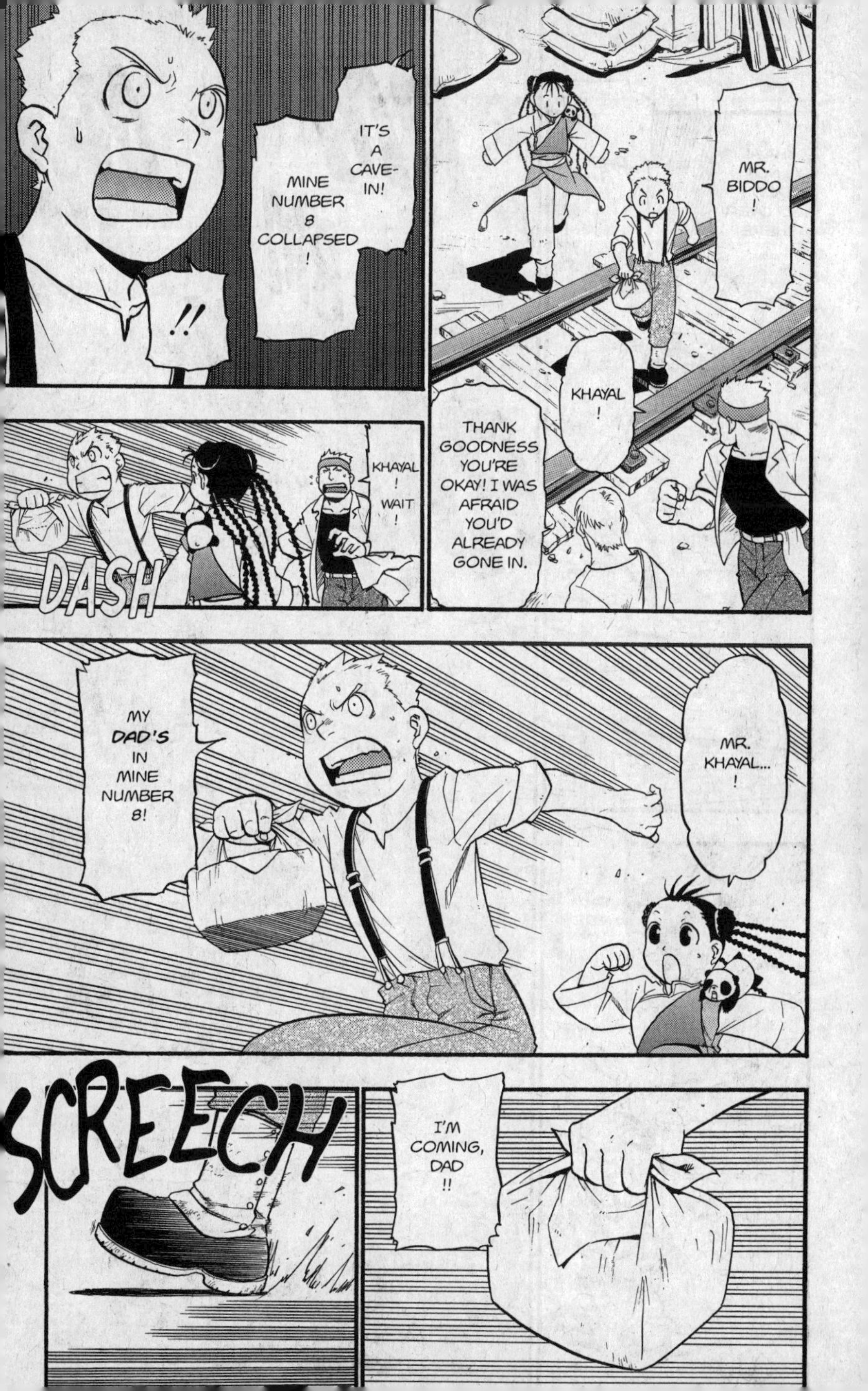
MR. BIDDO!
KHAYAL!
THANK GOODNESS YOU'RE OKAY! I WAS AFRAID YOU'D ALREADY GONE IN.
IT'S A CAVE-IN!
MINE NUMBER 8 COLLAPSED!
!!
KHAYAL! WAIT!
DASH
MR. KHAYAL...!
MY DAD'S IN MINE NUMBER 8!
I'M COMING, DAD!!
SCREECH

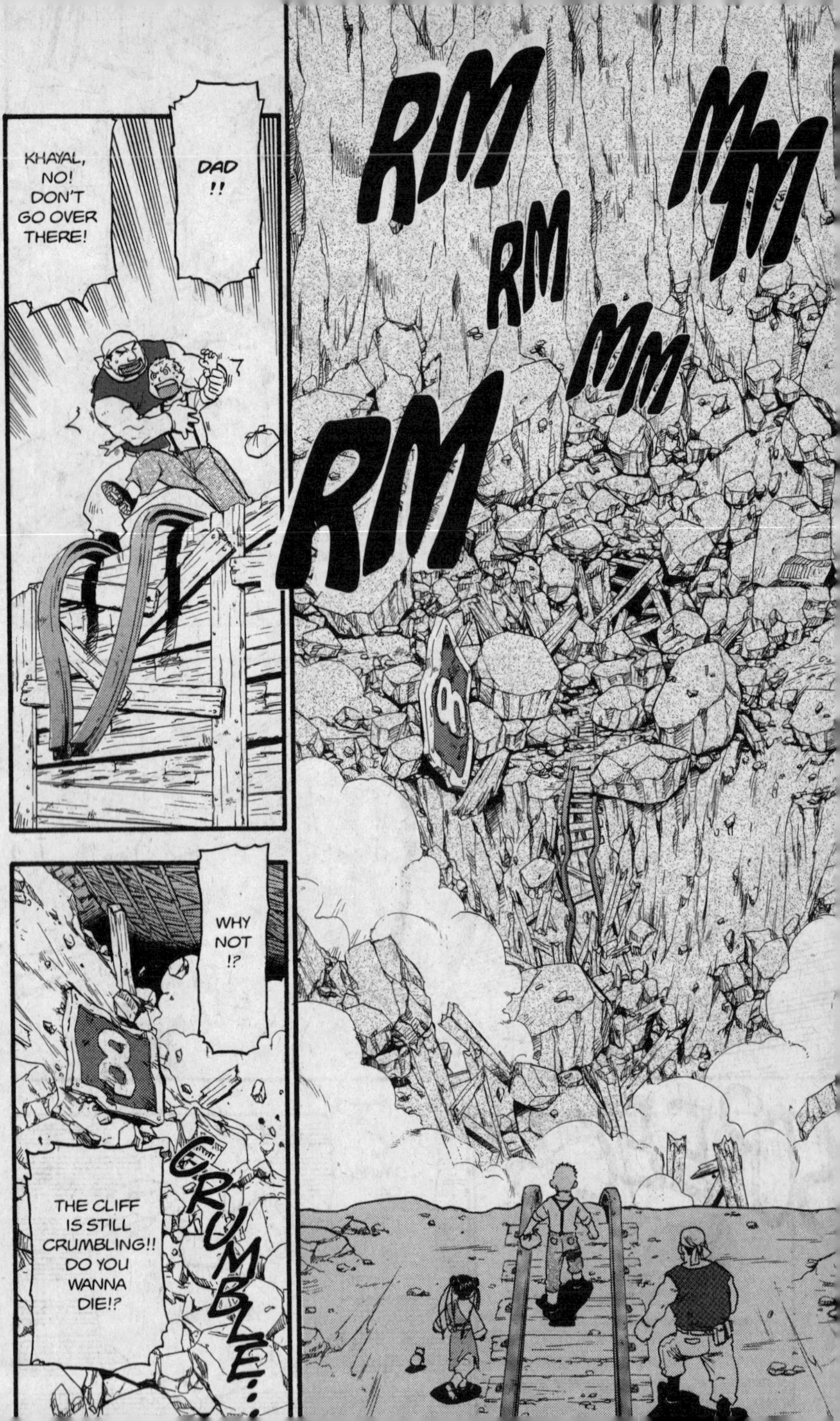
RM
MM
RM
MM
RM
DAD!!
KHAYAL, NO! DON'T GO OVER THERE!
WHY NOT!?
THE CLIFF IS STILL CRUMBLING!! DO YOU WANNA DIE!?
CRUMBLE...

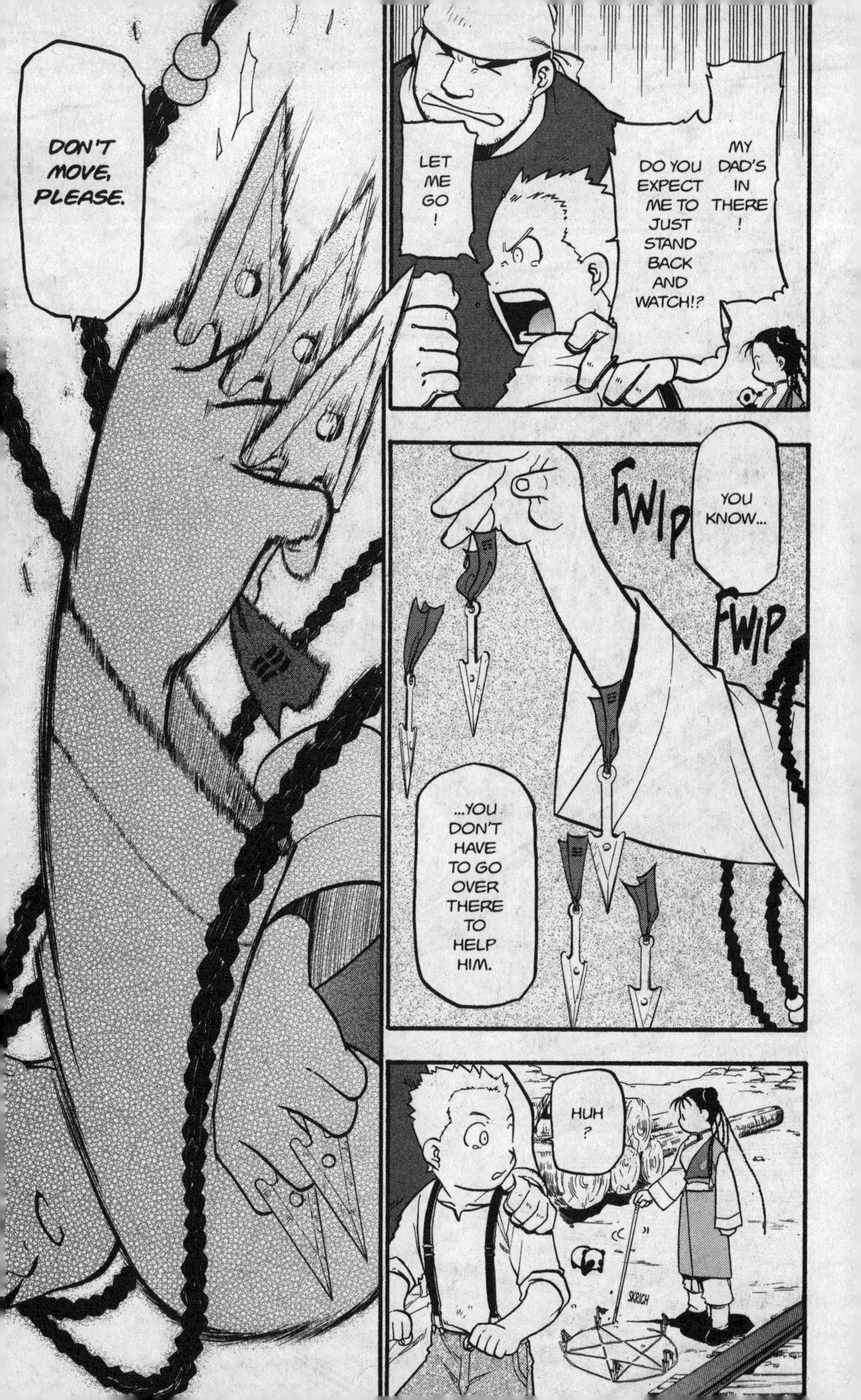
MY DAD'S IN THERE!
DO YOU EXPECT ME TO JUST STAND BACK AND WATCH!?
LET ME GO!
FWIP
FWIP
YOU KNOW...
...YOU DON'T HAVE TO GO OVER THERE TO HELP HIM.
HUH?
SKRICH
DON'T MOVE, PLEASE.

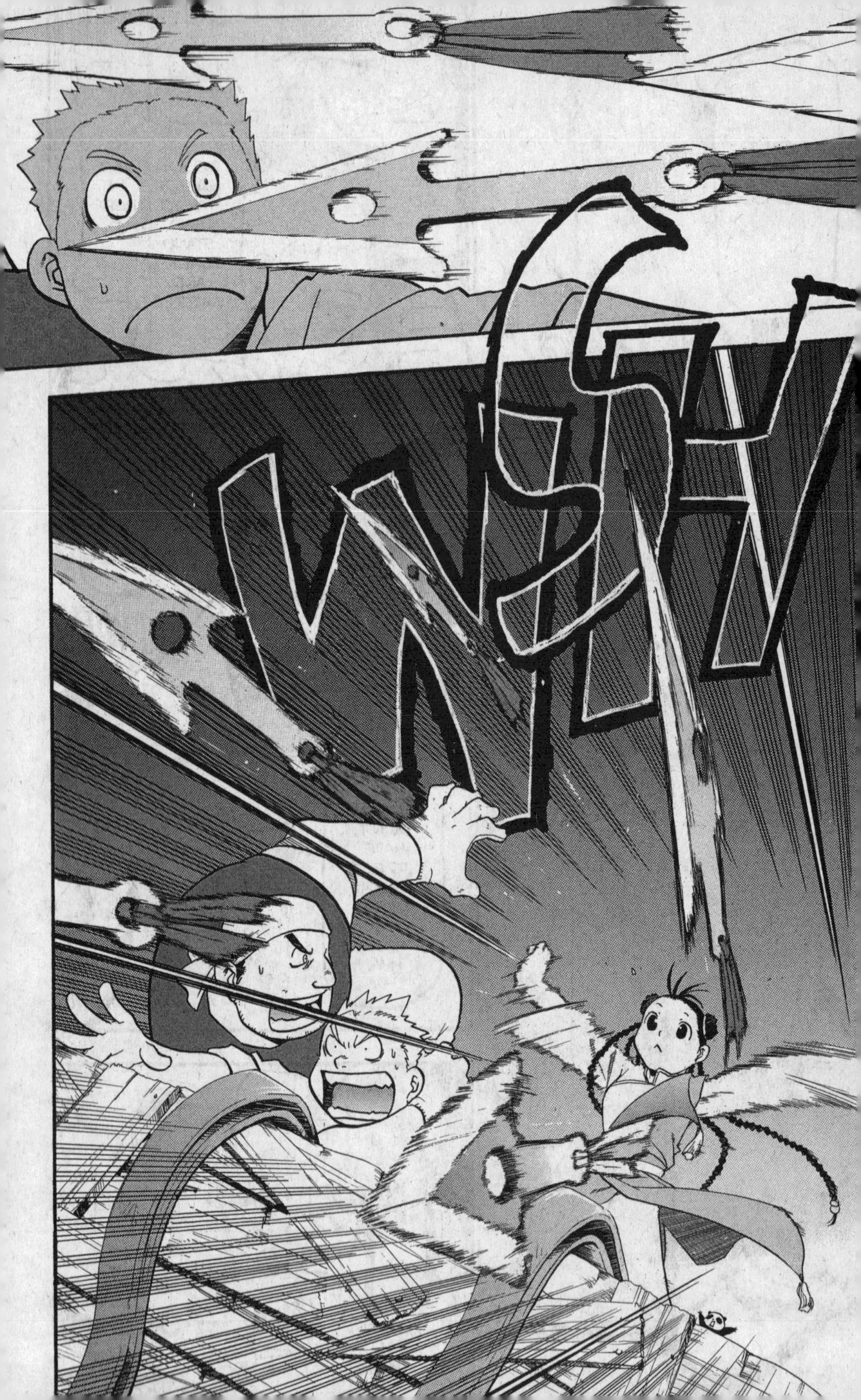
WSSH

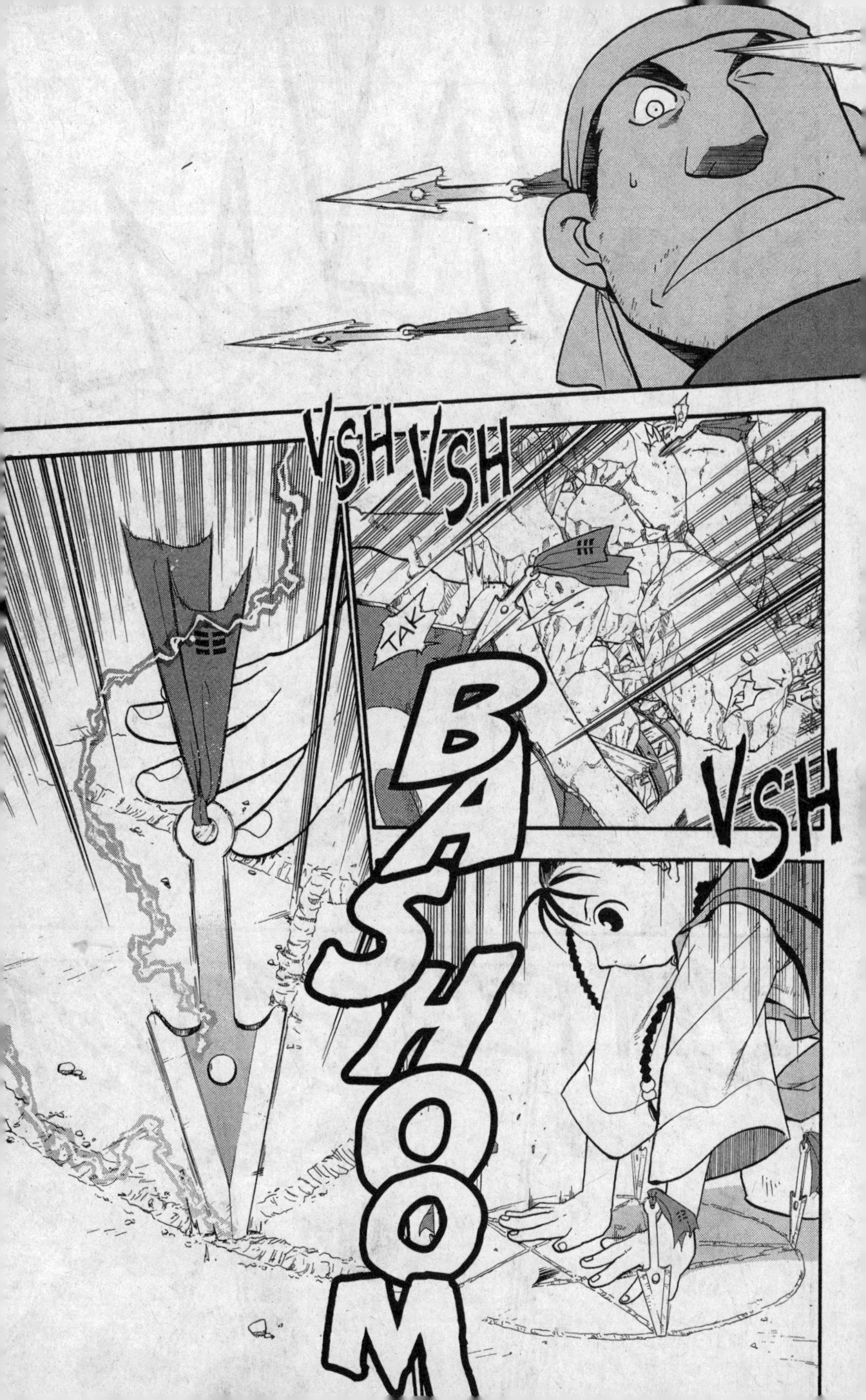
VSH VSH
TAK
VSH
BASHOOM

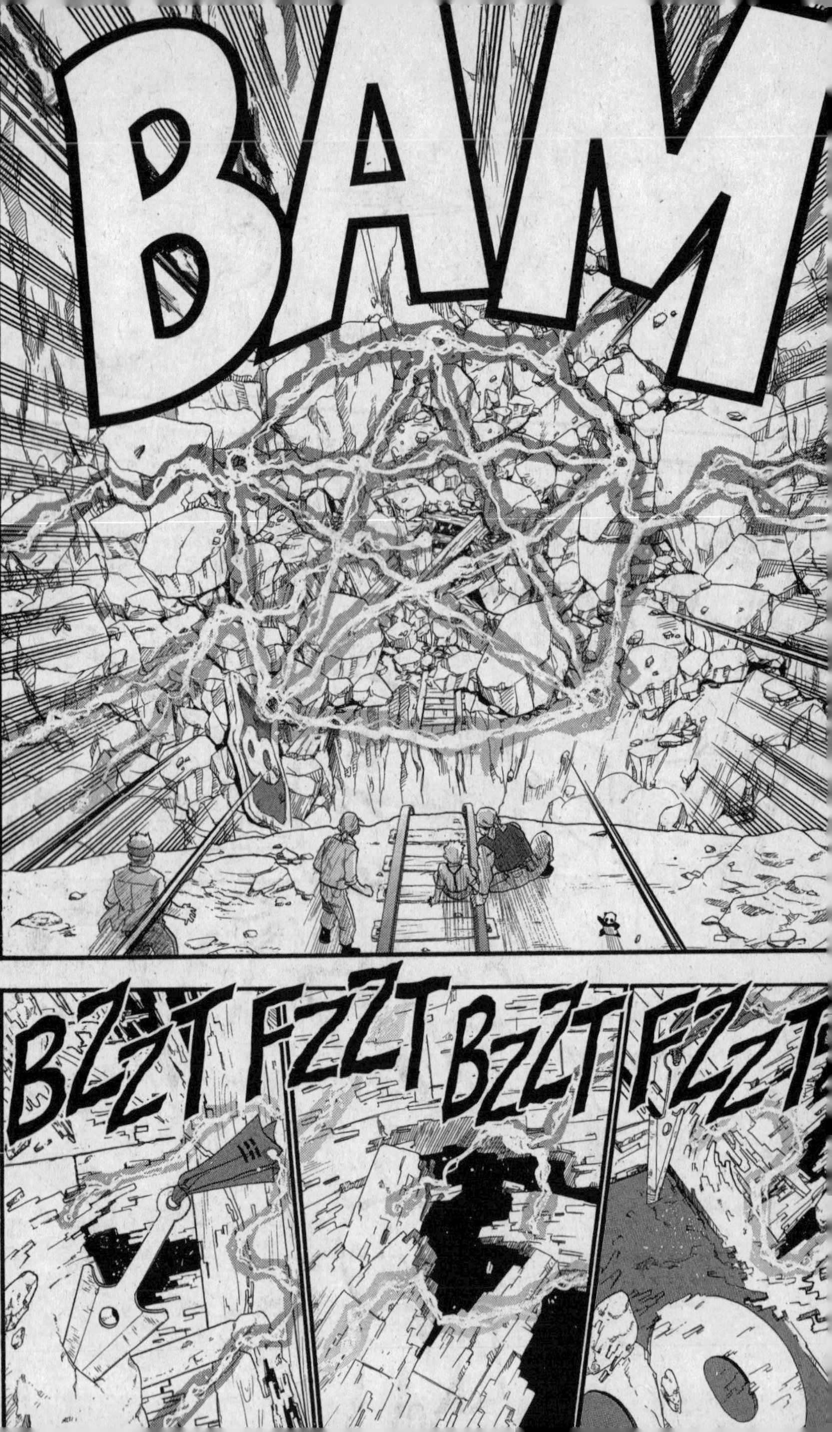
BAM
BZZT FZZT BZZT FZZT

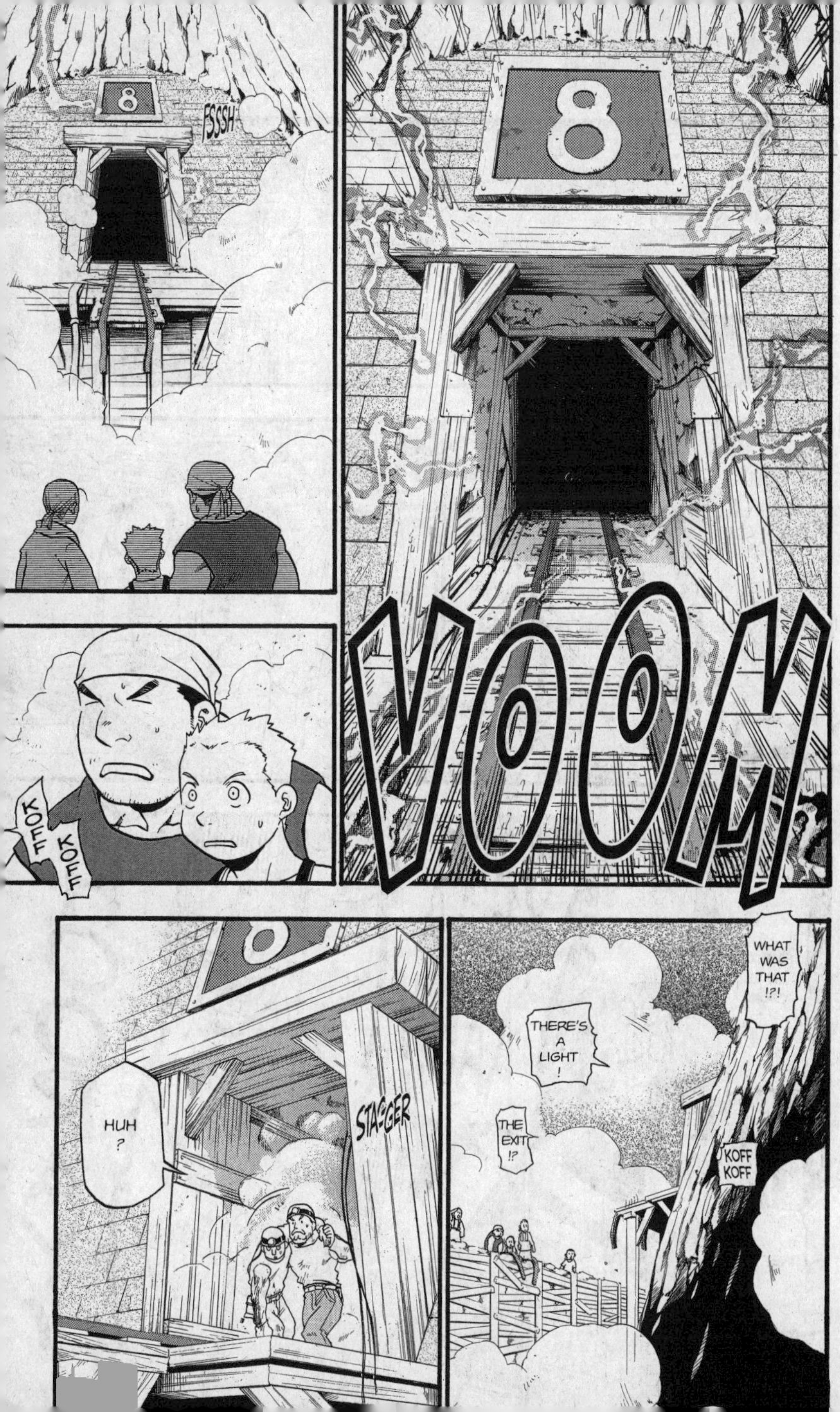
VOOM
FSSSH
KOFF KOFF
WHAT WAS THAT !?!
THERE'S A LIGHT !
THE EXIT !?
KOFF KOFF
STAGGER
HUH ?

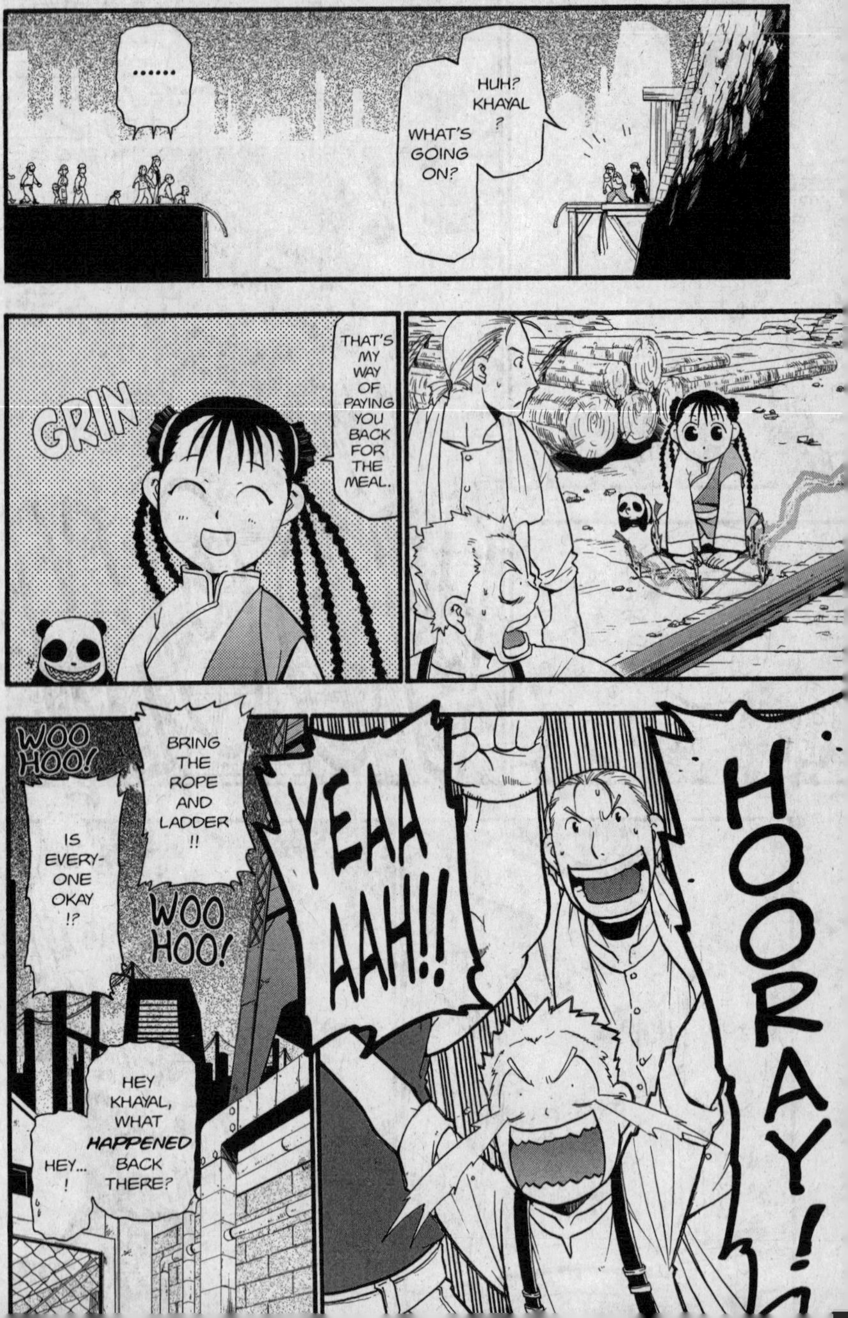
HUH? KHAYAL?
WHAT'S GOING ON?
....
THAT'S MY WAY OF PAYING YOU BACK FOR THE MEAL.
GRIN
HOORAY!!
YEAAAAH!!
BRING THE ROPE AND LADDER!!
WOO HOO!
IS EVERYONE OKAY!?
WOO HOO!
HEY KHAYAL, WHAT HAPPENED BACK THERE?
HEY...!

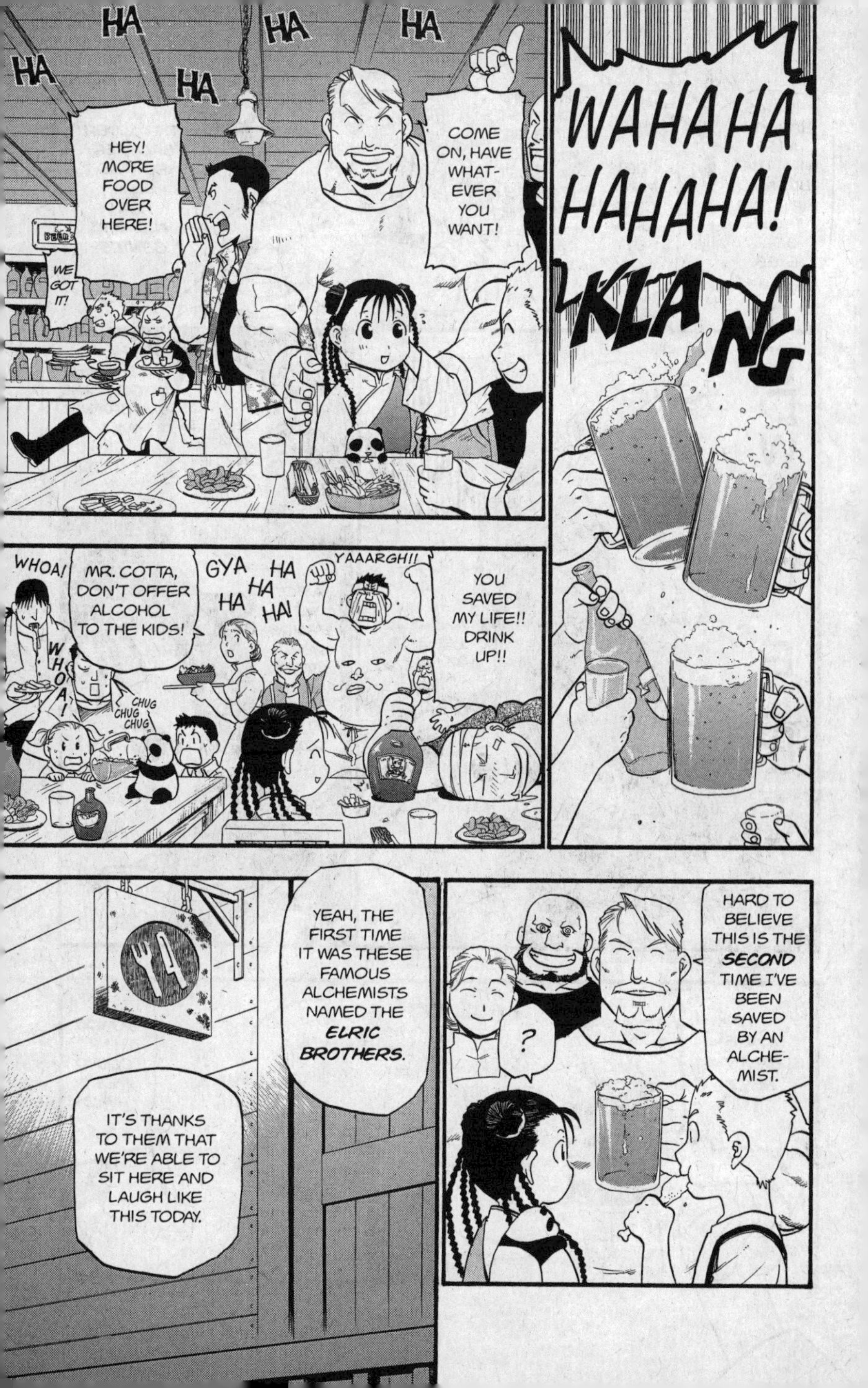
WAHAHA HAHAHA!
KLANG
HA HA HA HA HA
COME ON, HAVE WHATEVER YOU WANT!
HEY! MORE FOOD OVER HERE!
WE GOT IT!
YOU SAVED MY LIFE!! DRINK UP!!
YAAARGH!!
GYA HA HA HA HA!
MR. COTTA, DON'T OFFER ALCOHOL TO THE KIDS!
WHOA!
WHOA!
CHUG CHUG CHUG
HARD TO BELIEVE THIS IS THE SECOND TIME I'VE BEEN SAVED BY AN ALCHEMIST.
?
YEAH, THE FIRST TIME IT WAS THESE FAMOUS ALCHEMISTS NAMED THE ELRIC BROTHERS.
IT'S THANKS TO THEM THAT WE'RE ABLE TO SIT HERE AND LAUGH LIKE THIS TODAY.

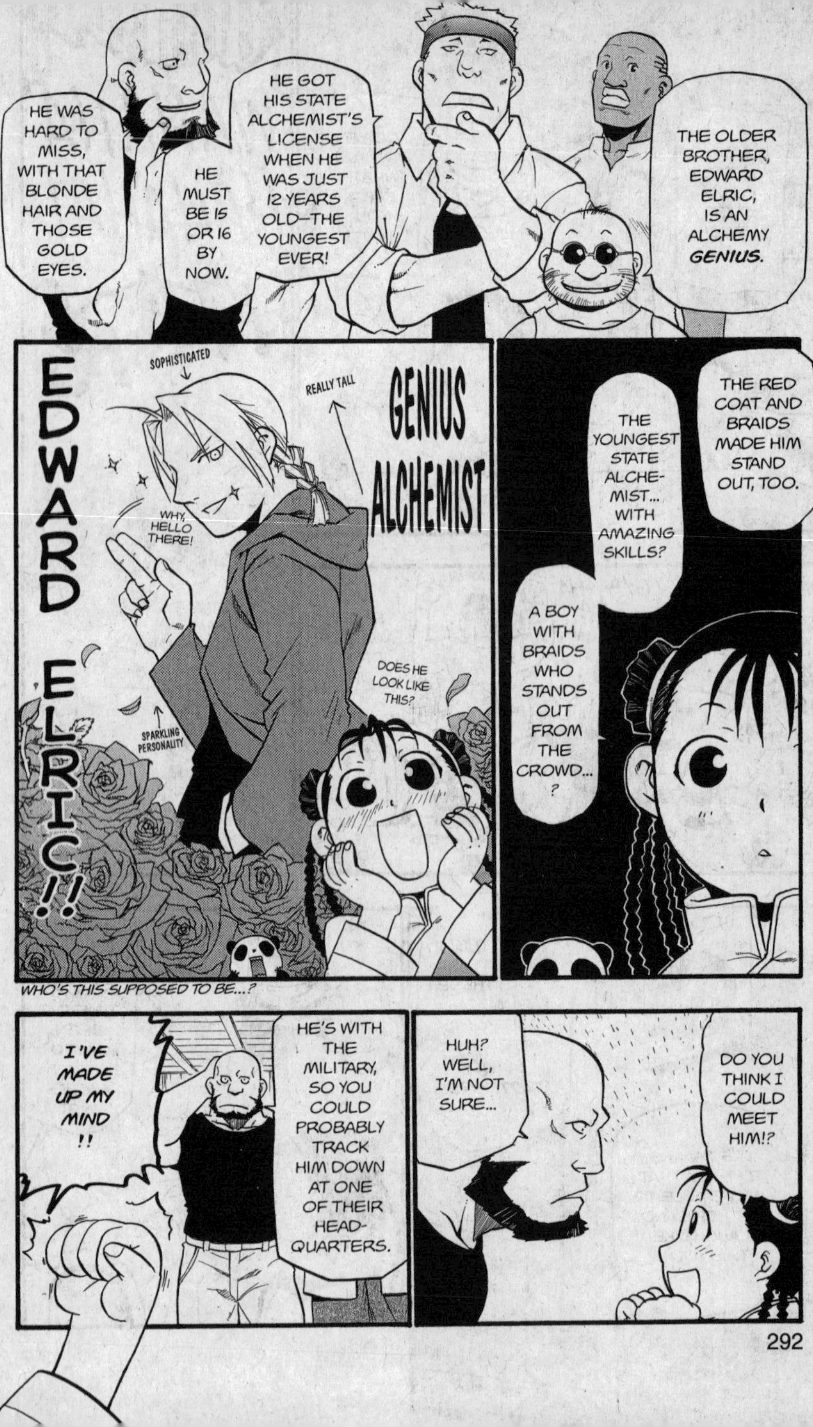
THE OLDER BROTHER, EDWARD ELRIC, IS AN ALCHEMY GENIUS.
HE GOT HIS STATE ALCHEMIST'S LICENSE WHEN HE WAS JUST 12 YEARS OLD—THE YOUNGEST EVER!
HE MUST BE 15 OR 16 BY NOW.
HE WAS HARD TO MISS, WITH THAT BLONDE HAIR AND THOSE GOLD EYES.
THE RED COAT AND BRAIDS MADE HIM STAND OUT, TOO.
THE YOUNGEST STATE ALCHEMIST... WITH AMAZING SKILLS?
A BOY WITH BRAIDS WHO STANDS OUT FROM THE CROWD...?
EDWARD ELRIC!!
GENIUS ALCHEMIST
SOPHISTICATED
REALLY TALL
WHY, HELLO THERE!
SPARKLING PERSONALITY
DOES HE LOOK LIKE THIS?
WHO'S THIS SUPPOSED TO BE...?
DO YOU THINK I COULD MEET HIM!?
HUH? WELL, I'M NOT SURE...
HE'S WITH THE MILITARY, SO YOU COULD PROBABLY TRACK HIM DOWN AT ONE OF THEIR HEAD-QUARTERS.
I'VE MADE UP MY MIND!!

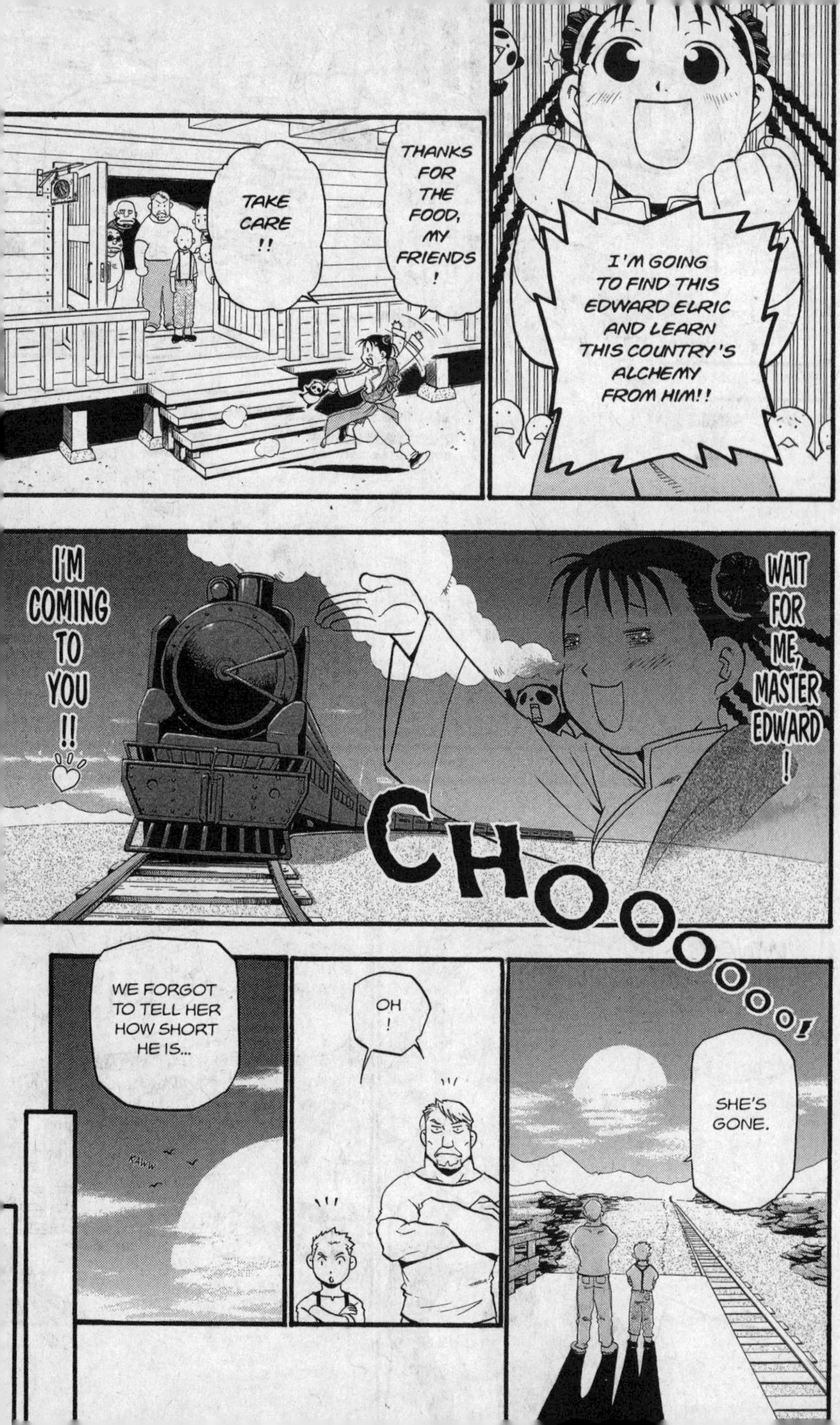
I'M GOING TO FIND THIS EDWARD ELRIC AND LEARN THIS COUNTRY'S ALCHEMY FROM HIM!!
THANKS FOR THE FOOD, MY FRIENDS!
TAKE CARE!!
WAIT FOR ME, MASTER EDWARD!
I'M COMING TO YOU!!
CHOOOOOOO!
SHE'S GONE.
OH!
WE FORGOT TO TELL HER HOW SHORT HE IS...
KAWW

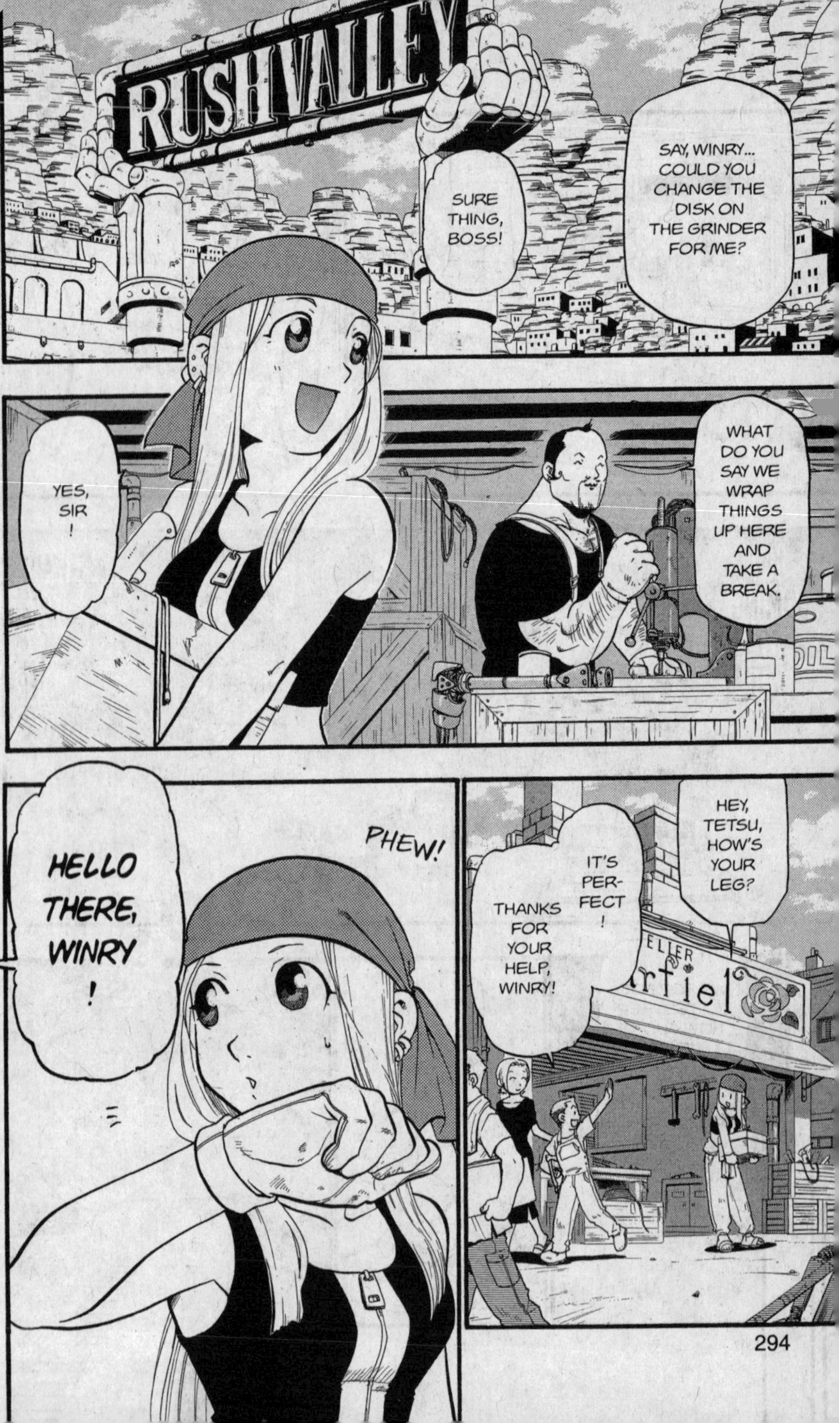
RUSH VALLEY
SAY, WINRY... COULD YOU CHANGE THE DISK ON THE GRINDER FOR ME?
SURE THING, BOSS!
WHAT DO YOU SAY WE WRAP THINGS UP HERE AND TAKE A BREAK.
YES, SIR!
HEY, TETSU, HOW'S YOUR LEG?
IT'S PER-FECT!
THANKS FOR YOUR HELP, WINRY!
PHEW!
HELLO THERE, WINRY!

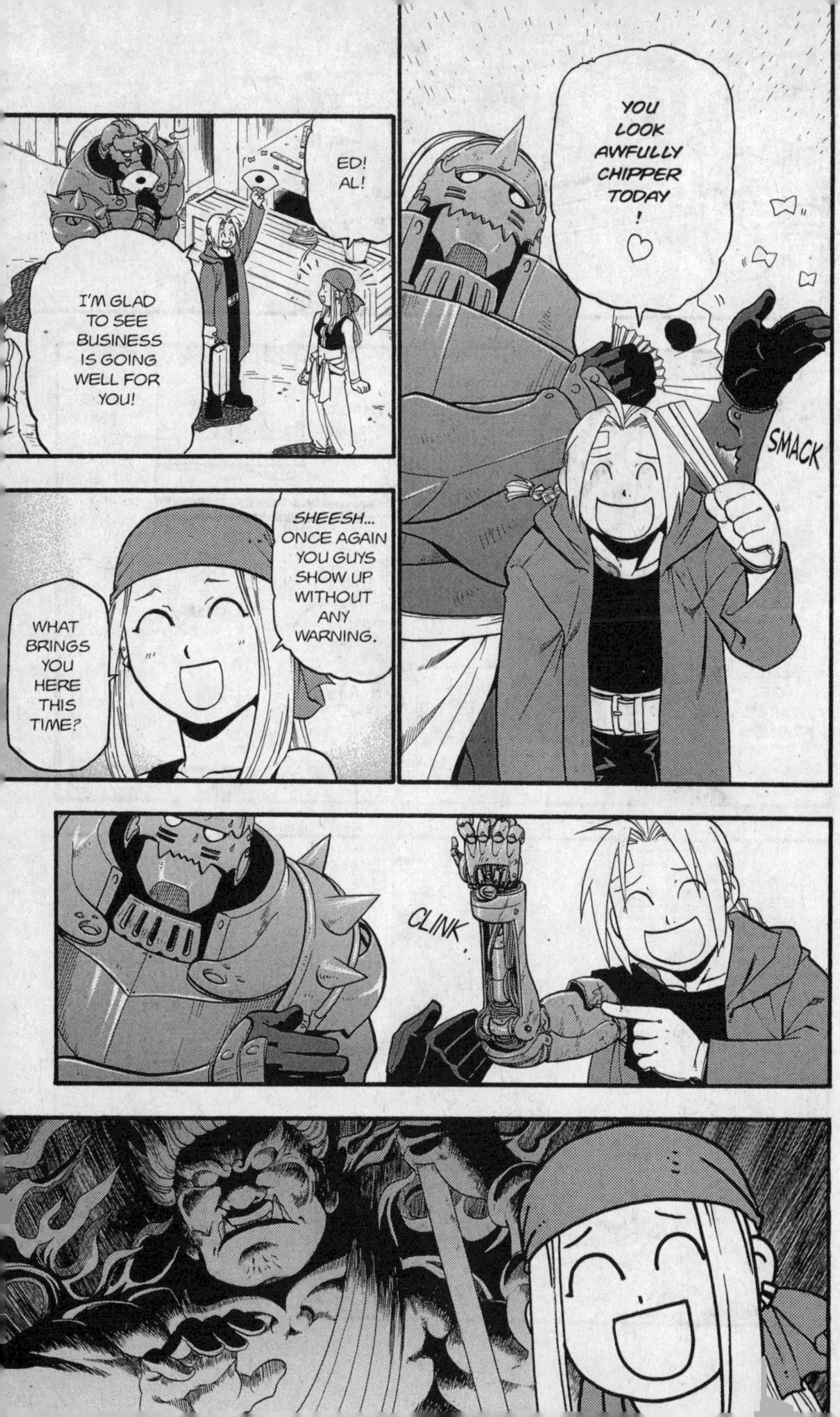
YOU LOOK AWFULLY CHIPPER TODAY! ♡
SMACK
ED! AL!
I'M GLAD TO SEE BUSINESS IS GOING WELL FOR YOU!
SHEESH... ONCE AGAIN YOU GUYS SHOW UP WITHOUT ANY WARNING.
WHAT BRINGS YOU HERE THIS TIME?
CLINK

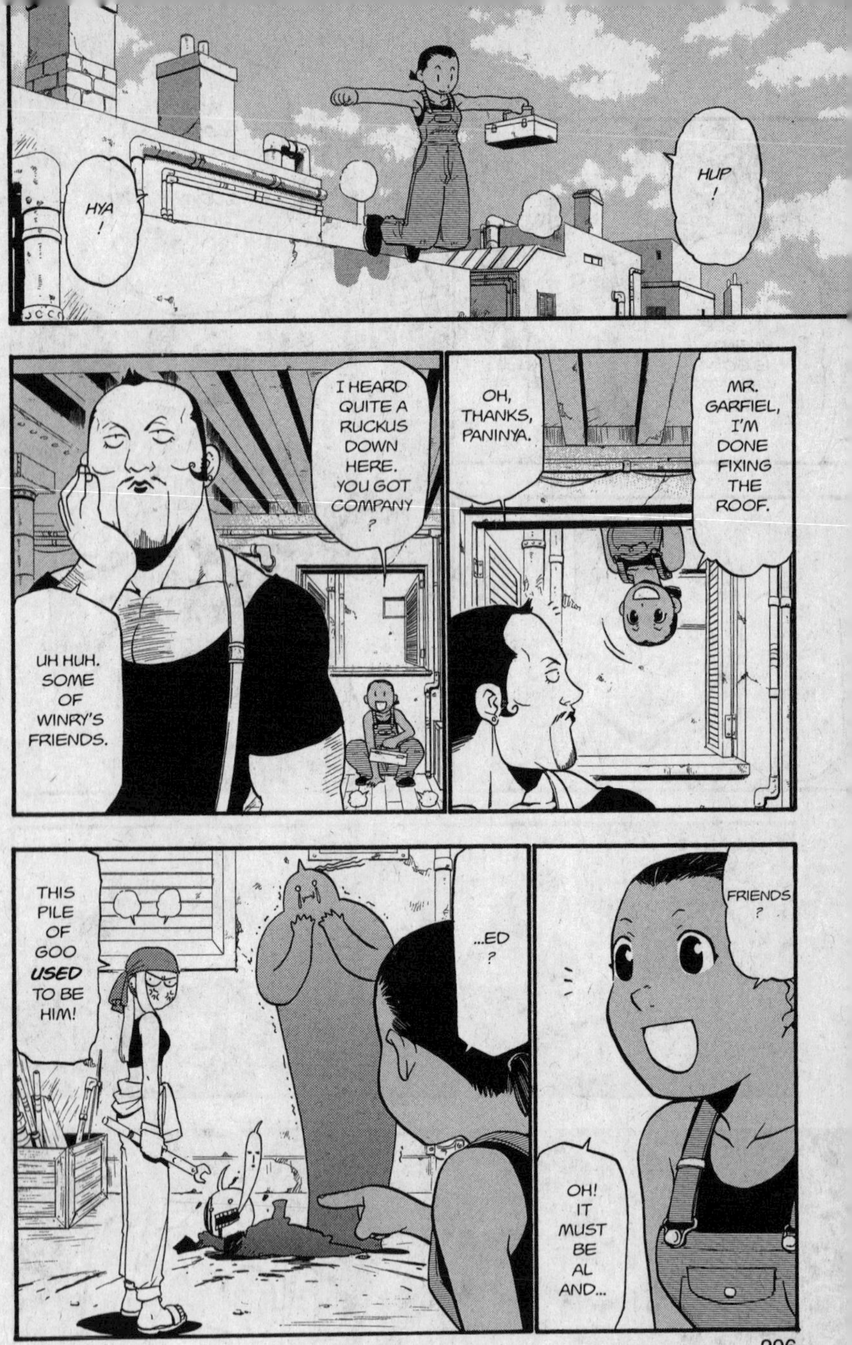
HUP!
HYA!
MR. GARFIEL, I'M DONE FIXING THE ROOF.
OH, THANKS, PANINYA.
I HEARD QUITE A RUCKUS DOWN HERE. YOU GOT COMPANY?
UH HUH. SOME OF WINRY'S FRIENDS.
FRIENDS?
OH! IT MUST BE AL AND...
...ED?
THIS PILE OF GOO **USED** TO BE HIM!

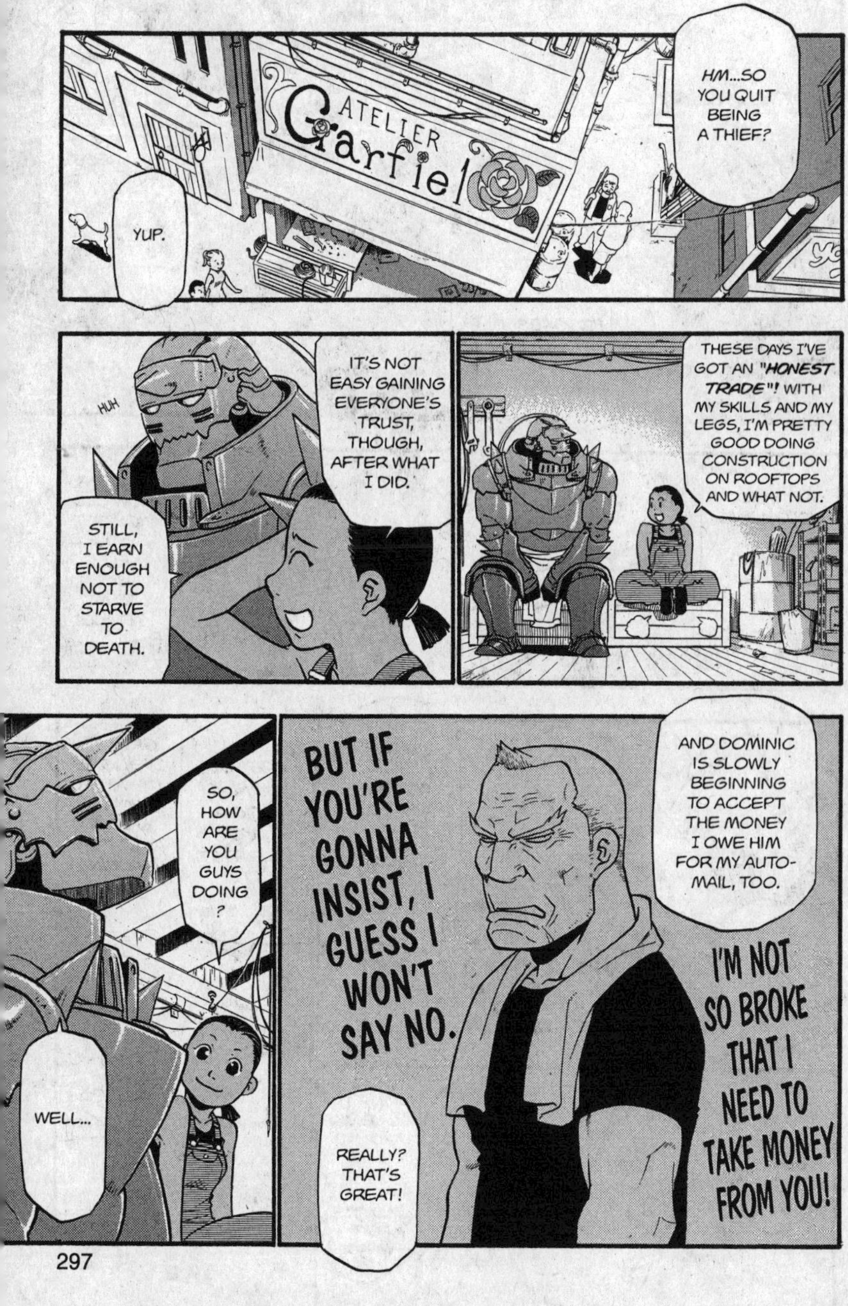
HM...SO YOU QUIT BEING A THIEF?
ATELIER Garfiel
YUP.
THESE DAYS I'VE GOT AN "HONEST TRADE"! WITH MY SKILLS AND MY LEGS, I'M PRETTY GOOD DOING CONSTRUCTION ON ROOFTOPS AND WHAT NOT.
IT'S NOT EASY GAINING EVERYONE'S TRUST, THOUGH, AFTER WHAT I DID.
HUH
STILL, I EARN ENOUGH NOT TO STARVE TO DEATH.
AND DOMINIC IS SLOWLY BEGINNING TO ACCEPT THE MONEY I OWE HIM FOR MY AUTO-MAIL, TOO.
I'M NOT SO BROKE THAT I NEED TO TAKE MONEY FROM YOU!
BUT IF YOU'RE GONNA INSIST, I GUESS I WON'T SAY NO.
REALLY? THAT'S GREAT!
SO, HOW ARE YOU GUYS DOING?
WELL...

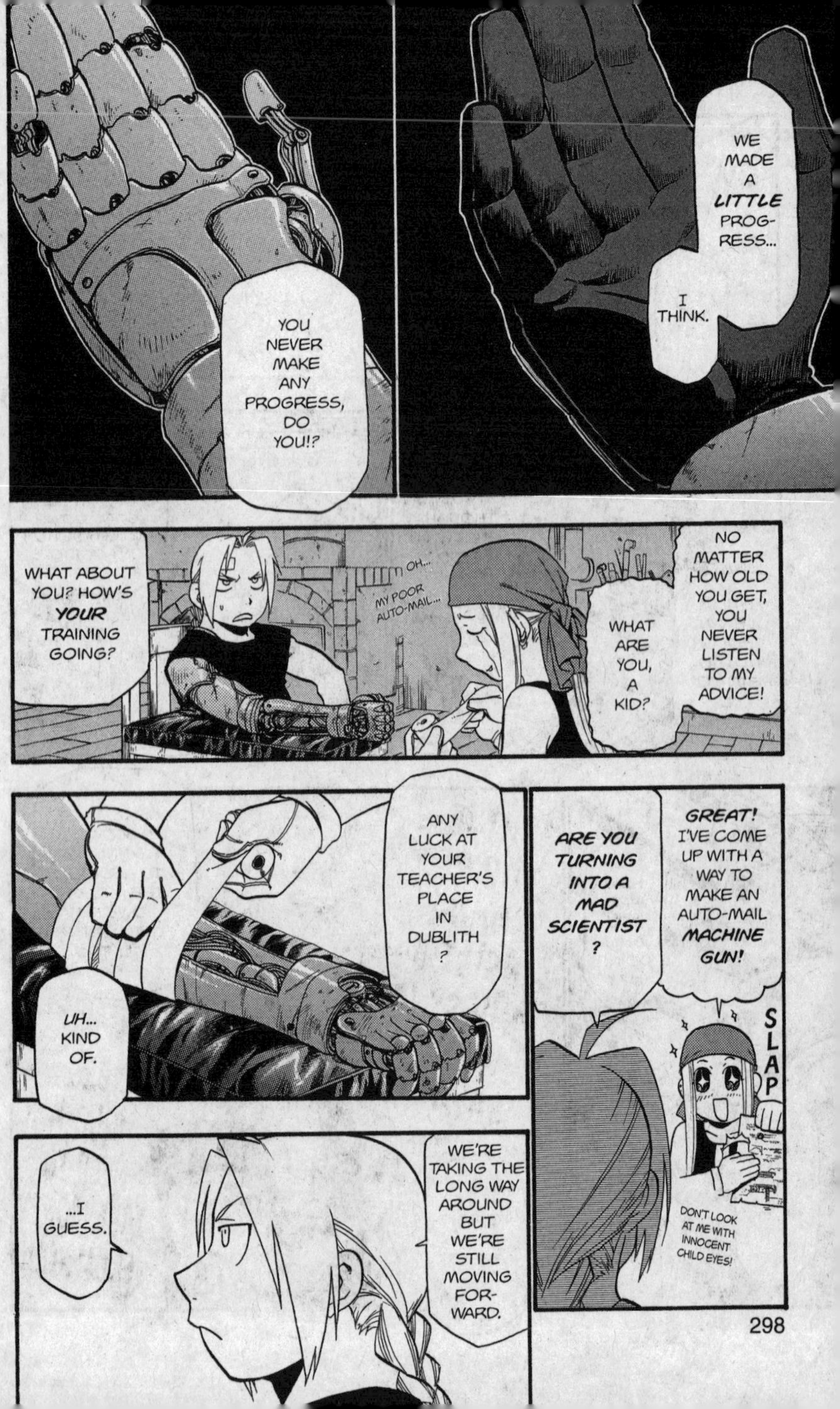
WE MADE A LITTLE PROGRESS...
I THINK.
YOU NEVER MAKE ANY PROGRESS, DO YOU!?
NO MATTER HOW OLD YOU GET, YOU NEVER LISTEN TO MY ADVICE!
WHAT ARE YOU, A KID?
OH... MY POOR AUTO-MAIL...
WHAT ABOUT YOU? HOW'S YOUR TRAINING GOING?
GREAT! I'VE COME UP WITH A WAY TO MAKE AN AUTO-MAIL MACHINE GUN!
ARE YOU TURNING INTO A MAD SCIENTIST?
SLAP
DON'T LOOK AT ME WITH INNOCENT CHILD EYES!
ANY LUCK AT YOUR TEACHER'S PLACE IN DUBLITH?
UH... KIND OF.
WE'RE TAKING THE LONG WAY AROUND BUT WE'RE STILL MOVING FOR-WARD.
...I GUESS.

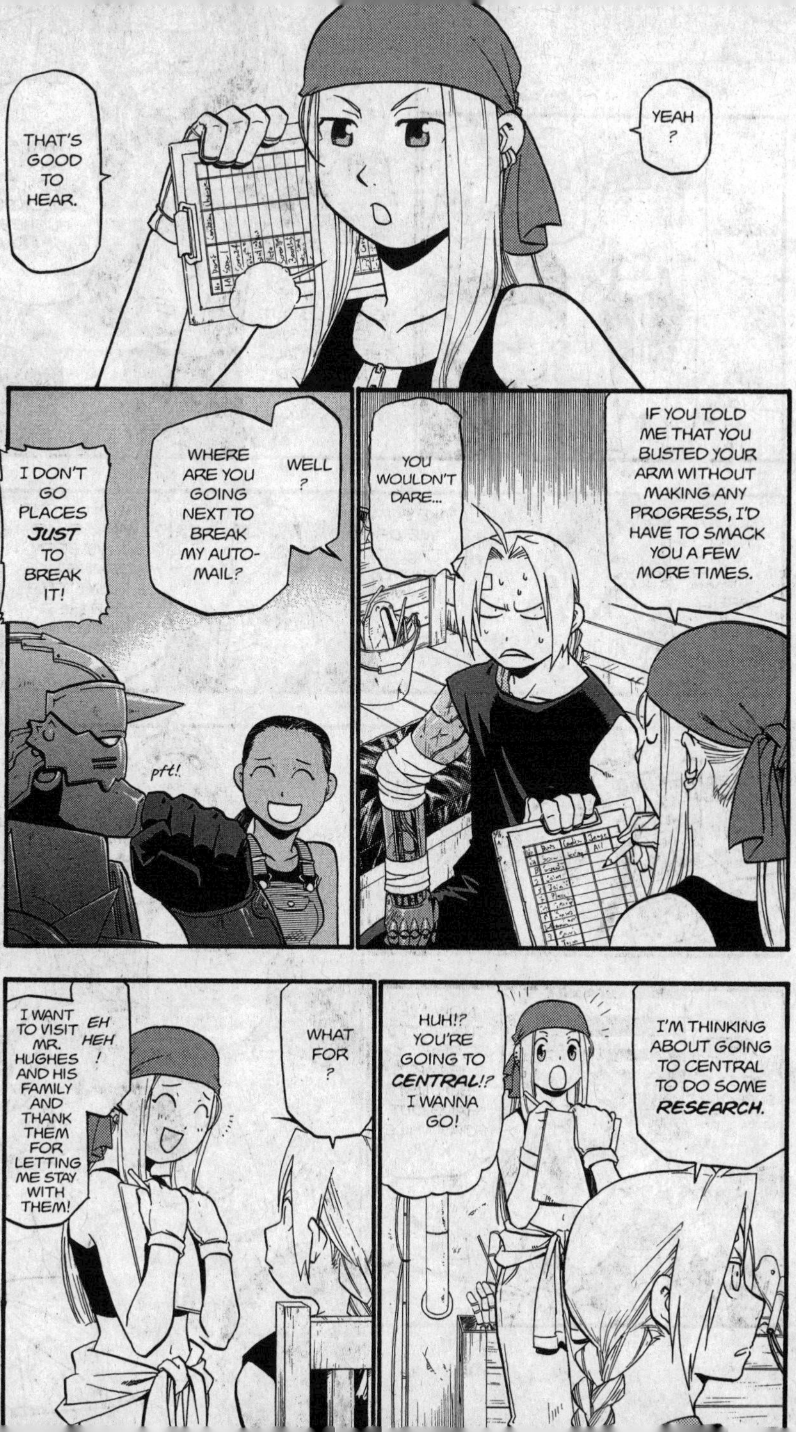
YEAH?
THAT'S GOOD TO HEAR.
IF YOU TOLD ME THAT YOU BUSTED YOUR ARM WITHOUT MAKING ANY PROGRESS, I'D HAVE TO SMACK YOU A FEW MORE TIMES.
YOU WOULDN'T DARE...
WELL?
WHERE ARE YOU GOING NEXT TO BREAK MY AUTO-MAIL?
I DON'T GO PLACES **JUST** TO BREAK IT!
pft!
I'M THINKING ABOUT GOING TO CENTRAL TO DO SOME **RESEARCH.**
HUH!? YOU'RE GOING TO **CENTRAL!?** I WANNA GO!
WHAT FOR?
EH HEH!
I WANT TO VISIT MR. HUGHES AND HIS FAMILY AND THANK THEM FOR LETTING ME STAY WITH THEM!

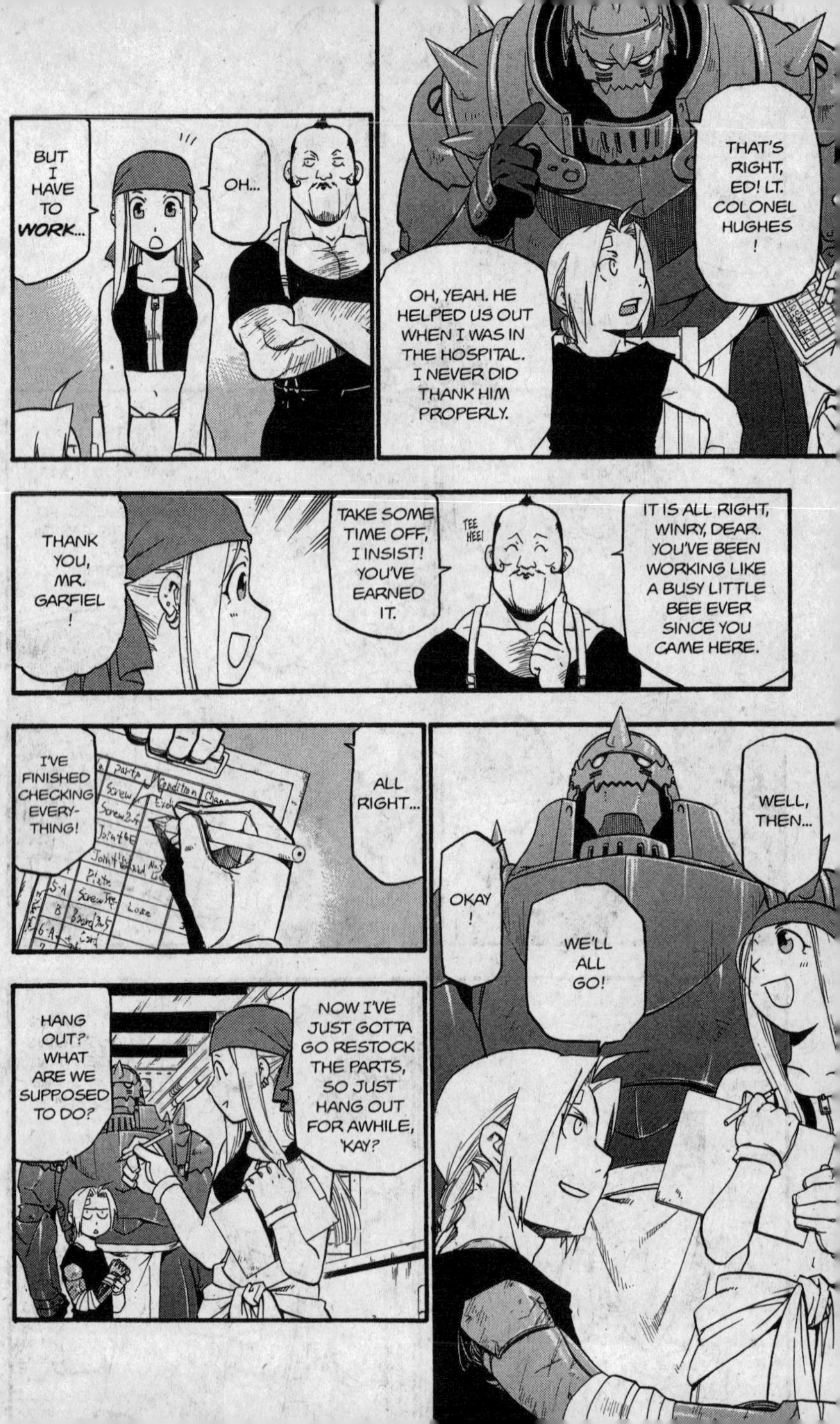
THAT'S RIGHT, ED! LT. COLONEL HUGHES!
OH, YEAH. HE HELPED US OUT WHEN I WAS IN THE HOSPITAL. I NEVER DID THANK HIM PROPERLY.
OH...
BUT I HAVE TO *WORK*...
IT IS ALL RIGHT, WINRY, DEAR. YOU'VE BEEN WORKING LIKE A BUSY LITTLE BEE EVER SINCE YOU CAME HERE.
TEE HEE!
TAKE SOME TIME OFF, I INSIST! YOU'VE EARNED IT.
THANK YOU, MR. GARFIEL!
WELL, THEN...
OKAY!
WE'LL ALL GO!
ALL RIGHT...
I'VE FINISHED CHECKING EVERYTHING!
NOW I'VE JUST GOTTA GO RESTOCK THE PARTS, SO JUST HANG OUT FOR AWHILE, 'KAY?
HANG OUT? WHAT ARE WE SUPPOSED TO DO?

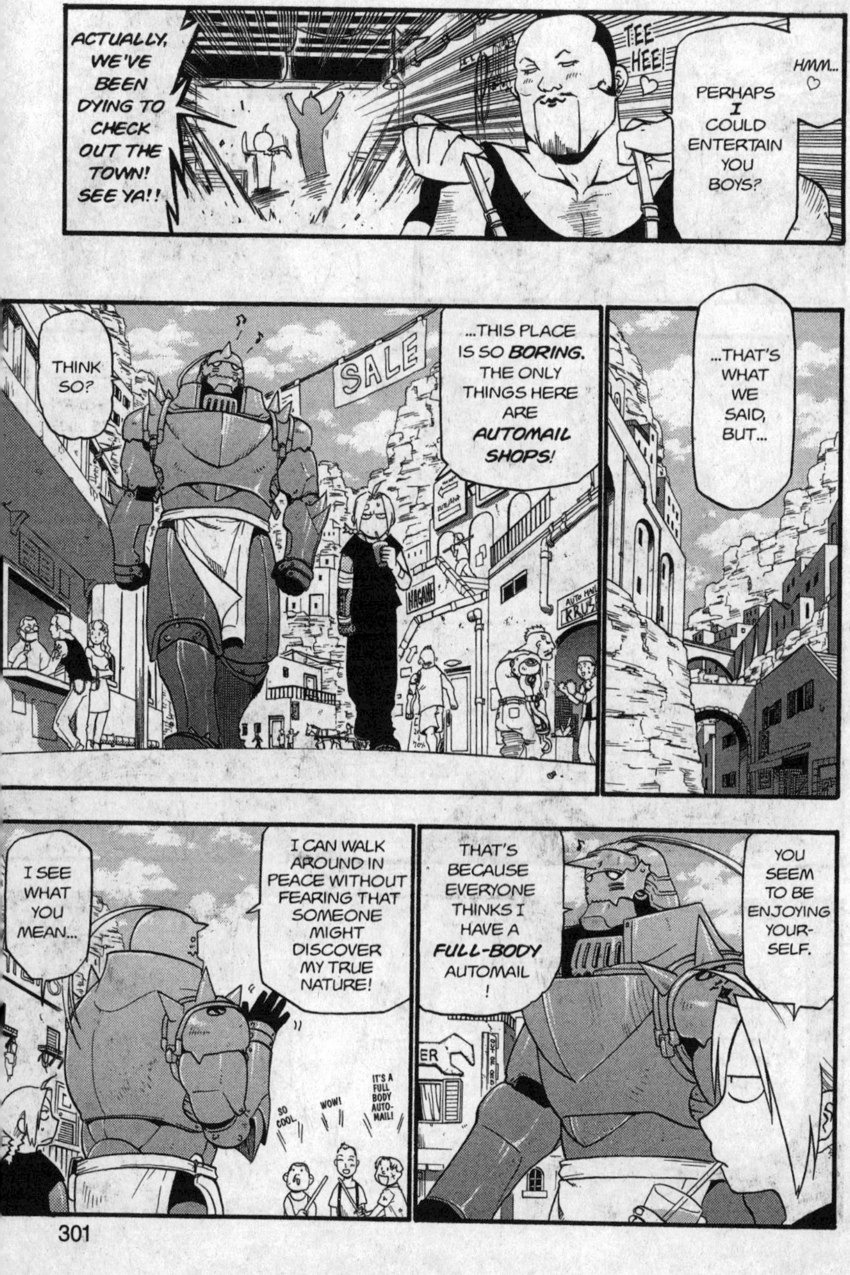
HMM... ♡
PERHAPS I COULD ENTERTAIN YOU BOYS?
TEE HEE!
ACTUALLY, WE'VE BEEN DYING TO CHECK OUT THE TOWN! SEE YA!!
...THAT'S WHAT WE SAID, BUT...
...THIS PLACE IS SO BORING. THE ONLY THINGS HERE ARE AUTOMAIL SHOPS!
SALE
HAGANE
THINK SO?
YOU SEEM TO BE ENJOYING YOUR-SELF.
THAT'S BECAUSE EVERYONE THINKS I HAVE A FULL-BODY AUTOMAIL!
I CAN WALK AROUND IN PEACE WITHOUT FEARING THAT SOMEONE MIGHT DISCOVER MY TRUE NATURE!
I SEE WHAT YOU MEAN...
IT'S A FULL BODY AUTO-MAIL!
WOW!
SO COOL.

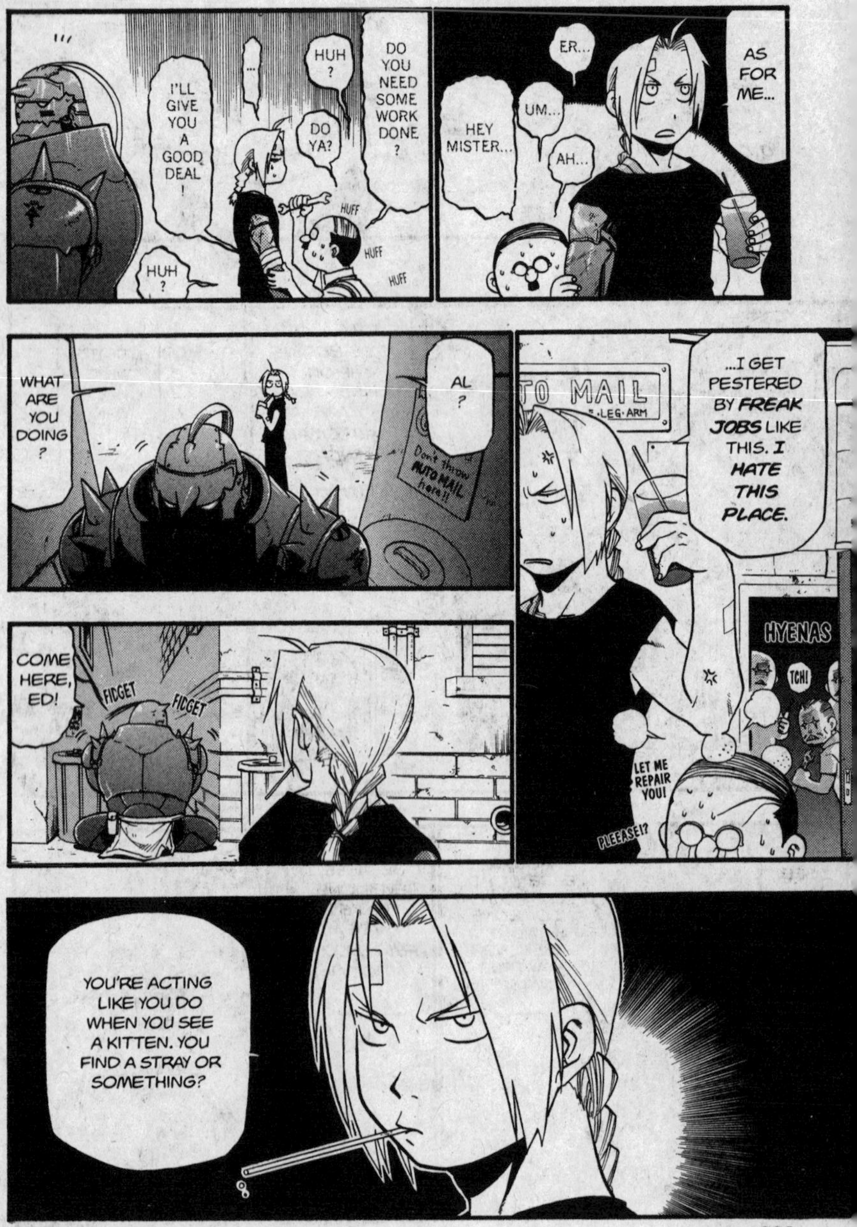
AS FOR ME...
ER...
UM...
HEY MISTER...
AH...
DO YOU NEED SOME WORK DONE?
HUH?
DO YA?
...
I'LL GIVE YOU A GOOD DEAL!
HUFF
HUFF
HUFF
HUH?
TO MAIL
LEG·ARM
...I GET PESTERED BY **FREAK JOBS** LIKE THIS. I **HATE THIS PLACE.**
HYENAS
TCH!
LET ME REPAIR YOU!
PLEEASE!?
AL?
WHAT ARE YOU DOING?
Don't throw AUTO MAIL here!!
COME HERE, ED!
FIDGET
FIDGET
YOU'RE ACTING LIKE YOU DO WHEN YOU SEE A KITTEN. YOU FIND A STRAY OR SOMETHING?

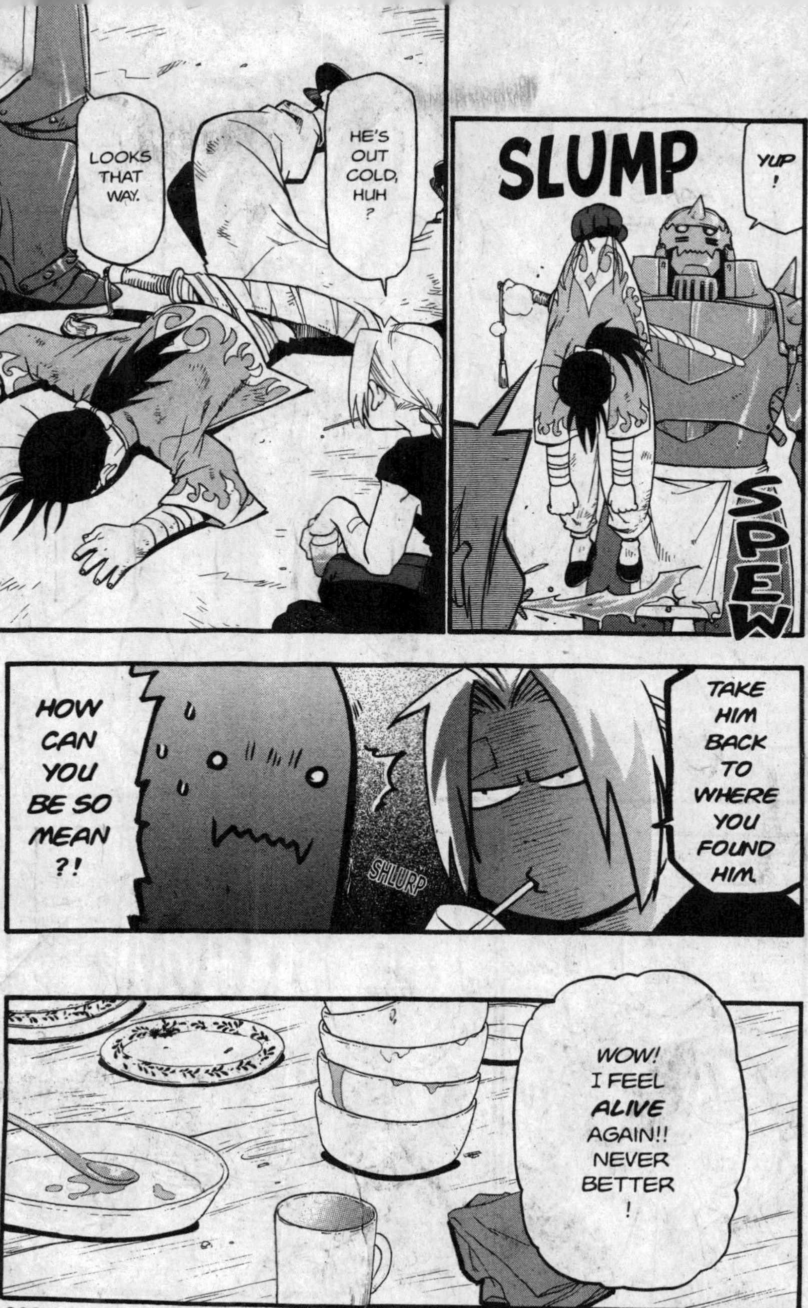
SLUMP
YUP!
SPEW
HE'S OUT COLD, HUH?
LOOKS THAT WAY.
TAKE HIM BACK TO WHERE YOU FOUND HIM.
SHLURP
HOW CAN YOU BE SO MEAN?!
WOW! I FEEL **ALIVE** AGAIN!! NEVER BETTER!

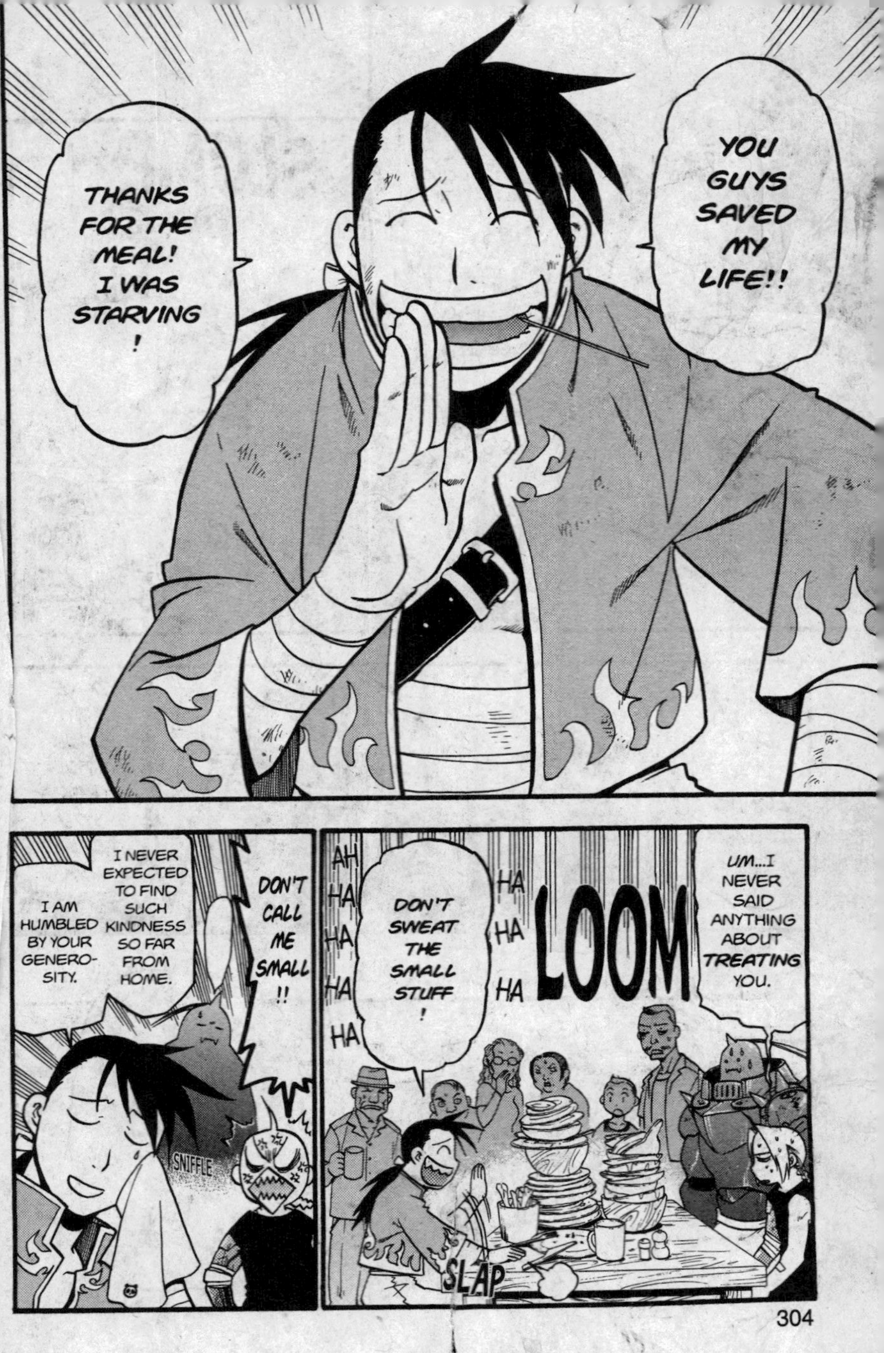
YOU GUYS SAVED MY LIFE!!
THANKS FOR THE MEAL! I WAS STARVING!
UM...I NEVER SAID ANYTHING ABOUT TREATING YOU.
LOOM
HA HA HA
AH HA HA HA HA
DON'T SWEAT THE SMALL STUFF!
SLAP
DON'T CALL ME SMALL!!
I NEVER EXPECTED TO FIND SUCH KINDNESS SO FAR FROM HOME.
I AM HUMBLED BY YOUR GENERO-SITY.
SNIFFLE

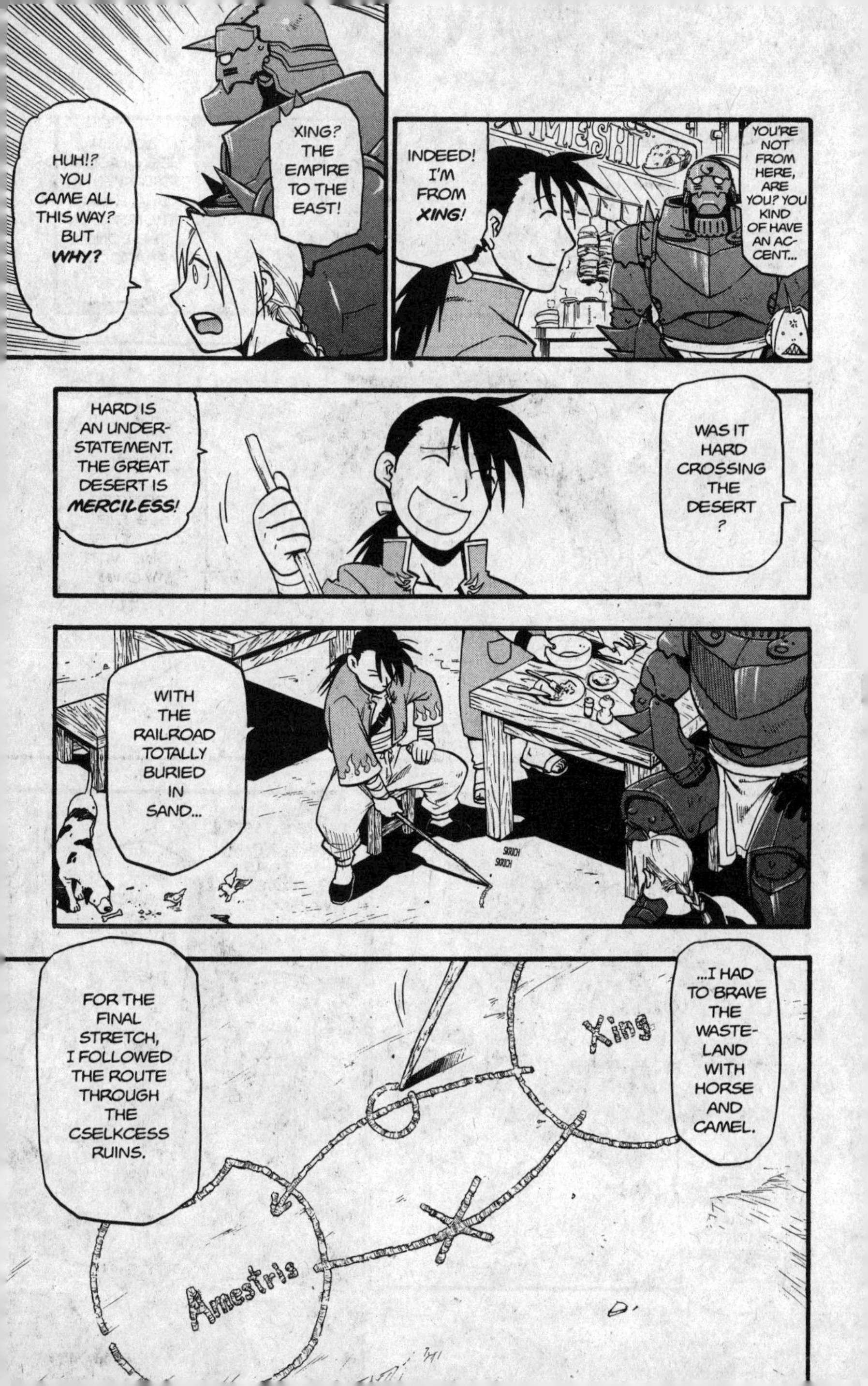
YOU'RE NOT FROM HERE, ARE YOU? YOU KIND OF HAVE AN ACCENT...
MESHI
INDEED! I'M FROM **XING**!
XING? THE EMPIRE TO THE EAST!
HUH!? YOU CAME ALL THIS WAY? BUT **WHY?**
WAS IT HARD CROSSING THE DESERT?
HARD IS AN UNDER-STATEMENT. THE GREAT DESERT IS ***MERCILESS!***
WITH THE RAILROAD TOTALLY BURIED IN SAND...
SKRICH SKRICH
...I HAD TO BRAVE THE WASTE-LAND WITH HORSE AND CAMEL.
Xing
FOR THE FINAL STRETCH, I FOLLOWED THE ROUTE THROUGH THE CSELKCESS RUINS.
Amestris

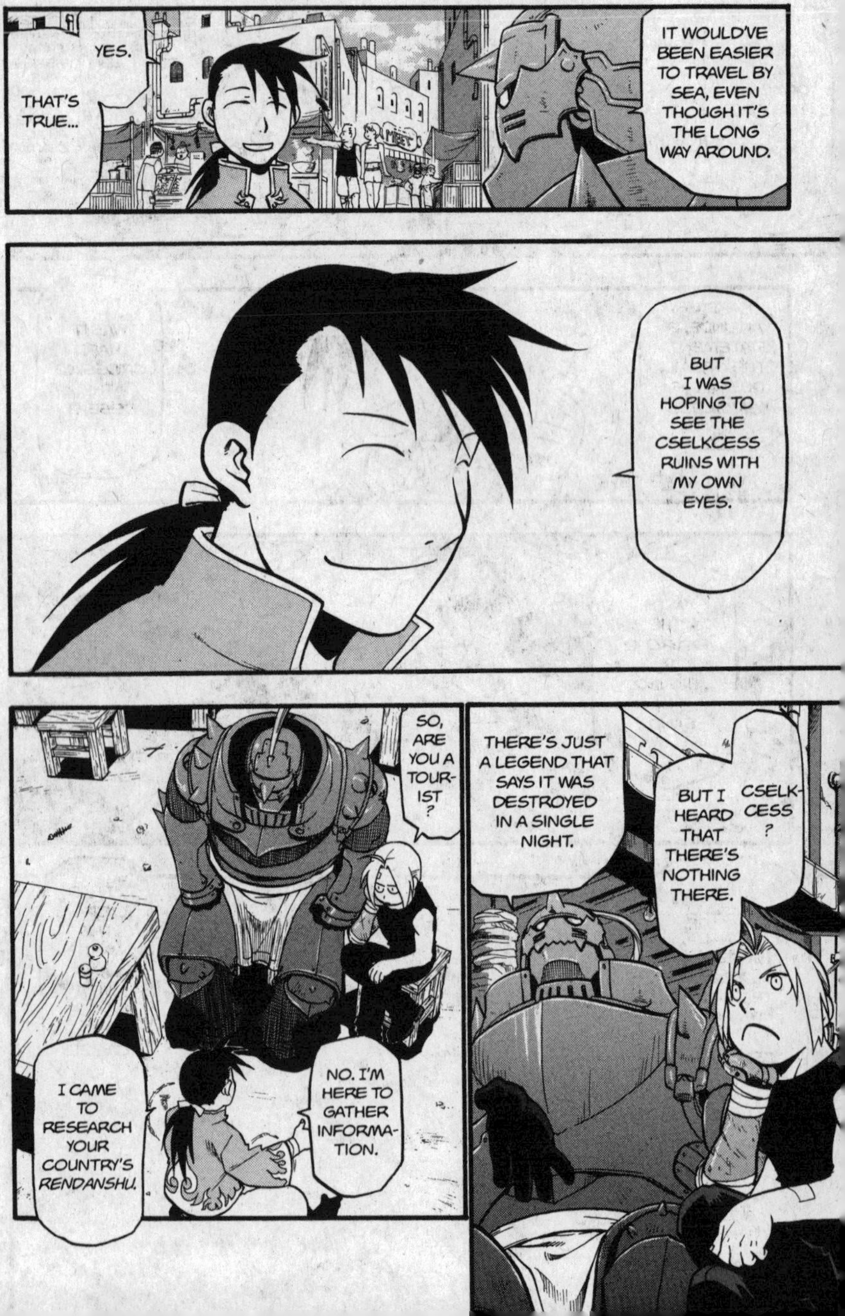
IT WOULD'VE BEEN EASIER TO TRAVEL BY SEA, EVEN THOUGH IT'S THE LONG WAY AROUND.
YES.
THAT'S TRUE...
MEET
BUT I WAS HOPING TO SEE THE CSELKCESS RUINS WITH MY OWN EYES.
CSELK-CESS?
BUT I HEARD THAT THERE'S NOTHING THERE.
THERE'S JUST A LEGEND THAT SAYS IT WAS DESTROYED IN A SINGLE NIGHT.
SO, ARE YOU A TOUR-IST?
NO. I'M HERE TO GATHER INFORMA-TION.
I CAME TO RESEARCH YOUR COUNTRY'S RENDANSHU.

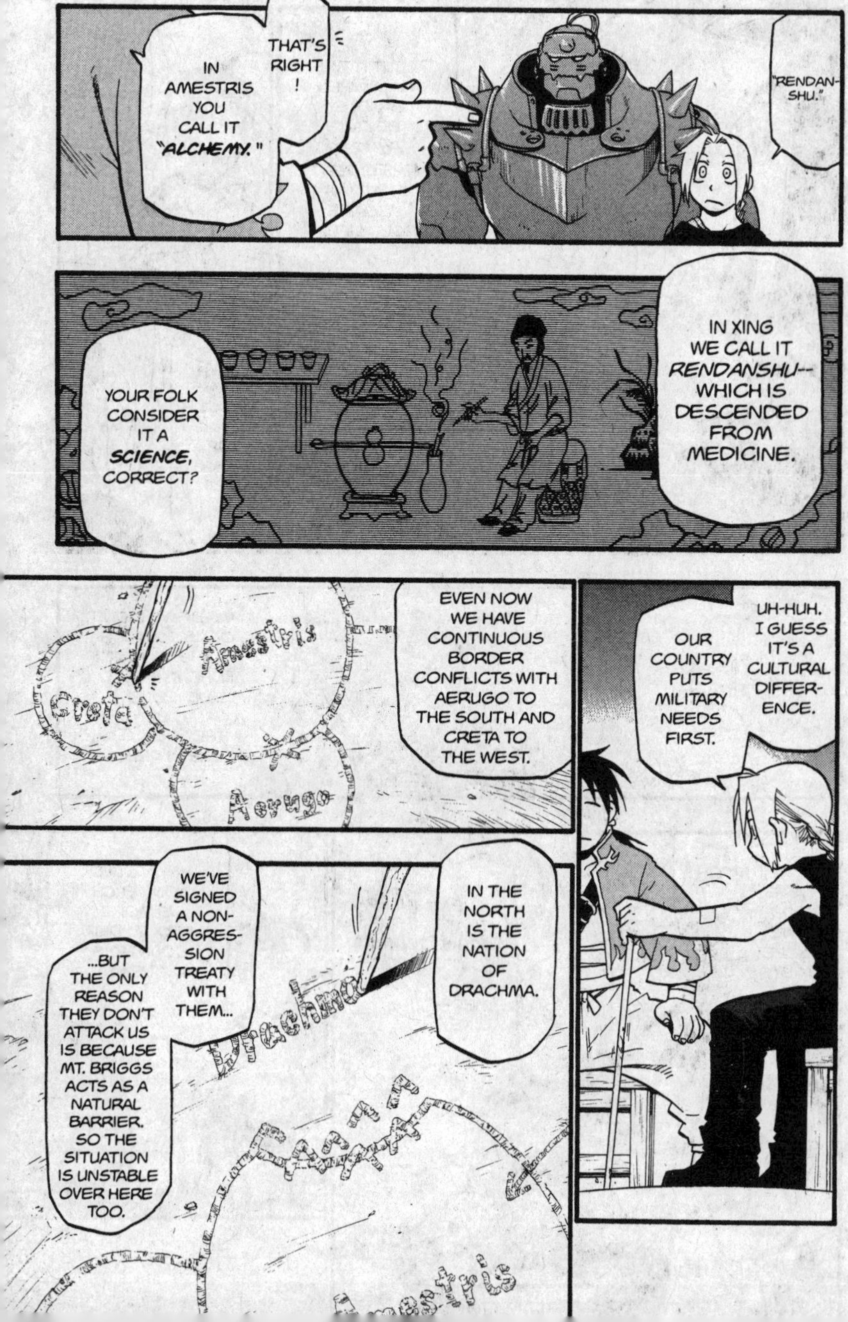
"RENDANSHU."
THAT'S RIGHT!
IN AMESTRIS YOU CALL IT "ALCHEMY."
IN XING WE CALL IT RENDANSHU-- WHICH IS DESCENDED FROM MEDICINE.
YOUR FOLK CONSIDER IT A SCIENCE, CORRECT?
UH-HUH. I GUESS IT'S A CULTURAL DIFFER-ENCE.
OUR COUNTRY PUTS MILITARY NEEDS FIRST.
EVEN NOW WE HAVE CONTINUOUS BORDER CONFLICTS WITH AERUGO TO THE SOUTH AND CRETA TO THE WEST.
Amestris
Creta
Aerugo
IN THE NORTH IS THE NATION OF DRACHMA.
WE'VE SIGNED A NON-AGGRES-SION TREATY WITH THEM...
...BUT THE ONLY REASON THEY DON'T ATTACK US IS BECAUSE MT. BRIGGS ACTS AS A NATURAL BARRIER. SO THE SITUATION IS UNSTABLE OVER HERE TOO.
Drachma
Amestris

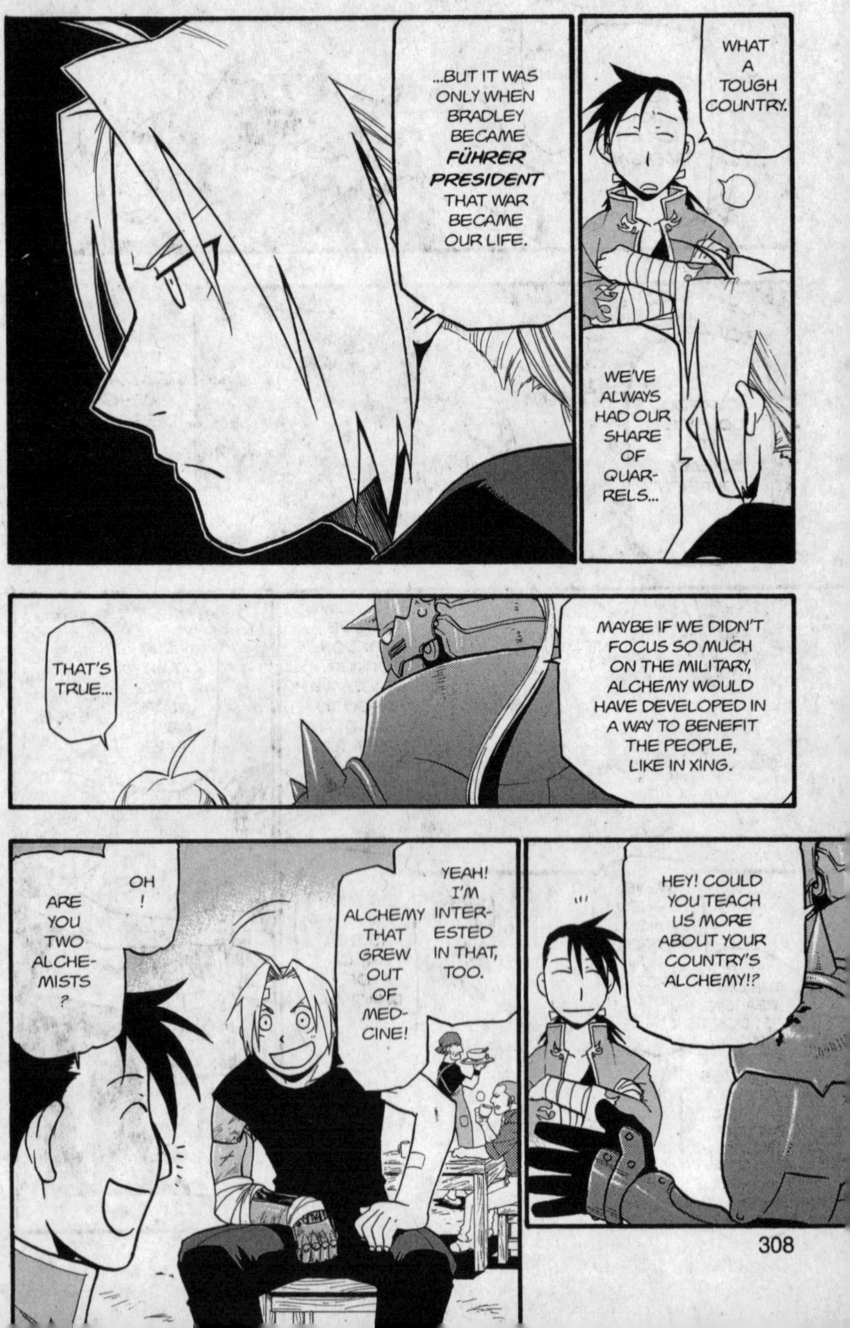
WHAT A TOUGH COUNTRY.
WE'VE ALWAYS HAD OUR SHARE OF QUARRELS...
...BUT IT WAS ONLY WHEN BRADLEY BECAME FÜHRER PRESIDENT THAT WAR BECAME OUR LIFE.
MAYBE IF WE DIDN'T FOCUS SO MUCH ON THE MILITARY, ALCHEMY WOULD HAVE DEVELOPED IN A WAY TO BENEFIT THE PEOPLE, LIKE IN XING.
THAT'S TRUE...
HEY! COULD YOU TEACH US MORE ABOUT YOUR COUNTRY'S ALCHEMY!?
YEAH! I'M INTERESTED IN THAT, TOO.
ALCHEMY THAT GREW OUT OF MEDICINE!
OH!
ARE YOU TWO ALCHEMISTS?

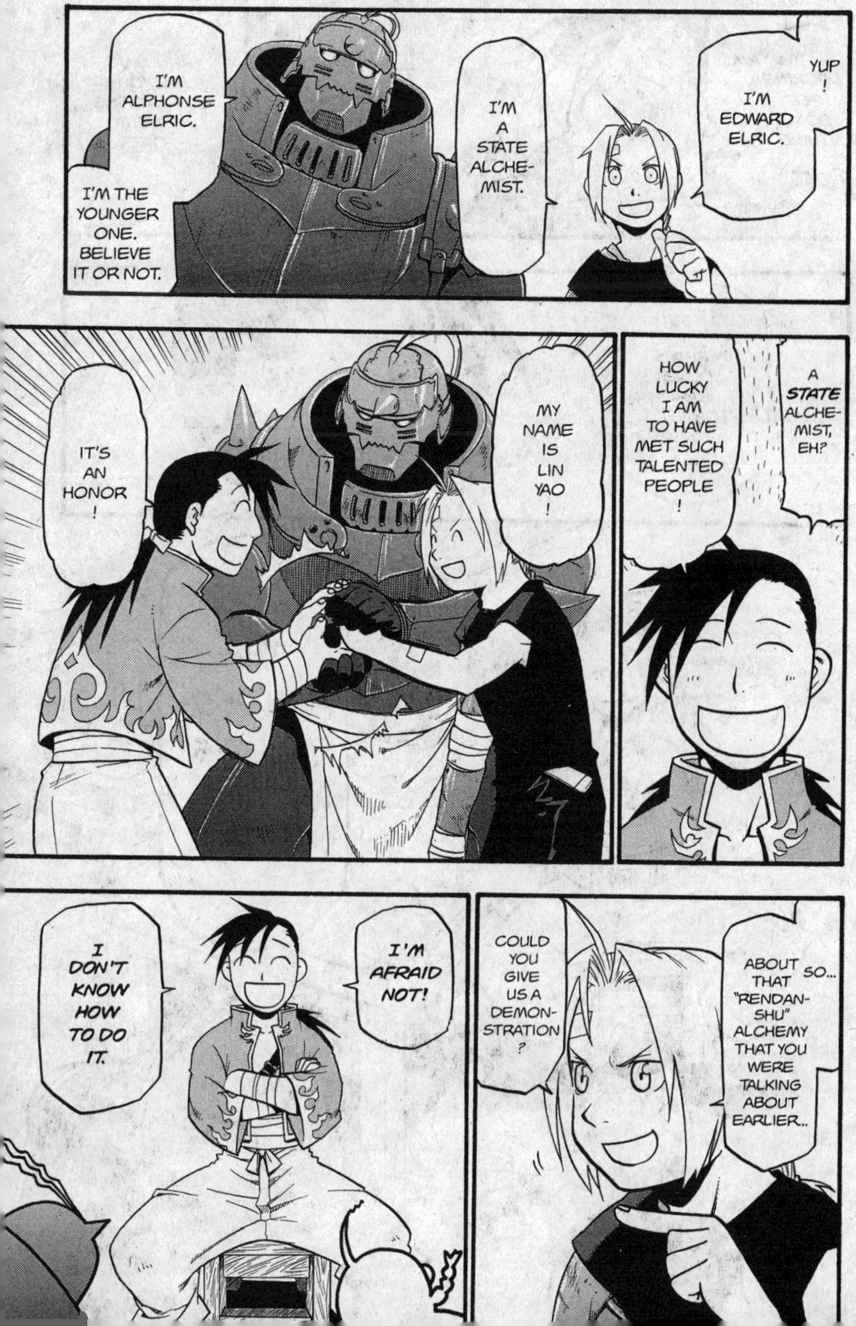
YUP!
I'M EDWARD ELRIC.
I'M A STATE ALCHEMIST.
I'M ALPHONSE ELRIC.
I'M THE YOUNGER ONE. BELIEVE IT OR NOT.
A STATE ALCHEMIST, EH?
HOW LUCKY I AM TO HAVE MET SUCH TALENTED PEOPLE!
MY NAME IS LIN YAO!
IT'S AN HONOR!
SO...
ABOUT THAT "RENDAN-SHU" ALCHEMY THAT YOU WERE TALKING ABOUT EARLIER...
COULD YOU GIVE US A DEMONSTRATION?
I'M AFRAID NOT!
I DON'T KNOW HOW TO DO IT.

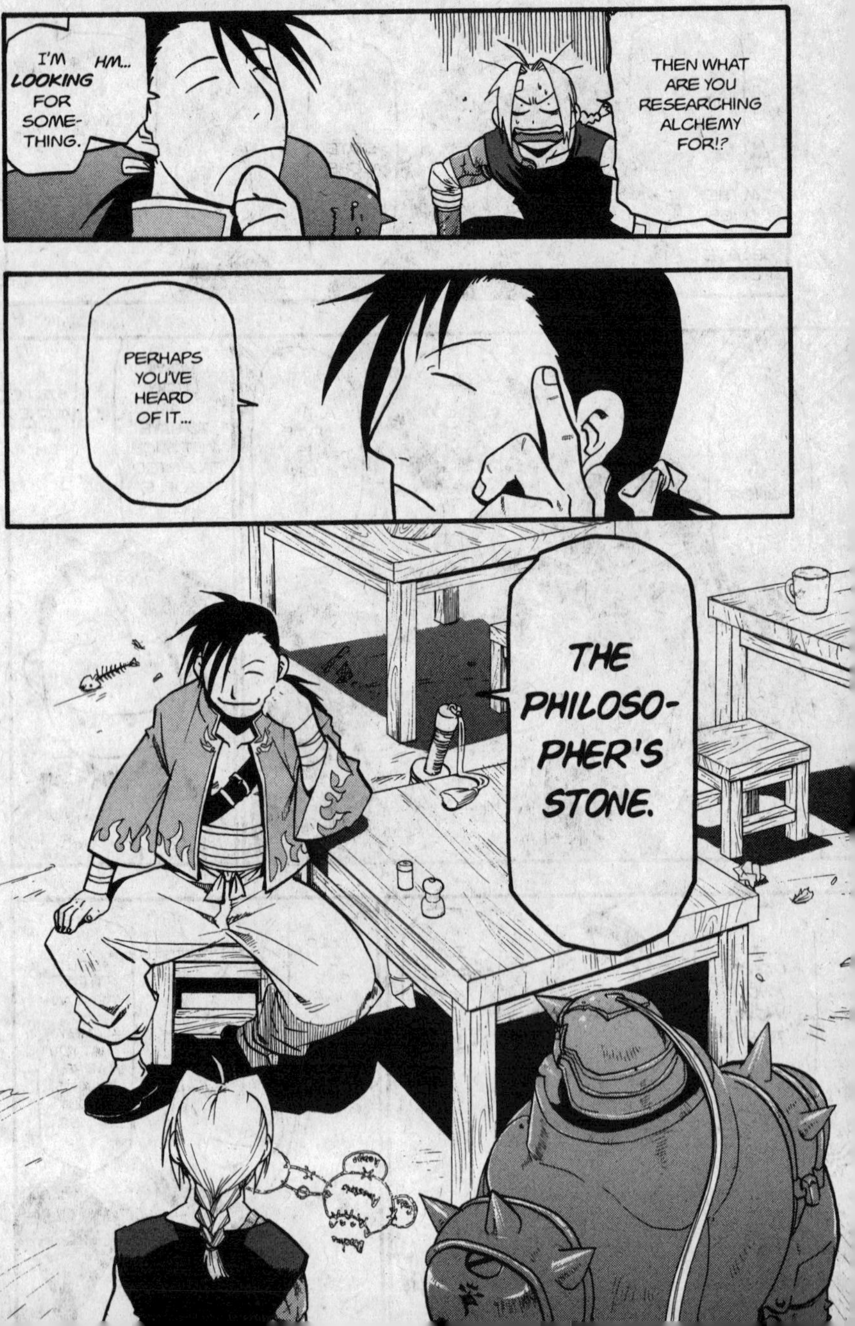
THEN WHAT ARE YOU RESEARCHING ALCHEMY FOR!?
HM...
I'M LOOKING FOR SOME-THING.
PERHAPS YOU'VE HEARD OF IT...
THE PHILOSO-PHER'S STONE.

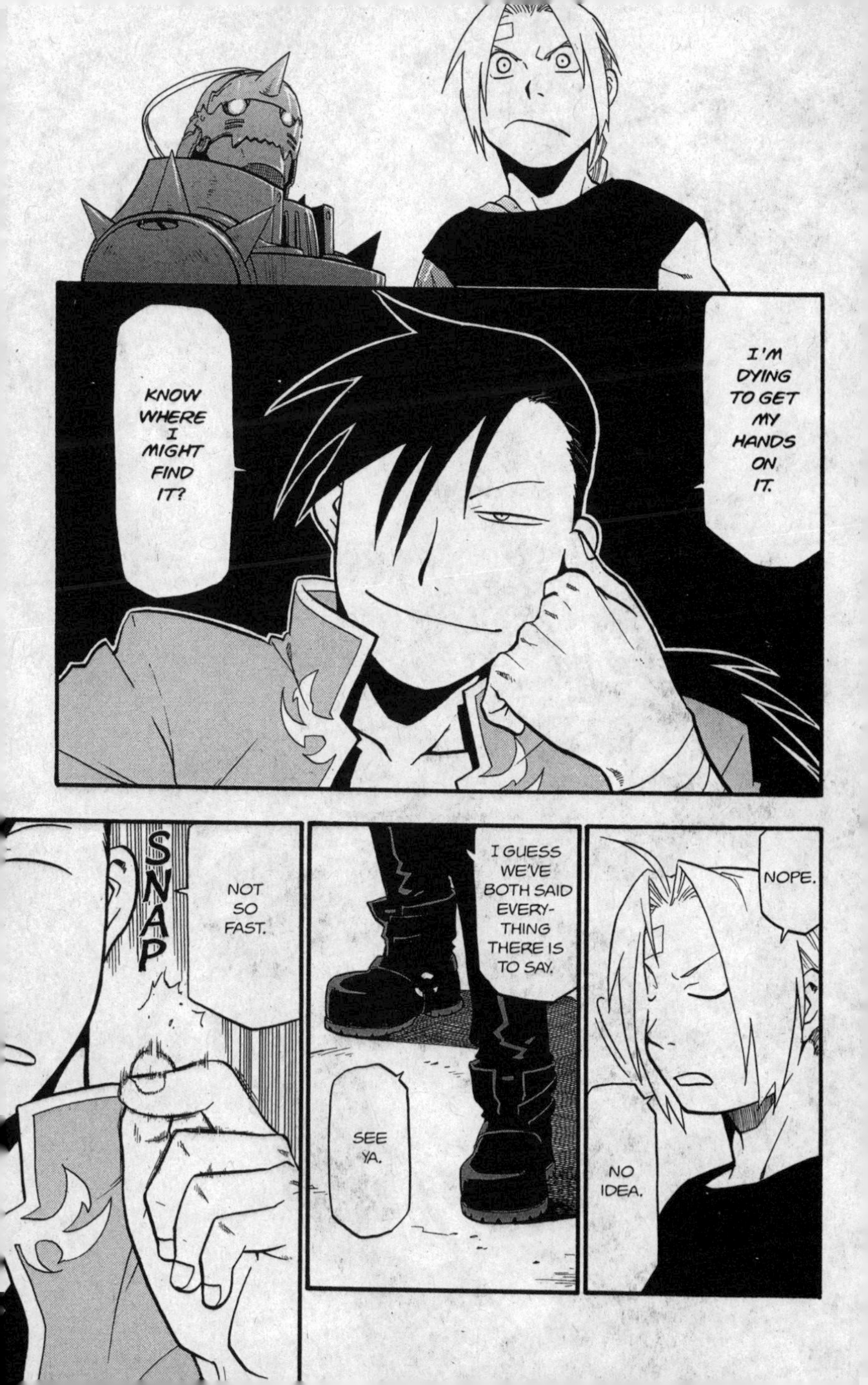
I'M DYING TO GET MY HANDS ON IT.
KNOW WHERE I MIGHT FIND IT?
NOPE.
NO IDEA.
I GUESS WE'VE BOTH SAID EVERY-THING THERE IS TO SAY.
SEE YA.
SNAP
NOT SO FAST.

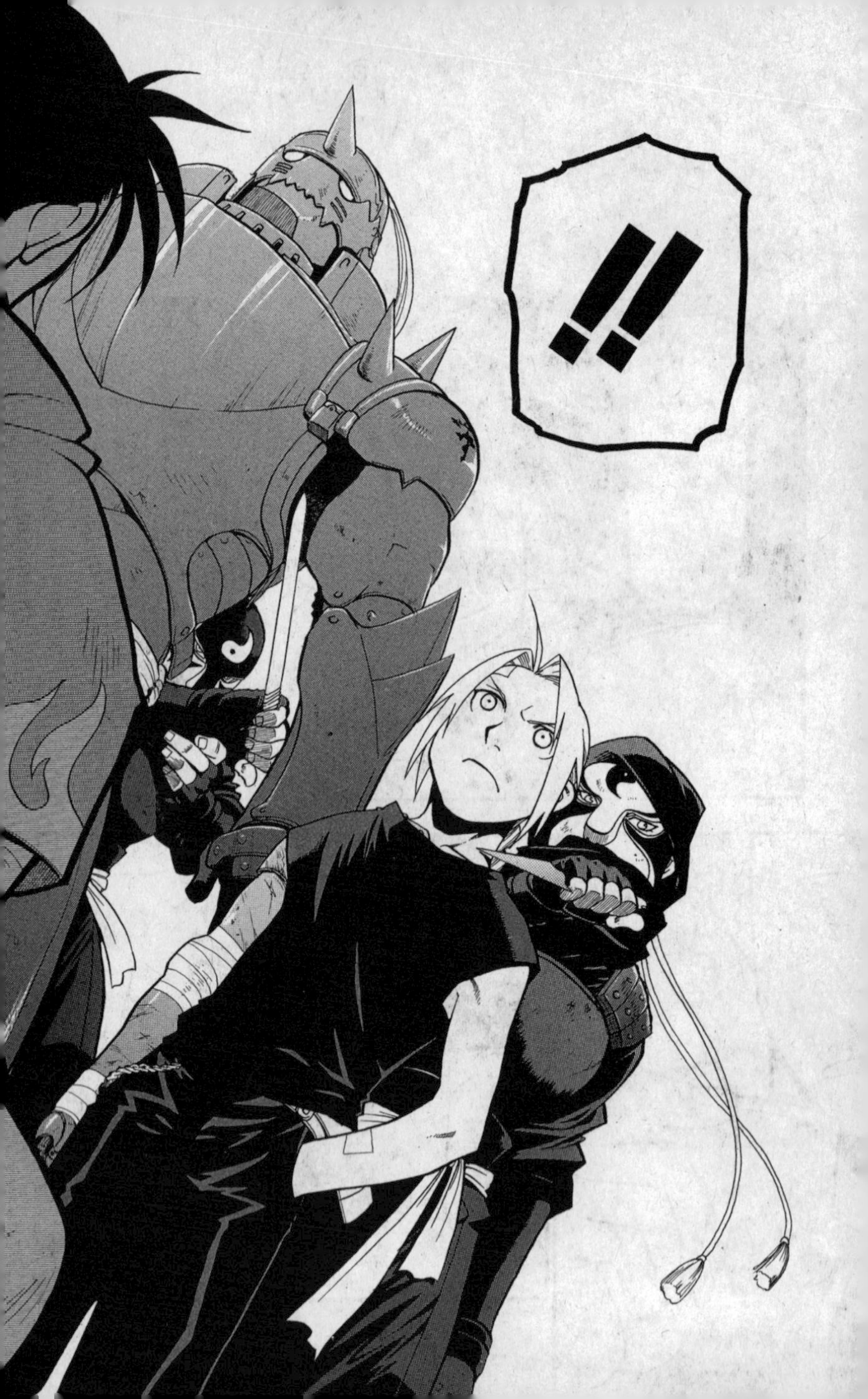
!!

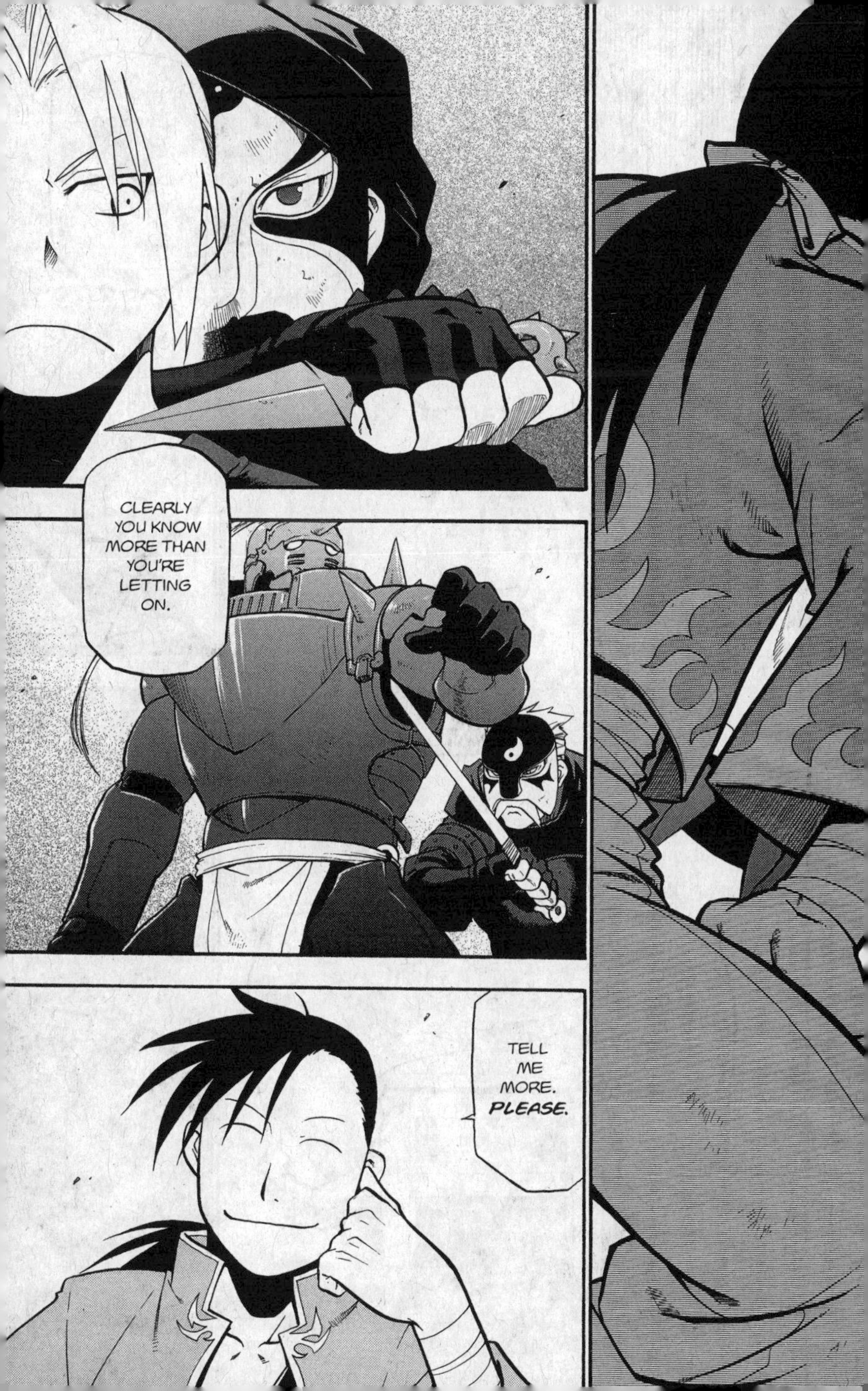
CLEARLY YOU KNOW MORE THAN YOU'RE LETTING ON.
TELL ME MORE. PLEASE.

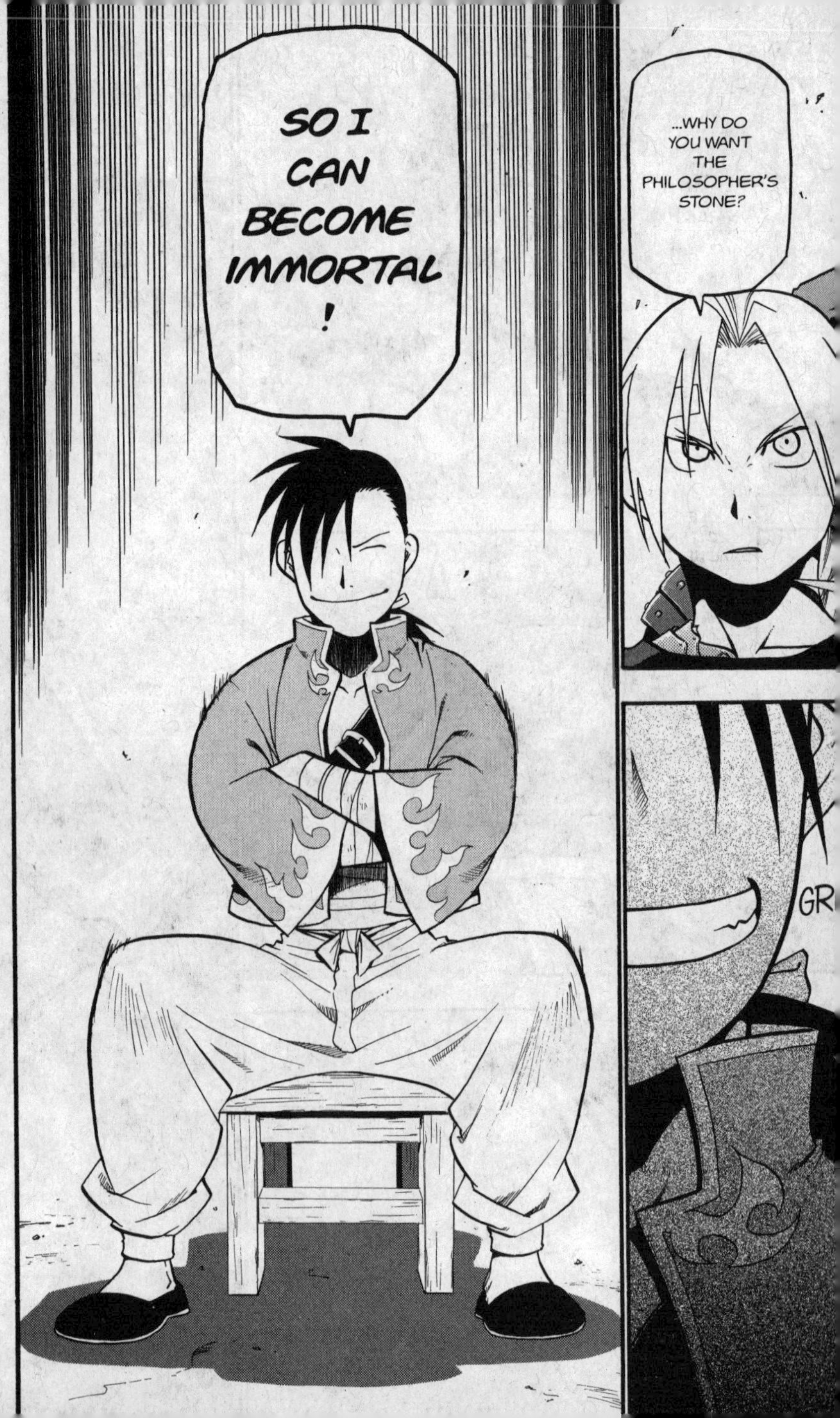
...WHY DO YOU WANT THE PHILOSOPHER'S STONE?
GR
SO I CAN BECOME IMMORTAL!

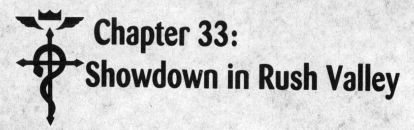

Chapter 33: Showdown in Rush Valley

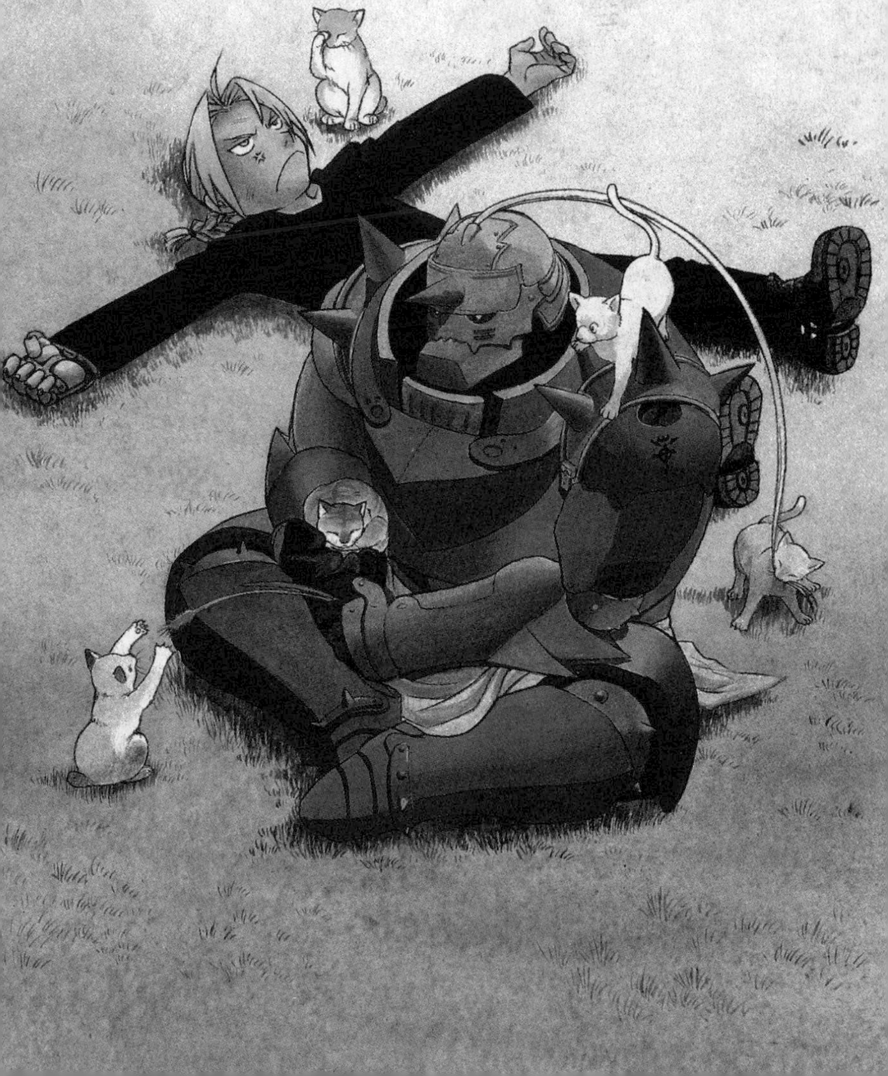

FULLMETAL
ALCHEMIST

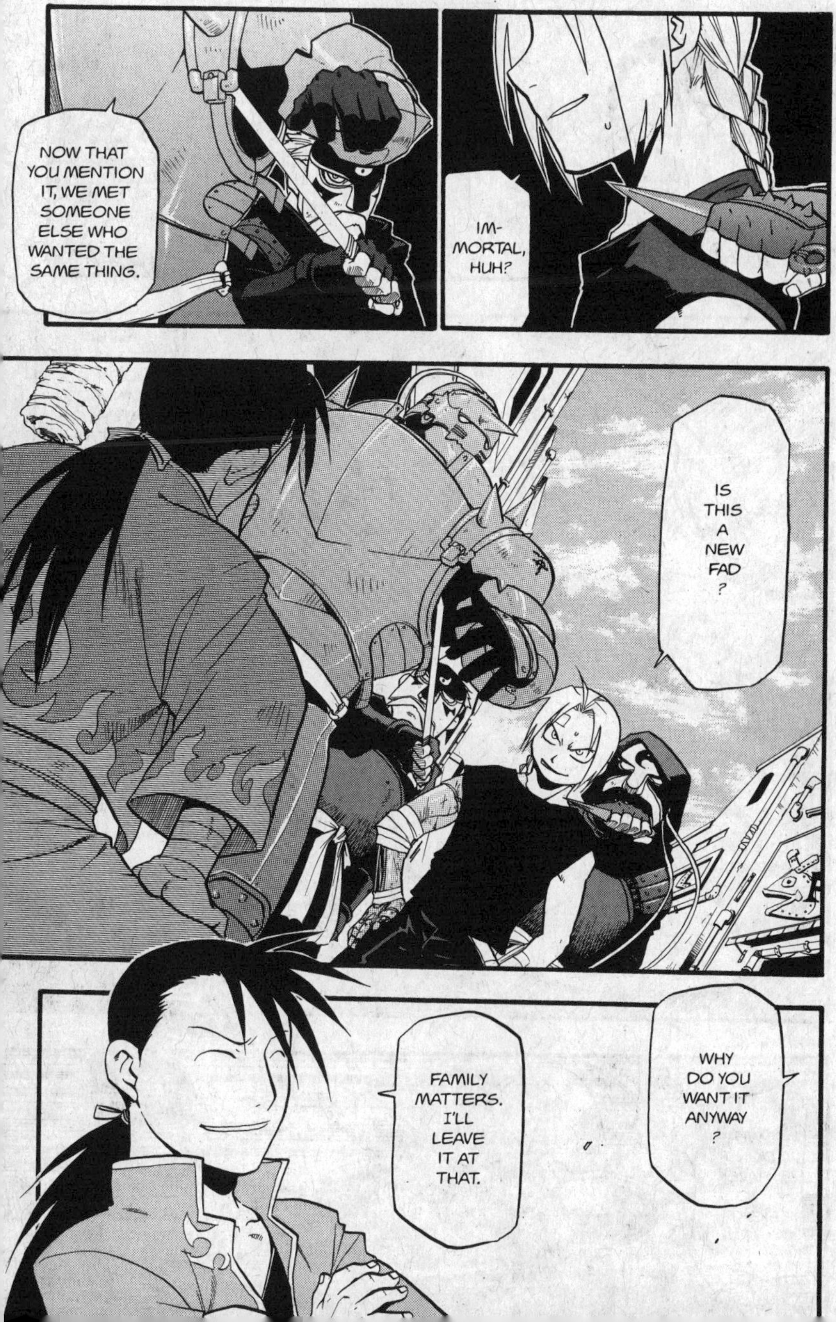
IM-MORTAL, HUH?
NOW THAT YOU MENTION IT, WE MET SOMEONE ELSE WHO WANTED THE SAME THING.
IS THIS A NEW FAD?
WHY DO YOU WANT IT ANYWAY?
FAMILY MATTERS. I'LL LEAVE IT AT THAT.

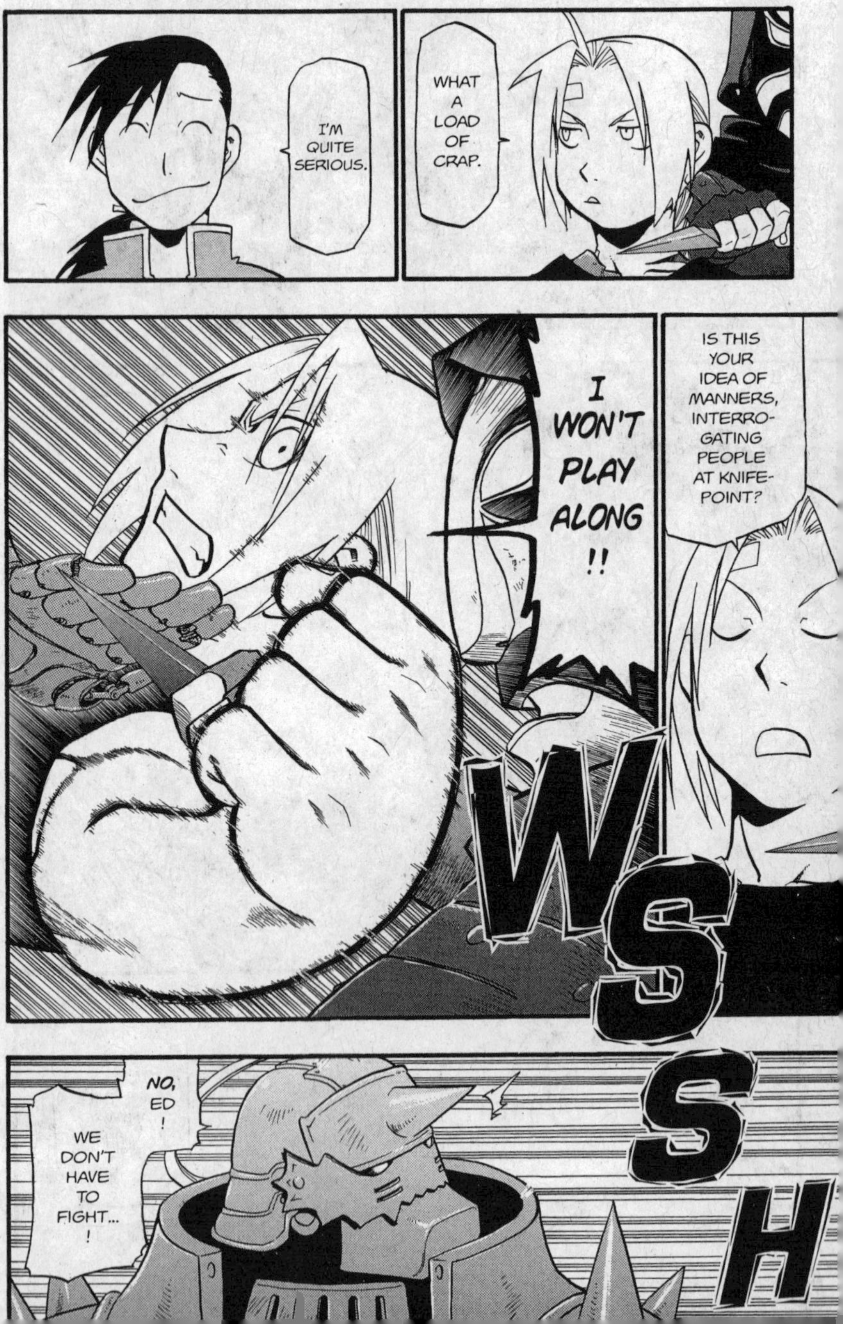
WHAT A LOAD OF CRAP.
I'M QUITE SERIOUS.
IS THIS YOUR IDEA OF MANNERS, INTERROGATING PEOPLE AT KNIFE-POINT?
I WON'T PLAY ALONG!!
WSSH
NO, ED!
WE DON'T HAVE TO FIGHT...!

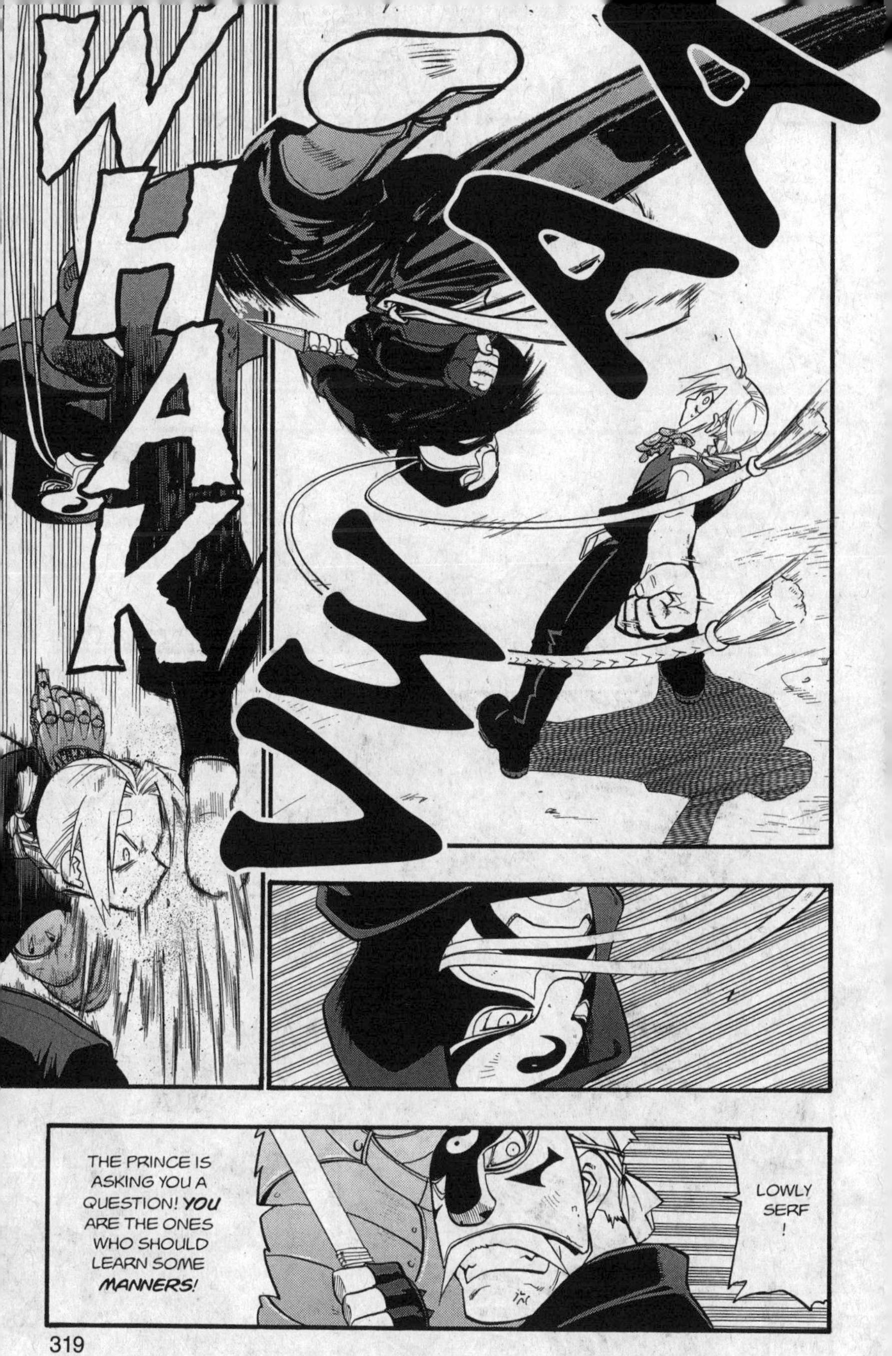
WHAK
WAA
LOWLY SERF!
THE PRINCE IS ASKING YOU A QUESTION! ***YOU*** ARE THE ONES WHO SHOULD LEARN SOME ***MANNERS!***

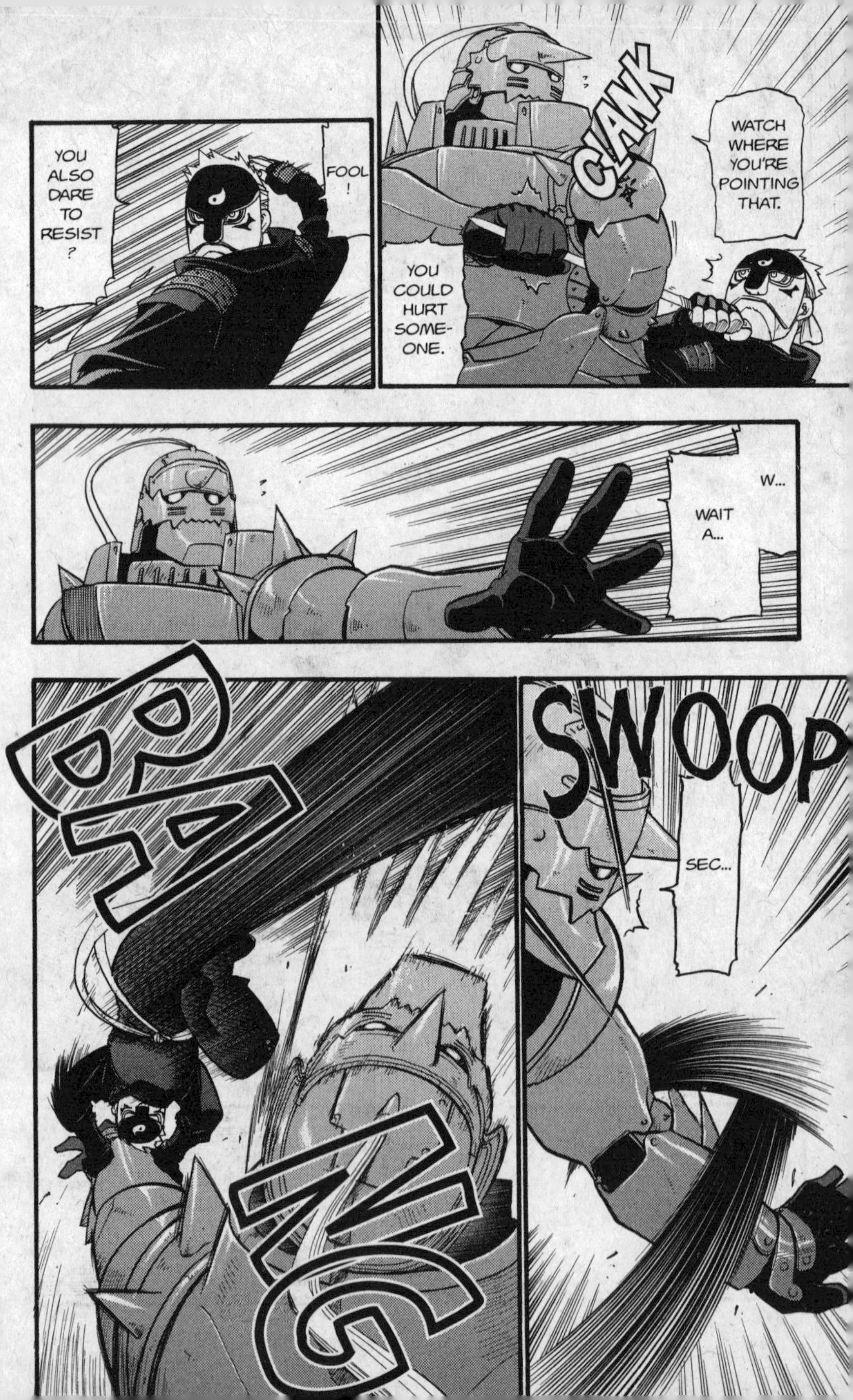
CLANK
WATCH WHERE YOU'RE POINTING THAT.
YOU COULD HURT SOME-ONE.
FOOL!
YOU ALSO DARE TO RESIST?
W...
WAIT A...
SWOOP
SEC...
BANG

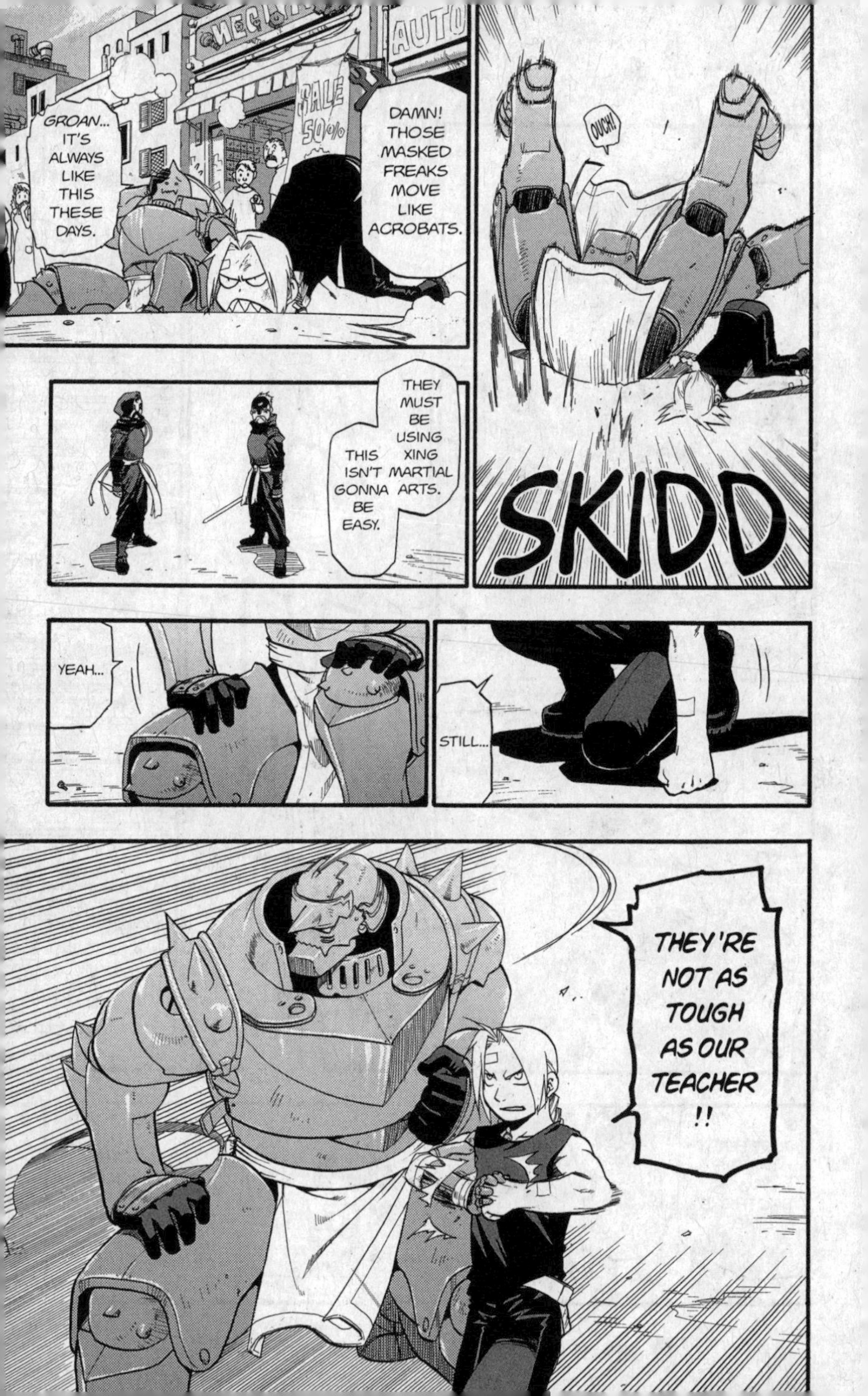
OUCH!
SKIDD
DAMN! THOSE MASKED FREAKS MOVE LIKE ACROBATS.
GROAN... IT'S ALWAYS LIKE THIS THESE DAYS.
THEY MUST BE USING XING MARTIAL ARTS.
THIS ISN'T GONNA BE EASY.
STILL...
YEAH...
THEY'RE NOT AS TOUGH AS OUR TEACHER!!

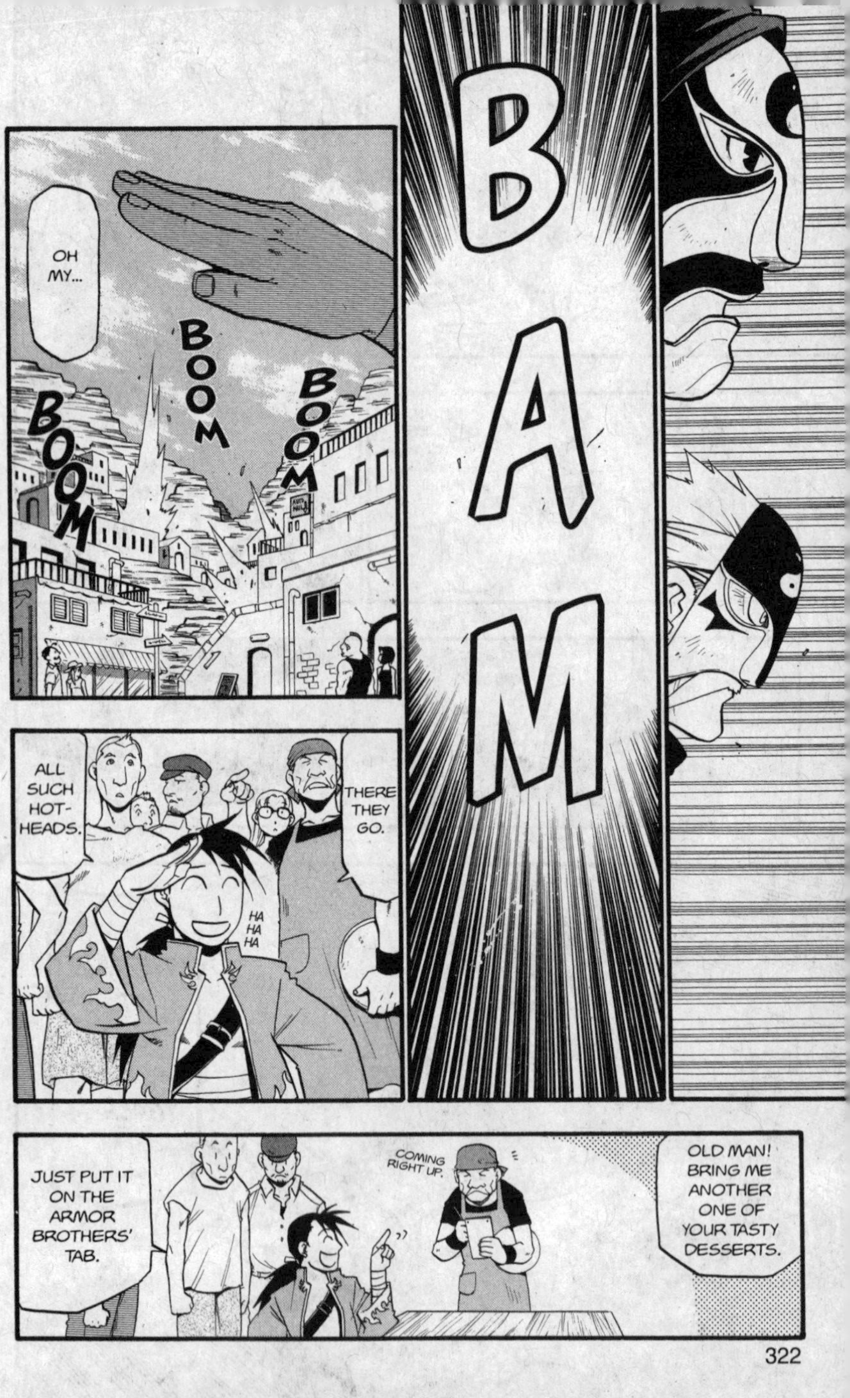
BAM
BOOM
BOOM
OH MY...
BOOM
THERE THEY GO.
ALL SUCH HOT-HEADS.
HA HA HA
OLD MAN! BRING ME ANOTHER ONE OF YOUR TASTY DESSERTS.
COMING RIGHT UP.
JUST PUT IT ON THE ARMOR BROTHERS' TAB.

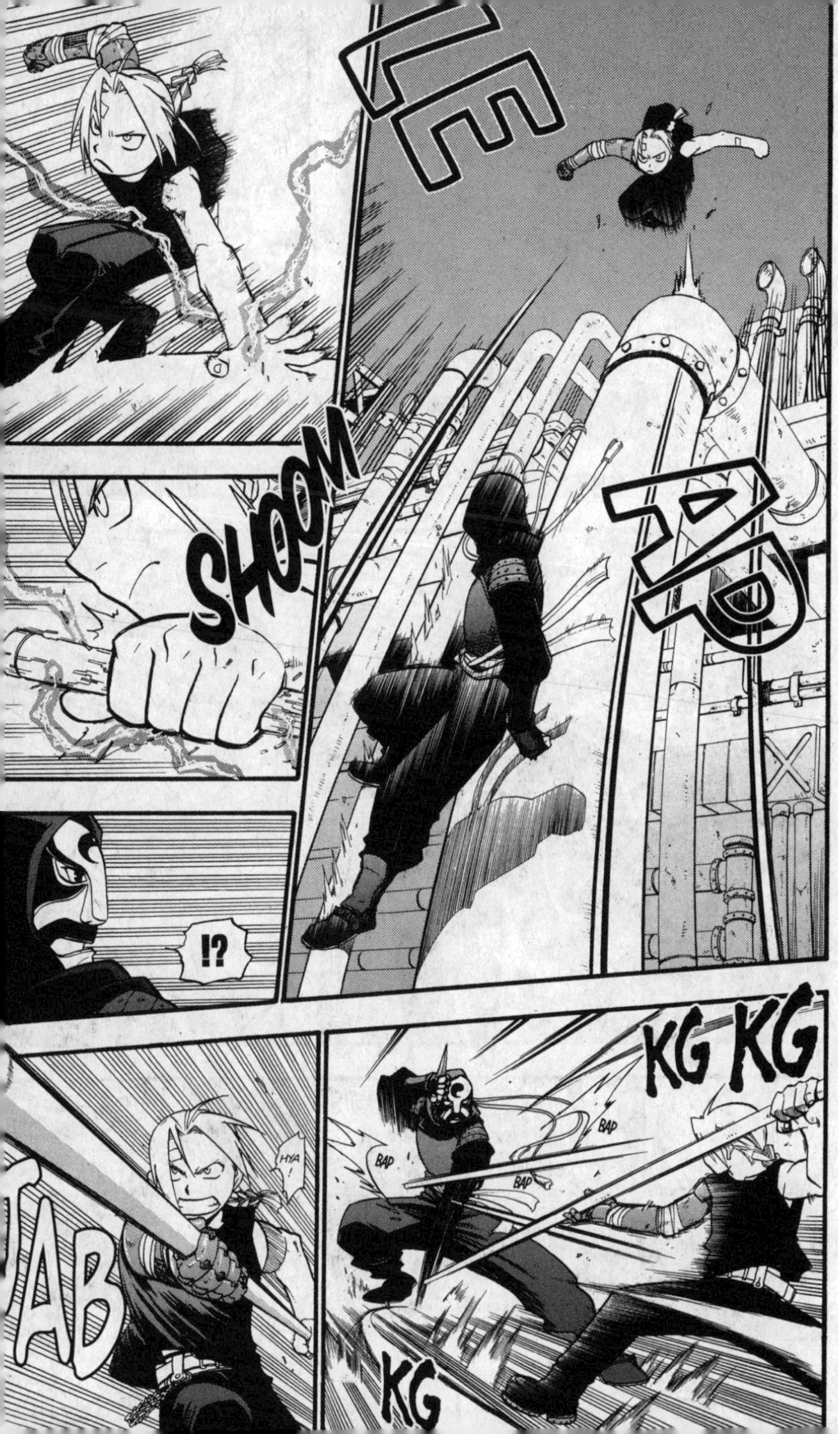
LE
AP
SHOOM
!?
KG KG
BAP
BAP
BAP
KG
HYA!
AB

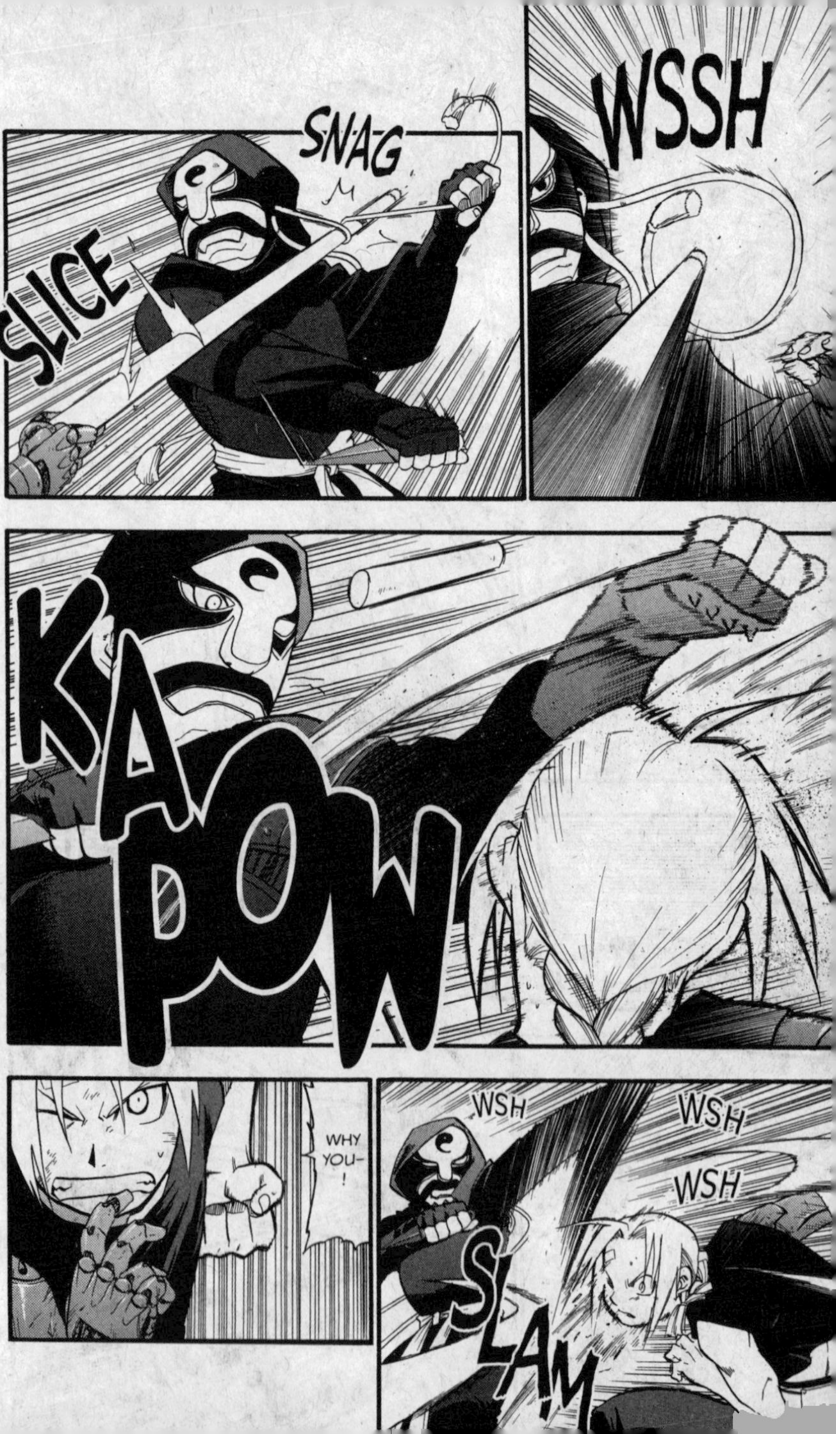
WSSH
SNAG
SLICE
KAPOW
WSH
WSH
WSH
SLAM
WHY YOU- !

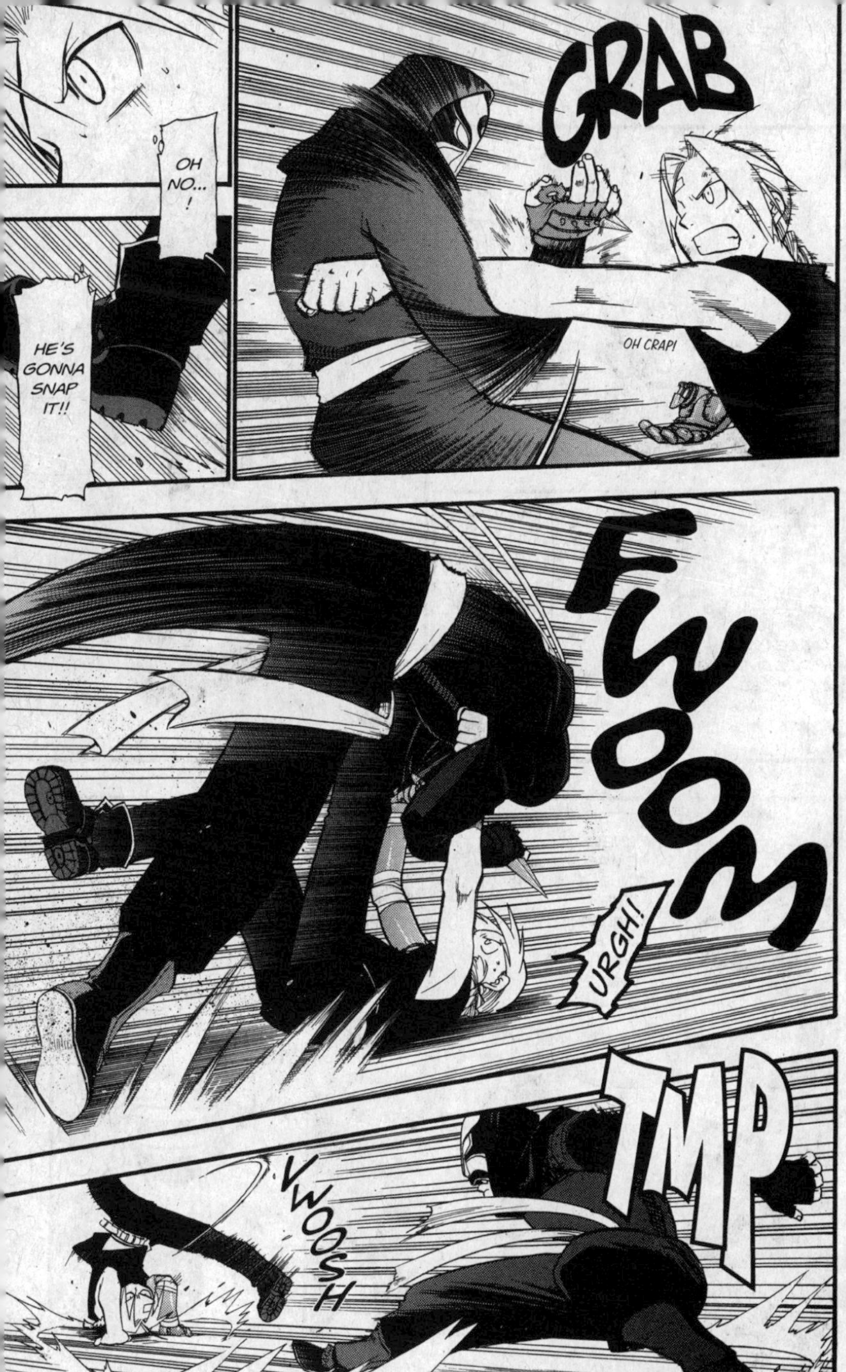
GRAB
OH CRAP!
OH NO... !
HE'S GONNA SNAP IT!!
FWOOM
URGH!
TMP
VWOOSH

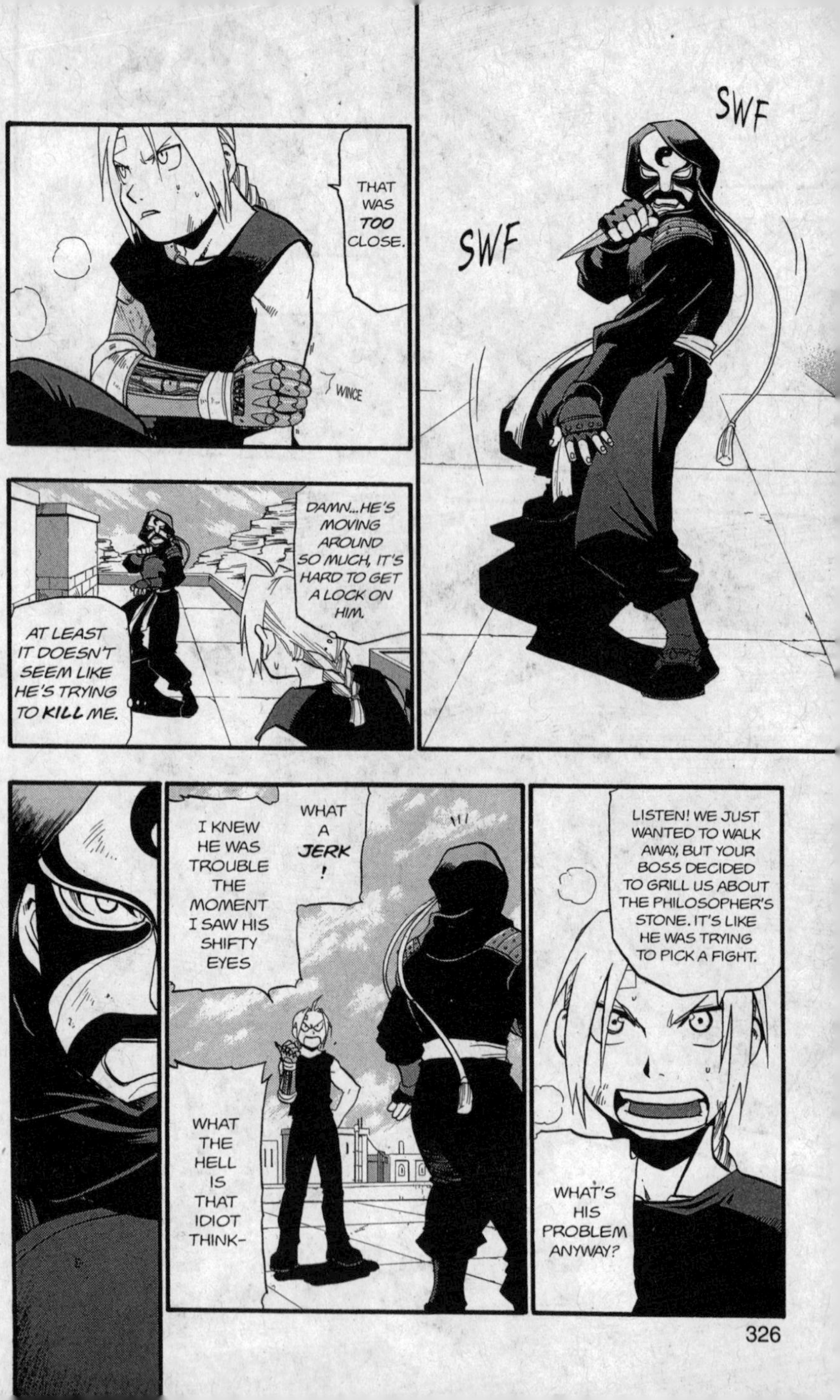
SWF
SWF
THAT WAS TOO CLOSE.
WINCE
DAMN...HE'S MOVING AROUND SO MUCH, IT'S HARD TO GET A LOCK ON HIM.
AT LEAST IT DOESN'T SEEM LIKE HE'S TRYING TO KILL ME.
LISTEN! WE JUST WANTED TO WALK AWAY, BUT YOUR BOSS DECIDED TO GRILL US ABOUT THE PHILOSOPHER'S STONE. IT'S LIKE HE WAS TRYING TO PICK A FIGHT.
WHAT'S HIS PROBLEM ANYWAY?
WHAT A JERK!
I KNEW HE WAS TROUBLE THE MOMENT I SAW HIS SHIFTY EYES
WHAT THE HELL IS THAT IDIOT THINK-

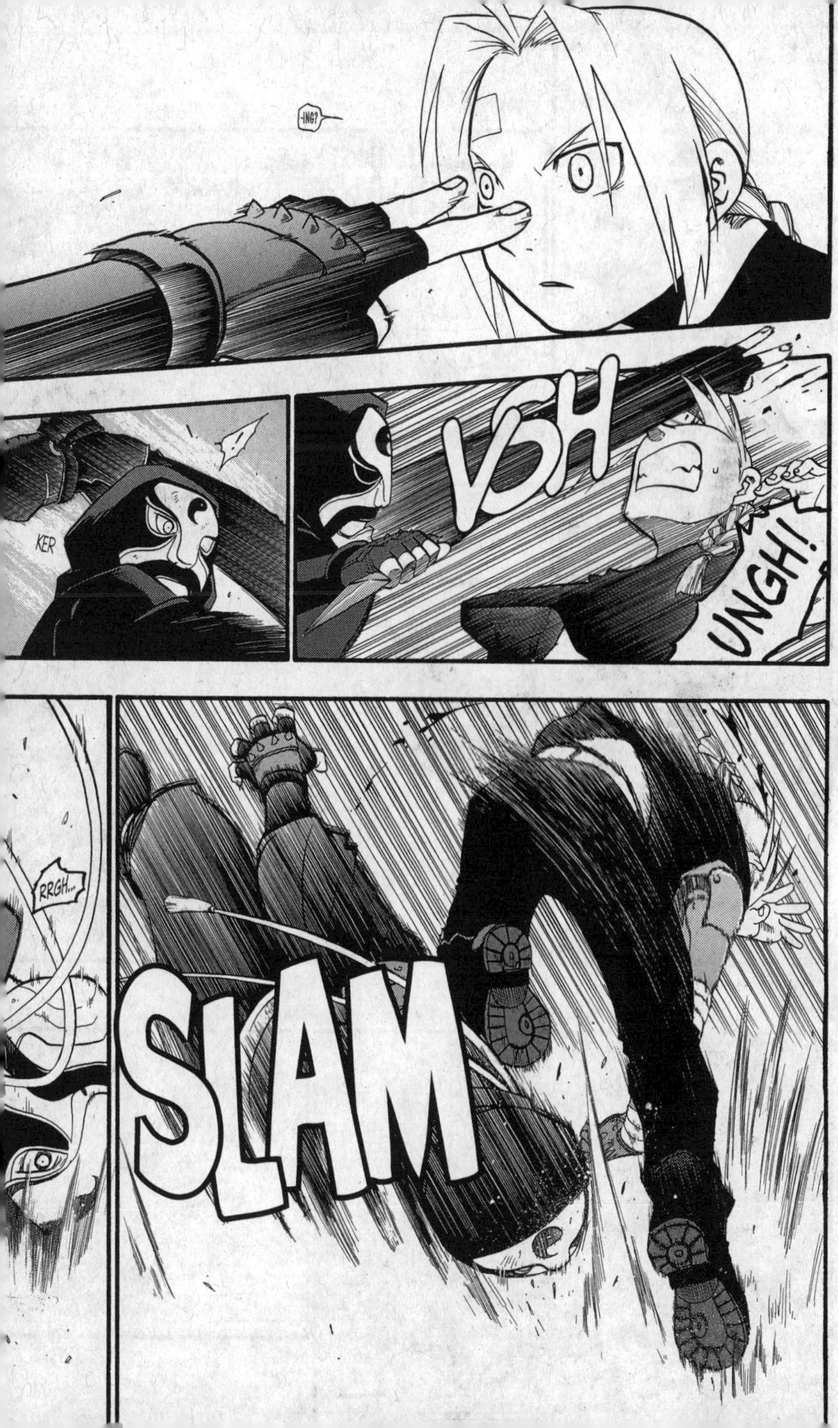
-ING?
VSH
UNGH!
KER
SLAM
RRGH...

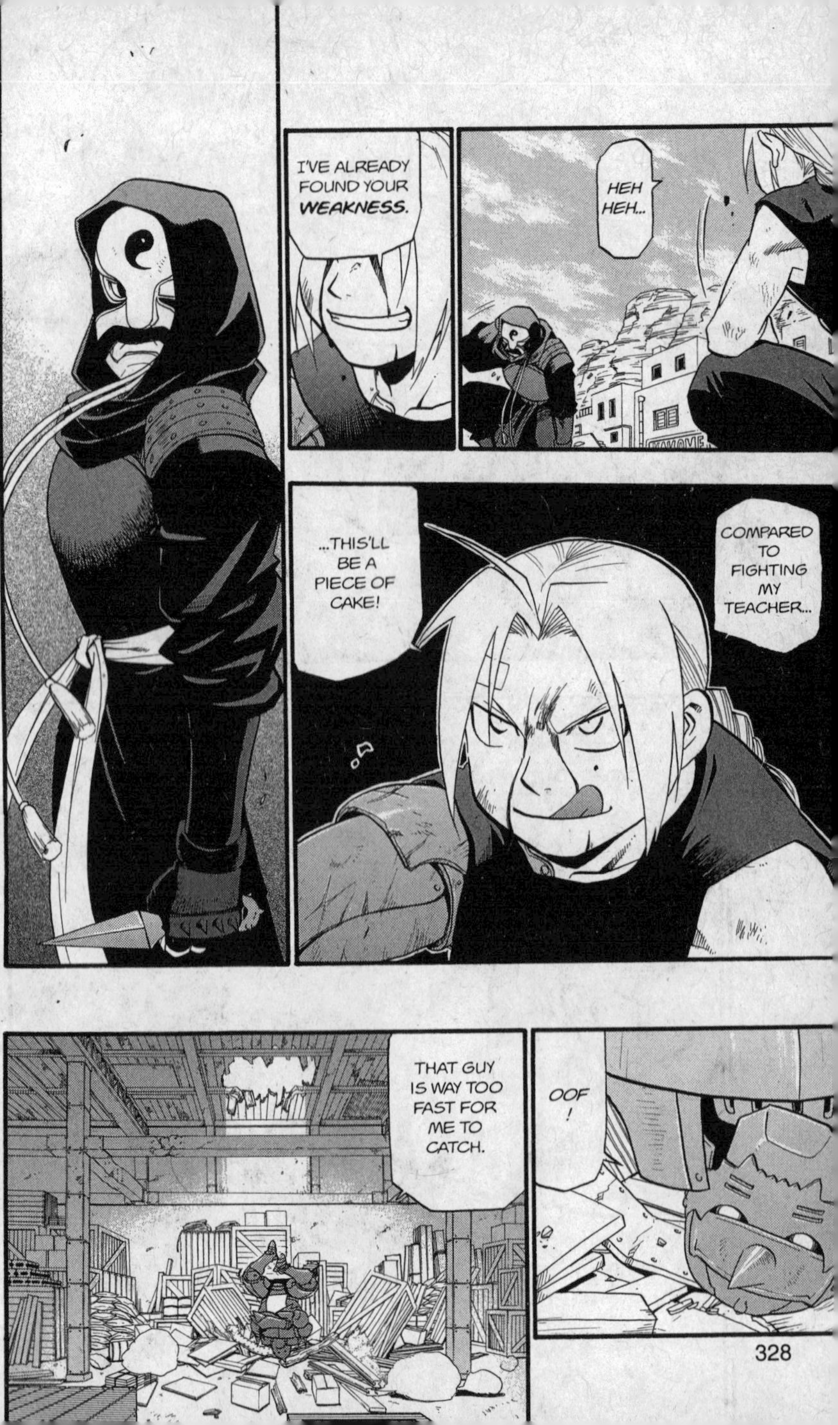
HEH HEH...
I'VE ALREADY FOUND YOUR **WEAKNESS.**
COMPARED TO FIGHTING MY TEACHER...
...THIS'LL BE A PIECE OF CAKE!
OOF!
THAT GUY IS WAY TOO FAST FOR ME TO CATCH.

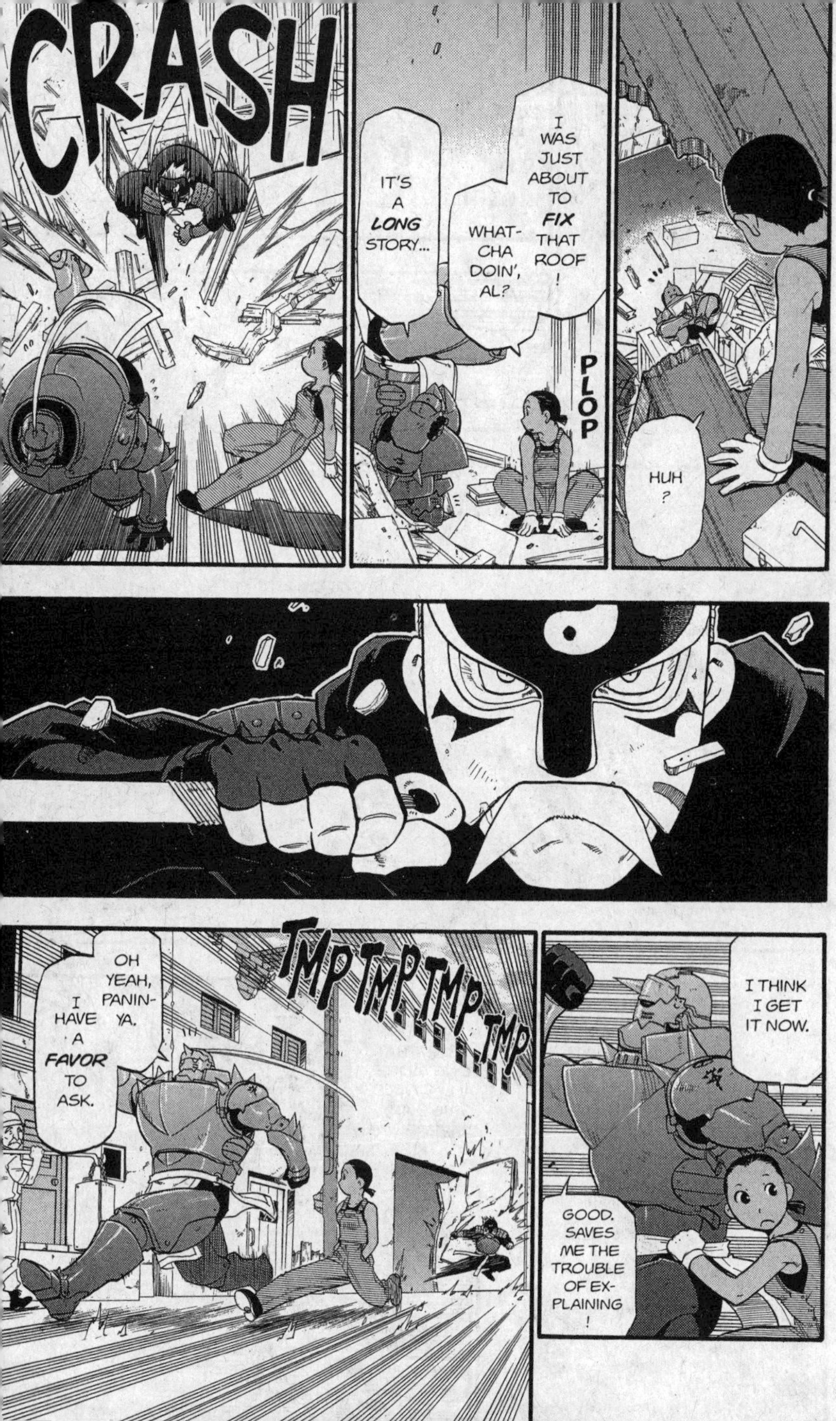
HUH?
I WAS JUST ABOUT TO FIX THAT ROOF!
WHATCHA DOIN', AL?
IT'S A LONG STORY...
PLOP
CRASH
I THINK I GET IT NOW.
GOOD. SAVES ME THE TROUBLE OF EXPLAINING!
TMP TMP TMP TMP
OH YEAH, PANINYA.
I HAVE A FAVOR TO ASK.

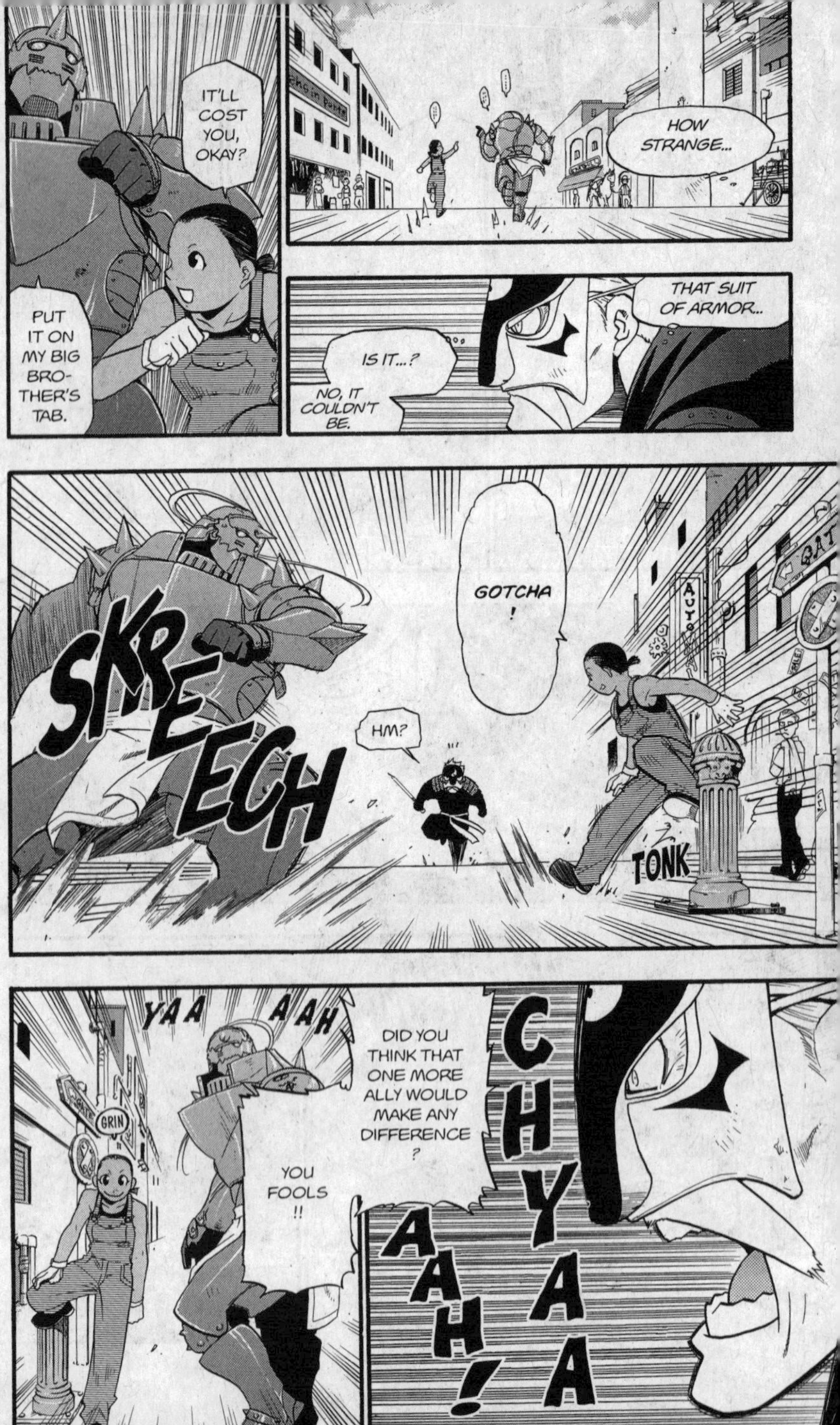
HOW STRANGE...
THAT SUIT OF ARMOR...
IS IT...?
NO, IT COULDN'T BE.
IT'LL COST YOU, OKAY?
PUT IT ON MY BIG BROTHER'S TAB.
GOTCHA
!
TONK
HM?
SKREECH
CHYAA
DID YOU THINK THAT ONE MORE ALLY WOULD MAKE ANY DIFFERENCE
?
YOU FOOLS
!!
AAH!
YAA AAH
GRIN

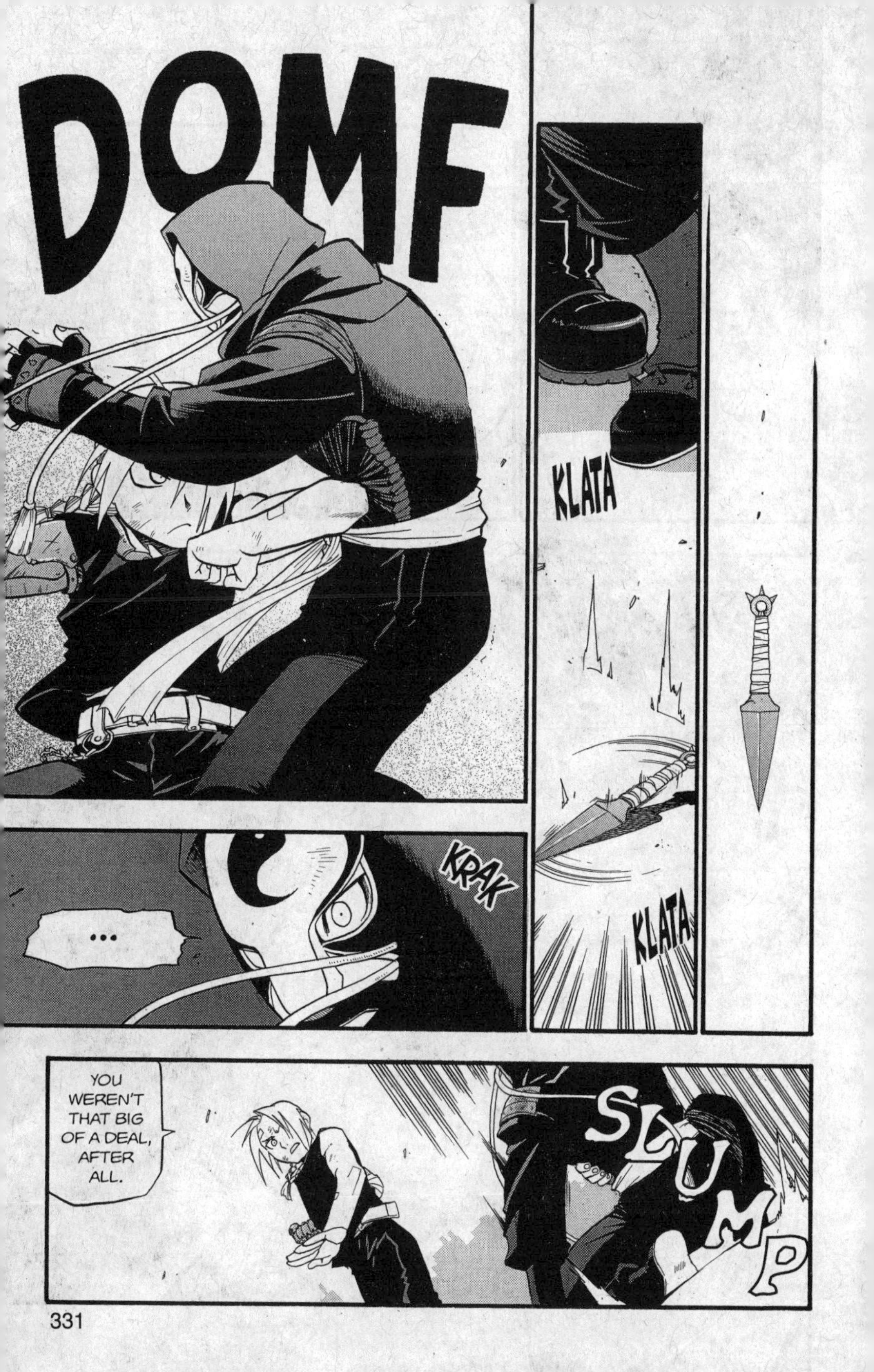
KLATA
KLATA
DOMF
KRAK
...
SLUMP
YOU WEREN'T THAT BIG OF A DEAL, AFTER ALL.

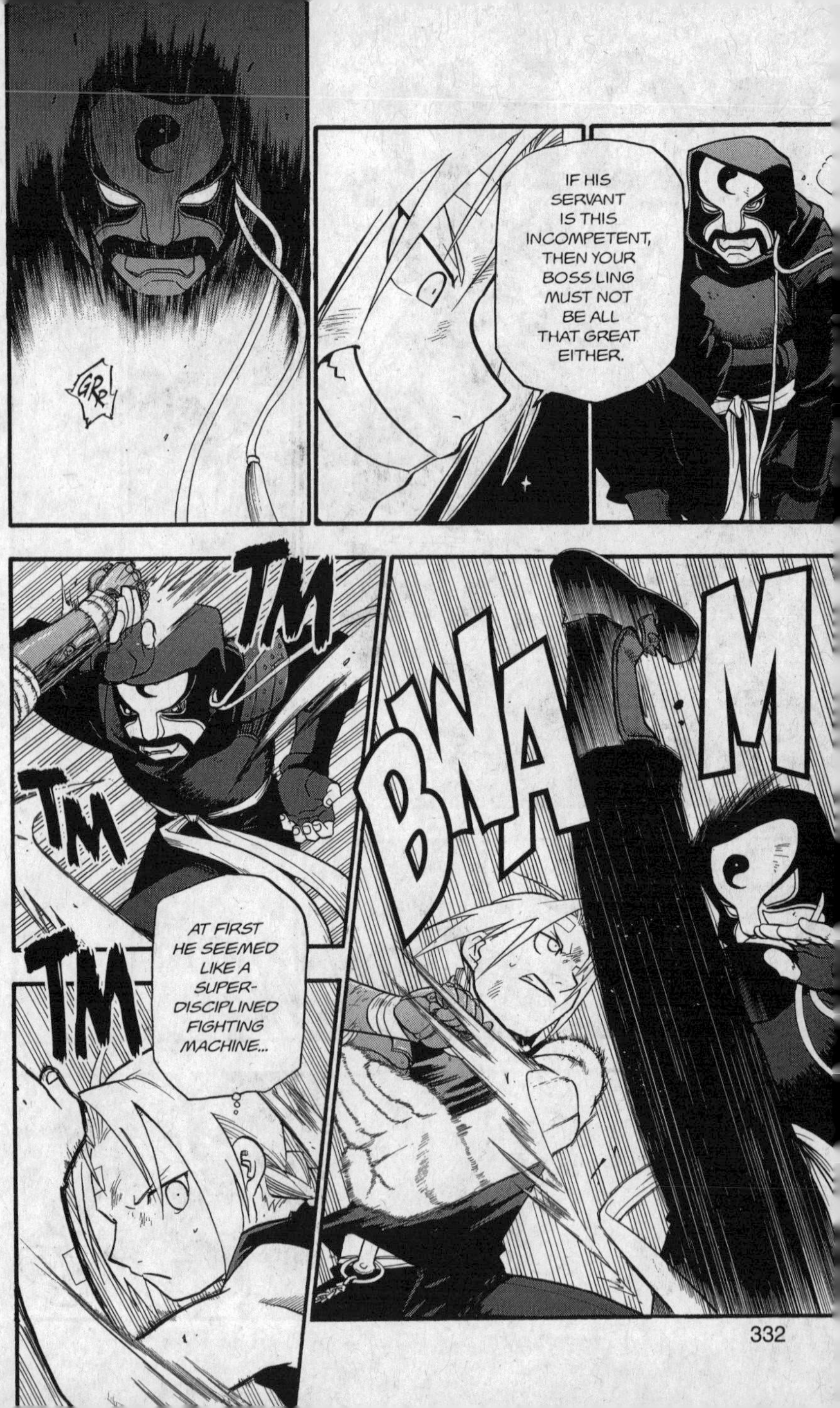
IF HIS SERVANT IS THIS INCOMPETENT, THEN YOUR BOSS LING MUST NOT BE ALL THAT GREAT EITHER.
GRR
BWAM
TM
TM
TM
AT FIRST HE SEEMED LIKE A SUPER-DISCIPLINED FIGHTING MACHINE...

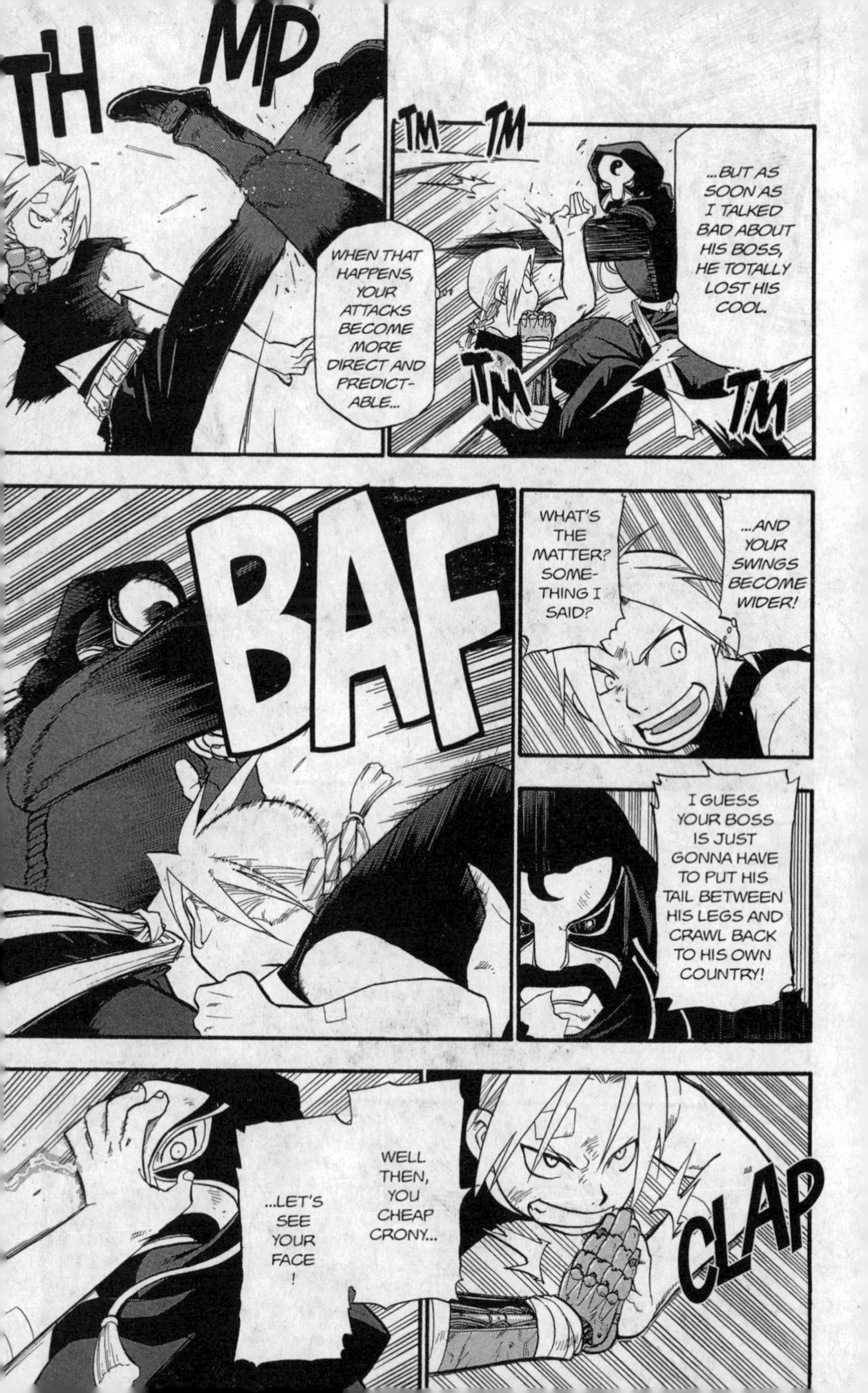
TM TM
...BUT AS SOON AS I TALKED BAD ABOUT HIS BOSS, HE TOTALLY LOST HIS COOL.
TM TM
THUMP
WHEN THAT HAPPENS, YOUR ATTACKS BECOME MORE DIRECT AND PREDICT-ABLE...
...AND YOUR SWINGS BECOME WIDER!
WHAT'S THE MATTER? SOME-THING I SAID?
I GUESS YOUR BOSS IS JUST GONNA HAVE TO PUT HIS TAIL BETWEEN HIS LEGS AND CRAWL BACK TO HIS OWN COUNTRY!
BAF
CLAP
WELL THEN, YOU CHEAP CRONY...
...LET'S SEE YOUR FACE!

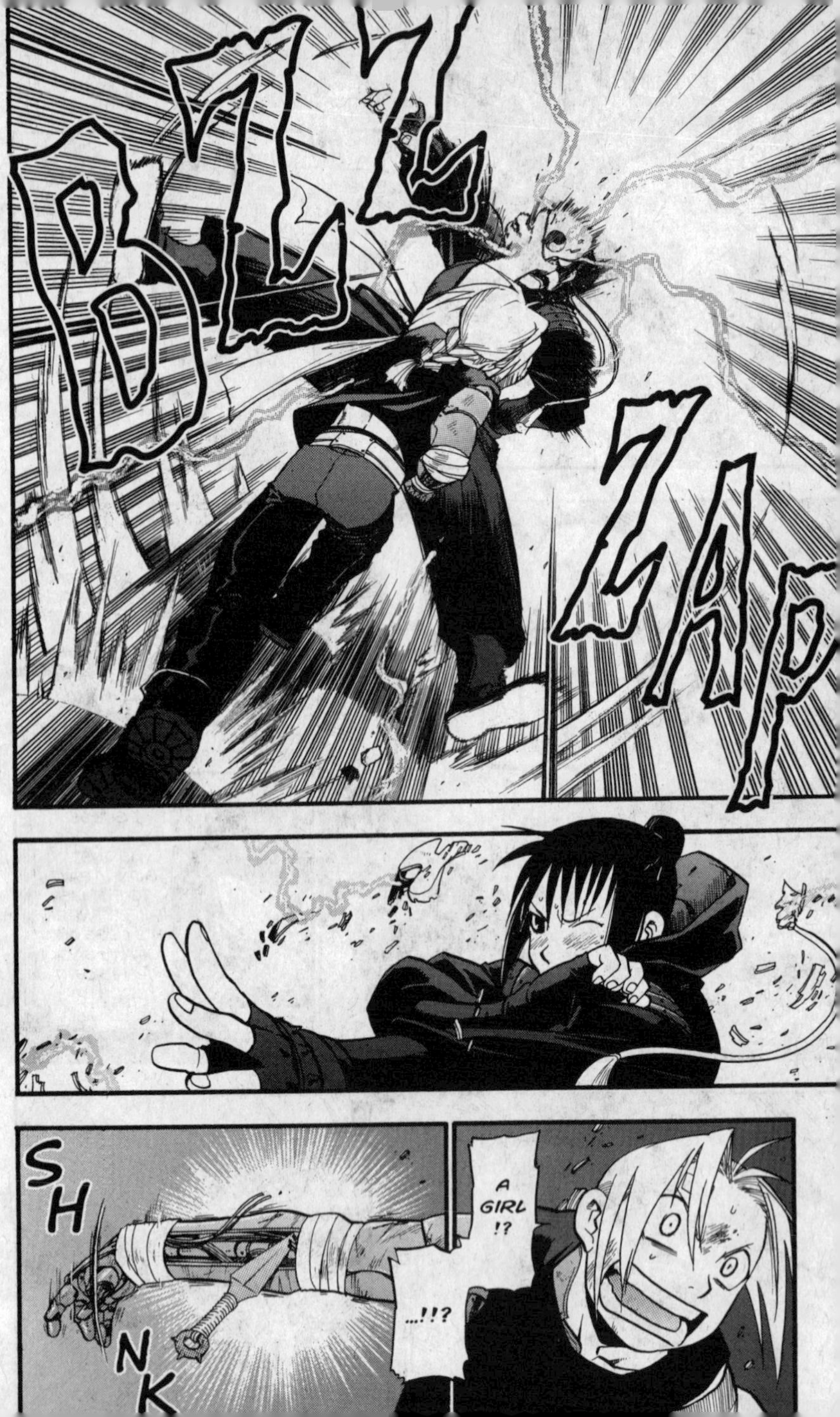
ZAP
A GIRL !?
...!!?
SHNK

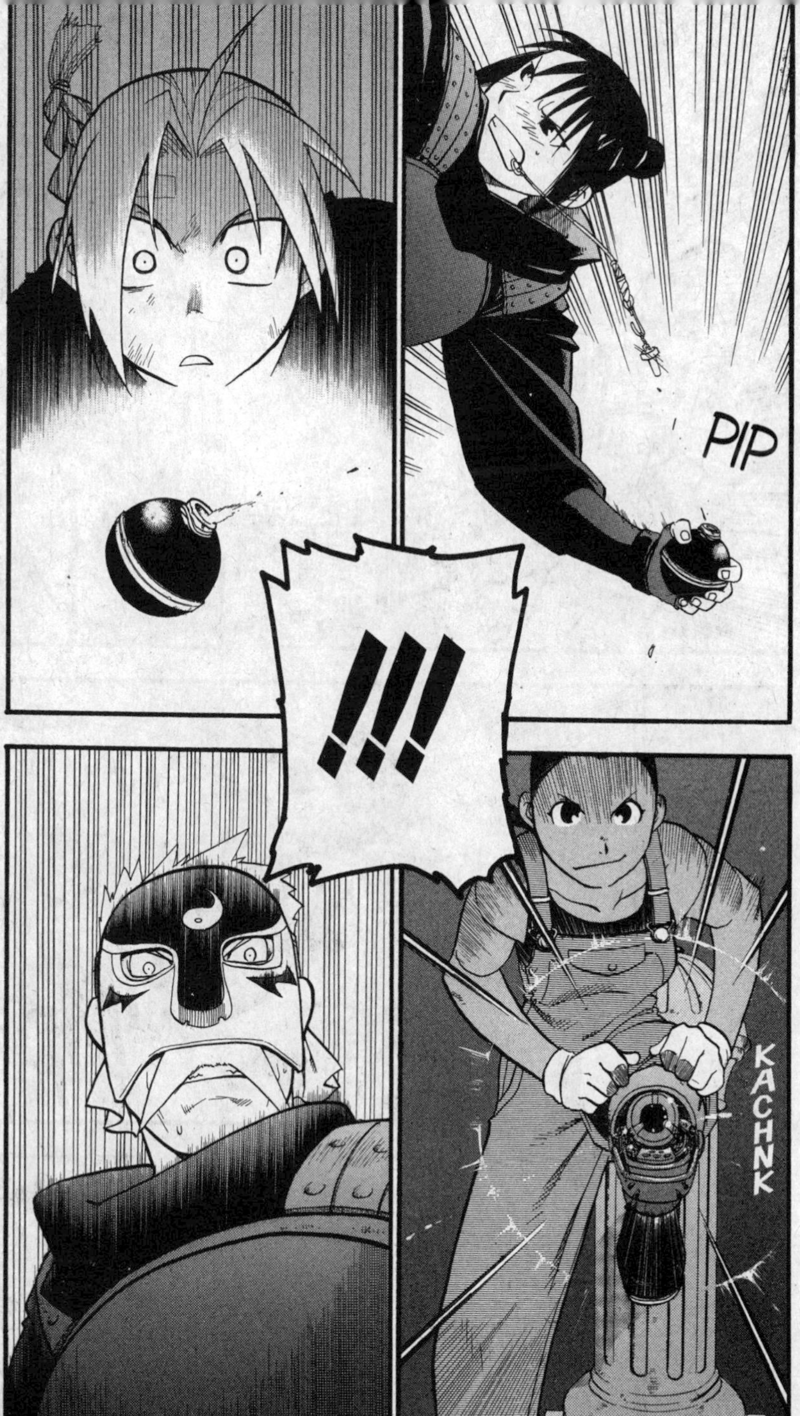
PIP
!!!
KACHNK

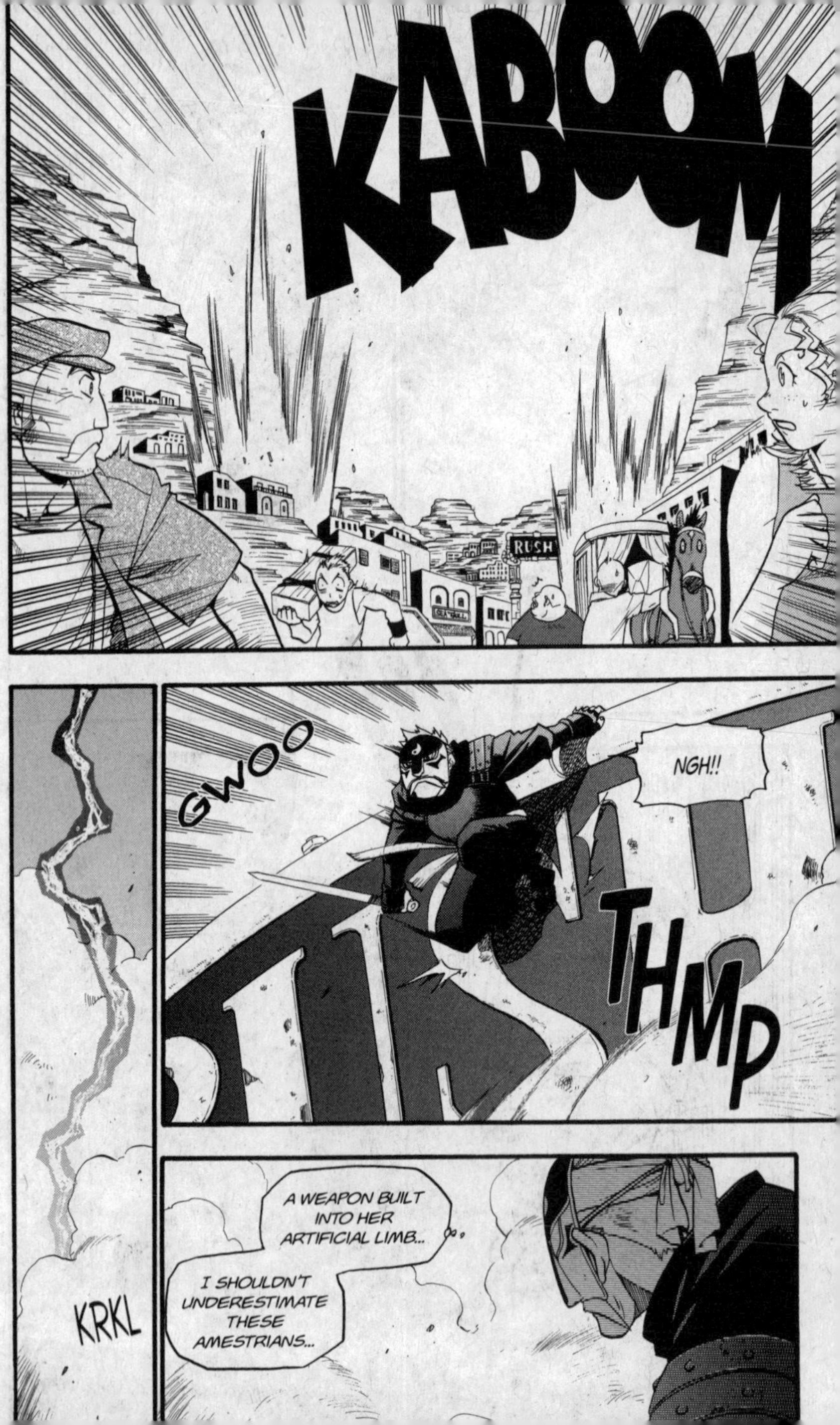
KABOOM
RUSH
SEA GULL
NGH!!
GWOO
THMP
A WEAPON BUILT INTO HER ARTIFICIAL LIMB...
I SHOULDN'T UNDERESTIMATE THESE AMESTRIANS...
KRKL

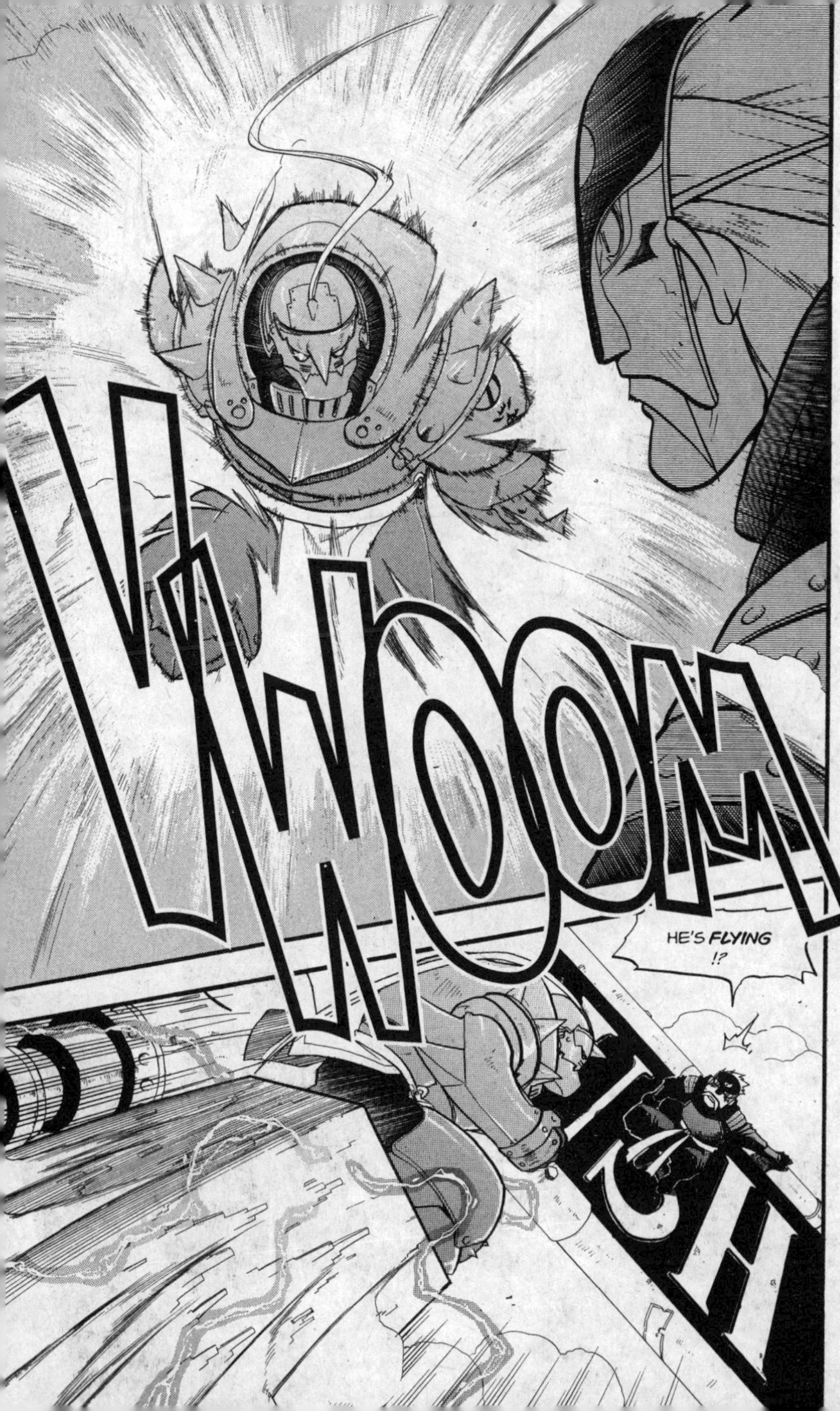
VWOOM
HE'S FLYING !?

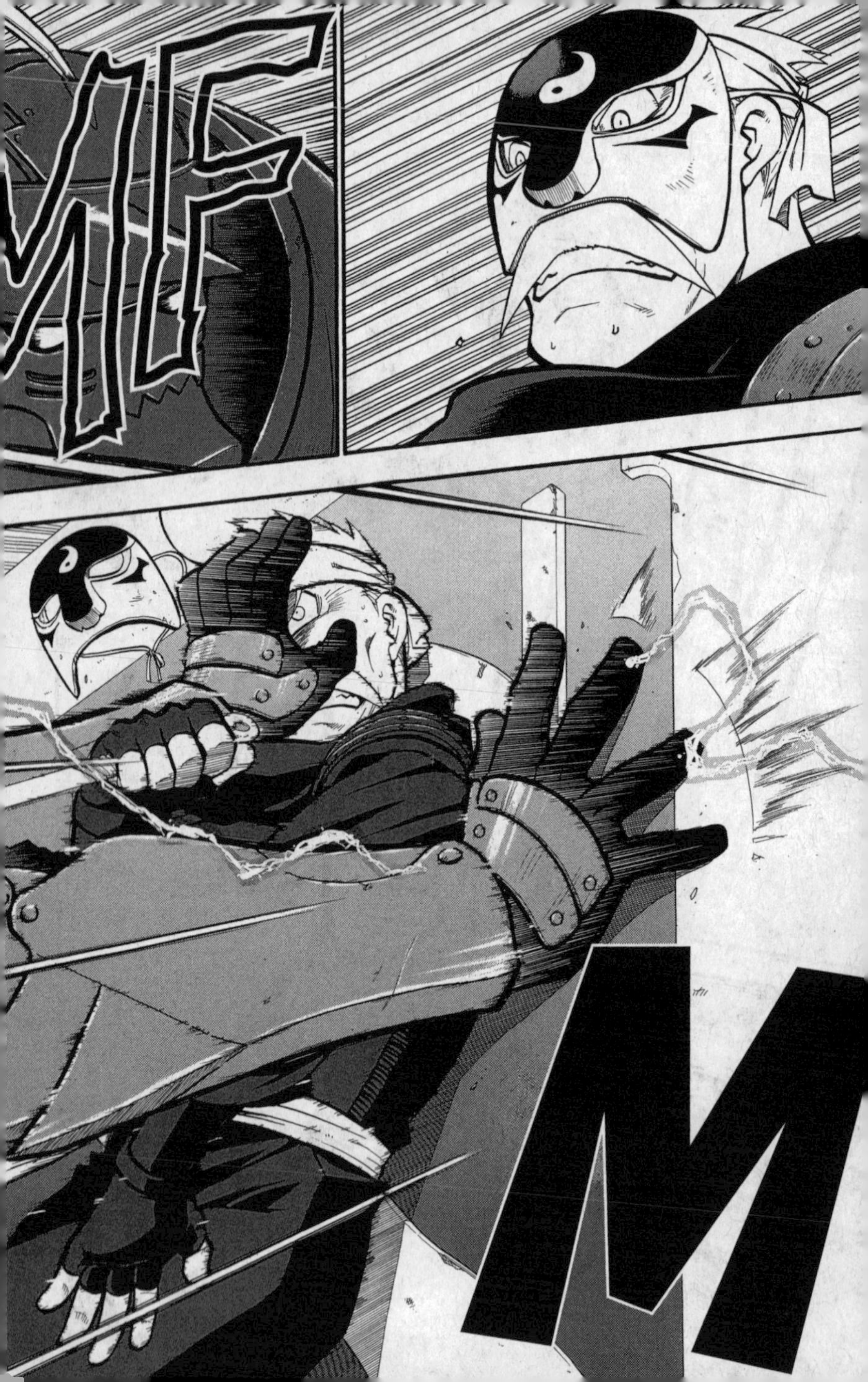
M

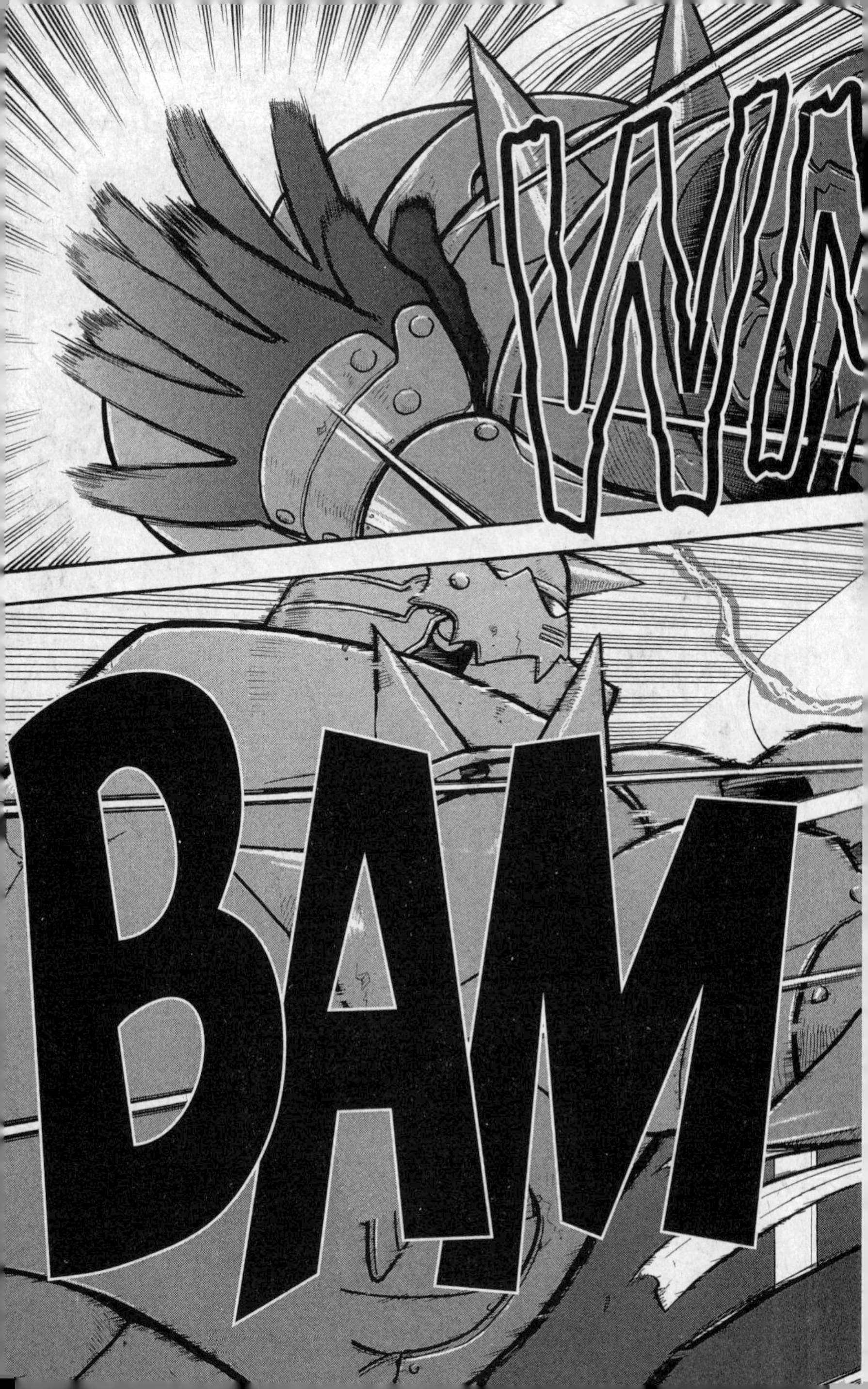
WOM
BAM

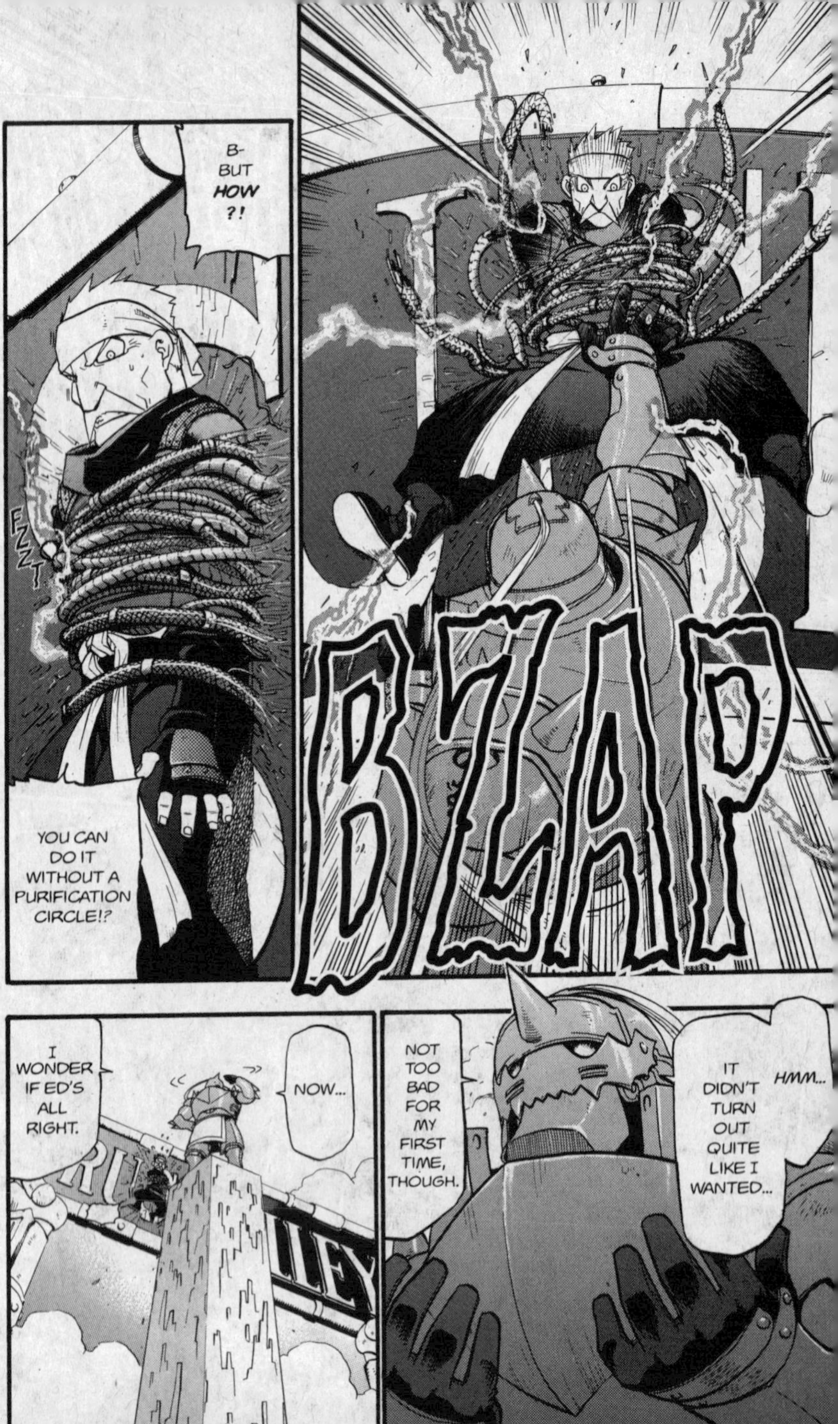
BZZAP
B- BUT HOW?!
FZZT
YOU CAN DO IT WITHOUT A PURIFICATION CIRCLE!?
HMM...
IT DIDN'T TURN OUT QUITE LIKE I WANTED...
NOT TOO BAD FOR MY FIRST TIME, THOUGH.
NOW...
I WONDER IF ED'S ALL RIGHT.

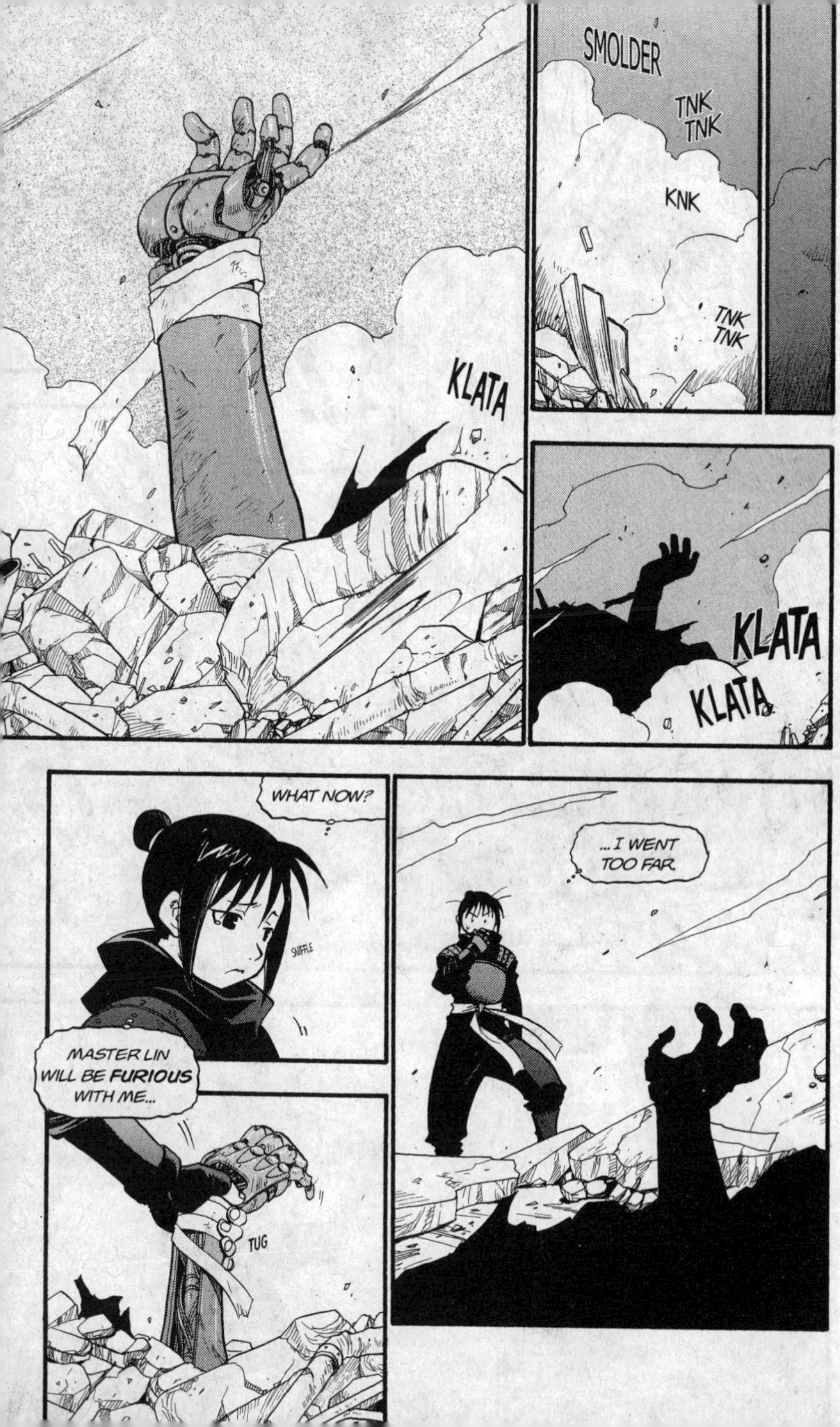
SMOLDER
TNK TNK
KNK
TNK TNK
KLATA
KLATA
KLATA
...I WENT TOO FAR.
WHAT NOW?
SNIFFLE
MASTER LIN WILL BE FURIOUS WITH ME...
TUG

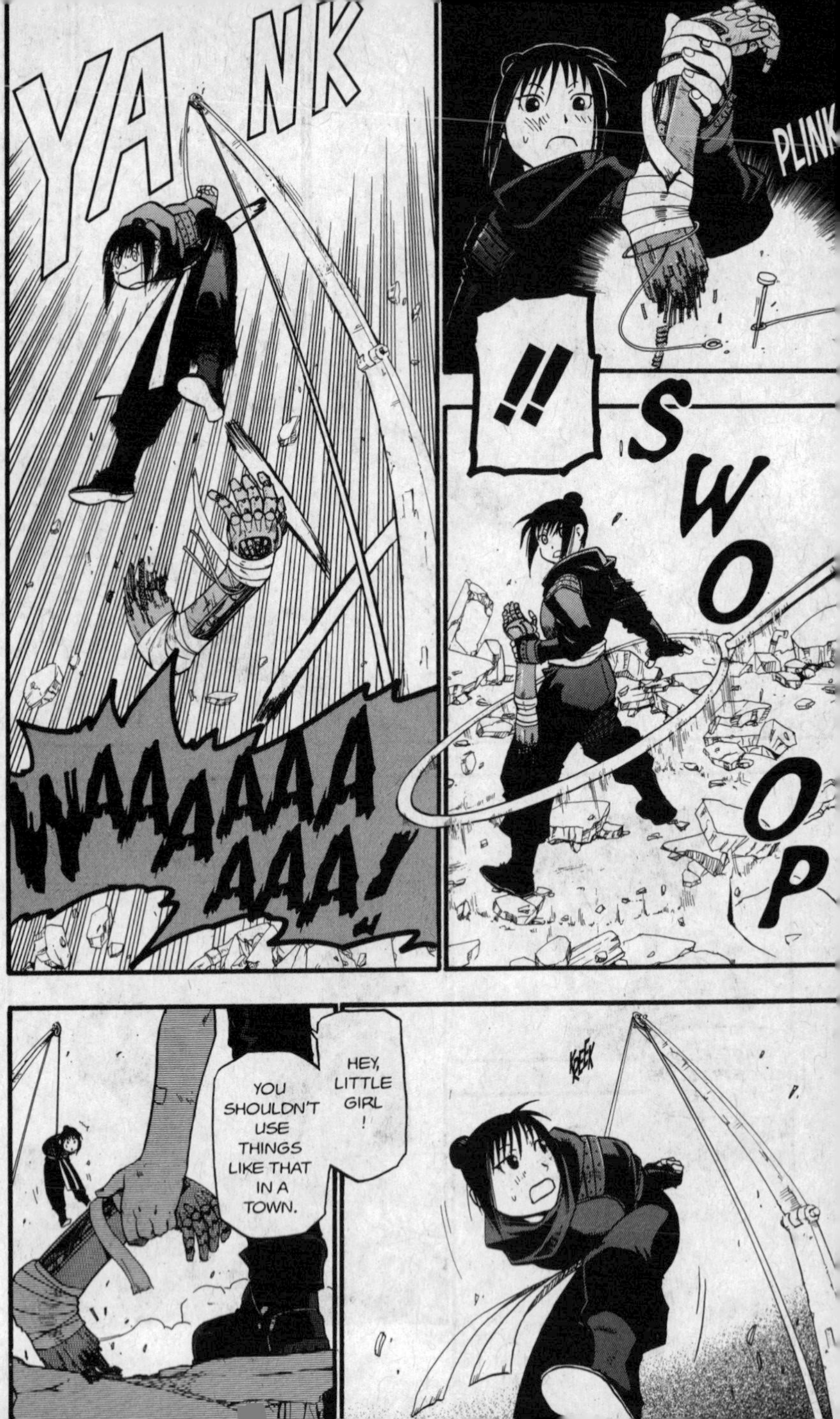
PLINK
!!
SWOOP
YANK
WAAAAAAAAA!
KREEK
HEY, LITTLE GIRL!
YOU SHOULDN'T USE THINGS LIKE THAT IN A TOWN.

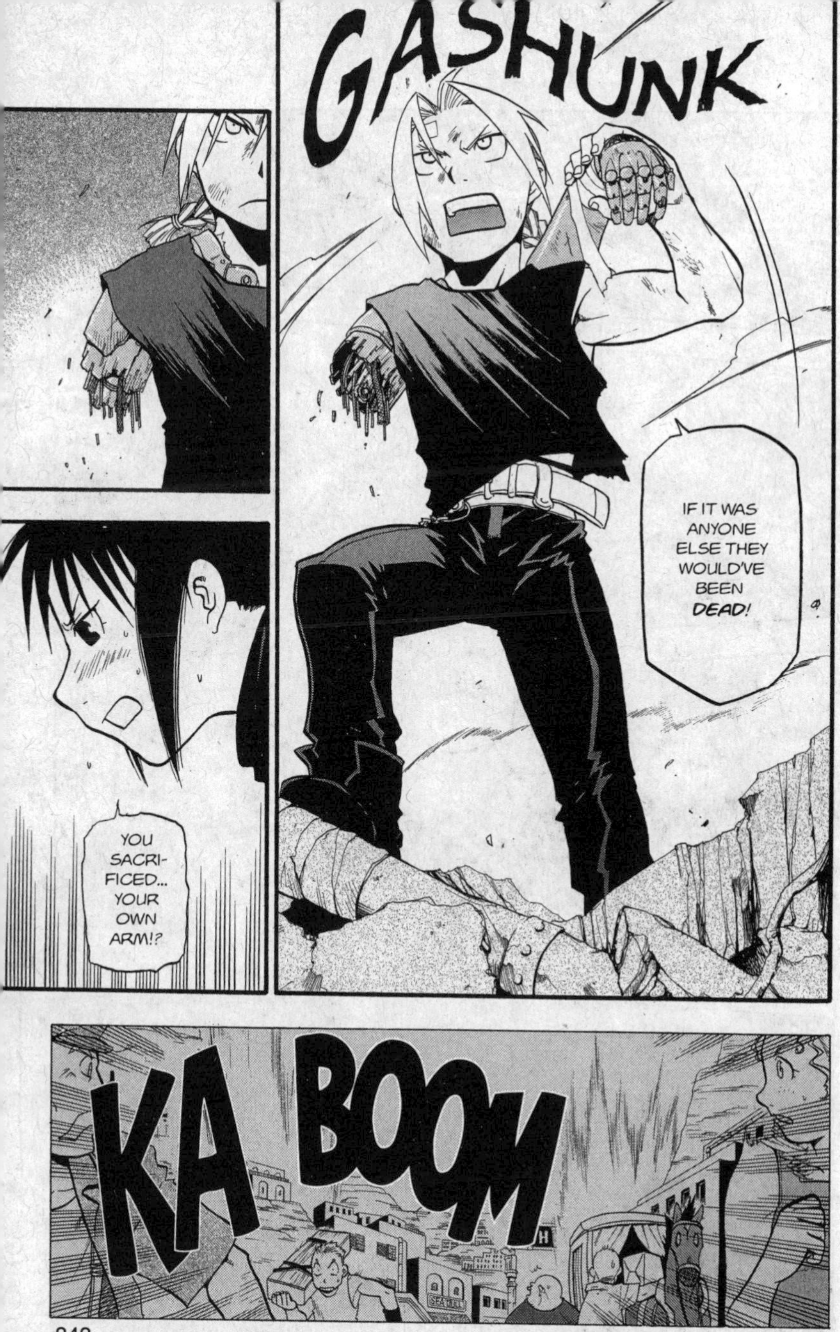
GASHUNK
IF IT WAS ANYONE ELSE THEY WOULD'VE BEEN **DEAD!**
YOU SACRIFICED... YOUR OWN ARM!?
KA BOOM

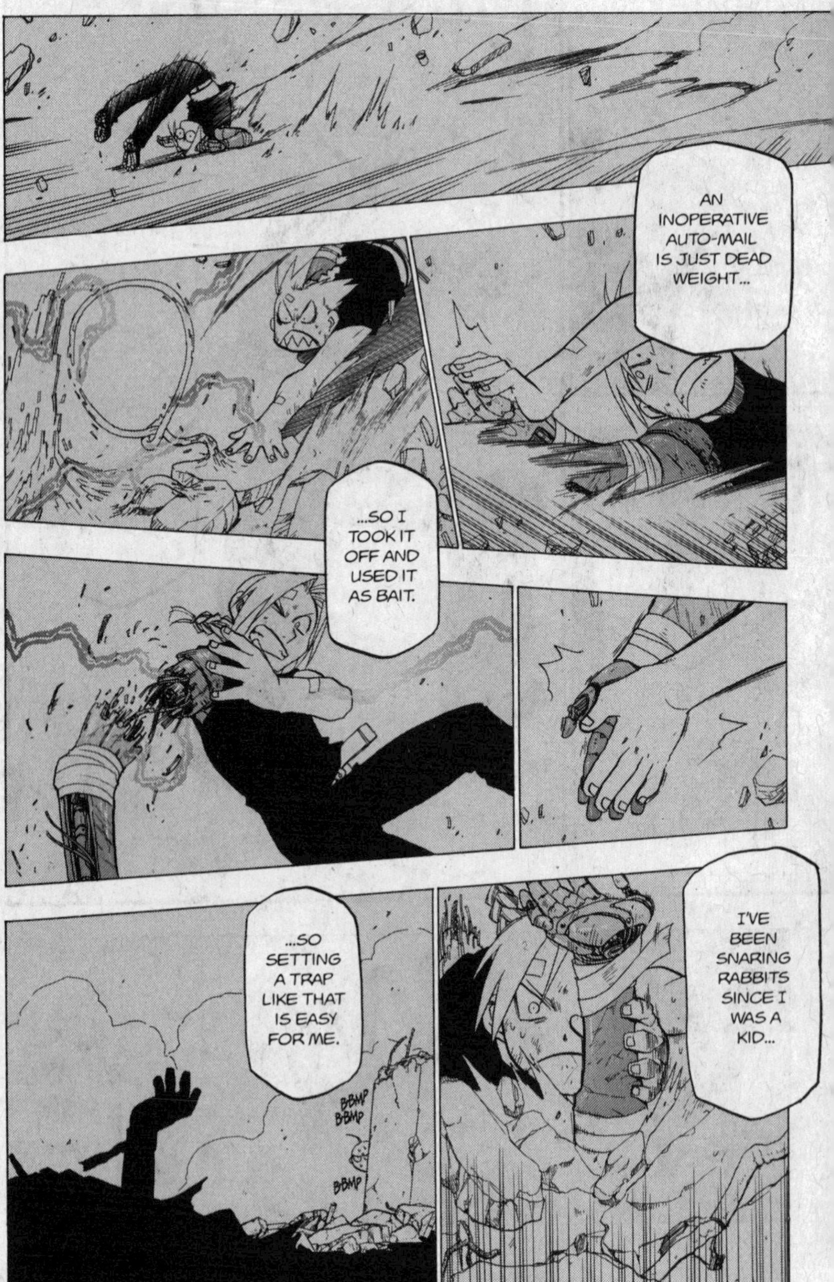
AN INOPERATIVE AUTO-MAIL IS JUST DEAD WEIGHT...
...SO I TOOK IT OFF AND USED IT AS BAIT.
I'VE BEEN SNARING RABBITS SINCE I WAS A KID...
...SO SETTING A TRAP LIKE THAT IS EASY FOR ME.
B-BMP
B-BMP
B-BMP

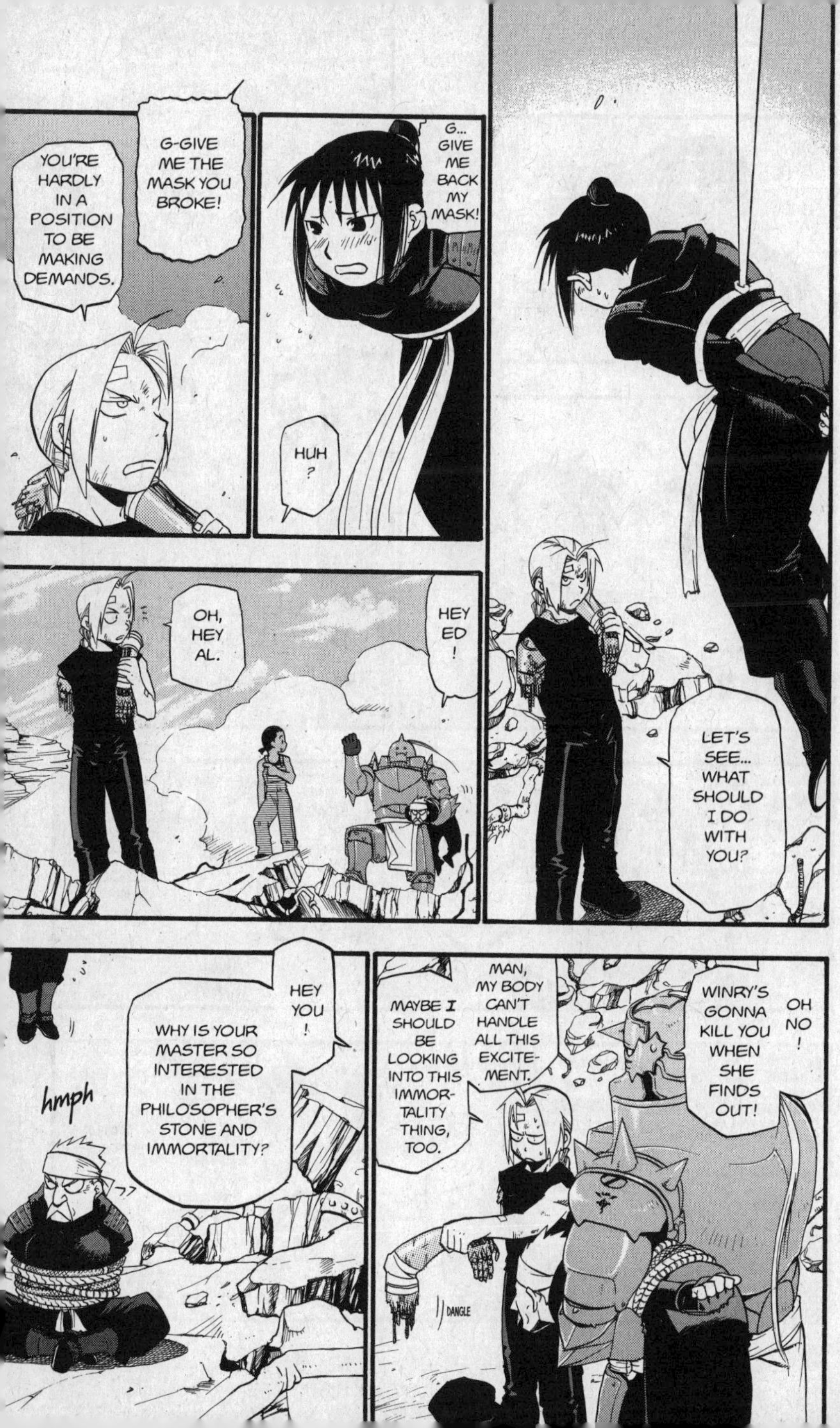
LET'S SEE... WHAT SHOULD I DO WITH YOU?
G... GIVE ME BACK MY MASK!
HUH?
G-GIVE ME THE MASK YOU BROKE!
YOU'RE HARDLY IN A POSITION TO BE MAKING DEMANDS.
HEY ED!
OH, HEY AL.
OH NO!
WINRY'S GONNA KILL YOU WHEN SHE FINDS OUT!
MAN, MY BODY CAN'T HANDLE ALL THIS EXCITEMENT.
MAYBE I SHOULD BE LOOKING INTO THIS IMMORTALITY THING, TOO.
DANGLE
HEY YOU!
WHY IS YOUR MASTER SO INTERESTED IN THE PHILOSOPHER'S STONE AND IMMORTALITY?
hmph

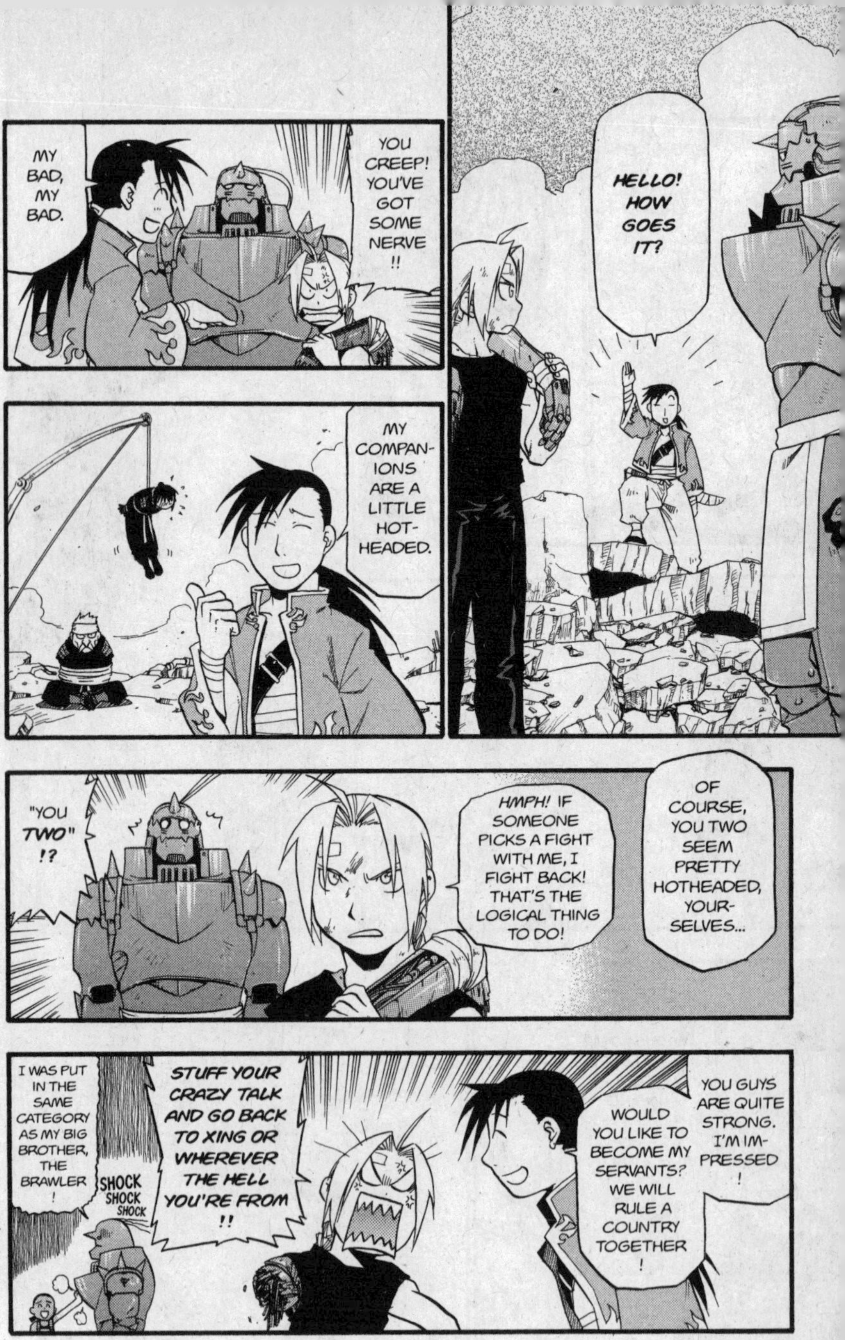
HELLO! HOW GOES IT?
YOU CREEP! YOU'VE GOT SOME NERVE !!
MY BAD, MY BAD.
MY COMPANIONS ARE A LITTLE HOT-HEADED.
OF COURSE, YOU TWO SEEM PRETTY HOTHEADED, YOURSELVES...
HMPH! IF SOMEONE PICKS A FIGHT WITH ME, I FIGHT BACK! THAT'S THE LOGICAL THING TO DO!
"YOU TWO" !?
YOU GUYS ARE QUITE STRONG. I'M IMPRESSED !
WOULD YOU LIKE TO BECOME MY SERVANTS? WE WILL RULE A COUNTRY TOGETHER !
STUFF YOUR CRAZY TALK AND GO BACK TO XING OR WHEREVER THE HELL YOU'RE FROM !!
I WAS PUT IN THE SAME CATEGORY AS MY BIG BROTHER, THE BRAWLER !
SHOCK SHOCK SHOCK

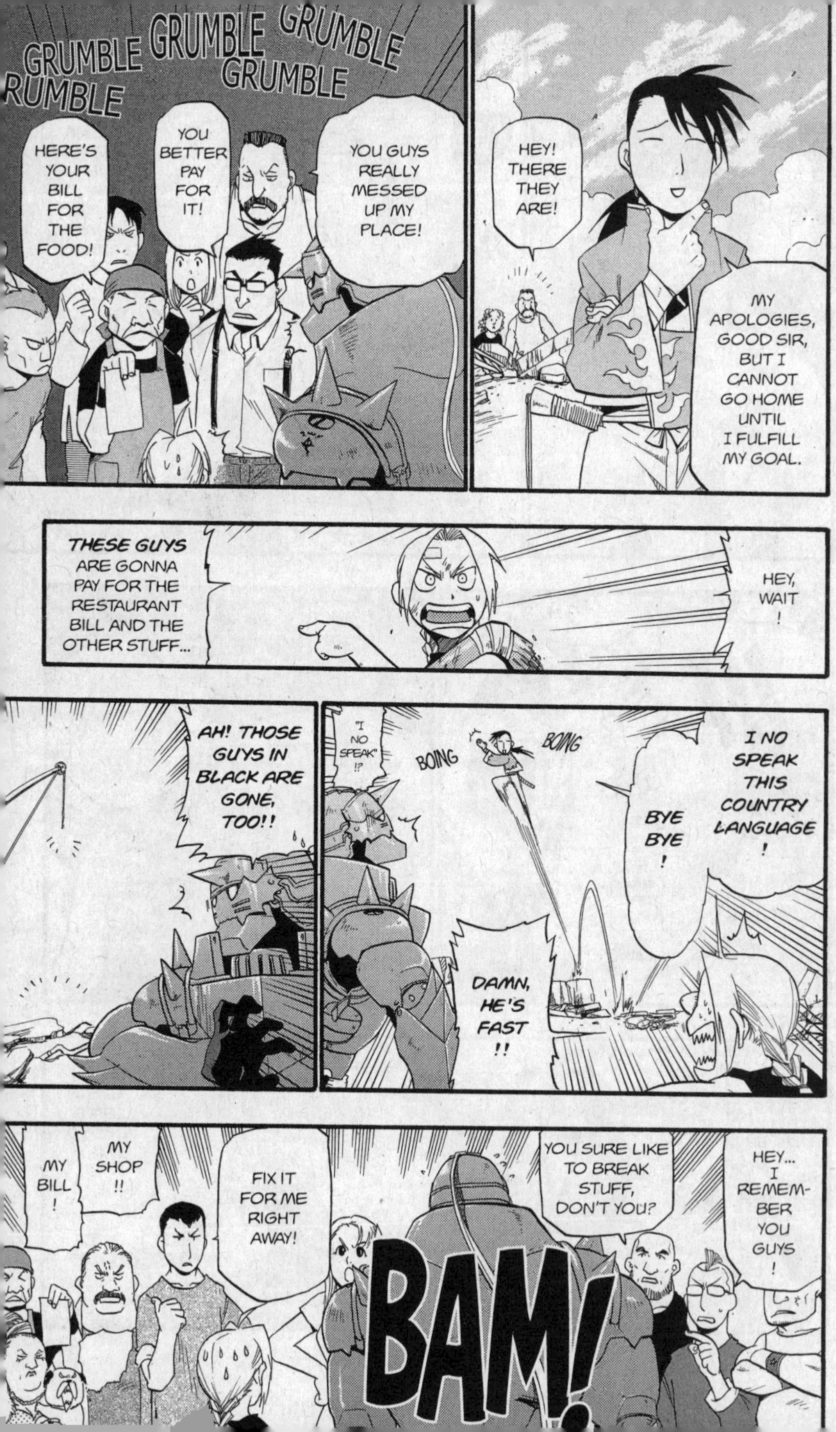
HEY! THERE THEY ARE!
MY APOLOGIES, GOOD SIR, BUT I CANNOT GO HOME UNTIL I FULFILL MY GOAL.
GRUMBLE GRUMBLE
GRUMBLE GRUMBLE
RUMBLE
YOU GUYS REALLY MESSED UP MY PLACE!
YOU BETTER PAY FOR IT!
HERE'S YOUR BILL FOR THE FOOD!
HEY, WAIT!
THESE GUYS ARE GONNA PAY FOR THE RESTAURANT BILL AND THE OTHER STUFF...
I NO SPEAK THIS COUNTRY LANGUAGE!
BYE BYE!
BOING
BOING
"I NO SPEAK"!?
DAMN, HE'S FAST!!
AH! THOSE GUYS IN BLACK ARE GONE, TOO!!
HEY... I REMEMBER YOU GUYS!
YOU SURE LIKE TO BREAK STUFF, DON'T YOU?
FIX IT FOR ME RIGHT AWAY!
MY SHOP!!
MY BILL!
BAM!

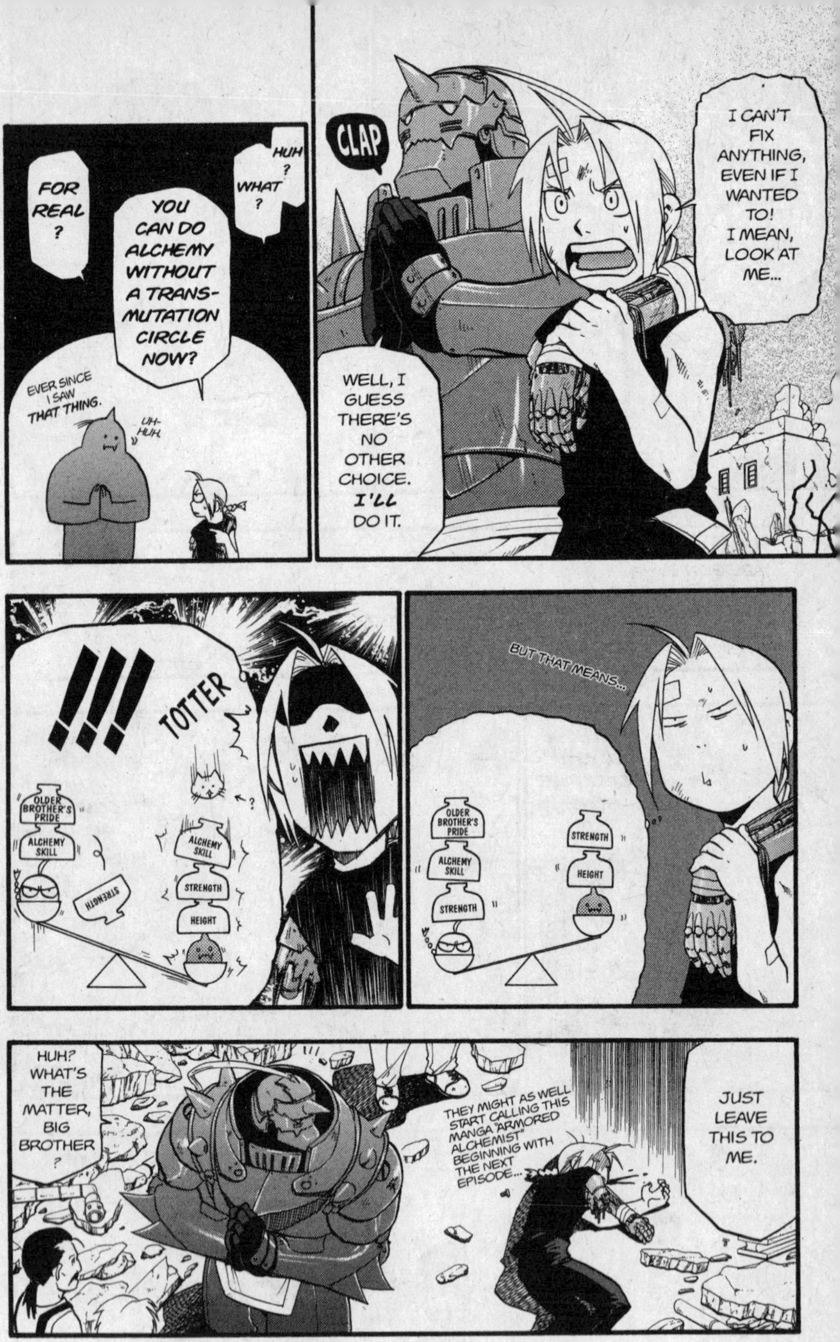
I CAN'T FIX ANYTHING, EVEN IF I WANTED TO! I MEAN, LOOK AT ME...
CLAP
WELL, I GUESS THERE'S NO OTHER CHOICE. I'LL DO IT.
HUH? WHAT?
YOU CAN DO ALCHEMY WITHOUT A TRANSMUTATION CIRCLE NOW?
FOR REAL?
EVER SINCE I SAW THAT THING.
UH-HUH.
BUT THAT MEANS...
STRENGTH
HEIGHT
OLDER BROTHER'S PRIDE
ALCHEMY SKILL
STRENGTH
!!!
TOTTER
ALCHEMY SKILL
STRENGTH
HEIGHT
OLDER BROTHER'S PRIDE
ALCHEMY SKILL
STRENGTH
JUST LEAVE THIS TO ME.
THEY MIGHT AS WELL START CALLING THIS MANGA "ARMORED ALCHEMIST" BEGINNING WITH THE NEXT EPISODE...
HUH? WHAT'S THE MATTER, BIG BROTHER?

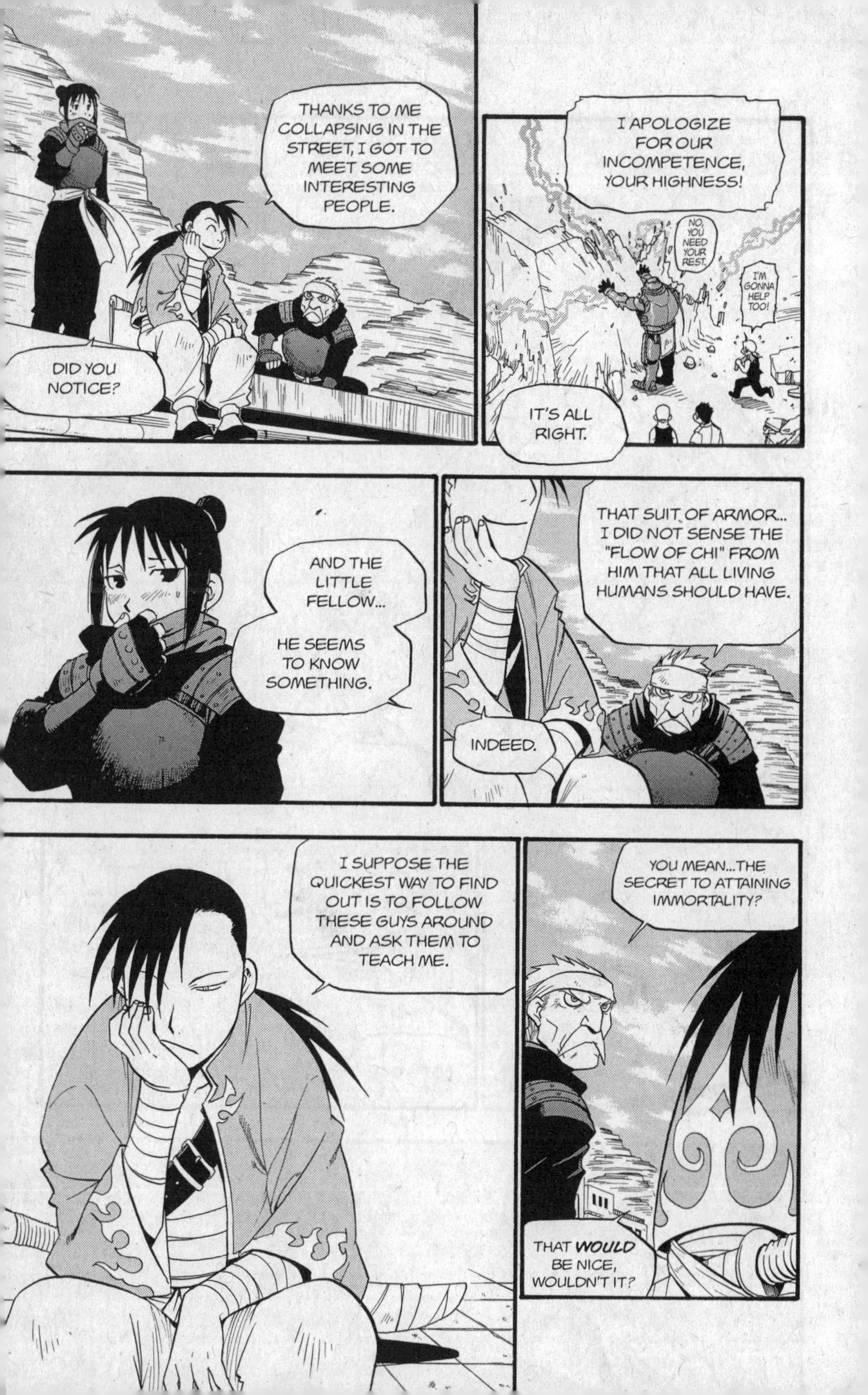
I APOLOGIZE FOR OUR INCOMPETENCE, YOUR HIGHNESS!
NO, YOU NEED YOUR REST.
I'M GONNA HELP TOO!
IT'S ALL RIGHT.
THANKS TO ME COLLAPSING IN THE STREET, I GOT TO MEET SOME INTERESTING PEOPLE.
DID YOU NOTICE?
THAT SUIT OF ARMOR... I DID NOT SENSE THE "FLOW OF CHI" FROM HIM THAT ALL LIVING HUMANS SHOULD HAVE.
INDEED.
AND THE LITTLE FELLOW...
HE SEEMS TO KNOW SOMETHING.
YOU MEAN...THE SECRET TO ATTAINING IMMORTALITY?
THAT ***WOULD*** BE NICE, WOULDN'T IT?
I SUPPOSE THE QUICKEST WAY TO FIND OUT IS TO FOLLOW THESE GUYS AROUND AND ASK THEM TO TEACH ME.

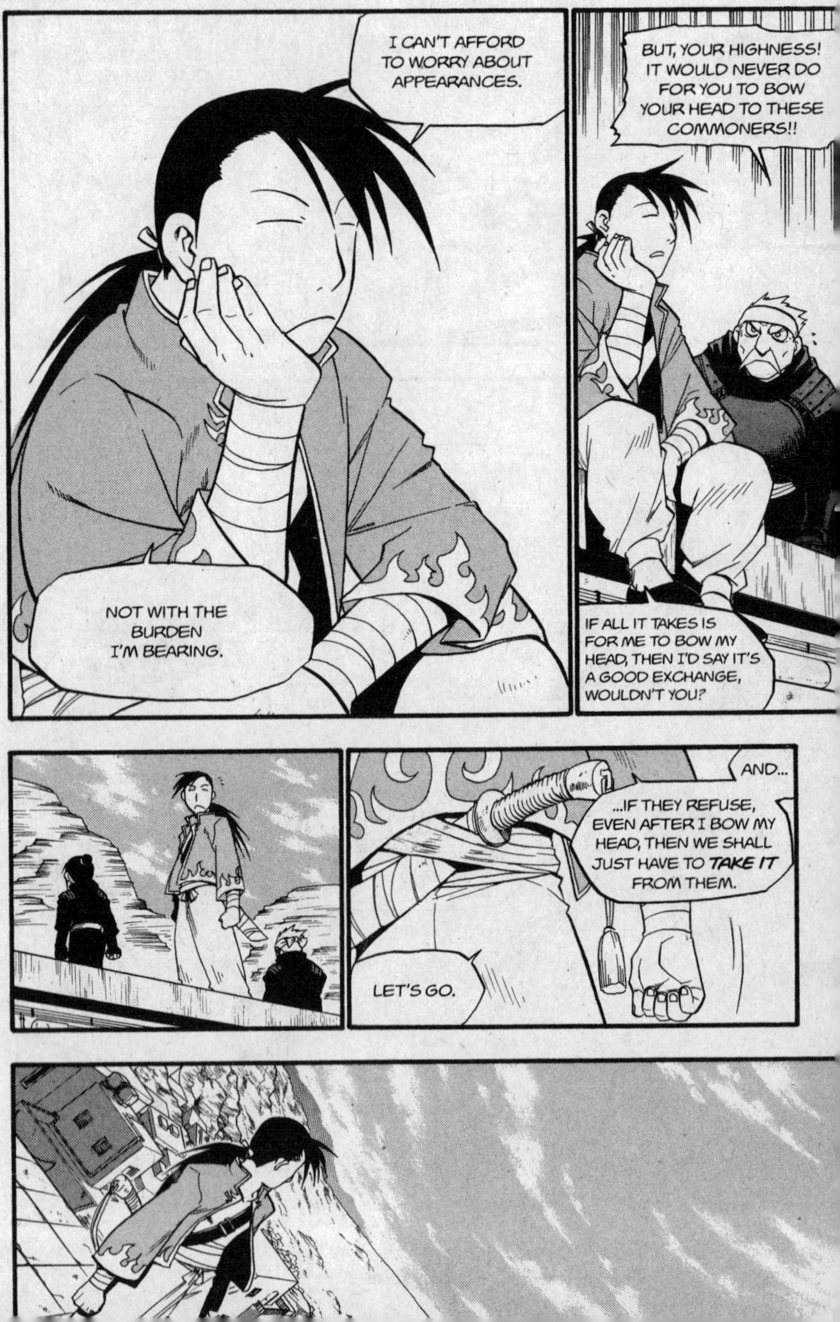
BUT, YOUR HIGHNESS! IT WOULD NEVER DO FOR YOU TO BOW YOUR HEAD TO THESE COMMONERS!!
IF ALL IT TAKES IS FOR ME TO BOW MY HEAD, THEN I'D SAY IT'S A GOOD EXCHANGE, WOULDN'T YOU?
I CAN'T AFFORD TO WORRY ABOUT APPEARANCES.
NOT WITH THE BURDEN I'M BEARING.
AND...
...IF THEY REFUSE, EVEN AFTER I BOW MY HEAD, THEN WE SHALL JUST HAVE TO *TAKE IT* FROM THEM.
LET'S GO.

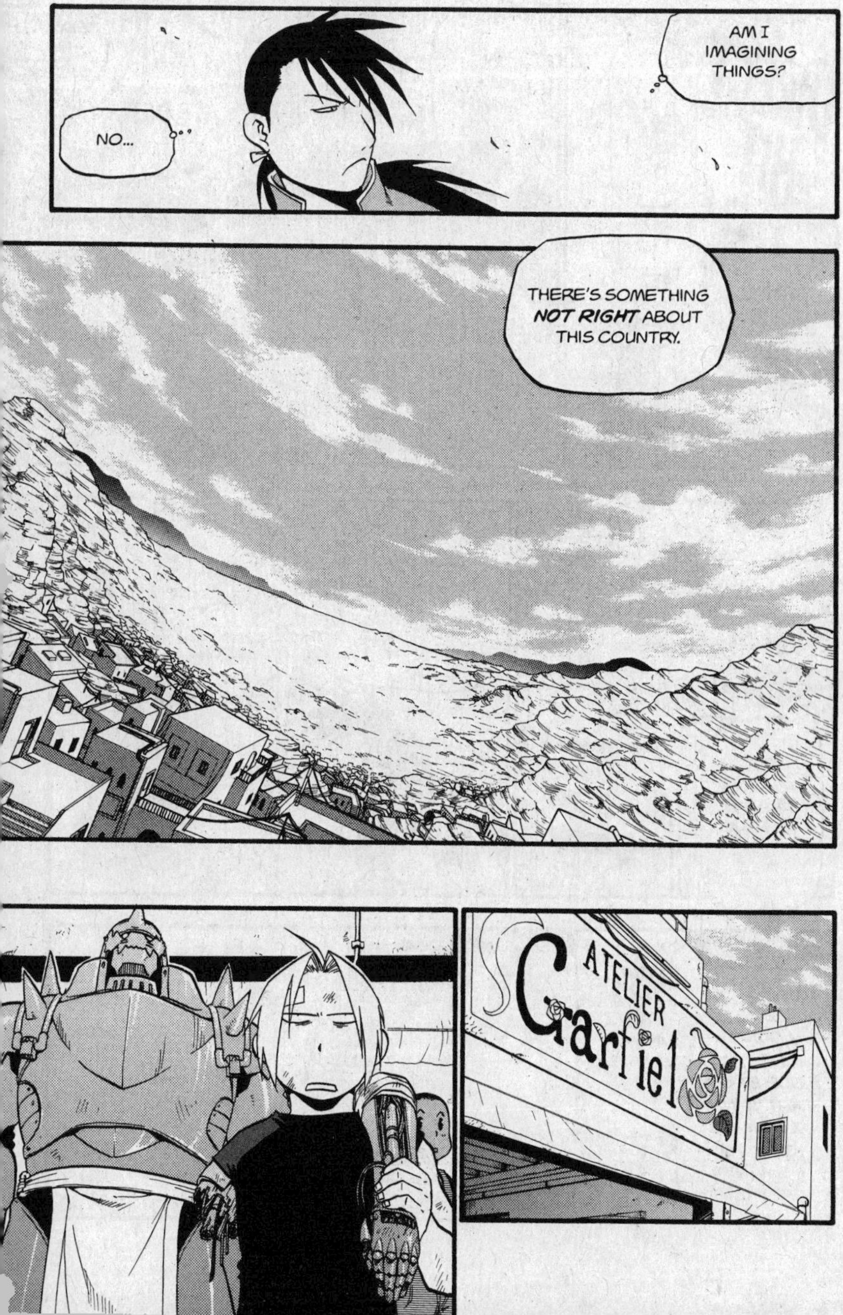

AM I IMAGINING THINGS?
NO...
THERE'S SOMETHING **NOT RIGHT** ABOUT THIS COUNTRY.
ATELIER
Garfiel

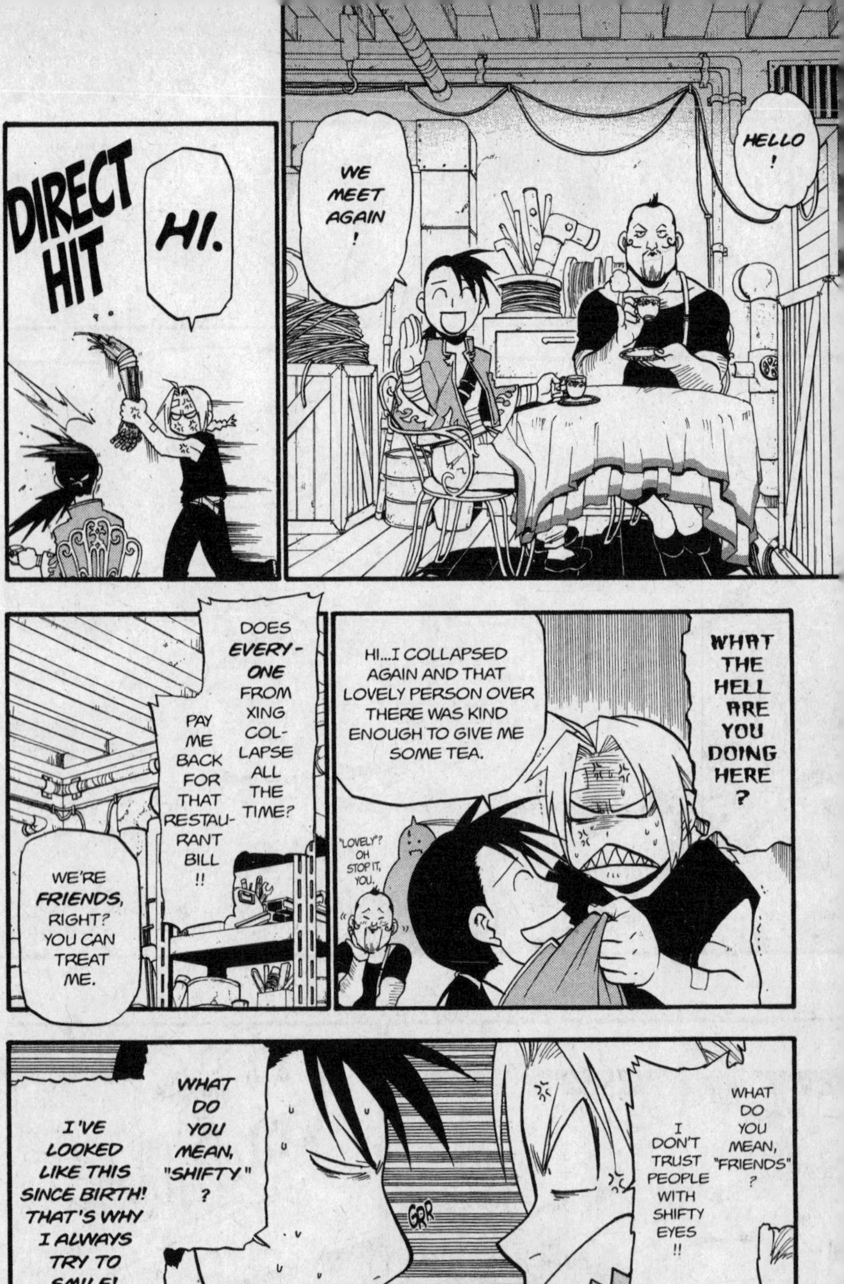
HELLO!
WE MEET AGAIN!
HI.
DIRECT HIT
WHAT THE HELL ARE YOU DOING HERE?
HI...I COLLAPSED AGAIN AND THAT LOVELY PERSON OVER THERE WAS KIND ENOUGH TO GIVE ME SOME TEA.
"LOVELY"? OH STOP IT, YOU.
DOES EVERYONE FROM XING COLLAPSE ALL THE TIME?
PAY ME BACK FOR THAT RESTAURANT BILL!!
WE'RE FRIENDS, RIGHT? YOU CAN TREAT ME.
WHAT DO YOU MEAN, "FRIENDS"?
I DON'T TRUST PEOPLE WITH SHIFTY EYES!!
GRR
WHAT DO YOU MEAN, "SHIFTY"?
I'VE LOOKED LIKE THIS SINCE BIRTH! THAT'S WHY I ALWAYS TRY TO SMILE!

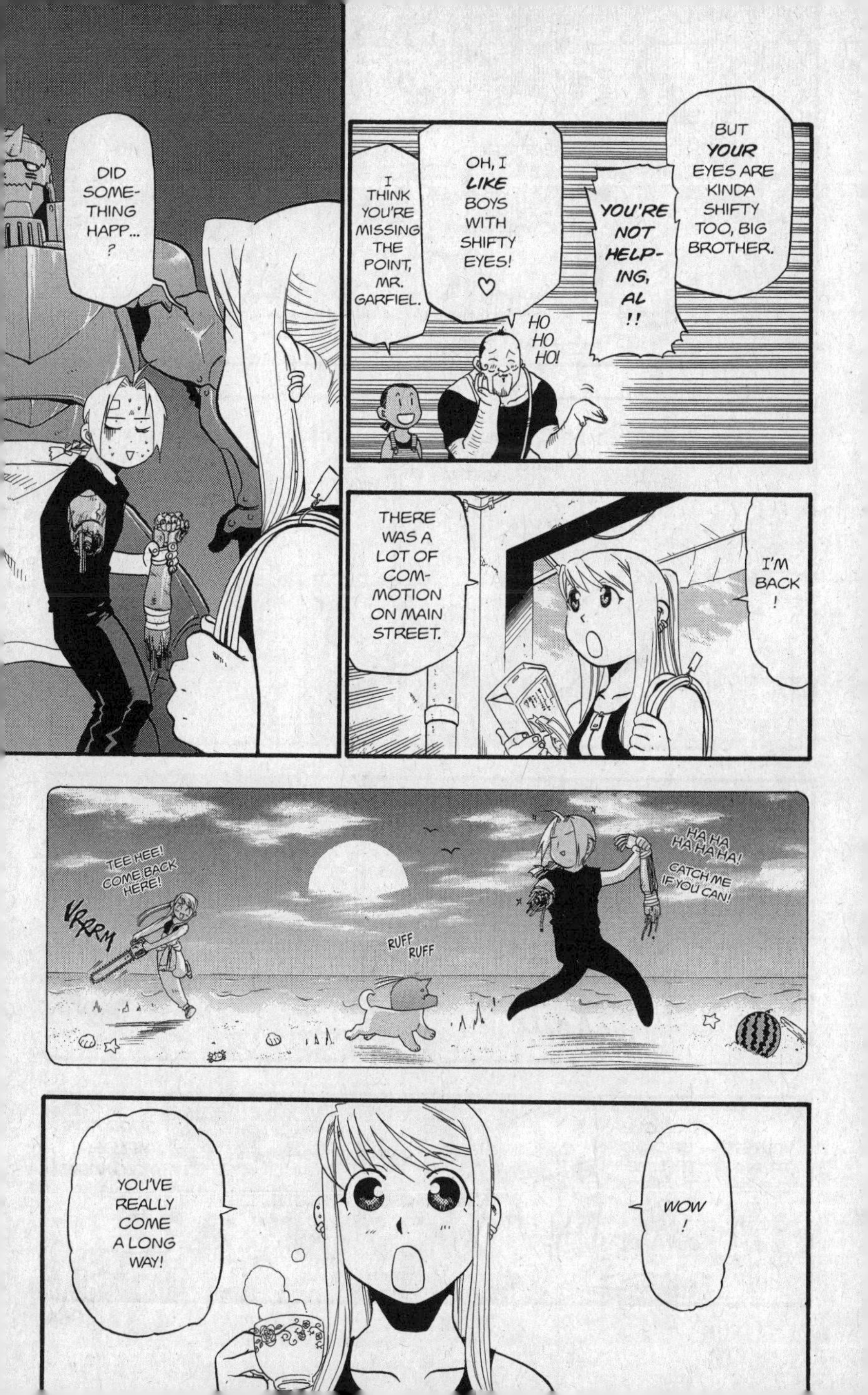
BUT YOUR EYES ARE KINDA SHIFTY TOO, BIG BROTHER.
YOU'RE NOT HELPING, AL!!
OH, I LIKE BOYS WITH SHIFTY EYES! ♡
HO HO HO!
I THINK YOU'RE MISSING THE POINT, MR. GARFIEL.
I'M BACK!
THERE WAS A LOT OF COMMOTION ON MAIN STREET.
DID SOMETHING HAPP...?
HA HA HA HA HA! CATCH ME IF YOU CAN!
RUFF RUFF
TEE HEE! COME BACK HERE!
VRRRM
WOW!
YOU'VE REALLY COME A LONG WAY!

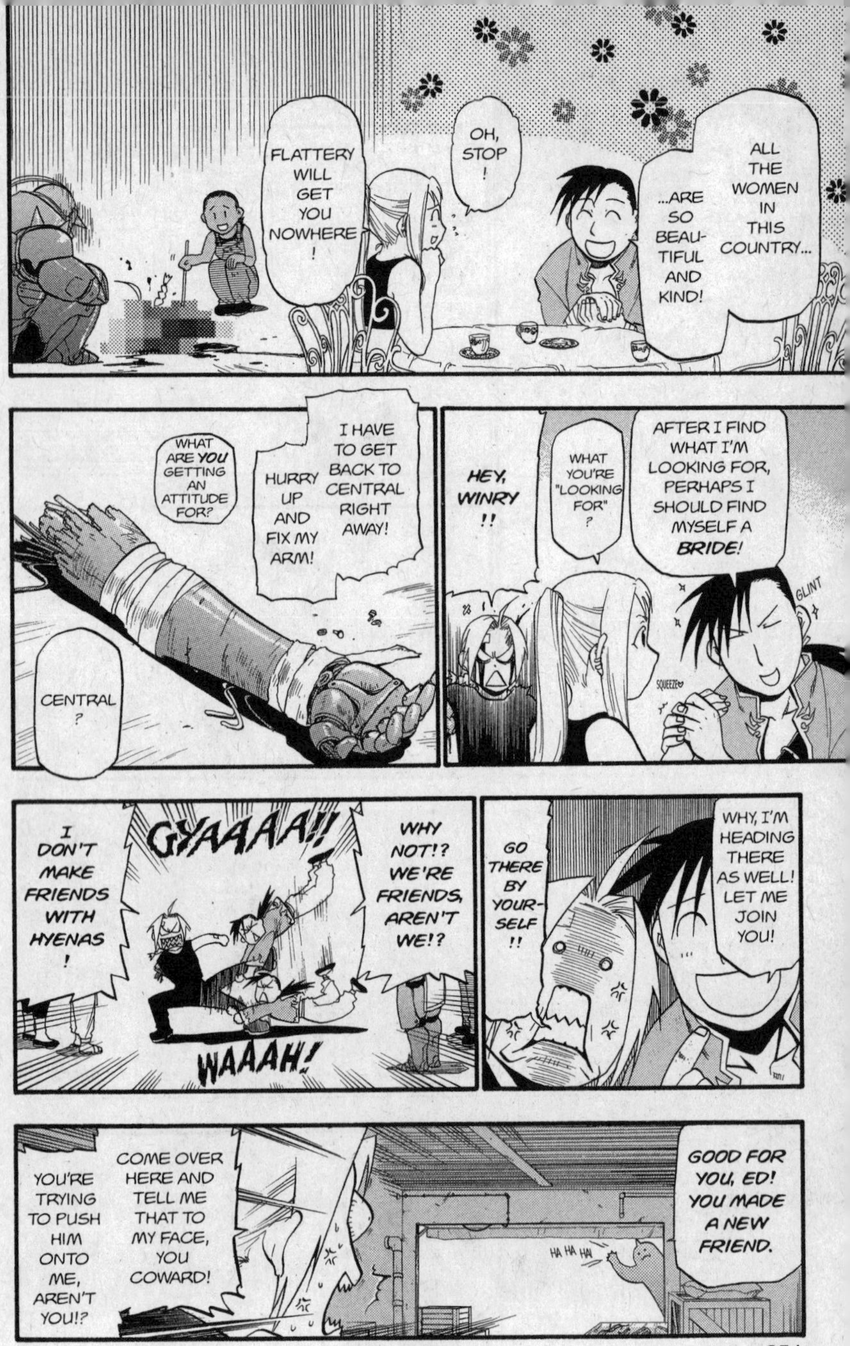
ALL THE WOMEN IN THIS COUNTRY...
...ARE SO BEAUTIFUL AND KIND!
OH, STOP!
FLATTERY WILL GET YOU NOWHERE!
AFTER I FIND WHAT I'M LOOKING FOR, PERHAPS I SHOULD FIND MYSELF A BRIDE!
GLINT
WHAT YOU'RE "LOOKING FOR"?
HEY, WINRY!!
SQUEEZE
I HAVE TO GET BACK TO CENTRAL RIGHT AWAY!
HURRY UP AND FIX MY ARM!
WHAT ARE YOU GETTING AN ATTITUDE FOR?
CENTRAL?
WHY, I'M HEADING THERE AS WELL! LET ME JOIN YOU!
GO THERE BY YOURSELF!!
WHY NOT!? WE'RE FRIENDS, AREN'T WE!?
GYAAAA!!
I DON'T MAKE FRIENDS WITH HYENAS!
WAAAH!
GOOD FOR YOU, ED! YOU MADE A NEW FRIEND.
HA HA HA!
COME OVER HERE AND TELL ME THAT TO MY FACE, YOU COWARD!
YOU'RE TRYING TO PUSH HIM ONTO ME, AREN'T YOU!?

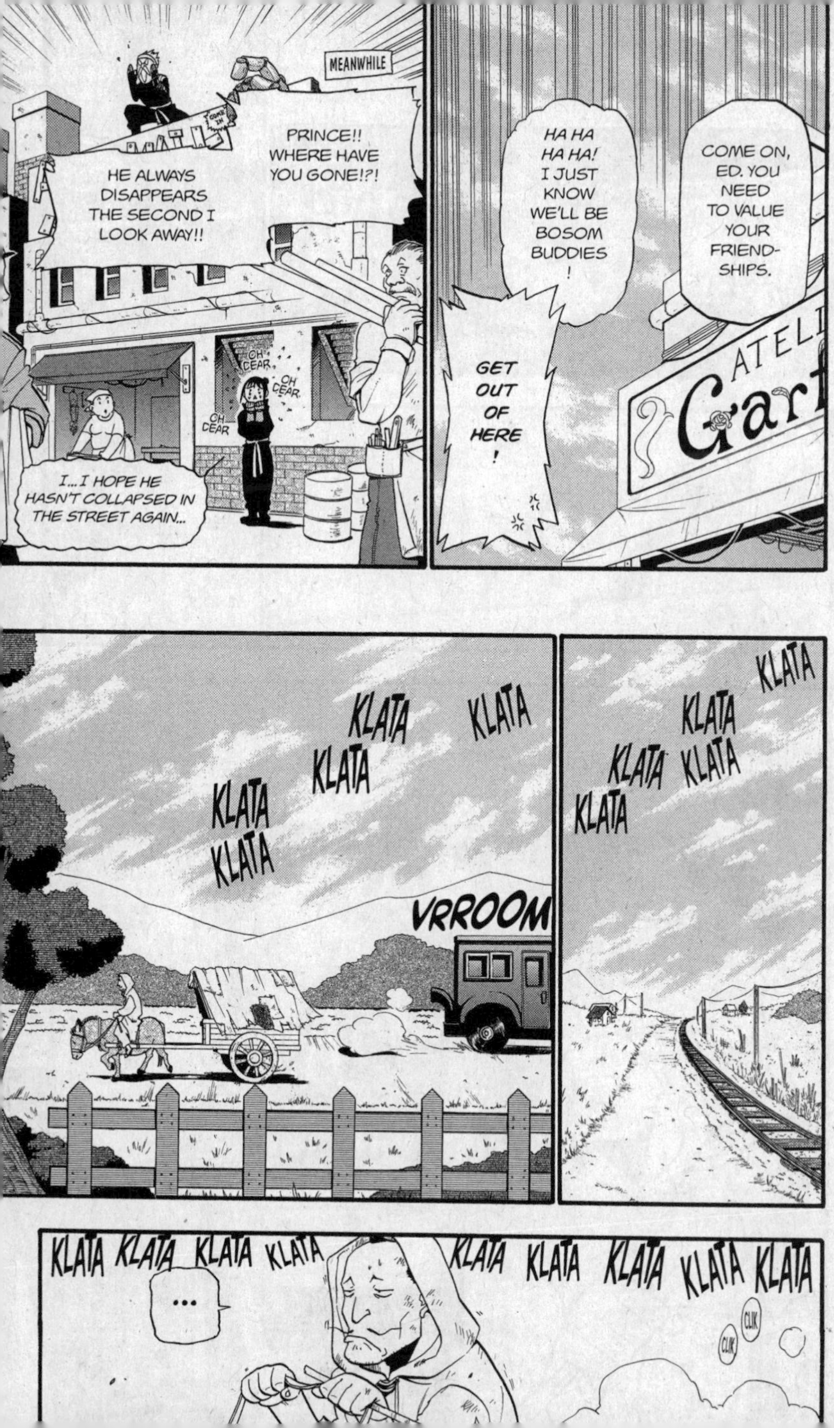
COME ON, ED. YOU NEED TO VALUE YOUR FRIENDSHIPS.
HA HA HA HA! I JUST KNOW WE'LL BE BOSOM BUDDIES!
GET OUT OF HERE!
MEANWHILE
PRINCE!! WHERE HAVE YOU GONE!?!
HE ALWAYS DISAPPEARS THE SECOND I LOOK AWAY!!
COME IN
OH DEAR OH DEAR OH DEAR
I...I HOPE HE HASN'T COLLAPSED IN THE STREET AGAIN...
KLATA KLATA KLATA KLATA KLATA
KLATA KLATA KLATA KLATA KLATA
VRROOM
KLATA KLATA KLATA KLATA KLATA KLATA KLATA KLATA KLATA
...
CLIK CLIK

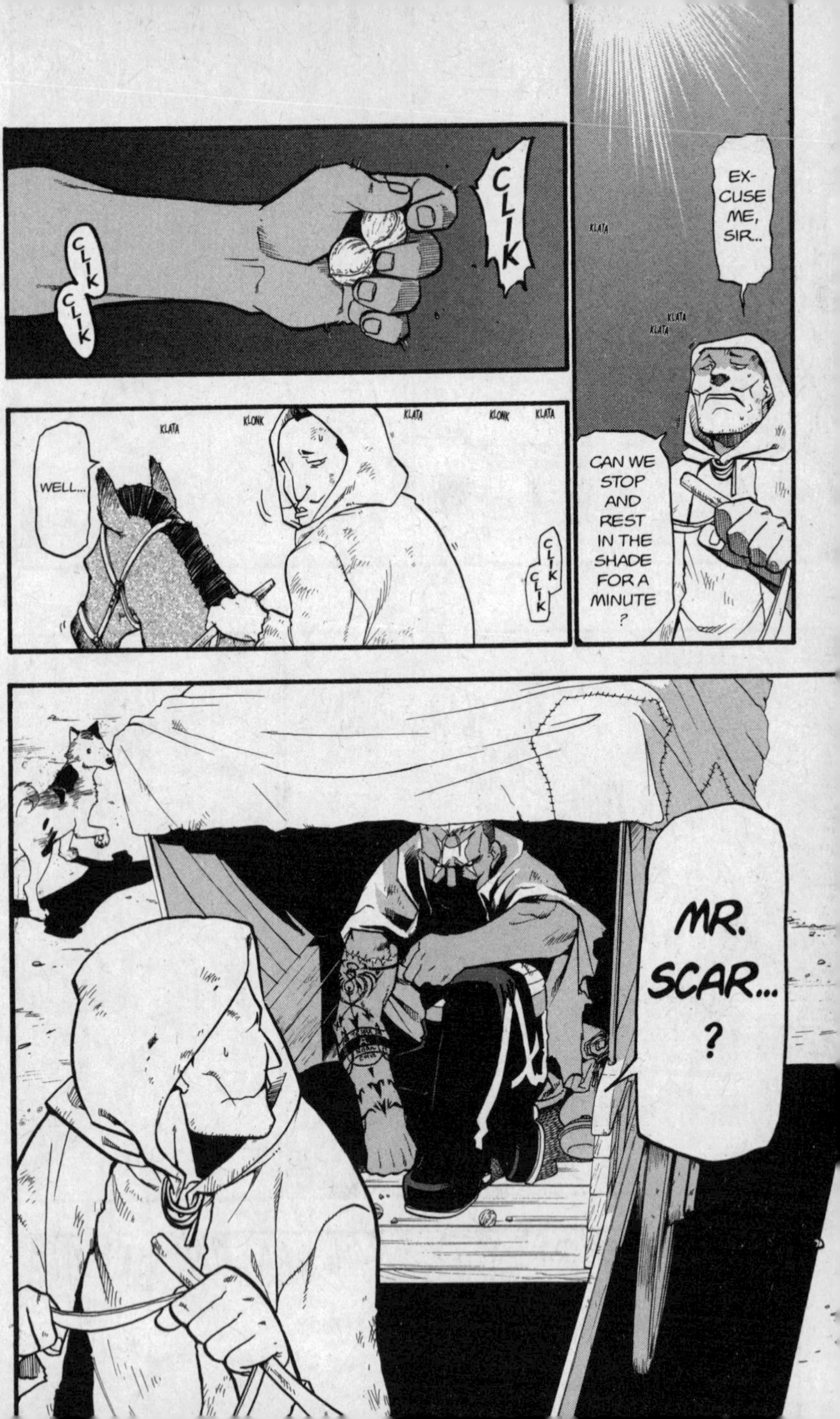

EX-CUSE ME, SIR...
KLATA
KLATA KLATA
CAN WE STOP AND REST IN THE SHADE FOR A MINUTE?
CLIK
CLIK CLIK
KLATA KLONK KLATA
KLONK KLATA
WELL...
CLIK CLIK
MR. SCAR...?

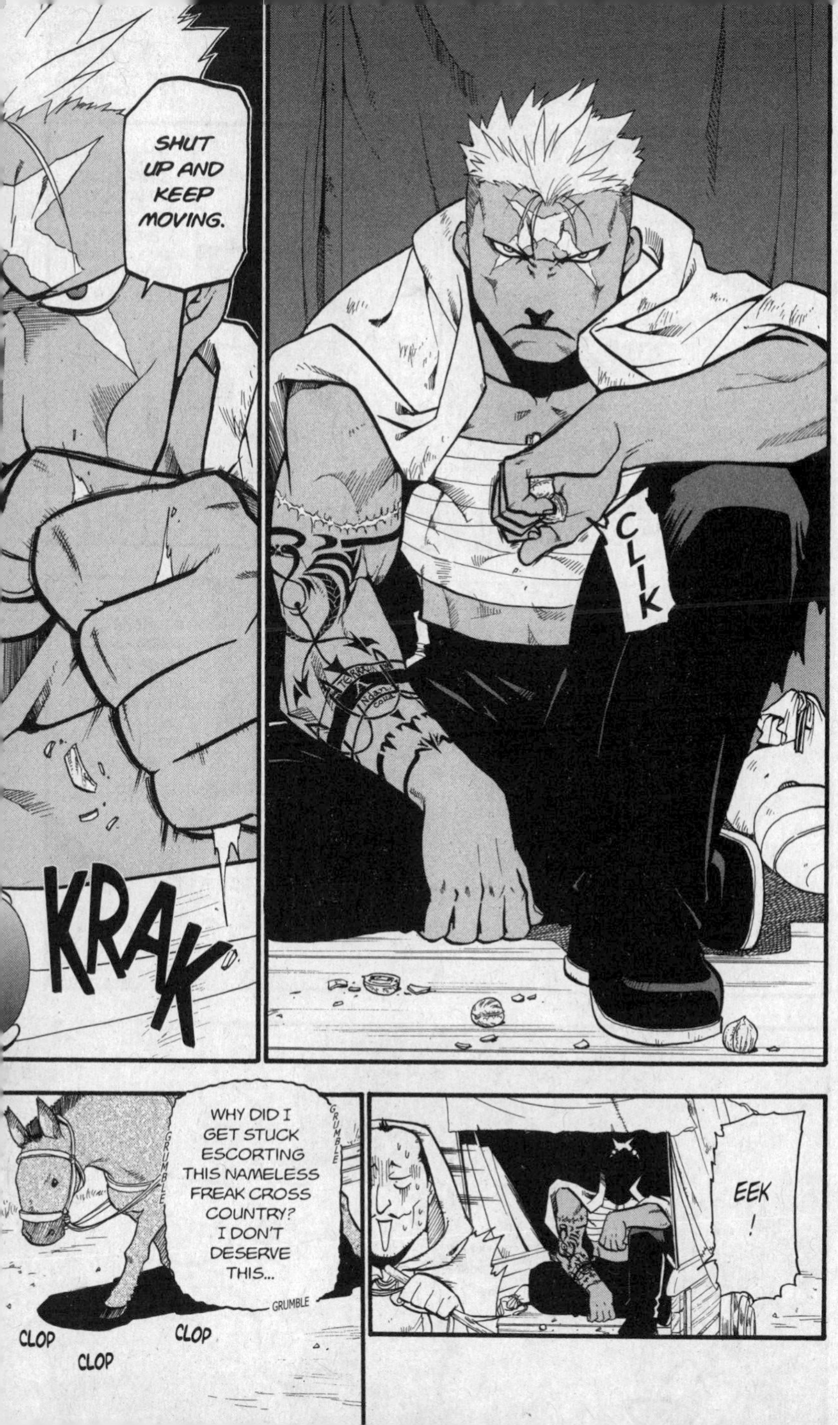
CLIK
SHUT UP AND KEEP MOVING.
KRAK
EEK!
GRUMBLE
WHY DID I GET STUCK ESCORTING THIS NAMELESS FREAK CROSS COUNTRY? I DON'T DESERVE THIS...
GRUMBLE
CLOP
CLOP
CLOP

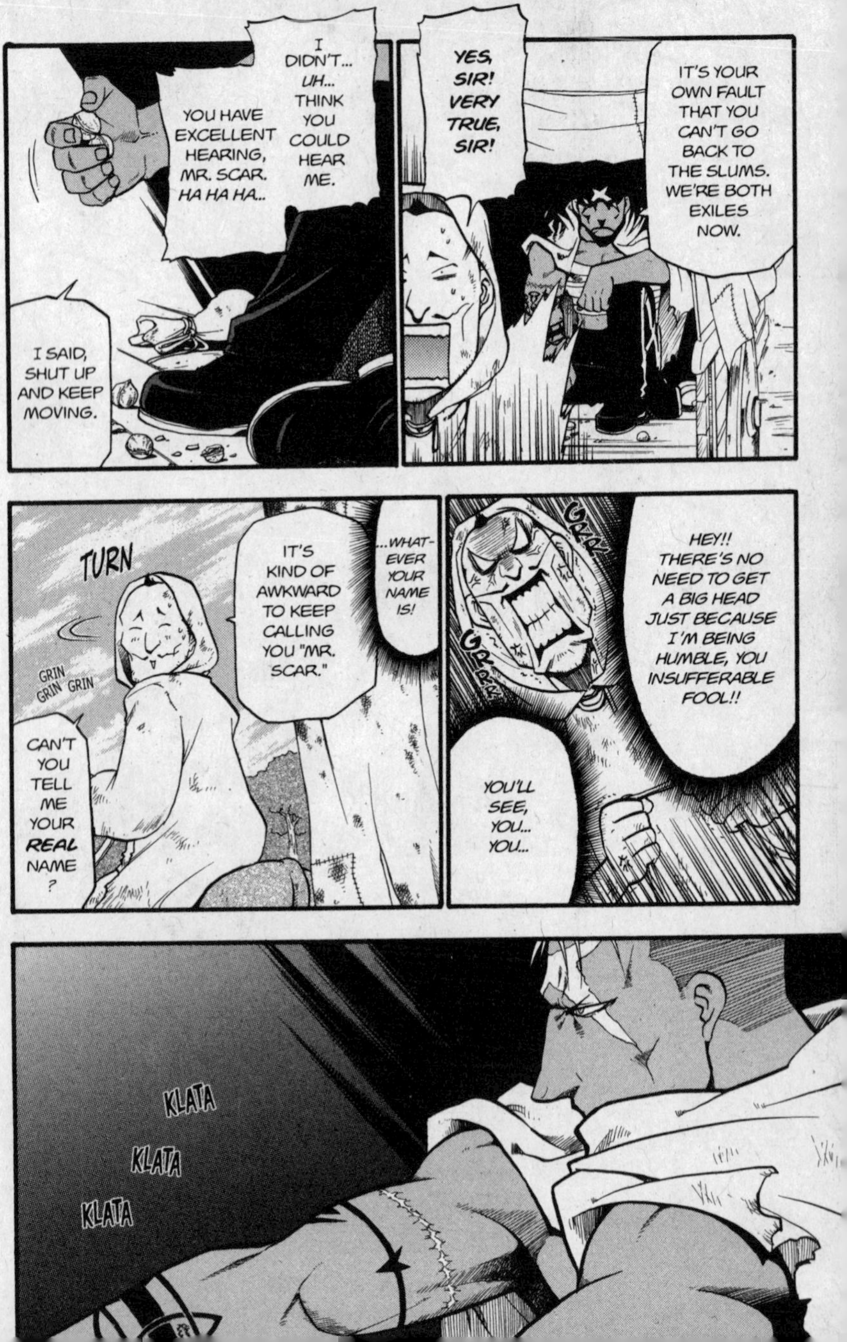
IT'S YOUR OWN FAULT THAT YOU CAN'T GO BACK TO THE SLUMS. WE'RE BOTH EXILES NOW.
YES, SIR! VERY TRUE, SIR!
I DIDN'T... UH... THINK YOU COULD HEAR ME.
YOU HAVE EXCELLENT HEARING, MR. SCAR. HA HA HA...
I SAID, SHUT UP AND KEEP MOVING.
HEY!! THERE'S NO NEED TO GET A BIG HEAD JUST BECAUSE I'M BEING HUMBLE, YOU INSUFFERABLE FOOL!!
GRRR
GRRR
YOU'LL SEE, YOU... YOU...
...WHATEVER YOUR NAME IS!
IT'S KIND OF AWKWARD TO KEEP CALLING YOU "MR. SCAR."
TURN
GRIN GRIN GRIN
CAN'T YOU TELL ME YOUR REAL NAME ?
KLATA
KLATA
KLATA

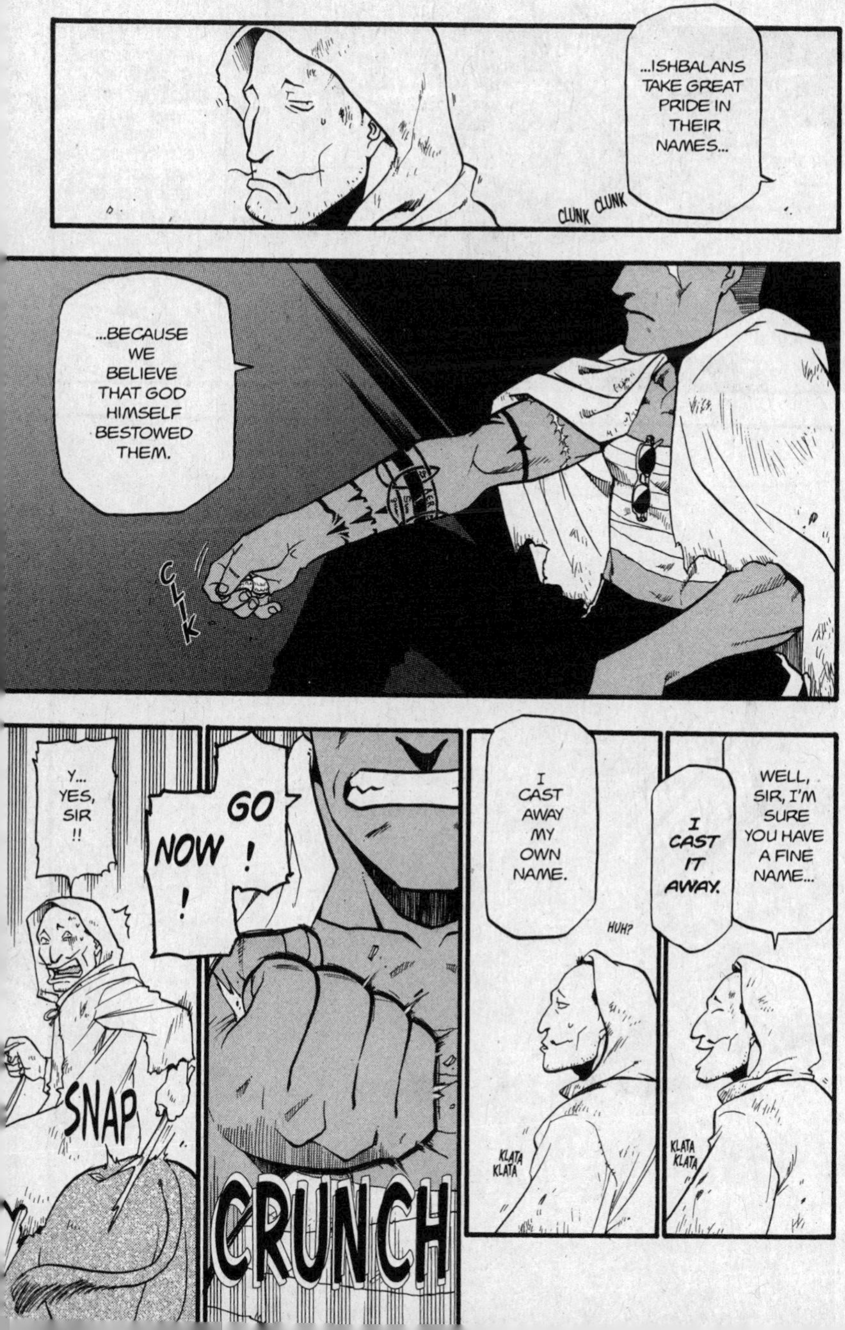
...ISHBALANS TAKE GREAT PRIDE IN THEIR NAMES...
CLUNK CLUNK
...BECAUSE WE BELIEVE THAT GOD HIMSELF BESTOWED THEM.
CLIK
WELL, SIR, I'M SURE YOU HAVE A FINE NAME...
I CAST IT AWAY.
KLATA KLATA
HUH?
I CAST AWAY MY OWN NAME.
KLATA KLATA
GO NOW!!
CRUNCH
Y... YES, SIR!!
SNAP

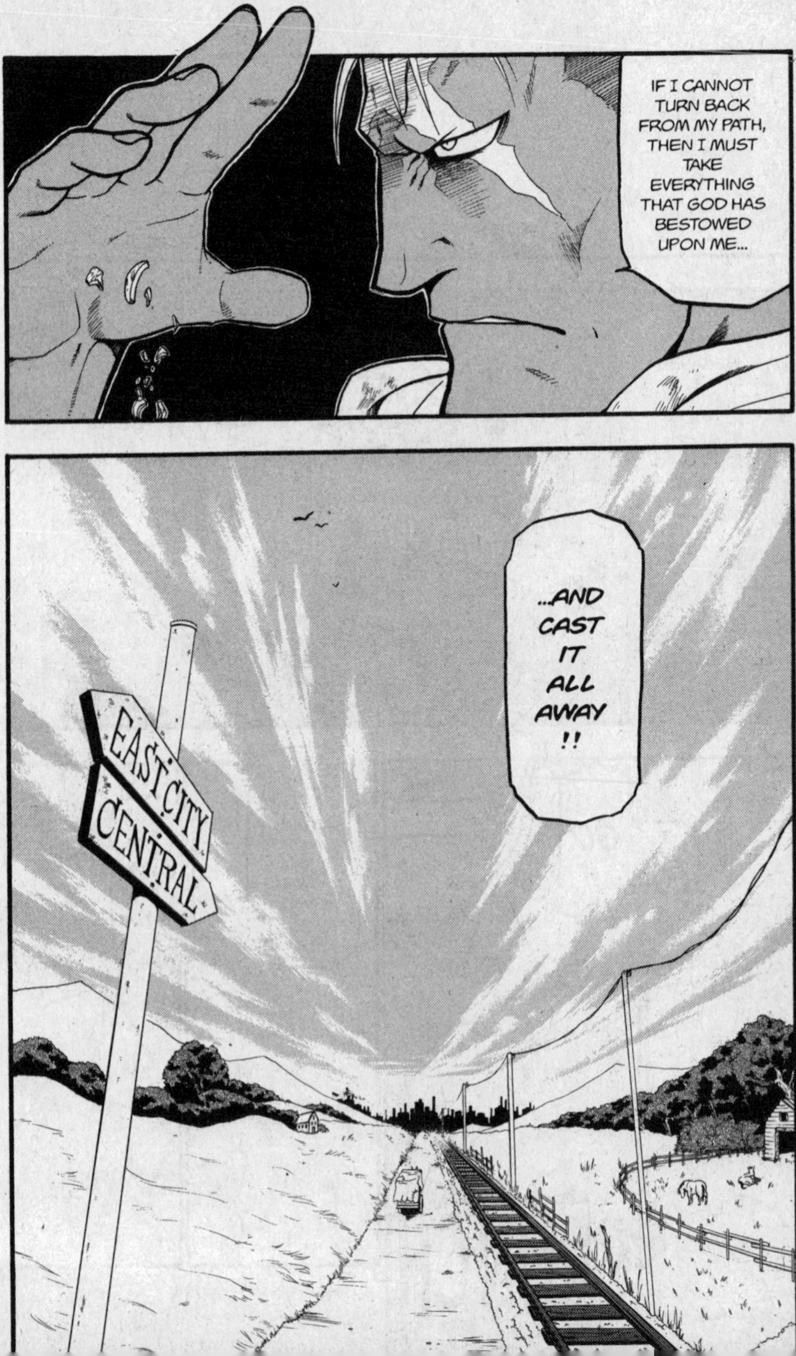
IF I CANNOT TURN BACK FROM MY PATH, THEN I MUST TAKE EVERYTHING THAT GOD HAS BESTOWED UPON ME...
...AND CAST IT ALL AWAY !!
EAST CITY
CENTRAL

FULLMETAL
ALCHEMIST

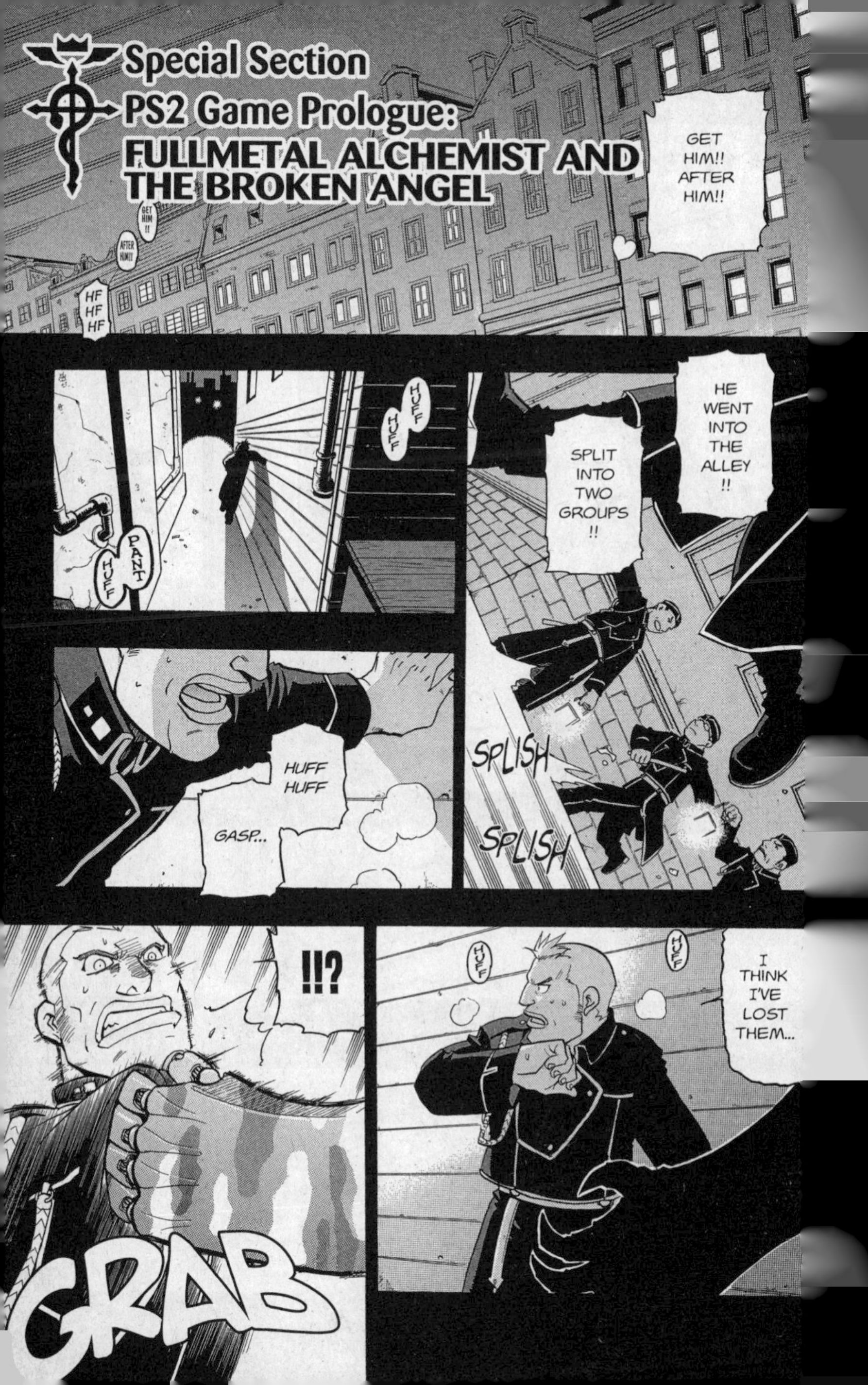
Special Section
PS2 Game Prologue:
FULLMETAL ALCHEMIST AND THE BROKEN ANGEL
GET HIM!! AFTER HIM!!
GET HIM !!
AFTER HIM!!
HF HF HF
HE WENT INTO THE ALLEY !!
SPLIT INTO TWO GROUPS !!
SPLISH
SPLISH
HUFF HUFF
PANT HUFF HUFF
HUFF HUFF
GASP...
HUFF
HUFF
I THINK I'VE LOST THEM...
!!?
GRAB

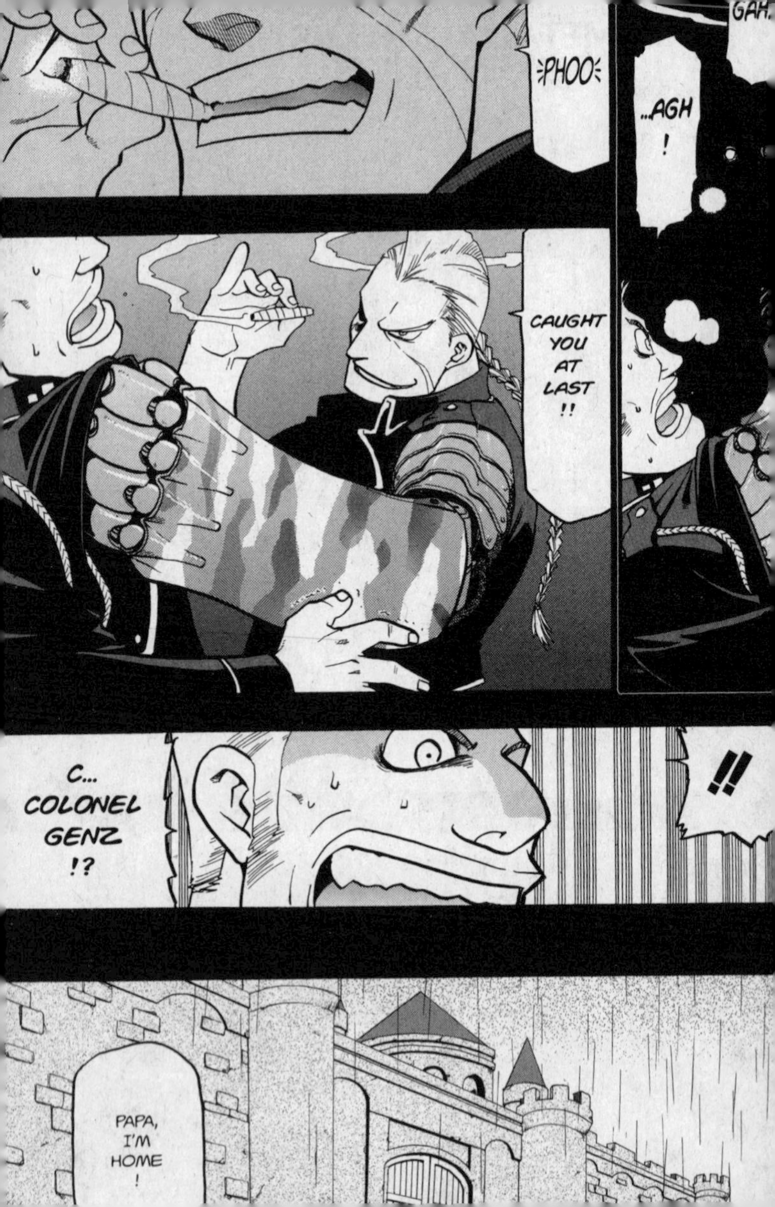
GAH.
...AGH !
PHOO
CAUGHT YOU AT LAST !!
!!
C... COLONEL GENZ !?
PAPA, I'M HOME !

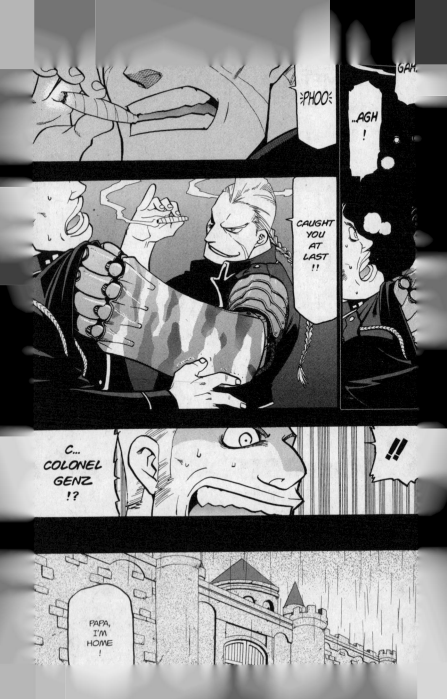

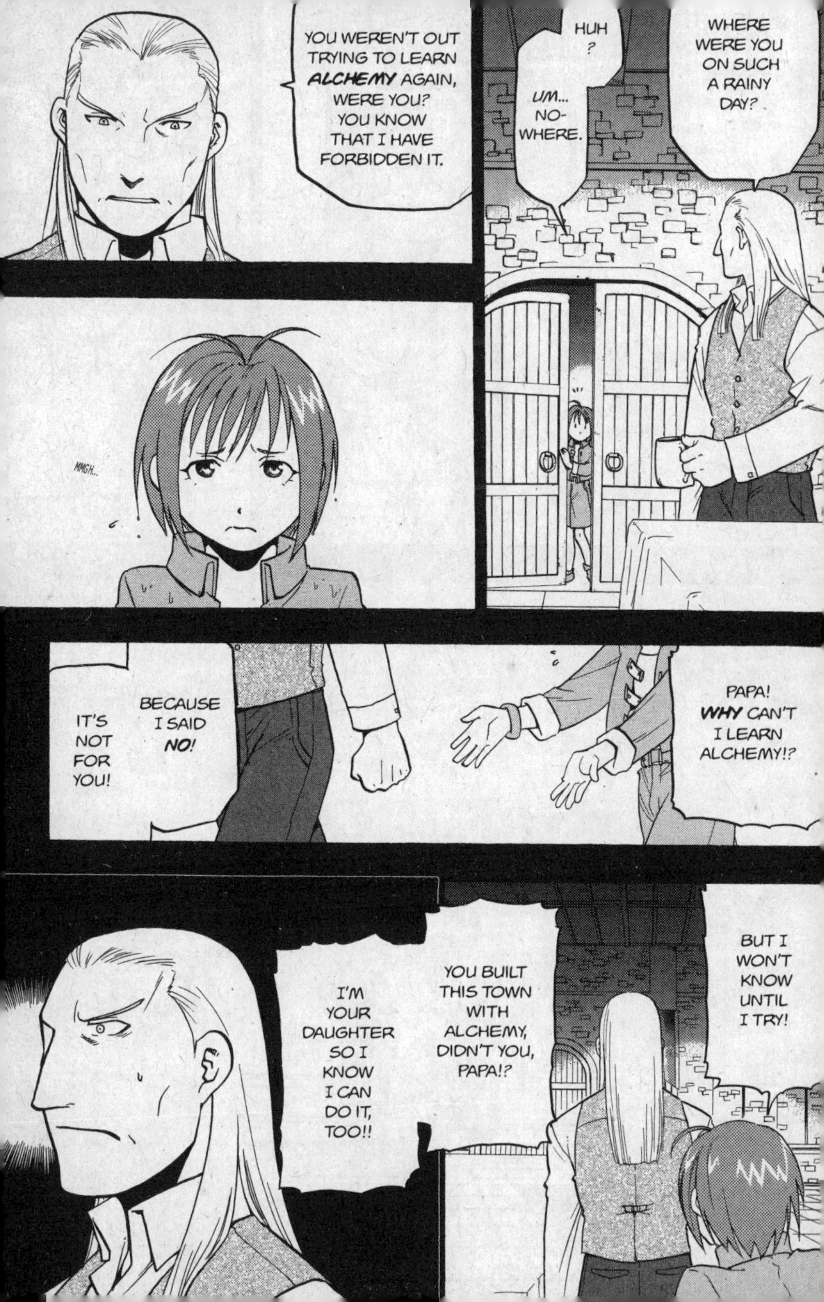
WHERE WERE YOU ON SUCH A RAINY DAY?
HUH?
UM... NO-WHERE.
YOU WEREN'T OUT TRYING TO LEARN ALCHEMY AGAIN, WERE YOU? YOU KNOW THAT I HAVE FORBIDDEN IT.
MMGH..
PAPA! WHY CAN'T I LEARN ALCHEMY!?
BECAUSE I SAID NO!
IT'S NOT FOR YOU!
BUT I WON'T KNOW UNTIL I TRY!
YOU BUILT THIS TOWN WITH ALCHEMY, DIDN'T YOU, PAPA!?
I'M YOUR DAUGHTER SO I KNOW I CAN DO IT, TOO!!

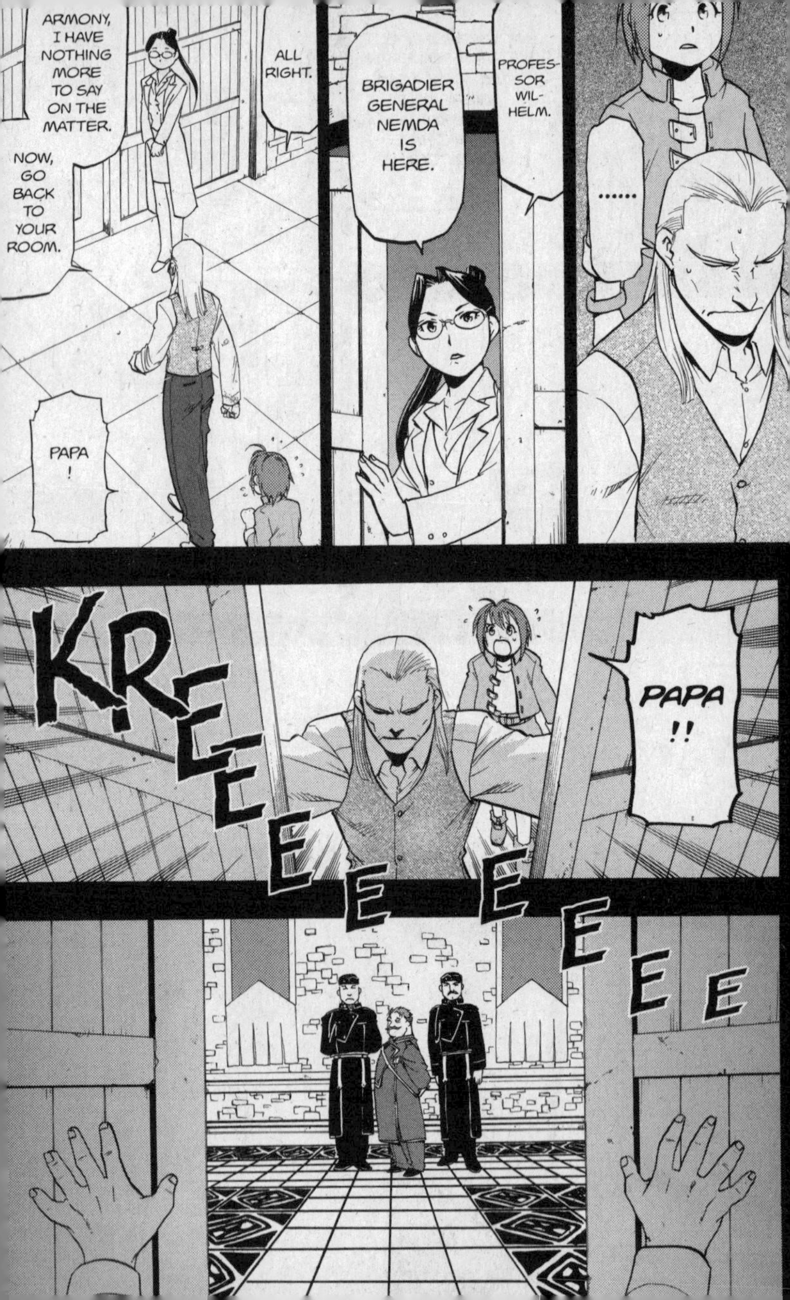
......
PROFESSOR WILHELM.
BRIGADIER GENERAL NEMDA IS HERE.
ALL RIGHT.
ARMONY, I HAVE NOTHING MORE TO SAY ON THE MATTER.
NOW, GO BACK TO YOUR ROOM.
PAPA!
PAPA!!
KREEEEEEEEE

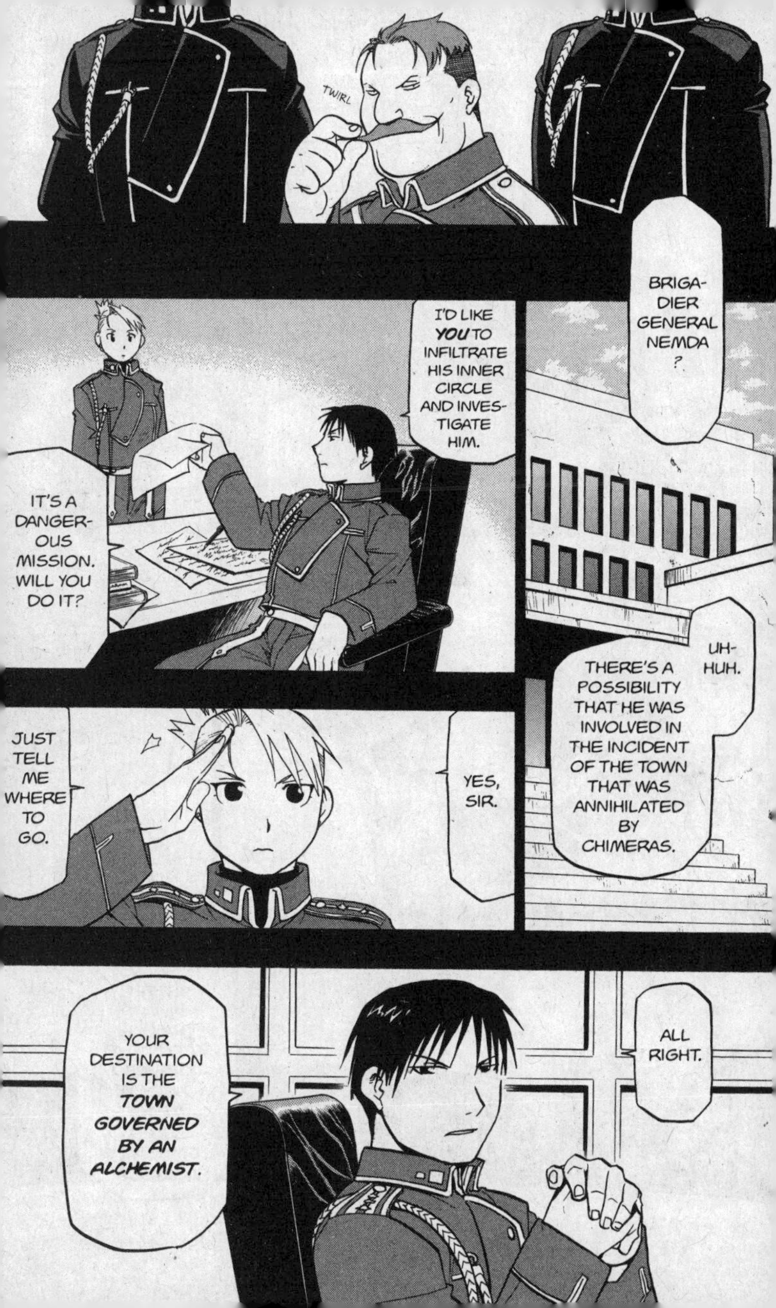
TWIRL
BRIGADIER GENERAL NEMDA?
UH-HUH.
THERE'S A POSSIBILITY THAT HE WAS INVOLVED IN THE INCIDENT OF THE TOWN THAT WAS ANNIHILATED BY CHIMERAS.
I'D LIKE YOU TO INFILTRATE HIS INNER CIRCLE AND INVESTIGATE HIM.
IT'S A DANGEROUS MISSION. WILL YOU DO IT?
YES, SIR.
JUST TELL ME WHERE TO GO.
ALL RIGHT.
YOUR DESTINATION IS THE TOWN GOVERNED BY AN ALCHEMIST.

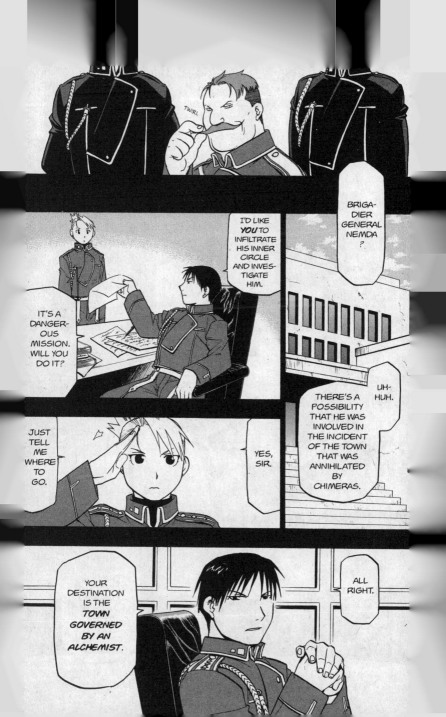

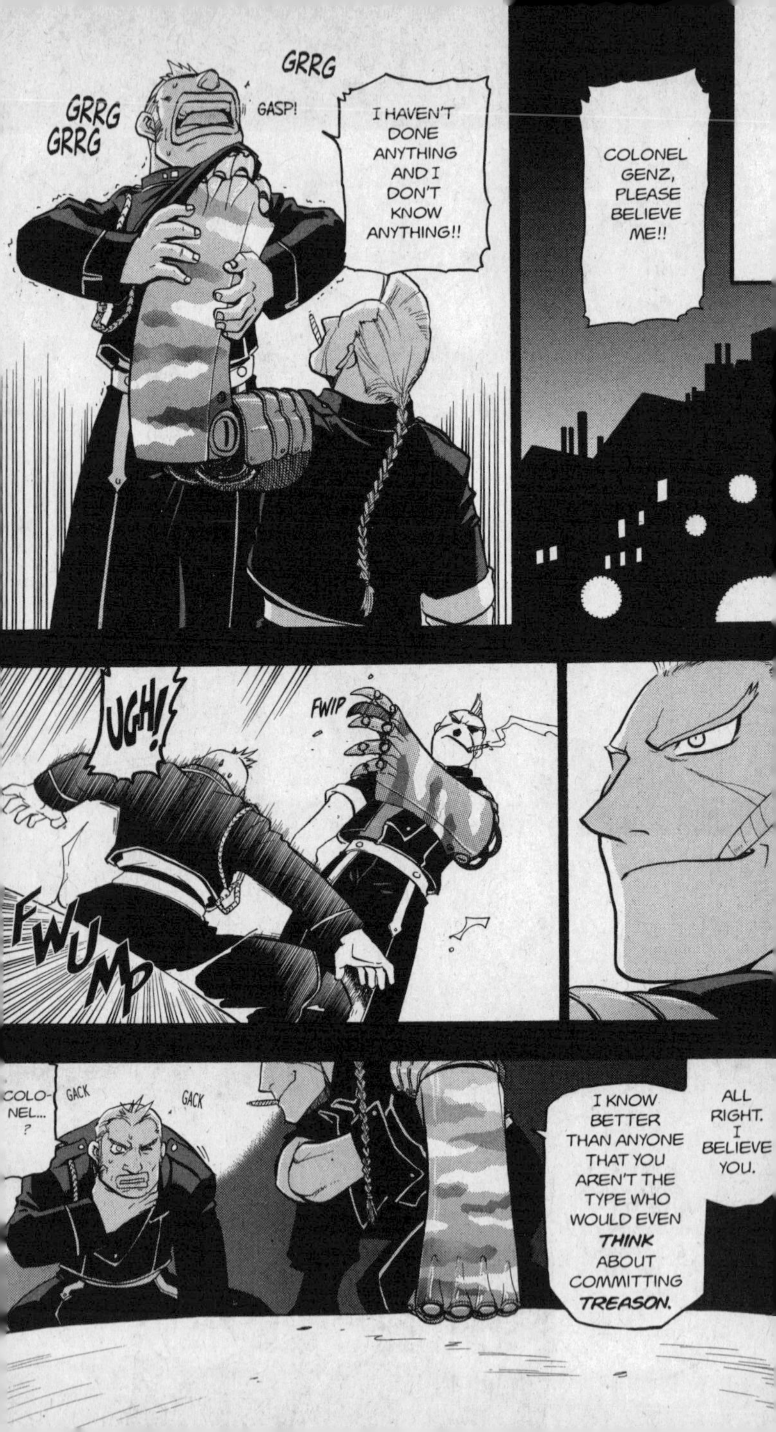
COLONEL GENZ, PLEASE BELIEVE ME!!
GRRG
I HAVEN'T DONE ANYTHING AND I DON'T KNOW ANYTHING!!
GASP!
GRRG GRRG
FWIP
UGH!
FWUMP
ALL RIGHT. I BELIEVE YOU.
I KNOW BETTER THAN ANYONE THAT YOU AREN'T THE TYPE WHO WOULD EVEN **THINK** ABOUT COMMITTING **TREASON.**
GACK
GACK
COLONEL...?

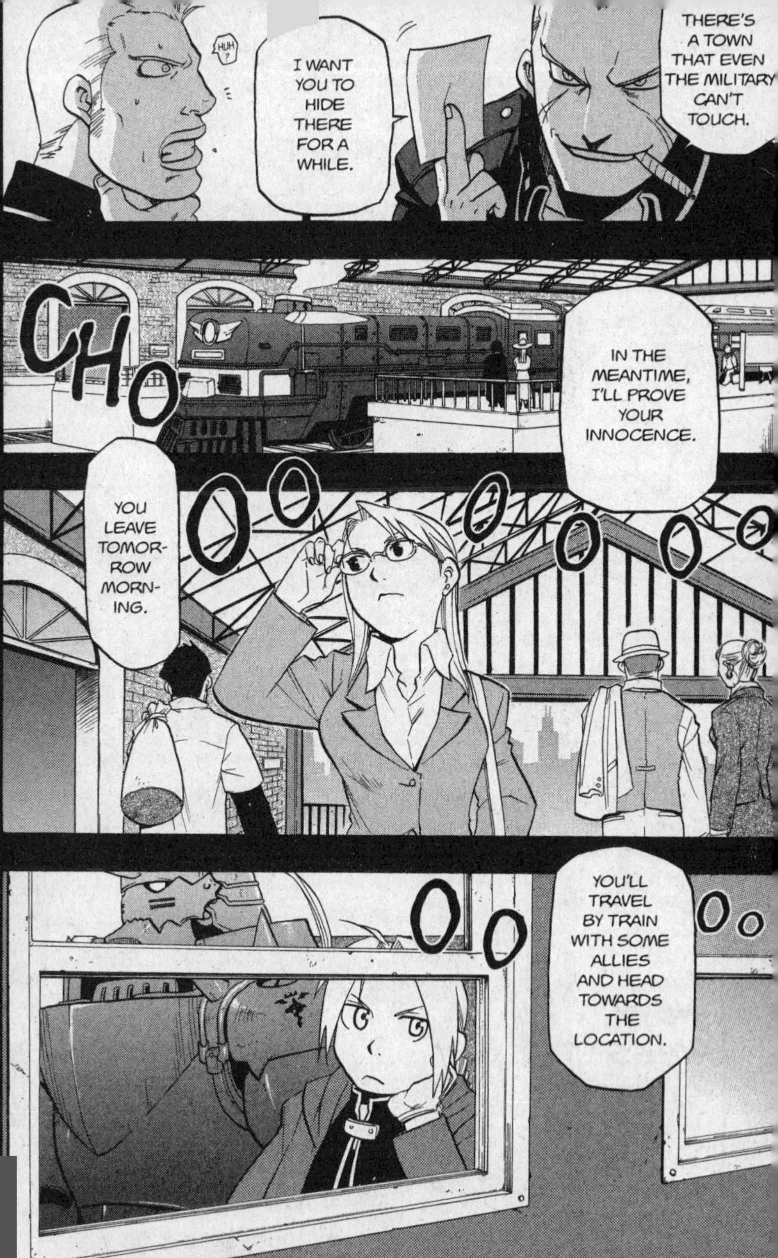
THERE'S A TOWN THAT EVEN THE MILITARY CAN'T TOUCH.
HUH?
I WANT YOU TO HIDE THERE FOR A WHILE.
CHO
IN THE MEANTIME, I'LL PROVE YOUR INNOCENCE.
OOOOOOOO
YOU LEAVE TOMORROW MORNING.
YOU'LL TRAVEL BY TRAIN WITH SOME ALLIES AND HEAD TOWARDS THE LOCATION.
OOOo

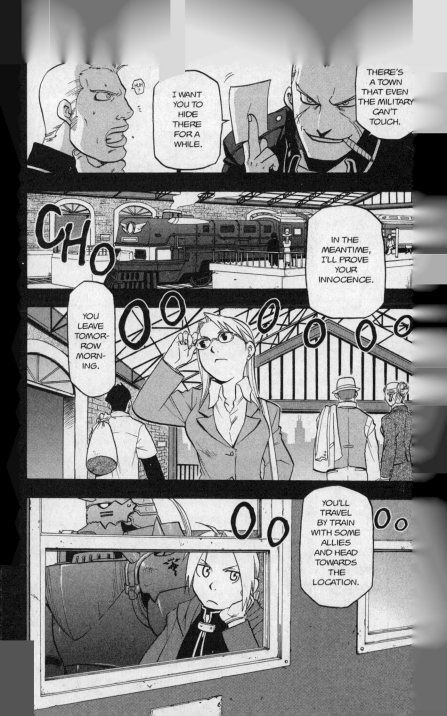

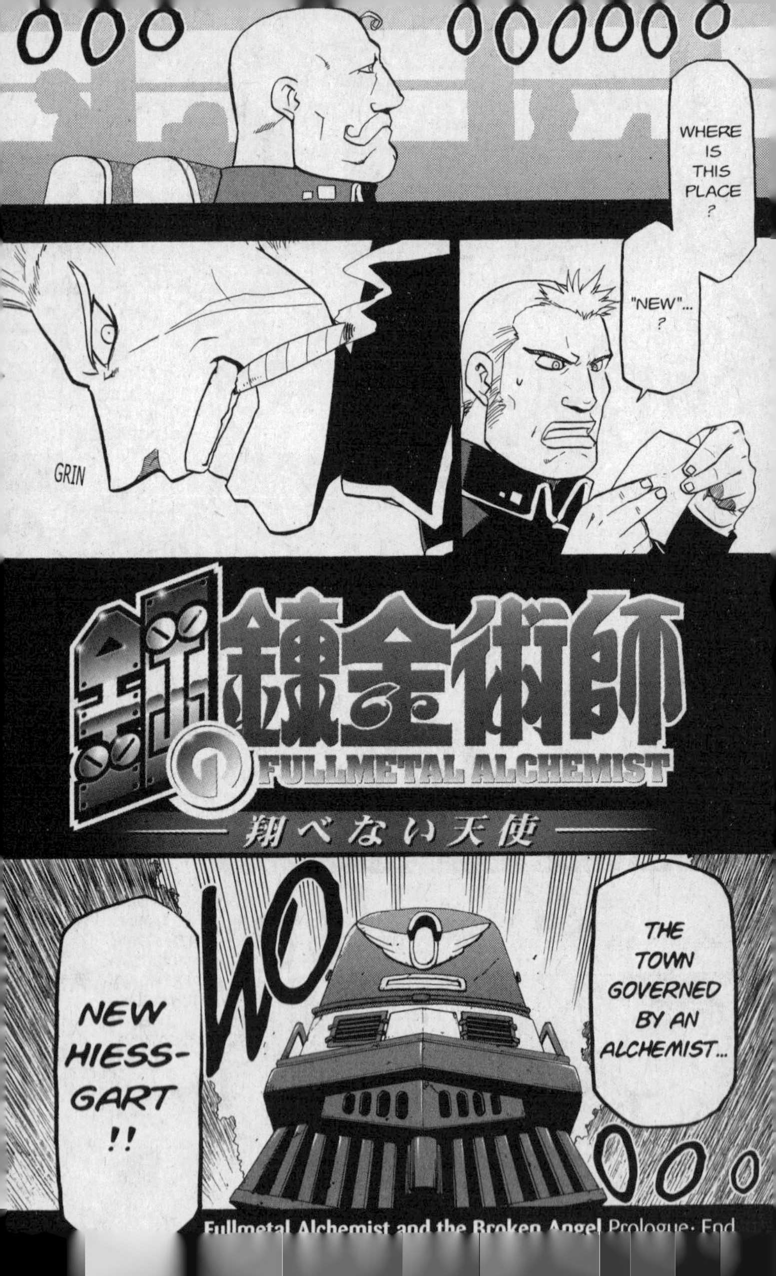
WHERE IS THIS PLACE ?
"NEW"... ?
GRIN
鋼の錬金術師
FULLMETAL ALCHEMIST
翔べない天使
THE TOWN GOVERNED BY AN ALCHEMIST...
WO
NEW HIESS-GART !!

Fullmetal Alchemist and the Broken Angel Prologue: End

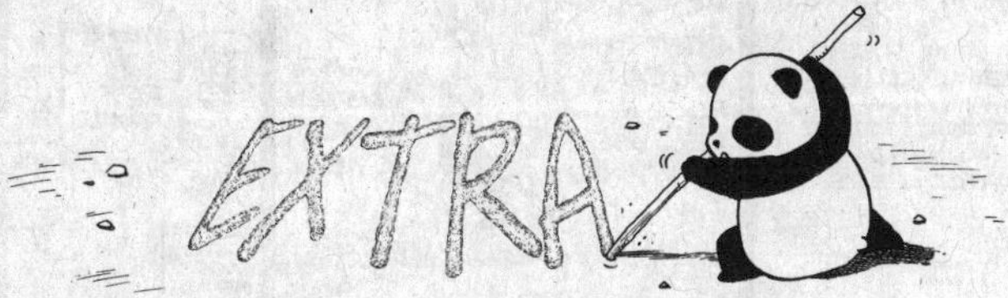
EXTRA

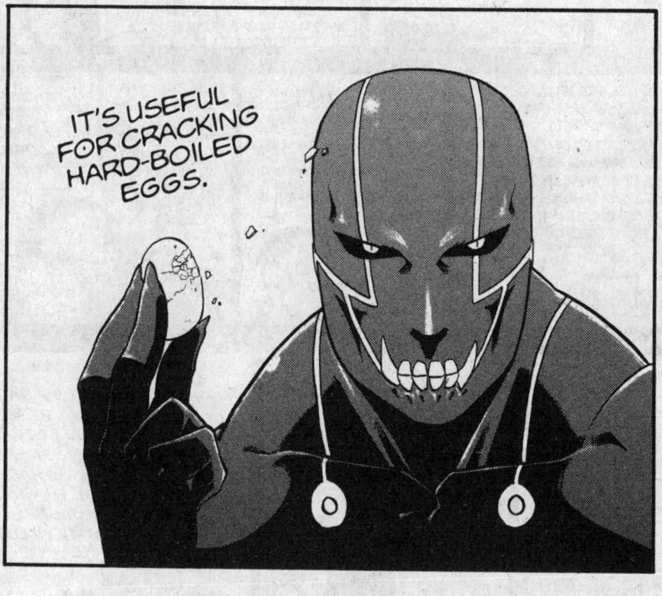
IT'S USEFUL FOR CRACKING HARD-BOILED EGGS.

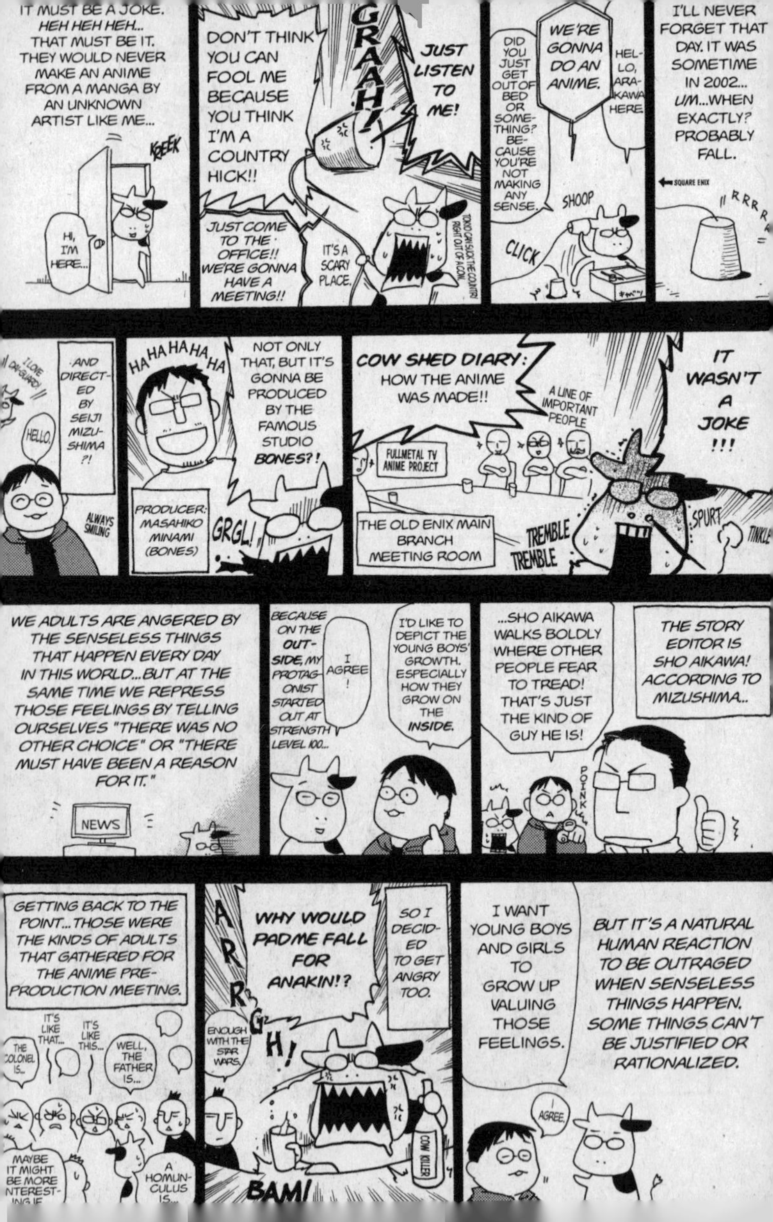
I'LL NEVER FORGET THAT DAY. IT WAS SOMETIME IN 2002... UM...WHEN EXACTLY? PROBABLY FALL.
SQUARE ENIX
RRRRR
HEL-LO, ARA-KAWA HERE.
WE'RE GONNA DO AN ANIME.
DID YOU JUST GET OUT OF BED OR SOME-THING? BE-CAUSE YOU'RE NOT MAKING ANY SENSE.
SHOOP
CLICK
GRAAH!
JUST LISTEN TO ME!
DON'T THINK YOU CAN FOOL ME BECAUSE YOU THINK I'M A COUNTRY HICK!!
JUST COME TO THE OFFICE!! WE'RE GONNA HAVE A MEETING!!
IT'S A SCARY PLACE.
TOKYO CAN SUCK THE COUNTRY RIGHT OUT OF A COW.
IT MUST BE A JOKE. HEH HEH HEH... THAT MUST BE IT. THEY WOULD NEVER MAKE AN ANIME FROM A MANGA BY AN UNKNOWN ARTIST LIKE ME...
KREEK
HI, I'M HERE...
IT WASN'T A JOKE!!!
SPURT
TINKLE
TREMBLE TREMBLE
COW SHED DIARY: HOW THE ANIME WAS MADE!!
A LINE OF IMPORTANT PEOPLE
FULLMETAL TV ANIME PROJECT
THE OLD ENIX MAIN BRANCH MEETING ROOM
HAHAHAHAHAHA
NOT ONLY THAT, BUT IT'S GONNA BE PRODUCED BY THE FAMOUS STUDIO BONES?!
PRODUCER: MASAHIKO MINAMI (BONES)
GRGL!
AND DIRECT-ED BY SEIJI MIZU-SHIMA ?!
I LOVE DAYGUARD!
HELLO.
ALWAYS SMILING
THE STORY EDITOR IS SHO AIKAWA! ACCORDING TO MIZUSHIMA...
...SHO AIKAWA WALKS BOLDLY WHERE OTHER PEOPLE FEAR TO TREAD! THAT'S JUST THE KIND OF GUY HE IS!
POINK
I'D LIKE TO DEPICT THE YOUNG BOYS' GROWTH. ESPECIALLY HOW THEY GROW ON THE INSIDE.
I AGREE!
BECAUSE ON THE OUT-SIDE, MY PROTAG-ONIST STARTED OUT AT STRENGTH LEVEL 100...
WE ADULTS ARE ANGERED BY THE SENSELESS THINGS THAT HAPPEN EVERY DAY IN THIS WORLD...BUT AT THE SAME TIME WE REPRESS THOSE FEELINGS BY TELLING OURSELVES "THERE WAS NO OTHER CHOICE" OR "THERE MUST HAVE BEEN A REASON FOR IT."
NEWS
BUT IT'S A NATURAL HUMAN REACTION TO BE OUTRAGED WHEN SENSELESS THINGS HAPPEN. SOME THINGS CAN'T BE JUSTIFIED OR RATIONALIZED.
I WANT YOUNG BOYS AND GIRLS TO GROW UP VALUING THOSE FEELINGS.
I AGREE.
SO I DECID-ED TO GET ANGRY TOO.
WHY WOULD PADME FALL FOR ANAKIN!?
ARRRGH!
ENOUGH WITH THE STAR WARS.
COW KILLER
BAM!
GETTING BACK TO THE POINT...THOSE WERE THE KINDS OF ADULTS THAT GATHERED FOR THE ANIME PRE-PRODUCTION MEETING.
IT'S LIKE THAT...
IT'S LIKE THIS...
THE COLONEL IS...
WELL, THE FATHER IS...
MAYBE IT MIGHT BE MORE INTEREST-
A HOMUN-CULUS IS...

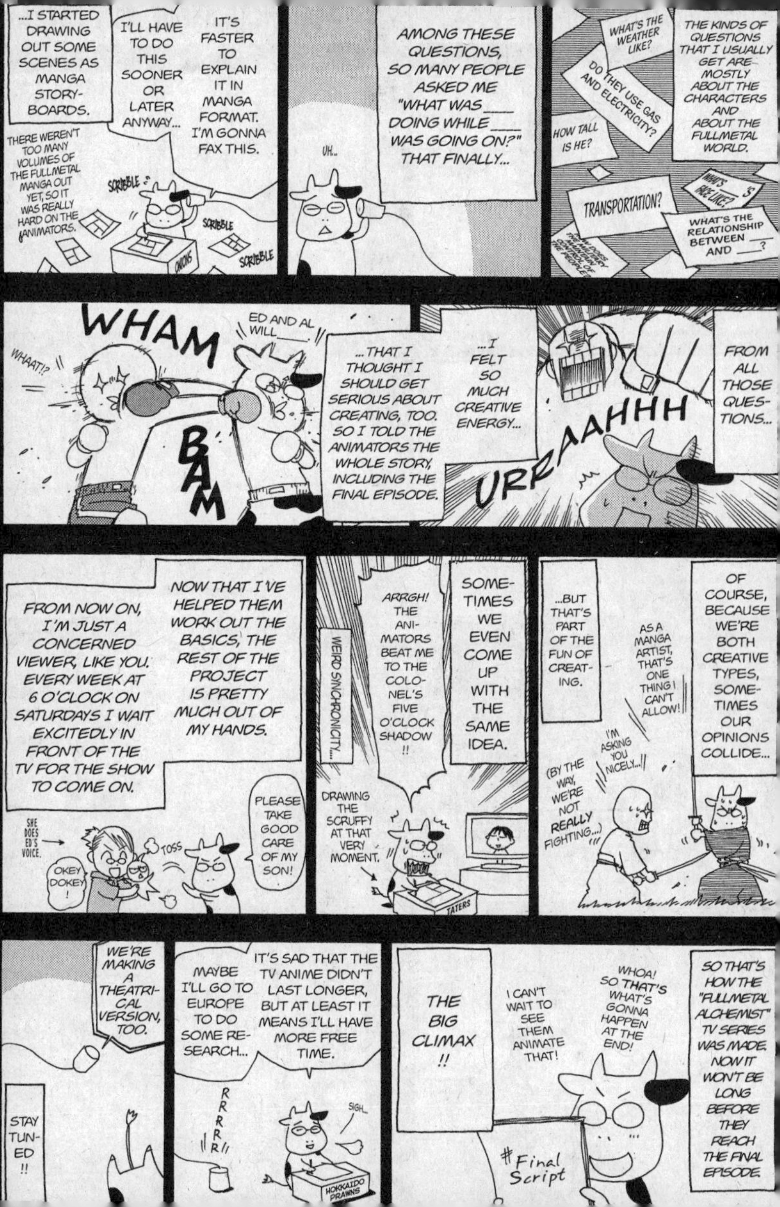
THE KINDS OF QUESTIONS THAT I USUALLY GET ARE MOSTLY ABOUT THE CHARACTERS AND ABOUT THE FULLMETAL WORLD.
WHAT'S THE WEATHER LIKE?
DO THEY USE GAS AND ELECTRICITY?
HOW TALL IS HE?
WHAT'S ___'S FACE LIKE?
TRANSPORTATION?
WHAT'S THE RELATIONSHIP BETWEEN ___ AND ___?
AMONG THESE QUESTIONS, SO MANY PEOPLE ASKED ME "WHAT WAS ___ DOING WHILE ___ WAS GOING ON?" THAT FINALLY...
UH...
IT'S FASTER TO EXPLAIN IT IN MANGA FORMAT. I'M GONNA FAX THIS.
I'LL HAVE TO DO THIS SOONER OR LATER ANYWAY...
...I STARTED DRAWING OUT SOME SCENES AS MANGA STORY-BOARDS.
THERE WEREN'T TOO MANY VOLUMES OF THE FULLMETAL MANGA OUT YET, SO IT WAS REALLY HARD ON THE ANIMATORS.
SCRIBBLE
SCRIBBLE
SCRIBBLE
ONIONS
FROM ALL THOSE QUES-TIONS...
URRAAHHH
...I FELT SO MUCH CREATIVE ENERGY...
...THAT I THOUGHT I SHOULD GET SERIOUS ABOUT CREATING, TOO. SO I TOLD THE ANIMATORS THE WHOLE STORY, INCLUDING THE FINAL EPISODE.
ED AND AL WILL___.
WHAM
WHAAT!?
BAM
OF COURSE, BECAUSE WE'RE BOTH CREATIVE TYPES, SOME-TIMES OUR OPINIONS COLLIDE...
AS A MANGA ARTIST, THAT'S ONE THING I CAN'T ALLOW!
...BUT THAT'S PART OF THE FUN OF CREAT-ING.
I'M ASKING YOU NICELY...
(BY THE WAY, WE'RE NOT REALLY FIGHTING...)
SOME-TIMES WE EVEN COME UP WITH THE SAME IDEA.
ARRGH! THE ANI-MATORS BEAT ME TO THE COLO-NEL'S FIVE O'CLOCK SHADOW!!
WEIRD SYNCHRONICITY...
DRAWING THE SCRUFFY AT THAT VERY MOMENT.
TATERS
NOW THAT I'VE HELPED THEM WORK OUT THE BASICS, THE REST OF THE PROJECT IS PRETTY MUCH OUT OF MY HANDS.
FROM NOW ON, I'M JUST A CONCERNED VIEWER, LIKE YOU. EVERY WEEK AT 6 O'CLOCK ON SATURDAYS I WAIT EXCITEDLY IN FRONT OF THE TV FOR THE SHOW TO COME ON.
PLEASE TAKE GOOD CARE OF MY SON!
TOSS
SHE DOES ED'S VOICE.
OKEY DOKEY!
SO THAT'S HOW THE "FULLMETAL ALCHEMIST" TV SERIES WAS MADE. NOW IT WON'T BE LONG BEFORE THEY REACH THE FINAL EPISODE.
WHOA! SO THAT'S WHAT'S GONNA HAPPEN AT THE END!
I CAN'T WAIT TO SEE THEM ANIMATE THAT!
THE BIG CLIMAX!!
#Final Script
IT'S SAD THAT THE TV ANIME DIDN'T LAST LONGER, BUT AT LEAST IT MEANS I'LL HAVE MORE FREE TIME.
MAYBE I'LL GO TO EUROPE TO DO SOME RE-SEARCH...
SIGH...
RRRRRR
HOKKAIDO PRAWNS
WE'RE MAKING A THEATRI-CAL VERSION, TOO.
STAY TUN-ED!!

MEAT, MEAT, ARMOR, MEAT, MEAT

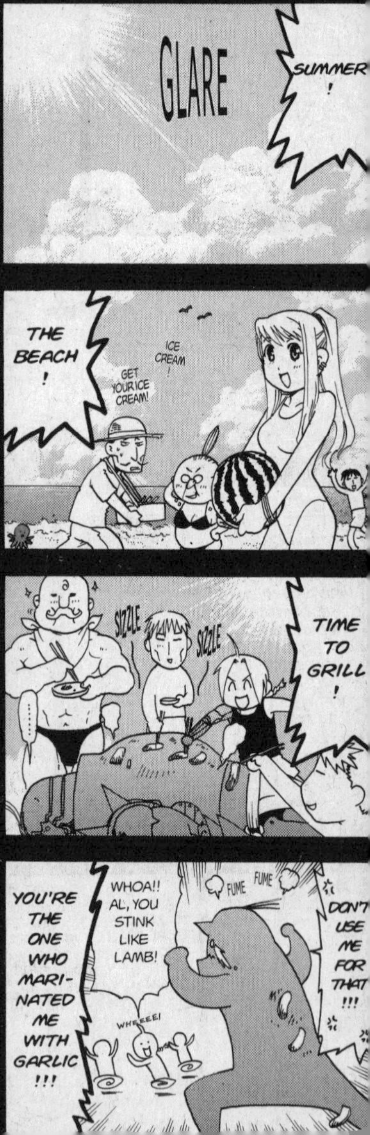
SUMMER!
GLARE
ICE CREAM!
THE BEACH!
GET YOUR ICE CREAM!
TIME TO GRILL!
SIZZLE
SIZZLE
DON'T USE ME FOR THAT!!!
FUME
FUME
WHOA!! AL, YOU STINK LIKE LAMB!
YOU'RE THE ONE WHO MARINATED ME WITH GARLIC!!!
WHEEEE!

THE WONDERFUL WORLD OF DOGS

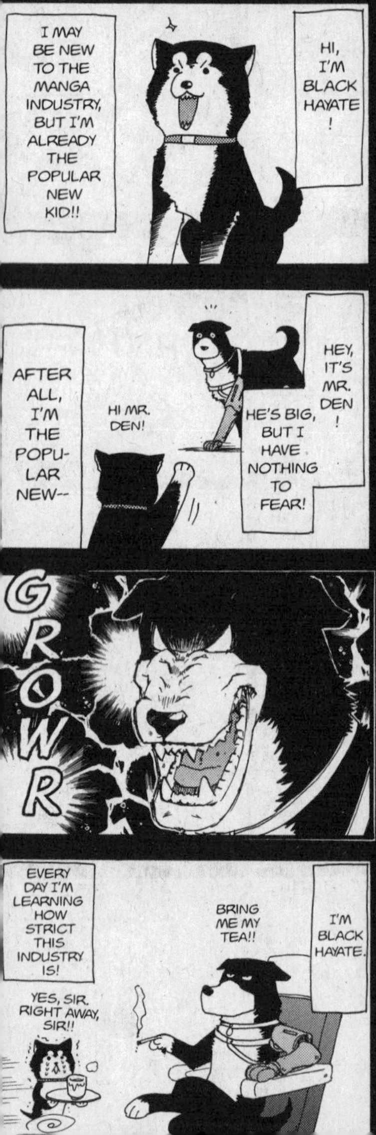
HI, I'M BLACK HAYATE!
I MAY BE NEW TO THE MANGA INDUSTRY, BUT I'M ALREADY THE POPULAR NEW KID!!
HEY, IT'S MR. DEN!
HE'S BIG, BUT I HAVE NOTHING TO FEAR!
HI MR. DEN!
AFTER ALL, I'M THE POPULAR NEW--
GROWR
I'M BLACK HAYATE.
BRING ME MY TEA!!
EVERY DAY I'M LEARNING HOW STRICT THIS INDUSTRY IS!
YES, SIR. RIGHT AWAY, SIR!!

DEATHTRAP

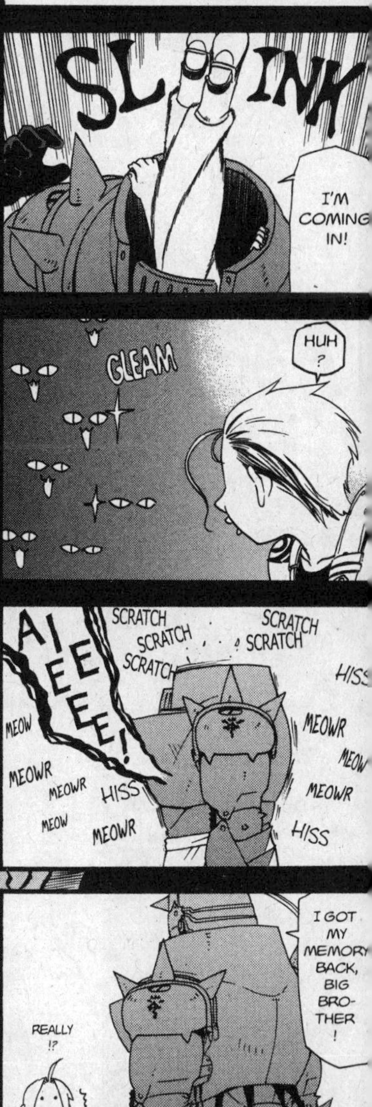
SLINK
I'M COMING IN!
HUH ?
GLEAM
AIEEEEE!
SCRATCH SCRATCH SCRATCH
SCRATCH SCRATCH
HISS
MEOW
MEOWR
MEOWR
MEOW
HISS
MEOWR
MEOWR
MEOW
MEOWR
HISS
I GOT MY MEMORY BACK, BIG BROTHER!
REALLY !?
GUSH

FULLMETAL ALCHEMIST 8

SPECIAL THANKS TO...

KEISUI TAKAEDA-SAN
SANKICHI HINODEYA-SAN
MASANARI YUBEKA-SAN
JUNSHI BABA-SAN
AIYAABALL-SAN
JUN TOKO-SAN
YOICHI SHIMOMURA-SHI (MANAGER)
AND YOU !!

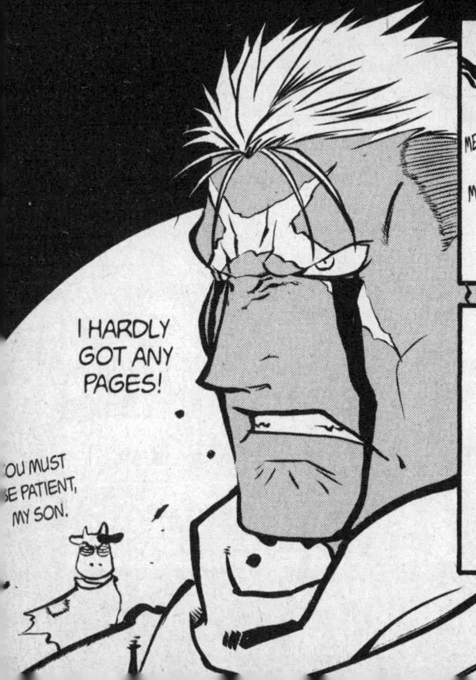
I HARDLY GOT ANY PAGES!
OU MUST
E PATIENT,
MY SON.

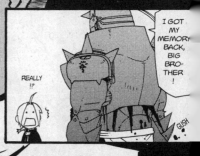

Image change

side
part

Third grade
Group two
Masuda

Aww
geez

In Memoriam

Image change 2

Image
change
3

HE CUT HIS
BANGS. NOW
IT'S A
DISASTER.

Note: This is an Izakaya

Puffer fish liver | Filet | Eel | Chicken with leeks

juice   juice

juice   juice

When my comic artist friends and I gather at an izakaya (pub), we always have lively conversations about manga. Sometimes we talk so much that we miss the last train. Some people might think, "What are a bunch of grown-ups doing wasting time like that?" But when I hear my friends saying things like, "This is the kind of manga that I want to do!!" I really feel reenergized. This time Mr. Moritaishi, who is a passionate and talented fellow of the best sort, was kind enough to do the bonus comic for this volume. Yaaay!! (Bliss)

—*Hiromu Arakawa, 2004*

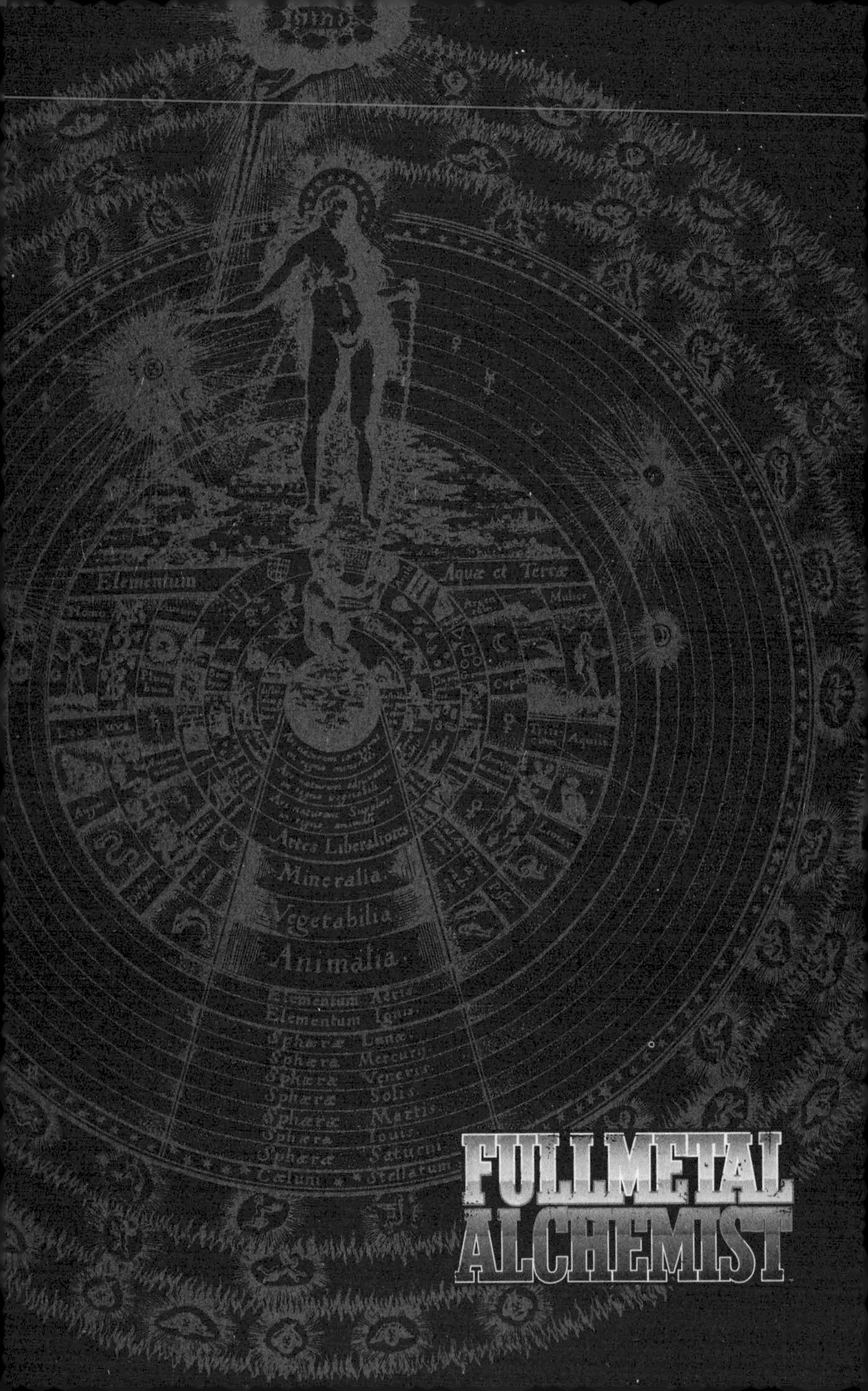
Elementum
Aquæ et Terræ
Artes Liberales
Mineralia
Vegetabilia
Animalia
Elementum Aeris
Elementum Ignis
Sphæra Lunæ
Sphæra Mercurij
Sphæra Veneris
Sphæra Solis
Sphæra Martis
Sphæra Iouis
Sphæra Saturni
Cœlum Stellatum
FULLMETAL ALCHEMIST

鋼の錬金術師

FULLMETAL ALCHEMIST

HIROMU ARAKAWA

荒川弘

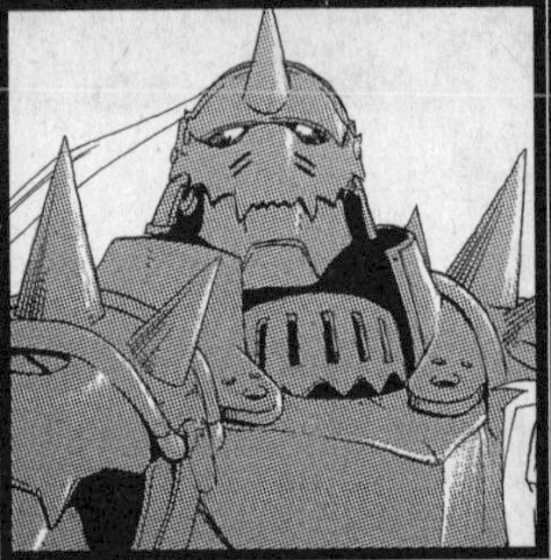

■アルフォンス・エルリック

Alphonse Elric

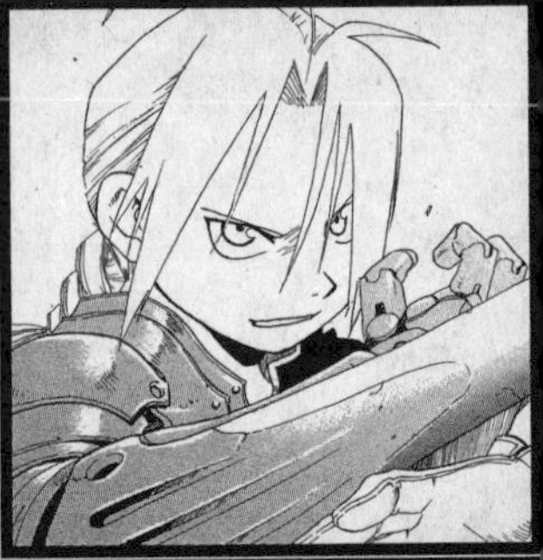

■エドワード・エルリック

Edward Elric

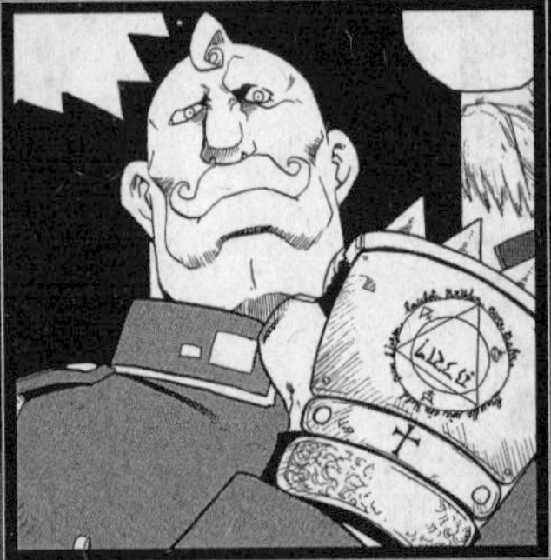

■アレックス・ルイ・アームストロング

Alex Louis Armstrong

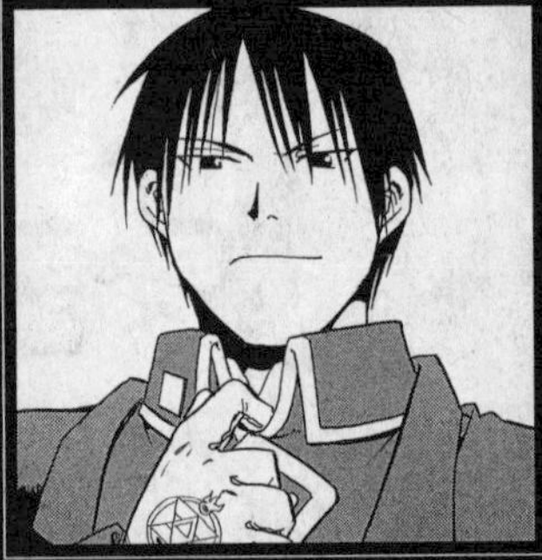

■ロイ・マスタング

Roy Mustang

OUTLINE
FULLMETAL ALCHEMIST

Using a forbidden alchemical ritual, the Elric Brothers attempted to bring their dead mother back to life. But the ritual went wrong, consuming Edward Elric's leg and Alphonse Elric's entire body. At the cost of his arm, Edward was able to graft brother's soul into a suit of armor. Equipped with mechanical "auto-mail" to repla his missing limbs, Edward becomes a state alchemist, serving the military on deac missions. Now, the two brothers roam the world in search of the philosopher, the legendary substance with the power to restore what they have lost...

After a traumatic visit to Dublith and a run-in with the rogue homunculus Greed, Al's memory of "the truth" is unlocked. Now, like his brother and their teacher Izu the younger Elric can perform alchemy without a transmutation circle. The trauma battle left Ed's auto-mail broken, so once again they go to Winry for repairs. In Ru Valley, the Elric brothers are joined by Lin, a prince from Xing who also seeks the philosopher's stone. As they set off for central, Winry joins the boys in the hopes visiting Lt. Colonel Hughes. Little do they know that Hughes was murdered shortly

鋼の錬金術師
FULLMETAL ALCHEMIST

CHARACTERS
FULLMETAL ALCHEMIST

■ ウィンリィ・ロックベル

Winry Rockbell

■ マリア・ロス

Maria Ross

■ グラトニー

Gluttony

■ ラスト

Lust

■ 66

■ エンヴィー

66

Envy

CONTENTS

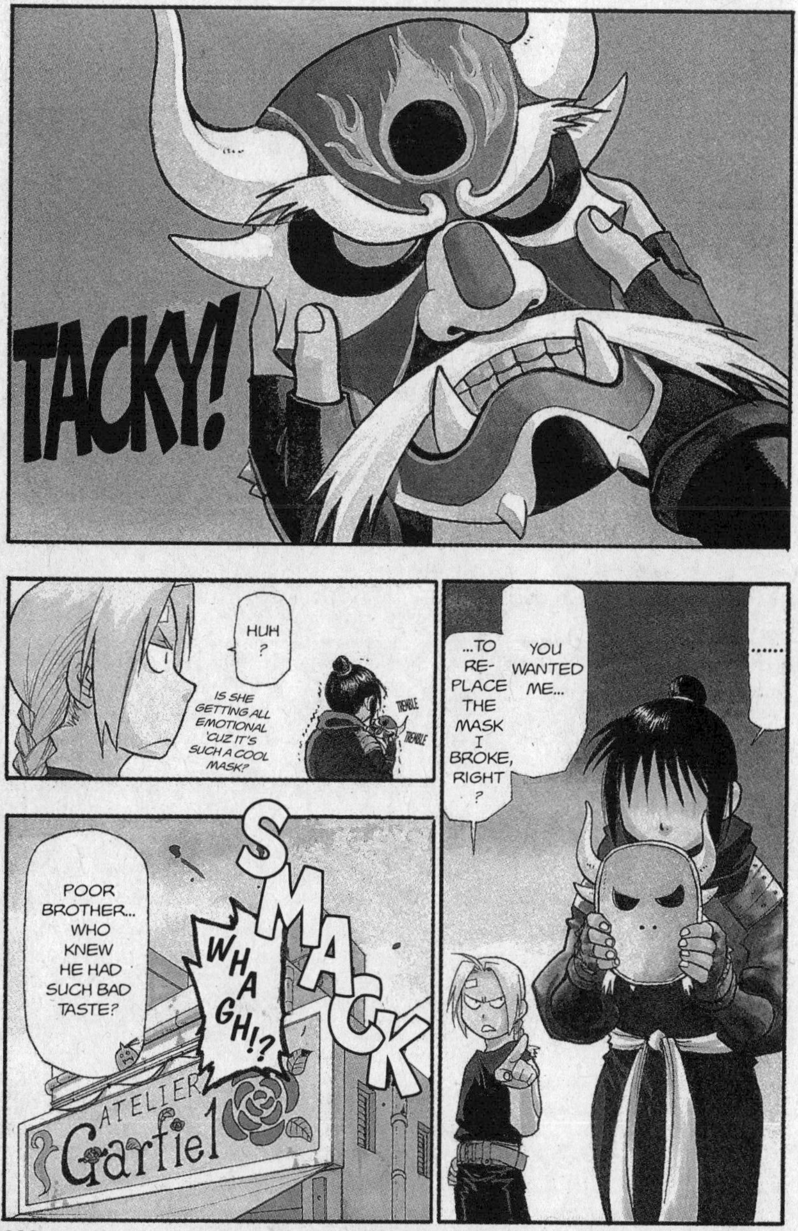
TACKY!
......
YOU WANTED ME...
...TO RE-PLACE THE MASK I BROKE, RIGHT?
HUH?
IS SHE GETTING ALL EMOTIONAL 'CUZ IT'S SUCH A COOL MASK?
TREMBLE
TREMBLE
SMACK
WHAGH!?
POOR BROTHER... WHO KNEW HE HAD SUCH BAD TASTE?
ATELIER Garfiel

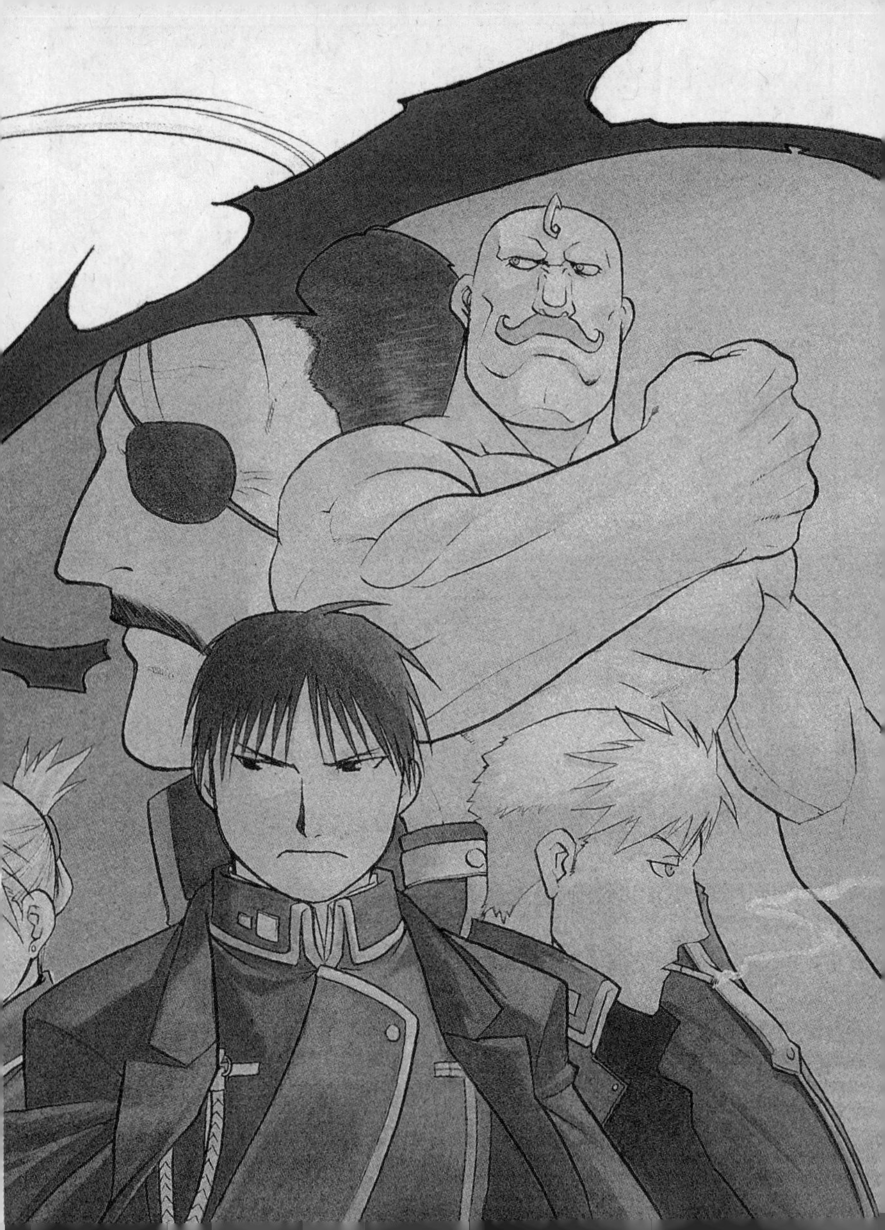

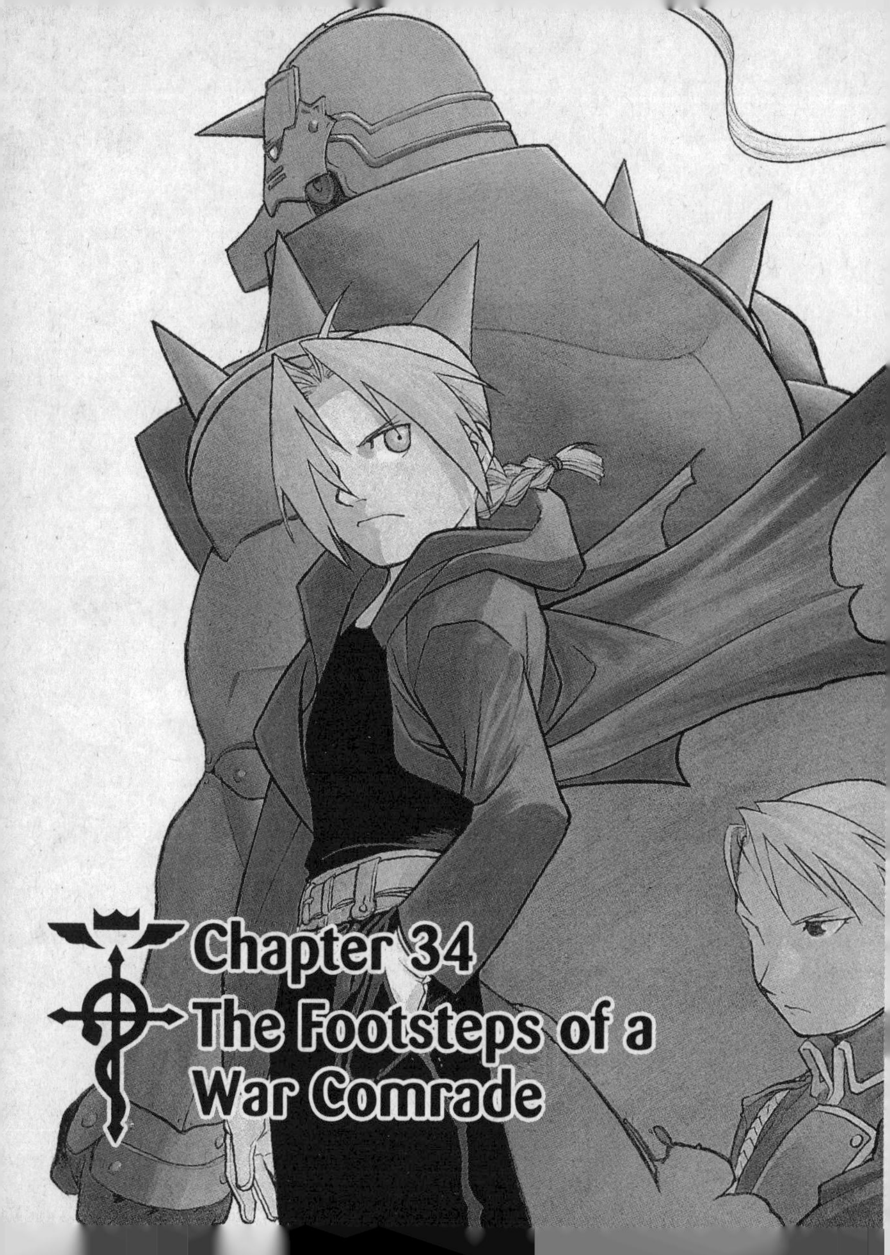
Chapter 34
The Footsteps of a War Comrade

FULLMETAL
ALCHEMIST

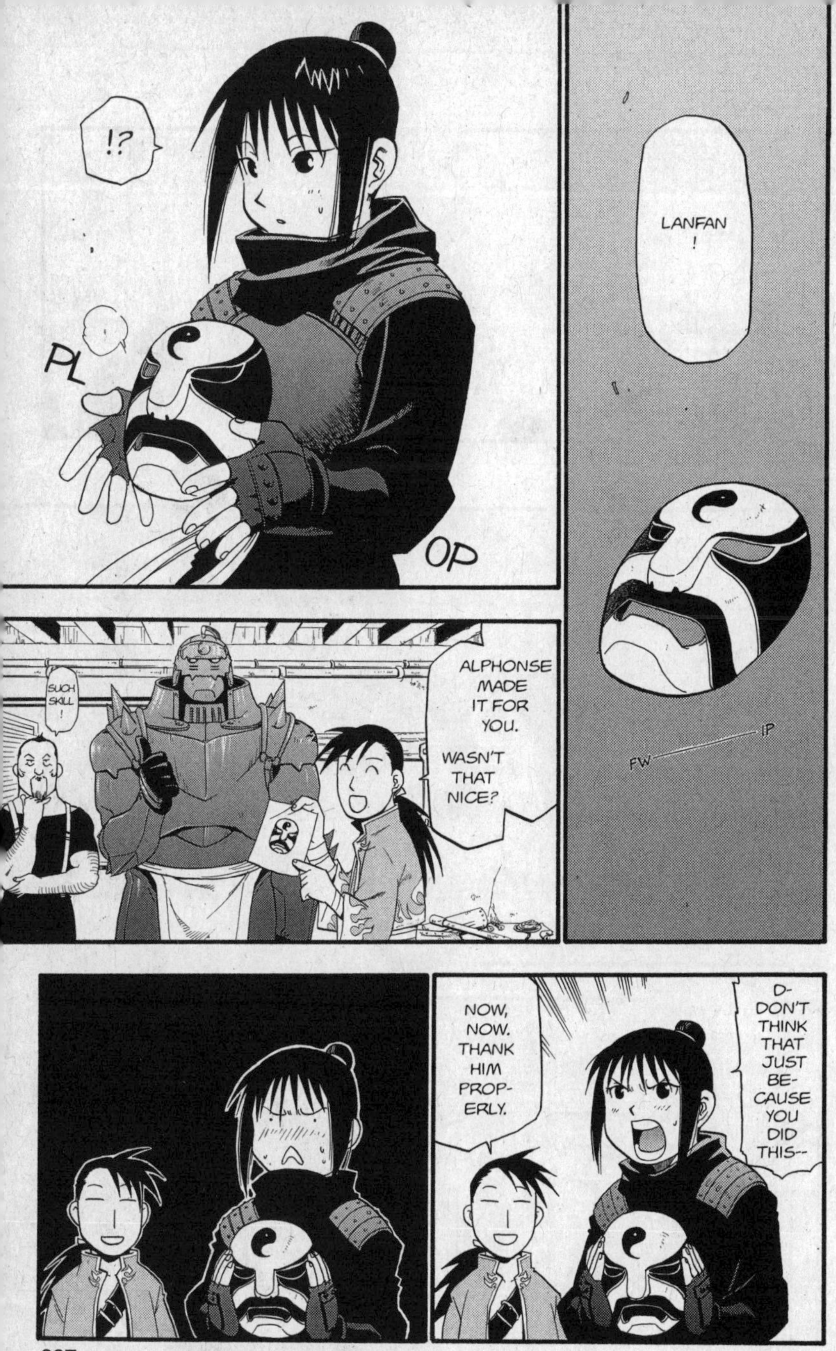
LANFAN!
FWIP
!?
PLOP
ALPHONSE MADE IT FOR YOU.
WASN'T THAT NICE?
SUCH SKILL!
D-DON'T THINK THAT JUST BE-CAUSE YOU DID THIS--
NOW, NOW. THANK HIM PROP-ERLY.

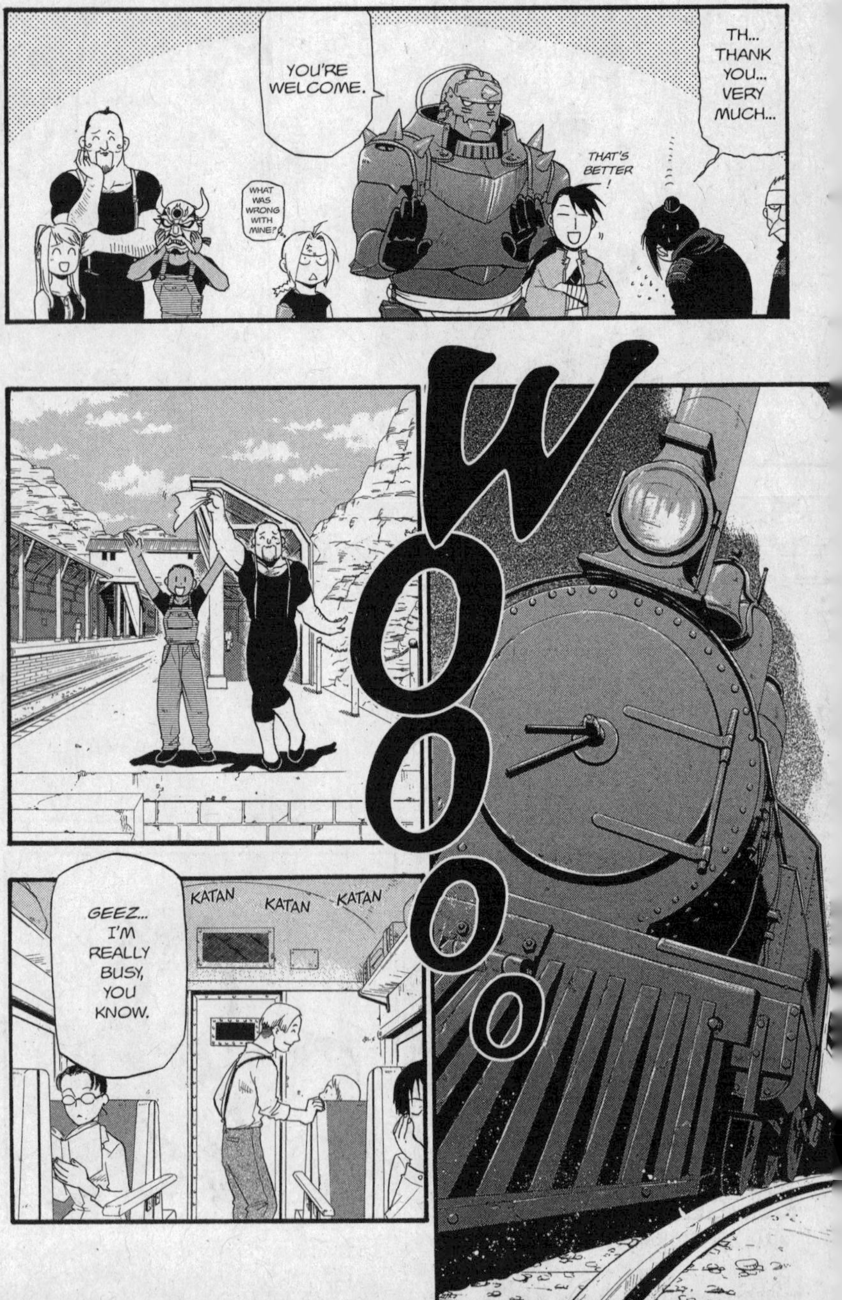
TH... THANK YOU... VERY MUCH...
THAT'S BETTER!
YOU'RE WELCOME.
WHAT WAS WRONG WITH MINE?
WOOOOO
KATAN KATAN KATAN
GEEZ... I'M REALLY BUSY, YOU KNOW.

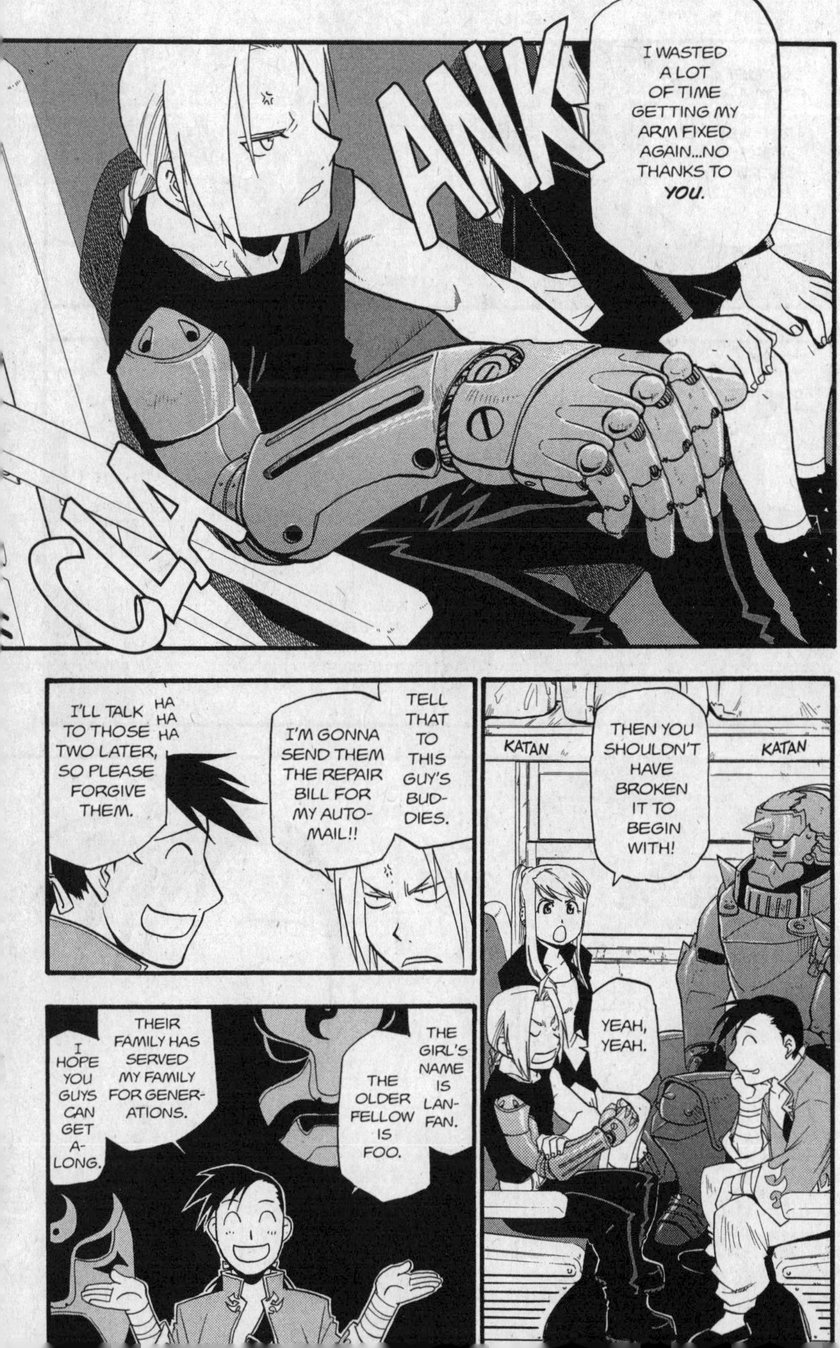
I WASTED A LOT OF TIME GETTING MY ARM FIXED AGAIN...NO THANKS TO *YOU*.
ANK
CLA
KATAN
KATAN
THEN YOU SHOULDN'T HAVE BROKEN IT TO BEGIN WITH!
YEAH, YEAH.
TELL THAT TO THIS GUY'S BUD-DIES.
I'M GONNA SEND THEM THE REPAIR BILL FOR MY AUTO-MAIL!!
HA HA HA
I'LL TALK TO THOSE TWO LATER, SO PLEASE FORGIVE THEM.
THE GIRL'S NAME IS LAN-FAN.
THE OLDER FELLOW IS FOO.
THEIR FAMILY HAS SERVED MY FAMILY FOR GENER-ATIONS.
I HOPE YOU GUYS CAN GET A-LONG.

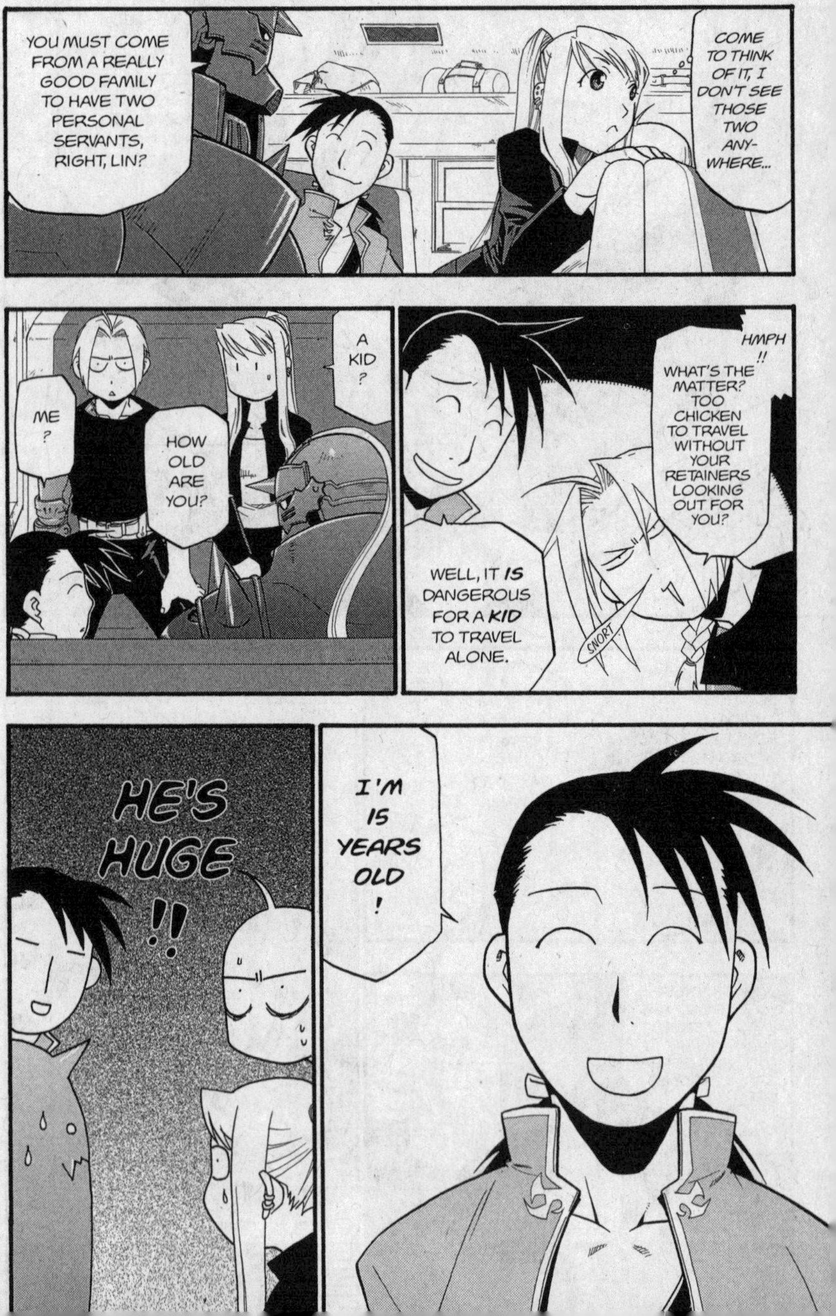
COME TO THINK OF IT, I DON'T SEE THOSE TWO ANYWHERE...
YOU MUST COME FROM A REALLY GOOD FAMILY TO HAVE TWO PERSONAL SERVANTS, RIGHT, LIN?
HMPH!!
WHAT'S THE MATTER? TOO CHICKEN TO TRAVEL WITHOUT YOUR RETAINERS LOOKING OUT FOR YOU?
SNORT
WELL, IT IS DANGEROUS FOR A KID TO TRAVEL ALONE.
A KID?
ME?
HOW OLD ARE YOU?
I'M 15 YEARS OLD!
HE'S HUGE!!

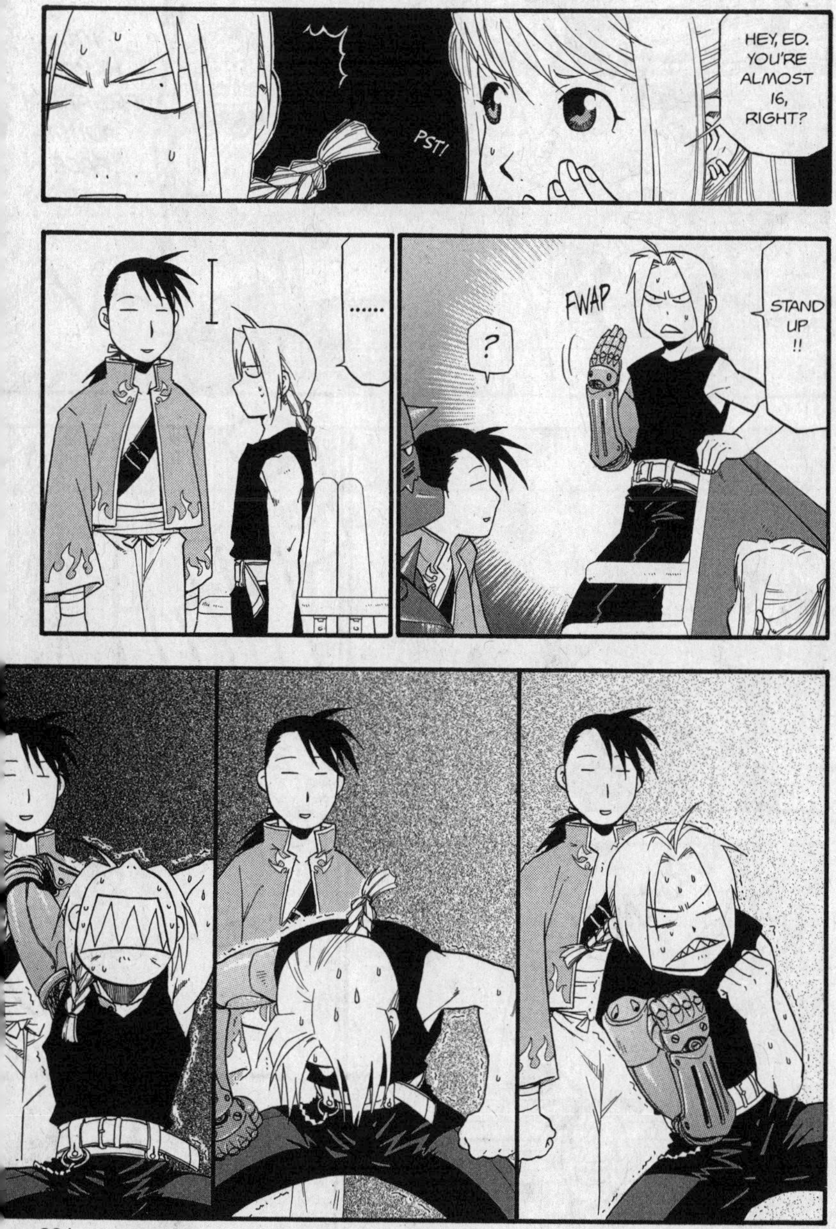
HEY, ED. YOU'RE ALMOST 16, RIGHT?
PST!
STAND UP !!
FWAP
?
......

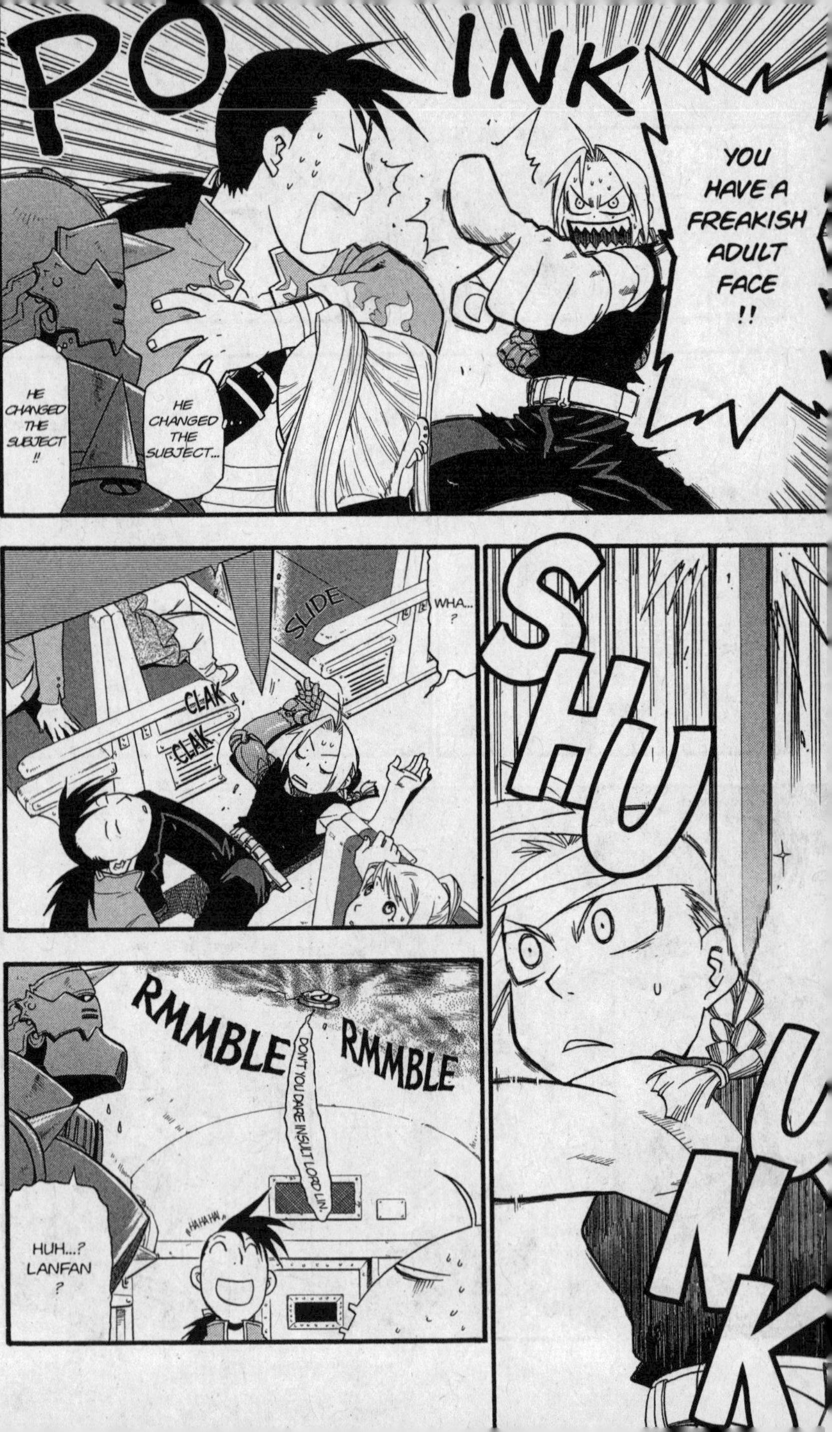
POINK
YOU HAVE A FREAKISH ADULT FACE !!
HE CHANGED THE SUBJECT...
HE CHANGED THE SUBJECT !!
SHUNK
WHA...?
SLIDE
CLAK
CLAK
RMMBLE RMMBLE
DON'T YOU DARE INSULT LORD LIN.
HA HA HA
HUH...? LANFAN ?

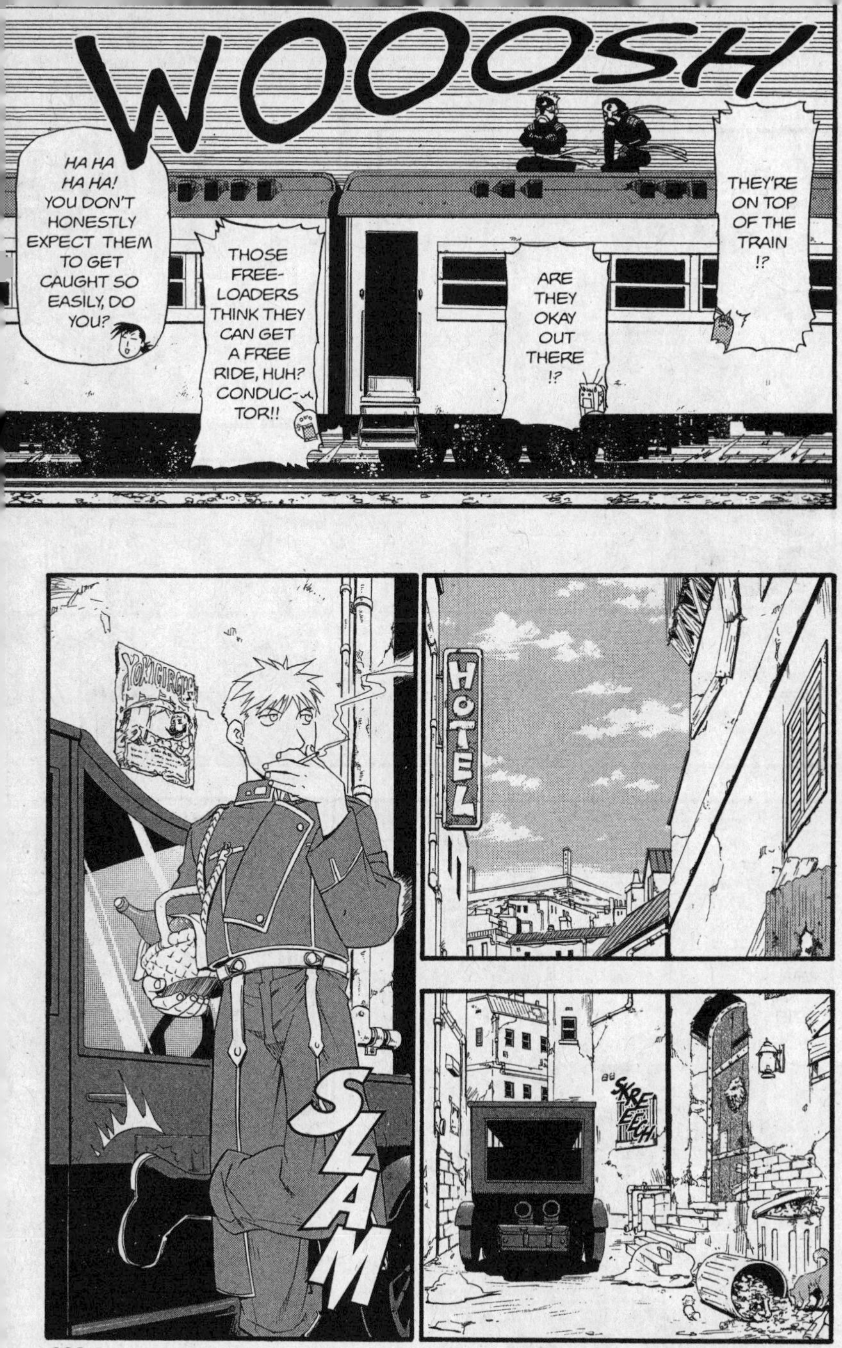
WOOOSH
THEY'RE ON TOP OF THE TRAIN !?
ARE THEY OKAY OUT THERE !?
THOSE FREE-LOADERS THINK THEY CAN GET A FREE RIDE, HUH? CONDUC-TOR!!
HA HA HA HA! YOU DON'T HONESTLY EXPECT THEM TO GET CAUGHT SO EASILY, DO YOU?
HOTEL
SKREEEECH
SLAM

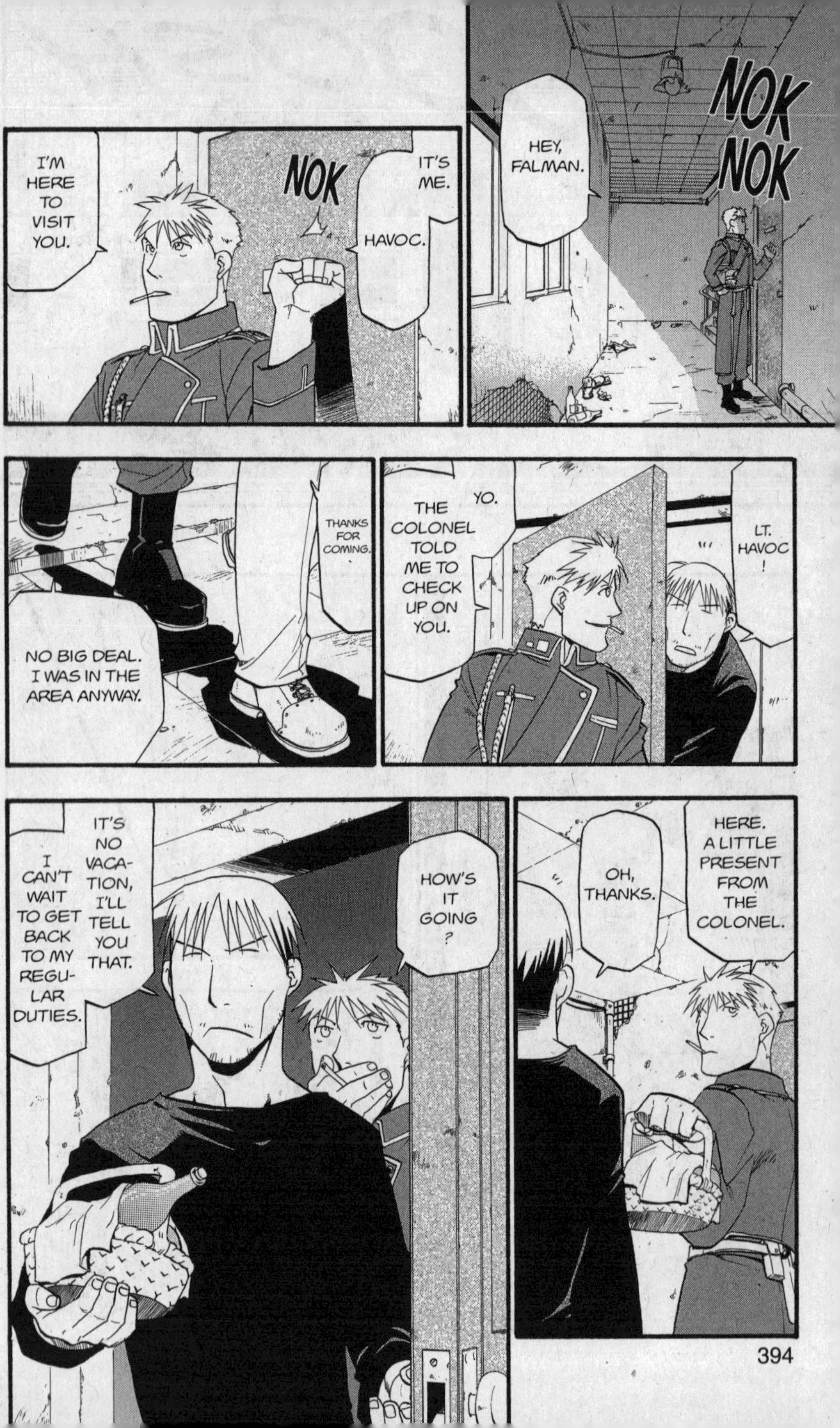
NOK NOK
HEY, FALMAN.
IT'S ME.
HAVOC.
NOK
I'M HERE TO VISIT YOU.
LT. HAVOC!
YO.
THE COLONEL TOLD ME TO CHECK UP ON YOU.
THANKS FOR COMING.
NO BIG DEAL. I WAS IN THE AREA ANYWAY.
HERE. A LITTLE PRESENT FROM THE COLONEL.
OH, THANKS.
HOW'S IT GOING?
IT'S NO VACATION, I'LL TELL YOU THAT.
I CAN'T WAIT TO GET BACK TO MY REGULAR DUTIES.

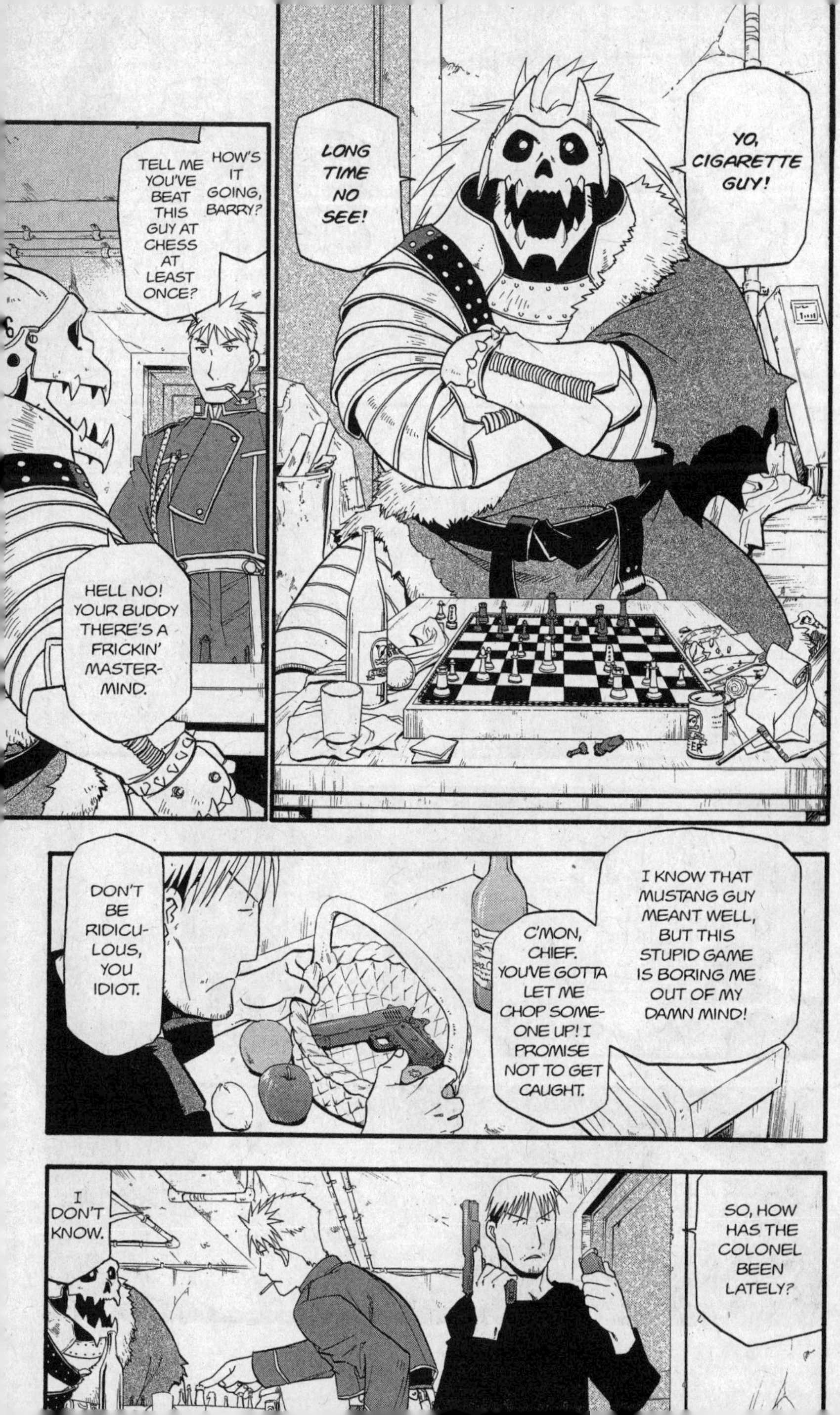
YO, CIGARETTE GUY!
LONG TIME NO SEE!
HOW'S IT GOING, BARRY?
TELL ME YOU'VE BEAT THIS GUY AT CHESS AT LEAST ONCE?
HELL NO! YOUR BUDDY THERE'S A FRICKIN' MASTER-MIND.
I KNOW THAT MUSTANG GUY MEANT WELL, BUT THIS STUPID GAME IS BORING ME OUT OF MY DAMN MIND!
C'MON, CHIEF. YOU'VE GOTTA LET ME CHOP SOME-ONE UP! I PROMISE NOT TO GET CAUGHT.
DON'T BE RIDICULOUS, YOU IDIOT.
SO, HOW HAS THE COLONEL BEEN LATELY?
I DON'T KNOW.

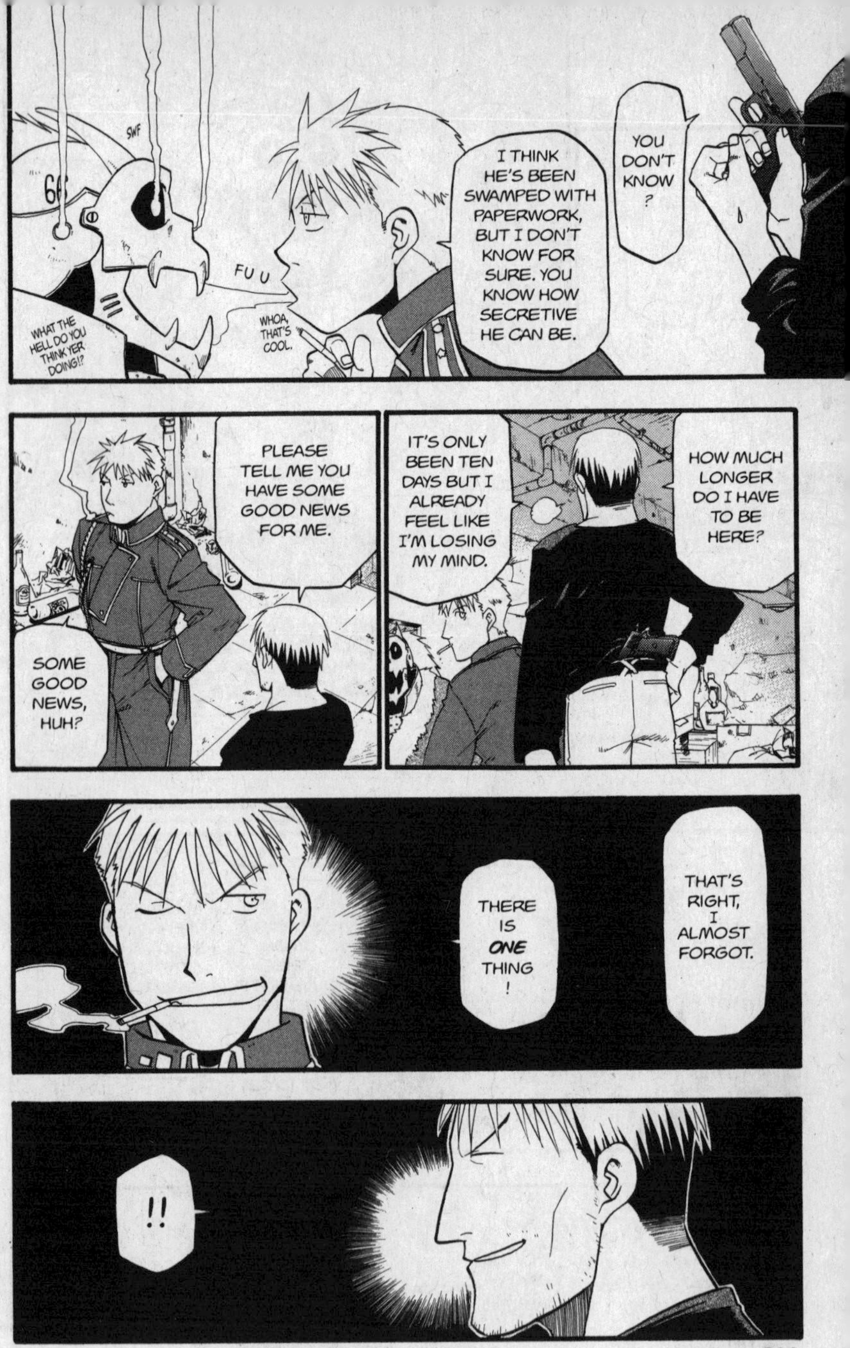
YOU DON'T KNOW?
I THINK HE'S BEEN SWAMPED WITH PAPERWORK, BUT I DON'T KNOW FOR SURE. YOU KNOW HOW SECRETIVE HE CAN BE.
FU U
WHOA, THAT'S COOL.
SWF
WHAT THE HELL DO YOU THINK YER DOING!?
HOW MUCH LONGER DO I HAVE TO BE HERE?
IT'S ONLY BEEN TEN DAYS BUT I ALREADY FEEL LIKE I'M LOSING MY MIND.
PLEASE TELL ME YOU HAVE SOME GOOD NEWS FOR ME.
SOME GOOD NEWS, HUH?
THAT'S RIGHT, I ALMOST FORGOT.
THERE IS ***ONE*** THING!
!!

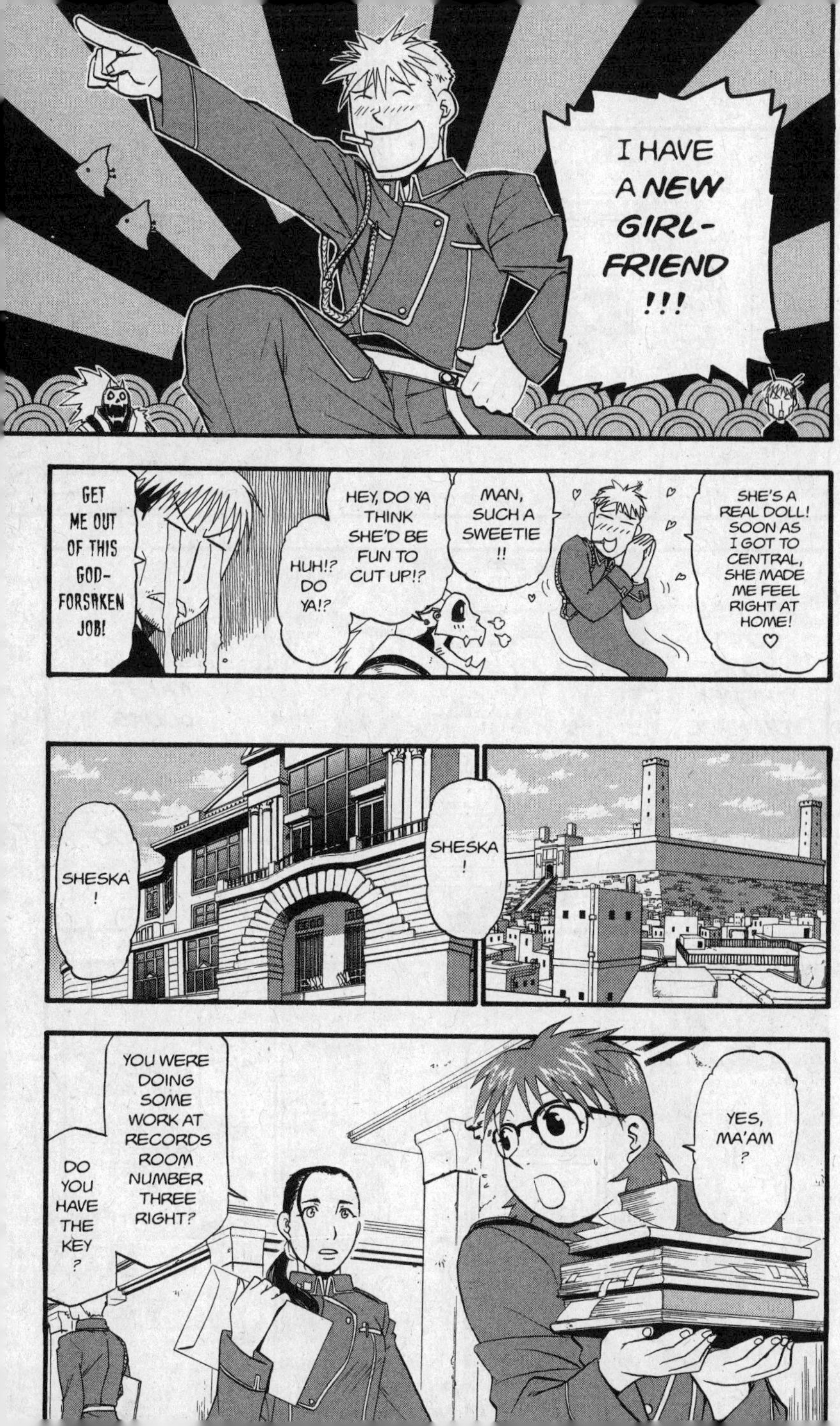
I HAVE A NEW GIRL-FRIEND!!!
SHE'S A REAL DOLL! SOON AS I GOT TO CENTRAL, SHE MADE ME FEEL RIGHT AT HOME! ♥
MAN, SUCH A SWEETIE!!
HEY, DO YA THINK SHE'D BE FUN TO CUT UP!?
HUH!? DO YA!?
GET ME OUT OF THIS GOD-FORSAKEN JOB!
SHESKA!
SHESKA!
YES, MA'AM?
YOU WERE DOING SOME WORK AT RECORDS ROOM NUMBER THREE RIGHT?
DO YOU HAVE THE KEY?

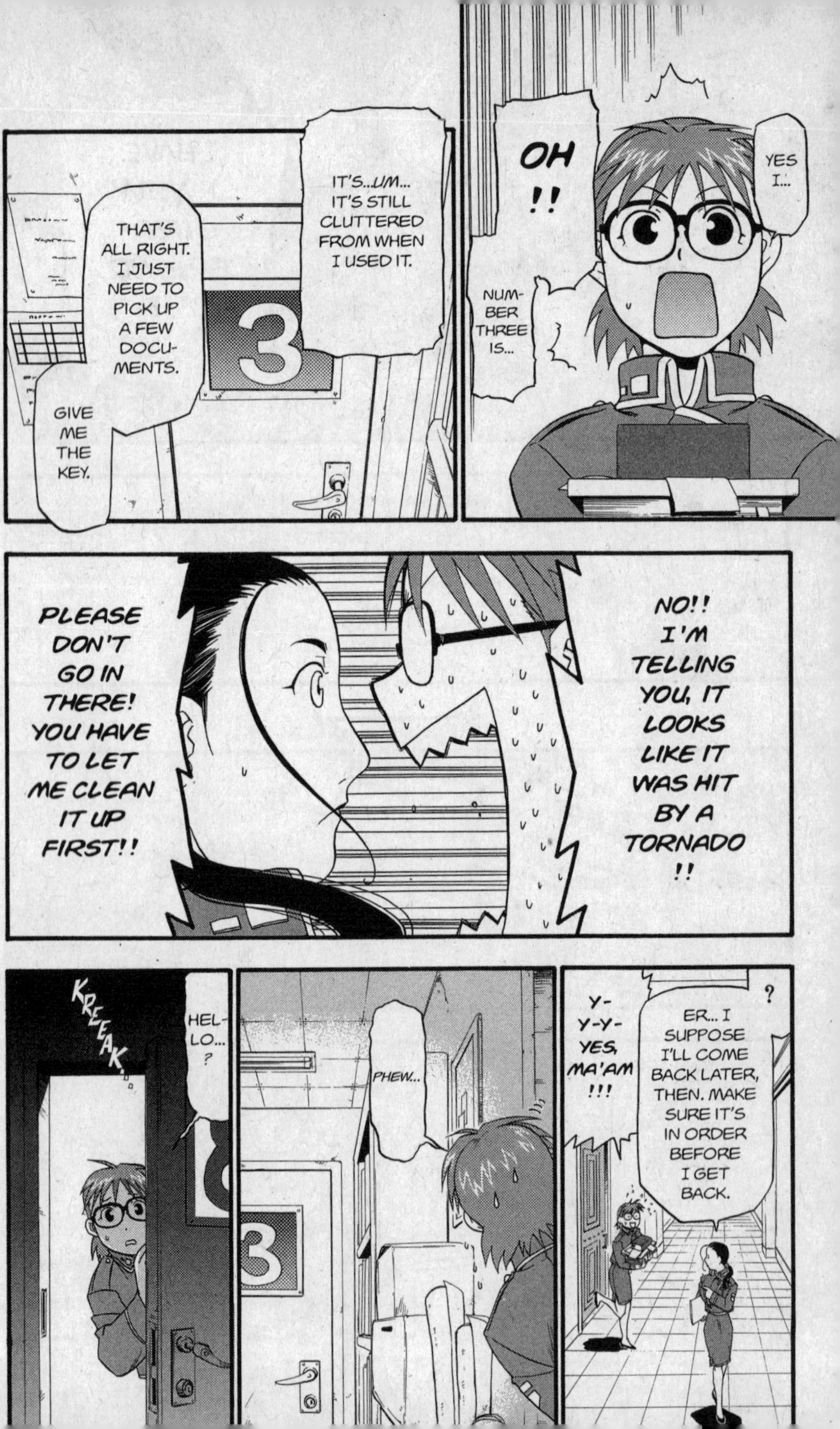
YES I...
OH!!
NUMBER THREE IS...
IT'S...UM... IT'S STILL CLUTTERED FROM WHEN I USED IT.
THAT'S ALL RIGHT. I JUST NEED TO PICK UP A FEW DOCUMENTS.
GIVE ME THE KEY.
NO!! I'M TELLING YOU, IT LOOKS LIKE IT WAS HIT BY A TORNADO!!
PLEASE DON'T GO IN THERE! YOU HAVE TO LET ME CLEAN IT UP FIRST!!
?
ER... I SUPPOSE I'LL COME BACK LATER, THEN. MAKE SURE IT'S IN ORDER BEFORE I GET BACK.
Y-Y-Y-YES, MA'AM!!!
PHEW...
HELLO...?
KREEAK...

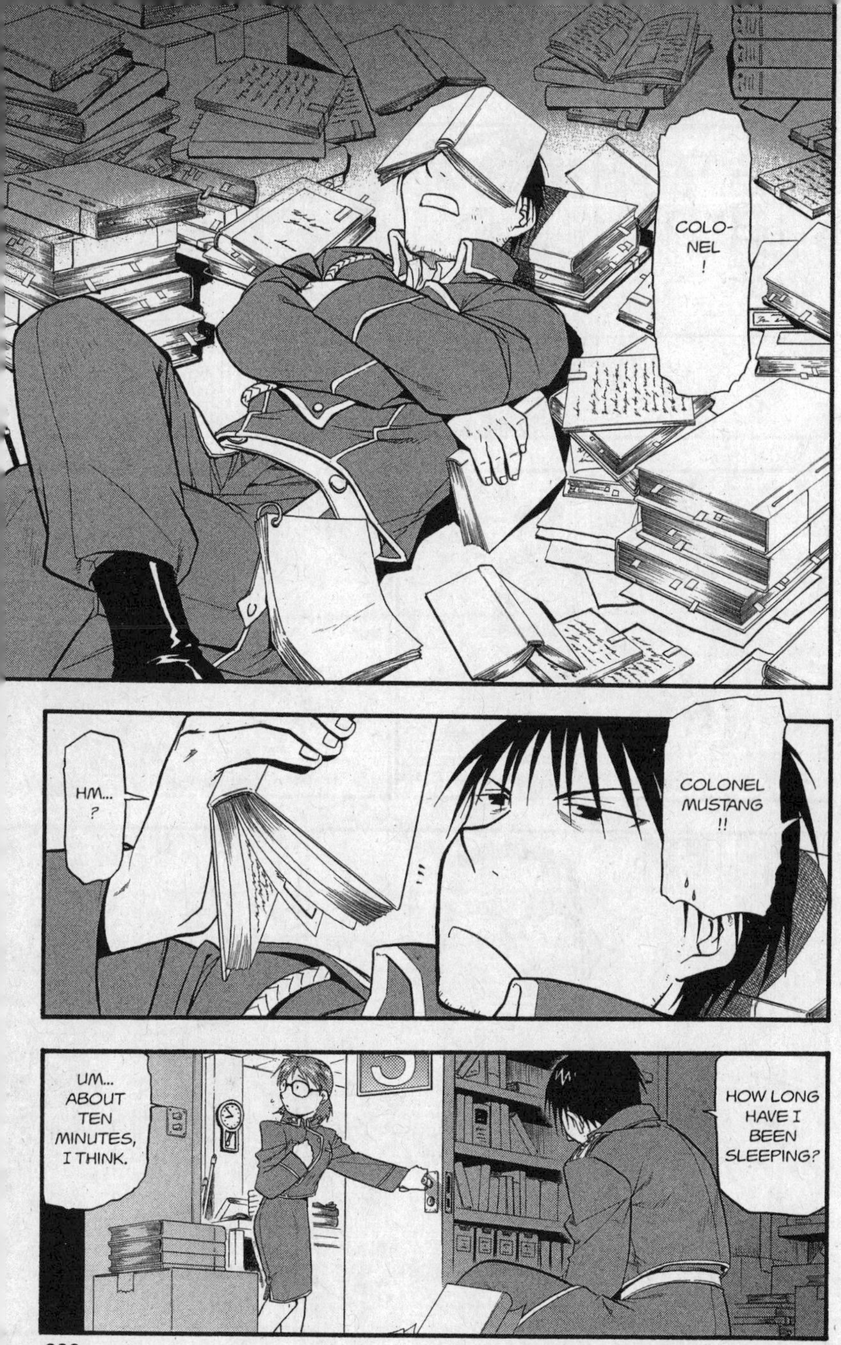
COLO-
NEL
!
COLONEL
MUSTANG
!!
HM...
?
HOW LONG
HAVE I
BEEN
SLEEPING?
UM...
ABOUT
TEN
MINUTES,
I THINK.

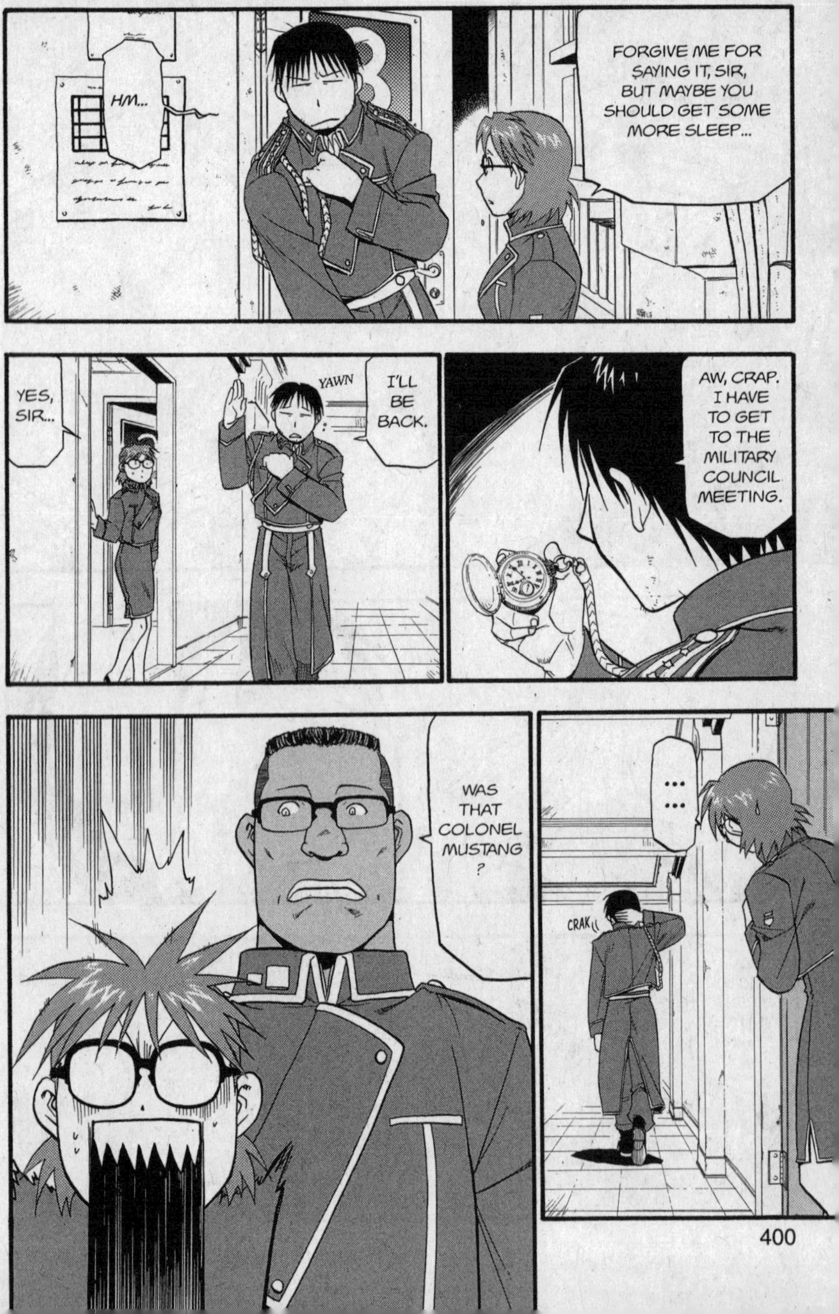
FORGIVE ME FOR SAYING IT, SIR, BUT MAYBE YOU SHOULD GET SOME MORE SLEEP...
HM...
AW, CRAP. I HAVE TO GET TO THE MILITARY COUNCIL MEETING.
I'LL BE BACK.
YAWN
YES, SIR...
......
CRAK
WAS THAT COLONEL MUSTANG?

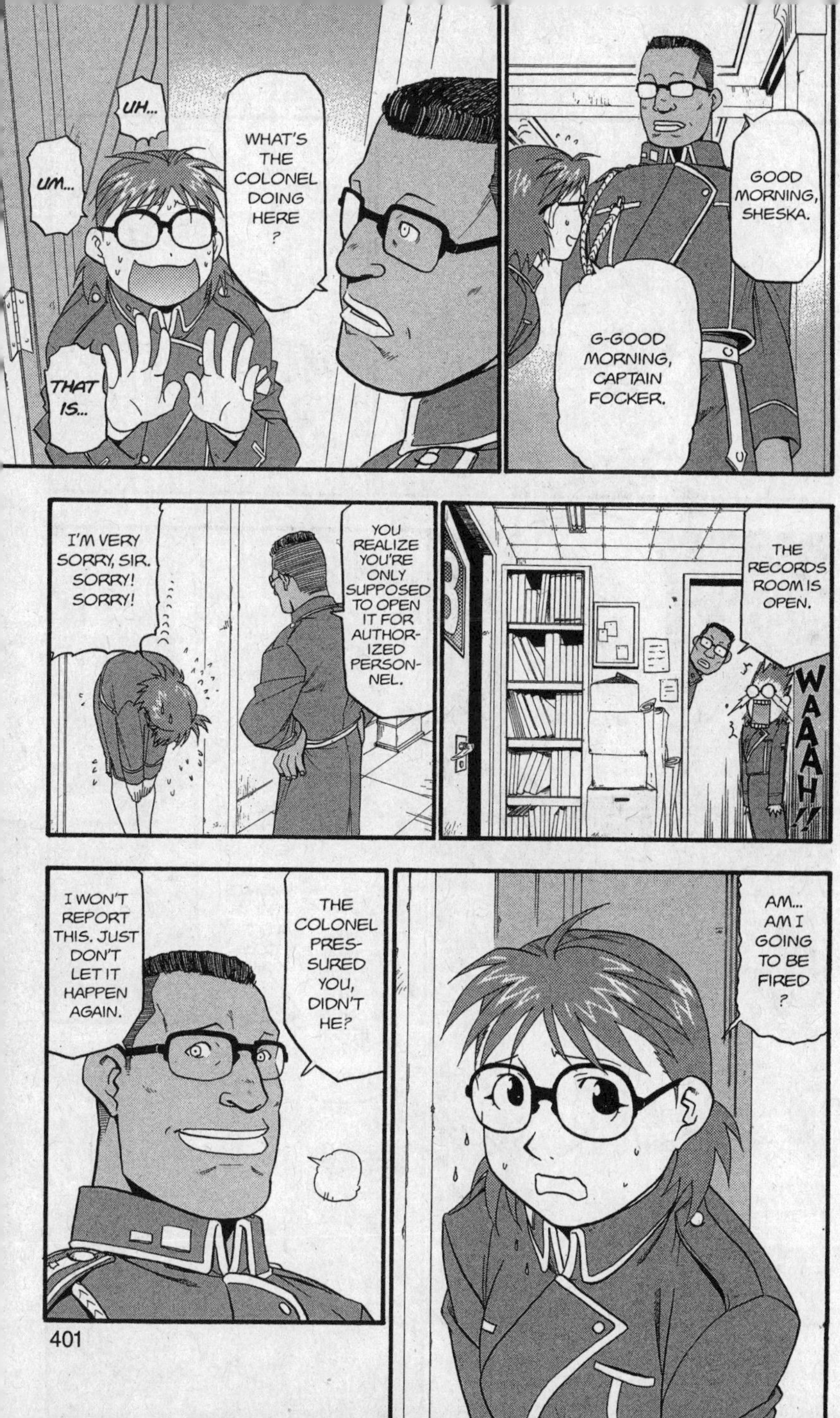
GOOD MORNING, SHESKA.
G-GOOD MORNING, CAPTAIN FOCKER.
WHAT'S THE COLONEL DOING HERE?
UH...
UM...
THAT IS...
THE RECORDS ROOM IS OPEN.
WAAAH!!
YOU REALIZE YOU'RE ONLY SUPPOSED TO OPEN IT FOR AUTHOR-IZED PERSON-NEL.
I'M VERY SORRY, SIR. SORRY! SORRY!
AM... AM I GOING TO BE FIRED?
THE COLONEL PRES-SURED YOU, DIDN'T HE?
I WON'T REPORT THIS. JUST DON'T LET IT HAPPEN AGAIN.

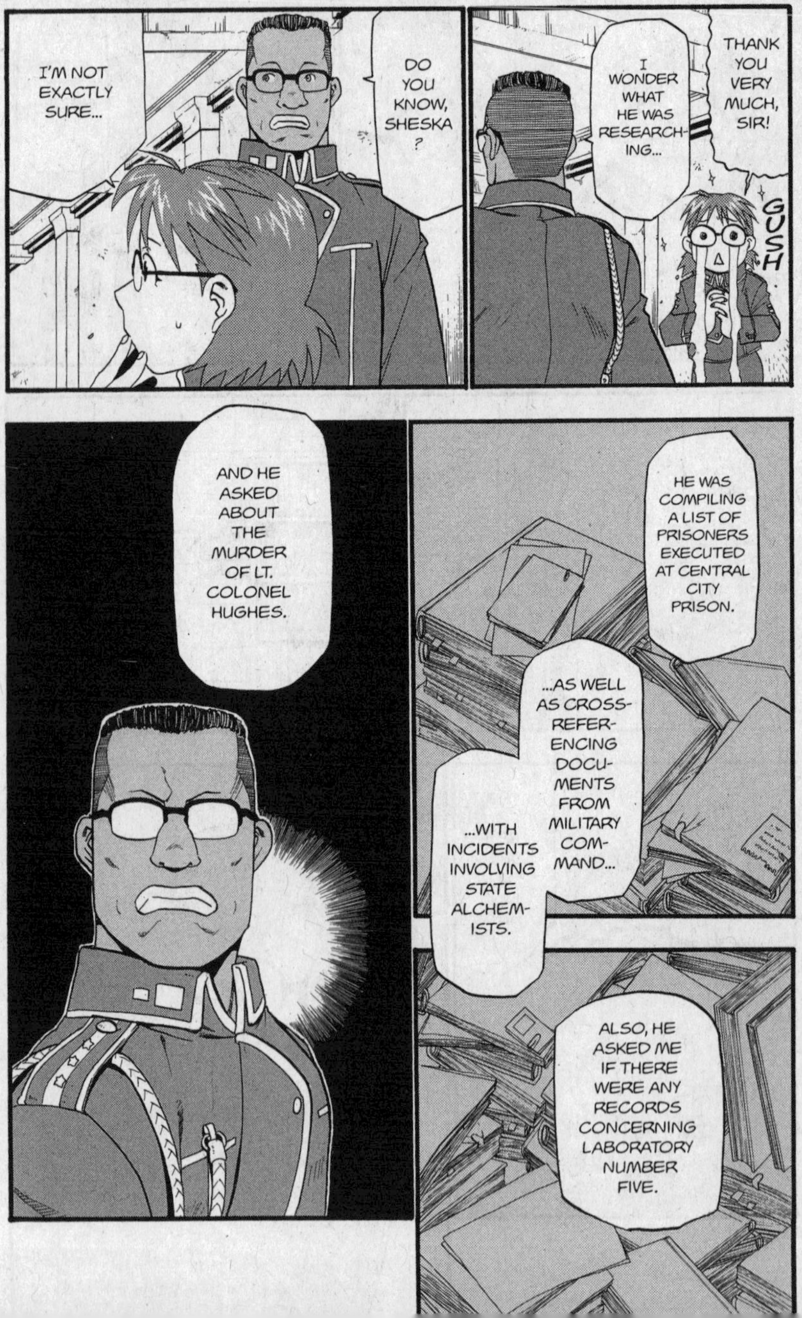
THANK YOU VERY MUCH, SIR!
I WONDER WHAT HE WAS RESEARCHING...
GUSH
DO YOU KNOW, SHESKA?
I'M NOT EXACTLY SURE...
HE WAS COMPILING A LIST OF PRISONERS EXECUTED AT CENTRAL CITY PRISON.
...AS WELL AS CROSS-REFERENCING DOCUMENTS FROM MILITARY COMMAND...
...WITH INCIDENTS INVOLVING STATE ALCHEMISTS.
ALSO, HE ASKED ME IF THERE WERE ANY RECORDS CONCERNING LABORATORY NUMBER FIVE.
AND HE ASKED ABOUT THE MURDER OF LT. COLONEL HUGHES.

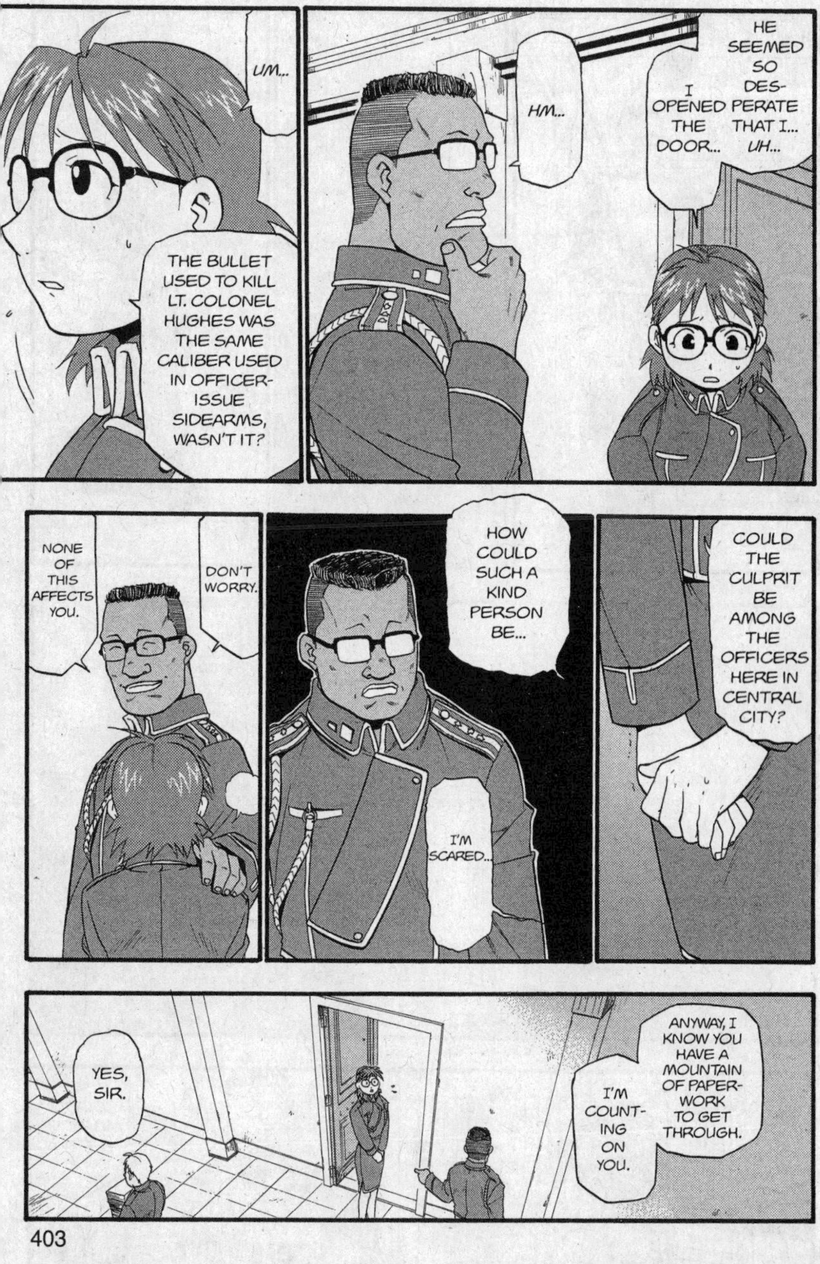
HE SEEMED SO DESPERATE THAT I... UH...
I OPENED THE DOOR...
HM...
UM...
THE BULLET USED TO KILL LT. COLONEL HUGHES WAS THE SAME CALIBER USED IN OFFICER-ISSUE SIDEARMS, WASN'T IT?
COULD THE CULPRIT BE AMONG THE OFFICERS HERE IN CENTRAL CITY?
HOW COULD SUCH A KIND PERSON BE...
I'M SCARED...
DON'T WORRY.
NONE OF THIS AFFECTS YOU.
ANYWAY, I KNOW YOU HAVE A MOUNTAIN OF PAPERWORK TO GET THROUGH.
I'M COUNTING ON YOU.
YES, SIR.

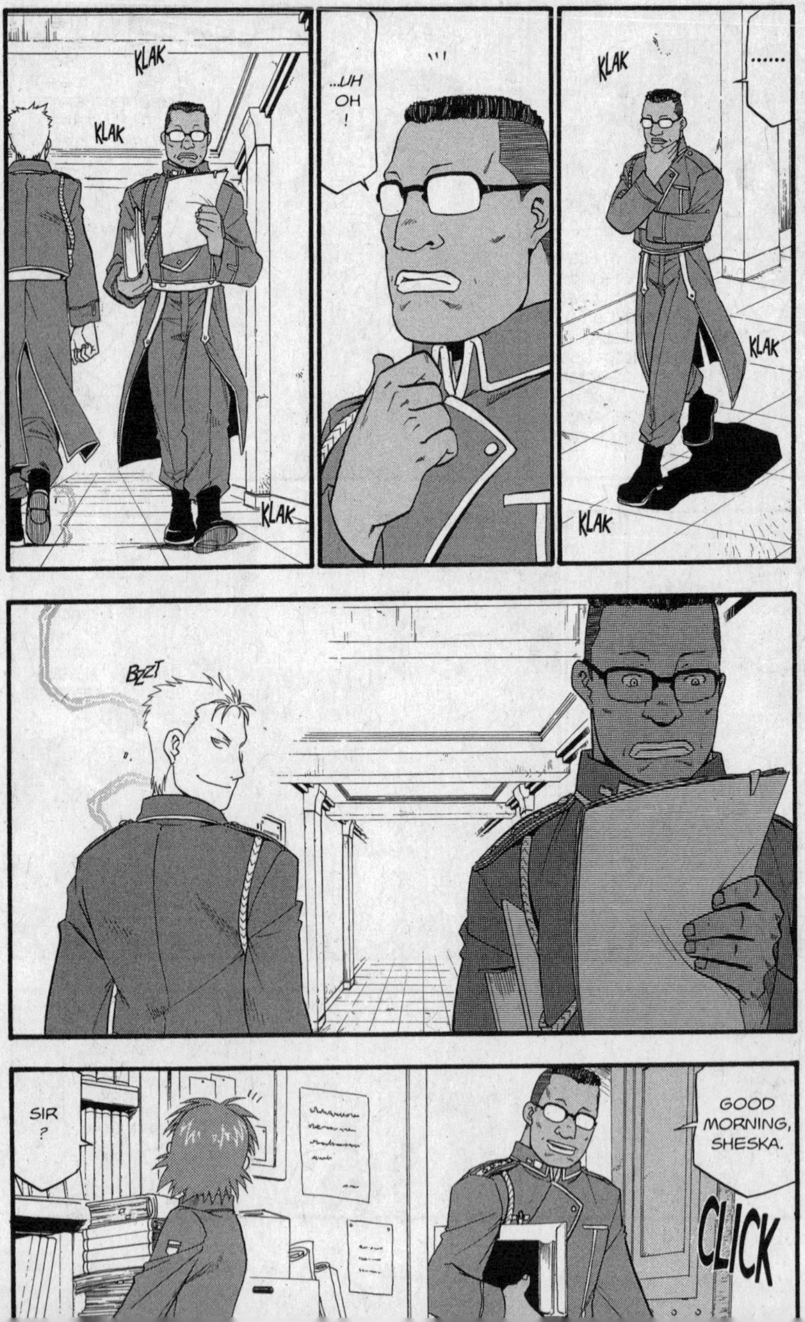
KLAK
......
KLAK
KLAK
...UH OH!
KLAK
KLAK
KLAK
BZZT
GOOD MORNING, SHESKA.
CLICK
SIR?

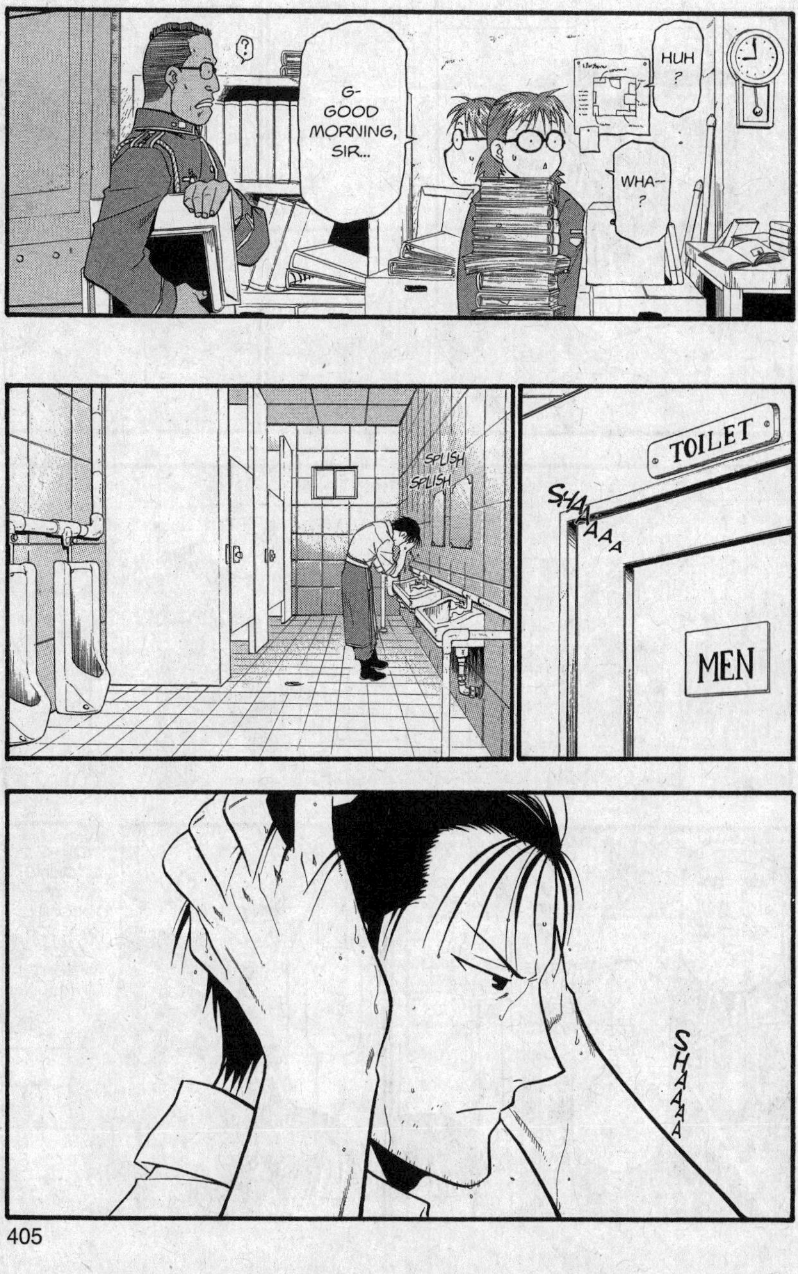
HUH ?
?
G-GOOD MORNING, SIR...
WHA-- ?
TOILET
SHAAAAAA
MEN
SPLISH
SPLISH
SHAAAAA

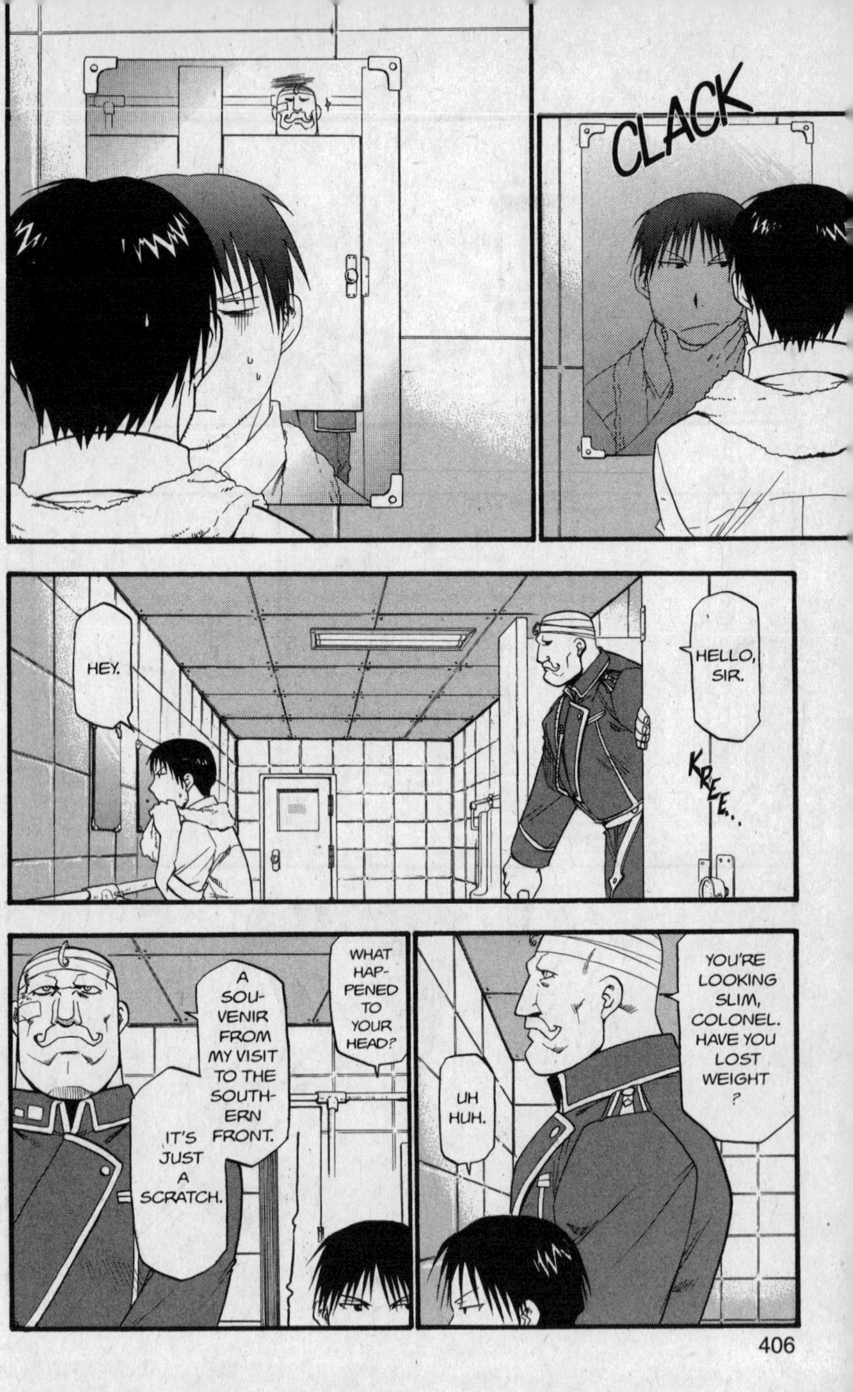
CLACK
HELLO, SIR.
KREEE...
HEY.
YOU'RE LOOKING SLIM, COLONEL. HAVE YOU LOST WEIGHT?
UH HUH.
WHAT HAPPENED TO YOUR HEAD?
A SOUVENIR FROM MY VISIT TO THE SOUTHERN FRONT.
IT'S JUST A SCRATCH.

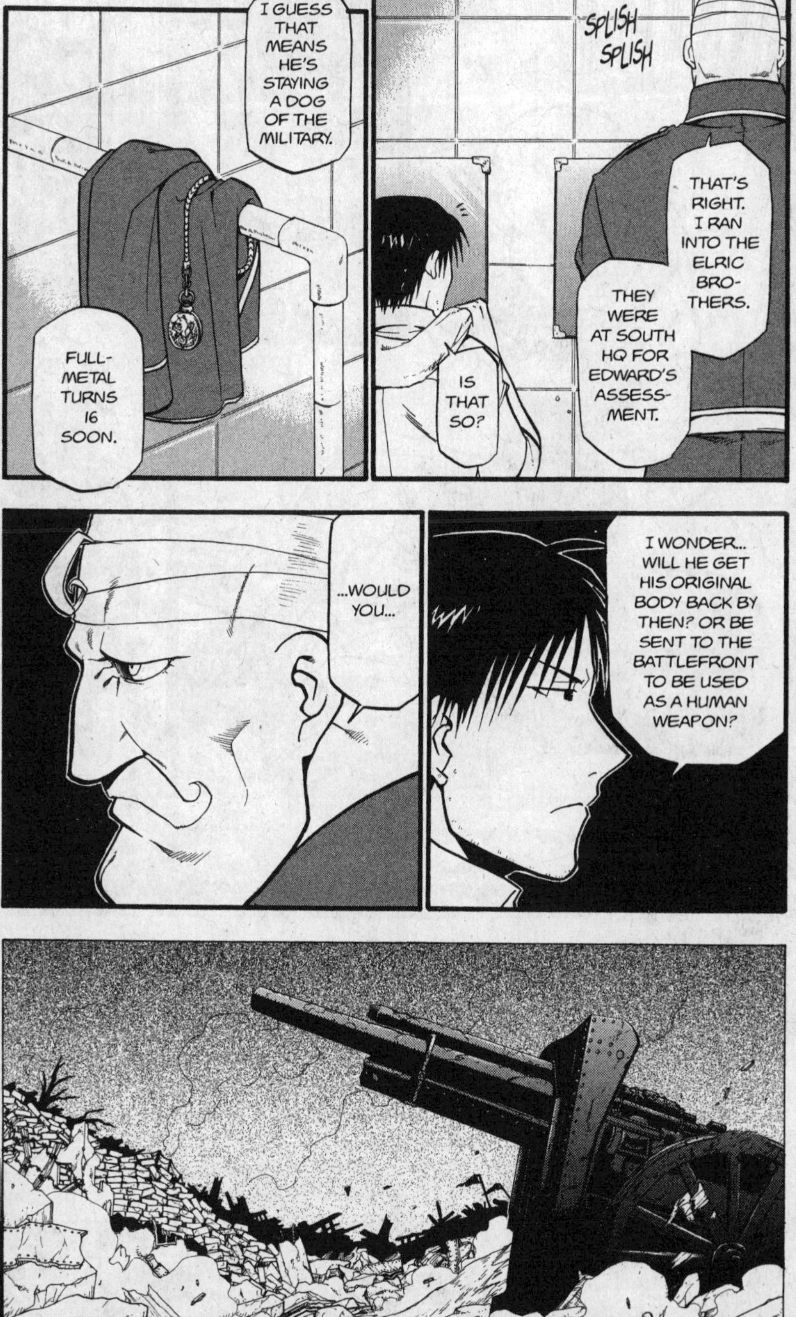
SPLISH SPLISH
THAT'S RIGHT. I RAN INTO THE ELRIC BROTHERS.
THEY WERE AT SOUTH HQ FOR EDWARD'S ASSESSMENT.
IS THAT SO?
I GUESS THAT MEANS HE'S STAYING A DOG OF THE MILITARY.
FULL-METAL TURNS 16 SOON.
I WONDER... WILL HE GET HIS ORIGINAL BODY BACK BY THEN? OR BE SENT TO THE BATTLEFRONT TO BE USED AS A HUMAN WEAPON?
...WOULD YOU...

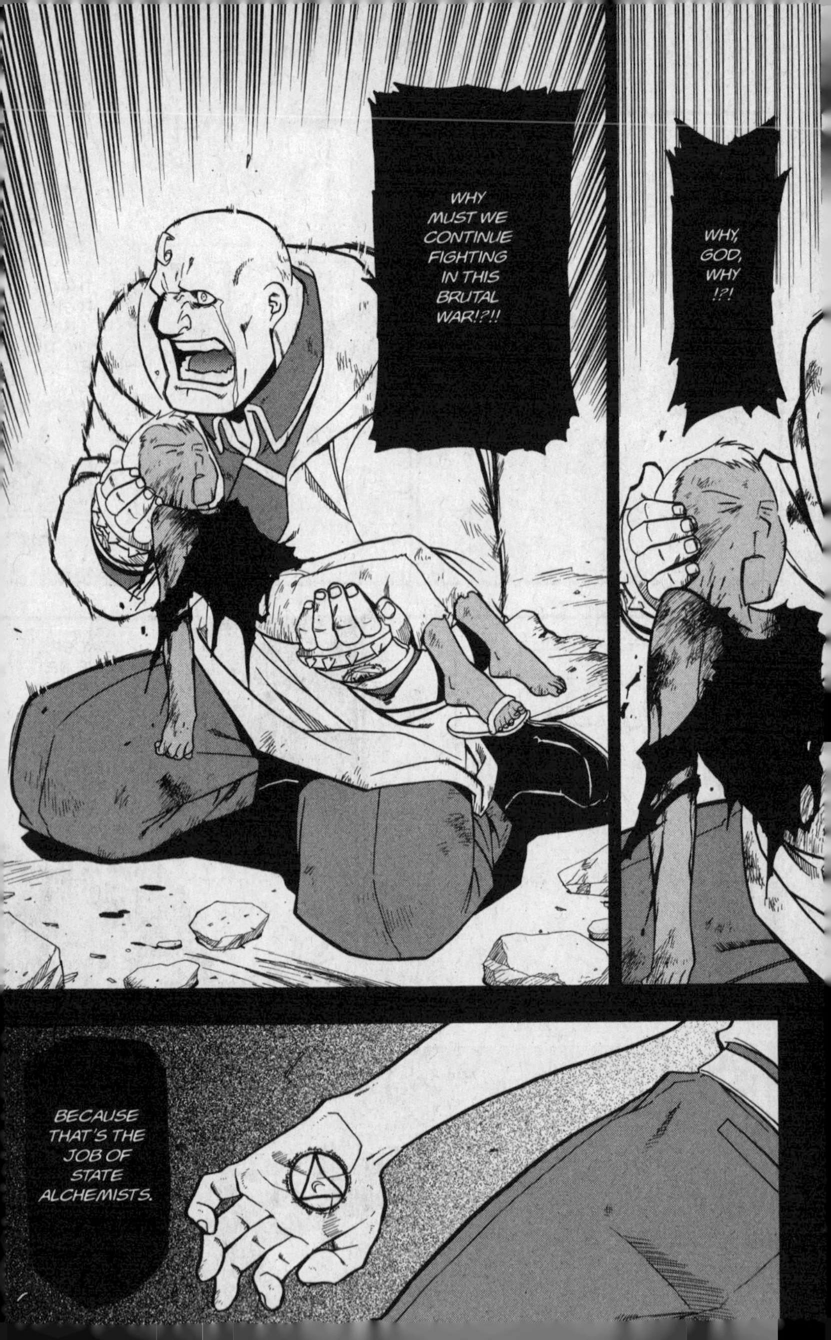
WHY, GOD, WHY !?!
WHY MUST WE CONTINUE FIGHTING IN THIS BRUTAL WAR!?!!
BECAUSE THAT'S THE JOB OF STATE ALCHEMISTS.

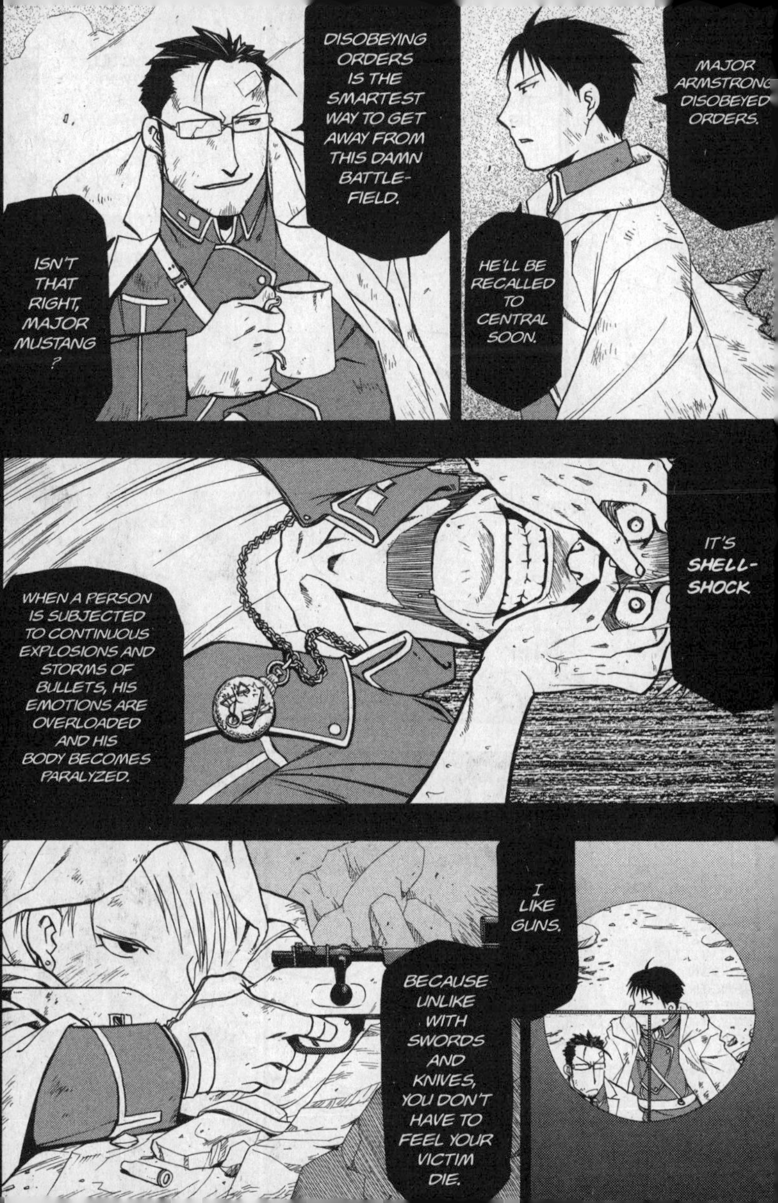
MAJOR ARMSTRONG DISOBEYED ORDERS.
HE'LL BE RECALLED TO CENTRAL SOON.
DISOBEYING ORDERS IS THE SMARTEST WAY TO GET AWAY FROM THIS DAMN BATTLE-FIELD.
ISN'T THAT RIGHT, MAJOR MUSTANG ?
IT'S SHELL-SHOCK.
WHEN A PERSON IS SUBJECTED TO CONTINUOUS EXPLOSIONS AND STORMS OF BULLETS, HIS EMOTIONS ARE OVERLOADED AND HIS BODY BECOMES PARALYZED.
I LIKE GUNS.
BECAUSE UNLIKE WITH SWORDS AND KNIVES, YOU DON'T HAVE TO FEEL YOUR VICTIM DIE.

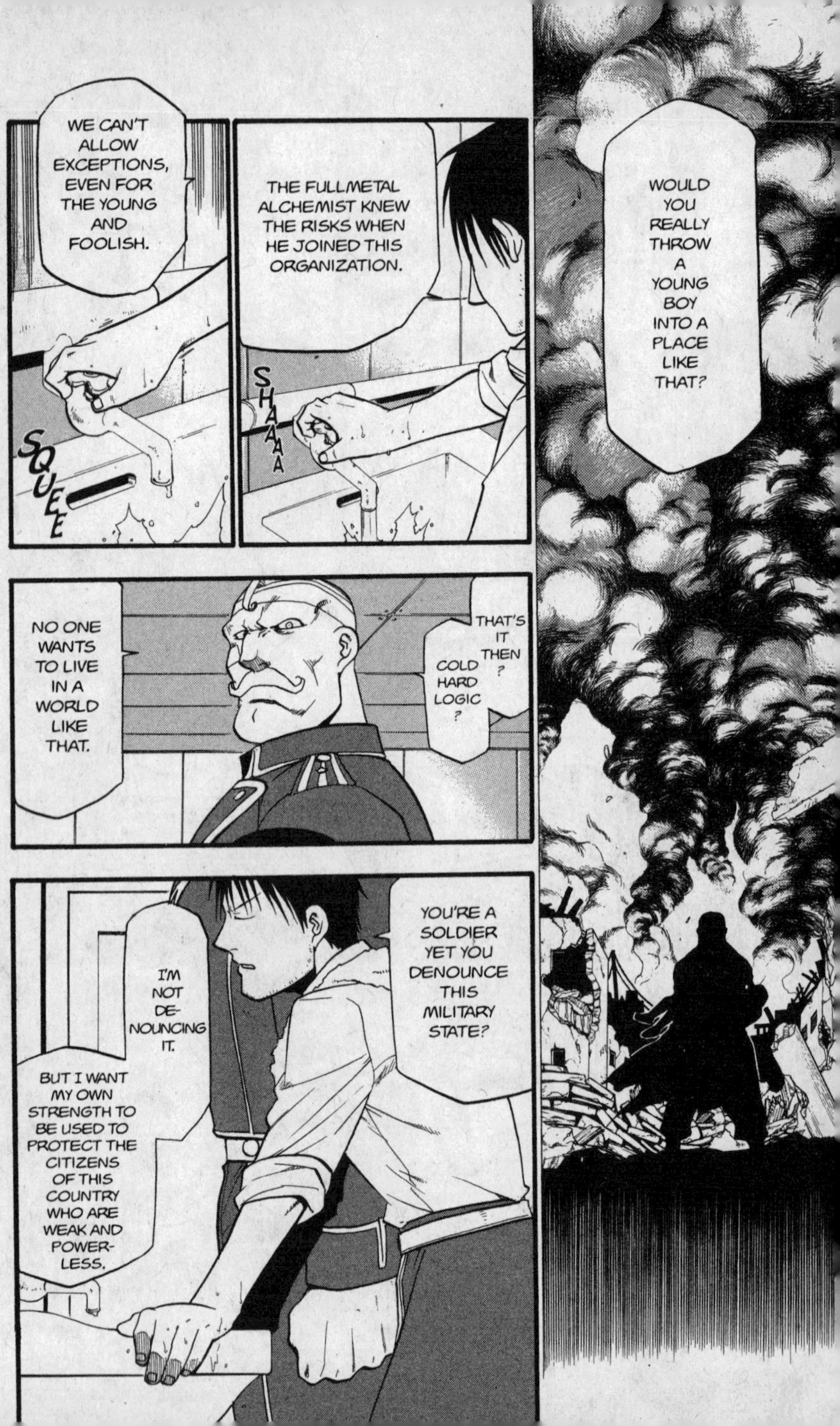
WOULD YOU REALLY THROW A YOUNG BOY INTO A PLACE LIKE THAT?
THE FULLMETAL ALCHEMIST KNEW THE RISKS WHEN HE JOINED THIS ORGANIZATION.
SHAAAA
WE CAN'T ALLOW EXCEPTIONS, EVEN FOR THE YOUNG AND FOOLISH.
SQUEE
THAT'S IT THEN?
COLD HARD LOGIC?
NO ONE WANTS TO LIVE IN A WORLD LIKE THAT.
YOU'RE A SOLDIER YET YOU DENOUNCE THIS MILITARY STATE?
I'M NOT DE-NOUNCING IT.
BUT I WANT MY OWN STRENGTH TO BE USED TO PROTECT THE CITIZENS OF THIS COUNTRY WHO ARE WEAK AND POWER-LESS.

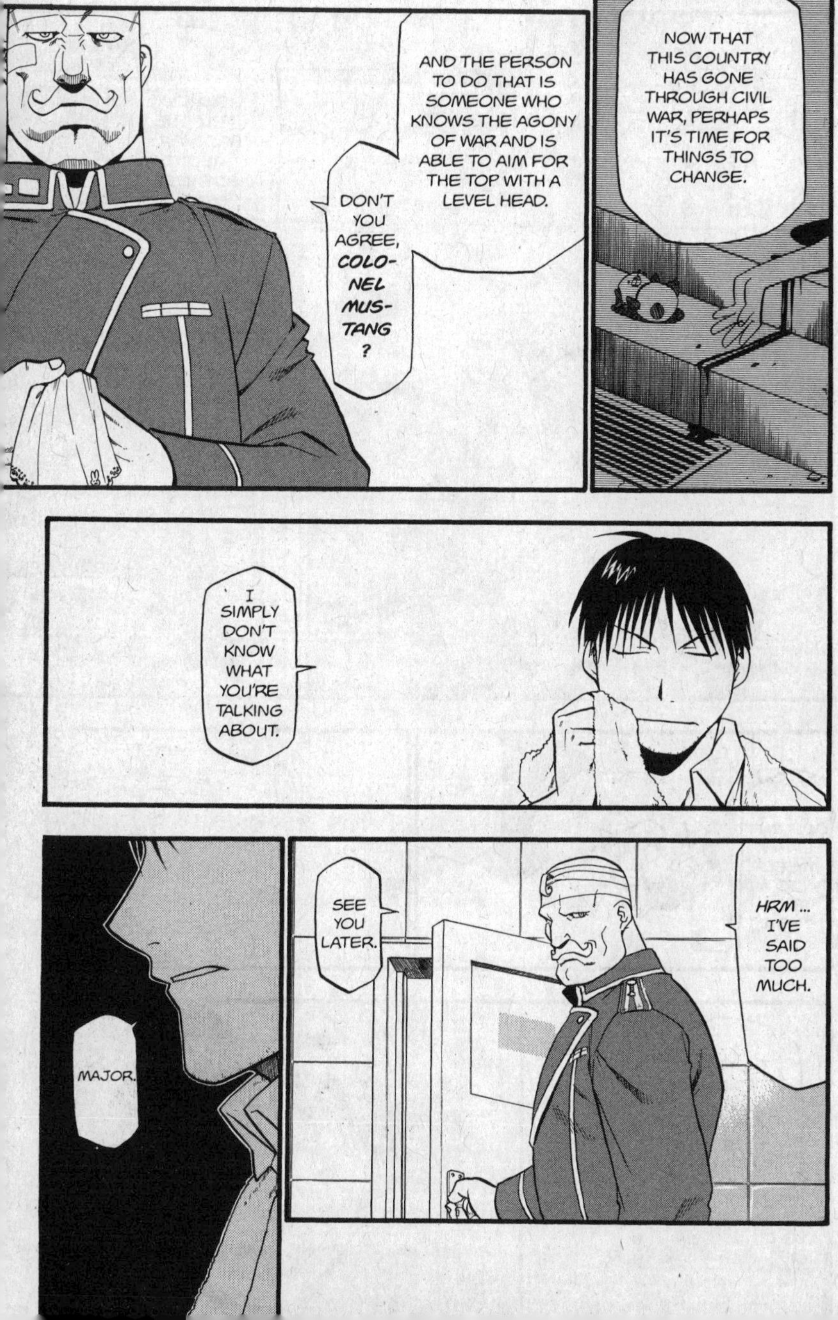
NOW THAT THIS COUNTRY HAS GONE THROUGH CIVIL WAR, PERHAPS IT'S TIME FOR THINGS TO CHANGE.
AND THE PERSON TO DO THAT IS SOMEONE WHO KNOWS THE AGONY OF WAR AND IS ABLE TO AIM FOR THE TOP WITH A LEVEL HEAD.
DON'T YOU AGREE, *COLONEL MUSTANG?*
I SIMPLY DON'T KNOW WHAT YOU'RE TALKING ABOUT.
HRM ... I'VE SAID TOO MUCH.
SEE YOU LATER.
MAJOR.

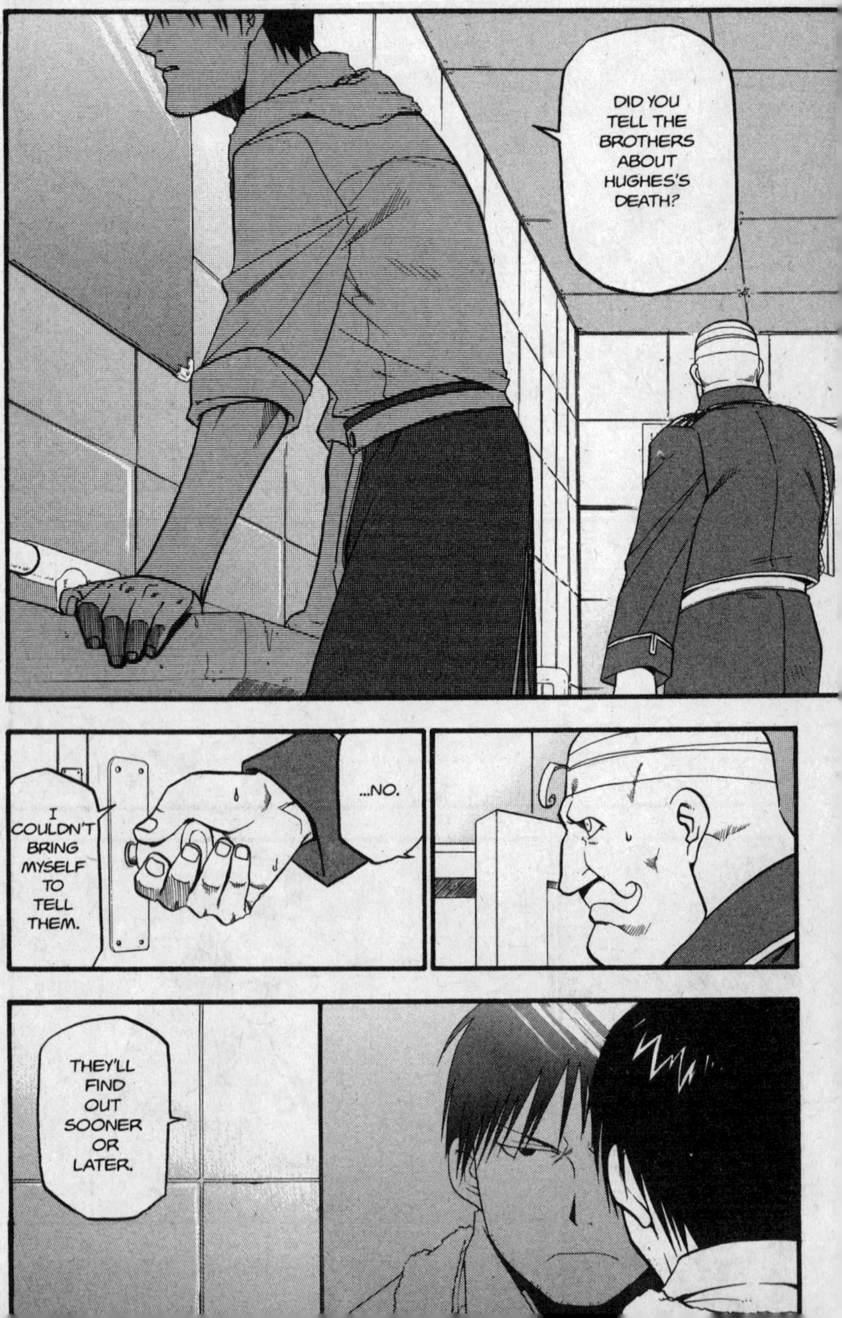
DID YOU TELL THE BROTHERS ABOUT HUGHES'S DEATH?
...NO.
I COULDN'T BRING MYSELF TO TELL THEM.
THEY'LL FIND OUT SOONER OR LATER.

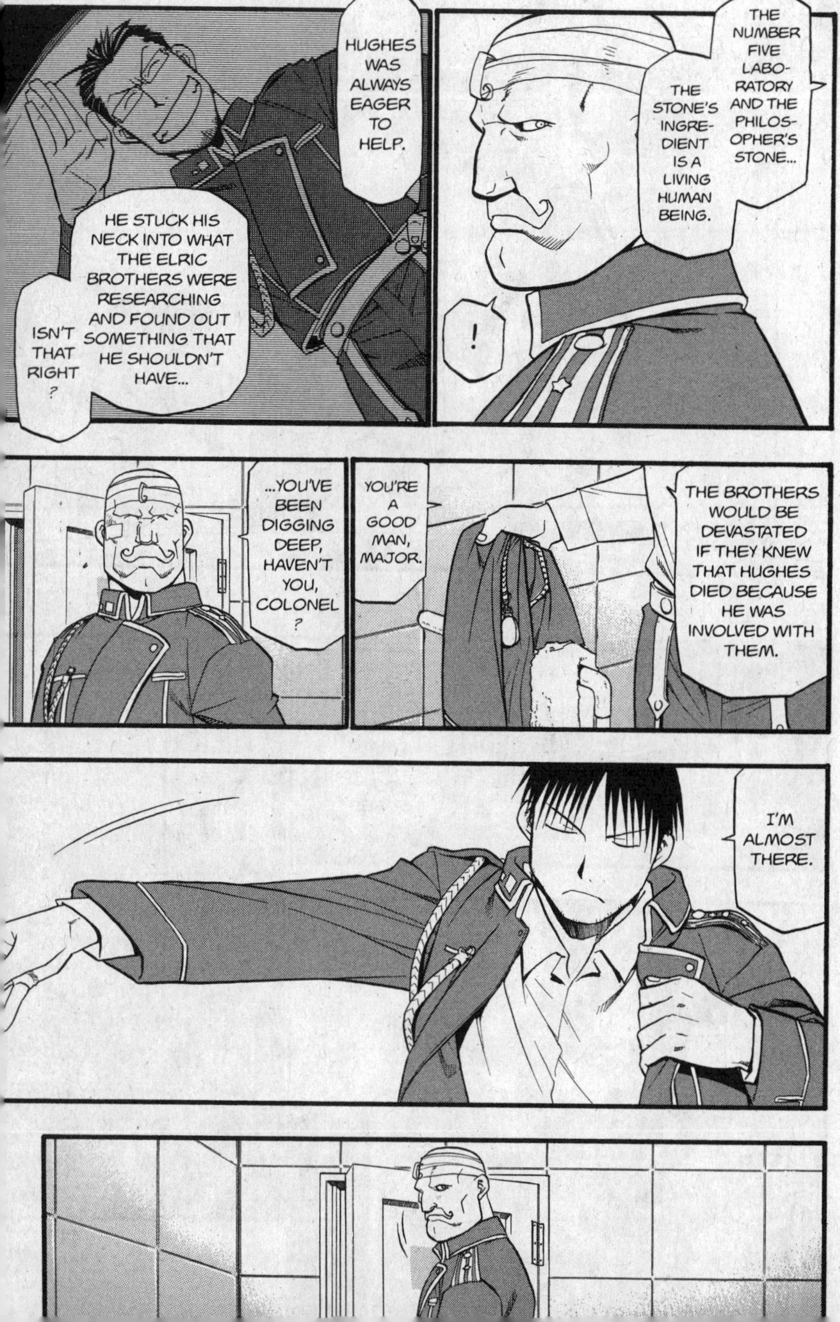
THE NUMBER FIVE LABORATORY AND THE PHILOSOPHER'S STONE...
THE STONE'S INGREDIENT IS A LIVING HUMAN BEING.
!
HUGHES WAS ALWAYS EAGER TO HELP.
HE STUCK HIS NECK INTO WHAT THE ELRIC BROTHERS WERE RESEARCHING AND FOUND OUT SOMETHING THAT HE SHOULDN'T HAVE...
ISN'T THAT RIGHT?
THE BROTHERS WOULD BE DEVASTATED IF THEY KNEW THAT HUGHES DIED BECAUSE HE WAS INVOLVED WITH THEM.
YOU'RE A GOOD MAN, MAJOR.
...YOU'VE BEEN DIGGING DEEP, HAVEN'T YOU, COLONEL?
I'M ALMOST THERE.

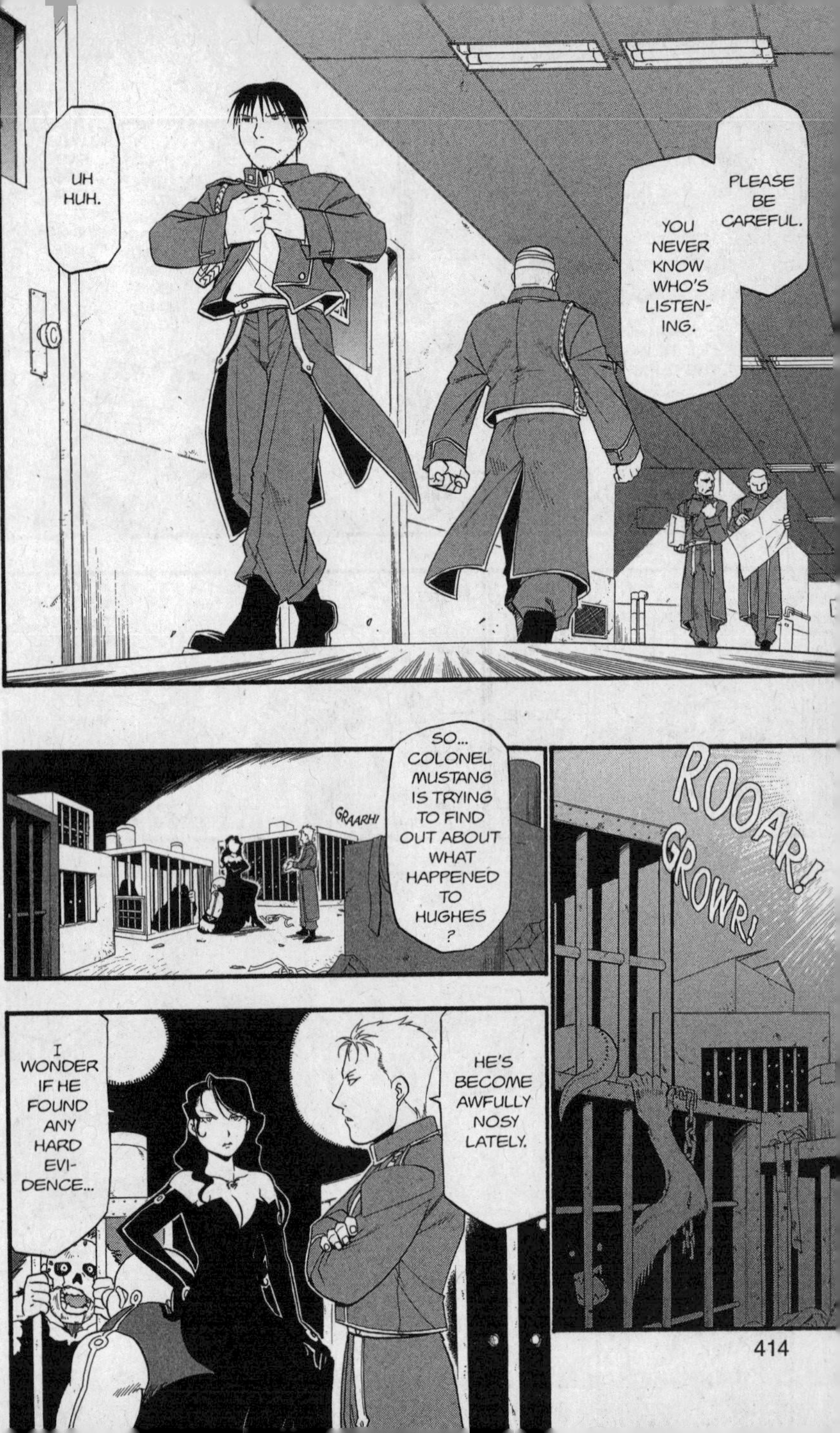
PLEASE BE CAREFUL.
YOU NEVER KNOW WHO'S LISTEN-ING.
UH HUH.
ROOAR!
GROWR!
SO... COLONEL MUSTANG IS TRYING TO FIND OUT ABOUT WHAT HAPPENED TO HUGHES ?
GRAARH!
HE'S BECOME AWFULLY NOSY LATELY.
I WONDER IF HE FOUND ANY HARD EVI-DENCE...

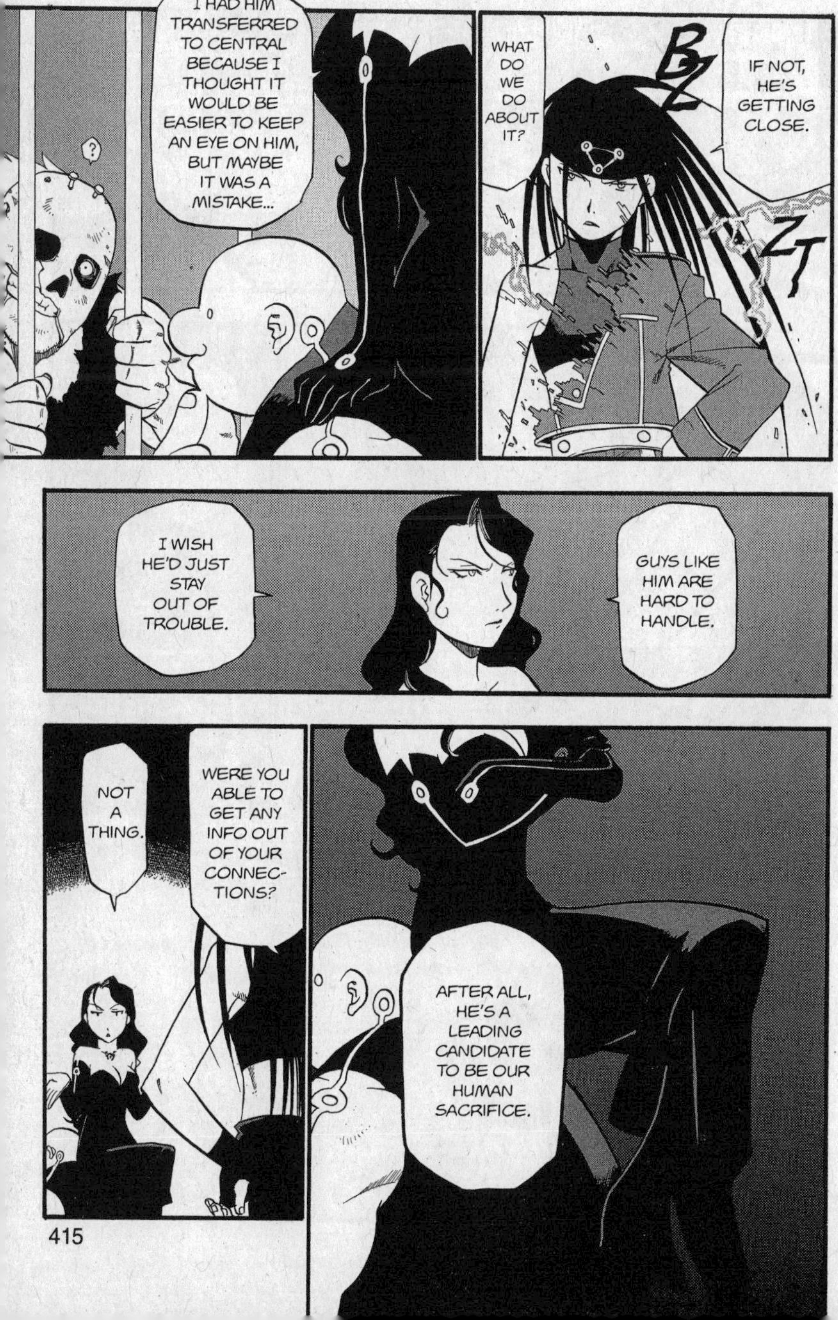
BZZT
IF NOT, HE'S GETTING CLOSE.
WHAT DO WE DO ABOUT IT?
I HAD HIM TRANSFERRED TO CENTRAL BECAUSE I THOUGHT IT WOULD BE EASIER TO KEEP AN EYE ON HIM, BUT MAYBE IT WAS A MISTAKE...
?
GUYS LIKE HIM ARE HARD TO HANDLE.
I WISH HE'D JUST STAY OUT OF TROUBLE.
AFTER ALL, HE'S A LEADING CANDIDATE TO BE OUR HUMAN SACRIFICE.
WERE YOU ABLE TO GET ANY INFO OUT OF YOUR CONNECTIONS?
NOT A THING.

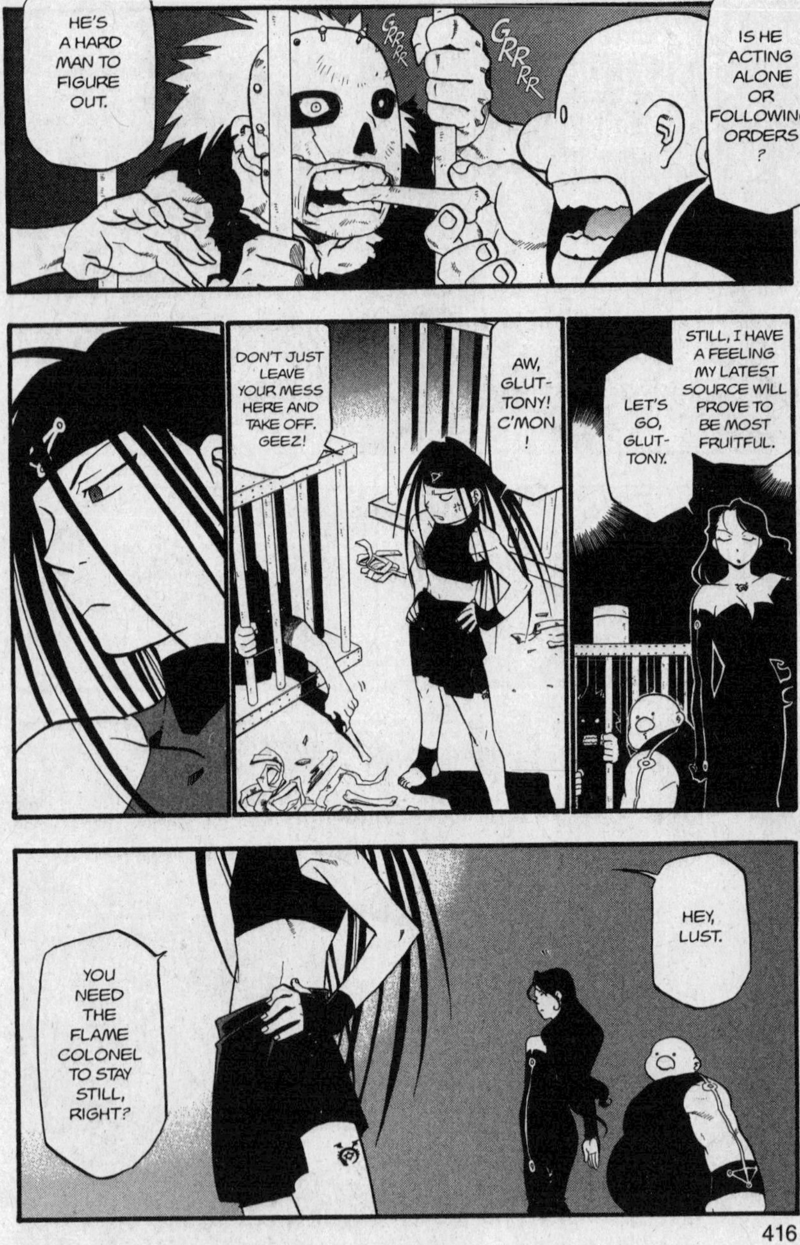
IS HE ACTING ALONE OR FOLLOWING ORDERS?
GRRRR
GRRRR
HE'S A HARD MAN TO FIGURE OUT.
STILL, I HAVE A FEELING MY LATEST SOURCE WILL PROVE TO BE MOST FRUITFUL.
LET'S GO, GLUTTONY.
AW, GLUTTONY! C'MON!
DON'T JUST LEAVE YOUR MESS HERE AND TAKE OFF. GEEZ!
HEY, LUST.
YOU NEED THE FLAME COLONEL TO STAY STILL, RIGHT?

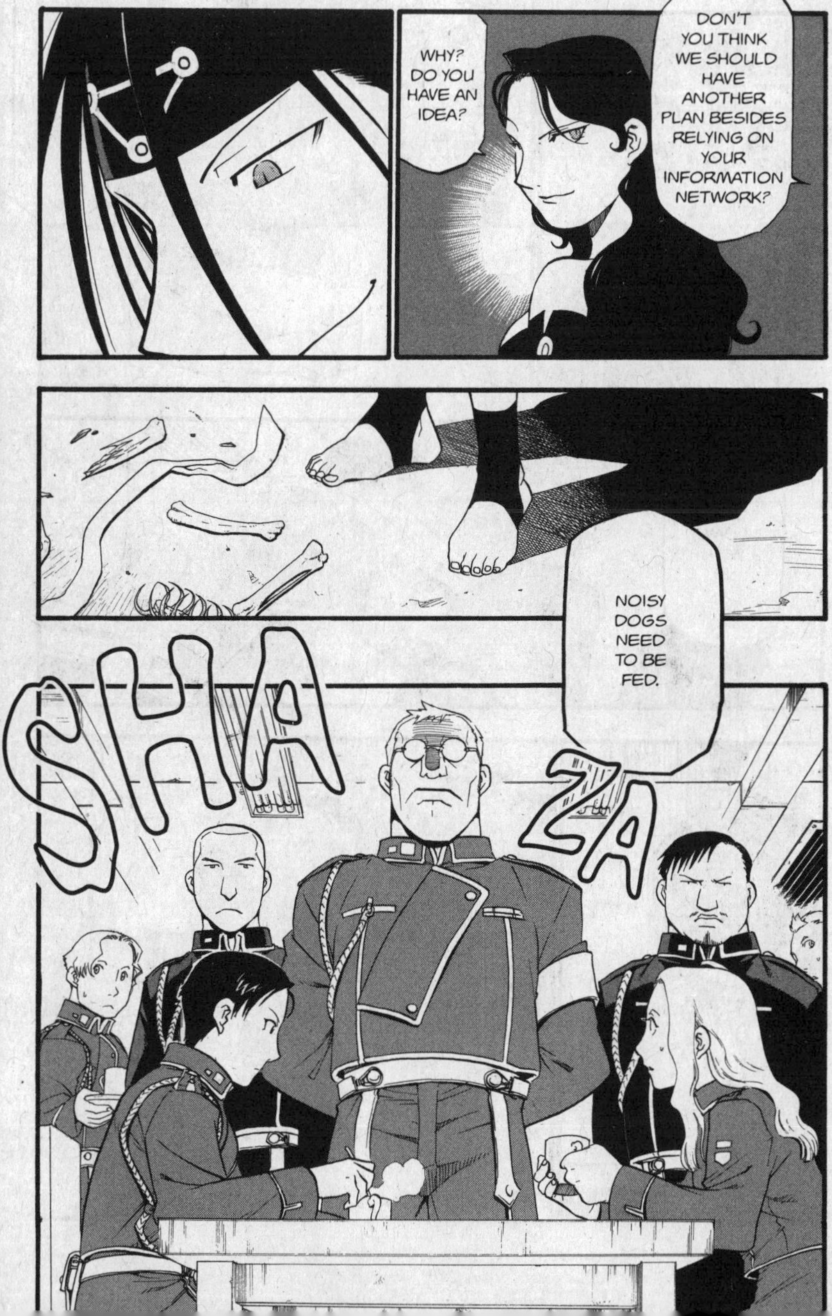
DON'T YOU THINK WE SHOULD HAVE ANOTHER PLAN BESIDES RELYING ON YOUR INFORMATION NETWORK?
WHY? DO YOU HAVE AN IDEA?
NOISY DOGS NEED TO BE FED.
SHA
ZA

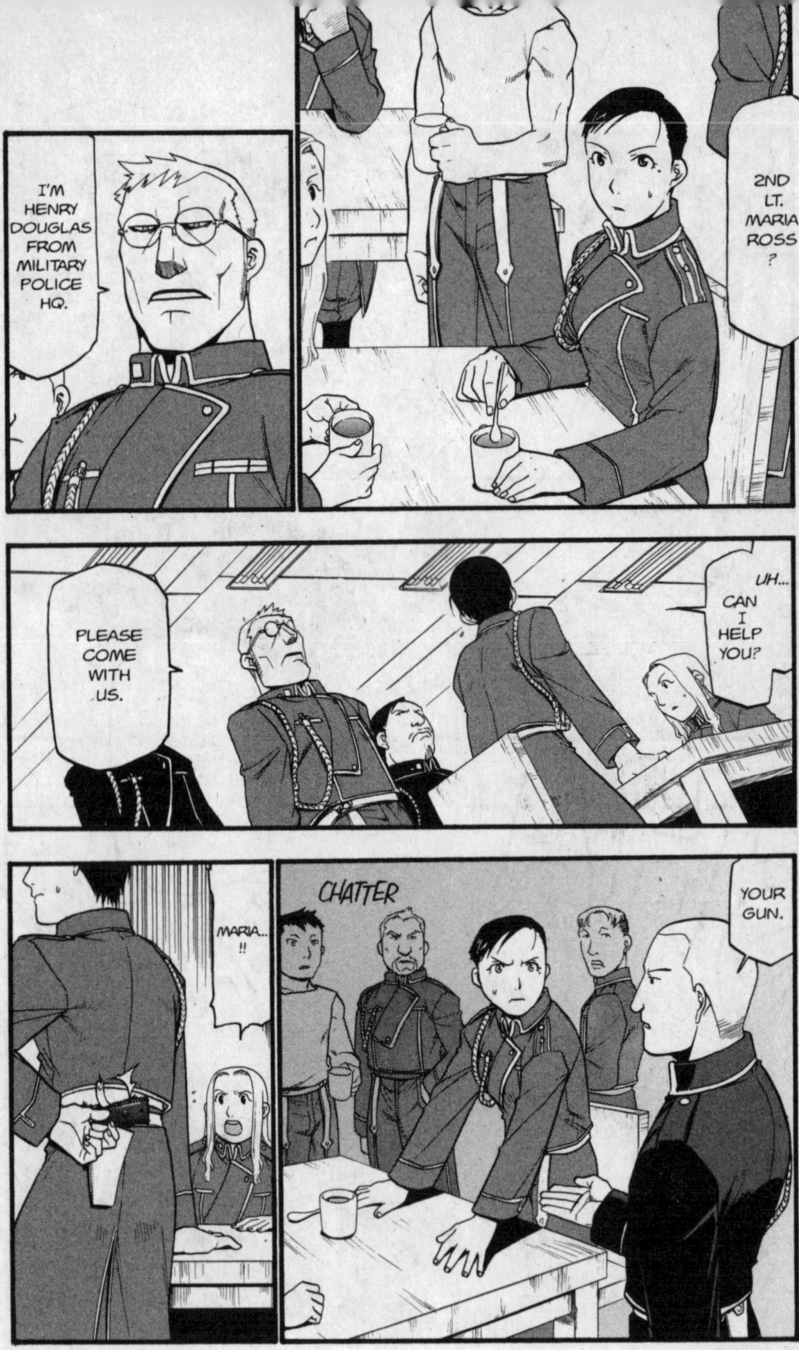
2ND LT. MARIA ROSS?
I'M HENRY DOUGLAS FROM MILITARY POLICE HQ.
UH... CAN I HELP YOU?
PLEASE COME WITH US.
YOUR GUN.
CHATTER
MARIA...!!

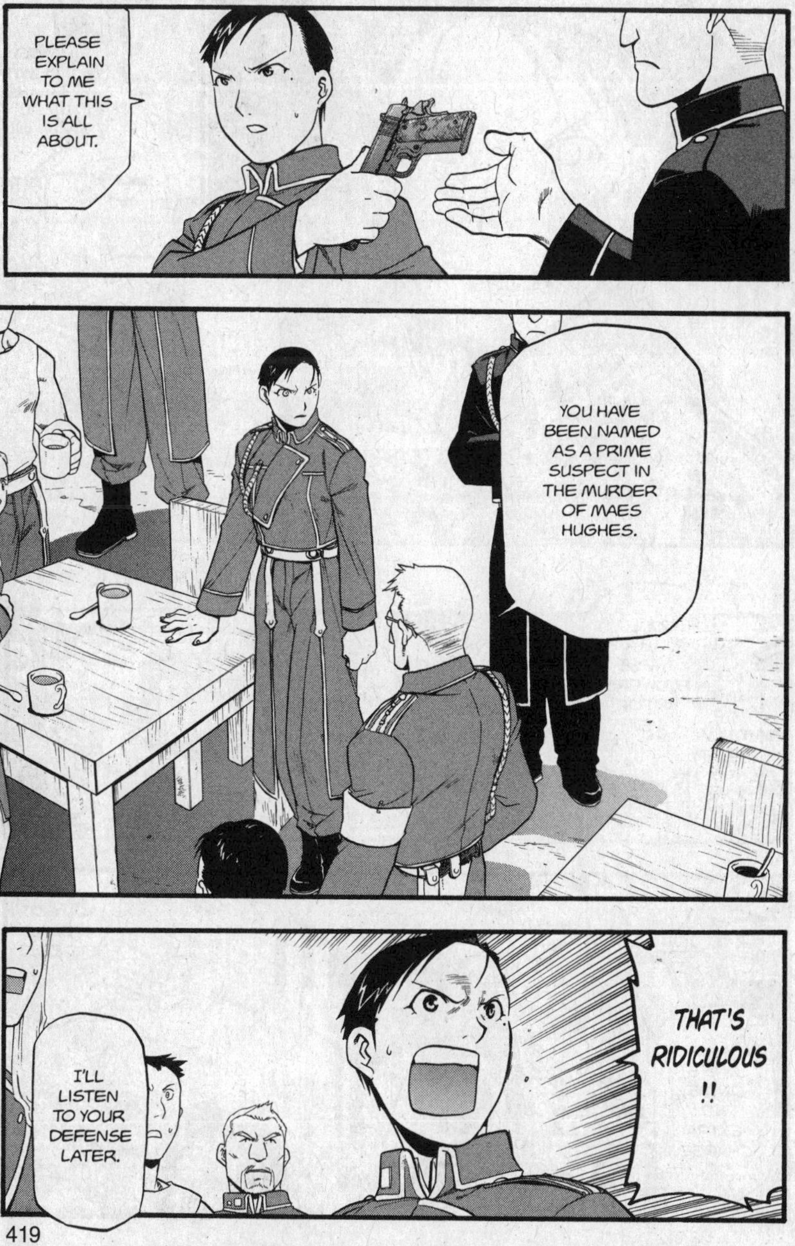
PLEASE EXPLAIN TO ME WHAT THIS IS ALL ABOUT.
YOU HAVE BEEN NAMED AS A PRIME SUSPECT IN THE MURDER OF MAES HUGHES.
THAT'S RIDICULOUS !!
I'LL LISTEN TO YOUR DEFENSE LATER.

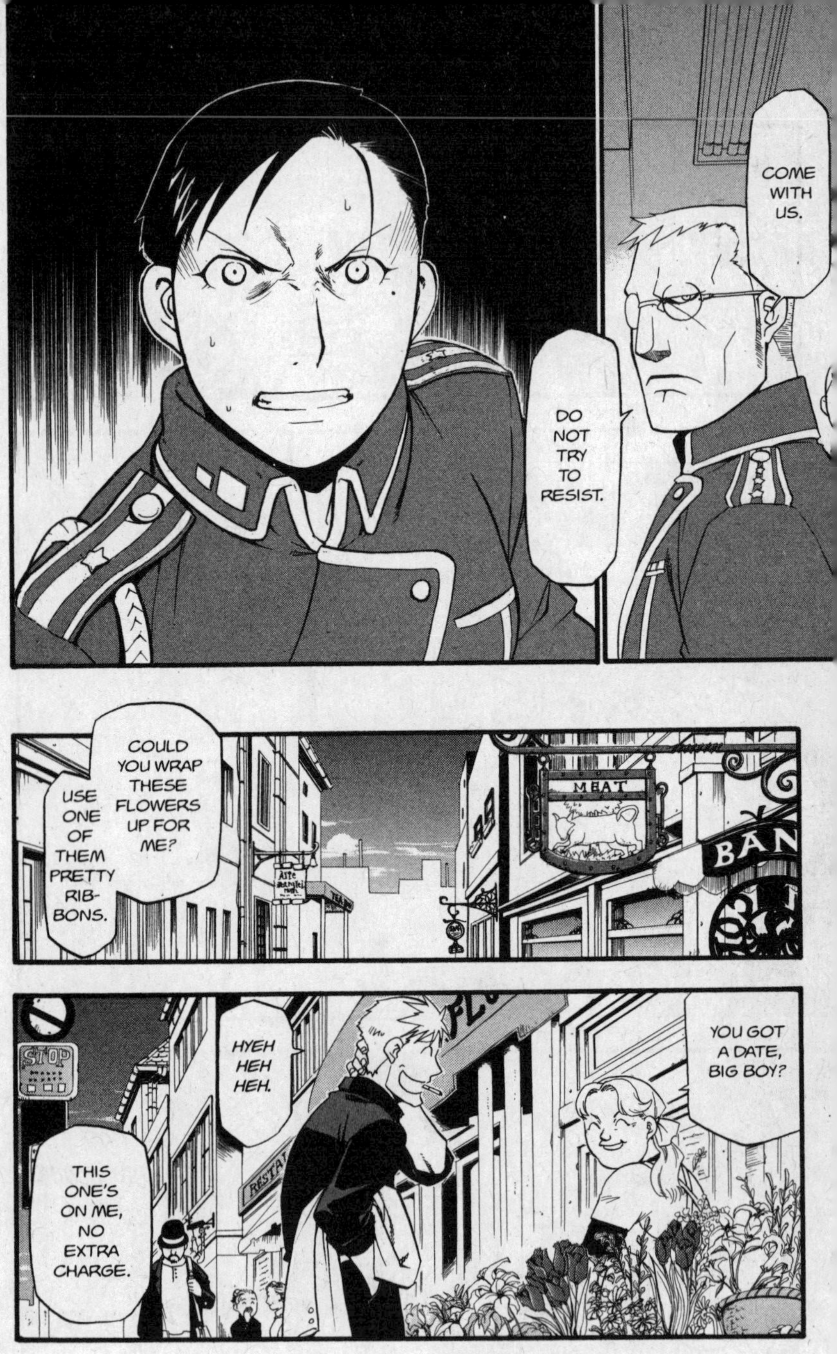
COME WITH US.
DO NOT TRY TO RESIST.
MEAT
COULD YOU WRAP THESE FLOWERS UP FOR ME?
USE ONE OF THEM PRETTY RIB-BONS.
YOU GOT A DATE, BIG BOY?
HYEH HEH HEH.
STOP
THIS ONE'S ON ME, NO EXTRA CHARGE.

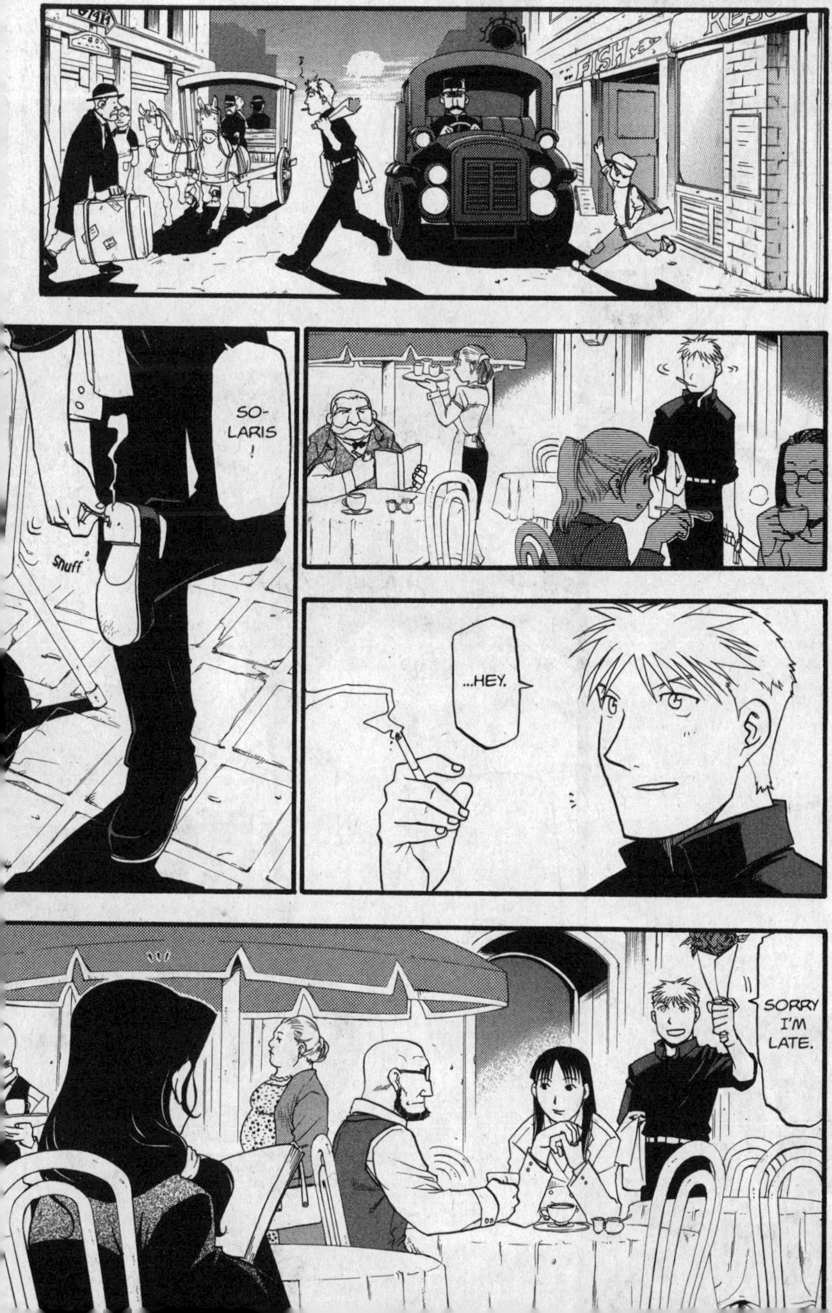
FISH
...HEY.
SO-LARIS!
snuff
SORRY I'M LATE.

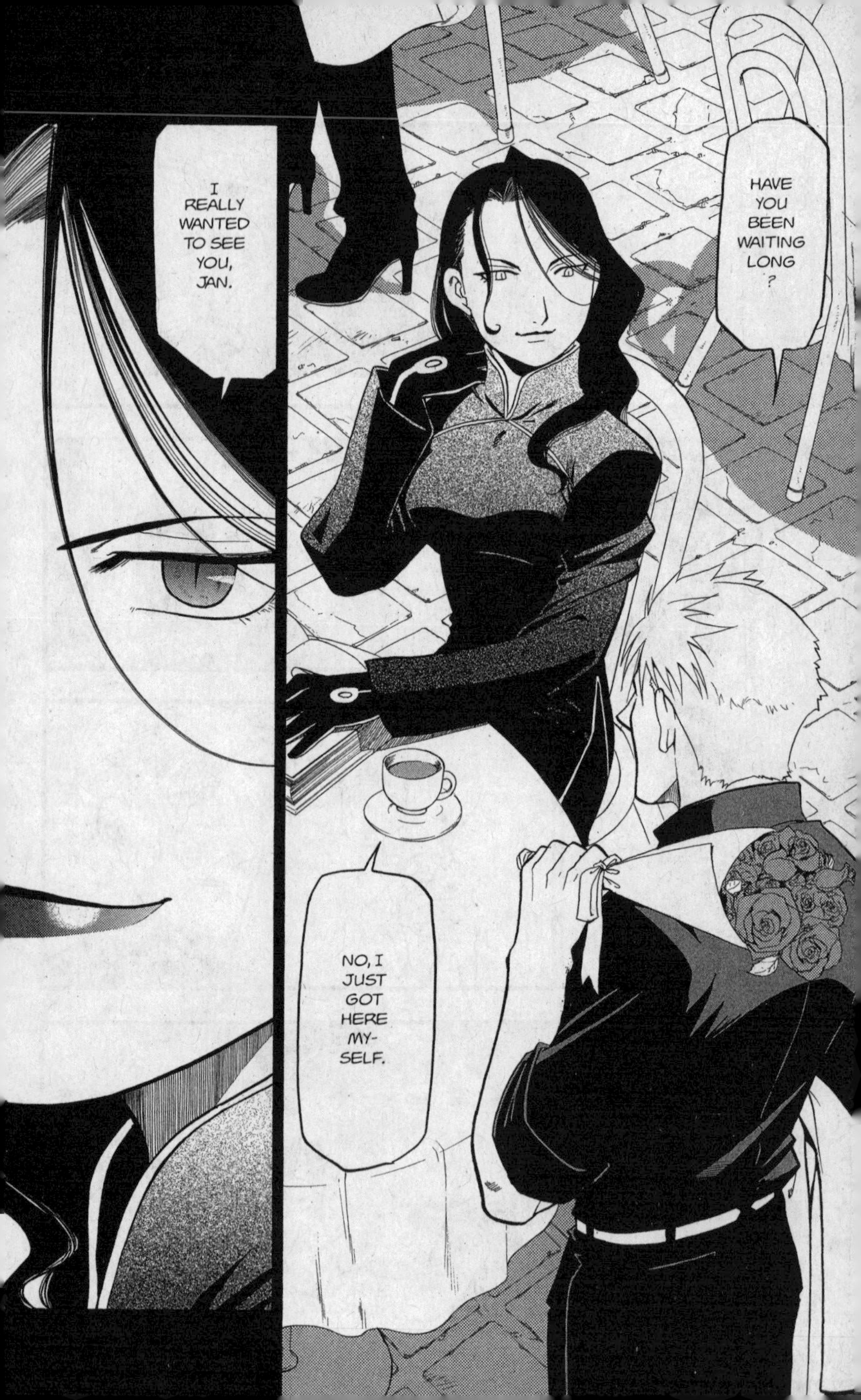
HAVE YOU BEEN WAITING LONG?
NO, I JUST GOT HERE MY-SELF.
I REALLY WANTED TO SEE YOU, JAN.

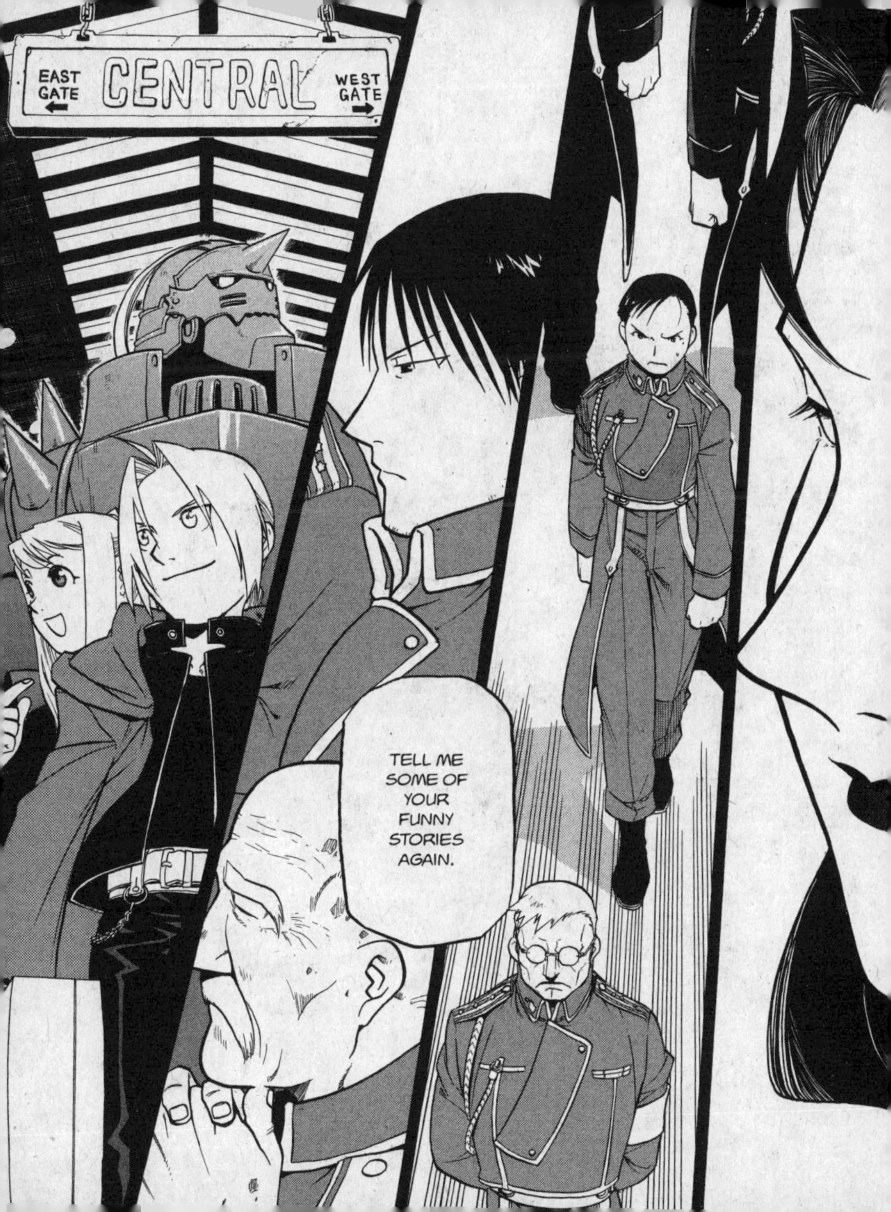
EAST GATE
CENTRAL
WEST GATE
TELL ME SOME OF YOUR FUNNY STORIES AGAIN.

FULLMETAL
ALCHEMIST

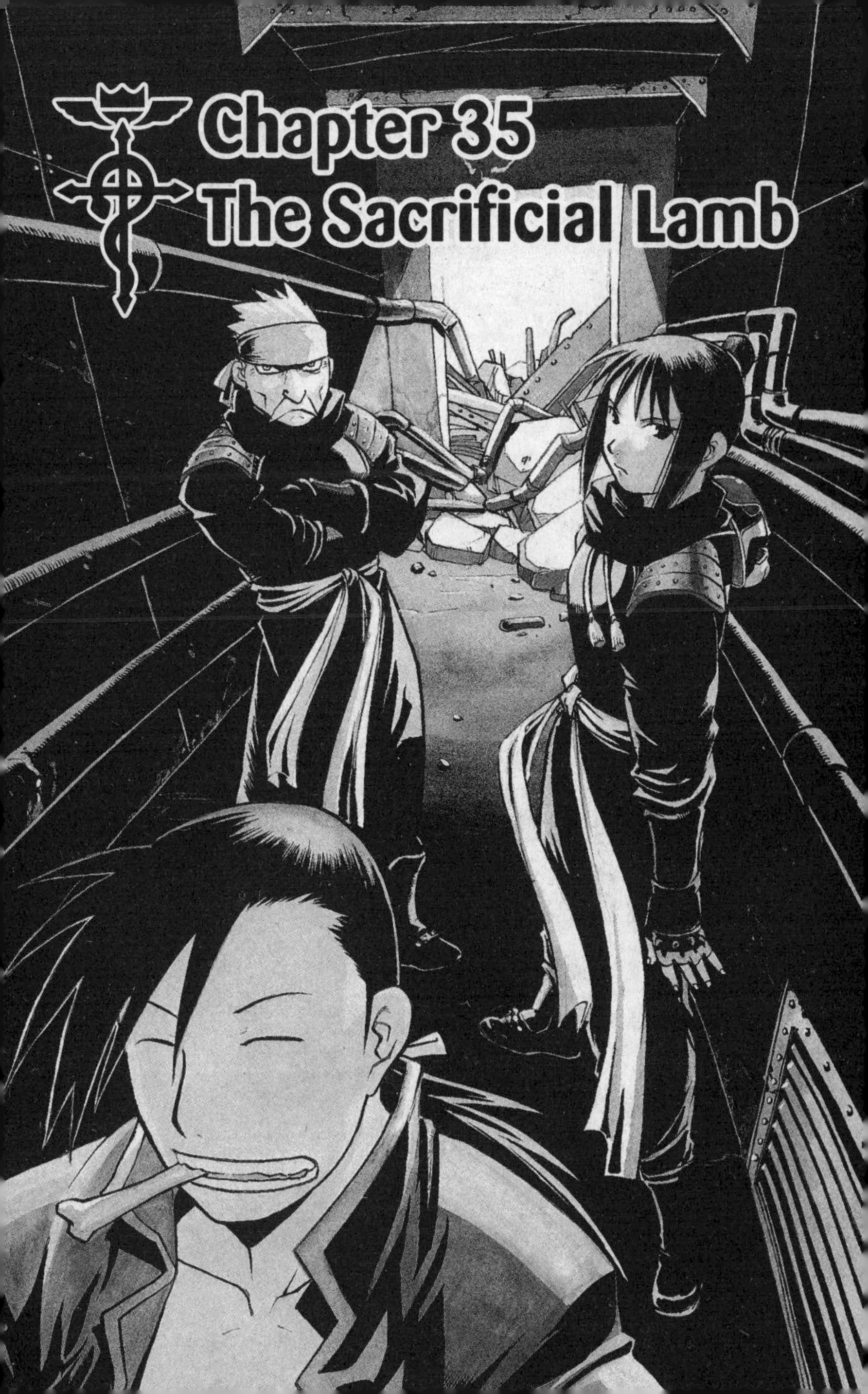
Chapter 35
The Sacrificial Lamb

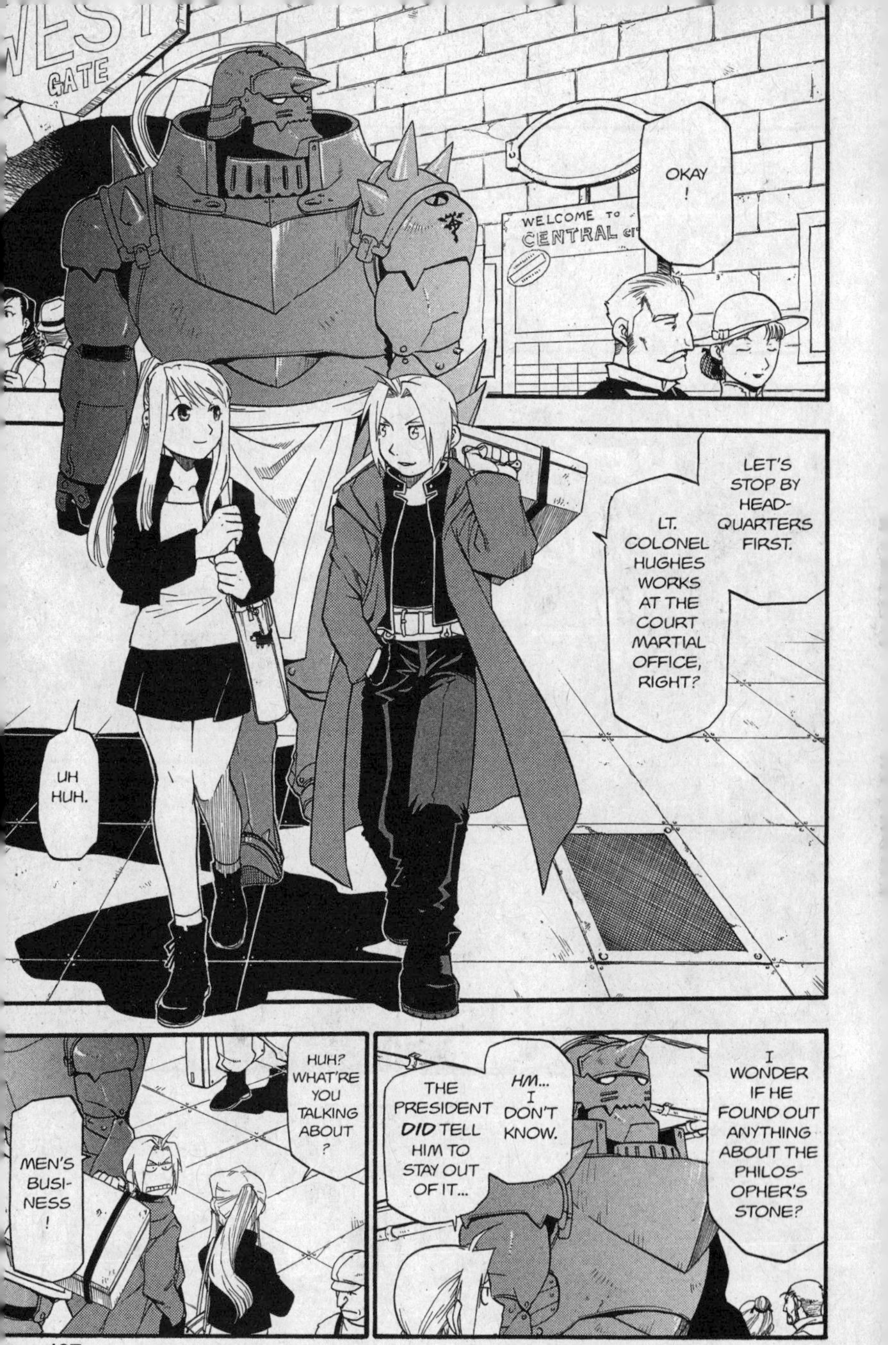
WEST GATE
WELCOME TO CENTRAL
OKAY!
LET'S STOP BY HEAD-QUARTERS FIRST.
LT. COLONEL HUGHES WORKS AT THE COURT MARTIAL OFFICE, RIGHT?
UH HUH.
I WONDER IF HE FOUND OUT ANYTHING ABOUT THE PHILOSOPHER'S STONE?
HM... I DON'T KNOW.
THE PRESIDENT **DID** TELL HIM TO STAY OUT OF IT...
HUH? WHAT'RE YOU TALKING ABOUT?
MEN'S BUSINESS!

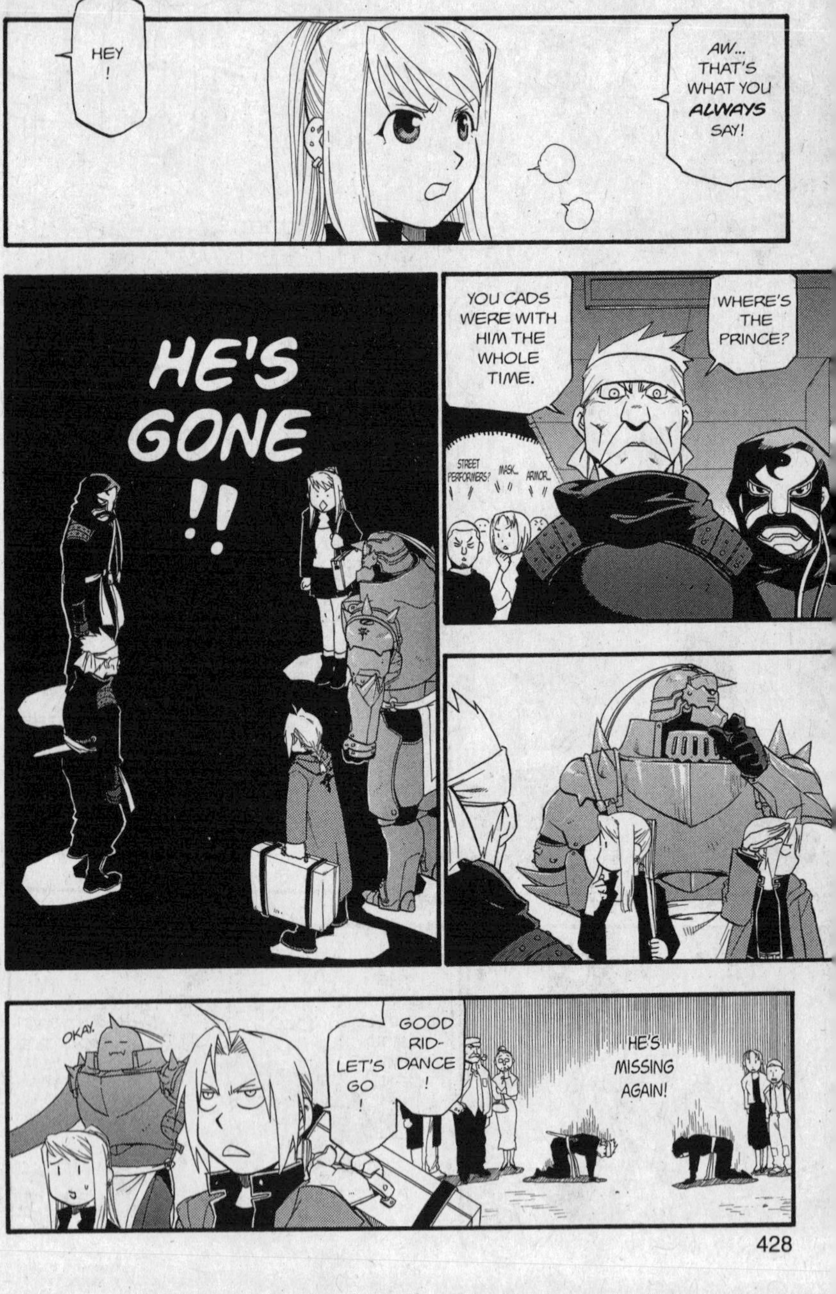
AW... THAT'S WHAT YOU ALWAYS SAY!
HEY!
WHERE'S THE PRINCE?
YOU CADS WERE WITH HIM THE WHOLE TIME.
ARMOR...
MASK...
STREET PERFORMERS?
HE'S GONE!!
HE'S MISSING AGAIN!
GOOD RID-DANCE!
LET'S GO!
OKAY.

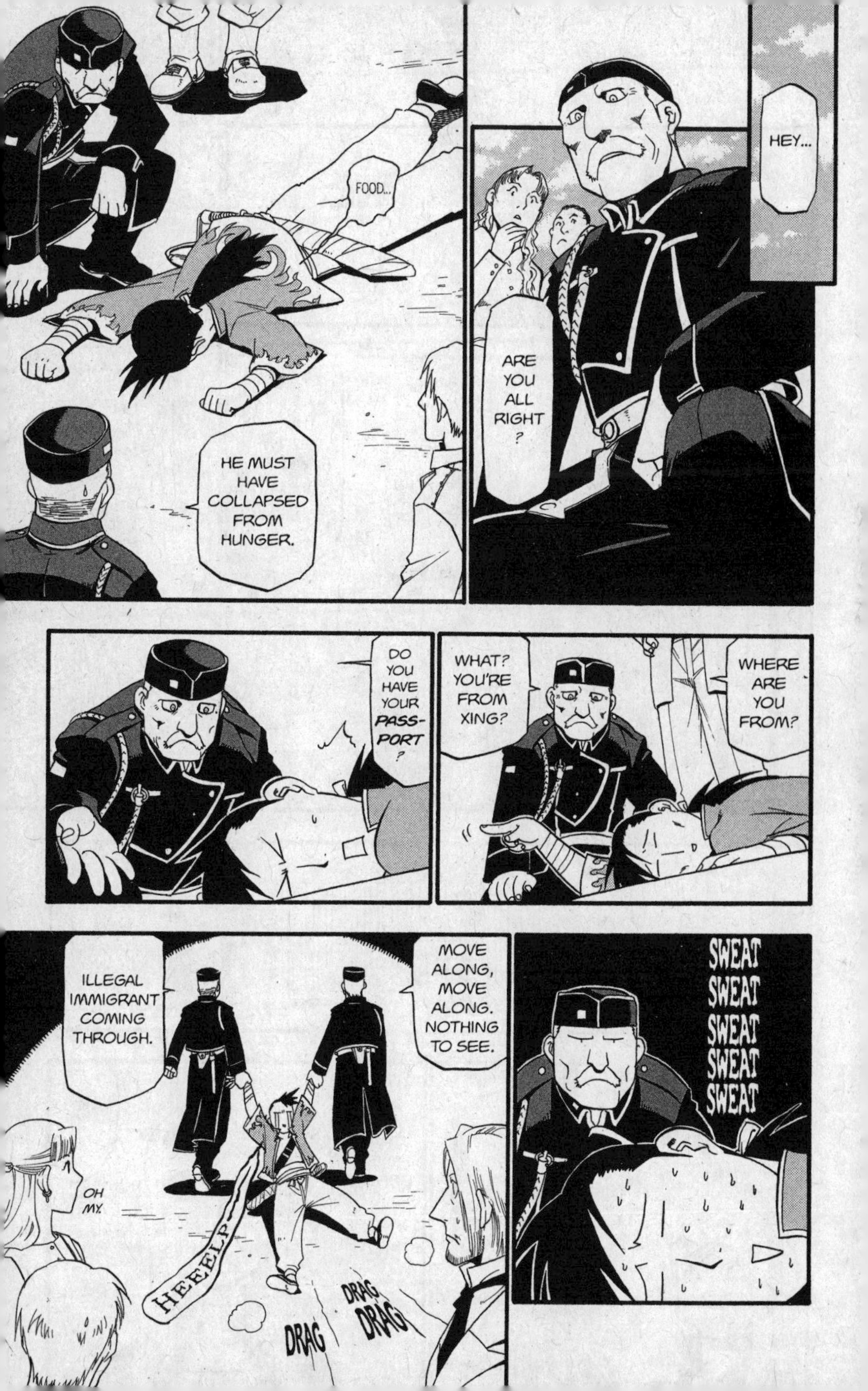
HEY...
ARE YOU ALL RIGHT?
FOOD...
HE MUST HAVE COLLAPSED FROM HUNGER.
WHERE ARE YOU FROM?
WHAT? YOU'RE FROM XING?
DO YOU HAVE YOUR PASSPORT?
SWEAT SWEAT SWEAT SWEAT SWEAT
MOVE ALONG, MOVE ALONG. NOTHING TO SEE.
ILLEGAL IMMIGRANT COMING THROUGH.
OH MY.
HEEELP
DRAG DRAG
DRAG

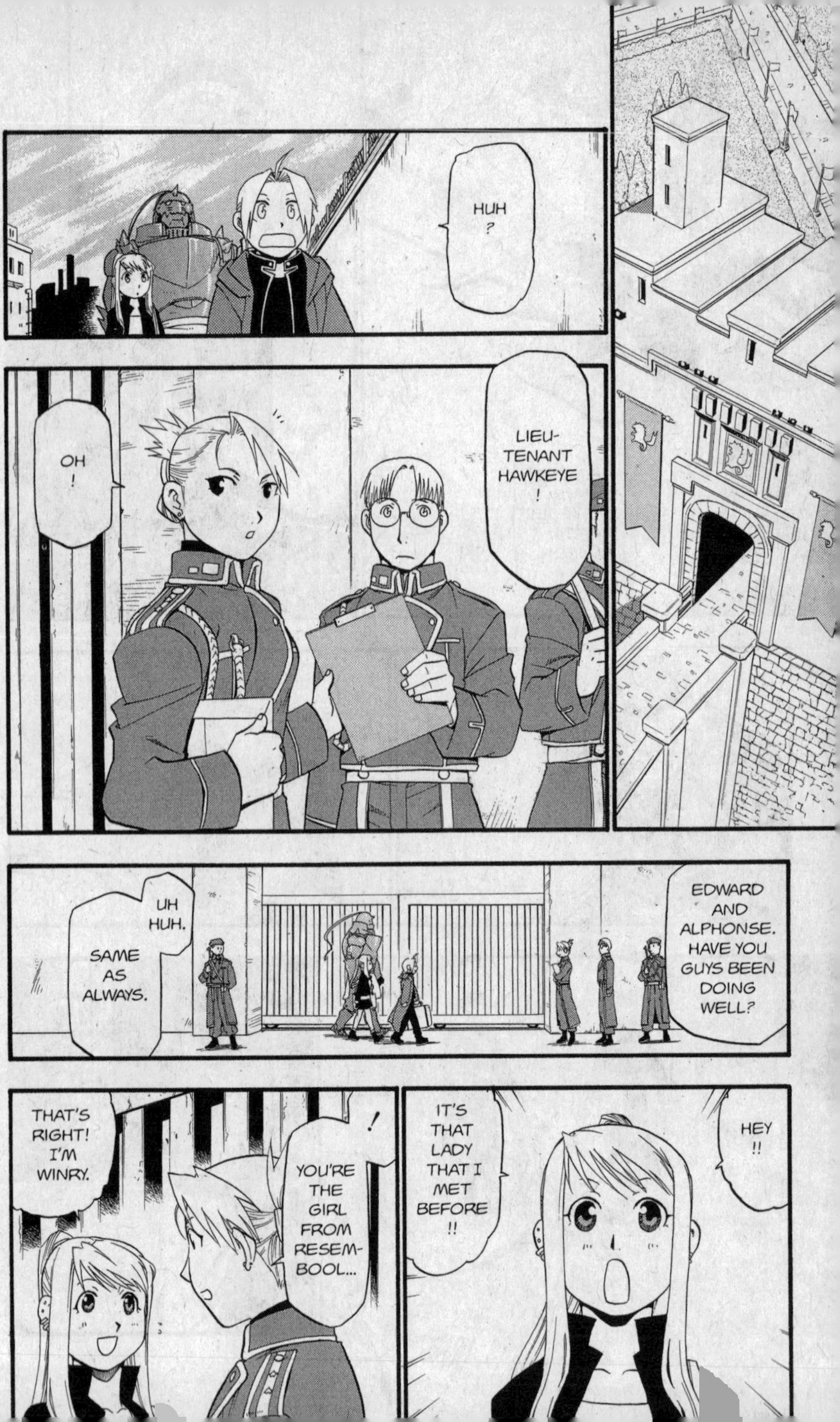
HUH?
LIEUTENANT HAWKEYE!
OH!
EDWARD AND ALPHONSE. HAVE YOU GUYS BEEN DOING WELL?
UH HUH.
SAME AS ALWAYS.
HEY!!
IT'S THAT LADY THAT I MET BEFORE!!
!
YOU'RE THE GIRL FROM RESEMBOOL...
THAT'S RIGHT! I'M WINRY.

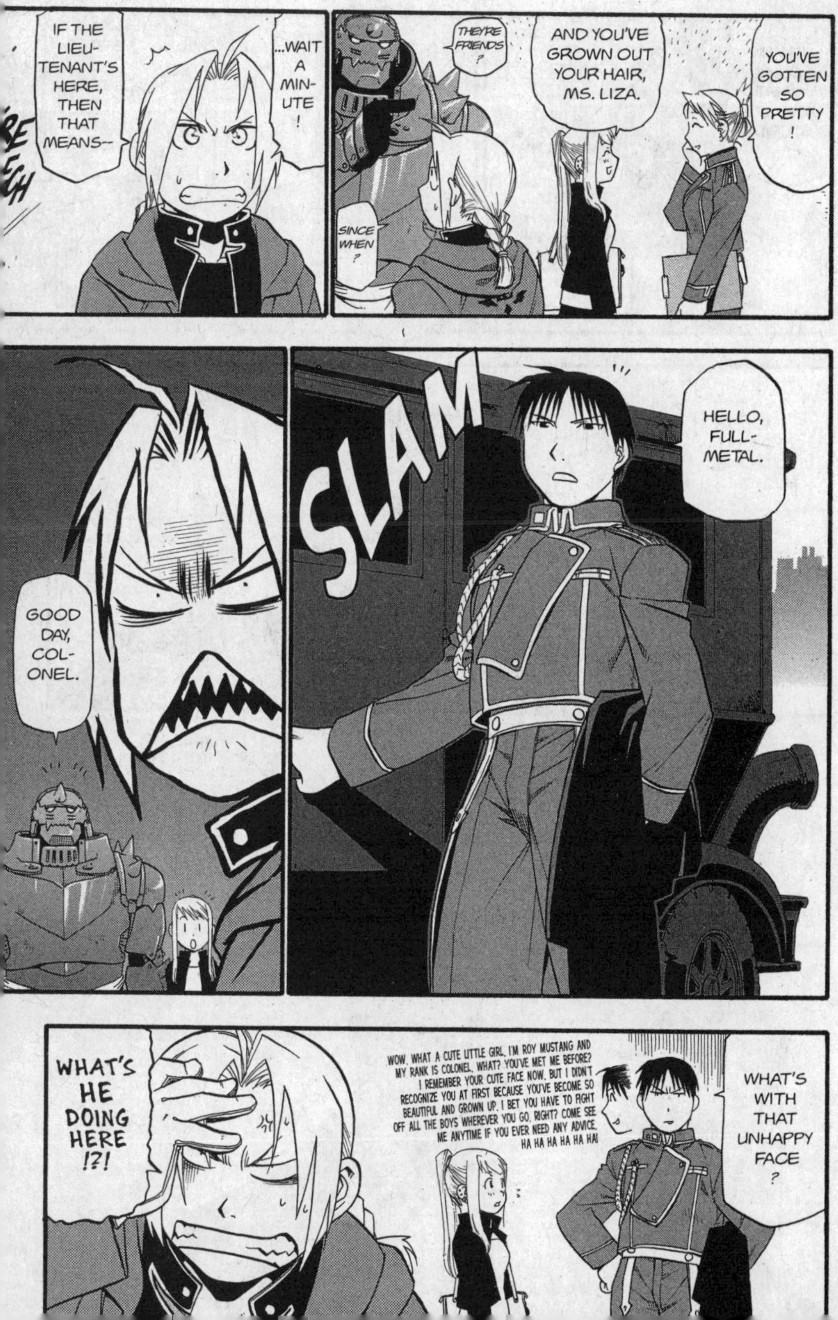
YOU'VE GOTTEN SO PRETTY!
AND YOU'VE GROWN OUT YOUR HAIR, MS. LIZA.
THEY'RE FRIENDS?
SINCE WHEN?
...WAIT A MINUTE!
IF THE LIEUTENANT'S HERE, THEN THAT MEANS--
HELLO, FULLMETAL.
SLAM
GOOD DAY, COLONEL.
WHAT'S WITH THAT UNHAPPY FACE?
WOW, WHAT A CUTE LITTLE GIRL. I'M ROY MUSTANG AND MY RANK IS COLONEL. WHAT? YOU'VE MET ME BEFORE? I REMEMBER YOUR CUTE FACE NOW, BUT I DIDN'T RECOGNIZE YOU AT FIRST BECAUSE YOU'VE BECOME SO BEAUTIFUL AND GROWN UP. I BET YOU HAVE TO FIGHT OFF ALL THE BOYS WHEREVER YOU GO, RIGHT? COME SEE ME ANYTIME IF YOU EVER NEED ANY ADVICE. HA HA HA HA HA HA!
WHAT'S HE DOING HERE!?!

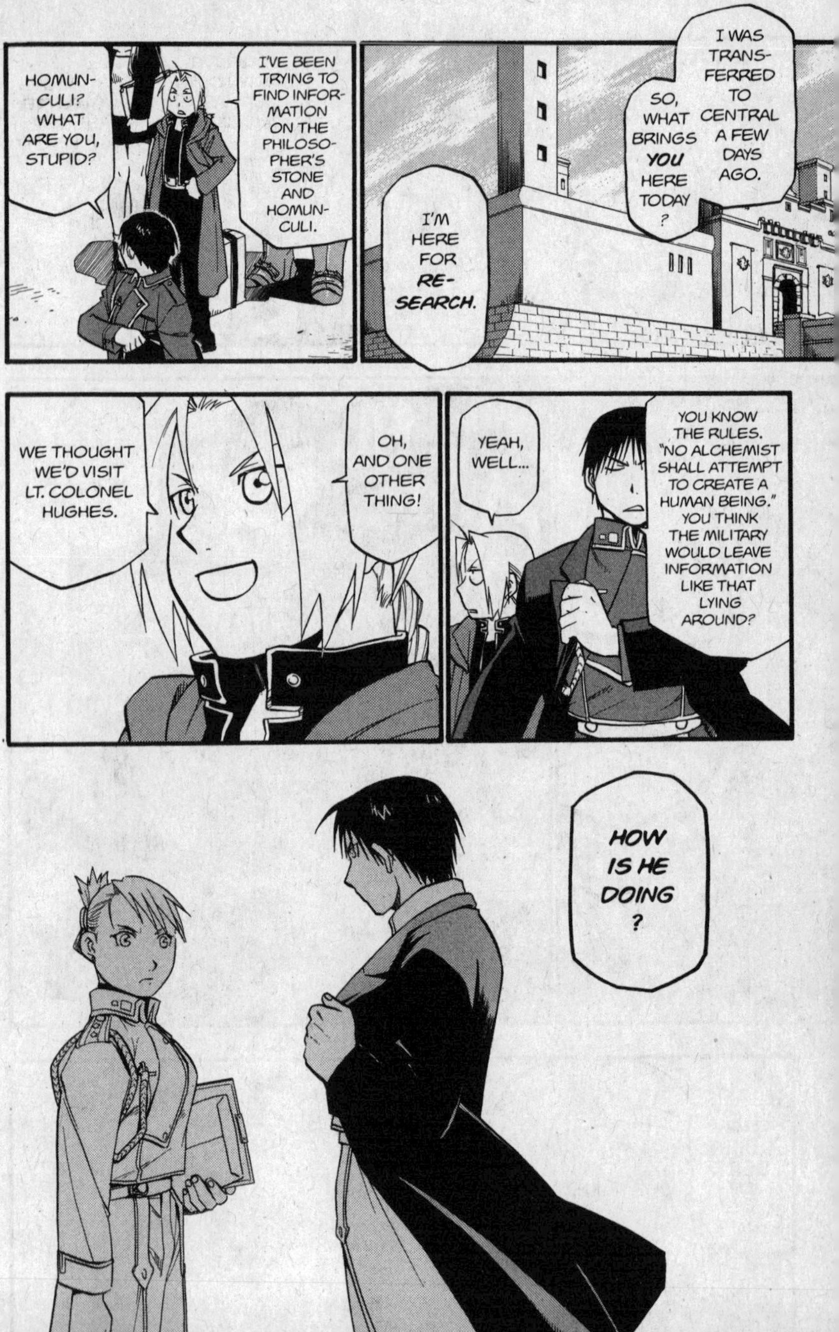
I WAS TRANSFERRED TO CENTRAL A FEW DAYS AGO.
SO, WHAT BRINGS *YOU* HERE TODAY?
I'M HERE FOR *RESEARCH*.
I'VE BEEN TRYING TO FIND INFORMATION ON THE PHILOSOPHER'S STONE AND HOMUNCULI.
HOMUNCULI? WHAT ARE YOU, STUPID?
YOU KNOW THE RULES. "NO ALCHEMIST SHALL ATTEMPT TO CREATE A HUMAN BEING." YOU THINK THE MILITARY WOULD LEAVE INFORMATION LIKE THAT LYING AROUND?
YEAH, WELL...
OH, AND ONE OTHER THING!
WE THOUGHT WE'D VISIT LT. COLONEL HUGHES.
HOW IS HE DOING?

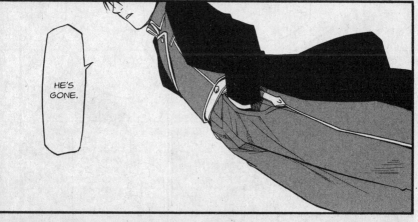

HE'S
GONE.

HUH
?

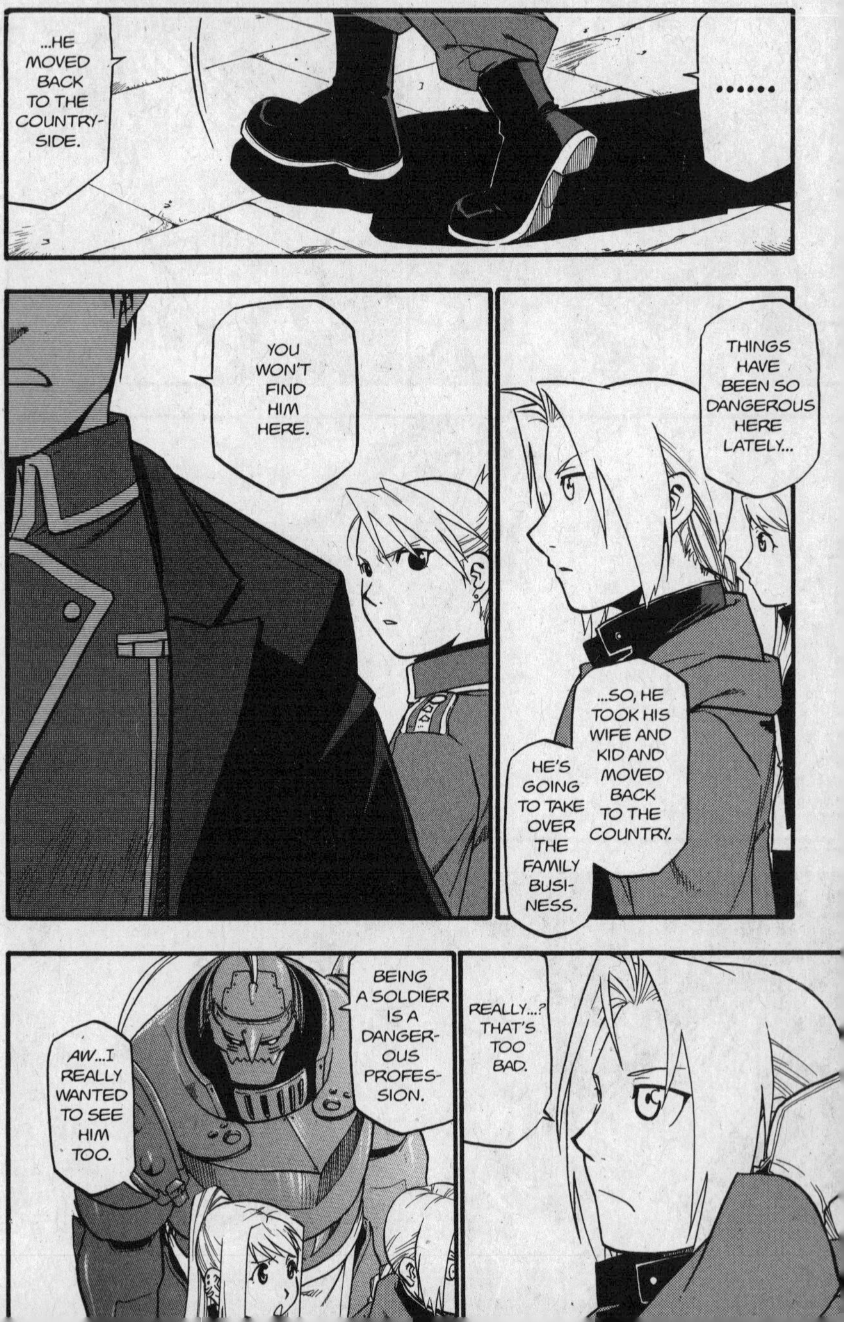
......
...HE MOVED BACK TO THE COUNTRYSIDE.
THINGS HAVE BEEN SO DANGEROUS HERE LATELY...
...SO, HE TOOK HIS WIFE AND KID AND MOVED BACK TO THE COUNTRY.
HE'S GOING TO TAKE OVER THE FAMILY BUSINESS.
YOU WON'T FIND HIM HERE.
REALLY...? THAT'S TOO BAD.
BEING A SOLDIER IS A DANGEROUS PROFESSION.
AW...I REALLY WANTED TO SEE HIM TOO.

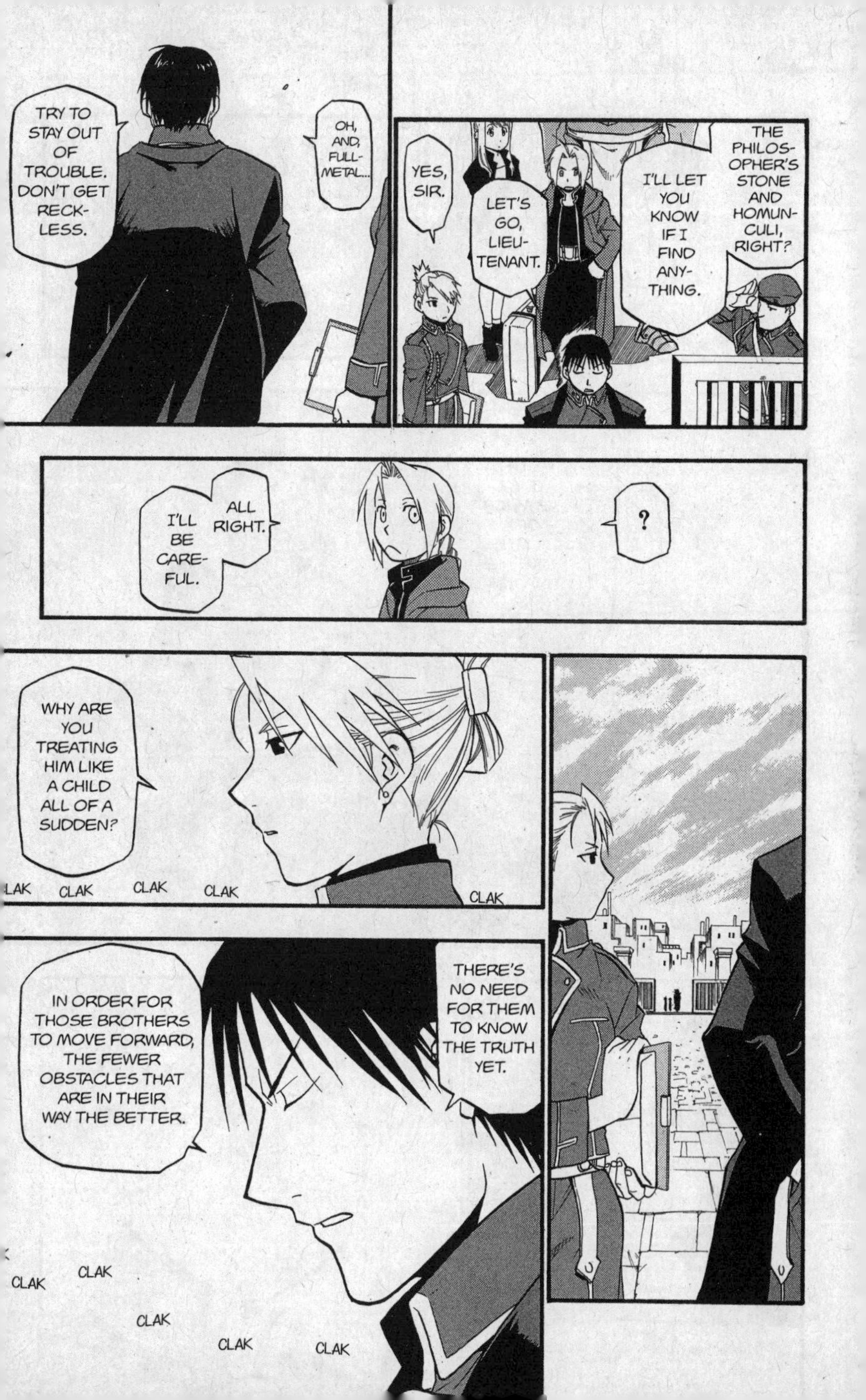
THE PHILOSOPHER'S STONE AND HOMUNCULI, RIGHT?
I'LL LET YOU KNOW IF I FIND ANYTHING.
LET'S GO, LIEUTENANT.
YES, SIR.
OH, AND, FULLMETAL...
TRY TO STAY OUT OF TROUBLE. DON'T GET RECKLESS.
?
ALL RIGHT. I'LL BE CAREFUL.
WHY ARE YOU TREATING HIM LIKE A CHILD ALL OF A SUDDEN?
CLAK
CLAK
CLAK
CLAK
LAK
THERE'S NO NEED FOR THEM TO KNOW THE TRUTH YET.
IN ORDER FOR THOSE BROTHERS TO MOVE FORWARD, THE FEWER OBSTACLES THAT ARE IN THEIR WAY THE BETTER.
CLAK
CLAK
CLAK
CLAK
CLAK

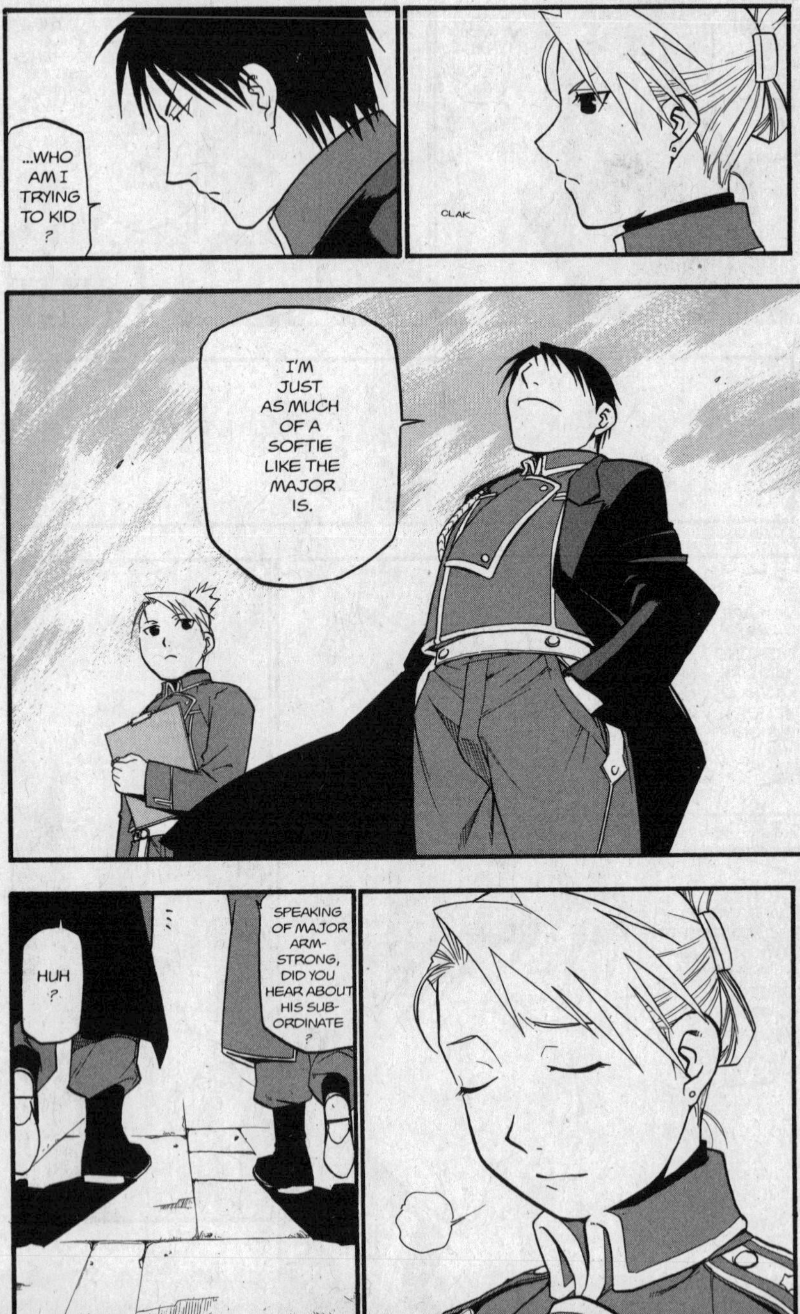
CLAK...
...WHO AM I TRYING TO KID?
I'M JUST AS MUCH OF A SOFTIE LIKE THE MAJOR IS.
SPEAKING OF MAJOR ARM-STRONG, DID YOU HEAR ABOUT HIS SUB-ORDINATE?
...
HUH?

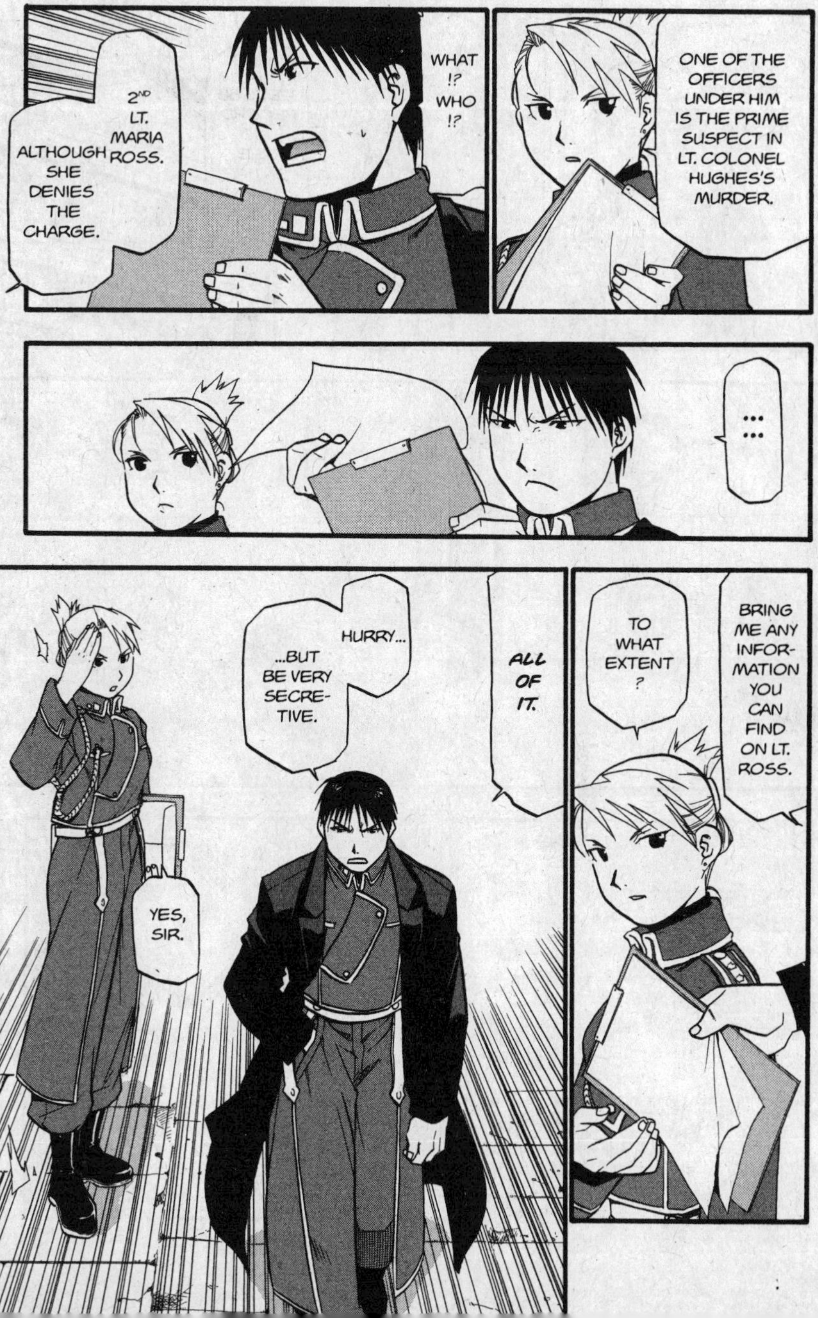
ONE OF THE OFFICERS UNDER HIM IS THE PRIME SUSPECT IN LT. COLONEL HUGHES'S MURDER.
WHAT!? WHO!?
2ND LT. MARIA ROSS.
ALTHOUGH SHE DENIES THE CHARGE.
......
BRING ME ANY INFORMATION YOU CAN FIND ON LT. ROSS.
TO WHAT EXTENT?
ALL OF IT.
HURRY...
...BUT BE VERY SECRETIVE.
YES, SIR.

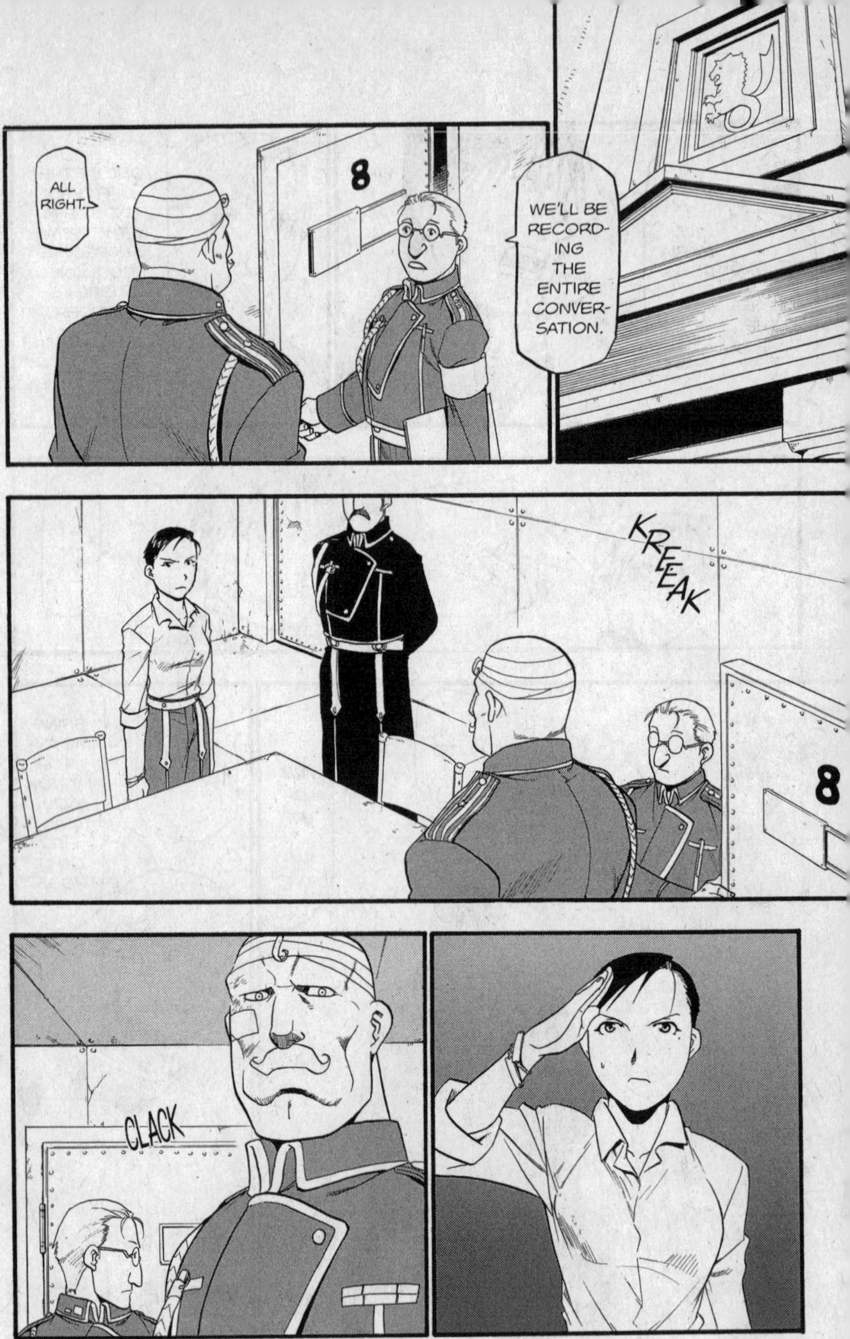
WE'LL BE RECORDING THE ENTIRE CONVERSATION.
ALL RIGHT.
KREEAK
CLACK

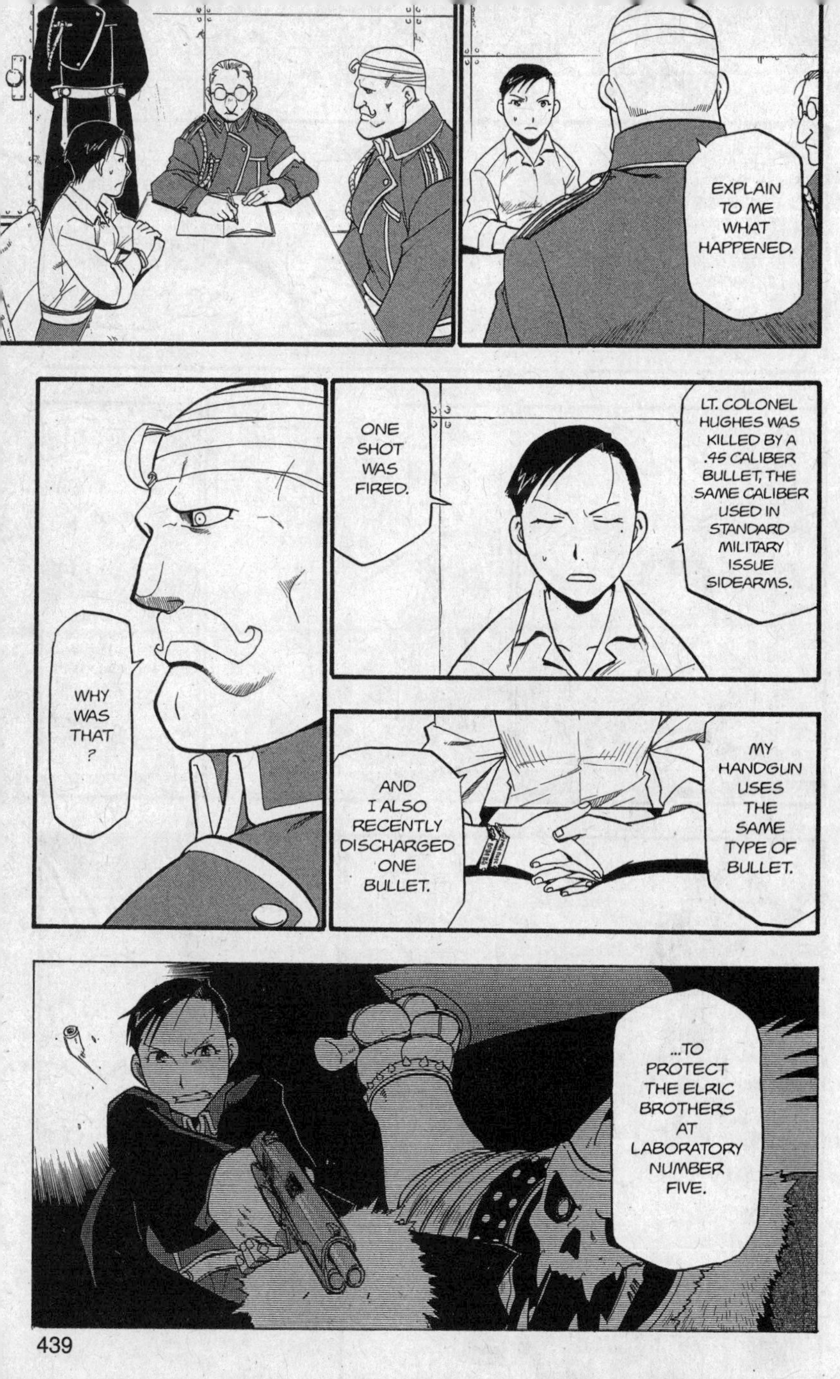
EXPLAIN TO ME WHAT HAPPENED.
LT. COLONEL HUGHES WAS KILLED BY A .45 CALIBER BULLET, THE SAME CALIBER USED IN STANDARD MILITARY ISSUE SIDEARMS.
ONE SHOT WAS FIRED.
MY HANDGUN USES THE SAME TYPE OF BULLET.
AND I ALSO RECENTLY DISCHARGED ONE BULLET.
WHY WAS THAT?
...TO PROTECT THE ELRIC BROTHERS AT LABORATORY NUMBER FIVE.

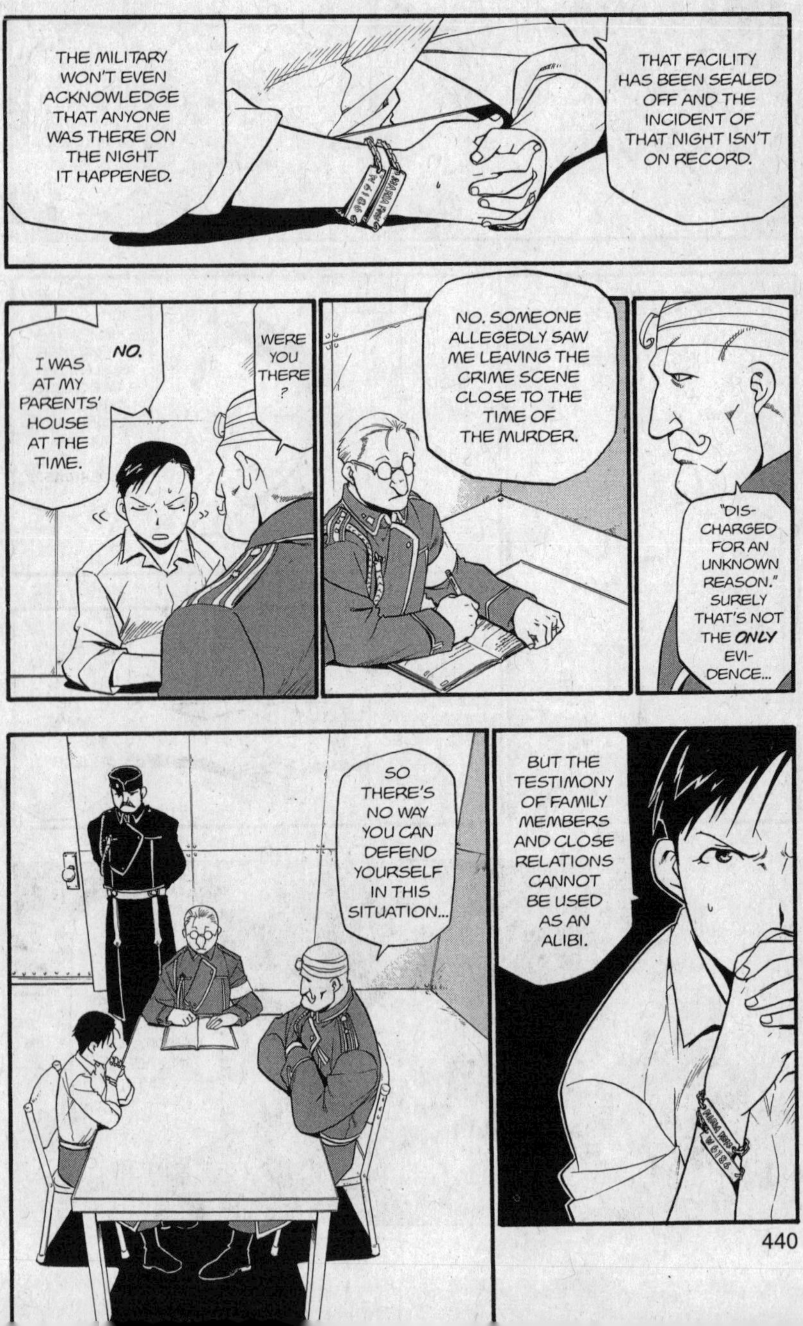
THAT FACILITY HAS BEEN SEALED OFF AND THE INCIDENT OF THAT NIGHT ISN'T ON RECORD.
THE MILITARY WON'T EVEN ACKNOWLEDGE THAT ANYONE WAS THERE ON THE NIGHT IT HAPPENED.
"DIS-CHARGED FOR AN UNKNOWN REASON." SURELY THAT'S NOT THE *ONLY* EVI-DENCE...
NO. SOMEONE ALLEGEDLY SAW ME LEAVING THE CRIME SCENE CLOSE TO THE TIME OF THE MURDER.
WERE YOU THERE?
NO.
I WAS AT MY PARENTS' HOUSE AT THE TIME.
BUT THE TESTIMONY OF FAMILY MEMBERS AND CLOSE RELATIONS CANNOT BE USED AS AN ALIBI.
SO THERE'S NO WAY YOU CAN DEFEND YOURSELF IN THIS SITUATION...

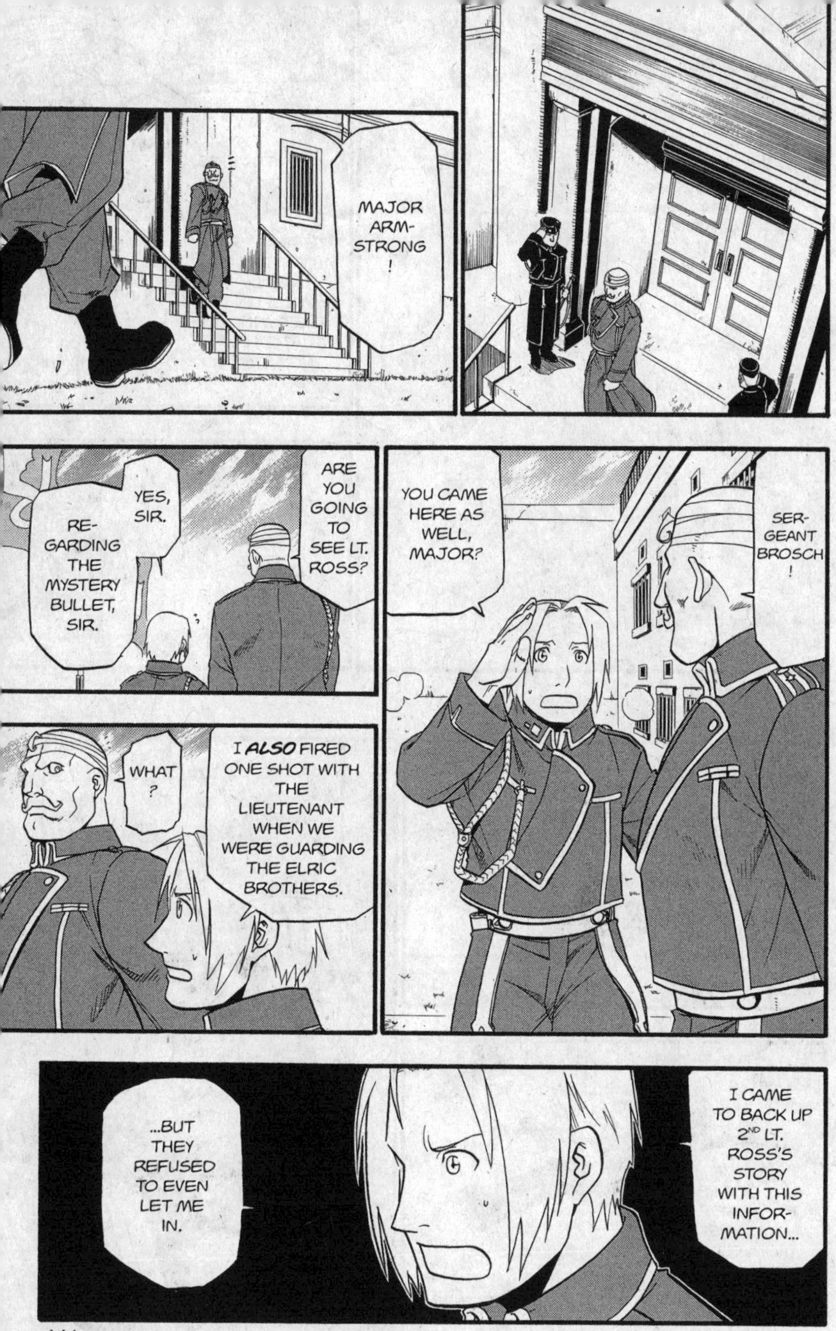
MAJOR ARMSTRONG!
SERGEANT BROSCH!
YOU CAME HERE AS WELL, MAJOR?
ARE YOU GOING TO SEE LT. ROSS?
YES, SIR.
REGARDING THE MYSTERY BULLET, SIR.
I ALSO FIRED ONE SHOT WITH THE LIEUTENANT WHEN WE WERE GUARDING THE ELRIC BROTHERS.
WHAT?
I CAME TO BACK UP 2ND LT. ROSS'S STORY WITH THIS INFORMATION...
...BUT THEY REFUSED TO EVEN LET ME IN.

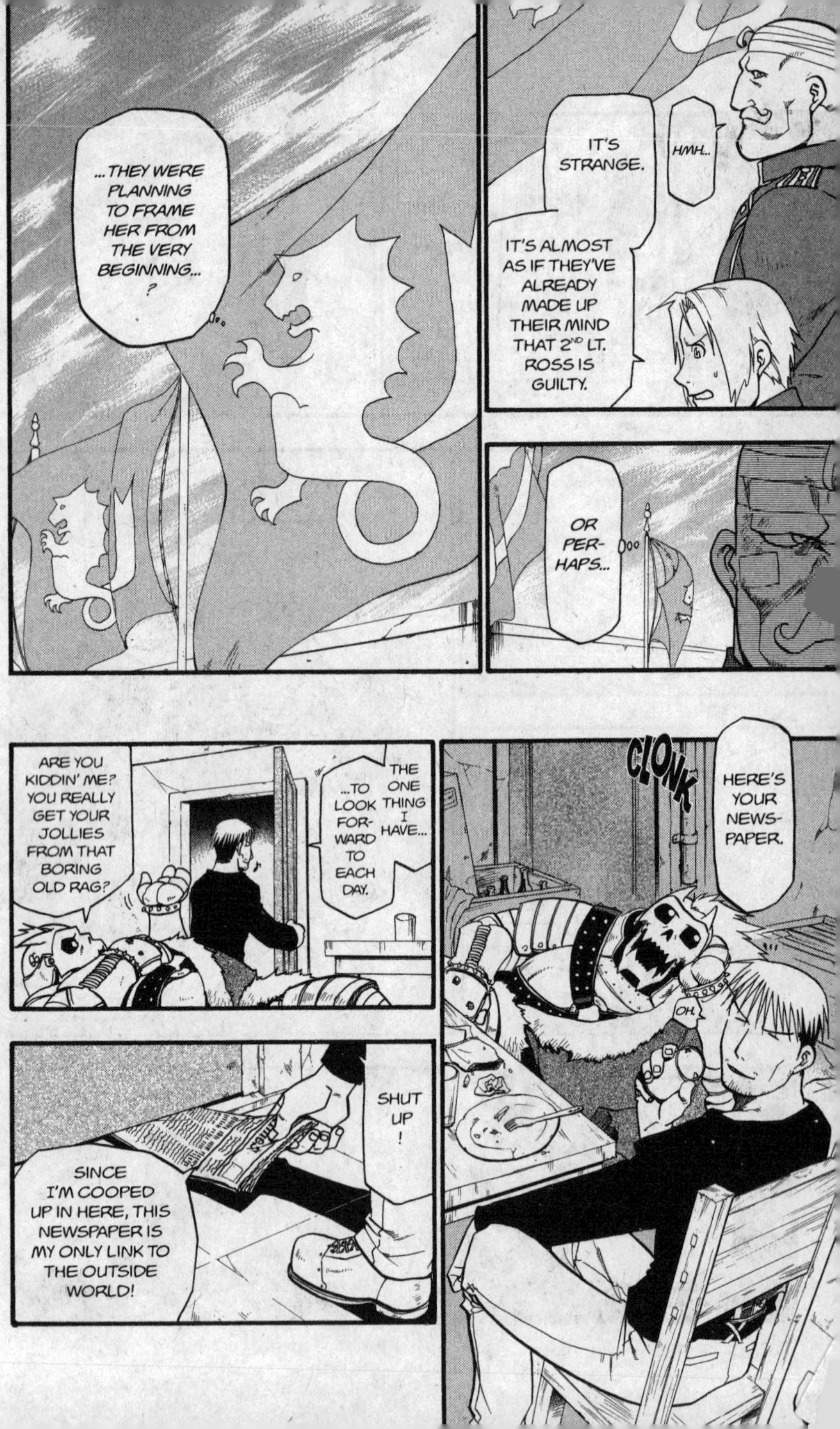
HMH...
IT'S STRANGE.
IT'S ALMOST AS IF THEY'VE ALREADY MADE UP THEIR MIND THAT 2ND LT. ROSS IS GUILTY.
OR PERHAPS...
...THEY WERE PLANNING TO FRAME HER FROM THE VERY BEGINNING...?
HERE'S YOUR NEWSPAPER.
CLONK
OH.
THE ONE THING I HAVE...
...TO LOOK FORWARD TO EACH DAY.
ARE YOU KIDDIN' ME? YOU REALLY GET YOUR JOLLIES FROM THAT BORING OLD RAG?
SHUT UP!
SINCE I'M COOPED UP IN HERE, THIS NEWSPAPER IS MY ONLY LINK TO THE OUTSIDE WORLD!

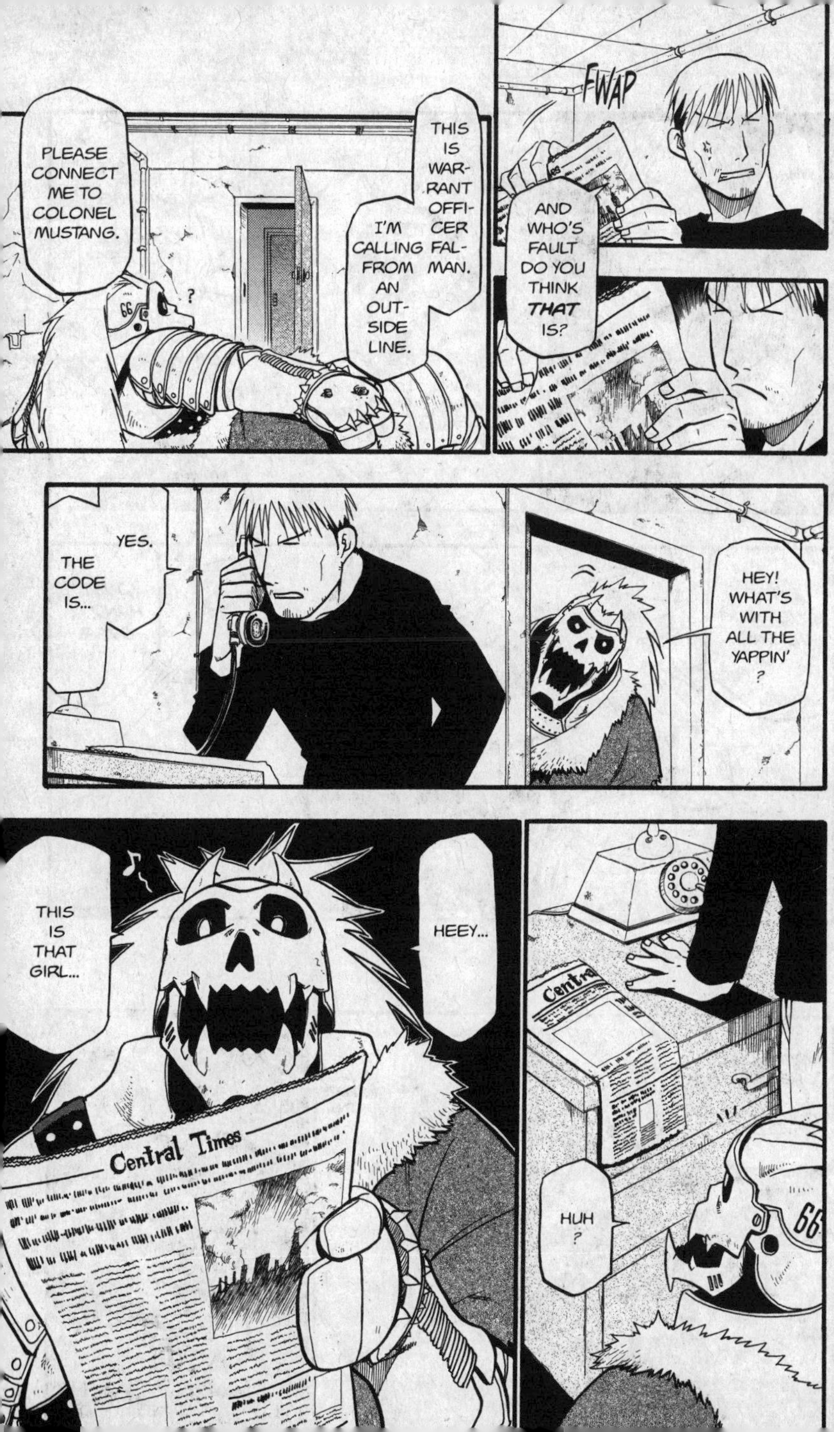

FWAP
AND WHO'S FAULT DO YOU THINK *THAT* IS?
THIS IS WARRANT OFFICER FALMAN.
I'M CALLING FROM AN OUTSIDE LINE.
PLEASE CONNECT ME TO COLONEL MUSTANG.
?
HEY! WHAT'S WITH ALL THE YAPPIN'?
YES.
THE CODE IS...
HUH?
HEEY...
THIS IS THAT GIRL...
Central Times

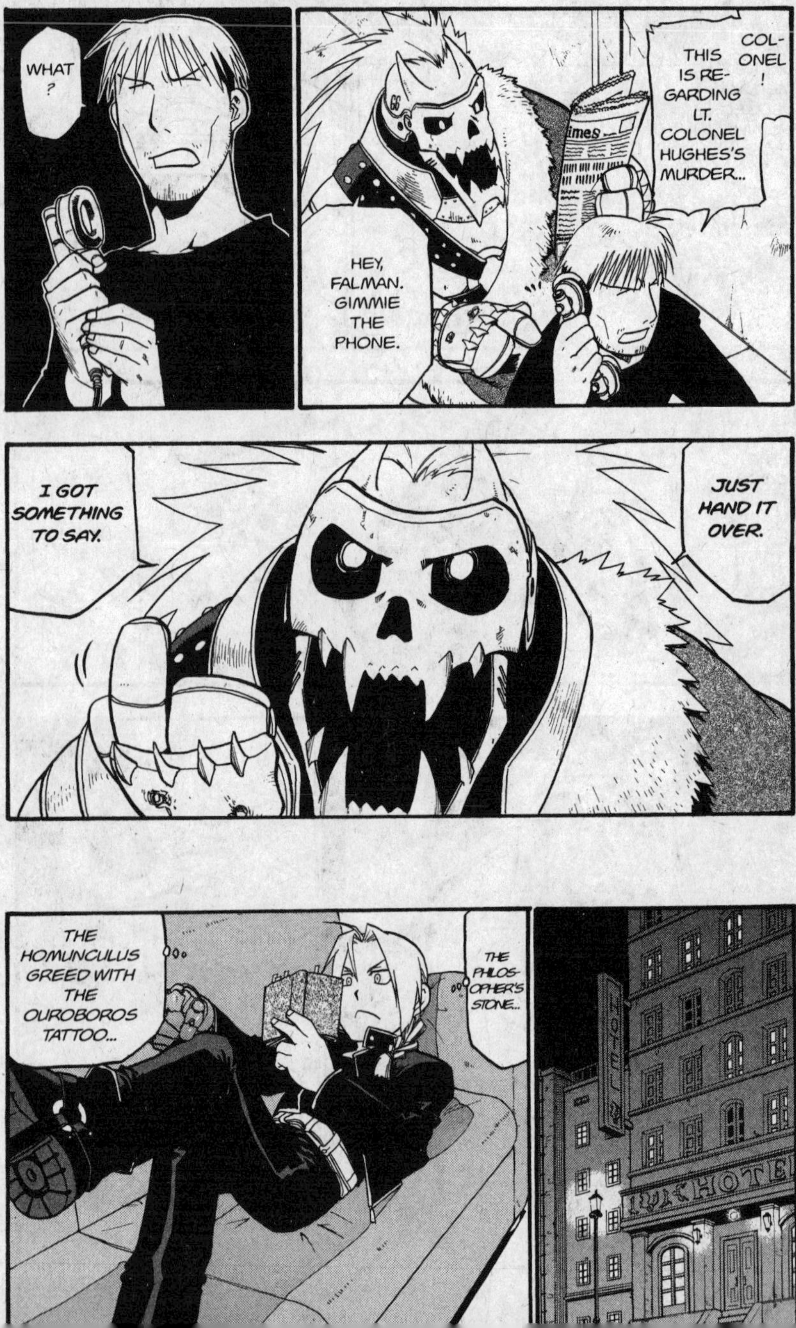
COLONEL!
THIS IS REGARDING LT. COLONEL HUGHES'S MURDER...
HEY, FALMAN. GIMMIE THE PHONE.
WHAT?
JUST HAND IT OVER.
I GOT SOMETHING TO SAY.
HOTEL
THE PHILOSOPHER'S STONE...
THE HOMUNCULUS GREED WITH THE OUROBOROS TATTOO...

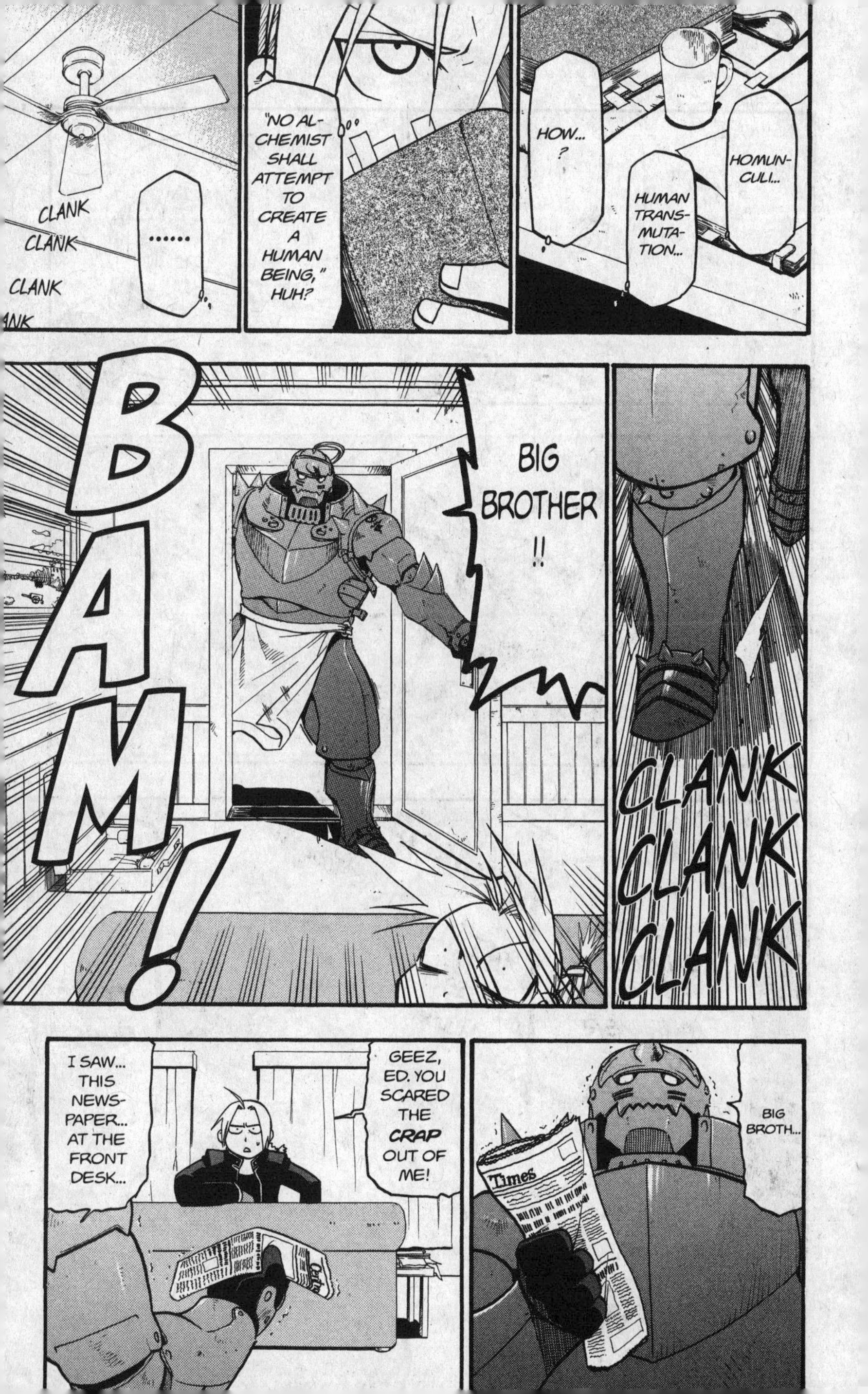
HOMUN-CULI...
HUMAN TRANS-MUTA-TION...
HOW... ?
"NO AL-CHEMIST SHALL ATTEMPT TO CREATE A HUMAN BEING," HUH?
......
CLANK
CLANK
CLANK
ANK
CLANK CLANK CLANK
BIG BROTHER !!
BAM!
BIG BROTH...
GEEZ, ED. YOU SCARED THE CRAP OUT OF ME!
I SAW... THIS NEWS-PAPER... AT THE FRONT DESK...
Times

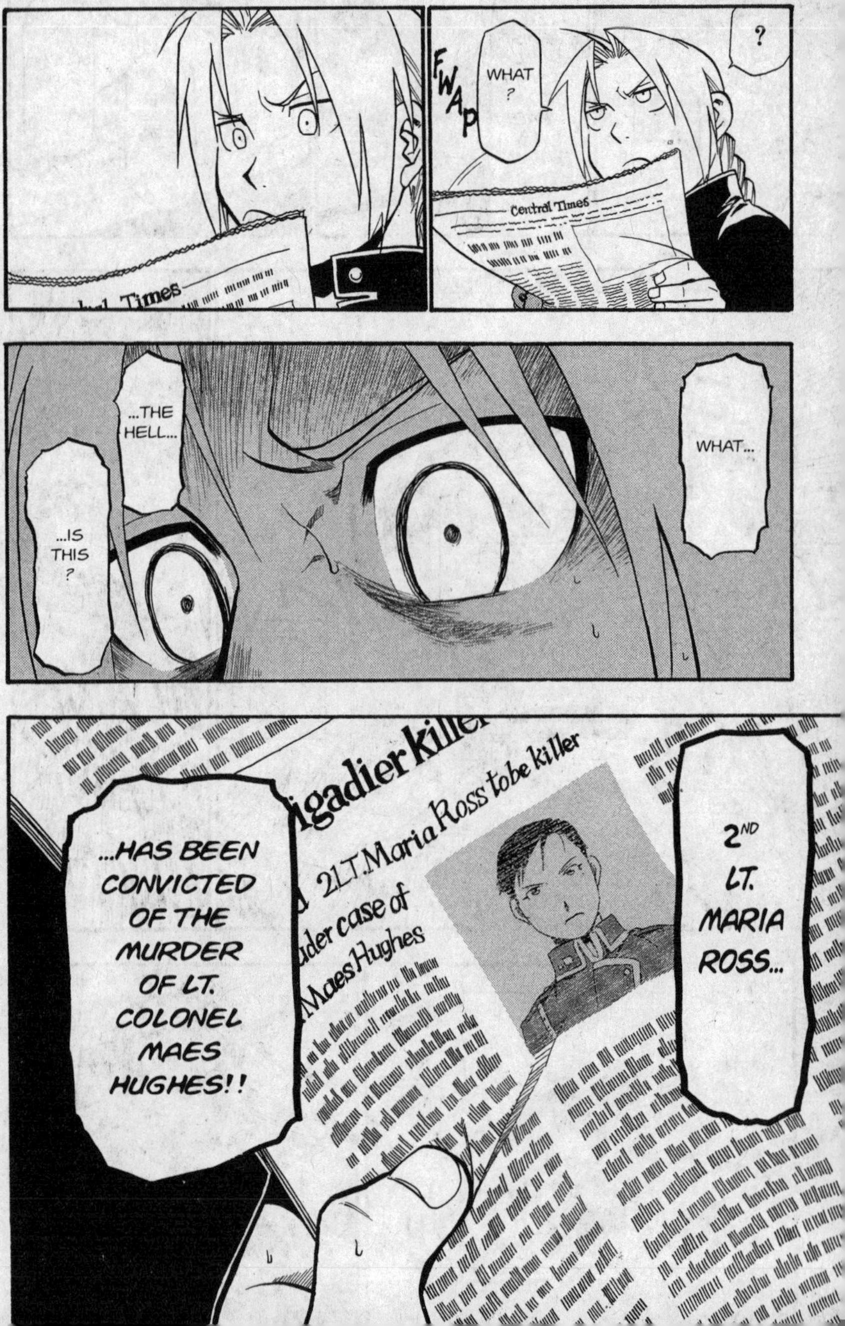
?
WHAT?
FWAP
Central Times
WHAT...
...THE HELL...
...IS THIS?
2ND LT. MARIA ROSS...
...HAS BEEN CONVICTED OF THE MURDER OF LT. COLONEL MAES HUGHES!!
2LT. Maria Ross tobe killer
Maes Hughes

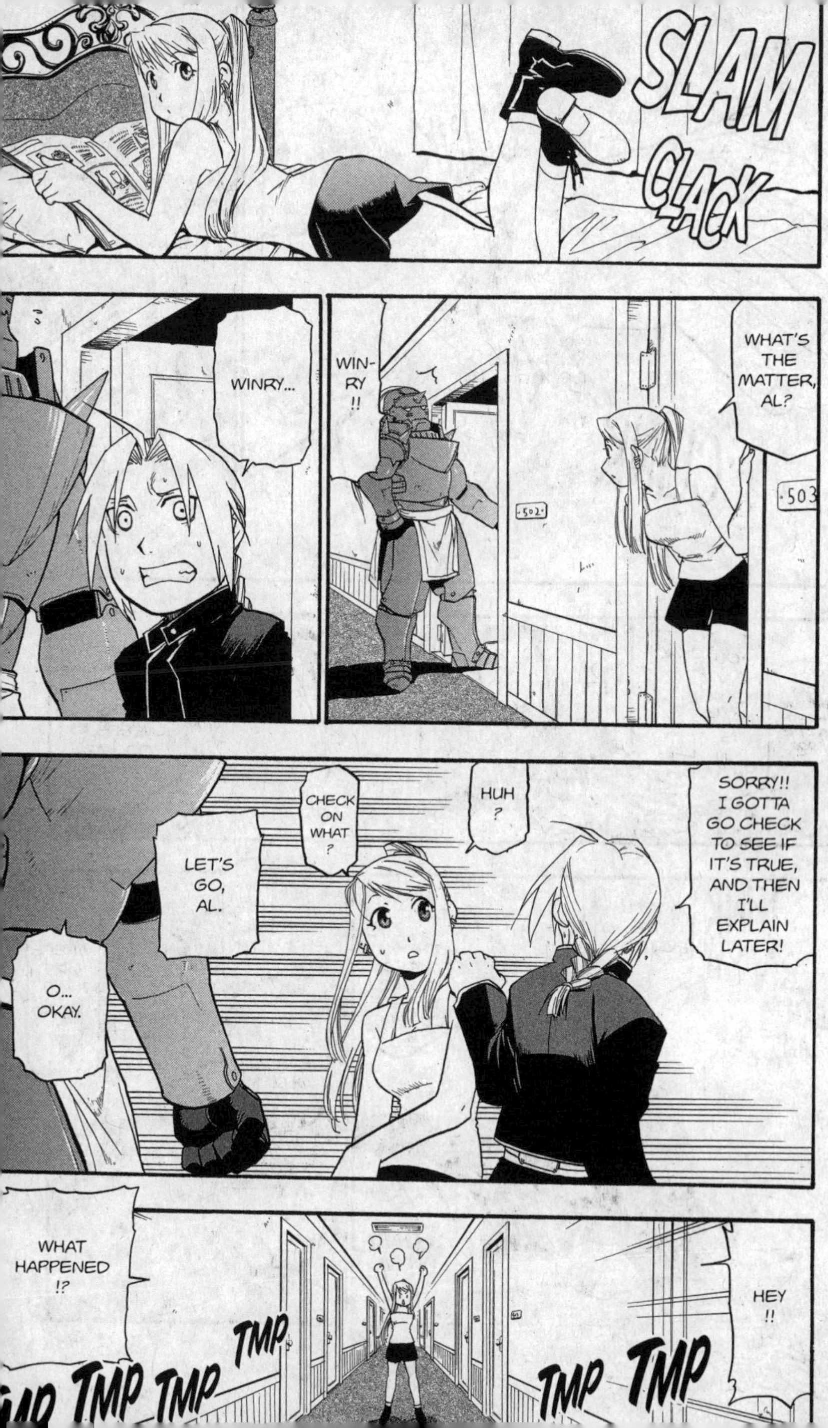
SLAM
CLACK
WHAT'S THE MATTER, AL?
WIN-RY !!
WINRY...
SORRY!! I GOTTA GO CHECK TO SEE IF IT'S TRUE, AND THEN I'LL EXPLAIN LATER!
HUH ?
CHECK ON WHAT ?
LET'S GO, AL.
O... OKAY.
HEY !!
TMP TMP
WHAT HAPPENED !?
TMP
TMP TMP

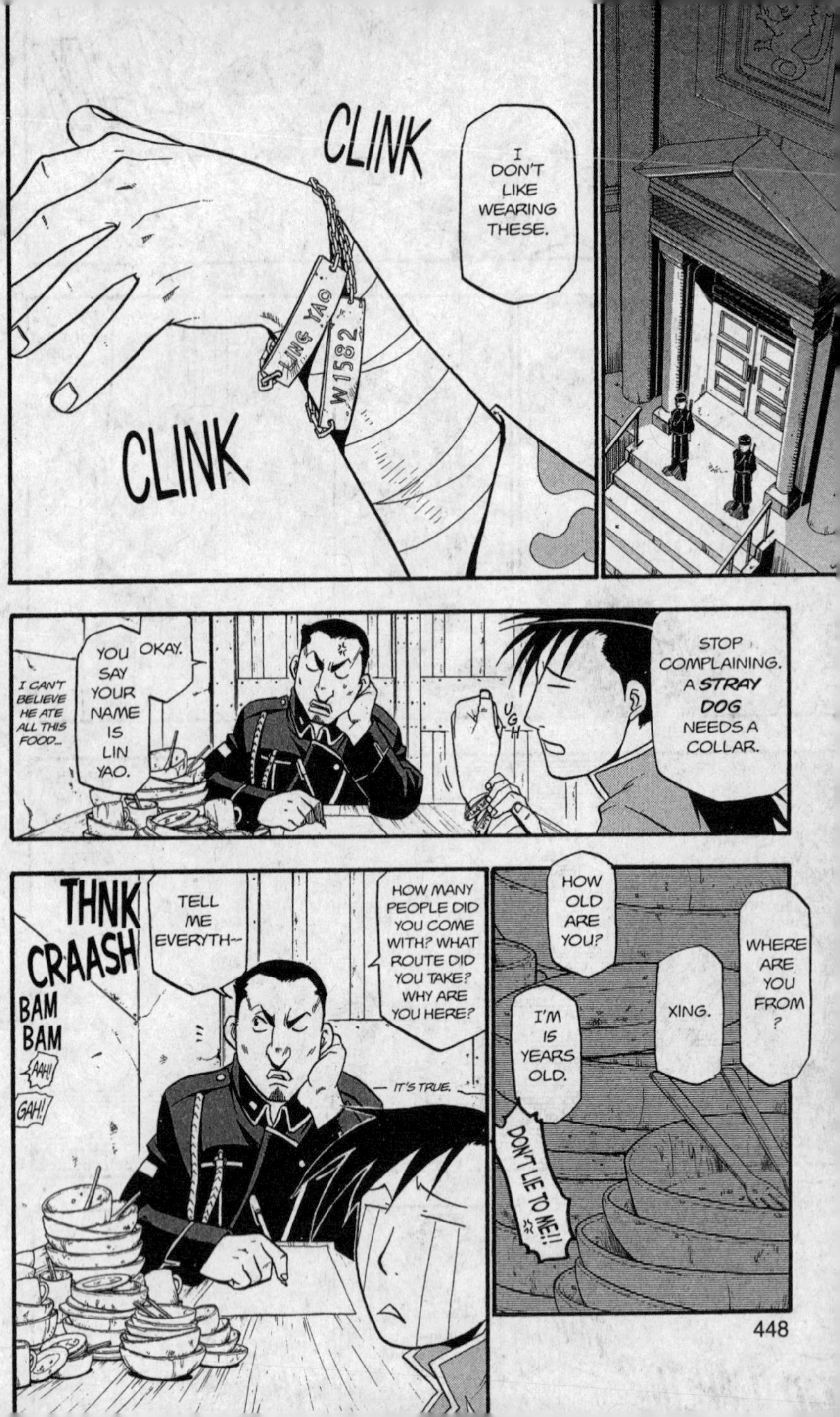
I DON'T LIKE WEARING THESE.
CLINK
LING YAO
W1582
CLINK
STOP COMPLAINING. A **STRAY DOG** NEEDS A COLLAR.
UGH
OKAY.
YOU SAY YOUR NAME IS LIN YAO.
I CAN'T BELIEVE HE ATE ALL THIS FOOD...
WHERE ARE YOU FROM?
XING.
HOW OLD ARE YOU?
I'M 15 YEARS OLD.
DON'T LIE TO ME!!
HOW MANY PEOPLE DID YOU COME WITH? WHAT ROUTE DID YOU TAKE? WHY ARE YOU HERE?
TELL ME EVERYTH--
— IT'S TRUE.
THNK
CRAASH
BAM BAM
AAH!
GAH!

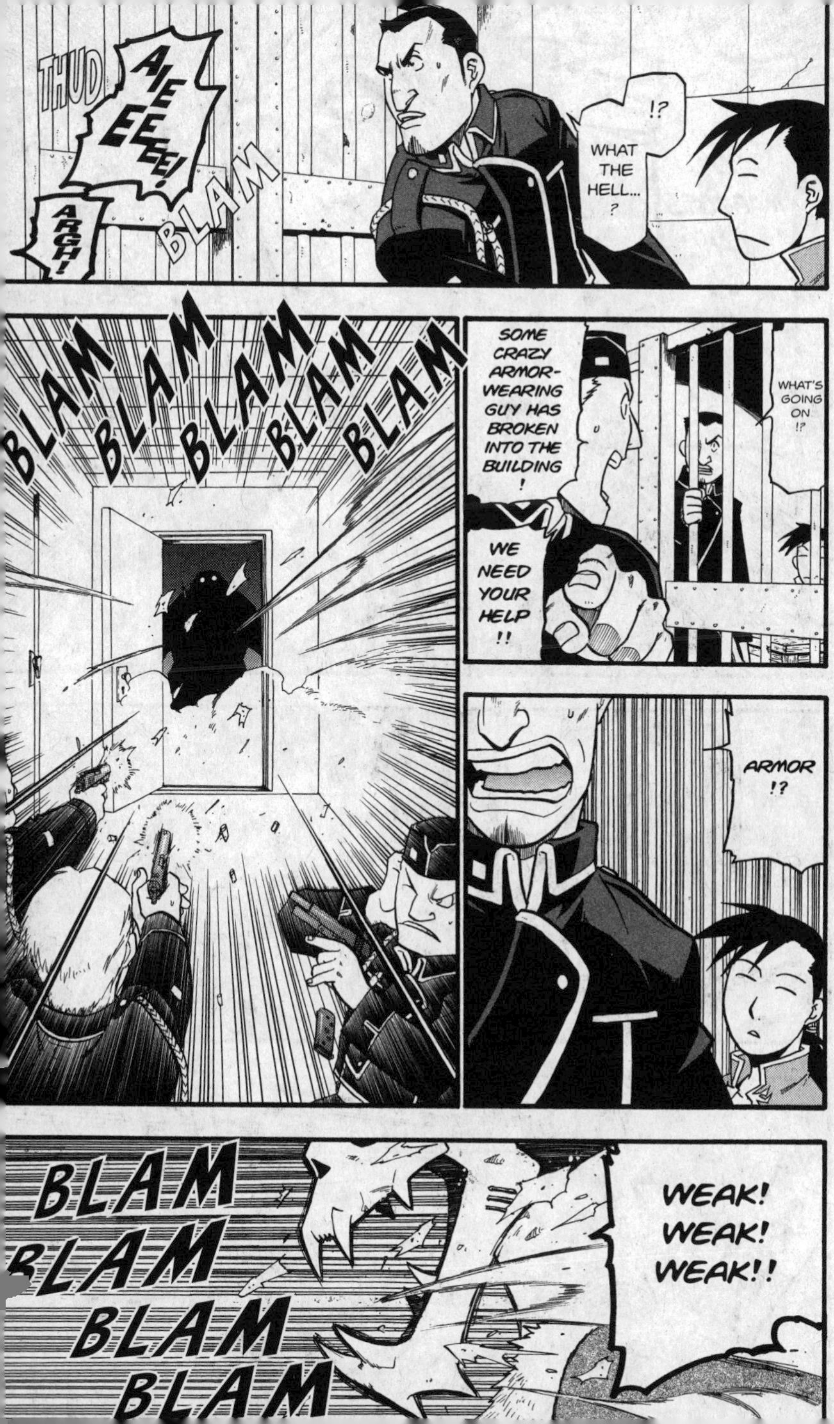
!?
WHAT THE HELL...?
BLAM
AIEEEEEE!
THUD
ARGH!
WHAT'S GOING ON!?
SOME CRAZY ARMOR-WEARING GUY HAS BROKEN INTO THE BUILDING!
WE NEED YOUR HELP!!
ARMOR!?
BLAM BLAM BLAM BLAM BLAM
WEAK! WEAK! WEAK!!
BLAM BLAM BLAM BLAM

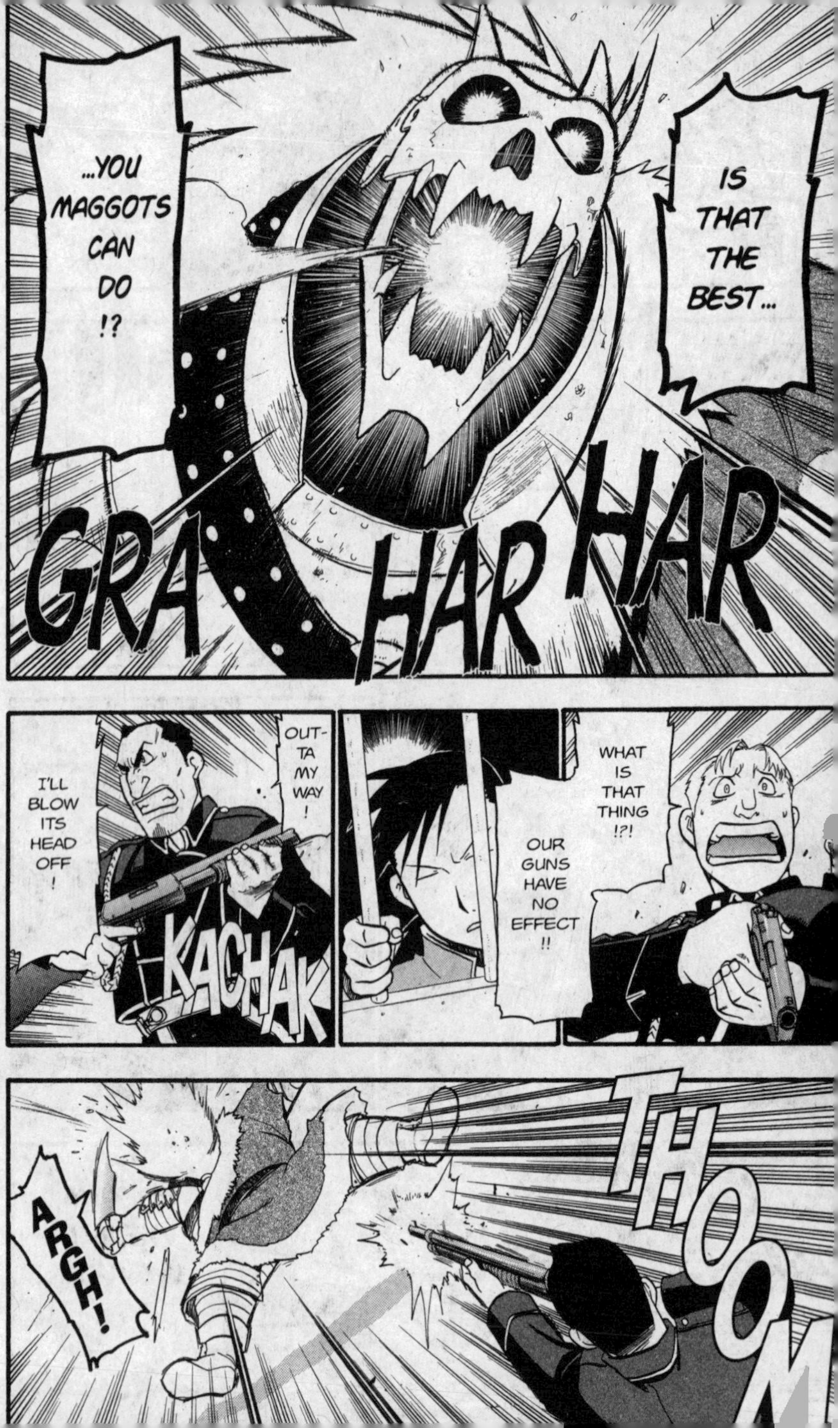
IS THAT THE BEST...
...YOU MAGGOTS CAN DO !?
GRA HAR HAR
WHAT IS THAT THING !?!
OUR GUNS HAVE NO EFFECT !!
OUT-TA MY WAY !
I'LL BLOW ITS HEAD OFF !
KACHAK
THOOM
ARGH!

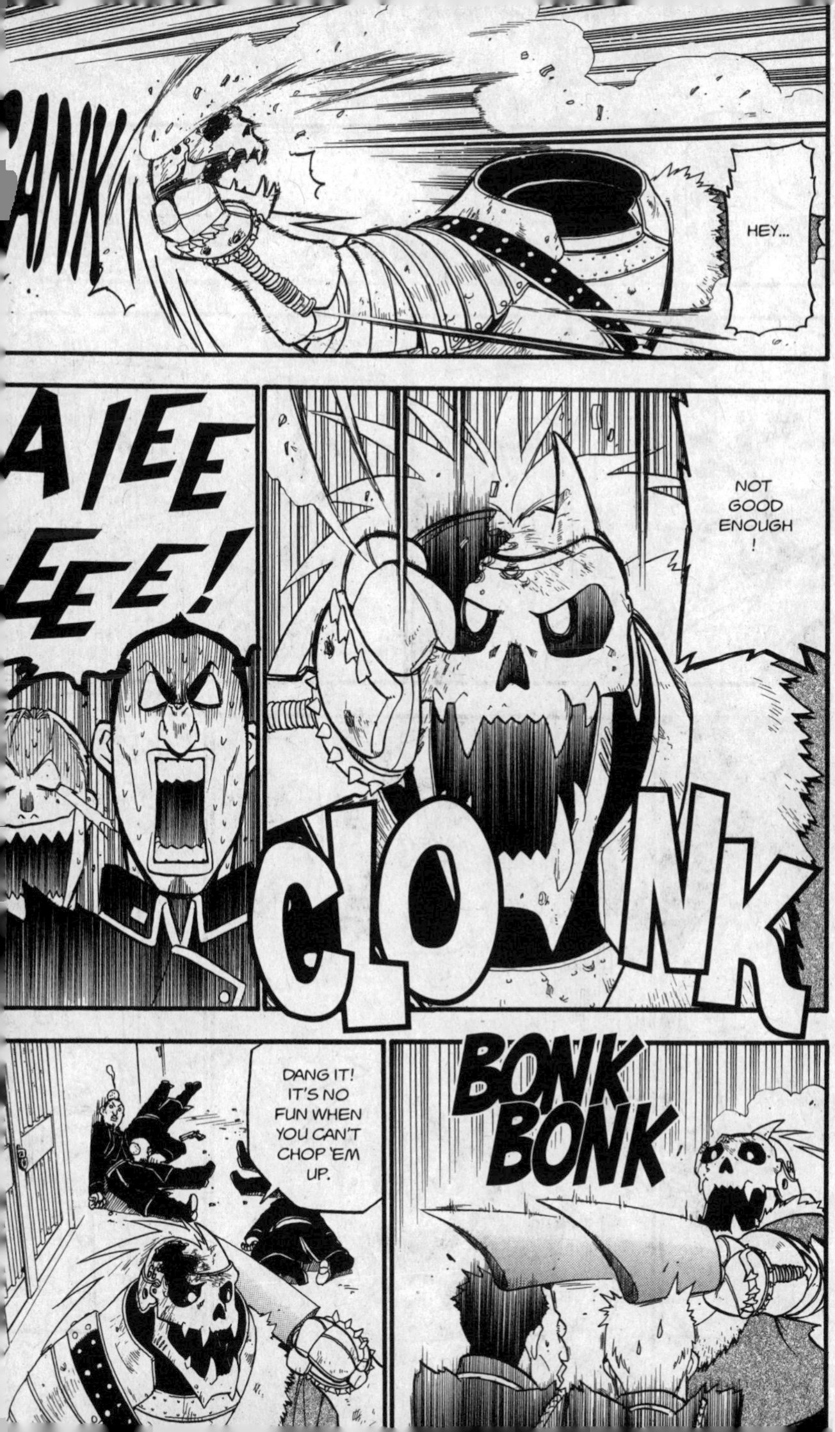
HEY...
CANK
NOT GOOD ENOUGH!
CLONK
AIEEEEE!
BONK BONK
DANG IT! IT'S NO FUN WHEN YOU CAN'T CHOP 'EM UP.

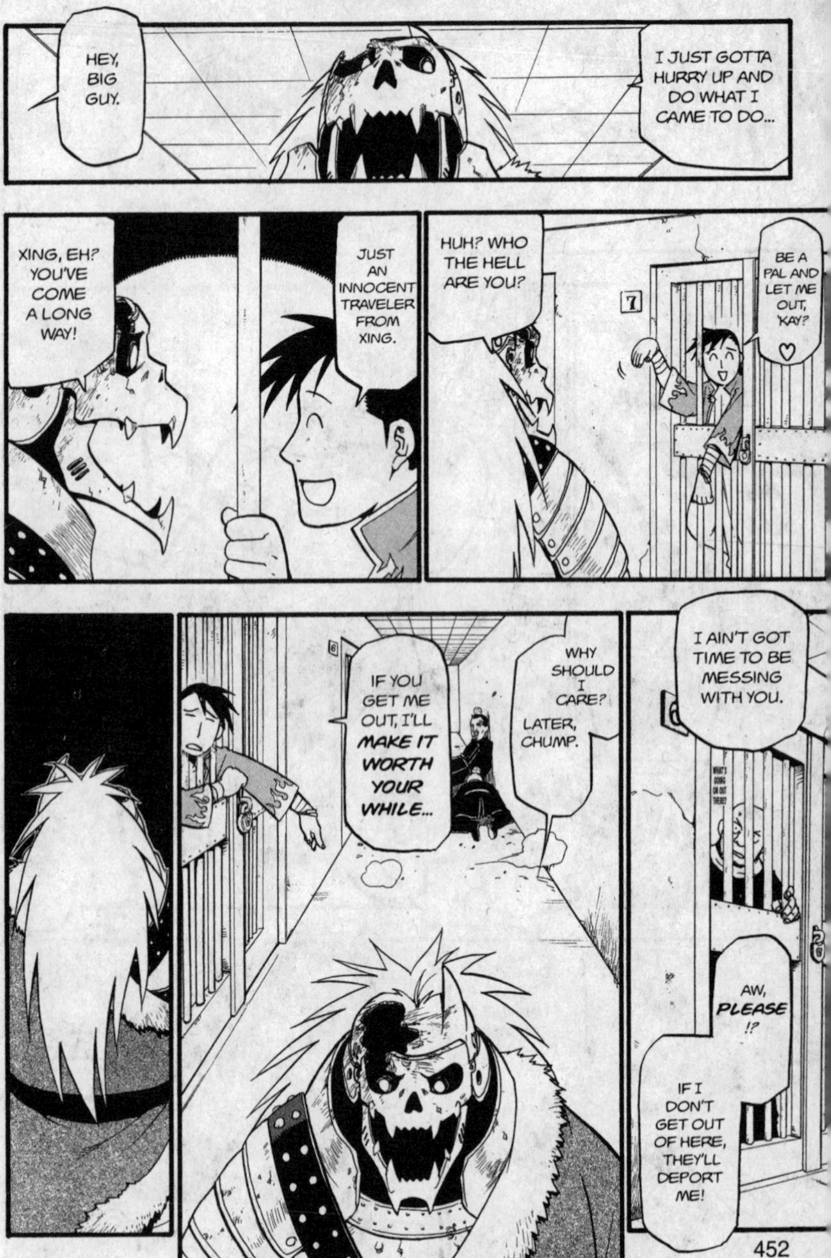
I JUST GOTTA HURRY UP AND DO WHAT I CAME TO DO...
HEY, BIG GUY.
BE A PAL AND LET ME OUT, 'KAY? ♡
HUH? WHO THE HELL ARE YOU?
JUST AN INNOCENT TRAVELER FROM XING.
XING, EH? YOU'VE COME A LONG WAY!
I AIN'T GOT TIME TO BE MESSING WITH YOU.
WHAT'S GOING ON OUT THERE?
AW, **PLEASE**!?
IF I DON'T GET OUT OF HERE, THEY'LL DEPORT ME!
WHY SHOULD I CARE?
LATER, CHUMP.
IF YOU GET ME OUT, I'LL ***MAKE IT WORTH YOUR WHILE...***

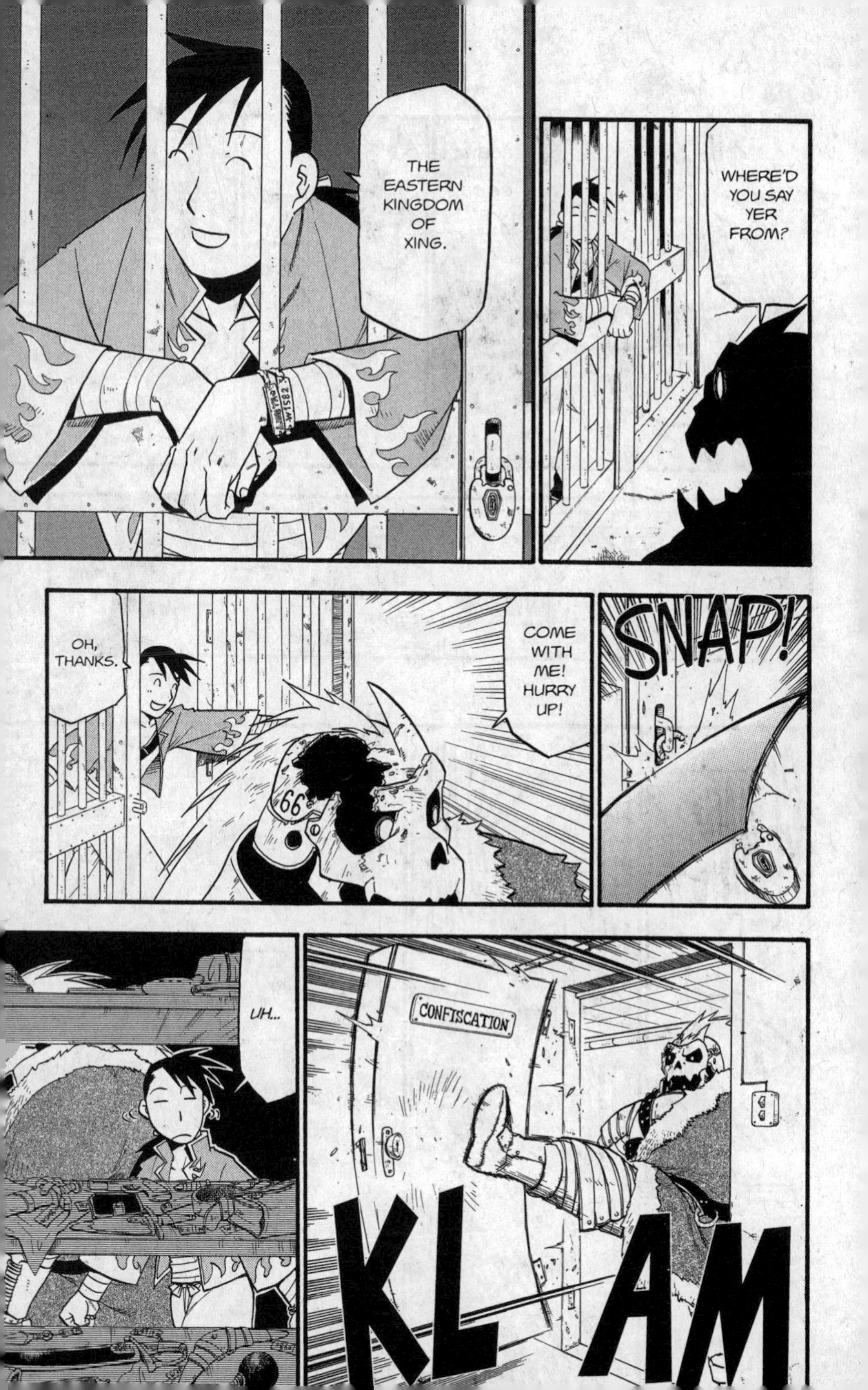
WHERE'D YOU SAY YER FROM?
THE EASTERN KINGDOM OF XING.
SNAP!
COME WITH ME! HURRY UP!
OH, THANKS.
CONFISCATION
KLAM
UH...

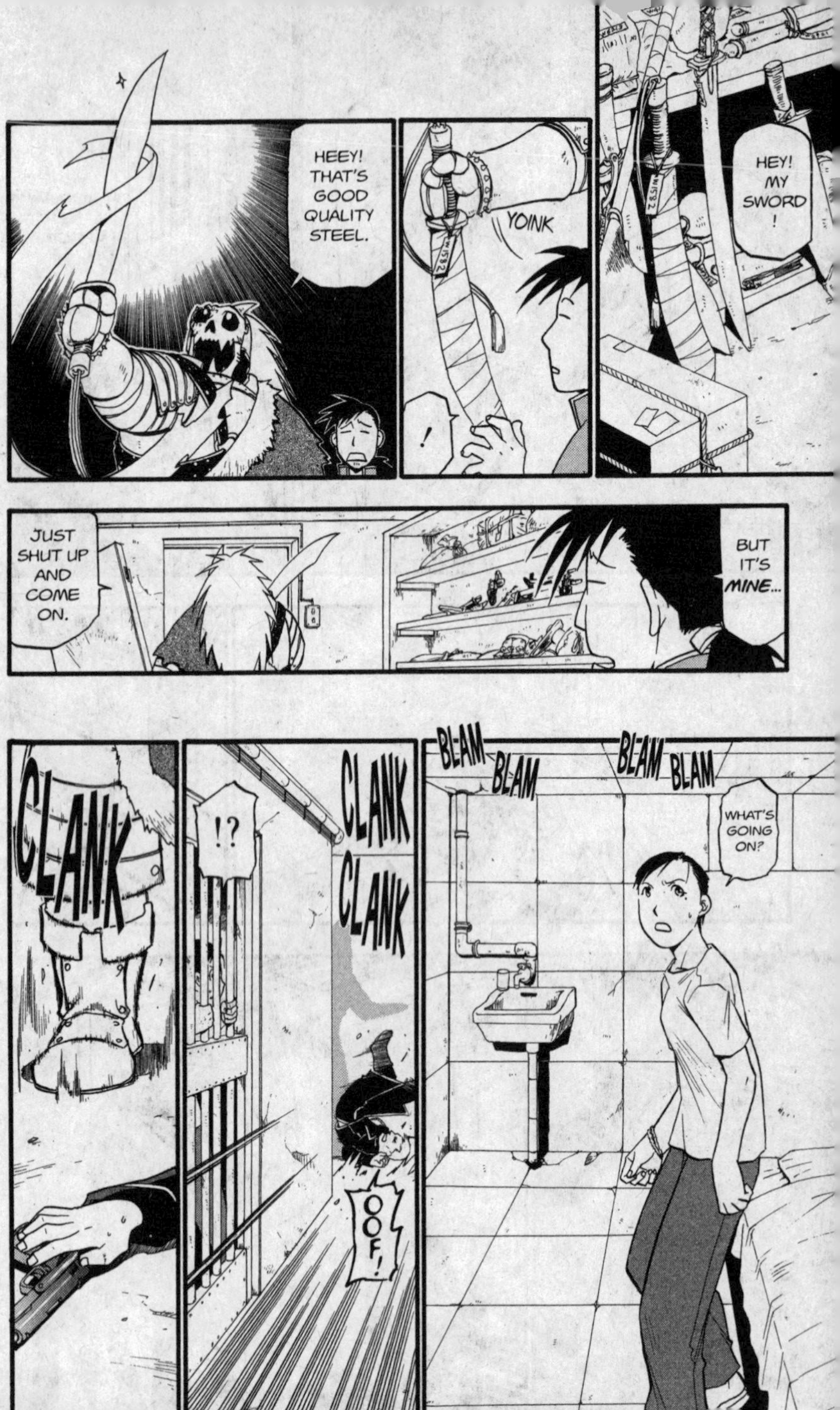
HEY! MY SWORD !
YOINK
!
HEEY! THAT'S GOOD QUALITY STEEL.
BUT IT'S *MINE*...
JUST SHUT UP AND COME ON.
BLAM BLAM
BLAM BLAM
WHAT'S GOING ON?
CLANK
CLANK
OOF!
!?
CLANK

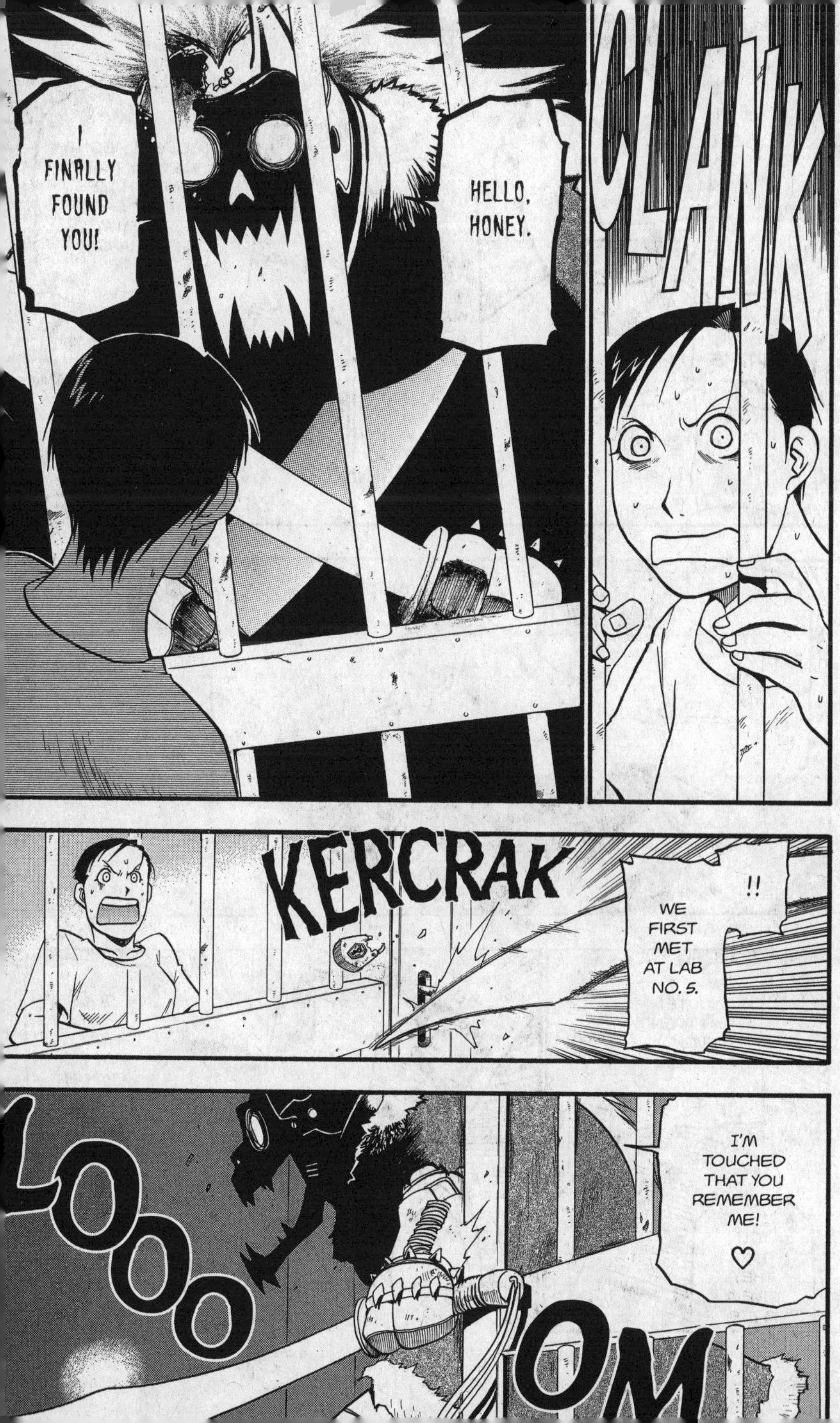
CLANK
HELLO, HONEY.
I FINALLY FOUND YOU!
!!
WE FIRST MET AT LAB NO. 5.
KERCRAK
I'M TOUCHED THAT YOU REMEMBER ME! ♥
LOOOOOM

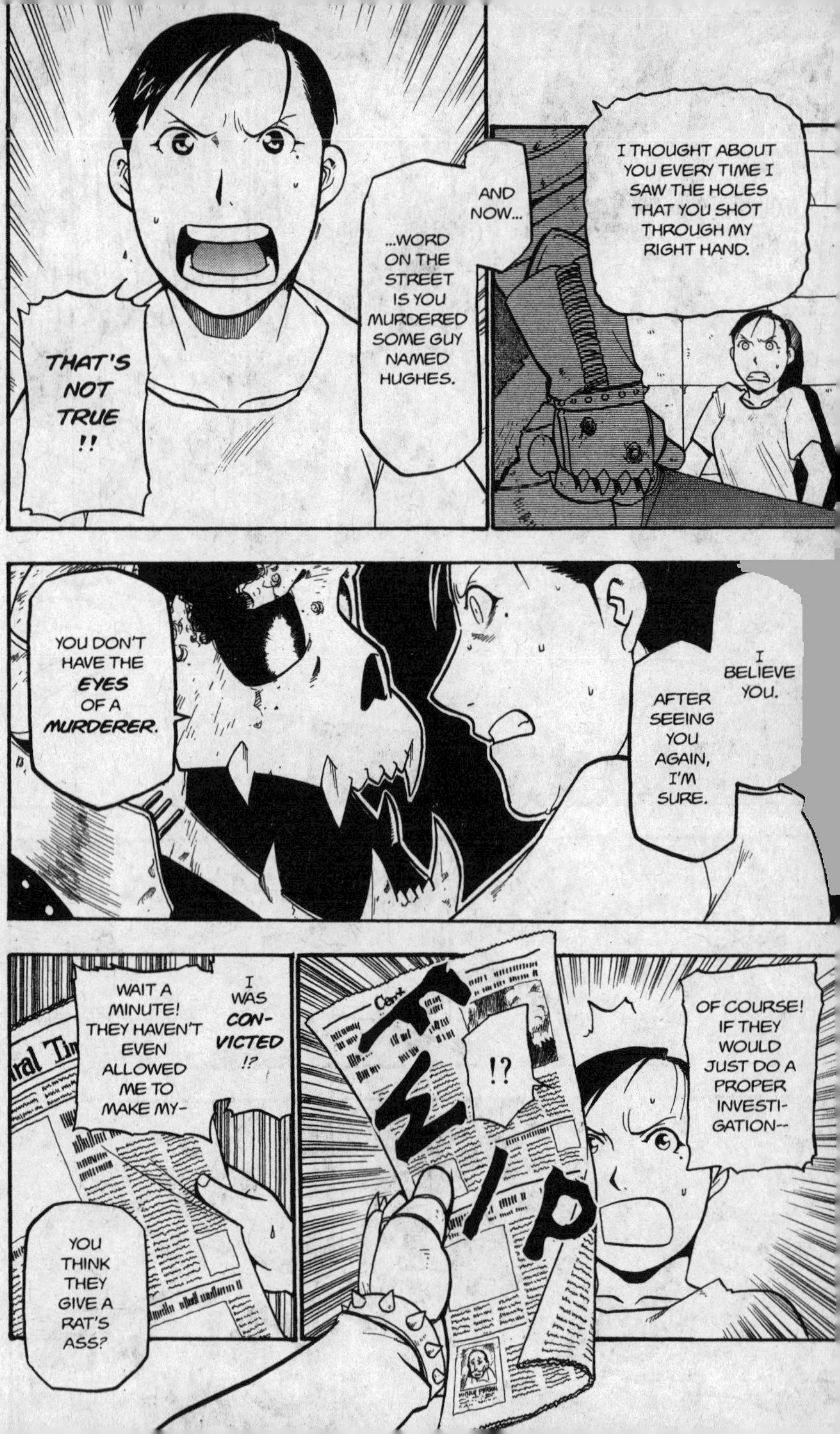
I THOUGHT ABOUT YOU EVERY TIME I SAW THE HOLES THAT YOU SHOT THROUGH MY RIGHT HAND.
AND NOW...
...WORD ON THE STREET IS YOU MURDERED SOME GUY NAMED HUGHES.
THAT'S NOT TRUE !!
I BELIEVE YOU.
AFTER SEEING YOU AGAIN, I'M SURE.
YOU DON'T HAVE THE EYES OF A MURDERER.
OF COURSE! IF THEY WOULD JUST DO A PROPER INVESTIGATION--
FWIP
!?
I WAS CONVICTED !?
WAIT A MINUTE! THEY HAVEN'T EVEN ALLOWED ME TO MAKE MY-
YOU THINK THEY GIVE A RAT'S ASS?

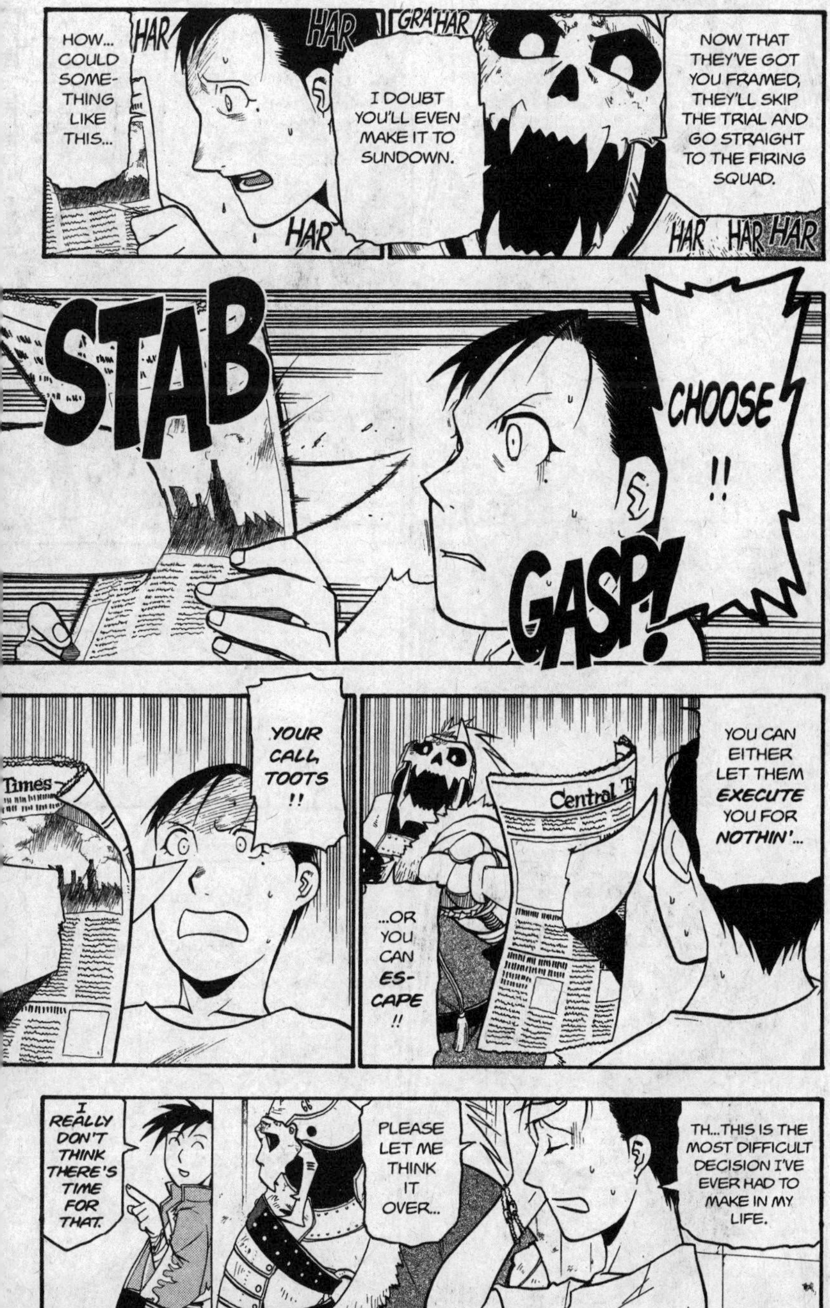

NOW THAT THEY'VE GOT YOU FRAMED, THEY'LL SKIP THE TRIAL AND GO STRAIGHT TO THE FIRING SQUAD.
GRA HAR
HAR HAR HAR
I DOUBT YOU'LL EVEN MAKE IT TO SUNDOWN.
HAR
HAR
HAR
HOW... COULD SOME-THING LIKE THIS...
CHOOSE !!
GASP!
STAB
YOU CAN EITHER LET THEM EXECUTE YOU FOR NOTHIN'...
...OR YOU CAN ES-CAPE !!
Central T
YOUR CALL, TOOTS !!
Times
TH...THIS IS THE MOST DIFFICULT DECISION I'VE EVER HAD TO MAKE IN MY LIFE.
PLEASE LET ME THINK IT OVER...
I REALLY DON'T THINK THERE'S TIME FOR THAT.

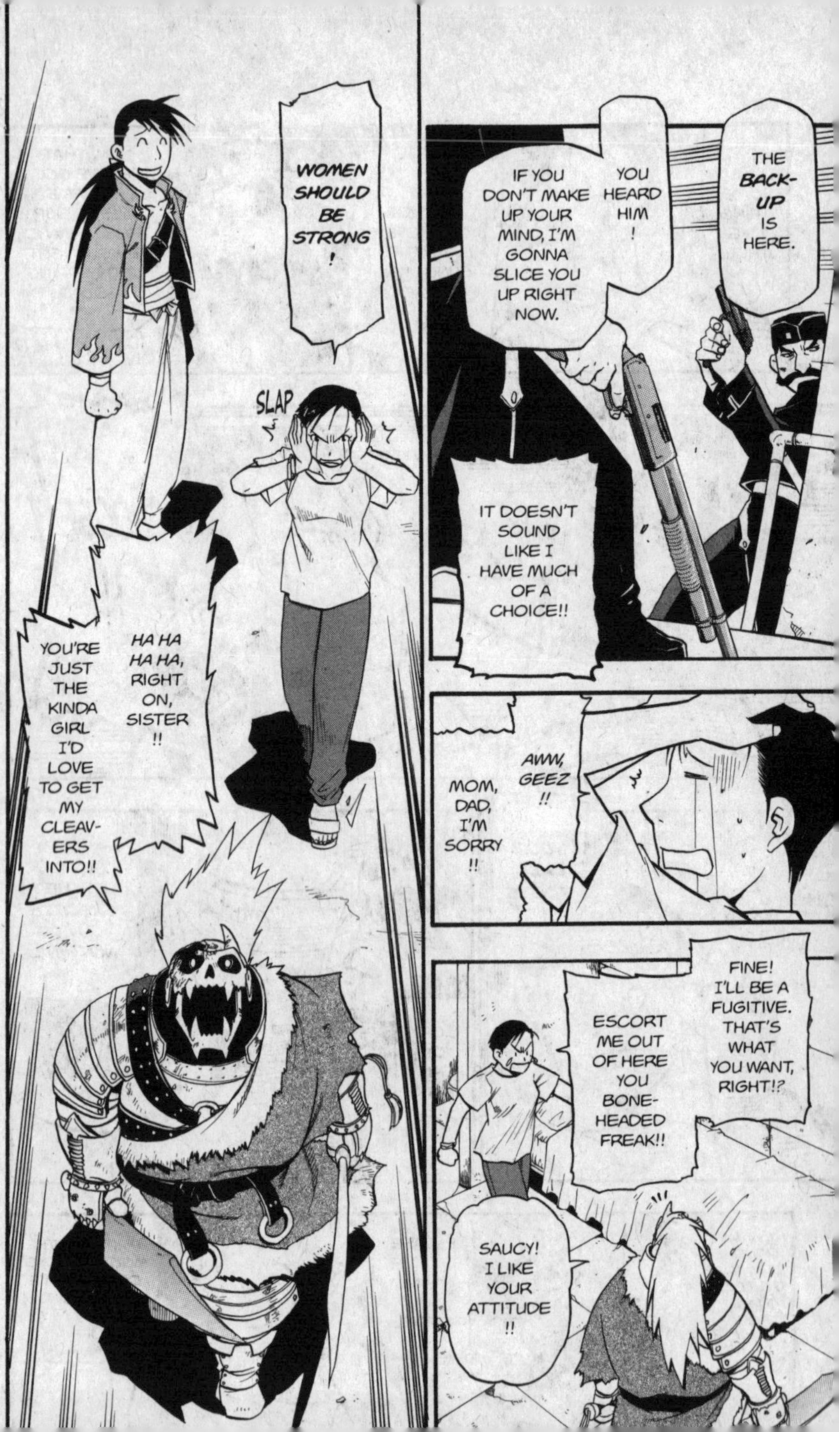
THE BACK-UP IS HERE.
YOU HEARD HIM!
IF YOU DON'T MAKE UP YOUR MIND, I'M GONNA SLICE YOU UP RIGHT NOW.
IT DOESN'T SOUND LIKE I HAVE MUCH OF A CHOICE!!
AWW, GEEZ!!
MOM, DAD, I'M SORRY!!
FINE! I'LL BE A FUGITIVE. THAT'S WHAT YOU WANT, RIGHT!?
ESCORT ME OUT OF HERE YOU BONE-HEADED FREAK!!
SAUCY! I LIKE YOUR ATTITUDE!!
WOMEN SHOULD BE STRONG!
SLAP
HA HA HA HA, RIGHT ON, SISTER!!
YOU'RE JUST THE KINDA GIRL I'D LOVE TO GET MY CLEAVERS INTO!!

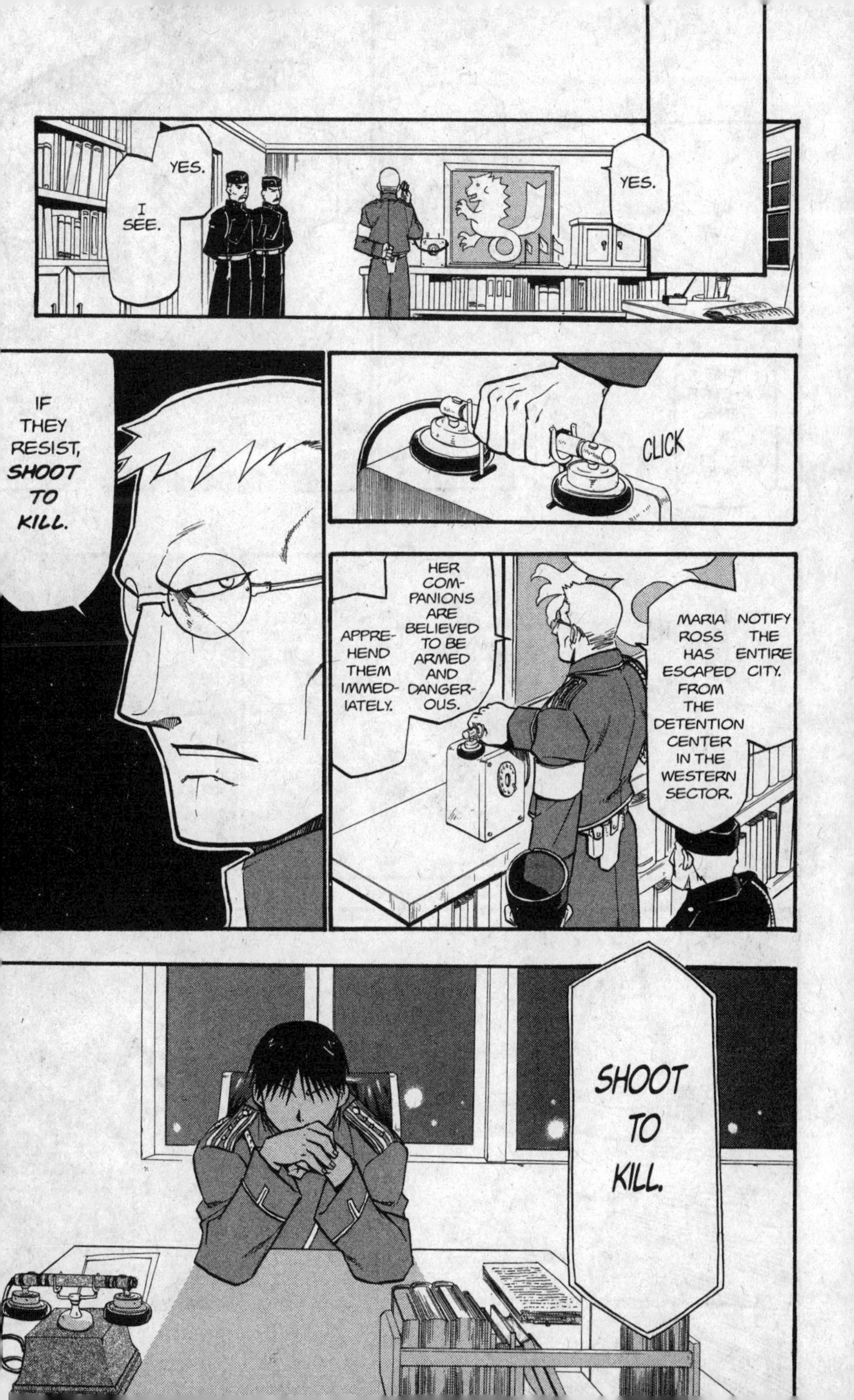
YES.
YES. I SEE.
CLICK
MARIA ROSS HAS ESCAPED FROM THE DETENTION CENTER IN THE WESTERN SECTOR. NOTIFY THE ENTIRE CITY.
HER COMPANIONS ARE BELIEVED TO BE ARMED AND DANGEROUS. APPREHEND THEM IMMEDIATELY.
IF THEY RESIST, **SHOOT TO KILL.**
SHOOT TO KILL.

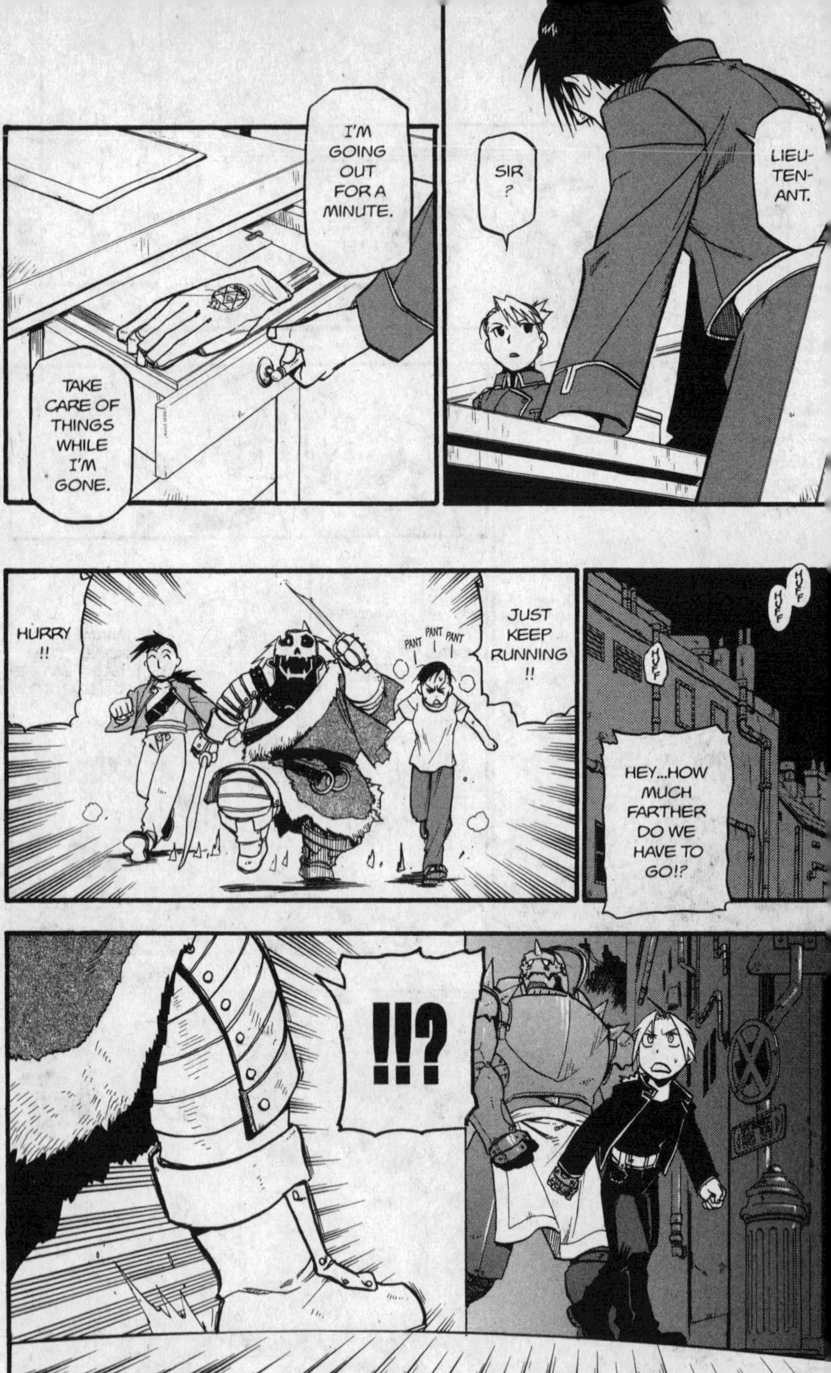
LIEU-TEN-ANT.
SIR ?
I'M GOING OUT FOR A MINUTE.
TAKE CARE OF THINGS WHILE I'M GONE.
HUFF HUFF HUFF
HUFF
HEY...HOW MUCH FARTHER DO WE HAVE TO GO!?
JUST KEEP RUNNING !!
PANT PANT PANT
HURRY !!
!!?

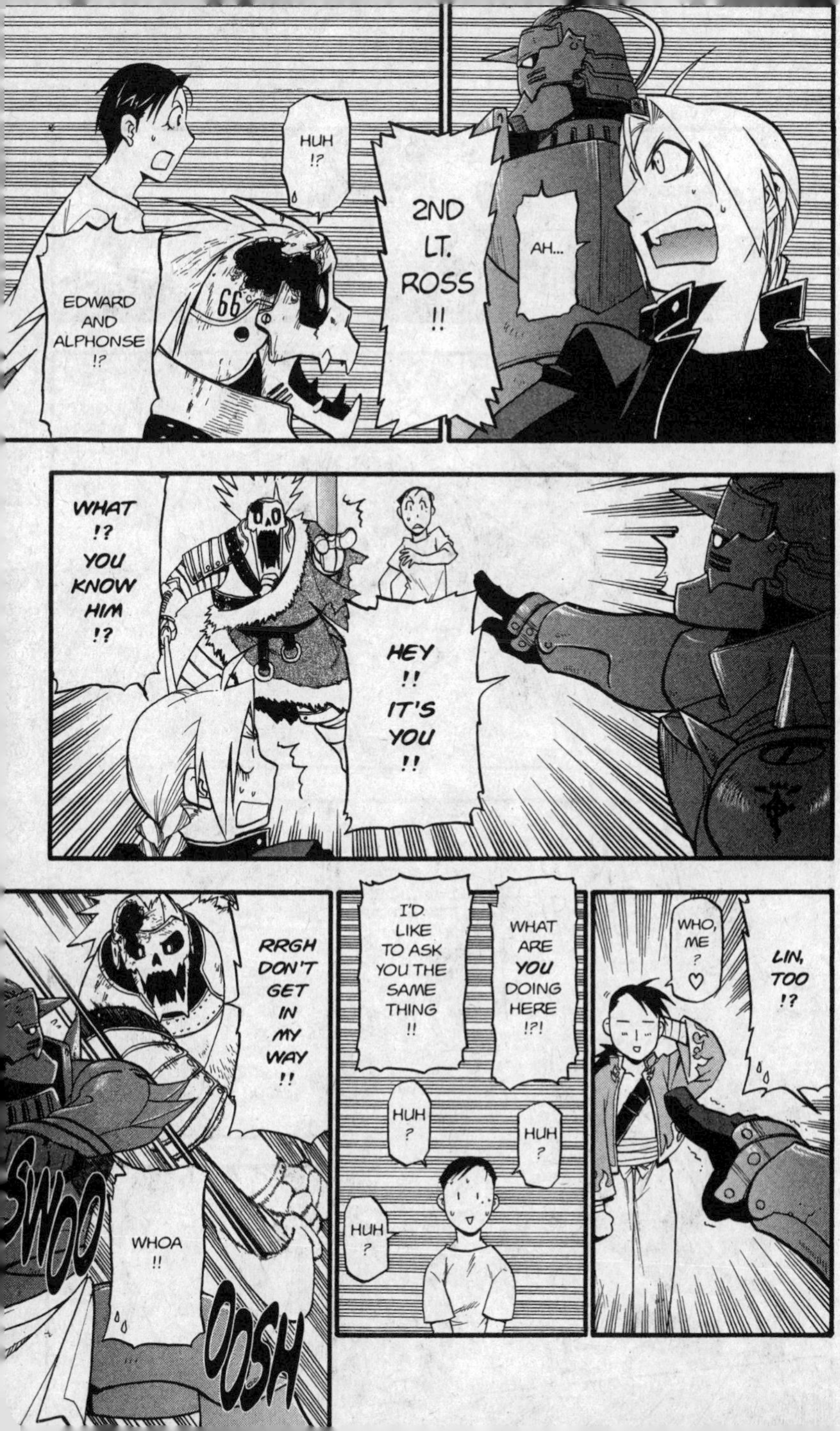
AH...
2ND LT. ROSS !!
HUH !?
EDWARD AND ALPHONSE !?
HEY !! IT'S YOU !!
WHAT !? YOU KNOW HIM !?
LIN, TOO !?
WHO, ME ? ♡
WHAT ARE YOU DOING HERE !?!
I'D LIKE TO ASK YOU THE SAME THING !!
HUH ?
HUH ?
HUH ?
RRGH DON'T GET IN MY WAY !!
SWOOOOSH
WHOA !!

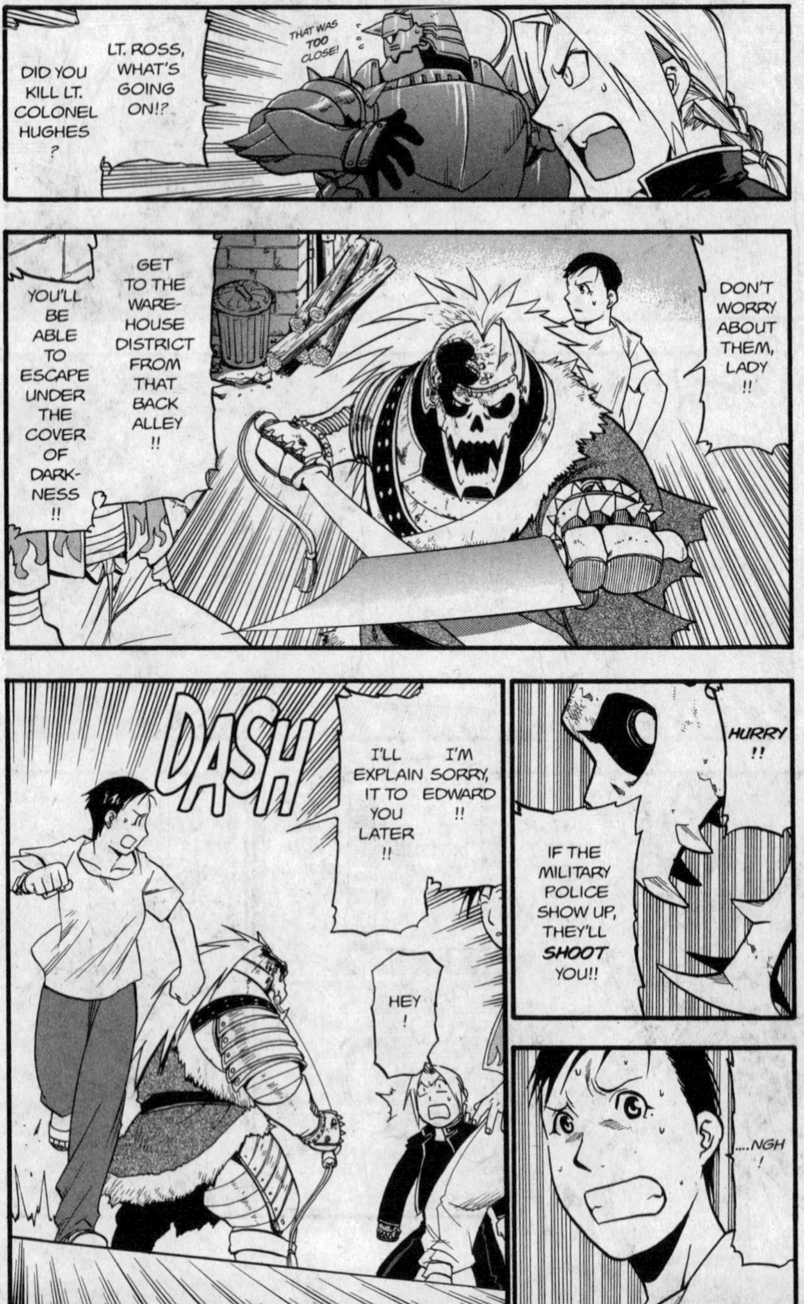
THAT WAS TOO CLOSE!
LT. ROSS, WHAT'S GOING ON!?
DID YOU KILL LT. COLONEL HUGHES?
DON'T WORRY ABOUT THEM, LADY!!
GET TO THE WARE-HOUSE DISTRICT FROM THAT BACK ALLEY!!
YOU'LL BE ABLE TO ESCAPE UNDER THE COVER OF DARK-NESS!!
HURRY!!
IF THE MILITARY POLICE SHOW UP, THEY'LL SHOOT YOU!!
....NGH!
I'M SORRY, EDWARD!!
I'LL EXPLAIN IT TO YOU LATER!!
DASH
HEY!

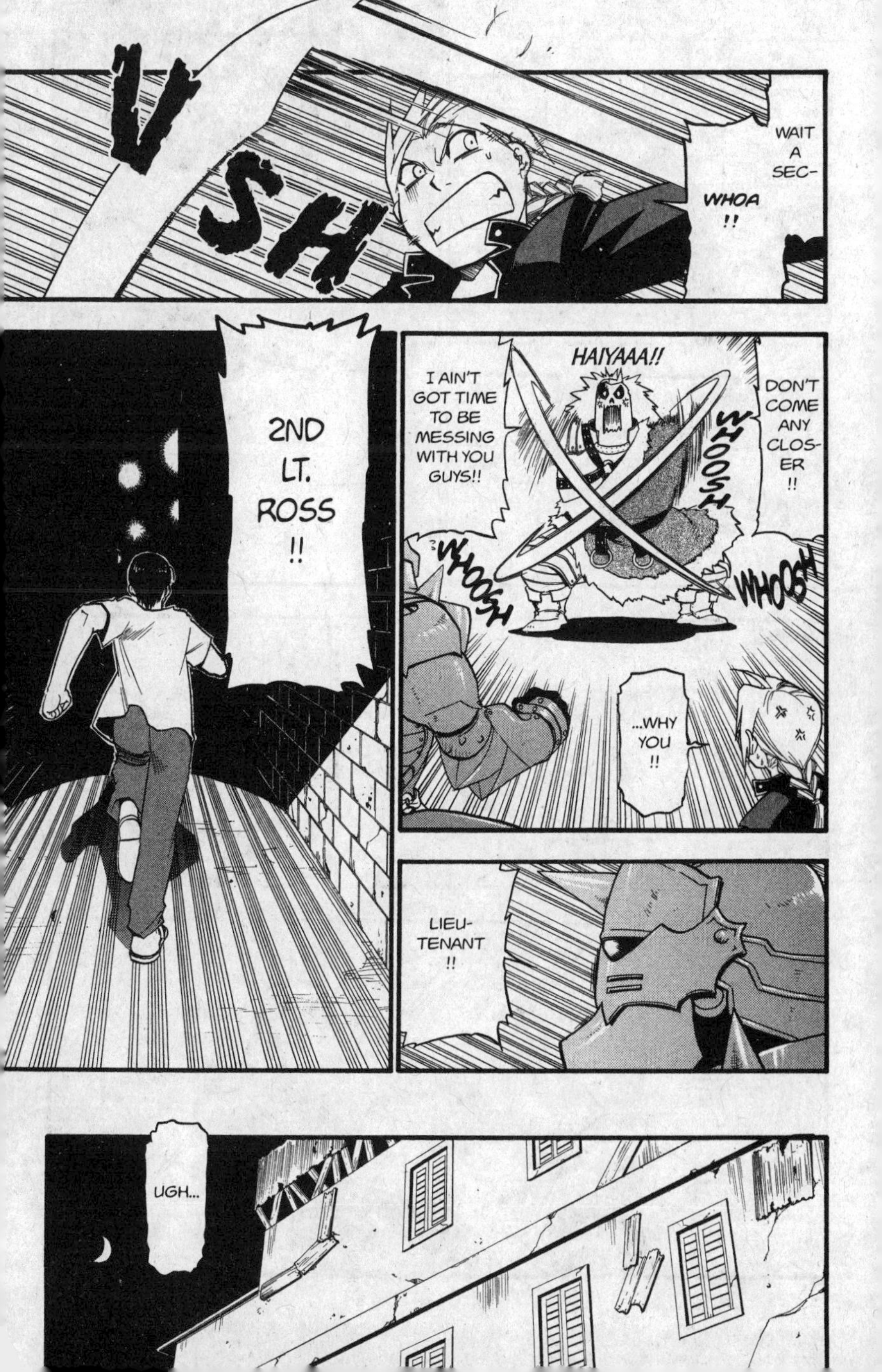
WAIT A SEC-
WHOA!!
VSH
DON'T COME ANY CLOSER!!
HAIYAAA!!
WHOOSH
I AIN'T GOT TIME TO BE MESSING WITH YOU GUYS!!
WHOOSH
WHOOSH
...WHY YOU!!
LIEUTENANT!!
2ND LT. ROSS!!
UGH...

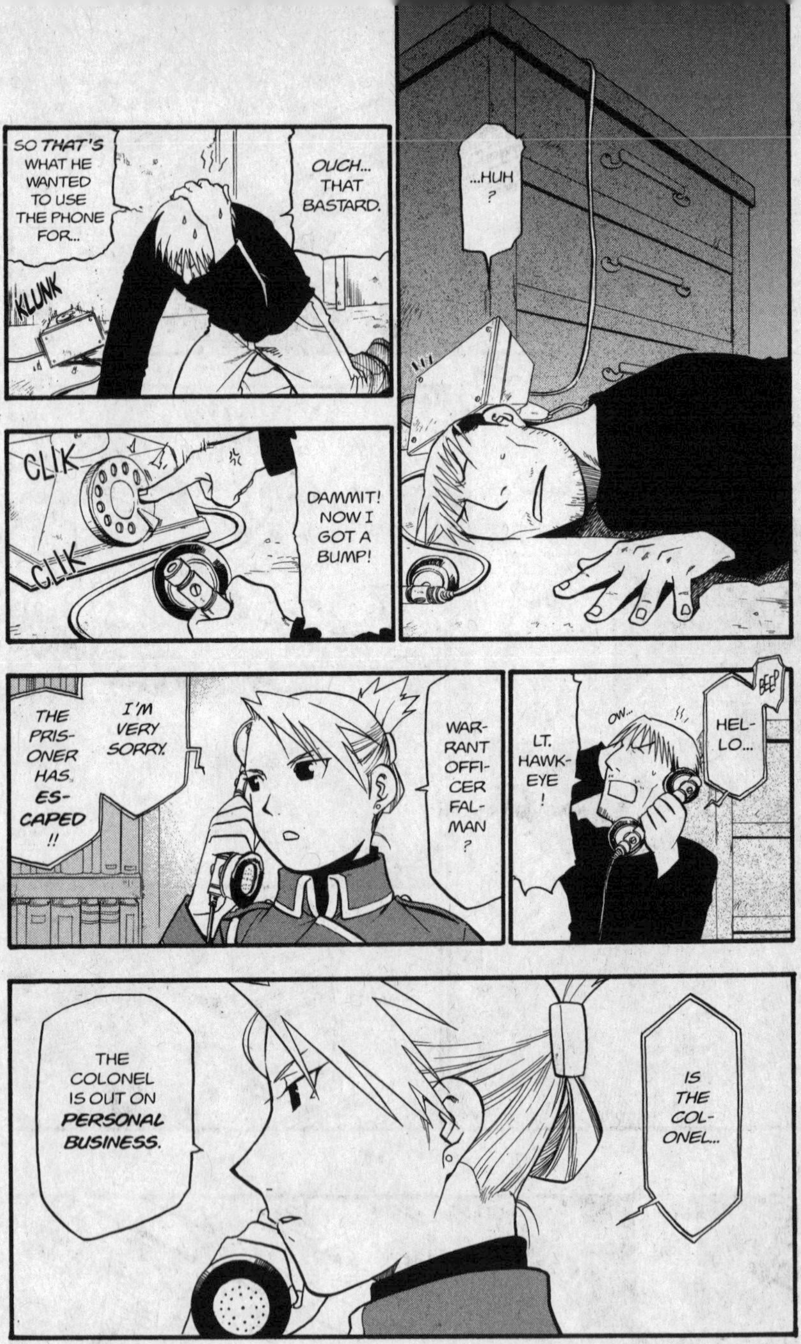
...HUH?
OUCH... THAT BASTARD.
SO *THAT'S* WHAT HE WANTED TO USE THE PHONE FOR...
KLUNK
DAMMIT! NOW I GOT A BUMP!
CLIK
CLIK
BEEP
HEL-LO...
LT. HAWK-EYE!
OW...
WAR-RANT OFFI-CER FAL-MAN?
I'M VERY SORRY.
THE PRIS-ONER HAS ES-CAPED!!
IS THE COL-ONEL...
THE COLONEL IS OUT ON **PERSONAL BUSINESS.**

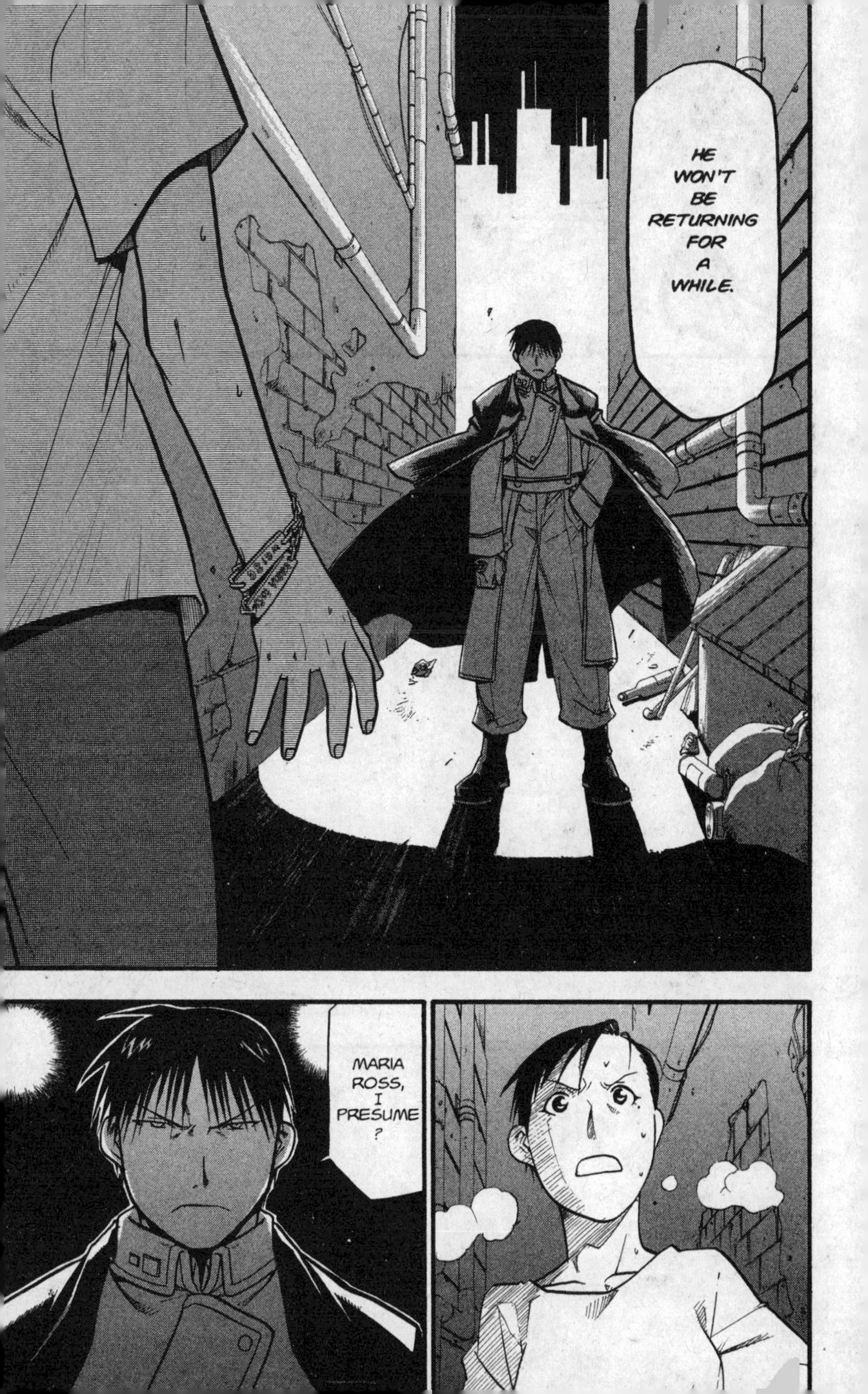
HE WON'T BE RETURNING FOR A WHILE.
MARIA ROSS, I PRESUME?

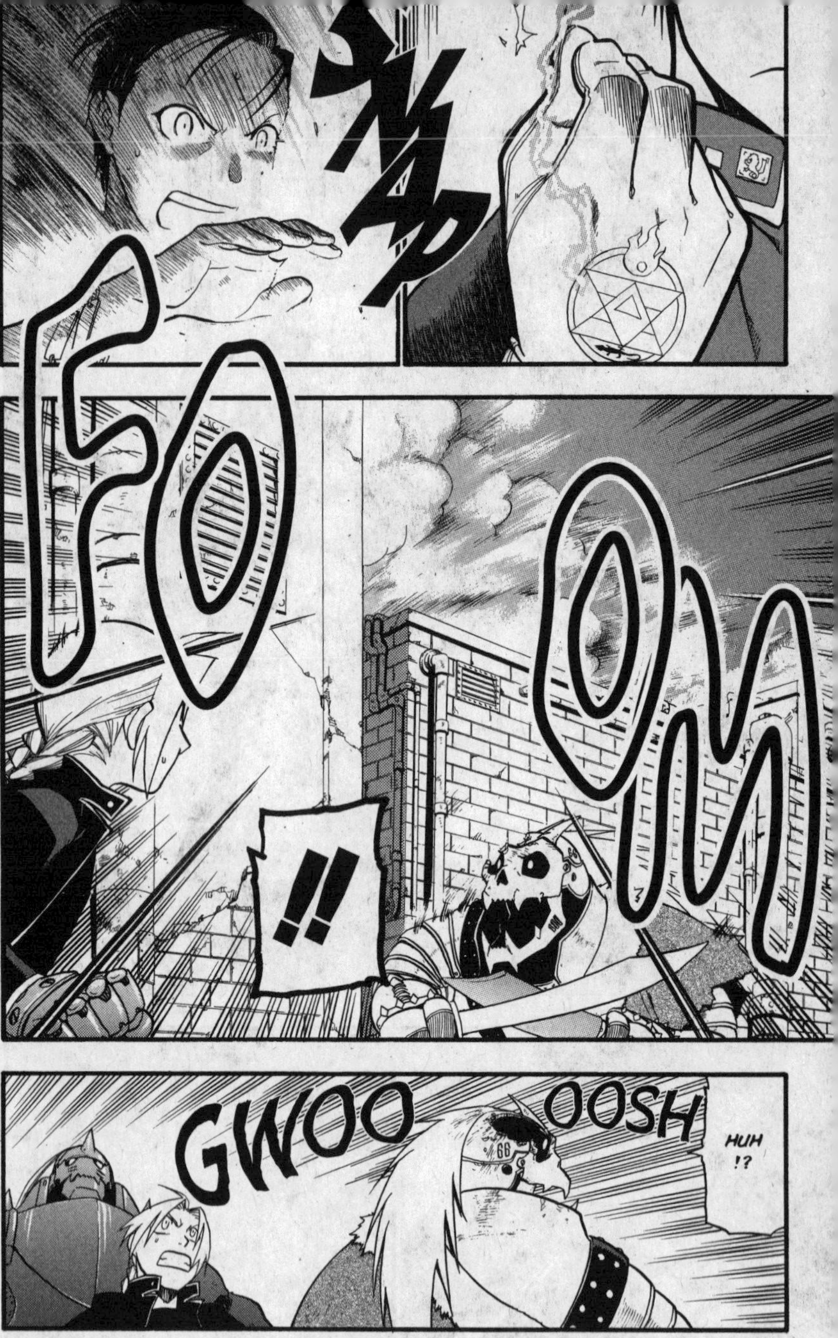
SNAP
FOOM
!!
HUH !?
GWOO OOSH

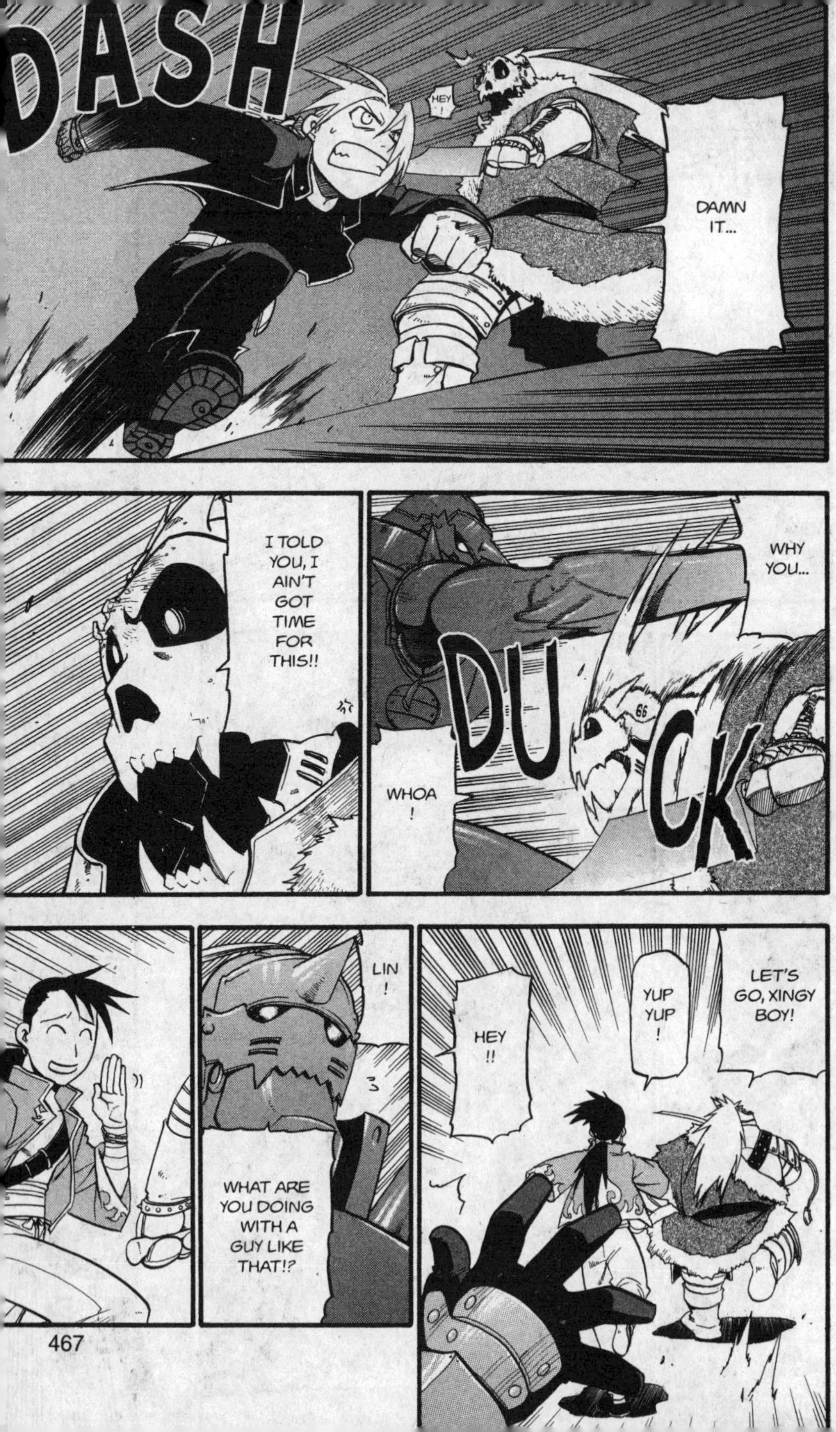
DAMN IT...
HEY!
DASH
WHY YOU...
DUCK
WHOA!
I TOLD YOU, I AIN'T GOT TIME FOR THIS!!
LET'S GO, XINGY BOY!
YUP YUP!
HEY!!
LIN!
WHAT ARE YOU DOING WITH A GUY LIKE THAT!?

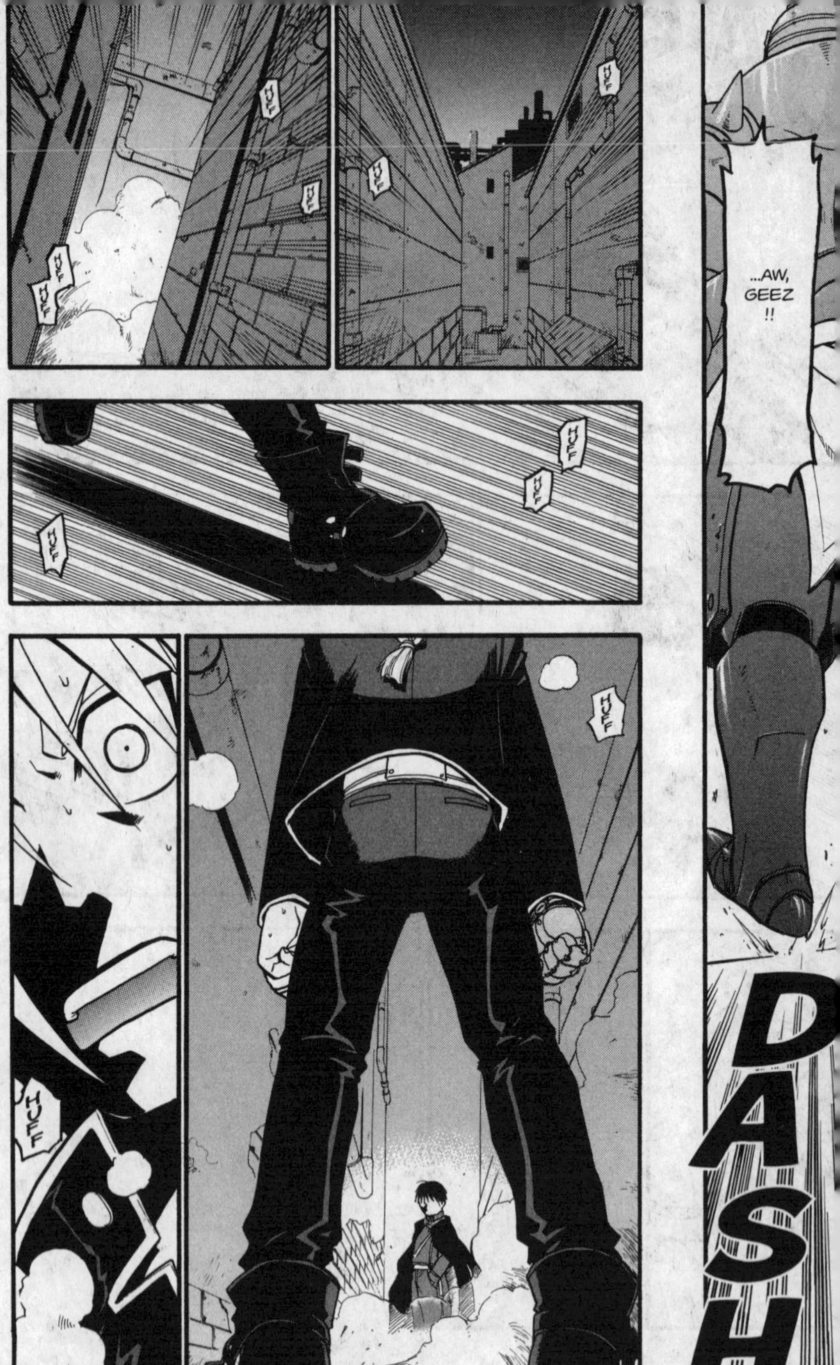
...AW, GEEZ !!
DASH
HUFF
HUFF
HUFF
HUFF
HUFF
HUFF
HUFF
HUFF
HUFF
HUFF
HUFF
HUFF

...FULL-METAL.

WELL, HELLO...

...UGH...

WHAT'S THE... MEANING... OF THIS?

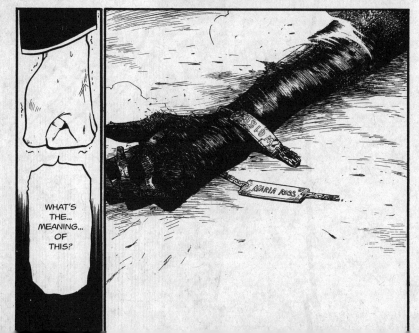

MARIA ROSS

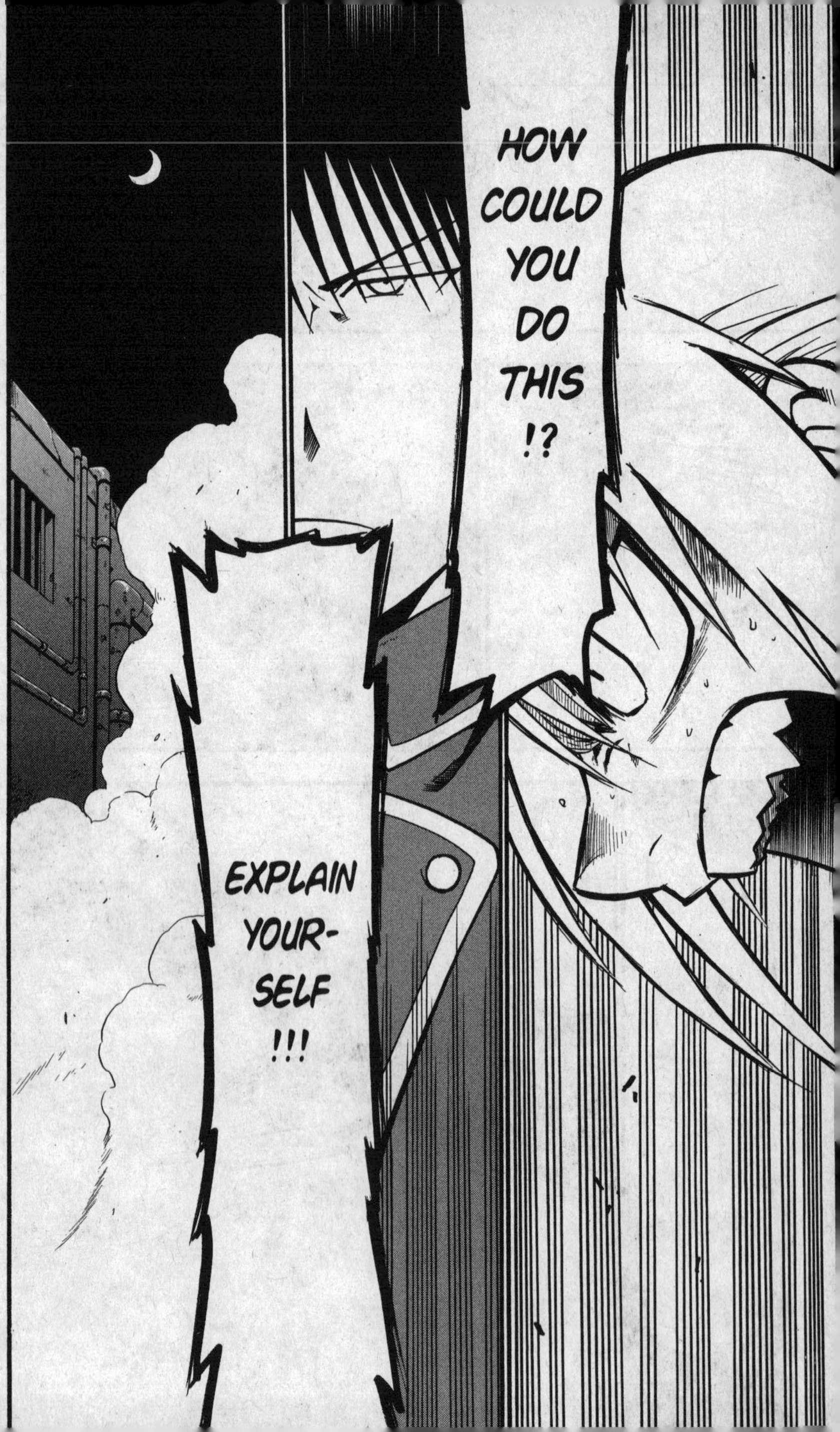
HOW COULD YOU DO THIS !?
EXPLAIN YOUR-SELF !!!

FULLMETAL
ALCHEMIST

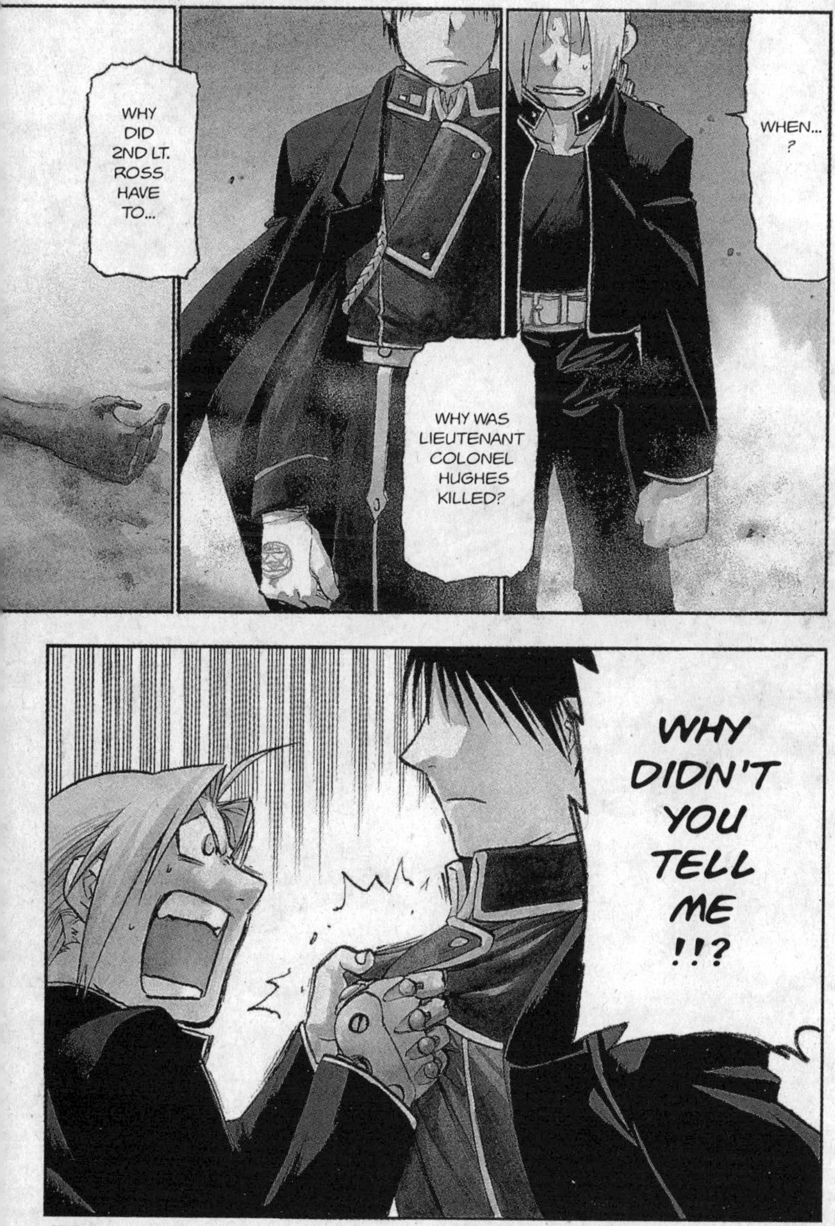
WHEN... ?
WHY WAS LIEUTENANT COLONEL HUGHES KILLED?
WHY DID 2ND LT. ROSS HAVE TO...
WHY DIDN'T YOU TELL ME !!?

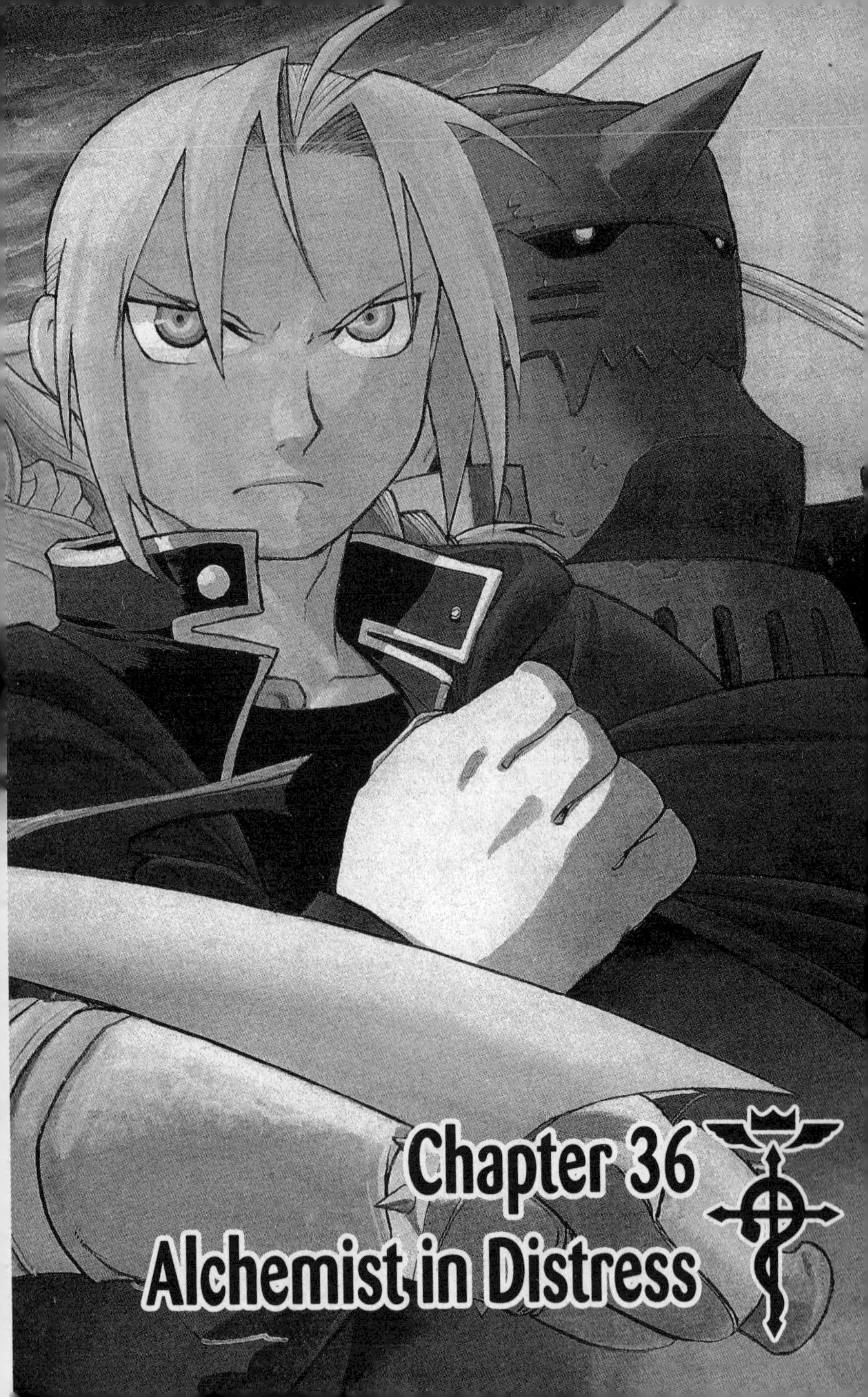
Chapter 36
Alchemist in Distress

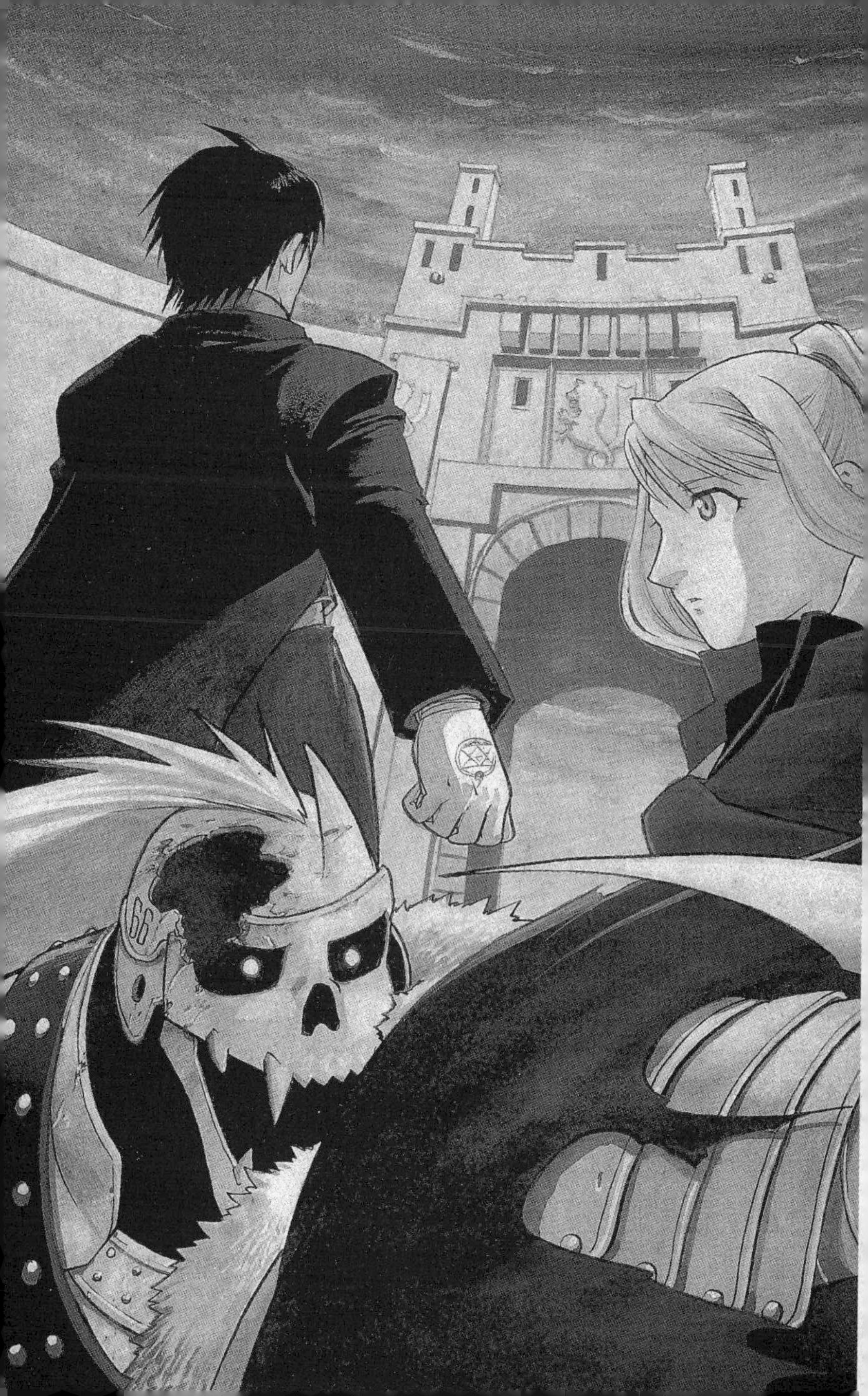

FULLMETAL
ALCHEMIST

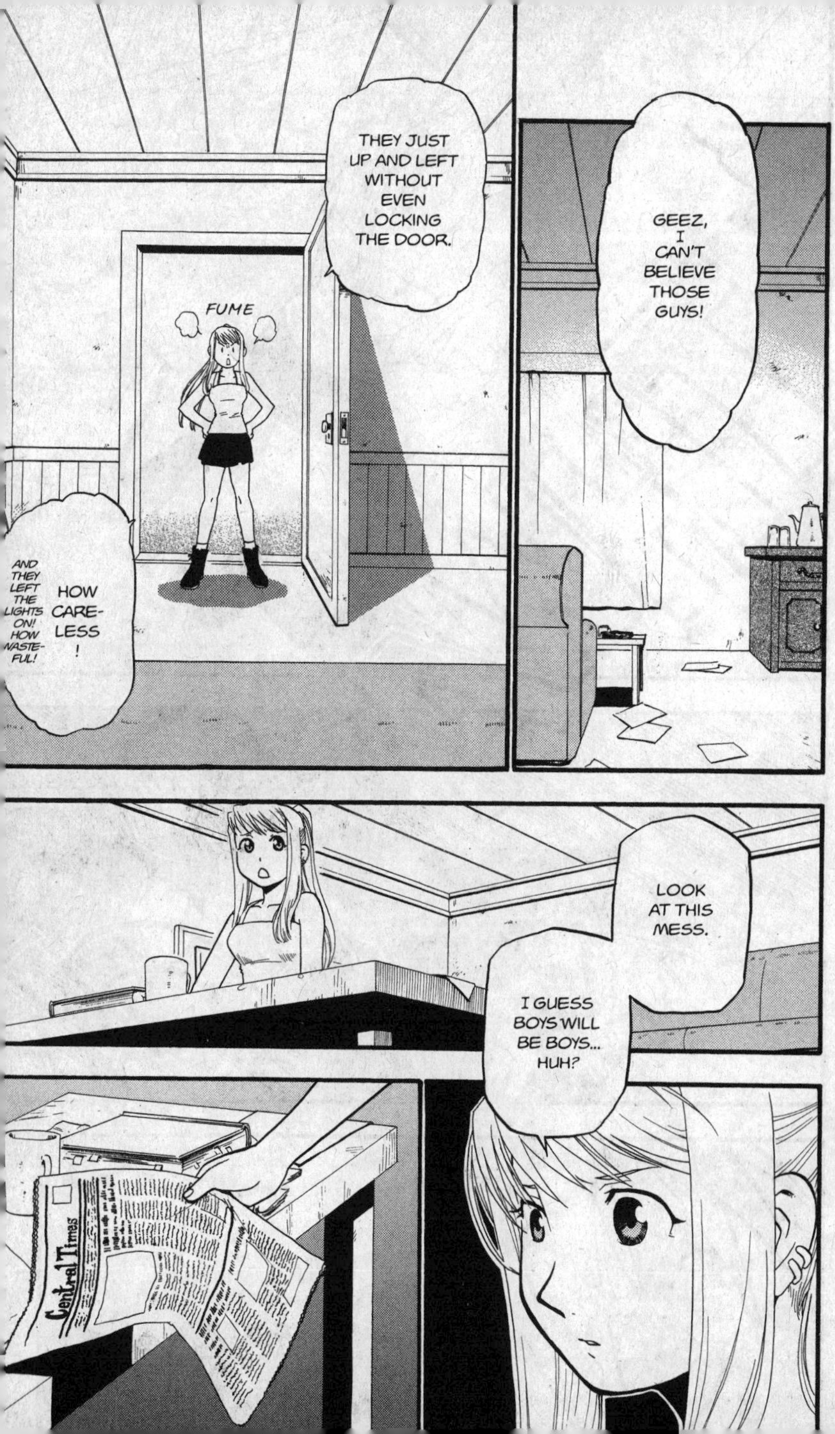
GEEZ, I CAN'T BELIEVE THOSE GUYS!
THEY JUST UP AND LEFT WITHOUT EVEN LOCKING THE DOOR.
FUME
HOW CARE-LESS!
AND THEY LEFT THE LIGHTS ON! HOW WASTE-FUL!
LOOK AT THIS MESS.
I GUESS BOYS WILL BE BOYS... HUH?
Central Times

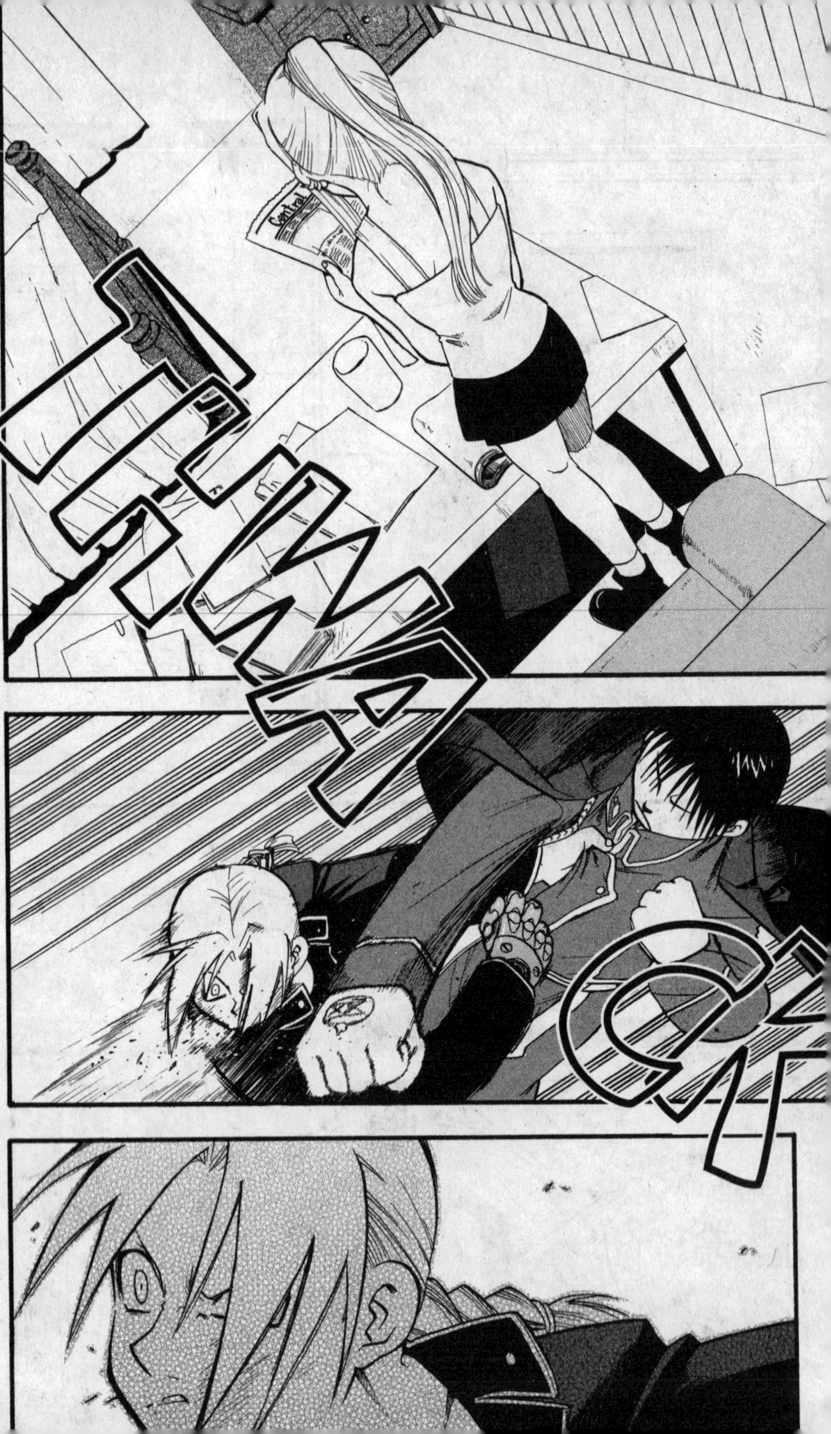
Central
THWA

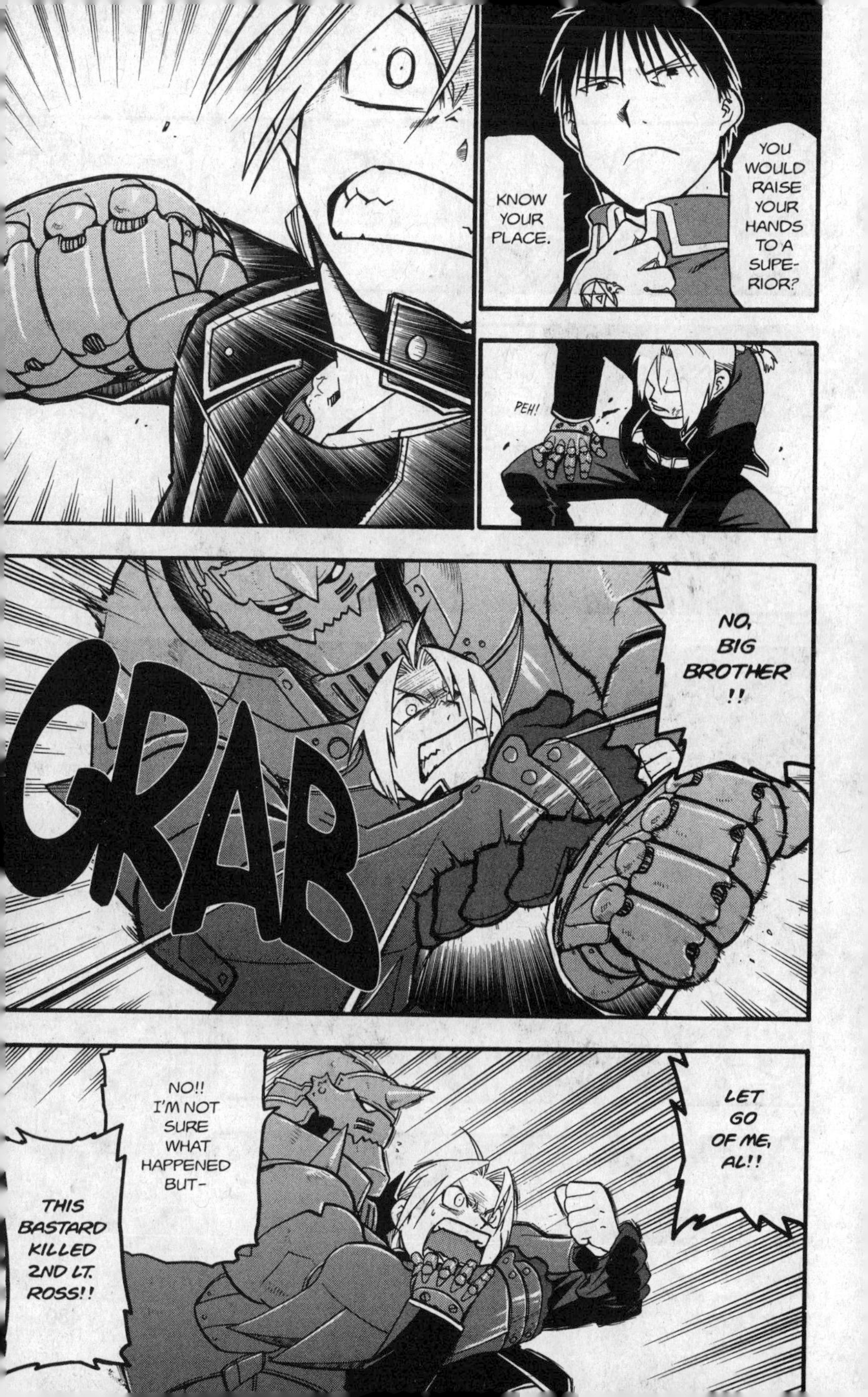
YOU WOULD RAISE YOUR HANDS TO A SUPER-RIOR?
KNOW YOUR PLACE.
PEH!
NO, BIG BROTHER !!
GRAB
LET GO OF ME, AL!!
NO!! I'M NOT SURE WHAT HAPPENED BUT-
THIS BASTARD KILLED 2ND LT. ROSS!!

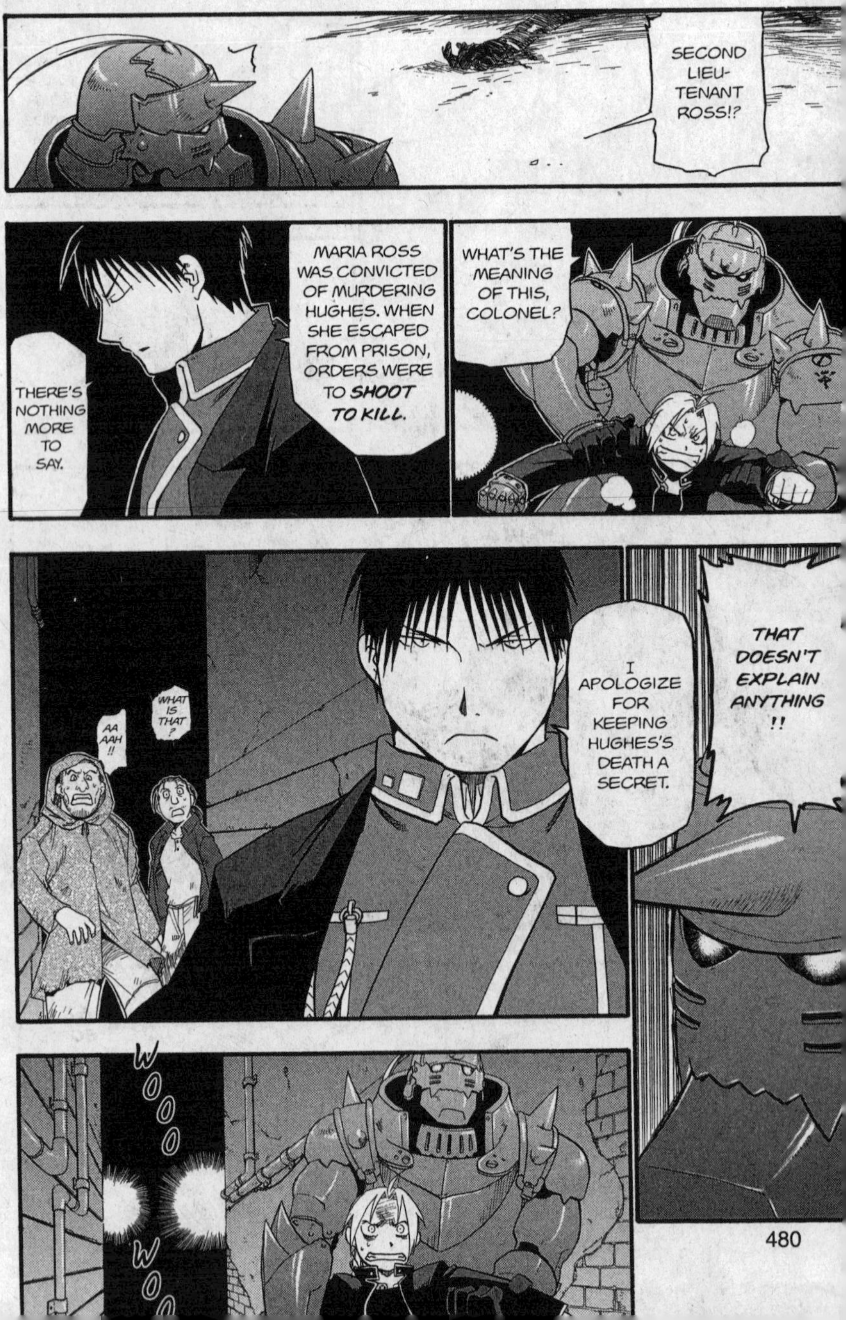
SECOND LIEU-TENANT ROSS!?
WHAT'S THE MEANING OF THIS, COLONEL?
MARIA ROSS WAS CONVICTED OF MURDERING HUGHES. WHEN SHE ESCAPED FROM PRISON, ORDERS WERE TO SHOOT TO KILL.
THERE'S NOTHING MORE TO SAY.
THAT DOESN'T EXPLAIN ANYTHING!!
I APOLOGIZE FOR KEEPING HUGHES'S DEATH A SECRET.
WHAT IS THAT?
AAAAH!!
WOOOO
WOO

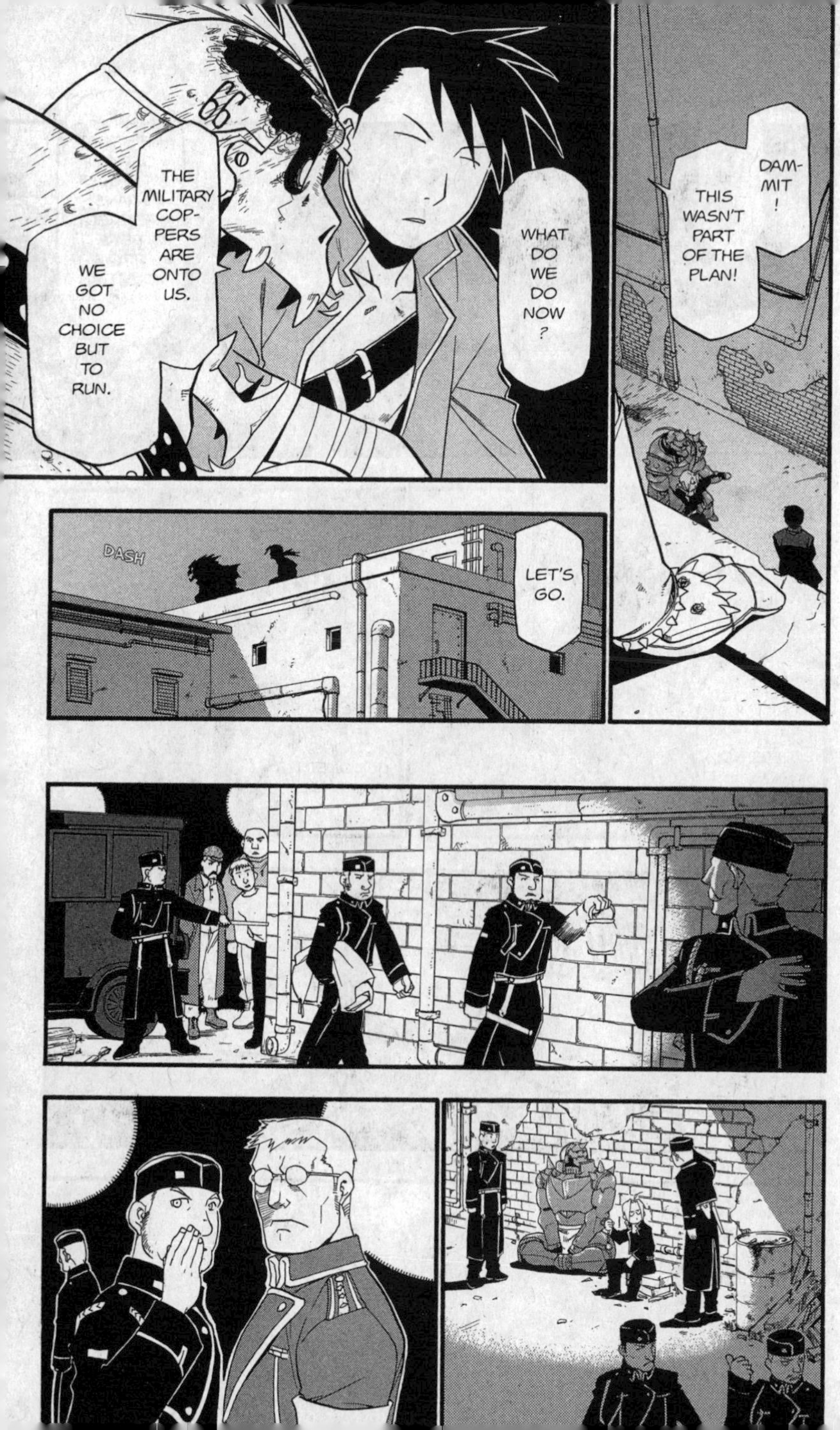
DAMMIT!
THIS WASN'T PART OF THE PLAN!
WHAT DO WE DO NOW?
THE MILITARY COPPERS ARE ONTO US.
WE GOT NO CHOICE BUT TO RUN.
LET'S GO.
DASH

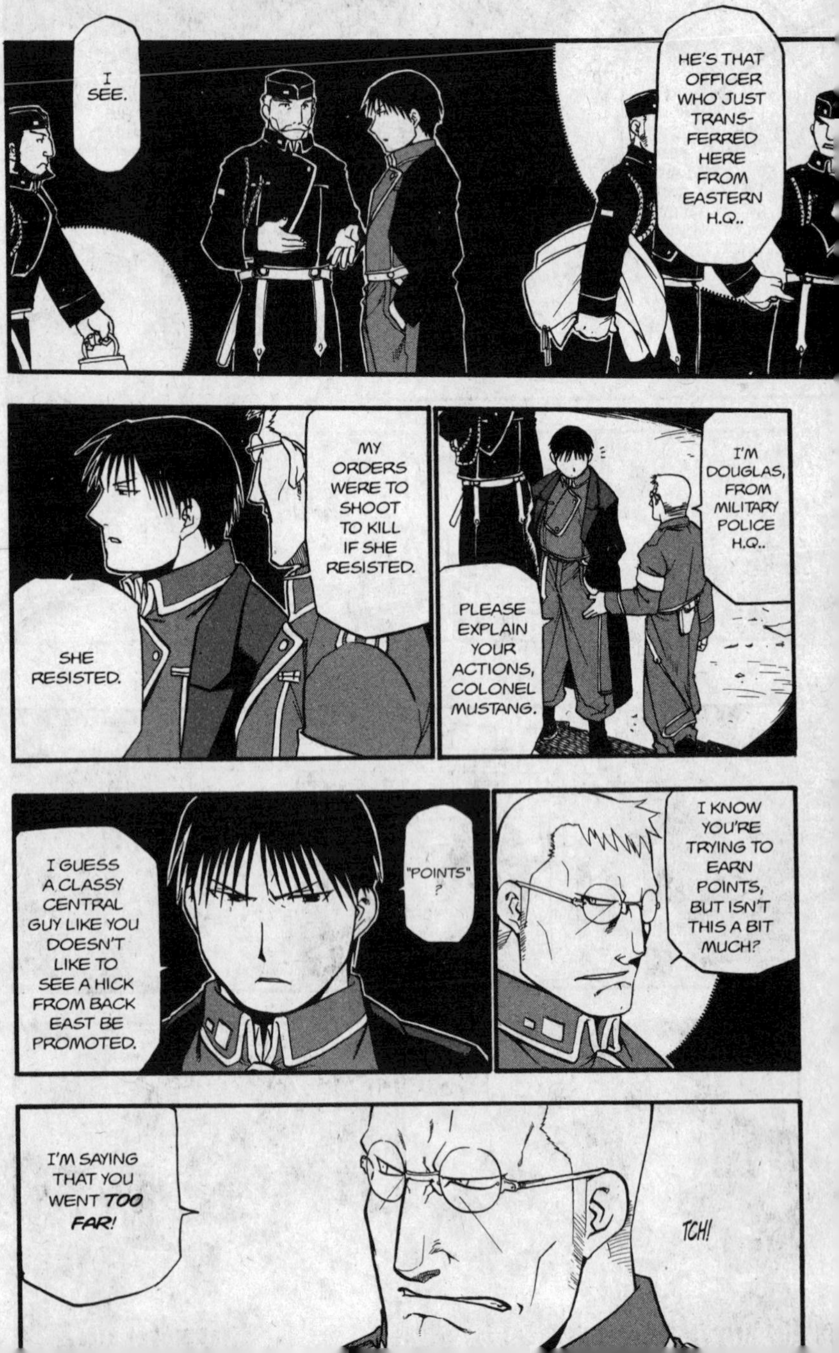
HE'S THAT OFFICER WHO JUST TRANS-FERRED HERE FROM EASTERN H.Q..
I SEE.
I'M DOUGLAS, FROM MILITARY POLICE H.Q..
PLEASE EXPLAIN YOUR ACTIONS, COLONEL MUSTANG.
MY ORDERS WERE TO SHOOT TO KILL IF SHE RESISTED.
SHE RESISTED.
I KNOW YOU'RE TRYING TO EARN POINTS, BUT ISN'T THIS A BIT MUCH?
"POINTS"?
I GUESS A CLASSY CENTRAL GUY LIKE YOU DOESN'T LIKE TO SEE A HICK FROM BACK EAST BE PROMOTED.
I'M SAYING THAT YOU WENT ***TOO FAR!***
TCH!

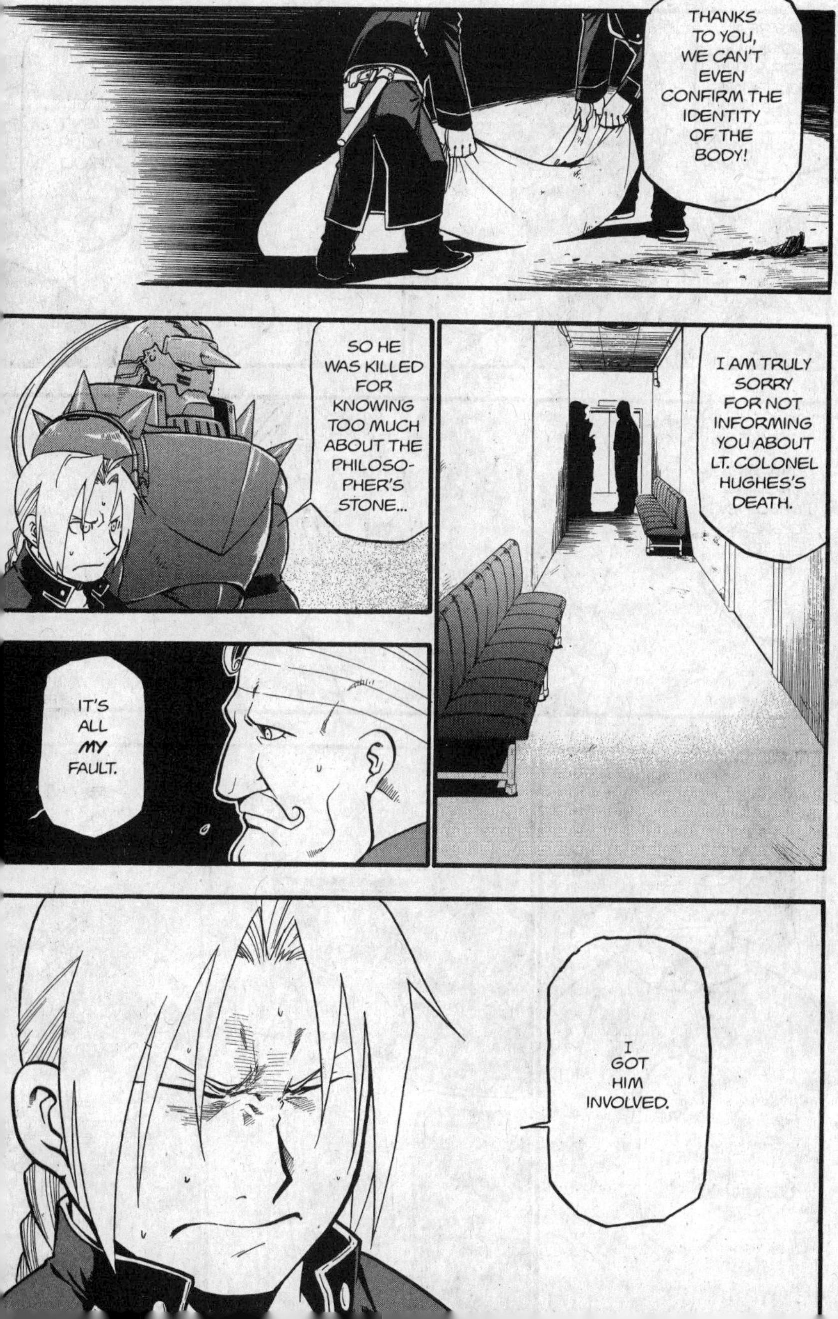
THANKS TO YOU, WE CAN'T EVEN CONFIRM THE IDENTITY OF THE BODY!
I AM TRULY SORRY FOR NOT INFORMING YOU ABOUT LT. COLONEL HUGHES'S DEATH.
SO HE WAS KILLED FOR KNOWING TOO MUCH ABOUT THE PHILOSO-PHER'S STONE...
IT'S ALL *MY* FAULT.
I GOT HIM INVOLVED.

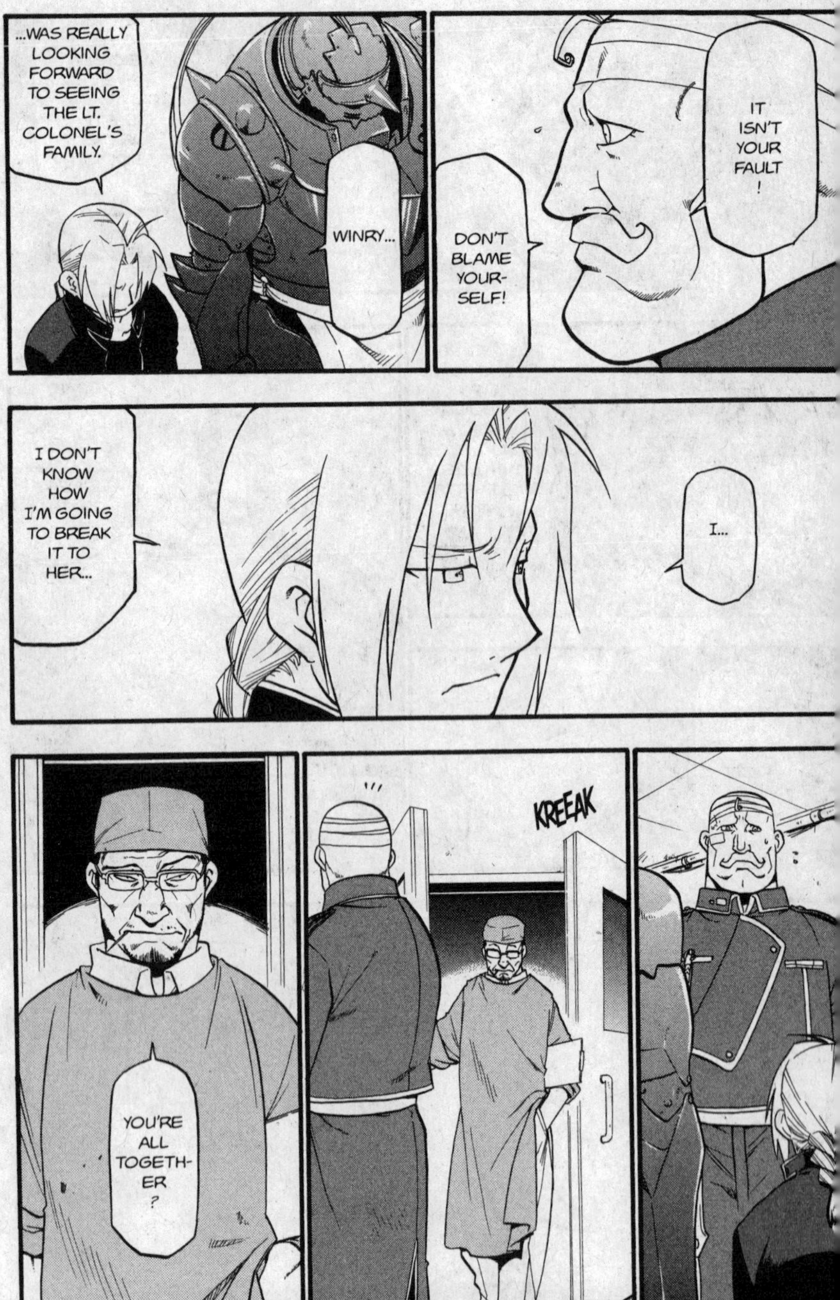
IT ISN'T YOUR FAULT!
DON'T BLAME YOUR-SELF!
WINRY...
...WAS REALLY LOOKING FORWARD TO SEEING THE LT. COLONEL'S FAMILY.
I...
I DON'T KNOW HOW I'M GOING TO BREAK IT TO HER...
KREEAK
YOU'RE ALL TOGETH-ER?

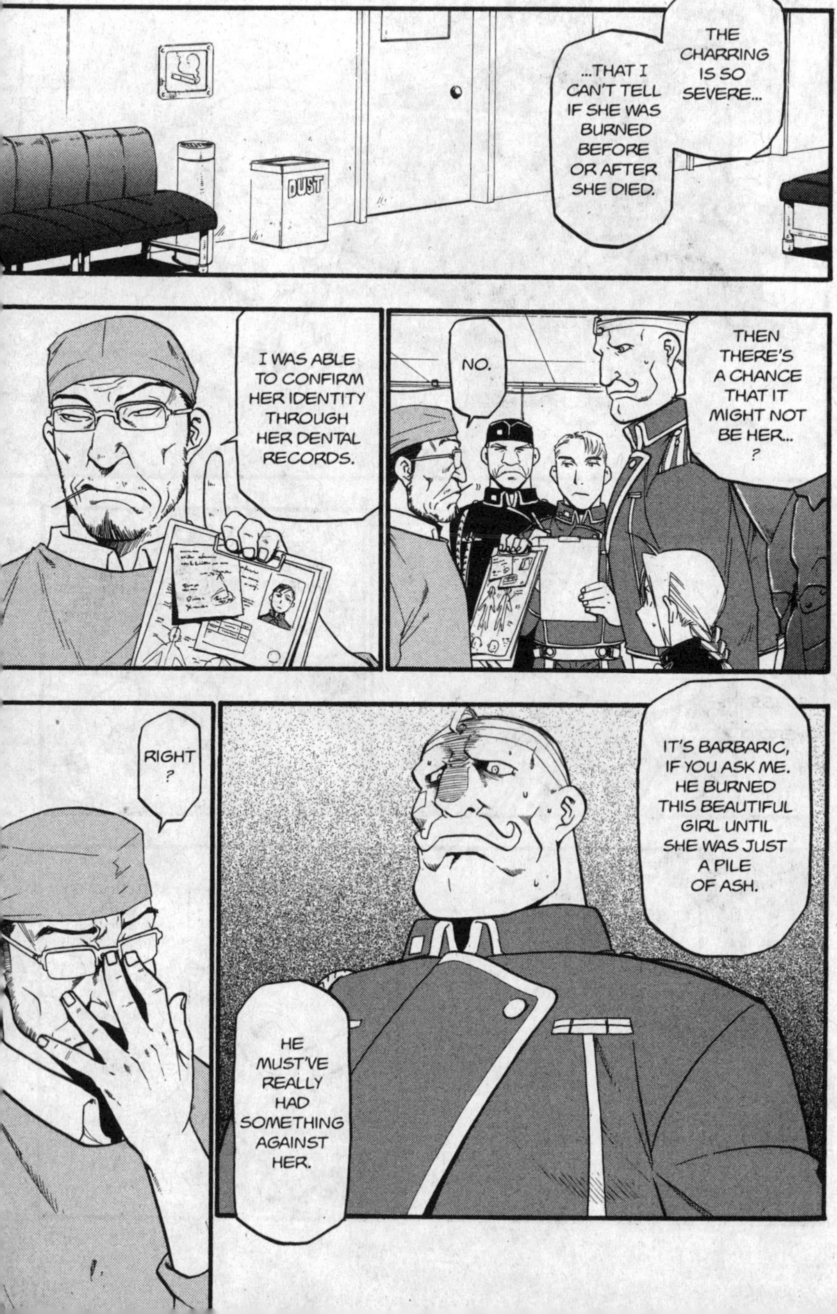
THE CHARRING IS SO SEVERE...
...THAT I CAN'T TELL IF SHE WAS BURNED BEFORE OR AFTER SHE DIED.
DUST
THEN THERE'S A CHANCE THAT IT MIGHT NOT BE HER... ?
NO.
I WAS ABLE TO CONFIRM HER IDENTITY THROUGH HER DENTAL RECORDS.
IT'S BARBARIC, IF YOU ASK ME. HE BURNED THIS BEAUTIFUL GIRL UNTIL SHE WAS JUST A PILE OF ASH.
HE MUST'VE REALLY HAD SOMETHING AGAINST HER.
RIGHT ?

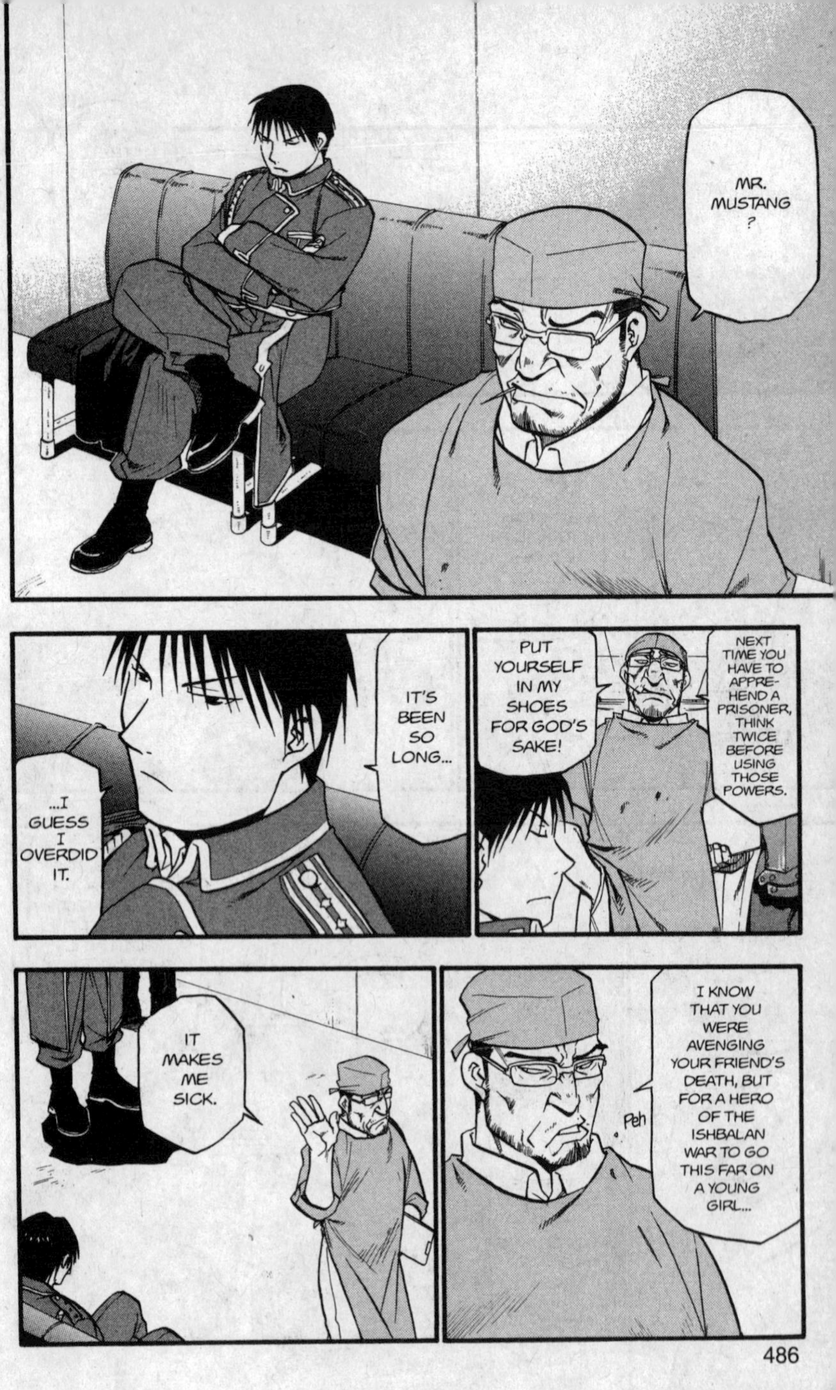
MR. MUSTANG ?
NEXT TIME YOU HAVE TO APPRE-HEND A PRISONER, THINK TWICE BEFORE USING THOSE POWERS.
PUT YOURSELF IN MY SHOES FOR GOD'S SAKE!
IT'S BEEN SO LONG...
...I GUESS I OVERDID IT.
I KNOW THAT YOU WERE AVENGING YOUR FRIEND'S DEATH, BUT FOR A HERO OF THE ISHBALAN WAR TO GO THIS FAR ON A YOUNG GIRL...
Peh
IT MAKES ME SICK.

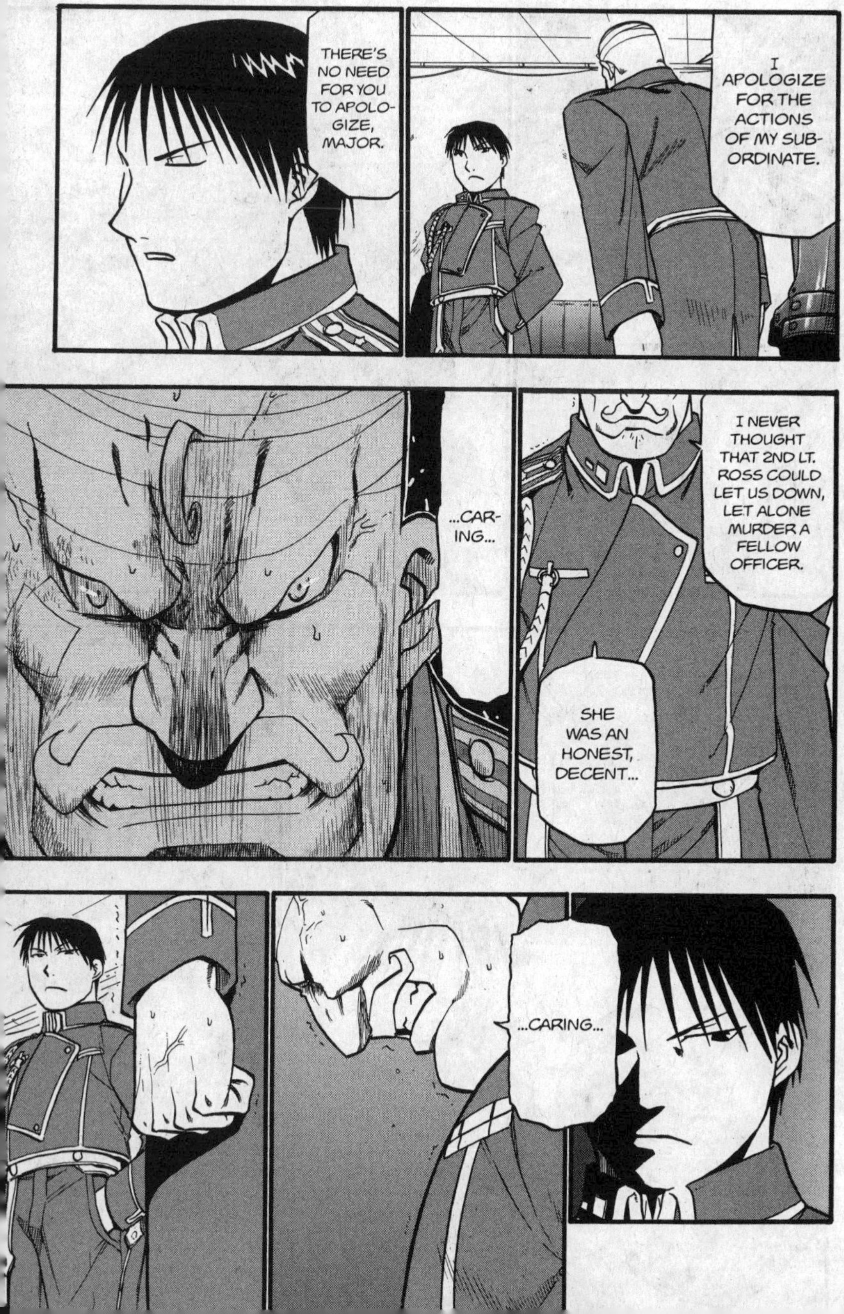
I APOLOGIZE FOR THE ACTIONS OF MY SUB-ORDINATE.
THERE'S NO NEED FOR YOU TO APOLO-GIZE, MAJOR.
I NEVER THOUGHT THAT 2ND LT. ROSS COULD LET US DOWN, LET ALONE MURDER A FELLOW OFFICER.
SHE WAS AN HONEST, DECENT...
...CAR-ING...
...CARING...

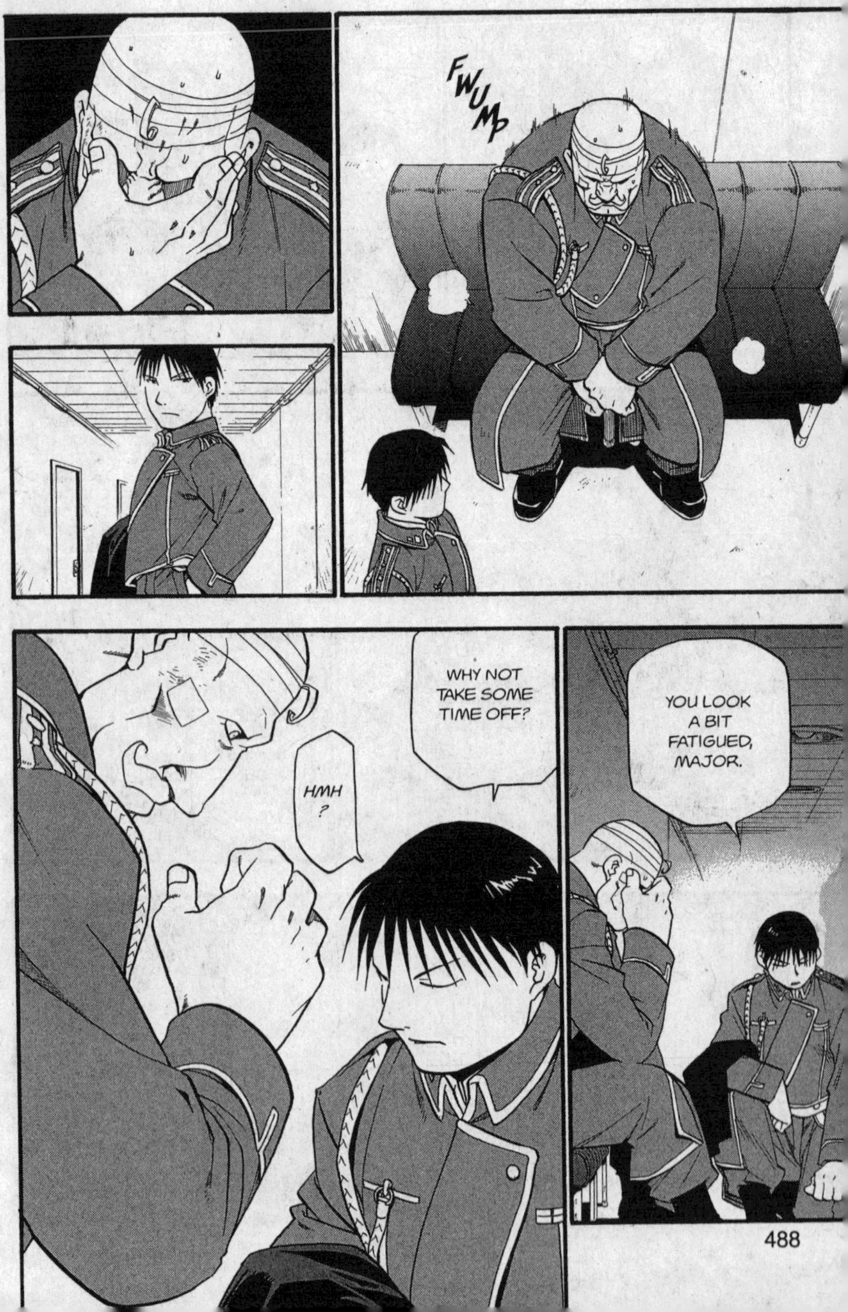
FWUMP
YOU LOOK A BIT FATIGUED, MAJOR.
WHY NOT TAKE SOME TIME OFF?
HMH ?

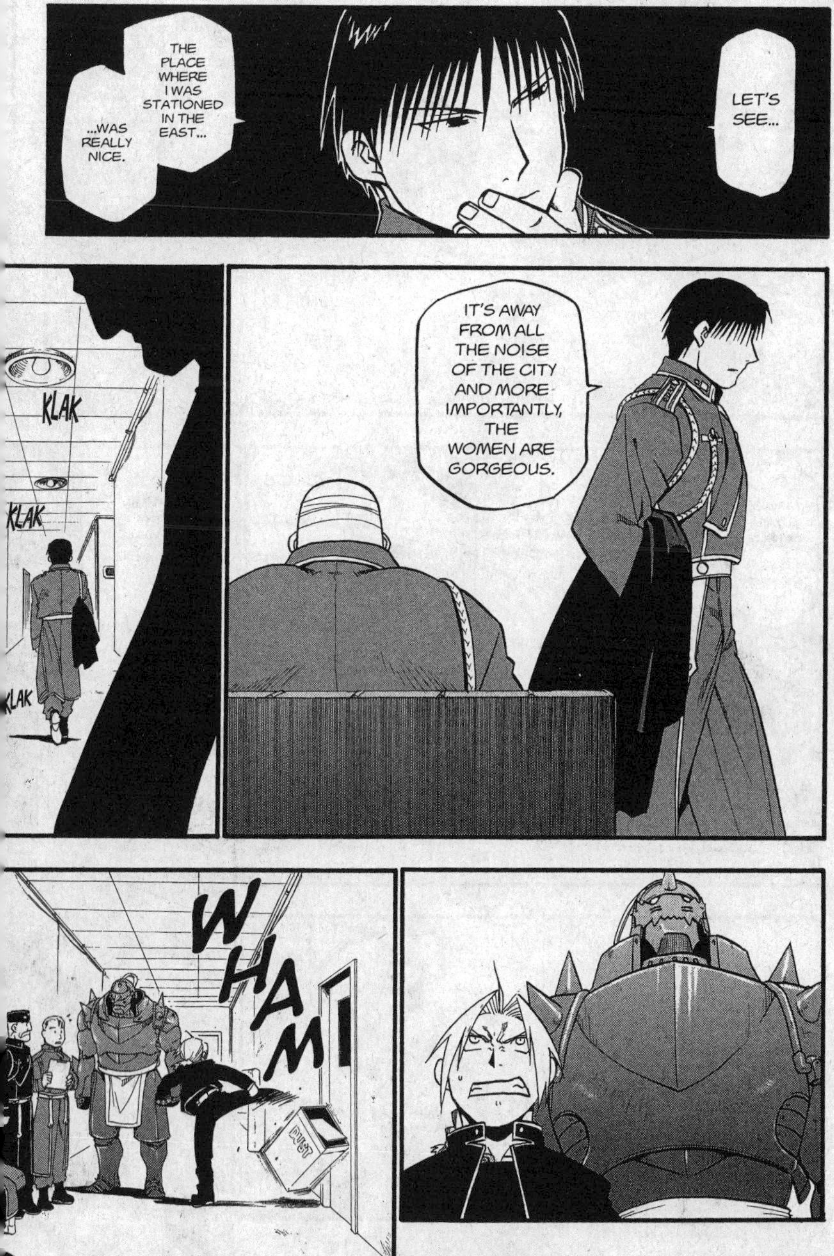
LET'S SEE...
THE PLACE WHERE I WAS STATIONED IN THE EAST...
...WAS REALLY NICE.
IT'S AWAY FROM ALL THE NOISE OF THE CITY AND MORE IMPORTANTLY, THE WOMEN ARE GORGEOUS.
KLAK
KLAK
KLAK
WHAM
DUST

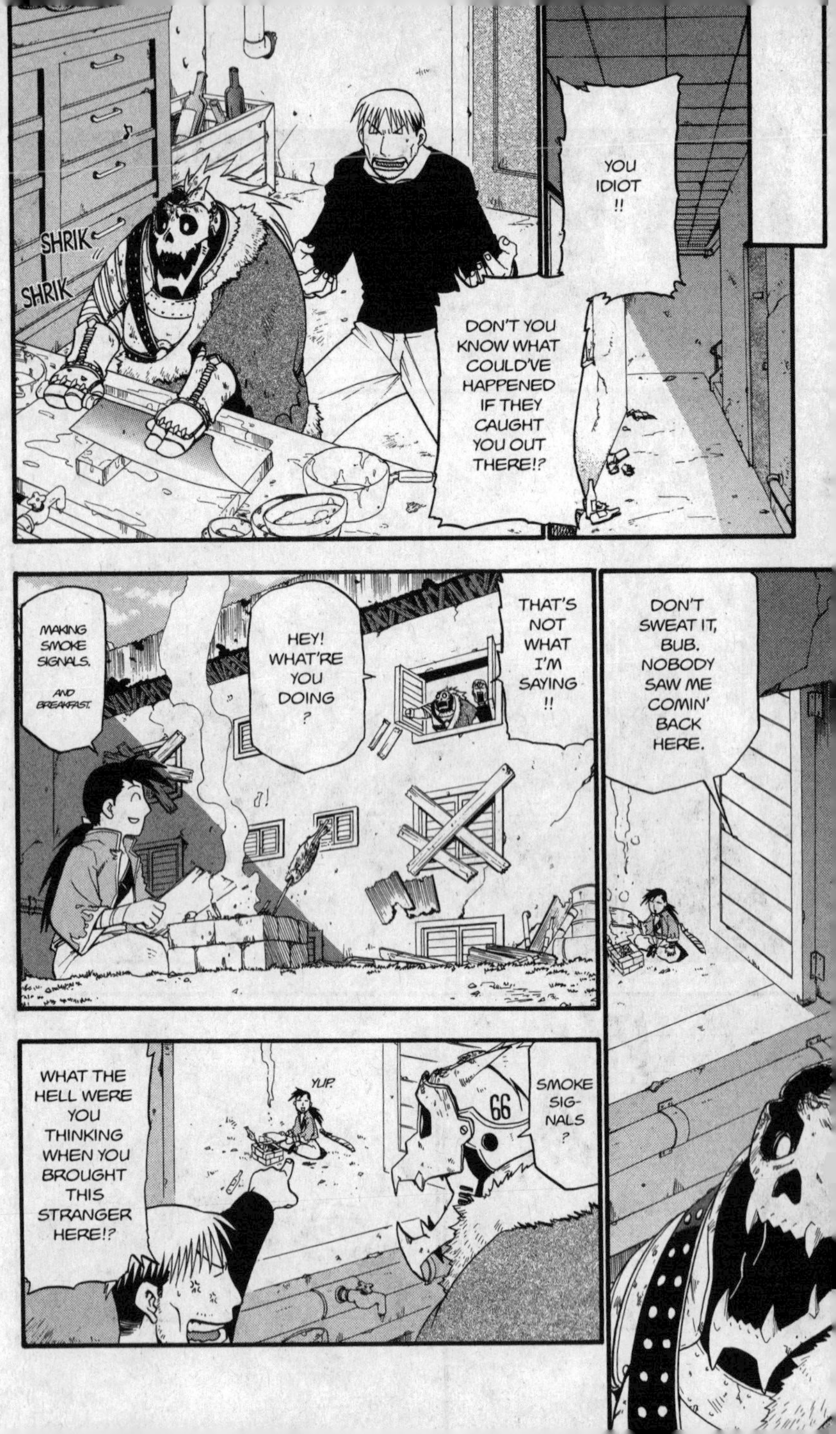
YOU IDIOT !!
SHRIK
SHRIK
DON'T YOU KNOW WHAT COULD'VE HAPPENED IF THEY CAUGHT YOU OUT THERE!?
DON'T SWEAT IT, BUB. NOBODY SAW ME COMIN' BACK HERE.
THAT'S NOT WHAT I'M SAYING !!
HEY! WHAT'RE YOU DOING ?
MAKING SMOKE SIGNALS.
AND BREAKFAST.
SMOKE SIG-NALS ?
YUP.
WHAT THE HELL WERE YOU THINKING WHEN YOU BROUGHT THIS STRANGER HERE!?

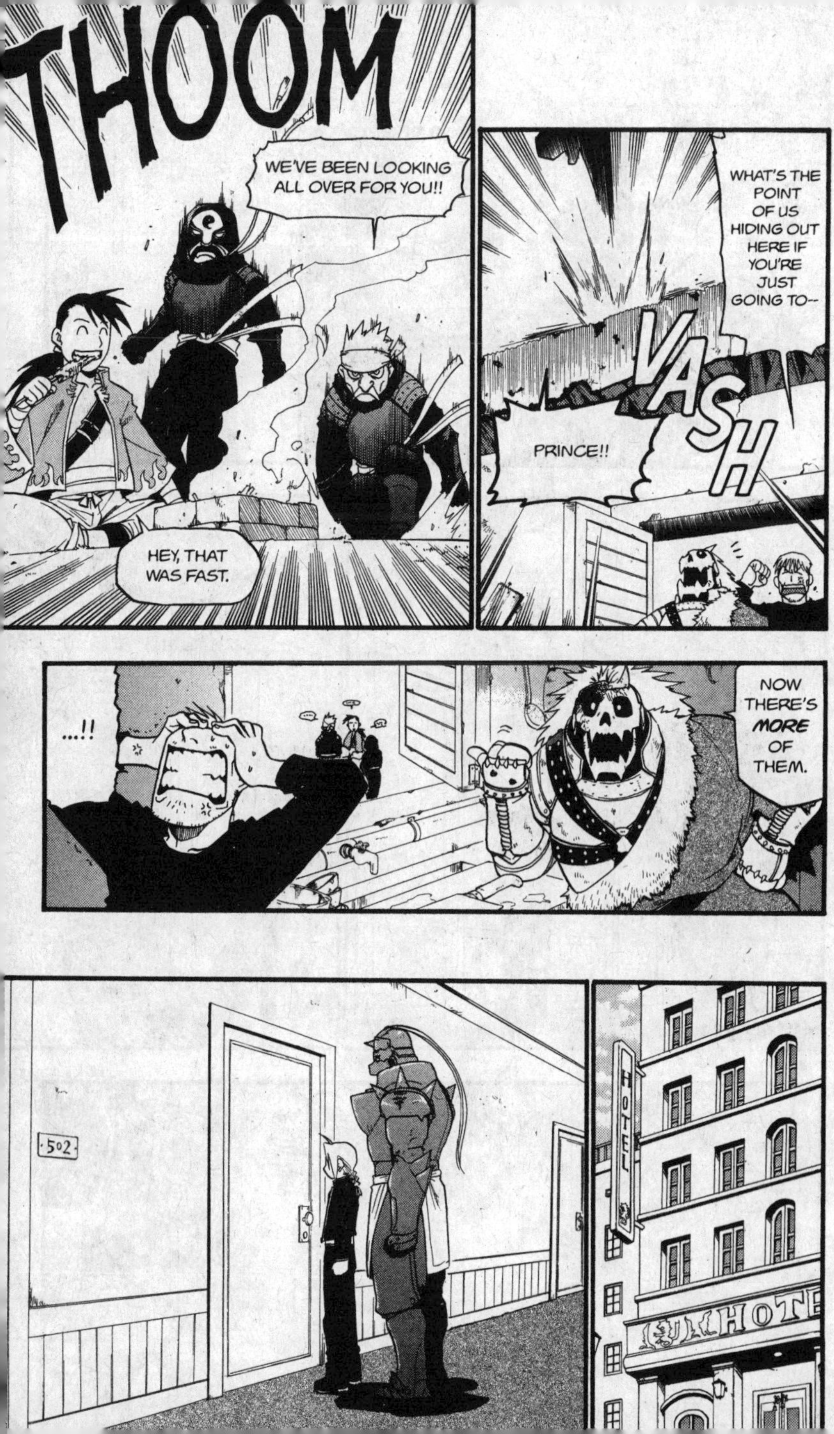

WHAT'S THE POINT OF US HIDING OUT HERE IF YOU'RE JUST GOING TO--
VASH
PRINCE!!
THOOM
WE'VE BEEN LOOKING ALL OVER FOR YOU!!
HEY, THAT WAS FAST.
NOW THERE'S *MORE* OF THEM.
...!!
HOTEL
HOTE
502

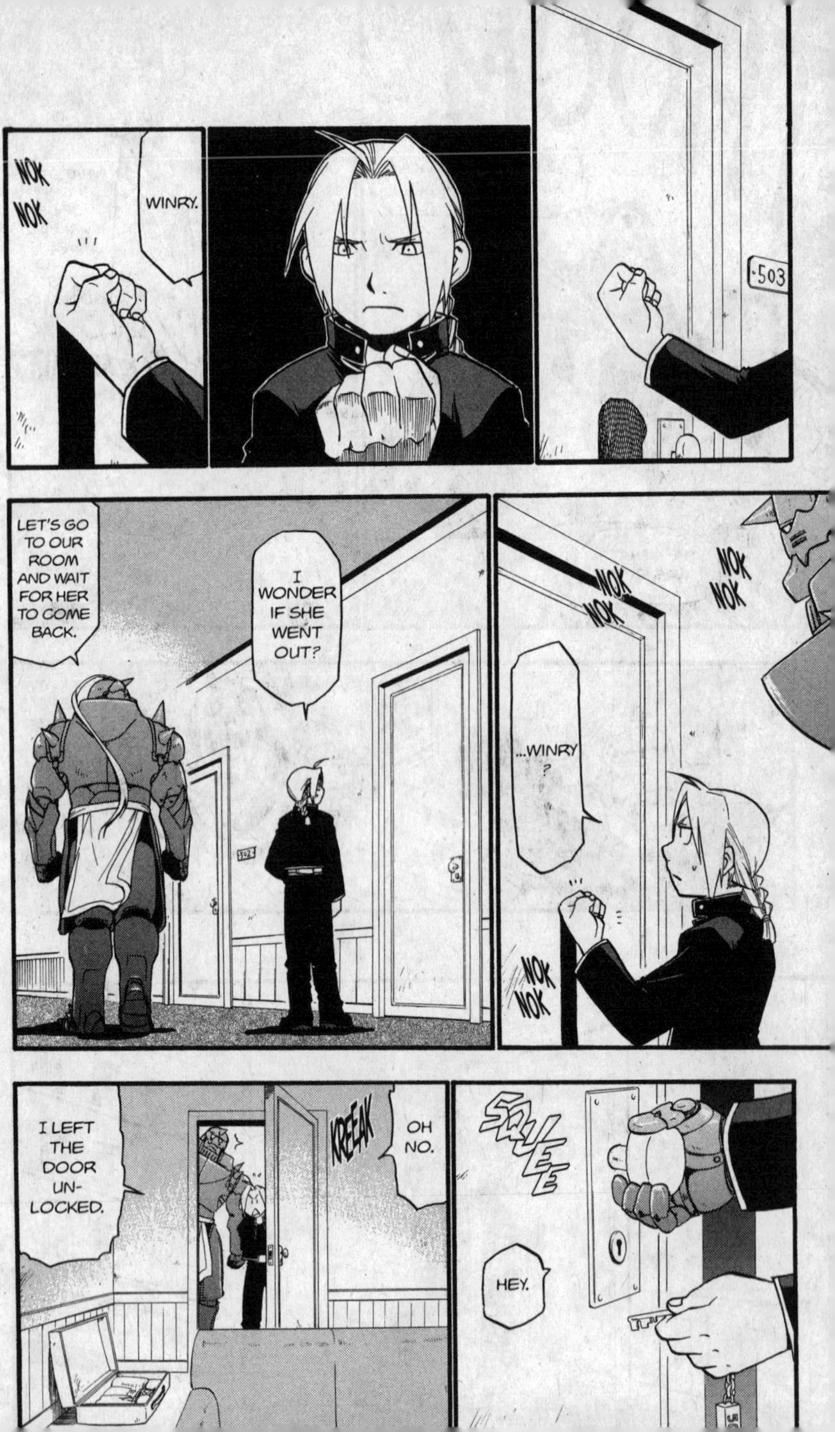

503
WINRY.
NOK NOK
NOK NOK
NOK NOK
...WINRY?
NOK NOK
I WONDER IF SHE WENT OUT?
LET'S GO TO OUR ROOM AND WAIT FOR HER TO COME BACK.
SQUEE
HEY.
OH NO.
KREEAK
I LEFT THE DOOR UNLOCKED.

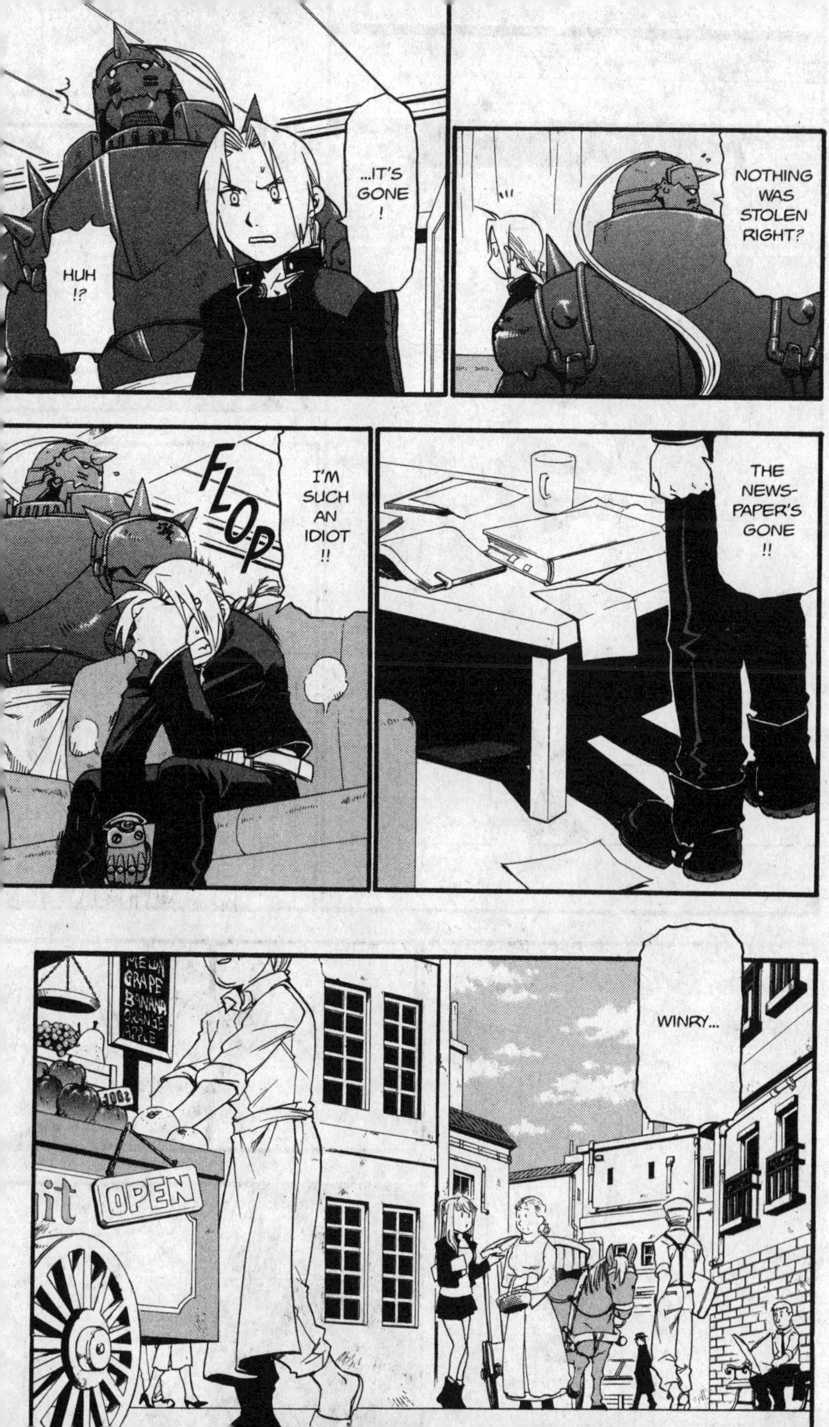
NOTHING WAS STOLEN RIGHT?
...IT'S GONE !
HUH !?
THE NEWS-PAPER'S GONE !!
I'M SUCH AN IDIOT !!
FLOP
WINRY...
MELON GRAPE BANANA ORANGE APPLE
OPEN

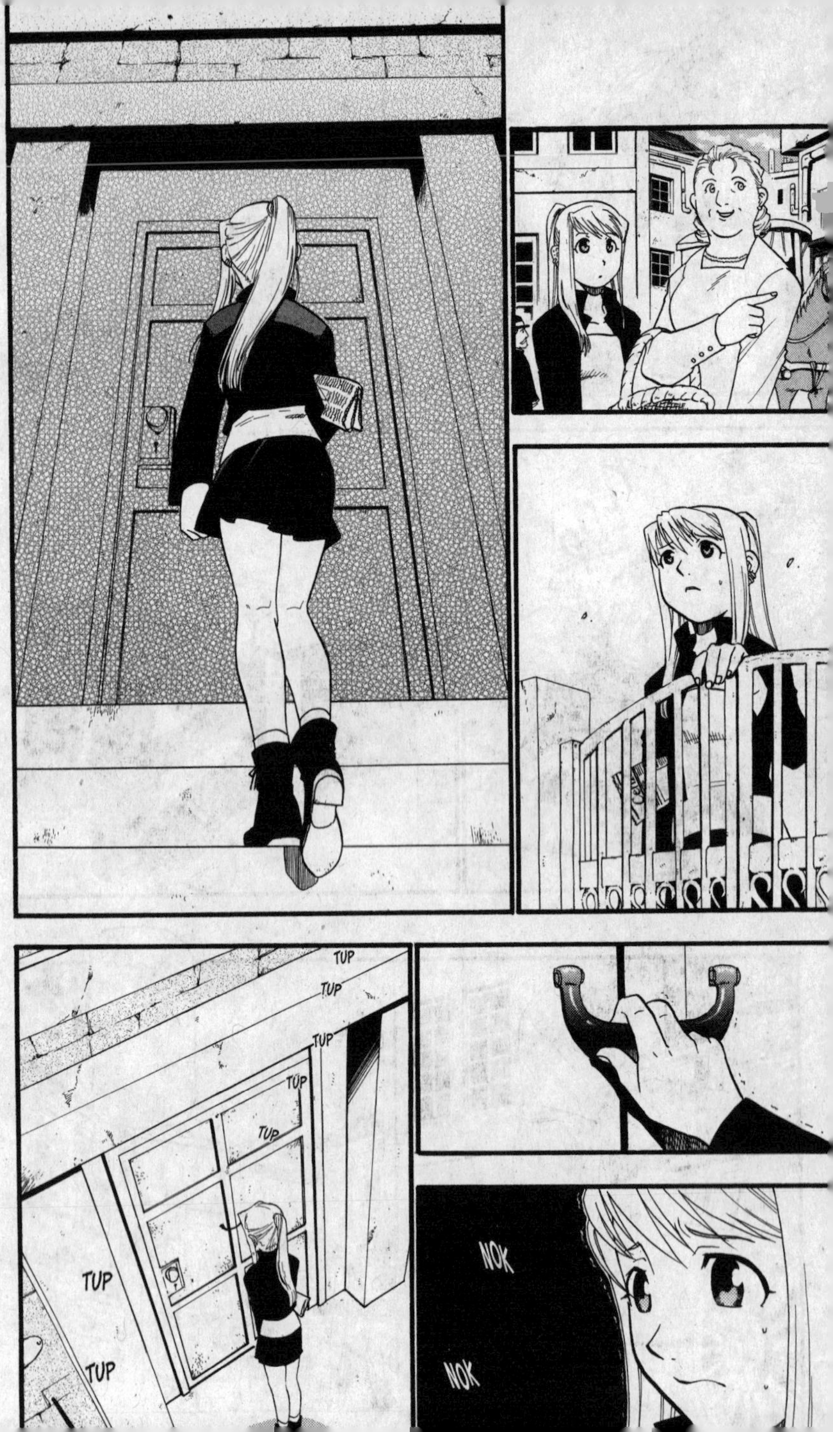
NOK
NOK
TUP
TUP
TUP
TUP
TUP
TUP
TUP

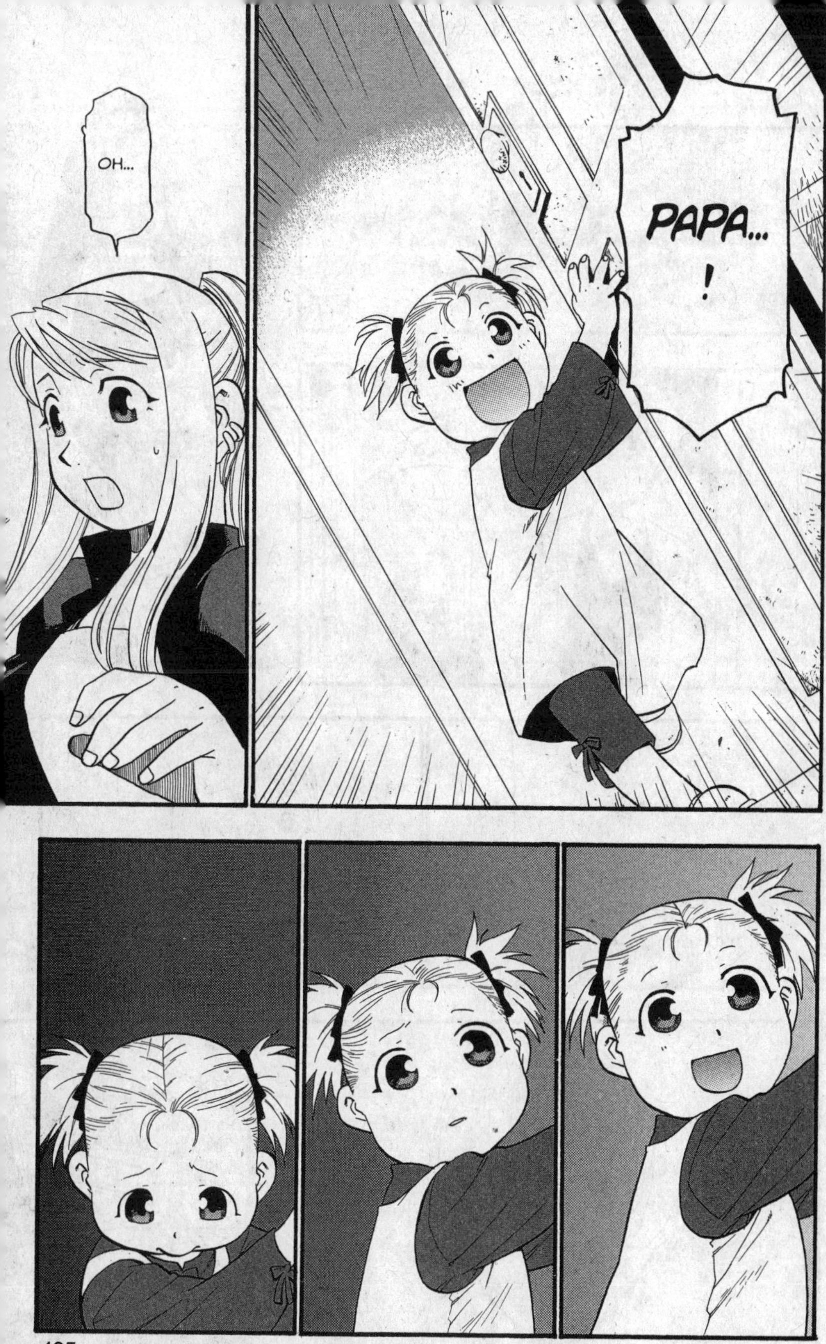
PAPA... !
OH...

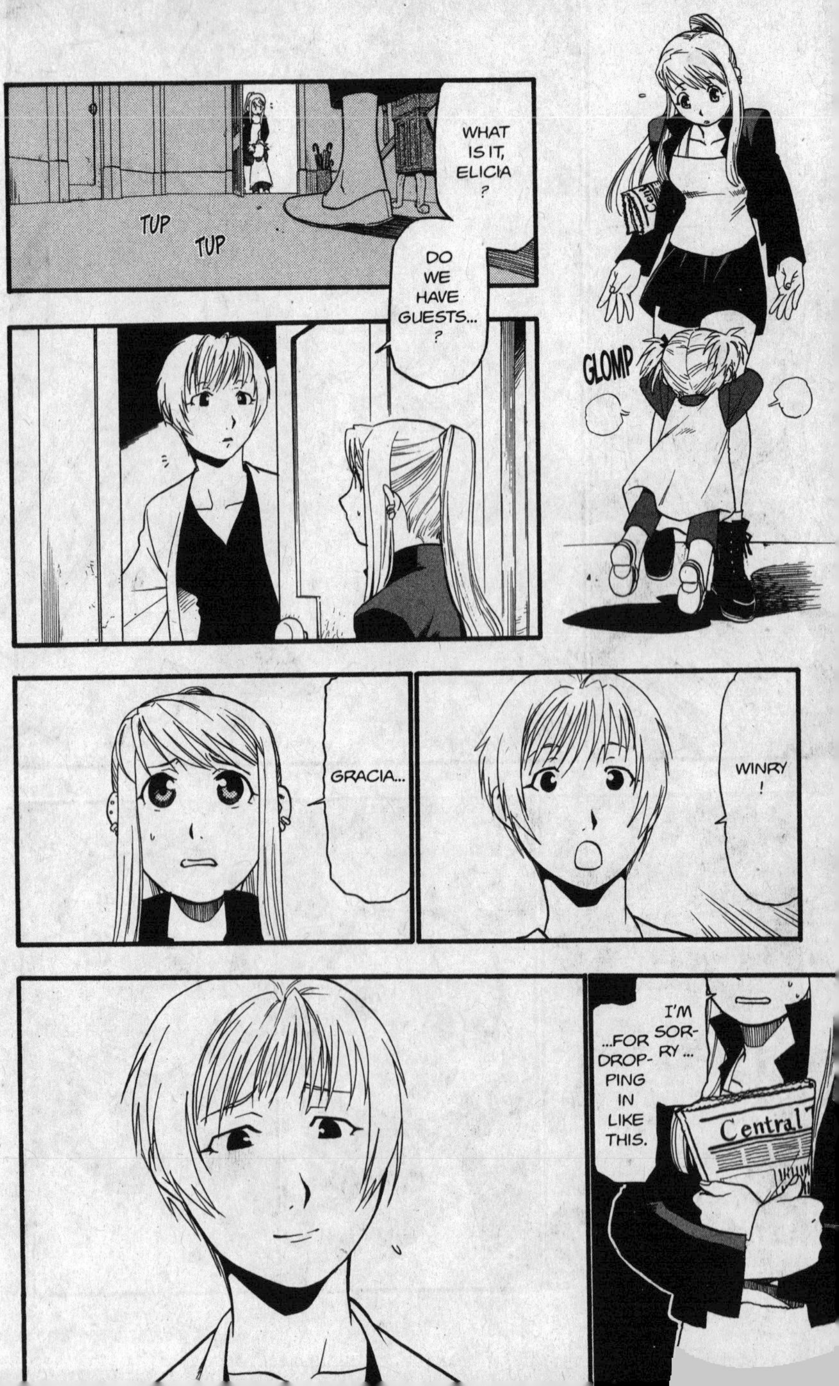
GLOMP
Cent
WHAT IS IT, ELICIA?
TUP
TUP
DO WE HAVE GUESTS...?
WINRY!
GRACIA...
I'M SORRY...
...FOR DROPPING IN LIKE THIS.
Central

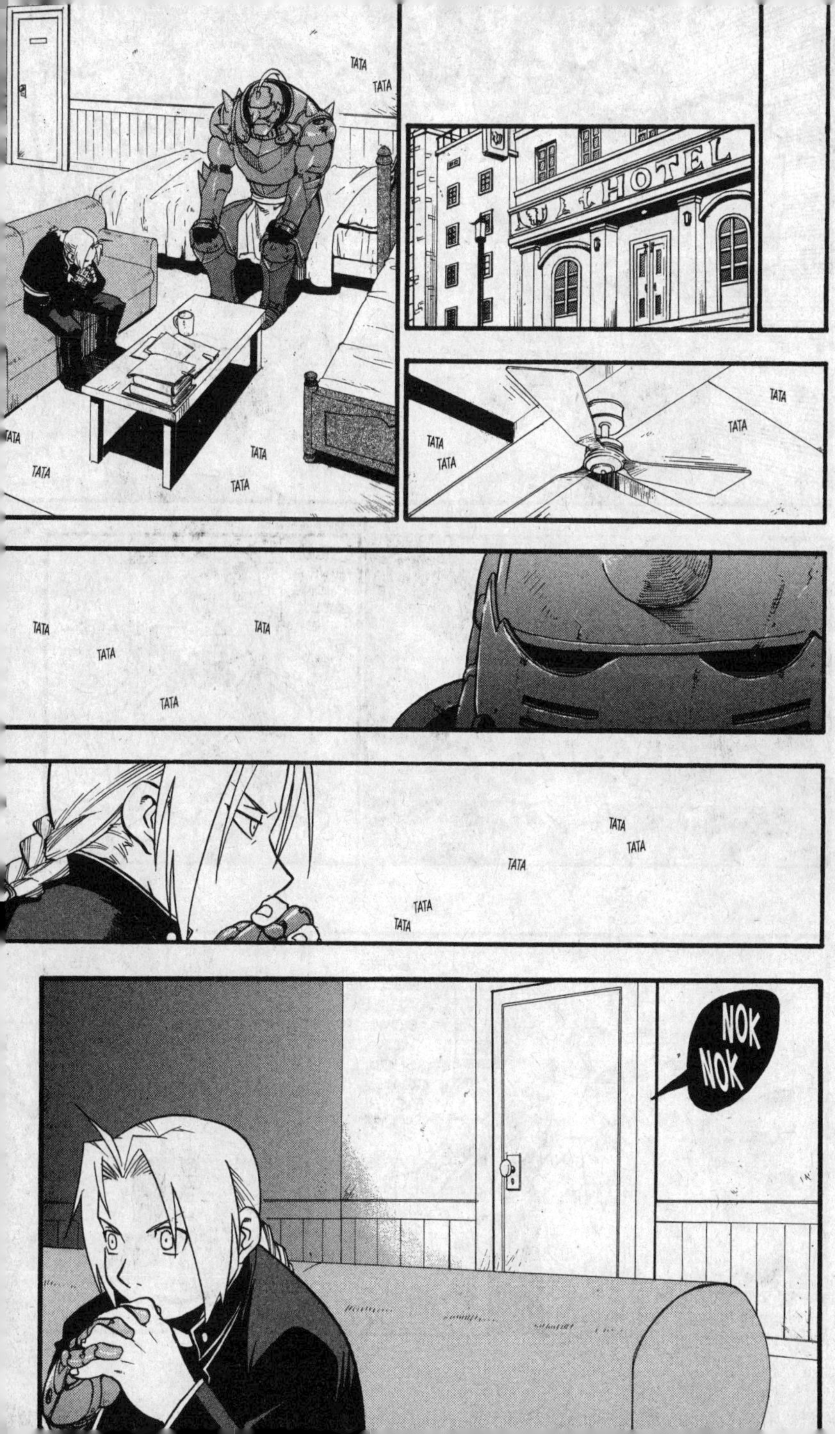
HOTEL
TATA
TATA
TATA
TATA
TATA
TATA
TATA
TATA
TATA
TATA
TATA
TATA
TATA
TATA
TATA
TATA
TATA
TATA
TATA
TATA
TATA
NOK NOK

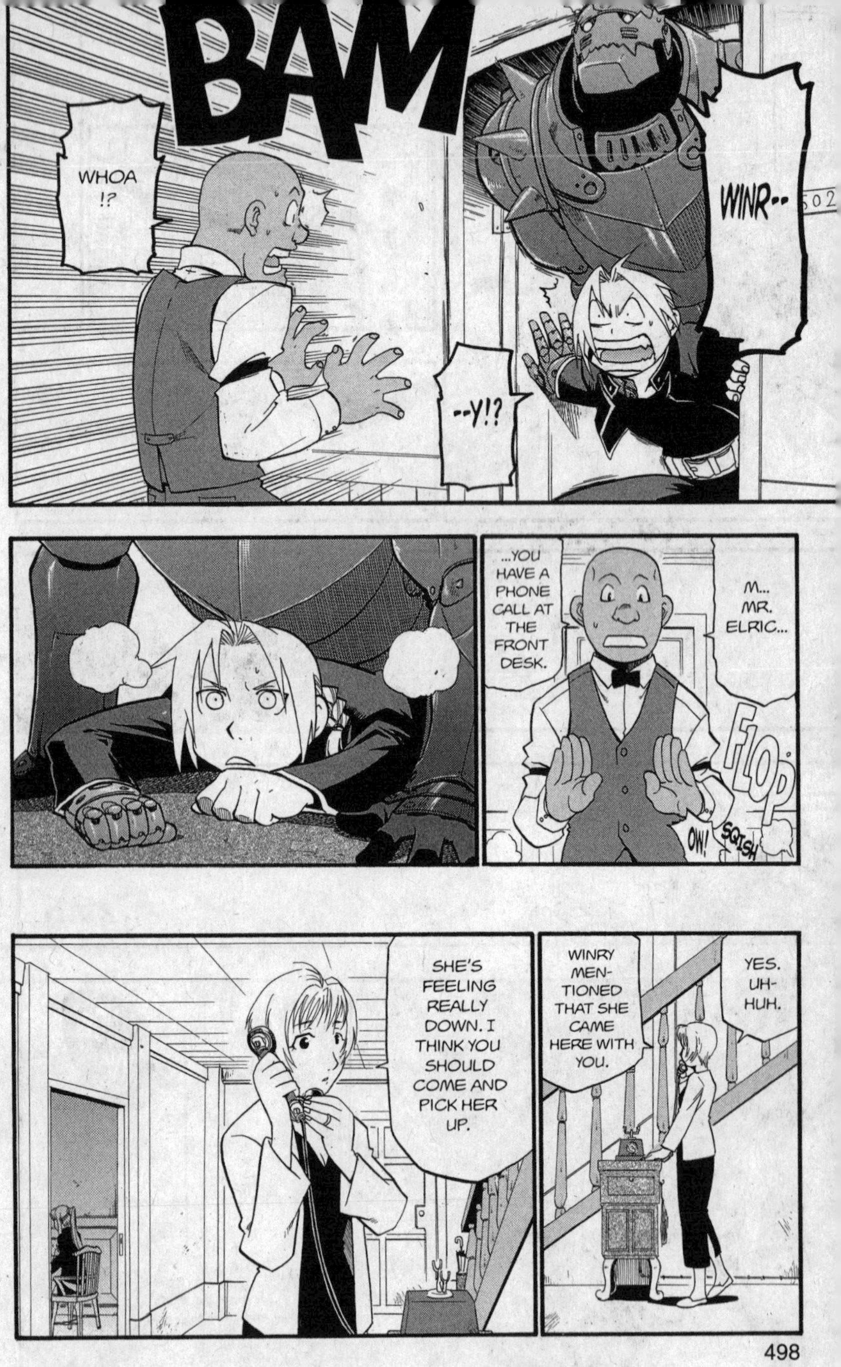
BAM
WINR--
502
--Y!?
WHOA !?
M... MR. ELRIC...
...YOU HAVE A PHONE CALL AT THE FRONT DESK.
FLOP
OW!
SQISH
YES. UH-HUH.
WINRY MENTIONED THAT SHE CAME HERE WITH YOU.
SHE'S FEELING REALLY DOWN. I THINK YOU SHOULD COME AND PICK HER UP.

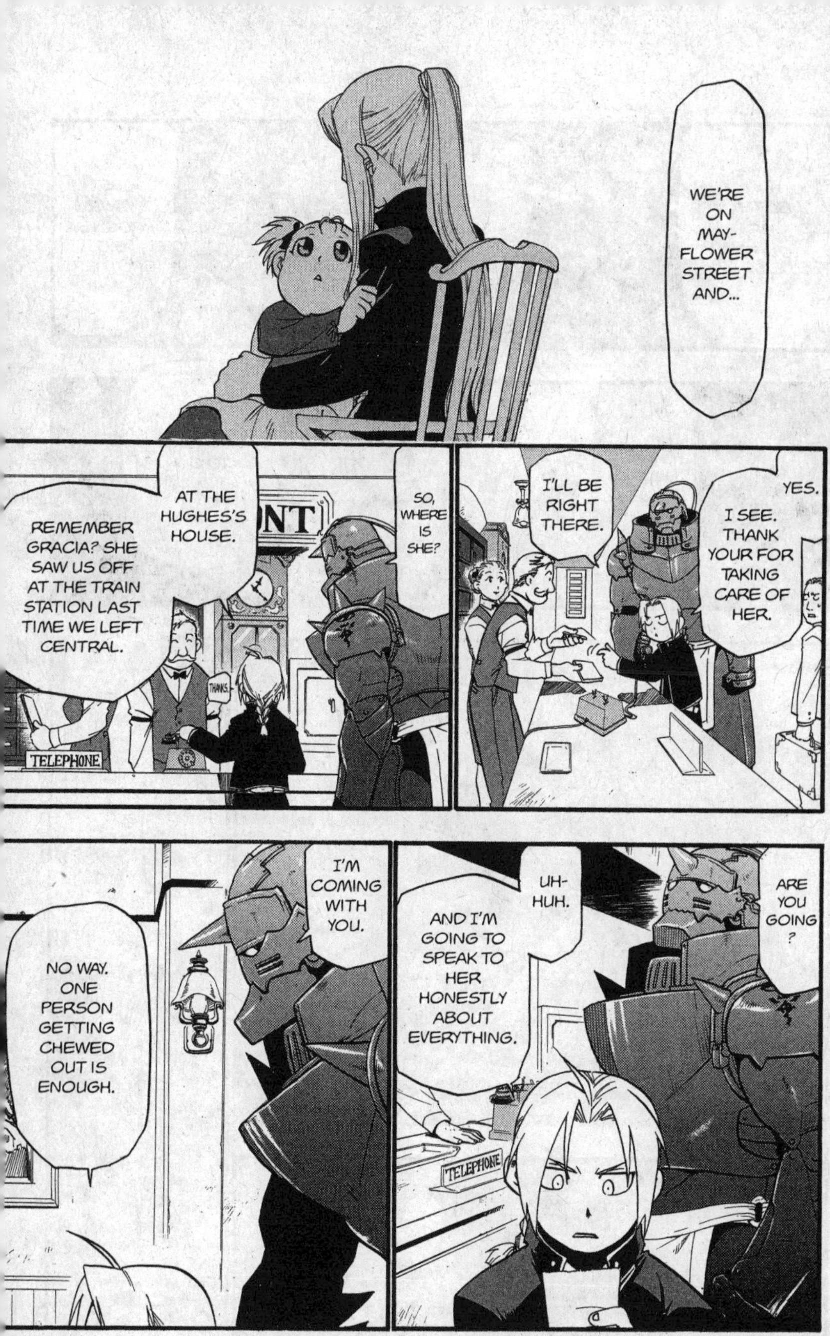
WE'RE ON MAY-FLOWER STREET AND...
YES.
I SEE. THANK YOUR FOR TAKING CARE OF HER.
I'LL BE RIGHT THERE.
SO, WHERE IS SHE?
AT THE HUGHES'S HOUSE.
REMEMBER GRACIA? SHE SAW US OFF AT THE TRAIN STATION LAST TIME WE LEFT CENTRAL.
ONT
THANKS.
TELEPHONE
ARE YOU GOING?
UH-HUH.
AND I'M GOING TO SPEAK TO HER HONESTLY ABOUT EVERYTHING.
TELEPHONE
I'M COMING WITH YOU.
NO WAY. ONE PERSON GETTING CHEWED OUT IS ENOUGH.

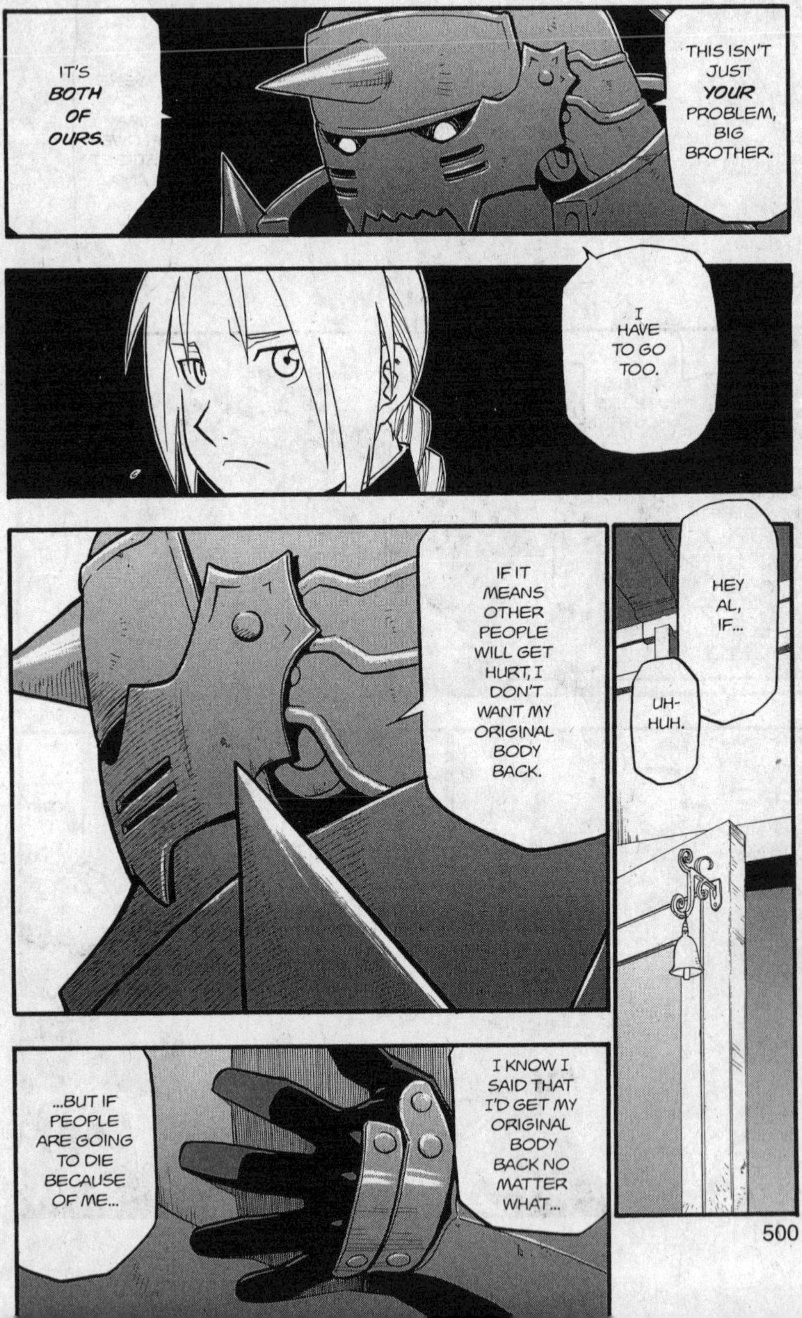
THIS ISN'T JUST YOUR PROBLEM, BIG BROTHER.
IT'S BOTH OF OURS.
I HAVE TO GO TOO.
HEY AL, IF...
UH-HUH.
IF IT MEANS OTHER PEOPLE WILL GET HURT, I DON'T WANT MY ORIGINAL BODY BACK.
I KNOW I SAID THAT I'D GET MY ORIGINAL BODY BACK NO MATTER WHAT...
...BUT IF PEOPLE ARE GOING TO DIE BECAUSE OF ME...

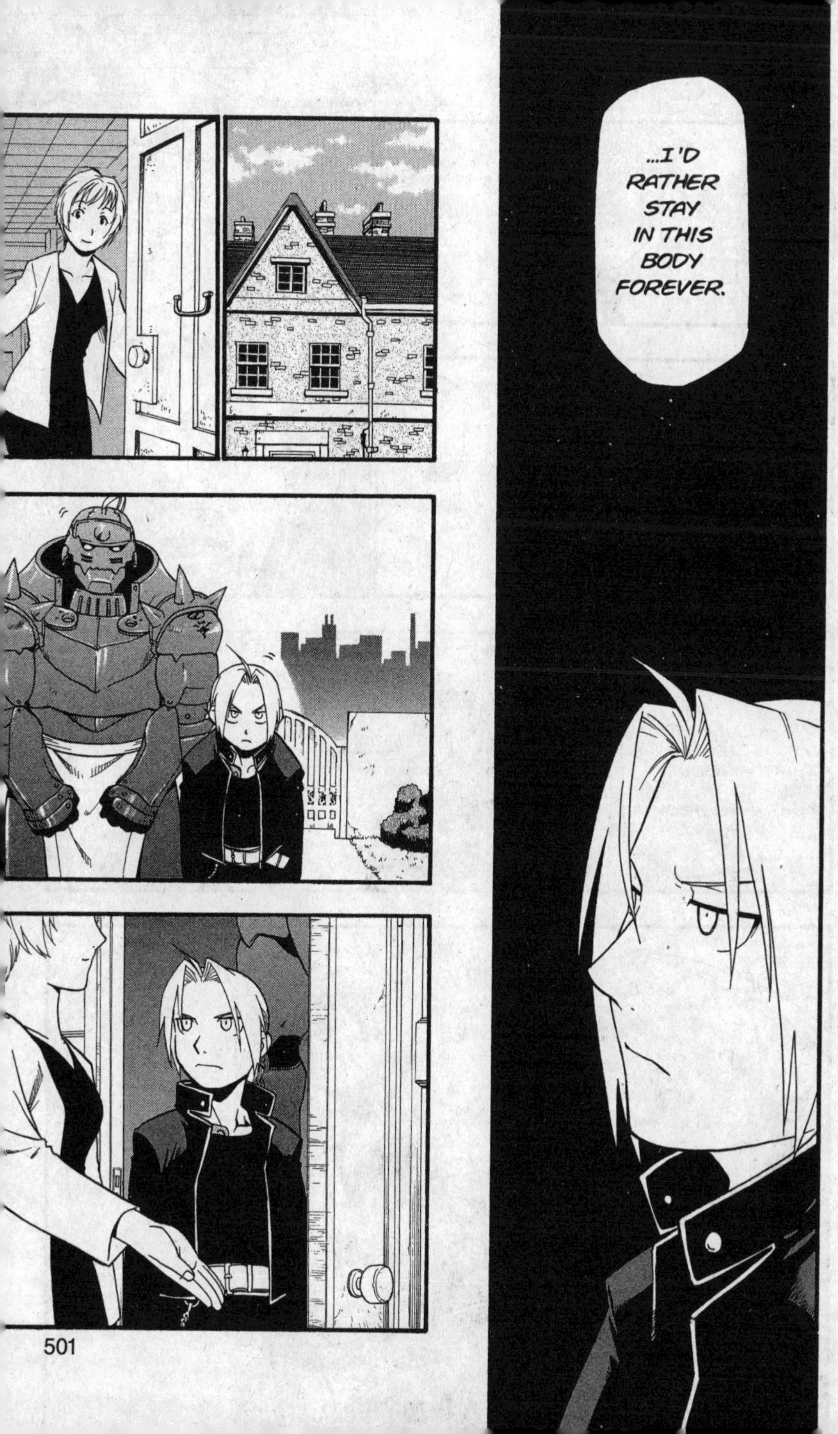
...I'D RATHER STAY IN THIS BODY FOREVER.

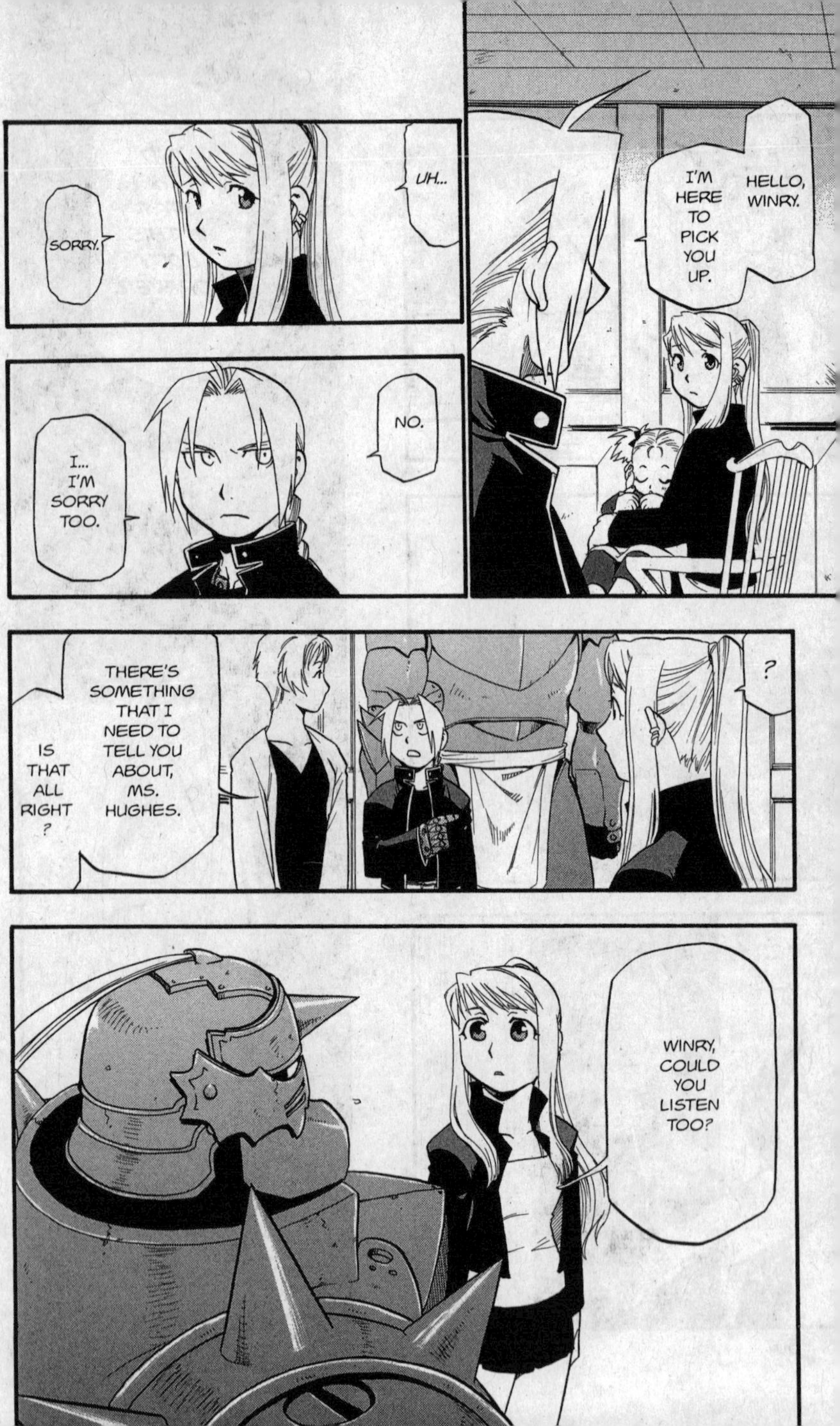
HELLO, WINRY.
I'M HERE TO PICK YOU UP.
UH...
SORRY.
NO.
I... I'M SORRY TOO.
?
THERE'S SOMETHING THAT I NEED TO TELL YOU ABOUT, MS. HUGHES.
IS THAT ALL RIGHT?
WINRY, COULD YOU LISTEN TOO?

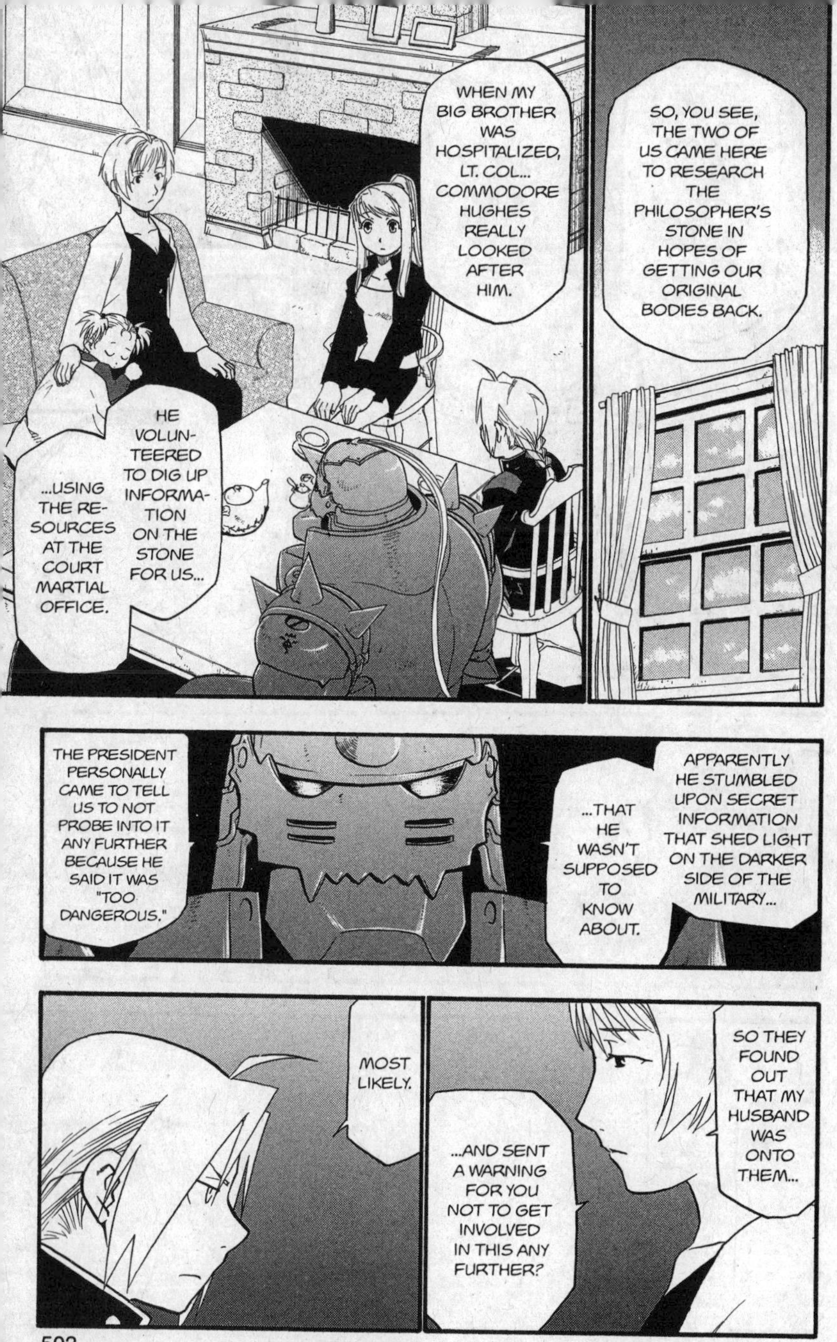
SO, YOU SEE, THE TWO OF US CAME HERE TO RESEARCH THE PHILOSOPHER'S STONE IN HOPES OF GETTING OUR ORIGINAL BODIES BACK.
WHEN MY BIG BROTHER WAS HOSPITALIZED, LT. COL... COMMODORE HUGHES REALLY LOOKED AFTER HIM.
HE VOLUNTEERED TO DIG UP INFORMATION ON THE STONE FOR US...
...USING THE RESOURCES AT THE COURT MARTIAL OFFICE.
APPARENTLY HE STUMBLED UPON SECRET INFORMATION THAT SHED LIGHT ON THE DARKER SIDE OF THE MILITARY...
...THAT HE WASN'T SUPPOSED TO KNOW ABOUT.
THE PRESIDENT PERSONALLY CAME TO TELL US TO NOT PROBE INTO IT ANY FURTHER BECAUSE HE SAID IT WAS "TOO DANGEROUS."
SO THEY FOUND OUT THAT MY HUSBAND WAS ONTO THEM...
...AND SENT A WARNING FOR YOU NOT TO GET INVOLVED IN THIS ANY FURTHER?
MOST LIKELY.

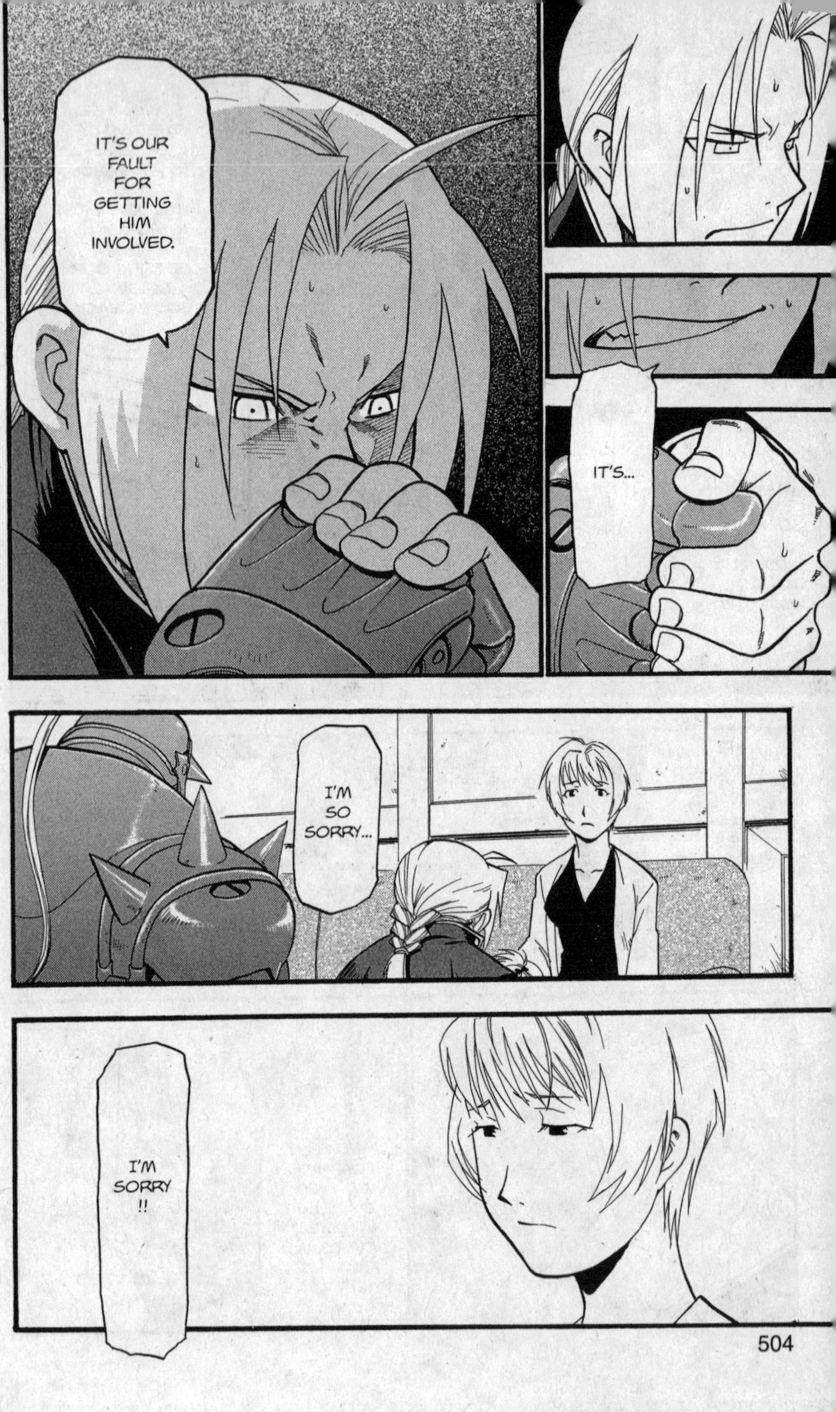
IT'S...
IT'S OUR FAULT FOR GETTING HIM INVOLVED.
I'M SO SORRY...
I'M SORRY !!

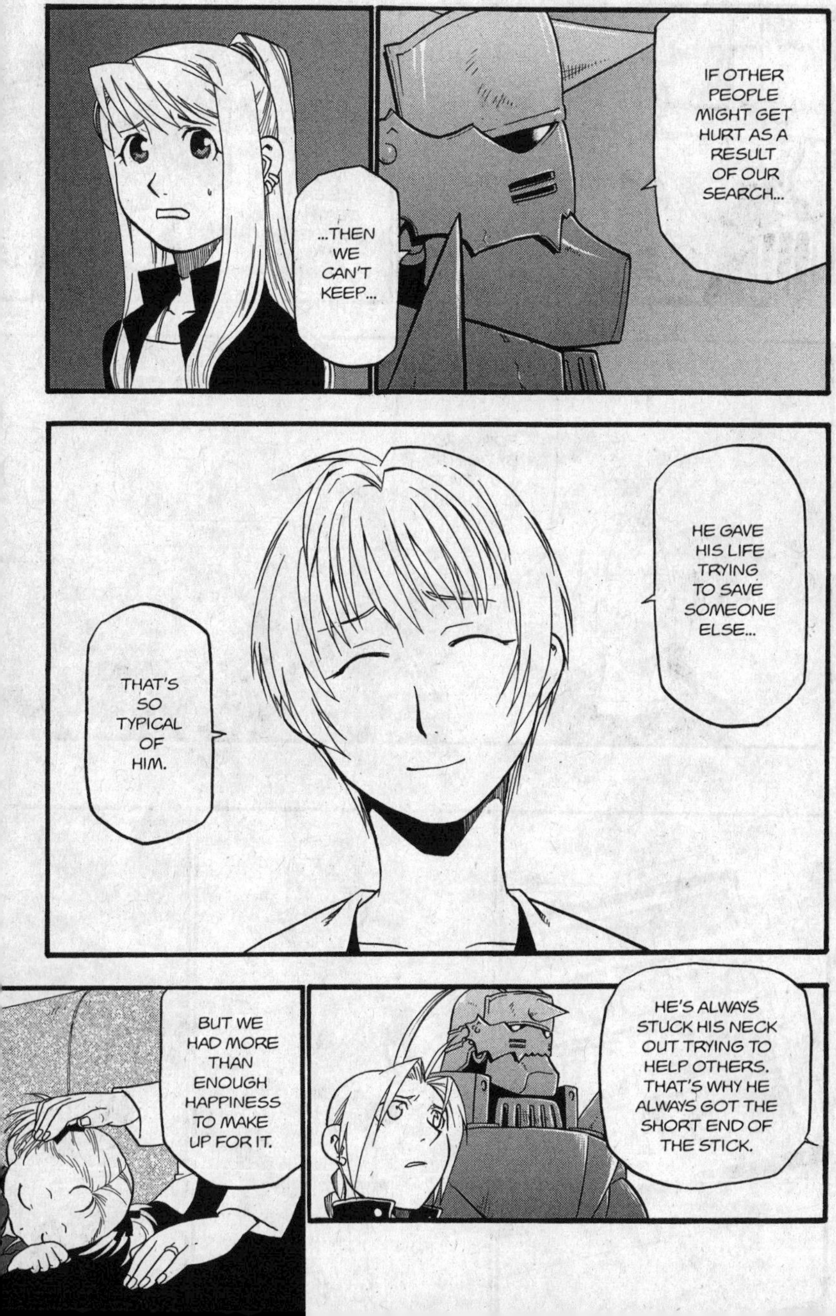
IF OTHER PEOPLE MIGHT GET HURT AS A RESULT OF OUR SEARCH...
...THEN WE CAN'T KEEP...
HE GAVE HIS LIFE TRYING TO SAVE SOMEONE ELSE...
THAT'S SO TYPICAL OF HIM.
HE'S ALWAYS STUCK HIS NECK OUT TRYING TO HELP OTHERS. THAT'S WHY HE ALWAYS GOT THE SHORT END OF THE STICK.
BUT WE HAD MORE THAN ENOUGH HAPPINESS TO MAKE UP FOR IT.

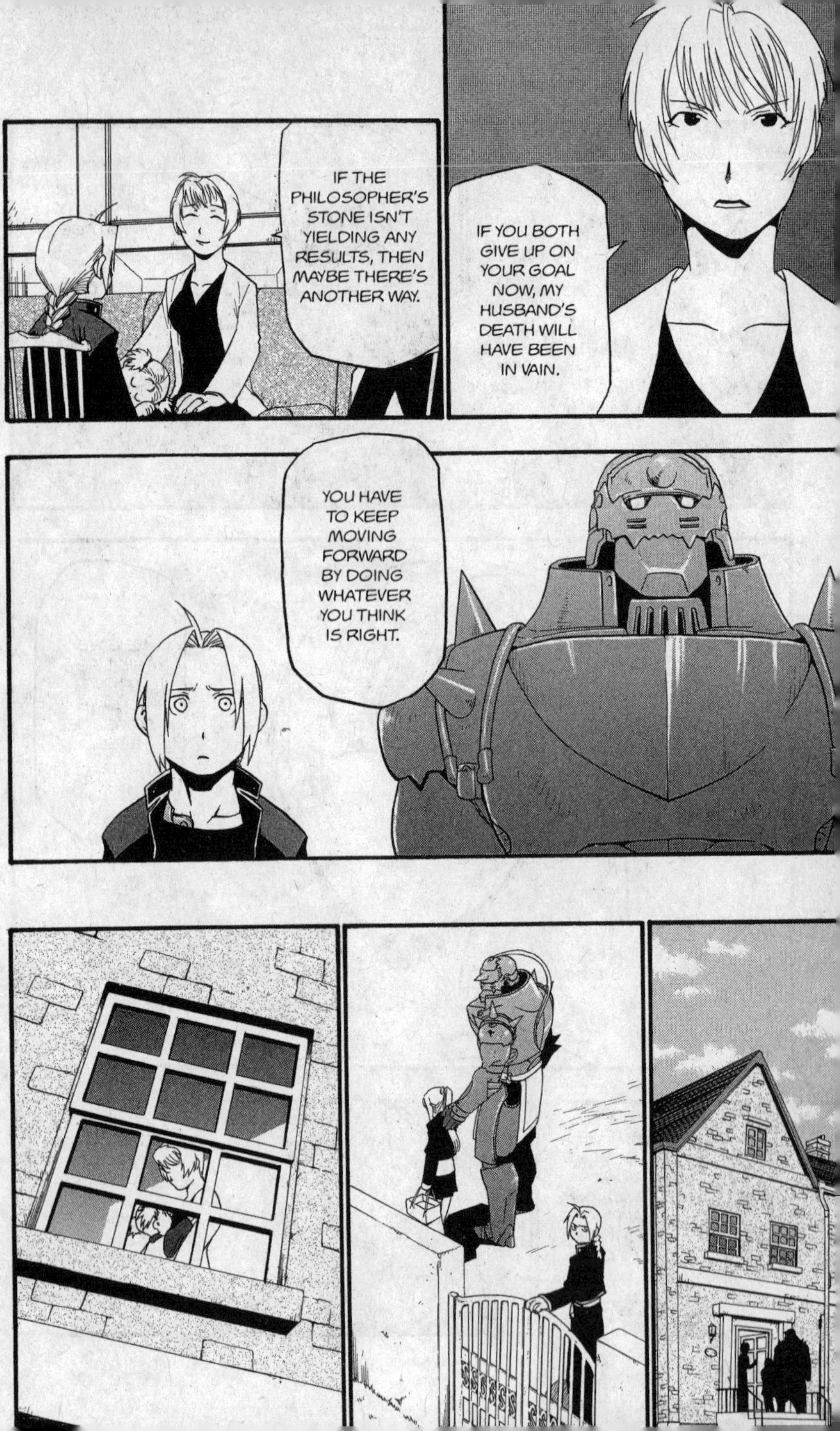
IF YOU BOTH GIVE UP ON YOUR GOAL NOW, MY HUSBAND'S DEATH WILL HAVE BEEN IN VAIN.
IF THE PHILOSOPHER'S STONE ISN'T YIELDING ANY RESULTS, THEN MAYBE THERE'S ANOTHER WAY.
YOU HAVE TO KEEP MOVING FORWARD BY DOING WHATEVER YOU THINK IS RIGHT.

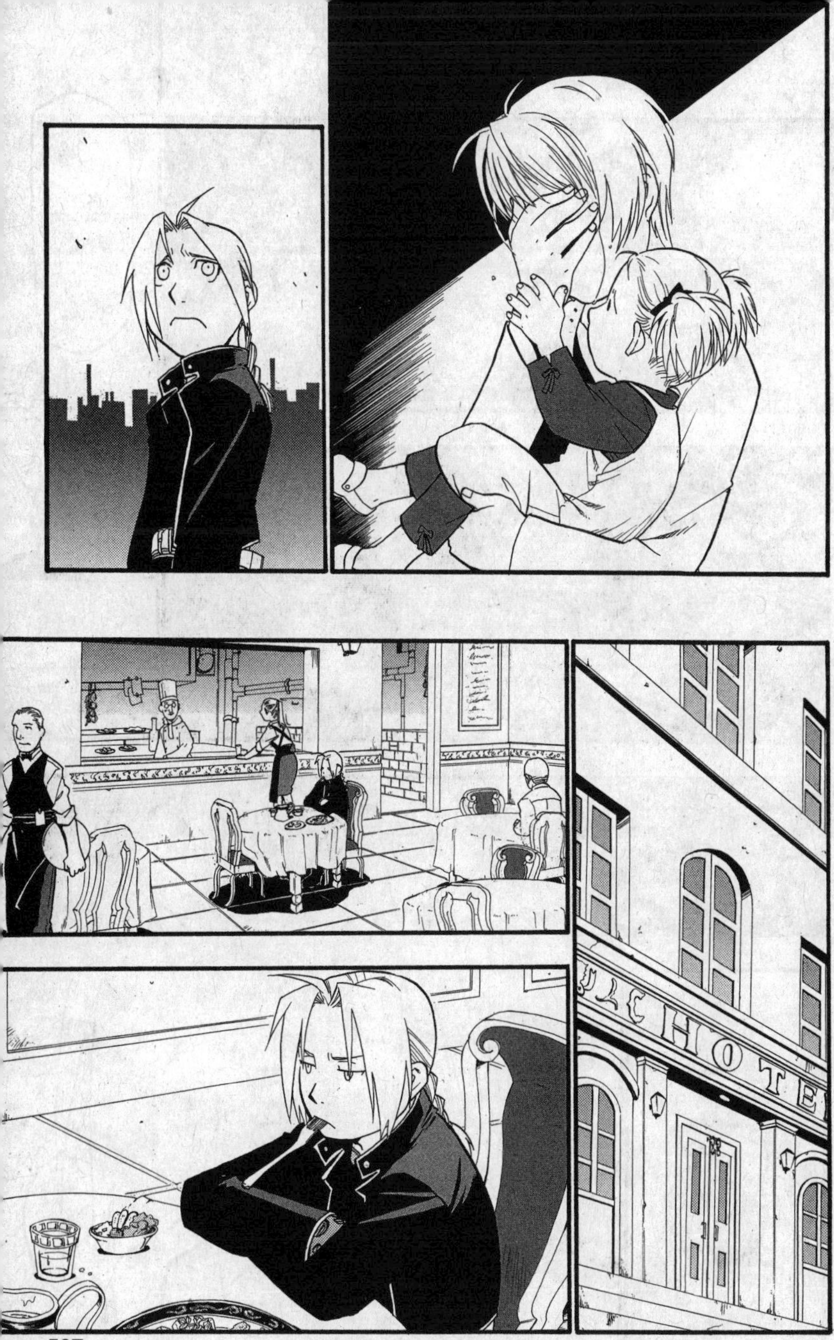

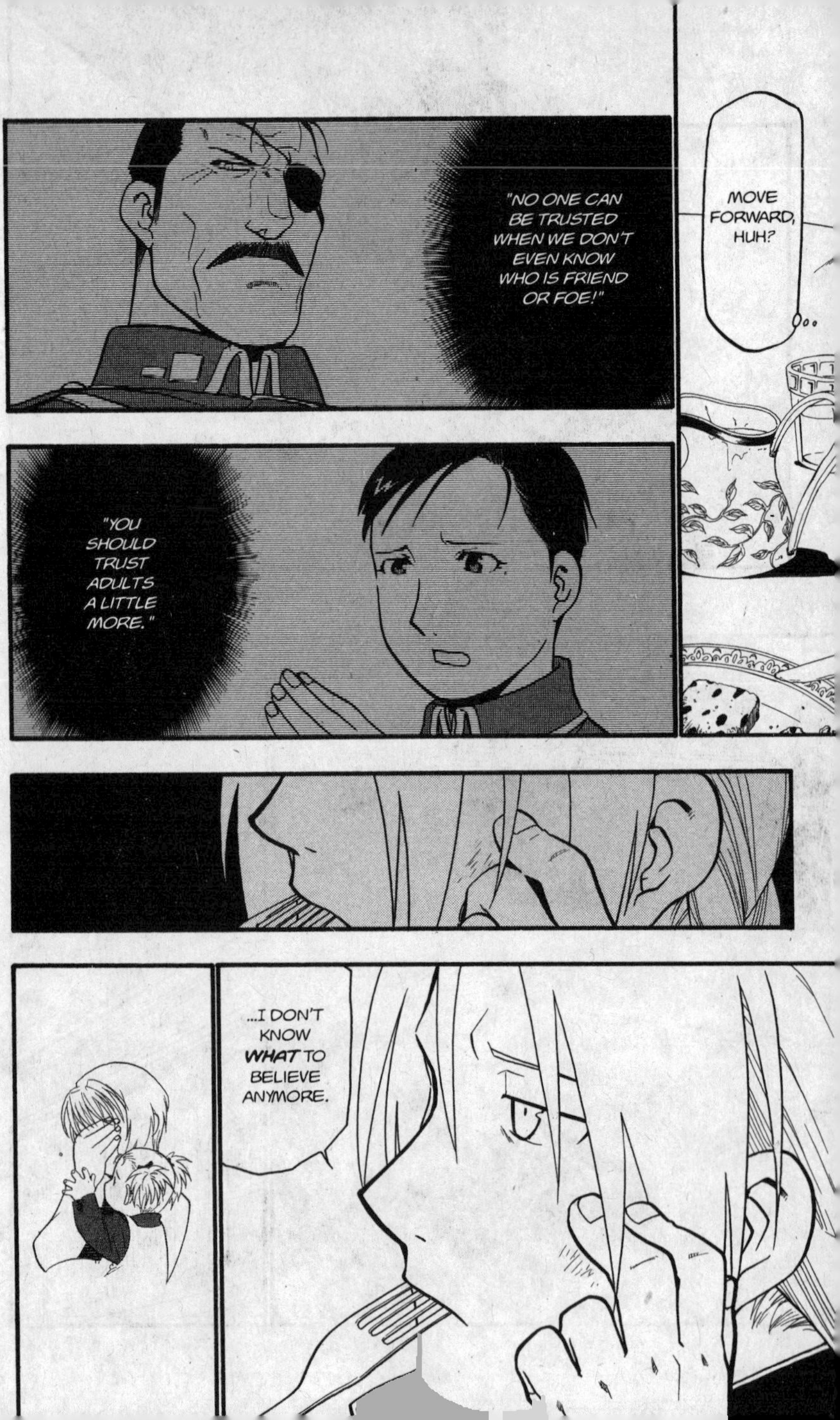
MOVE FORWARD, HUH?
"NO ONE CAN BE TRUSTED WHEN WE DON'T EVEN KNOW WHO IS FRIEND OR FOE!"
"YOU SHOULD TRUST ADULTS A LITTLE MORE."
...I DON'T KNOW ***WHAT*** TO BELIEVE ANYMORE.

KONK
CLACK
AW, GEEZ...
SIR?
ARE YOU FEELING SICK, SIR?
SIR?
IT WOULD'VE BEEN EASIER...
...IF SHE HAD JUST CHEWED ME OUT.
NOK
NOK
NOK
NOK
503
NOK

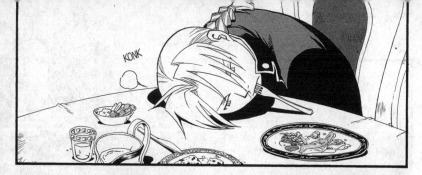

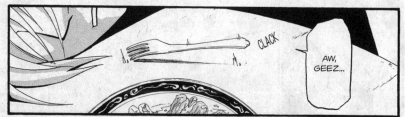

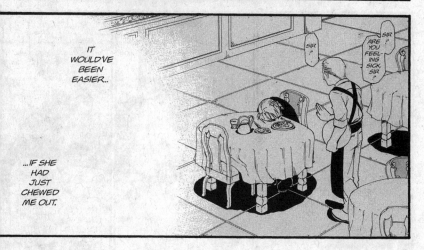

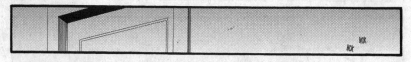

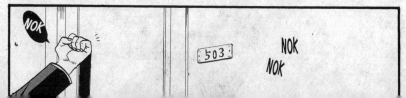

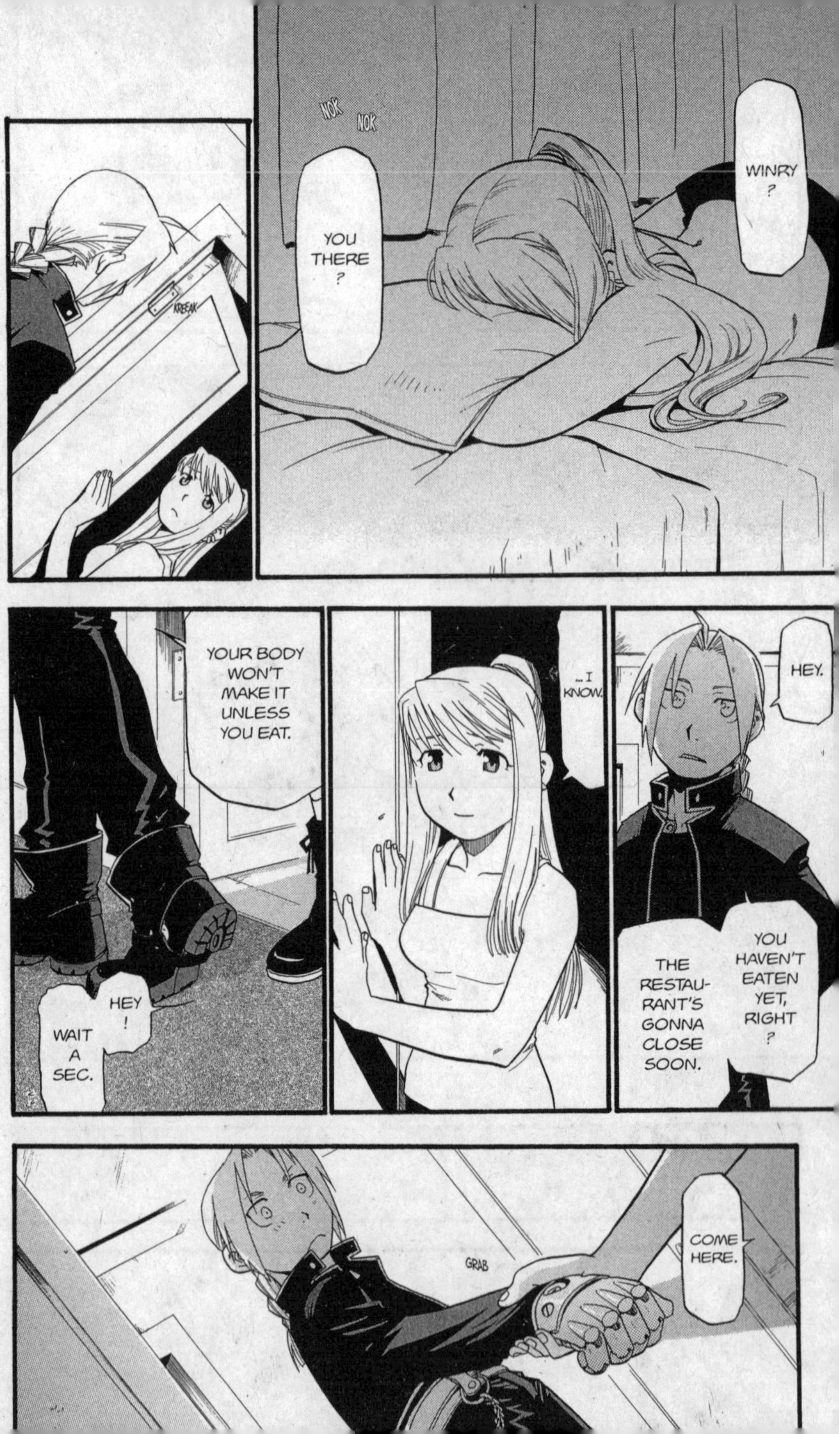
NOK NOK
WINRY ?
YOU THERE ?
KREEAK
HEY.
YOU HAVEN'T EATEN YET, RIGHT ?
THE RESTAU-RANT'S GONNA CLOSE SOON.
...I KNOW.
YOUR BODY WON'T MAKE IT UNLESS YOU EAT.
HEY !
WAIT A SEC.
COME HERE.
GRAB

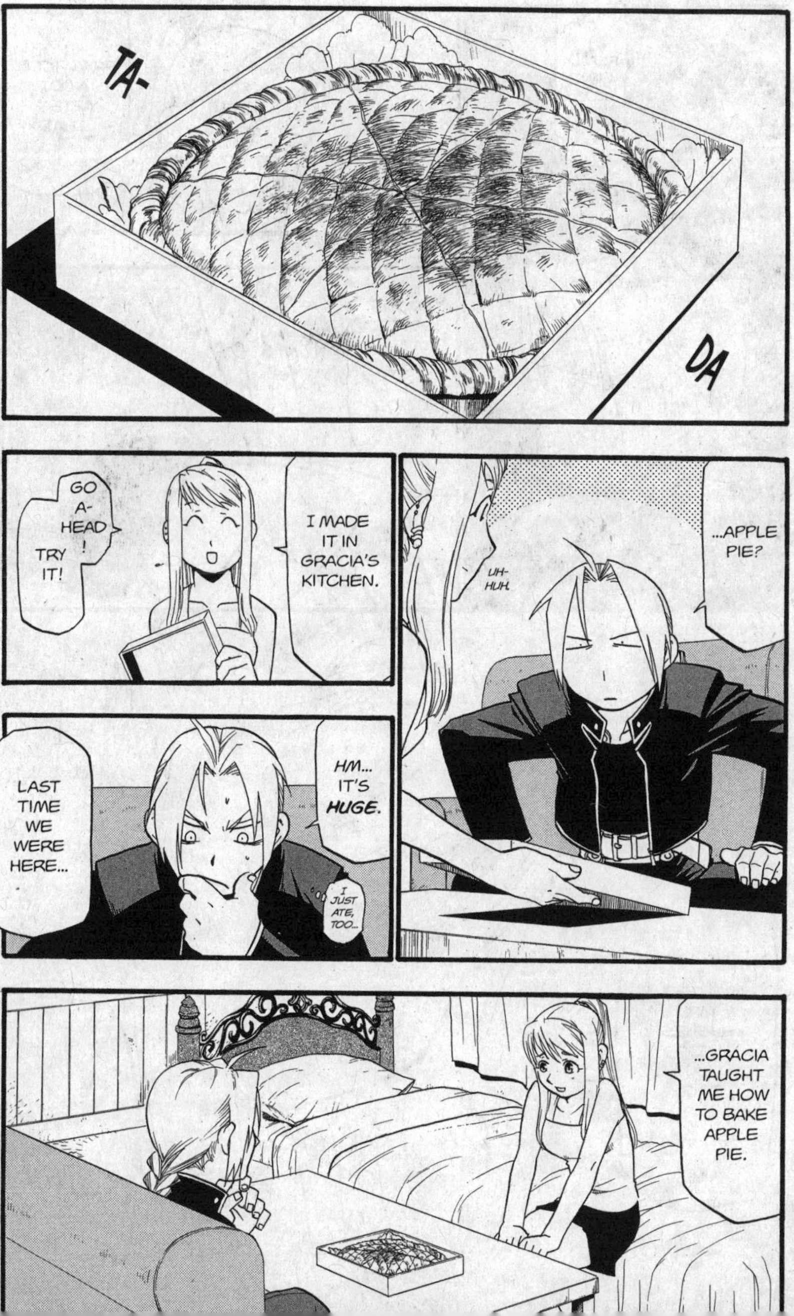
TA-
DA
...APPLE PIE?
UH-HUH.
I MADE IT IN GRACIA'S KITCHEN.
GO A-HEAD! TRY IT!
HM... IT'S **HUGE**.
I JUST ATE, TOO...
LAST TIME WE WERE HERE...
...GRACIA TAUGHT ME HOW TO BAKE APPLE PIE.

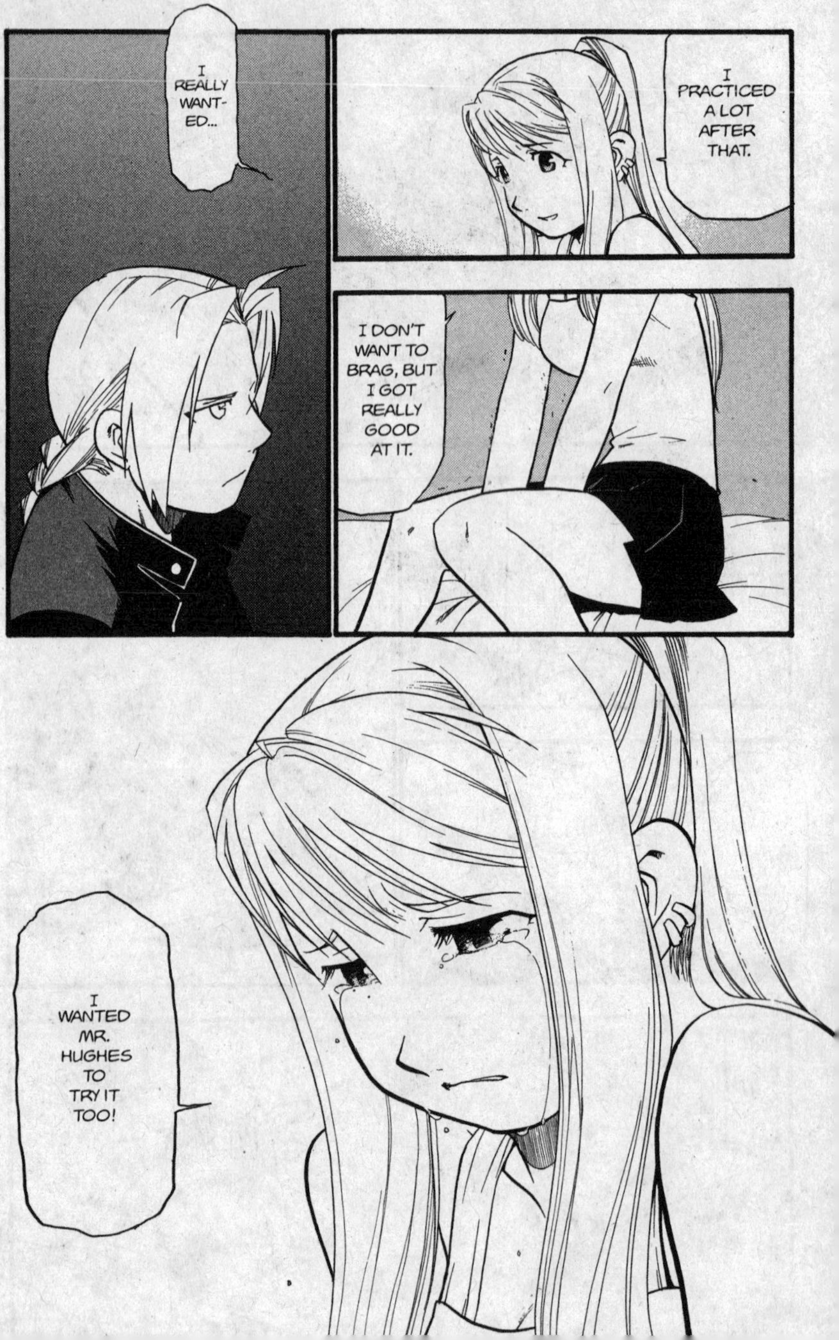
I PRACTICED A LOT AFTER THAT.
I DON'T WANT TO BRAG, BUT I GOT REALLY GOOD AT IT.
I REALLY WANT-ED...
I WANTED MR. HUGHES TO TRY IT TOO!

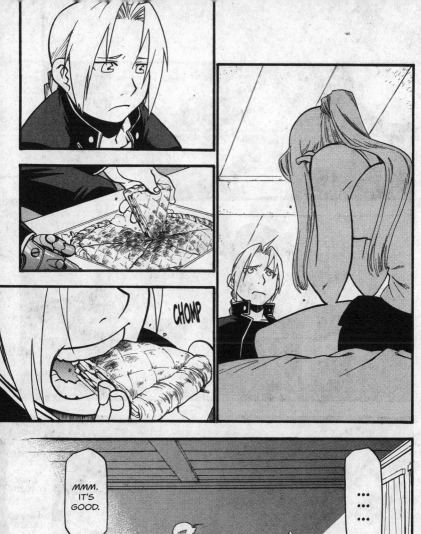

CHOMP

MMM.
IT'S
GOOD.

...
...
...

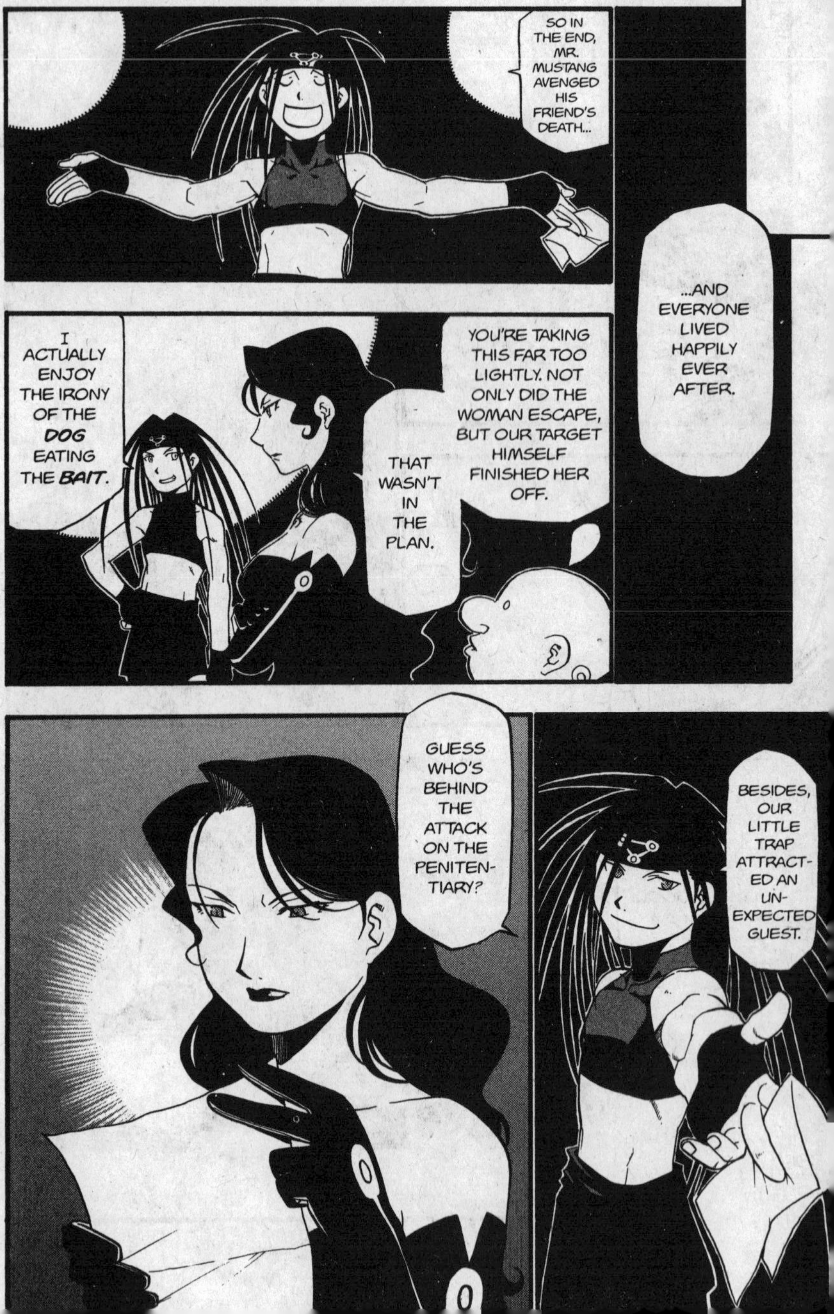
SO IN THE END, MR. MUSTANG AVENGED HIS FRIEND'S DEATH...
...AND EVERYONE LIVED HAPPILY EVER AFTER.
YOU'RE TAKING THIS FAR TOO LIGHTLY. NOT ONLY DID THE WOMAN ESCAPE, BUT OUR TARGET HIMSELF FINISHED HER OFF.
THAT WASN'T IN THE PLAN.
I ACTUALLY ENJOY THE IRONY OF THE *DOG* EATING THE *BAIT*.
BESIDES, OUR LITTLE TRAP ATTRACT-ED AN UN-EXPECTED GUEST.
GUESS WHO'S BEHIND THE ATTACK ON THE PENITEN-TIARY?

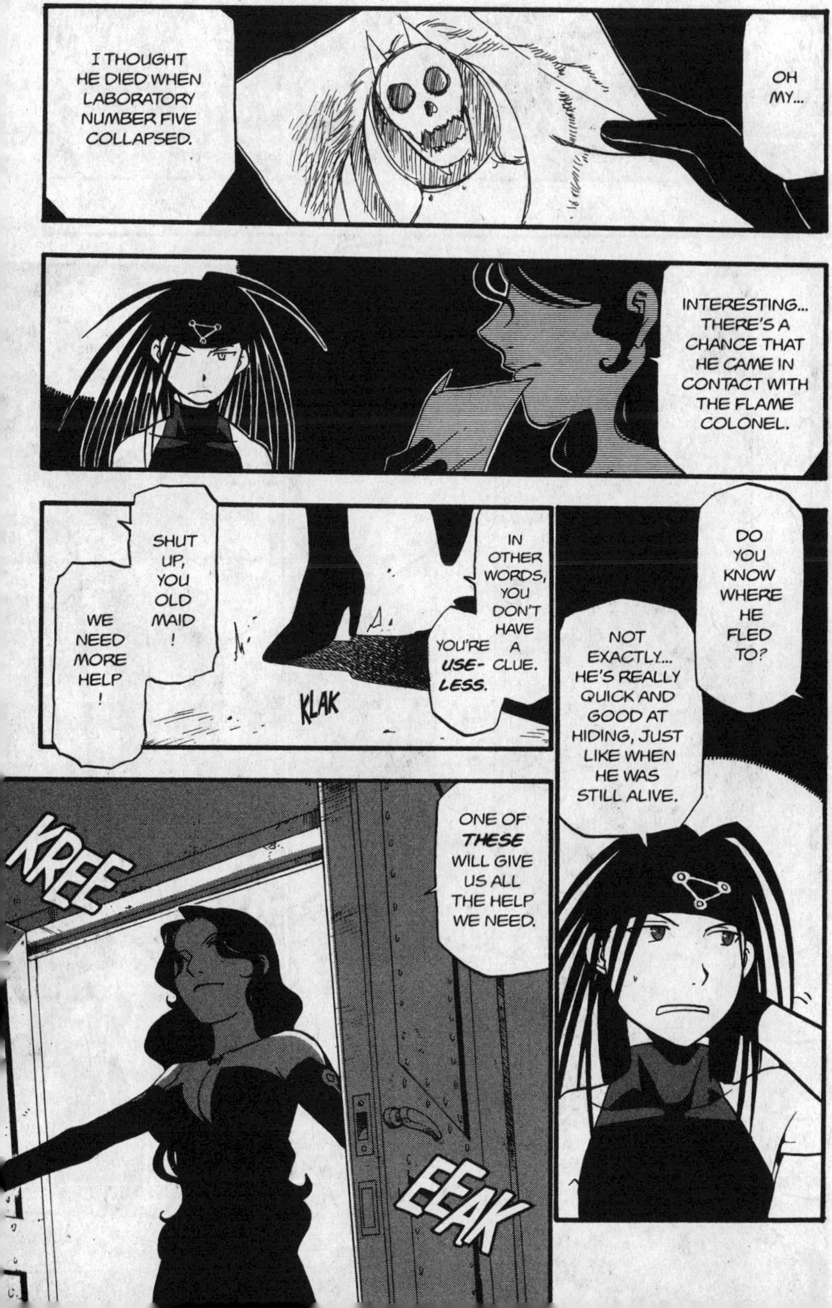
OH MY...
I THOUGHT HE DIED WHEN LABORATORY NUMBER FIVE COLLAPSED.
INTERESTING... THERE'S A CHANCE THAT HE CAME IN CONTACT WITH THE FLAME COLONEL.
DO YOU KNOW WHERE HE FLED TO?
NOT EXACTLY... HE'S REALLY QUICK AND GOOD AT HIDING, JUST LIKE WHEN HE WAS STILL ALIVE.
IN OTHER WORDS, YOU DON'T HAVE A CLUE.
YOU'RE USE-LESS.
KLAK
SHUT UP, YOU OLD MAID!
WE NEED MORE HELP!
ONE OF THESE WILL GIVE US ALL THE HELP WE NEED.
KREE
EEAK

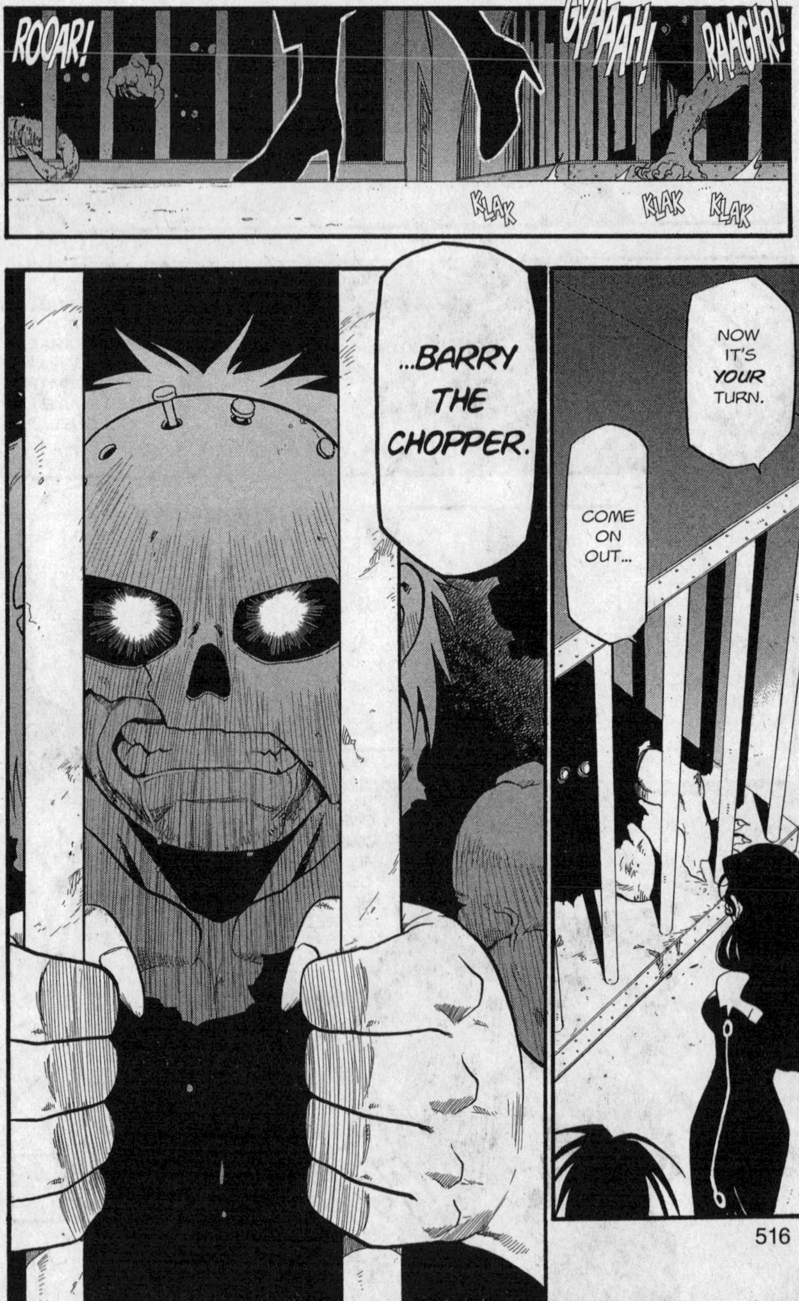
RAAGHR!
GYAAAH!
ROOAR!
KLAK
KLAK
KLAK
NOW IT'S YOUR TURN.
COME ON OUT...
...BARRY THE CHOPPER.

FULLMETAL
ALCHEMIST

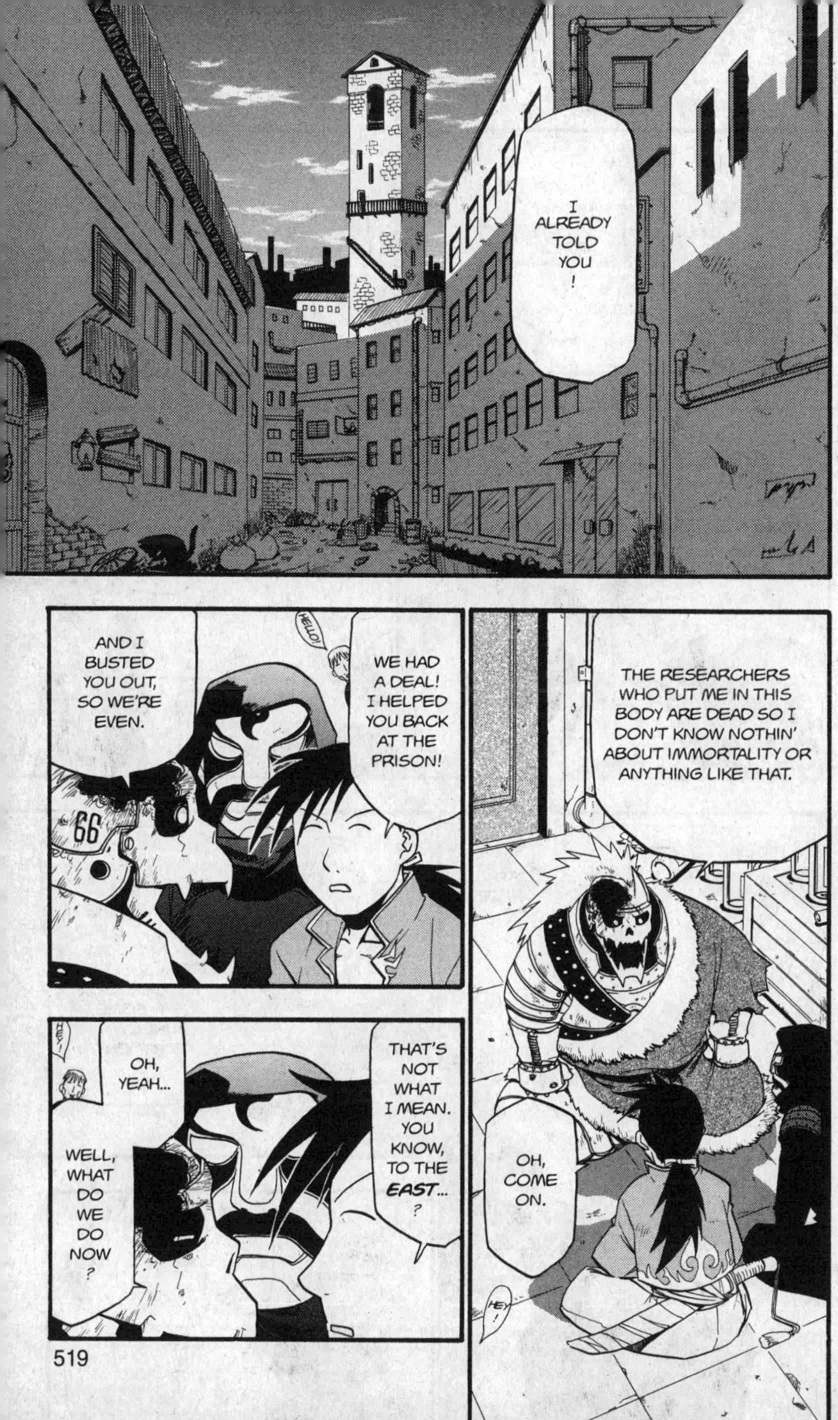
I ALREADY TOLD YOU!
THE RESEARCHERS WHO PUT ME IN THIS BODY ARE DEAD SO I DON'T KNOW NOTHIN' ABOUT IMMORTALITY OR ANYTHING LIKE THAT.
OH, COME ON.
HEY!
WE HAD A DEAL! I HELPED YOU BACK AT THE PRISON!
HELLO!
AND I BUSTED YOU OUT, SO WE'RE EVEN.
THAT'S NOT WHAT I MEAN. YOU KNOW, TO THE *EAST*...?
OH, YEAH...
HEY!
WELL, WHAT DO WE DO NOW?

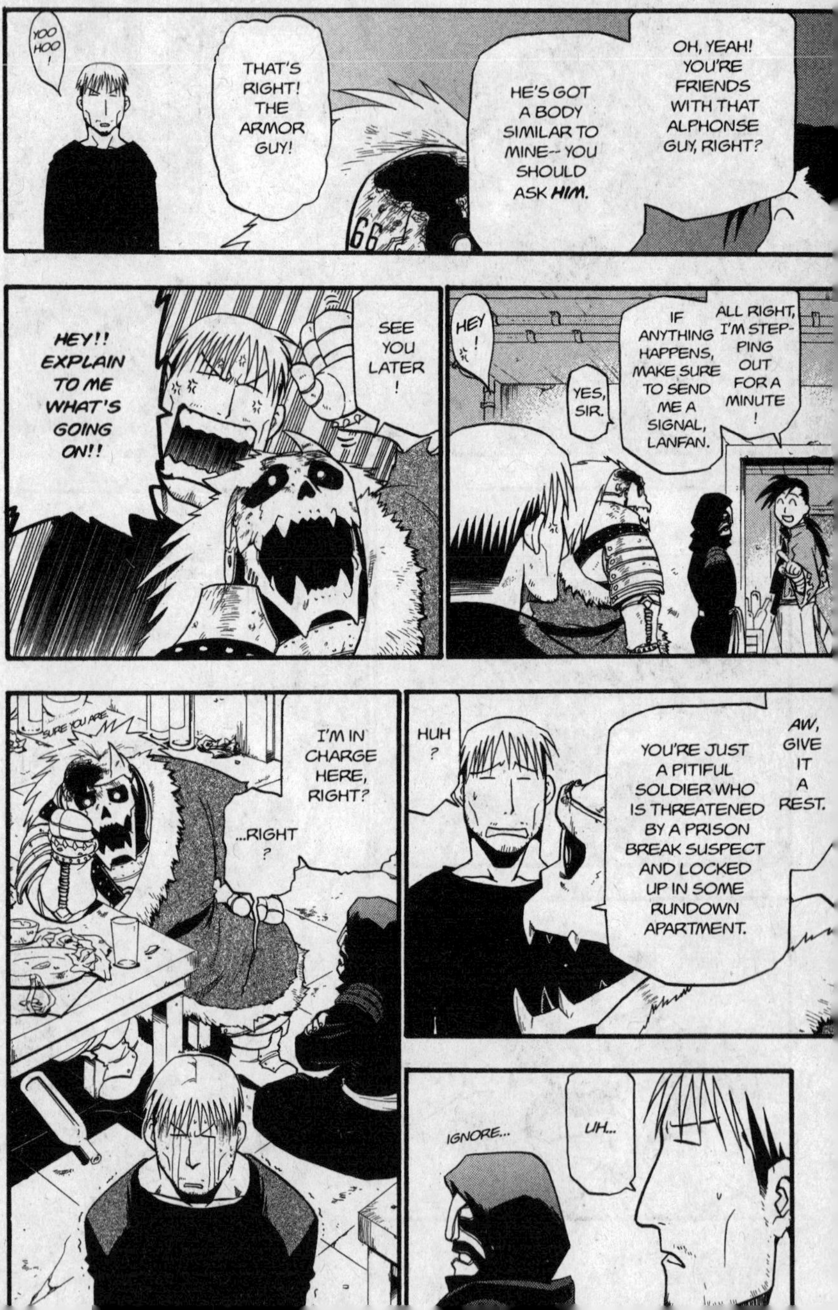
OH, YEAH! YOU'RE FRIENDS WITH THAT ALPHONSE GUY, RIGHT?
HE'S GOT A BODY SIMILAR TO MINE-- YOU SHOULD ASK **HIM**.
THAT'S RIGHT! THE ARMOR GUY!
YOO HOO!
ALL RIGHT, I'M STEPPING OUT FOR A MINUTE!
IF ANYTHING HAPPENS, MAKE SURE TO SEND ME A SIGNAL, LANFAN.
YES, SIR.
HEY!
SEE YOU LATER!
HEY!! EXPLAIN TO ME WHAT'S GOING ON!!
AW, GIVE IT A REST.
YOU'RE JUST A PITIFUL SOLDIER WHO IS THREATENED BY A PRISON BREAK SUSPECT AND LOCKED UP IN SOME RUNDOWN APARTMENT.
HUH?
UH...
IGNORE...
I'M IN CHARGE HERE, RIGHT?
...RIGHT?
SURE YOU ARE.

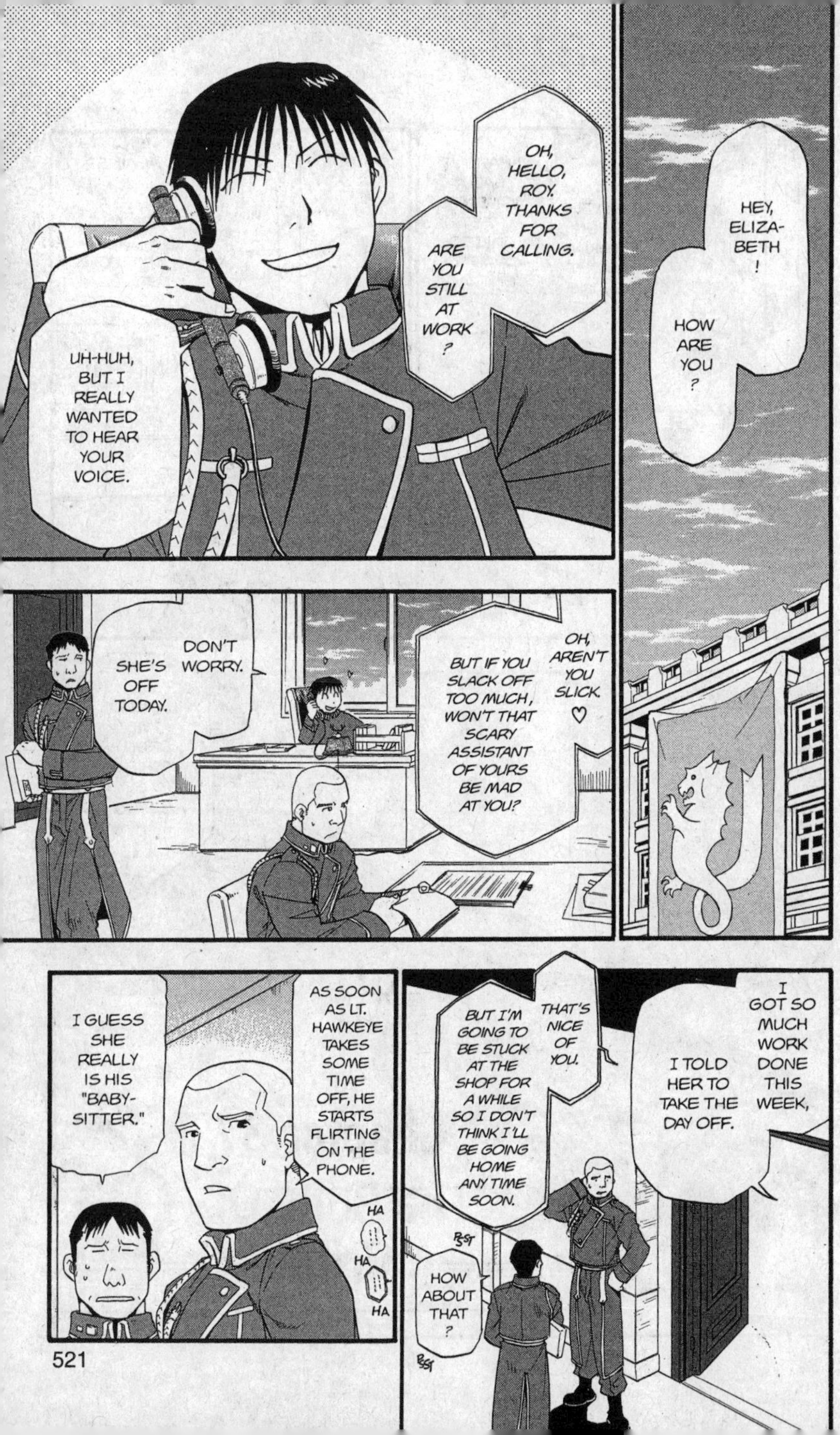
HEY, ELIZA-BETH!
HOW ARE YOU?
OH, HELLO, ROY. THANKS FOR CALLING.
ARE YOU STILL AT WORK?
UH-HUH, BUT I REALLY WANTED TO HEAR YOUR VOICE.
OH, AREN'T YOU SLICK. ♡
BUT IF YOU SLACK OFF TOO MUCH, WON'T THAT SCARY ASSISTANT OF YOURS BE MAD AT YOU?
DON'T WORRY.
SHE'S OFF TODAY.
I GOT SO MUCH WORK DONE THIS WEEK,
I TOLD HER TO TAKE THE DAY OFF.
THAT'S NICE OF YOU.
BUT I'M GOING TO BE STUCK AT THE SHOP FOR A WHILE SO I DON'T THINK I'LL BE GOING HOME ANY TIME SOON.
PSST
HOW ABOUT THAT?
PSST
AS SOON AS LT. HAWKEYE TAKES SOME TIME OFF, HE STARTS FLIRTING ON THE PHONE.
I GUESS SHE REALLY IS HIS "BABY-SITTER."
HA
HA
HA

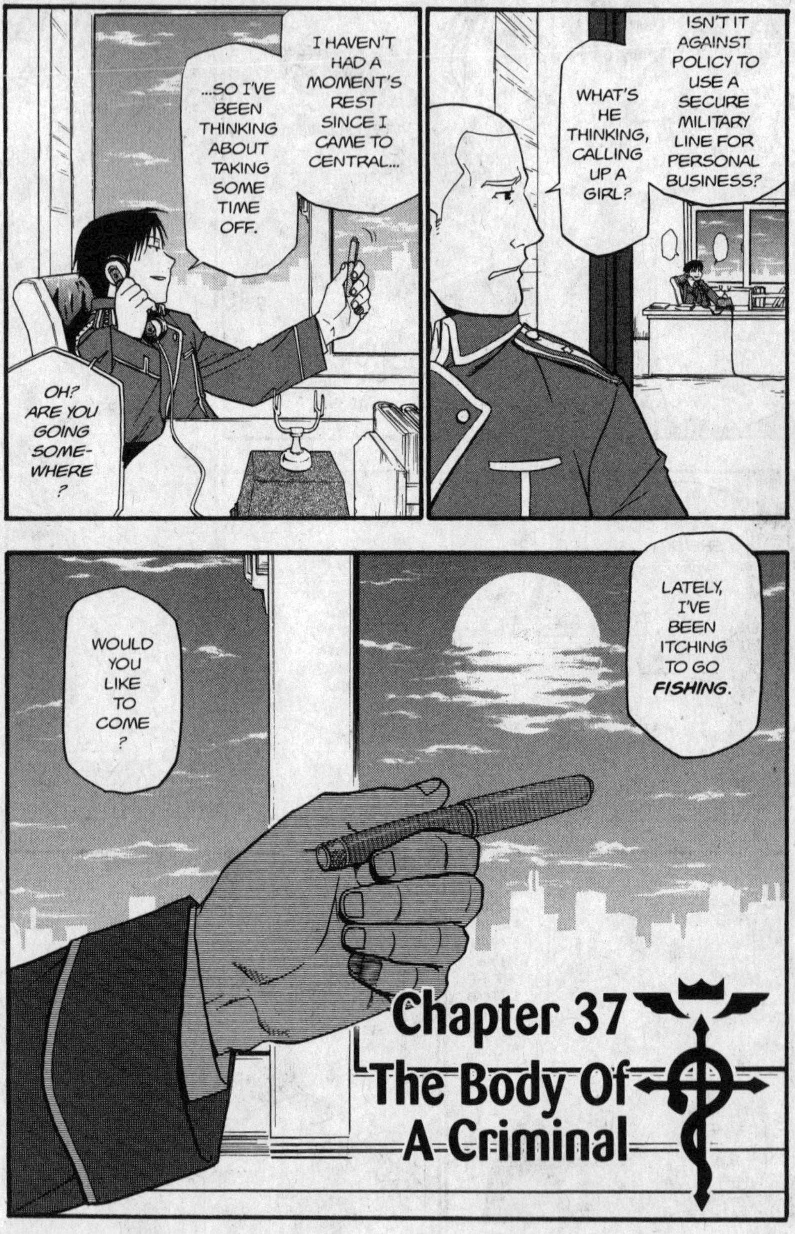
ISN'T IT AGAINST POLICY TO USE A SECURE MILITARY LINE FOR PERSONAL BUSINESS?
WHAT'S HE THINKING, CALLING UP A GIRL?
I HAVEN'T HAD A MOMENT'S REST SINCE I CAME TO CENTRAL...
...SO I'VE BEEN THINKING ABOUT TAKING SOME TIME OFF.
OH? ARE YOU GOING SOME-WHERE?
LATELY, I'VE BEEN ITCHING TO GO **FISHING**.
WOULD YOU LIKE TO COME?
Chapter 37
The Body Of A Criminal

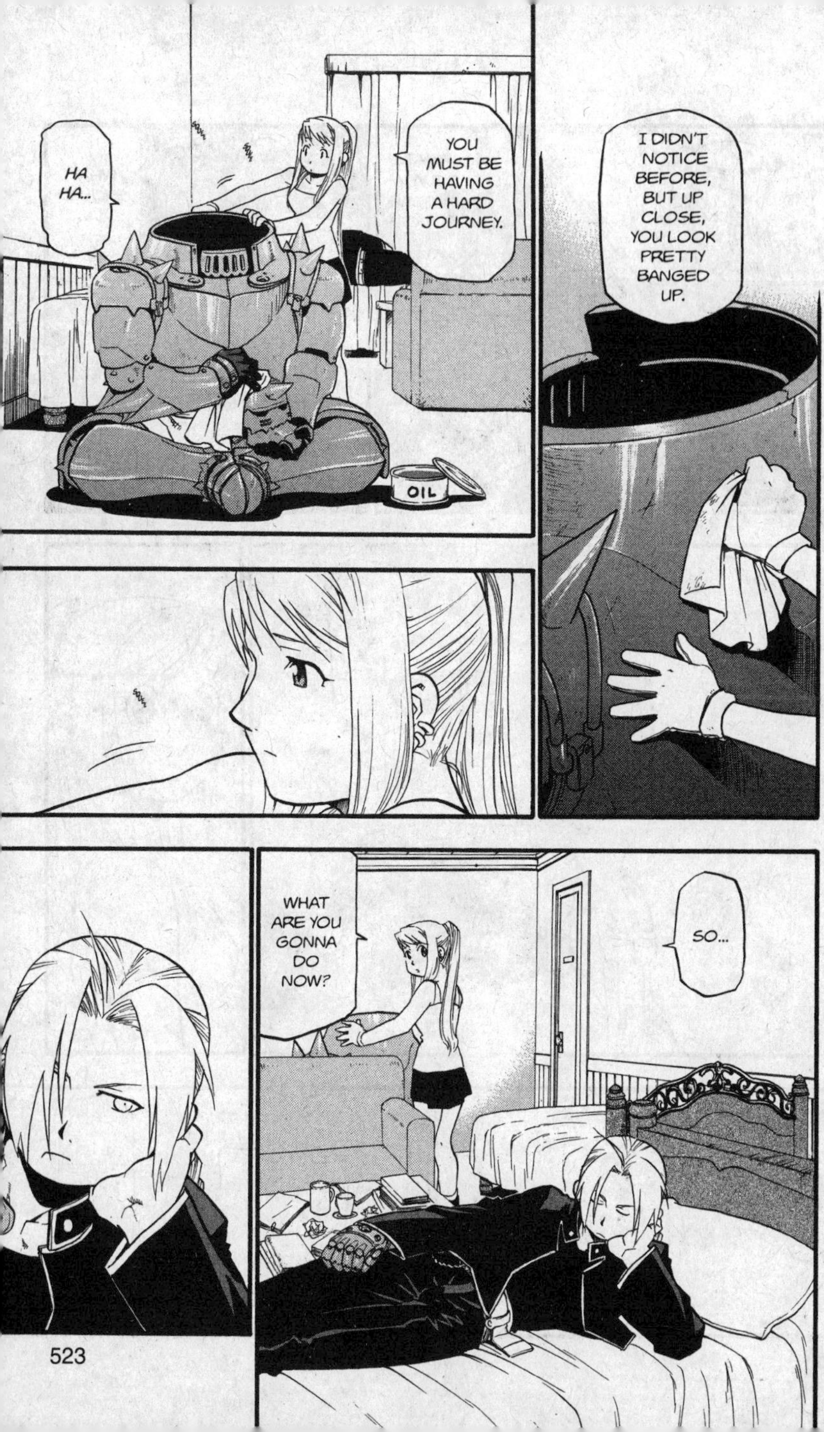
I DIDN'T NOTICE BEFORE, BUT UP CLOSE, YOU LOOK PRETTY BANGED UP.
YOU MUST BE HAVING A HARD JOURNEY.
HA HA...
OIL
SO...
WHAT ARE YOU GONNA DO NOW?

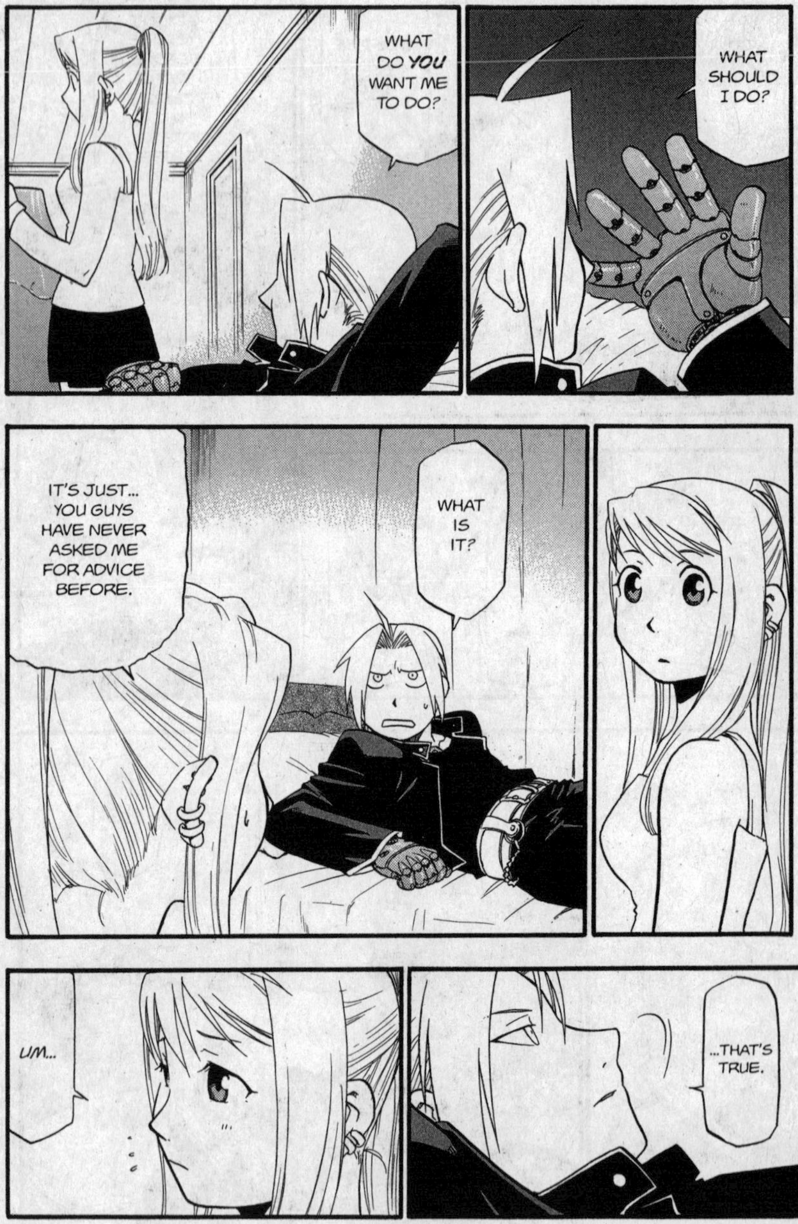
WHAT SHOULD I DO?
WHAT DO *YOU* WANT ME TO DO?
WHAT IS IT?
IT'S JUST... YOU GUYS HAVE NEVER ASKED ME FOR ADVICE BEFORE.
...THAT'S TRUE.
UM...

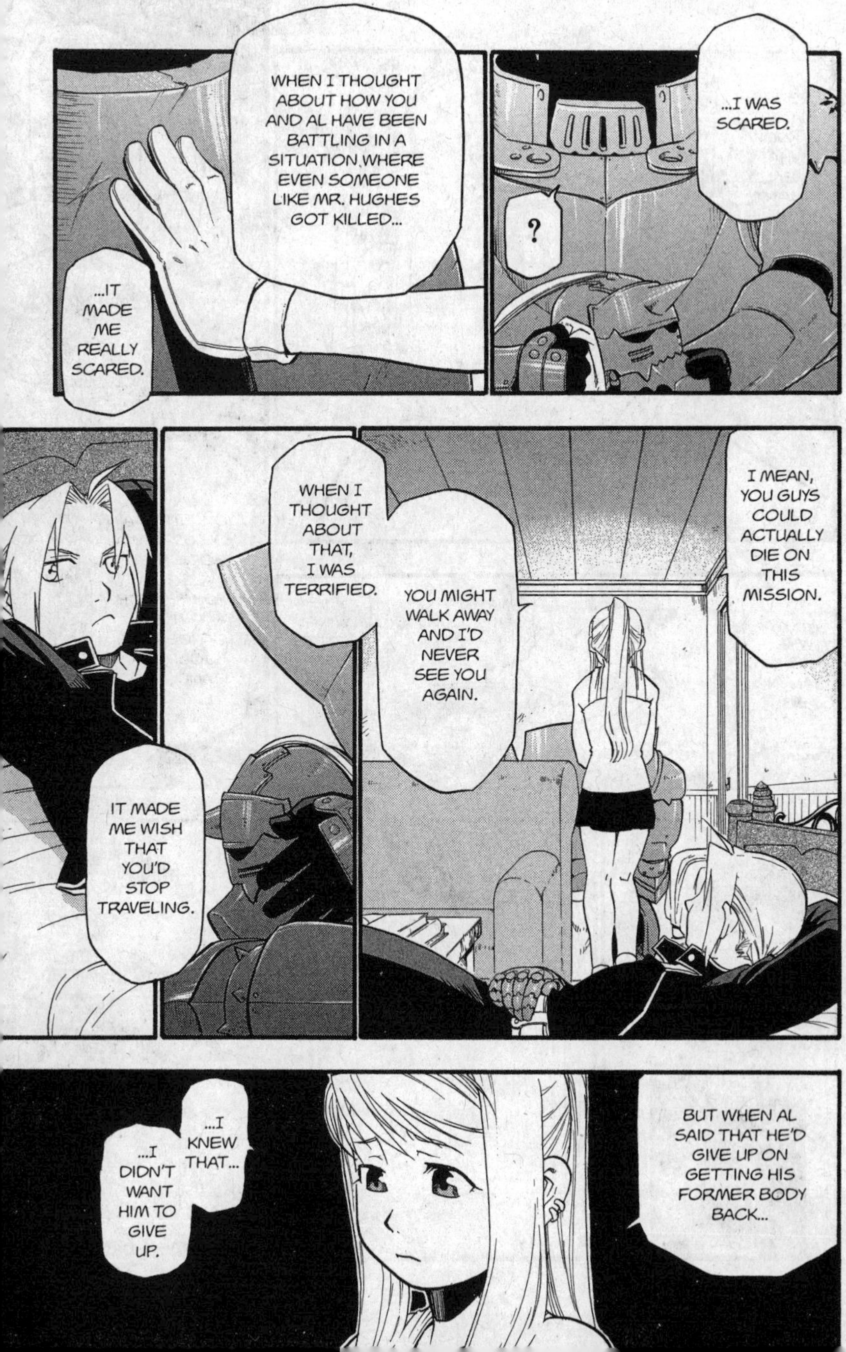
...I WAS SCARED.
?
WHEN I THOUGHT ABOUT HOW YOU AND AL HAVE BEEN BATTLING IN A SITUATION WHERE EVEN SOMEONE LIKE MR. HUGHES GOT KILLED...
...IT MADE ME REALLY SCARED.
I MEAN, YOU GUYS COULD ACTUALLY DIE ON THIS MISSION.
WHEN I THOUGHT ABOUT THAT, I WAS TERRIFIED.
YOU MIGHT WALK AWAY AND I'D NEVER SEE YOU AGAIN.
IT MADE ME WISH THAT YOU'D STOP TRAVELING.
BUT WHEN AL SAID THAT HE'D GIVE UP ON GETTING HIS FORMER BODY BACK...
...I KNEW THAT...
...I DIDN'T WANT HIM TO GIVE UP.

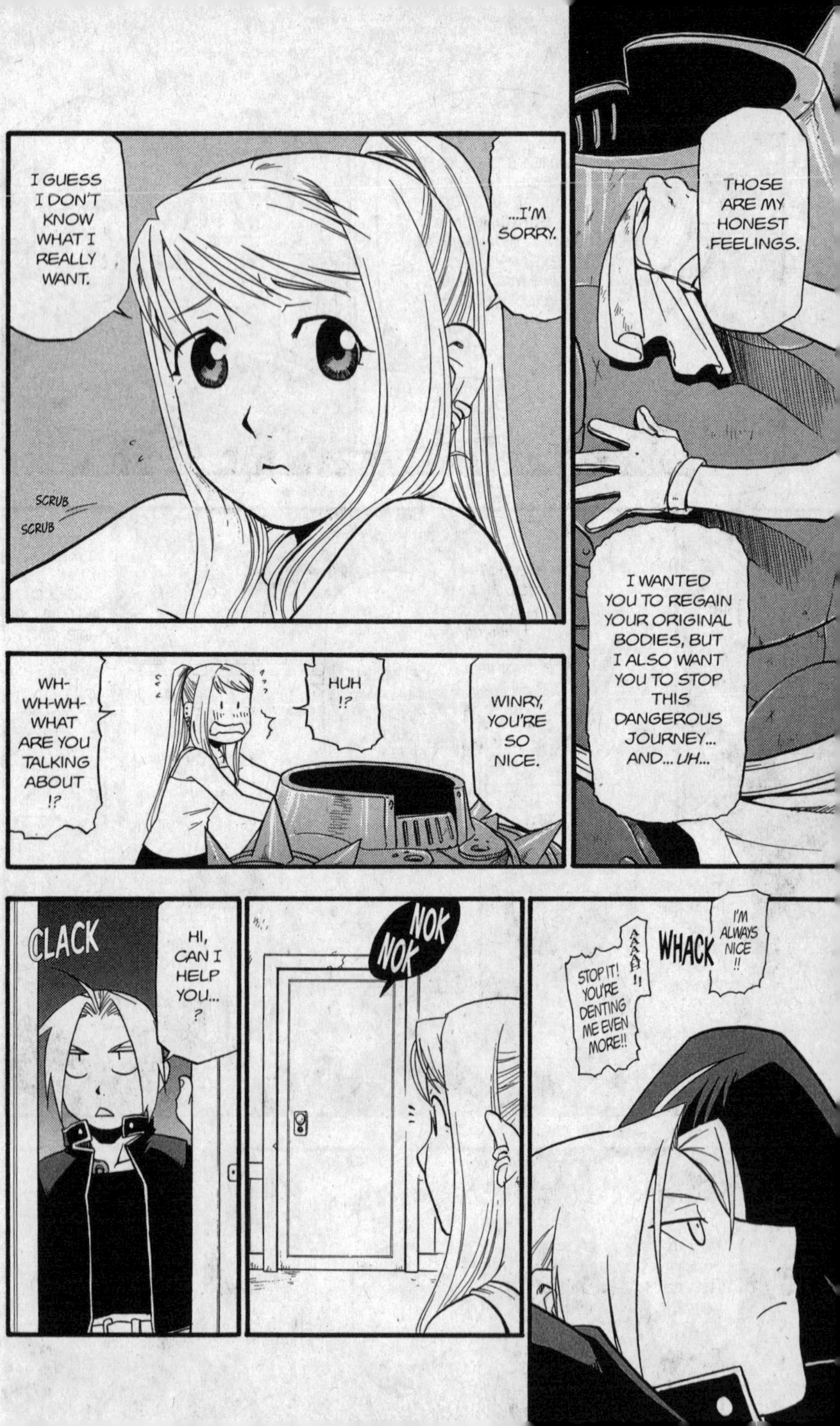
THOSE ARE MY HONEST FEELINGS.
I WANTED YOU TO REGAIN YOUR ORIGINAL BODIES, BUT I ALSO WANT YOU TO STOP THIS DANGEROUS JOURNEY... AND... *UH*...
...I'M SORRY.
I GUESS I DON'T KNOW WHAT I REALLY WANT.
SCRUB
SCRUB
WINRY, YOU'RE SO NICE.
HUH!?
WH-WH-WH-WHAT ARE YOU TALKING ABOUT!?
I'M ALWAYS NICE!!
WHACK
AAAAH!!
STOP IT! YOU'RE DENTING ME EVEN MORE!!
NOK NOK
CLACK
HI, CAN I HELP YOU...?

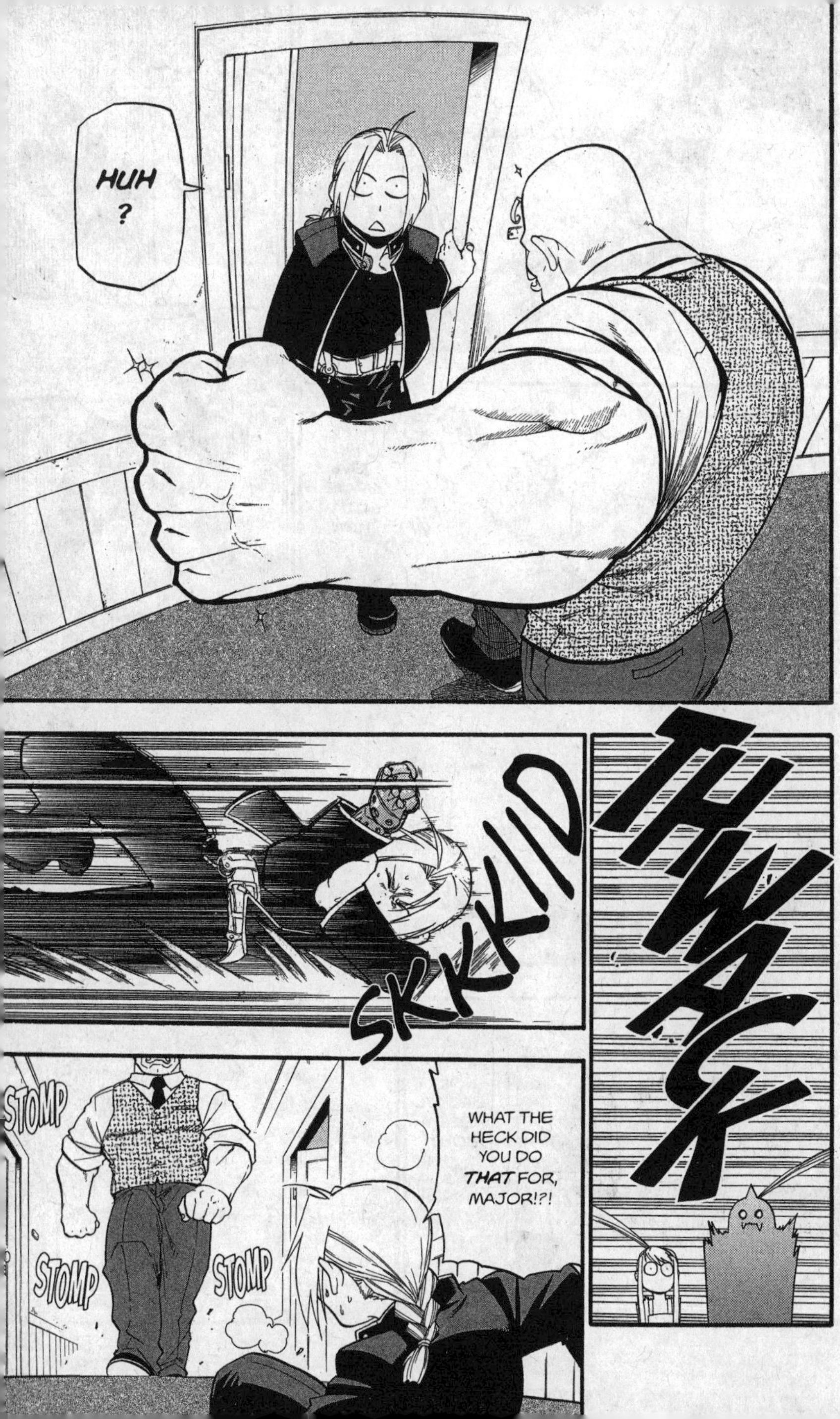
HUH ?
THWACK
SKKID
WHAT THE HECK DID YOU DO *THAT* FOR, MAJOR!?!
STOMP
STOMP
STOMP

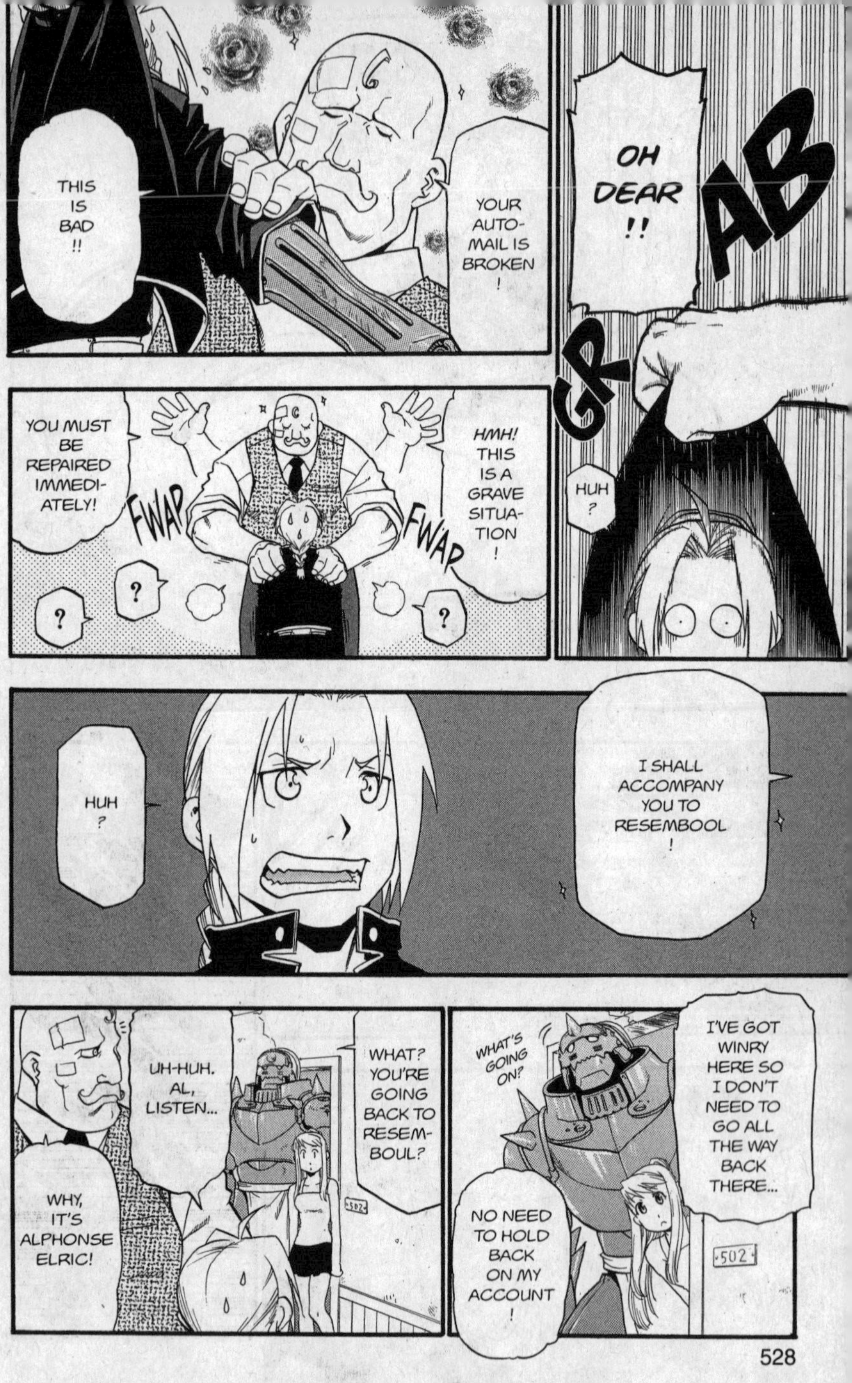
OH DEAR !!
GRAB
HUH ?
YOUR AUTO-MAIL IS BROKEN !
THIS IS BAD !!
HMH! THIS IS A GRAVE SITUATION !
FWAP
FWAP
YOU MUST BE REPAIRED IMMEDIATELY!
?
?
?
I SHALL ACCOMPANY YOU TO RESEMBOOL !
HUH ?
I'VE GOT WINRY HERE SO I DON'T NEED TO GO ALL THE WAY BACK THERE...
WHAT'S GOING ON?
502
NO NEED TO HOLD BACK ON MY ACCOUNT !
WHAT? YOU'RE GOING BACK TO RESEMBOUL?
UH-HUH. AL, LISTEN...
502
WHY, IT'S ALPHONSE ELRIC!

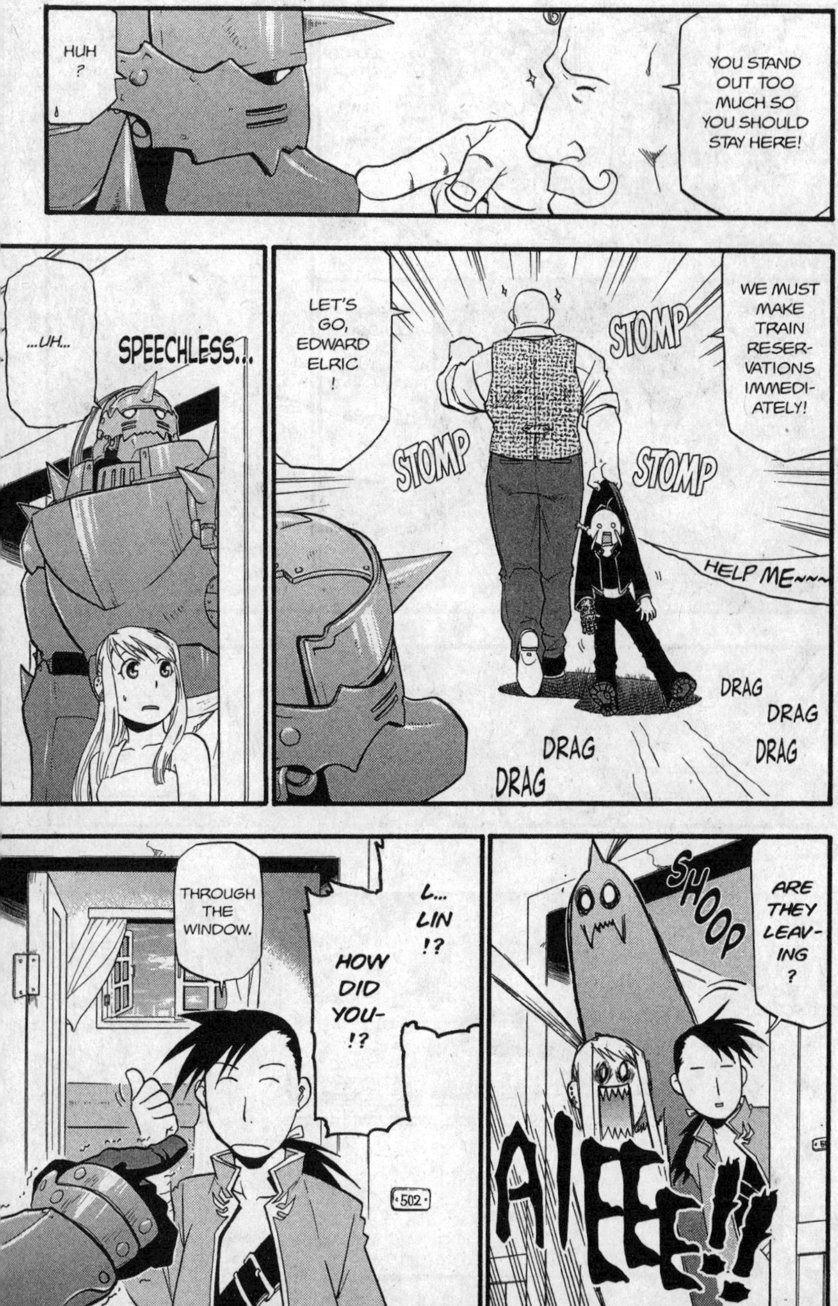
YOU STAND OUT TOO MUCH SO YOU SHOULD STAY HERE!
HUH ?
WE MUST MAKE TRAIN RESER-VATIONS IMMEDI-ATELY!
STOMP
LET'S GO, EDWARD ELRIC !
STOMP
STOMP
HELP ME~~~
DRAG
DRAG
DRAG
DRAG
DRAG
...UH...
SPEECHLESS...
ARE THEY LEAV-ING ?
SHOOP
AIEEE!!
L... LIN !?
HOW DID YOU- !?
THROUGH THE WINDOW.

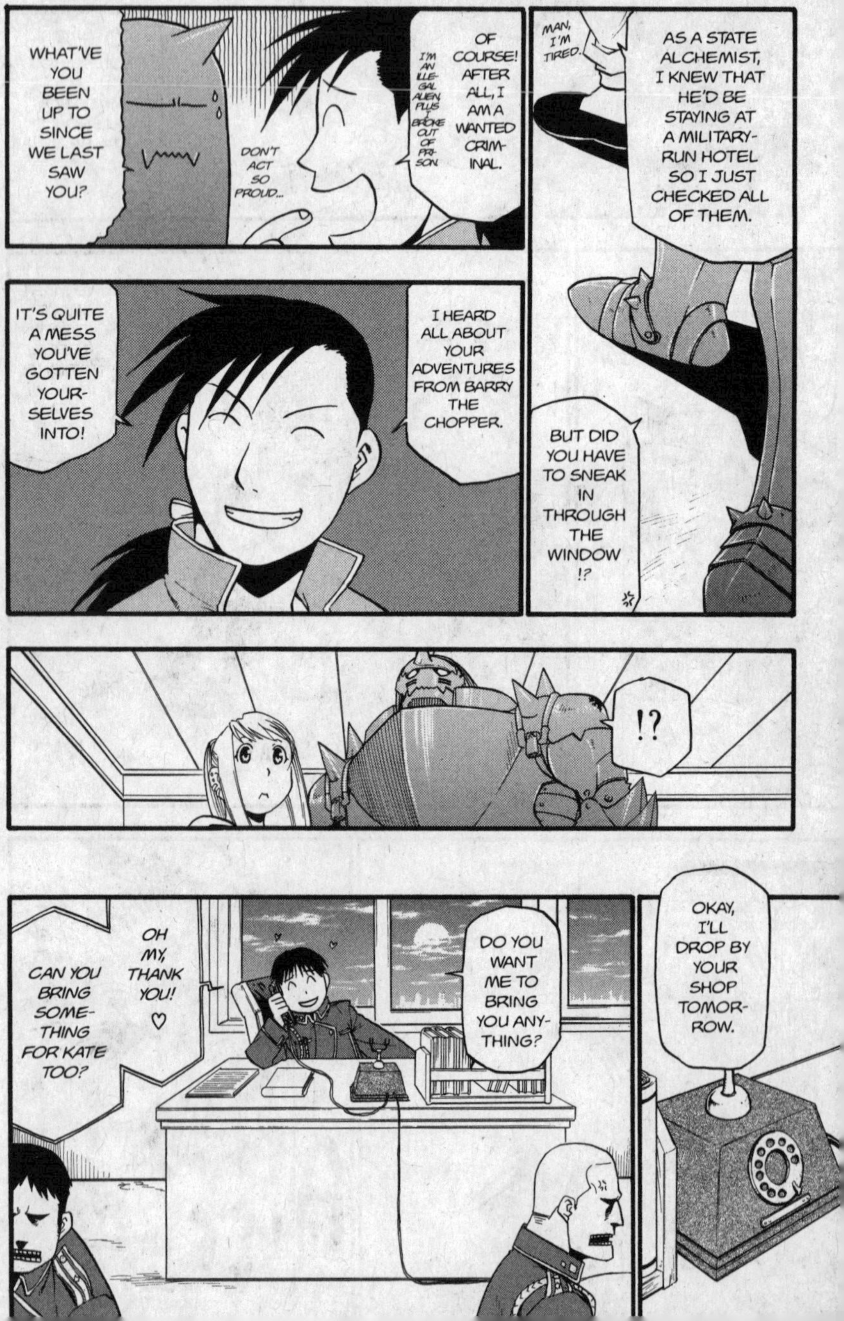
MAN, I'M TIRED.
AS A STATE ALCHEMIST, I KNEW THAT HE'D BE STAYING AT A MILITARY-RUN HOTEL SO I JUST CHECKED ALL OF THEM.
BUT DID YOU HAVE TO SNEAK IN THROUGH THE WINDOW !?
OF COURSE! AFTER ALL, I AM A WANTED CRIMINAL.
I'M AN ILLEGAL ALIEN, PLUS I BROKE OUT OF PRISON.
DON'T ACT SO PROUD...
WHAT'VE YOU BEEN UP TO SINCE WE LAST SAW YOU?
I HEARD ALL ABOUT YOUR ADVENTURES FROM BARRY THE CHOPPER.
IT'S QUITE A MESS YOU'VE GOTTEN YOURSELVES INTO!
!?
OKAY, I'LL DROP BY YOUR SHOP TOMORROW.
DO YOU WANT ME TO BRING YOU ANYTHING?
OH MY, THANK YOU! ♡
CAN YOU BRING SOMETHING FOR KATE TOO?

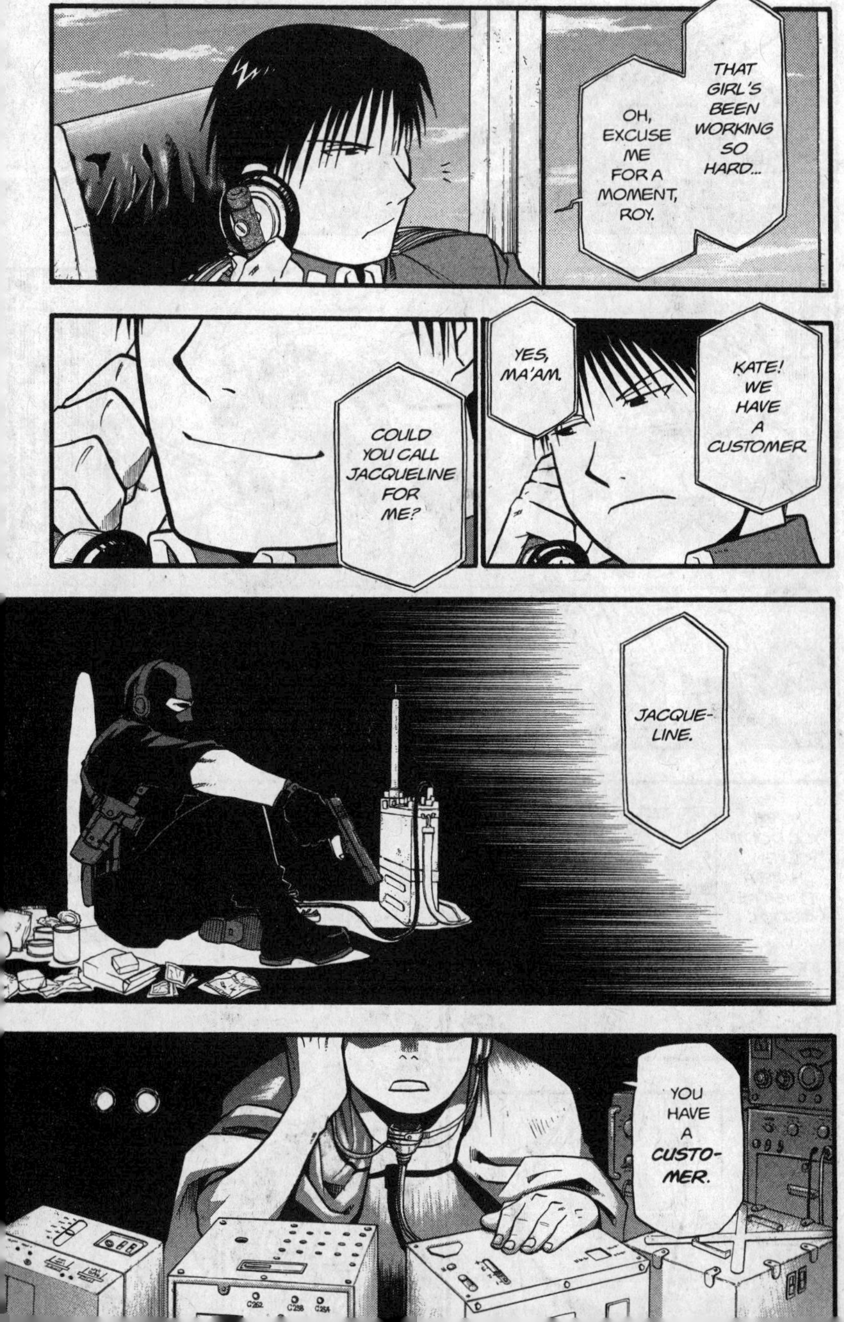
THAT GIRL'S BEEN WORKING SO HARD...
OH, EXCUSE ME FOR A MOMENT, ROY.
KATE! WE HAVE A CUSTOMER.
YES, MA'AM.
COULD YOU CALL JACQUELINE FOR ME?
JACQUE-LINE.
YOU HAVE A CUSTO-MER.

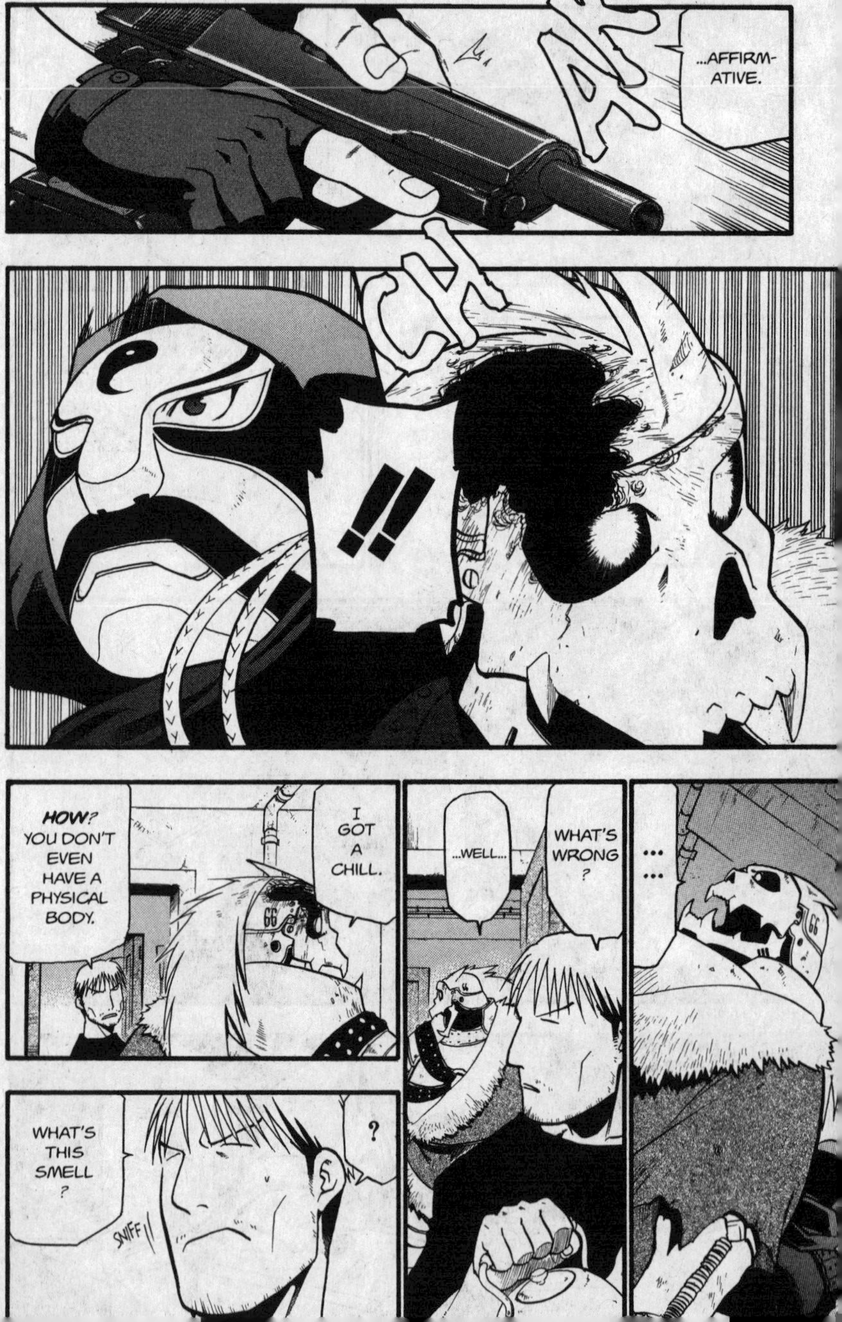

...AFFIRM-ATIVE.
CHAK
!!
...
...
WHAT'S WRONG ?
...WELL...
I GOT A CHILL.
HOW? YOU DON'T EVEN HAVE A PHYSICAL BODY.
?
WHAT'S THIS SMELL ?
SNIFF

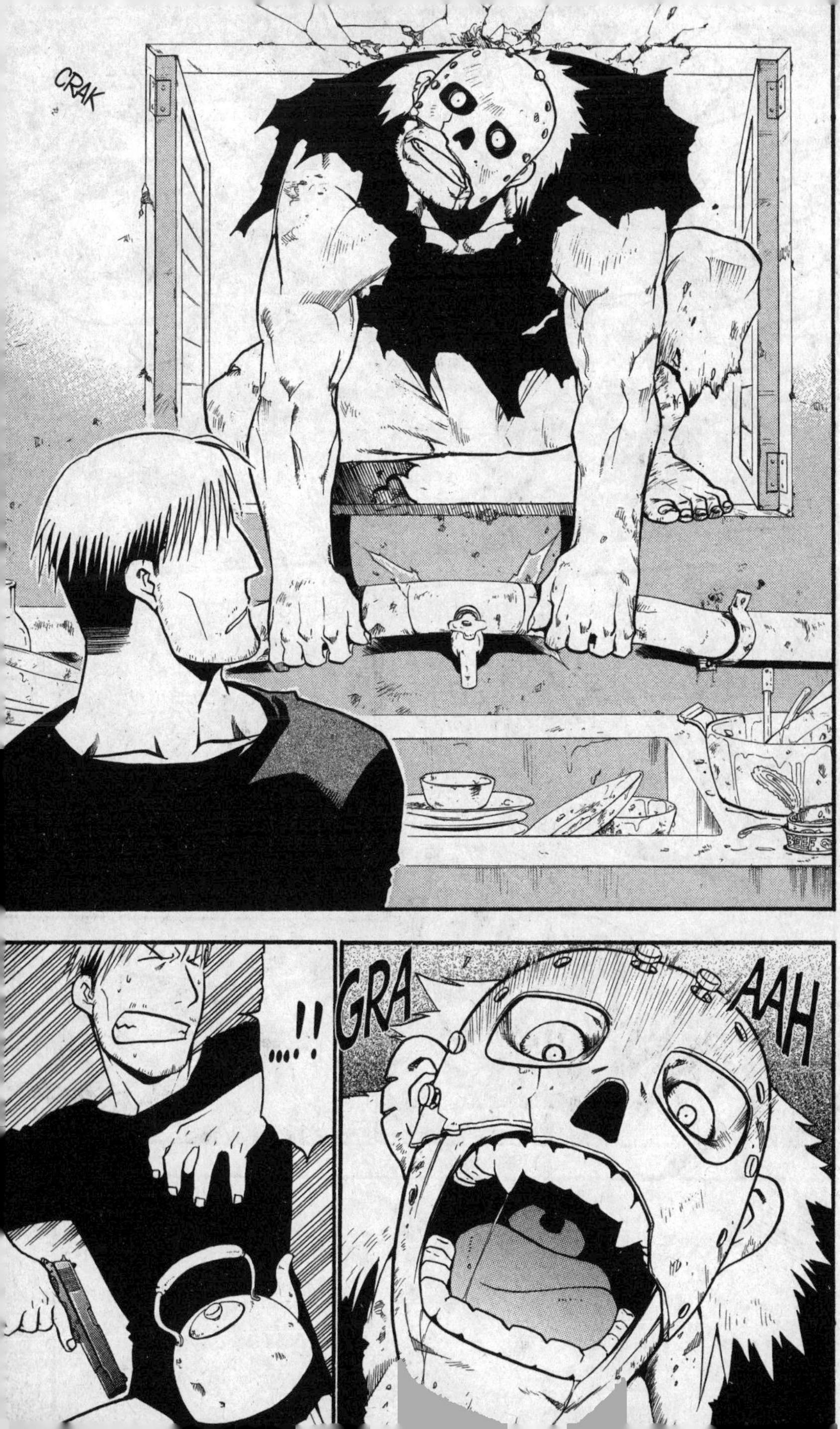
CRAK
GRA
AAH
...!!

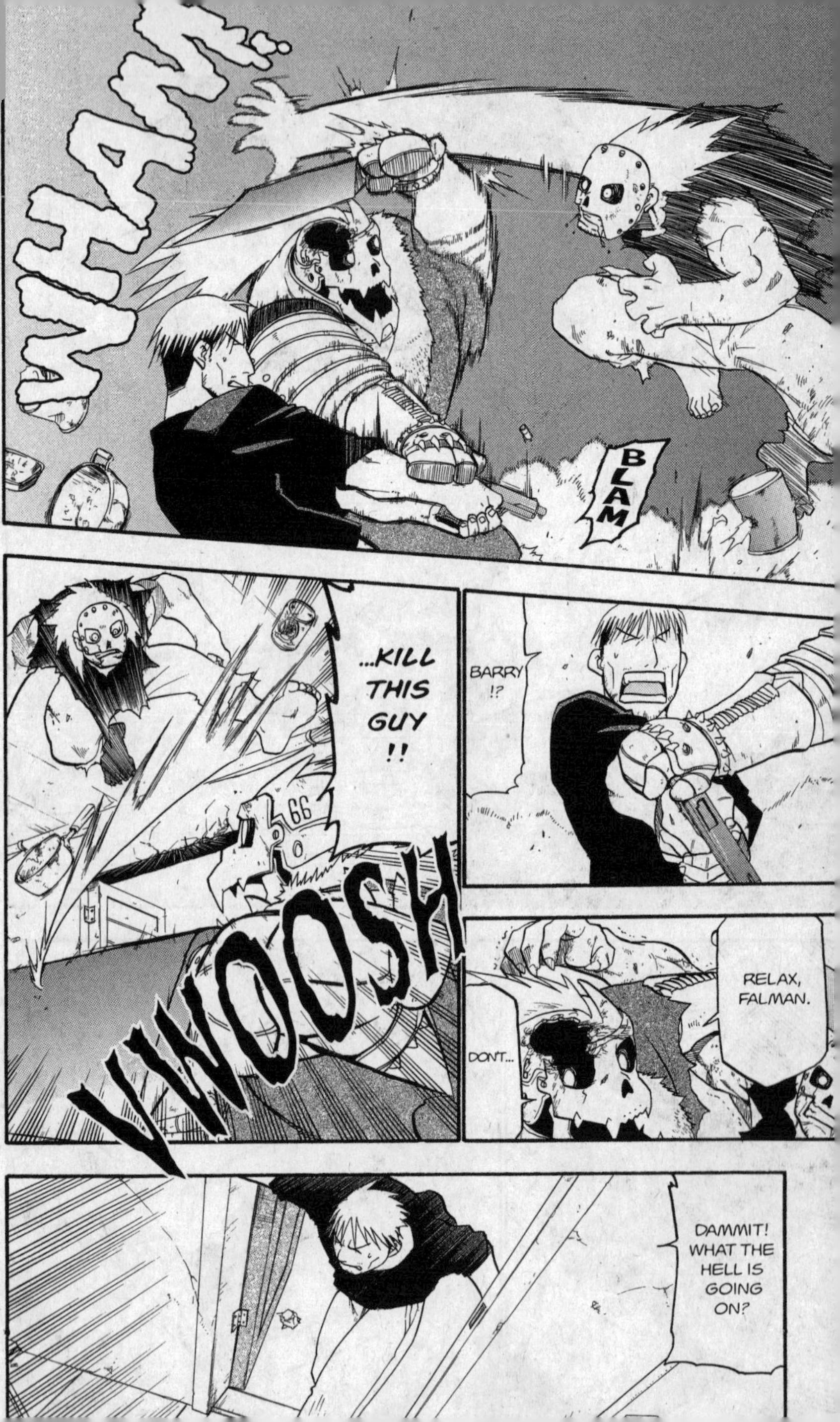
WHAM!!
BLAM
BARRY !?
RELAX, FALMAN.
DON'T...
...KILL THIS GUY !!
WHOOSH
DAMMIT! WHAT THE HELL IS GOING ON?

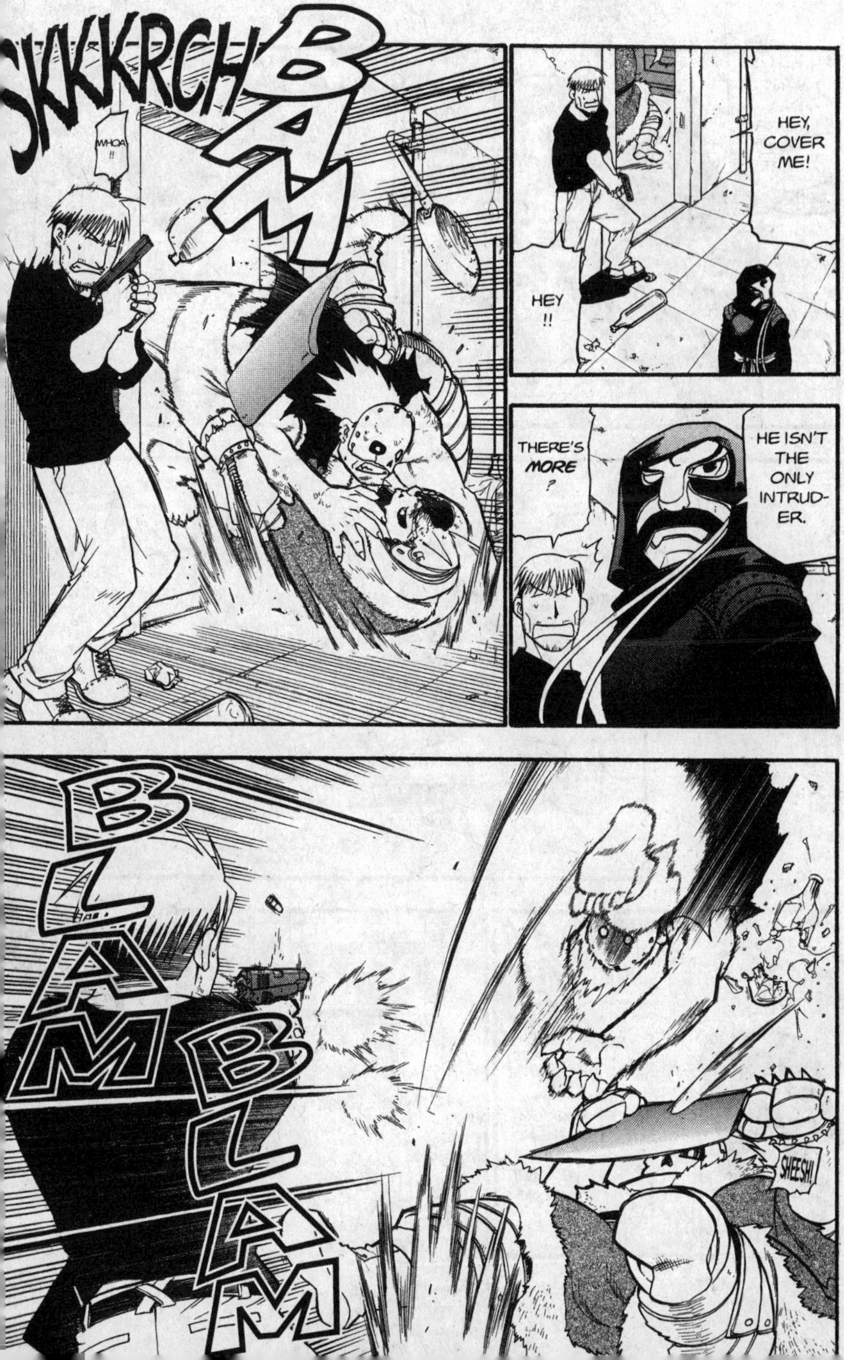
HEY, COVER ME!
HEY !!
HE ISN'T THE ONLY INTRUDER.
THERE'S *MORE* ?
SKKKRCH
BAM
WHOA !!
BLAM
BLAM
SHEESH!

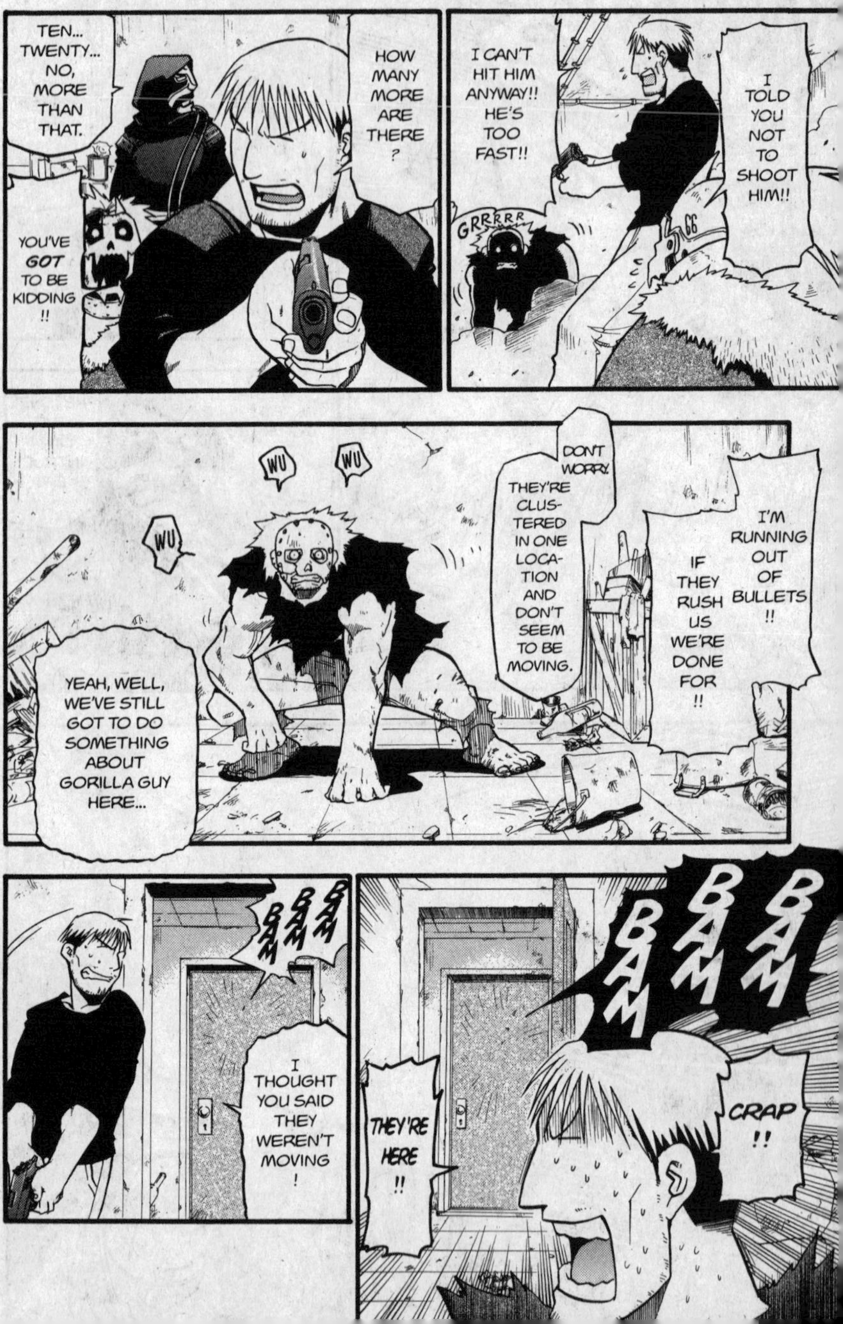
I TOLD YOU NOT TO SHOOT HIM!!
I CAN'T HIT HIM ANYWAY!! HE'S TOO FAST!!
GRRRRR
HOW MANY MORE ARE THERE?
TEN... TWENTY... NO, MORE THAN THAT.
YOU'VE *GOT* TO BE KIDDING!!
I'M RUNNING OUT OF BULLETS!!
IF THEY RUSH US WE'RE DONE FOR!!
DONT WORRY. THEY'RE CLUSTERED IN ONE LOCATION AND DON'T SEEM TO BE MOVING.
WU
WU
WU
YEAH, WELL, WE'VE STILL GOT TO DO SOMETHING ABOUT GORILLA GUY HERE...
BAM BAM BAM
CRAP!!
THEY'RE HERE!!
BAM BAM BAM
I THOUGHT YOU SAID THEY WEREN'T MOVING!

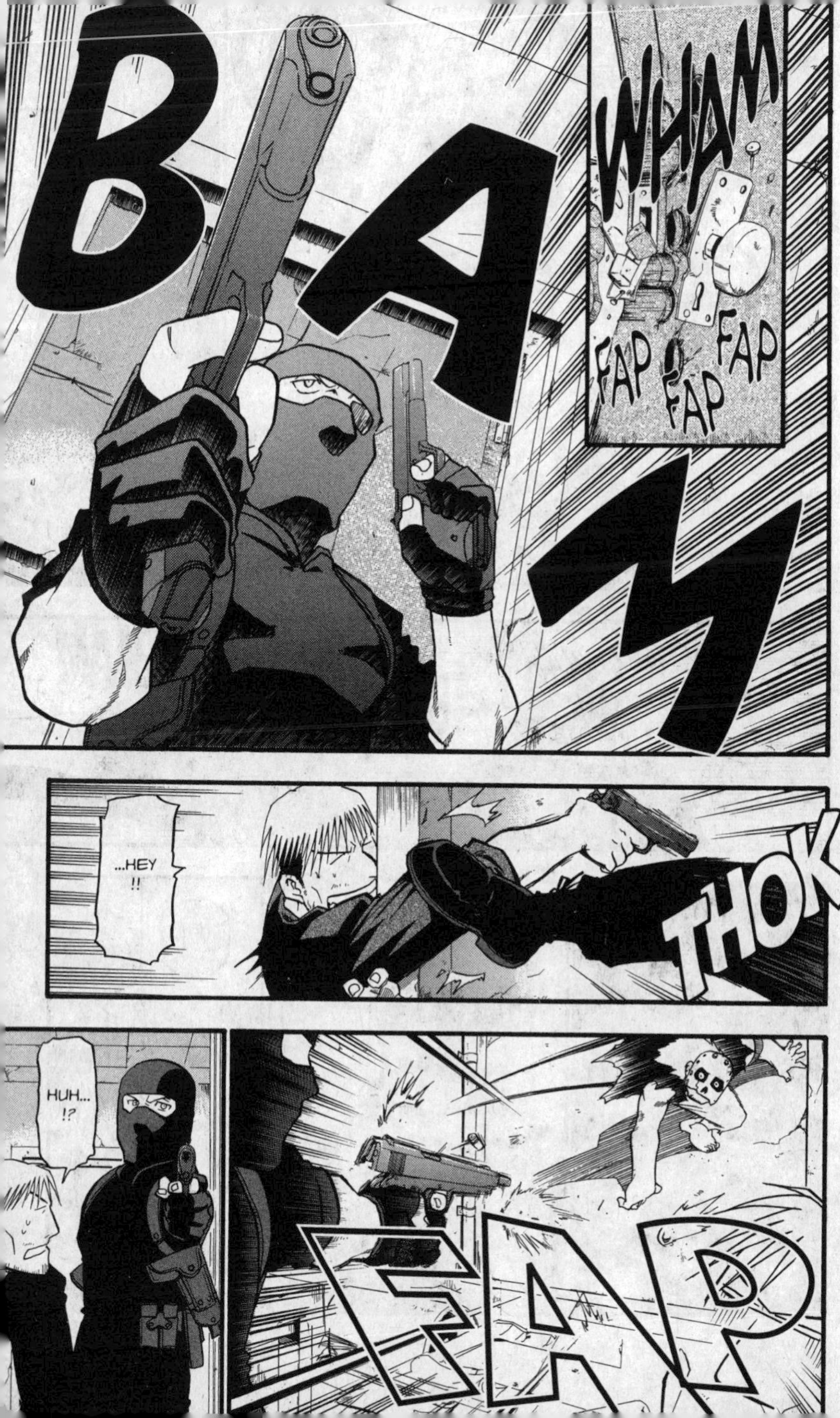
WHAM
FAP
FAP
FAP
BAM
THOK
...HEY !!
FAP
HUH... !?

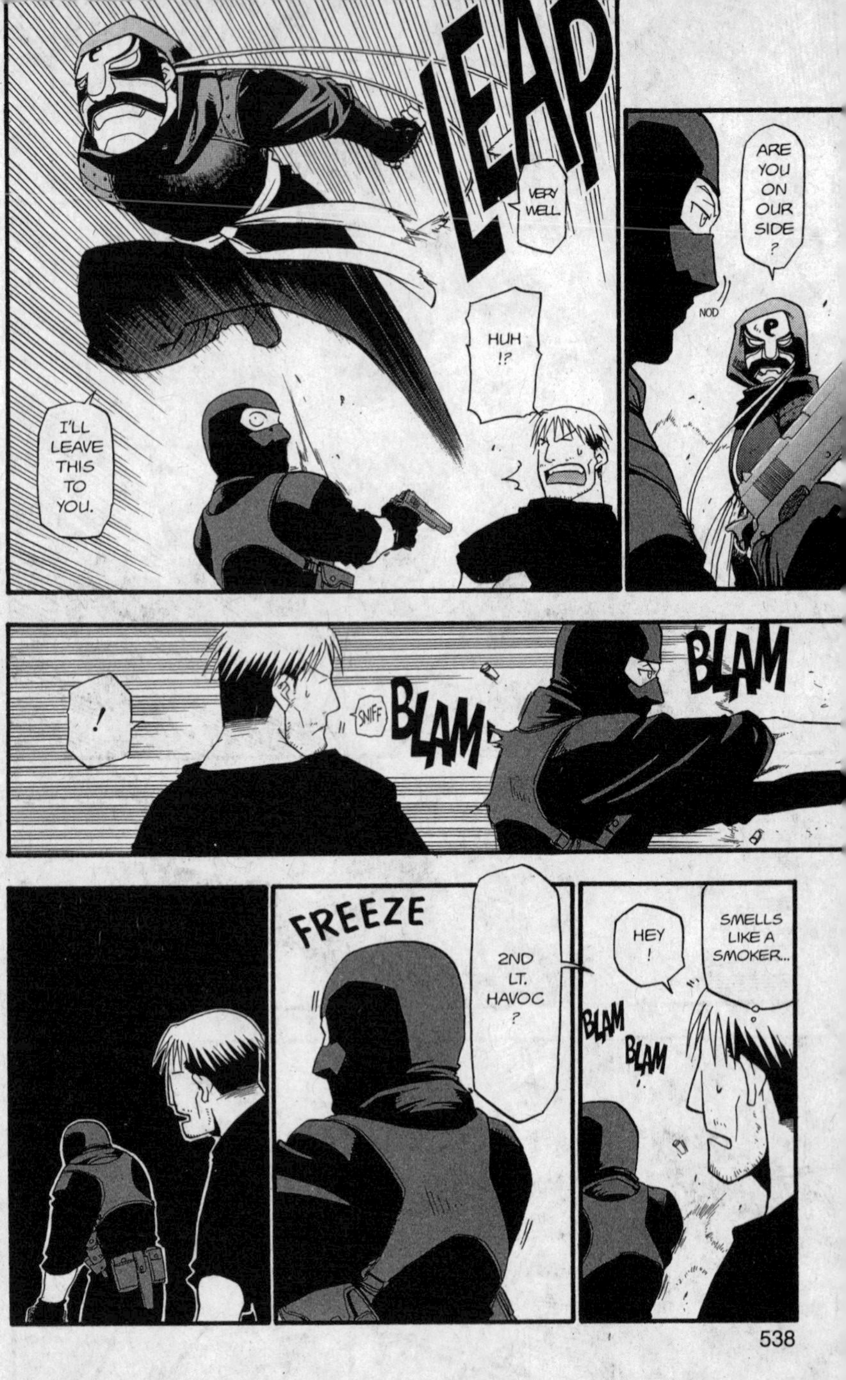
ARE YOU ON OUR SIDE ?
NOD
LEAP
VERY WELL.
HUH !?
I'LL LEAVE THIS TO YOU.
BLAM
BLAM
SNIFF
!
SMELLS LIKE A SMOKER...
HEY !
BLAM
BLAM
2ND LT. HAVOC ?
FREEZE

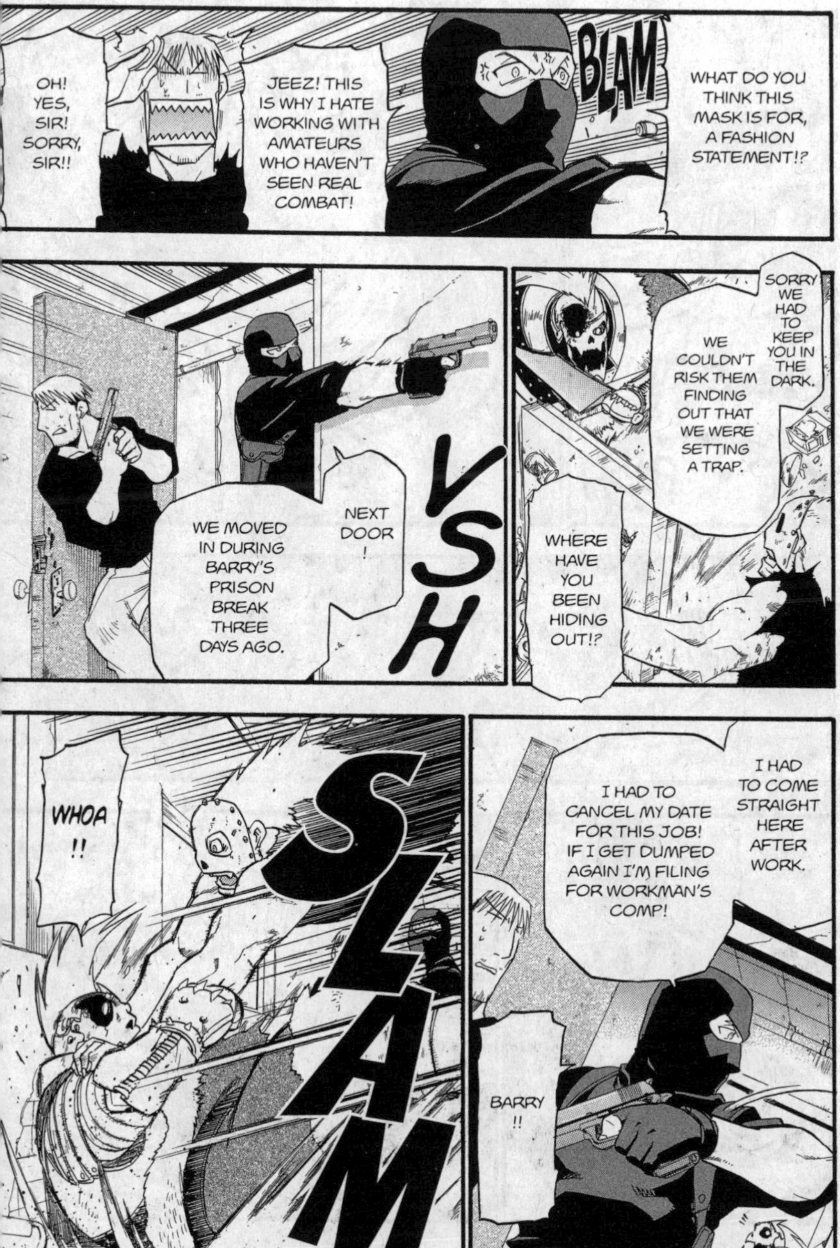
WHAT DO YOU THINK THIS MASK IS FOR, A FASHION STATEMENT!?
BLAM
JEEZ! THIS IS WHY I HATE WORKING WITH AMATEURS WHO HAVEN'T SEEN REAL COMBAT!
OH! YES, SIR! SORRY, SIR!!
SORRY WE HAD TO KEEP YOU IN THE DARK.
WE COULDN'T RISK THEM FINDING OUT THAT WE WERE SETTING A TRAP.
WHERE HAVE YOU BEEN HIDING OUT!?
VSH
NEXT DOOR!
WE MOVED IN DURING BARRY'S PRISON BREAK THREE DAYS AGO.
I HAD TO COME STRAIGHT HERE AFTER WORK.
I HAD TO CANCEL MY DATE FOR THIS JOB! IF I GET DUMPED AGAIN I'M FILING FOR WORKMAN'S COMP!
BARRY!!
SLAM
WHOA!!

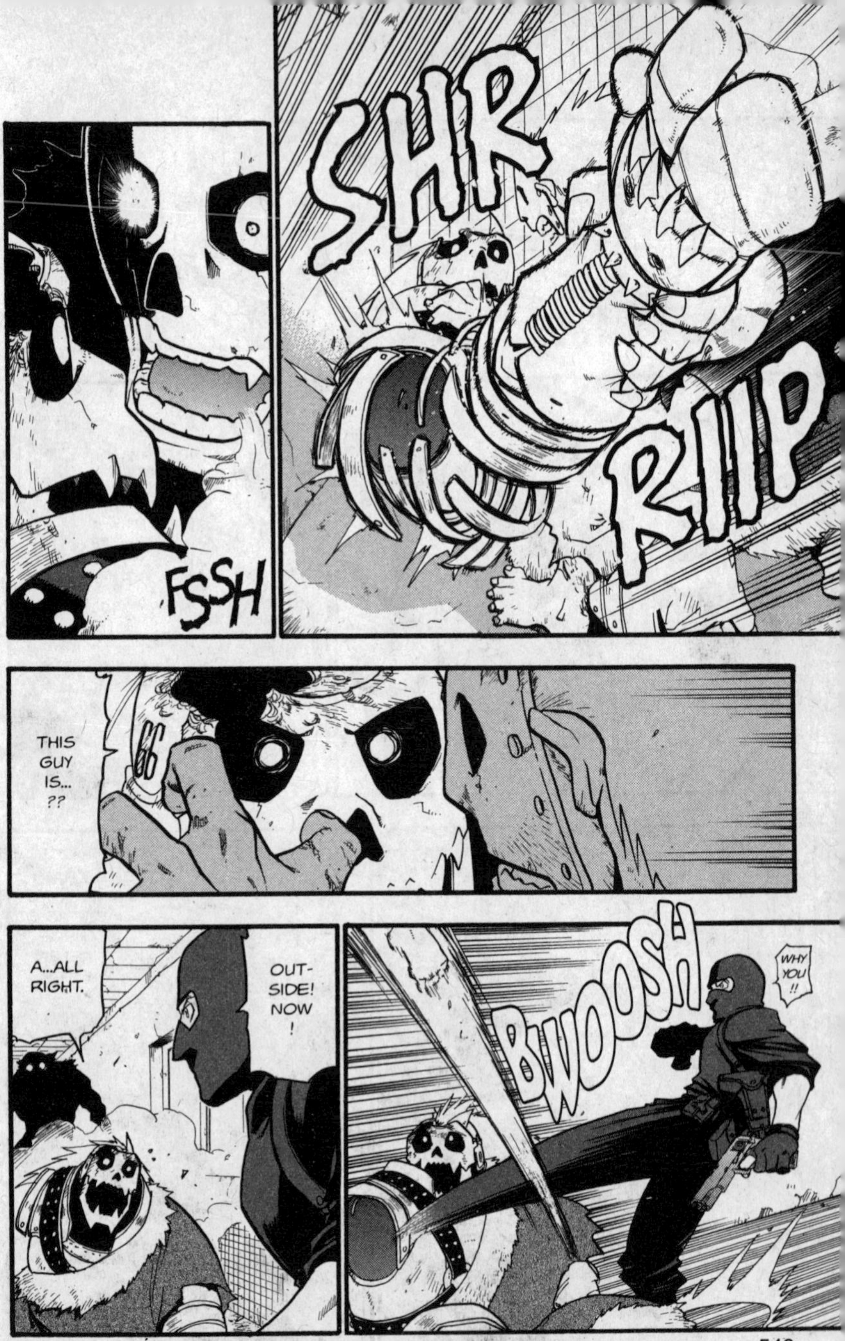
SHR
RIIP
FSSH
THIS GUY IS... ??
BWOOSH
WHY YOU !!
OUT-SIDE! NOW!
A...ALL RIGHT.

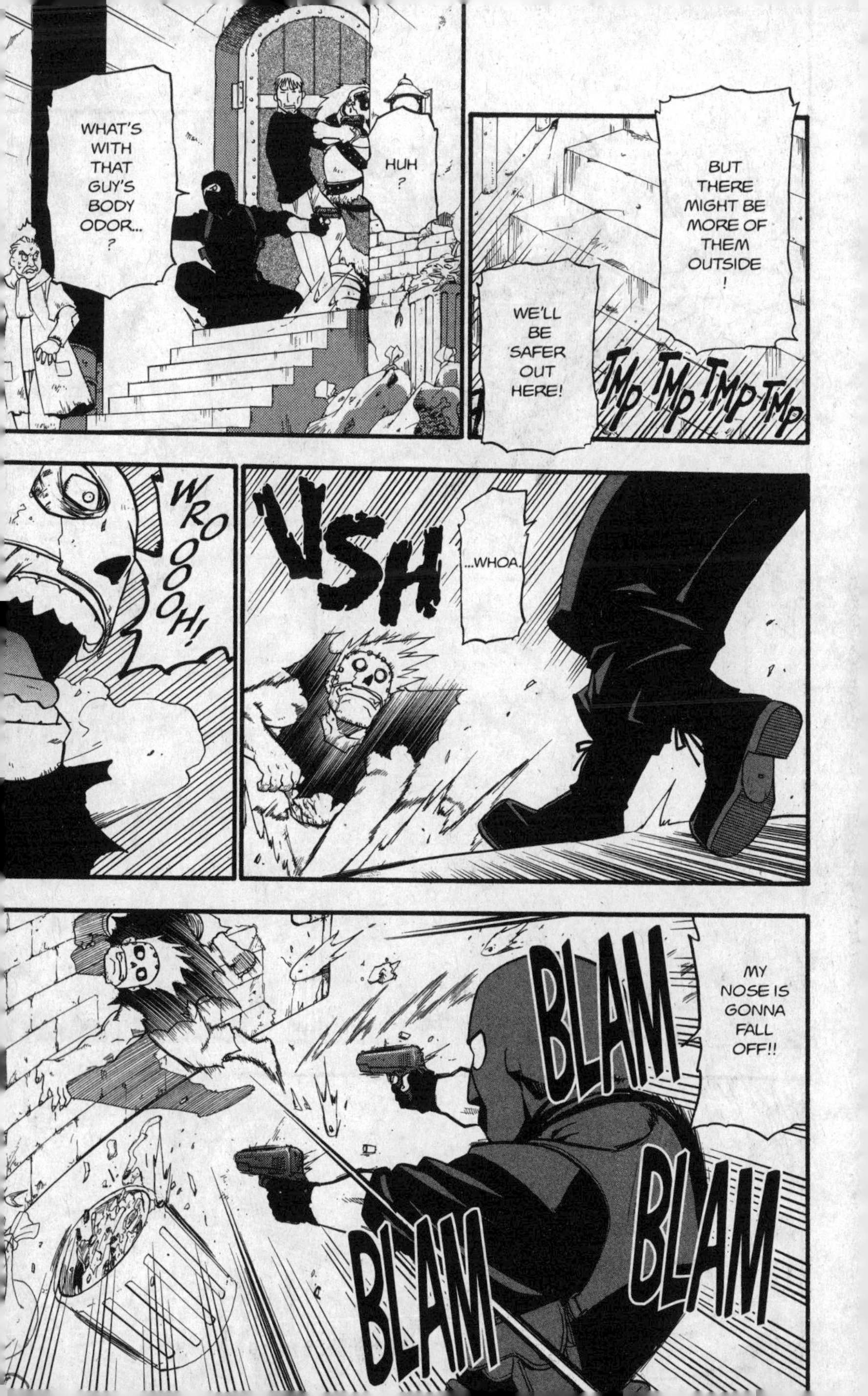
BUT THERE MIGHT BE MORE OF THEM OUTSIDE!
WE'LL BE SAFER OUT HERE!
TMP TMP TMP TMP
HUH?
WHAT'S WITH THAT GUY'S BODY ODOR...?
...WHOA.
VSH
WROOOOOH!
MY NOSE IS GONNA FALL OFF!!
BLAM
BLAM
BLAM

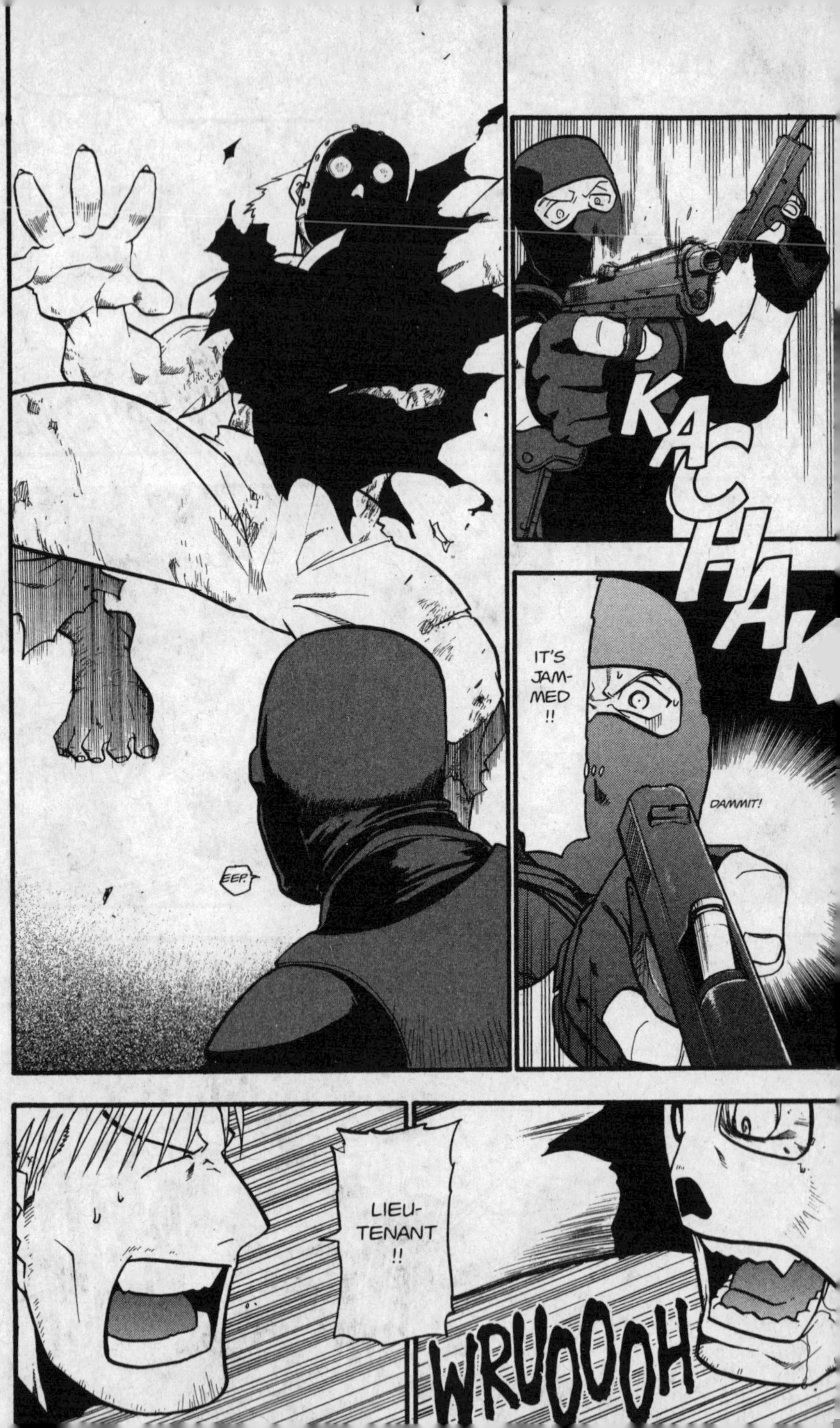
KACHAK
IT'S JAM-MED !!
DAMMIT!
EEP.
WRUOOOH
LIEU-TENANT !!

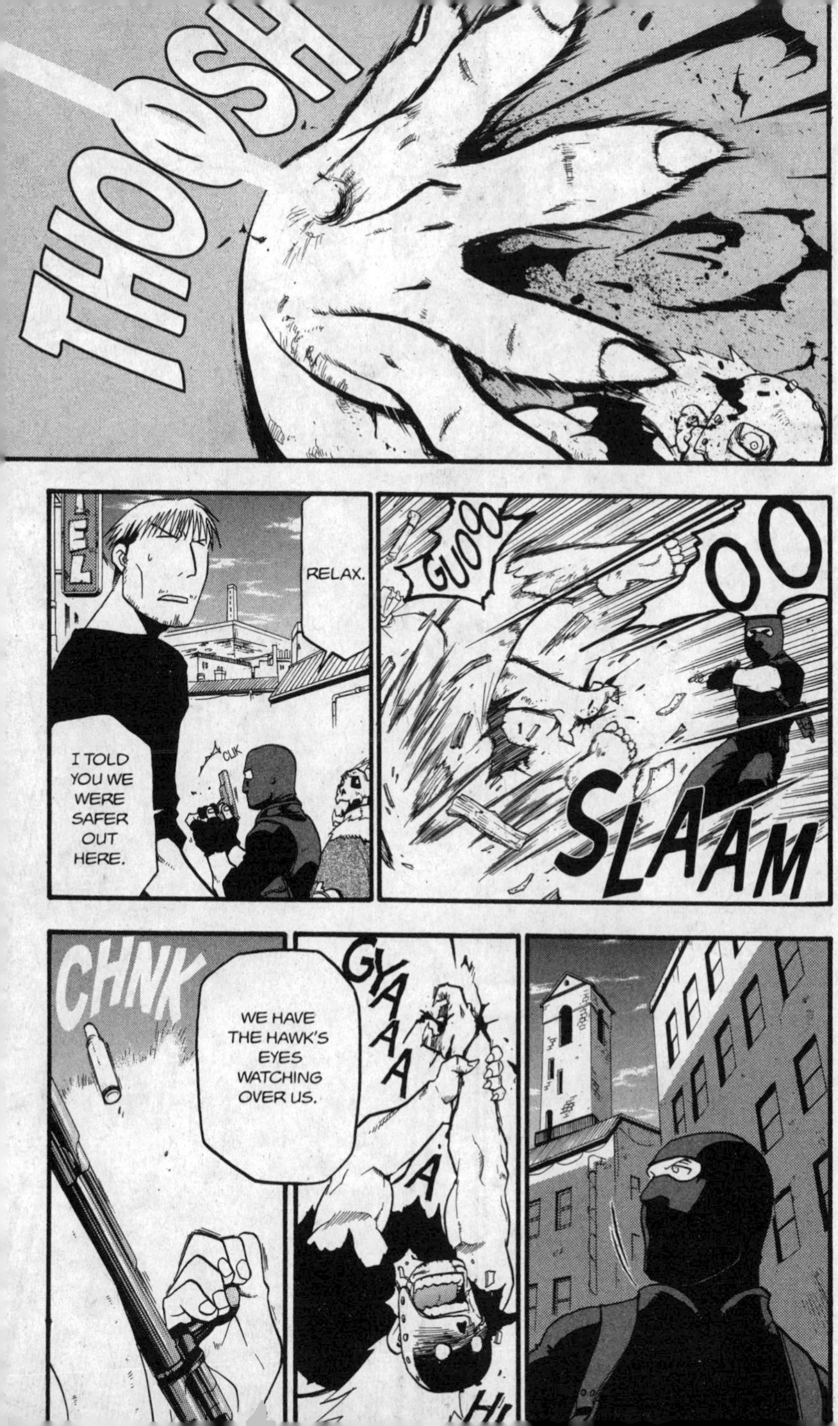
THOOSH
GUOOO
OO
SLAAM
RELAX.
CLIK
I TOLD YOU WE WERE SAFER OUT HERE.
GYAAAAA
WE HAVE THE HAWK'S EYES WATCHING OVER US.
CHNK

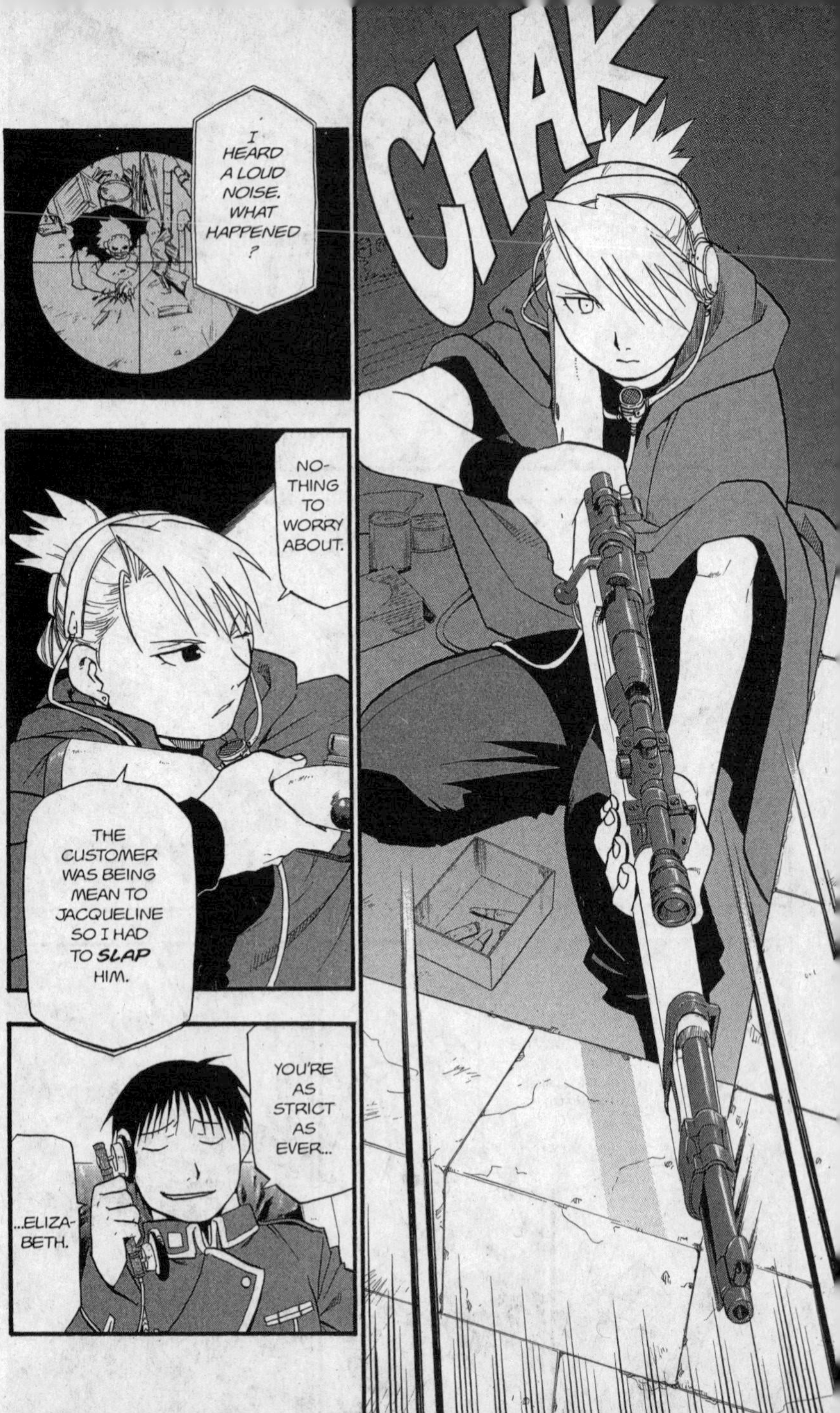
CHAK
I HEARD A LOUD NOISE. WHAT HAPPENED?
NO-THING TO WORRY ABOUT.
THE CUSTOMER WAS BEING MEAN TO JACQUELINE SO I HAD TO **SLAP** HIM.
YOU'RE AS STRICT AS EVER...
...ELIZA-BETH.

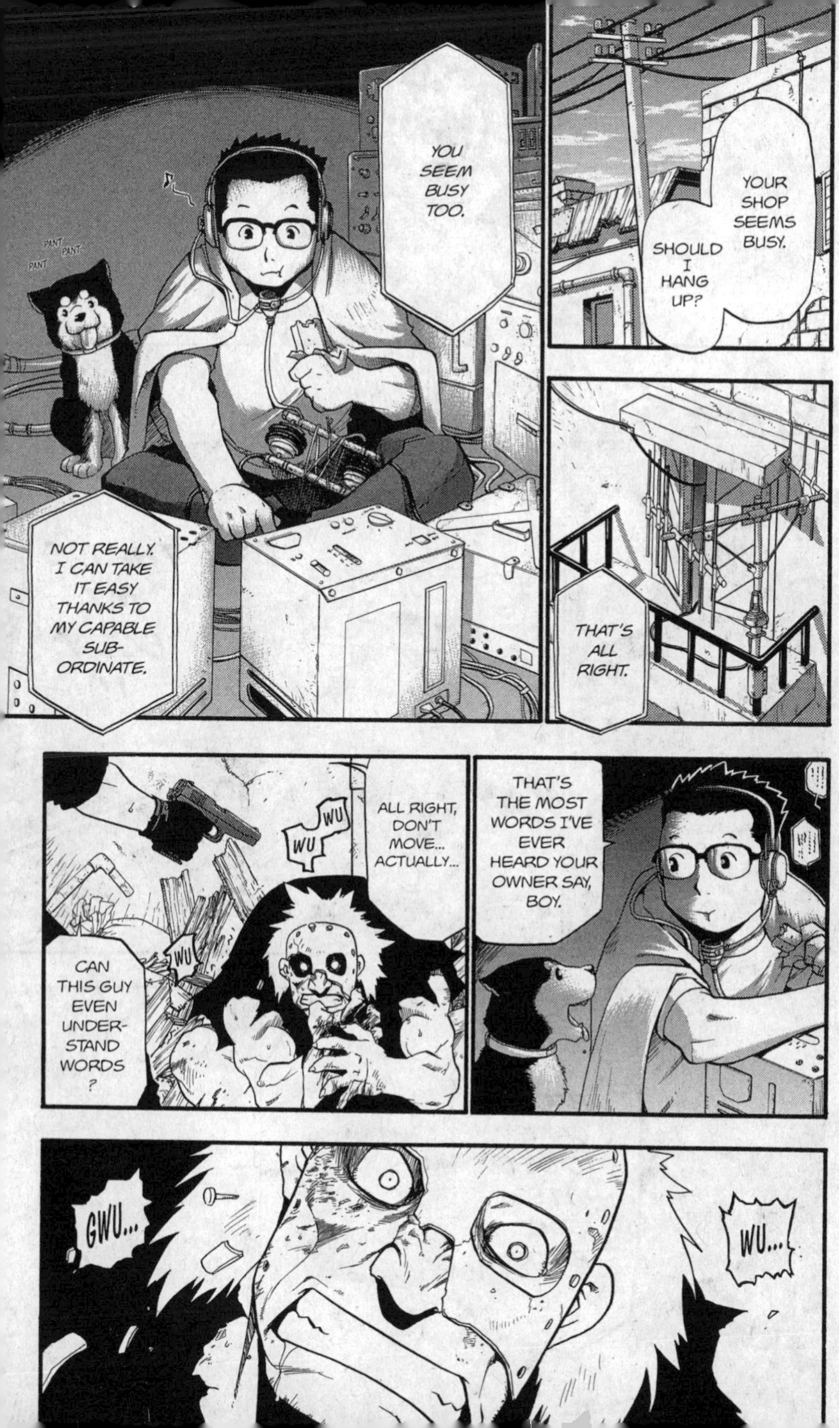
YOUR SHOP SEEMS BUSY.
SHOULD I HANG UP?
THAT'S ALL RIGHT.
YOU SEEM BUSY TOO.
PANT PANT PANT
NOT REALLY. I CAN TAKE IT EASY THANKS TO MY CAPABLE SUB-ORDINATE.
THAT'S THE MOST WORDS I'VE EVER HEARD YOUR OWNER SAY, BOY.
ALL RIGHT, DON'T MOVE... ACTUALLY...
WU WU
WU
CAN THIS GUY EVEN UNDER-STAND WORDS?
WU...
GWU...

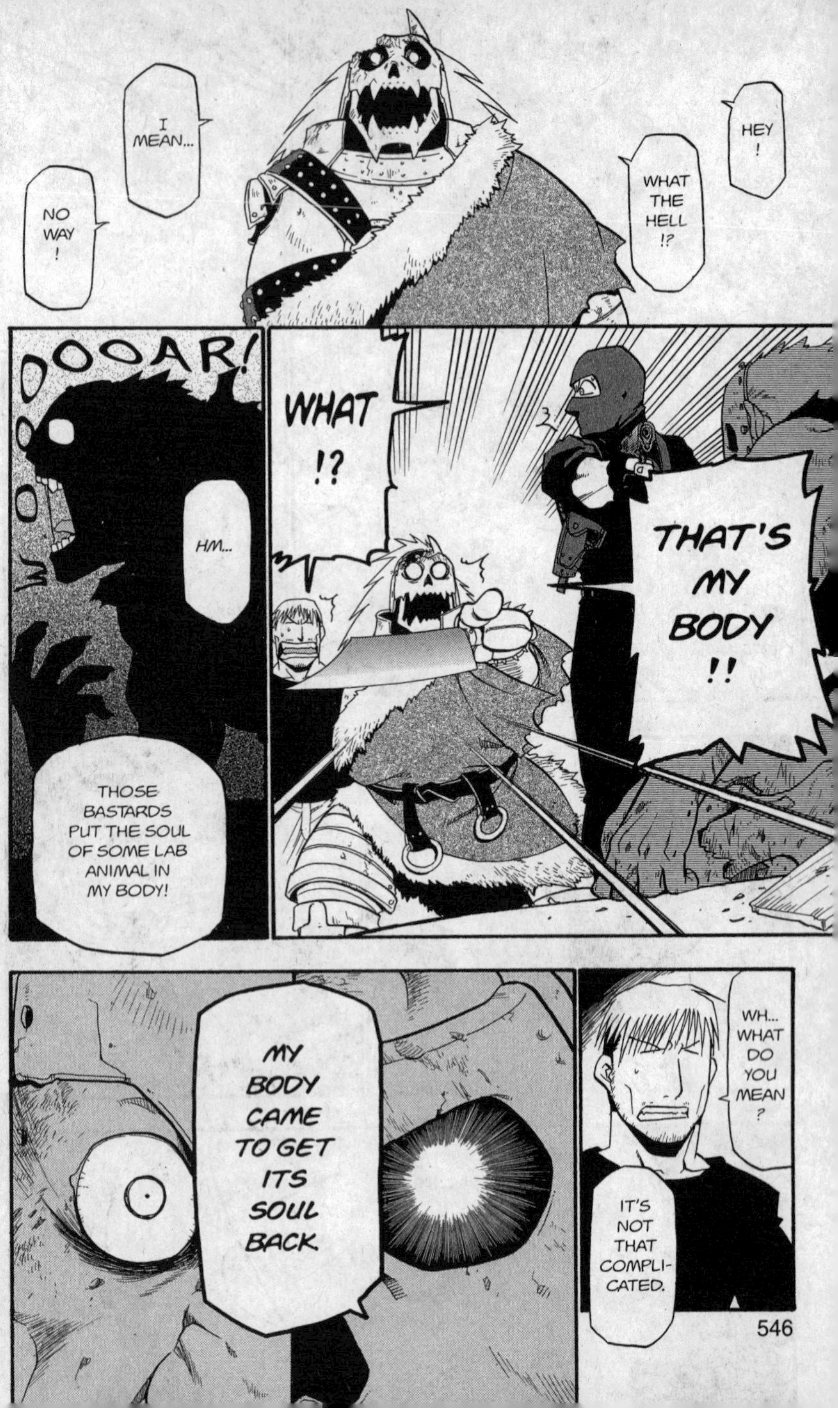
HEY !
WHAT THE HELL !?
I MEAN...
NO WAY !
THAT'S MY BODY !!
WHAT !?
WOOOOOAR!
HM...
THOSE BASTARDS PUT THE SOUL OF SOME LAB ANIMAL IN MY BODY!
WH... WHAT DO YOU MEAN ?
IT'S NOT THAT COMPLICATED.
MY BODY CAME TO GET ITS SOUL BACK.

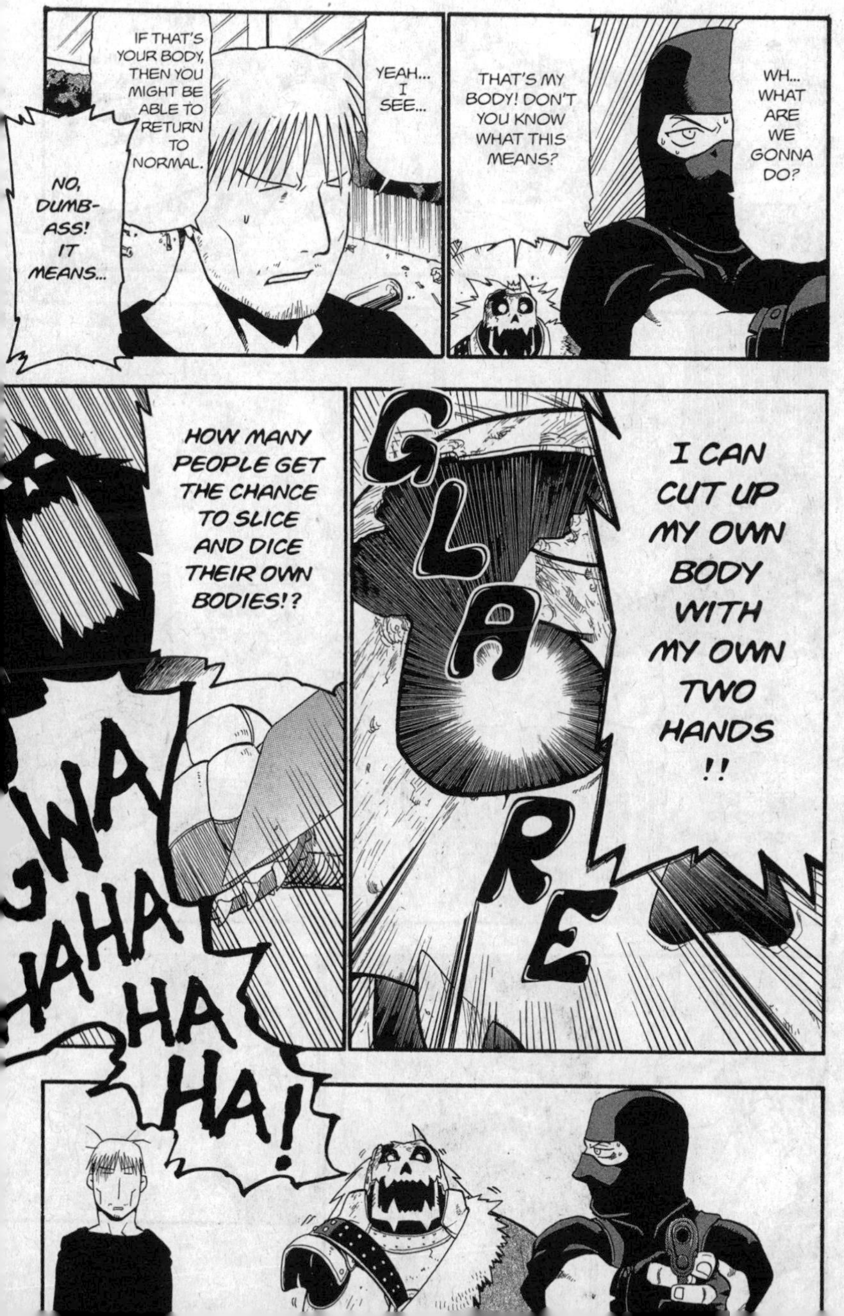
WH... WHAT ARE WE GONNA DO?
THAT'S MY BODY! DON'T YOU KNOW WHAT THIS MEANS?
YEAH... I SEE...
IF THAT'S YOUR BODY, THEN YOU MIGHT BE ABLE TO RETURN TO NORMAL.
NO, DUMB-ASS! IT MEANS...
I CAN CUT UP MY OWN BODY WITH MY OWN TWO HANDS!!
GLARE
HOW MANY PEOPLE GET THE CHANCE TO SLICE AND DICE THEIR OWN BODIES!?
GWAHAHAHAHA!

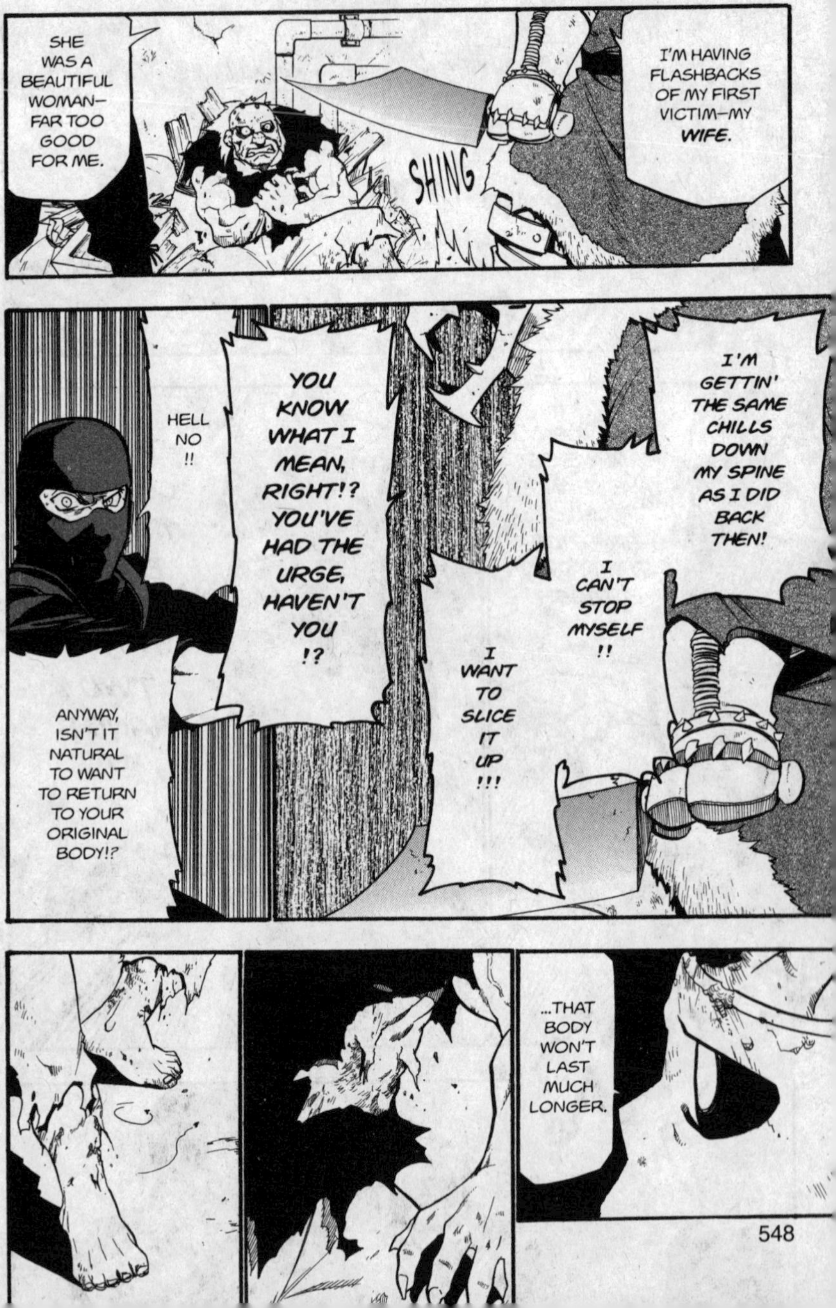
I'M HAVING FLASHBACKS OF MY FIRST VICTIM—MY WIFE.
SHING
SHE WAS A BEAUTIFUL WOMAN—FAR TOO GOOD FOR ME.
I'M GETTIN' THE SAME CHILLS DOWN MY SPINE AS I DID BACK THEN!
I CAN'T STOP MYSELF!!
I WANT TO SLICE IT UP!!!
YOU KNOW WHAT I MEAN, RIGHT!? YOU'VE HAD THE URGE, HAVEN'T YOU!?
HELL NO!!
ANYWAY, ISN'T IT NATURAL TO WANT TO RETURN TO YOUR ORIGINAL BODY!?
...THAT BODY WON'T LAST MUCH LONGER.

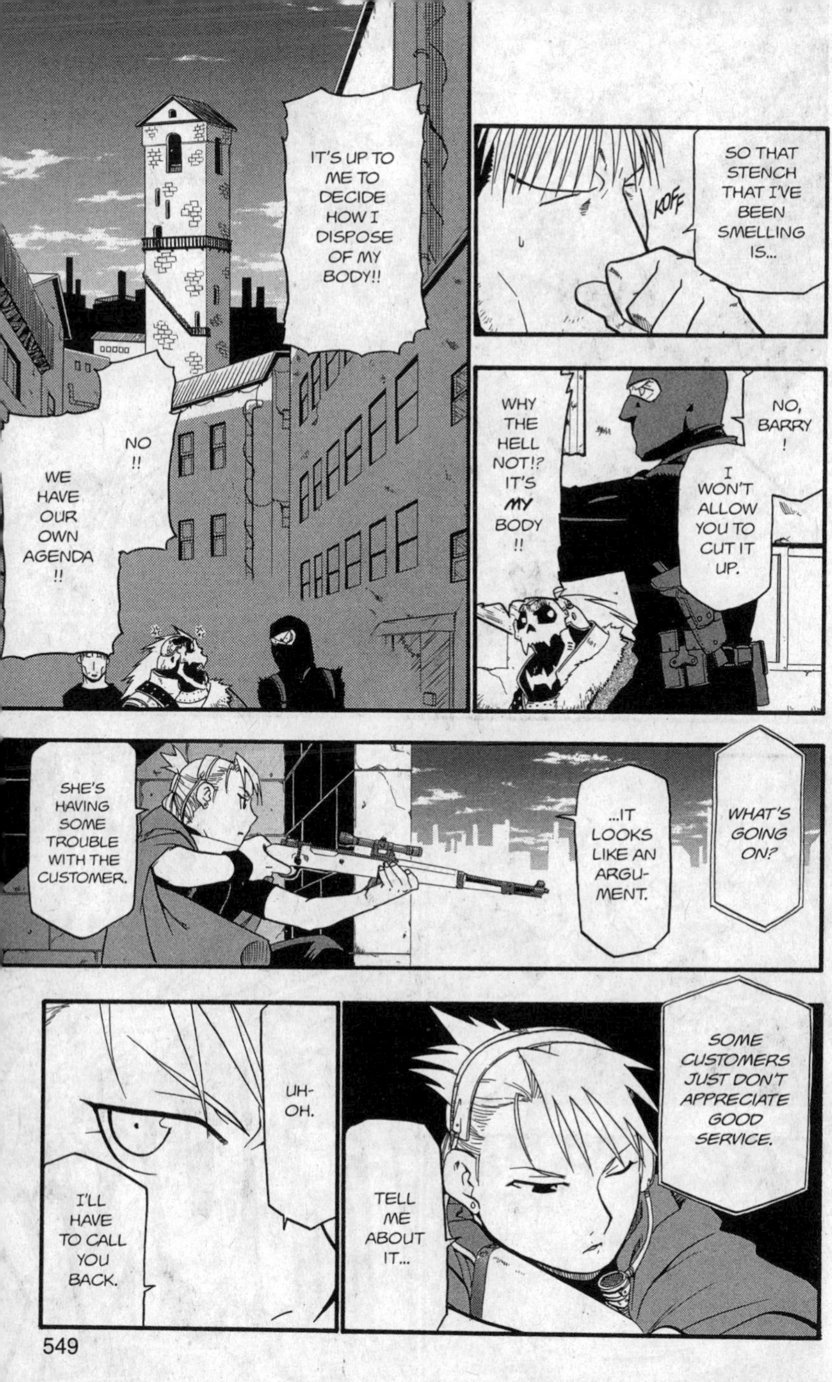

KOFF
SO THAT STENCH THAT I'VE BEEN SMELLING IS...
NO, BARRY! I WON'T ALLOW YOU TO CUT IT UP.
WHY THE HELL NOT!? IT'S *MY* BODY!!
IT'S UP TO ME TO DECIDE HOW I DISPOSE OF MY BODY!!
NO!!
WE HAVE OUR OWN AGENDA!!
WHAT'S GOING ON?
...IT LOOKS LIKE AN ARGUMENT.
SHE'S HAVING SOME TROUBLE WITH THE CUSTOMER.
SOME CUSTOMERS JUST DON'T APPRECIATE GOOD SERVICE.
TELL ME ABOUT IT...
UH-OH.
I'LL HAVE TO CALL YOU BACK.

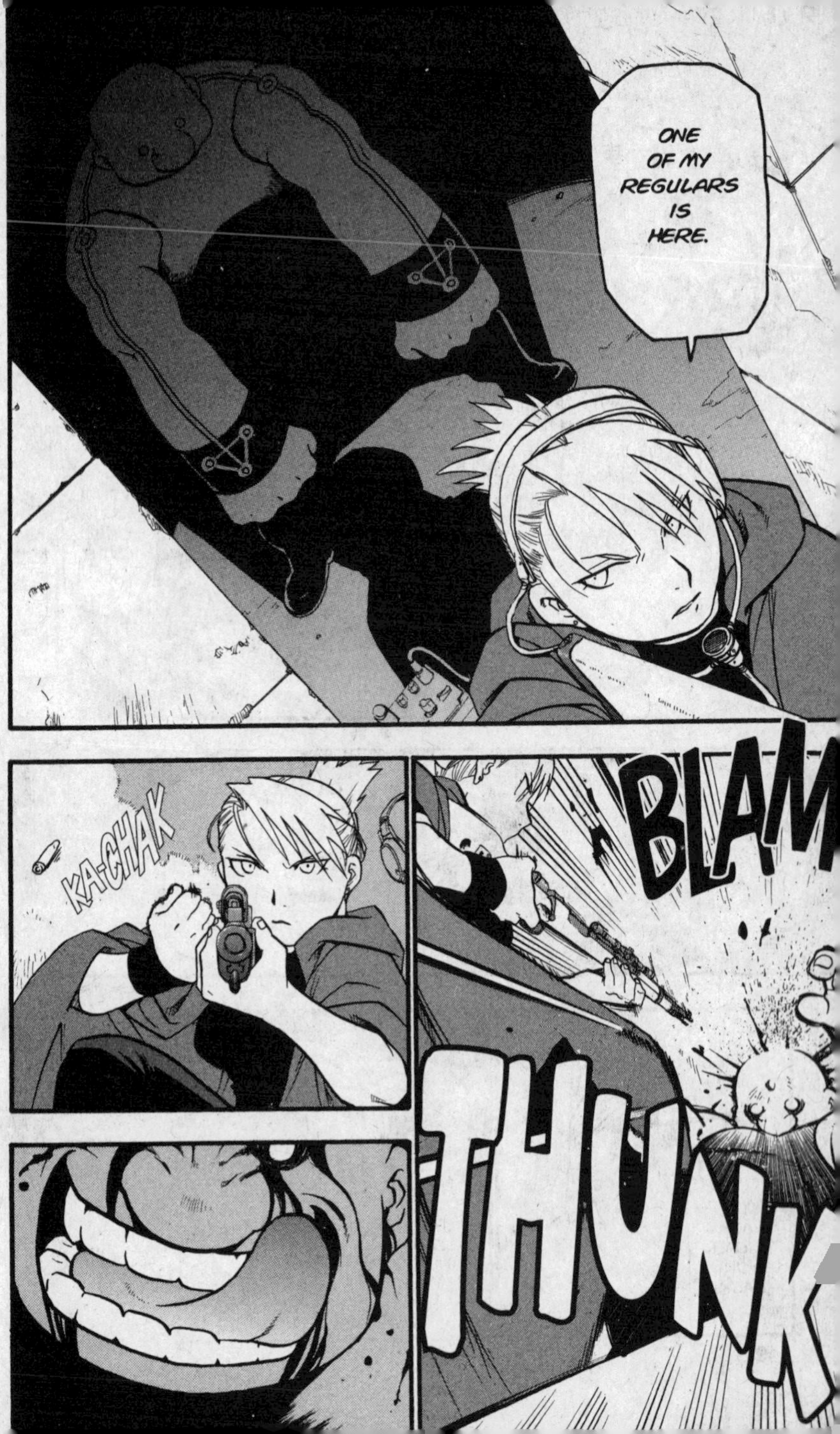
ONE OF MY REGULARS IS HERE.
BLAM
KA-CHAK
THUNK

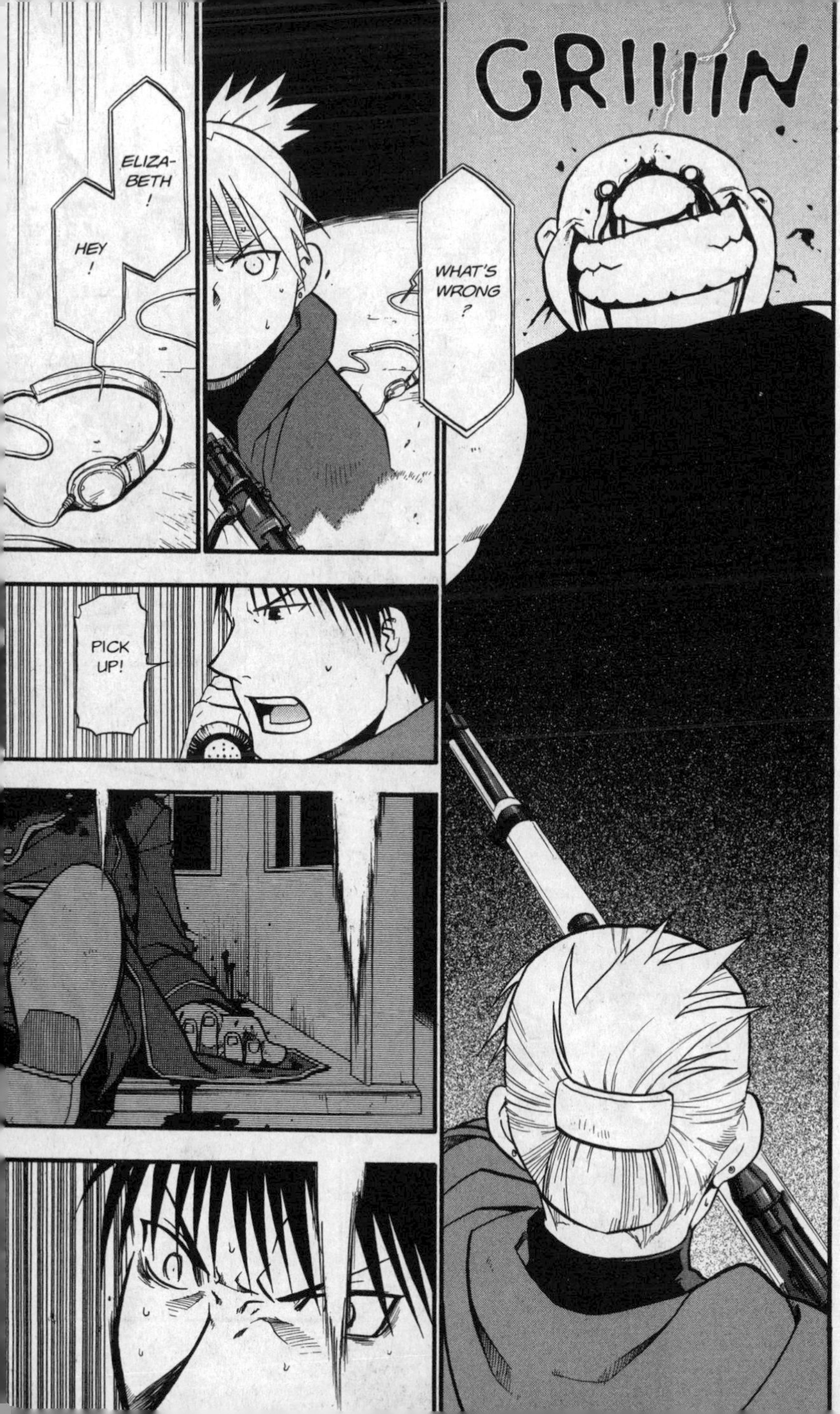
GRIIIN
WHAT'S WRONG?
ELIZA-BETH!
HEY!
PICK UP!

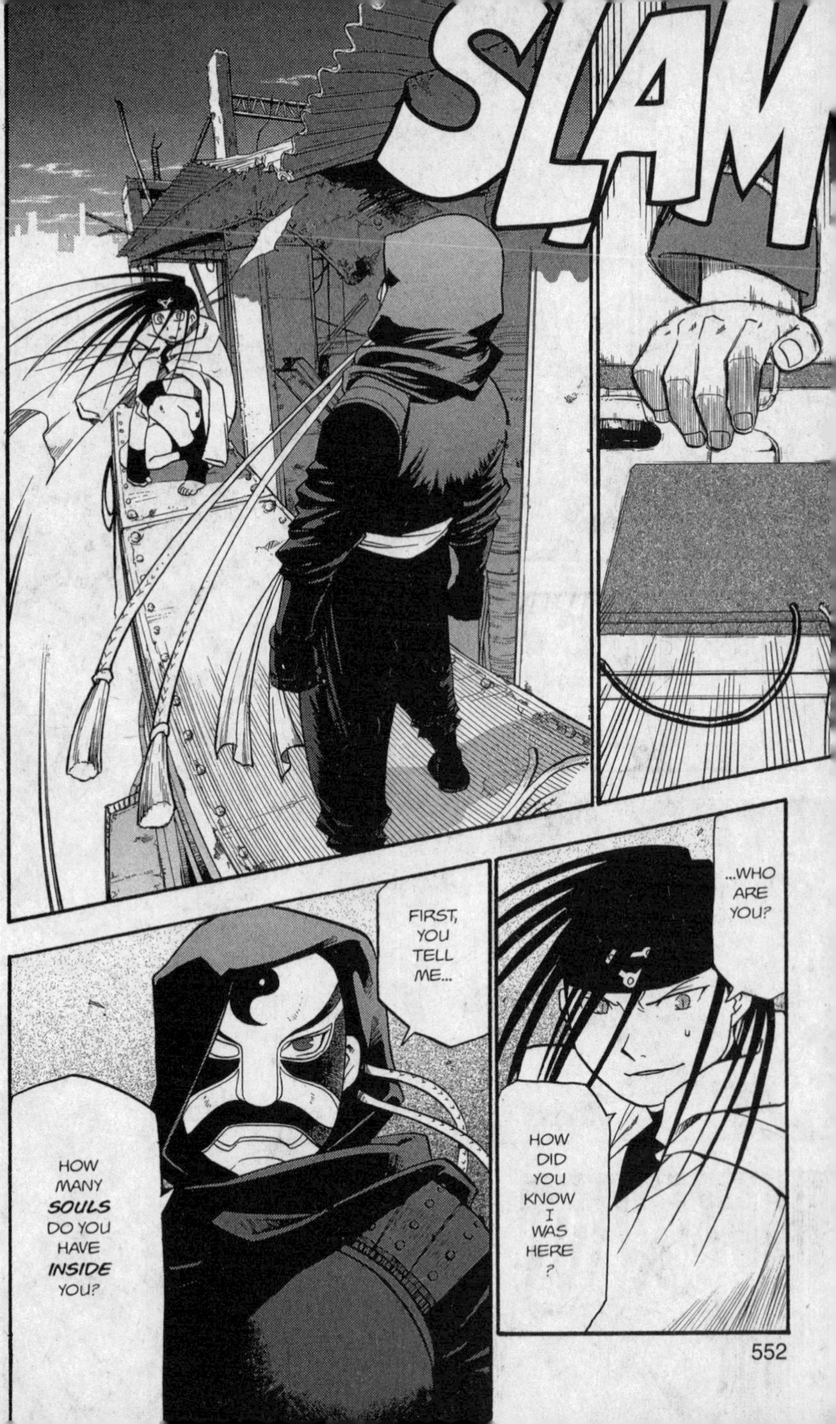
SLAM
...WHO ARE YOU?
HOW DID YOU KNOW I WAS HERE?
FIRST, YOU TELL ME...
HOW MANY **SOULS** DO YOU HAVE **INSIDE** YOU?

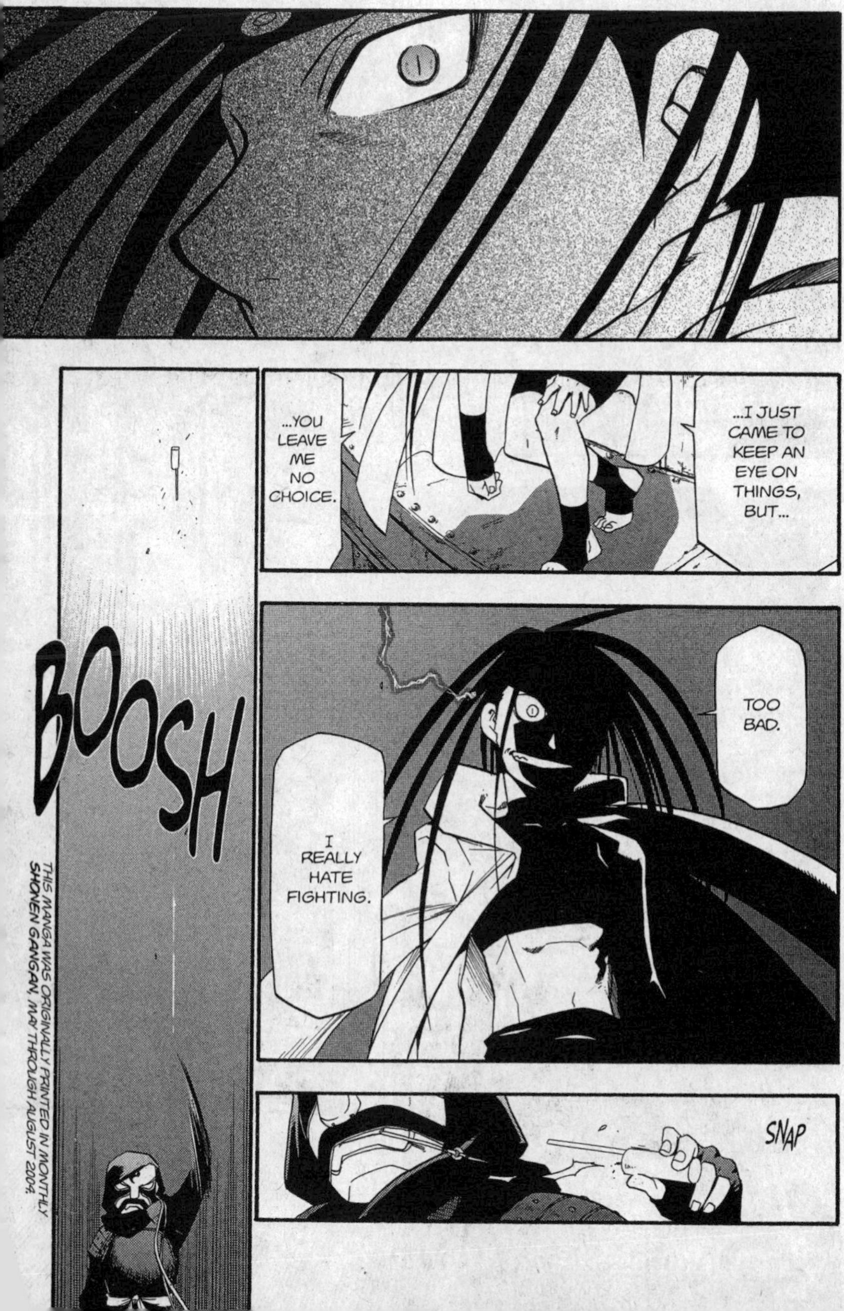
...I JUST CAME TO KEEP AN EYE ON THINGS, BUT...
...YOU LEAVE ME NO CHOICE.
TOO BAD.
I REALLY HATE FIGHTING.
SNAP
BOOSH

THIS MANGA WAS ORIGINALLY PRINTED IN MONTHLY SHONEN GANGAN, MAY THROUGH AUGUST 2004.

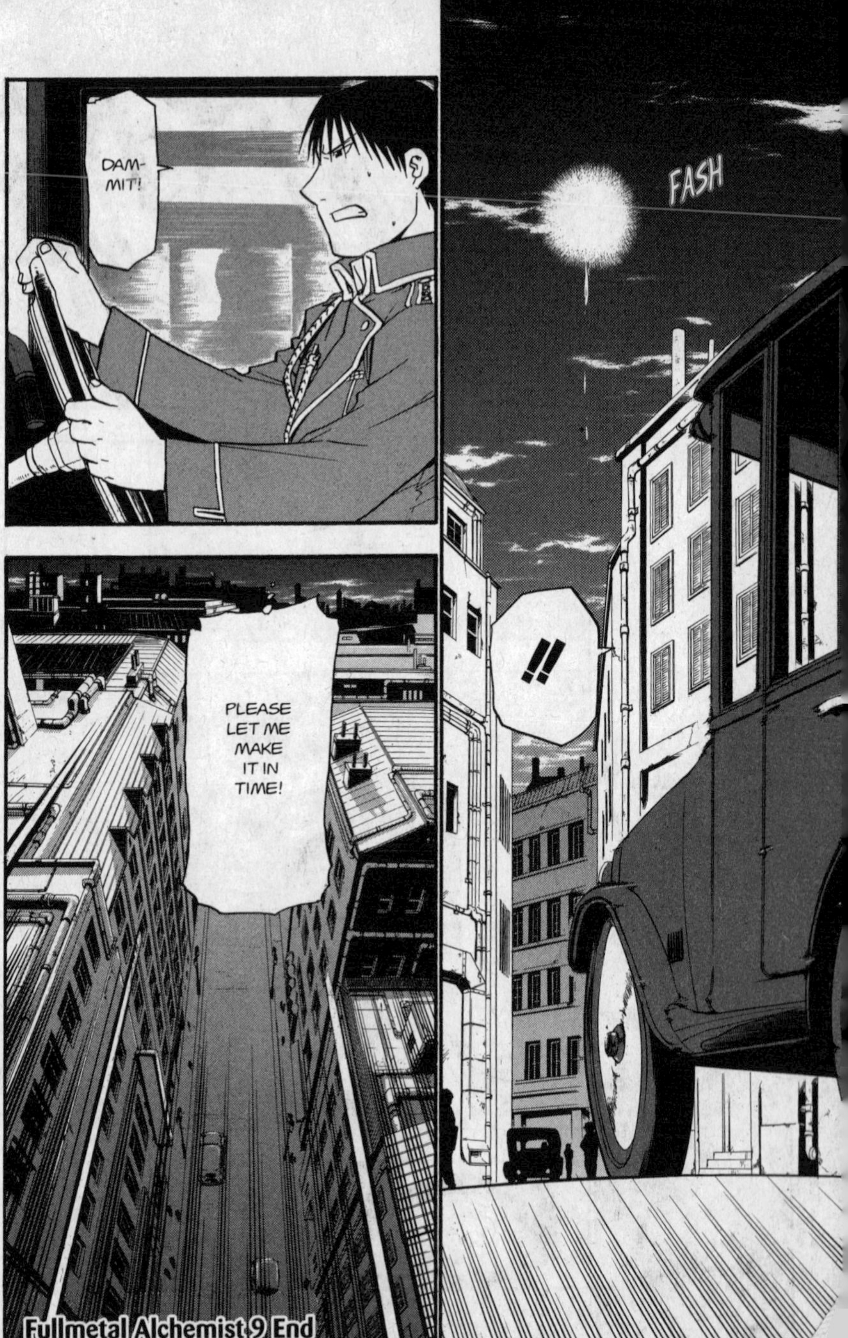
FASH
!!
DAM-MIT!
PLEASE LET ME MAKE IT IN TIME!
Fullmetal Alchemist 9 End

FULLMETAL
ALCHEMIST

EXTRAS

In the Next Volumn (Not)

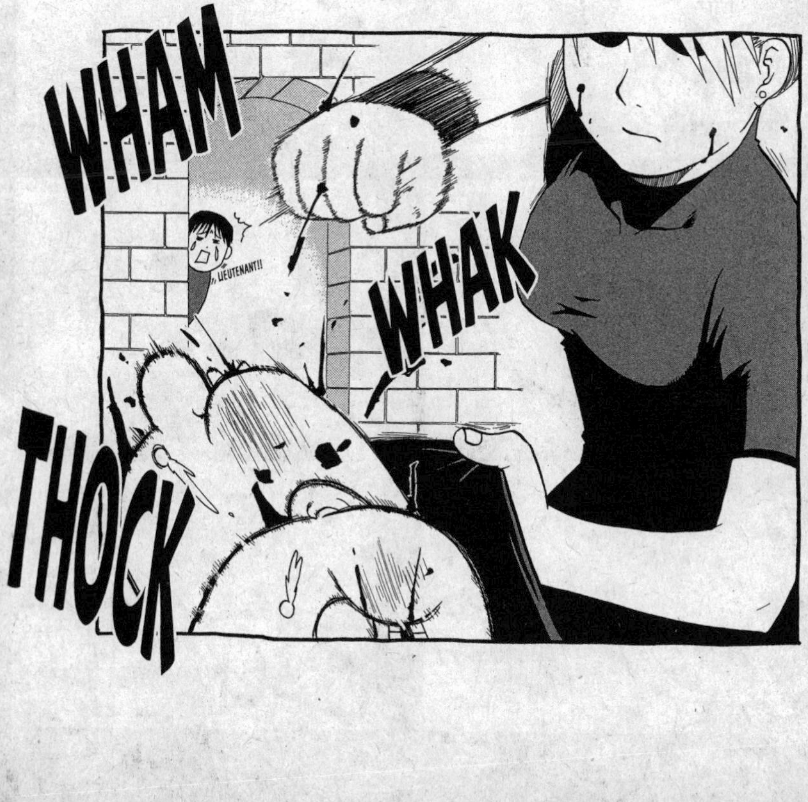

WHAM
WHAK
LIEUTENANT!!
THOCK

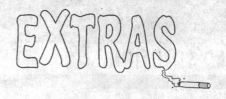

CRAMPED

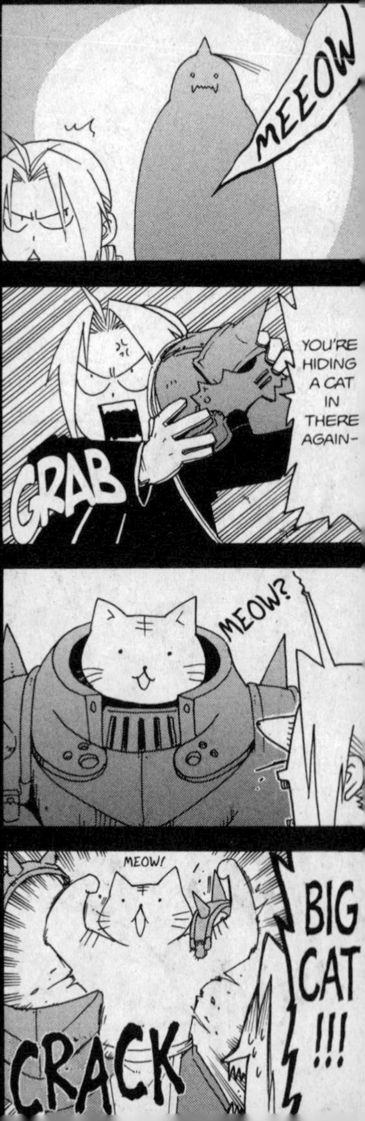
MEEOW
YOU'RE HIDING A CAT IN THERE AGAIN-
GRAB
MEOW?
BIG CAT!!!
MEOW!
CRACK

A BAD SOLUTION

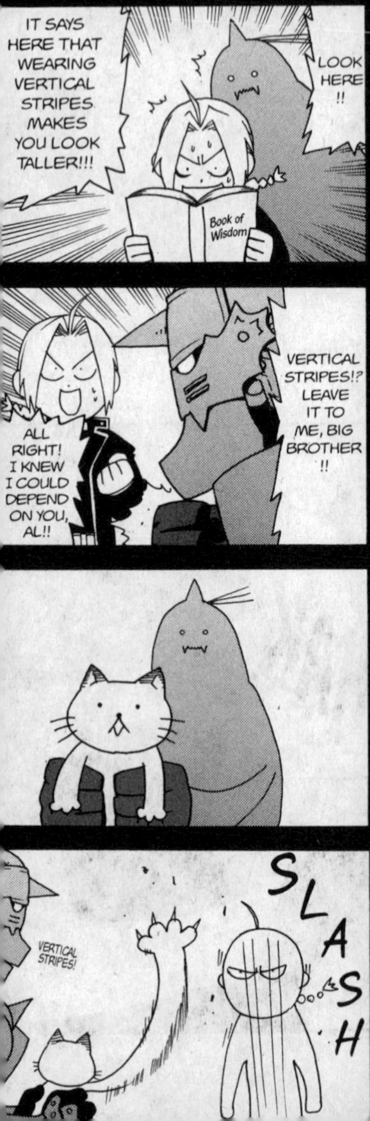
LOOK HERE!!
IT SAYS HERE THAT WEARING VERTICAL STRIPES MAKES YOU LOOK TALLER!!!
Book of Wisdom
VERTICAL STRIPES!? LEAVE IT TO ME, BIG BROTHER!!
ALL RIGHT! I KNEW I COULD DEPEND ON YOU, AL!!
SLASH
VERTICAL STRIPES!

LIFELINE

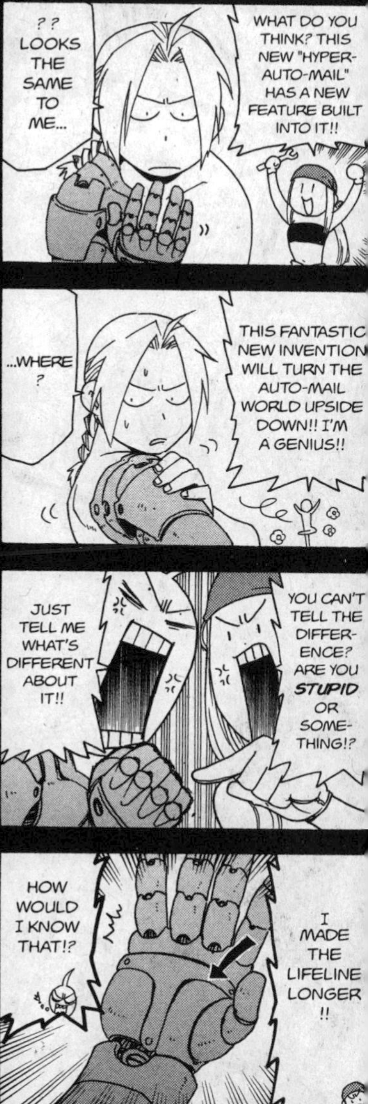
WHAT DO YOU THINK? THIS NEW "HYPER-AUTO-MAIL" HAS A NEW FEATURE BUILT INTO IT!!
? ? LOOKS THE SAME TO ME...
THIS FANTASTIC NEW INVENTION WILL TURN THE AUTO-MAIL WORLD UPSIDE DOWN!! I'M A GENIUS!!
...WHERE ?
YOU CAN'T TELL THE DIFFER-ENCE? ARE YOU **STUPID** OR SOME-THING!?
JUST TELL ME WHAT'S DIFFERENT ABOUT IT!!
I MADE THE LIFELINE LONGER !!
HOW WOULD I KNOW THAT!?

FULLMETAL ALCHEMIST 9

SPECIAL THANKS

MR. KEISUI TAKAEDA
MR. SANKICHI HINODEYA
MR. MASANARI YUZUKA
MR. JUNSHI BABA
MR. AIYAABALL
MR. JUN TOKO
MS. RIKA SUGIYAMA
MORITAISHI SENSEI

MANAGER—MR. YOICHI SHIMOMURA

AND YOU!!

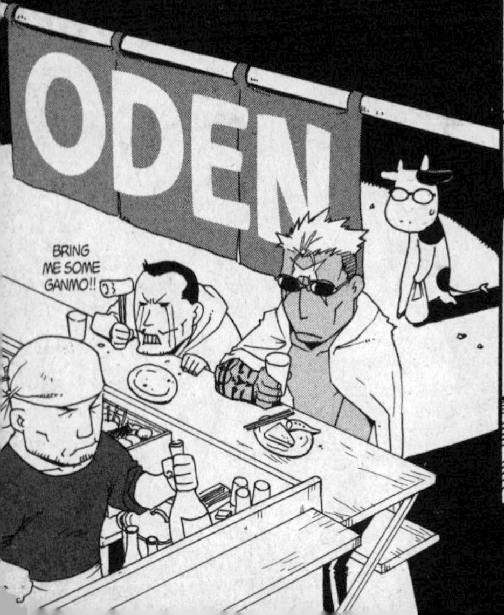
ODEN
BRING ME SOME GANMO!!

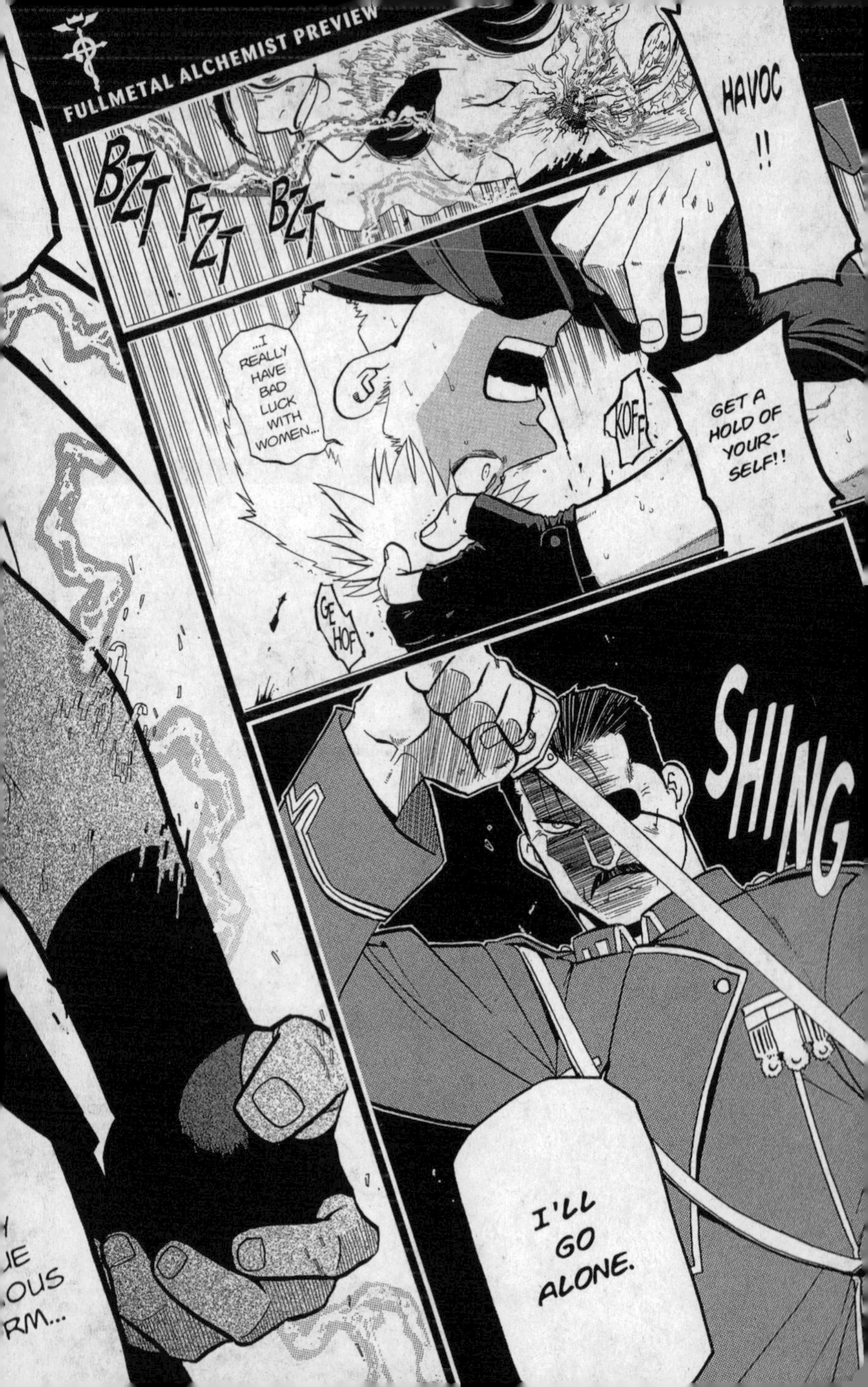
HAVOC !!
BZT FZT BZT
GET A HOLD OF YOUR-SELF!!
KOFF
...I REALLY HAVE BAD LUCK WITH WOMEN...
GEHOF
SHING
I'LL GO ALONE.

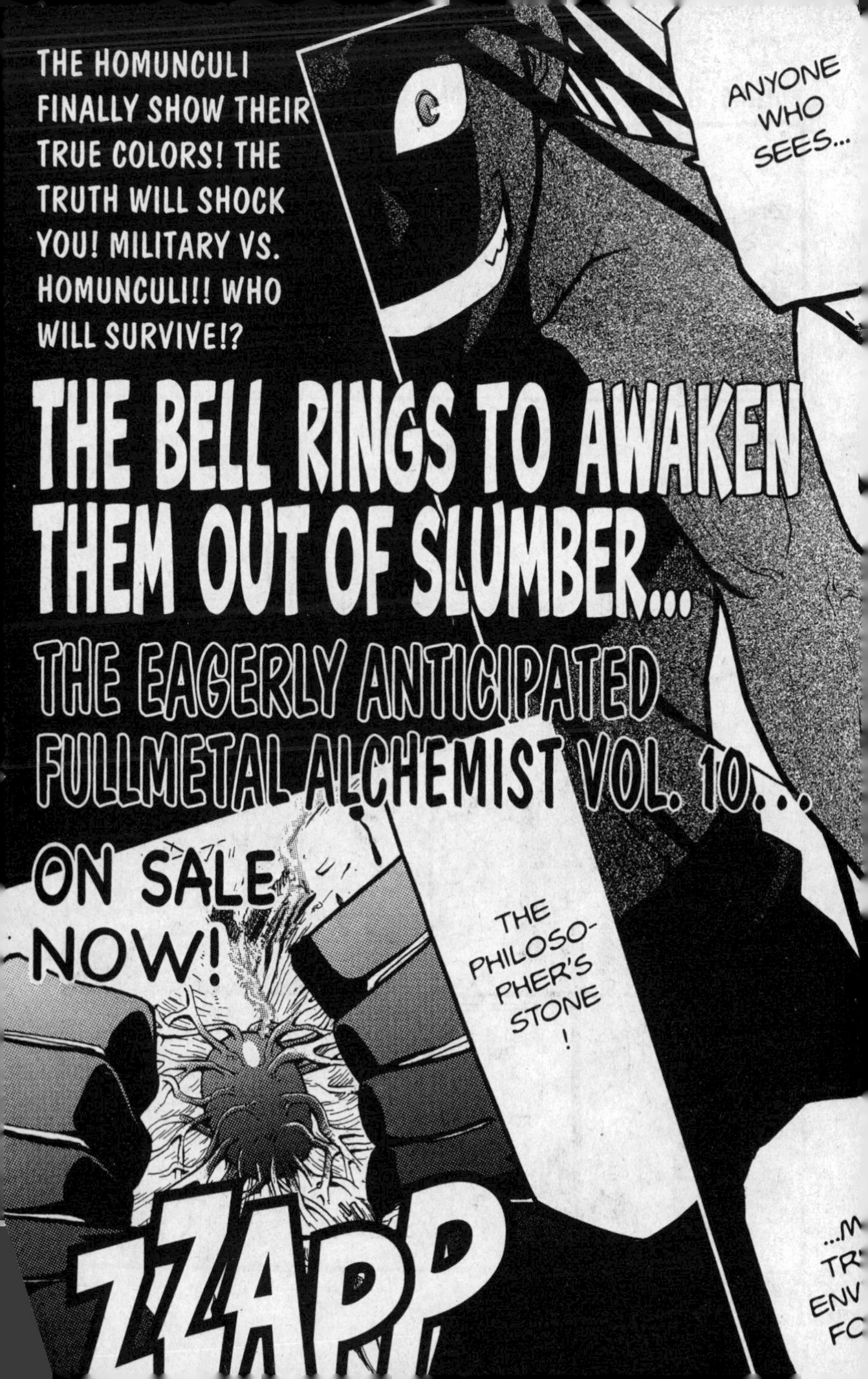

THE HOMUNCULI FINALLY SHOW THEIR TRUE COLORS! THE TRUTH WILL SHOCK YOU! MILITARY VS. HOMUNCULI!! WHO WILL SURVIVE!?
THE BELL RINGS TO AWAKEN THEM OUT OF SLUMBER...
THE EAGERLY ANTICIPATED FULLMETAL ALCHEMIST VOL. 10...
ON SALE NOW!
ANYONE WHO SEES...
THE PHILOSOPHER'S STONE!
ZZAPP

Fullmetal Alchemist 9 Special Guest Comic: On Location

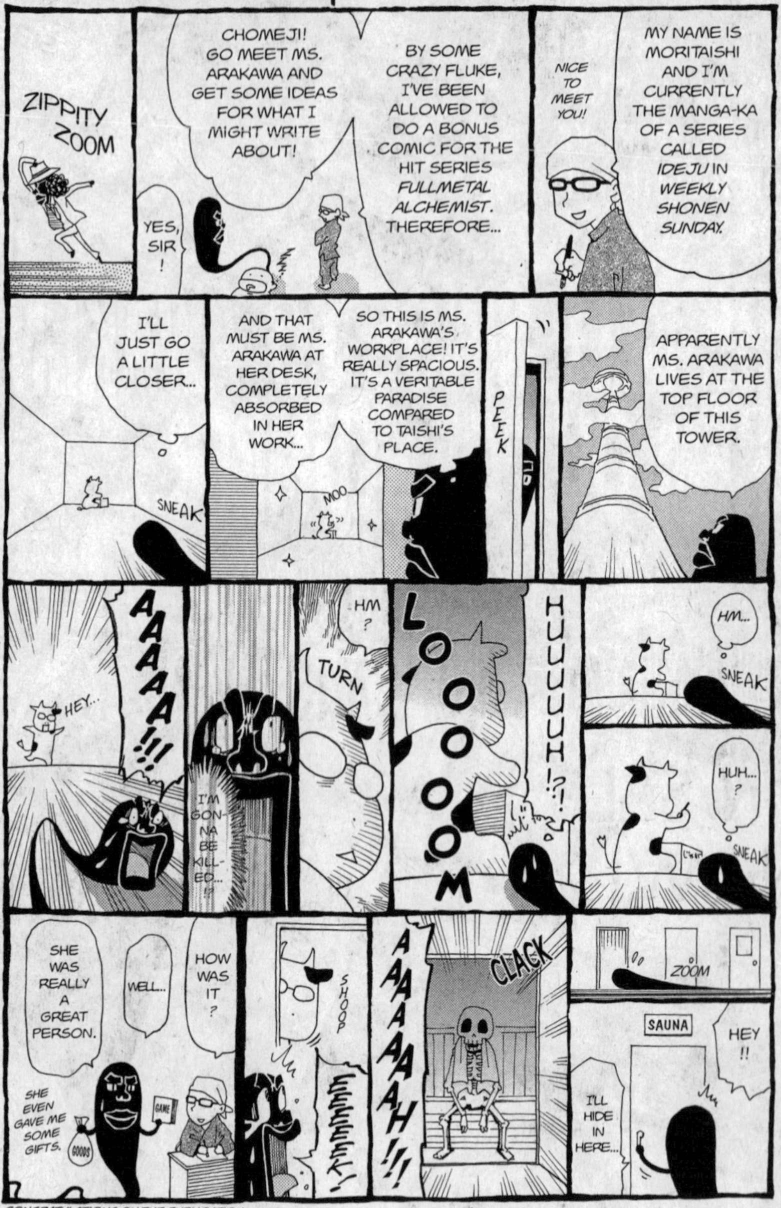

MY NAME IS MORITAISHI AND I'M CURRENTLY THE MANGA-KA OF A SERIES CALLED *IDEJU* IN WEEKLY SHONEN SUNDAY.
NICE TO MEET YOU!
BY SOME CRAZY FLUKE, I'VE BEEN ALLOWED TO DO A BONUS COMIC FOR THE HIT SERIES *FULLMETAL ALCHEMIST*. THEREFORE...
CHOMEJI! GO MEET MS. ARAKAWA AND GET SOME IDEAS FOR WHAT I MIGHT WRITE ABOUT!
YES, SIR!
ZIPPITY ZOOM
APPARENTLY MS. ARAKAWA LIVES AT THE TOP FLOOR OF THIS TOWER.
PEEK
SO THIS IS MS. ARAKAWA'S WORKPLACE! IT'S REALLY SPACIOUS. IT'S A VERITABLE PARADISE COMPARED TO TAISHI'S PLACE.
AND THAT MUST BE MS. ARAKAWA AT HER DESK, COMPLETELY ABSORBED IN HER WORK...
MOO
I'LL JUST GO A LITTLE CLOSER...
SNEAK
HM...
SNEAK
HUH...?
SNEAK
LOOOOOOM
HUUUUUH!?!
HM?
TURN
I'M GONNA BE KILLED...!?
AAAAAA!!!
HEY...
ZOOM
SAUNA
HEY!!
I'LL HIDE IN HERE...
CLACK
AAAAAAAH!!!
SHOOP
EEEEEEK!
HOW WAS IT?
WELL...
SHE WAS REALLY A GREAT PERSON.
SHE EVEN GAVE ME SOME GIFTS.
GAME
GOODS

CONGRATULATIONS ON THE PUBLICATION OF VOLUME 9, MS. ARAKAWA!

↑ *TRUE STORY.*

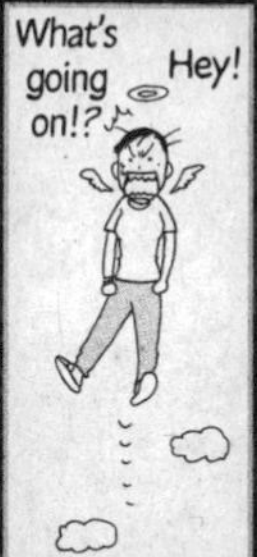
What's going on!?
Hey!

In Memoriam

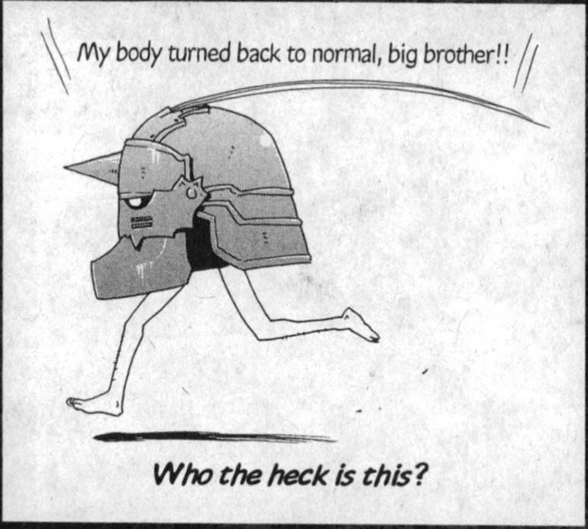
My body turned back to normal, big brother!!
Who the heck is this?

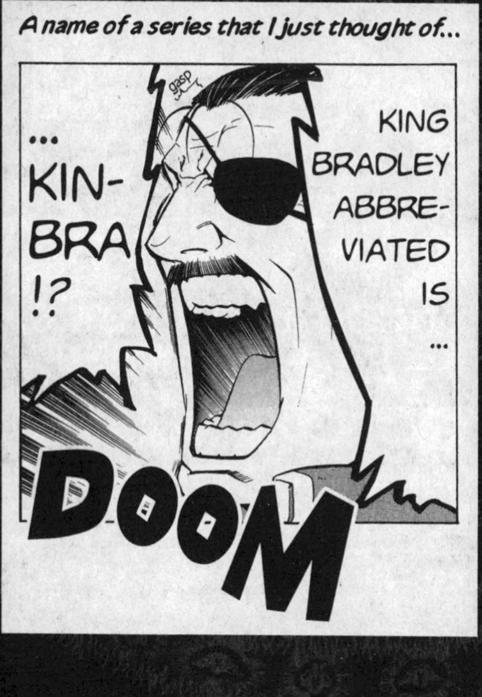
A name of a series that I just thought of...
KING BRADLEY ABBRE-VIATED IS ...
gasp
... KIN-BRA !?
DOOM

Hey! You're Reading in the Wrong Direction!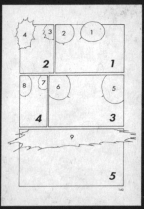

This is the **end** of this graphic novel!

To properly enjoy this VIZ graphic novel, please turn it around and begin reading from **right to left**. Unlike English, Japanese is read right to left, so Japanese comics are read in reverse order from the way English comics are typically read.

Follow the action this way

This book has been printed in the original Japanese format in order to preserve the orientation of the original artwork. Have fun with it!

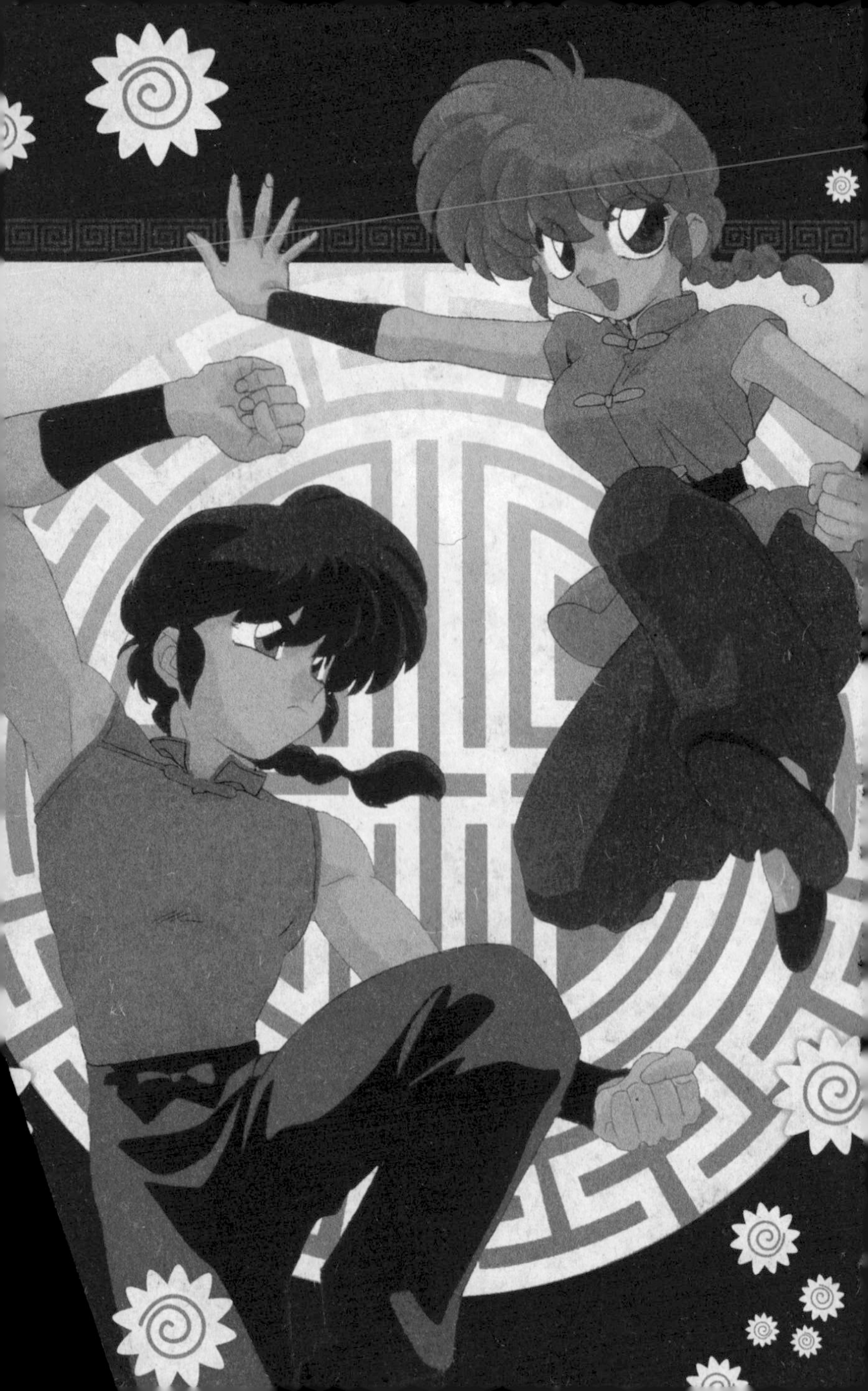